P9-CRS-612

# LITTLE WOMEN:

## COMPLETE SERIES –
## 4 NOVELS IN ONE EDITION:
## LITTLE WOMEN,
## GOOD WIVES,
## LITTLE MEN AND
## JO'S BOYS

ORIGINAL ILLUSTRATIONS

## LOUISA MAY ALCOTT

## CONTENTS

LIST OF ILLUSTRATIONS.

# BOOK ONE

# LITTLE WOMEN

# OR

# MEG, JO, BETH, AND AMY

*"Go then, my little Book, and show to all*
*That entertain and bid thee welcome shall,*
*What thou dost keep close shut up in thy breast;*
*And wish what thou dost show them may be blest*
*To them for good, may make them choose to be*
*Pilgrims better, by far, than thee or me.*
*Tell them of Mercy; she is one*
*Who early hath her pilgrimage begun.*
*Yea, let young damsels learn of her to prize*
*The world which is to come, and so be wise;*
*For little tripping maids may follow God*
*Along the ways which saintly feet have trod."*
Adapted from JOHN BUNYAN.

I.

## PLAYING PILGRIMS.

"CHRISTMAS won't be Christmas without any presents," grumbled Jo, lying on the rug.

"It's so dreadful to be poor!" sighed Meg, looking down at her old dress.

"I don't think it's fair for some girls to have plenty of pretty things, and other girls nothing at all," added little Amy, with an injured sniff.

"We've got father and mother and each other," said Beth contentedly, from her corner.

The four young faces on which the firelight shone brightened at the cheerful words, but darkened again as Jo said sadly,—

"We haven't got father, and shall not have him for a long time." She didn't say "perhaps never," but each silently added it, thinking of father far away, where the fighting was.

Nobody spoke for a minute; then Meg said in an altered tone,—

"You know the reason mother proposed not having any presents this Christmas was because it is going to be a hard winter for every one; and she thinks we ought not to spend money for pleasure, when our men are suffering so in the army. We can't do much, but we can make our little sacrifices, and ought to do it gladly. But I am afraid I don't;" and Meg shook her head, as she thought regretfully of all the pretty things she wanted.

"But I don't think the little we should spend would do any good. We've each got a dollar, and the army wouldn't be much helped by our giving that. I agree not to expect anything from mother or you, but I do want to buy Undine and Sintram for myself; I've wanted it *so* long," said Jo, who was a bookworm.

"I planned to spend mine in new music," said Beth, with a little sigh, which no one heard but the hearth-brush and kettle-holder.

"I shall get a nice box of Faber's drawing-pencils; I really need them," said Amy decidedly.

"Mother didn't say anything about our money, and she won't wish us to give up everything. Let's each buy what we want, and have a little fun; I'm sure we work hard enough to earn it," cried Jo, examining the heels of her shoes in a gentlemanly manner.

"I know *I* do,—teaching those tiresome children nearly all day, when I'm longing to enjoy myself at home," began Meg, in the complaining tone again.

"You don't have half such a hard time as I do," said Jo. "How would you like to be shut up for hours with a nervous, fussy old lady, who keeps you trotting, is never satisfied, and worries you till you're ready to fly out of the window or cry?"

"It's naughty to fret; but I do think washing dishes and keeping things tidy is the worst work in the world. It makes me cross; and my hands get so stiff, I can't practise well at all;" and Beth looked at her rough hands with a sigh that any one could hear that time.

"I don't believe any of you suffer as I do," cried Amy; "for you don't have to go to school with impertinent girls, who plague you if you don't know your lessons, and laugh at your dresses, and label your father if he isn't rich, and insult you when your nose isn't nice."

"If you mean *libel*, I'd say so, and not talk about *labels*, as if papa was a pickle-bottle," advised Jo, laughing.

"I know what I mean, and you needn't be *statirical* about it. It's proper to use good words, and improve your *vocabilary*," returned Amy, with dignity.

"Don't peck at one another, children. Don't you wish we had the money papa lost when we were little, Jo? Dear me! how happy and good we'd be, if we had no worries!" said Meg, who could remember better times.

"You said the other day, you thought we were a deal happier than the King children, for they were fighting and fretting all the time, in spite of their money."

"So I did, Beth. Well, I think we are; for, though we do have to work, we make fun for ourselves, and are a pretty jolly set, as Jo would say."

"Jo does use such slang words!" observed Amy, with a reproving look at the long figure stretched on the rug. Jo immediately sat up, put her hands in her pockets, and began to whistle.

"Don't, Jo; it's so boyish!"

"That's why I do it."

"I detest rude, unlady-like girls!"

"I hate affected, niminy-piminy chits!"

"'Birds in their little nests agree,'" sang Beth, the peace-maker, with such a funny face that both sharp voices softened to a laugh, and the "pecking" ended for that time.

"Really, girls, you are both to be blamed," said Meg, beginning to lecture in her elder-sisterly fashion. "You are old enough to leave off boyish tricks, and to behave better, Josephine. It didn't matter so much when you were a little girl; but now you are so tall, and turn up your hair, you should remember that you are a young lady."

"I'm not! and if turning up my hair makes me one, I'll wear it in two tails till I'm twenty," cried Jo, pulling off her net, and shaking down a chestnut mane. "I hate to think I've got to grow up, and be Miss March, and wear long gowns, and look as prim as a China-aster! It's bad enough to be a girl, anyway, when I like boys' games and work and manners! I can't get over my disappointment in not being a boy; and it's worse than ever now, for I'm dying to go and fight with papa, and I can only stay at home and knit, like a poky old woman!" And Jo shook the blue army-sock till the needles rattled like castanets, and her ball bounded across the room.

"Poor Jo! It's too bad, but it can't be helped; so you must try to be contented with making your name boyish, and playing brother to us girls," said Beth, stroking the rough head at her knee with a hand that all the dish-washing and dusting in the world could not make ungentle in its touch.

"As for you, Amy," continued Meg, "you are altogether too particular and prim. Your airs are funny now; but you'll grow up an affected little goose, if you don't take care. I like your nice manners and refined ways of speaking, when you don't try to be elegant; but your absurd words are as bad as Jo's slang."

"If Jo is a tom-boy and Amy a goose, what am I, please?" asked Beth, ready to share the lecture.

"You're a dear, and nothing else," answered Meg warmly; and no one contradicted her, for the "Mouse" was the pet of the family.

As young readers like to know "how people look," we will take this moment to give them a little sketch of the four sisters, who sat knitting away in the twilight, while the December snow fell quietly without, and the fire crackled cheerfully within. It was a comfortable old room, though the carpet was faded and the furniture very plain; for a good picture or two hung on the walls, books filled the recesses, chrysanthemums and Christmas roses bloomed in the windows, and a pleasant atmosphere of home-peace pervaded it.

Margaret, the eldest of the four, was sixteen, and very pretty, being plump and fair, with large eyes, plenty of soft, brown hair, a sweet mouth, and white hands, of which she was rather vain. Fifteen-year-old Jo was very tall, thin, and brown, and reminded one of a colt; for she never seemed to know what to do with her long limbs, which were very much in her way. She had a decided mouth, a comical nose, and sharp, gray eyes, which appeared to see everything, and were by turns fierce, funny, or thoughtful. Her long, thick hair was her one beauty; but it was usually bundled into a net, to be out of her way. Round shoulders had Jo, big hands and feet, a fly-away look to her clothes, and the uncomfortable appearance of a girl who was rapidly shooting up into a woman, and didn't like it. Elizabeth—or Beth, as every one called her—was a rosy, smooth-haired, bright-eyed girl of thirteen, with a shy manner, a timid voice, and a peaceful expression, which was seldom disturbed. Her father called her "Little Tranquillity," and the name suited her excellently; for she seemed to live in a happy world of her own, only venturing out to meet the few whom she trusted and loved. Amy, though the youngest, was a most important person,—in her own opinion at least. A regular snow-maiden, with blue eyes, and yellow hair, curling on her shoulders, pale and slender, and always carrying herself like a young lady mindful of her manners. What the characters of the four sisters were we will leave to be found out.

The clock struck six; and, having swept up the hearth, Beth put a pair of slippers down to warm. Somehow the sight of the old shoes had a good effect upon the girls; for mother was coming, and every one brightened to welcome her. Meg stopped lecturing, and lighted the lamp, Amy got out of the easy-chair without being asked, and Jo forgot how tired she was as she sat up to hold the slippers nearer to the blaze.

"They are quite worn out; Marmee must have a new pair."

"I thought I'd get her some with my dollar," said Beth.

"No, I shall!" cried Amy.

"I'm the oldest," began Meg, but Jo cut in with a decided—

"I'm the man of the family now papa is away, and *I* shall provide the slippers, for he told me to take special care of mother while he was gone."

"I'll tell you what we'll do," said Beth; "let's each get her something for Christmas, and not get anything for ourselves."

"That's like you, dear! What will we get?" exclaimed Jo.

Every one thought soberly for a minute; then Meg announced, as if the idea was suggested by the sight of her own pretty hands, "I shall give her a nice pair of gloves."

"Army shoes, best to be had," cried Jo.

"Some handkerchiefs, all hemmed," said Beth.

"I'll get a little bottle of cologne; she likes it, and it won't cost much, so I'll have some left to buy my pencils," added Amy.

"How will we give the things?" asked Meg.

"Put them on the table, and bring her in and see her open the bundles. Don't you remember how we used to do on our birthdays?" answered Jo.

"I used to be *so* frightened when it was my turn to sit in the big chair with the crown on, and see you all come marching round to give the presents, with a kiss. I liked the things and the kisses, but it was dreadful to have you sit looking at me while I opened the bundles," said Beth, who was toasting her face and the bread for tea, at the same time.

"Let Marmee think we are getting things for ourselves, and then surprise her. We must go shopping to-morrow afternoon, Meg; there is so much to do about the play for Christmas night," said Jo, marching up and down, with her hands behind her back and her nose in the air.

"I don't mean to act any more after this time; I'm getting too old for such things," observed Meg, who was as much a child as ever about "dressing-up" frolics.

"You won't stop, I know, as long as you can trail round in a white gown with your hair down, and wear gold-paper jewelry. You are the best actress we've got, and there'll be an end of everything if you quit the boards," said Jo. "We ought to rehearse to-night. Come here, Amy, and do the fainting scene, for you are as stiff as a poker in that."

"I can't help it; I never saw any one faint, and I don't choose to make myself all black and blue, tumbling flat as you do. If I can go down easily, I'll drop; if I can't, I shall fall into a chair and be graceful; I don't care if Hugo does come at me with a pistol," returned Amy, who was not gifted with dramatic power, but was chosen because she was small enough to be borne out shrieking by the villain of the piece.

"Do it this way; clasp your hands so, and stagger across the room, crying frantically, 'Roderigo! save me! save me!'" and away went Jo, with a melodramatic scream which was truly thrilling.

Amy followed, but she poked her hands out stiffly before her, and jerked herself along as if she went by machinery; and her "Ow!" was more suggestive of pins being run into her than of fear and anguish. Jo gave a despairing groan, and Meg laughed outright, while Beth let her bread burn as she watched the fun, with interest.

"It's no use! Do the best you can when the time comes, and if the audience laugh, don't blame me. Come on, Meg."

Then things went smoothly, for Don Pedro defied the world in a speech of two pages without a single break; Hagar, the witch, chanted an awful incantation over her kettleful of simmering toads, with weird effect; Roderigo rent his chains asunder manfully, and Hugo died in agonies of remorse and arsenic, with a wild "Ha! ha!"

"It's the best we've had yet," said Meg, as the dead villain sat up and rubbed his elbows.

"I don't see how you can write and act such splendid things, Jo. You're a regular Shakespeare!" exclaimed Beth, who firmly believed that her sisters were gifted with wonderful genius in all things.

"Not quite," replied Jo modestly. "I do think 'The Witch's Curse, an Operatic Tragedy,' is rather a nice thing; but I'd like to try Macbeth, if we only had a trap-door for Banquo. I always wanted to do the killing part. 'Is that a dagger that I see before me?'" muttered Jo, rolling her eyes and clutching at the air, as she had seen a famous tragedian do.

"No, it's the toasting fork, with mother's shoe on it instead of the bread. Beth's stage-struck!" cried Meg, and the rehearsal ended in a general burst of laughter.

"Glad to find you so merry, my girls," said a cheery voice at the door, and actors and audience turned to welcome a tall, motherly lady, with a "can-I-help-you" look about her which was truly delightful. She was not elegantly dressed, but a noble-looking woman, and the girls thought the gray cloak and unfashionable bonnet covered the most splendid mother in the world.

"Well, dearies, how have you got on to-day? There was so much to do, getting the boxes ready to go to-morrow, that I didn't come home to dinner. Has any one called, Beth? How is your cold, Meg? Jo, you look tired to death. Come and kiss me, baby."

While making these maternal inquiries Mrs. March got her wet things off, her warm slippers on, and sitting down in the easy-chair, drew Amy to her lap, preparing to enjoy the happiest hour of her busy day. The girls flew about, trying to make things comfortable, each in her own way. Meg arranged the tea-table; Jo brought wood and set chairs, dropping, overturning, and clattering everything she touched; Beth trotted to and fro between parlor and kitchen, quiet and busy; while Amy gave directions to every one, as she sat with her hands folded.

As they gathered about the table, Mrs. March said, with a particularly happy face, "I've got a treat for you after supper."

A quick, bright smile went round like a streak of sunshine. Beth clapped her hands, regardless of the biscuit she held, and Jo tossed up her napkin, crying, "A letter! a letter! Three cheers for father!"

"Yes, a nice long letter. He is well, and thinks he shall get through the cold season better than we feared. He sends all sorts of loving wishes for Christmas, and an especial message to you girls," said Mrs. March, patting her pocket as if she had got a treasure there.

"Hurry and get done! Don't stop to quirk your little finger, and simper over your plate, Amy," cried Jo, choking in her tea, and dropping her bread, butter side down, on the carpet, in her haste to get at the treat.

Beth ate no more, but crept away, to sit in her shadowy corner and brood over the delight to come, till the others were ready.

"I think it was so splendid in father to go as a chaplain when he was too old to be drafted, and not strong enough for a soldier," said Meg warmly.

"Don't I wish I could go as a drummer, a *vivan*—what's its name? or a nurse, so I could be near him and help him," exclaimed Jo, with a groan.

"It must be very disagreeable to sleep in a tent, and eat all sorts of bad-tasting things, and drink out of a tin mug," sighed Amy.

"When will he come home, Marmee?" asked Beth, with a little quiver in her voice.

"Not for many months, dear, unless he is sick. He will stay and do his work faithfully as long as he can, and we won't ask for him back a minute sooner than he can be spared. Now come and hear the letter."

They all drew to the fire, mother in the big chair with Beth at her feet, Meg and Amy perched on either arm of the chair, and Jo leaning on the back, where no one would see any sign of emotion if the letter should happen to be touching.

Very few letters were written in those hard times that were not touching, especially those which fathers sent home. In this one little was said of the hardships endured, the dangers faced, or the homesickness conquered; it was a cheerful, hopeful letter, full of lively descriptions of camp life, marches, and military news; and only at the end did the writer's heart overflow with fatherly love and longing for the little girls at home.

"Give them all my dear love and a kiss. Tell them I think of them by day, pray for them by night, and find my best comfort in their affection at all times. A year seems very long to wait before I see them, but remind them that while we wait we may all work, so that these hard days need not be wasted. I know they will remember all I said to them, that they will be loving children to you, will do their duty faithfully, fight their bosom enemies bravely, and conquer themselves so beautifully, that when I come back to them I may be fonder and prouder than ever of my little women."

Everybody sniffed when they came to that part; Jo wasn't ashamed of the great tear that dropped off the end of her nose, and Amy never minded the rumpling of her curls as she hid her face on her mother's shoulder and sobbed out, "I *am* a selfish girl! but I'll truly try to be better, so he mayn't be disappointed in me by and by."

"We all will!" cried Meg. "I think too much of my looks, and hate to work, but won't any more, if I can help it."

"I'll try and be what he loves to call me, 'a little woman,' and not be rough and wild; but do my duty here instead of wanting to be somewhere else," said Jo, thinking that keeping her temper at home was a much harder task than facing a rebel or two down South.

Beth said nothing, but wiped away her tears with the blue army-sock, and began to knit with all her might, losing no time in doing the duty that lay nearest her, while she resolved in her quiet little soul to be all that father hoped to find her when the year brought round the happy coming home.

Mrs. March broke the silence that followed Jo's words, by saying in her cheery voice, "Do you remember how you used to play Pilgrim's Progress when you were little things? Nothing delighted you more than to have me tie my piece-bags on your backs for burdens, give you hats and sticks and rolls of paper, and let you travel through the house from the cellar, which was the City of Destruction, up, up, to the house-top, where you had all the lovely things you could collect to make a Celestial City."

"What fun it was, especially going by the lions, fighting Apollyon, and passing through the Valley where the hobgoblins were!" said Jo.

"I liked the place where the bundles fell off and tumbled down stairs," said Meg.

"My favorite part was when we came out on the flat roof where our flowers and arbors and pretty things were, and all stood and sung for joy up there in the sunshine," said Beth, smiling, as if that pleasant moment had come back to her.

"I don't remember much about it, except that I was afraid of the cellar and the dark entry, and always liked the cake and milk we had up at the top. If I wasn't too old for such things, I'd rather like to play it over again," said Amy, who began to talk of renouncing childish things at the mature age of twelve.

"We never are too old for this, my dear, because it is a play we are playing all the time in one way or another. Our burdens are here, our road is before us, and the longing for goodness and happiness is the guide that leads us through many troubles and mistakes to the peace which is a true Celestial City. Now, my little pilgrims, suppose you begin again, not in play, but in earnest, and see how far on you can get before father comes home."

"Really, mother? Where are our bundles?" asked Amy, who was a very literal young lady.

"Each of you told what your burden was just now, except Beth; I rather think she hasn't got any," said her mother.

"Yes, I have; mine is dishes and dusters, and envying girls with nice pianos, and being afraid of people."

Beth's bundle was such a funny one that everybody wanted to laugh; but nobody did, for it would have hurt her feelings very much.

"Let us do it," said Meg thoughtfully. "It is only another name for trying to be good, and the story may help us; for though we do want to be good, it's hard work, and we forget, and don't do our best."

"We were in the Slough of Despond to-night, and mother came and pulled us out as Help did in the book. We ought to have our roll of directions, like Christian. What shall we do about that?" asked Jo, delighted with the fancy which lent a little romance to the very dull task of doing her duty.

"Look under your pillows, Christmas morning, and you will find your guide-book," replied Mrs. March.

They talked over the new plan while old Hannah cleared the table; then out came the four little work-baskets, and the needles flew as the girls made sheets for Aunt March. It was uninteresting sewing, but to-night no one grumbled. They adopted Jo's plan of dividing the long seams into four parts, and calling the quarters Europe, Asia, Africa, and America, and in that way got on capitally, especially when they talked about the different countries as they stitched their way through them.

At nine they stopped work, and sung, as usual, before they went to bed. No one but Beth could get much music out of the old piano; but she had a way of softly touching the yellow keys, and making a pleasant accompaniment to the simple songs they sung. Meg had a voice like a flute, and she and her mother led the little choir. Amy chirped like a cricket, and Jo wandered through the airs at her own sweet will, always coming out at the wrong place with a croak or a quaver that spoilt the most pensive tune. They had always done this from the time they could lisp

"Crinkle, crinkle, 'ittle 'tar,"

and it had become a household custom, for the mother was a born singer. The first sound in the morning was her voice, as she went about the house singing like a lark; and the last sound at night was the same cheery sound, for the girls never grew too old for that familiar lullaby.

II.

## A MERRY CHRISTMAS.

JO was the first to wake in the gray dawn of Christmas morning. No stockings hung at the fireplace, and for a moment she felt as much disappointed as she did long ago, when her little sock fell down because it was so crammed with goodies. Then she remembered her mother's promise, and, slipping her hand under her pillow, drew out a little crimson-covered book. She knew it very well, for it was that beautiful old story of the best life ever lived, and Jo felt that it was a true guide-book for any pilgrim going the long journey. She woke Meg with a "Merry Christmas," and bade her see what was under her pillow. A green-covered book appeared, with the same picture inside, and a few words written by their mother, which made their one present very precious in their eyes. Presently Beth and Amy woke, to rummage and find their little books also,—one dove-colored, the other blue; and all sat looking at and talking about them, while the east grew rosy with the coming day.

In spite of her small vanities, Margaret had a sweet and pious nature, which unconsciously influenced her sisters, especially Jo, who loved her very tenderly, and obeyed her because her advice was so gently given.

"Girls," said Meg seriously, looking from the tumbled head beside her to the two little night-capped ones in the room beyond, "mother wants us to read and love and mind these books, and we must begin at once. We used to be faithful about it; but since father went away, and all this war trouble unsettled us, we have neglected many things. You can do as you please; but *I* shall keep my book on the table here, and read a little every morning as soon as I wake, for I know it will do me good, and help me through the day."

Then she opened her new book and began to read. Jo put her arm round her, and, leaning cheek to cheek, read also, with the quiet expression so seldom seen on her restless face.

"How good Meg is! Come, Amy, let's do as they do. I'll help you with the hard words, and they'll explain things if we don't understand," whispered Beth, very much impressed by the pretty books and her sisters' example.

"I'm glad mine is blue," said Amy; and then the rooms were very still while the pages were softly turned, and the winter sunshine crept in to touch the bright heads and serious faces with a Christmas greeting.

"Where is mother?" asked Meg, as she and Jo ran down to thank her for their gifts, half an hour later.

"Goodness only knows. Some poor creeter come a-beggin', and your ma went straight off to see what was needed. There never *was* such a woman for givin' away vittles and drink, clothes and firin'," replied Hannah, who had lived with the family since Meg was born, and was considered by them all more as a friend than a servant.

"She will be back soon, I think; so fry your cakes, and have everything ready," said Meg, looking over the presents which were collected in a basket and kept under the sofa, ready to be produced at the proper time. "Why, where is Amy's bottle of cologne?" she added, as the little flask did not appear.

"She took it out a minute ago, and went off with it to put a ribbon on it, or some such notion," replied Jo, dancing about the room to take the first stiffness off the new army-slippers.

"How nice my handkerchiefs look, don't they? Hannah washed and ironed them for me, and I marked them all myself," said Beth, looking proudly at the somewhat uneven letters which had cost her such labor.

"Bless the child! she's gone and put 'Mother' on them instead of 'M. March.' How funny!" cried Jo, taking up one.

"Isn't it right? I thought it was better to do it so, because Meg's initials are 'M. M.,' and I don't want any one to use these but Marmee," said Beth, looking troubled.

"It's all right, dear, and a very pretty idea,—quite sensible, too, for no one can ever mistake now. It will please her very much, I know," said Meg, with a frown for Jo and a smile for Beth.

"There's mother. Hide the basket, quick!" cried Jo, as a door slammed, and steps sounded in the hall.

Amy came in hastily, and looked rather abashed when she saw her sisters all waiting for her.

"Where have you been, and what are you hiding behind you?" asked Meg, surprised to see, by her hood and cloak, that lazy Amy had been out so early.

"Don't laugh at me, Jo! I didn't mean any one should know till the time came. I only meant to change the little bottle for a big one, and I gave *all* my money to get it, and I'm truly trying not to be selfish any more."

As she spoke, Amy showed the handsome flask which replaced the cheap one; and looked so earnest and humble in her little effort to forget herself that Meg hugged her on the spot, and Jo pronounced her "a trump," while Beth ran to the window, and picked her finest rose to ornament the stately bottle.

"You see I felt ashamed of my present, after reading and talking about being good this morning, so I ran round the corner and changed it the minute I was up: and I'm *so* glad, for mine is the handsomest now."

Another bang of the street-door sent the basket under the sofa, and the girls to the table, eager for breakfast.

"Merry Christmas, Marmee! Many of them! Thank you for our books; we read some, and mean to every day," they cried, in chorus.

"Merry Christmas, little daughters! I'm glad you began at once, and hope you will keep on. But I want to say one word before we sit down. Not far away from here lies a poor woman with a little new-born baby. Six children are huddled into one bed to keep from freezing, for they have no fire. There is nothing to eat over there; and the oldest boy came to tell me they were suffering hunger and cold. My girls, will you give them your breakfast as a Christmas present?"

They were all unusually hungry, having waited nearly an hour, and for a minute no one spoke; only a minute, for Jo exclaimed impetuously,—

"I'm so glad you came before we began!"

"May I go and help carry the things to the poor little children?" asked Beth, eagerly.

"*I* shall take the cream and the muffins," added Amy, heroically giving up the articles she most liked.

Meg was already covering the buckwheats, and piling the bread into one big plate.

"I thought you'd do it," said Mrs. March, smiling as if satisfied. "You shall all go and help me, and when we come back we will have bread and milk for breakfast, and make it up at dinner-time."

They were soon ready, and the procession set out. Fortunately it was early, and they went through back streets, so few people saw them, and no one laughed at the queer party.

A poor, bare, miserable room it was, with broken windows, no fire, ragged bed-clothes, a sick mother, wailing baby, and a group of pale, hungry children cuddled under one old quilt, trying to keep warm.

How the big eyes stared and the blue lips smiled as the girls went in!

"Ach, mein Gott! it is good angels come to us!" said the poor woman, crying for joy.

"Funny angels in hoods and mittens," said Jo, and set them laughing.

In a few minutes it really did seem as if kind spirits had been at work there. Hannah, who had carried wood, made a fire, and stopped up the broken panes with old hats and her own cloak. Mrs. March gave the mother tea and gruel, and comforted her with promises of help, while she dressed the little baby as tenderly as if it had been her own. The girls, meantime, spread the table, set the children round the fire, and fed them like so many hungry birds,—laughing, talking, and trying to understand the funny broken English.

"Das ist gut!" "Die Engel-kinder!" cried the poor things, as they ate, and warmed their purple hands at the comfortable blaze.

The girls had never been called angel children before, and thought it very agreeable, especially Jo, who had been considered a "Sancho" ever since she was born. That was a very happy breakfast, though they didn't get any of it; and when they went away, leaving comfort behind, I think there were not in all the city four merrier people than the hungry little girls who gave away their breakfasts and contented themselves with bread and milk on Christmas morning.

"That's loving our neighbor better than ourselves, and I like it," said Meg, as they set out their presents, while their mother was upstairs collecting clothes for the poor Hummels.

Not a very splendid show, but there was a great deal of love done up in the few little bundles; and the tall vase of red roses, white chrysanthemums, and trailing vines, which stood in the middle, gave quite an elegant air to the table.

"She's coming! Strike up, Beth! Open the door, Amy! Three cheers for Marmee!" cried Jo, prancing about, while Meg went to conduct mother to the seat of honor.

Beth played her gayest march, Amy threw open the door, and Meg enacted escort with great dignity. Mrs. March was both surprised and touched; and smiled with her eyes full as she examined her presents, and read the little notes which accompanied them. The slippers went on at once, a new handkerchief was slipped into her pocket, well scented with Amy's cologne, the rose was fastened in her bosom, and the nice gloves were pronounced a "perfect fit."

There was a good deal of laughing and kissing and explaining, in the simple, loving fashion which makes these home-festivals so pleasant at the time, so sweet to remember long afterward, and then all fell to work.

The morning charities and ceremonies took so much time that the rest of the day was devoted to preparations for the evening festivities. Being still too young to go often to the theatre, and not rich enough to afford any great outlay for private performances, the girls put their wits to work, and—necessity being the mother of invention,—made whatever they needed. Very clever were some of their productions,—pasteboard guitars, antique lamps made of old-fashioned butter-boats covered with silver paper, gorgeous robes of old cotton, glittering with tin spangles from a pickle factory, and armor covered with the same useful diamond-shaped bits, left in sheets when the lids of tin preserve-pots were cut out. The furniture was used to being turned topsy-turvy, and the big chamber was the scene of many innocent revels.

No gentlemen were admitted; so Jo played male parts to her heart's content, and took immense satisfaction in a pair of russet-leather boots given her by a friend, who knew a lady who knew an actor. These boots, an old foil, and a slashed doublet once used by an artist for some picture, were Jo's chief treasures, and appeared on all occasions. The smallness of the company made it necessary for the two principal actors to take several parts apiece; and they certainly deserved some credit for the hard work they did in learning three or four different parts, whisking in and out of various costumes, and managing the stage besides. It was excellent drill for their memories, a harmless amusement, and employed many hours which otherwise would have been idle, lonely, or spent in less profitable society.

On Christmas night, a dozen girls piled on to the bed which was the dress-circle, and sat before the blue and yellow chintz curtains in a most flattering state of expectancy. There was a good deal of rustling and whispering behind the curtain, a trifle of lamp-smoke, and an occasional giggle from Amy, who was apt to get hysterical in the excitement of the moment. Presently a bell sounded, the curtains flew apart, and the Operatic Tragedy began.

"A gloomy wood," according to the one play-bill, was represented by a few shrubs in pots, green baize on the floor, and a cave in the distance. This cave was made with a clothes-horse for a roof, bureaus for walls; and in it was a small furnace in full blast, with a black pot on it, and an old witch bending over it. The stage was dark, and the glow of the furnace had a fine effect, especially as real steam issued from the kettle when the witch took off the cover. A moment was allowed for the first thrill to subside; then Hugo, the villain, stalked in with a clanking sword at his side, a slouched hat, black beard, mysterious cloak, and the boots. After pacing to and fro in much agitation, he struck his forehead, and burst out in a wild strain, singing of his hatred to Roderigo, his love for Zara, and his pleasing resolution to kill the one and win the other. The gruff tones of Hugo's voice, with an occasional shout when his feelings overcame him, were very impressive, and the audience applauded the moment he paused for breath. Bowing with the air of one accustomed to public praise, he stole to the cavern, and ordered Hagar to come forth with a commanding "What ho, minion! I need thee!"

Out came Meg, with gray horse-hair hanging about her face, a red and black robe, a staff, and cabalistic signs upon her cloak. Hugo demanded a potion to make Zara adore him, and one to destroy Roderigo. Hagar, in a fine dramatic melody, promised both, and proceeded to call up the spirit who would bring the love philter:—

"Hither, hither, from thy home,
Airy sprite, I bid thee come!
Born of roses, fed on dew,
Charms and potions canst thou brew?
Bring me here, with elfin speed,
The fragrant philter which I need;
Make it sweet and swift and strong,
Spirit, answer now my song!"

A soft strain of music sounded, and then at the back of the cave appeared a little figure in cloudy white, with glittering wings, golden hair, and a garland of roses on its head. Waving a wand, it sang,—

"Hither I come,
From my airy home,
Afar in the silver moon.
Take the magic spell,
And use it well,
Or its power will vanish soon!"

And, dropping a small, gilded bottle at the witch's feet, the spirit vanished. Another chant from Hagar produced another apparition,—not a lovely one; for, with a bang, an ugly black imp appeared, and, having croaked a reply, tossed a dark bottle at Hugo, and disappeared with a mocking laugh. Having warbled his thanks and put the potions in his boots, Hugo departed; and Hagar informed the audience that, as he had killed a few of her friends in times past, she has cursed him, and intends to thwart his plans, and be revenged on him. Then the curtain fell, and the audience reposed and ate candy while discussing the merits of the play.

A good deal of hammering went on before the curtain rose again; but when it became evident what a masterpiece of stage-carpentering had been got up, no one murmured at the delay. It was truly superb! A tower rose to the ceiling; half-way up appeared a window, with a lamp burning at it, and behind the white curtain appeared Zara in a lovely blue and silver dress, waiting for Roderigo. He came in gorgeous array, with plumed cap, red cloak, chestnut love-locks, a guitar, and the boots, of course. Kneeling at the foot of the tower, he sang a serenade in melting tones. Zara replied, and, after a musical dialogue, consented to fly. Then came the grand effect of the play. Roderigo produced a rope-ladder, with five steps to it, threw up one end, and invited Zara to descend. Timidly she crept from her lattice, put her hand on Roderigo's shoulder, and was about to leap gracefully down, when, "Alas! alas for Zara!" she forgot her train,—it caught in the window; the tower tottered, leaned forward, fell with a crash, and buried the unhappy lovers in the ruins!

A universal shriek arose as the russet boots waved wildly from the wreck, and a golden head emerged, exclaiming, "I told you so! I told you so!" With wonderful presence of mind, Don Pedro, the cruel sire, rushed in, dragged out his daughter, with a hasty aside,—

"Don't laugh! Act as if it was all right!"—and, ordering Roderigo up, banished him from the kingdom with wrath and scorn. Though decidedly shaken by the fall of the tower upon him, Roderigo defied the old gentleman, and refused to stir. This dauntless example fired Zara: she also defied her sire, and he ordered them both to the deepest dungeons of the castle. A stout little retainer came in with chains, and led them away, looking very much frightened, and evidently forgetting the speech he ought to have made.

Act third was the castle hall; and here Hagar appeared, having come to free the lovers and finish Hugo. She hears him coming, and hides; sees him put the potions into two cups of wine, and bid the timid little servant "Bear them to the captives in their cells, and tell them I shall come anon." The servant takes Hugo aside to tell him something, and Hagar changes the cups for two others which are harmless. Ferdinando, the "minion," carries them away, and Hagar puts back the cup which holds the poison meant for Roderigo. Hugo, getting thirsty after a long warble, drinks it, loses his wits, and, after a good deal of clutching and stamping, falls flat and dies; while Hagar informs him what she has done in a song of exquisite power and melody.

This was a truly thrilling scene, though some persons might have thought that the sudden tumbling down of a quantity of long hair rather marred the effect of the villain's death. He was called before the curtain, and with great propriety appeared, leading Hagar, whose singing was considered more wonderful than all the rest of the performance put together.

Act fourth displayed the despairing Roderigo on the point of stabbing himself, because he has been told that Zara has deserted him. Just as the dagger is at his heart, a lovely song is sung under his window, informing him that Zara is true, but in danger, and he can save her, if he will. A key is thrown in, which unlocks the door, and in a spasm of rapture he tears off his chains, and rushes away to find and rescue his lady-love.

Act fifth opened with a stormy scene between Zara and Don Pedro. He wishes her to go into a convent, but she won't hear of it; and, after a touching appeal, is about to faint, when Roderigo dashes in and demands her hand. Don Pedro refuses, because he is not rich. They shout and gesticulate tremendously, but cannot agree, and Roderigo is about to bear away the exhausted Zara, when the timid servant enters with a letter and a bag from Hagar, who has mysteriously disappeared. The latter informs the party that she bequeaths untold wealth to the young pair, and an awful doom to Don Pedro, if he doesn't make them happy. The bag is opened, and several quarts of tin money shower down upon the stage, till it is quite glorified with the glitter. This entirely softens the "stern sire": he consents without a murmur, all join in a joyful chorus, and the curtain falls upon the lovers kneeling to receive Don Pedro's blessing in attitudes of the most romantic grace.

Tumultuous applause followed, but received an unexpected check; for the cot-bed, on which the "dress-circle" was built, suddenly shut up, and extinguished the enthusiastic audience. Roderigo and Don Pedro flew to the rescue, and all were taken out unhurt, though many were speechless with laughter. The excitement had hardly subsided, when Hannah appeared, with "Mrs. March's compliments, and would the ladies walk down to supper."

This was a surprise, even to the actors; and, when they saw the table, they looked at one another in rapturous amazement. It was like Marmee to get up a little treat for them; but anything so fine as this was unheard-of since the departed days of plenty. There was ice-cream,—actually two dishes of it, pink and white,—and cake and fruit and distracting French bonbons, and, in the middle of the table, four great bouquets of hot-house flowers!

It quite took their breath away; and they stared first at the table and then at their mother, who looked as if she enjoyed it immensely.

"Is it fairies?" asked Amy,

"It's Santa Claus," said Beth.

"Mother did it"; and Meg smiled her sweetest, in spite of her gray beard and white eyebrows.

"Aunt March had a good fit, and sent the supper," cried Jo, with a sudden inspiration.

"All wrong. Old Mr. Laurence sent it," replied Mrs. March.

"The Laurence boy's grandfather! What in the world put such a thing into his head? We don't know him!" exclaimed Meg.

"Hannah told one of his servants about your breakfast party. He is an odd old gentleman, but that pleased him. He knew my father, years ago; and he sent me a polite note this afternoon, saying he hoped I would allow him to express his friendly feeling toward my children by sending them a few trifles in honor of the day. I could not refuse; and so you have a little feast at night to make up for the bread-and-milk breakfast."

"That boy put it into his head, I know he did! He's a capital fellow, and I wish we could get acquainted. He looks as if he'd like to know us; but he's bashful, and Meg is so prim she won't let me speak to him when we pass," said Jo, as the plates went round, and the ice began to melt out of sight, with "Ohs!" and "Ahs!" of satisfaction.

"You mean the people who live in the big house next door, don't you?" asked one of the girls. "My mother knows old Mr. Laurence; but says he's very proud, and doesn't like to mix with his neighbors. He keeps his grandson shut up, when he isn't riding or walking with his tutor, and makes him study very hard. We invited him to our party, but he didn't come. Mother says he's very nice, though he never speaks to us girls."

"Our cat ran away once, and he brought her back, and we talked over the fence, and were getting on capitally,—all about cricket, and so on,—when he saw Meg coming, and walked off. I mean to know him some day; for he needs fun, I'm sure he does," said Jo decidedly.

"I like his manners, and he looks like a little gentleman; so I've no objection to your knowing him, if a proper opportunity comes. He brought the flowers himself; and I should have asked him in, if I had been sure what was going on upstairs. He looked so wistful as he went away, hearing the frolic, and evidently having none of his own."

"It's a mercy you didn't, mother!" laughed Jo, looking at her boots. "But we'll have another play, some time, that he *can* see. Perhaps he'll help act; wouldn't that be jolly?"

"I never had such a fine bouquet before! How pretty it is!" And Meg examined her flowers with great interest.

"They *are* lovely! But Beth's roses are sweeter to me," said Mrs. March, smelling the half-dead posy in her belt.

Beth nestled up to her, and whispered softly, "I wish I could send my bunch to father. I'm afraid he isn't having such a merry Christmas as we are."

III.

## THE LAURENCE BOY.

"JO! JO! where are you?" cried Meg, at the foot of the garret stairs.

"Here!" answered a husky voice from above; and, running up, Meg found her sister eating apples and crying over the "Heir of Redclyffe," wrapped up in a comforter on an old three-legged sofa by the sunny window. This was Jo's favorite refuge; and here she loved to retire with half a dozen russets and a nice book, to enjoy the quiet and the society of a pet rat who lived near by, and didn't mind her a particle. As Meg appeared, Scrabble whisked into his hole. Jo shook the tears off her cheeks, and waited to hear the news.

"Such fun! only see! a regular note of invitation from Mrs. Gardiner for to-morrow night!" cried Meg, waving the precious paper, and then proceeding to read it, with girlish delight.

"'Mrs. Gardiner would be happy to see Miss March and Miss Josephine at a little dance on New-Year's Eve.' Marmee is willing we should go; now what *shall* we wear?"

"What's the use of asking that, when you know we shall wear our poplins, because we haven't got anything else?" answered Jo, with her mouth full.

"If I only had a silk!" sighed Meg. "Mother says I may when I'm eighteen, perhaps; but two years is an everlasting time to wait."

"I'm sure our pops look like silk, and they are nice enough for us. Yours is as good as new, but I forgot the burn and the tear in mine. Whatever shall I do? the burn shows badly, and I can't take any out."

"You must sit still all you can, and keep your back out of sight; the front is all right. I shall have a new ribbon for my hair, and Marmee will lend me her little pearl pin, and my new slippers are lovely, and my gloves will do, though they aren't as nice as I'd like."

"Mine are spoilt with lemonade, and I can't get any new ones, so I shall have to go without," said Jo, who never troubled herself much about dress.

"You *must* have gloves, or I won't go," cried Meg decidedly. "Gloves are more important than anything else; you can't dance without them, and if you don't I should be *so* mortified."

"Then I'll stay still. I don't care much for company dancing; it's no fun to go sailing round; I like to fly about and cut capers."

"You can't ask mother for new ones, they are so expensive, and you are so careless. She said, when you spoilt the others, that she shouldn't get you any more this winter. Can't you make them do?" asked Meg anxiously.

"I can hold them crumpled up in my hand, so no one will know how stained they are; that's all I can do. No! I'll tell you how we can manage—each wear one good one and carry a bad one; don't you see?"

"Your hands are bigger than mine, and you will stretch my glove dreadfully," began Meg, whose gloves were a tender point with her.

"Then I'll go without. I don't care what people say!" cried Jo, taking up her book.

"You may have it, you may! only don't stain it, and do behave nicely. Don't put your hands behind you, or stare, or say 'Christopher Columbus!' will you?"

"Don't worry about me; I'll be as prim as I can, and not get into any scrapes, if I can help it. Now go and answer your note, and let me finish this splendid story."

So Meg went away to "accept with thanks," look over her dress, and sing blithely as she did up her one real lace frill; while Jo finished her story, her four apples, and had a game of romps with Scrabble.

On New-Year's Eve the parlor was deserted, for the two younger girls played dressing-maids, and the two elder were absorbed in the all-important business of "getting ready for the party." Simple as the toilets were, there was a great deal of running up and down, laughing and talking, and at one time a strong smell of burnt hair pervaded the house. Meg wanted a few curls about her face, and Jo undertook to pinch the papered locks with a pair of hot tongs.

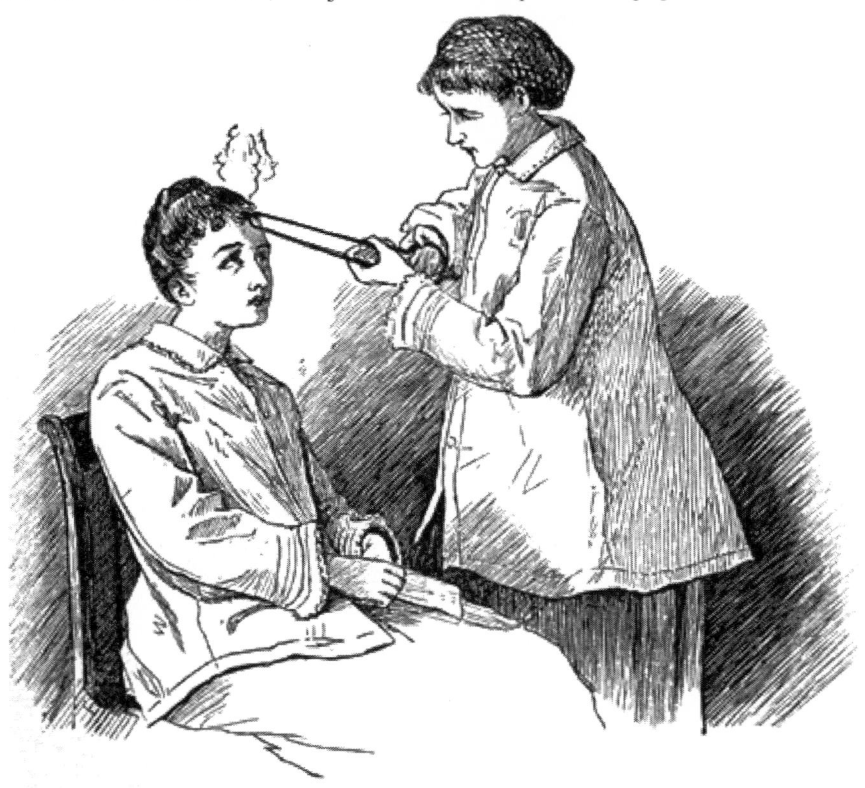

"Ought they to smoke like that?" asked Beth, from her perch on the bed.

"It's the dampness drying," replied Jo.

"What a queer smell! it's like burnt feathers," observed Amy, smoothing her own pretty curls with a superior air.

"There, now I'll take off the papers and you'll see a cloud of little ringlets," said Jo, putting down the tongs.

She did take off the papers, but no cloud of ringlets appeared, for the hair came with the papers, and the horrified hair-dresser laid a row of little scorched bundles on the bureau before her victim.

"Oh, oh, oh! what *have* you done? I'm spoilt! I can't go! My hair, oh, my hair!" wailed Meg, looking with despair at the uneven frizzle on her forehead.

"Just my luck! you shouldn't have asked me to do it; I always spoil everything. I'm so sorry, but the tongs were too hot, and so I've made a mess," groaned poor Jo, regarding the black pancakes with tears of regret.

"It isn't spoilt; just frizzle it, and tie your ribbon so the ends come on your forehead a bit, and it will look like the last fashion. I've seen many girls do it so," said Amy consolingly.

"Serves me right for trying to be fine. I wish I'd let my hair alone," cried Meg petulantly.

"So do I, it was so smooth and pretty. But it will soon grow out again," said Beth, coming to kiss and comfort the shorn sheep.

After various lesser mishaps, Meg was finished at last, and by the united exertions of the family Jo's hair was got up and her dress on. They looked very well in their simple suits,—Meg in silvery drab, with a blue velvet snood, lace frills, and the pearl pin; Jo in maroon, with a stiff, gentlemanly linen collar, and a white chrysanthemum or two for her only ornament. Each put on one nice light glove, and carried one soiled one, and all pronounced the effect "quite easy and fine." Meg's high-heeled slippers were very tight, and hurt her, though she would not own it, and Jo's nineteen hair-pins all seemed stuck straight into her head, which was not exactly comfortable; but, dear me, let us be elegant or die!

"Have a good time, dearies!" said Mrs. March, as the sisters went daintily down the walk. "Don't eat much supper, and come away at eleven, when I send Hannah for you." As the gate clashed behind them, a voice cried from a window,—

"Girls, girls! *have* you both got nice pocket-handkerchiefs?"

"Yes, yes, spandy nice, and Meg has cologne on hers," cried Jo, adding, with a laugh, as they went on, "I do believe Marmee would ask that if we were all running away from an earthquake."

"It is one of her aristocratic tastes, and quite proper, for a real lady is always known by neat boots, gloves, and handkerchief," replied Meg, who had a good many little "aristocratic tastes" of her own.

"Now don't forget to keep the bad breadth out of sight, Jo. Is my sash right? and does my hair look *very* bad?" said Meg, as she turned from the glass in Mrs. Gardiner's dressing-room, after a prolonged prink.

"I know I shall forget. If you see me doing anything wrong, just remind me by a wink, will you?" returned Jo, giving her collar a twitch and her head a hasty brush.

"No, winking isn't lady-like; I'll lift my eyebrows if anything is wrong, and nod if you are all right. Now hold your shoulders straight, and take short steps, and don't shake hands if you are introduced to any one: it isn't the thing."

"How *do* you learn all the proper ways? I never can. Isn't that music gay?"

Down they went, feeling a trifle timid, for they seldom went to parties, and, informal as this little gathering was, it was an event to them. Mrs. Gardiner, a stately old lady, greeted them kindly, and handed them over to the eldest of her six daughters. Meg knew Sallie, and was at her ease very soon; but Jo, who didn't care much for girls or girlish gossip, stood about, with her back carefully against the wall, and felt as much out of place as a colt in a flower-garden. Half a dozen jovial lads were talking about skates in another part of the room, and she longed to go and join them, for skating was one of the joys of her life. She telegraphed her wish to Meg, but the eyebrows went up so alarmingly that she dared not stir. No one came to talk to her, and one by one the group near her dwindled away, till she was left alone. She could not roam about and amuse herself, for the burnt breadth would show, so she stared at people rather forlornly till the dancing began. Meg was asked at once, and the tight slippers tripped about so briskly that none would have guessed the pain their wearer suffered smilingly. Jo saw a big red-headed youth approaching her corner, and fearing he meant to engage her, she slipped into a curtained recess, intending to peep and enjoy herself in peace.

Unfortunately, another bashful person had chosen the same refuge; for, as the curtain fell behind her, she found herself face to face with the "Laurence boy."

"Dear me, I didn't know any one was here!" stammered Jo, preparing to back out as speedily as she had bounced in.

But the boy laughed, and said pleasantly, though he looked a little startled,—

"Don't mind me; stay, if you like."

"Sha'n't I disturb you?"

"Not a bit; I only came here because I don't know many people, and felt rather strange at first, you know."

"So did I. Don't go away, please, unless you'd rather."

The boy sat down again and looked at his pumps, till Jo said, trying to be polite and easy,—

"I think I've had the pleasure of seeing you before; you live near us, don't you?"

"Next door"; and he looked up and laughed outright, for Jo's prim manner was rather funny when he remembered how they had chatted about cricket when he brought the cat home.

That put Jo at her ease; and she laughed too, as she said, in her heartiest way,—

"We did have such a good time over your nice Christmas present."

"Grandpa sent it."

"But you put it into his head, didn't you, now?"

"How is your cat, Miss March?" asked the boy, trying to look sober, while his black eyes shone with fun.

"Nicely, thank you, Mr. Laurence; but I am not Miss March, I'm only Jo," returned the young lady.

"I'm not Mr. Laurence, I'm only Laurie."

"Laurie Laurence,—what an odd name!"

"My first name is Theodore, but I don't like it, for the fellows called me Dora, so I made them say Laurie instead."

"I hate my name, too—so sentimental! I wish every one would say Jo, instead of Josephine. How did you make the boys stop calling you Dora?"

"I thrashed 'em."

"I can't thrash Aunt March, so I suppose I shall have to bear it"; and Jo resigned herself with a sigh.

"Don't you like to dance, Miss Jo?" asked Laurie, looking as if he thought the name suited her.

"I like it well enough if there is plenty of room, and every one is lively. In a place like this I'm sure to upset something, tread on people's toes, or do something dreadful, so I keep out of mischief, and let Meg sail about. Don't you dance?"

"Sometimes; you see I've been abroad a good many years, and haven't been into company enough yet to know how you do things here."

"Abroad!" cried Jo. "Oh, tell me about it! I love dearly to hear people describe their travels."

Laurie didn't seem to know where to begin; but Jo's eager questions soon set him going, and he told her how he had been at school in Vevay, where the boys never wore hats, and had a fleet of boats on the lake, and for holiday fun went walking trips about Switzerland with their teachers.

"Don't I wish I'd been there!" cried Jo. "Did you go to Paris?"

"We spent last winter there."

"Can you talk French?"

"We were not allowed to speak any thing else at Vevay."

"Do say some! I can read it, but can't pronounce."

"Quel nom a cette jeune demoiselle en les pantoufles jolis?" said Laurie good-naturedly.

"How nicely you do it! Let me see,—you said, 'Who is the young lady in the pretty slippers,' didn't you?"

"Oui, mademoiselle."

"It's my sister Margaret, and you knew it was! Do you think she is pretty?"

"Yes; she makes me think of the German girls, she looks so fresh and quiet, and dances like a lady."

Jo quite glowed with pleasure at this boyish praise of her sister, and stored it up to repeat to Meg. Both peeped and criticised and chatted, till they felt like old acquaintances. Laurie's bashfulness soon wore off; for Jo's gentlemanly demeanor amused and set him at his ease, and Jo was her merry self again, because her dress was forgotten, and nobody lifted their eyebrows at her. She liked the "Laurence boy" better than ever, and took several good looks at him, so that she might describe him to the girls; for they had no brothers, very few male cousins, and boys were almost unknown creatures to them.

"Curly black hair; brown skin; big, black eyes; handsome nose; fine teeth; small hands and feet; taller than I am; very polite, for a boy, and altogether jolly. Wonder how old he is?"

It was on the tip of Jo's tongue to ask; but she checked herself in time, and, with unusual tact, tried to find out in a roundabout way.

"I suppose you are going to college soon? I see you pegging away at your books,—no, I mean studying hard"; and Jo blushed at the dreadful "pegging" which had escaped her.

Laurie smiled, but didn't seem shocked, and answered, with a shrug,—

"Not for a year or two; I won't go before seventeen, anyway."

"Aren't you but fifteen?" asked Jo, looking at the tall lad, whom she had imagined seventeen already.

"Sixteen, next month."

"How I wish I was going to college! You don't look as if you liked it."

"I hate it! Nothing but grinding or skylarking. And I don't like the way fellows do either, in this country."

"What do you like?"

"To live in Italy, and to enjoy myself in my own way."

Jo wanted very much to ask what his own way was; but his black brows looked rather threatening as he knit them; so she changed the subject by saying, as her foot kept time, "That's a splendid polka! Why don't you go and try it?"

"If you will come too," he answered, with a gallant little bow.

"I can't; for I told Meg I wouldn't, because—" There Jo stopped, and looked undecided whether to tell or to laugh.

"Because what?" asked Laurie curiously.

"You won't tell?"

"Never!"

"Well, I have a bad trick of standing before the fire, and so I burn my frocks, and I scorched this one; and, though it's nicely mended, it shows, and Meg told me to keep still, so no one would see it. You may laugh, if you want to; it is funny, I know."

But Laurie didn't laugh; he only looked down a minute, and the expression of his face puzzled Jo, when he said very gently,—

"Never mind that; I'll tell you how we can manage: there's a long hall out there, and we can dance grandly, and no one will see us. Please come?"

Jo thanked him, and gladly went, wishing she had two neat gloves, when she saw the nice, pearl-colored ones her partner wore. The hall was empty, and they had a grand polka; for Laurie danced well, and taught her the German step, which delighted Jo, being full of swing and spring. When the music stopped, they sat down on the stairs to get their breath; and Laurie was in the midst of an account of a students' festival at Heidelberg, when Meg appeared in search of her sister. She beckoned, and Jo reluctantly followed her into a side-room, where she found her on a sofa, holding her foot, and looking pale.

"I've sprained my ankle. That stupid high heel turned, and gave me a sad wrench. It aches so, I can hardly stand, and I don't know how I'm ever going to get home," she said, rocking to and fro in pain.

"I knew you'd hurt your feet with those silly shoes. I'm sorry. But I don't see what you can do, except get a carriage, or stay here all night," answered Jo, softly rubbing the poor ankle as she spoke.

"I can't have a carriage, without its costing ever so much. I dare say I can't get one at all; for most people come in their own, and it's a long way to the stable, and no one to send."

"I'll go."

"No, indeed! It's past nine, and dark as Egypt. I can't stop here, for the house is full. Sallie has some girls staying with her. I'll rest till Hannah comes, and then do the best I can."

"I'll ask Laurie; he will go," said Jo, looking relieved as the idea occurred to her.

"Mercy, no! Don't ask or tell any one. Get me my rubbers, and put these slippers with our things. I can't dance any more; but as soon as supper is over, watch for Hannah, and tell me the minute she comes."

"They are going out to supper now. I'll stay with you; I'd rather."

"No, dear, run along, and bring me some coffee. I'm so tired, I can't stir!"

So Meg reclined, with rubbers well hidden, and Jo went blundering away to the dining-room, which she found after going into a china-closet, and opening the door of a room where old Mr. Gardiner was taking a little private refreshment. Making a dart at the table, she secured the coffee, which she immediately spilt, thereby making the front of her dress as bad as the back.

"Oh, dear, what a blunderbuss I am!" exclaimed Jo, finishing Meg's glove by scrubbing her gown with it.

"Can I help you?" said a friendly voice; and there was Laurie, with a full cup in one hand and a plate of ice in the other.

"I was trying to get something for Meg, who is very tired, and some one shook me; and here I am, in a nice state," answered Jo, glancing dismally from the stained skirt to the coffee-colored glove.

"Too bad! I was looking for some one to give this to. May I take it to your sister?"

"Oh, thank you! I'll show you where she is. I don't offer to take it myself, for I should only get into another scrape if I did."

Jo led the way; and, as if used to waiting on ladies, Laurie drew up a little table, brought a second instalment of coffee and ice for Jo, and was so obliging that even particular Meg pronounced him a "nice boy." They had a merry time over the bonbons and mottoes, and were in the midst of a quiet game of "Buzz," with two or three other young people who had strayed in, when Hannah appeared. Meg forgot her foot, and rose so quickly that she was forced to catch hold of Jo, with an exclamation of pain.

"Hush! Don't say anything," she whispered, adding aloud, "It's nothing. I turned my foot a little, that's all"; and limped up-stairs to put her things on.

Hannah scolded, Meg cried, and Jo was at her wits' end, till she decided to take things into her own hands. Slipping out, she ran down, and, finding a servant, asked if he could get her a carriage. It happened to be a hired waiter, who knew nothing about the neighborhood; and Jo was looking round for help, when Laurie, who had heard what she said, came up, and offered his grandfather's carriage, which had just come for him, he said.

"It's so early! You can't mean to go yet?" began Jo, looking relieved, but hesitating to accept the offer.

"I always go early,—I do, truly! Please let me take you home? It's all on my way, you know, and it rains, they say."

That settled it; and, telling him of Meg's mishap, Jo gratefully accepted, and rushed up to bring down the rest of the party. Hannah hated rain as much as a cat does; so she made no trouble, and they rolled away in the luxurious close carriage, feeling very festive and elegant. Laurie went on the box, so Meg could keep her foot up, and the girls talked over their party in freedom.

"I had a capital time. Did you?" asked Jo, rumpling up her hair, and making herself comfortable.

"Yes, till I hurt myself. Sallie's friend, Annie Moffat, took a fancy to me, and asked me to come and spend a week with her, when Sallie does. She is going in the spring, when the opera comes; and it will be perfectly splendid, if mother only lets me go," answered Meg, cheering up at the thought.

"I saw you dancing with the red-headed man I ran away from. Was he nice?"

"Oh, very! His hair is auburn, not red; and he was very polite, and I had a delicious redowa with him."

"He looked like a grasshopper in a fit, when he did the new step. Laurie and I couldn't help laughing. Did you hear us?"

"No; but it was very rude. What *were* you about all that time, hidden away there?"

Jo told her adventures, and, by the time she had finished, they were at home. With many thanks, they said "Good night," and crept in, hoping to disturb no one; but the instant their door creaked, two little night-caps bobbed up, and two sleepy but eager voices cried out,—

"Tell about the party! tell about the party!"

With what Meg called "a great want of manners," Jo had saved some bonbons for the little girls; and they soon subsided, after hearing the most thrilling events of the evening.

"I declare, it really seems like being a fine young lady, to come home from the party in a carriage, and sit in my dressing-gown, with a maid to wait on me," said Meg, as Jo bound up her foot with arnica, and brushed her hair.

"I don't believe fine young ladies enjoy themselves a bit more than we do, in spite of our burnt hair, old gowns, one glove apiece, and tight slippers that sprain our ankles when we are silly enough to wear them." And I think Jo was quite right.

IV.

## BURDENS.

"OH dear, how hard it does seem to take up our packs and go on," sighed Meg, the morning after the party; for, now the holidays were over, the week of merry-making did not fit her for going on easily with the task she never liked.

"I wish it was Christmas or New-Year all the time; wouldn't it be fun?" answered Jo, yawning dismally.

"We shouldn't enjoy ourselves half so much as we do now. But it does seem so nice to have little suppers and bouquets, and go to parties, and drive home, and read and rest, and not work. It's like other people, you know, and I always envy girls who do such things; I'm so fond of luxury," said Meg, trying to decide which of two shabby gowns was the least shabby.

"Well, we can't have it, so don't let us grumble, but shoulder our bundles and trudge along as cheerfully as Marmee does. I'm sure Aunt March is a regular Old Man of the Sea to me, but I suppose when I've learned to carry her without complaining, she will tumble off, or get so light that I sha'n't mind her."

This idea tickled Jo's fancy, and put her in good spirits; but Meg didn't brighten, for her burden, consisting of four spoilt children, seemed heavier than ever. She hadn't heart enough even to make herself pretty, as usual, by putting on a blue neck-ribbon, and dressing her hair in the most becoming way.

"Where's the use of looking nice, when no one sees me but those cross midgets, and no one cares whether I'm pretty or not?" she muttered, shutting her drawer with a jerk. "I shall have to toil and moil all my days, with only little bits of fun now and then, and get old and ugly and sour, because I'm poor, and can't enjoy my life as other girls do. It's a shame!"

So Meg went down, wearing an injured look, and wasn't at all agreeable at breakfast-time. Every one seemed rather out of sorts, and inclined to croak. Beth had a headache, and lay on the sofa, trying to comfort herself with the cat and three kittens; Amy was fretting because her lessons were not learned, and she couldn't find her rubbers; Jo *would* whistle and make a great racket getting ready; Mrs. March was very busy trying to finish a letter, which must go at once; and Hannah had the grumps, for being up late didn't suit her.

"There never *was* such a cross family!" cried Jo, losing her temper when she had upset an inkstand, broken both boot-lacings, and sat down upon her hat.

"You're the crossest person in it!" returned Amy, washing out the sum, that was all wrong, with the tears that had fallen on her slate.

"Beth, if you don't keep these horrid cats down cellar I'll have them drowned," exclaimed Meg angrily, as she tried to get rid of the kitten, which had scrambled up her back, and stuck like a burr just out of reach.

Jo laughed, Meg scolded, Beth implored, and Amy wailed, because she couldn't remember how much nine times twelve was.

"Girls, girls, do be quiet one minute! I *must* get this off by the early mail, and you drive me distracted with your worry," cried Mrs. March, crossing out the third spoilt sentence in her letter.

There was a momentary lull, broken by Hannah, who stalked in, laid two hot turn-overs on the table, and stalked out again. These turn-overs were an institution; and the girls called them "muffs," for they had no others, and found the hot pies very comforting to their hands on cold mornings. Hannah never forgot to make them, no matter how busy or grumpy she might be, for the walk was long and bleak; the poor things got no other lunch, and were seldom home before two.

"Cuddle your cats, and get over your headache, Bethy. Good-by, Marmee; we are a set of rascals this morning, but we'll come home regular angels. Now then, Meg!" and Jo tramped away, feeling that the pilgrims were not setting out as they ought to do.

They always looked back before turning the corner, for their mother was always at the window, to nod and smile, and wave her hand to them. Somehow it seemed as if they couldn't have got through the day without that; for, whatever their mood might be, the last glimpse of that motherly face was sure to affect them like sunshine.

"If Marmee shook her fist instead of kissing her hand to us, it would serve us right, for more ungrateful wretches than we are were never seen," cried Jo, taking a remorseful satisfaction in the snowy walk and bitter wind.

"Don't use such dreadful expressions," said Meg, from the depths of the vail in which she had shrouded herself like a nun sick of the world.

"I like good strong words, that mean something," replied Jo, catching her hat as it took a leap off her head, preparatory to flying away altogether.

"Call yourself any names you like; but *I* am neither a rascal nor a wretch, and I don't choose to be called so."

"You're a blighted being, and decidedly cross to-day because you can't sit in the lap of luxury all the time. Poor dear, just wait till I make my fortune, and you shall revel in carriages and ice-cream and high-heeled slippers and posies and red-headed boys to dance with."

"How ridiculous you are, Jo!" but Meg laughed at the nonsense, and felt better in spite of herself.

"Lucky for you I am; for if I put on crushed airs, and tried to be dismal, as you do, we should be in a nice state. Thank goodness, I can always find something funny to keep me up. Don't croak any more, but come home jolly, there's a dear."

Jo gave her sister an encouraging pat on the shoulder as they parted for the day, each going a different way, each hugging her little warm turn-over, and each trying to be cheerful in spite of wintry weather, hard work, and the unsatisfied desires of pleasure-loving youth.

When Mr. March lost his property in trying to help an unfortunate friend, the two oldest girls begged to be allowed to do something toward their own support, at least. Believing that they could not begin too early to cultivate energy, industry, and independence, their parents consented, and both fell to work with the hearty good-will which in spite of all obstacles, is sure to succeed at last. Margaret found a place as nursery governess, and felt rich with her small salary. As she said, she *was* "fond of luxury," and her chief trouble was poverty. She found it harder to bear than the others, because she could remember a time when home was beautiful, life full of ease and pleasure, and want of any kind unknown. She tried not to be envious or discontented, but it was very natural that the young girl should long for pretty things, gay friends, accomplishments, and a happy life. At the Kings' she daily saw all she wanted, for the children's older sisters were just out, and Meg caught frequent glimpses of dainty ball-dresses and bouquets, heard lively gossip about theatres, concerts, sleighing parties, and merry-makings of all kinds, and saw money lavished on trifles which would have been so precious to her. Poor Meg seldom complained, but a sense of injustice made her feel bitter toward every one sometimes, for she had not yet learned to know how rich she was in the blessings which alone can make life happy.

Jo happened to suit Aunt March, who was lame, and needed an active person to wait upon her. The childless old lady had offered to adopt one of the girls when the troubles came, and was much offended because her offer was declined. Other friends told the Marches that they had lost all chance of being remembered in the rich old lady's will; but the unworldly Marches only said,—

"We can't give up our girls for a dozen fortunes. Rich or poor, we will keep together and be happy in one another."

The old lady wouldn't speak to them for a time, but happening to meet Jo at a friend's, something in her comical face and blunt manners struck the old lady's fancy, and she proposed to take her for a companion. This did not suit Jo at all; but she accepted the place since nothing better appeared, and, to every one's surprise, got on remarkably well with her irascible relative. There was an occasional tempest, and once Jo had marched home, declaring she couldn't bear it any longer; but Aunt March always cleared up quickly, and sent for her back again with such urgency that she could not refuse, for in her heart she rather liked the peppery old lady.

I suspect that the real attraction was a large library of fine books, which was left to dust and spiders since Uncle March died. Jo remembered the kind old gentleman, who used to let her build railroads and bridges with his big dictionaries, tell her stories about the queer pictures in his Latin books, and buy her cards of gingerbread whenever he met her in the street. The dim, dusty room, with the busts staring down from the tall book-cases, the cosy chairs, the globes, and, best of all, the wilderness of books, in which she could wander where she liked, made the library a region of bliss to her. The moment Aunt March took her nap, or was busy with company, Jo hurried to this quiet place, and, curling herself up in the easy-chair, devoured poetry, romance, history, travels, and pictures, like a regular book-worm. But, like all happiness, it did not last long; for as sure as she had just reached the heart of the story, the sweetest verse of the song, or the most perilous adventure of her traveller, a shrill voice called, "Josy-phine! Josy-phine!" and she had to leave her paradise to wind yarn, wash the poodle, or read Belsham's Essays by the hour together.

Jo's ambition was to do something very splendid; what it was she had no idea, as yet, but left it for time to tell her; and, meanwhile, found her greatest affliction in the fact that she couldn't read, run, and ride as much as she liked. A quick temper, sharp tongue, and restless spirit were always getting her into scrapes, and her life was a series of ups and downs, which were both comic and pathetic. But the training she received at Aunt March's was just what she needed; and the thought that she was doing something to support herself made her happy, in spite of the perpetual "Josy-phine!"

Beth was too bashful to go to school; it had been tried, but she suffered so much that it was given up, and she did her lessons at home, with her father. Even when he went away, and her mother was called to devote her skill and energy to Soldiers' Aid Societies, Beth went faithfully on by herself, and did the best she could. She was a housewifely little creature, and helped Hannah keep home neat and comfortable for the workers, never thinking of any reward but to be loved. Long, quiet days she spent, not lonely nor idle, for her little world was peopled with imaginary friends, and she was by nature a busy bee. There were six dolls to be taken up and dressed every morning, for Beth was a child still, and loved her pets as well as ever. Not one whole or handsome one among them; all were outcasts till Beth took them in; for, when her sisters outgrew these idols, they passed to her, because Amy would have nothing old or ugly. Beth cherished them all the more tenderly for that very reason, and set up a hospital for infirm dolls. No pins were ever stuck into their cotton vitals; no harsh words or blows were ever given them; no neglect ever saddened the heart of the most repulsive: but all were fed and clothed, nursed and caressed, with an affection which never failed. One forlorn fragment of *dollanity* had belonged to Jo; and, having led a tempestuous life, was left a wreck in the rag-bag, from which dreary poorhouse it was rescued by Beth, and taken to her refuge. Having no top to its head, she tied on a neat little cap, and, as both arms and legs were gone, she hid these deficiencies by folding it in a blanket, and devoting her best bed to this chronic invalid. If any one had known the care lavished on that dolly, I think it would have touched their hearts, even while they laughed. She brought it bits of bouquets; she read to it, took it out to breathe the air, hidden under her coat; she sung it lullabys, and never went to bed without kissing its dirty face, and whispering tenderly, "I hope you'll have a good night, my poor dear."

Beth had her troubles as well as the others; and not being an angel, but a very human little girl, she often "wept a little weep," as Jo said, because she couldn't take music lessons and have a fine piano. She loved music so dearly, tried so hard to learn, and practised away so patiently at the jingling old instrument, that it did seem as if some one (not to hint Aunt March) ought to help her. Nobody did, however, and nobody saw Beth wipe the tears off the yellow keys, that wouldn't keep in tune, when she was all alone. She sang like a little lark about her work, never was too tired to play for Marmee and the girls, and day after day said hopefully to herself, "I know I'll get my music some time, if I'm good."

There are many Beths in the world, shy and quiet, sitting in corners till needed, and living for others so cheerfully that no one sees the sacrifices till the little cricket on the hearth stops chirping, and the sweet, sunshiny presence vanishes, leaving silence and shadow behind.

If anybody had asked Amy what the greatest trial of her life was, she would have answered at once, "My nose." When she was a baby, Jo had accidentally dropped her into the coal-hod, and Amy insisted that the fall had ruined her nose forever. It was not big, nor red, like poor "Petrea's"; it was only rather flat, and all the pinching in the world could not give it an aristocratic point. No one minded it but herself, and it was doing its best to grow, but Amy felt deeply the want of a Grecian nose, and drew whole sheets of handsome ones to console herself.

"Little Raphael," as her sisters called her, had a decided talent for drawing, and was never so happy as when copying flowers, designing fairies, or illustrating stories with queer specimens of art. Her teachers complained that, instead of doing her sums, she covered her slate with animals; the blank pages of her atlas were used to copy maps on; and caricatures of the most ludicrous description came fluttering out of all her books at unlucky moments. She got through her lessons as well as she could, and managed to escape reprimands by being a model of deportment. She was a great favorite with her mates, being good-tempered, and possessing the happy art of pleasing without effort. Her little airs and graces were much admired, so were her accomplishments; for beside her drawing, she could play twelve tunes, crochet, and read French without mispronouncing more than two thirds of the words. She had a plaintive way of saying, "When papa was rich we did so-and-so," which was very touching; and her long words were considered "perfectly elegant" by the girls.

Amy was in a fair way to be spoilt; for every one petted her, and her small vanities and selfishnesses were growing nicely. One thing, however, rather quenched the vanities; she had to wear her cousin's clothes. Now Florence's mamma hadn't a particle of taste, and Amy suffered deeply at having to wear a red instead of a blue bonnet, unbecoming gowns, and fussy aprons that did not fit. Everything was good, well made, and little worn; but Amy's artistic eyes were much afflicted, especially this winter, when her school dress was a dull purple, with yellow dots, and no trimming.

"My only comfort," she said to Meg, with tears in her eyes, "is, that mother don't take tucks in my dresses whenever I'm naughty, as Maria Parks' mother does. My dear, it's really dreadful; for sometimes she is so bad, her frock is up to her knees, and she can't come to school. When I think of this *deggerredation*, I feel that I can bear even my flat nose and purple gown, with yellow sky-rockets on it."

Meg was Amy's confidant and monitor, and, by some strange attraction of opposites, Jo was gentle Beth's. To Jo alone did the shy child tell her thoughts; and over her big, harum-scarum sister, Beth unconsciously exercised more influence than any one in the family. The two older girls were a great deal to one another, but each took one of the younger into her keeping, and watched over her in her own way; "playing mother" they called it, and put their sisters in the places of discarded dolls, with the maternal instinct of little women.

"Has anybody got anything to tell? It's been such a dismal day I'm really dying for some amusement," said Meg, as they sat sewing together that evening.

"I had a queer time with aunt to-day, and, as I got the best of it, I'll tell you about it," began Jo, who dearly loved to tell stories. "I was reading that everlasting Belsham, and droning away as I always do, for aunt soon drops off, and then I take out some nice book, and read like fury till she wakes up. I actually made myself sleepy; and, before she began to nod, I gave such a gape that she asked me what I meant by opening my mouth wide enough to take the whole book in at once.

"'I wish I could, and be done with it,' said I, trying not to be saucy.

"Then she gave me a long lecture on my sins, and told me to sit and think them over while she just 'lost' herself for a moment. She never finds herself very soon; so the minute her cap began to bob, like a top-heavy dahlia, I whipped the 'Vicar of Wakefield' out of my pocket, and read away, with one eye on him, and one on aunt. I'd just got to where they all tumbled into the water, when I forgot, and laughed out loud. Aunt woke up; and, being more good-natured after her nap, told me to read a bit, and show what frivolous work I preferred to the worthy and instructive Belsham. I did my very best, and she liked it, though she only said,—

"'I don't understand what it's all about. Go back and begin it, child.'

"Back I went, and made the Primroses as interesting as ever I could. Once I was wicked enough to stop in a thrilling place, and say meekly, 'I'm afraid it tires you, ma'am; sha'n't I stop now?'

"She caught up her knitting, which had dropped out of her hands, gave me a sharp look through her specs, and said, in her short way,—

"'Finish the chapter, and don't be impertinent, miss.'"

"Did she own she liked it?" asked Meg.

"Oh, bless you, no! but she let old Belsham rest; and, when I ran back after my gloves this afternoon, there she was, so hard at the Vicar that she didn't hear me laugh as I danced a jig in the hall, because of the good time coming. What a pleasant life she might have, if she only chose. I don't envy her much, in spite of her money, for after all rich people have about as many worries as poor ones, I think," added Jo.

"That reminds me," said Meg, "that I've got something to tell. It isn't funny, like Jo's story, but I thought about it a good deal as I came home. At the Kings to-day I found everybody in a flurry, and one of the children said that her oldest brother had done something dreadful, and papa had sent him away. I heard Mrs. King crying and Mr. King talking very loud, and Grace and Ellen turned away their faces when they passed me, so I shouldn't see how red their eyes were. I didn't ask any questions, of course; but I felt so sorry for them, and was rather glad I hadn't any wild brothers to do wicked things and disgrace the family."

"I think being disgraced in school is a great deal try*inger* than anything bad boys can do," said Amy, shaking her head, as if her experience of life had been a deep one. "Susie Perkins came to school to-day with a lovely red carnelian ring; I wanted it dreadfully, and wished I was her with all my might. Well, she drew a picture of Mr. Davis, with a monstrous nose and a hump, and the words, 'Young ladies, my eye is upon you!' coming out of his mouth in a balloon thing. We were laughing over it, when all of a sudden his eye *was* on us, and he ordered Susie to bring up her slate. She was *parry*lized with fright, but she went, and oh, what *do* you think he did? He took her by the ear, the ear! just fancy how horrid!—and led her to the recitation platform, and made her stand there half an hour, holding that slate so every one could see."

"Didn't the girls laugh at the picture?" asked Jo, who relished the scrape.

"Laugh? Not one! They sat as still as mice; and Susie cried quarts, I know she did. I didn't envy her then; for I felt that millions of carnelian rings wouldn't have made me happy, after that. I never, never should have got over such a agonizing mortification." And Amy went on with her work, in the proud consciousness of virtue, and the successful utterance of two long words in a breath.

"I saw something that I liked this morning, and I meant to tell it at dinner, but I forgot," said Beth, putting Jo's topsy-turvy basket in order as she talked. "When I went to get some oysters for Hannah, Mr. Laurence was in the fish-shop; but he didn't see me, for I kept behind a barrel, and he was busy with Mr. Cutter, the fish-man. A poor woman came in, with a pail and a mop, and asked Mr. Cutter if he would let her do some scrubbing for a bit of fish, because she hadn't any dinner for her children, and had been disappointed of a day's work. Mr. Cutter was in a hurry, and said 'No,' rather crossly; so she was going away, looking hungry and sorry, when Mr. Laurence hooked up a big fish with the crooked end of his cane, and held it out to her. She was so glad and surprised, she took it right in her arms, and thanked him over and over. He told her to 'go along and cook it,' and she hurried off, so happy! Wasn't it good of him? Oh, she did look so funny, hugging the big, slippery fish, and hoping Mr. Laurence's bed in heaven would be 'aisy.'"

When they had laughed at Beth's story, they asked their mother for one; and, after a moment's thought, she said soberly,—

"As I sat cutting out blue flannel jackets to-day, at the rooms, I felt very anxious about father, and thought how lonely and helpless we should be, if anything happened to him. It was not a wise thing to do; but I kept on worrying, till an old man came in, with an order for some clothes. He sat down near me, and I began to talk to him; for he looked poor and tired and anxious.

"'Have you sons in the army?' I asked; for the note he brought was not to me.

"'Yes, ma'am. I had four, but two were killed, one is a prisoner, and I'm going to the other, who is very sick in a Washington hospital,' he answered quietly.

"'You have done a great deal for your country, sir,' I said, feeling respect now, instead of pity.

"'Not a mite more than I ought, ma'am. I'd go myself, if I was any use; as I ain't, I give my boys, and give 'em free.'

"He spoke so cheerfully, looked so sincere, and seemed so glad to give his all, that I was ashamed of myself. I'd given one man, and thought it too much, while he gave four, without grudging them. I had all my girls to comfort me at home; and his last son was waiting, miles away, to say 'good by' to him, perhaps! I felt so rich, so happy, thinking of my blessings, that I made him a nice bundle, gave him some money, and thanked him heartily for the lesson he had taught me."

"Tell another story, mother,— one with a moral to it, like this. I like to think about them afterwards, if they are real, and not too preachy," said Jo, after a minute's silence.

Mrs. March smiled, and began at once; for she had told stories to this little audience for many years, and knew how to please them.

"Once upon a time, there were four girls, who had enough to eat and drink and wear, a good many comforts and pleasures, kind friends and parents, who loved them dearly, and yet they were not contented." (Here the listeners stole sly looks at one another, and began to sew diligently.) "These girls were anxious to be good, and made many excellent resolutions; but they did not keep them very well, and were constantly saying, 'If we only had this,' or 'If we could only do that,' quite forgetting how much they already had, and how many pleasant things they actually could do. So they asked an old woman what spell they could use to make them happy, and she said, 'When you feel discontented, think over your blessings, and be grateful.'" (Here Jo looked up quickly, as if about to speak, but changed her mind, seeing that the story was not done yet.)

"Being sensible girls, they decided to try her advice, and soon were surprised to see how well off they were. One discovered that money couldn't keep shame and sorrow out of rich people's houses; another that, though she was poor, she was a great deal happier, with her youth, health, and good spirits, than a certain fretful, feeble old lady, who couldn't enjoy her comforts; a third that, disagreeable as it was to help get dinner, it was harder still to have to go begging for it; and the fourth, that even carnelian rings were not so valuable as good behavior. So they agreed to stop complaining, to enjoy the blessings already possessed, and try to deserve them, lest they should be taken away entirely, instead of increased; and I believe they were never disappointed, or sorry that they took the old woman's advice."

"Now, Marmee, that is very cunning of you to turn our own stories against us, and give us a sermon instead of a romance!" cried Meg.

"I like that kind of sermon. It's the sort father used to tell us," said Beth thoughtfully, putting the needles straight on Jo's cushion.

"I don't complain near as much as the others do, and I shall be more careful than ever now; for I've had warning from Susie's downfall," said Amy morally.

"We needed that lesson, and we won't forget it. If we do, you just say to us, as old Chloe did in 'Uncle Tom,' 'Tink ob yer marcies, chillen! tink ob yer marcies!'" added Jo, who could not, for the life of her, help getting a morsel of fun out of the little sermon, though she took it to heart as much as any of them.

V.

# BEING NEIGHBORLY.

"WHAT in the world are you going to do now, Jo?" asked Meg, one snowy afternoon, as her sister came tramping through the hall, in rubber boots, old sack and hood, with a broom in one hand and a shovel in the other.

"Going out for exercise," answered Jo, with a mischievous twinkle in her eyes.

"I should think two long walks this morning would have been enough! It's cold and dull out; and I advise you to stay, warm and dry, by the fire, as I do," said Meg, with a shiver.

"Never take advice! Can't keep still all day, and, not being a pussycat, I don't like to doze by the fire. I like adventures, and I'm going to find some."

Meg went back to toast her feet and read "Ivanhoe"; and Jo began to dig paths with great energy. The snow was light, and with her broom she soon swept a path all round the garden, for Beth to walk in when the sun came out; and the invalid dolls needed air. Now, the garden separated the Marches' house from that of Mr. Laurence. Both stood in a suburb of the city, which was still country-like, with groves and lawns, large gardens, and quiet streets. A low hedge parted the two estates. On one side was an old, brown house, looking rather bare and shabby, robbed of the vines that in summer covered its walls, and the flowers which then surrounded it. On the other side was a stately stone mansion, plainly betokening every sort of comfort and luxury, from the big coach-house and well-kept grounds to the conservatory and the glimpses of lovely things one caught between the rich curtains. Yet it seemed a lonely, lifeless sort of house; for no children frolicked on the lawn, no motherly face ever smiled at the windows, and few people went in and out, except the old gentleman and his grandson.

To Jo's lively fancy, this fine house seemed a kind of enchanted palace, full of splendors and delights, which no one enjoyed. She had long wanted to behold these hidden glories, and to know the "Laurence boy," who looked as if he would like to be known, if he only knew how to begin. Since the party, she had been more eager than ever, and had planned many ways of making friends with him; but he had not been seen lately, and Jo began to think he had gone away, when she one day spied a brown face at an upper window, looking wistfully down into their garden, where Beth and Amy were snow-balling one another.

"That boy is suffering for society and fun," she said to herself. "His grandpa does not know what's good for him, and keeps him shut up all alone. He needs a party of jolly boys to play with, or somebody young and lively. I've a great mind to go over and tell the old gentleman so!"

The idea amused Jo, who liked to do daring things, and was always scandalizing Meg by her queer performances. The plan of "going over" was not forgotten; and when the snowy afternoon came, Jo resolved to try what could be done. She saw Mr. Laurence drive off, and then sallied out to dig her way down to the hedge, where she paused, and took a survey. All quiet,—curtains down at the lower windows; servants out of sight, and nothing human visible but a curly black head leaning on a thin hand at the upper window.

"There he is," thought Jo, "poor boy! all alone and sick this dismal day. It's a shame! I'll toss up a snow-ball, and make him look out, and then say a kind word to him."

Up went a handful of soft snow, and the head turned at once, showing a face which lost its listless look in a minute, as the big eyes brightened and the mouth began to smile. Jo nodded and laughed, and flourished her broom as she called out,—

"How do you do? Are you sick?"

Laurie opened the window, and croaked out as hoarsely as a raven,—

"Better, thank you. I've had a bad cold, and been shut up a week."

"I'm sorry. What do you amuse yourself with?"

"Nothing; it's as dull as tombs up here."

"Don't you read?"

"Not much; they won't let me."

"Can't somebody read to you?"

"Grandpa does, sometimes; but my books don't interest him, and I hate to ask Brooke all the time."

"Have some one come and see you, then."

"There isn't any one I'd like to see. Boys make such a row, and my head is weak."

"Isn't there some nice girl who'd read and amuse you? Girls are quiet, and like to play nurse."

"Don't know any."

"You know us," began Jo, then laughed, and stopped.

"So I do! Will you come, please?" cried Laurie.

"I'm not quiet and nice; but I'll come, if mother will let me. I'll go ask her. Shut that window, like a good boy, and wait till I come."

With that, Jo shouldered her broom and marched into the house, wondering what they would all say to her. Laurie was in a flutter of excitement at the idea of having company, and flew about to get ready; for, as Mrs. March said, he was "a little gentleman," and did honor to the coming guest by brushing his curly pate, putting on a fresh collar, and trying to tidy up the room, which, in spite of half a dozen servants, was anything but neat. Presently there came a loud ring, then a decided voice, asking for "Mr. Laurie," and a surprised-looking servant came running up to announce a young lady.

"All right, show her up, it's Miss Jo," said Laurie, going to the door of his little parlor to meet Jo, who appeared, looking rosy and kind and quite at her ease, with a covered dish in one hand and Beth's three kittens in the other.

"Here I am, bag and baggage," she said briskly. "Mother sent her love, and was glad if I could do anything for you. Meg wanted me to bring some of her blanc-mange; she makes it very nicely, and Beth thought her cats would be comforting. I knew you'd laugh at them, but I couldn't refuse, she was so anxious to do something."

It so happened that Beth's funny loan was just the thing; for, in laughing over the kits, Laurie forgot his bashfulness, and grew sociable at once.

"That looks too pretty to eat," he said, smiling with pleasure, as Jo uncovered the dish, and showed the blanc-mange, surrounded by a garland of green leaves, and the scarlet flowers of Amy's pet geranium.

"It isn't anything, only they all felt kindly, and wanted to show it. Tell the girl to put it away for your tea: it's so simple, you can eat it; and, being soft, it will slip down without hurting your sore throat. What a cosy room this is!"

"It might be if it was kept nice; but the maids are lazy, and I don't know how to make them mind. It worries me, though."

"I'll right it up in two minutes; for it only needs to have the hearth brushed, so,—and the things made straight on the mantel-piece so,—and the books put here, and the bottles there, and your sofa turned from the light, and the pillows plumped up a bit. Now, then, you're fixed."

And so he was; for, as she laughed and talked, Jo had whisked things into place, and given quite a different air to the room. Laurie watched her in respectful silence; and when she beckoned him to his sofa, he sat down with a sigh of satisfaction, saying gratefully,—

"How kind you are! Yes, that's what it wanted. Now please take the big chair, and let me do something to amuse my company."

"No; I came to amuse you. Shall I read aloud?" and Jo looked affectionately toward some inviting books near by.

"Thank you; I've read all those, and if you don't mind, I'd rather talk," answered Laurie.

"Not a bit; I'll talk all day if you'll only set me going. Beth says I never know when to stop."

"Is Beth the rosy one, who stays at home a good deal, and sometimes goes out with a little basket?" asked Laurie, with interest.

"Yes, that's Beth; she's my girl, and a regular good one she is, too."

"The pretty one is Meg, and the curly-haired one is Amy, I believe?"

"How did you find that out?"

Laurie colored up, but answered frankly, "Why, you see, I often hear you calling to one another, and when I'm alone up here, I can't help looking over at your house, you always seem to be having such good times. I beg your pardon for being so rude, but sometimes you forget to put down the curtain at the window where the flowers are; and when the lamps are lighted, it's like looking at a picture to see the fire, and you all round the table with your mother; her face is right opposite, and it looks so sweet behind the flowers, I can't help watching it. I haven't got any mother, you know;" and Laurie poked the fire to hide a little twitching of the lips that he could not control.

The solitary, hungry look in his eyes went straight to Jo's warm heart. She had been so simply taught that there was no nonsense in her head, and at fifteen she was as innocent and frank as any child. Laurie was sick and lonely; and, feeling how rich she was in home-love and happiness, she gladly tried to share it with him. Her face was very friendly and her sharp voice unusually gentle as she said,—

"We'll never draw that curtain any more, and I give you leave to look as much as you like. I just wish, though, instead of peeping, you'd come over and see us. Mother is so splendid, she'd do you heaps of good, and Beth would sing to you if *I* begged her to, and Amy would dance; Meg and I would make you laugh over our funny stage properties, and we'd have jolly times. Wouldn't your grandpa let you?"

"I think he would, if your mother asked him. He's very kind, though he does not look so; and he lets me do what I like, pretty much, only he's afraid I might be a bother to strangers," began Laurie, brightening more and more.

"We are not strangers, we are neighbors, and you needn't think you'd be a bother. We *want* to know you, and I've been trying to do it this ever so long. We haven't been here a great while, you know, but we have got acquainted with all our neighbors but you."

"You see grandpa lives among his books, and doesn't mind much what happens outside. Mr. Brooke, my tutor, doesn't stay here, you know, and I have no one to go about with me, so I just stop at home and get on as I can."

"That's bad. You ought to make an effort, and go visiting everywhere you are asked; then you'll have plenty of friends, and pleasant places to go to. Never mind being bashful; it won't last long if you keep going."

Laurie turned red again, but wasn't offended at being accused of bashfulness; for there was so much good-will in Jo, it was impossible not to take her blunt speeches as kindly as they were meant.

"Do you like your school?" asked the boy, changing the subject, after a little pause, during which he stared at the fire, and Jo looked about her, well pleased.

"Don't go to school; I'm a business man—girl, I mean. I go to wait on my great-aunt, and a dear, cross old soul she is, too," answered Jo.

Laurie opened his mouth to ask another question; but remembering just in time that it wasn't manners to make too many inquiries into people's affairs, he shut it again, and looked uncomfortable. Jo liked his good breeding, and didn't mind having a laugh at Aunt March, so she gave him a lively description of the fidgety old lady, her fat poodle, the parrot that talked Spanish, and the library where she revelled. Laurie enjoyed that immensely; and when she told about the prim old gentleman who came once to woo Aunt March, and, in the middle of a fine speech, how Poll had tweaked his wig off to his great dismay, the boy lay back and laughed till the tears ran down his cheeks, and a maid popped her head in to see what was the matter.

"Oh! that does me no end of good. Tell on, please," he said, taking his face out of the sofa-cushion, red and shining with merriment.

Much elated with her success, Jo did "tell on," all about their plays and plans, their hopes and fears for father, and the most interesting events of the little world in which the sisters lived. Then they got to talking about books; and to Jo's delight, she found that Laurie loved them as well as she did, and had read even more than herself.

"If you like them so much, come down and see ours. Grandpa is out, so you needn't be afraid," said Laurie, getting up.

"I'm not afraid of anything," returned Jo, with a toss of the head.

"I don't believe you are!" exclaimed the boy, looking at her with much admiration, though he privately thought she would have good reason to be a trifle afraid of the old gentleman, if she met him in some of his moods.

The atmosphere of the whole house being summer-like, Laurie led the way from room to room, letting Jo stop to examine whatever struck her fancy; and so at last they came to the library, where she clapped her hands, and pranced, as she always did when especially delighted. It was lined with books, and there were pictures and statues, and distracting little cabinets full of coins and curiosities, and sleepy-hollow chairs, and queer tables, and bronzes; and, best of all, a great open fireplace, with quaint tiles all round it.

"What richness!" sighed Jo, sinking into the depth of a velvet chair, and gazing about her with an air of intense satisfaction. "Theodore Laurence, you ought to be the happiest boy in the world," she added impressively.

"A fellow can't live on books," said Laurie, shaking his head, as he perched on a table opposite.

Before he could say more, a bell rung, and Jo flew up, exclaiming with alarm, "Mercy me! it's your grandpa!"

"Well, what if it is? You are not afraid of anything, you know," returned the boy, looking wicked.

"I think I am a little bit afraid of him, but I don't know why I should be. Marmee said I might come, and I don't think you're any the worse for it," said Jo, composing herself, though she kept her eyes on the door.

"I'm a great deal better for it, and ever so much obliged. I'm only afraid you are very tired talking to me; it was *so* pleasant, I couldn't bear to stop," said Laurie gratefully.

"The doctor to see you, sir," and the maid beckoned as she spoke.

"Would you mind if I left you for a minute? I suppose I must see him," said Laurie.

"Don't mind me. I'm as happy as a cricket here," answered Jo.

Laurie went away, and his guest amused herself in her own way. She was standing before a fine portrait of the old gentleman, when the door opened again, and, without turning, she said decidedly, "I'm sure now that I shouldn't be afraid of him, for he's got kind eyes, though his mouth is grim, and he looks as if he had a tremendous will of his own. He isn't as handsome as *my* grandfather, but I like him."

"Thank you, ma'am," said a gruff voice behind her; and there, to her great dismay, stood old Mr. Laurence.

Poor Jo blushed till she couldn't blush any redder, and her heart began to beat uncomfortably fast as she thought what she had said. For a minute a wild desire to run away possessed her; but that was cowardly, and the girls would laugh at her: so she resolved to stay, and get out of the scrape as she could. A second look showed her that the living eyes, under the bushy gray eyebrows, were kinder even than the painted ones; and there was a sly twinkle in them, which lessened her fear a good deal. The gruff voice was gruffer than ever, as the old gentleman said abruptly, after that dreadful pause, "So you're not afraid of me, hey?"

"Not much, sir."

"And you don't think me as handsome as your grandfather?"

"Not quite, sir."

"And I've got a tremendous will, have I?"

"I only said I thought so."

"But you like me, in spite of it?"

"Yes, I do, sir."

That answer pleased the old gentleman; he gave a short laugh, shook hands with her, and, putting his finger under her chin, turned up her face, examined it gravely, and let it go, saying, with a nod, "You've got your grandfather's spirit, if you haven't his face. He *was* a fine man, my dear; but, what is better, he was a brave and an honest one, and I was proud to be his friend."

"Thank you, sir;" and Jo was quite comfortable after that, for it suited her exactly.

"What have you been doing to this boy of mine, hey?" was the next question, sharply put.

"Only trying to be neighborly, sir;" and Jo told how her visit came about.

"You think he needs cheering up a bit, do you?"

"Yes, sir; he seems a little lonely, and young folks would do him good perhaps. We are only girls, but we should be glad to help if we could, for we don't forget the splendid Christmas present you sent us," said Jo eagerly.

"Tut, tut, tut! that was the boy's affair. How is the poor woman?"

"Doing nicely, sir;" and off went Jo, talking very fast, as she told all about the Hummels, in whom her mother had interested richer friends than they were.

"Just her father's way of doing good. I shall come and see your mother some fine day. Tell her so. There's the tea-bell; we have it early, on the boy's account. Come down, and go on being neighborly."

"If you'd like to have me, sir."

"Shouldn't ask you, if I didn't;" and Mr. Laurence offered her his arm with old-fashioned courtesy.

"What *would* Meg say to this?" thought Jo, as she was marched away, while her eyes danced with fun as she imagined herself telling the story at home.

"Hey! Why, what the dickens has come to the fellow?" said the old gentleman, as Laurie came running down stairs, and brought up with a start of surprise at the astonishing sight of Jo arm-in-arm with his redoubtable grandfather.

"I didn't know you'd come, sir," he began, as Jo gave him a triumphant little glance.

"That's evident, by the way you racket down stairs. Come to your tea, sir, and behave like a gentleman;" and having pulled the boy's hair by way of a caress, Mr. Laurence walked on, while Laurie went through a series of comic evolutions behind their backs, which nearly produced an explosion of laughter from Jo.

The old gentleman did not say much as he drank his four cups of tea, but he watched the young people, who soon chatted away like old friends, and the change in his grandson did not escape him. There was color, light, and life in the boy's face now, vivacity in his manner, and genuine merriment in his laugh.

"She's right; the lad *is* lonely. I'll see what these little girls can do for him," thought Mr. Laurence, as he looked and listened. He liked Jo, for her odd, blunt ways suited him; and she seemed to understand the boy almost as well as if she had been one herself.

If the Laurences had been what Jo called "prim and poky," she would not have got on at all, for such people always made her shy and awkward; but finding them free and easy, she was so herself, and made a good impression. When they rose she proposed to go, but Laurie said he had something more to show her, and took her away to the conservatory, which had been lighted for her benefit. It seemed quite fairylike to Jo, as she went up and down the walks, enjoying the blooming walls on either side, the soft light, the damp sweet air, and the wonderful vines and trees that hung above her,—while her new friend cut the finest flowers till his hands were full; then he tied them up, saying, with the happy look Jo liked to see, "Please give these to your mother, and tell her I like the medicine she sent me very much."

They found Mr. Laurence standing before the fire in the great drawing-room, but Jo's attention was entirely absorbed by a grand piano, which stood open.

"Do you play?" she asked, turning to Laurie with a respectful expression.

"Sometimes," he answered modestly.

"Please do now. I want to hear it, so I can tell Beth."

"Won't you first?"

"Don't know how; too stupid to learn, but I love music dearly."

So Laurie played, and Jo listened, with her nose luxuriously buried in heliotrope and tea-roses. Her respect and regard for the "Laurence boy" increased very much, for he played remarkably well, and didn't put on any airs. She wished Beth could hear him, but she did not say so; only praised him till he was quite abashed, and his grandfather came to the rescue. "That will do, that will do, young lady. Too many sugar-plums are not good for him. His music isn't bad, but I hope he will do as well in more important things. Going? Well, I'm much obliged to you, and I hope you'll come again. My respects to your mother. Good-night, Doctor Jo."

He shook hands kindly, but looked as if something did not please him. When they got into the hall, Jo asked Laurie if she had said anything amiss. He shook his head.

"No, it was me; he doesn't like to hear me play."

"Why not?"

"I'll tell you some day. John is going home with you, as I can't."

"No need of that; I am not a young lady, and it's only a step. Take care of yourself, won't you?"

"Yes; but you will come again, I hope?"

"If you promise to come and see us after you are well."

"I will."

"Good-night, Laurie!"

"Good-night, Jo, good-night!"

When all the afternoon's adventures had been told, the family felt inclined to go visiting in a body, for each found something very attractive in the big house on the other side of the hedge. Mrs. March wanted to talk of her father with the old man who had not forgotten him; Meg longed to walk in the conservatory; Beth sighed for the grand piano; and Amy was eager to see the fine pictures and statues.

"Mother, why didn't Mr. Laurence like to have Laurie play?" asked Jo, who was of an inquiring disposition.

"I am not sure, but I think it was because his son, Laurie's father, married an Italian lady, a musician, which displeased the old man, who is very proud. The lady was good and lovely and accomplished, but he did not like her, and never saw his son after he married. They both died when Laurie was a little child, and then his grandfather took him home. I fancy the boy, who was born in Italy, is not very strong, and the old man is afraid of losing him, which makes him so careful. Laurie comes naturally by his love of music, for he is like his mother, and I dare say his grandfather fears that he may want to be a musician; at any rate, his skill reminds him of the woman he did not like, and so he 'glowered,' as Jo said."

"Dear me, how romantic!" exclaimed Meg.

"How silly!" said Jo. "Let him be a musician, if he wants to, and not plague his life out sending him to college, when he hates to go."

"That's why he has such handsome black eyes and pretty manners, I suppose. Italians are always nice," said Meg, who was a little sentimental.

"What do you know about his eyes and his manners? You never spoke to him, hardly," cried Jo, who was *not* sentimental.

"I saw him at the party, and what you tell shows that he knows how to behave. That was a nice little speech about the medicine mother sent him."

"He meant the blanc-mange, I suppose."

"How stupid you are, child! He meant you, of course."

"Did he?" and Jo opened her eyes as if it had never occurred to her before.

"I never saw such a girl! You don't know a compliment when you get it," said Meg, with the air of a young lady who knew all about the matter.

"I think they are great nonsense, and I'll thank you not to be silly, and spoil my fun. Laurie's a nice boy, and I like him, and I won't have any sentimental stuff about compliments and such rubbish. We'll all be good to him, because he hasn't got any mother, and he *may* come over and see us, mayn't he, Marmee?"

"Yes, Jo, your little friend is very welcome, and I hope Meg will remember that children should be children as long as they can."

"I don't call myself a child, and I'm not in my teens yet," observed Amy. "What do you say, Beth?"

"I was thinking about our 'Pilgrim's Progress,'" answered Beth, who had not heard a word. "How we got out of the Slough and through the Wicket Gate by resolving to be good, and up the steep hill by trying; and that maybe the house over there, full of splendid things, is going to be our Palace Beautiful."

"We have got to get by the lions, first," said Jo, as if she rather liked the prospect.

## VI.

# BETH FINDS THE PALACE BEAUTIFUL.

THE big house did prove a Palace Beautiful, though it took some time for all to get in, and Beth found it very hard to pass the lions. Old Mr. Laurence was the biggest one; but after he had called, said something funny or kind to each one of the girls, and talked over old times with their mother, nobody felt much afraid of him, except timid Beth. The other lion was the fact that they were poor and Laurie rich; for this made them shy of accepting favors which they could not return. But, after a while, they found that he considered them the benefactors, and could not do enough to show how grateful he was for Mrs. March's motherly welcome, their cheerful society, and the comfort he took in that humble home of theirs. So they soon forgot their pride, and interchanged kindnesses without stopping to think which was the greater.

All sorts of pleasant things happened about that time; for the new friendship flourished like grass in spring. Every one liked Laurie, and he privately informed his tutor that "the Marches were regularly splendid girls." With the delightful enthusiasm of youth, they took the solitary boy into their midst, and made much of him, and he found something very charming in the innocent companionship of these simple-hearted girls. Never having known mother or sisters, he was quick to feel the influences they brought about him; and their busy, lively ways made him ashamed of the indolent life he led. He was tired of books, and found people so interesting now that Mr. Brooke was obliged to make very unsatisfactory reports; for Laurie was always playing truant, and running over to the Marches.

"Never mind; let him take a holiday, and make it up afterwards," said the old gentleman. "The good lady next door says he is studying too hard, and needs young society, amusement, and exercise. I suspect she is right, and that I've been coddling the fellow as if I'd been his grandmother. Let him do what he likes, as long as he is happy. He can't get into mischief in that little nunnery over there; and Mrs. March is doing more for him than we can."

What good times they had, to be sure! Such plays and tableaux, such sleigh-rides and skating frolics, such pleasant evenings in the old parlor, and now and then such gay little parties at the great house. Meg could walk in the conservatory whenever she liked, and revel in bouquets; Jo browsed over the new library voraciously, and convulsed the old gentleman with her criticisms; Amy copied pictures, and enjoyed beauty to her heart's content; and Laurie played "lord of the manor" in the most delightful style.

But Beth, though yearning for the grand piano, could not pluck up courage to go to the "Mansion of Bliss," as Meg called it. She went once with Jo; but the old gentleman, not being aware of her infirmity, stared at her so hard from under his heavy eyebrows, and said "Hey!" so loud, that he frightened her so much her "feet chattered on the floor," she told her mother; and she ran away, declaring she would never go there any more, not even for the dear piano. No persuasions or enticements could overcome her fear, till, the fact coming to Mr. Laurence's ear in some mysterious way, he set about mending matters. During one of the brief calls he made, he artfully led the conversation to music, and talked away about great singers whom he had seen, fine organs he had heard, and told such charming anecdotes that Beth found it impossible to stay in her distant corner, but crept nearer and nearer, as if fascinated. At the back of his chair she stopped, and stood listening, with her great eyes wide open, and her cheeks red with the excitement of this unusual performance. Taking no more notice of her than if she had been a fly, Mr. Laurence talked on about Laurie's lessons and teachers; and presently, as if the idea had just occurred to him, he said to Mrs. March,—

"The boy neglects his music now, and I'm glad of it, for he was getting too fond of it. But the piano suffers for want of use. Wouldn't some of your girls like to run over, and practise on it now and then, just to keep it in tune, you know, ma'am?"

Beth took a step forward, and pressed her hands tightly together to keep from clapping them, for this was an irresistible temptation; and the thought of practising on that splendid instrument quite took her breath away. Before Mrs. March could reply, Mr. Laurence went on with an odd little nod and smile,—

"They needn't see or speak to any one, but run in at any time; for I'm shut up in my study at the other end of the house, Laurie is out a great deal, and the servants are never near the drawing-room after nine o'clock."

Here he rose, as if going, and Beth made up her mind to speak, for that last arrangement left nothing to be desired. "Please tell the young ladies what I say; and if they don't care to come, why, never mind." Here a little hand slipped into his, and Beth looked up at him with a face full of gratitude, as she said, in her earnest yet timid way,—

"O sir, they do care, very, very much!"

"Are you the musical girl?" he asked, without any startling "Hey!" as he looked down at her very kindly.

"I'm Beth. I love it dearly, and I'll come, if you are quite sure nobody will hear me—and be disturbed," she added, fearing to be rude, and trembling at her own boldness as she spoke.

"Not a soul, my dear. The house is empty half the day; so come, and drum away as much as you like, and I shall be obliged to you."

"How kind you are, sir!"

Beth blushed like a rose under the friendly look he wore; but she was not frightened now, and gave the big hand a grateful squeeze, because she had no words to thank him for the precious gift he had given her. The old gentleman softly stroked the hair off her forehead, and, stooping down, he kissed her, saying, in a tone few people ever heard,—

"I had a little girl once, with eyes like these. God bless you, my dear! Good day, madam;" and away he went, in a great hurry.

Beth had a rapture with her mother, and then rushed up to impart the glorious news to her family of invalids, as the girls were not at home. How blithely she sung that evening, and how they all laughed at her, because she woke Amy in the night by playing the piano on her face in her sleep. Next day, having seen both the old and young gentleman out of the house, Beth, after two or three retreats, fairly got in at the side-door, and made her way, as noiselessly as any mouse, to the drawing-room, where her idol stood. Quite by accident, of course, some pretty, easy music lay on the piano; and, with trembling fingers, and frequent stops to listen and look about, Beth at last touched the great instrument, and straightway forgot her fear, herself, and everything else but the unspeakable delight which the music gave her, for it was like the voice of a beloved friend.

She stayed till Hannah came to take her home to dinner; but she had no appetite, and could only sit and smile upon every one in a general state of beatitude.

After that, the little brown hood slipped through the hedge nearly every day, and the great drawing-room was haunted by a tuneful spirit that came and went unseen. She never knew that Mr. Laurence often opened his study-door to hear the old-fashioned airs he liked; she never saw Laurie mount guard in the hall to warn the servants away; she never suspected that the exercise-books and new songs which she found in the rack were put there for her especial benefit; and when he talked to her about music at home, she only thought how kind he was to tell things that helped her so much. So she enjoyed herself heartily, and found, what isn't always the case, that her granted wish was all she had hoped. Perhaps it was because she was so grateful for this blessing that a greater was given her; at any rate, she deserved both.

"Mother, I'm going to work Mr. Laurence a pair of slippers. He is so kind to me, I must thank him, and I don't know any other way. Can I do it?" asked Beth, a few weeks after that eventful call of his.

"Yes, dear. It will please him very much, and be a nice way of thanking him. The girls will help you about them, and I will pay for the making up," replied Mrs. March, who took peculiar pleasure in granting Beth's requests, because she so seldom asked anything for herself.

After many serious discussions with Meg and Jo, the pattern was chosen, the materials bought, and the slippers begun. A cluster of grave yet cheerful pansies, on a deeper purple ground, was pronounced very appropriate and pretty; and Beth worked away early and late, with occasional lifts over hard parts. She was a nimble little needle-woman, and they were finished before any one got tired of them. Then she wrote a very short, simple note, and, with Laurie's help, got them smuggled on to the study-table one morning before the old gentleman was up.

When this excitement was over, Beth waited to see what would happen. All that day passed, and a part of the next, before any acknowledgment arrived, and she was beginning to fear she had offended her crotchety friend. On the afternoon of the second day, she went out to do an errand, and give poor Joanna, the invalid doll, her daily exercise. As she came up the street, on her return, she saw three, yes, four, heads popping in and out of the parlor windows, and the moment they saw her, several hands were waved, and several joyful voices screamed,—

"Here's a letter from the old gentleman! Come quick, and read it!"

"O Beth, he's sent you—" began Amy, gesticulating with unseemly energy; but she got no further, for Jo quenched her by slamming down the window.

Beth hurried on in a flutter of suspense. At the door, her sisters seized and bore her to the parlor in a triumphal procession, all pointing, and all saying at once, "Look there! look there!" Beth did look, and turned pale with delight and surprise; for there stood a little cabinet-piano, with a letter lying on the glossy lid, directed, like a sign-board, to "Miss Elizabeth March."

"For me?" gasped Beth, holding on to Jo, and feeling as if she should tumble down, it was such an overwhelming thing altogether.

"Yes; all for you, my precious! Isn't it splendid of him? Don't you think he's the dearest old man in the world? Here's the key in the letter. We didn't open it, but we are dying to know what he says," cried Jo, hugging her sister, and offering the note.

"You read it! I can't, I feel so queer! Oh, it is too lovely!" and Beth hid her face in Jo's apron, quite upset by her present.

Jo opened the paper, and began to laugh, for the first words she saw were,—

"MISS MARCH:

"*Dear Madam,—*"

"How nice it sounds! I wish some one would write to me so!" said Amy, who thought the old-fashioned address very elegant.

"'I have had many pairs of slippers in my life, but I never had any that suited me so well as yours,'" continued Jo. "'Heart's-ease is my favorite flower, and these will always remind me of the gentle giver. I like to pay my debts; so I know you will allow "the old gentleman" to send you something which once belonged to the little granddaughter he lost. With hearty thanks and best wishes, I remain,

"'Your grateful friend and humble servant,

"'JAMES LAURENCE.'"

"There, Beth, that's an honor to be proud of, I'm sure! Laurie told me how fond Mr. Laurence used to be of the child who died, and how he kept all her little things carefully. Just think, he's given you her piano. That comes of having big blue eyes and loving music," said Jo, trying to soothe Beth, who trembled, and looked more excited than she had ever been before.

"See the cunning brackets to hold candles, and the nice green silk, puckered up, with a gold rose in the middle, and the pretty rack and stool, all complete," added Meg, opening the instrument and displaying its beauties.

"'Your humble servant, James Laurence'; only think of his writing that to you. I'll tell the girls. They'll think it's splendid," said Amy, much impressed by the note.

"Try it, honey. Let's hear the sound of the baby-pianny," said Hannah, who always took a share in the family joys and sorrows.

So Beth tried it; and every one pronounced it the most remarkable piano ever heard. It had evidently been newly tuned and put in apple-pie order; but, perfect as it was, I think the real charm of it lay in the happiest of all happy faces which leaned over it, as Beth lovingly touched the beautiful black and white keys and pressed the bright pedals.

"You'll have to go and thank him," said Jo, by way of a joke; for the idea of the child's really going never entered her head.

"Yes, I mean to. I guess I'll go now, before I get frightened thinking about it." And, to the utter amazement of the assembled family, Beth walked deliberately down the garden, through the hedge, and in at the Laurences' door.

"Well, I wish I may die if it ain't the queerest thing I ever see! The pianny has turned her head! She'd never have gone in her right mind," cried Hannah, staring after her, while the girls were rendered quite speechless by the miracle.

They would have been still more amazed if they had seen what Beth did afterward. If you will believe me, she went and knocked at the study-door before she gave herself time to think; and when a gruff voice called out, "Come in!" she did go in, right up to Mr. Laurence, who looked quite taken aback, and held out her hand, saying, with only a small quaver in her voice, "I came to thank you, sir, for—" But she didn't finish; for he looked so friendly that she forgot her speech, and, only remembering that he had lost the little girl he loved, she put both arms round his neck, and kissed him.

If the roof of the house had suddenly flown off, the old gentleman wouldn't have been more astonished; but he liked it,—oh, dear, yes, he liked it amazingly!—and was so touched and pleased by that confiding little kiss that all his crustiness vanished; and he just set her on his knee, and laid his wrinkled cheek against her rosy one, feeling as if he had got his own little granddaughter back again. Beth ceased to fear him from that moment, and sat there talking to him as cosily as if she had known him all her life; for love casts out fear, and gratitude can conquer pride. When she went home, he walked with her to her own gate, shook hands cordially, and touched his hat as he marched back again, looking very stately and erect, like a handsome, soldierly old gentleman, as he was.

When the girls saw that performance, Jo began to dance a jig, by way of expressing her satisfaction; Amy nearly fell out of the window in her surprise; and Meg exclaimed, with uplifted hands, "Well, I do believe the world is coming to an end!"

VII.

# AMY'S VALLEY OF HUMILIATION.

"THAT boy is a perfect Cyclops, isn't he?" said Amy, one day, as Laurie clattered by on horseback, with a flourish of his whip as he passed.

"How dare you say so, when he's got both his eyes? and very handsome ones they are, too," cried Jo, who resented any slighting remarks about her friend.

"I didn't say anything about his eyes, and I don't see why you need fire up when I admire his riding."

"Oh, my goodness! that little goose means a centaur, and she called him a Cyclops," exclaimed Jo, with a burst of laughter.

"You needn't be so rude; it's only a 'lapse of lingy,' as Mr. Davis says," retorted Amy, finishing Jo with her Latin. "I just wish I had a little of the money Laurie spends on that horse," she added, as if to herself, yet hoping her sisters would hear.

"Why?" asked Meg kindly, for Jo had gone off in another laugh at Amy's second blunder.

"I need it so much; I'm dreadfully in debt, and it won't be my turn to have the rag-money for a month."

"In debt, Amy? What do you mean?" and Meg looked sober.

"Why, I owe at least a dozen pickled limes, and I can't pay them, you know, till I have money, for Marmee forbade my having anything charged at the shop."

"Tell me all about it. Are limes the fashion now? It used to be pricking bits of rubber to make balls;" and Meg tried to keep her countenance, Amy looked so grave and important.

"Why, you see, the girls are always buying them, and unless you want to be thought mean, you must do it, too. It's nothing but limes now, for every one is sucking them in their desks in school-time, and trading them off for pencils, bead-rings, paper dolls, or something else, at recess. If one girl likes another, she gives her a lime; if she's mad with her, she eats one before her face, and don't offer even a suck. They treat by turns; and I've had ever so many, but haven't returned them; and I ought, for they are debts of honor, you know."

"How much will pay them off, and restore your credit?" asked Meg, taking out her purse.

"A quarter would more than do it, and leave a few cents over for a treat for you. Don't you like limes?"

"Not much; you may have my share. Here's the money. Make it last as long as you can, for it isn't very plenty, you know."

"Oh, thank you! It must be so nice to have pocket-money! I'll have a grand feast, for I haven't tasted a lime this week. I felt delicate about taking any, as I couldn't return them, and I'm actually suffering for one."

Next day Amy was rather late at school; but could not resist the temptation of displaying, with pardonable pride, a moist brown-paper parcel, before she consigned it to the inmost recesses of her desk. During the next few minutes the rumor that Amy March had got twenty-four delicious limes (she ate one on the way), and was going to treat, circulated through her "set," and the attentions of her friends became quite overwhelming. Katy Brown invited her to her next party on the spot; Mary Kingsley insisted on lending her her watch till recess; and Jenny Snow, a satirical young lady, who had basely twitted Amy upon her limeless state, promptly buried the hatchet, and offered to furnish answers to certain appalling sums. But Amy had not forgotten Miss Snow's cutting remarks about "some persons whose noses were not too flat to smell other people's limes, and stuck-up people, who were not too proud to ask for them;" and she instantly crushed "that Snow girl's" hopes by the withering telegram, "You needn't be so polite all of a sudden, for you won't get any."

A distinguished personage happened to visit the school that morning, and Amy's beautifully drawn maps received praise, which honor to her foe rankled in the soul of Miss Snow, and caused Miss March to assume the airs of a studious young peacock. But, alas, alas! pride goes before a fall, and the revengeful Snow turned the tables with disastrous success. No sooner had the guest paid the usual stale compliments, and bowed himself out, than Jenny, under pretence of asking an important question, informed Mr. Davis, the teacher, that Amy March had pickled limes in her desk.

Now Mr. Davis had declared limes a contraband article, and solemnly vowed to publicly ferrule the first person who was found breaking the law. This much-enduring man had succeeded in banishing chewing-gum after a long and stormy war, had made a bonfire of the confiscated novels and newspapers, had suppressed a private post-office, had forbidden distortions of the face, nicknames, and caricatures, and done all that one man could do to keep half a hundred rebellious girls in order. Boys are trying enough to human patience, goodness knows! but girls are infinitely more so, especially to nervous gentlemen, with tyrannical tempers, and no more talent for teaching than Dr. Blimber. Mr. Davis knew any quantity of Greek, Latin, Algebra, and ologies of all sorts, so he was called a fine teacher; and manners, morals, feelings, and examples were not considered of any particular importance. It was a most unfortunate moment for denouncing Amy, and Jenny knew it. Mr. Davis had evidently taken his coffee too strong that morning; there was an east wind, which always affected his neuralgia; and his pupils had not done him the credit which he felt he deserved: therefore, to use the expressive, if not elegant, language of a school-girl, "he was as nervous as a witch and as cross as a bear." The word "limes" was like fire to powder; his yellow face flushed, and he rapped on his desk with an energy which made Jenny skip to her seat with unusual rapidity.

"Young ladies, attention, if you please!"

At the stern order the buzz ceased, and fifty pairs of blue, black, gray, and brown eyes were obediently fixed upon his awful countenance.

"Miss March, come to the desk."

Amy rose to comply with outward composure, but a secret fear oppressed her, for the limes weighed upon her conscience.

"Bring with you the limes you have in your desk," was the unexpected command which arrested her before she got out of her seat.

"Don't take all," whispered her neighbor, a young lady of great presence of mind.

Amy hastily shook out half a dozen, and laid the rest down before Mr. Davis, feeling that any man possessing a human heart would relent when that delicious perfume met his nose. Unfortunately, Mr. Davis particularly detested the odor of the fashionable pickle, and disgust added to his wrath.

"Is that all?"

"Not quite," stammered Amy.

"Bring the rest immediately."

With a despairing glance at her set, she obeyed.

"You are sure there are no more?"

"I never lie, sir."

"So I see. Now take these disgusting things two by two, and throw them out of the window."

There was a simultaneous sigh, which created quite a little gust, as the last hope fled, and the treat was ravished from their longing lips. Scarlet with shame and anger, Amy went to and fro six dreadful times; and as each doomed couple—looking oh! so plump and juicy—fell from her reluctant hands, a shout from the street completed the anguish of the girls, for it told them that their feast was being exulted over by the little Irish children, who were their sworn foes. This—this was too much; all flashed indignant or appealing glances at the inexorable Davis, and one passionate lime-lover burst into tears.

As Amy returned from her last trip, Mr. Davis gave a portentous "Hem!" and said, in his most impressive manner,—

"Young ladies, you remember what I said to you a week ago. I am sorry this has happened, but I never allow my rules to be infringed, and I *never* break my word. Miss March, hold out your hand."

Amy started, and put both hands behind her, turning on him an imploring look which pleaded for her better than the words she could not utter. She was rather a favorite with "old Davis," as, of course, he was called, and it's my private belief that he *would* have broken his word if the indignation of one irrepressible young lady had not found vent in a hiss. That hiss, faint as it was, irritated the irascible gentleman, and sealed the culprit's fate.

"Your hand, Miss March!" was the only answer her mute appeal received; and, too proud to cry or beseech, Amy set her teeth, threw back her head defiantly, and bore without flinching several tingling blows on her little palm. They were neither many nor heavy, but that made no difference to her. For the first time in her life she had been struck; and the disgrace, in her eyes, was as deep as if he had knocked her down.

"You will now stand on the platform till recess," said Mr. Davis, resolved to do the thing thoroughly, since he had begun.

That was dreadful. It would have been bad enough to go to her seat, and see the pitying faces of her friends, or the satisfied ones of her few enemies; but to face the whole school, with that shame fresh upon her, seemed impossible, and for a second she felt as if she could only drop down where she stood, and break her heart with crying. A bitter sense of wrong, and the thought of Jenny Snow, helped her to bear it; and, taking the ignominious place, she fixed her eyes on the stove-funnel above what now seemed a sea of faces, and stood there, so motionless and white that the girls found it very hard to study, with that pathetic figure before them.

During the fifteen minutes that followed, the proud and sensitive little girl suffered a shame and pain which she never forgot. To others it might seem a ludicrous or trivial affair, but to her it was a hard experience; for during the twelve years of her life she had been governed by love alone, and a blow of that sort had never touched her before. The smart of her hand and the ache of her heart were forgotten in the sting of the thought,—

"I shall have to tell at home, and they will be so disappointed in me!"

The fifteen minutes seemed an hour; but they came to an end at last, and the word "Recess!" had never seemed so welcome to her before.

"You can go, Miss March," said Mr. Davis, looking, as he felt, uncomfortable.

He did not soon forget the reproachful glance Amy gave him, as she went, without a word to any one, straight into the ante-room, snatched her things, and left the place "forever," as she passionately declared to herself. She was in a sad state when she got home; and when the older girls arrived, some time later, an indignation meeting was held at once. Mrs. March did not say much, but looked disturbed, and comforted her afflicted little daughter in her tenderest manner. Meg bathed the insulted hand with glycerine and tears; Beth felt that even her beloved kittens would fail as a balm for griefs like this; Jo wrathfully proposed that Mr. Davis be arrested without delay; and Hannah shook her fist at the "villain," and pounded potatoes for dinner as if she had him under her pestle.

No notice was taken of Amy's flight, except by her mates; but the sharp-eyed demoiselles discovered that Mr. Davis was quite benignant in the afternoon, also unusually nervous. Just before school closed, Jo appeared, wearing a grim expression, as she stalked up to the desk, and delivered a letter from her mother; then collected Amy's property, and departed, carefully scraping the mud from her boots on the door-mat, as if she shook the dust of the place off her feet.

"Yes, you can have a vacation from school, but I want you to study a little every day, with Beth," said Mrs. March, that evening. "I don't approve of corporal punishment, especially for girls. I dislike Mr. Davis's manner of teaching, and don't think the girls you associate with are doing you any good, so I shall ask your father's advice before I send you anywhere else."

"That's good! I wish all the girls would leave, and spoil his old school. It's perfectly maddening to think of those lovely limes," sighed Amy, with the air of a martyr.

"I am not sorry you lost them, for you broke the rules, and deserved some punishment for disobedience," was the severe reply, which rather disappointed the young lady, who expected nothing but sympathy.

"Do you mean you are glad I was disgraced before the whole school?" cried Amy.

"I should not have chosen that way of mending a fault," replied her mother; "but I'm not sure that it won't do you more good than a milder method. You are getting to be rather conceited, my dear, and it is quite time you set about correcting it. You have a good many little gifts and virtues, but there is no need of parading them, for conceit spoils the finest genius. There is not much danger that real talent or goodness will be overlooked long; even if it is, the consciousness of possessing and using it well should satisfy one, and the great charm of all power is modesty."

"So it is!" cried Laurie, who was playing chess in a corner with Jo. "I knew a girl, once, who had a really remarkable talent for music, and she didn't know it; never guessed what sweet little things she composed when she was alone, and wouldn't have believed it if any one had told her."

"I wish I'd known that nice girl; maybe she would have helped me, I'm so stupid," said Beth, who stood beside him, listening eagerly.

"You do know her, and she helps you better than any one else could," answered Laurie, looking at her with such mischievous meaning in his merry black eyes, that Beth suddenly turned very red, and hid her face in the sofa-cushion, quite overcome by such an unexpected discovery.

Jo let Laurie win the game, to pay for that praise of her Beth, who could not be prevailed upon to play for them after her compliment. So Laurie did his best, and sung delightfully, being in a particularly lively humor, for to the Marches he seldom showed the moody side of his character. When he was gone, Amy, who had been pensive all the evening, said suddenly, as if busy over some new idea,—

"Is Laurie an accomplished boy?"

"Yes; he has had an excellent education, and has much talent; he will make a fine man, if not spoilt by petting," replied her mother.

"And he isn't conceited, is he?" asked Amy.

"Not in the least; that is why he is so charming, and we all like him so much."

"I see; it's nice to have accomplishments, and be elegant; but not to show off, or get perked up," said Amy thoughtfully.

"These things are always seen and felt in a person's manner and conversation, if modestly used; but it is not necessary to display them," said Mrs. March.

"Any more than it's proper to wear all your bonnets and gowns and ribbons at once, that folks may know you've got them," added Jo; and the lecture ended in a laugh.

VIII.

## JO MEETS APOLLYON.

"GIRLS, where are you going?" asked Amy, coming into their room one Saturday afternoon, and finding them getting ready to go out, with an air of secrecy which excited her curiosity.

"Never mind; little girls shouldn't ask questions," returned Jo sharply.

Now if there *is* anything mortifying to our feelings, when we are young, it is to be told that; and to be bidden to "run away, dear," is still more trying to us. Amy bridled up at this insult, and determined to find out the secret, if she teased for an hour. Turning to Meg, who never refused her anything very long, she said coaxingly, "Do tell me! I should think you might let me go, too; for Beth is fussing over her piano, and I haven't got anything to do, and am *so* lonely."

"I can't, dear, because you aren't invited," began Meg; but Jo broke in impatiently, "Now, Meg, be quiet, or you will spoil it all. You can't go, Amy; so don't be a baby, and whine about it."

"You are going somewhere with Laurie, I know you are; you were whispering and laughing together, on the sofa, last night, and you stopped when I came in. Aren't you going with him?"

"Yes, we are; now do be still, and stop bothering."

Amy held her tongue, but used her eyes, and saw Meg slip a fan into her pocket.

"I know! I know! you're going to the theatre to see the 'Seven Castles!'" she cried; adding resolutely, "and I *shall* go, for mother said I might see it; and I've got my rag-money, and it was mean not to tell me in time."

"Just listen to me a minute, and be a good child," said Meg soothingly. "Mother doesn't wish you to go this week, because your eyes are not well enough yet to bear the light of this fairy piece. Next week you can go with Beth and Hannah, and have a nice time."

"I don't like that half as well as going with you and Laurie. Please let me; I've been sick with this cold so long, and shut up, I'm dying for some fun. Do, Meg! I'll be ever so good," pleaded Amy, looking as pathetic as she could.

"Suppose we take her. I don't believe mother would mind, if we bundle her up well," began Meg.

"If *she* goes *I* sha'n't; and if I don't, Laurie won't like it; and it will be very rude, after he invited only us, to go and drag in Amy. I should think she'd hate to poke herself where she isn't wanted," said Jo crossly, for she disliked the trouble of overseeing a fidgety child, when she wanted to enjoy herself.

Her tone and manner angered Amy, who began to put her boots on, saying, in her most aggravating way, "I *shall* go; Meg says I may; and if I pay for myself, Laurie hasn't anything to do with it."

"You can't sit with us, for our seats are reserved, and you mustn't sit alone; so Laurie will give you his place, and that will spoil our pleasure; or he'll get another seat for you, and that isn't proper, when you weren't asked. You sha'n't stir a step; so you may just stay where you are," scolded Jo, crosser than ever, having just pricked her finger in her hurry.

Sitting on the floor, with one boot on, Amy began to cry, and Meg to reason with her, when Laurie called from below, and the two girls hurried down, leaving their sister wailing; for now and then she forgot her grown-up ways, and acted like a spoilt child. Just as the party was setting out, Amy called over the banisters, in a threatening tone, "You'll be sorry for this, Jo March; see if you ain't."

"Fiddlesticks!" returned Jo, slamming the door.

They had a charming time, for "The Seven Castles of the Diamond Lake" were as brilliant and wonderful as heart could wish. But, in spite of the comical red imps, sparkling elves, and gorgeous princes and princesses, Jo's pleasure had a drop of bitterness in it; the fairy queen's yellow curls reminded her of Amy; and between the acts she amused herself with wondering what her sister would do to make her "sorry for it." She and Amy had had many lively skirmishes in the course of their lives, for both had quick tempers, and were apt to be violent when fairly roused. Amy teased Jo, and Jo irritated Amy, and semi-occasional explosions occurred, of which both were much ashamed afterward. Although the oldest, Jo had the least self-control, and had hard times trying to curb the fiery spirit which was continually getting her into trouble; her anger never lasted long, and, having humbly confessed her fault, she sincerely repented, and tried to do better. Her sisters used to say that they rather liked to get Jo into a fury, because she was such an angel afterward. Poor Jo tried desperately to be good, but her bosom enemy was always ready to flame up and defeat her; and it took years of patient effort to subdue it.

When they got home, they found Amy reading in the parlor. She assumed an injured air as they came in; never lifted her eyes from her book, or asked a single question. Perhaps curiosity might have conquered resentment, if Beth had not been there to inquire, and receive a glowing description of the play. On going up to put away her best hat, Jo's first look was toward the bureau; for, in their last quarrel, Amy had soothed her feelings by turning Jo's top drawer upside down on the floor. Everything was in its place, however; and after a hasty glance into her various closets, bags, and boxes, Jo decided that Amy had forgiven and forgotten her wrongs.

There Jo was mistaken; for next day she made a discovery which produced a tempest. Meg, Beth, and Amy were sitting together, late in the afternoon, when Jo burst into the room, looking excited, and demanding breathlessly, "Has any one taken my book?"

Meg and Beth said "No," at once, and looked surprised; Amy poked the fire, and said nothing. Jo saw her color rise, and was down upon her in a minute.

"Amy, you've got it?"

"No, I haven't."

"You know where it is, then?"

"No, I don't."

"That's a fib!" cried Jo, taking her by the shoulders, and looking fierce enough to frighten a much braver child than Amy.

"It isn't. I haven't got it, don't know where it is now, and don't care."

"You know something about it, and you'd better tell at once, or I'll make you," and Jo gave her a slight shake.

"Scold as much as you like, you'll never see your silly old book again," cried Amy, getting excited in her turn.

"Why not?"

"I burnt it up."

"What! my little book I was so fond of, and worked over, and meant to finish before father got home? Have you really burnt it?" said Jo, turning very pale, while her eyes kindled and her hands clutched Amy nervously.

"Yes, I did! I told you I'd make you pay for being so cross yesterday, and I have, so—"

Amy got no farther, for Jo's hot temper mastered her, and she shook Amy till her teeth chattered in her head; crying, in a passion of grief and anger,—

"You wicked, wicked girl! I never can write it again, and I'll never forgive you as long as I live."

Meg flew to rescue Amy, and Beth to pacify Jo, but Jo was quite beside herself; and, with a parting box on her sister's ear, she rushed out of the room up to the old sofa in the garret, and finished her fight alone.

The storm cleared up below, for Mrs. March came home, and, having heard the story, soon brought Amy to a sense of the wrong she had done her sister. Jo's book was the pride of her heart, and was regarded by her family as a literary sprout of great promise. It was only half a dozen little fairy tales, but Jo had worked over them patiently, putting her whole heart into her work, hoping to make something good enough to print. She had just copied them with great care, and had destroyed the old manuscript, so that Amy's bonfire had consumed the loving work of several years. It seemed a small loss to others, but to Jo it was a dreadful calamity, and she felt that it never could be made up to her. Beth mourned as for a departed kitten, and Meg refused to defend her pet; Mrs. March looked grave and grieved, and Amy felt that no one would love her till she had asked pardon for the act which she now regretted more than any of them.

When the tea-bell rung, Jo appeared, looking so grim and unapproachable that it took all Amy's courage to say meekly,—

"Please forgive me, Jo; I'm very, very sorry."

"I never shall forgive you," was Jo's stern answer; and, from that moment, she ignored Amy entirely.

No one spoke of the great trouble,—not even Mrs. March,—for all had learned by experience that when Jo was in that mood words were wasted; and the wisest course was to wait till some little accident, or her own generous nature, softened Jo's resentment, and healed the breach. It was not a happy evening; for, though they sewed as usual, while their mother read aloud from Bremer, Scott, or Edgeworth, something was wanting, and the sweet home-peace was disturbed. They felt this most when singing-time came; for Beth could only play, Jo stood dumb as a stone, and Amy broke down, so Meg and mother sung alone. But, in spite of their efforts to be as cheery as larks, the flute-like voices did not seem to chord as well as usual, and all felt out of tune.

As Jo received her good-night kiss, Mrs. March whispered gently,—

"My dear, don't let the sun go down upon your anger; forgive each other, help each other, and begin again to-morrow."

Jo wanted to lay her head down on that motherly bosom, and cry her grief and anger all away; but tears were an unmanly weakness, and she felt so deeply injured that she really *couldn't* quite forgive yet. So she winked hard, shook her head, and said, gruffly because Amy was listening,—

"It was an abominable thing, and she don't deserve to be forgiven."

With that she marched off to bed, and there was no merry or confidential gossip that night.

Amy was much offended that her overtures of peace had been repulsed, and began to wish she had not humbled herself, to feel more injured than ever, and to plume herself on her superior virtue in a way which was particularly exasperating. Jo still looked like a thunder-cloud, and nothing went well all day. It was bitter cold in the morning; she dropped her precious turn-over in the gutter, Aunt March had an attack of fidgets, Meg was pensive, Beth *would* look grieved and wistful when she got home, and Amy kept making remarks about people who were always talking about being good, and yet wouldn't try, when other people set them a virtuous example.

"Everybody is so hateful, I'll ask Laurie to go skating. He is always kind and jolly, and will put me to rights, I know," said Jo to herself, and off she went.

Amy heard the clash of skates, and looked out with an impatient exclamation,—

"There! she promised I should go next time, for this is the last ice we shall have. But it's no use to ask such a cross-patch to take me."

"Don't say that; you *were* very naughty, and it *is* hard to forgive the loss of her precious little book; but I think she might do it now, and I guess she will, if you try her at the right minute," said Meg. "Go after them; don't say anything till Jo has got good-natured with Laurie, then take a quiet minute, and just kiss her, or do some kind thing, and I'm sure she'll be friends again, with all her heart."

"I'll try," said Amy, for the advice suited her; and, after a flurry to get ready, she ran after the friends, who were just disappearing over the hill.

It was not far to the river, but both were ready before Amy reached them. Jo saw her coming, and turned her back; Laurie did not see, for he was carefully skating along the shore, sounding the ice, for a warm spell had preceded the cold snap.

"I'll go on to the first bend, and see if it's all right, before we begin to race," Amy heard him say, as he shot away, looking like a young Russian, in his fur-trimmed coat and cap.

Jo heard Amy panting after her run, stamping her feet and blowing her fingers, as she tried to put her skates on; but Jo never turned, and went slowly zigzagging down the river, taking a bitter, unhappy sort of satisfaction in her sister's troubles. She had cherished her anger till it grew strong, and took possession of her, as evil thoughts and feelings always do, unless cast out at once. As Laurie turned the bend, he shouted back,—

"Keep near the shore; it isn't safe in the middle."

Jo heard, but Amy was just struggling to her feet, and did not catch a word. Jo glanced over her shoulder, and the little demon she was harboring said in her ear,—

"No matter whether she heard or not, let her take care of herself."

Laurie had vanished round the bend; Jo was just at the turn, and Amy, far behind, striking out toward the smoother ice in the middle of the river. For a minute Jo stood still, with a strange feeling at her heart; then she resolved to go on, but something held and turned her round, just in time to see Amy throw up her hands and go down, with the sudden crash of rotten ice, the splash of water, and a cry that made Jo's heart stand still with fear. She tried to call Laurie, but her voice was gone; she tried to rush forward, but her feet seemed to have no strength in them; and, for a second, she could only stand motionless, staring, with a terror-stricken face, at the little blue hood above the black water. Something rushed swiftly by her, and Laurie's voice cried out,—

"Bring a rail; quick, quick!"

How she did it, she never knew; but for the next few minutes she worked as if possessed, blindly obeying Laurie, who was quite self-possessed, and, lying flat, held Amy up by his arm and hockey till Jo dragged a rail from the fence, and together they got the child out, more frightened than hurt.

"Now then, we must walk her home as fast as we can; pile our things on her, while I get off these confounded skates," cried Laurie, wrapping his coat round Amy, and tugging away at the straps, which never seemed so intricate before.

Shivering, dripping, and crying, they got Amy home; and, after an exciting time of it, she fell asleep, rolled in blankets, before a hot fire. During the bustle Jo had scarcely spoken; but flown about, looking pale and wild, with her things half off, her dress torn, and her hands cut and bruised by ice and rails, and refractory buckles. When Amy was comfortably asleep, the house quiet, and Mrs. March sitting by the bed, she called Jo to her, and began to bind up the hurt hands.

"Are you sure she is safe?" whispered Jo, looking remorsefully at the golden head, which might have been swept away from her sight forever under the treacherous ice.

"Quite safe, dear; she is not hurt, and won't even take cold, I think, you were so sensible in covering and getting her home quickly," replied her mother cheerfully.

"Laurie did it all; I only let her go. Mother, if she *should* die, it would be my fault"; and Jo dropped down beside the bed, in a passion of penitent tears, telling all that had happened, bitterly condemning her hardness of heart, and sobbing out her gratitude for being spared the heavy punishment which might have come upon her.

"It's my dreadful temper! I try to cure it; I think I have, and then it breaks out worse than ever. O mother, what shall I do? what shall I do?" cried poor Jo, in despair.

"Watch and pray, dear; never get tired of trying; and never think it is impossible to conquer your fault," said Mrs. March, drawing the blowzy head to her shoulder, and kissing the wet cheek so tenderly that Jo cried harder than ever.

"You don't know, you can't guess how bad it is! It seems as if I could do anything when I'm in a passion; I get so savage, I could hurt any one, and enjoy it. I'm afraid I *shall* do something dreadful some day, and spoil my life, and make everybody hate me. O mother, help me, do help me!"

"I will, my child, I will. Don't cry so bitterly, but remember this day, and resolve, with all your soul, that you will never know another like it. Jo, dear, we all have our temptations, some far greater than yours, and it often takes us all our lives to conquer them. You think your temper is the worst in the world; but mine used to be just like it."

"Yours, mother? Why, you are never angry!" and, for the moment, Jo forgot remorse in surprise.

"I've been trying to cure it for forty years, and have only succeeded in controlling it. I am angry nearly every day of my life, Jo; but I have learned not to show it; and I still hope to learn not to feel it, though it may take me another forty years to do so."

The patience and the humility of the face she loved so well was a better lesson to Jo than the wisest lecture, the sharpest reproof. She felt comforted at once by the sympathy and confidence given her; the knowledge that her mother had a fault like hers, and tried to mend it, made her own easier to bear and strengthened her resolution to cure it; though forty years seemed rather a long time to watch and pray, to a girl of fifteen.

"Mother, are you angry when you fold your lips tight together, and go out of the room sometimes, when Aunt March scolds, or people worry you?" asked Jo, feeling nearer and dearer to her mother than ever before.

"Yes, I've learned to check the hasty words that rise to my lips; and when I feel that they mean to break out against my will, I just go away a minute, and give myself a little shake, for being so weak and wicked," answered Mrs. March, with a sigh and a smile, as she smoothed and fastened up Jo's dishevelled hair.

"How did you learn to keep still? That is what troubles me—for the sharp words fly out before I know what I'm about; and the more I say the worse I get, till it's a pleasure to hurt people's feelings, and say dreadful things. Tell me how you do it, Marmee dear."

"My good mother used to help me—"

"As you do us—" interrupted Jo, with a grateful kiss.

"But I lost her when I was a little older than you are, and for years had to struggle on alone, for I was too proud to confess my weakness to any one else. I had a hard time, Jo, and shed a good many bitter tears over my failures; for, in spite of my efforts, I never seemed to get on. Then your father came, and I was so happy that I found it easy to be good. But by and by, when I had four little daughters round me, and we were poor, then the old trouble began again; for I am not patient by nature, and it tried me very much to see my children wanting anything."

"Poor mother! what helped you then?"

"Your father, Jo. He never loses patience,—never doubts or complains,—but always hopes, and works and waits so cheerfully, that one is ashamed to do otherwise before him. He helped and comforted me, and showed me that I must try to practise all the virtues I would have my little girls possess, for I was their example. It was easier to try for your sakes than for my own; a startled or surprised look from one of you, when I spoke sharply, rebuked me more than any words could have done; and the love, respect, and confidence of my children was the sweetest reward I could receive for my efforts to be the woman I would have them copy."

"O mother, if I'm ever half as good as you, I shall be satisfied," cried Jo, much touched.

"I hope you will be a great deal better, dear; but you must keep watch over your 'bosom enemy,' as father calls it, or it may sadden, if not spoil your life. You have had a warning; remember it, and try with heart and soul to master this quick temper, before it brings you greater sorrow and regret than you have known to-day."

"I will try, mother; I truly will. But you must help me, remind me, and keep me from flying out. I used to see father sometimes put his finger on his lips, and look at you with a very kind, but sober face, and you always folded your lips tight or went away: was he reminding you then?" asked Jo softly.

"Yes; I asked him to help me so, and he never forgot it, but saved me from many a sharp word by that little gesture and kind look."

Jo saw that her mother's eyes filled and her lips trembled, as she spoke; and, fearing that she had said too much, she whispered anxiously, "Was it wrong to watch you, and to speak of it? I didn't mean to be rude, but it's so comfortable to say all I think to you, and feel so safe and happy here."

"My Jo, you may say anything to your mother, for it is my greatest happiness and pride to feel that my girls confide in me, and know how much I love them."

"I thought I'd grieved you."

"No, dear; but speaking of father reminded me how much I miss him, how much I owe him, and how faithfully I should watch and work to keep his little daughters safe and good for him."

"Yet you told him to go, mother, and didn't cry when he went, and never complain now, or seem as if you needed any help," said Jo, wondering.

"I gave my best to the country I love, and kept my tears till he was gone. Why should I complain, when we both have merely done our duty and will surely be the happier for it in the end? If I don't seem to need help, it is because I have a better friend, even than father, to comfort and sustain me. My child, the troubles and temptations of your life are beginning, and may be many; but you can overcome and outlive them all if you learn to feel the strength and tenderness of your Heavenly Father as you do that of your earthly one. The more you love and trust Him, the nearer you will feel to Him, and the less you will depend on human power and wisdom. His love and care never tire or change, can never be taken from you, but may become the source of life-long peace, happiness, and strength. Believe this heartily, and go to God with all your little cares, and hopes, and sins, and sorrows, as freely and confidingly as you come to your mother."

Jo's only answer was to hold her mother close, and, in the silence which followed, the sincerest prayer she had ever prayed left her heart without words; for in that sad, yet happy hour, she had learned not only the bitterness of remorse and despair, but the sweetness of self-denial and self-control; and, led by her mother's hand, she had drawn nearer to the Friend who welcomes every child with a love stronger than that of any father, tenderer than that of any mother.

Amy stirred, and sighed in her sleep; and, as if eager to begin at once to mend her fault, Jo looked up with an expression on her face which it had never worn before.

"I let the sun go down on my anger; I wouldn't forgive her, and to-day, if it hadn't been for Laurie, it might have been too late! How could I be so wicked?" said Jo, half aloud, as she leaned over her sister, softly stroking the wet hair scattered on the pillow.

As if she heard, Amy opened her eyes, and held out her arms, with a smile that went straight to Jo's heart. Neither said a word, but they hugged one another close, in spite of the blankets, and everything was forgiven and forgotten in one hearty kiss.

---

IX.

## MEG GOES TO VANITY FAIR.

"I DO think it was the most fortunate thing in the world that those children should have the measles just now," said Meg, one April day, as she stood packing the "go abroady" trunk in her room, surrounded by her sisters.

"And so nice of Annie Moffat not to forget her promise. A whole fortnight of fun will be regularly splendid," replied Jo, looking like a windmill, as she folded skirts with her long arms.

"And such lovely weather; I'm so glad of that," added Beth, tidily sorting neck and hair ribbons in her best box, lent for the great occasion.

"I wish I was going to have a fine time, and wear all these nice things," said Amy, with her mouth full of pins, as she artistically replenished her sister's cushion.

"I wish you were all going; but, as you can't, I shall keep my adventures to tell you when I come back. I'm sure it's the least I can do, when you have been so kind, lending me things, and helping me get ready," said Meg, glancing round the room at the very simple outfit, which seemed nearly perfect in their eyes.

"What did mother give you out of the treasure-box?" asked Amy, who had not been present at the opening of a certain cedar chest, in which Mrs. March kept a few relics of past splendor, as gifts for her girls when the proper time came.

"A pair of silk stockings, that pretty carved fan, and a lovely blue sash. I wanted the violet silk; but there isn't time to make it over, so I must be contented with my old tarlatan."

"It will look nicely over my new muslin skirt, and the sash will set it off beautifully. I wish I hadn't smashed my coral bracelet, for you might have had it," said Jo, who loved to give and lend, but whose possessions were usually too dilapidated to be of much use.

"There is a lovely old-fashioned pearl set in the treasure-box; but mother said real flowers were the prettiest ornament for a young girl, and Laurie promised to send me all I want," replied Meg. "Now, let me see; there's my new gray walking-suit—just curl up the feather in my hat, Beth,—then my poplin, for Sunday, and the small party,—it looks heavy for spring, doesn't it? The violet silk would be so nice; oh, dear!"

"Never mind; you've got the tarlatan for the big party, and you always look like an angel in white," said Amy, brooding over the little store of finery in which her soul delighted.

"It isn't low-necked, and it doesn't sweep enough, but it will have to do. My blue house-dress looks so well, turned and freshly trimmed, that I feel as if I'd got a new one. My silk sacque isn't a bit the fashion, and my bonnet doesn't look like Sallie's; I didn't like to say anything, but I was sadly disappointed in my umbrella. I told mother black, with a white handle, but she forgot, and bought a green one, with a yellowish handle. It's strong and neat, so I ought not to complain, but I know I shall feel ashamed of it beside Annie's silk one with a gold top," sighed Meg, surveying the little umbrella with great disfavor.

"Change it," advised Jo.

"I won't be so silly, or hurt Marmee's feelings, when she took so much pains to get my things. It's a nonsensical notion of mine, and I'm not going to give up to it. My silk stockings and two pairs of new gloves are my comfort. You are a dear, to lend me yours, Jo. I feel so rich, and sort of elegant, with two new pairs, and the old ones cleaned up for common;" and Meg took a refreshing peep at her glove-box.

"Annie Moffat has blue and pink bows on her night-caps; would you put some on mine?" she asked, as Beth brought up a pile of snowy muslins, fresh from Hannah's hands.

"No, I wouldn't; for the smart caps won't match the plain gowns, without any trimming on them. Poor folks shouldn't rig," said Jo decidedly.

"I wonder if I shall *ever* be happy enough to have real lace on my clothes, and bows on my caps?" said Meg impatiently.

"You said the other day that you'd be perfectly happy if you could only go to Annie Moffat's," observed Beth, in her quiet way.

"So I did! Well, I *am* happy, and I *won't* fret; but it does seem as if the more one gets the more one wants, doesn't it? There, now, the trays are ready, and everything in but my ball-dress, which I shall leave for mother to pack," said Meg, cheering up, as she glanced from the half-filled trunk to the many-times pressed and mended white tarlatan, which she called her "ball-dress," with an important air.

The next day was fine, and Meg departed, in style, for a fortnight of novelty and pleasure. Mrs. March had consented to the visit rather reluctantly, fearing that Margaret would come back more discontented than she went. But she had begged so hard, and Sallie had promised to take good care of her, and a little pleasure seemed so delightful after a winter of irksome work, that the mother yielded, and the daughter went to take her first taste of fashionable life.

The Moffats *were* very fashionable, and simple Meg was rather daunted, at first, by the splendor of the house and the elegance of its occupants. But they were kindly people, in spite of the frivolous life they led, and soon put their guest at her ease. Perhaps Meg felt, without understanding why, that they were not particularly cultivated or intelligent people, and that all their gilding could not quite conceal the ordinary material of which they were made. It certainly was agreeable to fare sumptuously, drive in a fine carriage, wear her best frock every day, and do nothing but enjoy herself. It suited her exactly; and soon she began to imitate the manners and conversation of those about her; to put on little airs and graces, use French phrases, crimp her hair, take in her dresses, and talk about the fashions as well as she could. The more she saw of Annie Moffat's pretty things, the more she envied her, and sighed to be rich. Home now looked bare and dismal as she thought of it, work grew harder than ever, and she felt that she was a very destitute and much-injured girl, in spite of the new gloves and silk stockings.

She had not much time for repining, however, for the three young girls were busily employed in "having a good time." They shopped, walked, rode, and called all day; went to theatres and operas, or frolicked at home in the evening; for Annie had many friends, and knew how to entertain them. Her older sisters were very fine young ladies, and one was engaged, which was extremely interesting and romantic, Meg thought. Mr. Moffat was a fat, jolly old gentleman, who knew her father; and Mrs. Moffat, a fat, jolly old lady, who took as great a fancy to Meg as her daughter had done. Every one petted her; and "Daisy," as they called her, was in a fair way to have her head turned.

When the evening for the "small party" came, she found that the poplin wouldn't do at all, for the other girls were putting on thin dresses, and making themselves very fine indeed; so out came the tarlatan, looking older, limper, and shabbier than ever beside Sallie's crisp new one. Meg saw the girls glance at it and then at one another, and her cheeks began to burn, for, with all her gentleness, she was very proud. No one said a word about it, but Sallie offered to dress her hair, and Annie to tie her sash, and Belle, the engaged sister, praised her white arms; but in their kindness Meg saw only pity for her poverty, and her heart felt very heavy as she stood by herself, while the others laughed, chattered, and flew about like gauzy butterflies. The hard, bitter feeling was getting pretty bad, when the maid brought in a box of flowers. Before she could speak, Annie had the cover off, and all were exclaiming at the lovely roses, heath, and fern within.

"It's for Belle, of course; George always sends her some, but these are altogether ravishing," cried Annie, with a great sniff.

"They are for Miss March, the man said. And here's a note," put in the maid, holding it to Meg.

"What fun! Who are they from? Didn't know you had a lover," cried the girls, fluttering about Meg in a high state of curiosity and surprise.

"The note is from mother, and the flowers from Laurie," said Meg simply, yet much gratified that he had not forgotten her.

"Oh, indeed!" said Annie, with a funny look, as Meg slipped the note into her pocket, as a sort of talisman against envy, vanity, and false pride; for the few loving words had done her good, and the flowers cheered her up by their beauty.

Feeling almost happy again, she laid by a few ferns and roses for herself, and quickly made up the rest in dainty bouquets for the breasts, hair, or skirts of her friends, offering them so prettily that Clara, the elder sister, told her she was "the sweetest little thing she ever saw;" and they looked quite charmed with her small attention. Somehow the kind act finished her despondency; and when all the rest went to show themselves to Mrs. Moffat, she saw a happy, bright-eyed face in the mirror, as she laid her ferns against her rippling hair, and fastened the roses in the dress that didn't strike her as so *very* shabby now.

She enjoyed herself very much that evening, for she danced to her heart's content; every one was very kind, and she had three compliments. Annie made her sing, and some one said she had a remarkably fine voice; Major Lincoln asked who "the fresh little girl, with the beautiful eyes," was; and Mr. Moffat insisted on dancing with her, because she "didn't dawdle, but had some spring in her," as he gracefully expressed it. So, altogether, she had a very nice time, till she overheard a bit of a conversation, which disturbed her extremely. She was sitting just inside the conservatory, waiting for her partner to bring her an ice, when she heard a voice ask, on the other side of the flowery wall,—

"How old is he?"

"Sixteen or seventeen, I should say," replied another voice.

"It would be a grand thing for one of those girls, wouldn't it? Sallie says they are very intimate now, and the old man quite dotes on them."

"Mrs M. has made her plans, I dare say, and will play her cards well, early as it is. The girl evidently doesn't think of it yet," said Mrs. Moffat.

"She told that fib about her mamma, as if she did know, and colored up when the flowers came, quite prettily. Poor thing! she'd be so nice if she was only got up in style. Do you think she'd be offended if we offered to lend her a dress for Thursday?" asked another voice.

"She's proud, but I don't believe she'd mind, for that dowdy tarlatan is all she has got. She may tear it to-night, and that will be a good excuse for offering a decent one."

"We'll see. I shall ask young Laurence, as a compliment to her, and we'll have fun about it afterward."

Here Meg's partner appeared, to find her looking much flushed and rather agitated. She *was* proud, and her pride was useful just then, for it helped her hide her mortification, anger, and disgust at what she had just heard; for, innocent and unsuspicious as she was, she could not help understanding the gossip of her friends. She tried to forget it, but could not, and kept repeating to herself, "Mrs. M. has made her plans," "that fib about her mamma," and "dowdy tarlatan," till she was ready to cry, and rush home to tell her troubles and ask for advice. As that was impossible, she did her best to seem gay; and, being rather excited, she succeeded so well that no one dreamed what an effort she was making. She was very glad when it was all over, and she was quiet in her bed, where she could think and wonder and fume till her head ached and her hot cheeks were cooled by a few natural tears. Those foolish, yet well-meant words, had opened a new world to Meg, and much disturbed the peace of the old one, in which, till now, she had lived as happily as a child.

Her innocent friendship with Laurie was spoilt by the silly speeches she had overheard; her faith in her mother was a little shaken by the worldly plans attributed to her by Mrs. Moffat, who judged others by herself; and the sensible resolution to be contented with the simple wardrobe which suited a poor man's daughter, was weakened by the unnecessary pity of girls who thought a shabby dress one of the greatest calamities under heaven.

Poor Meg had a restless night, and got up heavy-eyed, unhappy, half resentful toward her friends, and half ashamed of herself for not speaking out frankly, and setting everything right. Everybody dawdled that morning, and it was noon before the girls found energy enough even to take up their worsted work. Something in the manner of her friends struck Meg at once; they treated her with more respect, she thought; took quite a tender interest in what she said, and looked at her with eyes that plainly betrayed curiosity. All this surprised and flattered her, though she did not understand it till Miss Belle looked up from her writing, and said, with a sentimental air,—

"Daisy, dear, I've sent an invitation to your friend, Mr. Laurence, for Thursday. We should like to know him, and it's only a proper compliment to you."

Meg colored, but a mischievous fancy to tease the girls made her reply demurely,—

"You are very kind, but I'm afraid he won't come."

"Why not, *chérie*?" asked Miss Belle.

"He's too old."

"My child, what do you mean? What is his age, I beg to know!" cried Miss Clara.

"Nearly seventy, I believe," answered Meg, counting stitches, to hide the merriment in her eyes.

"You sly creature! Of course we meant the young man," exclaimed Miss Belle, laughing.

"There isn't any; Laurie is only a little boy," and Meg laughed also at the queer look which the sisters exchanged as she thus described her supposed lover.

"About your age," Nan said.

"Nearer my sister Jo's; *I* am seventeen in August," returned Meg, tossing her head.

"It's very nice of him to send you flowers, isn't it?" said Annie, looking wise about nothing.

"Yes, he often does, to all of us; for their house is full, and we are so fond of them. My mother and old Mr. Laurence are friends, you know, so it is quite natural that we children should play together;" and Meg hoped they would say no more.

"It's evident Daisy isn't out yet," said Miss Clara to Belle, with a nod.

"Quite a pastoral state of innocence all round," returned Miss Belle, with a shrug.

"I'm going out to get some little matters for my girls; can I do anything for you, young ladies?" asked Mrs. Moffat, lumbering in, like an elephant, in silk and lace.

"No, thank you, ma'am," replied Sallie. "I've got my new pink silk for Thursday, and don't want a thing."

"Nor I,—" began Meg, but stopped, because it occurred to her that she *did* want several things, and could not have them.

"What shall you wear?" asked Sallie.

"My old white one again, if I can mend it fit to be seen; it got sadly torn last night," said Meg, trying to speak quite easily, but feeling very uncomfortable.

"Why don't you send home for another?" said Sallie, who was not an observing young lady.

"I haven't got any other." It cost Meg an effort to say that, but Sallie did not see it, and exclaimed, in amiable surprise,—

"Only that? How funny—" She did not finish her speech, for Belle shook her head at her, and broke in, saying kindly,—

"Not at all; where is the use of having a lot of dresses when she isn't out? There's no need of sending home, Daisy, even if you had a dozen, for I've got a sweet blue silk laid away, which I've outgrown, and you shall wear it, to please me, won't you, dear?"

"You are very kind, but I don't mind my old dress, if you don't; it does well enough for a little girl like me," said Meg.

"Now do let me please myself by dressing you up in style. I admire to do it, and you'd be a regular little beauty, with a touch here and there. I sha'n't let any one see you till you are done, and then we'll burst upon them like Cinderella and her godmother, going to the ball," said Belle, in her persuasive tone.

Meg couldn't refuse the offer so kindly made, for a desire to see if she would be "a little beauty" after touching up, caused her to accept, and forget all her former uncomfortable feelings towards the Moffats.

On the Thursday evening, Belle shut herself up with her maid; and, between them, they turned Meg into a fine lady. They crimped and curled her hair, they polished her neck and arms with some fragrant powder, touched her lips with coralline salve, to make them redder, and Hortense would have added "a *soupçon* of rouge," if Meg had not rebelled. They laced her into a sky-blue dress, which was so tight she could hardly breathe, and so low in the neck that modest Meg blushed at herself in the mirror. A set of silver filagree was added, bracelets, necklace, brooch, and even ear-rings, for Hortense tied them on, with a bit of pink silk, which did not show. A cluster of tea-rosebuds at the bosom, and a *ruche*, reconciled Meg to the display of her pretty white shoulders, and a pair of high-heeled blue silk boots satisfied the last wish of her heart. A laced handkerchief, a plumy fan, and a bouquet in a silver holder finished her off; and Miss Belle surveyed her with the satisfaction of a little girl with a newly dressed doll.

"Mademoiselle is charmante, très jolie, is she not?" cried Hortense, clasping her hands in an affected rapture.

"Come and show yourself," said Miss Belle, leading the way to the room where the others were waiting.

As Meg went rustling after, with her long skirts trailing, her ear-rings tinkling, her curls waving, and her heart beating, she felt as if her "fun" had really begun at last, for the mirror had plainly told her that she *was* "a little beauty." Her friends repeated the pleasing phrase enthusiastically; and, for several minutes, she stood, like the jackdaw in the fable, enjoying her borrowed plumes, while the rest chattered like a party of magpies.

"While I dress, do you drill her, Nan, in the management of her skirt, and those French heels, or she will trip herself up. Take your silver butterfly, and catch up that long curl on the left side of her head, Clara, and don't any of you disturb the charming work of my hands," said Belle, as she hurried away, looking well pleased with her success.

"I'm afraid to go down, I feel so queer and stiff and half-dressed," said Meg to Sallie, as the bell rang, and Mrs. Moffat sent to ask the young ladies to appear at once.

"You don't look a bit like yourself, but you are very nice. I'm nowhere beside you, for Belle has heaps of taste, and you're quite French, I assure you. Let your flowers hang; don't be so careful of them, and be sure you don't trip," returned Sallie, trying not to care that Meg was prettier than herself.

Keeping that warning carefully in mind, Margaret got safely down stairs, and sailed into the drawing-rooms, where the Moffats and a few early guests were assembled. She very soon discovered that there is a charm about fine clothes which attracts a certain class of people, and secures their respect. Several young ladies, who had taken no notice of her before, were very affectionate all of a sudden; several young gentlemen, who had only stared at her at the other party, now not only stared, but asked to be introduced, and said all manner of foolish but agreeable things to her; and several old ladies, who sat on sofas, and criticised the rest of the party, inquired who she was, with an air of interest. She heard Mrs. Moffat reply to one of them,—

"Daisy March—father a colonel in the army—one of our first families, but reverses of fortune, you know; intimate friends of the Laurences; sweet creature, I assure you; my Ned is quite wild about her."

"Dear me!" said the old lady, putting up her glass for another observation of Meg, who tried to look as if she had not heard, and been rather shocked at Mrs. Moffat's fibs.

The "queer feeling" did not pass away, but she imagined herself acting the new part of fine lady, and so got on pretty well, though the tight dress gave her a side-ache, the train kept getting under her feet, and she was in constant fear lest her ear-rings should fly off, and get lost or broken. She was flirting her fan and laughing at the feeble jokes of a young gentleman who tried to be witty, when she suddenly stopped laughing and looked confused; for, just opposite, she saw Laurie. He was staring at her with undisguised surprise, and disapproval also, she thought; for, though he bowed and smiled, yet something in his honest eyes made her blush, and wish she had her old dress on. To complete her confusion, she saw Belle nudge Annie, and both glance from her to Laurie, who, she was happy to see, looked unusually boyish and shy.

"Silly creatures, to put such thoughts into my head! I won't care for it, or let it change me a bit," thought Meg, and rustled across the room to shake hands with her friend.

"I'm glad you came, I was afraid you wouldn't," she said, with her most grown-up air.

"Jo wanted me to come, and tell her how you looked, so I did;" answered Laurie, without turning his eyes upon her, though he half smiled at her maternal tone.

"What shall you tell her?" asked Meg, full of curiosity to know his opinion of her, yet feeling ill at ease with him, for the first time.

"I shall say I didn't know you; for you look so grown-up, and unlike yourself, I'm quite afraid of you," he said, fumbling at his glove-button.

"How absurd of you! The girls dressed me up for fun, and I rather like it. Wouldn't Jo stare if she saw me?" said Meg, bent on making him say whether he thought her improved or not.

"Yes, I think she would," returned Laurie gravely.

"Don't you like me so?" asked Meg.

"No, I don't," was the blunt reply.

"Why not?" in an anxious tone.

He glanced at her frizzled head, bare shoulders, and fantastically trimmed dress, with an expression that abashed her more than his answer, which had not a particle of his usual politeness about it.

"I don't like fuss and feathers."

That was altogether too much from a lad younger than herself; and Meg walked away, saying petulantly,—

"You are the rudest boy I ever saw."

Feeling very much ruffled, she went and stood at a quiet window, to cool her cheeks, for the tight dress gave her an uncomfortably brilliant color. As she stood there, Major Lincoln passed by; and, a minute after, she heard him saying to his mother,—

"They are making a fool of that little girl; I wanted you to see her, but they have spoilt her entirely; she's nothing but a doll, to-night."

"Oh, dear!" sighed Meg; "I wish I'd been sensible, and worn my own things; then I should not have disgusted other people, or felt so uncomfortable and ashamed myself."

She leaned her forehead on the cool pane, and stood half hidden by the curtains, never minding that her favorite waltz had begun, till some one touched her; and, turning, she saw Laurie, looking penitent, as he said, with his very best bow, and his hand out,—

"Please forgive my rudeness, and come and dance with me."

"I'm afraid it will be too disagreeable to you," said Meg, trying to look offended, and failing entirely.

"Not a bit of it; I'm dying to do it. Come, I'll be good; I don't like your gown, but I do think you are—just splendid;" and he waved his hands, as if words failed to express his admiration.

Meg smiled and relented, and whispered, as they stood waiting to catch the time,—

"Take care my skirt don't trip you up; it's the plague of my life, and I was a goose to wear it."

"Pin it round your neck, and then it will be useful," said Laurie, looking down at the little blue boots, which he evidently approved of.

Away they went, fleetly and gracefully; for, having practised at home, they were well matched, and the blithe young couple were a pleasant sight to see, as they twirled merrily round and round, feeling more friendly than ever after their small tiff.

"Laurie, I want you to do me a favor; will you?" said Meg, as he stood fanning her, when her breath gave out, which it did very soon, though she would not own why.

"Won't I!" said Laurie, with alacrity.

"Please don't tell them at home about my dress to-night. They won't understand the joke, and it will worry mother."

"Then why did you do it?" said Laurie's eyes, so plainly that Meg hastily added,—

"I shall tell them, myself, all about it, and "fess' to mother how silly I've been. But I'd rather do it myself; so you'll not tell, will you?"

"I give you my word I won't; only what shall I say when they ask me?"

"Just say I looked pretty well, and was having a good time."

"I'll say the first, with all my heart; but how about the other? You don't look as if you were having a good time; are you?" and Laurie looked at her with an expression which made her answer, in a whisper,—

"No; not just now. Don't think I'm horrid; I only wanted a little fun, but this sort doesn't pay, I find, and I'm getting tired of it."

"Here comes Ned Moffat; what does he want?" said Laurie, knitting his black brows, as if he did not regard his young host in the light of a pleasant addition to the party.

"He put his name down for three dances, and I suppose he's coming for them. What a bore!" said Meg, assuming a languid air, which amused Laurie immensely.

He did not speak to her again till supper-time, when he saw her drinking champagne with Ned and his friend Fisher, who were behaving "like a pair of fools," as Laurie said to himself, for he felt a brotherly sort of right to watch over the Marches, and fight their battles whenever a defender was needed.

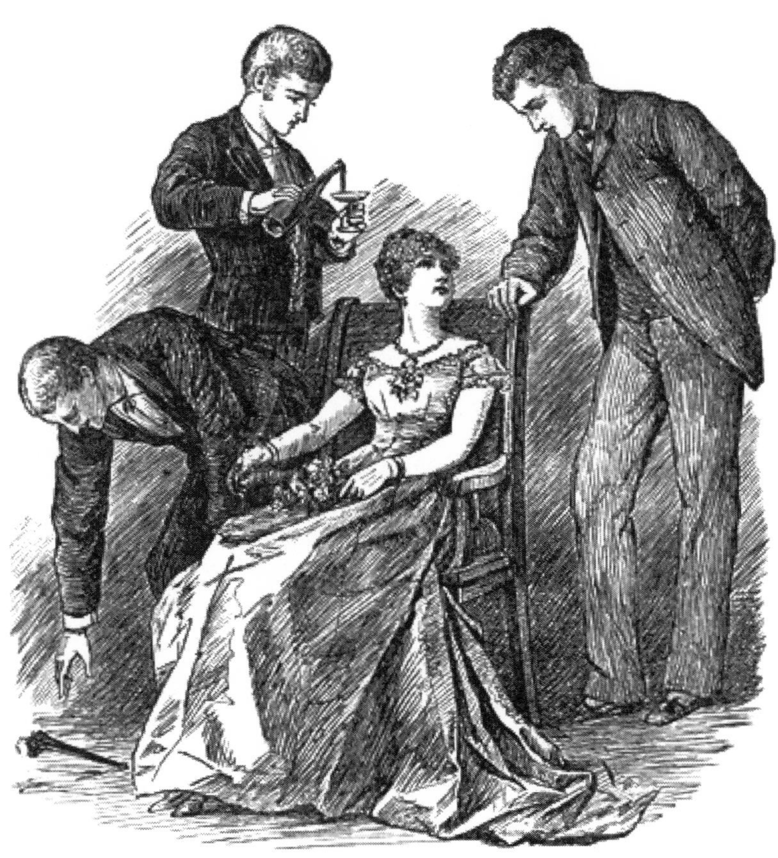

"You'll have a splitting headache to-morrow, if you drink much of that. I wouldn't Meg; your mother doesn't like it, you know," he whispered, leaning over her chair, as Ned turned to refill her glass, and Fisher stooped to pick up her fan.

"I'm not Meg, to-night; I'm 'a doll,' who does all sorts of crazy things. To-morrow I shall put away my 'fuss and feathers,' and be desperately good again," she answered, with an affected little laugh.

"Wish to-morrow was here, then," muttered Laurie, walking off, ill-pleased at the change he saw in her.

Meg danced and flirted, chattered and giggled, as the other girls did; after supper she undertook the German, and blundered through it, nearly upsetting her partner with her long skirt, and romping in a way that scandalized Laurie, who looked on and meditated a lecture. But he got no chance to deliver it, for Meg kept away from him till he came to say good-night.

"Remember!" she said, trying to smile, for the splitting headache had already begun.

"Silence à la mort," replied Laurie, with a melodramatic flourish, as he went away.

This little bit of by-play excited Annie's curiosity; but Meg was too tired for gossip, and went to bed, feeling as if she had been to a masquerade, and hadn't enjoyed herself as much as she expected. She was sick all the next day, and on Saturday went home, quite used up with her fortnight's fun, and feeling that she had "sat in the lap of luxury" long enough.

"It does seem pleasant to be quiet, and not have company manners on all the time. Home *is* a nice place, though it isn't splendid," said Meg, looking about her with a restful expression, as she sat with her mother and Jo on the Sunday evening.

"I'm glad to hear you say so, dear, for I was afraid home would seem dull and poor to you, after your fine quarters," replied her mother, who had given her many anxious looks that day; for motherly eyes are quick to see any change in children's faces.

Meg had told her adventures gayly, and said over and over what a charming time she had had; but something still seemed to weigh upon her spirits, and, when the younger girls were gone to bed, she sat thoughtfully staring at the fire, saying little, and looking worried. As the clock struck nine, and Jo proposed bed, Meg suddenly left her chair, and, taking Beth's stool, leaned her elbows on her mother's knee, saying bravely,—

"Marmee, I want to "fess.'"

"I thought so; what is it, dear?"

"Shall I go away?" asked Jo discreetly.

"Of course not; don't I always tell you everything? I was ashamed to speak of it before the children, but I want you to know all the dreadful things I did at the Moffat's."

"We are prepared," said Mrs. March, smiling, but looking a little anxious.

"I told you they dressed me up, but I didn't tell you that they powdered and squeezed and frizzled, and made me look like a fashion-plate. Laurie thought I wasn't proper; I know he did, though he didn't say so, and one man called me 'a doll.' I knew it was silly, but they flattered me, and said I was a beauty, and quantities of nonsense, so I let them make a fool of me."

"Is that all?" asked Jo, as Mrs. March looked silently at the downcast face of her pretty daughter, and could not find it in her heart to blame her little follies.

"No; I drank champagne and romped and tried to flirt, and was altogether abominable," said Meg self-reproachfully.

"There is something more, I think;" and Mrs. March smoothed the soft cheek, which suddenly grew rosy, as Meg answered slowly,—

"Yes; it's very silly, but I want to tell it, because I hate to have people say and think such things about us and Laurie."

Then she told the various bits of gossip she had heard at the Moffats; and, as she spoke, Jo saw her mother fold her lips tightly, as if ill pleased that such ideas should be put into Meg's innocent mind.

"Well, if that isn't the greatest rubbish I ever heard," cried Jo indignantly. "Why didn't you pop out and tell them so, on the spot?"

"I couldn't, it was so embarrassing for me. I couldn't help hearing, at first, and then I was so angry and ashamed, I didn't remember that I ought to go away."

"Just wait till *I* see Annie Moffat, and I'll show you how to settle such ridiculous stuff. The idea of having 'plans,' and being kind to Laurie, because he's rich, and may marry us by and by! Won't he shout, when I tell him what those silly things say about us poor children?" and Jo laughed, as if, on second thoughts, the thing struck her as a good joke.

"If you tell Laurie, I'll never forgive you! She mustn't, must she, mother?" said Meg, looking distressed.

"No; never repeat that foolish gossip, and forget it as soon as you can," said Mrs. March gravely. "I was very unwise to let you go among people of whom I know so little,—kind, I dare say, but worldly, ill-bred, and full of these vulgar ideas about young people. I am more sorry than I can express for the mischief this visit may have done you, Meg."

"Don't be sorry, I won't let it hurt me; I'll forget all the bad, and remember only the good; for I did enjoy a great deal, and thank you very much for letting me go. I'll not be sentimental or dissatisfied, mother; I know I'm a silly little girl, and I'll stay with you till I'm fit to take care of myself. But it *is* nice to be praised and admired, and I can't help saying I like it," said Meg, looking half ashamed of the confession.

"That is perfectly natural, and quite harmless, if the liking does not become a passion, and lead one to do foolish or unmaidenly things. Learn to know and value the praise which is worth having, and to excite the admiration of excellent people by being modest as well as pretty, Meg."

Margaret sat thinking a moment, while Jo stood with her hands behind her, looking both interested and a little perplexed; for it was a new thing to see Meg blushing and talking about admiration, lovers, and things of that sort; and Jo felt as if, during that fortnight, her sister had grown up amazingly, and was drifting away from her into a world where she could not follow.

"Mother, do you have 'plans,' as Mrs. Moffat said?" asked Meg bashfully.

"Yes, my dear, I have a great many; all mothers do, but mine differ somewhat from Mrs. Moffat's, I suspect. I will tell you some of them, for the time has come when a word may set this romantic little head and heart of yours right, on a very serious subject. You are young, Meg, but not too young to understand me; and mothers' lips are the fittest to speak of such things to girls like you. Jo, your turn will come in time, perhaps, so listen to my 'plans,' and help me carry them out, if they are good."

Jo went and sat on one arm of the chair, looking as if she thought they were about to join in some very solemn affair. Holding a hand of each, and watching the two young faces wistfully, Mrs. March said, in her serious yet cheery way,—

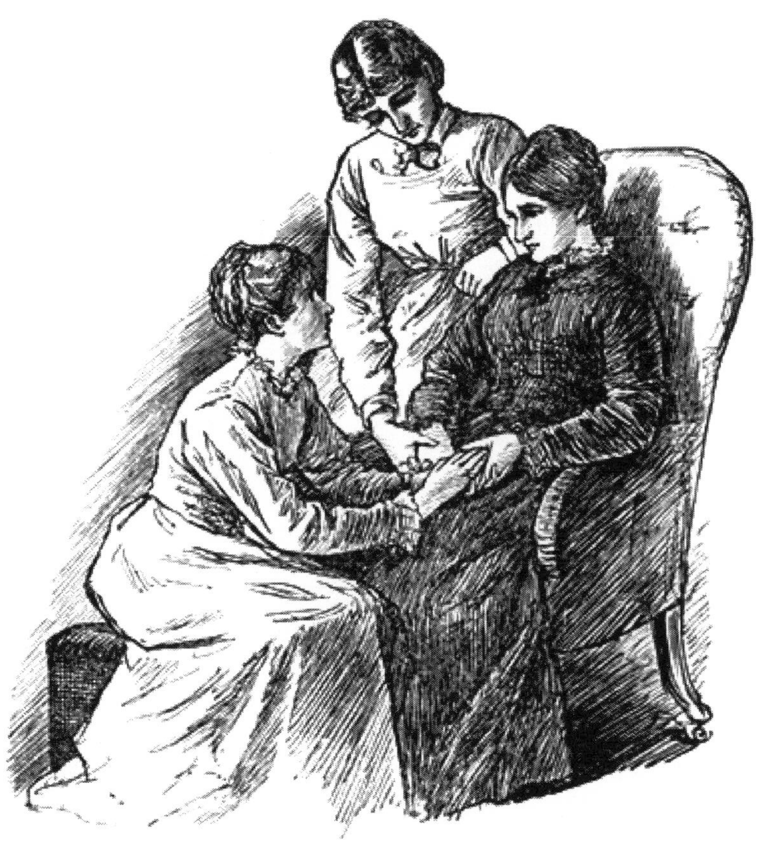

"I want my daughters to be beautiful, accomplished, and good; to be admired, loved, and respected; to have a happy youth, to be well and wisely married, and to lead useful, pleasant lives, with as little care and sorrow to try them as God sees fit to send. To be loved and chosen by a good man is the best and sweetest thing which can happen to a woman; and I sincerely hope my girls may know this beautiful experience. It is natural to think of it, Meg; right to hope and wait for it, and wise to prepare for it; so that, when the happy time comes, you may feel ready for the duties and worthy of the joy. My dear girls, I *am* ambitious for you, but not to have you make a dash in the world,—marry rich men merely because they are rich, or have splendid houses, which are not homes because love is wanting. Money is a needful and precious thing,—and, when well used, a noble thing,—but I never want you to think it is the first or only prize to strive for. I'd rather see you poor men's wives, if you were happy, beloved, contented, than queens on thrones, without self-respect and peace."

"Poor girls don't stand any chance, Belle says, unless they put themselves forward," sighed Meg.

"Then we'll be old maids," said Jo stoutly.

"Right, Jo; better be happy old maids than unhappy wives, or unmaidenly girls, running about to find husbands," said Mrs. March decidedly. "Don't be troubled, Meg; poverty seldom daunts a sincere lover. Some of the best and most honored women I know were poor girls, but so love-worthy that they were not allowed to be old maids. Leave these things to time; make this home happy, so that you may be fit for homes of your own, if they are offered you, and contented here if they are not. One thing remember, my girls: mother is always ready to be your confidant, father to be your friend; and both of us trust and hope that our daughters, whether married or single, will be the pride and comfort of our lives."

"We will, Marmee, we will!" cried both, with all their hearts, as she bade them good-night.

X.

# THE P. C. AND P. O.

AS spring came on, a new set of amusements became the fashion, and the lengthening days gave long afternoons for work and play of all sorts. The garden had to be put in order, and each sister had a quarter of the little plot to do what she liked with. Hannah used to say, "I'd know which each of them gardings belonged to, ef I see 'em in Chiny;" and so she might, for the girls' tastes differed as much as their characters. Meg's had roses and heliotrope, myrtle, and a little orange-tree in it. Jo's bed was never alike two seasons, for she was always trying experiments; this year it was to be a plantation of sun-flowers, the seeds of which cheerful and aspiring plant were to feed "Aunt Cockle-top" and her family of chicks. Beth had old-fashioned, fragrant flowers in her garden,—sweet peas and mignonette, larkspur, pinks, pansies, and southernwood, with chickweed for the bird, and catnip for the pussies. Amy had a bower in hers,—rather small and earwiggy, but very pretty to look at,—with honeysuckles and morning-glories hanging their colored horns and bells in graceful wreaths all over it; tall, white lilies, delicate ferns, and as many brilliant, picturesque plants as would consent to blossom there.

Gardening, walks, rows on the river, and flower-hunts employed the fine days; and for rainy ones, they had house diversions,—some old, some new,—all more or less original. One of these was the "P. C."; for, as secret societies were the fashion, it was thought proper to have one; and, as all of the girls admired Dickens, they called themselves the Pickwick Club. With a few interruptions, they had kept this up for a year, and met every Saturday evening in the big garret, on which occasions the ceremonies were as follows: Three chairs were arranged in a row before a table, on which was a lamp, also four white badges, with a big "P. C." in different colors on each, and the weekly newspaper, called "The Pickwick Portfolio," to which all contributed something; while Jo, who revelled in pens and ink, was the editor. At seven o'clock, the four members ascended to the club-room, tied their badges round their heads, and took their seats with great solemnity. Meg, as the eldest, was Samuel Pickwick; Jo, being of a literary turn, Augustus Snodgrass; Beth, because she was round and rosy, Tracy Tupman, and Amy, who was always trying to do what she couldn't, was Nathaniel Winkle. Pickwick, the president, read the paper, which was filled with original tales, poetry, local news, funny advertisements, and hints, in which they good-naturedly reminded each other of their faults and short-comings.

On one occasion, Mr. Pickwick put on a pair of spectacles without any glasses, rapped upon the table, hemmed, and, having stared hard at Mr. Snodgrass, who was tilting back in his chair, till he arranged himself properly, began to read:—

---

**"The Pickwick Portfolio."**
MAY , —

---

## ANNIVERSARY ODE.

Again we meet to celebrate
With badge and solemn rite,
Our fifty-second anniversary,
In Pickwick Hall, to-night.

We all are here in perfect health,
None gone from our small band;
Again we see each well-known face,
And press each friendly hand.

Our Pickwick, always at his post,
With reverence we greet,
As, spectacles on nose, he reads
Our well-filled weekly sheet.

Although he suffers from a cold,
We joy to hear him speak,
For words of wisdom from him fall,
In spite of croak or squeak.

Old six-foot Snodgrass looms on high,
With elephantine grace,
And beams upon the company,
With brown and jovial face.

Poetic fire lights up his eye,
He struggles 'gainst his lot.
Behold ambition on his brow,
And on his nose a blot!

Next our peaceful Tupman comes,
So rosy, plump, and sweet.
Who chokes with laughter at the puns,
And tumbles off his seat.

Prim little Winkle too is here,
With every hair in place,
A model of propriety,
Though he hates to wash his face.

The year is gone, we still unite
To joke and laugh and read,
And tread the path of literature
That doth to glory lead.

Long may our paper prosper well,
Our club unbroken be,
And coming years their blessings pour
On the useful, gay "P. C."

A. SNODGRASS.

## THE MASKED MARRIAGE.
## A TALE OF VENICE.

Gondola after gondola swept up to the marble steps, and left its lovely load to swell the brilliant throng that filled the stately halls of Count de Adelon. Knights and ladies, elves and pages, monks and flower-girls, all mingled gayly in the dance. Sweet voices and rich melody filled the air; and so with mirth and music the masquerade went on.

"Has your Highness seen the Lady Viola to-night?" asked a gallant troubadour of the fairy queen who floated down the hall upon his arm.

"Yes; is she not lovely, though so sad! Her dress is well chosen, too, for in a week she weds Count Antonio, whom she passionately hates."

"By my faith, I envy him. Yonder he comes, arrayed like a bridegroom, except the black mask. When that is off we shall see how he regards the fair maid whose heart he cannot win, though her stern father bestows her hand," returned the troubadour.

"'Tis whispered that she loves the young English artist who haunts her steps, and is spurned by the old count," said the lady, as they joined the dance.

The revel was at its height when a priest appeared, and, withdrawing the young pair to an alcove hung with purple velvet, he motioned them to kneel. Instant silence fell upon the gay throng; and not a sound, but the dash of fountains or the rustle of orange-groves sleeping in the moonlight, broke the hush, as Count de Adelon spoke thus:—

"My lords and ladies, pardon the ruse by which I have gathered you here to witness the marriage of my daughter. Father, we wait your services."

All eyes turned toward the bridal party, and a low murmur of amazement went through the throng, for neither bride nor groom removed their masks. Curiosity and wonder possessed all hearts, but respect restrained all tongues till the holy rite was over. Then the eager spectators gathered round the count, demanding an explanation.

"Gladly would I give it if I could; but I only know that it was the whim of my timid Viola, and I yielded to it. Now, my children, let the play end. Unmask, and receive my blessing."

But neither bent the knee; for the young bridegroom replied, in a tone that startled all listeners, as the mask fell, disclosing the noble face of Ferdinand Devereux, the artist lover; and, leaning on the breast where now flashed the star of an English earl, was the lovely Viola, radiant with joy and beauty.

"My lord, you scornfully bade me claim your daughter when I could boast as high a name and vast a fortune as the Count Antonio. I can do more; for even your ambitious soul cannot refuse the Earl of Devereux and De Vere, when he gives his ancient name and boundless wealth in return for the beloved hand of this fair lady, now my wife."

The count stood like one changed to stone; and, turning to the bewildered crowd, Ferdinand added, with a gay smile of triumph, "To you, my gallant friends, I can only wish that your wooing may prosper as mine has done; and that you may all win as fair a bride as I have, by this masked marriage."

S. PICKWICK.

---

Why is the P. C. like the Tower of Babel? It is full of unruly members.

---

THE HISTORY OF A SQUASH.

---

Once upon a time a farmer planted a little seed in his garden, and after a while it sprouted and became a vine, and bore many squashes. One day in October, when they were ripe, he picked one and took it to market. A grocerman bought and put it in his shop. That same morning, a little girl, in a brown hat and blue dress, with a round face and snub nose, went and bought it for her mother. She lugged it home, cut it up, and boiled it in the big pot; mashed some of it, with salt and butter, for dinner; and to the rest she added a pint of milk, two eggs, four spoons of sugar, nutmeg, and some crackers; put it in a deep dish, and baked it till it was brown and nice; and next day it was eaten by a family named March.

T. TUPMAN.

---

MR. PICKWICK, *Sir*:—

I address you upon the subject of sin the sinner I mean is a man named Winkle who makes trouble in his club by laughing and sometimes won't write his piece in this fine paper I hope you will pardon his badness and let him send a French fable because he can't write out of his head as he has so many lessons to do and no brains in future I will try to take time by the fetlock and prepare some work which will be all *commy la fo* that means all right I am in haste as it is nearly school time

Yours respectably,

N. WINKLE.

[The above is a manly and handsome acknowledgment of past misdemeanors. If our young friend studied punctuation, it would be well.]

## A SAD ACCIDENT.

On Friday last, we were startled by a violent shock in our basement, followed by cries of distress. On rushing, in a body, to the cellar, we discovered our beloved President prostrate upon the floor, having tripped and fallen while getting wood for domestic purposes. A perfect scene of ruin met our eyes; for in his fall Mr. Pickwick had plunged his head and shoulders into a tub of water, upset a keg of soft soap upon his manly form, and torn his garments badly. On being removed from this perilous situation, it was discovered that he had suffered no injury but several bruises; and, we are happy to add, is now doing well.

ED.

## THE PUBLIC BEREAVEMENT.

It is our painful duty to record the sudden and mysterious disappearance of our cherished friend, Mrs. Snowball Pat Paw. This lovely and beloved cat was the pet of a large circle of warm and admiring friends; for her beauty attracted all eyes, her graces and virtues endeared her to all hearts, and her loss is deeply felt by the whole community.

When last seen, she was sitting at the gate, watching the butcher's cart; and it is feared that some villain, tempted by her charms, basely stole her. Weeks have passed, but no trace of her has been discovered; and we relinquish all hope, tie a black ribbon to her basket, set aside her dish, and weep for her as one lost to us forever.

---

A sympathizing friend sends the following gem:—

### A LAMENT
### FOR S. B. PAT PAW.

We mourn the loss of our little pet,
And sigh o'er her hapless fate,
For never more by the fire she'll sit,
Nor play by the old green gate.

The little grave where her infant sleeps,
Is 'neath the chestnut tree;
But o'er *her* grave we may not weep,
We know not where it may be.

Her empty bed, her idle ball,
Will never see her more;
No gentle tap, no loving purr
Is heard at the parlor-door.

Another cat comes after her mice,
A cat with a dirty face;
But she does not hunt as our darling did,
Nor play with her airy grace.

Her stealthy paws tread the very hall
Where Snowball used to play,
But she only spits at the dogs our pet
So gallantly drove away.

She is useful and mild, and does her best,
But she is not fair to see;
And we cannot give her your place, dear,
Nor worship her as we worship thee.

A. S.

---

## ADVERTISEMENTS.

---

MISS ORANTHY BLUGGAGE, the accomplished Strong-Minded Lecturer, will deliver her famous Lecture on "WOMAN AND HER POSITION," at Pickwick Hall, next Saturday Evening, after the usual performances.

---

A WEEKLY MEETING will be held at Kitchen Place, to teach young ladies how to cook. Hannah Brown will preside; and all are invited to attend.

---

THE DUSTPAN SOCIETY will meet on Wednesday next, and parade in the upper story of the Club House. All members to appear in uniform and shoulder their brooms at nine precisely.

---

MRS. BETH BOUNCER will open her new assortment of Doll's Millinery next week. The latest Paris Fashions have arrived, and orders are respectfully solicited.

---

A NEW PLAY will appear at the Barnville Theatre, in the course of a few weeks, which will surpass anything ever seen on the American stage. "THE GREEK SLAVE, or Constantine the Avenger," is the name of this thrilling drama!!!

---

HINTS.

If S. P. didn't use so much soap on his hands, he wouldn't always be late at breakfast. A. S. is requested not to whistle in the street. T. T. please don't forget Amy's napkin. N. W. must not fret because his dress has not nine tucks.

---

WEEKLY REPORT.

Meg—Good.
Jo—Bad.
Beth—Very good.
Amy—Middling.

---

As the President finished reading the paper (which I beg leave to assure my readers is a *bona fide* copy of one written by *bona fide* girls once upon a time), a round of applause followed, and then Mr. Snodgrass rose to make a proposition.

"Mr. President and gentlemen," he began, assuming a parliamentary attitude and tone, "I wish to propose the admission of a new member,—one who highly deserves the honor, would be deeply grateful for it, and would add immensely to the spirit of the club, the literary value of the paper, and be no end jolly and nice. I propose Mr. Theodore Laurence as an honorary member of the P. C. Come now, do have him."

Jo's sudden change of tone made the girls laugh; but all looked rather anxious, and no one said a word, as Snodgrass took his seat.

"We'll put it to vote," said the President. "All in favor of this motion please to manifest it by saying 'Ay.'"

A loud response from Snodgrass, followed, to everybody's surprise, by a timid one from Beth.

"Contrary minded say 'No.'"

Meg and Amy were contrary minded; and Mr. Winkle rose to say, with great elegance, "We don't wish any boys; they only joke and bounce about. This is a ladies' club, and we wish to be private and proper."

"I'm afraid he'll laugh at our paper, and make fun of us afterward," observed Pickwick, pulling the little curl on her forehead, as she always did when doubtful.

Up rose Snodgrass, very much in earnest. "Sir, I give you my word as a gentleman, Laurie won't do anything of the sort. He likes to write, and he'll give a tone to our contributions, and keep us from being sentimental, don't you see? We can do so little for him, and he does so much for us, I think the least we can do is to offer him a place here, and make him welcome if he comes."

This artful allusion to benefits conferred brought Tupman to his feet, looking as if he had quite made up his mind.

"Yes, we ought to do it, even if we *are* afraid. I say he *may* come, and his grandpa, too, if he likes."

This spirited burst from Beth electrified the club, and Jo left her seat to shake hands approvingly. "Now then, vote again. Everybody remember it's our Laurie, and say 'Ay!'" cried Snodgrass excitedly.

"Ay! ay! ay!" replied three voices at once.

"Good! Bless you! Now, as there's nothing like 'taking time by the *fetlock*,' as Winkle characteristically observes, allow me to present the new member;" and, to the dismay of the rest of the club, Jo threw open the door of the closet, and displayed Laurie sitting on a rag-bag, flushed and twinkling with suppressed laughter.

"You rogue! you traitor! Jo, how could you?" cried the three girls, as Snodgrass led her friend triumphantly forth; and, producing both a chair and a badge, installed him in a jiffy.

"The coolness of you two rascals is amazing," began Mr. Pickwick, trying to get up an awful frown, and only succeeding in producing an amiable smile. But the new member was equal to the occasion; and, rising, with a grateful salutation to the Chair, said, in the most engaging manner, "Mr. President and ladies,—I beg pardon, gentlemen,—allow me to introduce myself as Sam Weller, the very humble servant of the club."

"Good! good!" cried Jo, pounding with the handle of the old warming-pan on which she leaned.

"My faithful friend and noble patron," continued Laurie, with a wave of the hand, "who has so flatteringly presented me, is not to be blamed for the base stratagem of to-night. I planned it, and she only gave in after lots of teasing."

"Come now, don't lay it all on yourself; you know I proposed the cupboard," broke in Snodgrass, who was enjoying the joke amazingly.

"Never you mind what she says. I'm the wretch that did it, sir," said the new member, with a Welleresque nod to Mr. Pickwick. "But on my honor, I never will do so again, and henceforth *dewote* myself to the interest of this immortal club."

"Hear! hear!" cried Jo, clashing the lid of the warming-pan like a cymbal.

"Go on, go on!" added Winkle and Tupman, while the President bowed benignly.

"I merely wish to say, that as a slight token of my gratitude for the honor done me, and as a means of promoting friendly relations between adjoining nations, I have set up a post-office in the hedge in the lower corner of the garden; a fine, spacious building, with padlocks on the doors, and every convenience for the mails,—also the females, if I may be allowed the expression. It's the old martin-house; but I've stopped up the door, and made the roof open, so it will hold all sorts of things, and save our valuable time. Letters, manuscripts, books, and bundles can be passed in there; and, as each nation has a key, it will be uncommonly nice, I fancy. Allow me to present the club key; and, with many thanks for your favor, take my seat."

Great applause as Mr. Weller deposited a little key on the table, and subsided; the warming-pan clashed and waved wildly, and it was some time before order could be restored. A long discussion followed, and every one came out surprising, for every one did her best; so it was an unusually lively meeting, and did not adjourn till a late hour, when it broke up with three shrill cheers for the new member.

No one ever regretted the admittance of Sam Weller, for a more devoted, well-behaved, and jovial member no club could have. He certainly did add "spirit" to the meetings, and "a tone" to the paper; for his orations convulsed his hearers, and his contributions were excellent, being patriotic, classical, comical, or dramatic, but never sentimental. Jo regarded them as worthy of Bacon, Milton, or Shakespeare; and remodelled her own works with good effect, she thought.

The P. O. was a capital little institution, and flourished wonderfully, for nearly as many queer things passed through it as through the real office. Tragedies and cravats, poetry and pickles, garden-seeds and long letters, music and gingerbread, rubbers, invitations, scoldings and puppies. The old gentleman liked the fun, and amused himself by sending odd bundles, mysterious messages, and funny telegrams; and his gardener, who was smitten with Hannah's charms, actually sent a love-letter to Jo's care. How they laughed when the secret came out, never dreaming how many love-letters that little post-office would hold in the years to come!

# XI.

## EXPERIMENTS.

"THE first of June! The Kings are off to the seashore to-morrow, and I'm free. Three months' vacation,—how I shall enjoy it!" exclaimed Meg, coming home one warm day to find Jo laid upon the sofa in an unusual state of exhaustion, while Beth took off her dusty boots, and Amy made lemonade for the refreshment of the whole party.

"Aunt March went to-day, for which, oh, be joyful!" said Jo. "I was mortally afraid she'd ask me to go with her; if she had, I should have felt as if I ought to do it; but Plumfield is about as gay as a churchyard, you know, and I'd rather be excused. We had a flurry getting the old lady off, and I had a fright every time she spoke to me, for I was in such a hurry to be through that I was uncommonly helpful and sweet, and feared she'd find it impossible to part from me. I quaked till she was fairly in the carriage, and had a final fright, for, as it drove off, she popped out her head, saying, 'Josy-phine, won't you—?' I didn't hear any more, for I basely turned and fled; I did actually run, and whisked round the corner, where I felt safe."

"Poor old Jo! she came in looking as if bears were after her," said Beth, as she cuddled her sister's feet with a motherly air.

"Aunt March is a regular samphire, is she not?" observed Amy, tasting her mixture critically.

"She means *vampire*, not sea-weed; but it doesn't matter; it's too warm to be particular about one's parts of speech," murmured Jo.

"What shall you do all your vacation?" asked Amy, changing the subject, with tact.

"I shall lie abed late, and do nothing," replied Meg, from the depths of the rocking-chair. "I've been routed up early all winter, and had to spend my days working for other people; so now I'm going to rest and revel to my heart's content."

"No," said Jo; "that dozy way wouldn't suit me. I've laid in a heap of books, and I'm going to improve my shining hours reading on my perch in the old apple-tree, when I'm not having l———"

"Don't say 'larks!'" implored Amy, as a return snub for the "samphire" correction.

"I'll say 'nightingales,' then, with Laurie; that's proper and appropriate, since he's a warbler."

"Don't let us do any lessons, Beth, for a while, but play all the time, and rest, as the girls mean to," proposed Amy.

"Well, I will, if mother doesn't mind. I want to learn some new songs, and my children need fitting up for the summer; they are dreadfully out of order, and really suffering for clothes."

"May we, mother?" asked Meg, turning to Mrs. March, who sat sewing, in what they called "Marmee's corner."

"You may try your experiment for a week, and see how you like it. I think by Saturday night you will find that all play and no work is as bad as all work and no play."

"Oh, dear, no! it will be delicious, I'm sure," said Meg complacently.

"I now propose a toast, as my 'friend and pardner, Sairy Gamp,' says. Fun forever, and no grubbing!" cried Jo, rising, glass in hand, as the lemonade went round.

They all drank it merrily, and began the experiment by lounging for the rest of the day. Next morning, Meg did not appear till ten o'clock; her solitary breakfast did not taste nice, and the room seemed lonely and untidy; for Jo had not filled the vases, Beth had not dusted, and Amy's books lay scattered about. Nothing was neat and pleasant but "Marmee's corner," which looked as usual; and there Meg sat, to "rest and read," which meant yawn, and imagine what pretty summer dresses she would get with her salary. Jo spent the morning on the river, with Laurie, and the afternoon reading and crying over "The Wide, Wide World," up in the apple-tree. Beth began by rummaging everything out of the big closet, where her family resided; but, getting tired before half done, she left her establishment topsy-turvy, and went to her music, rejoicing that she had no dishes to wash. Amy arranged her bower, put on her best white frock, smoothed her curls, and sat down to draw, under the honeysuckles, hoping some one would see and inquire who the young artist was. As no one appeared but an inquisitive daddy-long-legs, who examined her work with interest, she went to walk, got caught in a shower, and came home dripping.

At tea-time they compared notes, and all agreed that it had been a delightful, though unusually long day. Meg, who went shopping in the afternoon, and got a "sweet blue muslin," had discovered, after she had cut the breadths off, that it wouldn't wash, which mishap made her slightly cross. Jo had burnt the skin off her nose boating, and got a raging headache by reading too long. Beth was worried by the confusion of her closet, and the difficulty of learning three or four songs at once; and Amy deeply regretted the damage done her frock, for Katy Brown's party was to be the next day; and now, like Flora McFlimsey, she had "nothing to wear." But these were mere trifles; and they assured their mother that the experiment was working finely. She smiled, said nothing, and, with Hannah's help, did their neglected work, keeping home pleasant, and the domestic machinery running smoothly. It was astonishing what a peculiar and uncomfortable state of things was produced by the "resting and revelling" process. The days kept getting longer and longer; the weather was unusually variable, and so were tempers; an unsettled feeling possessed every one, and Satan found plenty of mischief for the idle hands to do. As the height of luxury, Meg put out some of her sewing, and then found time hang so heavily that she fell to snipping and spoiling her clothes, in her attempts to furbish them up à la Moffat. Jo read till her eyes gave out, and she was sick of books; got so fidgety that even good-natured Laurie had a quarrel with her, and so reduced in spirits that she desperately wished she had gone with Aunt March. Beth got on pretty well, for she was constantly forgetting that it was to be *all play, and no work*, and fell back into her old ways now and then; but something in the air affected her, and, more than once, her tranquillity was much disturbed; so much so, that, on one occasion, she actually shook poor dear Joanna, and told her she was "a fright." Amy fared worst of all, for her resources were small; and when her sisters left her to amuse and care for herself, she soon found that accomplished and important little self a great burden. She didn't like dolls, fairy-tales were childish, and one couldn't draw all the time; tea-parties didn't amount to much, neither did picnics, unless very well conducted. "If one could have a fine house, full of nice girls, or go travelling, the summer would be delightful; but to stay at home with three selfish sisters and a grown-up boy was enough to try the patience of a Boaz," complained Miss Malaprop, after several days devoted to pleasure, fretting, and *ennui.*

No one would own that they were tired of the experiment; but, by Friday night, each acknowledged to herself that she was glad the week was nearly done. Hoping to impress the lesson more deeply, Mrs. March, who had a good deal of humor, resolved to finish off the trial in an appropriate manner; so she gave Hannah a holiday, and let the girls enjoy the full effect of the play system.

When they got up on Saturday morning, there was no fire in the kitchen, no breakfast in the dining-room, and no mother anywhere to be seen.

"Mercy on us! what *has* happened?" cried Jo, staring about her in dismay.

Meg ran upstairs, and soon came back again, looking relieved, but rather bewildered, and a little ashamed.

"Mother isn't sick, only very tired, and she says she is going to stay quietly in her room all day, and let us do the best we can. It's a very queer thing for her to do, she doesn't act a bit like herself; but she says it has been a hard week for her, so we mustn't grumble, but take care of ourselves."

"That's easy enough, and I like the idea; I'm aching for something to do—that is, some new amusement, you know," added Jo quickly.

In fact it *was* an immense relief to them all to have a little work, and they took hold with a will, but soon realized the truth of Hannah's saying, "Housekeeping ain't no joke." There was plenty of food in the larder, and, while Beth and Amy set the table, Meg and Jo got breakfast, wondering, as they did so, why servants ever talked about hard work.

"I shall take some up to mother, though she said we were not to think of her, for she'd take care of herself," said Meg, who presided, and felt quite matronly behind the teapot.

So a tray was fitted out before any one began, and taken up, with the cook's compliments. The boiled tea was very bitter, the omelette scorched, and the biscuits speckled with saleratus; but Mrs. March received her repast with thanks, and laughed heartily over it after Jo was gone.

"Poor little souls, they will have a hard time, I'm afraid; but they won't suffer, and it will do them good," she said, producing the more palatable viands with which she had provided herself, and disposing of the bad breakfast, so that their feelings might not be hurt,—a motherly little deception, for which they were grateful.

Many were the complaints below, and great the chagrin of the head cook at her failures. "Never mind, I'll get the dinner, and be servant; you be mistress, keep your hands nice, see company, and give orders," said Jo, who knew still less than Meg about culinary affairs.

This obliging offer was gladly accepted; and Margaret retired to the parlor, which she hastily put in order by whisking the litter under the sofa, and shutting the blinds, to save the trouble of dusting. Jo, with perfect faith in her own powers, and a friendly desire to make up the quarrel, immediately put a note in the office, inviting Laurie to dinner.

"You'd better see what you have got before you think of having company," said Meg, when informed of the hospitable but rash act.

"Oh, there's corned beef and plenty of potatoes; and I shall get some asparagus, and a lobster, 'for a relish,' as Hannah says. We'll have lettuce, and make a salad. I don't know how, but the book tells. I'll have blanc-mange and strawberries for dessert; and coffee, too, if you want to be elegant."

"Don't try too many messes, Jo, for you can't make anything but gingerbread and molasses candy, fit to eat. I wash my hands of the dinner-party; and, since you have asked Laurie on your own responsibility, you may just take care of him."

"I don't want you to do anything but be civil to him, and help to the pudding. You'll give me your advice if I get in a muddle, won't you?" asked Jo, rather hurt.

"Yes; but I don't know much, except about bread, and a few trifles. You had better ask mother's leave before you order anything," returned Meg prudently.

"Of course I shall; I'm not a fool," and Jo went off in a huff at the doubts expressed of her powers.

"Get what you like, and don't disturb me; I'm going out to dinner, and can't worry about things at home," said Mrs. March, when Jo spoke to her. "I never enjoyed housekeeping, and I'm going to take a vacation to-day, and read, write, go visiting, and amuse myself."

The unusual spectacle of her busy mother rocking comfortably, and reading, early in the morning, made Jo feel as if some natural phenomenon had occurred, for an eclipse, an earthquake, or a volcanic eruption would hardly have seemed stranger.

"Everything is out of sorts, somehow," she said to herself, going down stairs. "There's Beth crying; that's a sure sign that something is wrong with this family. If Amy is bothering, I'll shake her."

Feeling very much out of sorts herself, Jo hurried into the parlor to find Beth sobbing over Pip, the canary, who lay dead in the cage, with his little claws pathetically extended, as if imploring the food for want of which he had died.

"It's all my fault—I forgot him—there isn't a seed or a drop left. O Pip! O Pip! how could I be so cruel to you?" cried Beth, taking the poor thing in her hands, and trying to restore him.

Jo peeped into his half-open eye, felt his little heart, and finding him stiff and cold, shook her head, and offered her domino-box for a coffin.

"Put him in the oven, and maybe he will get warm and revive," said Amy hopefully.

"He's been starved, and he sha'n't be baked, now he's dead. I'll make him a shroud, and he shall be buried in the garden; and I'll never have another bird, never, my Pip! for I am too bad to own one," murmured Beth, sitting on the floor with her pet folded in her hands.

"The funeral shall be this afternoon, and we will all go. Now, don't cry, Bethy; it's a pity, but nothing goes right this week, and Pip has had the worst of the experiment. Make the shroud, and lay him in my box; and, after the dinner-party, we'll have a nice little funeral," said Jo, beginning to feel as if she had undertaken a good deal.

Leaving the others to console Beth, she departed to the kitchen, which was in a most discouraging state of confusion. Putting on a big apron, she fell to work, and got the dishes piled up ready for washing, when she discovered that the fire was out.

"Here's a sweet prospect!" muttered Jo, slamming the stove-door open, and poking vigorously among the cinders.

Having rekindled the fire, she thought she would go to market while the water heated. The walk revived her spirits; and, flattering herself that she had made good bargains, she trudged home again, after buying a very young lobster, some very old asparagus, and two boxes of acid strawberries. By the time she got cleared up, the dinner arrived, and the stove was red-hot. Hannah had left a pan of bread to rise, Meg had worked it up early, set it on the hearth for a second rising, and forgotten it. Meg was entertaining Sallie Gardiner in the parlor, when the door flew open, and a floury, crocky, flushed, and dishevelled figure appeared, demanding tartly,—

"I say, isn't bread 'riz' enough when it runs over the pans?"

Sallie began to laugh; but Meg nodded, and lifted her eyebrows as high as they would go, which caused the apparition to vanish, and put the sour bread into the oven without further delay. Mrs. March went out, after peeping here and there to see how matters went, also saying a word of comfort to Beth, who sat making a winding-sheet, while the dear departed lay in state in the domino-box. A strange sense of helplessness fell upon the girls as the gray bonnet vanished round the corner; and despair seized them, when, a few minutes later, Miss Crocker appeared, and said she'd come to dinner. Now, this lady was a thin, yellow spinster, with a sharp nose and inquisitive eyes, who saw everything, and gossiped about all she saw. They disliked her, but had been taught to be kind to her, simply because she was old and poor, and had few friends. So Meg gave her the easy-chair, and tried to entertain her, while she asked questions, criticised everything, and told stories of the people whom she knew.

Language cannot describe the anxieties, experiences, and exertions which Jo underwent that morning; and the dinner she served up became a standing joke. Fearing to ask any more advice, she did her best alone, and discovered that something more than energy and good-will is necessary to make a cook. She boiled the asparagus for an hour, and was grieved to find the heads cooked off and the stalks harder than ever. The bread burnt black; for the salad-dressing so aggravated her, that she let everything else go till she had convinced herself that she could not make it fit to eat. The lobster was a scarlet mystery to her, but she hammered and poked, till it was unshelled, and its meagre proportions concealed in a grove of lettuce-leaves. The potatoes had to be hurried, not to keep the asparagus waiting, and were not done at last. The blanc-mange was lumpy, and the strawberries not as ripe as they looked, having been skilfully "deaconed."

"Well, they can eat beef, and bread and butter, if they are hungry; only it's mortifying to have to spend your whole morning for nothing," thought Jo, as she rang the bell half an hour later than usual, and stood, hot, tired, and dispirited, surveying the feast spread for Laurie, accustomed to all sorts of elegance, and Miss Crocker, whose curious eyes would mark all failures, and whose tattling tongue would report them far and wide.

Poor Jo would gladly have gone under the table, as one thing after another was tasted and left; while Amy giggled, Meg looked distressed, Miss Crocker pursed up her lips, and Laurie talked and laughed with all his might, to give a cheerful tone to the festive scene. Jo's one strong point was the fruit, for she had sugared it well, and had a pitcher of rich cream to eat with it. Her hot cheeks cooled a trifle, and she drew a long breath, as the pretty glass plates went round, and every one looked graciously at the little rosy islands floating in a sea of cream. Miss Crocker tasted first, made a wry face, and drank some water hastily. Jo, who had refused, thinking there might not be enough, for they dwindled sadly after the picking over, glanced at Laurie, but he was eating away manfully, though there was a slight pucker about his mouth, and he kept his eye fixed on his plate. Amy, who was fond of delicate fare, took a heaping spoonful, choked, hid her face in her napkin, and left the table precipitately.

"Oh, what is it?" exclaimed Jo trembling.

"Salt instead of sugar, and the cream is sour," replied Meg, with a tragic gesture.

Jo uttered a groan, and fell back in her chair; remembering that she had given a last hasty powdering to the berries out of one of the two boxes on the kitchen table, and had neglected to put the milk in the refrigerator. She turned scarlet, and was on the verge of crying, when she met Laurie's eyes, which *would* look merry in spite of his heroic efforts; the comical side of the affair suddenly struck her, and she laughed till the tears ran down her cheeks. So did every one else, even "Croaker," as the girls called the old lady; and the unfortunate dinner ended gayly, with bread and butter, olives and fun.

"I haven't strength of mind enough to clear up now, so we will sober ourselves with a funeral," said Jo, as they rose; and Miss Crocker made ready to go, being eager to tell the new story at another friend's dinner-table.

They did sober themselves, for Beth's sake; Laurie dug a grave under the ferns in the grove, little Pip was laid in, with many tears, by his tender-hearted mistress, and covered with moss, while a wreath of violets and chickweed was hung on the stone which bore his epitaph, composed by Jo, while she struggled with the dinner:—

"Here lies Pip March,
Who died the th of June;
Loved and lamented sore,
And not forgotten soon."

At the conclusion of the ceremonies, Beth retired to her room, overcome with emotion and lobster; but there was no place of repose, for the beds were not made, and she found her grief much assuaged by beating up pillows and putting things in order. Meg helped Jo clear away the remains of the feast, which took half the afternoon, and left them so tired that they agreed to be contented with tea and toast for supper. Laurie took Amy to drive, which was a deed of charity, for the sour cream seemed to have had a bad effect upon her temper. Mrs. March came home to find the three older girls hard at work in the middle of the afternoon; and a glance at the closet gave her an idea of the success of one part of the experiment.

Before the housewives could rest, several people called, and there was a scramble to get ready to see them; then tea must be got, errands done; and one or two necessary bits of sewing neglected till the last minute. As twilight fell, dewy and still, one by one they gathered in the porch where the June roses were budding beautifully, and each groaned or sighed as she sat down, as if tired or troubled.

"What a dreadful day this has been!" begun Jo, usually the first to speak.

"It has seemed shorter than usual, but *so* uncomfortable," said Meg.

"Not a bit like home," added Amy.

"It can't seem so without Marmee and little Pip," sighed Beth, glancing, with full eyes, at the empty cage above her head.

"Here's mother, dear, and you shall have another bird to-morrow, if you want it."

As she spoke, Mrs. March came and took her place among them, looking as if her holiday had not been much pleasanter than theirs.

"Are you satisfied with your experiment, girls, or do you want another week of it?" she asked, as Beth nestled up to her, and the rest turned toward her with brightening faces, as flowers turn toward the sun.

"I don't!" cried Jo decidedly.

"Nor I," echoed the others.

"You think, then, that it is better to have a few duties, and live a little for others, do you?"

"Lounging and larking doesn't pay," observed Jo, shaking her head. "I'm tired of it, and mean to go to work at something right off."

"Suppose you learn plain cooking; that's a useful accomplishment, which no woman should be without," said Mrs. March, laughing inaudibly at the recollection of Jo's dinner-party; for she had met Miss Crocker, and heard her account of it.

"Mother, did you go away and let everything be, just to see how we'd get on?" cried Meg, who had had suspicions all day.

"Yes; I wanted you to see how the comfort of all depends on each doing her share faithfully. While Hannah and I did your work, you got on pretty well, though I don't think you were very happy or amiable; so I thought, as a little lesson, I would show you what happens when every one thinks only of herself. Don't you feel that it is pleasanter to help one another, to have daily duties which make leisure sweet when it comes, and to bear and forbear, that home may be comfortable and lovely to us all?"

"We do, mother, we do!" cried the girls.

"Then let me advise you to take up your little burdens again; for though they seem heavy sometimes, they are good for us, and lighten as we learn to carry them. Work is wholesome, and there is plenty for every one; it keeps us from *ennui* and mischief, is good for health and spirits, and gives us a sense of power and independence better than money or fashion."

"We'll work like bees, and love it too; see if we don't!" said Jo. "I'll learn plain cooking for my holiday task; and the next dinner-party I have shall be a success."

"I'll make the set of shirts for father, instead of letting you do it, Marmee. I can and I will, though I'm not fond of sewing; that will be better than fussing over my own things, which are plenty nice enough as they are," said Meg.

"I'll do my lessons every day, and not spend so much time with my music and dolls. I am a stupid thing, and ought to be studying, not playing," was Beth's resolution; while Amy followed their example by heroically declaring, "I shall learn to make button-holes, and attend to my parts of speech."

"Very good! then I am quite satisfied with the experiment, and fancy that we shall not have to repeat it; only don't go to the other extreme, and delve like slaves. Have regular hours for work and play; make each day both useful and pleasant, and prove that you understand the worth of time by employing it well. Then youth will be delightful, old age will bring few regrets, and life become a beautiful success, in spite of poverty."

"We'll remember, mother!" and they did

XII.

# CAMP LAURENCE.

BETH was post-mistress, for, being most at home, she could attend to it regularly, and dearly liked the daily task of unlocking the little door and distributing the mail. One July day she came in with her hands full, and went about the house leaving letters and parcels, like the penny post.

"Here's your posy, mother! Laurie never forgets that," she said, putting the fresh nosegay in the vase that stood in "Marmee's corner," and was kept supplied by the affectionate boy.

"Miss Meg March, one letter and a glove," continued Beth, delivering the articles to her sister, who sat near her mother, stitching wristbands.

"Why, I left a pair over there, and here is only one," said Meg, looking at the gray cotton glove.

"Didn't you drop the other in the garden?"

"No, I'm sure I didn't; for there was only one in the office."

"I hate to have odd gloves! Never mind, the other may be found. My letter is only a translation of the German song I wanted; I think Mr. Brooke did it, for this isn't Laurie's writing."

Mrs. March glanced at Meg, who was looking very pretty in her gingham morning-gown, with the little curls blowing about her forehead, and very womanly, as she sat sewing at her little work-table, full of tidy white rolls; so unconscious of the thought in her mother's mind as she sewed and sung, while her fingers flew, and her thoughts were busied with girlish fancies as innocent and fresh as the pansies in her belt, that Mrs. March smiled, and was satisfied.

"Two letters for Doctor Jo, a book, and a funny old hat, which covered the whole post-office, stuck outside," said Beth, laughing, as she went into the study, where Jo sat writing.

"What a sly fellow Laurie is! I said I wished bigger hats were the fashion, because I burn my face every hot day. He said, 'Why mind the fashion? Wear a big hat, and be comfortable!' I said I would if I had one, and he has sent me this, to try me. I'll wear it, for fun, and show him I *don't* care for the fashion;" and, hanging the antique broad-brim on a bust of Plato, Jo read her letters.

One from her mother made her cheeks glow and her eyes fill, for it said to her,—

"MY DEAR:

"I write a little word to tell you with how much satisfaction I watch your efforts to control your temper. You say nothing about your trials, failures, or successes, and think, perhaps, that no one sees them but the Friend whose help you daily ask, if I may trust the well-worn cover of your guide-book. *I*, too, have seen them all, and heartily believe in the sincerity of your resolution, since it begins to bear fruit. Go on, dear, patiently and bravely, and always believe that no one sympathizes more tenderly with you than your loving

"MOTHER."

"That does me good! that's worth millions of money and pecks of praise. O Marmee, I do try! I will keep on trying, and not get tired, since I have you to help me."

Laying her head on her arms, Jo wet her little romance with a few happy tears, for she *had* thought that no one saw and appreciated her efforts to be good; and this assurance was doubly precious, doubly encouraging, because unexpected, and from the person whose commendation she most valued. Feeling stronger than ever to meet and subdue her Apollyon, she pinned the note inside her frock, as a shield and a reminder, lest she be taken unaware, and proceeded to open her other letter, quite ready for either good or bad news. In a big, dashing hand, Laurie wrote,—

"DEAR JO,

What ho!

Some English girls and boys are coming to see me to-morrow and I want to have a jolly time. If it's fine, I'm going to pitch my tent in Longmeadow, and row up the whole crew to lunch and croquet,—have a fire, make messes, gypsy fashion, and all sorts of larks. They are nice people, and like such things. Brooke will go, to keep us boys steady, and Kate Vaughn will play propriety for the girls. I want you all to come; can't let Beth off, at any price, and nobody shall worry her. Don't bother about rations,—I'll see to that, and everything else,—only do come, there's a good fellow!

"In a tearing hurry,

Yours ever, LAURIE."

"Here's richness!" cried Jo, flying in to tell the news to Meg.

"Of course we can go, mother? it will be such a help to Laurie, for I can row, and Meg see to the lunch, and the children be useful in some way."

"I hope the Vaughns are not fine, grown-up people. Do you know anything about them, Jo?" asked Meg.

"Only that there are four of them. Kate is older than you, Fred and Frank (twins) about my age, and a little girl (Grace), who is nine or ten. Laurie knew them abroad, and liked the boys; I fancied, from the way he primmed up his mouth in speaking of her, that he didn't admire Kate much."

"I'm so glad my French print is clean; it's just the thing, and so becoming!" observed Meg complacently. "Have you anything decent, Jo?"

"Scarlet and gray boating suit, good enough for me. I shall row and tramp about, so I don't want any starch to think of. You'll come, Bethy?"

"If you won't let any of the boys talk to me."

"Not a boy!"

"I like to please Laurie; and I'm not afraid of Mr. Brooke, he is so kind; but I don't want to play, or sing, or say anything. I'll work hard, and not trouble any one; and you'll take care of me, Jo, so I'll go."

"That's my good girl; you do try to fight off your shyness, and I love you for it. Fighting faults isn't easy, as I know; and a cheery word kind of gives a lift. Thank you, mother," and Jo gave the thin cheek a grateful kiss, more precious to Mrs. March than if it had given back the rosy roundness of her youth.

"I had a box of chocolate drops, and the picture I wanted to copy," said Amy, showing her mail.

"And I got a note from Mr. Laurence, asking me to come over and play to him to-night, before the lamps are lighted, and I shall go," added Beth, whose friendship with the old gentleman prospered finely.

"Now let's fly round, and do double duty to-day, so that we can play to-morrow with free minds," said Jo, preparing to replace her pen with a broom.

When the sun peeped into the girls' room early next morning, to promise them a fine day, he saw a comical sight. Each had made such preparation for the fête as seemed necessary and proper. Meg had an extra row of little curl-papers across her forehead, Jo had copiously anointed her afflicted face with cold cream, Beth had taken Joanna to bed with her to atone for the approaching separation, and Amy had capped the climax by putting a clothes-pin on her nose, to uplift the offending feature. It was one of the kind artists use to hold the paper on their drawing-boards, therefore quite appropriate and effective for the purpose to which it was now put. This funny spectacle appeared to amuse the sun, for he burst out with such radiance that Jo woke up, and roused all her sisters by a hearty laugh at Amy's ornament.

Sunshine and laughter were good omens for a pleasure party, and soon a lively bustle began in both houses. Beth, who was ready first, kept reporting what went on next door, and enlivened her sisters' toilets by frequent telegrams from the window.

"There goes the man with the tent! I see Mrs. Barker doing up the lunch in a hamper and a great basket. Now Mr. Laurence is looking up at the sky, and the weathercock; I wish he would go, too. There's Laurie, looking like a sailor,—nice boy! Oh, mercy me! here's a carriage full of people—a tall lady, a little girl, and two dreadful boys. One is lame; poor thing, he's got a crutch. Laurie didn't tell us that. Be quick, girls! it's getting late. Why, there is Ned Moffat, I do declare. Look, Meg, isn't that the man who bowed to you one day, when we were shopping?"

"So it is. How queer that he should come. I thought he was at the Mountains. There is Sallie; I'm glad she got back in time. Am I all right, Jo?" cried Meg, in a flutter.

"A regular daisy. Hold up your dress and put your hat straight; it looks sentimental tipped that way, and will fly off at the first puff. Now, then, come on!"

"O Jo, you are not going to wear that awful hat? It's too absurd! You shall *not* make a guy of yourself," remonstrated Meg, as Jo tied down, with a red ribbon, the broad-brimmed, old-fashioned Leghorn Laurie had sent for a joke.

"I just will, though, for it's capital,—so shady, light, and big. It will make fun; and I don't mind being a guy if I'm comfortable." With that Jo marched straight away, and the rest followed,—a bright little band of sisters, all looking their best, in summer suits, with happy faces under the jaunty hat-brims.

Laurie ran to meet, and present them to his friends, in the most cordial manner. The lawn was the reception-room, and for several minutes a lively scene was enacted there. Meg was grateful to see that Miss Kate, though twenty, was dressed with a simplicity which American girls would do well to imitate; and she was much flattered by Mr. Ned's assurances that he came especially to see her. Jo understood why Laurie "primmed up his mouth" when speaking of Kate, for that young lady had a stand-off-don't-touch-me air, which contrasted strongly with the free and easy demeanor of the other girls. Beth took an observation of the new boys, and decided that the lame one was not "dreadful," but gentle and feeble, and she would be kind to him on that account. Amy found Grace a well-mannered, merry little person; and after staring dumbly at one another for a few minutes, they suddenly became very good friends.

Tents, lunch, and croquet utensils having been sent on beforehand, the party was soon embarked, and the two boats pushed off together, leaving Mr. Laurence waving his hat on the shore. Laurie and Jo rowed one boat; Mr. Brooke and Ned the other; while Fred Vaughn, the riotous twin, did his best to upset both by paddling about in a wherry like a disturbed water-bug. Jo's funny hat deserved a vote of thanks, for it was of general utility; it broke the ice in the beginning, by producing a laugh; it created quite a refreshing breeze, flapping to and fro, as she rowed, and would make an excellent umbrella for the whole party, if a shower came up, she said. Kate looked rather amazed at Jo's proceedings, especially as she exclaimed "Christopher Columbus!" when she lost her oar; and Laurie said, "My dear fellow, did I hurt you?" when he tripped over her feet in taking his place. But after putting up her glass to examine the queer girl several times, Miss Kate decided that she was "odd, but rather clever," and smiled upon her from afar.

Meg, in the other boat, was delightfully situated, face to face with the rowers, who both admired the prospect, and feathered their oars with uncommon "skill and dexterity." Mr. Brooke was a grave, silent young man, with handsome brown eyes and a pleasant voice. Meg liked his quiet manners, and considered him a walking encyclopædia of useful knowledge. He never talked to her much; but he looked at her a good deal, and she felt sure that he did not regard her with aversion. Ned, being in college, of course put on all the airs which Freshmen think it their bounden duty to assume; he was not very wise, but very good-natured, and altogether an excellent person to carry on a picnic. Sallie Gardiner was absorbed in keeping her white piqué dress clean, and chattering with the ubiquitous Fred, who kept Beth in constant terror by his pranks.

It was not far to Longmeadow; but the tent was pitched and the wickets down by the time they arrived. A pleasant green field, with three wide-spreading oaks in the middle, and a smooth strip of turf for croquet.

"Welcome to Camp Laurence!" said the young host, as they landed, with exclamations of delight.

"Brooke is commander-in-chief; I am commissary-general; the other fellows are staff-officers; and you, ladies, are company. The tent is for your especial benefit, and that oak is your drawing-room; this is the mess-room, and the third is the camp-kitchen. Now, let's have a game before it gets hot, and then we'll see about dinner."

Frank, Beth, Amy, and Grace sat down to watch the game played by the other eight. Mr. Brooke chose Meg, Kate, and Fred; Laurie took Sallie, Jo, and Ned. The Englishers played well; but the Americans played better, and contested every inch of the ground as strongly as if the spirit of ' inspired them. Jo and Fred had several skirmishes, and once narrowly escaped high words. Jo was through the last wicket, and had missed the stroke, which failure ruffled her a good deal. Fred was close behind her, and his turn came before hers; he gave a stroke, his ball hit the wicket, and stopped an inch on the wrong side. No one was very near; and running up to examine, he gave it a sly nudge with his toe, which put it just an inch on the right side.

"I'm through! Now, Miss Jo, I'll settle you, and get in first," cried the young gentleman, swinging his mallet for another blow.

"You pushed it; I saw you; it's my turn now," said Jo sharply.

"Upon my word, I didn't move it; it rolled a bit, perhaps, but that is allowed; so stand off, please, and let me have a go at the stake."

"We don't cheat in America, but you can, if you choose," said Jo angrily.

"Yankees are a deal the most tricky, everybody knows. There you go!" returned Fred, croqueting her ball far away.

Jo opened her lips to say something rude, but checked herself in time, colored up to her forehead, and stood a minute, hammering down a wicket with all her might, while Fred hit the stake, and declared himself out with much exultation. She went off to get her ball, and was a long time finding it, among the bushes; but she came back, looking cool and quiet, and waited her turn patiently. It took several strokes to regain the place she had lost; and, when she got there, the other side had nearly won, for Kate's ball was the last but one, and lay near the stake.

"By George, it's all up with us! Good-by, Kate. Miss Jo owes me one, so you are finished," cried Fred excitedly, as they all drew near to see the finish.

"Yankees have a trick of being generous to their enemies," said Jo, with a look that made the lad redden, "especially when they beat them," she added, as, leaving Kate's ball untouched, she won the game by a clever stroke.

Laurie threw up his hat; then remembered that it wouldn't do to exult over the defeat of his guests, and stopped in the middle of a cheer to whisper to his friend,—

"Good for you, Jo! He did cheat, I saw him; we can't tell him so, but he won't do it again, take my word for it."

Meg drew her aside, under pretence of pinning up a loose braid, and said approvingly,—

"It was dreadfully provoking; but you kept your temper, and I'm so glad, Jo."

"Don't praise me, Meg, for I could box his ears this minute. I should certainly have boiled over if I hadn't stayed among the nettles till I got my rage under enough to hold my tongue. It's simmering now, so I hope he'll keep out of my way," returned Jo, biting her lips, as she glowered at Fred from under her big hat.

"Time for lunch," said Mr. Brooke, looking at his watch. "Commissary-general, will you make the fire and get water, while Miss March, Miss Sallie, and I spread the table? Who can make good coffee?"

"Jo can," said Meg, glad to recommend her sister. So Jo, feeling that her late lessons in cookery were to do her honor, went to preside over the coffee-pot, while the children collected dry sticks, and the boys made a fire, and got water from a spring near by. Miss Kate sketched, and Frank talked to Beth, who was making little mats of braided rushes to serve as plates.

The commander-in-chief and his aids soon spread the table-cloth with an inviting array of eatables and drinkables, prettily decorated with green leaves. Jo announced that the coffee was ready, and every one settled themselves to a hearty meal; for youth is seldom dyspeptic, and exercise develops wholesome appetites. A very merry lunch it was; for everything seemed fresh and funny, and frequent peals of laughter startled a venerable horse who fed near by. There was a pleasing inequality in the table, which produced many mishaps to cups and plates; acorns dropped into the milk, little black ants partook of the refreshments without being invited, and fuzzy caterpillars swung down from the tree, to see what was going on. Three white-headed children peeped over the fence, and an objectionable dog barked at them from the other side of the river with all his might and main.

**"A very merry lunch it was."—Page .**

"There's salt here, if you prefer it," said Laurie, as he handed Jo a saucer of berries.

"Thank you, I prefer spiders," she replied, fishing up two unwary little ones who had gone to a creamy death. "How dare you remind me of that horrid dinner-party, when yours is so nice in every way?" added Jo, as they both laughed, and ate out of one plate, the china having run short.

"I had an uncommonly good time that day, and haven't got over it yet. This is no credit to me, you know; I don't do anything; it's you and Meg and Brooke who make it go, and I'm no end obliged to you. What shall we do when we can't eat any more?" asked Laurie, feeling that his trump card had been played when lunch was over.

"Have games, till it's cooler. I brought 'Authors,' and I dare say Miss Kate knows something new and nice. Go and ask her; she's company, and you ought to stay with her more."

"Aren't you company too? I thought she'd suit Brooke; but he keeps talking to Meg, and Kate just stares at them through that ridiculous glass of hers. I'm going, so you needn't try to preach propriety, for you can't do it, Jo."

Miss Kate did know several new games; and as the girls would not, and the boys could not, eat any more, they all adjourned to the drawing-room to play "Rigmarole."

"One person begins a story, any nonsense you like, and tells as long as he pleases, only taking care to stop short at some exciting point, when the next takes it up and does the same. It's very funny when well done, and makes a perfect jumble of tragical comical stuff to laugh over. Please start it, Mr. Brooke," said Kate, with a commanding air, which surprised Meg, who treated the tutor with as much respect as any other gentleman.

Lying on the grass at the feet of the two young ladies, Mr. Brooke obediently began the story, with the handsome brown eyes steadily fixed upon the sunshiny river.

"Once on a time, a knight went out into the world to seek his fortune, for he had nothing but his sword and his shield. He travelled a long while, nearly eight-and-twenty years, and had a hard time of it, till he came to the palace of a good old king, who had offered a reward to any one who would tame and train a fine but unbroken colt, of which he was very fond. The knight agreed to try, and got on slowly but surely; for the colt was a gallant fellow, and soon learned to love his new master, though he was freakish and wild. Every day, when he gave his lessons to this pet of the king's, the knight rode him through the city; and, as he rode, he looked everywhere for a certain beautiful face, which he had seen many times in his dreams, but never found. One day, as he went prancing down a quiet street, he saw at the window of a ruinous castle the lovely face. He was delighted, inquired who lived in this old castle, and was told that several captive princesses were kept there by a spell, and spun all day to lay up money to buy their liberty. The knight wished intensely that he could free them; but he was poor, and could only go by each day, watching for the sweet face, and longing to see it out in the sunshine. At last, he resolved to get into the castle and ask how he could help them. He went and knocked; the great door flew open, and he beheld—"

"A ravishingly lovely lady, who exclaimed, with a cry of rapture, 'At last! at last!'" continued Kate, who had read French novels, and admired the style. "'Tis she!' cried Count Gustave, and fell at her feet in an ecstasy of joy. 'Oh, rise!' she said, extending a hand of marble fairness. 'Never! till you tell me how I may rescue you,' swore the knight, still kneeling. 'Alas, my cruel fate condemns me to remain here till my tyrant is destroyed.' 'Where is the villain?' 'In the mauve salon. Go, brave heart, and save me from despair.' 'I obey, and return victorious or dead!' With these thrilling words he rushed away, and flinging open the door of the mauve salon, was about to enter, when he received—"

"A stunning blow from the big Greek lexicon, which an old fellow in a black gown fired at him," said Ned.

"Instantly Sir What's-his-name recovered himself, pitched the tyrant out of the window, and turned to join the lady, victorious, but with a bump on his brow; found the door locked, tore up the curtains, made a rope ladder, got half-way down when the ladder broke, and he went head first into the moat, sixty feet below. Could swim like a duck, paddled round the castle till he came to a little door guarded by two stout fellows; knocked their heads together till they cracked like a couple of nuts, then, by a trifling exertion of his prodigious strength, he smashed in the door, went up a pair of stone steps covered with dust a foot thick, toads as big as your fist, and spiders that would frighten you into hysterics, Miss March. At the top of these steps he came plump upon a sight that took his breath away and chilled his blood—"

"A tall figure, all in white with a veil over its face and a lamp in its wasted hand," went on Meg. "It beckoned, gliding noiselessly before him down a corridor as dark and cold as any tomb. Shadowy effigies in armor stood on either side, a dead silence reigned, the lamp burned blue, and the ghostly figure ever and anon turned its face toward him, showing the glitter of awful eyes through its white veil. They reached a curtained door, behind which sounded lovely music; he sprang forward to enter, but the spectre plucked him back, and waved threateningly before him a—"

"Snuff-box," said Jo, in a sepulchral tone, which convulsed the audience. "'Thankee,' said the knight politely, as he took a pinch, and sneezed seven times so violently that his head fell off. 'Ha! ha!' laughed the ghost; and having peeped through the key-hole at the princesses spinning away for dear life, the evil spirit picked up her victim and put him in a large tin box, where there were eleven other knights packed together without their heads, like sardines, who all rose and began to—"

"Dance a hornpipe," cut in Fred, as Jo paused for breath; "and, as they danced, the rubbishy old castle turned to a man-of-war in full sail. 'Up with the jib, reef the tops'l halliards, helm hard a lee, and man the guns!' roared the captain, as a Portuguese pirate hove in sight, with a flag black as ink flying from her foremast. 'Go in and win, my hearties!' says the captain; and a tremendous fight begun. Of course the British beat; they always do."

"No, they don't!" cried Jo, aside.

"Having taken the pirate captain prisoner, sailed slap over the schooner, whose decks were piled with dead, and whose lee-scuppers ran blood, for the order had been 'Cutlasses, and die hard!' 'Bosen's mate, take a bight of the flying-jib sheet, and start this villain if he don't confess his sins double quick,' said the British captain. The Portuguese held his tongue like a brick, and walked the plank, while the jolly tars cheered like mad. But the sly dog dived, came up under the man-of-war, scuttled her, and down she went, with all sail set, 'To the bottom of the sea, sea, sea,' where—"

"Oh, gracious! what *shall* I say?" cried Sallie, as Fred ended his rigmarole, in which he had jumbled together, pell-mell, nautical phrases and facts, out of one of his favorite books. "Well they went to the bottom, and a nice mermaid welcomed them, but was much grieved on finding the box of headless knights, and kindly pickled them in brine, hoping to discover the mystery about them; for, being a woman, she was curious. By and by a diver came down, and the mermaid said, 'I'll give you this box of pearls if you can take it up;' for she wanted to restore the poor things to life, and couldn't raise the heavy load herself. So the diver hoisted it up, and was much disappointed, on opening it, to find no pearls. He left it in a great lonely field, where it was found by a—"

"Little goose-girl, who kept a hundred fat geese in the field," said Amy, when Sallie's invention gave out. "The little girl

was sorry for them, and asked an old woman what she should do to help them. 'Your geese will tell you, they know everything,' said the old woman. So she asked what she should use for new heads, since the old ones were lost, and all the geese opened their hundred mouths and screamed—"

"'Cabbages!'" continued Laurie promptly. "'Just the thing,' said the girl, and ran to get twelve fine ones from her garden. She put them on, the knights revived at once, thanked her, and went on their way rejoicing, never knowing the difference, for there were so many other heads like them in the world that no one thought anything of it. The knight in whom I'm interested went back to find the pretty face, and learned that the princesses had spun themselves free, and all gone to be married, but one. He was in a great state of mind at that; and mounting the colt, who stood by him through thick and thin, rushed to the castle to see which was left. Peeping over the hedge, he saw the queen of his affections picking flowers in her garden. 'Will you give me a rose?' said he. 'You must come and get it. I can't come to you; it isn't proper,' said she, as sweet as honey. He tried to climb over the hedge, but it seemed to grow higher and higher; then he tried to push through, but it grew thicker and thicker, and he was in despair. So he patiently broke twig after twig, till he had made a little hole, through which he peeped, saying imploringly, 'Let me in! let me in!' But the pretty princess did not seem to understand, for she picked her roses quietly, and left him to fight his way in. Whether he did or not, Frank will tell you."

"I can't; I'm not playing, I never do," said Frank, dismayed at the sentimental predicament out of which he was to rescue the absurd couple. Beth had disappeared behind Jo, and Grace was asleep.

"So the poor knight is to be left sticking in the hedge, is he?" asked Mr. Brooke, still watching the river, and playing with the wild rose in his button-hole.

"I guess the princess gave him a posy, and opened the gate, after a while," said Laurie, smiling to himself, as he threw acorns at his tutor.

"What a piece of nonsense we have made! With practice we might do something quite clever. Do you know 'Truth'?" asked Sallie, after they had laughed over their story.

"I hope so," said Meg soberly.

"The game, I mean?"

"What is it?" said Fred.

"Why, you pile up your hands, choose a number, and draw out in turn, and the person who draws at the number has to answer truly any questions put by the rest. It's great fun."

"Let's try it," said Jo, who liked new experiments.

Miss Kate and Mr. Brooke, Meg, and Ned declined, but Fred, Sallie, Jo, and Laurie piled and drew; and the lot fell to Laurie.

"Who are your heroes?" asked Jo.

"Grandfather and Napoleon."

"Which lady here do you think prettiest?" said Sallie.

"Margaret."

"Which do you like best?" from Fred.
"Jo, of course."
"What silly questions you ask!" and Jo gave a disdainful shrug as the rest laughed at Laurie's matter-of-fact tone.
"Try again; Truth isn't a bad game," said Fred.
"It's a very good one for you," retorted Jo, in a low voice.
Her turn came next.
"What is your greatest fault?" asked Fred, by way of testing in her the virtue he lacked himself.
"A quick temper."
"What do you most wish for?" said Laurie.
"A pair of boot-lacings," returned Jo, guessing and defeating his purpose.
"Not a true answer; you must say what you really do want most."
"Genius; don't you wish you could give it to me, Laurie?" and she slyly smiled in his disappointed face.
"What virtues do you most admire in a man?" asked Sallie.
"Courage and honesty."
"Now my turn," said Fred, as his hand came last.
"Let's give it to him," whispered Laurie to Jo, who nodded, and asked at once,—
"Didn't you cheat at croquet?"
"Well, yes, a little bit."
"Good! Didn't you take your story out of 'The Sea-Lion?'" said Laurie.
"Rather."
"Don't you think the English nation perfect in every respect?" asked Sallie.
"I should be ashamed of myself if I didn't."
"He's a true John Bull. Now, Miss Sallie, you shall have a chance without waiting to draw. I'll harrow up your feelings first, by asking if you don't think you are something of a flirt," said Laurie, as Jo nodded to Fred, as a sign that peace was declared.
"You impertinent boy! of course I'm not," exclaimed Sallie, with an air that proved the contrary.
"What do you hate most?" asked Fred.
"Spiders and rice-pudding."
"What do you like best?" asked Jo.
"Dancing and French gloves."
"Well, *I* think Truth is a very silly play; let's have a sensible game of Authors, to refresh our minds," proposed Jo.
Ned, Frank, and the little girls joined in this, and, while it went on, the three elders sat apart, talking. Miss Kate took out her sketch again, and Margaret watched her, while Mr. Brooke lay on the grass, with a book, which he did not read.
"How beautifully you do it! I wish I could draw," said Meg, with mingled admiration and regret in her voice.
"Why don't you learn? I should think you had taste and talent for it," replied Miss Kate graciously.
"I haven't time."
"Your mamma prefers other accomplishments, I fancy. So did mine; but I proved to her that I had talent, by taking a few lessons privately, and then she was quite willing I should go on. Can't you do the same with your governess?"
"I have none."
"I forgot; young ladies in America go to school more than with us. Very fine schools they are, too, papa says. You go to a private one, I suppose?"
"I don't go at all; I am a governess myself."
"Oh, indeed!" said Miss Kate; but she might as well have said, "Dear me, how dreadful!" for her tone implied it, and something in her face made Meg color, and wish she had not been so frank.
Mr. Brooke looked up, and said quickly, "Young ladies in America love independence as much as their ancestors did, and are admired and respected for supporting themselves."
"Oh, yes; of course it's very nice and proper in them to do so. We have many most respectable and worthy young women, who do the same and are employed by the nobility, because, being the daughters of gentlemen, they are both well-bred and accomplished, you know," said Miss Kate, in a patronizing tone, that hurt Meg's pride, and made her work seem not only more distasteful, but degrading.
"Did the German song suit, Miss March?" inquired Mr. Brooke, breaking an awkward pause.
"Oh, yes! it was very sweet, and I'm much obliged to whoever translated it for me;" and Meg's downcast face brightened as she spoke.
"Don't you read German?" asked Miss Kate, with a look of surprise.

"Not very well. My father, who taught me, is away, and I don't get on very fast alone, for I've no one to correct my pronunciation."

"Try a little now; here is Schiller's 'Mary Stuart,' and a tutor who loves to teach," and Mr. Brooke laid his book on her lap, with an inviting smile.

"It's so hard I'm afraid to try," said Meg, grateful, but bashful in the presence of the accomplished young lady beside her.

"I'll read a bit to encourage you;" and Miss Kate read one of the most beautiful passages, in a perfectly correct but perfectly expressionless manner.

Mr. Brooke made no comment, as she returned the book to Meg, who said innocently,—

"I thought it was poetry."

"Some of it is. Try this passage."

There was a queer smile about Mr. Brooke's mouth as he opened at poor Mary's lament.

Meg, obediently following the long grass-blade which her new tutor used to point with, read slowly and timidly, unconsciously making poetry of the hard words by the soft intonation of her musical voice. Down the page went the green guide, and presently, forgetting her listener in the beauty of the sad scene, Meg read as if alone, giving a little touch of tragedy to the words of the unhappy queen. If she had seen the brown eyes then, she would have stopped short; but she never looked up, and the lesson was not spoiled for her.

"Very well indeed!" said Mr. Brooke, as she paused, quite ignoring her many mistakes, and looking as if he did, indeed, "love to teach."

Miss Kate put up her glass, and, having taken a survey of the little tableau before her, shut her sketch-book, saying, with condescension,—

"You've a nice accent, and, in time, will be a clever reader. I advise you to learn, for German is a valuable accomplishment to teachers. I must look after Grace, she is romping;" and Miss Kate strolled away, adding to herself, with a shrug, "I didn't come to chaperone a governess, though she *is* young and pretty. What odd people these Yankees are; I'm afraid Laurie will be quite spoilt among them."

"I forgot that English people rather turn up their noses at governesses, and don't treat them as we do," said Meg, looking after the retreating figure with an annoyed expression.

"Tutors, also, have rather a hard time of it there, as I know to my sorrow. There's no place like America for us workers, Miss Margaret;" and Mr. Brooke looked so contented and cheerful, that Meg was ashamed to lament her hard lot.

"I'm glad I live in it then. I don't like my work, but I get a good deal of satisfaction out of it after all, so I won't complain; I only wish I liked teaching as you do."

"I think you would if you had Laurie for a pupil. I shall be very sorry to lose him next year," said Mr. Brooke, busily punching holes in the turf.

"Going to college, I suppose?" Meg's lips asked that question, but her eyes added, "And what becomes of you?"

"Yes; it's high time he went, for he is ready; and as soon as he is off, I shall turn soldier. I am needed."

"I am glad of that!" exclaimed Meg. "I should think every young man would want to go; though it is hard for the mothers and sisters who stay at home," she added sorrowfully.

"I have neither, and very few friends, to care whether I live or die," said Mr. Brooke, rather bitterly, as he absently put the dead rose in the hole he had made and covered it up, like a little grave.

"Laurie and his grandfather would care a great deal, and we should all be very sorry to have any harm happen to you," said Meg heartily.

"Thank you; that sounds pleasant," began Mr. Brooke, looking cheerful again; but before he could finish his speech, Ned, mounted on the old horse, came lumbering up to display his equestrian skill before the young ladies, and there was no more quiet that day.

"Don't you love to ride?" asked Grace of Amy, as they stood resting, after a race round the field with the others, led by Ned.

"I dote upon it; my sister Meg used to ride when papa was rich, but we don't keep any horses now, except Ellen Tree," added Amy, laughing.

"Tell me about Ellen Tree; is it a donkey?" asked Grace curiously.

"Why, you see, Jo is crazy about horses, and so am I, but we've only got an old side-saddle, and no horse. Out in our garden is an apple-tree, that has a nice low branch; so Jo put the saddle on it, fixed some reins on the part that turns up, and we bounce away on Ellen Tree whenever we like."

"How funny!" laughed Grace. "I have a pony at home, and ride nearly every day in the park, with Fred and Kate; it's very nice, for my friends go too, and the Row is full of ladies and gentlemen."

"Dear, how charming! I hope I shall go abroad some day; but I'd rather go to Rome than the Row," said Amy, who had not the remotest idea what the Row was, and wouldn't have asked for the world.

Frank, sitting just behind the little girls, heard what they were saying, and pushed his crutch away from him with an impatient gesture as he watched the active lads going through all sorts of comical gymnastics. Beth, who was collecting the scattered Author-cards, looked up, and said, in her shy yet friendly way,—

"I'm afraid you are tired; can I do anything for you?"

"Talk to me, please; it's dull, sitting by myself," answered Frank, who had evidently been used to being made much of at home.

If he had asked her to deliver a Latin oration, it would not have seemed a more impossible task to bashful Beth; but there was no place to run to, no Jo to hide behind now, and the poor boy looked so wistfully at her, that she bravely resolved to try.

"What do you like to talk about?" she asked, fumbling over the cards, and dropping half as she tried to tie them up.

"Well, I like to hear about cricket and boating and hunting," said Frank, who had not yet learned to suit his amusements to his strength.

"My heart! what shall I do? I don't know anything about them," thought Beth; and, forgetting the boy's misfortune in her flurry, she said, hoping to make him talk, "I never saw any hunting, but I suppose you know all about it."

"I did once; but I can never hunt again, for I got hurt leaping a confounded five-barred gate; so there are no more horses and hounds for me," said Frank, with a sigh that made Beth hate herself for her innocent blunder.

"Your deer are much prettier than our ugly buffaloes," she said, turning to the prairies for help, and feeling glad that she had read one of the boys' books in which Jo delighted.

Buffaloes proved soothing and satisfactory; and, in her eagerness to amuse another, Beth forgot herself, and was quite unconscious of her sisters' surprise and delight at the unusual spectacle of Beth talking away to one of the dreadful boys, against whom she had begged protection.

"Bless her heart! She pities him, so she is good to him," said Jo, beaming at her from the croquet-ground.

"I always said she was a little saint," added Meg, as if there could be no further doubt of it.

"I haven't heard Frank laugh so much for ever so long," said Grace to Amy, as they sat discussing dolls, and making tea-sets out of the acorn-cups.

"My sister Beth is a very *fastidious* girl, when she likes to be," said Amy, well pleased at Beth's success. She meant "fascinating," but as Grace didn't know the exact meaning of either word, "fastidious" sounded well, and made a good impression.

An impromptu circus, fox and geese, and an amicable game of croquet, finished the afternoon. At sunset the tent was struck, hampers packed, wickets pulled up, boats loaded, and the whole party floated down the river, singing at the tops of their voices. Ned, getting sentimental, warbled a serenade with the pensive refrain,—

"Alone, alone, ah! woe, alone,"

and at the lines—

"We each are young, we each have a heart,
Oh, why should we stand thus coldly apart?"

he looked at Meg with such a lackadaisical expression that she laughed outright and spoilt his song.

"How can you be so cruel to me?" he whispered, under cover of a lively chorus. "You've kept close to that starched-up Englishwoman all day, and now you snub me."

"I didn't mean to; but you looked so funny I really couldn't help it," replied Meg, passing over the first part of his reproach; for it was quite true that she *had* shunned him, remembering the Moffat party and the talk after it.

Ned was offended, and turned to Sallie for consolation, saying to her rather pettishly, "There isn't a bit of flirt in that girl, is there?"

"Not a particle; but she's a dear," returned Sallie, defending her friend even while confessing her short-comings.

"She's not a stricken deer, any way," said Ned, trying to be witty, and succeeding as well as very young gentlemen usually do.

On the lawn, where it had gathered, the little party separated with cordial good-nights and good-byes, for the Vaughns were going to Canada. As the four sisters went home through the garden, Miss Kate looked after them, saying, without the patronizing tone in her voice, "In spite of their demonstrative manners, American girls are very nice when one knows them."

"I quite agree with you," said Mr. Brooke.

XIII.

## CASTLES IN THE AIR.

LAURIE lay luxuriously swinging to and fro in his hammock, one warm September afternoon, wondering what his neighbors were about, but too lazy to go and find out. He was in one of his moods; for the day had been both unprofitable and unsatisfactory, and he was wishing he could live it over again. The hot weather made him indolent, and he had shirked his studies, tried Mr. Brooke's patience to the utmost, displeased his grandfather by practising half the afternoon, frightened the maid-servants half out of their wits, by mischievously hinting that one of his dogs was going mad, and, after high words with the stable-man about some fancied neglect of his horse, he had flung himself into his hammock, to fume over the stupidity of the world in general, till the peace of the lovely day quieted him in spite of himself. Staring up into the green gloom of the horse-chestnut trees above him, he dreamed dreams of all sorts, and was just imagining himself tossing on the ocean, in a voyage round the world, when the sound of voices brought him ashore in a flash. Peeping through the meshes of the hammock, he saw the Marches coming out, as if bound on some expedition.

"What in the world are those girls about now?" thought Laurie, opening his sleepy eyes to take a good look, for there was something rather peculiar in the appearance of his neighbors. Each wore a large, flapping hat, a brown linen pouch slung over one shoulder, and carried a long staff. Meg had a cushion, Jo a book, Beth a basket, and Amy a portfolio. All walked quietly through the garden, out at the little back gate, and began to climb the hill that lay between the house and river.

"Well, that's cool!" said Laurie to himself, "to have a picnic and never ask me. They can't be going in the boat, for they haven't got the key. Perhaps they forgot it; I'll take it to them, and see what's going on."

Though possessed of half a dozen hats, it took him some time to find one; then there was a hunt for the key, which was at last discovered in his pocket; so that the girls were quite out of sight when he leaped the fence and ran after them. Taking the shortest way to the boat-house, he waited for them to appear: but no one came, and he went up the hill to take an observation. A grove of pines covered one part of it, and from the heart of this green spot came a clearer sound than the soft sigh of the pines or the drowsy chirp of the crickets.

"Here's a landscape!" thought Laurie, peeping through the bushes, and looking wide-awake and good-natured already.

It *was* rather a pretty little picture; for the sisters sat together in the shady nook, with sun and shadow flickering over them, the aromatic wind lifting their hair and cooling their hot cheeks, and all the little wood-people going on with their affairs as if these were no strangers, but old friends. Meg sat upon her cushion, sewing daintily with her white hands, and looking as fresh and sweet as a rose, in her pink dress, among the green. Beth was sorting the cones that lay thick under the hemlock near by, for she made pretty things of them. Amy was sketching a group of ferns, and Jo was knitting as she read aloud. A shadow passed over the boy's face as he watched them, feeling that he ought to go away, because uninvited; yet lingering, because home seemed very lonely, and this quiet party in the woods most attractive to his restless spirit. He stood so still that a squirrel, busy with its harvesting, ran down a pine close beside him, saw him suddenly and skipped back, scolding so shrilly that Beth looked up, espied the wistful face behind the birches, and beckoned with a reassuring smile.

"May I come in, please? or shall I be a bother?" he asked, advancing slowly.

Meg lifted her eyebrows, but Jo scowled at her defiantly, and said, at once, "Of course you may. We should have asked you before, only we thought you wouldn't care for such a girl's game as this."

"I always liked your games; but if Meg doesn't want me, I'll go away."

"I've no objection, if you do something; it's against the rules to be idle here," replied Meg, gravely but graciously.

"Much obliged; I'll do anything if you'll let me stop a bit, for it's as dull as the Desert of Sahara down there. Shall I sew, read, cone, draw, or do all at once? Bring on your bears; I'm ready," and Laurie sat down, with a submissive expression delightful to behold.

"Finish this story while I set my heel," said Jo, handing him the book.

"Yes'm," was the meek answer, as he began, doing his best to prove his gratitude for the favor of an admission into the "Busy Bee Society."

The story was not a long one, and, when it was finished, he ventured to ask a few questions as a reward of merit.

"Please, ma'am, could I inquire if this highly instructive and charming institution is a new one?"

"Would you tell him?" asked Meg of her sisters.

"He'll laugh," said Amy warningly.

"Who cares?" said Jo.

"I guess he'll like it," added Beth.

"Of course I shall! I give you my word I won't laugh. Tell away, Jo, and don't be afraid."

"The idea of being afraid of you! Well, you see we used to play 'Pilgrim's Progress,' and we have been going on with it in earnest, all winter and summer."

"Yes, I know," said Laurie, nodding wisely.

"Who told you?" demanded Jo.

"Spirits."

"No, I did; I wanted to amuse him one night when you were all away, and he was rather dismal. He did like it, so don't scold, Jo," said Beth meekly.

"You can't keep a secret. Never mind; it saves trouble now."

"Go on, please," said Laurie, as Jo became absorbed in her work, looking a trifle displeased.

"Oh, didn't she tell you about this new plan of ours? Well, we have tried not to waste our holiday, but each has had a task, and worked at it with a will. The vacation is nearly over, the stints are all done, and we are ever so glad that we didn't dawdle."

"Yes, I should think so;" and Laurie thought regretfully of his own idle days.

"Mother likes to have us out of doors as much as possible; so we bring our work here, and have nice times. For the fun of it we bring our things in these bags, wear the old hats, use poles to climb the hill, and play pilgrims, as we used to do years ago. We call this hill the 'Delectable Mountain,' for we can look far away and see the country where we hope to live some time."

Jo pointed, and Laurie sat up to examine; for through an opening in the wood one could look across the wide, blue river, the meadows on the other side, far over the outskirts of the great city, to the green hills that rose to meet the sky. The sun was low, and the heavens glowed with the splendor of an autumn sunset. Gold and purple clouds lay on the hill-tops; and rising high into the ruddy light were silvery white peaks, that shone like the airy spires of some Celestial City.

"How beautiful that is!" said Laurie softly, for he was quick to see and feel beauty of any kind.

"It's often so; and we like to watch it, for it is never the same, but always splendid," replied Amy, wishing she could paint it.

"Jo talks about the country where we hope to live some time,—the real country, she means, with pigs and chickens, and haymaking. It would be nice, but I wish the beautiful country up there was real, and we could ever go to it," said Beth musingly.

"There is a lovelier country even than that, where we *shall* go, by and by, when we are good enough," answered Meg, with her sweet voice.

"It seems so long to wait, so hard to do; I want to fly away at once, as those swallows fly, and go in at that splendid gate."

"You'll get there, Beth, sooner or later; no fear of that," said Jo; "I'm the one that will have to fight and work, and climb and wait, and maybe never get in after all."

"You'll have me for company, if that's any comfort. I shall have to do a deal of travelling before I come in sight of your Celestial City. If I arrive late, you'll say a good word for me, won't you, Beth?"

Something in the boy's face troubled his little friend; but she said cheerfully, with her quiet eyes on the changing clouds, "If people really want to go, and really try all their lives, I think they will get in; for I don't believe there are any locks on that door, or any guards at the gate. I always imagine it is as it is in the picture, where the shining ones stretch out their hands to welcome poor Christian as he comes up from the river."

"Wouldn't it be fun if all the castles in the air which we make could come true, and we could live in them?" said Jo, after a little pause.

"I've made such quantities it would be hard to choose which I'd have," said Laurie, lying flat, and throwing cones at the squirrel who had betrayed him.

"You'd have to take your favorite one. What is it?" asked Meg.

"If I tell mine, will you tell yours?"

"Yes, if the girls will too."

"We will. Now, Laurie."

"After I'd seen as much of the world as I want to, I'd like to settle in Germany, and have just as much music as I choose. I'm to be a famous musician myself, and all creation is to rush to hear me; and I'm never to be bothered about money or business, but just enjoy myself, and live for what I like. That's my favorite castle. What's yours, Meg?"

Margaret seemed to find it a little hard to tell hers, and waved a brake before her face, as if to disperse imaginary gnats, while she said slowly, "I should like a lovely house, full of all sorts of luxurious things,—nice food, pretty clothes, handsome furniture, pleasant people, and heaps of money. I am to be mistress of it, and manage it as I like, with plenty of servants, so I never need work a bit. How I should enjoy it! for I wouldn't be idle, but do good, and make every one love me dearly."

"Wouldn't you have a master for your castle in the air?" asked Laurie slyly.

"I said 'pleasant people,' you know;" and Meg carefully tied up her shoe as she spoke, so that no one saw her face.

"Why don't you say you'd have a splendid, wise, good husband, and some angelic little children? You know your castle wouldn't be perfect without," said blunt Jo, who had no tender fancies yet, and rather scorned romance, except in books.

"You'd have nothing but horses, inkstands, and novels in yours," answered Meg petulantly.

"Wouldn't I, though? I'd have a stable full of Arabian steeds, rooms piled with books, and I'd write out of a magic inkstand, so that my works should be as famous as Laurie's music. I want to do something splendid before I go into my castle,—something heroic or wonderful, that won't be forgotten after I'm dead. I don't know what, but I'm on the watch for it, and mean to astonish you all, some day. I think I shall write books, and get rich and famous: that would suit me, so that is *my* favorite dream."

"Mine is to stay at home safe with father and mother, and help take care of the family," said Beth contentedly.

"Don't you wish for anything else?" asked Laurie.

"Since I had my little piano, I am perfectly satisfied. I only wish we may all keep well and be together; nothing else."

"I have ever so many wishes; but the pet one is to be an artist, and go to Rome, and do fine pictures, and be the best artist in the whole world," was Amy's modest desire.

"We're an ambitious set, aren't we? Every one of us, but Beth, wants to be rich and famous, and gorgeous in every respect. I do wonder if any of us will ever get our wishes," said Laurie, chewing grass, like a meditative calf.

"I've got the key to my castle in the air; but whether I can unlock the door remains to be seen," observed Jo mysteriously.

"I've got the key to mine, but I'm not allowed to try it. Hang college!" muttered Laurie, with an impatient sigh.

"Here's mine!" and Amy waved her pencil.

"I haven't got any," said Meg forlornly.

"Yes, you have," said Laurie at once.

"Where?"

"In your face."

"Nonsense; that's of no use."

"Wait and see if it doesn't bring you something worth having," replied the boy, laughing at the thought of a charming little secret which he fancied he knew.

Meg colored behind the brake, but asked no questions, and looked across the river with the same expectant expression which Mr. Brooke had worn when he told the story of the knight.

"If we are all alive ten years hence, let's meet, and see how many of us have got our wishes, or how much nearer we are then than now," said Jo, always ready with a plan.

"Bless me! how old I shall be,—twenty-seven!" exclaimed Meg who felt grown up already, having just reached seventeen.

"You and I shall be twenty-six, Teddy, Beth twenty-four, and Amy twenty-two. What a venerable party!" said Jo.

"I hope I shall have done something to be proud of by that time; but I'm such a lazy dog, I'm afraid I shall 'dawdle,' Jo."

"You need a motive, mother says; and when you get it, she is sure you'll work splendidly."

"Is she? By Jupiter I will, if I only get the chance!" cried Laurie, sitting up with sudden energy. "I ought to be satisfied to please grandfather, and I do try, but it's working against the grain, you see, and comes hard. He wants me to be an India merchant, as he was, and I'd rather be shot. I hate tea and silk and spices, and every sort of rubbish his old ships bring, and I don't care how soon they go to the bottom when I own them. Going to college ought to satisfy him, for if I give him four years he ought to let me off from the business; but he's set, and I 've got to do just as he did, unless I break away and please myself, as my father did. If there was any one left to stay with the old gentleman, I'd do it to-morrow."

Laurie spoke excitedly, and looked ready to carry his threat into execution on the slightest provocation; for he was growing up very fast, and, in spite of his indolent ways, had a young man's hatred of subjection, a young man's restless longing to try the world for himself.

"I advise you to sail away in one of your ships, and never come home again till you have tried your own way," said Jo, whose imagination was fired by the thought of such a daring exploit, and whose sympathy was excited by what she called "Teddy's wrongs."

"That's not right, Jo; you mustn't talk in that way, and Laurie mustn't take your bad advice. You should do just what your grandfather wishes, my dear boy," said Meg, in her most maternal tone. "Do your best at college, and, when he sees that you try to please him, I'm sure he won't be hard or unjust to you. As you say, there is no one else to stay with and love him, and you'd never forgive yourself if you left him without his permission. Don't be dismal or fret, but do your duty; and you'll get your reward, as good Mr. Brooke has, by being respected and loved."

"What do you know about him?" asked Laurie, grateful for the good advice, but objecting to the lecture, and glad to turn the conversation from himself, after his unusual outbreak.

"Only what your grandpa told us about him,—how he took good care of his own mother till she died, and wouldn't go abroad as tutor to some nice person, because he wouldn't leave her; and how he provides now for an old woman who nursed his mother; and never tells any one, but is just as generous and patient and good as he can be."

"So he is, dear old fellow!" said Laurie heartily, as Meg paused, looking flushed and earnest with her story. "It's like grandpa to find out all about him, without letting him know, and to tell all his goodness to others, so that they might like him. Brooke couldn't understand why your mother was so kind to him, asking him over with me, and treating him in her beautiful friendly way. He thought she was just perfect, and talked about it for days and days, and went on about you all in flaming style. If ever I do get my wish, you see what I'll do for Brooke."

"Begin to do something now, by not plaguing his life out," said Meg sharply.

"How do you know I do, miss?"

"I can always tell by his face, when he goes away. If you have been good, he looks satisfied and walks briskly; if you have plagued him, he's sober and walks slowly, as if he wanted to go back and do his work better."

"Well, I like that! So you keep an account of my good and bad marks in Brooke's face, do you? I see him bow and smile as he passes your window, but I didn't know you'd got up a telegraph."

"We haven't; don't be angry, and oh, don't tell him I said anything! It was only to show that I cared how you get on, and what is said here is said in confidence, you know," cried Meg, much alarmed at the thought of what might follow from her careless speech.

"*I* don't tell tales," replied Laurie, with his "high and mighty" air, as Jo called a certain expression which he occasionally wore. "Only if Brooke is going to be a thermometer, I must mind and have fair weather for him to report."

"Please don't be offended. I didn't mean to preach or tell tales or be silly; I only thought Jo was encouraging you in a feeling which you'd be sorry for, by and by. You are so kind to us, we feel as if you were our brother, and say just what we think. Forgive me, I meant it kindly." And Meg offered her hand with a gesture both affectionate and timid.

Ashamed of his momentary pique, Laurie squeezed the kind little hand, and said frankly, "I'm the one to be forgiven; I'm cross, and have been out of sorts all day. I like to have you tell me my faults and be sisterly, so don't mind if I am grumpy sometimes; I thank you all the same."

Bent on showing that he was not offended, he made himself as agreeable as possible,—wound cotton for Meg, recited poetry to please Jo, shook down cones for Beth, and helped Amy with her ferns, proving himself a fit person to belong to the "Busy Bee Society." In the midst of an animated discussion on the domestic habits of turtles (one of those amiable creatures having strolled up from the river), the faint sound of a bell warned them that Hannah had put the tea "to draw," and they would just have time to get home to supper.

"May I come again?" asked Laurie.

"Yes, if you are good, and love your book, as the boys in the primer are told to do," said Meg smiling.

"I'll try."

"Then you may come, and I'll teach you to knit as the Scotchmen do; there's a demand for socks just now," added Jo, waving hers, like a big blue worsted banner, as they parted at the gate.

That night, when Beth played to Mr. Laurence in the twilight, Laurie, standing in the shadow of the curtain, listened to the little David, whose simple music always quieted his moody spirit, and watched the old man, who sat with his gray head on his hand, thinking tender thoughts of the dead child he had loved so much. Remembering the conversation of the afternoon, the boy said to himself, with the resolve to make the sacrifice cheerfully, "I'll let my castle go, and stay with the dear old gentleman while he needs me, for I am all he has."

XIV.

## SECRETS.

JO was very busy in the garret, for the October days began to grow chilly, and the afternoons were short. For two or three hours the sun lay warmly in the high window, showing Jo seated on the old sofa, writing busily, with her papers spread out upon a trunk before her, while Scrabble, the pet rat, promenaded the beams overhead, accompanied by his oldest son, a fine young fellow, who was evidently very proud of his whiskers. Quite absorbed in her work, Jo scribbled away till the last page was filled, when she signed her name with a flourish, and threw down her pen, exclaiming,—

"There, I've done my best! If this won't suit I shall have to wait till I can do better."

Lying back on the sofa, she read the manuscript carefully through, making dashes here and there, and putting in many exclamation points, which looked like little balloons; then she tied it up with a smart red ribbon, and sat a minute looking at it with a sober, wistful expression, which plainly showed how earnest her work had been. Jo's desk up here was an old tin kitchen, which hung against the wall. In it she kept her papers and a few books, safely shut away from Scrabble, who, being likewise of a literary turn, was fond of making a circulating library of such books as were left in his way, by eating the leaves. From this tin receptacle Jo produced another manuscript; and, putting both in her pocket, crept quietly down stairs, leaving her friends to nibble her pens and taste her ink.

She put on her hat and jacket as noiselessly as possible, and, going to the back entry window, got out upon the roof of a low porch, swung herself down to the grassy bank, and took a roundabout way to the road. Once there, she composed herself, hailed a passing omnibus, and rolled away to town, looking very merry and mysterious.

If any one had been watching her, he would have thought her movements decidedly peculiar; for, on alighting, she went off at a great pace till she reached a certain number in a certain busy street; having found the place with some difficulty, she went into the door-way, looked up the dirty stairs, and, after standing stock still a minute, suddenly dived into the street, and walked away as rapidly as she came. This manœuvre she repeated several times, to the great amusement of a black-eyed young gentleman lounging in the window of a building opposite. On returning for the third time, Jo gave herself a shake, pulled her hat over her eyes, and walked up the stairs, looking as if she were going to have all her teeth out.

There was a dentist's sign, among others, which adorned the entrance, and, after staring a moment at the pair of artificial jaws which slowly opened and shut to draw attention to a fine set of teeth, the young gentleman put on his coat, took his hat, and went down to post himself in the opposite door-way, saying, with a smile and a shiver,—

"It's like her to come alone, but if she has a bad time she'll need some one to help her home."

In ten minutes Jo came running down stairs with a very red face, and the general appearance of a person who had just passed through a trying ordeal of some sort. When she saw the young gentleman she looked anything but pleased, and passed him with a nod; but he followed, asking with an air of sympathy,—

"Did you have a bad time?"

"Not very."

"You got through quickly."

"Yes, thank goodness!"

"Why did you go alone?"

"Didn't want any one to know."

"You're the oddest fellow I ever saw. How many did you have out?"

Jo looked at her friend as if she did not understand him; then began to laugh, as if mightily amused at something.

"There are two which I want to have come out, but I must wait a week."

"What are you laughing at? You are up to some mischief, Jo," said Laurie, looking mystified.

"So are you. What were you doing, sir, up in that billiard saloon?"

"Begging your pardon, ma'am, it wasn't a billiard saloon, but a gymnasium, and I was taking a lesson in fencing."

"I'm glad of that."

"Why?"

"You can teach me, and then when we play Hamlet, you can be Laertes, and we'll make a fine thing of the fencing scene."

Laurie burst out with a hearty boy's laugh, which made several passers-by smile in spite of themselves.

"I'll teach you whether we play Hamlet or not; it's grand fun, and will straighten you up capitally. But I don't believe that was your only reason for saying 'I'm glad,' in that decided way; was it, now?"

"No, I was glad that you were not in the saloon, because I hope you never go to such places. Do you?"

"Not often."

"I wish you wouldn't."

"It's no harm, Jo. I have billiards at home, but it's no fun unless you have good players; so, as I'm fond of it, I come sometimes and have a game with Ned Moffat or some of the other fellows."

"Oh dear, I'm so sorry, for you'll get to liking it better and better, and will waste time and money, and grow like those dreadful boys. I did hope you'd stay respectable, and be a satisfaction to your friends," said Jo, shaking her head.

"Can't a fellow take a little innocent amusement now and then without losing his respectability?" asked Laurie, looking nettled.

"That depends upon how and where he takes it. I don't like Ned and his set, and wish you'd keep out of it. Mother won't let us have him at our house, though he wants to come; and if you grow like him she won't be willing to have us frolic together as we do now."

"Won't she?" asked Laurie anxiously.

"No, she can't bear fashionable young men, and she'd shut us all up in bandboxes rather than have us associate with them."

"Well, she needn't get out her bandboxes yet; I'm not a fashionable party, and don't mean to be; but I do like harmless larks now and then, don't you?"

"Yes, nobody minds them, so lark away, but don't get wild, will you? or there will be an end of all our good times."

"I'll be a double-distilled saint."

"I can't bear saints: just be a simple, honest, respectable boy, and we'll never desert you. I don't know what I *should* do if you acted like Mr. King's son; he had plenty of money, but didn't know how to spend it, and got tipsy and gambled, and ran away, and forged his father's name, I believe, and was altogether horrid."

"You think I'm likely to do the same? Much obliged."

"No, I don't—oh, *dear*, no!—but I hear people talking about money being such a temptation, and I sometimes wish you were poor; I shouldn't worry then."

"Do you worry about me, Jo?"

"A little, when you look moody or discontented, as you sometimes do; for you've got such a strong will, if you once get started wrong, I'm afraid it would be hard to stop you."

Laurie walked in silence a few minutes, and Jo watched him, wishing she had held her tongue, for his eyes looked angry, though his lips still smiled as if at her warnings.

"Are you going to deliver lectures all the way home?" he asked presently.

"Of course not; why?"

"Because if you are, I'll take a 'bus; if you are not, I'd like to walk with you, and tell you something very interesting."

"I won't preach any more, and I'd like to hear the news immensely."

"Very well, then; come on. It's a secret, and if I tell you, you must tell me yours."

"I haven't got any," began Jo, but stopped suddenly, remembering that she had.

"You know you have,—you can't hide anything; so up and 'fess, or I won't tell," cried Laurie.

"Is your secret a nice one?"

"Oh, isn't it! all about people you know, and such fun! You ought to hear it, and I've been aching to tell it this long time. Come, you begin."

"You'll not say anything about it at home, will you?"
"Not a word."
"And you won't tease me in private?"
"I never tease."
"Yes, you do; you get everything you want out of people. I don't know how you do it, but you are a born wheedler."
"Thank you; fire away."
"Well, I've left two stories with a newspaper man, and he's to give his answer next week," whispered Jo, in her confidant's ear.

"Hurrah for Miss March, the celebrated American authoress!" cried Laurie, throwing up his hat and catching it again, to the great delight of two ducks, four cats, five hens, and half a dozen Irish children; for they were out of the city now.
"Hush! It won't come to anything, I dare say; but I couldn't rest till I had tried, and I said nothing about it, because I didn't want any one else to be disappointed."
"It won't fail. Why, Jo, your stories are works of Shakespeare, compared to half the rubbish that is published every day. Won't it be fun to see them in print; and sha'n't we feel proud of our authoress?"
Jo's eyes sparkled, for it is always pleasant to be believed in; and a friend's praise is always sweeter than a dozen newspaper puffs.
"Where's *your* secret? Play fair, Teddy, or I'll never believe you again," she said, trying to extinguish the brilliant hopes that blazed up at a word of encouragement.
"I may get into a scrape for telling; but I didn't promise not to, so I will, for I never feel easy in my mind till I've told you any plummy bit of news I get. I know where Meg's glove is."
"Is that all?" said Jo, looking disappointed, as Laurie nodded and twinkled, with a face full of mysterious intelligence.
"It's quite enough for the present, as you'll agree when I tell you where it is."
"Tell, then."
Laurie bent, and whispered three words in Jo's ear, which produced a comical change. She stood and stared at him for a minute, looking both surprised and displeased, then walked on, saying sharply, "How do you know?"
"Saw it."
"Where?"
"Pocket."
"All this time?"
"Yes; isn't that romantic?"
"No, it's horrid."
"Don't you like it?"
"Of course I don't. It's ridiculous; it won't be allowed. My patience! what would Meg say?"
"You are not to tell any one; mind that."
"I didn't promise."
"That was understood, and I trusted you."
"Well, I won't for the present, any way; but I'm disgusted, and wish you hadn't told me."
"I thought you'd be pleased."
"At the idea of anybody coming to take Meg away? No, thank you."
"You'll feel better about it when somebody comes to take you away."
"I'd like to see any one try it," cried Jo fiercely.
"So should I!" and Laurie chuckled at the idea.
"I don't think secrets agree with me; I feel rumpled up in my mind since you told me that," said Jo, rather ungratefully.
"Race down this hill with me, and you'll be all right," suggested Laurie.

No one was in sight; the smooth road sloped invitingly before her; and finding the temptation irresistible, Jo darted away, soon leaving hat and comb behind her, and scattering hair-pins as she ran. Laurie reached the goal first, and was quite satisfied with the success of his treatment; for his Atalanta came panting up, with flying hair, bright eyes, ruddy cheeks, and no signs of dissatisfaction in her face.

"I wish I was a horse; then I could run for miles in this splendid air, and not lose my breath. It was capital; but see what a guy it's made me. Go, pick up my things, like a cherub as you are," said Jo, dropping down under a maple-tree, which was carpeting the bank with crimson leaves.

Laurie leisurely departed to recover the lost property, and Jo bundled up her braids, hoping no one would pass by till she was tidy again. But some one did pass, and who should it be but Meg, looking particularly ladylike in her state and festival suit, for she had been making calls.

"What in the world are you doing here?" she asked, regarding her dishevelled sister with well-bred surprise.

"Getting leaves," meekly answered Jo, sorting the rosy handful she had just swept up.

"And hair-pins," added Laurie, throwing half a dozen into Jo's lap. "They grow on this road, Meg; so do combs and brown straw hats."

"You have been running, Jo; how could you? When *will* you stop such romping ways?" said Meg reprovingly, as she settled her cuffs, and smoothed her hair, with which the wind had taken liberties.

"Never till I'm stiff and old, and have to use a crutch. Don't try to make me grow up before my time, Meg: it's hard enough to have you change all of a sudden; let me be a little girl as long as I can."

As she spoke, Jo bent over the leaves to hide the trembling of her lips; for lately she had felt that Margaret was fast getting to be a woman, and Laurie's secret made her dread the separation which must surely come some time, and now seemed very near. He saw the trouble in her face, and drew Meg's attention from it by asking quickly, "Where have you been calling, all so fine?"

"At the Gardiners', and Sallie has been telling me all about Belle Moffat's wedding. It was very splendid, and they have gone to spend the winter in Paris. Just think how delightful that must be!"

"Do you envy her, Meg?" said Laurie.

"I'm afraid I do."

"I'm glad of it!" muttered Jo, tying on her hat with a jerk.

"Why?" asked Meg, looking surprised.

"Because if you care much about riches, you will never go and marry a poor man," said Jo, frowning at Laurie, who was mutely warning her to mind what she said.

"I shall never '*go* and marry' any one," observed Meg, walking on with great dignity, while the others followed, laughing, whispering, skipping stones, and "behaving like children," as Meg said to herself, though she might have been tempted to join them if she had not had her best dress on.

For a week or two, Jo behaved so queerly that her sisters were quite bewildered. She rushed to the door when the postman rang; was rude to Mr. Brooke whenever they met; would sit looking at Meg with a woe-begone face, occasionally jumping up to shake, and then to kiss her, in a very mysterious manner; Laurie and she were always making signs to one another, and talking about "Spread Eagles," till the girls declared they had both lost their wits. On the second Saturday after Jo got out of the window, Meg, as she sat sewing at her window, was scandalized by the sight of Laurie chasing Jo all over the garden, and finally capturing her in Amy's bower. What went on there, Meg could not see; but shrieks of laughter were heard, followed by the murmur of voices and a great flapping of newspapers.

"What shall we do with that girl? She never *will* behave like a young lady," sighed Meg, as she watched the race with a disapproving face.

"I hope she won't; she is so funny and dear as she is," said Beth, who had never betrayed that she was a little hurt at Jo's having secrets with any one but her.

"It's very trying, but we never can make her *commy la fo*," added Amy, who sat making some new frills for herself, with her curls tied up in a very becoming way,—two agreeable things, which made her feel unusually elegant and ladylike.

In a few minutes Jo bounced in, laid herself on the sofa, and affected to read.

"Have you anything interesting there?" asked Meg, with condescension.

"Nothing but a story; won't amount to much, I guess," returned Jo, carefully keeping the name of the paper out of sight.

"You'd better read it aloud; that will amuse us and keep you out of mischief," said Amy, in her most grown-up tone.

"What's the name?" asked Beth, wondering why Jo kept her face behind the sheet.

"The Rival Painters."

"That sounds well; read it," said Meg.

With a loud "Hem!" and a long breath, Jo began to read very fast. The girls listened with interest, for the tale was romantic, and somewhat pathetic, as most of the characters died in the end.

"I like that about the splendid picture," was Amy's approving remark, as Jo paused.

"I prefer the lovering part. Viola and Angelo are two of our favorite names; isn't that queer?" said Meg, wiping her eyes, for the "lovering part" was tragical.

"Who wrote it?" asked Beth, who had caught a glimpse of Jo's face.

The reader suddenly sat up, cast away the paper, displaying a flushed countenance, and, with a funny mixture of solemnity and excitement, replied in a loud voice, "Your sister."

"You?" cried Meg, dropping her work.

"It's very good," said Amy critically.

"I knew it! I knew it! O my Jo, I *am* so proud!" and Beth ran to hug her sister, and exult over this splendid success.

Dear me, how delighted they all were, to be sure! how Meg wouldn't believe it till she saw the words, "Miss Josephine March," actually printed in the paper; how graciously Amy criticised the artistic parts of the story, and offered hints for a sequel, which unfortunately couldn't be carried out, as the hero and heroine were dead; how Beth got excited, and skipped and sung with joy; how Hannah came in to exclaim "Sakes alive, well I never!" in great astonishment at "that Jo's doin's;" how proud Mrs. March was when she knew it; how Jo laughed, with tears in her eyes, as she declared she might as well be a peacock and done with it; and how the "Spread Eagle" might be said to flap his wings triumphantly over the House of March, as the paper passed from hand to hand.

"Tell us all about it." "When did it come?" "How much did you get for it?" "What *will* father say?" "Won't Laurie laugh?" cried the family, all in one breath, as they clustered about Jo; for these foolish, affectionate people made a jubilee of every little household joy.

"Stop jabbering, girls, and I'll tell you everything," said Jo, wondering if Miss Burney felt any grander over her "Evelina" than she did over her "Rival Painters." Having told how she disposed of her tales, Jo added, "And when I went to get my answer, the man said he liked them both, but didn't pay beginners, only let them print in his paper, and noticed the stories. It was good practice, he said; and when the beginners improved, any one would pay. So I let him have the two stories, and to-day this was sent to me, and Laurie caught me with it, and insisted on seeing it, so I let him; and he said it was good, and I shall write more, and he's going to get the next paid for, and I *am* so happy, for in time I may be able to support myself and help the girls."

Jo's breath gave out here; and, wrapping her head in the paper, she bedewed her little story with a few natural tears; for to be independent, and earn the praise of those she loved were the dearest wishes of her heart, and this seemed to be the first step toward that happy end.

XV.

## A TELEGRAM.

"NOVEMBER is the most disagreeable month in the whole year," said Margaret, standing at the window one dull afternoon, looking out at the frost-bitten garden.

"That's the reason I was born in it," observed Jo pensively, quite unconscious of the blot on her nose.

"If something very pleasant should happen now, we should think it a delightful month," said Beth, who took a hopeful view of everything, even November.

"I dare say; but nothing pleasant ever *does* happen in this family," said Meg, who was out of sorts. "We go grubbing along day after day, without a bit of change, and very little fun. We might as well be in a treadmill."

"My patience, how blue we are!" cried Jo. "I don't much wonder, poor dear, for you see other girls having splendid times, while you grind, grind, year in and year out. Oh, don't I wish I could manage things for you as I do for my heroines! You're pretty enough and good enough already, so I'd have some rich relation leave you a fortune unexpectedly; then you'd dash out as an heiress, scorn every one who has slighted you, go abroad, and come home my Lady Something, in a blaze of splendor and elegance."

"People don't have fortunes left them in that style now-a-days; men have to work, and women to marry for money. It's a dreadfully unjust world," said Meg bitterly.

"Jo and I are going to make fortunes for you all; just wait ten years, and see if we don't," said Amy, who sat in a corner, making mud pies, as Hannah called her little clay models of birds, fruit, and faces.

"Can't wait, and I'm afraid I haven't much faith in ink and dirt, though I'm grateful for your good intentions."

Meg sighed, and turned to the frost-bitten garden again; Jo groaned, and leaned both elbows on the table in a despondent attitude, but Amy spatted away energetically; and Beth, who sat at the other window, said, smiling, "Two pleasant things are going to happen right away: Marmee is coming down the street, and Laurie is tramping through the garden as if he had something nice to tell."

In they both came, Mrs. March with her usual question, "Any letter from father, girls?" and Laurie to say in his persuasive way, "Won't some of you come for a drive? I've been working away at mathematics till my head is in a muddle, and I'm going to freshen my wits by a brisk turn. It's a dull day, but the air isn't bad, and I'm going to take Brooke home, so it will be gay inside, if it isn't out. Come, Jo, you and Beth will go, won't you?"

"Of course we will."

"Much obliged, but I'm busy;" and Meg whisked out her work-basket, for she had agreed with her mother that it was best, for her at least, not to drive often with the young gentleman.

"We three will be ready in a minute," cried Amy, running away to wash her hands.

"Can I do anything for you, Madam Mother?" asked Laurie, leaning over Mrs. March's chair, with the affectionate look and tone he always gave her.

"No, thank you, except call at the office, if you'll be so kind, dear. It's our day for a letter, and the postman hasn't been. Father is as regular as the sun, but there's some delay on the way, perhaps."

A sharp ring interrupted her, and a minute after Hannah came in with a letter.

"It's one of them horrid telegraph things, mum," she said, handing it as if she was afraid it would explode and do some damage.

At the word "telegraph," Mrs. March snatched it, read the two lines it contained, and dropped back into her chair as white as if the little paper had sent a bullet to her heart. Laurie dashed down stairs for water, while Meg and Hannah supported her, and Jo read aloud, in a frightened voice,—

"MRS. MARCH:

"Your husband is very ill. Come at once.

S. HALE,

"Blank Hospital, Washington"

How still the room was as they listened breathlessly, how strangely the day darkened outside, and how suddenly the whole world seemed to change, as the girls gathered about their mother, feeling as if all the happiness and support of their lives was about to be taken from them. Mrs. March was herself again directly; read the message over, and stretched out her arms to her daughters, saying, in a tone they never forgot, "I shall go at once, but it may be too late. O children, children, help me to bear it!"

For several minutes there was nothing but the sound of sobbing in the room, mingled with broken words of comfort, tender assurances of help, and hopeful whispers that died away in tears. Poor Hannah was the first to recover, and with unconscious wisdom she set all the rest a good example; for, with her, work was the panacea for most afflictions.

"The Lord keep the dear man! I won't waste no time a cryin', but git your things ready right away, mum," she said, heartily, as she wiped her face on her apron, gave her mistress a warm shake of the hand with her own hard one, and went away, to work like three women in one.

"She's right; there's no time for tears now. Be calm, girls, and let me think."

They tried to be calm, poor things, as their mother sat up, looking pale, but steady, and put away her grief to think and plan for them.

"Where's Laurie?" she asked presently, when she had collected her thoughts, and decided on the first duties to be done.

"Here, ma'am. Oh, let me do something!" cried the boy, hurrying from the next room, whither he had withdrawn, feeling that their first sorrow was too sacred for even his friendly eyes to see.

"Send a telegram saying I will come at once. The next train goes early in the morning. I'll take that."

"What else? The horses are ready; I can go anywhere, do anything," he said, looking ready to fly to the ends of the earth.

"Leave a note at Aunt March's. Jo, give me that pen and paper."

Tearing off the blank side of one of her newly copied pages, Jo drew the table before her mother, well knowing that money for the long, sad journey must be borrowed, and feeling as if she could do anything to add a little to the sum for her father.

"Now go, dear; but don't kill yourself driving at a desperate pace; there is no need of that."

Mrs. March's warning was evidently thrown away; for five minutes later Laurie tore by the window on his own fleet horse, riding as if for his life.

"Jo, run to the rooms, and tell Mrs. King that I can't come. On the way get these things. I'll put them down; they'll be needed, and I must go prepared for nursing. Hospital stores are not always good. Beth, go and ask Mr. Laurence for a couple of bottles of old wine: I'm not too proud to beg for father; he shall have the best of everything. Amy, tell Hannah to get down the black trunk; and, Meg, come and help me find my things, for I'm half bewildered."

Writing, thinking, and directing, all at once, might well bewilder the poor lady, and Meg begged her to sit quietly in her room for a little while, and let them work. Every one scattered like leaves before a gust of wind; and the quiet, happy household was broken up as suddenly as if the paper had been an evil spell.

Mr. Laurence came hurrying back with Beth, bringing every comfort the kind old gentleman could think of for the invalid, and friendliest promises of protection for the girls during the mother's absence, which comforted her very much. There was nothing he didn't offer, from his own dressing-gown to himself as escort. But that last was impossible. Mrs. March would not hear of the old gentleman's undertaking the long journey; yet an expression of relief was visible when he spoke of it, for anxiety ill fits one for travelling. He saw the look, knit his heavy eyebrows, rubbed his hands, and marched abruptly away, saying he'd be back directly. No one had time to think of him again till, as Meg ran through the entry, with a pair of rubbers in one hand and a cup of tea in the other, she came suddenly upon Mr. Brooke.

"I'm very sorry to hear of this, Miss March," he said, in the kind, quiet tone which sounded very pleasantly to her perturbed spirit. "I came to offer myself as escort to your mother. Mr. Laurence has commissions for me in Washington, and it will give me real satisfaction to be of service to her there."

Down dropped the rubbers, and the tea was very near following, as Meg put out her hand, with a face so full of gratitude, that Mr. Brooke would have felt repaid for a much greater sacrifice than the trifling one of time and comfort which he was about to make.

"How kind you all are! Mother will accept, I'm sure; and it will be such a relief to know that she has some one to take care of her. Thank you very, very much!"

Meg spoke earnestly, and forgot herself entirely till something in the brown eyes looking down at her made her remember the cooling tea, and lead the way into the parlor, saying she would call her mother.

Everything was arranged by the time Laurie returned with a note from Aunt March, enclosing the desired sum, and a few lines repeating what she had often said before,—that she had always told them it was absurd for March to go into the army, always predicted that no good would come of it, and she hoped they would take her advice next time. Mrs. March put the note in the fire, the money in her purse, and went on with her preparations, with her lips folded tightly, in a way which Jo would have understood if she had been there.

The short afternoon wore away; all the other errands were done, and Meg and her mother busy at some necessary needle-work, while Beth and Amy got tea, and Hannah finished her ironing with what she called a "slap and a bang," but still Jo did not come. They began to get anxious; and Laurie went off to find her, for no one ever knew what freak Jo might take into her head. He missed her, however, and she came walking in with a very queer expression of countenance, for there was a mixture of fun and fear, satisfaction and regret, in it, which puzzled the family as much as did the roll of bills she laid before her mother, saying, with a little choke in her voice, "That's my contribution towards making father comfortable and bringing him home!"

"My dear, where did you get it? Twenty-five dollars! Jo, I hope you haven't done anything rash?

"No, it's mine honestly; I didn't beg, borrow, or steal it. I earned it; and I don't think you'll blame me, for I only sold what was my own."

As she spoke, Jo took off her bonnet, and a general outcry arose, for all her abundant hair was cut short.

"Your hair! Your beautiful hair!" "O Jo, how could you? Your one beauty." "My dear girl, there was no need of this." "She doesn't look like my Jo any more, but I love her dearly for it!"

As every one exclaimed, and Beth hugged the cropped head tenderly, Jo assumed an indifferent air, which did not deceive any one a particle, and said, rumpling up the brown bush, and trying to look as if she liked it, "It doesn't affect the fate of the nation, so don't wail, Beth. It will be good for my vanity; I was getting too proud of my wig. It will do my brains good to have that mop taken off; my head feels deliciously light and cool, and the barber said I could soon have a curly crop, which will be boyish, becoming, and easy to keep in order. I'm satisfied; so please take the money, and let's have supper."

"Tell me all about it, Jo. *I* am not quite satisfied, but I can't blame you, for I know how willingly you sacrificed your vanity, as you call it, to your love. But, my dear, it was not necessary, and I'm afraid you will regret it, one of these days," said Mrs. March.

"No, I won't!" returned Jo stoutly, feeling much relieved that her prank was not entirely condemned.

"What made you do it?" asked Amy, who would as soon have thought of cutting off her head as her pretty hair.

"Well, I was wild to do something for father," replied Jo, as they gathered about the table, for healthy young people can eat even in the midst of trouble. "I hate to borrow as much as mother does, and I knew Aunt March would croak; she always does, if you ask for a ninepence. Meg gave all her quarterly salary toward the rent, and I only got some clothes with mine, so I felt wicked, and was bound to have some money, if I sold the nose off my face to get it."

"You needn't feel wicked, my child: you had no winter things, and got the simplest with your own hard earnings," said Mrs. March, with a look that warmed Jo's heart.

"I hadn't the least idea of selling my hair at first, but as I went along I kept thinking what I could do, and feeling as if I'd like to dive into some of the rich stores and help myself. In a barber's window I saw tails of hair with the prices marked; and one black tail, not so thick as mine, was forty dollars. It came over me all of a sudden that I had one thing to make money out of, and without stopping to think, I walked in, asked if they bought hair, and what they would give for mine."

"I don't see how you dared to do it," said Beth, in a tone of awe.

"Oh, he was a little man who looked as if he merely lived to oil his hair. He rather stared, at first, as if he wasn't used to having girls bounce into his shop and ask him to buy their hair. He said he didn't care about mine, it wasn't the fashionable color, and he never paid much for it in the first place; the work put into it made it dear, and so on. It was getting late, and I was afraid, if it wasn't done right away, that I shouldn't have it done at all, and you know when I start to do a thing, I hate to give it up; so I begged him to take it, and told him why I was in such a hurry. It was silly, I dare say, but it changed his mind, for I got rather excited, and told the story in my topsy-turvy way, and his wife heard, and said so kindly,—

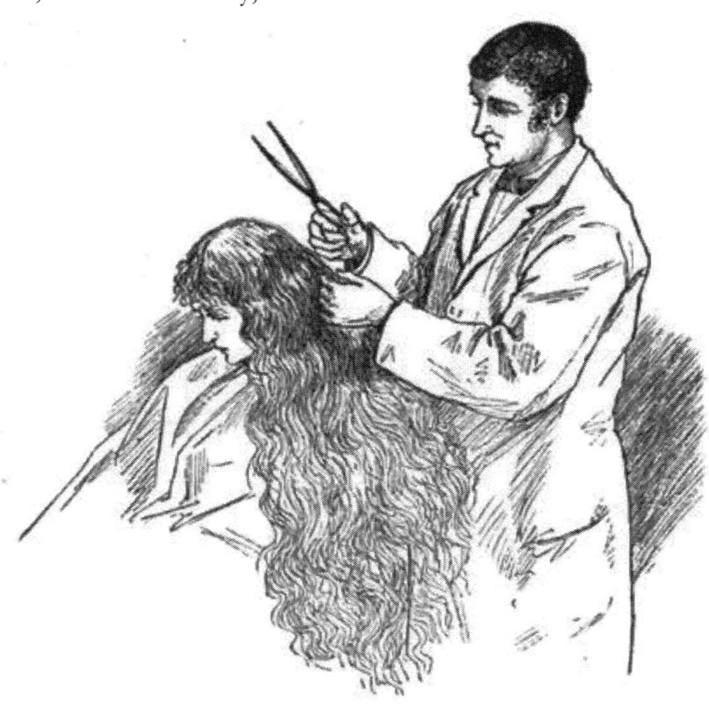

"'Take it, Thomas, and oblige the young lady; I'd do as much for our Jimmy any day if I had a spire of hair worth selling.'"

"Who was Jimmy?" asked Amy, who liked to have things explained as they went along.

"Her son, she said, who was in the army. How friendly such things make strangers feel, don't they? She talked away all the time the man clipped, and diverted my mind nicely."

"Didn't you feel dreadfully when the first cut came?" asked Meg, with a shiver.

"I took a last look at my hair while the man got his things, and that was the end of it. I never snivel over trifles like that; I will confess, though, I felt queer when I saw the dear old hair laid out on the table, and felt only the short, rough ends on my head. It almost seemed as if I'd an arm or a leg off. The woman saw me look at it, and picked out a long lock for me to keep. I'll give it to you, Marmee, just to remember past glories by; for a crop is so comfortable I don't think I shall ever have a mane again."

Mrs. March folded the wavy, chestnut lock, and laid it away with a short gray one in her desk. She only said "Thank you, deary," but something in her face made the girls change the subject, and talk as cheerfully as they could about Mr. Brooke's kindness, the prospect of a fine day to-morrow, and the happy times they would have when father came home to be nursed.

No one wanted to go to bed, when, at ten o'clock, Mrs. March put by the last finished job, and said, "Come, girls." Beth went to the piano and played the father's favorite hymn; all began bravely, but broke down one by one, till Beth was left alone, singing with all her heart, for to her music was always a sweet consoler.

"Go to bed and don't talk, for we must be up early, and shall need all the sleep we can get. Good-night, my darlings," said Mrs. March, as the hymn ended, for no one cared to try another.

They kissed her quietly, and went to bed as silently as if the dear invalid lay in the next room. Beth and Amy soon fell asleep in spite of the great trouble, but Meg lay awake, thinking the most serious thoughts she had ever known in her short life. Jo lay motionless, and her sister fancied that she was asleep, till a stifled sob made her exclaim, as she touched a wet cheek,—

"Jo, dear, what is it? Are you crying about father?"

"No, not now."

"What then?"

"My—my hair!" burst out poor Jo, trying vainly to smother her emotion in the pillow.

It did not sound at all comical to Meg, who kissed and caressed the afflicted heroine in the tenderest manner.

"I'm not sorry," protested Jo, with a choke. "I'd do it again to-morrow, if I could. It's only the vain, selfish part of me that goes and cries in this silly way. Don't tell any one, it's all over now. I thought you were asleep, so I just made a little private moan for my one beauty. How came you to be awake?"

"I can't sleep, I'm so anxious," said Meg.

"Think about something pleasant, and you'll soon drop off."

"I tried it, but felt wider awake than ever."

"What did you think of?"

"Handsome faces,—eyes particularly," answered Meg, smiling to herself, in the dark.

"What color do you like best?"

"Brown—that is, sometimes; blue are lovely."

Jo laughed, and Meg sharply ordered her not to talk, then amiably promised to make her hair curl, and fell asleep to dream of living in her castle in the air.

The clocks were striking midnight, and the rooms were very still, as a figure glided quietly from bed to bed, smoothing a coverlid here, settling a pillow there, and pausing to look long and tenderly at each unconscious face, to kiss each with lips that mutely blessed, and to pray the fervent prayers which only mothers utter. As she lifted the curtain to look out into the dreary night, the moon broke suddenly from behind the clouds, and shone upon her like a bright, benignant face, which seemed to whisper in the silence, "Be comforted, dear soul! There is always light behind the clouds."

XVI.

# LETTERS.

IN the cold gray dawn the sisters lit their lamp, and read their chapter with an earnestness never felt before; for now the shadow of a real trouble had come, the little books were full of help and comfort; and, as they dressed, they agreed to say good-by cheerfully and hopefully, and send their mother on her anxious journey unsaddened by tears or complaints from them. Everything seemed very strange when they went down,—so dim and still outside, so full of light and bustle within. Breakfast at that early hour seemed odd, and even Hannah's familiar face looked unnatural as she flew about her kitchen with her night-cap on. The big trunk stood ready in the hall, mother's cloak and bonnet lay on the sofa, and mother herself sat trying to eat, but looking so pale and worn with sleeplessness and anxiety that the girls found it very hard to keep their resolution. Meg's eyes kept filling in spite of herself; Jo was obliged to hide her face in the kitchen roller more than once; and the little girls' wore a grave, troubled expression, as if sorrow was a new experience to them.

Nobody talked much, but as the time drew very near, and they sat waiting for the carriage, Mrs. March said to the girls, who were all busied about her, one folding her shawl, another smoothing out the strings of her bonnet, a third putting on her overshoes, and a fourth fastening up her travelling bag,—

"Children, I leave you to Hannah's care and Mr. Laurence's protection. Hannah is faithfulness itself, and our good neighbor will guard you as if you were his own. I have no fears for you, yet I am anxious that you should take this trouble rightly. Don't grieve and fret when I am gone, or think that you can comfort yourselves by being idle and trying to forget. Go on with your work as usual, for work is a blessed solace. Hope and keep busy; and whatever happens, remember that you never can be fatherless."

"Yes, mother."

"Meg, dear, be prudent, watch over your sisters, consult Hannah, and, in any perplexity, go to Mr. Laurence. Be patient, Jo, don't get despondent or do rash things; write to me often, and be my brave girl, ready to help and cheer us all. Beth, comfort yourself with your music, and be faithful to the little home duties; and you, Amy, help all you can, be obedient, and keep happy safe at home."

"We will, mother! we will!"

The rattle of an approaching carriage made them all start and listen. That was the hard minute, but the girls stood it well: no one cried, no one ran away or uttered a lamentation, though their hearts were very heavy as they sent loving messages to father, remembering, as they spoke, that it might be too late to deliver them. They kissed their mother quietly, clung about her tenderly, and tried to wave their hands cheerfully when she drove away.

Laurie and his grandfather came over to see her off, and Mr. Brooke looked so strong and sensible and kind that the girls christened him "Mr. Greatheart" on the spot.

"Good-by, my darlings! God bless and keep us all!" whispered Mrs. March, as she kissed one dear little face after the other, and hurried into the carriage.

As she rolled away, the sun came out, and, looking back, she saw it shining on the group at the gate, like a good omen. They saw it also, and smiled and waved their hands; and the last thing she beheld, as she turned the corner, was the four bright faces, and behind them, like a body-guard, old Mr. Laurence, faithful Hannah, and devoted Laurie.

"How kind every one is to us!" she said, turning to find fresh proof of it in the respectful sympathy of the young man's face.

"I don't see how they can help it," returned Mr. Brooke, laughing so infectiously that Mrs. March could not help smiling; and so the long journey began with the good omens of sunshine, smiles, and cheerful words.

"I feel as if there had been an earthquake," said Jo, as their neighbors went home to breakfast, leaving them to rest and refresh themselves.

"It seems as if half the house was gone," added Meg forlornly.

Beth opened her lips to say something, but could only point to the pile of nicely-mended hose which lay on mother's table, showing that even in her last hurried moments she had thought and worked for them. It was a little thing, but it went straight to their hearts; and, in spite of their brave resolutions, they all broke down, and cried bitterly.

Hannah wisely allowed them to relieve their feelings, and, when the shower showed signs of clearing up, she came to the rescue, armed with a coffee-pot.

"Now, my dear young ladies, remember what your ma said, and don't fret. Come and have a cup of coffee all round, and then let's fall to work, and be a credit to the family."

Coffee was a treat, and Hannah showed great tact in making it that morning. No one could resist her persuasive nods, or the fragrant invitation issuing from the nose of the coffee-pot. They drew up to the table, exchanged their handkerchiefs for napkins, and in ten minutes were all right again.

"'Hope and keep busy;' that's the motto for us, so let's see who will remember it best. I shall go to Aunt March, as usual. Oh, won't she lecture though!" said Jo, as she sipped with returning spirit.

"I shall go to my Kings, though I'd much rather stay at home and attend to things here," said Meg, wishing she hadn't made her eyes so red.

"No need of that; Beth and I can keep house perfectly well," put in Amy, with an important air.

"Hannah will tell us what to do; and we'll have everything nice when you come home," added Beth, getting out her mop and dish-tub without delay.

"I think anxiety is very interesting," observed Amy, eating sugar, pensively.

The girls couldn't help laughing, and felt better for it, though Meg shook her head at the young lady who could find consolation in a sugar-bowl.

The sight of the turn-overs made Jo sober again; and when the two went out to their daily tasks, they looked sorrowfully back at the window where they were accustomed to see their mother's face. It was gone; but Beth had remembered the little household ceremony, and there she was, nodding away at them like a rosy-faced mandarin.

"That's so like my Beth!" said Jo, waving her hat, with a grateful face. "Good-by, Meggy; I hope the Kings won't train to-day. Don't fret about father, dear," she added, as they parted.

"And I hope Aunt March won't croak. Your hair *is* becoming, and it looks very boyish and nice," returned Meg, trying not to smile at the curly head, which looked comically small on her tall sister's shoulders.

"That's my only comfort;" and, touching her hat *à la* Laurie, away went Jo, feeling like a shorn sheep on a wintry day.

News from their father comforted the girls very much; for, though dangerously ill, the presence of the best and tenderest of nurses had already done him good. Mr. Brooke sent a bulletin every day, and, as the head of the family, Meg insisted on reading the despatches, which grew more and more cheering as the week passed. At first, every one was eager to write, and plump envelopes were carefully poked into the letter-box by one or other of the sisters, who felt rather important with their Washington correspondence. As one of these packets contained characteristic notes from the party, we will rob an imaginary mail, and read them:—

"MY DEAREST MOTHER,—

"It is impossible to tell you how happy your last letter made us, for the news was so good we couldn't help laughing and crying over it. How very kind Mr. Brooke is, and how fortunate that Mr. Laurence's business detains him near you so long, since he is so useful to you and father. The girls are all as good as gold. Jo helps me with the sewing, and insists on doing all sorts of hard jobs. I should be afraid she might overdo, if I didn't know that her 'moral fit' wouldn't last long. Beth is as regular about her tasks as a clock, and never forgets what you told her. She grieves about father, and looks sober except when she is at her little piano. Amy minds me nicely, and I take great care of her. She does her own hair, and I am teaching her to make button-holes and mend her stockings. She tries very hard, and I know you will be pleased with her improvement when you come. Mr. Laurence watches over us like a motherly old hen, as Jo says; and Laurie is very kind and neighborly. He and Jo keep us merry, for we get pretty blue sometimes, and feel like orphans, with you so far away. Hannah is a perfect saint; she does not scold at all, and always calls me Miss 'Margaret,' which is quite proper, you know, and treats me with respect. We are all well and busy; but we long, day and night, to have you back. Give my dearest love to father, and believe me, ever your own

"MEG."

This note, prettily written on scented paper, was a great contrast to the next, which was scribbled on a big sheet of thin foreign paper, ornamented with blots and all manner of flourishes and curly-tailed letters:—

"MY PRECIOUS MARMEE,—

"Three cheers for dear father! Brooke was a trump to telegraph right off, and let us know the minute he was better. I rushed up garret when the letter came, and tried to thank God for being so good to us; but I could only cry, and say, 'I'm glad! I'm glad!' Didn't that do as well as a regular prayer? for I felt a great many in my heart. We have such funny times; and now I can enjoy them, for every one is so desperately good, it's like living in a nest of turtle-doves. You'd laugh to see Meg head the table and try to be motherish. She gets prettier every day, and I'm in love with her sometimes. The children are regular archangels, and I—well, I'm Jo, and never shall be anything else. Oh, I must tell you that I came near having a quarrel with Laurie. I freed my mind about a silly little thing, and he was offended. I was right, but didn't speak as I ought, and he marched home, saying he wouldn't come again till I begged pardon. I declared I wouldn't, and got mad. It lasted all day; I felt bad, and wanted you very much. Laurie and I are both so proud, it's hard to beg pardon; but I thought he'd come to it, for I *was* in the right. He didn't come; and just at night I remembered what you said when Amy fell into the river. I read my little book, felt better, resolved not to let the sun set on *my* anger, and ran over to tell Laurie I was sorry. I met him at the gate, coming for the same thing. We both laughed, begged each other's pardon, and felt all good and comfortable again.

"I made a 'pome' yesterday, when I was helping Hannah wash; and, as father likes my silly little things, I put it in to amuse him. Give him the lovingest hug that ever was, and kiss yourself a dozen times for your

"TOPSY-TURVY JO."

---

"A SONG FROM THE SUDS.

"Queen of my tub, I merrily sing,  
While the white foam rises high;  
And sturdily wash and rinse and wring,  
And fasten the clothes to dry;

Then out in the free fresh air they swing,
Under the sunny sky.

"I wish we could wash from our hearts and souls
The stains of the week away,
And let water and air by their magic make
Ourselves as pure as they;
Then on the earth there would be indeed
A glorious washing-day!

"Along the path of a useful life,
Will heart's-ease ever bloom;
The busy mind has no time to think
Of sorrow or care or gloom;
And anxious thoughts may be swept away,
As we bravely wield a broom.

"I am glad a task to me is given,
To labor at day by day;
For it brings me health and strength and hope,
And I cheerfully learn to say,—
'Head, you may think, Heart, you may feel,
But, Hand, you shall work alway!'"

"DEAR MOTHER,—

"There is only room for me to send my love, and some pressed pansies from the root I have been keeping safe in the house for father to see. I read every morning, try to be good all day, and sing myself to sleep with father's tune. I can't sing 'Land of the Leal' now; it makes me cry. Every one is very kind, and we are as happy as we can be without you. Amy wants the rest of the page, so I must stop. I didn't forget to cover the holders, and I wind the clock and air the rooms every day.

"Kiss dear father on the cheek he calls mine. Oh, do come soon to your loving

"LITTLE BETH."

---

"MA CHERE MAMMA,—

"We are all well I do my lessons always and never corroberate the girls—Meg says I mean contradick so I put in both words and you can take the properest. Meg is a great comfort to me and lets me have jelly every night at tea its so good for me Jo says because it keeps me sweet tempered. Laurie is not as respeckful as he ought to be now I am almost in my teens, he calls me Chick and hurts my feelings by talking French to me very fast when I say Merci or Bon jour as Hattie King does. The sleeves of my blue dress were all worn out, and Meg put in new ones, but the full front came wrong and they are more blue than the dress. I felt bad but did not fret I bear my troubles well but I do wish Hannah would put more starch in my aprons and have buckwheats every day. Can't she? Didn't I make that interrigation point nice? Meg says my punchtuation and spelling are disgraceful and I am mortyfied but dear me I have so many things to do, I can't stop. Adieu, I send heaps of love to Papa.

"Your affectionate daughter,

"AMY CURTIS MARCH."

"DEAR MIS MARCH,—

"I jes drop a line to say we git on fust rate. The girls is clever and fly round right smart. Miss Meg is going to make a proper good housekeeper; she hes the liking for it, and gits the hang of things surprisin quick. Jo doos beat all for goin ahead, but she don't stop to cal'k'late fust, and you never know where she's like to bring up. She done out a tub of clothes on Monday, but she starched 'em afore they was wrenched, and blued a pink calico dress till I thought I should a died a laughin. Beth is the best of little creeters, and a sight of help to me, bein so forehanded and dependable. She tries to learn everything, and really goes to market beyond her years; likewise keeps accounts, with my help, quite wonderful. We have got on very economical so fur; I don't let the girls hev coffee only once a week, accordin to your wish, and keep em on plain wholesome vittles. Amy does well about frettin, wearin her best clothes and eatin sweet stuff. Mr. Laurie is as full of didoes as usual, and turns the house upside down frequent; but he heartens up the girls, and so I let em hev full swing. The old gentleman sends heaps of things, and is rather wearin, but means wal, and it aint my place to say nothin. My bread is riz, so no more at this time. I send my duty to Mr. March, and hope he's seen the last of his Pewmonia.

"Yours Respectful,
"HANNAH MULLET."

---

"HEAD NURSE OF WARD NO. ,—

"All serene on the Rappahannock, troops in fine condition, commissary department well conducted, the Home Guard under Colonel Teddy always on duty, Commander-in-chief General Laurence reviews the army daily, Quartermaster Mullett keeps order in camp, and Major Lion does picket duty at night. A salute of twenty-four guns was fired on receipt of good news from Washington, and a dress parade took place at head-quarters. Commander-in-chief sends best wishes, in which he is heartily joined by

"COLONEL TEDDY."

---

"DEAR MADAM,—

"The little girls are all well; Beth and my boy report daily; Hannah is a model servant, and guards pretty Meg like a dragon. Glad the fine weather holds; pray make Brooke useful, and draw on me for funds if expenses exceed your estimate. Don't let your husband want anything. Thank God he is mending.

"Your sincere friend and servant,
"JAMES LAURENCE."

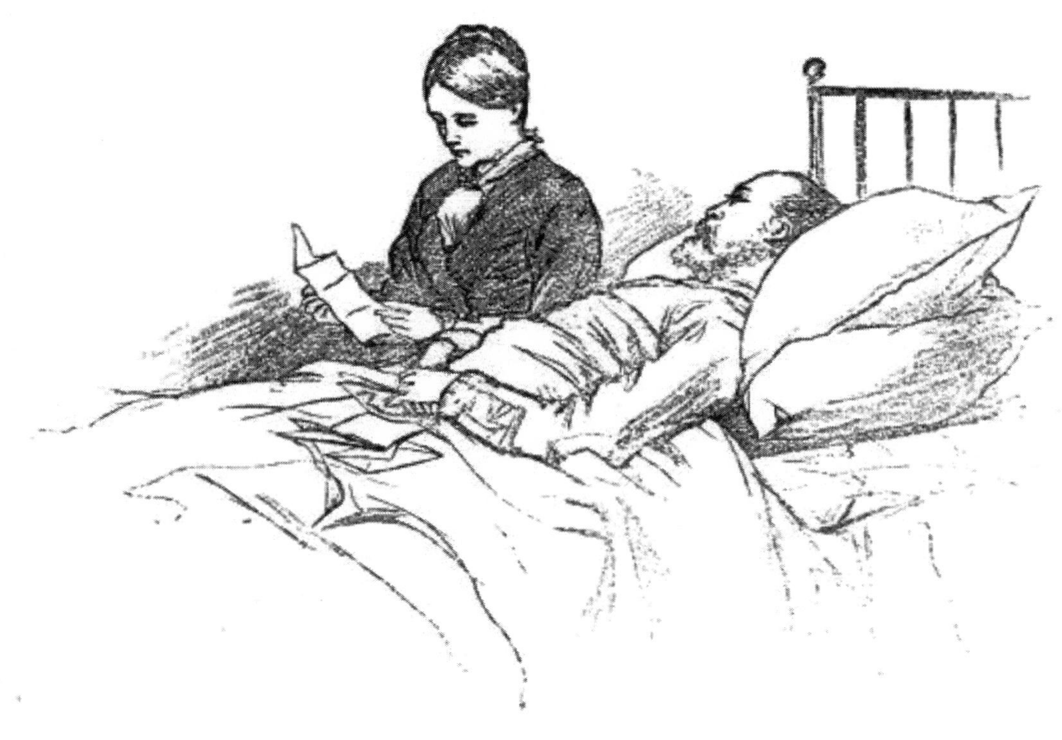

XVII.

## LITTLE FAITHFUL.

FOR a week the amount of virtue in the old house would have supplied the neighborhood. It was really amazing, for every one seemed in a heavenly frame of mind, and self-denial was all the fashion. Relieved of their first anxiety about their father, the girls insensibly relaxed their praiseworthy efforts a little, and began to fall back into the old ways. They did not forget their motto, but hoping and keeping busy seemed to grow easier; and after such tremendous exertions, they felt that Endeavor deserved a holiday, and gave it a good many.

Jo caught a bad cold through neglect to cover the shorn head enough, and was ordered to stay at home till she was better, for Aunt March didn't like to hear people read with colds in their heads. Jo liked this, and after an energetic rummage from garret to cellar, subsided on the sofa to nurse her cold with arsenicum and books. Amy found that housework and art did not go well together, and returned to her mud pies. Meg went daily to her pupils, and sewed, or thought she did, at home, but much time was spent in writing long letters to her mother, or reading the Washington despatches over and over. Beth kept on, with only slight relapses into idleness or grieving. All the little duties were faithfully done each day, and many of her sisters' also, for they were forgetful, and the house seemed like a clock whose pendulum was gone a-visiting. When her heart got heavy with longings for mother or fears for father, she went away into a certain closet, hid her face in the folds of a certain dear old gown, and made her little moan and prayed her little prayer quietly by herself. Nobody knew what cheered her up after a sober fit, but every one felt how sweet and helpful Beth was, and fell into a way of going to her for comfort or advice in their small affairs.

All were unconscious that this experience was a test of character; and, when the first excitement was over, felt that they had done well, and deserved praise. So they did; but their mistake was in ceasing to do well, and they learned this lesson through much anxiety and regret.

"Meg, I wish you'd go and see the Hummels; you know mother told us not to forget them," said Beth, ten days after Mrs. March's departure.

"I'm too tired to go this afternoon," replied Meg, rocking comfortably as she sewed.

"Can't you, Jo?" asked Beth.

"Too stormy for me with my cold."

"I thought it was almost well."

"It's well enough for me to go out with Laurie, but not well enough to go to the Hummels'," said Jo, laughing, but looking a little ashamed of her inconsistency.

"Why don't you go yourself?" asked Meg.

"I *have* been every day, but the baby is sick, and I don't know what to do for it. Mrs. Hummel goes away to work, and Lottchen takes care of it; but it gets sicker and sicker, and I think you or Hannah ought to go."

Beth spoke earnestly, and Meg promised she would go to-morrow.

"Ask Hannah for some nice little mess, and take it round, Beth; the air will do you good," said Jo, adding apologetically, "I'd go, but I want to finish my writing."

"My head aches and I'm tired, so I thought may be some of you would go," said Beth.

"Amy will be in presently, and she will run down for us," suggested Meg.

"Well, I'll rest a little and wait for her."

So Beth lay down on the sofa, the others returned to their work, and the Hummels were forgotten. An hour passed: Amy did not come; Meg went to her room to try on a new dress; Jo was absorbed in her story, and Hannah was sound asleep before the kitchen fire, when Beth quietly put on her hood, filled her basket with odds and ends for the poor children, and went out into the chilly air, with a heavy head, and a grieved look in her patient eyes. It was late when she came back, and no one saw her creep upstairs and shut herself into her mother's room. Half an hour after Jo went to "mother's closet" for something, and there found Beth sitting on the medicine chest, looking very grave, with red eyes, and a camphor-bottle in her hand.

"Christopher Columbus! What's the matter?" cried Jo, as Beth put out her hand as if to warn her off, and asked quickly,—

"You've had the scarlet fever, haven't you?"

"Years ago, when Meg did. Why?"

"Then I'll tell you. Oh, Jo, the baby's dead!"

"What baby?"

"Mrs. Hummel's; it died in my lap before she got home," cried Beth, with a sob.

"My poor dear, how dreadful for you! I ought to have gone," said Jo, taking her sister in her arms as she sat down in her mother's big chair, with a remorseful face.

"It wasn't dreadful, Jo, only so sad! I saw in a minute that it was sicker, but Lottchen said her mother had gone for a doctor, so I took baby and let Lotty rest. It seemed asleep, but all of a sudden it gave a little cry, and trembled, and then lay very still. I tried to warm its feet, and Lotty gave it some milk, but it didn't stir, and I knew it was dead."

"Don't cry, dear! What did you do?"

"I just sat and held it softly till Mrs. Hummel came with the doctor. He said it was dead, and looked at Heinrich and Minna, who have got sore throats. 'Scarlet fever, ma'am. Ought to have called me before,' he said crossly. Mrs. Hummel told him she was poor, and had tried to cure baby herself, but now it was too late, and she could only ask him to help the others, and trust to charity for his pay. He smiled then, and was kinder; but it was very sad, and I cried with them till he turned round, all of a sudden, and told me to go home and take belladonna right away, or I'd have the fever."

"No, you won't!" cried Jo, hugging her close, with a frightened look. "O Beth, if you should be sick I never could forgive myself! What *shall* we do?"

"Don't be frightened, I guess I shan't have it badly. I looked in mother's book, and saw that it begins with headache, sore throat, and queer feelings like mine, so I did take some belladonna, and I feel better," said Beth, laying her cold hands on her hot forehead, and trying to look well.

"If mother was only at home!" exclaimed Jo, seizing the book, and feeling that Washington was an immense way off. She read a page, looked at Beth, felt her head, peeped into her throat, and then said gravely; "You've been over the baby every day for more than a week, and among the others who are going to have it; so I'm afraid *you* are going to have it, Beth. I'll call Hannah, she knows all about sickness."

"Don't let Amy come; she never had it, and I should hate to give it to her. Can't you and Meg have it over again?" asked Beth, anxiously.

"I guess not; don't care if I do; serve me right, selfish pig, to let you go, and stay writing rubbish myself!" muttered Jo, as she went to consult Hannah.

The good soul was wide awake in a minute, and took the lead at once, assuring Jo that there was no need to worry; every one had scarlet fever, and, if rightly treated, nobody died,—all of which Jo believed, and felt much relieved as they went up to call Meg.

"Now I'll tell you what we'll do," said Hannah, when she had examined and questioned Beth; "we will have Dr. Bangs, just to take a look at you, dear, and see that we start right; then we'll send Amy off to Aunt March's, for a spell, to keep her out of harm's way, and one of you girls can stay at home and amuse Beth for a day or two."

"I shall stay, of course; I'm oldest," began Meg, looking anxious and self-reproachful.

"*I* shall, because it's my fault she is sick; I told mother I'd do the errands, and I haven't," said Jo decidedly.

"Which will you have, Beth? there ain't no need of but one," said Hannah.

"Jo, please;" and Beth leaned her head against her sister, with a contented look, which effectually settled that point.

"I'll go and tell Amy," said Meg, feeling a little hurt, yet rather relieved, on the whole, for she did not like nursing, and Jo did.

Amy rebelled outright, and passionately declared that she had rather have the fever than go to Aunt March. Meg reasoned, pleaded, and commanded: all in vain. Amy protested that she would *not* go; and Meg left her in despair, to ask Hannah what should be done. Before she came back, Laurie walked into the parlor to find Amy sobbing, with her head in the sofa-cushions. She told her story, expecting to be consoled; but Laurie only put his hands in his pockets and walked about the room, whistling softly, as he knit his brows in deep thought. Presently he sat down beside her, and said, in his most wheedlesome tone, "Now be a sensible little woman, and do as they say. No, don't cry, but hear what a jolly plan I've got. You go to Aunt March's, and I'll come and take you out every day, driving or walking, and we'll have capital times. Won't that be better than moping here?"

"I don't wish to be sent off as if I was in the way," began Amy, in an injured voice.

"Bless your heart, child, it's to keep you well. You don't want to be sick, do you?"

"No, I'm sure I don't; but I dare say I shall be, for I've been with Beth all the time."

"That's the very reason you ought to go away at once, so that you may escape it. Change of air and care will keep you well, I dare say; or, if it does not entirely, you will have the fever more lightly. I advise you to be off as soon as you can, for scarlet fever is no joke, miss."

"But it's dull at Aunt March's, and she is so cross," said Amy, looking rather frightened.

"It won't be dull with me popping in every day to tell you how Beth is, and take you out gallivanting. The old lady likes me, and I'll be as sweet as possible to her, so she won't peck at us, whatever we do."

"Will you take me out in the trotting wagon with Puck?"

"On my honor as a gentleman."

"And come every single day?"

"See if I don't."

"And bring me back the minute Beth is well?"

"The identical minute."

"And go to the theatre, truly?"

"A dozen theatres, if we may."

"Well—I guess—I will," said Amy slowly.

"Good girl! Call Meg, and tell her you'll give in," said Laurie, with an approving pat, which annoyed Amy more than the "giving in."

Meg and Jo came running down to behold the miracle which had been wrought; and Amy, feeling very precious and self-sacrificing, promised to go, if the doctor said Beth was going to be ill.

"How is the little dear?" asked Laurie; for Beth was his especial pet, and he felt more anxious about her than he liked to show.

"She is lying down on mother's bed, and feels better. The baby's death troubled her, but I dare say she has only got cold. Hannah *says* she thinks so; but she *looks* worried, and that makes me fidgety," answered Meg.

"What a trying world it is!" said Jo, rumpling up her hair in a fretful sort of way. "No sooner do we get out of one trouble than down comes another. There doesn't seem to be anything to hold on to when mother's gone; so I'm all at sea."

"Well, don't make a porcupine of yourself, it isn't becoming. Settle your wig, Jo, and tell me if I shall telegraph to your mother, or do anything?" asked Laurie, who never had been reconciled to the loss of his friend's one beauty.

"That is what troubles me," said Meg. "I think we ought to tell her if Beth is really ill, but Hannah says we mustn't, for mother can't leave father, and it will only make them anxious. Beth won't be sick long, and Hannah knows just what to do, and mother said we were to mind her, so I suppose we must, but it doesn't seem quite right to me."

"Hum, well, I can't say; suppose you ask grandfather after the doctor has been."

"We will. Jo, go and get Dr. Bangs at once," commanded Meg; "we can't decide anything till he has been."

"Stay where you are, Jo; I'm errand-boy to this establishment," said Laurie, taking up his cap.

"I'm afraid you are busy," began Meg.

"No, I've done my lessons for the day."

"Do you study in vacation time?" asked Jo.

"I follow the good example my neighbors set me," was Laurie's answer, as he swung himself out of the room.

"I have great hopes of my boy," observed Jo, watching him fly over the fence with an approving smile.

"He does very well—for a boy," was Meg's somewhat ungracious answer, for the subject did not interest her.

Dr. Bangs came, said Beth had symptoms of the fever, but thought she would have it lightly, though he looked sober over the Hummel story. Amy was ordered off at once, and provided with something to ward off danger, she departed in great state, with Jo and Laurie as escort.

Aunt March received them with her usual hospitality.

"What do you want now?" she asked, looking sharply over her spectacles, while the parrot, sitting on the back of her chair, called out,—

"Go away. No boys allowed here."

Laurie retired to the window, and Jo told her story.

"No more than I expected, if you are allowed to go poking about among poor folks. Amy can stay and make herself useful if she isn't sick, which I've no doubt she will be,—looks like it now. Don't cry, child, it worries me to hear people sniff."

Amy *was* on the point of crying, but Laurie slyly pulled the parrot's tail, which caused Polly to utter an astonished croak, and call out,—

"Bless my boots!" in such a funny way, that she laughed instead.

"What do you hear from your mother?" asked the old lady gruffly.

"Father is much better," replied Jo, trying to keep sober.

"Oh, is he? Well, that won't last long, I fancy; March never had any stamina," was the cheerful reply.

"Ha, ha! never say die, take a pinch of snuff, good by, good by!" squalled Polly, dancing on her perch, and clawing at the old lady's cap as Laurie tweaked him in the rear.

"Hold your tongue, you disrespectful old bird! and, Jo, you'd better go at once; it isn't proper to be gadding about so late with a rattle-pated boy like—"

"Hold your tongue, you disrespectful old bird!" cried Polly, tumbling off the chair with a bounce, and running to peck the "rattle-pated" boy, who was shaking with laughter at the last speech.

"I don't think I *can* bear it, but I'll try," thought Amy, as she was left alone with Aunt March.

"Get along, you fright!" screamed Polly; and at that rude speech Amy could not restrain a sniff.

## XVIII.

## DARK DAYS.

BETH did have the fever, and was much sicker than any one but Hannah and the doctor suspected. The girls knew nothing about illness, and Mr. Laurence was not allowed to see her, so Hannah had everything all her own way, and busy Dr. Bangs did his best, but left a good deal to the excellent nurse. Meg stayed at home, lest she should infect the Kings, and kept house, feeling very anxious and a little guilty when she wrote letters in which no mention was made of Beth's illness. She could not think it right to deceive her mother, but she had been bidden to mind Hannah, and Hannah wouldn't hear of "Mrs. March bein' told, and worried just for sech a trifle." Jo devoted herself to Beth day and night; not a hard task, for Beth was very patient, and bore her pain uncomplainingly as long as she could control herself. But there came a time when during the fever fits she began to talk in a hoarse, broken voice, to play on the coverlet, as if on her beloved little piano, and try to sing with a throat so swollen that there was no music left; a time when she did not know the familiar faces round her, but addressed them by wrong names, and called imploringly for her mother. Then Jo grew frightened, Meg begged to be allowed to write the truth, and even Hannah said she "would think of it, though there was no danger *yet*." A letter from Washington added to their trouble, for Mr. March had had a relapse, and could not think of coming home for a long while.

How dark the days seemed now, how sad and lonely the house, and how heavy were the hearts of the sisters as they worked and waited, while the shadow of death hovered over the once happy home! Then it was that Margaret, sitting alone with tears dropping often on her work, felt how rich she had been in things more precious than any luxuries money could buy,—in love, protection, peace, and health, the real blessings of life. Then it was that Jo, living in the darkened room, with that suffering little sister always before her eyes, and that pathetic voice sounding in her ears, learned to see the beauty and the sweetness of Beth's nature, to feel how deep and tender a place she filled in all hearts, and to acknowledge the worth of Beth's unselfish ambition, to live for others, and make home happy by the exercise of those simple virtues which all may possess, and which all should love and value more than talent, wealth, or beauty. And Amy, in her exile, longed eagerly to be at home, that she might work for Beth, feeling now that no service would be hard or irksome, and remembering, with regretful grief, how many neglected tasks those willing hands had done for her. Laurie haunted the house like a restless ghost, and Mr. Laurence locked the grand piano, because he could not bear to be reminded of the young neighbor who used to make the twilight pleasant for him. Every one missed Beth. The milkman, baker, grocer, and butcher inquired how she did; poor Mrs. Hummel came to beg pardon for her thoughtlessness, and to get a shroud for Minna; the neighbors sent all sorts of comforts and good wishes, and even those who knew her best were surprised to find how many friends shy little Beth had made.

Meanwhile she lay on her bed with old Joanna at her side, for even in her wanderings she did not forget her forlorn *protégé*. She longed for her cats, but would not have them brought, lest they should get sick; and, in her quiet hours, she was full of anxiety about Jo. She sent loving messages to Amy, bade them tell her mother that she would write soon; and often begged for pencil and paper to try to say a word, that father might not think she had neglected him. But soon even these intervals of consciousness ended, and she lay hour after hour, tossing to and fro, with incoherent words on her lips, or sank into a heavy sleep which brought her no refreshment. Dr. Bangs came twice a day, Hannah sat up at night, Meg kept a telegram in her desk all ready to send off at any minute, and Jo never stirred from Beth's side.

The first of December was a wintry day indeed to them, for a bitter wind blew, snow fell fast, and the year seemed getting ready for its death. When Dr. Bangs came that morning, he looked long at Beth, held the hot hand in both his own a minute, and laid it gently down, saying, in a low tone, to Hannah,—

"If Mrs. March *can* leave her husband, she'd better be sent for."

Hannah nodded without speaking, for her lips twitched nervously; Meg dropped down into a chair as the strength seemed to go out of her limbs at the sound of those words; and Jo, after standing with a pale face for a minute, ran to the parlor, snatched up the telegram, and, throwing on her things, rushed out into the storm. She was soon back, and, while noiselessly taking off her cloak, Laurie came in with a letter, saying that Mr. March was mending again. Jo read it thankfully, but the heavy weight did not seem lifted off her heart, and her face was so full of misery that Laurie asked quickly,—

"What is it? is Beth worse?"

"I've sent for mother," said Jo, tugging at her rubber boots with a tragical expression.

"Good for you, Jo! Did you do it on your own responsibility?" asked Laurie, as he seated her in the hall chair, and took off the rebellious boots, seeing how her hands shook.

"No, the doctor told us to."

"O Jo, it's not so bad as that?" cried Laurie, with a startled face.

"Yes, it is; she doesn't know us, she doesn't even talk about the flocks of green doves, as she calls the vine-leaves on the wall; she doesn't look like my Beth, and there's nobody to help us bear it; mother and father both gone, and God seems so far away I can't find Him."

As the tears streamed fast down poor Jo's cheeks, she stretched out her hand in a helpless sort of way, as if groping in the dark, and Laurie took it in his, whispering, as well as he could, with a lump in his throat,—

"I'm here. Hold on to me, Jo, dear!"

She could not speak, but she did "hold on," and the warm grasp of the friendly human hand comforted her sore heart, and seemed to lead her nearer to the Divine arm which alone could uphold her in her trouble. Laurie longed to say something tender and comfortable, but no fitting words came to him, so he stood silent, gently stroking her bent head as her mother used to do. It was the best thing he could have done; far more soothing than the most eloquent words, for Jo felt the unspoken sympathy, and, in the silence, learned the sweet solace which affection administers to sorrow. Soon she dried the tears which had relieved her, and looked up with a grateful face.

"Thank you, Teddy, I'm better now; I don't feel so forlorn, and will try to bear it if it comes."

"Keep hoping for the best; that will help you, Jo. Soon your mother will be here, and then everything will be right."

"I'm so glad father is better; now she won't feel so bad about leaving him. Oh, me! it does seem as if all the troubles came in a heap, and I got the heaviest part on my shoulders," sighed Jo, spreading her wet handkerchief over her knees to dry.

"Doesn't Meg pull fair?" asked Laurie, looking indignant.

"Oh, yes; she tries to, but she can't love Bethy as I do; and she won't miss her as I shall. Beth is my conscience, and I *can't* give her up. I can't! I can't!"

Down went Jo's face into the wet handkerchief, and she cried despairingly; for she had kept up bravely till now, and never shed a tear. Laurie drew his hand across his eyes, but could not speak till he had subdued the choky feeling in his throat and steadied his lips. It might be unmanly, but he couldn't help it, and I am glad of it. Presently, as Jo's sobs quieted, he said hopefully, "I don't think she will die; she's so good, and we all love her so much, I don't believe God will take her away yet."

"The good and dear people always do die," groaned Jo, but she stopped crying, for her friend's words cheered her up, in spite of her own doubts and fears.

"Poor girl, you're worn out. It isn't like you to be forlorn. Stop a bit; I'll hearten you up in a jiffy."

Laurie went off two stairs at a time, and Jo laid her wearied head down on Beth's little brown hood, which no one had thought of moving from the table where she left it. It must have possessed some magic, for the submissive spirit of its gentle owner seemed to enter into Jo; and, when Laurie came running down with a glass of wine, she took it with a smile, and said bravely, "I drink—Health to my Beth! You are a good doctor, Teddy, and *such* a comfortable friend; how can I ever pay you?" she added, as the wine refreshed her body, as the kind words had done her troubled mind.

"I'll send in my bill, by and by; and to-night I'll give you something that will warm the cockles of your heart better than quarts of wine," said Laurie, beaming at her with a face of suppressed satisfaction at something.

"What is it?" cried Jo, forgetting her woes for a minute, in her wonder.

"I telegraphed to your mother yesterday, and Brooke answered she'd come at once, and she'll be here to-night, and everything will be all right. Aren't you glad I did it?"

Laurie spoke very fast, and turned red and excited all in a minute, for he had kept his plot a secret, for fear of disappointing the girls or harming Beth. Jo grew quite white, flew out of her chair, and the moment he stopped speaking she electrified him by throwing her arms round his neck, and crying out, with a joyful cry, "O Laurie! O mother! I *am* so glad!" She did not weep again, but laughed hysterically, and trembled and clung to her friend as if she was a little bewildered by the sudden news. Laurie, though decidedly amazed, behaved with great presence of mind; he patted her back soothingly, and, finding that she was recovering, followed it up by a bashful kiss or two, which brought Jo round at once. Holding on to the banisters, she put him gently away, saying breathlessly, "Oh, don't! I didn't mean to; it was dreadful of me; but you were such a dear to go and do it in spite of Hannah that I couldn't help flying at you. Tell me all about it, and don't give me wine again; it makes me act so."

"I don't mind," laughed Laurie, as he settled his tie. "Why, you see I got fidgety, and so did grandpa. We thought Hannah was overdoing the authority business, and your mother ought to know. She'd never forgive us if Beth—well, if anything happened, you know. So I got grandpa to say it was high time we did something, and off I pelted to the office yesterday, for the doctor looked sober, and Hannah most took my head off when I proposed a telegram. I never *can* bear to be 'lorded over;' so that settled my mind, and I did it. Your mother will come, I know, and the late train is in at two, A.M. I shall go for her; and you've only got to bottle up your rapture, and keep Beth quiet, till that blessed lady gets here."

"Laurie, you're an angel! How shall I ever thank you?"

"Fly at me again; I rather like it," said Laurie, looking mischievous,—a thing he had not done for a fortnight.

"No, thank you. I'll do it by proxy, when your grandpa comes. Don't tease, but go home and rest, for you'll be up half the night. Bless you, Teddy, bless you!"

Jo had backed into a corner; and, as she finished her speech, she vanished precipitately into the kitchen, where she sat down upon a dresser, and told the assembled cats that she was "happy, oh, *so* happy!" while Laurie departed, feeling that he had made rather a neat thing of it.

"That's the interferingest chap I ever see; but I forgive him, and do hope Mrs. March is coming on right away," said Hannah, with an air of relief, when Jo told the good news.

Meg had a quiet rapture, and then brooded over the letter, while Jo set the sick-room in order, and Hannah "knocked up a couple of pies in case of company unexpected." A breath of fresh air seemed to blow through the house, and something better than sunshine brightened the quiet rooms. Everything appeared to feel the hopeful change; Beth's bird began to chirp again, and a half-blown rose was discovered on Amy's bush in the window; the fires seemed to burn with unusual cheeriness; and every time the girls met, their pale faces broke into smiles as they hugged one another, whispering encouragingly, "Mother's coming, dear! mother's coming!" Every one rejoiced but Beth; she lay in that heavy stupor, alike unconscious of hope and joy, doubt and danger. It was a piteous sight,—the once rosy face so changed and vacant, the once busy hands so weak and wasted, the once smiling lips quite dumb, and the once pretty, well-kept hair scattered rough and tangled on the pillow. All day she lay so, only rousing now and then to mutter, "Water!" with lips so parched they could hardly shape the word; all day Jo and Meg hovered over her, watching, waiting, hoping, and trusting in God and mother; and all day the snow fell, the bitter wind raged, and the hours dragged slowly by. But night came at last; and every time the clock struck, the sisters, still sitting on either side the bed, looked at each other with brightening eyes, for each hour brought help nearer. The doctor had been in to say that some change, for better or worse, would probably take place about midnight, at which time he would return.

Hannah, quite worn out, lay down on the sofa at the bed's foot, and fell fast asleep; Mr. Laurence marched to and fro in the parlor, feeling that he would rather face a rebel battery than Mrs. March's anxious countenance as she entered; Laurie lay on the rug, pretending to rest, but staring into the fire with the thoughtful look which made his black eyes beautifully soft and clear.

The girls never forgot that night, for no sleep came to them as they kept their watch, with that dreadful sense of powerlessness which comes to us in hours like those.

"If God spares Beth I never will complain again," whispered Meg earnestly.

"If God spares Beth I'll try to love and serve Him all my life," answered Jo, with equal fervor.

"I wish I had no heart, it aches so," sighed Meg, after a pause.

"If life is often as hard as this, I don't see how we ever shall get through it," added her sister despondently.

Here the clock struck twelve, and both forgot themselves in watching Beth, for they fancied a change passed over her wan face. The house was still as death, and nothing but the wailing of the wind broke the deep hush. Weary Hannah slept on, and no one but the sisters saw the pale shadow which seemed to fall upon the little bed. An hour went by, and nothing happened except Laurie's quiet departure for the station. Another hour,—still no one came; and anxious fears of delay in the storm, or accidents by the way, or, worst of all, a great grief at Washington, haunted the poor girls.

It was past two, when Jo, who stood at the window thinking how dreary the world looked in its winding-sheet of snow, heard a movement by the bed, and, turning quickly, saw Meg kneeling before their mother's easy-chair, with her face hidden. A dreadful fear passed coldly over Jo, as she thought, "Beth is dead, and Meg is afraid to tell me."

She was back at her post in an instant, and to her excited eyes a great change seemed to have taken place. The fever flush and the look of pain were gone, and the beloved little face looked so pale and peaceful in its utter repose, that Jo felt no desire to weep or to lament. Leaning low over this dearest of her sisters, she kissed the damp forehead with her heart on her lips, and softly whispered, "Good-by, my Beth; good-by!"

As if waked by the stir, Hannah started out of her sleep, hurried to the bed, looked at Beth, felt her hands, listened at her lips, and then, throwing her apron over her head, sat down to rock to and fro, exclaiming, under her breath, "The fever's turned; she's sleepin' nat'ral; her skin's damp, and she breathes easy. Praise be given! Oh, my goodness me!"

Before the girls could believe the happy truth, the doctor came to confirm it. He was a homely man, but they thought his face quite heavenly when he smiled, and said, with a fatherly look at them, "Yes, my dears, I think the little girl will pull through this time. Keep the house quiet; let her sleep, and when she wakes, give her—"

What they were to give, neither heard; for both crept into the dark hall, and, sitting on the stairs, held each other close, rejoicing with hearts too full for words. When they went back to be kissed and cuddled by faithful Hannah, they found Beth lying, as she used to do, with her cheek pillowed on her hand, the dreadful pallor gone, and breathing quietly, as if just fallen asleep.

"If mother would only come now!" said Jo, as the winter night began to wane.

"See," said Meg, coming up with a white, half-opened rose, "I thought this would hardly be ready to lay in Beth's hand to-morrow if she—went away from us. But it has blossomed in the night, and now I mean to put it in my vase here, so that when the darling wakes, the first thing she sees will be the little rose, and mother's face."

Never had the sun risen so beautifully, and never had the world seemed so lovely, as it did to the heavy eyes of Meg and Jo, as they looked out in the early morning, when their long, sad vigil was done.

"It looks like a fairy world," said Meg, smiling to herself, as she stood behind the curtain, watching the dazzling sight.

"Hark!" cried Jo, starting to her feet.

Yes, there was a sound of bells at the door below, a cry from Hannah, and then Laurie's voice saying, in a joyful whisper, "Girls, she's come! she's come!"

# XIX.

# AMY'S WILL.

WHILE these things were happening at home, Amy was having hard times at Aunt March's. She felt her exile deeply, and, for the first time in her life, realized how much she was beloved and petted at home. Aunt March never petted any one; she did not approve of it; but she meant to be kind, for the well-behaved little girl pleased her very much, and Aunt March had a soft place in her old heart for her nephew's children, though she didn't think proper to confess it. She really did her best to make Amy happy, but, dear me, what mistakes she made! Some old people keep young at heart in spite of wrinkles and gray hairs, can sympathize with children's little cares and joys, make them feel at home, and can hide wise lessons under pleasant plays, giving and receiving friendship in the sweetest way. But Aunt March had not this gift, and she worried Amy very much with her rules and orders, her prim ways, and long, prosy talks. Finding the child more docile and amiable than her sister, the old lady felt it her duty to try and counteract, as far as possible, the bad effects of home freedom and indulgence. So she took Amy in hand, and taught her as she herself had been taught sixty years ago,—a process which carried dismay to Amy's soul, and made her feel like a fly in the web of a very strict spider.

She had to wash the cups every morning, and polish up the old-fashioned spoons, the fat silver teapot, and the glasses, till they shone. Then she must dust the room, and what a trying job that was! Not a speck escaped Aunt March's eye, and all the furniture had claw legs, and much carving, which was never dusted to suit. Then Polly must be fed, the lap-dog combed, and a dozen trips upstairs and down, to get things, or deliver orders, for the old lady was very lame, and seldom left her big chair. After these tiresome labors, she must do her lessons, which was a daily trial of every virtue she possessed. Then she was allowed one hour for exercise or play, and didn't she enjoy it? Laurie came every day, and wheedled Aunt March, till Amy was allowed to go out with him, when they walked and rode, and had capital times. After dinner, she had to read aloud, and sit still while the old lady slept, which she usually did for an hour, as she dropped off over the first page. Then patchwork or towels appeared, and Amy sewed with outward meekness and inward rebellion till dusk, when she was allowed to amuse herself as she liked till tea-time. The evenings were the worst of all, for Aunt March fell to telling long stories about her youth, which were so unutterably dull that Amy was always ready to go to bed, intending to cry over her hard fate, but usually going to sleep before she had squeezed out more than a tear or two.

If it had not been for Laurie, and old Esther, the maid, she felt that she never could have got through that dreadful time. The parrot alone was enough to drive her distracted, for he soon felt that she did not admire him, and revenged himself by being as mischievous as possible. He pulled her hair whenever she came near him, upset his bread and milk to plague her when she had newly cleaned his cage, made Mop bark by pecking at him while Madam dozed; called her names before company, and behaved in all respects like a reprehensible old bird. Then she could not endure the dog,—a fat, cross beast, who snarled and yelped at her when she made his toilet, and who lay on his back, with all his legs in the air and a most idiotic expression of countenance when he wanted something to eat, which was about a dozen times a day. The cook was bad-tempered, the old coachman deaf, and Esther the only one who ever took any notice of the young lady.

Esther was a Frenchwoman, who had lived with "Madame," as she called her mistress, for many years, and who rather tyrannized over the old lady, who could not get along without her. Her real name was Estelle, but Aunt March ordered her to change it, and she obeyed, on condition that she was never asked to change her religion. She took a fancy to Mademoiselle, and amused her very much, with odd stories of her life in France, when Amy sat with her while she got up Madame's laces. She also allowed her to roam about the great house, and examine the curious and pretty things stored away in the big wardrobes and the ancient chests; for Aunt March hoarded like a magpie. Amy's chief delight was an Indian cabinet, full of queer drawers, little pigeon-holes, and secret places, in which were kept all sorts of ornaments, some precious, some merely curious, all more or less antique. To examine and arrange these things gave Amy great satisfaction, especially the jewel-cases, in which, on velvet cushions, reposed the ornaments which had adorned a belle forty years ago. There was the garnet set which Aunt March wore when she came out, the pearls her father gave her on her wedding-day, her lover's diamonds, the jet mourning rings and pins, the queer lockets, with portraits of dead friends, and weeping willows made of hair inside; the baby bracelets her one little daughter had worn; Uncle March's big watch, with the red seal so many childish hands had played with, and in a box, all by itself, lay Aunt March's wedding-ring, too small now for her fat finger, but put carefully away, like the most precious jewel of them all.

"Which would Mademoiselle choose if she had her will?" asked Esther, who always sat near to watch over and lock up the valuables.

"I like the diamonds best, but there is no necklace among them, and I'm fond of necklaces, they are so becoming. I should choose this if I might," replied Amy, looking with great admiration at a string of gold and ebony beads, from which hung a heavy cross of the same.

"I, too, covet that, but not as a necklace; ah, no! to me it is a rosary, and as such I should use it like a good Catholic," said Esther, eying the handsome thing wistfully.

"Is it meant to use as you use the string of good-smelling wooden beads hanging over your glass?" asked Amy.

"Truly, yes, to pray with. It would be pleasing to the saints if one used so fine a rosary as this, instead of wearing it as a vain bijou."

"You seem to take a great deal of comfort in your prayers, Esther, and always come down looking quiet and satisfied. I wish I could."

"If Mademoiselle was a Catholic, she would find true comfort; but, as that is not to be, it would be well if you went apart each day, to meditate and pray, as did the good mistress whom I served before Madame. She had a little chapel, and in it found solacement for much trouble."

"Would it be right for me to do so too?" asked Amy, who, in her loneliness, felt the need of help of some sort, and found that she was apt to forget her little book, now that Beth was not there to remind her of it.

"It would be excellent and charming; and I shall gladly arrange the little dressing-room for you if you like it. Say nothing to Madame, but when she sleeps go you and sit alone a while to think good thoughts, and pray the dear God to preserve your sister."

Esther was truly pious, and quite sincere in her advice; for she had an affectionate heart, and felt much for the sisters in their anxiety. Amy liked the idea, and gave her leave to arrange the light closet next her room, hoping it would do her good.

"I wish I knew where all these pretty things would go when Aunt March dies," she said, as she slowly replaced the shining rosary, and shut the jewel-cases one by one.

"To you and your sisters. I know it; Madame confides in me; I witnessed her will, and it is to be so," whispered Esther, smiling.

"How nice! but I wish she'd let us have them now. Pro-cras-ti-nation is not agreeable," observed Amy, taking a last look at the diamonds.

"It is too soon yet for the young ladies to wear these things. The first one who is affianced will have the pearls—Madame has said it; and I have a fancy that the little turquoise ring will be given to you when you go, for Madame approves your good behavior and charming manners."

"Do you think so? Oh, I'll be a lamb, if I can only have that lovely ring! It's ever so much prettier than Kitty Bryant's. I do like Aunt March, after all;" and Amy tried on the blue ring with a delighted face, and a firm resolve to earn it.

From that day she was a model of obedience, and the old lady complacently admired the success of her training. Esther fitted up the closet with a little table, placed a footstool before it, and over it a picture taken from one of the shut-up rooms. She thought it was of no great value, but, being appropriate, she borrowed it, well knowing that Madame would never know it, nor care if she did. It was, however, a very valuable copy of one of the famous pictures of the world, and Amy's beauty-loving eyes were never tired of looking up at the sweet face of the divine mother, while tender thoughts of her own were busy at her heart. On the table she laid her little Testament and hymn-book, kept a vase always full of the best flowers Laurie brought her, and came every day to "sit alone, thinking good thoughts, and praying the dear God to preserve her sister." Esther had given her a rosary of black beads, with a silver cross, but Amy hung it up and did not use it, feeling doubtful as to its fitness for Protestant prayers.

The little girl was very sincere in all this, for, being left alone outside the safe home-nest, she felt the need of some kind hand to hold by so sorely, that she instinctively turned to the strong and tender Friend, whose fatherly love most closely surrounds his little children. She missed her mother's help to understand and rule herself, but having been taught where to look, she did her best to find the way, and walk in it confidingly. But Amy was a young pilgrim, and just now her burden seemed very heavy. She tried to forget herself, to keep cheerful, and be satisfied with doing right, though no one saw or praised her for it. In her first effort at being very, very good, she decided to make her will, as Aunt March had done; so that if she *did* fall ill and die, her possessions might be justly and generously divided. It cost her a pang even to think of giving up the little treasures which in her eyes were as precious as the old lady's jewels.

During one of her play-hours she wrote out the important document as well as she could, with some help from Esther as to certain legal terms, and, when the good-natured Frenchwoman had signed her name, Amy felt relieved, and laid it by to show Laurie, whom she wanted as a second witness. As it was a rainy day, she went upstairs to amuse herself in one of the large chambers, and took Polly with her for company. In this room there was a wardrobe full of old-fashioned costumes, with which Esther allowed her to play, and it was her favorite amusement to array herself in the faded brocades, and parade up and down before the long mirror, making stately courtesies, and sweeping her train about, with a rustle which delighted her ears. So busy was she on this day that she did not hear Laurie's ring, nor see his face peeping in at her, as she gravely promenaded to and fro, flirting her fan and tossing her head, on which she wore a great pink turban, contrasting oddly with her blue brocade dress and yellow quilted petticoat. She was obliged to walk carefully, for she had on high-heeled shoes, and, as Laurie told Jo afterward, it was a comical sight to see her mince along in her gay suit, with Polly sidling and bridling just behind her, imitating her as well as he could, and occasionally stopping to laugh or exclaim, "Ain't we fine? Get along, you fright! Hold your tongue! Kiss me, dear! Ha! ha!"

Having with difficulty restrained an explosion of merriment, lest it should offend her majesty, Laurie tapped, and was graciously received.

"Sit down and rest while I put these things away; then I want to consult you about a very serious matter," said Amy, when she had shown her splendor, and driven Polly into a corner. "That bird is the trial of my life," she continued, removing the pink mountain from her head, while Laurie seated himself astride of a chair. "Yesterday, when aunt was asleep, and I was trying to be as still as a mouse, Polly began to squall and flap about in his cage; so I went to let him out, and found a big spider there. I poked it out, and it ran under the bookcase; Polly marched straight after it, stooped down and peeped under the bookcase, saying, in his funny way, with a cock of his eye, 'Come out and take a walk, my dear.' I *couldn't* help laughing, which made Poll swear, and aunt woke up and scolded us both."

"Did the spider accept the old fellow's invitation?" asked Laurie, yawning.

"Yes; out it came, and away ran Polly, frightened to death, and scrambled up on aunt's chair, calling out, 'Catch her! catch her! catch her!' as I chased the spider.

"That's a lie! Oh lor!" cried the parrot, pecking at Laurie's toes.

"I'd wring your neck if you were mine, you old torment," cried Laurie, shaking his fist at the bird, who put his head on one side, and gravely croaked, "Allyluyer! bless your buttons, dear!"

"Now I'm ready," said Amy, shutting the wardrobe, and taking a paper out of her pocket. "I want you to read that, please, and tell me if it is legal and right. I felt that I ought to do it, for life is uncertain and I don't want any ill-feeling over my tomb."

Laurie bit his lips, and turning a little from the pensive speaker, read the following document, with praiseworthy gravity, considering the spelling:—

"MY LAST WILL AND TESTIMENT.

"I, Amy Curtis March, being in my sane mind, do give and bequeethe all my earthly property—viz. to wit:—namely

"To my father, my best pictures, sketches, maps, and works of art, including frames. Also my $, to do what he likes with.

"To my mother, all my clothes, except the blue apron with pockets,—also my likeness, and my medal, with much love.

"To my dear sister Margaret, I give my turkquoise ring (if I get it), also my green box with the doves on it, also my piece of real lace for her neck, and my sketch of her as a memorial of her 'little girl.'

"To Jo I leave my breast-pin, the one mended with sealing wax, also my bronze inkstand—she lost the cover—and my most precious plaster rabbit, because I am sorry I burnt up her story.

"To Beth (if she lives after me) I give my dolls and the little bureau, my fan, my linen collars and my new slippers if she can wear them being thin when she gets well. And I herewith also leave her my regret that I ever made fun of old Joanna.

"To my friend and neighbor Theodore Laurence I bequeethe my paper marshay portfolio, my clay model of a horse though he did say it hadn't any neck. Also in return for his great kindness in the hour of affliction any one of my artistic works he likes, Noter Dame is the best.

"To our venerable benefactor Mr. Laurence I leave my purple box with a looking glass in the cover which will be nice for his pens and remind him of the departed girl who thanks him for his favors to her family, specially Beth.

"I wish my favorite playmate Kitty Bryant to have the blue silk apron and my gold-bead ring with a kiss.

"To Hannah I give the bandbox she wanted and all the patch work I leave hoping she 'will remember me, when it you see.'

"And now having disposed of my most valuable property I hope all will be satisfied and not blame the dead. I forgive every one, and trust we may all meet when the trump shall sound. Amen.

"To this will and testiment I set my hand and seal on this th day of Nov. Anni Domino .

"AMY CURTIS MARCH.

*"Witnesses:* { ESTELLE VALNOR,
THEODORE LAURENCE."

The last name was written in pencil, and Amy explained that he was to rewrite it in ink, and seal it up for her properly.

"What put it into your head? Did any one tell you about Beth's giving away her things?" asked Laurie soberly, as Amy laid a bit of red tape, with sealing-wax, a taper, and a standish before him.

She explained; and then asked anxiously, "What about Beth?"

"I'm sorry I spoke; but as I did, I'll tell you. She felt so ill one day that she told Jo she wanted to give her piano to Meg, her cats to you, and the poor old doll to Jo, who would love it for her sake. She was sorry she had so little to give, and left locks of hair to the rest of us, and her best love to grandpa. *She* never thought of a will."

Laurie was signing and sealing as he spoke, and did not look up till a great tear dropped on the paper. Amy's face was full of trouble; but she only said, "Don't people put sort of postscripts to their wills, sometimes?"

"Yes; 'codicils,' they call them."

"Put one in mine then—that I wish *all* my curls cut off, and given round to my friends. I forgot it; but I want it done, though it will spoil my looks."

Laurie added it, smiling at Amy's last and greatest sacrifice. Then he amused her for an hour, and was much interested in all her trials. But when he came to go, Amy held him back to whisper, with trembling lips, "Is there really any danger about Beth?"

"I'm afraid there is; but we must hope for the best, so don't cry, dear;" and Laurie put his arm about her with a brotherly gesture which was very comforting.

When he had gone, she went to her little chapel, and, sitting in the twilight, prayed for Beth, with streaming tears and an aching heart, feeling that a million turquoise rings would not console her for the loss of her gentle little sister.

XX.

# CONFIDENTIAL.

I DON'T think I have any words in which to tell the meeting of the mother and daughters; such hours are beautiful to live, but very hard to describe, so I will leave it to the imagination of my readers, merely saying that the house was full of genuine happiness, and that Meg's tender hope was realized; for when Beth woke from that long, healing sleep, the first objects on which her eyes fell *were* the little rose and mother's face. Too weak to wonder at anything, she only smiled, and nestled close into the loving arms about her, feeling that the hungry longing was satisfied at last. Then she slept again, and the girls waited upon their mother, for she would not unclasp the thin hand which clung to hers even in sleep. Hannah had "dished up" an astonishing breakfast for the traveller, finding it impossible to vent her excitement in any other way; and Meg and Jo fed their mother like dutiful young storks, while they listened to her whispered account of father's state, Mr. Brooke's promise to stay and nurse him, the delays which the storm occasioned on the homeward journey, and the unspeakable comfort Laurie's hopeful face had given her when she arrived, worn out with fatigue, anxiety, and cold.

What a strange, yet pleasant day that was! so brilliant and gay without, for all the world seemed abroad to welcome the first snow; so quiet and reposeful within, for every one slept, spent with watching, and a Sabbath stillness reigned through the house, while nodding Hannah mounted guard at the door. With a blissful sense of burdens lifted off, Meg and Jo closed their weary eyes, and lay at rest, like storm-beaten boats, safe at anchor in a quiet harbor. Mrs. March would not leave Beth's side, but rested in the big chair, waking often to look at, touch, and brood over her child, like a miser over some recovered treasure.

Laurie, meanwhile, posted off to comfort Amy, and told his story so well that Aunt March actually "sniffed" herself, and never once said, "I told you so." Amy came out so strong on this occasion that I think the good thoughts in the little chapel really began to bear fruit. She dried her tears quickly, restrained her impatience to see her mother, and never even thought of the turquoise ring, when the old lady heartily agreed in Laurie's opinion, that she behaved "like a capital little woman." Even Polly seemed impressed, for he called her "good girl," blessed her buttons, and begged her to "come and take a walk, dear," in his most affable tone. She would very gladly have gone out to enjoy the bright wintry weather; but, discovering that Laurie was dropping with sleep in spite of manful efforts to conceal the fact, she persuaded him to rest on the sofa, while she wrote a note to her mother. She was a long time about it; and, when she returned, he was stretched out, with both arms under his head, sound asleep, while Aunt March had pulled down the curtains, and sat doing nothing in an unusual fit of benignity.

After a while, they began to think he was not going to wake till night, and I'm not sure that he would, had he not been effectually roused by Amy's cry of joy at sight of her mother. There probably were a good many happy little girls in and about the city that day, but it is my private opinion that Amy was the happiest of all, when she sat in her mother's lap and told her trials, receiving consolation and compensation in the shape of approving smiles and fond caresses. They were alone together in the chapel, to which her mother did not object when its purpose was explained to her.

"On the contrary, I like it very much, dear," looking from the dusty rosary to the well-worn little book, and the lovely picture with its garland of evergreen. "It is an excellent plan to have some place where we can go to be quiet, when things vex or grieve us. There are a good many hard times in this life of ours, but we can always bear them if we ask help in the right way. I think my little girl is learning this?"

"Yes, mother; and when I go home I mean to have a corner in the big closet to put my books, and the copy of that picture which I've tried to make. The woman's face is not good,—it's too beautiful for me to draw,—but the baby is done better, and I love it very much. I like to think He was a little child once, for then I don't seem so far away, and that helps me."

As Amy pointed to the smiling Christ-child on his mother's knee, Mrs. March saw something on the lifted hand that made her smile. She said nothing, but Amy understood the look, and, after a minute's pause, she added gravely,—

"I wanted to speak to you about this, but I forgot it. Aunt gave me the ring to-day; she called me to her and kissed me, and put it on my finger, and said I was a credit to her, and she'd like to keep me always. She gave that funny guard to keep the turquoise on, as it's too big. I'd like to wear them, mother; can I?"

"They are very pretty, but I think you're rather too young for such ornaments, Amy," said Mrs. March, looking at the plump little hand, with the band of sky-blue stones on the forefinger, and the quaint guard, formed of two tiny, golden hands clasped together.

"I'll try not to be vain," said Amy. "I don't think I like it only because it's so pretty; but I want to wear it as the girl in the story wore her bracelet, to remind me of something."

"Do you mean Aunt March?" asked her mother, laughing.

"No, to remind me not to be selfish." Amy looked so earnest and sincere about it, that her mother stopped laughing, and listened respectfully to the little plan.

"I've thought a great deal lately about my 'bundle of naughties,' and being selfish is the largest one in it; so I'm going to try hard to cure it, if I can. Beth isn't selfish, and that's the reason every one loves her and feels so bad at the thoughts of losing her. People wouldn't feel half so bad about me if I was sick, and I don't deserve to have them; but I'd like to be loved and missed by a great many friends, so I'm going to try and be like Beth all I can. I'm apt to forget my resolutions; but if I had something always about me to remind me, I guess I should do better. May I try this way?"

"Yes; but I have more faith in the corner of the big closet. Wear your ring, dear, and do your best; I think you will prosper, for the sincere wish to be good is half the battle. Now I must go back to Beth. Keep up your heart, little daughter, and we will soon have you home again."

That evening, while Meg was writing to her father, to report the traveller's safe arrival, Jo slipped up stairs into Beth's room, and, finding her mother in her usual place, stood a minute twisting her fingers in her hair, with a worried gesture and an undecided look.

"What is it, deary?" asked Mrs. March, holding out her hand, with a face which invited confidence.

"I want to tell you something, mother."

"About Meg?"

"How quickly you guessed! Yes, it's about her, and though it's a little thing, it fidgets me."

"Beth is asleep; speak low, and tell me all about it. That Moffat hasn't been here, I hope?" asked Mrs. March rather sharply.

"No, I should have shut the door in his face if he had," said Jo, settling herself on the floor at her mother's feet. "Last summer Meg left a pair of gloves over at the Laurences', and only one was returned. We forgot all about it, till Teddy told me that Mr. Brooke had it. He kept it in his waistcoat pocket, and once it fell out, and Teddy joked him about it, and Mr. Brooke owned that he liked Meg, but didn't dare say so, she was so young and he so poor. Now, isn't it a *dread*ful state of things?"

"Do you think Meg cares for him?" asked Mrs. March, with an anxious look.

"Mercy me! I don't know anything about love and such nonsense!" cried Jo, with a funny mixture of interest and contempt. "In novels, the girls show it by starting and blushing, fainting away, growing thin, and acting like fools.

Now Meg does not do anything of the sort: she eats and drinks and sleeps, like a sensible creature: she looks straight in my face when I talk about that man, and only blushes a little bit when Teddy jokes about lovers. I forbid him to do it, but he doesn't mind me as he ought."

"Then you fancy that Meg is *not* interested in John?"

"Who?" cried Jo, staring.

"Mr. Brooke. I call him 'John' now; we fell into the way of doing so at the hospital, and he likes it."

"Oh, dear! I know you'll take his part: he's been good to father, and you won't send him away, but let Meg marry him, if she wants to. Mean thing! to go petting papa and helping you, just to wheedle you into liking him;" and Jo pulled her hair again with a wrathful tweak.

"My dear, don't get angry about it, and I will tell you how it happened. John went with me at Mr. Laurence's request, and was so devoted to poor father that we couldn't help getting fond of him. He was perfectly open and honorable about Meg, for he told us he loved her, but would earn a comfortable home before he asked her to marry him. He only wanted our leave to love her and work for her, and the right to make her love him if he could. He is a truly excellent young man, and we could not refuse to listen to him; but I will not consent to Meg's engaging herself so young."

"Of course not; it would be idiotic! I knew there was mischief brewing; I felt it; and now it's worse than I imagined. I just wish I could marry Meg myself, and keep her safe in the family."

This odd arrangement made Mrs. March smile; but she said gravely, "Jo, I confide in you, and don't wish you to say anything to Meg yet. When John comes back, and I see them together, I can judge better of her feelings toward him."

"She'll see his in those handsome eyes that she talks about, and then it will be all up with her. She's got such a soft heart, it will melt like butter in the sun if any one looks sentimentally at her. She read the short reports he sent more than she did your letters, and pinched me when I spoke of it, and likes brown eyes, and doesn't think John an ugly name, and she'll go and fall in love, and there's an end of peace and fun, and cosy times together. I see it all! they'll go lovering around the house, and we shall have to dodge; Meg will be absorbed, and no good to me any more; Brooke will scratch up a fortune somehow, carry her off, and make a hole in the family; and I shall break my heart, and everything will be abominably uncomfortable. Oh, dear me! why weren't we all boys, then there wouldn't be any bother."

Jo leaned her chin on her knees, in a disconsolate attitude, and shook her fist at the reprehensible John. Mrs. March sighed, and Jo looked up with an air of relief.

"You don't like it, mother? I'm glad of it. Let's send him about his business, and not tell Meg a word of it, but all be happy together as we always have been."

"I did wrong to sigh, Jo. It is natural and right you should all go to homes of your own, in time; but I do want to keep my girls as long as I can; and I am sorry that this happened so soon, for Meg is only seventeen, and it will be some years before John can make a home for her. Your father and I have agreed that she shall not bind herself in any way, nor be married, before twenty. If she and John love one another, they can wait, and test the love by doing so. She is conscientious, and I have no fear of her treating him unkindly. My pretty, tender-hearted girl! I hope things will go happily with her."

"Hadn't you rather have her marry a rich man?" asked Jo, as her mother's voice faltered a little over the last words.

"Money is a good and useful thing, Jo; and I hope my girls will never feel the need of it too bitterly, nor be tempted by too much. I should like to know that John was firmly established in some good business, which gave him an income large enough to keep free from debt and make Meg comfortable. I'm not ambitious for a splendid fortune, a fashionable position, or a great name for my girls. If rank and money come with love and virtue, also, I should accept them gratefully, and enjoy your good fortune; but I know, by experience, how much genuine happiness can be had in a plain little house, where the daily bread is earned, and some privations give sweetness to the few pleasures. I am content to see Meg begin humbly, for, if I am not mistaken, she will be rich in the possession of a good man's heart, and that is better than a fortune."

"I understand, mother, and quite agree; but I'm disappointed about Meg, for I'd planned to have her marry Teddy by and by, and sit in the lap of luxury all her days. Wouldn't it be nice?" asked Jo, looking up, with a brighter face.

"He is younger than she, you know," began Mrs. March; but Jo broke in,—

"Only a little; he's old for his age, and tall; and can be quite grown-up in his manners if he likes. Then he's rich and generous and good, and loves us all; and *I* say it's a pity my plan is spoilt."

"I'm afraid Laurie is hardly grown up enough for Meg, and altogether too much of a weathercock, just now, for any one to depend on. Don't make plans, Jo; but let time and their own hearts mate your friends. We can't meddle safely in such matters, and had better not get 'romantic rubbish,' as you call it, into our heads, lest it spoil our friendship."

"Well, I won't; but I hate to see things going all criss-cross and getting snarled up, when a pull here and a snip there would straighten it out. I wish wearing flat-irons on our heads would keep us from growing up. But buds will be roses, and kittens, cats,—more's the pity!"

"What's that about flat-irons and cats?" asked Meg, as she crept into the room, with the finished letter in her hand.

"Only one of my stupid speeches. I'm going to bed; come, Peggy," said Jo, unfolding herself, like an animated puzzle.

"Quite right, and beautifully written. Please add that I send my love to John," said Mrs. March, as she glanced over the letter, and gave it back.

"Do you call him 'John'?" asked Meg, smiling, with her innocent eyes looking down into her mother's.

"Yes; he has been like a son to us, and we are very fond of him," replied Mrs. March, returning the look with a keen one.

"I'm glad of that, he is so lonely. Good-night, mother, dear. It is so inexpressibly comfortable to have you here," was Meg's quiet answer.

The kiss her mother gave her was a very tender one; and, as she went away, Mrs. March said, with a mixture of satisfaction and regret, "She does not love John yet, but will soon learn to."

## XXI.

## LAURIE MAKES MISCHIEF, AND JO MAKES PEACE.

JO'S face was a study next day, for the secret rather weighed upon her, and she found it hard not to look mysterious and important. Meg observed it, but did not trouble herself to make inquiries, for she had learned that the best way to manage Jo was by the law of contraries, so she felt sure of being told everything if she did not ask. She was rather surprised, therefore, when the silence remained unbroken, and Jo assumed a patronizing air, which decidedly aggravated Meg, who in her turn assumed an air of dignified reserve, and devoted herself to her mother. This left Jo to her own devices; for Mrs. March had taken her place as nurse, and bade her rest, exercise, and amuse herself after her long confinement. Amy being gone, Laurie was her only refuge; and, much as she enjoyed his society, she rather dreaded him just then, for he was an incorrigible tease, and she feared he would coax her secret from her.

She was quite right, for the mischief-loving lad no sooner suspected a mystery than he set himself to find it out, and led Jo a trying life of it. He wheedled, bribed, ridiculed, threatened, and scolded; affected indifference, that he might surprise the truth from her; declared he knew, then that he didn't care; and, at last, by dint of perseverance, he satisfied himself that it concerned Meg and Mr. Brooke. Feeling indignant that he was not taken into his tutor's confidence, he set his wits to work to devise some proper retaliation for the slight.

Meg meanwhile had apparently forgotten the matter, and was absorbed in preparations for her father's return; but all of a sudden a change seemed to come over her, and, for a day or two, she was quite unlike herself. She started when spoken to, blushed when looked at, was very quiet, and sat over her sewing, with a timid, troubled look on her face. To her mother's inquiries she answered that she was quite well, and Jo's she silenced by begging to be let alone.

"She feels it in the air—love, I mean—and she's going very fast. She's got most of the symptoms,—is twittery and cross, doesn't eat, lies awake, and mopes in corners. I caught her singing that song he gave her, and once she said 'John,' as you do, and then turned as red as a poppy. Whatever shall we do?" said Jo, looking ready for any measures, however violent.

"Nothing but wait. Let her alone, be kind and patient, and father's coming will settle everything," replied her mother.

"Here's a note to you, Meg, all sealed up. How odd! Teddy never seals mine," said Jo, next day, as she distributed the contents of the little post-office.

Mrs. March and Jo were deep in their own affairs, when a sound from Meg made them look up to see her staring at her note, with a frightened face.

"My child, what is it?" cried her mother, running to her, while Jo tried to take the paper which had done the mischief.

"It's all a mistake—he didn't send it. O Jo, how could you do it?" and Meg hid her face in her hands, crying as if her heart was quite broken.

"Me! I've done nothing! What's she talking about?" cried Jo, bewildered.

Meg's mild eyes kindled with anger as she pulled a crumpled note from her pocket, and threw it at Jo, saying reproachfully,—

"You wrote it, and that bad boy helped you. How could you be so rude, so mean, and cruel to us both?"

Jo hardly heard her, for she and her mother were reading the note, which was written in a peculiar hand.

"MY DEAREST MARGARET,—

"I can no longer restrain my passion, and must know my fate before I return. I dare not tell your parents yet, but I think they would consent if they knew that we adored one another. Mr. Laurence will help me to some good place, and then, my sweet girl, you will make me happy. I implore you to say nothing to your family yet, but to send one word of hope through Laurie to

"Your devoted JOHN."

"Oh, the little villain! that's the way he meant to pay me for keeping my word to mother. I'll give him a hearty scolding, and bring him over to beg pardon," cried Jo, burning to execute immediate justice. But her mother held her back, saying, with a look she seldom wore,—

"Stop, Jo, you must clear yourself first. You have played so many pranks, that I am afraid you have had a hand in this."

"On my word, mother, I haven't! I never saw that note before, and don't know anything about it, as true as I live!" said Jo, so earnestly that they believed her. "If I *had* taken a part in it I'd have done it better than this, and have written a sensible note. I should think you'd have known Mr. Brooke wouldn't write such stuff as that," she added, scornfully tossing down the paper.

"It's like his writing," faltered Meg, comparing it with the note in her hand.

"O Meg, you didn't answer it?" cried Mrs. March quickly.

"Yes, I did!" and Meg hid her face again, overcome with shame.

"Here's a scrape! *Do* let me bring that wicked boy over to explain, and be lectured. I can't rest till I get hold of him;" and Jo made for the door again.

"Hush! let me manage this, for it is worse than I thought. Margaret, tell me the whole story," commanded Mrs. March, sitting down by Meg, yet keeping hold of Jo, lest she should fly off.

"I received the first letter from Laurie, who didn't look as if he knew anything about it," began Meg, without looking up. "I was worried at first, and meant to tell you; then I remembered how you liked Mr. Brooke, so I thought you wouldn't mind if I kept my little secret for a few days. I'm so silly that I liked to think no one knew; and, while I was deciding what to say, I felt like the girls in books, who have such things to do. Forgive me, mother, I'm paid for my silliness now; I never can look him in the face again."

"What did you say to him?" asked Mrs. March.

"I only said I was too young to do anything about it yet; that I didn't wish to have secrets from you, and he must speak to father. I was very grateful for his kindness, and would be his friend, but nothing more, for a long while."

Mrs. March smiled, as if well pleased, and Jo clapped her hands, exclaiming, with a laugh,—

"You are almost equal to Caroline Percy, who was a pattern of prudence! Tell on, Meg. What did he say to that?"

"He writes in a different way entirely, telling me that he never sent any love-letter at all, and is very sorry that my roguish sister, Jo, should take such liberties with our names. It's very kind and respectful, but think how dreadful for me!"

Meg leaned against her mother, looking the image of despair, and Jo tramped about the room, calling Laurie names. All of a sudden she stopped, caught up the two notes, and, after looking at them closely, said decidedly, "I don't believe Brooke ever saw either of these letters. Teddy wrote both, and keeps yours to crow over me with, because I wouldn't tell him my secret."

"Don't have any secrets, Jo; tell it to mother, and keep out of trouble, as I should have done," said Meg warningly.

"Bless you, child! Mother told me."

"That will do, Jo. I'll comfort Meg while you go and get Laurie. I shall sift the matter to the bottom, and put a stop to such pranks at once."

Away ran Jo, and Mrs. March gently told Meg Mr. Brooke's real feelings. "Now, dear, what are your own? Do you love him enough to wait till he can make a home for you, or will you keep yourself quite free for the present?"

"I've been so scared and worried, I don't want to have anything to do with lovers for a long while,—perhaps never," answered Meg petulantly. "If John *doesn't* know anything about this nonsense, don't tell him, and make Jo and Laurie hold their tongues. I won't be deceived and plagued and made a fool of,—it's a shame!"

Seeing that Meg's usually gentle temper was roused and her pride hurt by this mischievous joke, Mrs. March soothed her by promises of entire silence, and great discretion for the future. The instant Laurie's step was heard in the hall, Meg fled into the study, and Mrs. March received the culprit alone. Jo had not told him why he was wanted, fearing he wouldn't come; but he knew the minute he saw Mrs. March's face, and stood twirling his hat, with a guilty air which convicted him at once. Jo was dismissed, but chose to march up and down the hall like a sentinel, having some fear that the prisoner might bolt. The sound of voices in the parlor rose and fell for half an hour; but what happened during that interview the girls never knew.

When they were called in, Laurie was standing by their mother, with such a penitent face that Jo forgave him on the spot, but did not think it wise to betray the fact. Meg received his humble apology, and was much comforted by the assurance that Brooke knew nothing of the joke.

"I'll never tell him to my dying day,—wild horses sha'n't drag it out of me; so you'll forgive me, Meg, and I'll do anything to show how out-and-out sorry I am," he added, looking very much ashamed of himself.

"I'll try; but it was a very ungentlemanly thing to do. I didn't think you could be so sly and malicious, Laurie," replied Meg, trying to hide her maidenly confusion under a gravely reproachful air.

"It was altogether abominable, and I don't deserve to be spoken to for a month; but you will, though, won't you?" and Laurie folded his hands together with such an imploring gesture, as he spoke in his irresistibly persuasive tone, that it was impossible to frown upon him, in spite of his scandalous behavior. Meg pardoned him, and Mrs. March's grave face relaxed, in spite of her efforts to keep sober, when she heard him declare that he would atone for his sins by all sorts of penances, and abase himself like a worm before the injured damsel.

Jo stood aloof, meanwhile, trying to harden her heart against him, and succeeding only in primming up her face into an expression of entire disapprobation. Laurie looked at her once or twice, but, as she showed no sign of relenting, he felt injured, and turned his back on her till the others were done with him, when he made her a low bow, and walked off without a word.

As soon as he had gone, she wished she had been more forgiving; and when Meg and her mother went upstairs, she felt lonely, and longed for Teddy. After resisting for some time, she yielded to the impulse, and, armed with a book to return, went over to the big house.

"Is Mr. Laurence in?" asked Jo, of a housemaid, who was coming down stairs.

"Yes, miss; but I don't believe he's seeable just yet."

"Why not? is he ill?"

"La, no, miss, but he's had a scene with Mr. Laurie, who is in one of his tantrums about something, which vexes the old gentleman, so I dursn't go nigh him."

"Where is Laurie?"

"Shut up in his room, and he won't answer, though I've been a-tapping. I don't know what's to become of the dinner, for it's ready, and there's no one to eat it."

"I'll go and see what the matter is. I'm not afraid of either of them."

Up went Jo, and knocked smartly on the door of Laurie's little study.

"Stop that, or I'll open the door and make you!" called out the young gentleman, in a threatening tone.

Jo immediately knocked again; the door flew open, and in she bounced, before Laurie could recover from his surprise. Seeing that he really *was* out of temper, Jo, who knew how to manage him, assumed a contrite expression, and going artistically down upon her knees, said meekly, "Please forgive me for being so cross. I came to make it up, and can't go away till I have."

"It's all right. Get up, and don't be a goose, Jo," was the cavalier reply to her petition.

"Thank you; I will. Could I ask what's the matter? You don't look exactly easy in your mind."

"I've been shaken, and I won't bear it!" growled Laurie indignantly.

"Who did it?" demanded Jo.

"Grandfather; if it had been any one else I'd have—" and the injured youth finished his sentence by an energetic gesture of the right arm.

"That's nothing; I often shake you, and you don't mind," said Jo soothingly.

"Pooh! you're a girl, and it's fun; but I'll allow no man to shake *me*."

"I don't think any one would care to try it, if you looked as much like a thunder-cloud as you do now. Why were you treated so?"

"Just because I wouldn't say what your mother wanted me for. I'd promised not to tell, and of course I wasn't going to break my word."

"Couldn't you satisfy your grandpa in any other way?"

"No; he *would* have the truth, the whole truth, and nothing but the truth. I'd have told my part of the scrape, if I could without bringing Meg in. As I couldn't, I held my tongue, and bore the scolding till the old gentleman collared me. Then I got angry, and bolted, for fear I should forget myself."

"It wasn't nice, but he's sorry, I know; so go down and make up. I'll help you."

"Hanged if I do! I'm not going to be lectured and pummelled by every one, just for a bit of a frolic. I *was* sorry about Meg, and begged pardon like a man; but I won't do it again, when I wasn't in the wrong."

"He didn't know that."

"He ought to trust me, and not act as if I was a baby. It's no use, Jo; he's got to learn that I'm able to take care of myself, and don't need any one's apron-string to hold on by."

"What pepper-pots you are!" sighed Jo. "How do you mean to settle this affair?"

"Well, he ought to beg pardon, and believe me when I say I can't tell him what the fuss's about."

"Bless you! he won't do that."

"I won't go down till he does."

"Now, Teddy, be sensible; let it pass, and I'll explain what I can. You can't stay here, so what's the use of being melodramatic?"

"I don't intend to stay here long, any way. I'll slip off and take a journey somewhere, and when grandpa misses me he'll come round fast enough."

"I dare say; but you ought not to go and worry him."

"Don't preach. I'll go to Washington and see Brooke; it's gay there, and I'll enjoy myself after the troubles."

"What fun you'd have! I wish I could run off too," said Jo, forgetting her part of Mentor in lively visions of martial life at the capital.

"Come on, then! Why not? You go and surprise your father, and I'll stir up old Brooke. It would be a glorious joke; let's do it, Jo. We'll leave a letter saying we are all right, and trot off at once. I've got money enough; it will do you good, and be no harm, as you go to your father."

For a moment Jo looked as if she would agree; for, wild as the plan was, it just suited her. She was tired of care and confinement, longed for change, and thoughts of her father blended temptingly with the novel charms of camps and hospitals, liberty and fun. Her eyes kindled as they turned wistfully toward the window, but they fell on the old house opposite, and she shook her head with sorrowful decision.

"If I was a boy, we'd run away together, and have a capital time; but as I'm a miserable girl, I must be proper, and stop at home. Don't tempt me, Teddy, it's a crazy plan."

"That's the fun of it," began Laurie, who had got a wilful fit on him, and was possessed to break out of bounds in some way.

"Hold your tongue!" cried Jo, covering her ears. "'Prunes and prisms' are my doom, and I may as well make up my mind to it. I came here to moralize, not to hear about things that make me skip to think of."

"I know Meg would wet-blanket such a proposal, but I thought you had more spirit," began Laurie insinuatingly.

"Bad boy, be quiet! Sit down and think of your own sins, don't go making me add to mine. If I get your grandpa to apologize for the shaking, will you give up running away?" asked Jo seriously.

"Yes, but you won't do it," answered Laurie, who wished "to make up," but felt that his outraged dignity must be appeased first.

"If I can manage the young one I can the old one," muttered Jo, as she walked away, leaving Laurie bent over a railroad map, with his head propped up on both hands.

"Come in!" and Mr. Laurence's gruff voice sounded gruffer than ever, as Jo tapped at his door.

"It's only me, sir, come to return a book," she said blandly, as she entered.

"Want any more?" asked the old gentleman, looking grim and vexed, but trying not to show it.

"Yes, please. I like old Sam so well, I think I'll try the second volume," returned Jo, hoping to propitiate him by accepting a second dose of Boswell's "Johnson," as he had recommended that lively work.

The shaggy eyebrows unbent a little, as he rolled the steps toward the shelf where the Johnsonian literature was placed. Jo skipped up, and, sitting on the top step, affected to be searching for her book, but was really wondering how best to introduce the dangerous object of her visit. Mr. Laurence seemed to suspect that something was brewing in her mind; for, after taking several brisk turns about the room, he faced round on her, speaking so abruptly that "Rasselas" tumbled face downward on the floor.

"What has that boy been about? Don't try to shield him. I know he has been in mischief by the way he acted when he came home. I can't get a word from him; and when I threatened to shake the truth out of him he bolted upstairs, and locked himself into his room."

"He did do wrong, but we forgave him, and all promised not to say a word to any one," began Jo reluctantly.

"That won't do; he shall not shelter himself behind a promise from you soft-hearted girls. If he's done anything amiss, he shall confess, beg pardon, and be punished. Out with it, Jo, I won't be kept in the dark."

Mr. Laurence looked so alarming and spoke so sharply that Jo would have gladly run away, if she could, but she was perched aloft on the steps, and he stood at the foot, a lion in the path, so she had to stay and brave it out.

"Indeed, sir, I cannot tell; mother forbade it. Laurie has confessed, asked pardon, and been punished quite enough. We don't keep silence to shield him, but some one else, and it will make more trouble if you interfere. Please don't; it was partly my fault, but it's all right now; so let's forget it, and talk about the 'Rambler,' or something pleasant."

"Hang the 'Rambler!' come down and give me your word that this harum-scarum boy of mine hasn't done anything ungrateful or impertinent. If he has, after all your kindness to him, I'll thrash him with my own hands."

The threat sounded awful, but did not alarm Jo, for she knew the irascible old gentleman would never lift a finger against his grandson, whatever he might say to the contrary. She obediently descended, and made as light of the prank as she could without betraying Meg or forgetting the truth.

"Hum—ha—well, if the boy held his tongue because he promised, and not from obstinacy, I'll forgive him. He's a stubborn fellow, and hard to manage," said Mr. Laurence, rubbing up his hair till it looked as if he had been out in a gale, and smoothing the frown from his brow with an air of relief.

"So am I; but a kind word will govern me when all the king's horses and all the king's men couldn't," said Jo, trying to say a kind word for her friend, who seemed to get out of one scrape only to fall into another.

"You think I'm not kind to him, hey?" was the sharp answer.

"Oh, dear, no, sir; you are rather too kind sometimes, and then just a trifle hasty when he tries your patience. Don't you think you are?"

Jo was determined to have it out now, and tried to look quite placid, though she quaked a little after her bold speech. To her great relief and surprise, the old gentleman only threw his spectacles on to the table with a rattle, and exclaimed frankly,—

"You're right, girl, I am! I love the boy, but he tries my patience past bearing, and I don't know how it will end, if we go on so."

"I'll tell you, he'll run away." Jo was sorry for that speech the minute it was made; she meant to warn him that Laurie would not bear much restraint, and hoped he would be more forbearing with the lad.

Mr. Laurence's ruddy face changed suddenly, and he sat down, with a troubled glance at the picture of a handsome man, which hung over his table. It was Laurie's father, who *had* run away in his youth, and married against the imperious old man's will. Jo fancied he remembered and regretted the past, and she wished she had held her tongue.

"He won't do it unless he is very much worried, and only threatens it sometimes, when he gets tired of studying. I often think I should like to, especially since my hair was cut; so, if you ever miss us, you may advertise for two boys, and look among the ships bound for India."

She laughed as she spoke, and Mr. Laurence looked relieved, evidently taking the whole as a joke.

"You hussy, how dare you talk in that way? Where's your respect for me, and your proper bringing up? Bless the boys and girls! What torments they are; yet we can't do without them," he said, pinching her cheeks good-humoredly. "Go and bring that boy down to his dinner, tell him it's all right, and advise him not to put on tragedy airs with his grandfather. I won't bear it."

"He won't come, sir; he feels badly because you didn't believe him when he said he couldn't tell. I think the shaking hurt his feelings very much."

Jo tried to look pathetic, but must have failed, for Mr. Laurence began to laugh, and she knew the day was won.

"I'm sorry for that, and ought to thank him for not shaking *me,* I suppose. What the dickens does the fellow expect?" and the old gentleman looked a trifle ashamed of his own testiness.

"If I were you, I'd write him an apology, sir. He says he won't come down till he has one, and talks about Washington, and goes on in an absurd way. A formal apology will make him see how foolish he is, and bring him down quite amiable. Try it; he likes fun, and this way is better than talking. I'll carry it up, and teach him his duty."

Mr. Laurence gave her a sharp look, and put on his spectacles, saying slowly, "You're a sly puss, but I don't mind being managed by you and Beth. Here, give me a bit of paper, and let us have done with this nonsense."

The note was written in the terms which one gentleman would use to another after offering some deep insult. Jo dropped a kiss on the top of Mr. Laurence's bald head, and ran up to slip the apology under Laurie's door, advising him, through the key-hole, to be submissive, decorous, and a few other agreeable impossibilities. Finding the door locked again, she left the note to do its work, and was going quietly away, when the young gentleman slid down the banisters, and waited for her at the bottom, saying, with his most virtuous expression of countenance, "What a good fellow you are, Jo! Did you get blown up?" he added, laughing.

"No; he was pretty mild, on the whole."

"Ah! I got it all round; even you cast me off over there, and I felt just ready to go to the deuce," he began apologetically.

"Don't talk in that way; turn over a new leaf and begin again, Teddy, my son."

"I keep turning over new leaves, and spoiling them, as I used to spoil my copy-books; and I make so many beginnings there never will be an end," he said dolefully.

"Go and eat your dinner; you'll feel better after it. Men always croak when they are hungry," and Jo whisked out at the front door after that.

"That's a 'label' on my 'sect,'" answered Laurie, quoting Amy, as he went to partake of humble-pie dutifully with his grandfather, who was quite saintly in temper and overwhelmingly respectful in manner all the rest of the day.

Every one thought the matter ended and the little cloud blown over; but the mischief was done, for, though others forgot it, Meg remembered. She never alluded to a certain person, but she thought of him a good deal, dreamed dreams more than ever; and once Jo, rummaging her sister's desk for stamps, found a bit of paper scribbled over with the words, "Mrs. John Brooke;" whereat she groaned tragically, and cast it into the fire, feeling that Laurie's prank had hastened the evil day for her.

XXII.

## PLEASANT MEADOWS.

LIKE sunshine after storm were the peaceful weeks which followed. The invalids improved rapidly, and Mr. March began to talk of returning early in the new year. Beth was soon able to lie on the study sofa all day, amusing herself with the well-beloved cats, at first, and, in time, with doll's sewing, which had fallen sadly behindhand. Her once active limbs were so stiff and feeble that Jo took her a daily airing about the house in her strong arms. Meg cheerfully blackened and burnt her white hands cooking delicate messes for "the dear;" while Amy, a loyal slave of the ring, celebrated her return by giving away as many of her treasures as she could prevail on her sisters to accept.

As Christmas approached, the usual mysteries began to haunt the house, and Jo frequently convulsed the family by proposing utterly impossible or magnificently absurd ceremonies, in honor of this unusually merry Christmas. Laurie was equally impracticable, and would have had bonfires, sky-rockets, and triumphal arches, if he had had his own way. After many skirmishes and snubbings, the ambitious pair were considered effectually quenched, and went about with forlorn faces, which were rather belied by explosions of laughter when the two got together.

Several days of unusually mild weather fitly ushered in a splendid Christmas Day. Hannah "felt in her bones" that it was going to be an unusually fine day, and she proved herself a true prophetess, for everybody and everything seemed bound to produce a grand success. To begin with, Mr. March wrote that he should soon be with them; then Beth felt uncommonly well that morning, and, being dressed in her mother's gift,—a soft crimson merino wrapper,—was borne in triumph to the window to behold the offering of Jo and Laurie. The Unquenchables had done their best to be worthy of the name, for, like elves, they had worked by night, and conjured up a comical surprise. Out in the garden stood a stately snow-maiden, crowned with holly, bearing a basket of fruit and flowers in one hand, a great roll of new music in the other, a perfect rainbow of an Afghan round her chilly shoulders, and a Christmas carol issuing from her lips, on a pink paper streamer:—

"THE JUNGFRAU TO BETH.

"God bless you, dear Queen Bess!
May nothing you dismay,

But health and peace and happiness
Be yours, this Christmas Day.

"Here's fruit to feed our busy bee,
And flowers for her nose;
Here's music for her pianee,
An Afghan for her toes.

"A portrait of Joanna, see,
By Raphael No. ,
Who labored with great industry
To make it fair and true.

"Accept a ribbon red, I beg,
For Madam Purrer's tail;
And ice-cream made by lovely Peg,—
A Mont Blanc in a pail.

"Their dearest love my makers laid
Within my breast of snow:
Accept it, and the Alpine maid,
From Laurie and from Jo."

How Beth laughed when she saw it, how Laurie ran up and down to bring in the gifts, and what ridiculous speeches Jo made as she presented them!

"I'm so full of happiness, that, if father was only here, I couldn't hold one drop more," said Beth, quite sighing with contentment as Jo carried her off to the study to rest after the excitement, and to refresh herself with some of the delicious grapes the "Jungfrau" had sent her.

"So am I," added Jo, slapping the pocket wherein reposed the long-desired Undine and Sintram.

"I'm sure I am," echoed Amy, poring over the engraved copy of the Madonna and Child, which her mother had given her, in a pretty frame.

"Of course I am!" cried Meg, smoothing the silvery folds of her first silk dress; for Mr. Laurence had insisted on giving it.

"How can *I* be otherwise?" said Mrs. March gratefully, as her eyes went from her husband's letter to Beth's smiling face, and her hand caressed the brooch made of gray and golden, chestnut and dark brown hair, which the girls had just fastened on her breast.

Now and then, in this work-a-day world, things do happen in the delightful story-book fashion, and what a comfort that is. Half an hour after every one had said they were so happy they could only hold one drop more, the drop came. Laurie opened the parlor door, and popped his head in very quietly. He might just as well have turned a somersault and uttered an Indian war-whoop; for his face was so full of suppressed excitement and his voice so treacherously joyful, that every one jumped up, though he only said, in a queer, breathless voice, "Here's another Christmas present for the March family."

Before the words were well out of his mouth, he was whisked away somehow, and in his place appeared a tall man, muffled up to the eyes, leaning on the arm of another tall man, who tried to say something and couldn't. Of course there was a general stampede; and for several minutes everybody seemed to lose their wits, for the strangest things were done, and no one said a word. Mr. March became invisible in the embrace of four pairs of loving arms; Jo disgraced herself by nearly fainting away, and had to be doctored by Laurie in the china-closet; Mr. Brooke kissed Meg entirely by mistake, as he somewhat incoherently explained; and Amy, the dignified, tumbled over a stool, and, never stopping to get up, hugged and cried over her father's boots in the most touching manner. Mrs. March was the first to recover herself, and held up her hand with a warning, "Hush! remember Beth!"

But it was too late; the study door flew open, the little red wrapper appeared on the threshold,—joy put strength into the feeble limbs,—and Beth ran straight into her father's arms. Never mind what happened just after that; for the full hearts overflowed, washing away the bitterness of the past, and leaving only the sweetness of the present.

It was not at all romantic, but a hearty laugh set everybody straight again, for Hannah was discovered behind the door, sobbing over the fat turkey, which she had forgotten to put down when she rushed up from the kitchen. As the laugh subsided, Mrs. March began to thank Mr. Brooke for his faithful care of her husband, at which Mr. Brooke suddenly remembered that Mr. March needed rest, and, seizing Laurie, he precipitately retired. Then the two invalids were ordered to repose, which they did, by both sitting in one big chair, and talking hard.

Mr. March told how he had longed to surprise them, and how, when the fine weather came, he had been allowed by his doctor to take advantage of it; how devoted Brooke had been, and how he was altogether a most estimable and upright young man. Why Mr. March paused a minute just there, and, after a glance at Meg, who was violently poking the fire, looked at his wife with an inquiring lift of the eyebrows, I leave you to imagine; also why Mrs. March gently nodded her head, and asked, rather abruptly, if he wouldn't have something to eat. Jo saw and understood the look; and she stalked grimly away to get wine and beef-tea, muttering to herself, as she slammed the door, "I hate estimable young men with brown eyes!"

There never *was* such a Christmas dinner as they had that day. The fat turkey was a sight to behold, when Hannah sent him up, stuffed, browned, and decorated; so was the plum-pudding, which quite melted in one's mouth; likewise the jellies, in which Amy revelled like a fly in a honey-pot. Everything turned out well, which was a mercy, Hannah said, "For my mind was that flustered, mum, that it's a merrycle I didn't roast the pudding, and stuff the turkey with raisins, let alone bilin' of it in a cloth."

Mr. Laurence and his grandson dined with them, also Mr. Brooke,—at whom Jo glowered darkly, to Laurie's infinite amusement. Two easy-chairs stood side by side at the head of the table, in which sat Beth and her father, feasting modestly on chicken and a little fruit. They drank healths, told stories, sung songs, "reminisced," as the old folks say, and had a thoroughly good time. A sleigh-ride had been planned, but the girls would not leave their father; so the guests departed early, and, as twilight gathered, the happy family sat together round the fire.

"Just a year ago we were groaning over the dismal Christmas we expected to have. Do you remember?" asked Jo, breaking a short pause which had followed a long conversation about many things.

"Rather a pleasant year on the whole!" said Meg, smiling at the fire, and congratulating herself on having treated Mr. Brooke with dignity.

"I think it's been a pretty hard one," observed Amy, watching the light shine on her ring, with thoughtful eyes.

"I'm glad it's over, because we've got you back," whispered Beth, who sat on her father's knee.

"Rather a rough road for you to travel, my little pilgrims, especially the latter part of it. But you have got on bravely; and I think the burdens are in a fair way to tumble off very soon," said Mr. March, looking with fatherly satisfaction at the four young faces gathered round him.

"How do you know? Did mother tell you?" asked Jo.

"Not much; straws show which way the wind blows, and I've made several discoveries to-day."

"Oh, tell us what they are!" cried Meg, who sat beside him.

"Here is one;" and taking up the hand which lay on the arm of his chair, he pointed to the roughened forefinger, a burn on the back, and two or three little hard spots on the palm. "I remember a time when this hand was white and smooth, and your first care was to keep it so. It was very pretty then, but to me it is much prettier now,—for in these seeming blemishes I read a little history. A burnt-offering has been made of vanity; this hardened palm has earned something better than blisters; and I'm sure the sewing done by these pricked fingers will last a long time, so much good-will went into the stitches. Meg, my dear, I value the womanly skill which keeps home happy more than white hands or fashionable accomplishments. I'm proud to shake this good, industrious little hand, and hope I shall not soon be asked to give it away."

If Meg had wanted a reward for hours of patient labor, she received it in the hearty pressure of her father's hand and the approving smile he gave her.

"What about Jo? Please say something nice; for she has tried so hard, and been so very, very good to me," said Beth, in her father's ear.

He laughed, and looked across at the tall girl who sat opposite, with an unusually mild expression in her brown face.

"In spite of the curly crop, I don't see the 'son Jo' whom I left a year ago," said Mr. March. "I see a young lady who pins her collar straight, laces her boots neatly, and neither whistles, talks slang, nor lies on the rug as she used to do. Her face is rather thin and pale, just now, with watching and anxiety; but I like to look at it, for it has grown gentler, and her voice is lower; she doesn't bounce, but moves quietly, and takes care of a certain little person in a motherly way which delights me. I rather miss my wild girl; but if I get a strong, helpful, tender-hearted woman in her place, I shall feel quite satisfied. I don't know whether the shearing sobered our black sheep, but I do know that in all Washington I couldn't find anything beautiful enough to be bought with the five-and-twenty dollars which my good girl sent me."

Jo's keen eyes were rather dim for a minute, and her thin face grew rosy in the firelight, as she received her father's praise, feeling that she did deserve a portion of it.

"Now Beth," said Amy, longing for her turn, but ready to wait.

"There's so little of her, I'm afraid to say much, for fear she will slip away altogether, though she is not so shy as she used to be," began their father cheerfully; but recollecting how nearly he *had* lost her, he held her close, saying tenderly, with her cheek against his own, "I've got you safe, my Beth, and I'll keep you so, please God."

After a minute's silence, he looked down at Amy, who sat on the cricket at his feet, and said, with a caress of the shining hair,—

"I observed that Amy took drumsticks at dinner, ran errands for her mother all the afternoon, gave Meg her place to-night, and has waited on every one with patience and good-humor. I also observe that she does not fret much nor look in the glass, and has not even mentioned a very pretty ring which she wears; so I conclude that she has learned to think of other people more and of herself less, and has decided to try and mould her character as carefully as she moulds her little clay figures. I am glad of this; for though I should be very proud of a graceful statue made by her, I shall be infinitely prouder of a lovable daughter, with a talent for making life beautiful to herself and others."

"What are you thinking of, Beth?" asked Jo, when Amy had thanked her father and told about her ring.

"I read in 'Pilgrim's Progress' to-day, how, after many troubles, Christian and Hopeful came to a pleasant green meadow, where lilies bloomed all the year round, and there they rested happily, as we do now, before they went on to their journey's end," answered Beth; adding, as she slipped out of her father's arms, and went slowly to the instrument, "It's singing time now, and I want to be in my old place. I'll try to sing the song of the shepherd-boy which the Pilgrims heard. I made the music for father, because he likes the verses."

So, sitting at the dear little piano, Beth softly touched the keys, and, in the sweet voice they had never thought to hear again, sung to her own accompaniment the quaint hymn, which was a singularly fitting song for her:—

"He that is down need fear no fall,
He that is low no pride;
He that is humble ever shall
Have God to be his guide.

"I am content with what I have,
Little be it or much;
And, Lord! contentment still I crave,
Because Thou savest such.

"Fulness to them a burden is,
That go on pilgrimage;
Here little, and hereafter bliss,
Is best from age to age!"

**"He sat in the big chair by Beth's sofa with the other three close by."—Page .**

XXIII.

# AUNT MARCH SETTLES THE QUESTION.

LIKE bees swarming after their queen, mother and daughters hovered about Mr. March the next day, neglecting everything to look at, wait upon, and listen to the new invalid, who was in a fair way to be killed by kindness. As he sat propped up in a big chair by Beth's sofa, with the other three close by, and Hannah popping in her head now and then, "to peek at the dear man," nothing seemed needed to complete their happiness. But something *was* needed, and the elder ones felt it, though none confessed the fact. Mr. and Mrs. March looked at one another with an anxious expression, as their eyes followed Meg. Jo had sudden fits of sobriety, and was seen to shake her fist at Mr. Brooke's umbrella, which had been left in the hall; Meg was absent-minded, shy, and silent, started when the bell rang, and colored when John's name was mentioned; Amy said "Every one seemed waiting for something, and couldn't settle down, which was queer, since father was safe at home," and Beth innocently wondered why their neighbors didn't run over as usual.

Laurie went by in the afternoon, and, seeing Meg at the window, seemed suddenly possessed with a melodramatic fit, for he fell down upon one knee in the snow, beat his breast, tore his hair, and clasped his hands imploringly, as if begging some boon; and when Meg told him to behave himself and go away, he wrung imaginary tears out of his handkerchief, and staggered round the corner as if in utter despair.

"What does the goose mean?" said Meg, laughing, and trying to look unconscious.

"He's showing you how your John will go on by and by. Touching, isn't it?" answered Jo scornfully.

"Don't say *my John*, it isn't proper or true;" but Meg's voice lingered over the words as if they sounded pleasant to her. "Please don't plague me, Jo; I've told you I don't care *much* about him, and there isn't to be anything said, but we are all to be friendly, and go on as before."

"We can't, for something *has* been said, and Laurie's mischief has spoilt you for me. I see it, and so does mother; you are not like your old self a bit, and seem ever so far away from me. I don't mean to plague you, and will bear it like a man, but I do wish it was all settled. I hate to wait; so if you mean ever to do it, make haste and have it over quickly," said Jo pettishly.

"*I* can't say or do anything till he speaks, and he won't, because father said I was too young," began Meg, bending over her work, with a queer little smile, which suggested that she did not quite agree with her father on that point.

"If he did speak, you wouldn't know what to say, but would cry or blush, or let him have his own way, instead of giving a good, decided, No."

"I'm not so silly and weak as you think. I know just what I should say, for I've planned it all, so I needn't be taken unawares; there's no knowing what may happen, and I wished to be prepared."

Jo couldn't help smiling at the important air which Meg had unconsciously assumed, and which was as becoming as the pretty color varying in her cheeks.

"Would you mind telling me what you'd say?" asked Jo more respectfully.

"Not at all; you are sixteen now, quite old enough to be my confidant, and my experience will be useful to you by and by, perhaps, in your own affairs of this sort."

"Don't mean to have any; it's fun to watch other people philander, but I should feel like a fool doing it myself," said Jo, looking alarmed at the thought.

"I think not, if you liked any one very much, and he liked you." Meg spoke as if to herself, and glanced out at the lane, where she had often seen lovers walking together in the summer twilight.

"I thought you were going to tell your speech to that man," said Jo, rudely shortening her sister's little reverie.

"Oh, I should merely say, quite calmly and decidedly, 'Thank you, Mr. Brooke, you are very kind, but I agree with father that I am too young to enter into any engagement at present; so please say no more, but let us be friends as we were.'"

"Hum! that's stiff and cool enough. I don't believe you'll ever say it, and I know he won't be satisfied if you do. If he goes on like the rejected lovers in books, you'll give in, rather than hurt his feelings."

"No, I won't! I shall tell him I've made up my mind, and shall walk out of the room with dignity."

Meg rose as she spoke, and was just going to rehearse the dignified exit, when a step in the hall made her fly into her seat, and begin to sew as if her life depended on finishing that particular seam in a given time. Jo smothered a laugh at the sudden change, and, when some one gave a modest tap, opened the door with a grim aspect, which was anything but hospitable.

"Good afternoon. I came to get my umbrella,—that is, to see how your father finds himself to-day," said Mr. Brooke, getting a trifle confused as his eye went from one tell-tale face to the other.

"It's very well, he's in the rack, I'll get him, and tell it you are here," and having jumbled her father and the umbrella well together in her reply, Jo slipped out of the room to give Meg a chance to make her speech and air her dignity. But the instant she vanished, Meg began to sidle towards the door, murmuring,—

"Mother will like to see you. Pray sit down, I'll call her."

"Don't go; are you afraid of me, Margaret?" and Mr. Brooke looked so hurt that Meg thought she must have done something very rude. She blushed up to the little curls on her forehead, for he had never called her Margaret before, and she was surprised to find how natural and sweet it seemed to hear him say it. Anxious to appear friendly and at her ease, she put out her hand with a confiding gesture, and said gratefully,—

"How can I be afraid when you have been so kind to father? I only wish I could thank you for it."

"Shall I tell you how?" asked Mr. Brooke, holding the small hand fast in both his own, and looking down at Meg with so much love in the brown eyes, that her heart began to flutter, and she both longed to run away and to stop and listen.

"Oh no, please don't—I'd rather not," she said, trying to withdraw her hand, and looking frightened in spite of her denial.

"I won't trouble you, I only want to know if you care for me a little, Meg. I love you so much, dear," added Mr. Brooke tenderly.

This was the moment for the calm, proper speech, but Meg didn't make it; she forgot every word of it, hung her head, and answered, "I don't know," so softly, that John had to stoop down to catch the foolish little reply.

He seemed to think it was worth the trouble, for he smiled to himself as if quite satisfied, pressed the plump hand gratefully, and said, in his most persuasive tone, "Will you try and find out? I want to know *so* much; for I can't go to work with any heart until I learn whether I am to have my reward in the end or not."

"I'm too young," faltered Meg, wondering why she was so fluttered, yet rather enjoying it.

"I'll wait; and in the meantime, you could be learning to like me. Would it be a very hard lesson, dear?"

"Not if I chose to learn it, but—"

"Please choose to learn, Meg. I love to teach, and this is easier than German," broke in John, getting possession of the other hand, so that she had no way of hiding her face, as he bent to look into it.

His tone was properly beseeching; but, stealing a shy look at him, Meg saw that his eyes were merry as well as tender, and that he wore the satisfied smile of one who had no doubt of his success. This nettled her; Annie Moffat's foolish lessons in coquetry came into her mind, and the love of power, which sleeps in the bosoms of the best of little women, woke up all of a sudden and took possession of her. She felt excited and strange, and, not knowing what else to do, followed a capricious impulse, and, withdrawing her hands, said petulantly, "I *don't* choose. Please go away and let me be!"

Poor Mr. Brooke looked as if his lovely castle in the air was tumbling about his ears, for he had never seen Meg in such a mood before, and it rather bewildered him.

"Do you really mean that?" he asked anxiously, following her as she walked away.

"Yes, I do; I don't want to be worried about such things. Father says I needn't; it's too soon and I'd rather not."

"Mayn't I hope you'll change your mind by and by? I'll wait, and say nothing till you have had more time. Don't play with me, Meg. I didn't think that of you."

"Don't think of me at all. I'd rather you wouldn't," said Meg, taking a naughty satisfaction in trying her lover's patience and her own power.

He was grave and pale now, and looked decidedly more like the novel heroes whom she admired; but he neither slapped his forehead nor tramped about the room, as they did; he just stood looking at her so wistfully, so tenderly, that she found her heart relenting in spite of her. What would have happened next I cannot say, if Aunt March had not come hobbling in at this interesting minute.

The old lady couldn't resist her longing to see her nephew; for she had met Laurie as she took her airing, and, hearing of Mr. March's arrival, drove straight out to see him. The family were all busy in the back part of the house, and she had made her way quietly in, hoping to surprise them. She did surprise two of them so much that Meg started as if she had seen a ghost, and Mr. Brooke vanished into the study.

"Bless me, what's all this?" cried the old lady, with a rap of her cane, as she glanced from the pale young gentleman to the scarlet young lady.

"It's father's friend. I'm *so* surprised to see you!" stammered Meg, feeling that she was in for a lecture now.

"That's evident," returned Aunt March, sitting down. "But what is father's friend saying to make you look like a peony? There's mischief going on, and I insist upon knowing what it is," with another rap.

"We were merely talking. Mr. Brooke came for his umbrella," began Meg, wishing that Mr. Brooke and the umbrella were safely out of the house.

"Brooke? That boy's tutor? Ah! I understand now. I know all about it. Jo blundered into a wrong message in one of your father's letters, and I made her tell me. You haven't gone and accepted him, child?" cried Aunt March, looking scandalized.

"Hush! he'll hear. Sha'n't I call mother?" said Meg, much troubled.

"Not yet. I've something to say to you, and I must free my mind at once. Tell me, do you mean to marry this Cook? If you do, not one penny of my money ever goes to you. Remember that, and be a sensible girl," said the old lady impressively.

Now Aunt March possessed in perfection the art of rousing the spirit of opposition in the gentlest people, and enjoyed doing it. The best of us have a spice of perversity in us, especially when we are young and in love. If Aunt

March had begged Meg to accept John Brooke, she would probably have declared she couldn't think of it; but as she was peremptorily ordered *not* to like him, she immediately made up her mind that she would. Inclination as well as perversity made the decision easy, and, being already much excited, Meg opposed the old lady with unusual spirit.

"I shall marry whom I please, Aunt March, and you can leave your money to any one you like," she said, nodding her head with a resolute air.

"Highty tighty! Is that the way you take my advice, miss? You'll be sorry for it, by and by, when you've tried love in a cottage, and found it a failure."

"It can't be a worse one than some people find in big houses," retorted Meg.

Aunt March put on her glasses and took a look at the girl, for she did not know her in this new mood. Meg hardly knew herself, she felt so brave and independent,—so glad to defend John, and assert her right to love him, if she liked. Aunt March saw that she had begun wrong, and, after a little pause, made a fresh start, saying, as mildly as she could, "Now, Meg, my dear, be reasonable, and take my advice. I mean it kindly, and don't want you to spoil your whole life by making a mistake at the beginning. You ought to marry well, and help your family; it's your duty to make a rich match, and it ought to be impressed upon you."

"Father and mother don't think so; they like John, though he *is* poor."

"Your parents, my dear, have no more worldly wisdom than two babies."

"I'm glad of it," cried Meg stoutly.

Aunt March took no notice, but went on with her lecture. "This Rook is poor, and hasn't got any rich relations, has he?"

"No; but he has many warm friends."

"You can't live on friends; try it, and see how cool they'll grow. He hasn't any business, has he?"

"Not yet; Mr. Laurence is going to help him."

"That won't last long. James Laurence is a crotchety old fellow, and not to be depended on. So you intend to marry a man without money, position, or business, and go on working harder than you do now, when you might be comfortable all your days by minding me and doing better? I thought you had more sense, Meg."

"I couldn't do better if I waited half my life! John is good and wise; he's got heaps of talent; he's willing to work, and sure to get on, he's so energetic and brave. Every one likes and respects him, and I'm proud to think he cares for me, though I'm so poor and young and silly," said Meg, looking prettier than ever in her earnestness.

"He knows *you* have got rich relations, child; that's the secret of his liking, I suspect."

"Aunt March, how dare you say such a thing? John is above such meanness, and I won't listen to you a minute if you talk so," cried Meg indignantly, forgetting everything but the injustice of the old lady's suspicions. "My John wouldn't marry for money, anymore than I would. We are willing to work, and we mean to wait. I'm not afraid of being poor, for I've been happy so far, and I know I shall be with him, because he loves me, and I—"

Meg stopped there, remembering all of a sudden that she hadn't made up her mind; that she had told "her John" to go away, and that he might be overhearing her inconsistent remarks.

Aunt March was very angry, for she had set her heart on having her pretty niece make a fine match, and something in the girl's happy young face made the lonely old woman feel both sad and sour.

"Well, I wash my hands of the whole affair! You are a wilful child, and you've lost more than you know by this piece of folly. No, I won't stop; I'm disappointed in you, and haven't spirits to see your father now. Don't expect anything from me when you are married; your Mr. Book's friends must take care of you. I'm done with you forever."

And, slamming the door in Meg's face, Aunt March drove off in high dudgeon. She seemed to take all the girl's courage with her; for, when left alone, Meg stood a moment, undecided whether to laugh or cry. Before she could make up her mind, she was taken possession of by Mr. Brooke, who said, all in one breath, "I couldn't help hearing, Meg. Thank you for defending me, and Aunt March for proving that you *do* care for me a little bit."

"I didn't know how much, till she abused you," began Meg.

"And I needn't go away, but may stay and be happy, may I, dear?"

Here was another fine chance to make the crushing speech and the stately exit, but Meg never thought of doing either, and disgraced herself forever in Jo's eyes by meekly whispering, "Yes, John," and hiding her face on Mr. Brooke's waistcoat.

Fifteen minutes after Aunt March's departure, Jo came softly down stairs, paused an instant at the parlor door, and, hearing no sound within, nodded and smiled, with a satisfied expression, saying to herself, "She has sent him away as we planned, and that affair is settled. I'll go and hear the fun, and have a good laugh over it."

But poor Jo never got her laugh, for she was transfixed upon the threshold by a spectacle which held her there, staring with her mouth nearly as wide open as her eyes. Going in to exult over a fallen enemy, and to praise a strong-minded sister for the banishment of an objectionable lover, it certainly *was* a shock to behold the aforesaid enemy serenely sitting on the sofa, with the strong-minded sister enthroned upon his knee, and wearing an expression of the most abject submission. Jo gave a sort of gasp, as if a cold shower-bath had suddenly fallen upon her,—for such an unexpected turning of the tables actually took her breath away. At the odd sound, the lovers turned and saw her. Meg jumped up, looking both proud and shy; but "that man," as Jo called him, actually laughed, and said coolly, as he kissed the astonished new-comer, "Sister Jo, congratulate us!"

That was adding insult to injury,—it was altogether too much,—and, making some wild demonstration with her hands, Jo vanished without a word. Rushing upstairs, she startled the invalids by exclaiming tragically, as she burst into the room, "Oh, *do* somebody go down quick; John Brooke is acting dreadfully, and Meg likes it!"

Mr. and Mrs. March left the room with speed; and, casting herself upon the bed, Jo cried and scolded tempestuously as she told the awful news to Beth and Amy. The little girls, however, considered it a most agreeable and interesting event, and Jo got little comfort from them; so she went up to her refuge in the garret, and confided her troubles to the rats.

Nobody ever knew what went on in the parlor that afternoon; but a great deal of talking was done, and quiet Mr. Brooke astonished his friends by the eloquence and spirit with which he pleaded his suit, told his plans, and persuaded them to arrange everything just as he wanted it.

The tea-bell rang before he had finished describing the paradise which he meant to earn for Meg, and he proudly took her in to supper, both looking so happy that Jo hadn't the heart to be jealous or dismal. Amy was very much impressed by John's devotion and Meg's dignity. Beth beamed at them from a distance, while Mr. and Mrs. March surveyed the young couple with such tender satisfaction that it was perfectly evident Aunt March was right in calling them as "unworldly as a pair of babies." No one ate much, but every one looked very happy, and the old room seemed to brighten up amazingly when the first romance of the family began there.

"You can't say nothing pleasant ever happens now, can you, Meg?" said Amy, trying to decide how she would group the lovers in the sketch she was planning to take.

"No, I'm sure I can't. How much has happened since I said that! It seems a year ago," answered Meg, who was in a blissful dream, lifted far above such common things as bread and butter.

"The joys come close upon the sorrows this time, and I rather think the changes have begun," said Mrs. March. "In most families there comes, now and then, a year full of events; this has been such an one, but it ends well, after all."

"Hope the next will end better," muttered Jo, who found it very hard to see Meg absorbed in a stranger before her face; for Jo loved a few persons very dearly, and dreaded to have their affection lost or lessened in any way.

"I hope the third year from this *will* end better; I mean it shall, if I live to work out my plans," said Mr. Brooke, smiling at Meg, as if everything had become possible to him now.

"Doesn't it seem very long to wait?" asked Amy, who was in a hurry for the wedding.

"I've got so much to learn before I shall be ready, it seems a short time to me," answered Meg, with a sweet gravity in her face, never seen there before.

"You have only to wait; *I* am to do the work," said John, beginning his labors by picking up Meg's napkin, with an expression which caused Jo to shake her head, and then say to herself, with an air of relief, as the front door banged, "Here comes Laurie. Now we shall have a little sensible conversation."

But Jo was mistaken; for Laurie came prancing in, overflowing with spirits, bearing a great bridal-looking bouquet for "Mrs. John Brooke," and evidently laboring under the delusion that the whole affair had been brought about by his excellent management.

"I knew Brooke would have it all his own way, he always does; for when he makes up his mind to accomplish anything, it's done, though the sky falls," said Laurie, when he had presented his offering and his congratulations.

"Much obliged for that recommendation. I take it as a good omen for the future, and invite you to my wedding on the spot," answered Mr. Brooke, who felt at peace with all mankind, even his mischievous pupil.

"I'll come if I'm at the ends of the earth; for the sight of Jo's face alone, on that occasion, would be worth a long journey. You don't look festive, ma'am; what's the matter?" asked Laurie, following her into a corner of the parlor, whither all had adjourned to greet Mr. Laurence.

"I don't approve of the match, but I've made up my mind to bear it, and shall not say a word against it," said Jo solemnly. "You can't know how hard it is for me to give up Meg," she continued, with a little quiver in her voice.

"You don't give her up. You only go halves," said Laurie consolingly.

"It never can be the same again. I've lost my dearest friend," sighed Jo.

"You've got me, anyhow. I'm not good for much, I know; but I'll stand by you, Jo, all the days of my life; upon my word I will!" and Laurie meant what he said.

"I know you will, and I'm ever so much obliged; you are always a great comfort to me, Teddy," returned Jo, gratefully shaking hands.

"Well, now, don't be dismal, there's a good fellow. It's all right, you see. Meg is happy; Brooke will fly round and get settled immediately; grandpa will attend to him, and it will be very jolly to see Meg in her own little house. We'll have capital times after she is gone, for I shall be through college before long, and then we'll go abroad, or some nice trip or other. Wouldn't that console you?"

"I rather think it would; but there's no knowing what may happen in three years," said Jo thoughtfully.

"That's true. Don't you wish you could take a look forward, and see where we shall all be then? I do," returned Laurie.

"I think not, for I might see something sad; and every one looks so happy now, I don't believe they could be much improved," and Jo's eyes went slowly round the room, brightening as they looked, for the prospect was a pleasant one.

Father and mother sat together, quietly re-living the first chapter of the romance which for them began some twenty years ago. Amy was drawing the lovers, who sat apart in a beautiful world of their own, the light of which touched their faces with a grace the little artist could not copy. Beth lay on her sofa, talking cheerily with her old friend, who held her little hand as if he felt that it possessed the power to lead him along the peaceful way she walked. Jo lounged in her favorite low seat, with the grave, quiet look which best became her; and Laurie, leaning on the back of her chair, his chin on a level with her curly head, smiled with his friendliest aspect, and nodded at her in the long glass which reflected them both.

---

So grouped, the curtain falls upon Meg, Jo, Beth, and Amy. Whether it ever rises again, depends upon the reception given to the first act of the domestic drama called "LITTLE WOMEN."

**Home of the Little Women**

# BOOK TWO

# GOOD WIVES

**The Dove-Cote**

## I.

## GOSSIP.

IN order that we may start afresh, and go to Meg's wedding with free minds, it will be well to begin with a little gossip about the Marches. And here let me premise, that if any of the elders think there is too much "lovering" in the story, as I fear they may (I'm not afraid the young folks will make that objection), I can only say with Mrs. March, "What *can* you expect when I have four gay girls in the house, and a dashing young neighbor over the way?"

The three years that have passed have brought but few changes to the quiet family. The war is over, and Mr. March safely at home, busy with his books and the small parish which found in him a minister by nature as by grace,—a quiet, studious man, rich in the wisdom that is better than learning, the charity which calls all mankind "brother," the piety that blossoms into character, making it august and lovely.

These attributes, in spite of poverty and the strict integrity which shut him out from the more worldly successes, attracted to him many admirable persons, as naturally as sweet herbs draw bees, and as naturally he gave them the honey into which fifty years of hard experience had distilled no bitter drop. Earnest young men found the gray-headed scholar as young at heart as they; thoughtful or troubled women instinctively brought their doubts and sorrows to him, sure of finding the gentlest sympathy, the wisest counsel; sinners told their sins to the pure-hearted old man, and were both rebuked and saved; gifted men found a companion in him; ambitious men caught glimpses of nobler ambitions than their own; and even worldlings confessed that his beliefs were beautiful and true, although "they wouldn't pay."

To outsiders, the five energetic women seemed to rule the house, and so they did in many things; but the quiet scholar, sitting among his books, was still the head of the family, the household conscience, anchor, and comforter; for to him the busy, anxious women always turned in troublous times, finding him, in the truest sense of those sacred words, husband and father.

The girls gave their hearts into their mother's keeping, their souls into their father's; and to both parents, who lived and labored so faithfully for them, they gave a love that grew with their growth, and bound them tenderly together by the sweetest tie which blesses life and outlives death.

Mrs. March is as brisk and cheery, though rather grayer, than when we saw her last, and just now so absorbed in Meg's affairs that the hospitals and homes, still full of wounded "boys" and soldiers' widows, decidedly miss the motherly missionary's visits.

John Brooke did his duty manfully for a year, got wounded, was sent home, and not allowed to return. He received no stars or bars, but he deserved them, for he cheerfully risked all he had; and life and love are very precious when both are in full bloom. Perfectly resigned to his discharge, he devoted himself to getting well, preparing for business, and earning a home for Meg. With the good sense and sturdy independence that characterized him, he refused Mr. Laurence's more generous offers, and accepted the place of book-keeper feeling better satisfied to begin with an honestly-earned salary, than by running any risks with borrowed money.

Meg had spent the time in working as well as waiting, growing womanly in character, wise in housewifely arts, and prettier than ever; for love is a great beautifier. She had her girlish ambitions and hopes, and felt some disappointment at the humble way in which the new life must begin. Ned Moffat had just married Sallie Gardiner, and Meg couldn't help contrasting their fine house and carriage, many gifts, and splendid outfit, with her own, and secretly wishing she could have the same. But somehow envy and discontent soon vanished when she thought of all the patient love and labor John had put into the little home awaiting her; and when they sat together in the twilight, talking over their small plans, the future always grew so beautiful and bright that she forgot Sallie's splendor, and felt herself the richest, happiest girl in Christendom.

Jo never went back to Aunt March, for the old lady took such a fancy to Amy that she bribed her with the offer of drawing lessons from one of the best teachers going; and for the sake of this advantage, Amy would have served a far harder mistress. So she gave her mornings to duty, her afternoons to pleasure, and prospered finely. Jo, meantime, devoted herself to literature and Beth, who remained delicate long after the fever was a thing of the past. Not an invalid exactly, but never again the rosy, healthy creature she had been; yet always hopeful, happy, and serene, busy with the quiet duties she loved, every one's friend, and an angel in the house, long before those who loved her most had learned to know it.

As long as "The Spread Eagle" paid her a dollar a column for her "rubbish," as she called it, Jo felt herself a woman of means, and spun her little romances diligently. But great plans fermented in her busy brain and ambitious mind, and the old tin kitchen in the garret held a slowly increasing pile of blotted manuscript, which was one day to place the name of March upon the roll of fame.

Laurie, having dutifully gone to college to please his grandfather, was now getting through it in the easiest possible manner to please himself. A universal favorite, thanks to money, manners, much talent, and the kindest heart that ever got its owner into scrapes by trying to get other people out of them, he stood in great danger of being spoilt, and probably would have been, like many another promising boy, if he had not possessed a talisman against evil in the memory of the kind old man who was bound up in his success, the motherly friend who watched over him as if he were her son, and last, but not least by any means, the knowledge that four innocent girls loved, admired, and believed in him with all their hearts.

Being only "a glorious human boy," of course he frolicked and flirted, grew dandified, aquatic, sentimental, or gymnastic, as college fashions ordained; hazed and was hazed, talked slang, and more than once came perilously near suspension and expulsion. But as high spirits and the love of fun were the causes of these pranks, he always managed to save himself by frank confession, honorable atonement, or the irresistible power of persuasion which he possessed in perfection. In fact, he rather prided himself on his narrow escapes, and liked to thrill the girls with graphic accounts of his triumphs over wrathful tutors, dignified professors, and vanquished enemies. The "men of my class" were heroes in the eyes of the girls, who never wearied of the exploits of "our fellows," and were frequently allowed to bask in the smiles of these great creatures, when Laurie brought them home with him.

Amy especially enjoyed this high honor, and became quite a belle among them; for her ladyship early felt and learned to use the gift of fascination with which she was endowed. Meg was too much absorbed in her private and particular John to care for any other lords of creation, and Beth too shy to do more than peep at them, and wonder how Amy dared to order them about so; but Jo felt quite in her element, and found it very difficult to refrain from imitating the gentlemanly attitudes, phrases, and feats, which seemed more natural to her than the decorums prescribed for young ladies. They all liked Jo immensely, but never fell in love with her, though very few escaped without paying the tribute of a sentimental sigh or two at Amy's shrine. And speaking of sentiment brings us very naturally to the "Dove-cote."

That was the name of the little brown house which Mr. Brooke had prepared for Meg's first home. Laurie had christened it, saying it was highly appropriate to the gentle lovers, who "went on together like a pair of turtle-doves, with first a bill and then a coo." It was a tiny house, with a little garden behind, and a lawn about as big as a pocket-handkerchief in front. Here Meg meant to have a fountain, shrubbery, and a profusion of lovely flowers; though just at present, the fountain was represented by a weather-beaten urn, very like a dilapidated slop-bowl; the shrubbery consisted of several young larches, undecided whether to live or die; and the profusion of flowers was merely hinted by regiments of sticks, to show where seeds were planted. But inside, it was altogether charming, and the happy bride saw no fault from garret to cellar. To be sure, the hall was so narrow, it was fortunate that they had no piano, for one never could have been got in whole; the dining-room was so small that six people were a tight fit; and the kitchen stairs seemed built for the express purpose of precipitating both servants and china pell-mell into the coal-bin. But once get used to these slight blemishes, and nothing could be more complete, for good sense and good taste had presided over the furnishing, and the result was highly satisfactory. There were no marble-topped tables, long mirrors, or lace curtains in the little parlor, but simple furniture, plenty of books, a fine picture or two, a stand of flowers in the bay-window, and, scattered all about, the pretty gifts which came from friendly hands, and were the fairer for the loving messages they brought.

I don't think the Parian Psyche Laurie gave lost any of its beauty because John put up the bracket it stood upon; that any upholsterer could have draped the plain muslin curtains more gracefully than Amy's artistic hand; or that any store-room was ever better provided with good wishes, merry words, and happy hopes, than that in which Jo and her mother put away Meg's few boxes, barrels, and bundles; and I am morally certain that the spandy-new kitchen never *could* have looked so cosey and neat if Hannah had not arranged every pot and pan a dozen times over, and laid the fire all ready for lighting, the minute "Mis. Brooke came home." I also doubt if any young matron ever began life with so rich a supply of dusters, holders, and piece-bags; for Beth made enough to last till the silver wedding came round, and invented three different kinds of dishcloths for the express service of the bridal china.

People who hire all these things done for them never know what they lose; for the homeliest tasks get beautified if loving hands do them, and Meg found so many proofs of this, that everything in her small nest, from the kitchen roller to the silver vase on her parlor table, was eloquent of home love and tender forethought.

What happy times they had planning together, what solemn shopping excursions; what funny mistakes they made, and what shouts of laughter arose over Laurie's ridiculous bargains. In his love of jokes, this young gentleman, though nearly through college, was as much of a boy as ever. His last whim had been to bring with him, on his weekly visits, some new, useful, and ingenious article for the young housekeeper. Now a bag of remarkable clothes-pins; next, a wonderful nutmeg-grater, which fell to pieces at the first trial; a knife-cleaner that spoilt all the knives; or a sweeper that picked the nap neatly off the carpet, and left the dirt; labor-saving soap that took the skin off one's hands; infallible cements which stuck firmly to nothing but the fingers of the deluded buyer; and every kind of tin-ware, from a toy savings-bank for odd pennies, to a wonderful boiler which would wash articles in its own steam, with every prospect of exploding in the process.

In vain Meg begged him to stop. John laughed at him, and Jo called him "Mr. Toodles." He was possessed with a mania for patronizing Yankee ingenuity, and seeing his friends fitly furnished forth. So each week beheld some fresh absurdity.

Everything was done at last, even to Amy's arranging different colored soaps to match the different colored rooms, and Beth's setting the table for the first meal.

"Are you satisfied? Does it seem like home, and do you feel as if you should be happy here?" asked Mrs. March, as she and her daughter went through the new kingdom, arm-in-arm; for just then they seemed to cling together more tenderly than ever.

"Yes, mother, perfectly satisfied, thanks to you all, and *so* happy that I can't talk about it," answered Meg, with a look that was better than words.

"If she only had a servant or two it would be all right," said Amy, coming out of the parlor, where she had been trying to decide whether the bronze Mercury looked best on the whatnot or the mantle-piece.

"Mother and I have talked that over, and I have made up my mind to try her way first. There will be so little to do, that, with Lotty to run my errands and help me here and there, I shall only have enough work to keep me from getting lazy or homesick," answered Meg tranquilly.

"Sallie Moffat has four," began Amy.

"If Meg had four the house wouldn't hold them, and master and missis would have to camp in the garden," broke in Jo, who, enveloped in a big blue pinafore, was giving the last polish to the door-handles.

"Sallie isn't a poor man's wife, and many maids are in keeping with her fine establishment. Meg and John begin humbly, but I have a feeling that there will be quite as much happiness in the little house as in the big one. It's a great mistake for young girls like Meg to leave themselves nothing to do but dress, give orders, and gossip. When I was first married, I used to long for my new clothes to wear out or get torn, so that I might have the pleasure of mending them; for I got heartily sick of doing fancy work and tending my pocket handkerchief."

"Why didn't you go into the kitchen and make messes, as Sallie says she does, to amuse herself, though they never turn out well, and the servants laugh at her," said Meg.

"I did, after a while; not to 'mess,' but to learn of Hannah how things should be done, that my servants need *not* laugh at me. It was play then; but there came a time when I was truly grateful that I not only possessed the will but the power to cook wholesome food for my little girls, and help myself when I could no longer afford to hire help. You begin at the other end, Meg, dear; but the lessons you learn now will be of use to you by and by, when John is a richer man, for the mistress of a house, however splendid, should know how work ought to be done, if she wishes to be well and honestly served."

"Yes, mother, I'm sure of that," said Meg, listening respectfully to the little lecture; for the best of women will hold forth upon the all-absorbing subject of housekeeping. "Do you know I like this room most of all in my baby-house," added Meg, a minute after, as they went upstairs, and she looked into her well-stored linen-closet.

Beth was there, laying the snowy piles smoothly on the shelves, and exulting over the goodly array. All three laughed as Meg spoke; for that linen-closet was a joke. You see, having said that if Meg married "that Brooke" she shouldn't have a cent of her money, Aunt March was rather in a quandary, when time had appeased her wrath and made her repent her vow. She never broke her word, and was much exercised in her mind how to get round it, and at last devised a plan whereby she could satisfy herself. Mrs. Carrol, Florence's mamma, was ordered to buy, have made, and marked, a generous supply of house and table linen, and send it as *her* present, all of which was faithfully done; but the secret leaked out, and was greatly enjoyed by the family; for Aunt March tried to look utterly unconscious, and insisted that she could give nothing but the old-fashioned pearls, long promised to the first bride.

"That's a housewifely taste which I am glad to see. I had a young friend who set up housekeeping with six sheets, but she had finger bowls for company, and that satisfied her," said Mrs. March, patting the damask table-cloths, with a truly feminine appreciation of their fineness.

"I haven't a single finger-bowl, but this is a 'set out' that will last me all my days, Hannah says;" and Meg looked quite contented, as well she might.

"Toodles is coming," cried Jo from below; and they all went down to meet Laurie, whose weekly visit was an important event in their quiet lives.

A tall, broad-shouldered young fellow, with a cropped head, a felt-basin of a hat, and a fly-away coat, came tramping down the road at a great pace, walked over the low fence without stopping to open the gate, straight up to Mrs. March, with both hands out, and a hearty—

"Here I am, mother! Yes, it's all right."

The last words were in answer to the look the elder lady gave him; a kindly questioning look, which the handsome eyes met so frankly that the little ceremony closed, as usual, with a motherly kiss.

"For Mrs. John Brooke, with the maker's congratulations and compliments. Bless you, Beth! What a refreshing spectacle you are, Jo. Amy, you are getting altogether too handsome for a single lady."

As Laurie spoke, he delivered a brown paper parcel to Meg, pulled Beth's hair-ribbon, stared at Jo's big pinafore, and fell into an attitude of mock rapture before Amy, then shook hands all round, and every one began to talk.

"Where is John?" asked Meg anxiously.

"Stopped to get the license for to-morrow, ma'am."

"Which side won the last match, Teddy?" inquired Jo, who persisted in feeling an interest in manly sports, despite her nineteen years.

"Ours, of course. Wish you'd been there to see."

"How is the lovely Miss Randal?" asked Amy, with a significant smile.

"More cruel than ever; don't you see how I'm pining away?" and Laurie gave his broad chest a sounding slap and heaved a melodramatic sigh.

"What's the last joke? Undo the bundle and see, Meg," said Beth, eying the knobby parcel with curiosity.

"It's a useful thing to have in the house in case of fire or thieves," observed Laurie, as a watchman's rattle appeared, amid the laughter of the girls.

"Any time when John is away, and you get frightened, Mrs. Meg, just swing that out of the front window, and it will rouse the neighborhood in a jiffy. Nice thing, isn't it?" and Laurie gave them a sample of its powers that made them cover up their ears.

"There's gratitude for you! and speaking of gratitude reminds me to mention that you may thank Hannah for saving your wedding-cake from destruction. I saw it going into your house as I came by, and if she hadn't defended it manfully I'd have had a pick at it, for it looked like a remarkably plummy one."

"I wonder if you will ever grow up, Laurie," said Meg, in a matronly tone.

"I'm doing my best, ma'am, but can't get much higher, I'm afraid, as six feet is about all men can do in these degenerate days," responded the young gentleman, whose head was about level with the little chandelier. "I suppose it would be profanation to eat anything in this spick and span new bower, so, as I'm tremendously hungry, I propose an adjournment," he added presently.

"Mother and I are going to wait for John. There are some last things to settle," said Meg, bustling away.

"Beth and I are going over to Kitty Bryant's to get more flowers for to-morrow," added Amy, tying a picturesque hat over her picturesque curls, and enjoying the effect as much as anybody.

"Come, Jo, don't desert a fellow. I'm in such a state of exhaustion I can't get home without help. Don't take off your apron, whatever you do; it's peculiarly becoming," said Laurie, as Jo bestowed his especial aversion in her capacious pocket, and offered him her arm to support his feeble steps.

"Now, Teddy, I want to talk seriously to you about to-morrow," began Jo, as they strolled away together. "You *must* promise to behave well, and not cut up any pranks, and spoil our plans."

"Not a prank."

"And don't say funny things when we ought to be sober."

"I never do; you are the one for that."

"And I implore you not to look at me during the ceremony; I shall certainly laugh if you do."

"You won't see me; you'll be crying so hard that the thick fog round you will obscure the prospect."

"I never cry unless for some great affliction."

"Such as fellows going to college, hey?" cut in Laurie, with a suggestive laugh.

"Don't be a peacock. I only moaned a trifle to keep the girls company."

"Exactly. I say, Jo, how is grandpa this week; pretty amiable?"

"Very; why, have you got into a scrape, and want to know how he'll take it?" asked Jo rather sharply.

"Now, Jo, do you think I'd look your mother in the face, and say 'All right,' if it wasn't?" and Laurie stopped short, with an injured air.

"No, I don't."

"Then don't go and be suspicious; I only want some money," said Laurie, walking on again, appeased by her hearty tone.

"You spend a great deal, Teddy."

"Bless you, *I* don't spend it; it spends itself, somehow, and is gone before I know it."

"You are so generous and kind-hearted that you let people borrow, and can't say 'No' to any one. We heard about Henshaw, and all you did for him. If you always spent money in that way, no one would blame you," said Jo warmly.

"Oh, he made a mountain out of a mole-hill. You wouldn't have me let that fine fellow work himself to death, just for the want of a little help, when he is worth a dozen of us lazy chaps, would you?"

"Of course not; but I don't see the use of your having seventeen waistcoats, endless neckties, and a new hat every time you come home. I thought you'd got over the dandy period; but every now and then it breaks out in a new spot. Just now it's the fashion to be hideous,—to make your head look like a scrubbing-brush, wear a strait-jacket, orange gloves, and clumping, square-toed boots. If it was cheap ugliness, I'd say nothing; but it costs as much as the other, and I don't get any satisfaction out of it."

Laurie threw back his head, and laughed so heartily at this attack, that the felt-basin fell off, and Jo walked on it, which insult only afforded him an opportunity for expatiating on the advantages of a rough-and-ready costume, as he folded up the maltreated hat, and stuffed it into his pocket.

"Don't lecture any more, there's a good soul! I have enough all through the week, and like to enjoy myself when I come home. I'll get myself up regardless of expense, to-morrow, and be a satisfaction to my friends."

"I'll leave you in peace if you'll *only* let your hair grow. I'm not aristocratic, but I do object to being seen with a person who looks like a young prize-fighter," observed Jo severely.

"This unassuming style promotes study; that's why we adopt it," returned Laurie, who certainly could not be accused of vanity, having voluntarily sacrificed a handsome curly crop to the demand for quarter-of-an-inch-long stubble.

"By the way, Jo, I think that little Parker is really getting desperate about Amy. He talks of her constantly, writes poetry, and moons about in a most suspicious manner. He'd better nip his little passion in the bud, hadn't he?" added Laurie, in a confidential, elder-brotherly tone, after a minute's silence.

"Of course he had; we don't want any more marrying in this family for years to come. Mercy on us, what *are* the children thinking of?" and Jo looked as much scandalized as if Amy and little Parker were not yet in their teens.

"It's a fast age, and I don't know what we are coming to, ma'am. You are a mere infant, but you'll go next, Jo, and we'll be left lamenting," said Laurie, shaking his head over the degeneracy of the times.

"Don't be alarmed; I'm not one of the agreeable sort. Nobody will want me, and it's a mercy, for there should always be one old maid in a family."

"You won't give any one a chance," said Laurie, with a sidelong glance, and a little more color than before in his sunburnt face. "You won't show the soft side of your character; and if a fellow gets a peep at it by accident, and can't help showing that he likes it, you treat him as Mrs. Gummidge did her sweetheart,—throw cold water over him,—and get so thorny no one dares touch or look at you."

"I don't like that sort of thing; I'm too busy to be worried with nonsense, and I think it's dreadful to break up families so. Now don't say any more about it; Meg's wedding has turned all our heads, and we talk of nothing but lovers and such absurdities. I don't wish to get cross, so let's change the subject;" and Jo looked quite ready to fling cold water on the slightest provocation.

Whatever his feelings might have been, Laurie found a vent for them in a long low whistle, and the fearful prediction, as they parted at the gate, "Mark my words, Jo, you'll go next."

# II.

# THE FIRST WEDDING.

THE June roses over the porch were awake bright and early on that morning, rejoicing with all their hearts in the cloudless sunshine, like friendly little neighbors, as they were. Quite flushed with excitement were their ruddy faces, as they swung in the wind, whispering to one another what they had seen; for some peeped in at the dining-room windows, where the feast was spread, some climbed up to nod and smile at the sisters as they dressed the bride, others waved a welcome to those who came and went on various errands in garden, porch, and hall, and all, from the rosiest full-blown flower to the palest baby-bud, offered their tribute of beauty and fragrance to the gentle mistress who had loved and tended them so long.

Meg looked very like a rose herself; for all that was best and sweetest in heart and soul seemed to bloom into her face that day, making it fair and tender, with a charm more beautiful than beauty. Neither silk, lace, nor orange-flowers would she have. "I don't want to look strange or fixed up to-day," she said. "I don't want a fashionable wedding, but only those about me whom I love, and to them I wish to look and be my familiar self."

So she made her wedding gown herself, sewing into it the tender hopes and innocent romances of a girlish heart. Her sisters braided up her pretty hair, and the only ornaments she wore were the lilies of the valley, which "her John" liked best of all the flowers that grew.

"You *do* look just like our own dear Meg, only so very sweet and lovely that I should hug you if it wouldn't crumple your dress," cried Amy, surveying her with delight, when all was done.

"Then I am satisfied. But please hug and kiss me, every one, and don't mind my dress; I want a great many crumples of this sort put into it to-day;" and Meg opened her arms to her sisters, who clung about her with April faces for a minute, feeling that the new love had not changed the old.

"Now I'm going to tie John's cravat for him, and then to stay a few minutes with father quietly in the study;" and Meg ran down to perform these little ceremonies, and then to follow her mother wherever she went, conscious that, in spite of the smiles on the motherly face, there was a secret sorrow hid in the motherly heart at the flight of the first bird from the nest.

As the younger girls stand together, giving the last touches to their simple toilet, it may be a good time to tell of a few changes which three years have wrought in their appearance; for all are looking their best just now.

Jo's angles are much softened; she has learned to carry herself with ease, if not grace. The curly crop has lengthened into a thick coil, more becoming to the small head atop of the tall figure. There is a fresh color in her brown cheeks, a soft shine in her eyes, and only gentle words fall from her sharp tongue to-day.

Beth has grown slender, pale, and more quiet than ever; the beautiful, kind eyes are larger, and in them lies an expression that saddens one, although it is not sad itself. It is the shadow of pain which touches the young face with such pathetic patience; but Beth seldom complains, and always speaks hopefully of "being better soon."

Amy is with truth considered "the flower of the family;" for at sixteen she has the air and bearing of a full-grown woman—not beautiful, but possessed of that indescribable charm called grace. One saw it in the lines of her figure, the make and motion of her hands, the flow of her dress, the droop of her hair,—unconscious, yet harmonious, and as attractive to many as beauty itself. Amy's nose still afflicted her, for it never *would* grow Grecian; so did her mouth, being too wide, and having a decided chin. These offending features gave character to her whole face, but she never could see it, and consoled herself with her wonderfully fair complexion, keen blue eyes, and curls, more golden and abundant than ever.

All three wore suits of thin silver gray (their best gowns for the summer), with blush-roses in hair and bosom; and all three looked just what they were,—fresh-faced, happy-hearted girls, pausing a moment in their busy lives to read with wistful eyes the sweetest chapter in the romance of womanhood.

There were to be no ceremonious performances, everything was to be as natural and homelike as possible; so when Aunt March arrived, she was scandalized to see the bride come running to welcome and lead her in, to find the bridegroom fastening up a garland that had fallen down, and to catch a glimpse of the paternal minister marching upstairs with a grave countenance, and a wine-bottle under each arm.

"Upon my word, here's a state of things!" cried the old lady, taking the seat of honor prepared for her, and settling the folds of her lavender *moire* with a great rustle. "You oughtn't to be seen till the last minute, child."

"I'm not a show, aunty, and no one is coming to stare at me, to criticise my dress, or count the cost of my luncheon. I'm too happy to care what any one says or thinks, and I'm going to have my little wedding just as I like it. John, dear, here's your hammer;" and away went Meg to help "that man" in his highly improper employment.

Mr. Brooke didn't even say "Thank you," but as he stooped for the unromantic tool, he kissed his little bride behind the folding-door, with a look that made Aunt March whisk out her pocket-handkerchief, with a sudden dew in her sharp old eyes.

A crash, a cry, and a laugh from Laurie, accompanied by the indecorous exclamation, "Jupiter Ammon! Jo's upset the cake again!" caused a momentary flurry, which was hardly over when a flock of cousins arrived, and "the party came in," as Beth used to say when a child.

"Don't let that young giant come near me; he worries me worse than mosquitoes," whispered the old lady to Amy, as the rooms filled, and Laurie's black head towered above the rest.

"He has promised to be very good to-day, and he *can* be perfectly elegant if he likes," returned Amy, gliding away to warn Hercules to beware of the dragon, which warning caused him to haunt the old lady with a devotion that nearly distracted her.

There was no bridal procession, but a sudden silence fell upon the room as Mr. March and the young pair took their places under the green arch. Mother and sisters gathered close, as if loath to give Meg up; the fatherly voice broke more than once, which only seemed to make the service more beautiful and solemn; the bridegroom's hand trembled visibly, and no one heard his replies; but Meg looked straight up in her husband's eyes, and said, "I will!" with such tender trust in her own face and voice that her mother's heart rejoiced, and Aunt March sniffed audibly.

Jo did *not* cry, though she was very near it once, and was only saved from a demonstration by the consciousness that Laurie was staring fixedly at her, with a comical mixture of merriment and emotion in his wicked black eyes. Beth kept her face hidden on her mother's shoulder, but Amy stood like a graceful statue, with a most becoming ray of sunshine touching her white forehead and the flower in her hair.

It wasn't at all the thing, I'm afraid, but the minute she was fairly married, Meg cried, "The first kiss for Marmee!" and, turning, gave it with her heart on her lips. During the next fifteen minutes she looked more like a rose than ever, for every one availed themselves of their privileges to the fullest extent, from Mr. Laurence to old Hannah, who, adorned with a head-dress fearfully and wonderfully made, fell upon her in the hall, crying, with a sob and a chuckle, "Bless you, deary, a hundred times! The cake ain't hurt a mite, and everything looks lovely."

Everybody cleared up after that, and said something brilliant, or tried to, which did just as well, for laughter is ready when hearts are light. There was no display of gifts, for they were already in the little house, nor was there an elaborate breakfast, but a plentiful lunch of cake and fruit, dressed with flowers. Mr. Laurence and Aunt March shrugged and smiled at one another when water, lemonade, and coffee were found to be the only sorts of nectar which the three Hebes carried round. No one said anything, however, till Laurie, who insisted on serving the bride, appeared before her, with a loaded salver in his hand and a puzzled expression on his face.

"Has Jo smashed all the bottles by accident?" he whispered, "or am I merely laboring under a delusion that I saw some lying about loose this morning?"

"No; your grandfather kindly offered us his best, and Aunt March actually sent some, but father put away a little for Beth, and despatched the rest to the Soldiers' Home. You know he thinks that wine should be used only in illness, and mother says that neither she nor her daughters will ever offer it to any young man under her roof."

Meg spoke seriously, and expected to see Laurie frown or laugh; but he did neither, for after a quick look at her, he said, in his impetuous way, "I like that! for I've seen enough harm done to wish other women would think as you do."

"You are not made wise by experience, I hope?" and there was an anxious accent in Meg's voice.

"No; I give you my word for it. Don't think too well of me, either; this is not one of my temptations. Being brought up where wine is as common as water, and almost as harmless, I don't care for it; but when a pretty girl offers it, one doesn't like to refuse, you see."

"But you will, for the sake of others, if not for your own. Come, Laurie, promise, and give me one more reason to call this the happiest day of my life."

A demand so sudden and so serious made the young man hesitate a moment, for ridicule is often harder to bear than self-denial. Meg knew that if he gave the promise he would keep it at all costs; and, feeling her power, used it as a woman may for her friend's good. She did not speak, but she looked up at him with a face made very eloquent by happiness, and a smile which said, "No one can refuse me anything to-day." Laurie certainly could not; and, with an answering smile, he gave her his hand, saying heartily, "I promise, Mrs. Brooke!"

"I thank you, very, very much."

"And I drink 'long life to your resolution,' Teddy," cried Jo, baptizing him with a splash of lemonade, as she waved her glass, and beamed approvingly upon him.

So the toast was drunk, the pledge made, and loyally kept, in spite of many temptations; for, with instinctive wisdom, the girls had seized a happy moment to do their friend a service, for which he thanked them all his life.

After lunch, people strolled about, by twos and threes, through house and garden, enjoying the sunshine without and within. Meg and John happened to be standing together in the middle of the grass-plot, when Laurie was seized with an inspiration which put the finishing touch to this unfashionable wedding.

"All the married people take hands and dance round the new-made husband and wife, as the Germans do, while we bachelors and spinsters prance in couples outside!" cried Laurie, promenading down the path with Amy, with such infectious spirit and skill that every one else followed their example without a murmur. Mr. and Mrs. March, Aunt and Uncle Carrol, began it; others rapidly joined in; even Sallie Moffat, after a moment's hesitation, threw her train over her arm, and whisked Ned into the ring. But the crowning joke was Mr. Laurence and Aunt March; for when the stately old gentleman *chasséed* solemnly up to the old lady, she just tucked her cane under her arm, and hopped briskly away to join hands with the rest, and dance about the bridal pair, while the young folks pervaded the garden, like butterflies on a midsummer day.

Want of breath brought the impromptu ball to a close, and then people began to go.

"I wish you well, my dear, I heartily wish you well; but I think you'll be sorry for it," said Aunt March to Meg, adding to the bridegroom, as he led her to the carriage, "You've got a treasure, young man, see that you deserve it."

"That is the prettiest wedding I've been to for an age, Ned, and I don't see why, for there wasn't a bit of style about it," observed Mrs. Moffat to her husband, as they drove away.

"Laurie, my lad, if you ever want to indulge in this sort of thing, get one of those little girls to help you, and I shall be perfectly satisfied," said Mr. Laurence, settling himself in his easy-chair to rest, after the excitement of the morning.

"I'll do my best to gratify you, sir," was Laurie's unusually dutiful reply, as he carefully unpinned the posy Jo had put in his button-hole.

The little house was not far away, and the only bridal journey Meg had was the quiet walk with John, from the old home to the new. When she came down, looking like a pretty Quakeress in her dove-colored suit and straw bonnet tied with white, they all gathered about her to say "good-by," as tenderly as if she had been going to make the grand tour.

"Don't feel that I am separated from you, Marmee dear, or that I love you any the less for loving John so much," she said, clinging to her mother, with full eyes, for a moment. "I shall come every day, father, and expect to keep my old place in all your hearts, though I *am* married. Beth is going to be with me a great deal, and the other girls will drop in now and then to laugh at my housekeeping struggles. Thank you all for my happy wedding-day. Good-by, good-by!"

They stood watching her, with faces full of love and hope and tender pride, as she walked away, leaning on her husband's arm, with her hands full of flowers, and the June sunshine brightening her happy face,—and so Meg's married life began.

## III

## ARTISTIC ATTEMPTS.

IT takes people a long time to learn the difference between talent and genius, especially ambitious young men and women. Amy was learning this distinction through much tribulation; for, mistaking enthusiasm for inspiration, she attempted every branch of art with youthful audacity. For a long time there was a lull in the "mud-pie" business, and she devoted herself to the finest pen-and-ink drawing, in which she showed such taste and skill that her graceful handiwork proved both pleasant and profitable. But overstrained eyes soon caused pen and ink to be laid aside for a bold attempt at poker-sketching. While this attack lasted, the family lived in constant fear of a conflagration; for the odor of burning wood pervaded the house at all hours; smoke issued from attic and shed with alarming frequency, red-hot pokers lay about promiscuously, and Hannah never went to bed without a pail of water and the dinner-bell at her door, in case of fire. Raphael's face was found boldly executed on the under side of the moulding-board, and Bacchus on the head of a beer-barrel; a chanting cherub adorned the cover of the sugar-bucket, and attempts to portray Romeo and Juliet supplied kindlings for some time.

From fire to oil was a natural transition for burnt fingers, and Amy fell to painting with undiminished ardor. An artist friend fitted her out with his cast-off palettes, brushes, and colors; and she daubed away, producing pastoral and marine views such as were never seen on land or sea. Her monstrosities in the way of cattle would have taken prizes at an agricultural fair; and the perilous pitching of her vessels would have produced sea-sickness in the most nautical observer, if the utter disregard to all known rules of shipbuilding and rigging had not convulsed him with laughter at the first glance. Swarthy boys and dark-eyed Madonnas, staring at you from one corner of the studio, suggested Murillo; oily-brown shadows of faces, with a lurid streak in the wrong place, meant Rembrandt; buxom ladies and dropsical infants, Rubens; and Turner appeared in tempests of blue thunder, orange lightning, brown rain, and purple clouds, with a tomato-colored splash in the middle, which might be the sun or a buoy, a sailor's shirt or a king's robe, as the spectator pleased.

Charcoal portraits came next; and the entire family hung in a row, looking as wild and crocky as if just evoked from a coal-bin. Softened into crayon sketches, they did better; for the likenesses were good, and Amy's hair, Jo's nose, Meg's mouth, and Laurie's eyes were pronounced "wonderfully fine." A return to clay and plaster followed, and ghostly casts of her acquaintances haunted corners of the house, or tumbled off closet-shelves on to people's heads. Children were enticed in as models, till their incoherent accounts of her mysterious doings caused Miss Amy to be regarded in the light of a young ogress. Her efforts in this line, however, were brought to an abrupt close by an untoward accident, which quenched her ardor. Other models failing her for a time, she undertook to cast her own pretty foot, and the family were one day alarmed by an unearthly bumping and screaming, and running to the rescue, found the young enthusiast hopping wildly about the shed, with her foot held fast in a pan-full of plaster, which had hardened with unexpected rapidity. With much difficulty and some danger she was dug out; for Jo was so overcome with laughter while she excavated, that her knife went too far, cut the poor foot, and left a lasting memorial of one artistic attempt, at least.

After this Amy subsided, till a mania for sketching from nature set her to haunting river, field, and wood, for picturesque studies, and sighing for ruins to copy. She caught endless colds sitting on damp grass to book "a delicious bit," composed of a stone, a stump, one mushroom, and a broken mullein-stalk, or "a heavenly mass of clouds," that looked like a choice display of feather-beds when done. She sacrificed her complexion floating on the river in the midsummer sun, to study light and shade, and got a wrinkle over her nose, trying after "points of sight," or whatever the squint-and-string performance is called.

If "genius is eternal patience," as Michael Angelo affirms, Amy certainly had some claim to the divine attribute, for she persevered in spite of all obstacles, failures, and discouragements, firmly believing that in time she should do something worthy to be called "high art."

She was learning, doing, and enjoying other things, meanwhile, for she had resolved to be an attractive and accomplished woman, even if she never became a great artist. Here she succeeded better; for she was one of those happily created beings who please without effort, make friends everywhere, and take life so gracefully and easily that less fortunate souls are tempted to believe that such are born under a lucky star. Everybody liked her, for among her good gifts was tact. She had an instinctive sense of what was pleasing and proper, always said the right thing to the right person, did just what suited the time and place, and was so self-possessed that her sisters used to say, "If Amy went to court without any rehearsal beforehand, she'd know exactly what to do."

One of her weaknesses was a desire to move in "our best society," without being quite sure what the *best* really was. Money, position, fashionable accomplishments, and elegant manners were most desirable things in her eyes, and she liked to associate with those who possessed them, often mistaking the false for the true, and admiring what was not admirable. Never forgetting that by birth she was a gentlewoman, she cultivated her aristocratic tastes and feelings, so that when the opportunity came she might be ready to take the place from which poverty now excluded her.

"My lady," as her friends called her, sincerely desired to be a genuine lady, and was so at heart, but had yet to learn that money cannot buy refinement of nature, that rank does not always confer nobility, and that true breeding makes itself felt in spite of external drawbacks.

"I want to ask a favor of you, mamma," Amy said, coming in, with an important air, one day.

"Well, little girl, what is it?" replied her mother, in whose eyes the stately young lady still remained "the baby."

"Our drawing class breaks up next week, and before the girls separate for the summer, I want to ask them out here for a day. They are wild to see the river, sketch the broken bridge, and copy some of the things they admire in my book. They have been very kind to me in many ways, and I am grateful, for they are all rich, and know I am poor, yet they never made any difference."

"Why should they?" and Mrs. March put the question with what the girls called her "Maria Theresa air."

"You know as well as I that it *does* make a difference with nearly every one, so don't ruffle up, like a dear, motherly hen, when your chickens get pecked by smarter birds; the ugly duckling turned out a swan, you know;" and Amy smiled without bitterness, for she possessed a happy temper and hopeful spirit.

Mrs. March laughed, and smoothed down her maternal pride as she asked,—

"Well, my swan, what is your plan?"

"I should like to ask the girls out to lunch next week, to take them a drive to the places they want to see, a row on the river, perhaps, and make a little artistic *fête* for them."

"That looks feasible. What do you want for lunch? Cake, sandwiches, fruit, and coffee will be all that is necessary, I suppose?"

"Oh dear, no! we must have cold tongue and chicken, French chocolate and ice-cream, besides. The girls are used to such things, and I want my lunch to be proper and elegant, though I *do* work for my living."

"How many young ladies are there?" asked her mother, beginning to look sober.

"Twelve or fourteen in the class, but I dare say they won't all come."

"Bless me, child, you will have to charter an omnibus to carry them about."

"Why, mother, how *can* you think of such a thing? Not more than six or eight will probably come, so I shall hire a beach-wagon, and borrow Mr. Laurence's cherry-bounce." (Hannah's pronunciation of *char-à-banc.*)

"All this will be expensive, Amy."

"Not very; I've calculated the cost, and I'll pay for it myself."

"Don't you think, dear, that as these girls are used to such things, and the best we can do will be nothing new, that some simpler plan would be pleasanter to them, as a change, if nothing more, and much better for us than buying or borrowing what we don't need, and attempting a style not in keeping with our circumstances?"

"If I can't have it as I like, I don't care to have it at all. I know that I can carry it out perfectly well, if you and the girls will help a little; and I don't see why I can't if I'm willing to pay for it," said Amy, with the decision which opposition was apt to change into obstinacy.

Mrs. March knew that experience was an excellent teacher, and when it was possible she left her children to learn alone the lessons which she would gladly have made easier, if they had not objected to taking advice as much as they did salts and senna.

"Very well, Amy; if your heart is set upon it, and you see your way through without too great an outlay of money, time, and temper, I'll say no more. Talk it over with the girls, and whichever way you decide, I'll do my best to help you."

"Thanks, mother; you are always *so* kind;" and away went Amy to lay her plan before her sisters.

Meg agreed at once, and promised her aid, gladly offering anything she possessed, from her little house itself to her very best salt-spoons. But Jo frowned upon the whole project, and would have nothing to do with it at first.

"Why in the world should you spend your money, worry your family, and turn the house upside down for a parcel of girls who don't care a sixpence for you? I thought you had too much pride and sense to truckle to any mortal woman just because she wears French boots and rides in a *coupé*," said Jo, who, being called from the tragical climax of her novel, was not in the best mood for social enterprises.

"I *don't* truckle, and I hate being patronized as much as you do!" returned Amy indignantly, for the two still jangled when such questions arose. "The girls do care for me, and I for them, and there's a great deal of kindness and sense and talent among them, in spite of what you call fashionable nonsense. You don't care to make people like you, to go into good society, and cultivate your manners and tastes. I do, and I mean to make the most of every chance that comes. *You* can go through the world with your elbows out and your nose in the air, and call it independence, if you like. That's not my way."

When Amy whetted her tongue and freed her mind she usually got the best of it, for she seldom failed to have common sense on her side, while Jo carried her love of liberty and hate of conventionalities to such an unlimited extent that she naturally found herself worsted in an argument. Amy's definition of Jo's idea of independence was such a good hit that both burst out laughing, and the discussion took a more amiable turn. Much against her will, Jo at length consented to sacrifice a day to Mrs. Grundy, and help her sister through what she regarded as "a nonsensical business."

The invitations were sent, nearly all accepted, and the following Monday was set apart for the grand event. Hannah was out of humor because her week's work was deranged, and prophesied that "ef the washin' and ironin' warn't done reg'lar nothin' would go well anywheres." This hitch in the mainspring of the domestic machinery had a bad effect upon the whole concern; but Amy's motto was "Nil desperandum," and having made up her mind what to do, she proceeded to do it in spite of all obstacles. To begin with, Hannah's cooking didn't turn out well: the chicken was tough, the tongue too salt, and the chocolate wouldn't froth properly. Then the cake and ice cost more than Amy expected, so did the wagon; and various other expenses, which seemed trifling at the outset, counted up rather alarmingly afterward. Beth got cold and took to her bed, Meg had an unusual number of callers to keep her at home, and Jo was in such a divided state of mind that her breakages, accidents, and mistakes were uncommonly numerous, serious, and trying.

"If it hadn't been for mother I never should have got through," as Amy declared afterward, and gratefully remembered when "the best joke of the season" was entirely forgotten by everybody else.

If it was not fair on Monday, the young ladies were to come on Tuesday,—an arrangement which aggravated Jo and Hannah to the last degree. On Monday morning the weather was in that undecided state which is more exasperating than a steady pour. It drizzled a little, shone a little, blew a little, and didn't make up its mind till it was too late for any one else to make up theirs. Amy was up at dawn, hustling people out of their beds and through their breakfasts, that the house might be got in order. The parlor struck her as looking uncommonly shabby; but without stopping to sigh for what she had not, she skilfully made the best of what she had, arranging chairs over the worn places in the carpet, covering stains on the walls with pictures framed in ivy, and filling up empty corners with home-made statuary, which gave an artistic air to the room, as did the lovely vases of flowers Jo scattered about.

The lunch looked charmingly; and as she surveyed it, she sincerely hoped it would taste well, and that the borrowed glass, china, and silver would get safely home again. The carriages were promised, Meg and mother were all ready to do the honors, Beth was able to help Hannah behind the scenes, Jo had engaged to be as lively and amiable as an absent mind, an aching head, and a very decided disapproval of everybody and everything would allow, and, as she wearily dressed, Amy cheered herself with anticipations of the happy moment, when, lunch safely over, she should drive away with her friends for an afternoon of artistic delights; for the "cherry-bounce" and the broken bridge were her strong points.

Then came two hours of suspense, during which she vibrated from parlor to porch, while public opinion varied like the weathercock. A smart shower at eleven had evidently quenched the enthusiasm of the young ladies who were to arrive at twelve, for nobody came; and at two the exhausted family sat down in a blaze of sunshine to consume the perishable portions of the feast, that nothing might be lost.

"No doubt about the weather to-day; they will certainly come, so we must fly round and be ready for them," said Amy, as the sun woke her next morning. She spoke briskly, but in her secret soul she wished she had said nothing about Tuesday, for her interest, like her cake, was getting a little stale.

"I can't get any lobsters, so you will have to do without salad to-day," said Mr. March, coming in half an hour later, with an expression of placid despair.

"Use the chicken, then; the toughness won't matter in a salad," advised his wife.

"Hannah left it on the kitchen-table a minute, and the kittens got at it. I'm very sorry, Amy," added Beth, who was still a patroness of cats.

"Then I *must* have a lobster, for tongue alone won't do," said Amy decidedly.

"Shall I rush into town and demand one?" asked Jo, with the magnanimity of a martyr.

"You'd come bringing it home under your arm, without any paper, just to try me. I'll go myself," answered Amy, whose temper was beginning to fail.

Shrouded in a thick veil and armed with a genteel travelling-basket, she departed, feeling that a cool drive would soothe her ruffled spirit, and fit her for the labors of the day. After some delay, the object of her desire was procured, likewise a bottle of dressing, to prevent further loss of time at home, and off she drove again, well pleased with her own forethought.

As the omnibus contained only one other passenger, a sleepy old lady, Amy pocketed her veil, and beguiled the tedium of the way by trying to find out where all her money had gone to. So busy was she with her card full of refractory figures that she did not observe a new-comer, who entered without stopping the vehicle, till a masculine voice said, "Good-morning, Miss March," and, looking up, she beheld one of Laurie's most elegant college friends. Fervently hoping that he would get out before she did, Amy utterly ignored the basket at her feet, and, congratulating herself that she had on her new travelling dress, returned the young man's greeting with her usual suavity and spirit.

They got on excellently; for Amy's chief care was soon set at rest by learning that the gentleman would leave first, and she was chatting away in a peculiarly lofty strain, when the old lady got out. In stumbling to the door, she upset the basket, and—oh, horror!—the lobster, in all its vulgar size and brilliancy, was revealed to the highborn eyes of a Tudor.

"By Jove, she's forgotten her dinner!" cried the unconscious youth, poking the scarlet monster into its place with his cane, and preparing to hand out the basket after the old lady.

"Please don't—it's—it's mine," murmured Amy, with a face nearly as red as her fish.

"Oh, really, I beg pardon; it's an uncommonly fine one, isn't it?" said Tudor, with great presence of mind, and an air of sober interest that did credit to his breeding.

Amy recovered herself in a breath, set her basket boldly on the seat, and said, laughing,—

"Don't you wish you were to have some of the salad he's to make, and to see the charming young ladies who are to eat it?"

Now that was tact, for two of the ruling foibles of the masculine mind were touched: the lobster was instantly surrounded by a halo of pleasing reminiscences, and curiosity about "the charming young ladies" diverted his mind from the comical mishap.

"I suppose he'll laugh and joke over it with Laurie, but I sha'n't see them; that's a comfort," thought Amy, as Tudor bowed and departed.

She did not mention this meeting at home (though she discovered that, thanks to the upset, her new dress was much damaged by the rivulets of dressing that meandered down the skirt), but went through with the preparations which now seemed more irksome than before; and at twelve o'clock all was ready again. Feeling that the neighbors were interested in her movements, she wished to efface the memory of yesterday's failure by a grand success to-day; so she ordered the "cherry-bounce," and drove away in state to meet and escort her guests to the banquet.

"There's the rumble, they're coming! I'll go into the porch to meet them; it looks hospitable, and I want the poor child to have a good time after all her trouble," said Mrs. March, suiting the action to the word. But after one glance, she retired, with an indescribable expression, for, looking quite lost in the big carriage, sat Amy and one young lady.

"Run, Beth, and help Hannah clear half the things off the table; it will be too absurd to put a luncheon for twelve before a single girl," cried Jo, hurrying away to the lower regions, too excited to stop even for a laugh.

In came Amy, quite calm, and delightfully cordial to the one guest who had kept her promise; the rest of the family, being of a dramatic turn, played their parts equally well, and Miss Eliott found them a most hilarious set; for it was impossible to entirely control the merriment which possessed them. The remodelled lunch being gayly partaken of, the studio and garden visited, and art discussed with enthusiasm, Amy ordered a buggy (alas for the elegant cherry-bounce!) and drove her friend quietly about the neighborhood till sunset, when "the party went out."

As she came walking in, looking very tired, but as composed as ever, she observed that every vestige of the unfortunate *fête* had disappeared, except a suspicious pucker about the corners of Jo's mouth.

"You've had a lovely afternoon for your drive, dear," said her mother, as respectfully as if the whole twelve had come.

"Miss Eliott is a very sweet girl, and seemed to enjoy herself, I thought," observed Beth, with unusual warmth.

"Could you spare me some of your cake? I really need some, I have so much company, and I can't make such delicious stuff as yours," asked Meg soberly.

"Take it all; I'm the only one here who likes sweet things, and it will mould before I can dispose of it," answered Amy, thinking with a sigh of the generous store she had laid in for such an end as this.

"It's a pity Laurie isn't here to help us," began Jo, as they sat down to ice-cream and salad for the second time in two days.

A warning look from her mother checked any further remarks, and the whole family ate in heroic silence, till Mr. March mildly observed, "Salad was one of the favorite dishes of the ancients, and Evelyn"—here a general explosion of laughter cut short the "history of sallets," to the great surprise of the learned gentleman.

"Bundle everything into a basket and send it to the Hummels: Germans like messes. I'm sick of the sight of this; and there's no reason you should all die of a surfeit because I've been a fool," cried Amy, wiping her eyes.

"I thought I *should* have died when I saw you two girls rattling about in the what-you-call-it, like two little kernels in a very big nutshell, and mother waiting in state to receive the throng," sighed Jo, quite spent with laughter.

"I'm very sorry you were disappointed, dear, but we all did our best to satisfy you," said Mrs. March, in a tone full of motherly regret.

"I *am* satisfied; I've done what I undertook, and it's not my fault that it failed; I comfort myself with that," said Amy, with a little quiver in her voice. "I thank you all very much for helping me, and I'll thank you still more if you won't allude to it for a month, at least."

No one did for several months; but the word "*fête*" always produced a general smile, and Laurie's birthday gift to Amy was a tiny coral lobster in the shape of a charm for her watch-guard.

IV

## LITERARY LESSONS.

FORTUNE suddenly smiled upon Jo, and dropped a good-luck penny in her path. Not a golden penny, exactly, but I doubt if half a million would have given more real happiness than did the little sum that came to her in this wise.

Every few weeks she would shut herself up in her room, put on her scribbling suit, and "fall into a vortex," as she expressed it, writing away at her novel with all her heart and soul, for till that was finished she could find no peace. Her "scribbling suit" consisted of a black woollen pinafore on which she could wipe her pen at will, and a cap of the same material, adorned with a cheerful red bow, into which she bundled her hair when the decks were cleared for action. This cap was a beacon to the inquiring eyes of her family, who during these periods kept their distance, merely popping in their heads semi-occasionally, to ask, with interest, "Does genius burn, Jo?" They did not always venture even to ask this question, but took an observation of the cap, and judged accordingly. If this expressive article of dress was drawn low upon the forehead, it was a sign that hard work was going on; in exciting moments it was pushed rakishly askew; and when despair seized the author it was plucked wholly off, and cast upon the floor. At such times the intruder silently withdrew; and not until the red bow was seen gayly erect upon the gifted brow, did any one dare address Jo.

She did not think herself a genius by any means; but when the writing fit came on, she gave herself up to it with entire abandon, and led a blissful life, unconscious of want, care, or bad weather, while she sat safe and happy in an imaginary world, full of friends almost as real and dear to her as any in the flesh. Sleep forsook her eyes, meals stood untasted, day and night were all too short to enjoy the happiness which blessed her only at such times, and made these hours worth living, even if they bore no other fruit. The divine afflatus usually lasted a week or two, and then she emerged from her "vortex," hungry, sleepy, cross, or despondent.

She was just recovering from one of these attacks when she was prevailed upon to escort Miss Crocker to a lecture, and in return for her virtue was rewarded with a new idea. It was a People's Course, the lecture on the Pyramids, and Jo rather wondered at the choice of such a subject for such an audience, but took it for granted that some great social evil would be remedied or some great want supplied by unfolding the glories of the Pharaohs to an audience whose thoughts were busy with the price of coal and flour, and whose lives were spent in trying to solve harder riddles than that of the Sphinx.

They were early; and while Miss Crocker set the heel of her stocking, Jo amused herself by examining the faces of the people who occupied the seat with them. On her left were two matrons, with massive foreheads, and bonnets to match, discussing Woman's Rights and making tatting. Beyond sat a pair of humble lovers, artlessly holding each other by the hand, a sombre spinster eating peppermints out of a paper bag, and an old gentleman taking his preparatory nap behind a yellow bandanna. On her right, her only neighbor was a studious-looking lad absorbed in a newspaper.

It was a pictorial sheet, and Jo examined the work of art nearest her, idly wondering what unfortuitous concatenation of circumstances needed the melodramatic illustration of an Indian in full war costume, tumbling over a precipice with a wolf at his throat, while two infuriated young gentlemen, with unnaturally small feet and big eyes, were stabbing each other close by, and a dishevelled female was flying away in the background with her mouth wide open. Pausing to turn a page, the lad saw her looking, and, with boyish good-nature, offered half his paper, saying bluntly, "Want to read it? That's a first-rate story."

Jo accepted it with a smile, for she had never outgrown her liking for lads, and soon found herself involved in the usual labyrinth of love, mystery, and murder, for the story belonged to that class of light literature in which the passions have a holiday, and when the author's invention fails, a grand catastrophe clears the stage of one half the *dramatis personæ*, leaving the other half to exult over their downfall.

"Prime, isn't it?" asked the boy, as her eye went down the last paragraph of her portion.

"I think you and I could do as well as that if we tried," returned Jo, amused at his admiration of the trash.

"I should think I was a pretty lucky chap if I could. She makes a good living out of such stories, they say;" and he pointed to the name of Mrs. S. L. A. N. G. Northbury, under the title of the tale.

"Do you know her?" asked Jo, with sudden interest.

"No; but I read all her pieces, and I know a fellow who works in the office where this paper is printed."

"Do you say she makes a good living out of stories like this?" and Jo looked more respectfully at the agitated group and thickly-sprinkled exclamation-points that adorned the page.

"Guess she does! She knows just what folks like, and gets paid well for writing it."

Here the lecture began, but Jo heard very little of it, for while Prof. Sands was prosing away about Belzoni, Cheops, scarabei, and hieroglyphics, she was covertly taking down the address of the paper, and boldly resolving to try for the hundred-dollar prize offered in its columns for a sensational story. By the time the lecture ended and the audience awoke, she had built up a splendid fortune for herself (not the first founded upon paper), and was already deep in the concoction of her story, being unable to decide whether the duel should come before the elopement or after the murder.

She said nothing of her plan at home, but fell to work next day, much to the disquiet of her mother, who always looked a little anxious when "genius took to burning." Jo had never tried this style before, contenting herself with very mild romances for the "Spread Eagle." Her theatrical experience and miscellaneous reading were of service now, for they gave her some idea of dramatic effect, and supplied plot, language, and costumes. Her story was as full of desperation and despair as her limited acquaintance with those uncomfortable emotions enabled her to make it, and, having located it in Lisbon, she wound up with an earthquake, as a striking and appropriate *dénouement*. The manuscript was privately despatched, accompanied by a note, modestly saying that if the tale didn't get the prize, which the writer hardly dared expect, she would be very glad to receive any sum it might be considered worth.

Six weeks is a long time to wait, and a still longer time for a girl to keep a secret; but Jo did both, and was just beginning to give up all hope of ever seeing her manuscript again, when a letter arrived which almost took her breath away; for on opening it, a check for a hundred dollars fell into her lap. For a minute she stared at it as if it had been a snake, then she read her letter and began to cry. If the amiable gentleman who wrote that kindly note could have known what intense happiness he was giving a fellow-creature, I think he would devote his leisure hours, if he has any, to that amusement; for Jo valued the letter more than the money, because it was encouraging; and after years of effort it was *so* pleasant to find that she had learned to do something, though it was only to write a sensation story.

A prouder young woman was seldom seen than she, when, having composed herself, she electrified the family by appearing before them with the letter in one hand, the check in the other, announcing that she had won the prize. Of course there was a great jubilee, and when the story came every one read and praised it; though after her father had told her that the language was good, the romance fresh and hearty, and the tragedy quite thrilling, he shook his head, and said in his unworldly way,—

"You can do better than this, Jo. Aim at the highest, and never mind the money."

"*I* think the money is the best part of it. What *will* you do with such a fortune?" asked Amy, regarding the magic slip of paper with a reverential eye.

"Send Beth and mother to the seaside for a month or two," answered Jo promptly.

"Oh, how splendid! No, I can't do it, dear, it would be so selfish," cried Beth, who had clapped her thin hands, and taken a long breath, as if pining for fresh ocean-breezes; then stopped herself, and motioned away the check which her sister waved before her.

"Ah, but you shall go, I've set my heart on it; that's what I tried for, and that's why I succeeded. I never get on when I think of myself alone, so it will help me to work for you, don't you see? Besides, Marmee needs the change, and she won't leave you, so you *must* go. Won't it be fun to see you come home plump and rosy again? Hurrah for Dr. Jo, who always cures her patients!"

To the sea side they went, after much discussion; and though Beth didn't come home as plump and rosy as could be desired, she was much better, while Mrs. March declared she felt ten years younger; so Jo was satisfied with the investment of her prize money, and fell to work with a cheery spirit, bent on earning more of those delightful checks. She did earn several that year, and began to feel herself a power in the house; for by the magic of a pen, her "rubbish" turned into comforts for them all. "The Duke's Daughter" paid the butcher's bill, "A Phantom Hand" put down a new carpet, and the "Curse of the Coventrys" proved the blessing of the Marches in the way of groceries and gowns.

Wealth is certainly a most desirable thing, but poverty has its sunny side, and one of the sweet uses of adversity is the genuine satisfaction which comes from hearty work of head or hand; and to the inspiration of necessity, we owe half the wise, beautiful, and useful blessings of the world. Jo enjoyed a taste of this satisfaction, and ceased to envy richer girls, taking great comfort in the knowledge that she could supply her own wants, and need ask no one for a penny.

Little notice was taken of her stories, but they found a market; and, encouraged by this fact, she resolved to make a bold stroke for fame and fortune. Having copied her novel for the fourth time, read it to all her confidential friends, and submitted it with fear and trembling to three publishers, she at last disposed of it, on condition that she would cut it down one third, and omit all the parts which she particularly admired.

"Now I must either bundle it back into my tin-kitchen to mould, pay for printing it myself, or chop it up to suit purchasers, and get what I can for it. Fame is a very good thing to have in the house, but cash is more convenient; so I wish to take the sense of the meeting on this important subject," said Jo, calling a family council.

"Don't spoil your book, my girl, for there is more in it than you know, and the idea is well worked out. Let it wait and ripen," was her father's advice; and he practised as he preached, having waited patiently thirty years for fruit of his own to ripen, and being in no haste to gather it, even now, when it was sweet and mellow.

"It seems to me that Jo will profit more by making the trial than by waiting," said Mrs. March. "Criticism is the best test of such work, for it will show her both unsuspected merits and faults, and help her to do better next time. We are too partial; but the praise and blame of outsiders will prove useful, even if she gets but little money."

"Yes," said Jo, knitting her brows, "that's just it; I've been fussing over the thing so long, I really don't know whether it's good, bad, or indifferent. It will be a great help to have cool, impartial persons take a look at it, and tell me what they think of it."

"I wouldn't leave out a word of it; you'll spoil it if you do, for the interest of the story is more in the minds than in the actions of the people, and it will be all a muddle if you don't explain as you go on," said Meg, who firmly believed that this book was the most remarkable novel ever written.

"But Mr. Allen says, 'Leave out the explanations, make it brief and dramatic, and let the characters tell the story,'" interrupted Jo, turning to the publisher's note.

"Do as he tells you; he knows what will sell, and we don't. Make a good, popular book, and get as much money as you can. By and by, when, you've got a name, you can afford to digress, and have philosophical and metaphysical people in your novels," said Amy, who took a strictly practical view of the subject.

"Well," said Jo, laughing, "if my people *are* 'philosophical and metaphysical,' it isn't my fault, for I know nothing about such things, except what I hear father say, sometimes. If I've got some of his wise ideas jumbled up with my romance, so much the better for me. Now, Beth, what do you say?"

"I should so like to see it printed *soon*," was all Beth said, and smiled in saying it; but there was an unconscious emphasis on the last word, and a wistful look in the eyes that never lost their childlike candor, which chilled Jo's heart, for a minute, with a foreboding fear, and decided her to make her little venture "soon."

So, with Spartan firmness, the young authoress laid her first-born on her table, and chopped it up as ruthlessly as any ogre. In the hope of pleasing every one, she took every one's advice; and, like the old man and his donkey in the fable, suited nobody.

Her father liked the metaphysical streak which had unconsciously got into it; so that was allowed to remain, though she had her doubts about it. Her mother thought that there *was* a trifle too much description; out, therefore, it nearly all came, and with it many necessary links in the story. Meg admired the tragedy; so Jo piled up the agony to suit her, while Amy objected to the fun, and, with the best intentions in life, Jo quenched the sprightly scenes which relieved the sombre character of the story. Then, to complete the ruin, she cut it down one third, and confidingly sent the poor little romance, like a picked robin, out into the big, busy world, to try its fate.

Well, it was printed, and she got three hundred dollars for it; likewise plenty of praise and blame, both so much greater than she expected that she was thrown into a state of bewilderment, from which it took her some time to recover.

"You said, mother, that criticism would help me; but how can it, when it's so contradictory that I don't know whether I've written a promising book or broken all the ten commandments?" cried poor Jo, turning over a heap of notices, the perusal of which filled her with pride and joy one minute, wrath and dire dismay the next. "This man says 'An exquisite book, full of truth, beauty, and earnestness; all is sweet, pure, and healthy,'" continued the perplexed authoress. "The next, 'The theory of the book is bad, full of morbid fancies, spiritualistic ideas, and unnatural characters.' Now, as I had no theory of any kind, don't believe in Spiritualism, and copied my characters from life, I don't see how this critic *can* be right. Another says, 'It's one of the best American novels which has appeared for years' (I know better than that); and the next asserts that 'though it is original, and written with great force and feeling, it is a dangerous book.' 'Tisn't! Some make fun of it, some over-praise, and nearly all insist that I had a deep theory to expound, when I only wrote it for the pleasure and the money. I wish I'd printed it whole or not at all, for I do hate to be so misjudged."

Her family and friends administered comfort and commendation liberally; yet it was a hard time for sensitive, high-spirited Jo, who meant so well, and had apparently done so ill. But it did her good, for those whose opinion had real value gave her the criticism which is an author's best education; and when the first soreness was over, she could laugh at her poor little book, yet believe in it still, and feel herself the wiser and stronger for the buffeting she had received.

"Not being a genius, like Keats, it won't kill me," she said stoutly; "and I've got the joke on my side, after all; for the parts that were taken straight out of real life are denounced as impossible and absurd, and the scenes that I made up out of my own silly head are pronounced 'charmingly natural, tender, and true.' So I'll comfort myself with that; and when I'm ready, I'll up again and take another."

# V

## DOMESTIC EXPERIENCES.

LIKE most other young matrons, Meg began her married life with the determination to be a model housekeeper. John should find home a paradise; he should always see a smiling face, should fare sumptuously every day, and never know the loss of a button. She brought so much love, energy, and cheerfulness to the work that she could not but succeed, in spite of some obstacles. Her paradise was not a tranquil one; for the little woman fussed, was over-anxious to please, and bustled about like a true Martha, cumbered with many cares. She was too tired, sometimes, even to smile; John grew dyspeptic after a course of dainty dishes, and ungratefully demanded plain fare. As for buttons, she soon learned to wonder where they went, to shake her head over the carelessness of men, and to threaten to make him sew them on himself, and then see if *his* work would stand impatient tugs and clumsy fingers any better than hers.

They were very happy, even after they discovered that they couldn't live on love alone. John did not find Meg's beauty diminished, though she beamed at him from behind the familiar coffee-pot; nor did Meg miss any of the romance from the daily parting, when her husband followed up his kiss with the tender inquiry, "Shall I send home veal or mutton for dinner, darling?" The little house ceased to be a glorified bower, but it became a home, and the young couple soon felt that it was a change for the better. At first they played keep-house, and frolicked over it like children; then John took steadily to business, feeling the cares of the head of a family upon his shoulders; and Meg laid by her cambric wrappers, put on a big apron, and fell to work, as before said, with more energy than discretion.

While the cooking mania lasted she went through Mrs. Cornelius's Receipt Book as if it were a mathematical exercise, working out the problems with patience and care. Sometimes her family were invited in to help eat up a too bounteous feast of successes, or Lotty would be privately despatched with a batch of failures, which were to be concealed from all eyes in the convenient stomachs of the little Hummels. An evening with John over the account-books usually produced a temporary lull in the culinary enthusiasm, and a frugal fit would ensue, during which the poor man was put through a course of bread-pudding, hash, and warmed-over coffee, which tried his soul, although he bore it with praiseworthy fortitude. Before the golden mean was found, however, Meg added to her domestic possessions what young couples seldom get on long without,—a family jar.

Fired with a housewifely wish to see her store-room stocked with home-made preserves, she undertook to put up her own currant jelly. John was requested to order home a dozen or so of little pots, and an extra quantity of sugar, for their own currants were ripe, and were to be attended to at once. As John firmly believed that "my wife" was equal to anything, and took a natural pride in her skill, he resolved that she should be gratified, and their only crop of fruit laid by in a most pleasing form for winter use. Home came four dozen delightful little pots, half a barrel of sugar, and a small boy to pick the currants for her. With her pretty hair tucked into a little cap, arms bared to the elbow, and a checked apron which had a coquettish look in spite of the bib, the young housewife fell to work, feeling no doubts about her success; for hadn't she seen Hannah do it hundreds of times? The array of pots rather amazed her at first, but John was so fond of jelly, and the nice little jars would look so well on the top shelf, that Meg resolved to fill them all, and spent a long day picking, boiling, straining, and fussing over her jelly. She did her best; she asked advice of Mrs. Cornelius; she racked her brain to remember what Hannah did that she had left undone; she reboiled, resugared, and restrained, but that dreadful stuff wouldn't "*jell.*"

She longed to run home, bib and all, and ask mother to lend a hand, but John and she had agreed that they would never annoy any one with their private worries, experiments, or quarrels. They had laughed over that last word as if the idea it suggested was a most preposterous one; but they had held to their resolve, and whenever they could get on without help they did so, and no one interfered, for Mrs. March had advised the plan. So Meg wrestled alone with the refractory sweetmeats all that hot summer day, and at five o'clock sat down in her topsy-turvy kitchen, wrung her bedaubed hands, lifted up her voice and wept.

Now, in the first flush of the new life, she had often said,—

"My husband shall always feel free to bring a friend home whenever he likes. I shall always be prepared; there shall be no flurry, no scolding, no discomfort, but a neat house, a cheerful wife, and a good dinner. John, dear, never stop to ask my leave, invite whom you please, and be sure of a welcome from me."

How charming that was, to be sure! John quite glowed with pride to hear her say it, and felt what a blessed thing it was to have a superior wife. But, although they had had company from time to time, it never happened to be unexpected, and Meg had never had an opportunity to distinguish herself till now. It always happens so in this vale of tears; there is an inevitability about such things which we can only wonder at, deplore, and bear as we best can.

If John had not forgotten all about the jelly, it really would have been unpardonable in him to choose that day, of all the days in the year, to bring a friend home to dinner unexpectedly. Congratulating himself that a handsome repast had been ordered that morning, feeling sure that it would be ready to the minute, and indulging in pleasant anticipations of the charming effect it would produce, when his pretty wife came running out to meet him, he escorted his friend to his mansion, with the irrepressible satisfaction of a young host and husband.

It is a world of disappointments, as John discovered when he reached the Dove-cote. The front door usually stood hospitably open; now it was not only shut, but locked, and yesterday's mud still adorned the steps. The parlor-windows were closed and curtained, no picture of the pretty wife sewing on the piazza, in white, with a distracting little bow in her hair, or a bright-eyed hostess, smiling a shy welcome as she greeted her guest. Nothing of the sort, for not a soul appeared, but a sanguinary-looking boy asleep under the currant-bushes.

"I'm afraid something has happened. Step into the garden, Scott, while I look up Mrs. Brooke," said John, alarmed at the silence and solitude.

Round the house he hurried, led by a pungent smell of burnt sugar, and Mr. Scott strolled after him, with a queer look on his face. He paused discreetly at a distance when Brooke disappeared; but he could both see and hear, and, being a bachelor, enjoyed the prospect mightily.

In the kitchen reigned confusion and despair; one edition of jelly was trickled from pot to pot, another lay upon the floor, and a third was burning gayly on the stove. Lotty, with Teutonic phlegm, was calmly eating bread and currant wine, for the jelly was still in a hopelessly liquid state, while Mrs. Brooke, with her apron over her head, sat sobbing dismally.

"My dearest girl, what is the matter?" cried John, rushing in, with awful visions of scalded hands, sudden news of affliction, and secret consternation at the thought of the guest in the garden.

"O John, I *am* so tired and hot and cross and worried! I've been at it till I'm all worn out. Do come and help me or I *shall* die!" and the exhausted housewife cast herself upon his breast, giving him a sweet welcome in every sense of the word, for her pinafore had been baptized at the same time as the floor.

"What worries you, dear? Has anything dreadful happened?" asked the anxious John, tenderly kissing the crown of the little cap, which was all askew.

"Yes," sobbed Meg despairingly.

"Tell me quick, then. Don't cry, I can bear anything better than that. Out with it, love."

"The—the jelly won't jell and I don't know what to do!"

John Brooke laughed then as he never dared to laugh afterward; and the derisive Scott smiled involuntarily as he heard the hearty peal, which put the finishing stroke to poor Meg's woe.

"Is that all? Fling it out of window, and don't bother any more about it. I'll buy you quarts if you want it; but for heaven's sake don't have hysterics, for I've brought Jack Scott home to dinner, and—"

John got no further, for Meg cast him off, and clasped her hands with a tragic gesture as she fell into a chair, exclaiming in a tone of mingled indignation, reproach, and dismay,—

"A man to dinner, and everything in a mess! John Brooke, how *could* you do such a thing?"

"Hush, he's in the garden! I forgot the confounded jelly, but it can't be helped now," said John, surveying the prospect with an anxious eye.

"You ought to have sent word, or told me this morning, and you ought to have remembered how busy I was," continued Meg petulantly; for even turtle-doves will peck when ruffled.

"I didn't know it this morning, and there was no time to send word, for I met him on the way out. I never thought of asking leave, when you have always told me to do as I liked. I never tried it before, and hang me if I ever do again!" added John, with an aggrieved air.

"I should hope not! Take him away at once; I can't see him, and there isn't any dinner."

"Well, I like that! Where's the beef and vegetables I sent home, and the pudding you promised?" cried John, rushing to the larder.

"I hadn't time to cook anything; I meant to dine at mother's. I'm sorry, but I was *so* busy;" and Meg's tears began again.

John was a mild man, but he was human; and after a long day's work, to come home tired, hungry, and hopeful, to find a chaotic house, an empty table, and a cross wife was not exactly conducive to repose of mind or manner. He restrained himself, however, and the little squall would have blown over, but for one unlucky word.

"It's a scrape, I acknowledge; but if you will lend a hand, we'll pull through, and have a good time yet. Don't cry, dear, but just exert yourself a bit, and knock us up something to eat. We're both as hungry as hunters, so we sha'n't mind what it is. Give us the cold meat, and bread and cheese; we won't ask for jelly."

He meant it for a good-natured joke; but that one word sealed his fate. Meg thought it was *too* cruel to hint about her sad failure, and the last atom of patience vanished as he spoke.

"You must get yourself out of the scrape as you can; I'm too used up to 'exert' myself for any one. It's like a man to propose a bone and vulgar bread and cheese for company. I won't have anything of the sort in my house. Take that Scott up to mother's, and tell him I'm away, sick, dead,—anything. I won't see him, and you two can laugh at me and my jelly as much as you like: you won't have anything else here;" and having delivered her defiance all in one breath, Meg cast away her pinafore, and precipitately left the field to bemoan herself in her own room.

What those two creatures did in her absence, she never knew; but Mr. Scott was not taken "up to mother's," and when Meg descended, after they had strolled away together, she found traces of a promiscuous lunch which filled her with horror. Lotty reported that they had eaten "a much, and greatly laughed, and the master bid her throw away all the sweet stuff, and hide the pots."

Meg longed to go and tell mother; but a sense of shame at her own short-comings, of loyalty to John, "who might be cruel, but nobody should know it," restrained her; and after a summary clearing up, she dressed herself prettily, and sat down to wait for John to come and be forgiven.

Unfortunately, John didn't come, not seeing the matter in that light. He had carried it off as a good joke with Scott, excused his little wife as well as he could, and played the host so hospitably that his friend enjoyed the impromptu dinner, and promised to come again. But John was angry, though he did not show it; he felt that Meg had got him into a scrape, and then deserted him in his hour of need. "It wasn't fair to tell a man to bring folks home any time, with perfect freedom, and when he took you at your word, to flame up and blame him, and leave him in the lurch, to be laughed at or pitied. No, by George, it wasn't! and Meg must know it." He had fumed inwardly during the feast, but when the flurry was over, and he strolled home, after seeing Scott off, a milder mood came over him. "Poor little thing! it was hard upon her when she tried so heartily to please me. She was wrong, of course, but then she was young. I must be patient and teach her." He hoped she had not gone home—he hated gossip and interference. For a minute he was ruffled again at the mere thought of it; and then the fear that Meg would cry herself sick softened his heart, and sent him on at a quicker pace, resolving to be calm and kind, but firm, quite firm, and show her where she had failed in her duty to her spouse.

Meg likewise resolved to be "calm and kind, but firm," and show *him* his duty. She longed to run to meet him, and beg pardon, and be kissed and comforted, as she was sure of being; but, of course, she did nothing of the sort, and when she saw John coming, began to hum quite naturally, as she rocked and sewed, like a lady of leisure in her best parlor.

John was a little disappointed not to find a tender Niobe; but, feeling that his dignity demanded the first apology, he made none, only came leisurely in, and laid himself upon the sofa, with the singularly relevant remark,—

"We are going to have a new moon, my dear."

"I've no objection," was Meg's equally soothing remark.

A few other topics of general interest were introduced by Mr. Brooke, and wet-blanketed by Mrs. Brooke, and conversation languished. John went to one window, unfolded his paper, and wrapped himself in it, figuratively speaking. Meg went to the other window, and sewed as if new rosettes for her slippers were among the necessaries of life. Neither spoke; both looked quite "calm and firm," and both felt desperately uncomfortable.

"Oh dear," thought Meg, "married life is very trying, and does need infinite patience, as well as love, as mother says." The word "mother" suggested other maternal counsels, given long ago, and received with unbelieving protests.

"John is a good man, but he has his faults, and you must learn to see and bear with them, remembering your own. He is very decided, but never will be obstinate, if you reason kindly, not oppose impatiently. He is very accurate, and particular about the truth—a good trait, though you call him 'fussy.' Never deceive him by look or word, Meg, and he will give you the confidence you deserve, the support you need. He has a temper, not like ours,—one flash, and then all over,—but the white, still anger, that is seldom stirred, but once kindled, is hard to quench. Be careful, very careful, not to wake this anger against yourself, for peace and happiness depend on keeping his respect. Watch yourself, be the first to ask pardon if you both err, and guard against the little piques, misunderstandings, and hasty words that often pave the way for bitter sorrow and regret."

These words came back to Meg, as she sat sewing in the sunset, especially the last. This was the first serious disagreement; her own hasty speeches sounded both silly and unkind, as she recalled them, her own anger looked childish now, and thoughts of poor John coming home to such a scene quite melted her heart. She glanced at him with tears in her eyes, but he did not see them; she put down her work and got up, thinking, "I *will* be the first to say, 'Forgive me,'" but he did not seem to hear her; she went very slowly across the room, for pride was hard to swallow, and stood by him, but he did not turn his head. For a minute she felt as if she really couldn't do it; then came the thought, "This is the beginning, I'll do my part, and have nothing to reproach myself with," and stooping down, she softly kissed her husband on the forehead. Of course that settled it; the penitent kiss was better than a world of words, and John had her on his knee in a minute, saying tenderly,—

"It was too bad to laugh at the poor little jelly-pots. Forgive me, dear, I never will again!"

But he did, oh bless you, yes, hundreds of times, and so did Meg, both declaring that it was the sweetest jelly they ever made; for family peace was preserved in that little family jar.

After this, Meg had Mr. Scott to dinner by special invitation, and served him up a pleasant feast without a cooked wife for the first course; on which occasion she was so gay and gracious, and made everything go off so charmingly, that Mr. Scott told John he was a happy fellow, and shook his head over the hardships of bachelorhood all the way home.

In the autumn, new trials and experiences came to Meg. Sallie Moffat renewed her friendship, was always running out for a dish of gossip at the little house, or inviting "that poor dear" to come in and spend the day at the big house. It was pleasant, for in dull weather Meg often felt lonely; all were busy at home, John absent till night, and nothing to do but sew, or read, or potter about. So it naturally fell out that Meg got into the way of gadding and gossiping with her friend. Seeing Sallie's pretty things made her long for such, and pity herself because she had not got them. Sallie was very kind, and often offered her the coveted trifles; but Meg declined them, knowing that John wouldn't like it; and then this foolish little woman went and did what John disliked infinitely worse.

She knew her husband's income, and she loved to feel that he trusted her, not only with his happiness, but what some men seem to value more,—his money. She knew where it was, was free to take what she liked, and all he asked was that she should keep account of every penny, pay bills once a month, and remember that she was a poor man's wife. Till now, she had done well, been prudent and exact, kept her little account-books neatly, and showed them to him monthly without fear. But that autumn the serpent got into Meg's paradise, and tempted her, like many a modern Eve, not with apples, but with dress. Meg didn't like to be pitied and made to feel poor; it irritated her, but she was ashamed to confess it, and now and then she tried to console herself by buying something pretty, so that Sallie needn't think she had to economize. She always felt wicked after it, for the pretty things were seldom necessaries; but then they cost so little, it wasn't worth worrying about; so the trifles increased unconsciously, and in the shopping excursions she was no longer a passive looker-on.

But the trifles cost more than one would imagine; and when she cast up her accounts at the end of the month, the sum total rather scared her. John was busy that month, and left the bills to her; the next month he was absent; but the third he had a grand quarterly settling up, and Meg never forgot it. A few days before she had done a dreadful thing, and it weighed upon her conscience. Sallie had been buying silks, and Meg longed for a new one,—just a handsome light one for parties, her black silk was so common, and thin things for evening wear were only proper for girls. Aunt March usually gave the sisters a present of twenty-five dollars apiece at New Year; that was only a month to wait, and here was a lovely violet silk going at a bargain, and she had the money, if she only dared to take it. John always said what was his was hers; but would he think it right to spend not only the prospective five-and-twenty, but another five-and-twenty out of the household fund? That was the question. Sallie had urged her to do it, had offered to loan the money, and with the best intentions in life, had tempted Meg beyond her strength. In an evil moment the shopman held up the lovely, shimmering folds, and said, "A bargain, I assure you, ma'am." She answered, "I'll take it;" and it was cut off and paid for, and Sallie had exulted, and she had laughed as if it were a thing of no consequence, and driven away, feeling as if she had stolen something, and the police were after her.

When she got home, she tried to assuage the pangs of remorse by spreading forth the lovely silk; but it looked less silvery now, didn't become her, after all, and the words "fifty dollars" seemed stamped like a pattern down each breadth. She put it away; but it haunted her, not delightfully, as a new dress should, but dreadfully, like the ghost of a folly that was not easily laid. When John got out his books that night, Meg's heart sank, and for the first time in her married life, she was afraid of her husband. The kind, brown eyes looked as if they could be stern; and though he was unusually merry, she fancied he had found her out, but didn't mean to let her know it. The house-bills were all paid, the books all in order. John had praised her, and was undoing the old pocket-book which they called the "bank," when Meg, knowing that it was quite empty, stopped his hand, saying nervously,—

"You haven't seen my private expense book yet."

John never asked to see it; but she always insisted on his doing so, and used to enjoy his masculine amazement at the queer things women wanted, and made him guess what "piping" was, demand fiercely the meaning of a "hug-me-tight," or wonder how a little thing composed of three rosebuds, a bit of velvet, and a pair of strings, could possibly be a bonnet, and cost five or six dollars. That night he looked as if he would like the fun of quizzing her figures and pretending to be horrified at her extravagance, as he often did, being particularly proud of his prudent wife.

The little book was brought slowly out, and laid down before him. Meg got behind his chair under pretence of smoothing the wrinkles out of his tired forehead, and standing there, she said, with her panic increasing with every word,—

"John, dear, I'm ashamed to show you my book, for I've really been dreadfully extravagant lately. I go about so much I must have things, you know, and Sallie advised my getting it, so I did; and my New-Year's money will partly pay for it: but I was sorry after I'd done it, for I knew you'd think it wrong in me."

John laughed, and drew her round beside him, saying good-humoredly, "Don't go and hide. I won't beat you if you *have* got a pair of killing boots; I'm rather proud of my wife's feet, and don't mind if she does pay eight or nine dollars for her boots, if they are good ones."

That had been one of her last "trifles," and John's eye had fallen on it as he spoke. "Oh, what *will* he say when he comes to that awful fifty dollars!" thought Meg, with a shiver.

"It's worse than boots, it's a silk dress," she said, with the calmness of desperation, for she wanted the worst over.

"Well, dear, what is the 'dem'd total,' as Mr. Mantalini says?"

That didn't sound like John, and she knew he was looking up at her with the straightforward look that she had always been ready to meet and answer with one as frank till now. She turned the page and her head at the same time, pointing to the sum which would have been bad enough without the fifty, but which was appalling to her with that added. For a minute the room was very still; then John said slowly,—but she could feel it cost him an effort to express no displeasure,—

"Well, I don't know that fifty is much for a dress, with all the furbelows and notions you have to have to finish it off these days."

"It isn't made or trimmed," sighed Meg faintly, for a sudden recollection of the cost still to be incurred quite overwhelmed her.

"Twenty-five yards of silk seems a good deal to cover one small woman, but I've no doubt my wife will look as fine as Ned Moffat's when she gets it on," said John dryly.

"I know you are angry, John, but I can't help it. I don't mean to waste your money, and I didn't think those little things would count up so. I can't resist them when I see Sallie buying all she wants, and pitying me because I don't. I try to be contented, but it is hard, and I'm tired of being poor."

The last words were spoken so low she thought he did not hear them, but he did, and they wounded him deeply, for he had denied himself many pleasures for Meg's sake. She could have bitten her tongue out the minute she had said it, for John pushed the books away, and got up, saying, with a little quiver in his voice, "I was afraid of this; I do my best, Meg." If he had scolded her, or even shaken her, it would not have broken her heart like those few words. She ran to him and held him close, crying, with repentant tears, "O John, my dear, kind, hard-working boy, I didn't mean it! It was so wicked, so untrue and ungrateful, how could I say it! Oh, how could I say it!"

He was very kind, forgave her readily, and did not utter one reproach; but Meg knew that she had done and said a thing which would not be forgotten soon, although he might never allude to it again. She had promised to love him for better for worse; and then she, his wife, had reproached him with his poverty, after spending his earnings recklessly. It was dreadful; and the worst of it was John went on so quietly afterward, just as if nothing had happened, except that he stayed in town later, and worked at night when she had gone to cry herself to sleep. A week of remorse nearly made Meg sick; and the discovery that John had countermanded the order for his new great-coat reduced her to a state of despair which was pathetic to behold. He had simply said, in answer to her surprised inquiries as to the change, "I can't afford it, my dear."

Meg said no more, but a few minutes after he found her in the hall, with her face buried in the old great-coat, crying as if her heart would break.

They had a long talk that night, and Meg learned to love her husband better for his poverty, because it seemed to have made a man of him, given him the strength and courage to fight his own way, and taught him a tender patience with which to bear and comfort the natural longings and failures of those he loved.

Next day she put her pride in her pocket, went to Sallie, told the truth, and asked her to buy the silk as a favor. The good-natured Mrs. Moffat willingly did so, and had the delicacy not to make her a present of it immediately afterward. Then Meg ordered home the great-coat, and, when John arrived, she put it on, and asked him how he liked her new silk gown. One can imagine what answer he made, how he received his present, and what a blissful state of things ensued. John came home early, Meg gadded no more; and that great-coat was put on in the morning by a very happy husband, and taken off at night by a most devoted little wife. So the year rolled round, and at midsummer there came to Meg a new experience,—the deepest and tenderest of a woman's life.

Laurie came sneaking into the kitchen of the Dove-cote, one Saturday, with an excited face, and was received with the clash of cymbals; for Hannah clapped her hands with a saucepan in one and the cover in the other.

"How's the little mamma? Where is everybody? Why didn't you tell me before I came home?" began Laurie, in a loud whisper.

"Happy as a queen, the dear! Every soul of 'em is upstairs a worshipin'; we didn't want no hurrycanes round. Now you go into the parlor, and I'll send 'em down to you," with which somewhat involved reply Hannah vanished, chuckling ecstatically.

Presently Jo appeared, proudly bearing a flannel bundle laid forth upon a large pillow. Jo's face was very sober, but her eyes twinkled, and there was an odd sound in her voice of repressed emotion of some sort.

"Shut your eyes and hold out your arms," she said invitingly.

Laurie backed precipitately into a corner, and put his hands behind him with an imploring gesture: "No, thank you, I'd rather not. I shall drop it or smash it, as sure as fate."

"Then you sha'n't see your nevvy," said Jo decidedly, turning as if to go.

"I will, I will! only you must be responsible for damages;" and, obeying orders, Laurie heroically shut his eyes while something was put into his arms. A peal of laughter from Jo, Amy, Mrs. March, Hannah, and John caused him to open them the next minute, to find himself invested with two babies instead of one.

No wonder they laughed, for the expression of his face was droll enough to convulse a Quaker, as he stood and stared wildly from the unconscious innocents to the hilarious spectators, with such dismay that Jo sat down on the floor and screamed.

"Twins, by Jupiter!" was all he said for a minute; then, turning to the women with an appealing look that was comically piteous, he added, "Take 'em quick, somebody! I'm going to laugh, and I shall drop 'em."

John rescued his babies, and marched up and down, with one on each arm, as if already initiated into the mysteries of baby-tending, while Laurie laughed till the tears ran down his cheeks.

"It's the best joke of the season, isn't it? I wouldn't have you told, for I set my heart on surprising you, and I flatter myself I've done it," said Jo, when she got her breath.

"I never was more staggered in my life. Isn't it fun? Are they boys? What are you going to name them? Let's have another look. Hold me up, Jo; for upon my life it's one too many for me," returned Laurie, regarding the infants with the air of a big, benevolent Newfoundland looking at a pair of infantile kittens.

"Boy and girl. Aren't they beauties?" said the proud papa, beaming upon the little, red squirmers as if they were unfledged angels.

"Most remarkable children I ever saw. Which is which?" and Laurie bent like a well-sweep to examine the prodigies.

"Amy put a blue ribbon on the boy and a pink on the girl, French fashion, so you can always tell. Besides, one has blue eyes and one brown. Kiss them, Uncle Teddy," said wicked Jo.

"I'm afraid they mightn't like it," began Laurie, with unusual timidity in such matters.

"Of course they will; they are used to it now. Do it this minute, sir!" commanded Jo, fearing he might propose a proxy.

Laurie screwed up his face, and obeyed with a gingerly peck at each little cheek that produced another laugh, and made the babies squeal.

"There, I knew they didn't like it! That's the boy; see him kick; he hits out with his fists like a good one. Now then, young Brooke, pitch into a man of your own size, will you?" cried Laurie, delighted with a poke in the face from a tiny fist, flapping aimlessly about.

"He's to be named John Laurence, and the girl Margaret, after mother and grandmother. We shall call her Daisy, so as not to have two Megs, and I suppose the mannie will be Jack, unless we find a better name," said Amy, with aunt-like interest.

"Name him Demijohn, and call him 'Demi' for short," said Laurie.

"Daisy and Demi,—just the thing! I *knew* Teddy would do it," cried Jo, clapping her hands.

Teddy certainly had done it that time, for the babies were "Daisy" and "Demi" to the end of the chapter.

# VI.

# CALLS.

"COME, Jo, it's time."

"For what?"

"You don't mean to say you have forgotten that you promised to make half a dozen calls with me to-day?"

"I've done a good many rash and foolish things in my life, but I don't think I ever was mad enough to say I'd make six calls in one day, when a single one upsets me for a week."

"Yes, you did; it was a bargain between us. I was to finish the crayon of Beth for you, and you were to go properly with me, and return our neighbors' visits."

"If it was fair—that was in the bond; and I stand to the letter of my bond, Shylock. There is a pile of clouds in the east; it's *not* fair, and I don't go."

"Now, that's shirking. It's a lovely day, no prospect of rain, and you pride yourself on keeping promises; so be honorable; come and do your duty, and then be at peace for another six months."

At that minute Jo was particularly absorbed in dressmaking; for she was mantua-maker general to the family, and took especial credit to herself because she could use a needle as well as a pen. It was very provoking to be arrested in the act of a first trying-on, and ordered out to make calls in her best array, on a warm July day. She hated calls of the formal sort, and never made any till Amy compelled her with a bargain, bribe, or promise. In the present instance, there was no escape; and having clashed her scissors rebelliously, while protesting that she smelt thunder, she gave in, put away her work, and taking up her hat and gloves with an air of resignation, told Amy the victim was ready.

"Jo March, you are perverse enough to provoke a saint! You don't intend to make calls in that state, I hope," cried Amy, surveying her with amazement.

"Why not? I'm neat and cool and comfortable; quite proper for a dusty walk on a warm day. If people care more for my clothes than they do for me, I don't wish to see them. You can dress for both, and be as elegant as you please: it pays for you to be fine; it doesn't for me, and furbelows only worry me."

"Oh dear!" sighed Amy; "now she's in a contrary fit, and will drive me distracted before I can get her properly ready. I'm sure it's no pleasure to me to go to-day, but it's a debt we owe society, and there's no one to pay it but you and me. I'll do anything for you, Jo, if you'll only dress yourself nicely, and come and help me do the civil. You can talk so well, look so aristocratic in your best things, and behave so beautifully, if you try, that I'm proud of you. I'm afraid to go alone; do come and take care of me."

"You're an artful little puss to flatter and wheedle your cross old sister in that way. The idea of my being aristocratic and well-bred, and your being afraid to go anywhere alone! I don't know which is the most absurd. Well, I'll go if I must, and do my best. You shall be commander of the expedition, and I'll obey blindly; will that satisfy you?" said Jo, with a sudden change from perversity to lamb-like submission.

"You're a perfect cherub! Now put on all your best things, and I'll tell you how to behave at each place, so that you will make a good impression. I want people to like you, and they would if you'd only try to be a little more agreeable. Do your hair the pretty way, and put the pink rose in your bonnet; it's becoming, and you look too sober in your plain suit. Take your light gloves and the embroidered handkerchief. We'll stop at Meg's, and borrow her white sunshade, and then you can have my dove-colored one."

While Amy dressed, she issued her orders, and Jo obeyed them; not without entering her protest, however, for she sighed as she rustled into her new organdie, frowned darkly at herself as she tied her bonnet strings in an irreproachable bow, wrestled viciously with pins as she put on her collar, wrinkled up her features generally as she shook out the handkerchief, whose embroidery was as irritating to her nose as the present mission was to her feelings; and when she had squeezed her hands into tight gloves with three buttons and a tassel, as the last touch of elegance, she turned to Amy with an imbecile expression of countenance, saying meekly,—

"I'm perfectly miserable; but if you consider me presentable, I die happy."

"You are highly satisfactory; turn slowly round, and let me get a careful view." Jo revolved, and Amy gave a touch here and there, then fell back, with her head on one side, observing graciously, "Yes, you'll do; your head is all I could ask, for that white bonnet *with* the rose is quite ravishing. Hold back your shoulders, and carry your hands easily, no matter if your gloves do pinch. There's one thing you can do well, Jo, that is, wear a shawl—I can't; but it's very nice to see you, and I'm so glad Aunt March gave you that lovely one; it's simple, but handsome, and those folds over the arm are really artistic. Is the point of my mantle in the middle, and have I looped my dress evenly? I like to show my boots, for my feet *are* pretty, though my nose isn't."

"You are a thing of beauty and a joy forever," said Jo, looking through her hand with the air of a connoisseur at the blue feather against the gold hair. "Am I to drag my best dress through the dust, or loop it up, please, ma'am?"

"Hold it up when you walk, but drop it in the house; the sweeping style suits you best, and you must learn to trail your skirts gracefully. You haven't half buttoned one cuff; do it at once. You'll never look finished if you are not careful about the little details, for they make up the pleasing whole."

Jo sighed, and proceeded to burst the buttons off her glove, in doing up her cuff; but at last both were ready, and sailed away, looking as "pretty as picters," Hannah said, as she hung out of the upper window to watch them.

"Now, Jo dear, the Chesters consider themselves very elegant people, so I want you to put on your best deportment. Don't make any of your abrupt remarks, or do anything odd, will you? Just be calm, cool, and quiet,—that's safe and ladylike; and you can easily do it for fifteen minutes," said Amy, as they approached the first place, having borrowed the white parasol and been inspected by Meg, with a baby on each arm.

"Let me see. 'Calm, cool, and quiet,'—yes, I think I can promise that. I've played the part of a prim young lady on the stage, and I'll try it off. My powers are great, as you shall see; so be easy in your mind, my child."

Amy looked relieved, but naughty Jo took her at her word; for, during the first call, she sat with every limb gracefully composed, every fold correctly draped, calm as a summer sea, cool as a snow-bank, and as silent as a sphinx. In vain Mrs. Chester alluded to her "charming novel," and the Misses Chester introduced parties, picnics, the opera, and the fashions; each and all were answered by a smile, a bow, and a demure "Yes" or "No," with the chill on. In vain Amy telegraphed the word "Talk," tried to draw her out, and administered covert pokes with her foot. Jo sat as if blandly unconscious of it all, with deportment like Maud's face, "icily regular, splendidly null."

"What a haughty, uninteresting creature that oldest Miss March is!" was the unfortunately audible remark of one of the ladies, as the door closed upon their guests. Jo laughed noiselessly all through the hall, but Amy looked disgusted at the failure of her instructions, and very naturally laid the blame upon Jo.

"How could you mistake me so? I merely meant you to be properly dignified and composed, and you made yourself a perfect stock and stone. Try to be sociable at the Lambs', gossip as other girls do, and be interested in dress and flirtations and whatever nonsense comes up. They move in the best society, are valuable persons for us to know, and I wouldn't fail to make a good impression there for anything."

"I'll be agreeable; I'll gossip and giggle, and have horrors and raptures over any trifle you like. I rather enjoy this, and now I'll imitate what is called 'a charming girl;' I can do it, for I have May Chester as a model, and I'll improve upon her. See if the Lambs don't say, 'What a lively, nice creature that Jo March is!'"

Amy felt anxious, as well she might, for when Jo turned freakish there was no knowing where she would stop. Amy's face was a study when she saw her sister skim into the next drawing-room, kiss all the young ladies with effusion, beam graciously upon the young gentlemen, and join in the chat with a spirit which amazed the beholder. Amy was taken possession of by Mrs. Lamb, with whom she was a favorite, and forced to hear a long account of Lucretia's last attack, while three delightful young gentlemen hovered near, waiting for a pause when they might rush in and rescue her. So situated, she was powerless to check Jo, who seemed possessed by a spirit of mischief, and talked away as volubly as the old lady. A knot of heads gathered about her, and Amy strained her ears to hear what was going on; for broken sentences filled her with alarm, round eyes and uplifted hands tormented her with curiosity, and frequent peals of laughter made her wild to share the fun. One may imagine her suffering on overhearing fragments of this sort of conversation:—

"She rides splendidly,—who taught her?"

"No one; she used to practise mounting, holding the reins, and sitting straight on an old saddle in a tree. Now she rides anything, for she doesn't know what fear is, and the stable-man lets her have horses cheap, because she trains them to carry ladies so well. She has such a passion for it, I often tell her if everything else fails she can be a horse-breaker, and get her living so."

At this awful speech Amy contained herself with difficulty, for the impression was being given that she was rather a fast young lady, which was her especial aversion. But what could she do? for the old lady was in the middle of her story, and long before it was done Jo was off again, making more droll revelations, and committing still more fearful blunders.

"Yes, Amy was in despair that day, for all the good beasts were gone, and of three left, one was lame, one blind, and the other so balky that you had to put dirt in his mouth before he would start. Nice animal for a pleasure party, wasn't it?"

"Which did she choose?" asked one of the laughing gentlemen, who enjoyed the subject.

"None of them; she heard of a young horse at the farmhouse over the river, and, though a lady had never ridden him, she resolved to try, because he was handsome and spirited. Her struggles were really pathetic; there was no one to bring the horse to the saddle, so she took the saddle to the horse. My dear creature, she actually rowed it over the river, put it on her head, and marched up to the barn to the utter amazement of the old man!"

"Did she ride the horse?"

"Of course she did, and had a capital time. I expected to see her brought home in fragments, but she managed him perfectly, and was the life of the party."

"Well, I call that plucky!" and young Mr. Lamb turned an approving glance upon Amy, wondering what his mother could be saying to make the girl look so red and uncomfortable.

She was still redder and more uncomfortable a moment after, when a sudden turn in the conversation introduced the subject of dress. One of the young ladies asked Jo where she got the pretty drab hat she wore to the picnic; and stupid Jo, instead of mentioning the place where it was bought two years ago, must needs answer, with unnecessary frankness, "Oh, Amy painted it; you can't buy those soft shades, so we paint ours any color we like. It's a great comfort to have an artistic sister."

"Isn't that an original idea?" cried Miss Lamb, who found Jo great fun.

"That's nothing compared to some of her brilliant performances. There's nothing the child can't do. Why, she wanted a pair of blue boots for Sallie's party, so she just painted her soiled white ones the loveliest shade of sky-blue you ever saw, and they looked exactly like satin," added Jo, with an air of pride in her sister's accomplishments that exasperated Amy till she felt that it would be a relief to throw her card-case at her.

"We read a story of yours the other day, and enjoyed it very much," observed the elder Miss Lamb, wishing to compliment the literary lady, who did not look the character just then, it must be confessed.

Any mention of her "works" always had a bad effect upon Jo, who either grew rigid and looked offended, or changed the subject with a *brusque* remark, as now. "Sorry you could find nothing better to read. I write that rubbish because it sells, and ordinary people like it. Are you going to New York this winter?"

As Miss Lamb had "enjoyed" the story, this speech was not exactly grateful or complimentary. The minute it was made Jo saw her mistake; but, fearing to make the matter worse, suddenly remembered that it was for her to make the first move toward departure, and did so with an abruptness that left three people with half-finished sentences in their mouths.

"Amy, we *must* go. *Good*-by, dear; *do* come and see us; we are *pining* for a visit. I don't dare to ask *you*, Mr. Lamb; but if you *should* come, I don't think I shall have the heart to send you away."

Jo said this with such a droll imitation of May Chester's gushing style that Amy got out of the room as rapidly as possible, feeling a strong desire to laugh and cry at the same time.

"Didn't I do that well?" asked Jo, with a satisfied air, as they walked away.

"Nothing could have been worse," was Amy's crushing reply. "What possessed you to tell those stories about my saddle, and the hats and boots, and all the rest of it?"

"Why, it's funny, and amuses people. They know we are poor, so it's no use pretending that we have grooms, buy three or four hats a season, and have things as easy and fine as they do."

"You needn't go and tell them all our little shifts, and expose our poverty in that perfectly unnecessary way. You haven't a bit of proper pride, and never will learn when to hold your tongue and when to speak," said Amy despairingly.

Poor Jo looked abashed, and silently chafed the end of her nose with the stiff handkerchief, as if performing a penance for her misdemeanors.

"How shall I behave here?" she asked, as they approached the third mansion.

"Just as you please; I wash my hands of you," was Amy's short answer.

"Then I'll enjoy myself. The boys are at home, and we'll have a comfortable time. Goodness knows I need a little change, for elegance has a bad effect upon my constitution," returned Jo gruffly, being disturbed by her failures to suit.

An enthusiastic welcome from three big boys and several pretty children speedily soothed her ruffled feelings; and, leaving Amy to entertain the hostess and Mr. Tudor, who happened to be calling likewise, Jo devoted herself to the young folks, and found the change refreshing. She listened to college stories with deep interest, caressed pointers and poodles without a murmur, agreed heartily that "Tom Brown was a brick," regardless of the improper form of praise; and when one lad proposed a visit to his turtle-tank, she went with an alacrity which caused mamma to smile upon her, as that motherly lady settled the cap which was left in a ruinous condition by filial hugs, bear-like but affectionate, and dearer to her than the most faultless *coiffure* from the hands of an inspired Frenchwoman.

Leaving her sister to her own devices, Amy proceeded to enjoy herself to her heart's content. Mr. Tudor's uncle had married an English lady who was third cousin to a living lord, and Amy regarded the whole family with great respect; for, in spite of her American birth and breeding, she possessed that reverence for titles which haunts the best of us,—that unacknowledged loyalty to the early faith in kings which set the most democratic nation under the sun in a ferment at the coming of a royal yellow-haired laddie, some years ago, and which still has something to do with the love the young country bears the old, like that of a big son for an imperious little mother, who held him while she could, and let him go with a farewell scolding when he rebelled. But even the satisfaction of talking with a distant connection of the British nobility did not render Amy forgetful of time; and when the proper number of minutes had passed, she reluctantly tore herself from this aristocratic society, and looked about for Jo, fervently hoping that her incorrigible sister would not be found in any position which should bring disgrace upon the name of March.

It might have been worse, but Amy considered it bad; for Jo sat on the grass, with an encampment of boys about her, and a dirty-footed dog reposing on the skirt of her state and festival dress, as she related one of Laurie's pranks to her admiring audience. One small child was poking turtles with Amy's cherished parasol, a second was eating gingerbread over Jo's best bonnet, and a third playing ball with her gloves. But all were enjoying themselves; and when Jo collected her damaged property to go, her escort accompanied her, begging her to come again, "it was such fun to hear about Laurie's larks."

"Capital boys, aren't they? I feel quite young and brisk again after that," said Jo, strolling along with her hands behind her, partly from habit, partly to conceal the bespattered parasol.

"Why do you always avoid Mr. Tudor?" asked Amy, wisely refraining from any comment upon Jo's dilapidated appearance.

"Don't like him; he puts on airs, snubs his sisters, worries his father, and doesn't speak respectfully of his mother. Laurie says he is fast, and *I* don't consider him a desirable acquaintance; so I let him alone."

"You might treat him civilly, at least. You gave him a cool nod; and just now you bowed and smiled in the politest way to Tommy Chamberlain, whose father keeps a grocery store. If you had just reversed the nod and the bow, it would have been right," said Amy reprovingly.

"No, it wouldn't," returned perverse Jo; "I neither like, respect, nor admire Tudor, though his grandfather's uncle's nephew's niece *was* third cousin to a lord. Tommy is poor and bashful and good and very clever; I think well of him, and like to show that I do, for he *is* a gentleman in spite of the brown-paper parcels."

"It's no use trying to argue with you," began Amy.

"Not the least, my dear," interrupted Jo; "so let us look amiable, and drop a card here, as the Kings are evidently out, for which I'm deeply grateful."

The family card-case having done its duty, the girls walked on, and Jo uttered another thanksgiving on reaching the fifth house, and being told that the young ladies were engaged.

"Now let us go home, and never mind Aunt March to-day. We can run down there any time, and it's really a pity to trail through the dust in our best bibs and tuckers, when we are tired and cross."

"Speak for yourself, if you please. Aunt likes to have us pay her the compliment of coming in style, and making a formal call; it's a little thing to do, but it gives her pleasure, and I don't believe it will hurt your things half so much as letting dirty dogs and clumping boys spoil them. Stoop down, and let me take the crumbs off of your bonnet."

"What a good girl you are, Amy!" said Jo, with a repentant glance from her own damaged costume to that of her sister, which was fresh and spotless still. "I wish it was as easy for me to do little things to please people as it is for you. I think of them, but it takes too much time to do them; so I wait for a chance to confer a great favor, and let the small ones slip; but they tell best in the end, I fancy."

Amy smiled, and was mollified at once, saying with a maternal air,—

"Women should learn to be agreeable, particularly poor ones; for they have no other way of repaying the kindnesses they receive. If you'd remember that, and practise it, you'd be better liked than I am, because there is more of you."

"I'm a crotchety old thing, and always shall be, but I'm willing to own that you are right; only it's easier for me to risk my life for a person than to be pleasant to him when I don't feel like it. It's a great misfortune to have such strong likes and dislikes, isn't it?"

"It's a greater not to be able to hide them. I don't mind saying that I don't approve of Tudor any more than you do; but I'm not called upon to tell him so; neither are you, and there is no use in making yourself disagreeable because he is."

"But I think girls ought to show when they disapprove of young men; and how can they do it except by their manners? Preaching does not do any good, as I know to my sorrow, since I've had Teddy to manage; but there are many little ways in which I can influence him without a word, and I say we *ought* to do it to others if we can."

"Teddy is a remarkable boy, and can't be taken as a sample of other boys," said Amy, in a tone of solemn conviction, which would have convulsed the "remarkable boy," if he had heard it. "If we were belles, or women of wealth and position, we might do something, perhaps; but for us to frown at one set of young gentlemen because we don't approve of them, and smile upon another set because we do, wouldn't have a particle of effect, and we should only be considered odd and puritanical."

"So we are to countenance things and people which we detest, merely because we are not belles and millionaires, are we? That's a nice sort of morality."

"I can't argue about it, I only know that it's the way of the world; and people who set themselves against it only get laughed at for their pains. I don't like reformers, and I hope you will never try to be one."

"I do like them, and I shall be one if I can; for in spite of the laughing, the world would never get on without them. We can't agree about that, for you belong to the old set, and I to the new: you will get on the best, but I shall have the liveliest time of it. I should rather enjoy the brickbats and hooting, I think."

"Well, compose yourself now, and don't worry aunt with your new ideas."

"I'll try not to, but I'm always possessed to burst out with some particularly blunt speech or revolutionary sentiment before her; it's my doom, and I can't help it."

They found Aunt Carrol with the old lady, both absorbed in some very interesting subject; but they dropped it as the girls came in, with a conscious look which betrayed that they had been talking about their nieces. Jo was not in a good humor, and the perverse fit returned; but Amy, who had virtuously done her duty, kept her temper, and pleased everybody, was in a most angelic frame of mind. This amiable spirit was felt at once, and both the aunts "my deared" her affectionately, looking what they afterwards said emphatically,—"That child improves every day."

"Are you going to help about the fair, dear?" asked Mrs. Carrol, as Amy sat down beside her with the confiding air elderly people like so well in the young.

"Yes, aunt. Mrs. Chester asked me if I would, and I offered to tend a table, as I have nothing but my time to give."

"I'm not," put in Jo decidedly. "I hate to be patronized, and the Chesters think it's a great favor to allow us to help with their highly connected fair. I wonder you consented, Amy: they only want you to work."

"I am willing to work: it's for the freedmen as well as the Chesters, and I think it very kind of them to let me share the labor and the fun. Patronage does not trouble me when it is well meant."

"Quite right and proper. I like your grateful spirit, my dear; it's a pleasure to help people who appreciate our efforts: some do not, and that is trying," observed Aunt March, looking over her spectacles at Jo, who sat apart, rocking herself, with a somewhat morose expression.

If Jo had only known what a great happiness was wavering in the balance for one of them, she would have turned dovelike in a minute; but, unfortunately, we don't have windows in our breasts, and cannot see what goes on in the minds of our friends; better for us that we cannot as a general thing, but now and then it would be such a comfort, such a saving of time and temper. By her next speech, Jo deprived herself of several years of pleasure, and received a timely lesson in the art of holding her tongue.

"I don't like favors; they oppress and make me feel like a slave. I'd rather do everything for myself, and be perfectly independent."

"Ahem!" coughed Aunt Carrol softly, with a look at Aunt March.

"I told you so," said Aunt March, with a decided nod to Aunt Carrol.

Mercifully unconscious of what she had done, Jo sat with her nose in the air, and a revolutionary aspect which was anything but inviting.

"Do you speak French, dear?" asked Mrs. Carrol, laying her hand on Amy's.

"Pretty well, thanks to Aunt March, who lets Esther talk to me as often as I like," replied Amy, with a grateful look, which caused the old lady to smile affably.

"How are you about languages?" asked Mrs. Carrol of Jo.

"Don't know a word; I'm very stupid about studying anything; can't bear French, it's such a slippery, silly sort of language," was the *brusque* reply.

Another look passed between the ladies, and Aunt March said to Amy, "You are quite strong and well, now, dear, I believe? Eyes don't trouble you any more, do they?"

"Not at all, thank you, ma'am. I'm very well, and mean to do great things next winter, so that I may be ready for Rome, whenever that joyful time arrives."

"Good girl! You deserve to go, and I'm sure you will some day," said Aunt March, with an approving pat on the head, as Amy picked up her ball for her.

"Cross-patch, draw the latch,
Sit by the fire and spin,"

squalled Polly, bending down from his perch on the back of her chair to peep into Jo's face, with such a comical air of impertinent inquiry that it was impossible to help laughing.

"Most observing bird," said the old lady.

"Come and take a walk, my dear?" cried Polly, hopping toward the china-closet, with a look suggestive of lump-sugar.

"Thank you, I will. Come, Amy;" and Jo brought the visit to an end, feeling more strongly than ever that calls did have a bad effect upon her constitution. She shook hands in a gentlemanly manner, but Amy kissed both the aunts, and the girls departed, leaving behind them the impression of shadow and sunshine; which impression caused Aunt March to say, as they vanished,—

"You'd better do it, Mary; I'll supply the money," and Aunt Carrol to reply decidedly, "I certainly will, if her father and mother consent."

VII.

## CONSEQUENCES.

MRS. CHESTER'S fair was so very elegant and select that it was considered a great honor by the young ladies of the neighborhood to be invited to take a table, and every one was much interested in the matter. Amy was asked, but Jo was not, which was fortunate for all parties, as her elbows were decidedly akimbo at this period of her life, and it took a good many hard knocks to teach her how to get on easily. The "haughty, uninteresting creature" was let severely alone; but Amy's talent and taste were duly complimented by the offer of the art-table, and she exerted herself to prepare and secure appropriate and valuable contributions to it.

Everything went on smoothly till the day before the fair opened; then there occurred one of the little skirmishes which it is almost impossible to avoid, when some five and twenty women, old and young, with all their private piques and prejudices, try to work together.

May Chester was rather jealous of Amy because the latter was a greater favorite than herself, and, just at this time, several trifling circumstances occurred to increase the feeling. Amy's dainty pen-and-ink work entirely eclipsed May's painted vases,—that was one thorn; then the all-conquering Tudor had danced four times with Amy, at a late party, and only once with May,—that was thorn number two; but the chief grievance that rankled in her soul, and gave her an excuse for her unfriendly conduct, was a rumor which some obliging gossip had whispered to her, that the March girls had made fun of her at the Lambs'. All the blame of this should have fallen upon Jo, for her naughty imitation had been too lifelike to escape detection, and the frolicsome Lambs had permitted the joke to escape. No hint of this had reached the culprits, however, and Amy's dismay can be imagined, when, the very evening before the fair, as she was putting the last touches to her pretty table, Mrs. Chester, who, of course, resented the supposed ridicule of her daughter, said, in a bland tone, but with a cold look,—

"I find, dear, that there is some feeling among the young ladies about my giving this table to any one but my girls. As this is the most prominent, and some say the most attractive table of all, and they are the chief getters-up of the fair, it is thought best for them to take this place. I'm sorry, but I know you are too sincerely interested in the cause to mind a little personal disappointment, and you shall have another table if you like."

Mrs. Chester had fancied beforehand that it would be easy to deliver this little speech; but when the time came, she found it rather difficult to utter it naturally, with Amy's unsuspicious eyes looking straight at her, full of surprise and trouble.

Amy felt that there was something behind this, but could not guess what, and said quietly, feeling hurt, and showing that she did,—

"Perhaps you had rather I took no table at all?"

"Now, my dear, don't have any ill feeling, I beg; it's merely a matter of expediency, you see; my girls will naturally take the lead, and this table is considered their proper place. *I* think it very appropriate to you, and feel very grateful for your efforts to make it so pretty; but we must give up our private wishes, of course, and I will see that you have a good place elsewhere. Wouldn't you like the flower-table? The little girls undertook it, but they are discouraged. You could make a charming thing of it, and the flower-table is always attractive, you know."

"Especially to gentlemen," added May, with a look which enlightened Amy as to one cause of her sudden fall from favor. She colored angrily, but took no other notice of that girlish sarcasm, and answered, with unexpected amiability,—

"It shall be as you please, Mrs. Chester. I'll give up my place here at once, and attend to the flowers, if you like."

"You can put your own things on your own table, if you prefer," began May, feeling a little conscience-stricken, as she looked at the pretty racks, the painted shells, and quaint illuminations Amy had so carefully made and so gracefully arranged. She meant it kindly, but Amy mistook her meaning, and said quickly,—

"Oh, certainly, if they are in your way;" and sweeping her contributions into her apron, pell-mell, she walked off, feeling that herself and her works of art had been insulted past forgiveness.

"Now she's mad. Oh, dear, I wish I hadn't asked you to speak, mamma," said May, looking disconsolately at the empty spaces on her table.

"Girls' quarrels are soon over," returned her mother, feeling a trifle ashamed of her own part in this one, as well she might.

The little girls hailed Amy and her treasures with delight, which cordial reception somewhat soothed her perturbed spirit, and she fell to work, determined to succeed florally, if she could not artistically. But everything seemed against her: it was late, and she was tired; every one was too busy with their own affairs to help her; and the little girls were only hindrances, for the dears fussed and chattered like so many magpies, making a great deal of confusion in their artless efforts to preserve the most perfect order. The evergreen arch wouldn't stay firm after she got it up, but wiggled and threatened to tumble down on her head when the hanging baskets were filled; her best tile got a splash of water, which left a sepia tear on the Cupid's cheek; she bruised her hands with hammering, and got cold working in a draught, which last affliction filled her with apprehensions for the morrow. Any girl-reader who has suffered like afflictions will sympathize with poor Amy, and wish her well through with her task.

There was great indignation at home when she told her story that evening. Her mother said it was a shame, but told her she had done right; Beth declared she wouldn't go to the fair at all; and Jo demanded why she didn't take all her pretty things and leave those mean people to get on without her.

"Because they are mean is no reason why I should be. I hate such things, and though I think I've a right to be hurt, I don't intend to show it. They will feel that more than angry speeches or huffy actions, won't they, Marmee?"

"That's the right spirit, my dear; a kiss for a blow is always best, though it's not very easy to give it sometimes," said her mother, with the air of one who had learned the difference between preaching and practising.

In spite of various very natural temptations to resent and retaliate, Amy adhered to her resolution all the next day, bent on conquering her enemy by kindness. She began well, thanks to a silent reminder that came to her unexpectedly, but most opportunely. As she arranged her table that morning, while the little girls were in an ante-room filling the baskets, she took up her pet production,—a little book, the antique cover of which her father had found among his treasures, and in which, on leaves of vellum, she had beautifully illuminated different texts. As she turned the pages, rich in dainty devices, with very pardonable pride, her eye fell upon one verse that made her stop and think. Framed in a brilliant scroll-work of scarlet, blue, and gold, with little spirits of good-will helping one another up and down among the thorns and flowers, were the words, "Thou shalt love thy neighbor as thyself."

"I ought, but I don't," thought Amy, as her eye went from the bright page to May's discontented face behind the big vases, that could not hide the vacancies her pretty work had once filled. Amy stood a minute, turning the leaves in her hand, reading on each some sweet rebuke for all heart-burnings and uncharitableness of spirit. Many wise and true sermons are preached us every day by unconscious ministers in street, school, office, or home; even a fair-table may become a pulpit, if it can offer the good and helpful words which are never out of season. Amy's conscience preached her a little sermon from that text, then and there; and she did what many of us do not always do,—took the sermon to heart, and straightway put it in practice.

A group of girls were standing about May's table, admiring the pretty things, and talking over the change of saleswomen. They dropped their voices, but Amy knew they were speaking of her, hearing one side of the story, and judging accordingly. It was not pleasant, but a better spirit had come over her, and presently a chance offered for proving it. She heard May say sorrowfully,—

"It's too bad, for there is no time to make other things, and I don't want to fill up with odds and ends. The table was just complete then: now it's spoilt."

"I dare say she'd put them back if you asked her," suggested some one.

"How could I after all the fuss?" began May, but she did not finish, for Amy's voice came across the hall, saying pleasantly,—

"You may have them, and welcome, without asking, if you want them. I was just thinking I'd offer to put them back, for they belong to your table rather than mine. Here they are; please take them, and forgive me if I was hasty in carrying them away last night."

As she spoke, Amy returned her contribution, with a nod and a smile, and hurried away again, feeling that it was easier to do a friendly thing than it was to stay and be thanked for it.

"Now, I call that lovely of her, don't you?" cried one girl.

May's answer was inaudible; but another young lady, whose temper was evidently a little soured by making lemonade, added, with a disagreeable laugh, "Very lovely; for she knew she wouldn't sell them at her own table."

Now, that was hard; when we make little sacrifices we like to have them appreciated, at least; and for a minute Amy was sorry she had done it, feeling that virtue was not always its own reward. But it is,—as she presently discovered; for her spirits began to rise, and her table to blossom under her skilful hands; the girls were very kind, and that one little act seemed to have cleared the atmosphere amazingly.

It was a very long day, and a hard one to Amy, as she sat behind her table, often quite alone, for the little girls deserted very soon: few cared to buy flowers in summer, and her bouquets began to droop long before night.

The art-table *was* the most attractive in the room; there was a crowd about it all day long, and the tenders were constantly flying to and fro with important faces and rattling money-boxes. Amy often looked wistfully across, longing to be there, where she felt at home and happy, instead of in a corner with nothing to do. It might seem no hardship to some of us; but to a pretty, blithe young girl, it was not only tedious, but very trying; and the thought of being found there in the evening by her family, and Laurie and his friends, made it a real martyrdom.

She did not go home till night, and then she looked so pale and quiet that they knew the day had been a hard one, though she made no complaint, and did not even tell what she had done. Her mother gave her an extra cordial cup of tea, Beth helped her dress, and made a charming little wreath for her hair, while Jo astonished her family by getting herself up with unusual care, and hinting darkly that the tables were about to be turned.

"Don't do anything rude, pray, Jo. I won't have any fuss made, so let it all pass, and behave yourself," begged Amy, as she departed early, hoping to find a reinforcement of flowers to refresh her poor little table.

"I merely intend to make myself entrancingly agreeable to every one I know, and to keep them in your corner as long as possible. Teddy and his boys will lend a hand, and we'll have a good time yet," returned Jo, leaning over the gate to watch for Laurie. Presently the familiar tramp was heard in the dusk, and she ran out to meet him.

"Is that my boy?"

"As sure as this is my girl!" and Laurie tucked her hand under his arm, with the air of a man whose every wish was gratified.

"O Teddy, such doings!" and Jo told Amy's wrongs with sisterly zeal.

"A flock of our fellows are going to drive over by and by, and I'll be hanged if I don't make them buy every flower she's got, and camp down before her table afterward," said Laurie, espousing her cause with warmth.

"The flowers are not at all nice, Amy says, and the fresh ones may not arrive in time. I don't wish to be unjust or suspicious, but I shouldn't wonder if they never came at all. When people do one mean thing they are very likely to do another," observed Jo, in a disgusted tone.

"Didn't Hayes give you the best out of our gardens? I told him to."

"I didn't know that; he forgot, I suppose; and, as your grandpa was poorly, I didn't like to worry him by asking, though I did want some."

"Now, Jo, how could you think there was any need of asking! They are just as much yours as mine. Don't we always go halves in everything?" began Laurie, in the tone that always made Jo turn thorny.

"Gracious, I hope not! half of some of your things wouldn't suit me at all. But we mustn't stand philandering here; I've got to help Amy, so you go and make yourself splendid; and if you'll be so very kind as to let Hayes take a few nice flowers up to the Hall, I'll bless you forever."

"Couldn't you do it now?" asked Laurie, so suggestively that Jo shut the gate in his face with inhospitable haste, and called through the bars, "Go away, Teddy; I'm busy."

Thanks to the conspirators, the tables *were* turned that night; for Hayes sent up a wilderness of flowers, with a lovely basket, arranged in his best manner, for a centre-piece; then the March family turned out *en masse*, and Jo exerted herself to some purpose, for people not only came, but stayed, laughing at her nonsense, admiring Amy's taste, and apparently enjoying themselves very much. Laurie and his friends gallantly threw themselves into the breach, bought up the bouquets, encamped before the table, and made that corner the liveliest spot in the room. Amy was in her element now, and, out of gratitude, if nothing more, was as sprightly and gracious as possible,—coming to the conclusion, about that time, that virtue *was* its own reward, after all.

Jo behaved herself with exemplary propriety; and when Amy was happily surrounded by her guard of honor, Jo circulated about the hall, picking up various bits of gossip, which enlightened her upon the subject of the Chester change of base. She reproached herself for her share of the ill-feeling, and resolved to exonerate Amy as soon as possible; she also discovered what Amy had done about the things in the morning, and considered her a model of magnanimity. As she passed the art-table, she glanced over it for her sister's things, but saw no signs of them. "Tucked away out of sight, I dare say," thought Jo, who could forgive her own wrongs, but hotly resented any insult offered to her family.

"Good evening, Miss Jo. How does Amy get on?" asked May, with a conciliatory air, for she wanted to show that she also could be generous.

"She has sold everything she had that was worth selling, and now she is enjoying herself. The flower-table is always attractive, you know, 'especially to gentlemen.'"

Jo *couldn't* resist giving that little slap, but May took it so meekly she regretted it a minute after, and fell to praising the great vases, which still remained unsold.

"Is Amy's illumination anywhere about? I took a fancy to buy that for father," said Jo, very anxious to learn the fate of her sister's work.

"Everything of Amy's sold long ago; I took care that the right people saw them, and they made a nice little sum of money for us," returned May, who had overcome sundry small temptations, as well as Amy, that day.

Much gratified, Jo rushed back to tell the good news; and Amy looked both touched and surprised by the report of May's words and manner.

"Now, gentlemen, I want you to go and do your duty by the other tables as generously as you have by mine—especially the art-table," she said, ordering out "Teddy's Own," as the girls called the college friends.

"'Charge, Chester, charge!' is the motto for that table; but do your duty like men, and you'll get your money's worth of *art* in every sense of the word," said the irrepressible Jo, as the devoted phalanx prepared to take the field.

"To hear is to obey, but March is fairer far than May," said little Parker, making a frantic effort to be both witty and tender, and getting promptly quenched by Laurie, who said, "Very well, my son, for a small boy!" and walked him off, with a paternal pat on the head.

"Buy the vases," whispered Amy to Laurie, as a final heaping of coals of fire on her enemy's head.

To May's great delight, Mr. Laurence not only bought the vases, but pervaded the hall with one under each arm. The other gentlemen speculated with equal rashness in all sorts of frail trifles, and wandered helplessly about afterward, burdened with wax flowers, painted fans, filigree portfolios, and other useful and appropriate purchases.

Aunt Carrol was there, heard the story, looked pleased, and said something to Mrs. March in a corner, which made the latter lady beam with satisfaction, and watch Amy with a face full of mingled pride and anxiety, though she did not betray the cause of her pleasure till several days later.

The fair was pronounced a success; and when May bade Amy good night, she did not "gush" as usual, but gave her an affectionate kiss, and a look which said, "Forgive and forget." That satisfied Amy; and when she got home she found the vases paraded on the parlor chimney-piece, with a great bouquet in each. "The reward of merit for a magnanimous March," as Laurie announced with a flourish.

"You've a deal more principle and generosity and nobleness of character than I ever gave you credit for, Amy. You've behaved sweetly, and I respect you with all my heart," said Jo warmly, as they brushed their hair together late that night.

"Yes, we all do, and love her for being so ready to forgive. It must have been dreadfully hard, after working so long, and setting your heart on selling your own pretty things. I don't believe I could have done it as kindly as you did," added Beth from her pillow.

"Why, girls, you needn't praise me so; I only did as I'd be done by. You laugh at me when I say I want to be a lady, but I mean a true gentlewoman in mind and manners, and I try to do it as far as I know how. I can't explain exactly, but I want to be above the little meannesses and follies and faults that spoil so many women. I'm far from it now, but I do my best, and hope in time to be what mother is."

Amy spoke earnestly, and Jo said, with a cordial hug,—

"I understand now what you mean, and I'll never laugh at you again. You are getting on faster than you think, and I'll take lessons of you in true politeness, for you've learned the secret, I believe. Try away, deary; you'll get your reward some day, and no one will be more delighted than I shall."

A week later Amy did get her reward, and poor Jo found it hard to be delighted. A letter came from Aunt Carrol, and Mrs. March's face was illuminated to such a degree, when she read it, that Jo and Beth, who were with her, demanded what the glad tidings were.

"Aunt Carrol is going abroad next month, and wants—"

"Me to go with her!" burst in Jo, flying out of her chair in an uncontrollable rapture.

"No, dear, not you; it's Amy."

"O mother! she's too young; it's my turn first. I've wanted it so long—it would do me so much good, and be so altogether splendid—I *must* go."

"I'm afraid it's impossible, Jo. Aunt says Amy, decidedly, and it is not for us to dictate when she offers such a favor."

"It's always so. Amy has all the fun and I have all the work. It isn't fair, oh, it isn't fair!" cried Jo passionately.

"I'm afraid it is partly your own fault, dear. When Aunt spoke to me the other day, she regretted your blunt manners and too independent spirit; and here she writes, as if quoting something you had said,—'I planned at first to ask Jo; but as "favors burden her," and she "hates French," I think I won't venture to invite her. Amy is more docile, will make a good companion for Flo, and receive gratefully any help the trip may give her.'"

"Oh, my tongue, my abominable tongue! why can't I learn to keep it quiet?" groaned Jo, remembering words which had been her undoing. When she had heard the explanation of the quoted phrases, Mrs. March said sorrowfully,—

"I wish you could have gone, but there is no hope of it this time; so try to bear it cheerfully, and don't sadden Amy's pleasure by reproaches or regrets."

"I'll try," said Jo, winking hard, as she knelt down to pick up the basket she had joyfully upset. "I'll take a leaf out of her book, and try not only to seem glad, but to be so, and not grudge her one minute of happiness; but it won't be easy, for it is a dreadful disappointment;" and poor Jo bedewed the little fat pincushion she held with several very bitter tears.

"Jo, dear, I'm very selfish, but I couldn't spare you, and I'm glad you are not going quite yet," whispered Beth, embracing her, basket and all, with such a clinging touch and loving face, that Jo felt comforted in spite of the sharp regret that made her want to box her own ears, and humbly beg Aunt Carrol to burden her with this favor, and see how gratefully she would bear it.

By the time Amy came in, Jo was able to take her part in the family jubilation; not quite as heartily as usual, perhaps, but without repinings at Amy's good fortune. The young lady herself received the news as tidings of great joy, went about in a solemn sort of rapture, and began to sort her colors and pack her pencils that evening, leaving such trifles as clothes, money, and passports to those less absorbed in visions of art than herself.

"It isn't a mere pleasure trip to me, girls," she said impressively, as she scraped her best palette. "It will decide my career; for if I have any genius, I shall find it out in Rome, and will do something to prove it."

"Suppose you haven't?" said Jo, sewing away, with red eyes, at the new collars which were to be handed over to Amy.

"Then I shall come home and teach drawing for my living," replied the aspirant for fame, with philosophic composure; but she made a wry face at the prospect, and scratched away at her palette as if bent on vigorous measures before she gave up her hopes.

"No, you won't; you hate hard work, and you'll marry some rich man, and come home to sit in the lap of luxury all your days," said Jo.

"Your predictions sometimes come to pass, but I don't believe that one will. I'm sure I wish it would, for if I can't be an artist myself, I should like to be able to help those who are," said Amy, smiling, as if the part of Lady Bountiful would suit her better than that of a poor drawing-teacher.

"Hum!" said Jo, with a sigh; "if you wish it you'll have it, for your wishes are always granted—mine never."

"Would you like to go?" asked Amy, thoughtfully patting her nose with her knife.

"Rather!"

"Well, in a year or two I'll send for you, and we'll dig in the Forum for relics, and carry out all the plans we've made so many times."

"Thank you; I'll remind you of your promise when that joyful day comes, if it ever does," returned Jo, accepting the vague but magnificent offer as gratefully as she could.

There was not much time for preparation, and the house was in a ferment till Amy was off. Jo bore up very well till the last flutter of blue ribbon vanished, when she retired to her refuge, the garret, and cried till she couldn't cry any more. Amy likewise bore up stoutly till the steamer sailed; then, just as the gangway was about to be withdrawn, it suddenly came over her that a whole ocean was soon to roll between her and those who loved her best, and she clung to Laurie, the last lingerer, saying with a sob,—

"Oh, take care of them for me; and if anything should happen—"

"I will, dear, I will; and if anything happens, I'll come and comfort you," whispered Laurie, little dreaming that he would be called upon to keep his word.

So Amy sailed away to find the old world, which is always new and beautiful to young eyes, while her father and friend watched her from the shore, fervently hoping that none but gentle fortunes would befall the happy-hearted girl, who waved her hand to them till they could see nothing but the summer sunshine dazzling on the sea.

# VIII

## OUR FOREIGN CORRESPONDENT.

"LONDON.

"DEAREST PEOPLE,—

"Here I really sit at a front window of the Bath Hotel, Piccadilly. It's not a fashionable place, but uncle stopped here years ago, and won't go anywhere else; however, we don't mean to stay long, so it's no great matter. Oh, I can't begin to tell you how I enjoy it all! I never can, so I'll only give you bits out of my note-book, for I've done nothing but sketch and scribble since I started.

"I sent a line from Halifax, when I felt pretty miserable, but after that I got on delightfully, seldom ill, on deck all day, with plenty of pleasant people to amuse me. Every one was very kind to me, especially the officers. Don't laugh, Jo; gentlemen really are very necessary aboard ship, to hold on to, or to wait upon one; and as they have nothing to do, it's a mercy to make them useful, otherwise they would smoke themselves to death, I'm afraid.

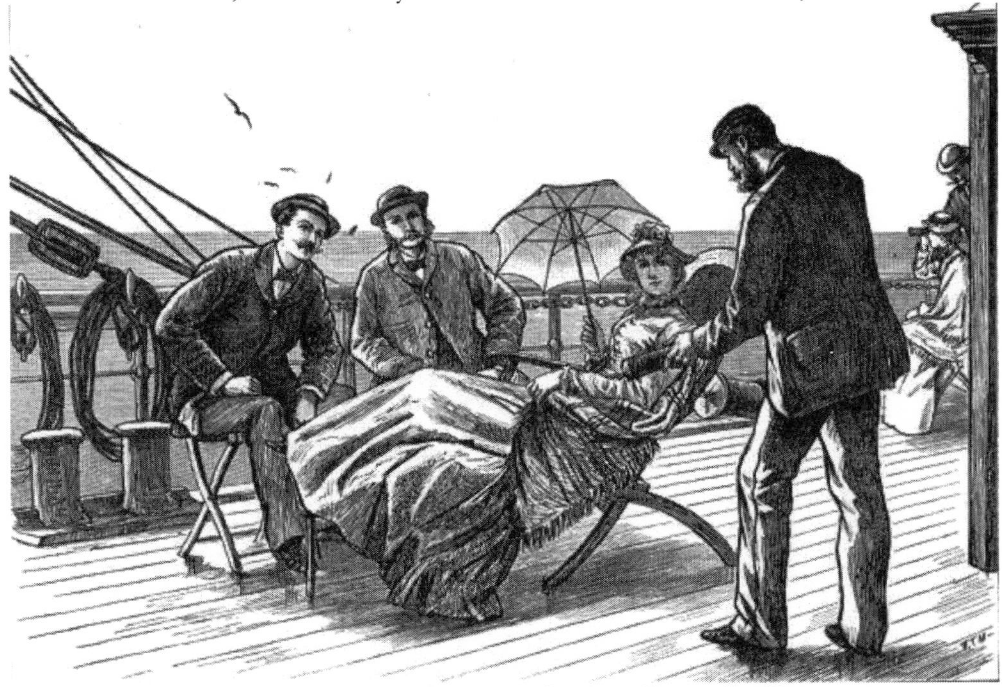

**"Every one was very kind, especially the officers."—Page .**

"Aunt and Flo were poorly all the way, and liked to be let alone, so when I had done what I could for them, I went and enjoyed myself. Such walks on deck, such sunsets, such splendid air and waves! It was almost as exciting as riding a fast horse, when we went rushing on so grandly. I wish Beth could have come, it would have done her so much good; as for Jo, she would have gone up and sat on the main-top jib, or whatever the high thing is called, made friends with the engineers, and tooted on the captain's speaking-trumpet, she'd have been in such a state of rapture.

"It was all heavenly, but I was glad to see the Irish coast, and found it very lovely, so green and sunny, with brown cabins here and there, ruins on some of the hills, and gentlemen's country-seats in the valleys, with deer feeding in the parks. It was early in the morning, but I didn't regret getting up to see it, for the bay was full of little boats, the shore *so* picturesque, and a rosy sky overhead. I never shall forget it.

"At Queenstown one of my new acquaintances left us,—Mr. Lennox,—and when I said something about the Lakes of Killarney, he sighed and sung, with a look at me,—

'Oh, have you e'er heard of Kate Kearney?
She lives on the banks of Killarney;
From the glance of her eye,
Shun danger and fly,
For fatal's the glance of Kate Kearney.'

Wasn't that nonsensical?

"We only stopped at Liverpool a few hours. It's a dirty, noisy place, and I was glad to leave it. Uncle rushed out and bought a pair of dog-skin gloves, some ugly, thick shoes, and an umbrella, and got shaved *à la* mutton-chop, the first thing. Then he flattered himself that he looked like a true Briton; but the first time he had the mud cleaned off his shoes, the little bootblack knew that an American stood in them, and said, with a grin, 'There yer har, sir. I've give 'em the latest Yankee shine.' It amused uncle immensely. Oh, I *must* tell you what that absurd Lennox did! He got his friend Ward, who came on with us, to order a bouquet for me, and the first thing I saw in my room was a lovely one, with 'Robert Lennox's compliments,' on the card. Wasn't that fun, girls? I like travelling.

"I never *shall* get to London if I don't hurry. The trip was like riding through a long picture-gallery, full of lovely landscapes. The farmhouses were my delight; with thatched roofs, ivy up to the eaves, latticed windows, and stout women with rosy children at the doors. The very cattle looked more tranquil than ours, as they stood knee-deep in clover, and the hens had a contented cluck, as if they never got nervous, like Yankee biddies. Such perfect color I never saw,—the grass so green, sky so blue, grain so yellow, woods so dark,—I was in a rapture all the way. So was Flo; and we kept bouncing from one side to the other, trying to see everything while we were whisking along at the rate of sixty miles an hour. Aunt was tired and went to sleep, but uncle read his guide-book, and wouldn't be astonished at anything. This is the way we went on: Amy, flying up,—'Oh, that must be Kenilworth, that gray place among the trees!' Flo, darting to my window,—'How sweet! We must go there some time, won't we, papa?' Uncle, calmly admiring his boots,—'No, my dear, not unless you want beer; that's a brewery.'

"A pause,—then Flo cried out, 'Bless me, there's a gallows and a man going up.' 'Where, where?' shrieks Amy, staring out at two tall posts with a cross-beam and some dangling chains. 'A colliery,' remarks uncle, with a twinkle of the eye. 'Here's a lovely flock of lambs all lying down,' says Amy. 'See, papa, aren't they pretty!' added Flo sentimentally. 'Geese, young ladies,' returns uncle, in a tone that keeps us quiet till Flo settles down to enjoy 'The Flirtations of Capt. Cavendish,' and I have the scenery all to myself.

"Of course it rained when we got to London, and there was nothing to be seen but fog and umbrellas. We rested, unpacked, and shopped a little between the showers. Aunt Mary got me some new things, for I came off in such a hurry I wasn't half ready. A white hat and blue feather, a muslin dress to match, and the loveliest mantle you ever saw. Shopping in Regent Street is perfectly splendid; things seem so cheap—nice ribbons only sixpence a yard. I laid in a stock, but shall get my gloves in Paris. Doesn't that sound sort of elegant and rich?

"Flo and I, for the fun of it, ordered a hansom cab, while aunt and uncle were out, and went for a drive, though we learned afterward that it wasn't the thing for young ladies to ride in them alone. It was so droll! for when we were shut in by the wooden apron, the man drove so fast that Flo was frightened, and told me to stop him. But he was up outside behind somewhere, and I couldn't get at him. He didn't hear me call, nor see me flap my parasol in front, and there we were, quite helpless, rattling away, and whirling around corners at a break-neck pace. At last, in my despair, I saw a little door in the roof, and on poking it open, a red eye appeared, and a beery voice said,—

"'Now then, mum?'

"I gave my order as soberly as I could, and slamming down the door, with an 'Aye, aye, mum,' the man made his horse walk, as if going to a funeral. I poked again, and said, 'A little faster;' then off he went, helter-skelter, as before, and we resigned ourselves to our fate.

"To-day was fair and we went to Hyde Park, close by, for we are more aristocratic than we look. The Duke of Devonshire lives near. I often see his footmen lounging at the back gate; and the Duke of Wellington's house is not far off. Such sights as I saw, my dear! It was as good as Punch, for there were fat dowagers rolling about in their red and yellow coaches, with gorgeous Jeameses in silk stockings and velvet coats, up behind, and powdered coachmen in front. Smart maids, with the rosiest children I ever saw; handsome girls, looking half asleep; dandies, in queer English hats and lavender kids, lounging about, and tall soldiers, in short red jackets and muffin caps stuck on one side, looking so funny I longed to sketch them.

"Rotten Row means '*Route de Roi*,' or the king's way; but now it's more like a riding-school than anything else. The horses are splendid, and the men, especially the grooms, ride well; but the women are stiff, and bounce, which isn't according to our rules. I longed to show them a tearing American gallop, for they trotted solemnly up and down, in their scant habits and high hats, looking like the women in a toy Noah's Ark. Every one rides,—old men, stout ladies, little children,—and the young folks do a deal of flirting here; I saw a pair exchange rosebuds, for it's the thing to wear one in the button-hole, and I thought it rather a nice little idea.

"In the P.M. to Westminster Abbey; but don't expect me to describe it, that's impossible—so I'll only say it was sublime! This evening we are going to see Fechter, which will be an appropriate end to the happiest day of my life.

---

"MIDNIGHT.

"It's very late, but I can't let my letter go in the morning without telling you what happened last evening. Who do you think came in, as we were at tea? Laurie's English friends, Fred and Frank Vaughn! I was *so* surprised, for I shouldn't have known them but for the cards. Both are tall fellows, with whiskers; Fred handsome in the English style, and Frank much better, for he only limps slightly, and uses no crutches. They had heard from Laurie where we were to be, and came to ask us to their house; but uncle won't go, so we shall return the call, and see them as we can. They went to the theatre with us, and we did have *such* a good time, for Frank devoted himself to Flo, and Fred and I talked over past, present, and future fun as if we had known each other all our days. Tell Beth Frank asked for her, and was sorry to hear of her ill health. Fred laughed when I spoke of Jo, and sent his 'respectful compliments to the big hat.' Neither of them had forgotten Camp Laurence, or the fun we had there. What ages ago it seems, doesn't it?

"Aunt is tapping on the wall for the third time, so I *must* stop. I really feel like a dissipated London fine lady, writing here so late, with my room full of pretty things, and my head a jumble of parks, theatres, new gowns, and gallant creatures who say 'Ah!' and twirl their blond mustaches with the true English lordliness. I long to see you all, and in spite of my nonsense am, as ever, your loving

AMY."

---

"PARIS"

"DEAR GIRLS,—

"In my last I told you about our London visit,—how kind the Vaughns were, and what pleasant parties they made for us. I enjoyed the trips to Hampton Court and the Kensington Museum more than anything else,—for at Hampton I saw Raphael's cartoons, and, at the Museum, rooms full of pictures by Turner, Lawrence, Reynolds, Hogarth, and the other great creatures. The day in Richmond Park was charming, for we had a regular English picnic, and I had more splendid oaks and groups of deer than I could copy; also heard a nightingale, and saw larks go up. We 'did' London to our hearts' content, thanks to Fred and Frank, and were sorry to go away; for, though English people are slow to take you in, when they once make up their minds to do it they cannot be outdone in hospitality, *I* think. The Vaughns hope to meet us in Rome next winter, and I shall be dreadfully disappointed if they don't, for Grace and I are great friends, and the boys very nice fellows,—especially Fred.

"Well, we were hardly settled here, when he turned up again, saying he had come for a holiday, and was going to Switzerland. Aunt looked sober at first, but he was so cool about it she couldn't say a word; and now we get on nicely, and are very glad he came, for he speaks French like a native, and I don't know what we should do without him. Uncle doesn't know ten words, and insists on talking English very loud, as if that would make people understand him. Aunt's pronunciation is old-fashioned, and Flo and I, though we flattered ourselves that we knew a good deal, find we don't, and are very grateful to have Fred do the '*parley vooing*,' as uncle calls it.

"Such delightful times as we are having! sight-seeing from morning till night, stopping for nice lunches in the gay *cafés*, and meeting with all sorts of droll adventures. Rainy days I spend in the Louvre, revelling in pictures. Jo would turn up her naughty nose at some of the finest, because she has no soul for art; but *I* have, and I'm cultivating eye and taste as fast as I can. She would like the relics of great people better, for I've seen her Napoleon's cocked hat and gray coat, his baby's cradle and his old toothbrush; also Marie Antoinette's little shoe, the ring of Saint Denis, Charlemagne's sword, and many other interesting things. I'll talk for hours about them when I come, but haven't time to write.

"The Palais Royale is a heavenly place,—so full of *bijouterie* and lovely things that I'm nearly distracted because I can't buy them. Fred wanted to get me some, but of course I didn't allow it. Then the Bois and the Champs Elysées are *très magnifique*. I've seen the imperial family several times,—the emperor an ugly, hard-looking man, the empress pale and pretty, but dressed in bad taste, *I* thought,—purple dress, green hat, and yellow gloves. Little Nap. is a handsome boy, who sits chatting to his tutor, and kisses his hand to the people as he passes in his four-horse barouche, with postilions in red satin jackets, and a mounted guard before and behind.

"We often walk in the Tuileries Gardens, for they are lovely, though the antique Luxembourg Gardens suit me better. Père la Chaise is very curious, for many of the tombs are like small rooms, and, looking in, one sees a table, with images or pictures of the dead, and chairs for the mourners to sit in when they come to lament. That is so Frenchy.

"Our rooms are on the Rue de Rivoli, and, sitting in the balcony, we look up and down the long, brilliant street. It is so pleasant that we spend our evenings talking there, when too tired with our day's work to go out. Fred is very entertaining, and is altogether the most agreeable young man I ever knew,—except Laurie, whose manners are more charming. I wish Fred was dark, for I don't fancy light men; however, the Vaughns are very rich, and come of an excellent family, so I won't find fault with their yellow hair, as my own is yellower.

"Next week we are off to Germany and Switzerland; and, as we shall travel fast, I shall only be able to give you hasty letters. I keep my diary, and try to 'remember correctly and describe clearly all that I see and admire,' as father advised. It is good practice for me, and, with my sketch-book, will give you a better idea of my tour than these scribbles.

"Adieu; I embrace you tenderly.

VOTRE AMIE."

---

"HEIDELBERG.

"MY DEAR MAMMA,—

"Having a quiet hour before we leave for Berne, I'll try to tell you what has happened, for some of it is very important, as you will see.

"The sail up the Rhine was perfect, and I just sat and enjoyed it with all my might. Get father's old guide-books, and read about it; I haven't words beautiful enough to describe it. At Coblentz we had a lovely time, for some students from Bonn, with whom Fred got acquainted on the boat, gave us a serenade. It was a moonlight night, and, about one o'clock, Flo and I were waked by the most delicious music under our windows. We flew up, and hid behind the curtains; but sly peeps showed us Fred and the students singing away down below. It was the most romantic thing I ever saw,—the river, the bridge of boats, the great fortress opposite, moonlight everywhere, and music fit to melt a heart of stone.

"When they were done we threw down some flowers, and saw them scramble for them, kiss their hands to the invisible ladies, and go laughing away,—to smoke and drink beer, I suppose. Next morning Fred showed me one of the crumpled flowers in his vest-pocket, and looked very sentimental. I laughed at him, and said I didn't throw it, but Flo, which seemed to disgust him, for he tossed it out of the window, and turned sensible again. I'm afraid I'm going to have trouble with that boy, it begins to look like it.

"The baths at Nassau were very gay, so was Baden-Baden, where Fred lost some money, and I scolded him. He needs some one to look after him when Frank is not with him. Kate said once she hoped he'd marry soon, and I quite agree with her that it would be well for him. Frankfort was delightful; I saw Goethe's house, Schiller's statue, and Dannecker's famous 'Ariadne.' It was very lovely, but I should have enjoyed it more if I had known the story better. I didn't like to ask, as every one knew it, or pretended they did. I wish Jo would tell me all about it; I ought to have read more, for I find I don't know anything, and it mortifies me.

"Now comes the serious part,—for it happened here, and Fred is just gone. He has been so kind and jolly that we all got quite fond of him; I never thought of anything but a travelling friendship, till the serenade night. Since then

I've begun to feel that the moonlight walks, balcony talks, and daily adventures were something more to him than fun. I haven't flirted, mother, truly, but remembered what you said to me, and have done my very best. I can't help it if people like me; I don't try to make them, and it worries me if I don't care for them, though Jo says I haven't got any heart. Now I know mother will shake her head, and the girls say, 'Oh, the mercenary little wretch!' but I've made up my mind, and, if Fred asks me, I shall accept him, though I'm not madly in love. I like him, and we get on comfortably together. He is handsome, young, clever enough, and very rich,—ever so much richer than the Laurences. I don't think his family would object, and I should be very happy, for they are all kind, well-bred, generous people, and they like me. Fred, as the eldest twin, will have the estate, I suppose, and such a splendid one as it is! A city house in a fashionable street, not so showy as our big houses, but twice as comfortable, and full of solid luxury, such as English people believe in. I like it, for it's genuine. I've seen the plate, the family jewels, the old servants, and pictures of the country place, with its park, great house, lovely grounds, and fine horses. Oh, it would be all I should ask! and I'd rather have it than any title such as girls snap up so readily, and find nothing behind. I may be mercenary, but I hate poverty, and don't mean to bear it a minute longer than I can help. One of us *must* marry well; Meg didn't, Jo won't, Beth can't yet, so I shall, and make everything cosey all round. I wouldn't marry a man I hated or despised. You may be sure of that; and, though Fred is not my model hero, he does very well, and, in time, I should get fond enough of him if he was very fond of me, and let me do just as I liked. So I've been turning the matter over in my mind the last week, for it was impossible to help seeing that Fred liked me. He said nothing, but little things showed it; he never goes with Flo, always gets on my side of the carriage, table, or promenade, looks sentimental when we are alone, and frowns at any one else who ventures to speak to me. Yesterday, at dinner, when an Austrian officer stared at us, and then said something to his friend,—a rakish-looking baron,—about '*ein wonderschönes Blöndchen*,' Fred looked as fierce as a lion, and cut his meat so savagely, it nearly flew off his plate. He isn't one of the cool, stiff Englishmen, but is rather peppery, for he has Scotch blood in him, as one might guess from his bonnie blue eyes.

"Well, last evening we went up to the castle about sunset,—at least all of us but Fred, who was to meet us there, after going to the Post Restante for letters. We had a charming time poking about the ruins, the vaults where the monster tun is, and the beautiful gardens made by the elector, long ago, for his English wife. I liked the great terrace best, for the view was divine; so, while the rest went to see the rooms inside, I sat there trying to sketch the gray stone lion's head on the wall, with scarlet woodbine sprays hanging round it. I felt as if I'd got into a romance, sitting there, watching the Neckar rolling through the valley, listening to the music of the Austrian band below, and waiting for my lover, like a real story-book girl. I had a feeling that something was going to happen, and I was ready for it. I didn't feel blushy or quakey, but quite cool, and only a little excited.

"By and by I heard Fred's voice, and then he came hurrying through the great arch to find me. He looked so troubled that I forgot all about myself, and asked what the matter was. He said he'd just got a letter begging him to come home, for Frank was very ill; so he was going at once, in the night train, and only had time to say good-by. I was very sorry for him, and disappointed for myself, but only for a minute, because he said, as he shook hands,—and said it in a way that I could not mistake,—'I shall soon come back; you won't forget me, Amy?'

"I didn't promise, but I looked at him, and he seemed satisfied, and there was no time for anything but messages and good-byes, for he was off in an hour, and we all miss him very much. I know he wanted to speak, but I think, from something he once hinted, that he had promised his father not to do anything of the sort yet awhile, for he is a rash boy, and the old gentleman dreads a foreign daughter-in-law. We shall soon meet in Rome; and then, if I don't change my mind, I'll say 'Yes, thank you,' when he says 'Will you, please?'

"Of course this is all *very private*, but I wished you to know what was going on. Don't be anxious about me; remember I am your 'prudent Amy,' and be sure I will do nothing rashly. Send me as much advice as you like; I'll use it if I can. I wish I could see you for a good talk, Marmee. Love and trust me.

"Ever your

AMY

## IX

## TENDER TROUBLES.

"JO, I'm anxious about Beth."

"Why, mother, she has seemed unusually well since the babies came."

"It's not her health that troubles me now; it's her spirits. I'm sure there is something on her mind, and I want you to discover what it is."

"What makes you think so, mother?"

"She sits alone a good deal, and doesn't talk to her father as much as she used. I found her crying over the babies the other day. When she sings, the songs are always sad ones, and now and then I see a look in her face that I don't understand. This isn't like Beth, and it worries me."

"Have you asked her about it?"

"I have tried once or twice; but she either evaded my questions, or looked so distressed that I stopped. I never force my children's confidence, and I seldom have to wait for it long."

Mrs. March glanced at Jo as she spoke, but the face opposite seemed quite unconscious of any secret disquietude but Beth's; and, after sewing thoughtfully for a minute, Jo said,—

"I think she is growing up, and so begins to dream dreams, and have hopes and fears and fidgets, without knowing why, or being able to explain them. Why, mother, Beth's eighteen, but we don't realize it, and treat her like a child, forgetting she's a woman."

"So she is. Dear heart, how fast you do grow up," returned her mother, with a sigh and a smile.

" Can't be helped, Marmee, so you must resign yourself to all sorts of worries, and let your birds hop out of the nest, one by one. I promise never to hop very far, if that is any comfort to you."

"It is a great comfort, Jo; I always feel strong when you are at home, now Meg is gone. Beth is too feeble and Amy too young to depend upon; but when the tug comes, you are always ready."

"Why, you know I don't mind hard jobs much, and there must always be one scrub in a family. Amy is splendid in fine works, and I'm not; but I feel in my element when all the carpets are to be taken up, or half the family fall sick at once. Amy is distinguishing herself abroad; but if anything is amiss at home, I'm your man."

"I leave Beth to your hands, then, for she will open her tender little heart to her Jo sooner than to any one else. Be very kind, and don't let her think any one watches or talks about her. If she only would get quite strong and cheerful again, I shouldn't have a wish in the world."

"Happy woman! I've got heaps."

"My dear, what are they?"

"I'll settle Bethy's troubles, and then I'll tell you mine. They are not very wearing, so they'll keep;" and Jo stitched away, with a wise nod which set her mother's heart at rest about her, for the present at least.

While apparently absorbed in her own affairs, Jo watched Beth; and, after many conflicting conjectures, finally settled upon one which seemed to explain the change in her. A slight incident gave Jo the clue to the mystery, she thought, and lively fancy, loving heart did the rest. She was affecting to write busily one Saturday afternoon, when she and Beth were alone together; yet as she scribbled, she kept her eye on her sister, who seemed unusually quiet. Sitting at the window, Beth's work often dropped into her lap, and she leaned her head upon her hand, in a dejected attitude, while her eyes rested on the dull, autumnal landscape. Suddenly some one passed below, whistling like an operatic blackbird, and a voice called out,—

"All serene! Coming in to-night."

Beth started, leaned forward, smiled and nodded, watched the passer-by till his quick tramp died away, then said softly, as if to herself,—

"How strong and well and happy that dear boy looks."

"Hum!" said Jo, still intent upon her sister's face; for the bright color faded as quickly as it came, the smile vanished, and presently a tear lay shining on the window-ledge. Beth whisked it off, and glanced apprehensively at Jo; but she was scratching away at a tremendous rate, apparently engrossed in "Olympia's Oath." The instant Beth turned, Jo began her watch again, saw Beth's hand go quietly to her eyes more than once, and, in her half-averted face, read a tender sorrow that made her own eyes fill. Fearing to betray herself, she slipped away, murmuring something about needing more paper.

"Mercy on me, Beth loves Laurie!" she said, sitting down in her own room, pale with the shock of the discovery which she believed she had just made. "I never dreamt of such a thing. What *will* mother say? I wonder if he—" there Jo stopped, and turned scarlet with a sudden thought. "If he shouldn't love back again, how dreadful it would be. He must; I'll make him!" and she shook her head threateningly at the picture of the mischievous-looking boy laughing at her from the wall. "Oh dear, we *are* growing up with a vengeance. Here's Meg married and a mamma, Amy flourishing away at Paris, and Beth in love. I'm the only one that has sense enough to keep out of mischief." Jo thought intently for a minute, with her eyes fixed on the picture; then she smoothed out her wrinkled forehead, and said, with a decided nod at the face opposite, "No, thank you, sir; you're very charming, but you've no more stability than a weathercock; so you needn't write touching notes, and smile in that insinuating way, for it won't do a bit of good, and I won't have it."

Then she sighed, and fell into a reverie, from which she did not wake till the early twilight sent her down to take new observations, which only confirmed her suspicion. Though Laurie flirted with Amy and joked with Jo, his manner to Beth had always been peculiarly kind and gentle, but so was everybody's; therefore, no one thought of imagining that he cared more for her than for the others. Indeed, a general impression had prevailed in the family, of late, that "our boy" was getting fonder than ever of Jo, who, however, wouldn't hear a word upon the subject, and scolded violently if any one dared to suggest it. If they had known the various tender passages of the past year, or rather attempts at tender passages which had been nipped in the bud, they would have had the immense satisfaction of saying, "I told you so." But Jo hated "philandering," and wouldn't allow it, always having a joke or a smile ready at the least sign of impending danger.

When Laurie first went to college, he fell in love about once a month; but these small flames were as brief as ardent, did no damage, and much amused Jo, who took great interest in the alternations of hope, despair, and resignation, which were confided to her in their weekly conferences. But there came a time when Laurie ceased to worship at many shrines, hinted darkly at one all-absorbing passion, and indulged occasionally in Byronic fits of gloom. Then he avoided the tender subject altogether, wrote philosophical notes to Jo, turned studious, and gave out that he was going to "dig," intending to graduate in a blaze of glory. This suited the young lady better than twilight confidences, tender pressures of the hand, and eloquent glances of the eye; for with Jo, brain developed earlier than heart, and she preferred imaginary heroes to real ones, because, when tired of them, the former could be shut up in the tin-kitchen till called for, and the latter were less manageable.

Things were in this state when the grand discovery was made, and Jo watched Laurie that night as she had never done before. If she had not got the new idea into her head, she would have seen nothing unusual in the fact that Beth was very quiet, and Laurie very kind to her. But having given the rein to her lively fancy, it galloped away with her at a great pace; and common sense, being rather weakened by a long course of romance writing, did not come to the rescue. As usual, Beth lay on the sofa, and Laurie sat in a low chair close by, amusing her with all sorts of gossip; for she depended on her weekly "spin," and he never disappointed her. But that evening, Jo fancied that Beth's eyes rested on the lively, dark face beside her with peculiar pleasure, and that she listened with intense interest to an account of some exciting cricket-match, though the phrases, "caught off a tice," "stumped off his ground," and "the leg hit for three," were as intelligible to her as Sanscrit. She also fancied, having set her heart upon seeing it, that she saw a certain increase of gentleness in Laurie's manner, that he dropped his voice now and then, laughed less than usual, was a little absent-minded, and settled the afghan over Beth's feet with an assiduity that was really almost tender.

"Who knows? stranger things have happened," thought Jo, as she fussed about the room. "She will make quite an angel of him, and he will make life delightfully easy and pleasant for the dear, if they only love each other. I don't see how he can help it; and I do believe he would if the rest of us were out of the way."

As every one *was* out of the way but herself, Jo began to feel that she ought to dispose of herself with all speed. But where should she go? and burning to lay herself upon the shrine of sisterly devotion, she sat down to settle that point.

Now, the old sofa was a regular patriarch of a sofa,—long, broad, well-cushioned, and low; a trifle shabby, as well it might be, for the girls had slept and sprawled on it as babies, fished over the back, rode on the arms, and had menageries under it as children, and rested tired heads, dreamed dreams, and listened to tender talk on it as young women. They all loved it, for it was a family refuge, and one corner had always been Jo's favorite lounging-place. Among the many pillows that adorned the venerable couch was one, hard, round, covered with prickly horsehair, and furnished with a knobby button at each end; this repulsive pillow was her especial property, being used as a weapon of defence, a barricade, or a stern preventive of too much slumber.

Laurie knew this pillow well, and had cause to regard it with deep aversion, having been unmercifully pummelled with it in former days, when romping was allowed, and now frequently debarred by it from taking the seat he most coveted, next to Jo in the sofa corner. If "the sausage" as they called it, stood on end, it was a sign that he might approach and repose; but if it lay flat across the sofa, woe to the man, woman, or child who dared disturb it! That evening Jo forgot to barricade her corner, and had not been in her seat five minutes, before a massive form appeared beside her, and, with both arms spread over the sofa-back, both long legs stretched out before him, Laurie exclaimed, with a sigh of satisfaction,—

"Now, *this* is filling at the price."

"No slang," snapped Jo, slamming down the pillow. But it was too late, there was no room for it; and, coasting on to the floor, it disappeared in a most mysterious manner.

"Come, Jo, don't be thorny. After studying himself to a skeleton all the week, a fellow deserves petting, and ought to get it."

"Beth will pet you; I'm busy."

"No, she's not to be bothered with me; but you like that sort of thing, unless you've suddenly lost your taste for it. Have you? Do you hate your boy, and want to fire pillows at him?"

Anything more wheedlesome than that touching appeal was seldom heard, but Jo quenched "her boy" by turning on him with the stern query,—

"How many bouquets have you sent Miss Randal this week?"

"Not one, upon my word. She's engaged. Now then."

"I'm glad of it; that's one of your foolish extravagances,—sending flowers and things to girls for whom you don't care two pins," continued Jo reprovingly.

"Sensible girls, for whom I do care whole papers of pins, won't let me send them 'flowers and things,' so what can I do? My feelings must have a *went*."

"Mother doesn't approve of flirting, even in fun; and you do flirt desperately, Teddy."

"I'd give anything if I could answer, 'So do you.' As I can't, I'll merely say that I don't see any harm in that pleasant little game, if all parties understand that it's only play."

"Well, it does look pleasant, but I can't learn how it's done. I've tried, because one feels awkward in company, not to do as everybody else is doing; but I don't seem to get on," said Jo, forgetting to play Mentor.

"Take lessons of Amy; she has a regular talent for it."

"Yes, she does it very prettily, and never seems to go too far. I suppose it's natural to some people to please without trying, and others to always say and do the wrong thing in the wrong place."

"I'm glad you can't flirt; it's really refreshing to see a sensible, straightforward girl, who can be jolly and kind without making a fool of herself. Between ourselves, Jo, some of the girls I know really do go on at such a rate I'm ashamed of them. They don't mean any harm, I'm sure; but if they knew how we fellows talked about them afterward, they'd mend their ways, I fancy."

"They do the same; and, as their tongues are the sharpest, you fellows get the worst of it, for you are as silly as they, every bit. If you behaved properly, they would; but, knowing you like their nonsense, they keep it up, and then you blame them."

"Much you know about it, ma'am," said Laurie, in a superior tone. "We don't like romps and flirts, though we may act as if we did sometimes. The pretty, modest girls are never talked about, except respectfully, among gentlemen. Bless your innocent soul! If you could be in my place for a month you'd see things that would astonish you a trifle. Upon my word, when I see one of those harum-scarum girls, I always want to say with our friend Cock Robin,—

"'Out upon you, fie upon you,
Bold-faced jig!'"

It was impossible to help laughing at the funny conflict between Laurie's chivalrous reluctance to speak ill of womankind, and his very natural dislike of the unfeminine folly of which fashionable society showed him many samples. Jo knew that "young Laurence" was regarded as a most eligible *parti* by worldly mammas, was much smiled upon by their daughters, and flattered enough by ladies of all ages to make a coxcomb of him; so she watched him rather jealously, fearing he would be spoilt, and rejoiced more than she confessed to find that he still believed in modest girls. Returning suddenly to her admonitory tone, she said, dropping her voice, "If you *must* have a 'went,' Teddy, go and devote yourself to one of the 'pretty, modest girls' whom you do respect, and not waste your time with the silly ones."

"You really advise it?" and Laurie looked at her with an odd mixture of anxiety and merriment in his face.

"Yes, I do; but you'd better wait till you are through college, on the whole, and be fitting yourself for the place meantime. You're not half good enough for—well, whoever the modest girl may be," and Jo looked a little queer likewise, for a name had almost escaped her.

"That I'm not!" acquiesced Laurie, with an expression of humility quite new to him, as he dropped his eyes, and absently wound Jo's apron-tassel round his finger.

"Mercy on us, this will never do," thought Jo; adding aloud, "Go and sing to me. I'm dying for some music, and always like yours."

"I'd rather stay here, thank you."

"Well, you can't; there isn't room. Go and make yourself useful, since you are too big to be ornamental. I thought you hated to be tied to a woman's apron-string?" retorted Jo, quoting certain rebellious words of his own.

"Ah, that depends on who wears the apron!" and Laurie gave an audacious tweak at the tassel.

"Are you going?" demanded Jo, diving for the pillow.

He fled at once, and the minute it was well "Up with the bonnets of bonnie Dundee," she slipped away, to return no more till the young gentleman had departed in high dudgeon.

Jo lay long awake that night, and was just dropping off when the sound of a stifled sob made her fly to Beth's bedside, with the anxious inquiry, "What is it, dear?"

"I thought you were asleep," sobbed Beth.

"Is it the old pain, my precious?"

"No; it's a new one; but I can bear it," and Beth tried to check her tears.

"Tell me all about it, and let me cure it as I often did the other."

"You can't; there is no cure." There Beth's voice gave way, and, clinging to her sister, she cried so despairingly that Jo was frightened.

"Where is it? Shall I call mother?"

Beth did not answer the first question; but in the dark one hand went involuntarily to her heart, as if the pain were there; with the other she held Jo fast, whispering eagerly, "No, no, don't call her, don't tell her. I shall be better soon. Lie down here and 'poor' my head. I'll be quiet, and go to sleep; indeed I will."

Jo obeyed; but as her hand went softly to and fro across Beth's hot forehead and wet eyelids, her heart was very full, and she longed to speak. But young as she was, Jo had learned that hearts, like flowers, cannot be rudely handled, but must open naturally; so, though she believed she knew the cause of Beth's new pain, she only said, in her tenderest tone, "Does anything trouble you, deary?"

"Yes, Jo," after a long pause.

"Wouldn't it comfort you to tell me what it is?"

"Not now, not yet."

"Then I won't ask; but remember, Bethy, that mother and Jo are always glad to hear and help you, if they can."

"I know it. I'll tell you by and by."

"Is the pain better now?"

"Oh, yes, much better; you are so comfortable, Jo!"

"Go to sleep, dear; I'll stay with you."

So cheek to cheek they fell asleep, and on the morrow Beth seemed quite herself again; for at eighteen, neither heads nor hearts ache long, and a loving word can medicine most ills.

But Jo had made up her mind, and, after pondering over a project for some days, she confided it to her mother.

"You asked me the other day what my wishes were. I'll tell you one of them, Marmee," she began, as they sat alone together. "I want to go away somewhere this winter for a change."

"Why, Jo?" and her mother looked up quickly, as if the words suggested a double meaning.

With her eyes on her work, Jo answered soberly, "I want something new; I feel restless, and anxious to be seeing, doing, and learning more than I am. I brood too much over my own small affairs, and need stirring up, so, as I can be spared this winter, I'd like to hop a little way, and try my wings."

"Where will you hop?"

"To New York. I had a bright idea yesterday, and this is it. You know Mrs. Kirke wrote to you for some respectable young person to teach her children and sew. It's rather hard to find just the thing, but I think I should suit if I tried."

"My dear, go out to service in that great boarding-house!" and Mrs. March looked surprised, but not displeased.

"It's not exactly going out to service; for Mrs. Kirke is your friend,—the kindest soul that ever lived,—and would make things pleasant for me, I know. Her family is separate from the rest, and no one knows me there. Don't care if they do; it's honest work, and I'm not ashamed of it."

"Nor I; but your writing?"

"All the better for the change. I shall see and hear new things, get new ideas, and, even if I haven't much time there, I shall bring home quantities of material for my rubbish."

"I have no doubt of it; but are these your only reasons for this sudden fancy?"

"No, mother."

"May I know the others?"

Jo looked up and Jo looked down, then said slowly, with sudden color in her cheeks, "It may be vain and wrong to say it, but—I'm afraid—Laurie is getting too fond of me."

"Then you don't care for him in the way it is evident he begins to care for you?" and Mrs. March looked anxious as she put the question.

"Mercy, no! I love the dear boy, as I always have, and am immensely proud of him; but as for anything more, it's out of the question."

"I'm glad of that, Jo."

"Why, please?"

"Because, dear, I don't think you suited to one another. As friends you are very happy, and your frequent quarrels soon blow over; but I fear you would both rebel if you were mated for life. You are too much alike and too fond of freedom, not to mention hot tempers and strong wills, to get on happily together, in a relation which needs infinite patience and forbearance, as well as love."

"That's just the feeling I had, though I couldn't express it. I'm glad you think he is only beginning to care for me. It would trouble me sadly to make him unhappy; for I couldn't fall in love with the dear old fellow merely out of gratitude, could I?"

"You are sure of his feeling for you?"

The color deepened in Jo's cheeks, as she answered, with the look of mingled pleasure, pride, and pain which young girls wear when speaking of first lovers,—

"I'm afraid it is so, mother; he hasn't said anything, but he looks a great deal. I think I had better go away before it comes to anything."

"I agree with you, and if it can be managed you shall go."

Jo looked relieved, and, after a pause, said, smiling, "How Mrs. Moffat would wonder at your want of management, if she knew; and how she will rejoice that Annie still may hope."

"Ah, Jo, mothers may differ in their management, but the hope is the same in all,—the desire to see their children happy. Meg is so, and I am content with her success. You I leave to enjoy your liberty till you tire of it; for only then will you find that there is something sweeter. Amy is my chief care now, but her good sense will help her. For Beth, I indulge no hopes except that she may be well. By the way, she seems brighter this last day or two. Have you spoken to her?"

"Yes; she owned she had a trouble, and promised to tell me by and by. I said no more, for I think I know it;" and Jo told her little story.

Mrs. March shook her head, and did not take so romantic a view of the case, but looked grave, and repeated her opinion that, for Laurie's sake, Jo should go away for a time.

"Let us say nothing about it to him till the plan is settled; then I'll run away before he can collect his wits and be tragical. Beth must think I'm going to please myself, as I am, for I can't talk about Laurie to her; but she can pet and comfort him after I'm gone, and so cure him of this romantic notion. He's been through so many little trials of the sort, he's used to it, and will soon get over his love-lornity."

Jo spoke hopefully, but could not rid herself of the foreboding fear that this "little trial" would be harder than the others, and that Laurie would not get over his "love-lornity" as easily as heretofore.

The plan was talked over in a family council, and agreed upon; for Mrs. Kirke gladly accepted Jo, and promised to make a pleasant home for her. The teaching would render her independent; and such leisure as she got might be made profitable by writing, while the new scenes and society would be both useful and agreeable. Jo liked the prospect and was eager to be gone, for the home-nest was growing too narrow for her restless nature and adventurous spirit. When all was settled, with fear and trembling she told Laurie; but to her surprise he took it very quietly. He had been graver than usual of late, but very pleasant; and, when jokingly accused of turning over a new leaf, he answered soberly, "So I am; and I mean this one shall stay turned."

Jo was very much relieved that one of his virtuous fits should come on just then, and made her preparations with a lightened heart,—for Beth seemed more cheerful,—and hoped she was doing the best for all.

"One thing I leave to your especial care," she said, the night before she left.

"You mean your papers?" asked Beth.

"No, my boy. Be very good to him, won't you?"

"Of course I will; but I can't fill your place, and he'll miss you sadly."

"It won't hurt him; so remember, I leave him in your charge, to plague, pet, and keep in order."

"I'll do my best, for your sake," promised Beth, wondering why Jo looked at her so queerly.

When Laurie said "Good-by," he whispered significantly, "It won't do a bit of good, Jo. My eye is on you; so mind what you do, or I'll come and bring you home."

# X

# JO'S JOURNAL.

"NEW YORK, November.

"DEAR MARMEE AND BETH,—

"I'm going to write you a regular volume, for I've got heaps to tell, though I'm not a fine young lady travelling on the continent. When I lost sight of father's dear old face, I felt a trifle blue, and might have shed a briny drop or two, if an Irish lady with four small children, all crying more or less, hadn't diverted my mind; for I amused myself by dropping gingerbread nuts over the seat every time they opened their mouths to roar.

"Soon the sun came out, and taking it as a good omen, I cleared up likewise, and enjoyed my journey with all my heart.

"Mrs. Kirke welcomed me so kindly I felt at home at once, even in that big house full of strangers. She gave me a funny little sky-parlor—all she had; but there is a stove in it, and a nice table in a sunny window, so I can sit here and write whenever I like. A fine view and a church-tower opposite atone for the many stairs, and I took a fancy to my den on the spot. The nursery, where I am to teach and sew, is a pleasant room next Mrs. Kirke's private parlor, and the two little girls are pretty children,—rather spoilt, I fancy, but they took to me after telling them 'The Seven Bad Pigs;' and I've no doubt I shall make a model governess.

"I am to have my meals with the children, if I prefer it to the great table, and for the present I do, for I *am* bashful, though no one will believe it.

"'Now, my dear, make yourself at home,' said Mrs. K. in her motherly way; 'I'm on the drive from morning to night, as you may suppose with such a family; but a great anxiety will be off my mind if I know the children are safe with you. My rooms are always open to you, and your own shall be as comfortable as I can make it. There are some pleasant people in the house if you feel sociable, and your evenings are always free. Come to me if anything goes wrong, and be as happy as you can. There's the tea-bell; I must run and change my cap;' and off she bustled, leaving me to settle myself in my new nest.

"As I went downstairs, soon after, I saw something I liked. The flights are very long in this tall house, and as I stood waiting at the head of the third one for a little servant girl to lumber up, I saw a gentleman come along behind her, take the heavy hod of coal out of her hand, carry it all the way up, put it down at a door near by, and walk away, saying, with a kind nod and a foreign accent,—

"'It goes better so. The little back is too young to haf such heaviness.'

"Wasn't it good of him? I like such things, for, as father says, trifles show character. When I mentioned it to Mrs. K., that evening, she laughed, and said,—

"'That must have been Professor Bhaer; he's always doing things of that sort.'

"Mrs. K. told me he was from Berlin; very learned and good, but poor as a church-mouse, and gives lessons to support himself and two little orphan nephews whom he is educating here, according to the wishes of his sister, who married an American. Not a very romantic story, but it interested me; and I was glad to hear that Mrs. K. lends him her parlor for some of his scholars. There is a glass door between it and the nursery, and I mean to peep at him, and then I'll tell you how he looks. He's almost forty, so it's no harm, Marmee.

"After tea and a go-to-bed romp with the little girls, I attacked the big work-basket, and had a quiet evening chatting with my new friend. I shall keep a journal-letter, and send it once a week; so good-night, and more to-morrow."

---

"*Tuesday Eve.*

"Had a lively time in my seminary, this morning, for the children acted like Sancho; and at one time I really thought I should shake them all round. Some good angel inspired me to try gymnastics, and I kept it up till they were glad to sit down and keep still. After luncheon, the girl took them out for a walk, and I went to my needle-work, like little Mabel, 'with a willing mind.' I was thanking my stars that I'd learned to make nice button-holes, when the parlor-door opened and shut, and some one began to hum,—

'Kennst du das land,'

like a big bumble-bee. It was dreadfully improper, I know, but I couldn't resist the temptation; and lifting one end of the curtain before the glass door, I peeped in. Professor Bhaer was there; and while he arranged his books, I took a good look at him. A regular German,—rather stout, with brown hair tumbled all over his head, a bushy beard, good nose, the kindest eyes I ever saw, and a splendid big voice that does one's ears good, after our sharp or slipshod American gabble. His clothes were rusty, his hands were large, and he hadn't a really handsome feature in his face, except his beautiful teeth; yet I liked him, for he had a fine head; his linen was very nice, and he looked like a gentleman, though two buttons were off his coat, and there was a patch on one shoe. He looked sober in spite of his humming, till he went to the window to turn the hyacinth bulbs toward the sun, and stroke the cat, who received him like an old friend. Then he smiled; and when a tap came at the door, called out in a loud, brisk tone,—

"'Herein!'

"I was just going to run, when I caught sight of a morsel of a child carrying a big book, and stopped to see what was going on.

"'Me wants my Bhaer,' said the mite, slamming down her book, and running to meet him.

"'Thou shalt haf thy Bhaer; come, then, and take a goot hug from him, my Tina,' said the Professor, catching her up, with a laugh, and holding her so high over his head that she had to stoop her little face to kiss him.

"'Now me mus tuddy my lessin,' went on the funny little thing; so he put her up at the table, opened the great dictionary she had brought, and gave her a paper and pencil, and she scribbled away, turning a leaf now and then, and passing her little fat finger down the page, as if finding a word, so soberly that I nearly betrayed myself by a laugh, while Mr. Bhaer stood stroking her pretty hair, with a fatherly look, that made me think she must be his own, though she looked more French than German.

"Another knock and the appearance of two young ladies sent me back to my work, and there I virtuously remained through all the noise and gabbling that went on next door. One of the girls kept laughing affectedly, and saying 'Now Professor,' in a coquettish tone, and the other pronounced her German with an accent that must have made it hard for him to keep sober.

"Both seemed to try his patience sorely; for more than once I heard him say emphatically, 'No, no, it is *not* so; you haf not attend to what I say;' and once there was a loud rap, as if he struck the table with his book, followed by the despairing exclamation, 'Prut! it all goes bad this day.'

"Poor man, I pitied him; and when the girls were gone, took just one more peep, to see if he survived it. He seemed to have thrown himself back in his chair, tired out, and sat there with his eyes shut till the clock struck two, when he jumped up, put his books in his pocket, as if ready for another lesson, and, taking little Tina, who had fallen asleep on the sofa, in his arms, he carried her quietly away. I fancy he has a hard life of it.

"Mrs. Kirke asked me if I wouldn't go down to the five o'clock dinner; and, feeling a little bit homesick, I thought I would, just to see what sort of people are under the same roof with me. So I made myself respectable, and tried to slip in behind Mrs. Kirke; but as she is short, and I'm tall, my efforts at concealment were rather a failure. She gave me a seat by her, and after my face cooled off, I plucked up courage, and looked about me. The long table was full, and every one intent on getting their dinner,—the gentlemen especially, who seemed to be eating on time, for they *bolted* in every sense of the word, vanishing as soon as they were done. There was the usual assortment of young men absorbed in themselves; young couples absorbed in each other; married ladies in their babies, and old gentlemen in politics. I don't think I shall care to have much to do with any of them, except one sweet-faced maiden lady, who looks as if she had something in her.

"Cast away at the very bottom of the table was the Professor, shouting answers to the questions of a very inquisitive, deaf old gentleman on one side, and talking philosophy with a Frenchman on the other. If Amy had been here, she'd have turned her back on him forever, because, sad to relate, he had a great appetite, and shovelled in his dinner in a manner which would have horrified 'her ladyship.' I didn't mind, for I like 'to see folks eat with a relish,' as Hannah says, and the poor man must have needed a deal of food after teaching idiots all day.

"As I went upstairs after dinner, two of the young men were settling their hats before the hall-mirror, and I heard one say low to the other, 'Who's the new party?'

"'Governess, or something of that sort.'

"'What the deuce is she at our table for?'

"'Friend of the old lady's.'

"'Handsome head, but no style.'

"'Not a bit of it. Give us a light and come on.'

"I felt angry at first, and then I didn't care, for a governess is as good as a clerk, and I've got sense, if I haven't style, which is more than some people have, judging from the remarks of the elegant beings who clattered away, smoking like bad chimneys. I hate ordinary people!"

---

"*Thursday.*

"Yesterday was a quiet day, spent in teaching, sewing, and writing in my little room, which is very cosey, with a light and fire. I picked up a few bits of news, and was introduced to the Professor. It seems that Tina is the child of the Frenchwoman who does the fine ironing in the laundry here. The little thing has lost her heart to Mr. Bhaer, and follows him about the house like a dog whenever he is at home, which delights him, as he is very fond of children, though a 'bacheldore.' Kitty and Minnie Kirke likewise regard him with affection, and tell all sorts of stories about the plays he invents, the presents he brings, and the splendid tales he tells. The young men quiz him, it seems, call him Old Fritz, Lager Beer, Ursa Major, and make all manner of jokes on his name. But he enjoys it like a boy, Mrs. K. says, and takes it so good-naturedly that they all like him, in spite of his foreign ways.

"The maiden lady is a Miss Norton,—rich, cultivated, and kind. She spoke to me at dinner to-day (for I went to table again, it's such fun to watch people), and asked me to come and see her at her room. She has fine books and pictures, knows interesting persons, and seems friendly; so I shall make myself agreeable, for I *do* want to get into good society, only it isn't the same sort that Amy likes.

"I was in our parlor last evening, when Mr. Bhaer came in with some newspapers for Mrs. Kirke. She wasn't there, but Minnie, who is a little old woman, introduced me very prettily: 'This is mamma's friend, Miss March.'

"'Yes; and she's jolly and we like her lots,' added Kitty, who is an *enfant terrible.*

"We both bowed, and then we laughed, for the prim introduction and the blunt addition were rather a comical contrast.

"'Ah, yes, I hear these naughty ones go to vex you, Mees Marsch. If so again, call at me and I come,' he said, with a threatening frown that delighted the little wretches.

"I promised I would, and he departed; but it seems as if I was doomed to see a good deal of him, for to-day, as I passed his door on my way out, by accident I knocked against it with my umbrella. It flew open, and there he stood in his dressing gown, with a big blue sock on one hand, and a darning-needle in the other; he didn't seem at all ashamed of it, for when I explained and hurried on, he waved his hand, sock and all, saying in his loud, cheerful way,—

"'You haf a fine day to make your walk. *Bon voyage, mademoiselle.*'

"I laughed all the way downstairs; but it was a little pathetic, also, to think of the poor man having to mend his own clothes. The German gentlemen embroider, I know; but darning hose is another thing, and not so pretty."

---

"*Saturday.*

"Nothing has happened to write about, except a call on Miss Norton, who has a room full of lovely things, and who was very charming, for she showed me all her treasures, and asked me if I would sometimes go with her to lectures and concerts, as her escort,—if I enjoyed them. She put it as a favor, but I'm sure Mrs. Kirke has told her about us, and she does it out of kindness to me. I'm as proud as Lucifer, but such favors from such people don't burden me, and I accepted gratefully.

"When I got back to the nursery there was such an uproar in the parlor that I looked in; and there was Mr. Bhaer down on his hands and knees, with Tina on his back, Kitty leading him with a jump-rope, and Minnie feeding two small boys with seed-cakes, as they roared and ramped in cages built of chairs.

"'We are playing *nargerie*,' explained Kitty.

"'Dis is mine effalunt!' added Tina, holding on by the Professor's hair.

"'Mamma always allows us to do what we like Saturday afternoon, when Franz and Emil come, doesn't she, Mr. Bhaer?' said Minnie.

"The 'effalunt' sat up, looking as much in earnest as any of them, and said soberly to me,—

"'I gif you my wort it is so. If we make too large a noise you shall say "Hush!" to us, and we go more softly.'

"I promised to do so, but left the door open, and enjoyed the fun as much as they did,—for a more glorious frolic I never witnessed. They played tag and soldiers, danced and sung, and when it began to grow dark they all piled on to the sofa about the Professor, while he told charming fairy stories of the storks on the chimney-tops, and the little 'kobolds,' who ride the snow-flakes as they fall. I wish Americans were as simple and natural as Germans, don't you?

"I'm so fond of writing, I should go spinning on forever if motives of economy didn't stop me, for though I've used thin paper and written fine, I tremble to think of the stamps this long letter will need. Pray forward Amy's as soon as you can spare them. My small news will sound very flat after her splendors, but you will like them, I know. Is Teddy studying so hard that he can't find time to write to his friends? Take good care of him for me, Beth, and tell me all about the babies, and give heaps of love to every one.

"From your faithful

JO.

"P. S. On reading over my letter it strikes me as rather Bhaery; but I am always interested in odd people, and I really had nothing else to write about. Bless you!"

---

"DECEMBER.

"MY PRECIOUS BETSEY,—

"As this is to be a scribble-scrabble letter, I direct it to you, for it may amuse you, and give you some idea of my goings on; for, though quiet, they are rather amusing, for which, oh, be joyful! After what Amy would call Herculaneum efforts, in the way of mental and moral agriculture, my young ideas begin to shoot and my little twigs to bend as I could wish. They are not so interesting to me as Tina and the boys, but I do my duty by them, and they are fond of me. Franz and Emil are jolly little lads, quite after my own heart; for the mixture of German and American spirit in them produces a constant state of effervescence. Saturday afternoons are riotous times, whether spent in the house or out; for on pleasant days they all go to walk, like a seminary, with the Professor and myself to keep order; and then such fun!

"We are very good friends now, and I've begun to take lessons. I really couldn't help it, and it all came about in such a droll way that I must tell you. To begin at the beginning, Mrs. Kirke called to me, one day, as I passed Mr. Bhaer's room, where she was rummaging.

"'Did you ever see such a den, my dear? Just come and help me put these books to rights, for I've turned everything upside down, trying to discover what he has done with the six new handkerchiefs I gave him not long ago.'

"I went in, and while we worked I looked about me, for it was 'a den,' to be sure. Books and papers everywhere; a broken meerschaum, and an old flute over the mantel-piece as if done with; a ragged bird, without any tail, chirped on one window-seat, and a box of white mice adorned the other; half-finished boats and bits of string lay among the manuscripts; dirty little boots stood drying before the fire; and traces of the dearly beloved boys, for whom he makes a slave of himself, were to be seen all over the room. After a grand rummage three of the missing articles were found,—one over the bird-cage, one covered with ink, and a third burnt brown, having been used as a holder.

"'Such a man!' laughed good-natured Mrs. K., as she put the relics in the rag-bag. 'I suppose the others are torn up to rig ships, bandage cut fingers, or make kite-tails. It's dreadful, but I can't scold him: he's so absent-minded and good-natured, he lets those boys ride over him rough-shod. I agreed to do his washing and mending, but he forgets to give out his things and I forget to look them over, so he comes to a sad pass sometimes.'

"'Let me mend them,' said I. 'I don't mind it, and he needn't know. I'd like to,—he's so kind to me about bringing my letters and lending books.'

"So I have got his things in order, and knit heels into two pairs of the socks,—for they were boggled out of shape with his queer darns. Nothing was said, and I hoped he wouldn't find it out, but one day last week he caught me at it. Hearing the lessons he gives to others has interested and amused me so much that I took a fancy to learn; for Tina runs in and out, leaving the door open, and I can hear. I had been sitting near this door, finishing off the last sock, and trying to understand what he said to a new scholar, who is as stupid as I am. The girl had gone, and I thought he had also, it was so still, and I was busily gabbling over a verb, and rocking to and fro in a most absurd way, when a little crow made me look up, and there was Mr. Bhaer looking and laughing quietly, while he made signs to Tina not to betray him.

"'So!' he said, as I stopped and stared like a goose, 'you peep at me, I peep at you, and that is not bad; but see, I am not pleasanting when I say, haf you a wish for German?'

"'Yes; but you are too busy. I am too stupid to learn,' I blundered out, as red as a peony.

"'Prut! we will make the time, and we fail not to find the sense. At efening I shall gif a little lesson with much gladness; for, look you, Mees Marsch, I haf this debt to pay,' and he pointed to my work. 'Yes, they say to one another, these so kind ladies, "he is a stupid old fellow; he will see not what we do; he will never opserve that his sock-heels go not in holes any more, he will think his buttons grow out new when they fall, and believe that strings make theirselves." Ah! but I haf an eye, and I see much. I haf a heart, and I feel the thanks for this. Come, a little lesson then and now, or no more good fairy works for me and mine.'

"Of course I couldn't say anything after that, and as it really is a splendid opportunity, I made the bargain, and we began. I took four lessons, and then I stuck fast in a grammatical bog. The Professor was very patient with me, but it must have been torment to him, and now and then he'd look at me with such an expression of mild despair that it was a toss-up with me whether to laugh or cry. I tried both ways; and when it came to a sniff of utter mortification and woe, he just threw the grammar on to the floor, and marched out of the room. I felt myself disgraced and deserted forever, but didn't blame him a particle, and was scrambling my papers together, meaning to rush upstairs and shake myself hard, when in he came, as brisk and beaming as if I'd covered myself with glory.

"'Now we shall try a new way. You and I will read these pleasant little Märchen together, and dig no more in that dry book, that goes in the corner for making us trouble.'

"He spoke so kindly, and opened Hans Andersen's fairy tales so invitingly before me, that I was more ashamed than ever, and went at my lesson in a neck-or-nothing style that seemed to amuse him immensely. I forgot my bashfulness, and pegged away (no other word will express it) with all my might, tumbling over long words, pronouncing according to the inspiration of the minute, and doing my very best. When I finished reading my first page, and stopped for breath, he clapped his hands and cried out, in his hearty way, 'Das ist gute! Now we go well! My turn. I do him in German; gif me your ear.' And away he went, rumbling out the words with his strong voice, and a relish which was good to see as well as hear. Fortunately the story was the 'Constant Tin Soldier,' which is droll, you know, so I could laugh,—and I did,—though I didn't understand half he read, for I couldn't help it, he was so earnest, I so excited, and the whole thing so comical.

"After that we got on better, and now I read my lessons pretty well; for this way of studying suits me, and I can see that the grammar gets tucked into the tales and poetry as one gives pills in jelly. I like it very much, and he doesn't seem tired of it yet,—which is very good of him, isn't it? I mean to give him something on Christmas, for I dare not offer money. Tell me something nice, Marmee.

"I'm glad Laurie seems so happy and busy, that he has given up smoking, and lets his hair grow. You see Beth manages him better than I did. I'm not jealous, dear; do your best, only don't make a saint of him. I'm afraid I couldn't like him without a spice of human naughtiness. Read him bits of my letters. I haven't time to write much, and that will do just as well. Thank Heaven Beth continues so comfortable."

---

"JANUARY.

"A Happy New Year to you all, my dearest family, which of course includes Mr. L. and a young man by the name of Teddy. I can't tell you how much I enjoyed your Christmas bundle, for I didn't get it till night, and had given up hoping. Your letter came in the morning, but you said nothing about a parcel, meaning it for a surprise; so I was disappointed, for I'd had a 'kind of a feeling' that you wouldn't forget me. I felt a little low in my mind, as I sat up in my room, after tea; and when the big, muddy, battered-looking bundle was brought to me, I just hugged it, and pranced. It was so *homey* and refreshing, that I sat down on the floor and read and looked and ate and laughed and cried, in my usual absurd way. The things were just what I wanted, and all the better for being made instead of bought. Beth's new 'ink-bib' was capital; and Hannah's box of hard gingerbread will be a treasure. I'll be sure and wear the nice flannels you sent, Marmee, and read carefully the books father has marked. Thank you all, heaps and heaps!

"Speaking of books reminds me that I'm getting rich in that line for, on New Year's Day, Mr. Bhaer gave me a fine Shakespeare. It is one he values much, and I've often admired it, set up in the place of honor, with his German Bible, Plato, Homer, and Milton; so you may imagine how I felt when he brought it down, without its cover, and showed me my name in it, 'from my friend Friedrich Bhaer.'

"'You say often you wish a library: here I gif you one; for between these lids (he meant covers) is many books in one. Read him well, and he will help you much; for the study of character in this book will help you to read it in the world and paint it with your pen.'

"I thanked him as well as I could, and talk now about 'my library,' as if I had a hundred books. I never knew how much there was in Shakespeare before; but then I never had a Bhaer to explain it to me. Now *don't* laugh at his horrid name; it isn't pronounced either Bear or Beer, as people *will* say it, but something between the two, as only Germans can give it. I'm glad you both like what I tell you about him, and hope you will know him some day. Mother would admire his warm heart, father his wise head. I admire both, and feel rich in my new 'friend Friedrich Bhaer.'

"Not having much money, or knowing what he'd like, I got several little things, and put them about the room, where he would find them unexpectedly. They were useful, pretty, or funny,—a new standish on his table, a little vase for his flower,—he always has one, or a bit of green in a glass, to keep him fresh, he says,—and a holder for his blower, so that he needn't burn up what Amy calls 'mouchoirs.' I made it like those Beth invented,—a big butterfly with a fat body, and black and yellow wings, worsted feelers, and bead eyes. It took his fancy immensely, and he put it on his mantel-piece as an article of *vertu*; so it was rather a failure after all. Poor as he is, he didn't forget a servant or a child in the house; and not a soul here, from the French laundry-woman to Miss Norton, forgot him. I was so glad of that.

"They got up a masquerade, and had a gay time New Year's Eve. I didn't mean to go down, having no dress; but at the last minute, Mrs. Kirke remembered some old brocades, and Miss Norton lent me lace and feathers; so I dressed up as Mrs. Malaprop, and sailed in with a mask on. No one knew me, for I disguised my voice, and no one dreamed of the silent, haughty Miss March (for they think I am very stiff and cool, most of them; and so I am to whipper-snappers) could dance and dress, and burst out into a 'nice derangement of epitaphs, like an allegory on the banks of the Nile.' I enjoyed it very much; and when we unmasked, it was fun to see them stare at me. I heard one of the young men tell another that he knew I'd been an actress; in fact, he thought he remembered seeing me at one of the minor theatres. Meg will relish that joke. Mr. Bhaer was Nick Bottom, and Tina was Titania,—a perfect little fairy in his arms. To see them dance was 'quite a landscape,' to use a Teddyism.

"I had a very happy New Year, after all; and when I thought it over in my room, I felt as if I was getting on a little in spite of my many failures; for I'm cheerful all the time now, work with a will, and take more interest in other people than I used to, which is satisfactory. Bless you all! Ever your loving

JO."

# XI

## A FRIEND.

THOUGH very happy in the social atmosphere about her, and very busy with the daily work that earned her bread, and made it sweeter for the effort, Jo still found time for literary labors. The purpose which now took possession of her was a natural one to a poor and ambitious girl; but the means she took to gain her end were not the best. She saw that money conferred power: money and power, therefore, she resolved to have; not to be used for herself alone, but for those whom she loved more than self.

The dream of filling home with comforts, giving Beth everything she wanted, from strawberries in winter to an organ in her bedroom; going abroad herself, and always having *more* than enough, so that she might indulge in the luxury of charity, had been for years Jo's most cherished castle in the air.

The prize-story experience had seemed to open a way which might, after long travelling and much up-hill work lead to this delightful *château en Espagne.* But the novel disaster quenched her courage for a time, for public opinion is a giant which has frightened stouter-hearted Jacks on bigger bean-stalks than hers. Like that immortal hero, she reposed awhile after the first attempt, which resulted in a tumble, and the least lovely of the giant's treasures, if I remember rightly. But the "up again and take another" spirit was as strong in Jo as in Jack; so she scrambled up, on the shady side this time, and got more booty, but nearly left behind her what was far more precious than the money-bags.

She took to writing sensation stories; for in those dark ages, even all-perfect America read rubbish. She told no one, but concocted a "thrilling tale," and boldly carried it herself to Mr. Dashwood, editor of the "Weekly Volcano." She had never read "Sartor Resartus," but she had a womanly instinct that clothes possess an influence more powerful over many than the worth of character or the magic of manners. So she dressed herself in her best, and, trying to persuade herself that she was neither excited nor nervous, bravely climbed two pairs of dark and dirty stairs to find herself in a disorderly room, a cloud of cigar-smoke, and the presence of three gentlemen, sitting with their heels rather higher than their hats, which articles of dress none of them took the trouble to remove on her appearance. Somewhat daunted by this reception, Jo hesitated on the threshold, murmuring in much embarrassment,—

"Excuse me, I was looking for the 'Weekly Volcano' office; I wished to see Mr. Dashwood."

Down went the highest pair of heels, up rose the smokiest gentleman, and, carefully cherishing his cigar between his fingers, he advanced, with a nod, and a countenance expressive of nothing but sleep. Feeling that she must get through the matter somehow, Jo produced her manuscript, and, blushing redder and redder with each sentence, blundered out fragments of the little speech carefully prepared for the occasion.

"A friend of mine desired me to offer—a story—just as an experiment—would like your opinion—be glad to write more if this suits."

While she blushed and blundered, Mr. Dashwood had taken the manuscript, and was turning over the leaves with a pair of rather dirty fingers, and casting critical glances up and down the neat pages.

"Not a first attempt, I take it?" observing that the pages were numbered, covered only on one side, and not tied up with a ribbon,—sure sign of a novice.

"No, sir; she has had some experience, and got a prize for a tale in the 'Blarneystone Banner.'"

"Oh, did she?" and Mr. Dashwood gave Jo a quick look, which seemed to take note of everything she had on, from the bow in her bonnet to the buttons on her boots. "Well, you can leave it, if you like. We've more of this sort of thing on hand than we know what to do with at present; but I'll run my eye over it, and give you an answer next week."

Now, Jo did *not* like to leave it, for Mr. Dashwood didn't suit her at all; but, under the circumstances, there was nothing for her to do but bow and walk away, looking particularly tall and dignified, as she was apt to do when nettled or abashed. Just then she was both; for it was perfectly evident, from the knowing glances exchanged among the gentlemen, that her little fiction of "my friend" was considered a good joke; and a laugh, produced by some inaudible remark of the editor, as he closed the door, completed her discomfiture. Half resolving never to return, she went home, and worked off her irritation by stitching pinafores vigorously; and in an hour or two was cool enough to laugh over the scene, and long for next week.

When she went again, Mr. Dashwood was alone, whereat she rejoiced; Mr. Dashwood was much wider awake than before, which was agreeable; and Mr. Dashwood was not too deeply absorbed in a cigar to remember his manners: so the second interview was much more comfortable than the first.

"We'll take this" (editors never say I), "if you don't object to a few alterations. It's too long, but omitting the passages I've marked will make it just the right length," he said, in a business-like tone.

Jo hardly knew her own MS. again, so crumpled and underscored were its pages and paragraphs; but, feeling as a tender parent might on being asked to cut off her baby's legs in order that it might fit into a new cradle, she looked at the marked passages, and was surprised to find that all the moral reflections—which she had carefully put in as ballast for much romance—had been stricken out.

"But, sir, I thought every story should have some sort of a moral, so I took care to have a few of my sinners repent."

Mr. Dashwood's editorial gravity relaxed into a smile, for Jo had forgotten her "friend," and spoken as only an author could.

"People want to be amused, not preached at, you know. Morals don't sell nowadays;" which was not quite a correct statement, by the way.

"You think it would do with these alterations, then?"

"Yes; it's a new plot, and pretty well worked up—language good, and so on," was Mr. Dashwood's affable reply.

"What do you—that is, what compensation—" began Jo, not exactly knowing how to express herself.

"Oh, yes, well, we give from twenty-five to thirty for things of this sort. Pay when it comes out," returned Mr. Dashwood, as if that point had escaped him; such trifles often do escape the editorial mind, it is said.

"Very well; you can have it," said Jo, handing back the story, with a satisfied air; for, after the dollar-a-column work, even twenty-five seemed good pay.

"Shall I tell my friend you will take another if she has one better than this?" asked Jo, unconscious of her little slip of the tongue, and emboldened by her success.

"Well, we'll look at it; can't promise to take it. Tell her to make it short and spicy, and never mind the moral. What name would your friend like to put to it?" in a careless tone.

"None at all, if you please; she doesn't wish her name to appear, and has no *nom de plume*," said Jo, blushing in spite of herself.

"Just as she likes, of course. The tale will be out next week; will you call for the money, or shall I send it?" asked Mr. Dashwood, who felt a natural desire to know who his new contributor might be.

"I'll call. Good morning, sir."

As she departed, Mr. Dashwood put up his feet, with the graceful remark, "Poor and proud, as usual, but she'll do."

Following Mr. Dashwood's directions, and making Mrs. Northbury her model, Jo rashly took a plunge into the frothy sea of sensational literature; but, thanks to the life-preserver thrown her by a friend, she came up again, not much the worse for her ducking.

Like most young scribblers, she went abroad for her characters and scenery; and banditti, counts, gypsies, nuns, and duchesses appeared upon her stage, and played their parts with as much accuracy and spirit as could be expected. Her readers were not particular about such trifles as grammar, punctuation, and probability, and Mr. Dashwood graciously permitted her to fill his columns at the lowest prices, not thinking it necessary to tell her that the real cause of his hospitality was the fact that one of his hacks, on being offered higher wages, had basely left him in the lurch.

She soon became interested in her work, for her emaciated purse grew stout, and the little hoard she was making to take Beth to the mountains next summer grew slowly but surely as the weeks passed. One thing disturbed her satisfaction, and that was that she did not tell them at home. She had a feeling that father and mother would not approve, and preferred to have her own way first, and beg pardon afterward. It was easy to keep her secret, for no name appeared with her stories; Mr. Dashwood had, of course, found it out very soon, but promised to be dumb; and, for a wonder, kept his word.

She thought it would do her no harm, for she sincerely meant to write nothing of which she should be ashamed, and quieted all pricks of conscience by anticipations of the happy minute when she should show her earnings and laugh over her well-kept secret.

But Mr. Dashwood rejected any but thrilling tales; and, as thrills could not be produced except by harrowing up the souls of the readers, history and romance, land and sea, science and art, police records and lunatic asylums, had to be ransacked for the purpose. Jo soon found that her innocent experience had given her but few glimpses of the tragic world which underlies society; so, regarding it in a business light, she set about supplying her deficiencies with characteristic energy. Eager to find material for stories, and bent on making them original in plot, if not masterly in execution, she searched newspapers for accidents, incidents, and crimes; she excited the suspicions of public librarians by asking for works on poisons; she studied faces in the street, and characters, good, bad, and indifferent, all about her; she delved in the dust of ancient times for facts or fictions so old that they were as good as new, and introduced herself to folly, sin, and misery, as well as her limited opportunities allowed. She thought she was prospering finely; but, unconsciously, she was beginning to desecrate some of the womanliest attributes of a woman's character. She was living in bad society; and, imaginary though it was, its influence affected her, for she was feeding heart and fancy on dangerous and unsubstantial food, and was fast brushing the innocent bloom from her nature by a premature acquaintance with the darker side of life, which comes soon enough to all of us.

She was beginning to feel rather than see this, for much describing of other people's passions and feelings set her to studying and speculating about her own,—a morbid amusement, in which healthy young minds do not voluntarily indulge. Wrong-doing always brings its own punishment; and, when Jo most needed hers, she got it.

I don't know whether the study of Shakespeare helped her to read character, or the natural instinct of a woman for what was honest, brave, and strong; but while endowing her imaginary heroes with every perfection under the sun, Jo was discovering a live hero, who interested her in spite of many human imperfections. Mr. Bhaer, in one of their conversations, had advised her to study simple, true, and lovely characters, wherever she found them, as good training for a writer. Jo took him at his word, for she coolly turned round and studied him,—a proceeding which would have much surprised him, had he known it, for the worthy Professor was very humble in his own conceit.

Why everybody liked him was what puzzled Jo, at first. He was neither rich nor great, young nor handsome; in no respect what is called fascinating, imposing, or brilliant; and yet he was as attractive as a genial fire, and people seemed to gather about him as naturally as about a warm hearth. He was poor, yet always appeared to be giving something away; a stranger, yet every one was his friend; no longer young, but as happy-hearted as a boy; plain and peculiar, yet his face looked beautiful to many, and his oddities were freely forgiven for his sake. Jo often watched him, trying to discover the charm, and, at last, decided that it was benevolence which worked the miracle. If he had any sorrow, "it sat with its head under its wing," and he turned only his sunny side to the world. There were lines upon his forehead, but Time seemed to have touched him gently, remembering how kind he was to others. The pleasant curves about his mouth were the memorials of many friendly words and cheery laughs; his eyes were never cold or hard, and his big hand had a warm, strong grasp that was more expressive than words.

His very clothes seemed to partake of the hospitable nature of the wearer. They looked as if they were at ease, and liked to make him comfortable; his capacious waistcoat was suggestive of a large heart underneath; his rusty coat had a social air, and the baggy pockets plainly proved that little hands often went in empty and came out full; his very boots were benevolent, and his collars never stiff and raspy like other people's.

"That's it!" said Jo to herself, when she at length discovered that genuine good-will towards one's fellow-men could beautify and dignify even a stout German teacher, who shovelled in his dinner, darned his own socks, and was burdened with the name of Bhaer.

Jo valued goodness highly, but she also possessed a most feminine respect for intellect, and a little discovery which she made about the Professor added much to her regard for him. He never spoke of himself, and no one ever knew that in his native city he had been a man much honored and esteemed for learning and integrity, till a countryman came to see him, and, in a conversation with Miss Norton, divulged the pleasing fact. From her Jo learned it, and liked it all the better because Mr. Bhaer had never told it. She felt proud to know that he was an honored Professor in Berlin, though only a poor language-master in America; and his homely, hard-working life was much beautified by the spice of romance which this discovery gave it.

Another and a better gift than intellect was shown her in a most unexpected manner. Miss Norton had the *entrée* into literary society, which Jo would have had no chance of seeing but for her. The solitary woman felt an interest in the ambitious girl, and kindly conferred many favors of this sort both on Jo and the Professor. She took them with her, one night, to a select symposium, held in honor of several celebrities.

Jo went prepared to bow down and adore the mighty ones whom she had worshipped with youthful enthusiasm afar off. But her reverence for genius received a severe shock that night, and it took her some time to recover from the discovery that the great creatures were only men and women after all. Imagine her dismay, on stealing a glance of timid admiration at the poet whose lines suggested an ethereal being fed on "spirit, fire, and dew," to behold him devouring his supper with an ardor which flushed his intellectual countenance. Turning as from a fallen idol, she made other discoveries which rapidly dispelled her romantic illusions. The great novelist vibrated between two decanters with the regularity of a pendulum; the famous divine flirted openly with one of the Madame de Staëls of the age, who looked daggers at another Corinne, who was amiably satirizing her, after out-manœuvring her in efforts to absorb the profound philosopher, who imbibed tea Johnsonianly and appeared to slumber, the loquacity of the lady rendering speech impossible. The scientific celebrities, forgetting their mollusks and glacial periods, gossiped about art, while devoting themselves to oysters and ices with characteristic energy; the young musician, who was charming the city like a second Orpheus, talked horses; and the specimen of the British nobility present happened to be the most ordinary man of the party.

Before the evening was half over, Jo felt so completely *désillusionée*, that she sat down in a corner to recover herself. Mr. Bhaer soon joined her, looking rather out of his element, and presently several of the philosophers, each mounted on his hobby, came ambling up to hold an intellectual tournament in the recess. The conversation was miles beyond Jo's comprehension, but she enjoyed it, though Kant and Hegel were unknown gods, the Subjective and Objective unintelligible terms; and the only thing "evolved from her inner consciousness," was a bad headache after it was all over. It dawned upon her gradually that the world was being picked to pieces, and put together on new, and, according to the talkers, on infinitely better principles than before; that religion was in a fair way to be reasoned into nothingness, and intellect was to be the only God. Jo knew nothing about philosophy or metaphysics of any sort, but a curious excitement, half pleasurable, half painful, came over her, as she listened with a sense of being turned adrift into time and space, like a young balloon out on a holiday.

She looked round to see how the Professor liked it, and found him looking at her with the grimmest expression she had ever seen him wear. He shook his head, and beckoned her to come away; but she was fascinated, just then, by the freedom of Speculative Philosophy, and kept her seat, trying to find out what the wise gentlemen intended to rely upon after they had annihilated all the old beliefs.

Now, Mr. Bhaer was a diffident man, and slow to offer his own opinions, not because they were unsettled, but too sincere and earnest to be lightly spoken. As he glanced from Jo to several other young people, attracted by the brilliancy of the philosophic pyrotechnics, he knit his brows, and longed to speak, fearing that some inflammable young soul would be led astray by the rockets, to find, when the display was over, that they had only an empty stick or a scorched hand.

He bore it as long as he could; but when he was appealed to for an opinion, he blazed up with honest indignation, and defended religion with all the eloquence of truth,—an eloquence which made his broken English musical, and his plain face beautiful. He had a hard fight, for the wise men argued well; but he didn't know when he was beaten, and stood to his colors like a man. Somehow, as he talked, the world got right again to Jo; the old beliefs, that had lasted so long, seemed better than the new; God was not a blind force, and immortality was not a pretty fable, but a blessed fact. She felt as if she had solid ground under her feet again; and when Mr. Bhaer paused, out-talked, but not one whit convinced, Jo wanted to clap her hands and thank him.

She did neither; but she remembered this scene, and gave the Professor her heartiest respect, for she knew it cost him an effort to speak out then and there, because his conscience would not let him be silent. She began to see that character is a better possession than money, rank, intellect, or beauty; and to feel that if greatness is what a wise man has defined it to be, "truth, reverence, and good-will," then her friend Friedrich Bhaer was not only good, but great.

This belief strengthened daily. She valued his esteem, she coveted his respect, she wanted to be worthy of his friendship; and, just when the wish was sincerest, she came near losing everything. It all grew out of a cocked hat; for one evening the Professor came in to give Jo her lesson, with a paper soldier-cap on his head, which Tina had put there, and he had forgotten to take off.

"It's evident he doesn't look in his glass before coming down," thought Jo, with a smile, as he said "Goot efening," and sat soberly down, quite unconscious of the ludicrous contrast between his subject and his head-gear, for he was going to read her the "Death of Wallenstein."

She said nothing at first, for she liked to hear him laugh out his big, hearty laugh, when anything funny happened, so she left him to discover it for himself, and presently forgot all about it; for to hear a German read Schiller is rather an absorbing occupation. After the reading came the lesson, which was a lively one, for Jo was in a gay mood that night, and the cocked-hat kept her eyes dancing with merriment. The Professor didn't know what to make of her, and stopped at last, to ask, with an air of mild surprise that was irresistible,—

"Mees Marsch, for what do you laugh in your master's face? Haf you no respect for me, that you go on so bad?"

"How can I be respectful, sir, when you forget to take your hat off?" said Jo.

Lifting his hand to his head, the absent-minded Professor gravely felt and removed the little cocked-hat, looked at it a minute, and then threw back his head, and laughed like a merry bass-viol.

"Ah! I see him now; it is that imp Tina who makes me a fool with my cap. Well, it is nothing; but see you, if this lesson goes not well, you too shall wear him."

But the lesson did not go at all for a few minutes, because Mr. Bhaer caught sight of a picture on the hat, and, unfolding it, said, with an air of great disgust,—

"I wish these papers did not come in the house; they are not for children to see, nor young people to read. It is not well, and I haf no patience with those who make this harm."

Jo glanced at the sheet, and saw a pleasing illustration composed of a lunatic, a corpse, a villain, and a viper. She did not like it; but the impulse that made her turn it over was not one of displeasure, but fear, because, for a minute, she fancied the paper was the "Volcano." It was not, however, and her panic subsided as she remembered that, even if it had been, and one of her own tales in it, there would have been no name to betray her. She had betrayed herself, however, by a look and a blush; for, though an absent man, the Professor saw a good deal more than people fancied. He knew that Jo wrote, and had met her down among the newspaper offices more than once; but as she never spoke of it, he asked no questions, in spite of a strong desire to see her work. Now it occurred to him that she was doing what she was ashamed to own, and it troubled him. He did not say to himself, "It is none of my business; I've no right to say anything," as many people would have done; he only remembered that she was young and poor, a girl far away from mother's love and father's care; and he was moved to help her with an impulse as quick and natural as that which would prompt him to put out his hand to save a baby from a puddle. All this flashed through his mind in a minute, but not a trace of it appeared in his face; and by the time the paper was turned, and Jo's needle threaded, he was ready to say quite naturally, but very gravely,—

"Yes, you are right to put it from you. I do not like to think that good young girls should see such things. They are made pleasant to some, but I would more rather give my boys gunpowder to play with than this bad trash."

"All may not be bad, only silly, you know; and if there is a demand for it, I don't see any harm in supplying it. Many very respectable people make an honest living out of what are called sensation stories," said Jo, scratching gathers so energetically that a row of little slits followed her pin.

"There is a demand for whiskey, but I think you and I do not care to sell it. If the respectable people knew what harm they did, they would not feel that the living *was* honest. They haf no right to put poison in the sugar-plum, and let the small ones eat it. No; they should think a little, and sweep mud in the street before they do this thing."

Mr. Bhaer spoke warmly, and walked to the fire, crumpling the paper in his hands. Jo sat still, looking as if the fire had come to her; for her cheeks burned long after the cocked hat had turned to smoke, and gone harmlessly up the chimney.

"I should like much to send all the rest after him," muttered the Professor, coming back with a relieved air.

Jo thought what a blaze her pile of papers upstairs would make, and her hard-earned money lay rather heavily on her conscience at that minute. Then she thought consolingly to herself, "Mine are not like that; they are only silly, never bad, so I won't be worried;" and taking up her book, she said, with a studious face,—

"Shall we go on, sir? I'll be very good and proper now."

"I shall hope so," was all he said, but he meant more than she imagined; and the grave, kind look he gave her made her feel as if the words "Weekly Volcano" were printed in large type on her forehead.

As soon as she went to her room, she got out her papers, and carefully re-read every one of her stories. Being a little short-sighted, Mr. Bhaer sometimes used eye-glasses, and Jo had tried them once, smiling to see how they magnified the fine print of her book; now she seemed to have got on the Professor's mental or moral spectacles also; for the faults of these poor stories glared at her dreadfully, and filled her with dismay.

"They *are* trash, and will soon be worse than trash if I go on; for each is more sensational than the last. I've gone blindly on, hurting myself and other people, for the sake of money; I know it's so, for I can't read this stuff in sober earnest without being horribly ashamed of it; and what *should* I do if they were seen at home, or Mr. Bhaer got hold of them?"

Jo turned hot at the bare idea, and stuffed the whole bundle into her stove, nearly setting the chimney afire with the blaze.

"Yes, that's the best place for such inflammable nonsense; I'd better burn the house down, I suppose, than let other people blow themselves up with my gunpowder," she thought, as she watched the "Demon of the Jura" whisk away, a little black cinder with fiery eyes.

But when nothing remained of all her three months' work except a heap of ashes, and the money in her lap, Jo looked sober, as she sat on the floor, wondering what she ought to do about her wages.

"I think I haven't done much harm *yet*, and may keep this to pay for my time," she said, after a long meditation, adding impatiently, "I almost wish I hadn't any conscience, it's so inconvenient. If I didn't care about doing right, and didn't feel uncomfortable when doing wrong, I should get on capitally. I can't help wishing sometimes, that father and mother hadn't been so particular about such things."

Ah, Jo, instead of wishing that, thank God that "father and mother *were* particular," and pity from your heart those who have no such guardians to hedge them round with principles which may seem like prison-walls to impatient youth, but which will prove sure foundations to build character upon in womanhood.

Jo wrote no more sensational stories, deciding that the money did not pay for her share of the sensation; but, going to the other extreme, as is the way with people of her stamp, she took a course of Mrs. Sherwood, Miss Edgeworth, and Hannah More; and then produced a tale which might have been more properly called an essay or a sermon, so intensely moral was it. She had her doubts about it from the beginning; for her lively fancy and girlish romance felt as ill at ease in the new style as she would have done masquerading in the stiff and cumbrous costume of the last century. She sent this didactic gem to several markets, but it found no purchaser; and she was inclined to agree with Mr. Dashwood, that morals didn't sell.

Then she tried a child's story, which she could easily have disposed of if she had not been mercenary enough to demand filthy lucre for it. The only person who offered enough to make it worth her while to try juvenile literature was a worthy gentleman who felt it his mission to convert all the world to his particular belief. But much as she liked to write for children, Jo could not consent to depict all her naughty boys as being eaten by bears or tossed by mad bulls, because they did not go to a particular Sabbath-school, nor all the good infants, who did go, as rewarded by every kind of bliss, from gilded gingerbread to escorts of angels, when they departed this life with psalms or sermons on their lisping tongues. So nothing came of these trials; and Jo corked up her inkstand, and said, in a fit of very wholesome humility,—

"I don't know anything; I'll wait till I do before I try again, and, meantime, 'sweep mud in the street,' if I can't do better; that's honest, at least;" which decision proved that her second tumble down the bean-stalk had done her some good.

While these internal revolutions were going on, her external life had been as busy and uneventful as usual; and if she sometimes looked serious or a little sad no one observed it but Professor Bhaer. He did it so quietly that Jo never knew he was watching to see if she would accept and profit by his reproof; but she stood the test, and he was satisfied;

for, though no words passed between them, he knew that she had given up writing. Not only did he guess it by the fact that the second finger of her right hand was no longer inky, but she spent her evenings downstairs now, was met no more among newspaper offices, and studied with a dogged patience, which assured him that she was bent on occupying her mind with something useful, if not pleasant.

He helped her in many ways, proving himself a true friend, and Jo was happy; for, while her pen lay idle, she was learning other lessons beside German, and laying a foundation for the sensation story of her own life.

It was a pleasant winter and a long one, for she did not leave Mrs. Kirke till June. Every one seemed sorry when the time came; the children were inconsolable, and Mr. Bhaer's hair stuck straight up all over his head, for he always rumpled it wildly when disturbed in mind.

"Going home? Ah, you are happy that you haf a home to go in," he said, when she told him, and sat silently pulling his beard, in the corner, while she held a little levee on that last evening.

She was going early, so she bade them all good-by over night; and when his turn came, she said warmly,—

"Now, sir, you won't forget to come and see us, if you ever travel our way, will you? I'll never forgive you if you do, for I want them all to know my friend."

"Do you? Shall I come?" he asked, looking down at her with an eager expression which she did not see.

"Yes, come next month; Laurie graduates then, and you'd enjoy Commencement as something new."

"That is your best friend, of whom you speak?" he said, in an altered tone.

"Yes, my boy Teddy; I'm very proud of him, and should like you to see him."

Jo looked up then, quite unconscious of anything but her own pleasure in the prospect of showing them to one another. Something in Mr. Bhaer's face suddenly recalled the fact that she might find Laurie more than a "best friend," and, simply because she particularly wished not to look as if anything was the matter, she involuntarily began to blush; and the more she tried not to, the redder she grew. If it had not been for Tina on her knee, she didn't know what would have become of her. Fortunately, the child was moved to hug her; so she managed to hide her face an instant, hoping the Professor did not see it. But he did, and his own changed again from that momentary anxiety to its usual expression, as he said cordially,—

"I fear I shall not make the time for that, but I wish the friend much success, and you all happiness. Gott bless you!" and with that, he shook hands warmly, shouldered Tina, and went away.

But after the boys were abed, he sat long before his fire, with the tired look on his face, and the "*heimweh*," or homesickness, lying heavy at his heart. Once, when he remembered Jo, as she sat with the little child in her lap and that new softness in her face, he leaned his head on his hands a minute, and then roamed about the room, as if in search of something that he could not find.

"It is not for me; I must not hope it now," he said to himself, with a sigh that was almost a groan; then, as if reproaching himself for the longing that he could not repress, he went and kissed the two towzled heads upon the pillow, took down his seldom-used meerschaum, and opened his Plato.

He did his best, and did it manfully; but I don't think he found that a pair of rampant boys, a pipe, or even the divine Plato, were very satisfactory substitutes for wife and child and home.

Early as it was, he was at the station, next morning, to see Jo off; and, thanks to him, she began her solitary journey with the pleasant memory of a familiar face smiling its farewell, a bunch of violets to keep her company, and, best of all, the happy thought,—

"Well, the winter's gone, and I've written no books, earned no fortune; but I've made a friend worth having, and I'll try to keep him all my life."

---

## XXXV.
## HEARTACHE.

WHATEVER his motive might have been, Laurie studied to some purpose that year, for he graduated with honor, and gave the Latin oration with the grace of a Phillips and the eloquence of a Demosthenes, so his friends said. They were all there, his grandfather,—oh, so proud!—Mr. and Mrs. March, John and Meg, Jo and Beth, and all exulted over him with the sincere admiration which boys make light of at the time, but fail to win from the world by any after-triumphs.

"I've got to stay for this confounded supper, but I shall be home early to-morrow; you'll come and meet me as usual, girls?" Laurie said, as he put the sisters into the carriage after the joys of the day were over. He said "girls," but he meant Jo, for she was the only one who kept up the old custom; she had not the heart to refuse her splendid, successful boy anything, and answered warmly,—

"I'll come, Teddy, rain or shine, and march before you, playing '*Hail the conquering hero comes*,' on a jews-harp."

Laurie thanked her with a look that made her think, in a sudden panic, "Oh, deary me! I know he'll say something, and then what shall I do?"

Evening meditation and morning work somewhat allayed her fears, and having decided that she wouldn't be vain enough to think people were going to propose when she had given them every reason to know what her answer would be, she set forth at the appointed time, hoping Teddy wouldn't do anything to make her hurt his poor little feelings. A call at Meg's, and a refreshing sniff and sip at the Daisy and Demijohn, still further fortified her for the *tête-à-tête*, but when she saw a stalwart figure looming in the distance, she had a strong desire to turn about and run away.

"Where's the jews-harp, Jo?" cried Laurie, as soon as he was within speaking distance.

"I forgot it;" and Jo took heart again, for that salutation could not be called lover-like.

She always used to take his arm on these occasions; now she did not, and he made no complaint, which was a bad sign, but talked on rapidly about all sorts of far-away subjects, till they turned from the road into the little path that led homeward through the grove. Then he walked more slowly, suddenly lost his fine flow of language, and, now and then, a dreadful pause occurred. To rescue the conversation from one of the wells of silence into which it kept falling, Jo said hastily,—

"Now you must have a good long holiday!"

"I intend to."

Something in his resolute tone made Jo look up quickly to find him looking down at her with an expression that assured her the dreaded moment had come, and made her put out her hand with an imploring,—

"No, Teddy, please don't!"

"I will, and you *must* hear me. It's no use, Jo; we've got to have it out, and the sooner the better for both of us," he answered, getting flushed and excited all at once.

"Say what you like, then; I'll listen," said Jo, with a desperate sort of patience.

Laurie was a young lover, but he was in earnest, and meant to "have it out," if he died in the attempt; so he plunged into the subject with characteristic impetuosity, saying in a voice that *would* get choky now and then, in spite of manful efforts to keep it steady,—

"I've loved you ever since I've known you, Jo; couldn't help it, you've been so good to me. I've tried to show it, but you wouldn't let me; now I'm going to make you hear, and give me an answer, for I *can't* go on so any longer."

"I wanted to save you this; I thought you'd understand—" began Jo, finding it a great deal harder than she expected.

"I know you did; but girls are so queer you never know what they mean. They say No when they mean Yes, and drive a man out of his wits just for the fun of it," returned Laurie, entrenching himself behind an undeniable fact.

"*I* don't. I never wanted to make you care for me so, and I went away to keep you from it if I could."

"I thought so; it was like you, but it was no use. I only loved you all the more, and I worked hard to please you, and I gave up billiards and everything you didn't like, and waited and never complained, for I hoped you'd love me, though I'm not half good enough—" here there was a choke that couldn't be controlled, so he decapitated buttercups while he cleared his "confounded throat."

"Yes, you are; you're a great deal too good for me, and I'm so grateful to you, and so proud and fond of you, I don't see why I can't love you as you want me to. I've tried, but I can't change the feeling, and it would be a lie to say I do when I don't."

"Really, truly, Jo?"

He stopped short, and caught both her hands as he put his question with a look that she did not soon forget.

"Really, truly, dear."

They were in the grove now, close by the stile; and when the last words fell reluctantly from Jo's lips, Laurie dropped her hands and turned as if to go on, but for once in his life that fence was too much for him; so he just laid his head down on the mossy post, and stood so still that Jo was frightened.

"O Teddy, I'm so sorry, so desperately sorry, I could kill myself if it would do any good! I wish you wouldn't take it so hard. I can't help it; you know it's impossible for people to make themselves love other people if they don't," cried Jo inelegantly but remorsefully, as she softly patted his shoulder, remembering the time when he had comforted her so long ago.

"They do sometimes," said a muffled voice from the post.

"I don't believe it's the right sort of love, and I'd rather not try it," was the decided answer.

There was a long pause, while a blackbird sung blithely on the willow by the river, and the tall grass rustled in the wind. Presently Jo said very soberly, as she sat down on the step of the stile,—

"Laurie, I want to tell you something."

He started as if he had been shot, threw up his head, and cried out, in a fierce tone—

"*Don't* tell me that, Jo; I can't bear it now!"

"Tell what?" she asked, wondering at his violence.

"That you love that old man."

"What old man?" demanded Jo, thinking he must mean his grandfather.

"That devilish Professor you were always writing about. If you say you love him, I know I shall do something desperate;" and he looked as if he would keep his word, as he clenched his hands, with a wrathful spark in his eyes.

Jo wanted to laugh, but restrained herself, and said warmly, for she, too, was getting excited with all this,—

"Don't swear, Teddy! He isn't old, nor anything bad, but good and kind, and the best friend I've got, next to you. Pray, don't fly into a passion; I want to be kind, but I know I shall get angry if you abuse my Professor. I haven't the least idea of loving him or anybody else."

"But you will after a while, and then what will become of me?"

"You'll love some one else too, like a sensible boy, and forget all this trouble."

"I *can't* love any one else; and I'll never forget you, Jo, never! never!" with a stamp to emphasize his passionate words.

"What *shall* I do with him?" sighed Jo, finding that emotions were more unmanageable than she expected. "You haven't heard what I wanted to tell you. Sit down and listen; for indeed I want to do right and make you happy," she said, hoping to soothe him with a little reason, which proved that she knew nothing about love.

Seeing a ray of hope in that last speech, Laurie threw himself down on the grass at her feet, leaned his arm on the lower step of the stile, and looked up at her with an expectant face. Now that arrangement was not conducive to calm speech or clear thought on Jo's part; for how *could* she say hard things to her boy while he watched her with eyes full of love and longing, and lashes still wet with the bitter drop or two her hardness of heart had wrung from him? She gently turned his head away, saying, as she stroked the wavy hair which had been allowed to grow for her sake,—how touching that was, to be sure!—

"I agree with mother that you and I are not suited to each other, because our quick tempers and strong wills would probably make us very miserable, if we were so foolish as to—" Jo paused a little over the last word, but Laurie uttered it with a rapturous expression,—

"Marry,—no, we shouldn't! If you loved me, Jo, I should be a perfect saint, for you could make me anything you like."

"No, I can't. I've tried it and failed, and I won't risk our happiness by such a serious experiment. We don't agree and we never shall; so we'll be good friends all our lives, but we won't go and do anything rash."

"Yes, we will if we get the chance," muttered Laurie rebelliously.

"Now do be reasonable, and take a sensible view of the case," implored Jo, almost at her wit's end.

"I won't be reasonable; I don't want to take what you call 'a sensible view;' it won't help me, and it only makes you harder. I don't believe you've got any heart."

"I wish I hadn't!"

There was a little quiver in Jo's voice, and, thinking it a good omen, Laurie turned round, bringing all his persuasive powers to bear as he said, in the wheedlesome tone that had never been so dangerously wheedlesome before,—

"Don't disappoint us, dear! Every one expects it. Grandpa has set his heart upon it, your people like it, and I can't get on without you. Say you will, and let's be happy. Do, do!"

Not until months afterward did Jo understand how she had the strength of mind to hold fast to the resolution she had made when she decided that she did not love her boy, and never could. It was very hard to do, but she did it, knowing that delay was both useless and cruel.

"I can't say 'Yes' truly, so I won't say it at all. You'll see that I'm right, by and by, and thank me for it"—she began solemnly.

"I'll be hanged if I do!" and Laurie bounced up off the grass, burning with indignation at the bare idea.

"Yes, you will!" persisted Jo; "you'll get over this after a while, and find some lovely, accomplished girl, who will adore you, and make a fine mistress for your fine house. I shouldn't. I'm homely and awkward and odd and old, and you'd be ashamed of me, and we should quarrel,—we can't help it even now, you see,—and I shouldn't like elegant society and you would, and you'd hate my scribbling, and I couldn't get on without it, and we should be unhappy, and wish we hadn't done it, and everything would be horrid!"

"Anything more?" asked Laurie, finding it hard to listen patiently to this prophetic burst.

"Nothing more, except that I don't believe I shall ever marry. I'm happy as I am, and love my liberty too well to be in any hurry to give it up for any mortal man."

"I know better!" broke in Laurie. "You think so now; but there'll come a time when you *will* care for somebody, and you'll love him tremendously, and live and die for him. I know you will, it's your way, and I shall have to stand by and see it;" and the despairing lover cast his hat upon the ground with a gesture that would have seemed comical, if his face had not been so tragical.

"Yes, I *will* live and die for him, if he ever comes and makes me love him in spite of myself, and you must do the best you can!" cried Jo, losing patience with poor Teddy. "I've done my best, but you *won't* be reasonable, and it's selfish of you to keep teasing for what I can't give. I shall always be fond of you, very fond indeed, as a friend, but I'll never marry you; and the sooner you believe it, the better for both of us,—so now!"

That speech was like fire to gunpowder. Laurie looked at her a minute as if he did not quite know what to do with himself, then turned sharply away, saying, in a desperate sort of tone,—

"You'll be sorry some day, Jo."

"Oh, where are you going?" she cried, for his face frightened her.

"To the devil!" was the consoling answer.

For a minute Jo's heart stood still, as he swung himself down the bank, toward the river; but it takes much folly, sin, or misery to send a young man to a violent death, and Laurie was not one of the weak sort who are conquered by a single failure. He had no thought of a melodramatic plunge, but some blind instinct led him to fling hat and coat into his boat, and row away with all his might, making better time up the river than he had done in many a race. Jo drew a long breath and unclasped her hands as she watched the poor fellow trying to outstrip the trouble which he carried in his heart.

"That will do him good, and he'll come home in such a tender, penitent state of mind, that I sha'n't dare to see him," she said; adding, as she went slowly home, feeling as if she had murdered some innocent thing, and buried it under the leaves,—

"Now I must go and prepare Mr. Laurence to be very kind to my poor boy. I wish he'd love Beth; perhaps he may, in time, but I begin to think I was mistaken about her. Oh dear! how can girls like to have lovers and refuse them. I think it's dreadful."

Being sure that no one could do it so well as herself, she went straight to Mr. Laurence, told the hard story bravely through, and then broke down, crying so dismally over her own insensibility that the kind old gentleman, though sorely disappointed, did not utter a reproach. He found it difficult to understand how any girl could help loving Laurie, and hoped she would change her mind, but he knew even better than Jo that love cannot be forced, so he shook his head sadly, and resolved to carry his boy out of harm's way; for Young Impetuosity's parting words to Jo disturbed him more than he would confess.

When Laurie came home, dead tired, but quite composed, his grandfather met him as if he knew nothing, and kept up the delusion very successfully for an hour or two. But when they sat together in the twilight, the time they used to enjoy so much, it was hard work for the old man to ramble on as usual, and harder still for the young one to listen to praises of the last year's success, which to him now seemed love's labor lost. He bore it as long as he could, then went to his piano, and began to play. The windows were open; and Jo, walking in the garden with Beth, for once understood music better than her sister, for he played the "Sonata Pathétique," and played it as he never did before.

"That's very fine, I dare say, but it's sad enough to make one cry; give us something gayer, lad," said Mr. Laurence, whose kind old heart was full of sympathy, which he longed to show, but knew not how.

Laurie dashed into a livelier strain, played stormily for several minutes, and would have got through bravely, if, in a momentary lull, Mrs. March's voice had not been heard calling,—

"Jo, dear, come in; I want you."

Just what Laurie longed to say, with a different meaning! As he listened, he lost his place; the music ended with a broken chord, and the musician sat silent in the dark.

"I can't stand this," muttered the old gentleman. Up he got, groped his way to the piano, laid a kind hand on either of the broad shoulders, and said, as gently as a woman,—

"I know, my boy, I know."

No answer for an instant; then Laurie asked sharply,—

"Who told you?"

"Jo herself."

"Then there's an end of it!" and he shook off his grandfather's hands with an impatient motion; for, though grateful for the sympathy, his man's pride could not bear a man's pity.

"Not quite; I want to say one thing, and then there shall be an end of it," returned Mr. Laurence, with unusual mildness. "You won't care to stay at home just now, perhaps?"

"I don't intend to run away from a girl. Jo can't prevent my seeing her, and I shall stay and do it as long as I like," interrupted Laurie, in a defiant tone.

"Not if you are the gentleman I think you. I'm disappointed, but the girl can't help it; and the only thing left for you to do is to go away for a time. Where will you go?"

"Anywhere. I don't care what becomes of me;" and Laurie got up, with a reckless laugh, that grated on his grandfather's ear.

"Take it like a man, and don't do anything rash, for God's sake. Why not go abroad, as you planned, and forget it?"

"I can't."

"But you've been wild to go, and I promised you should when you got through college."

"Ah, but I didn't mean to go alone!" and Laurie walked fast through the room, with an expression which it was well his grandfather did not see.

"I don't ask you to go alone; there's some one ready and glad to go with you, anywhere in the world."

"Who, sir?" stopping to listen.

"Myself."

Laurie came back as quickly as he went, and put out his hand, saying huskily,—

"I'm a selfish brute; but—you know—grandfather—"

"Lord help me, yes, I do know, for I've been through it all before, once in my own young days, and then with your father. Now, my dear boy, just sit quietly down, and hear my plan. It's all settled, and can be carried out at once," said Mr. Laurence, keeping hold of the young man, as if fearful that he would break away, as his father had done before him.

"Well, sir, what is it?" and Laurie sat down, without a sign of interest in face or voice.

"There is business in London that needs looking after; I meant you should attend to it; but I can do it better myself, and things here will get on very well with Brooke to manage them. My partners do almost everything; I'm merely holding on till you take my place, and can be off at any time."

"But you hate travelling, sir; I can't ask it of you at your age," began Laurie, who was grateful for the sacrifice, but much preferred to go alone, if he went at all.

The old gentleman knew that perfectly well, and particularly desired to prevent it; for the mood in which he found his grandson assured him that it would not be wise to leave him to his own devices. So, stifling a natural regret at the thought of the home comforts he would leave behind him, he said stoutly,—

"Bless your soul, I'm not superannuated yet. I quite enjoy the idea; it will do me good, and my old bones won't suffer, for travelling nowadays is almost as easy as sitting in a chair."

A restless movement from Laurie suggested that *his* chair was not easy, or that he did not like the plan, and made the old man add hastily,—

"I don't mean to be a marplot or a burden; I go because I think you'd feel happier than if I was left behind. I don't intend to gad about with you, but leave you free to go where you like, while I amuse myself in my own way. I've friends in London and Paris, and should like to visit them; meantime you can go to Italy, Germany, Switzerland, where you will, and enjoy pictures, music, scenery, and adventures to your heart's content."

Now, Laurie felt just then that his heart was entirely broken, and the world a howling wilderness; but at the sound of certain words which the old gentleman artfully introduced into his closing sentence, the broken heart gave an unexpected leap, and a green oasis or two suddenly appeared in the howling wilderness. He sighed, and then said, in a spiritless tone,—

"Just as you like, sir; it doesn't matter where I go or what I do."

"It does to me, remember that, my lad; I give you entire liberty, but I trust you to make an honest use of it. Promise me that, Laurie."

"Anything you like, sir."

"Good," thought the old gentleman. "You don't care now, but there'll come a time when that promise will keep you out of mischief, or I'm much mistaken."

Being an energetic individual, Mr. Laurence struck while the iron was hot; and before the blighted being recovered spirit enough to rebel, they were off. During the time necessary for preparation, Laurie bore himself as young gentlemen usually do in such cases. He was moody, irritable, and pensive by turns; lost his appetite, neglected his dress, and devoted much time to playing tempestuously on his piano; avoided Jo, but consoled himself by staring at her from his window, with a tragical face that haunted her dreams by night, and oppressed her with a heavy sense of guilt by day. Unlike some sufferers, he never spoke of his unrequited passion, and would allow no one, not even Mrs. March, to attempt consolation or offer sympathy. On some accounts, this was a relief to his friends; but the weeks before his departure were very uncomfortable, and every one rejoiced that the "poor, dear fellow was going away to forget his trouble, and come home happy." Of course, he smiled darkly at their delusion, but passed it by, with the sad superiority of one who knew that his fidelity, like his love, was unalterable.

When the parting came he affected high spirits, to conceal certain inconvenient emotions which seemed inclined to assert themselves. This gayety did not impose upon anybody, but they tried to look as if it did, for his sake, and he got on very well till Mrs. March kissed him, with a whisper full of motherly solicitude; then, feeling that he was going very fast, he hastily embraced them all round, not forgetting the afflicted Hannah, and ran downstairs as if for his life. Jo followed a minute after to wave her hand to him if he looked round. He did look round, came back, put his arms about her, as she stood on the step above him, and looked up at her with a face that made his short appeal both eloquent and pathetic.

"O Jo, can't you?"

"Teddy, dear, I wish I could!"

That was all, except a little pause; then Laurie straightened himself up, said "It's all right, never mind," and went away without another word. Ah, but it wasn't all right, and Jo *did* mind; for while the curly head lay on her arm a minute after her hard answer, she felt as if she had stabbed her dearest friend; and when he left her without a look behind him, she knew that the boy Laurie never would come again.

# XII

## BETH'S SECRET.

WHEN Jo came home that spring, she had been struck with the change in Beth. No one spoke of it or seemed aware of it, for it had come too gradually to startle those who saw her daily; but to eyes sharpened by absence, it was very plain; and a heavy weight fell on Jo's heart as she saw her sister's face. It was no paler and but little thinner than in the autumn; yet there was a strange, transparent look about it, as if the mortal was being slowly refined away, and the immortal shining through the frail flesh with an indescribably pathetic beauty. Jo saw and felt it, but said nothing at the time, and soon the first impression lost much of its power; for Beth seemed happy, no one appeared to doubt that she was better; and, presently, in other cares, Jo for a time forgot her fear.

But when Laurie was gone, and peace prevailed again, the vague anxiety returned and haunted her. She had confessed her sins and been forgiven; but when she showed her savings and proposed the mountain trip, Beth had thanked her heartily, but begged not to go so far away from home. Another little visit to the seashore would suit her better, and, as grandma could not be prevailed upon to leave the babies, Jo took Beth down to the quiet place, where she could live much in the open air, and let the fresh sea-breezes blow a little color into her pale cheeks.

It was not a fashionable place, but, even among the pleasant people there, the girls made few friends, preferring to live for one another. Beth was too shy to enjoy society, and Jo too wrapped up in her to care for any one else; so they were all in all to each other, and came and went, quite unconscious of the interest they excited in those about them, who watched with sympathetic eyes the strong sister and the feeble one, always together, as if they felt instinctively that a long separation was not far away.

They did feel it, yet neither spoke of it; for often between ourselves and those nearest and dearest to us there exists a reserve which it is very hard to overcome. Jo felt as if a veil had fallen between her heart and Beth's; but when she put out her hand to lift it up, there seemed something sacred in the silence, and she waited for Beth to speak. She wondered, and was thankful also, that her parents did not seem to see what she saw; and, during the quiet weeks, when the shadow grew so plain to her, she said nothing of it to those at home, believing that it would tell itself when Beth came back no better. She wondered still more if her sister really guessed the hard truth, and what thoughts were passing through her mind during the long hours when she lay on the warm rocks, with her head in Jo's lap, while the winds blew healthfully over her, and the sea made music at her feet.

One day Beth told her. Jo thought she was asleep, she lay so still; and, putting down her book, sat looking at her with wistful eyes, trying to see signs of hope in the faint color on Beth's cheeks. But she could not find enough to satisfy her, for the cheeks were very thin, and the hands seemed too feeble to hold even the rosy little shells they had been gathering. It came to her then more bitterly than ever that Beth was slowly drifting away from her, and her arms instinctively tightened their hold upon the dearest treasure she possessed. For a minute her eyes were too dim for seeing, and, when they cleared, Beth was looking up at her so tenderly that there was hardly any need for her to say,—

"Jo, dear, I'm glad you know it. I've tried to tell you, but I couldn't."

There was no answer except her sister's cheek against her own, not even tears; for when most deeply moved, Jo did not cry. She was the weaker, then, and Beth tried to comfort and sustain her, with her arms about her, and the soothing words she whispered in her ear.

"I've known it for a good while, dear, and, now I'm used to it, it isn't hard to think of or to bear. Try to see it so, and don't be troubled about me, because it's best; indeed it is."

"Is this what made you so unhappy in the autumn, Beth? You did not feel it then, and keep it to yourself so long, did you?" asked Jo, refusing to see or say that it *was* best, but glad to know that Laurie had no part in Beth's trouble.

"Yes, I gave up hoping then, but I didn't like to own it. I tried to think it was a sick fancy, and would not let it trouble any one. But when I saw you all so well and strong, and full of happy plans, it was hard to feel that I could never be like you, and then I was miserable, Jo."

"O Beth, and you didn't tell me, didn't let me comfort and help you! How could you shut me out, and bear it all alone?"

Jo's voice was full of tender reproach, and her heart ached to think of the solitary struggle that must have gone on while Beth learned to say good-by to health, love, and life, and take up her cross so cheerfully.

"Perhaps it was wrong, but I tried to do right; I wasn't sure, no one said anything, and I hoped I was mistaken. It would have been selfish to frighten you all when Marmee was so anxious about Meg, and Amy away, and you so happy with Laurie,—at least, I thought so then."

"And I thought that you loved him, Beth, and I went away because I couldn't," cried Jo, glad to say all the truth.

Beth looked so amazed at the idea that Jo smiled in spite of her pain, and added softly,—

"Then you didn't, deary? I was afraid it was so, and imagined your poor little heart full of love-lornity all that while."

"Why, Jo, how could I, when he was so fond of you?" asked Beth, as innocently as a child. "I do love him dearly; he is so good to me, how can I help it? But he never could be anything to me but my brother. I hope he truly will be, sometime."

"Not through me," said Jo decidedly. "Amy is left for him, and they would suit excellently; but I have no heart for such things, now. I don't care what becomes of anybody but you, Beth. You *must* get well."

"I want to, oh, so much! I try, but every day I lose a little, and feel more sure that I shall never gain it back. It's like the tide, Jo, when it turns, it goes slowly, but it can't be stopped."

"It *shall* be stopped, your tide must not turn so soon, nineteen is too young. Beth, I can't let you go. I'll work and pray and fight against it. I'll keep you in spite of everything; there must be ways, it can't be too late. God won't be so cruel as to take you from me," cried poor Jo rebelliously, for her spirit was far less piously submissive than Beth's.

Simple, sincere people seldom speak much of their piety; it shows itself in acts, rather than in words, and has more influence than homilies or protestations. Beth could not reason upon or explain the faith that gave her courage and patience to give up life, and cheerfully wait for death. Like a confiding child, she asked no questions, but left everything to God and nature, Father and mother of us all, feeling sure that they, and they only, could teach and strengthen heart and spirit for this life and the life to come. She did not rebuke Jo with saintly speeches, only loved her better for her passionate affection, and clung more closely to the dear human love, from which our Father never means us to be weaned, but through which He draws us closer to Himself. She could not say, "I'm glad to go," for life was very sweet to her; she could only sob out, "I try to be willing," while she held fast to Jo, as the first bitter wave of this great sorrow broke over them together.

By and by Beth said, with recovered serenity,—

"You'll tell them this when we go home?"

"I think they will see it without words," sighed Jo; for now it seemed to her that Beth changed every day.

"Perhaps not; I've heard that the people who love best are often blindest to such things. If they don't see it, you will tell them for me. I don't want any secrets, and it's kinder to prepare them. Meg has John and the babies to comfort her, but you must stand by father and mother, won't you, Jo?"

"If I can; but, Beth, I don't give up yet; I'm going to believe that it *is* a sick fancy, and not let you think it's true," said Jo, trying to speak cheerfully.

Beth lay a minute thinking, and then said in her quiet way,—

"I don't know how to express myself, and shouldn't try, to any one but you, because I can't speak out, except to my Jo. I only mean to say that I have a feeling that it never was intended I should live long. I'm not like the rest of you; I never made any plans about what I'd do when I grew up; I never thought of being married, as you all did. I couldn't seem to imagine myself anything but stupid little Beth, trotting about at home, of no use anywhere but there. I never wanted to go away, and the hard part now is the leaving you all. I'm not afraid, but it seems as if I should be homesick for you even in heaven."

Jo could not speak; and for several minutes there was no sound but the sigh of the wind and the lapping of the tide. A white-winged gull flew by, with the flash of sunshine on its silvery breast; Beth watched it till it vanished, and her eyes were full of sadness. A little gray-coated sand-bird came tripping over the beach, "peeping" softly to itself, as if enjoying the sun and sea; it came quite close to Beth, looked at her with a friendly eye, and sat upon a warm stone, dressing its wet feathers, quite at home. Beth smiled, and felt comforted, for the tiny thing seemed to offer its small friendship, and remind her that a pleasant world was still to be enjoyed.

"Dear little bird! See, Jo, how tame it is. I like peeps better than the gulls: they are not so wild and handsome, but they seem happy, confiding little things. I used to call them my birds, last summer; and mother said they reminded her of me,—busy, quaker-colored creatures, always near the shore, and always chirping that contented little song of theirs. You are the gull, Jo, strong and wild, fond of the storm and the wind, flying far out to sea, and happy all alone. Meg is the turtle-dove, and Amy is like the lark she writes about, trying to get up among the clouds, but always dropping down into its nest again. Dear little girl! she's so ambitious, but her heart is good and tender; and no matter how high she flies, she never will forget home. I hope I shall see her again, but she seems *so* far away."

"She is coming in the spring, and I mean that you shall be all ready to see and enjoy her. I'm going to have you well and rosy by that time," began Jo, feeling that of all the changes in Beth, the talking change was the greatest, for it seemed to cost no effort now, and she thought aloud in a way quite unlike bashful Beth.

"Jo, dear, don't hope any more; it won't do any good, I'm sure of that. We won't be miserable, but enjoy being together while we wait. We'll have happy times, for I don't suffer much, and I think the tide will go out easily, if you help me."

Jo leaned down to kiss the tranquil face; and with that silent kiss, she dedicated herself soul and body to Beth.

She was right: there was no need of any words when they got home, for father and mother saw plainly, now, what they had prayed to be saved from seeing. Tired with her short journey, Beth went at once to bed, saying how glad she was to be at home; and when Jo went down, she found that she would be spared the hard task of telling Beth's secret. Her father stood leaning his head on the mantel-piece, and did not turn as she came in; but her mother stretched out her arms as if for help, and Jo went to comfort her without a word.

## XIII

## NEW IMPRESSIONS.

AT three o'clock in the afternoon, all the fashionable world at Nice may be seen on the Promenade des Anglais,—a charming place; for the wide walk, bordered with palms, flowers, and tropical shrubs, is bounded on one side by the sea, on the other by the grand drive, lined with hotels and villas, while beyond lie orange-orchards and the hills. Many nations are represented, many languages spoken, many costumes worn; and, on a sunny day, the spectacle is as gay and brilliant as a carnival. Haughty English, lively French, sober Germans, handsome Spaniards, ugly Russians, meek Jews, free-and-easy Americans, all drive, sit, or saunter here, chatting over the news, and criticising the latest celebrity who has arrived,—Ristori or Dickens, Victor Emmanuel or the Queen of the Sandwich Islands. The equipages are as varied as the company, and attract as much attention, especially the low basket-barouches in which ladies drive themselves, with a pair of dashing ponies, gay nets to keep their voluminous flounces from overflowing the diminutive vehicles, and little grooms on the perch behind.

Along this walk, on Christmas Day, a tall young man walked slowly, with his hands behind him, and a somewhat absent expression of countenance. He looked like an Italian, was dressed like an Englishman, and had the independent air of an American,—a combination which caused sundry pairs of feminine eyes to look approvingly after him, and sundry dandies in black velvet suits, with rose-colored neckties, buff gloves, and orange-flowers in their button-holes, to shrug their shoulders, and then envy him his inches. There were plenty of pretty faces to admire, but the young man took little notice of them, except to glance, now and then, at some blonde girl, or lady in blue. Presently he strolled out of the promenade, and stood a moment at the crossing, as if undecided whether to go and listen to the band in the Jardin Publique, or to wander along the beach toward Castle Hill. The quick trot of ponies' feet made him look up, as one of the little carriages, containing a single lady, came rapidly down the street. The lady was young, blonde, and dressed in blue. He stared a minute, then his whole face woke up, and, waving his hat like a boy, he hurried forward to meet her.

"O Laurie, is it really you? I thought you'd never come!" cried Amy, dropping the reins, and holding out both hands, to the great scandalization of a French mamma, who hastened her daughter's steps, lest she should be demoralized by beholding the free manners of these "mad English."

"I was detained by the way, but I promised to spend Christmas with you, and here I am."

"How is your grandfather? When did you come? Where are you staying?"

"Very well—last night—at the Chauvain. I called at your hotel, but you were all out."

"I have so much to say, I don't know where to begin! Get in, and we can talk at our ease; I was going for a drive, and longing for company. Flo's saving up for to-night."

"What happens then, a ball?"

"A Christmas party at our hotel. There are many Americans there, and they give it in honor of the day. You'll go with us, of course? Aunt will be charmed."

"Thank you. Where now?" asked Laurie, leaning back and folding his arms, a proceeding which suited Amy, who preferred to drive; for her parasol-whip and blue reins over the white ponies' backs, afforded her infinite satisfaction.

"I'm going to the banker's first, for letters, and then to Castle Hill; the view is so lovely, and I like to feed the peacocks. Have you ever been there?"

"Often, years ago; but I don't mind having a look at it."

"Now tell me all about yourself. The last I heard of you, your grandfather wrote that he expected you from Berlin."

"Yes, I spent a month there, and then joined him in Paris, where he has settled for the winter. He has friends there, and finds plenty to amuse him; so I go and come, and we get on capitally."

"That's a sociable arrangement," said Amy, missing something in Laurie's manner, though she couldn't tell what.

"Why, you see he hates to travel, and I hate to keep still; so we each suit ourselves, and there is no trouble. I am often with him, and he enjoys my adventures, while I like to feel that some one is glad to see me when I get back from my wanderings. Dirty old hole, isn't it?" he added, with a look of disgust, as they drove along the boulevard to the Place Napoleon, in the old city.

"The dirt is picturesque, so I don't mind. The river and the hills are delicious, and these glimpses of the narrow cross-streets are my delight. Now we shall have to wait for that procession to pass; it's going to the Church of St. John."

While Laurie listlessly watched the procession of priests under their canopies, white-veiled nuns bearing lighted tapers, and some brotherhood in blue, chanting as they walked, Amy watched him, and felt a new sort of shyness steal over her; for he was changed, and she could not find the merry-faced boy she left in the moody-looking man beside her. He was handsomer than ever, and greatly improved, she thought; but now that the flush of pleasure at meeting her was over, he looked tired and spiritless,—not sick, nor exactly unhappy, but older and graver than a year or two of prosperous life should have made him. She couldn't understand it, and did not venture to ask questions; so she shook her head, and touched up her ponies, as the procession wound away across the arches of the Paglioni bridge, and vanished in the church.

"*Que pensez vous?*" she said, airing her French, which had improved in quantity, if not in quality, since she came abroad.

"That mademoiselle has made good use of her time, and the result is charming," replied Laurie, bowing, with his hand on his heart, and an admiring look.

She blushed with pleasure, but somehow the compliment did not satisfy her like the blunt praises he used to give her at home, when he promenaded round her on festival occasions, and told her she was "altogether jolly," with a hearty smile and an approving pat on the head. She didn't like the new tone; for, though not *blasé*, it sounded indifferent in spite of the look.

"If that's the way he's going to grow up, I wish he'd stay a boy," she thought, with a curious sense of disappointment and discomfort, trying meantime to seem quite easy and gay.

At Avigdor's she found the precious home-letters, and, giving the reins to Laurie, read them luxuriously as they wound up the shady road between green hedges, where tea-roses bloomed as freshly as in June.

"Beth is very poorly, mother says. I often think I ought to go home, but they all say 'stay;' so I do, for I shall never have another chance like this," said Amy, looking sober over one page.

"I think you are right, there; you could do nothing at home, and it is a great comfort to them to know that you are well and happy, and enjoying so much, my dear."

He drew a little nearer, and looked more like his old self, as he said that; and the fear that sometimes weighed on Amy's heart was lightened, for the look, the act, the brotherly "my dear," seemed to assure her that if any trouble did come, she would not be alone in a strange land. Presently she laughed, and showed him a small sketch of Jo in her scribbling-suit, with the bow rampantly erect upon her cap, and issuing from her mouth the words, "Genius burns!"

Laurie smiled, took it, put it in his vest-pocket, "to keep it from blowing away," and listened with interest to the lively letter Amy read him.

"This will be a regularly merry Christmas to me, with presents in the morning, you and letters in the afternoon, and a party at night," said Amy, as they alighted among the ruins of the old fort, and a flock of splendid peacocks came trooping about them, tamely waiting to be fed. While Amy stood laughing on the bank above him as she scattered crumbs to the brilliant birds, Laurie looked at her as she had looked at him, with a natural curiosity to see what changes time and absence had wrought. He found nothing to perplex or disappoint, much to admire and approve; for, overlooking a few little affectations of speech and manner, she was as sprightly and graceful as ever, with the addition of that indescribable something in dress and bearing which we call elegance. Always mature for her age, she had gained a certain *aplomb* in both carriage and conversation, which made her seem more of a woman of the world than she was; but her old petulance now and then showed itself, her strong will still held its own, and her native frankness was unspoiled by foreign polish.

Laurie did not read all this while he watched her feed the peacocks, but he saw enough to satisfy and interest him, and carried away a pretty little picture of a bright-faced girl standing in the sunshine, which brought out the soft hue of her dress, the fresh color of her cheeks, the golden gloss of her hair, and made her a prominent figure in the pleasant scene.

As they came up on to the stone plateau that crowns the hill, Amy waved her hand as if welcoming him to her favorite haunt, and said, pointing here and there,—

"Do you remember the Cathedral and the Corso, the fishermen dragging their nets in the bay, and the lovely road to Villa Franca, Schubert's Tower, just below, and, best of all, that speck far out to sea which they say is Corsica?"

"I remember; it's not much changed," he answered, without enthusiasm.

"What Jo would give for a sight of that famous speck!" said Amy, feeling in good spirits, and anxious to see him so also.

"Yes," was all he said, but he turned and strained his eyes to see the island which a greater usurper than even Napoleon now made interesting in his sight.

"Take a good look at it for her sake, and then come and tell me what you have been doing with yourself all this while," said Amy, seating herself, ready for a good talk.

But she did not get it; for, though he joined her, and answered all her questions freely, she could only learn that he had roved about the continent and been to Greece. So, after idling away an hour, they drove home again; and, having paid his respects to Mrs. Carrol, Laurie left them, promising to return in the evening.

It must be recorded of Amy that she deliberately "prinked" that night. Time and absence had done its work on both the young people; she had seen her old friend in a new light, not as "our boy," but as a handsome and agreeable man, and she was conscious of a very natural desire to find favor in his sight. Amy knew her good points, and made the most of them, with the taste and skill which is a fortune to a poor and pretty woman.

Tarlatan and tulle were cheap at Nice, so she enveloped herself in them on such occasions, and, following the sensible English fashion of simple dress for young girls, got up charming little toilettes with fresh flowers, a few trinkets, and all manner of dainty devices, which were both inexpensive and effective. It must be confessed that the artist sometimes got possession of the woman, and indulged in antique *coiffures*, statuesque attitudes, and classic draperies. But, dear heart, we all have our little weaknesses, and find it easy to pardon such in the young, who satisfy our eyes with their comeliness, and keep our hearts merry with their artless vanities.

"I do want him to think I look well, and tell them so at home," said Amy to herself, as she put on Flo's old white silk ball-dress, and covered it with a cloud of fresh illusion, out of which her white shoulders and golden head emerged with a most artistic effect. Her hair she had the sense to let alone, after gathering up the thick waves and curls into a Hebe-like knot at the back of her head.

"It's not the fashion, but it's becoming, and I can't afford to make a fright of myself," she used to say, when advised to frizzle, puff, or braid, as the latest style commanded.

Having no ornaments fine enough for this important occasion, Amy looped her fleecy skirts with rosy clusters of azalea, and framed the white shoulders in delicate green vines. Remembering the painted boots, she surveyed her white satin slippers with girlish satisfaction, and *chasséed* down the room, admiring her aristocratic feet all by herself.

"My new fan just matches my flowers, my gloves fit to a charm, and the real lace on aunt's *mouchoir* gives an air to my whole dress. If I only had a classical nose and mouth I should be perfectly happy," she said, surveying herself with a critical eye, and a candle in each hand.

In spite of this affliction, she looked unusually gay and graceful as she glided away; she seldom ran,—it did not suit her style, she thought, for, being tall, the stately and Junoesque was more appropriate than the sportive or piquante. She walked up and down the long saloon while waiting for Laurie, and once arranged herself under the chandelier, which had a good effect upon her hair; then she thought better of it, and went away to the other end of the room, as if ashamed of the girlish desire to have the first view a propitious one. It so happened that she could not have done a better thing, for Laurie came in so quietly she did not hear him; and, as she stood at the distant window, with her head half turned, and one hand gathering up her dress, the slender, white figure against the red curtains was as effective as a well-placed statue.

"Good evening, Diana!" said Laurie, with the look of satisfaction she liked to see in his eyes when they rested on her.

"Good evening, Apollo!" she answered, smiling back at him, for he, too, looked unusually *debonnaire*, and the thought of entering the ball-room on the arm of such a personable man caused Amy to pity the four plain Misses Davis from the bottom of her heart.

"Here are your flowers; I arranged them myself, remembering that you didn't like what Hannah calls a 'sot-bookay,'" said Laurie, handing her a delicate nosegay, in a holder that she had long coveted as she daily passed it in Cardiglia's window.

"How kind you are!" she exclaimed gratefully. "If I'd known you were coming I'd have had something ready for you to-day, though not as pretty as this, I'm afraid."

"Thank you; it isn't what it should be, but you have improved it," he added, as she snapped the silver bracelet on her wrist.

"Please don't."

"I thought you liked that sort of thing?"

"Not from you; it doesn't sound natural, and I like your old bluntness better."

"I'm glad of it," he answered, with a look of relief; then buttoned her gloves for her, and asked if his tie was straight, just as he used to do when they went to parties together, at home.

The company assembled in the long *salle à manger*, that evening, was such as one sees nowhere but on the Continent. The hospitable Americans had invited every acquaintance they had in Nice, and, having no prejudice against titles, secured a few to add lustre to their Christmas ball.

A Russian prince condescended to sit in a corner for an hour, and talk with a massive lady, dressed like Hamlet's mother, in black velvet, with a pearl bridle under her chin. A Polish count, aged eighteen, devoted himself to the ladies, who pronounced him "a fascinating dear," and a German Serene Something, having come for the supper alone, roamed vaguely about, seeking what he might devour. Baron Rothschild's private secretary, a large-nosed Jew, in tight boots, affably beamed upon the world, as if his master's name crowned him with a golden halo; a stout Frenchman, who knew the Emperor, came to indulge his mania for dancing, and Lady de Jones, a British matron, adorned the scene with her little family of eight. Of course, there were many light-footed, shrill-voiced American girls, handsome, lifeless-looking English ditto, and a few plain but piquante French demoiselles; likewise the usual set of travelling young gentlemen, who disported themselves gayly, while mammas of all nations lined the walls, and smiled upon them benignly when they danced with their daughters.

Any young girl can imagine Amy's state of mind when she "took the stage" that night, leaning on Laurie's arm. She knew she looked well, she loved to dance, she felt that her foot was on her native heath in a ball-room, and enjoyed the delightful sense of power which comes when young girls first discover the new and lovely kingdom they are born to rule by virtue of beauty, youth, and womanhood. She did pity the Davis girls, who were awkward, plain, and destitute of escort, except a grim papa and three grimmer maiden aunts, and she bowed to them in her friendliest manner as she passed; which was good of her, as it permitted them to see her dress, and burn with curiosity to know who her distinguished-looking friend might be. With the first burst of the band, Amy's color rose, her eyes began to sparkle, and her feet to tap the floor impatiently; for she danced well, and wanted Laurie to know it: therefore the shock she received can better be imagined than described, when he said, in a perfectly tranquil tone,—

"Do you care to dance?"

"One usually does at a ball."

Her amazed look and quick answer caused Laurie to repair his error as fast as possible.

"I meant the first dance. May I have the honor?"

"I can give you one if I put off the Count. He dances divinely; but he will excuse me, as you are an old friend," said Amy, hoping that the name would have a good effect, and show Laurie that she was not to be trifled with.

"Nice little boy, but rather a short Pole to support

"'A daughter of the gods,
Divinely tall, and most divinely fair,'"

was all the satisfaction she got, however.

The set in which they found themselves was composed of English, and Amy was compelled to walk decorously through a cotillon, feeling all the while as if she could dance the Tarantula with a relish. Laurie resigned her to the "nice little boy," and went to do his duty to Flo, without securing Amy for the joys to come, which reprehensible want of forethought was properly punished, for she immediately engaged herself till supper, meaning to relent if he then gave any signs of penitence. She showed him her ball-book with demure satisfaction when he strolled, instead of rushing, up to claim her for the next, a glorious polka-redowa; but his polite regrets didn't impose upon her, and when she gallopaded away with the Count, she saw Laurie sit down by her aunt with an actual expression of relief.

That was unpardonable; and Amy took no more notice of him for a long while, except a word now and then, when she came to her chaperon, between the dances, for a necessary pin or a moment's rest. Her anger had a good effect, however, for she hid it under a smiling face, and seemed unusually blithe and brilliant. Laurie's eyes followed her with pleasure, for she neither romped nor sauntered, but danced with spirit and grace, making the delightsome pastime what it should be. He very naturally fell to studying her from this new point of view; and, before the evening was half over, had decided that "little Amy was going to make a very charming woman."

It was a lively scene, for soon the spirit of the social season took possession of every one, and Christmas merriment made all faces shine, hearts happy, and heels light. The musicians fiddled, tooted, and banged as if they enjoyed it; everybody danced who could, and those who couldn't admired their neighbors with uncommon warmth. The air was dark with Davises, and many Joneses gambolled like a flock of young giraffes. The golden secretary darted through the room like a meteor, with a dashing Frenchwoman, who carpeted the floor with her pink satin train. The Serene Teuton found the supper-table, and was happy, eating steadily through the bill of fare, and dismayed the *garçons* by the ravages he committed. But the Emperor's friend covered himself with glory, for he danced everything, whether he knew it or not, and introduced impromptu pirouettes when the figures bewildered him. The boyish abandon of that stout man was charming to behold; for, though he "carried weight," he danced like an india-rubber ball. He ran, he flew, he pranced; his face glowed, his bald head shone; his coat-tails waved wildly, his pumps actually twinkled in the air, and when the music stopped, he wiped the drops from his brow, and beamed upon his fellow-men like a French Pickwick without glasses.

Amy and her Pole distinguished themselves by equal enthusiasm, but more graceful agility; and Laurie found himself involuntarily keeping time to the rhythmic rise and fall of the white slippers as they flew by as indefatigably as if winged. When little Vladimir finally relinquished her, with assurances that he was "desolated to leave so early," she was ready to rest, and see how her recreant knight had borne his punishment.

It had been successful; for, at three-and-twenty, blighted affections find a balm in friendly society, and young nerves will thrill, young blood dance, and healthy young spirits rise, when subjected to the enchantment of beauty, light, music, and motion. Laurie had a waked-up look as he rose to give her his seat; and when he hurried away to bring her some supper, she said to herself, with a satisfied smile,—

"Ah, I thought that would do him good!"

"You look like Balzac's 'Femme peinte par elle-même,'" he said, as he fanned her with one hand, and held her coffee-cup in the other.

"My rouge won't come off;" and Amy rubbed her brilliant cheek, and showed him her white glove with a sober simplicity that made him laugh outright.

"What do you call this stuff?" he asked, touching a fold of her dress that had blown over his knee.

"Illusion."

"Good name for it; it's very pretty—new thing, isn't it?"

"It's as old as the hills; you have seen it on dozens of girls, and you never found out that it was pretty till now—*stupide*!"

"I never saw it on you before, which accounts for the mistake, you see."

"None of that, it is forbidden; I'd rather take coffee than compliments just now. No, don't lounge, it makes me nervous."

Laurie sat bolt upright, and meekly took her empty plate, feeling an odd sort of pleasure in having "little Amy" order him about; for she had lost her shyness now, and felt an irresistible desire to trample on him, as girls have a delightful way of doing when lords of creation show any signs of subjection.

"Where did you learn all this sort of thing?" he asked, with a quizzical look.

"As 'this sort of thing' is rather a vague expression, would you kindly explain?" returned Amy, knowing perfectly well what he meant, but wickedly leaving him to describe what is indescribable.

"Well—the general air, the style, the self-possession, the—the—illusion—you know," laughed Laurie, breaking down, and helping himself out of his quandary with the new word.

Amy was gratified, but, of course, didn't show it, and demurely answered, "Foreign life polishes one in spite of one's self; I study as well as play; and as for this"—with a little gesture toward her dress—"why, tulle is cheap, posies to be had for nothing, and I am used to making the most of my poor little things."

Amy rather regretted that last sentence, fearing it wasn't in good taste; but Laurie liked her the better for it, and found himself both admiring and respecting the brave patience that made the most of opportunity, and the cheerful spirit that covered poverty with flowers. Amy did not know why he looked at her so kindly, nor why he filled up her book with his own name, and devoted himself to her for the rest of the evening, in the most delightful manner; but the impulse that wrought this agreeable change was the result of one of the new impressions which both of them were unconsciously giving and receiving.

## XXXVIII.
## ON THE SHELF.

IN France the young girls have a dull time of it till they are married, when "*Vive la liberté*" becomes their motto. In America, as every one knows, girls early sign the declaration of independence, and enjoy their freedom with republican zest; but the young matrons usually abdicate with the first heir to the throne, and go into a seclusion almost as close as a French nunnery, though by no means as quiet. Whether they like it or not, they are virtually put upon the shelf as soon as the wedding excitement is over, and most of them might exclaim, as did a very pretty woman the other day, "I'm as handsome as ever, but no one takes any notice of me because I'm married."

Not being a belle or even a fashionable lady, Meg did not experience this affliction till her babies were a year old, for in her little world primitive customs prevailed, and she found herself more admired and beloved than ever.

As she was a womanly little woman, the maternal instinct was very strong, and she was entirely absorbed in her children, to the utter exclusion of everything and everybody else. Day and night she brooded over them with tireless devotion and anxiety, leaving John to the tender mercies of the help, for an Irish lady now presided over the kitchen department. Being a domestic man, John decidedly missed the wifely attentions he had been accustomed to receive; but, as he adored his babies, he cheerfully relinquished his comfort for a time, supposing, with masculine ignorance, that peace would soon be restored. But three months passed, and there was no return of repose; Meg looked worn and nervous, the babies absorbed every minute of her time, the house was neglected, and Kitty, the cook, who took life "aisy," kept him on short commons. When he went out in the morning he was bewildered by small commissions for the captive mamma; if he came gayly in at night, eager to embrace his family, he was quenched by a "Hush! they are just asleep after worrying all day." If he proposed a little amusement at home, "No, it would disturb the babies." If he hinted at a lecture or concert, he was answered with a reproachful look, and a decided "Leave my children for pleasure, never!" His sleep was broken by infant wails and visions of a phantom figure pacing noiselessly to and fro in the watches of the night; his meals were interrupted by the frequent flight of the presiding genius, who deserted him, half-helped, if a muffled chirp sounded from the nest above; and when he read his paper of an evening, Demi's colic got into the shipping-list, and Daisy's fall affected the price of stocks, for Mrs. Brooke was only interested in domestic news.

The poor man was very uncomfortable, for the children had bereft him of his wife; home was merely a nursery, and the perpetual "hushing" made him feel like a brutal intruder whenever he entered the sacred precincts of Babyland. He bore it very patiently for six months, and, when no signs of amendment appeared, he did what other paternal exiles do,—tried to get a little comfort elsewhere. Scott had married and gone to housekeeping not far off, and John fell into the way of running over for an hour or two of an evening, when his own parlor was empty, and his own wife singing lullabies that seemed to have no end. Mrs. Scott was a lively, pretty girl, with nothing to do but be agreeable, and she performed her mission most successfully. The parlor was always bright and attractive, the chess-board ready, the piano in tune, plenty of gay gossip, and a nice little supper set forth in tempting style.

John would have preferred his own fireside if it had not been so lonely; but as it was, he gratefully took the next best thing, and enjoyed his neighbor's society.

Meg rather approved of the new arrangement at first, and found it a relief to know that John was having a good time instead of dozing in the parlor, or tramping about the house and waking the children. But by and by, when the teething worry was over, and the idols went to sleep at proper hours, leaving mamma time to rest, she began to miss John, and find her work-basket dull company, when he was not sitting opposite in his old dressing-gown, comfortably scorching his slippers on the fender. She would not ask him to stay at home, but felt injured because he did not know that she wanted him without being told, entirely forgetting the many evenings he had waited for her in vain. She was nervous and worn out with watching and worry, and in that unreasonable frame of mind which the best of mothers occasionally experience when domestic cares oppress them. Want of exercise robs them of cheerfulness, and too much devotion to that idol of American women, the teapot, makes them feel as if they were all nerve and no muscle.

"Yes," she would say, looking in the glass, "I'm getting old and ugly; John doesn't find me interesting any longer, so he leaves his faded wife and goes to see his pretty neighbor, who has no incumbrances. Well, the babies love me; they don't care if I am thin and pale, and haven't time to crimp my hair; they are my comfort, and some day John will see what I've gladly sacrificed for them, won't he, my precious?"

To which pathetic appeal Daisy would answer with a coo, or Demi with a crow, and Meg would put by her lamentations for a maternal revel, which soothed her solitude for the time being. But the pain increased as politics absorbed John, who was always running over to discuss interesting points with Scott, quite unconscious that Meg missed him. Not a word did she say, however, till her mother found her in tears one day, and insisted on knowing what the matter was, for Meg's drooping spirits had not escaped her observation.

"I wouldn't tell any one except you, mother; but I really do need advice, for, if John goes on so much longer I might as well be widowed," replied Mrs. Brooke, drying her tears on Daisy's bib, with an injured air.

"Goes on how, my dear?" asked her mother anxiously.

"He's away all day, and at night, when I want to see him, he is continually going over to the Scotts'. It isn't fair that I should have the hardest work, and never any amusement. Men are very selfish, even the best of them."

"So are women; don't blame John till you see where you are wrong yourself."

"But it can't be right for him to neglect me."

"Don't you neglect him?"

"Why, mother, I thought you'd take my part!"

"So I do, as far as sympathizing goes; but I think the fault is yours, Meg."

"I don't see how."

"Let me show you. Did John ever neglect you, as you call it, while you made it a point to give him your society of an evening, his only leisure time?"

"No; but I can't do it now, with two babies to tend."

"I think you could, dear; and I think you ought. May I speak quite freely, and will you remember that it's mother who blames as well as mother who sympathizes?"

"Indeed I will! Speak to me as if I were little Meg again. I often feel as if I needed teaching more than ever since these babies look to me for everything."

Meg drew her low chair beside her mother's, and, with a little interruption in either lap, the two women rocked and talked lovingly together, feeling that the tie of motherhood made them more one than ever.

"You have only made the mistake that most young wives make,—forgotten your duty to your husband in your love for your children. A very natural and forgivable mistake, Meg, but one that had better be remedied before you take to different ways; for children should draw you nearer than ever, not separate you, as if they were all yours, and John had nothing to do but support them. I've seen it for some weeks, but have not spoken, feeling sure it would come right in time."

"I'm afraid it won't. If I ask him to stay, he'll think I'm jealous; and I wouldn't insult him by such an idea. He doesn't see that I want him, and I don't know how to tell him without words."

"Make it so pleasant he won't want to go away. My dear, he's longing for his little home; but it isn't home without you, and you are always in the nursery."

"Oughtn't I to be there?"

"Not all the time; too much confinement makes you nervous, and then you are unfitted for everything. Besides, you owe something to John as well as to the babies; don't neglect husband for children, don't shut him out of the nursery, but teach him how to help in it. His place is there as well as yours, and the children need him; let him feel that he has his part to do, and he will do it gladly and faithfully, and it will be better for you all."

"You really think so, mother?"

"I know it, Meg, for I've tried it; and I seldom give advice unless I've proved its practicability. When you and Jo were little, I went on just as you are, feeling as if I didn't do my duty unless I devoted myself wholly to you. Poor father took to his books, after I had refused all offers of help, and left me to try my experiment alone. I struggled along as well as I could, but Jo was too much for me. I nearly spoilt her by indulgence. You were poorly, and I worried about you till I fell sick myself. Then father came to the rescue, quietly managed everything, and made himself so helpful that I saw my mistake, and never have been able to get on without him since. That is the secret of our home happiness: he does not let business wean him from the little cares and duties that affect us all, and I try not to let domestic worries destroy my interest in his pursuits. Each do our part alone in many things, but at home we work together, always."

"It is so, mother; and my great wish is to be to my husband and children what you have been to yours. Show me how; I'll do anything you say."

"You always were my docile daughter. Well, dear, if I were you, I'd let John have more to do with the management of Demi, for the boy needs training, and it's none too soon to begin. Then I'd do what I have often proposed, let Hannah come and help you; she is a capital nurse, and you may trust the precious babies to her while you do more housework. You need the exercise, Hannah would enjoy the rest, and John would find his wife again. Go out more; keep cheerful as well as busy, for you are the sunshine-maker of the family, and if you get dismal there is no fair weather. Then I'd try to take an interest in whatever John likes,—talk with him, let him read to you, exchange ideas, and help each other in that way. Don't shut yourself up in a bandbox because you are a woman, but understand what is going on, and educate yourself to take your part in the world's work, for it all affects you and yours."

"John is so sensible, I'm afraid he will think I'm stupid if I ask questions about politics and things."

"I don't believe he would; love covers a multitude of sins, and of whom could you ask more freely than of him? Try it, and see if he doesn't find your society far more agreeable than Mrs. Scott's suppers."

"I will. Poor John! I'm afraid I *have* neglected him sadly, but I thought I was right, and he never said anything."

"He tried not to be selfish, but he *has* felt rather forlorn, I fancy. This is just the time, Meg, when young married people are apt to grow apart, and the very time when they ought to be most together; for the first tenderness soon wears off, unless care is taken to preserve it; and no time is so beautiful and precious to parents as the first years of the little lives given them to train. Don't let John be a stranger to the babies, for they will do more to keep him safe and happy in this world of trial and temptation than anything else, and through them you will learn to know and love one another as you should. Now, dear, good-by; think over mother's preachment, act upon it if it seems good, and God bless you all!"

Meg did think it over, found it good, and acted upon it, though the first attempt was not made exactly as she planned to have it. Of course the children tyrannized over her, and ruled the house as so on as they found out that kicking and squalling brought them whatever they wanted. Mamma was an abject slave to their caprices, but papa was not so easily subjugated, and occasionally afflicted his tender spouse by an attempt at paternal discipline with his obstreperous son. For Demi inherited a trifle of his sire's firmness of character,—we won't call it obstinacy,—and when he made up his little mind to have or to do anything, all the king's horses and all the king's men could not change that pertinacious little mind. Mamma thought the dear too young to be taught to conquer his prejudices, but papa believed that it never was too soon to learn obedience; so Master Demi early discovered that when he undertook to "wrastle" with "parpar," he always got the worst of it; yet, like the Englishman, Baby respected the man who conquered him, and loved the father whose grave "No, no," was more impressive than all mamma's love-pats.

A few days after the talk with her mother, Meg resolved to try a social evening with John; so she ordered a nice supper, set the parlor in order, dressed herself prettily, and put the children to bed early, that nothing should interfere with her experiment. But, unfortunately, Demi's most unconquerable prejudice was against going to bed, and that night he decided to go on a rampage; so poor Meg sung and rocked, told stories and tried every sleep-provoking wile she could devise, but all in vain, the big eyes wouldn't shut; and long after Daisy had gone to byelow, like the chubby little bunch of good-nature she was, naughty Demi lay staring at the light, with the most discouragingly wide-awake expression of countenance.

"Will Demi lie still like a good boy, while mamma runs down and gives poor papa his tea?" asked Meg, as the hall-door softly closed, and the well-known step went tiptoeing into the dining-room.

"Me has tea!" said Demi, preparing to join in the revel.

"No; but I'll save you some little cakies for breakfast, if you'll go bye-by like Daisy. Will you, lovey?"

"Iss!" and Demi shut his eyes tight, as if to catch sleep and hurry the desired day.

Taking advantage of the propitious moment, Meg slipped away, and ran down to greet her husband with a smiling face, and the little blue bow in her hair which was his especial admiration. He saw it at once, and said, with pleased surprise,—

"Why, little mother, how gay we are to-night. Do you expect company?"

"Only you, dear."

"Is it a birthday, anniversary, or anything?"

"No; I'm tired of being a dowdy, so I dressed up as a change. You always make yourself nice for table, no matter how tired you are; so why shouldn't I when I have the time?"

"I do it out of respect to you, my dear," said old-fashioned John.

"Ditto, ditto, Mr. Brooke," laughed Meg, looking young and pretty again, as she nodded to him over the teapot.

"Well, it's altogether delightful, and like old times. This tastes right. I drink your health, dear." And John sipped his tea with an air of reposeful rapture, which was of very short duration, however; for, as he put down his cup, the door-handle rattled mysteriously, and a little voice was heard, saying impatiently,—

"Opy doy; me's tummin!"

"It's that naughty boy. I told him to go to sleep alone, and here he is, downstairs, getting his death a-cold pattering over that canvas," said Meg, answering the call.

"Mornin' now," announced Demi, in a joyful tone, as he entered, with his long night-gown gracefully festooned over his arm, and every curl bobbing gayly as he pranced about the table, eying the "cakies" with loving glances.

"No, it isn't morning yet. You must go to bed, and not trouble poor mamma; then you can have the little cake with sugar on it."

"Me loves parpar," said the artful one, preparing to climb the paternal knee, and revel in forbidden joys. But John shook his head, and said to Meg,—

"If you told him to stay up there, and go to sleep alone, make him do it, or he will never learn to mind you."

"Yes, of course. Come, Demi;" and Meg led her son away, feeling a strong desire to spank the little marplot who hopped beside her, laboring under the delusion that the bribe was to be administered as soon as they reached the nursery.

Nor was he disappointed; for that short-sighted woman actually gave him a lump of sugar, tucked him into his bed, and forbade any more promenades till morning.

"Iss!" said Demi the perjured, blissfully sucking his sugar, and regarding his first attempt as eminently successful.

Meg returned to her place, and supper was progressing pleasantly, when the little ghost walked again, and exposed the maternal delinquencies by boldly demanding,—

"More sudar, marmar."

"Now this won't do," said John, hardening his heart against the engaging little sinner. "We shall never know any peace till that child learns to go to bed properly. You have made a slave of yourself long enough; give him one lesson, and then there will be an end of it. Put him in his bed and leave him, Meg."

"He won't stay there; he never does, unless I sit by him."

"I'll manage him. Demi, go upstairs, and get into your bed, as mamma bids you."

"S'ant!" replied the young rebel, helping himself to the coveted "cakie," and beginning to eat the same with calm audacity.

"You must never say that to papa; I shall carry you if you don't go yourself."

"Go 'way; me don't love parpar;" and Demi retired to his mother's skirts for protection.

But even that refuge proved unavailing, for he was delivered over to the enemy, with a "Be gentle with him, John," which struck the culprit with dismay; for when mamma deserted him, then the judgment-day was at hand. Bereft of his cake, defrauded of his frolic, and borne away by a strong hand to that detested bed, poor Demi could not restrain his wrath, but openly defied papa, and kicked and screamed lustily all the way upstairs. The minute he was put into bed on one side, he rolled out on the other, and made for the door, only to be ignominiously caught up by the tail of his little toga, and put back again, which lively performance was kept up till the young man's strength gave out, when he devoted himself to roaring at the top of his voice. This vocal exercise usually conquered Meg; but John sat as unmoved as the post which is popularly believed to be deaf. No coaxing, no sugar, no lullaby, no story; even the light was put out, and only the red glow of the fire enlivened the "big dark" which Demi regarded with curiosity rather than fear. This new order of things disgusted him, and he howled dismally for "marmar," as his angry passions subsided, and recollections of his tender bondwoman returned to the captive autocrat. The plaintive wail which succeeded the passionate roar went to Meg's heart, and she ran up to say beseechingly,—

"Let me stay with him; he'll be good, now, John."

"No, my dear, I've told him he must go to sleep, as you bid him; and he must, if I stay here all night."

"But he'll cry himself sick," pleaded Meg, reproaching herself for deserting her boy.

"No, he won't, he's so tired he will soon drop off, and then the matter is settled; for he will understand that he has got to mind. Don't interfere; I'll manage him."

"He's my child, and I can't have his spirit broken by harshness."

"He's my child, and I won't have his temper spoilt by indulgence. Go down, my dear, and leave the boy to me."

When John spoke in that masterful tone, Meg always obeyed, and never regretted her docility.

"Please let me kiss him once, John?"

"Certainly. Demi, say 'good-night' to mamma, and let her go and rest, for she is very tired with taking care of you all day."

Meg always insisted upon it that the kiss won the victory; for after it was given, Demi sobbed more quietly, and lay quite still at the bottom of the bed, whither he had wriggled in his anguish of mind.

"Poor little man, he's worn out with sleep and crying. I'll cover him up, and then go and set Meg's heart at rest," thought John, creeping to the bedside, hoping to find his rebellious heir asleep.

But he wasn't; for the moment his father peeped at him, Demi's eyes opened, his little chin began to quiver, and he put up his arms, saying, with a penitent hiccough, "Me's dood, now."

Sitting on the stairs, outside, Meg wondered at the long silence which followed the uproar; and, after imagining all sorts of impossible accidents, she slipped into the room, to set her fears at rest. Demi lay fast asleep; not in his usual spread-eagle attitude, but in a subdued bunch, cuddled close in the circle of his father's arm and holding his father's finger, as if he felt that justice was tempered with mercy, and had gone to sleep a sadder and a wiser baby. So held, John had waited with womanly patience till the little hand relaxed its hold; and, while waiting, had fallen asleep, more tired by that tussle with his son than with his whole day's work.

As Meg stood watching the two faces on the pillow, she smiled to herself, and then slipped away again, saying, in a satisfied tone,—

"I never need fear that John will be too harsh with my babies: he *does* know how to manage them, and will be a great help, for Demi *is* getting too much for me."

When John came down at last, expecting to find a pensive or reproachful wife, he was agreeably surprised to find Meg placidly trimming a bonnet, and to be greeted with the request to read something about the election, if he was not too tired. John saw in a minute that a revolution of some kind was going on, but wisely asked no questions, knowing that Meg was such a transparent little person, she couldn't keep a secret to save her life, and therefore the clew would soon appear. He read a long debate with the most amiable readiness, and then explained it in his most lucid manner, while Meg tried to look deeply interested, to ask intelligent questions, and keep her thoughts from wandering from the state of the nation to the state of her bonnet. In her secret soul, however, she decided that politics were as bad as mathematics, and that the mission of politicians seemed to be calling each other names; but she kept these feminine ideas to herself, and when John paused, shook her head, and said with what she thought diplomatic ambiguity,—

"Well, I really don't see what we are coming to."

John laughed, and watched her for a minute, as she poised a pretty little preparation of lace and flowers on her hand, and regarded it with the genuine interest which his harangue had failed to waken.

"She is trying to like politics for my sake, so I'll try and like millinery for hers, that's only fair," thought John the Just, adding aloud,—

"That's very pretty; is it what you call a breakfast-cap?"

"My dear man, it's a bonnet! My very best go-to-concert-and-theatre bonnet."

"I beg your pardon; it was so small, I naturally mistook it for one of the fly-away things you sometimes wear. How do you keep it on?"

"These bits of lace are fastened under the chin with a rosebud, so;" and Meg illustrated by putting on the bonnet, and regarding him with an air of calm satisfaction that was irresistible.

"It's a love of a bonnet, but I prefer the face inside, for it looks young and happy again," and John kissed the smiling face, to the great detriment of the rosebud under the chin.

"I'm glad you like it, for I want you to take me to one of the new concerts some night; I really need some music to put me in tune. Will you, please?"

"Of course I will, with all my heart, or anywhere else you like. You have been shut up so long, it will do you no end of good, and I shall enjoy it, of all things. What put it into your head, little mother?"

"Well, I had a talk with Marmee the other day, and told her how nervous and cross and out of sorts I felt, and she said I needed change and less care; so Hannah is to help me with the children, and I'm to see to things about the house more, and now and then have a little fun, just to keep me from getting to be a fidgety, broken-down old woman before my time. It's only an experiment, John, and I want to try it for your sake as much as for mine, because I've neglected you shamefully lately, and I'm going to make home what it used to be, if I can. You don't object, I hope?"

Never mind what John said, or what a very narrow escape the little bonnet had from utter ruin; all that we have any business to know, is that John did *not* appear to object, judging from the changes which gradually took place in the house and its inmates. It was not all Paradise by any means, but every one was better for the division of labor system; the children throve under the paternal rule, for accurate, steadfast John brought order and obedience into Babydom, while Meg recovered her spirits and composed her nerves by plenty of wholesome exercise, a little pleasure, and much confidential conversation with her sensible husband. Home grew home-like again, and John had no wish to leave it, unless he took Meg with him. The Scotts came to the Brookes' now, and every one found the little house a cheerful place, full of happiness, content, and family love. Even gay Sallie Moffatt liked to go there. "It is always so quiet and pleasant here; it does me good, Meg," she used to say, looking about her with wistful eyes, as if trying to discover the charm, that she might use it in her great house, full of splendid loneliness; for there were no riotous, sunny-faced babies there, and Ned lived in a world of his own, where there was no place for her.

This household happiness did not come all at once, but John and Meg had found the key to it, and each year of married life taught them how to use it, unlocking the treasuries of real home-love and mutual helpfulness, which the poorest may possess, and the richest cannot buy. This is the sort of shelf on which young wives and mothers may consent to be laid, safe from the restless fret and fever of the world, finding loyal lovers in the little sons and daughters who cling to them, undaunted by sorrow, poverty, or age; walking side by side, through fair and stormy weather, with a faithful friend, who is, in the true sense of the good old Saxon word, the "house-band," and learning, as Meg learned, that a woman's happiest kingdom is home, her highest honor the art of ruling it, not as a queen, but a wise wife and mother.

# XIV

## LAZY LAURENCE.

LAURIE went to Nice intending to stay a week, and remained a month. He was tired of wandering about alone, and Amy's familiar presence seemed to give a home-like charm to the foreign scenes in which she bore a part. He rather missed the "petting" he used to receive, and enjoyed a taste of it again; for no attentions, however flattering, from strangers, were half so pleasant as the sisterly adoration of the girls at home. Amy never would pet him like the others, but she was very glad to see him now, and quite clung to him, feeling that he was the representative of the dear family for whom she longed more than she would confess. They naturally took comfort in each other's society, and were much together, riding, walking, dancing, or dawdling, for, at Nice, no one can be very industrious during the gay season. But, while apparently amusing themselves in the most careless fashion, they were half-consciously making discoveries and forming opinions about each other. Amy rose daily in the estimation of her friend, but he sunk in hers, and each felt the truth before a word was spoken. Amy tried to please, and succeeded, for she was grateful for the many pleasures he gave her, and repaid him with the little services to which womanly women know how to lend an indescribable charm. Laurie made no effort of any kind, but just let himself drift along as comfortably as possible, trying to forget, and feeling that all women owed him a kind word because one had been cold to him. It cost him no effort to be generous, and he would have given Amy all the trinkets in Nice if she would have taken them; but, at the same time, he felt that he could not change the opinion she was forming of him, and he rather dreaded the keen blue eyes that seemed to watch him with such half-sorrowful, half-scornful surprise.

"All the rest have gone to Monaco for the day; I preferred to stay at home and write letters. They are done now, and I am going to Valrosa to sketch; will you come?" said Amy, as she joined Laurie one lovely day when he lounged in as usual, about noon.

"Well, yes; but isn't it rather warm for such a long walk?" he answered slowly, for the shaded *salon* looked inviting, after the glare without.

"I'm going to have the little carriage, and Baptiste can drive, so you'll have nothing to do but hold your umbrella and keep your gloves nice," returned Amy, with a sarcastic glance at the immaculate kids, which were a weak point with Laurie.

"Then I'll go with pleasure;" and he put out his hand for her sketch-book. But she tucked it under her arm with a sharp—

"Don't trouble yourself; it's no exertion to me, but *you* don't look equal to it."

Laurie lifted his eyebrows, and followed at a leisurely pace as she ran downstairs; but when they got into the carriage he took the reins himself, and left little Baptiste nothing to do but fold his arms and fall asleep on his perch.

The two never quarrelled,—Amy was too well-bred, and just now Laurie was too lazy; so, in a minute he peeped under her hat-brim with an inquiring air; she answered with a smile, and they went on together in the most amicable manner.

It was a lovely drive, along winding roads rich in the picturesque scenes that delight beauty-loving eyes. Here an ancient monastery, whence the solemn chanting of the monks came down to them. There a bare-legged shepherd, in wooden shoes, pointed hat, and rough jacket over one shoulder, sat piping on a stone, while his goats skipped among the rocks or lay at his feet. Meek, mouse-colored donkeys, laden with panniers of freshly-cut grass, passed by, with a pretty girl in a *capaline* sitting between the green piles, or an old woman spinning with a distaff as she went. Brown, soft-eyed children ran out from the quaint stone hovels to offer nosegays, or bunches of oranges still on the bough. Gnarled olive-trees covered the hills with their dusky foliage, fruit hung golden in the orchard, and great scarlet anemones fringed the roadside; while beyond green slopes and craggy heights, the Maritime Alps rose sharp and white against the blue Italian sky.

Valrosa well deserved its name, for, in that climate of perpetual summer, roses blossomed everywhere. They overhung the archway, thrust themselves between the bars of the great gate with a sweet welcome to passers-by, and lined the avenue, winding through lemon-trees and feathery palms up to the villa on the hill. Every shadowy nook, where seats invited one to stop and rest, was a mass of bloom; every cool grotto had its marble nymph smiling from a veil of flowers, and every fountain reflected crimson, white, or pale pink roses, leaning down to smile at their own beauty. Roses covered the walls of the house, draped the cornices, climbed the pillars, and ran riot over the balustrade of the wide terrace, whence one looked down on the sunny Mediterranean, and the white-walled city on its shore.

"This is a regular honeymoon Paradise, isn't it? Did you ever see such roses?" asked Amy, pausing on the terrace to enjoy the view, and a luxurious whiff of perfume that came wandering by.

"No, nor felt such thorns," returned Laurie, with his thumb in his mouth, after a vain attempt to capture a solitary scarlet flower that grew just beyond his reach.

"Try lower down, and pick those that have no thorns," said Amy, gathering three of the tiny cream-colored ones that starred the wall behind her. She put them in his button-hole, as a peace-offering, and he stood a minute looking down at them with a curious expression, for in the Italian part of his nature there was a touch of superstition, and he was just then in that state of half-sweet, half-bitter melancholy, when imaginative young men find significance in trifles, and food for romance everywhere. He had thought of Jo in reaching after the thorny red rose, for vivid flowers became her, and she had often worn ones like that from the greenhouse at home. The pale roses Amy gave him were the sort that the Italians lay in dead hands, never in bridal wreaths, and, for a moment, he wondered if the omen was for Jo or for himself; but the next instant his American common-sense got the better of sentimentality, and he laughed a heartier laugh than Amy had heard since he came.

"It's good advice; you'd better take it and save your fingers," she said, thinking her speech amused him.

"Thank you, I will," he answered in jest, and a few months later he did it in earnest.

"Laurie, when are you going to your grandfather?" she asked presently, as she settled herself on a rustic seat.

"Very soon."

"You have said that a dozen times within the last three weeks."

"I dare say; short answers save trouble."

"He expects you, and you really ought to go."

"Hospitable creature! I know it."

"Then why don't you do it?"

"Natural depravity, I suppose."

"Natural indolence, you mean. It's really dreadful!" and Amy looked severe.

"Not so bad as it seems, for I should only plague him if I went, so I might as well stay, and plague you a little longer, you can bear it better; in fact, I think it agrees with you excellently;" and Laurie composed himself for a lounge on the broad ledge of the balustrade.

Amy shook her head, and opened her sketch-book with an air of resignation; but she had made up her mind to lecture "that boy," and in a minute she began again.

"What are you doing just now?"

"Watching lizards."

"No, no; I mean what do you intend and wish to do?"

"Smoke a cigarette, if you'll allow me."

"How provoking you are! I don't approve of cigars, and I will only allow it on condition that you let me put you into my sketch; I need a figure."

"With all the pleasure in life. How will you have me,—full-length or three-quarters, on my head or my heels? I should respectfully suggest a recumbent posture, then put yourself in also, and call it '*Dolce far niente.*'"

"Stay as you are, and go to sleep if you like. *I* intend to work hard," said Amy, in her most energetic tone.

"What delightful enthusiasm!" and he leaned against a tall urn with an air of entire satisfaction.

"What would Jo say if she saw you now?" asked Amy impatiently, hoping to stir him up by the mention of her still more energetic sister's name.

"As usual, 'Go away, Teddy, I'm busy!'" He laughed as he spoke, but the laugh was not natural, and a shade passed over his face, for the utterance of the familiar name touched the wound that was not healed yet. Both tone and shadow struck Amy, for she had seen and heard them before, and now she looked up in time to catch a new expression on Laurie's face,—a hard, bitter look, full of pain, dissatisfaction, and regret. It was gone before she could study it, and the listless expression back again. She watched him for a moment with artistic pleasure, thinking how like an Italian he looked, as he lay basking in the sun with uncovered head, and eyes full of southern dreaminess; for he seemed to have forgotten her, and fallen into a reverie.

"You look like the effigy of a young knight asleep on his tomb," she said, carefully tracing the well-cut profile defined against the dark stone.

"Wish I was!"

"That's a foolish wish, unless you have spoilt your life. You are so changed, I sometimes think—" there Amy stopped, with a half-timid, half-wistful look, more significant than her unfinished speech.

Laurie saw and understood the affectionate anxiety which she hesitated to express, and looking straight into her eyes, said, just as he used to say it to her mother,—

"It's all right, ma'am."

That satisfied her and set at rest the doubts that had begun to worry her lately. It also touched her, and she showed that it did, by the cordial tone in which she said,—

"I'm glad of that! I didn't think you'd been a very bad boy, but I fancied you might have wasted money at that wicked Baden-Baden, lost your heart to some charming Frenchwoman with a husband, or got into some of the scrapes that young men seem to consider a necessary part of a foreign tour. Don't stay out there in the sun; come and lie on the grass here, and 'let us be friendly,' as Jo used to say when we got in the sofa-corner and told secrets."

Laurie obediently threw himself down on the turf, and began to amuse himself by sticking daisies into the ribbons of Amy's hat, that lay there.

"I'm all ready for the secrets;" and he glanced up with a decided expression of interest in his eyes.

"I've none to tell; you may begin."

"Haven't one to bless myself with. I thought perhaps you'd had some news from home."

"You have heard all that has come lately. Don't you hear often? I fancied Jo would send you volumes."

"She's very busy; I'm roving about so, it's impossible to be regular, you know. When do you begin your great work of art, Raphaella?" he asked, changing the subject abruptly after another pause, in which he had been wondering if Amy knew his secret, and wanted to talk about it.

"Never," she answered, with a despondent but decided air. "Rome took all the vanity out of me; for after seeing the wonders there, I felt too insignificant to live, and gave up all my foolish hopes in despair."

"Why should you, with so much energy and talent?"

"That's just why,—because talent isn't genius, and no amount of energy can make it so. I want to be great, or nothing. I won't be a common-place dauber, so I don't intend to try any more."

"And what are you going to do with yourself now, if I may ask?"

"Polish up my other talents, and be an ornament to society, if I get the chance."

It was a characteristic speech, and sounded daring; but audacity becomes young people, and Amy's ambition had a good foundation. Laurie smiled, but he liked the spirit with which she took up a new purpose when a long-cherished one died, and spent no time lamenting.

"Good! and here is where Fred Vaughn comes in, I fancy."

Amy preserved a discreet silence, but there was a conscious look in her downcast face, that made Laurie sit up and say gravely,—

"Now I'm going to play brother, and ask questions. May I?"

"I don't promise to answer."

"Your face will, if your tongue won't. You aren't woman of the world enough yet to hide your feelings, my dear. I heard rumors about Fred and you last year, and it's my private opinion that, if he had not been called home so suddenly and detained so long, something would have come of it—hey?"

"That's not for me to say," was Amy's prim reply; but her lips would smile, and there was a traitorous sparkle of the eye, which betrayed that she knew her power and enjoyed the knowledge.

"You are not engaged, I hope?" and Laurie looked very elder-brotherly and grave all of a sudden.

"No."

"But you will be, if he comes back and goes properly down upon his knees, won't you?"

"Very likely."

"Then you are fond of old Fred?"

"I could be, if I tried."

"But you don't intend to try till the proper moment? Bless my soul, what unearthly prudence! He's a good fellow, Amy, but not the man I fancied you'd like."

"He is rich, a gentleman, and has delightful manners," began Amy, trying to be quite cool and dignified, but feeling a little ashamed of herself, in spite of the sincerity of her intentions.

"I understand; queens of society can't get on without money, so you mean to make a good match, and start in that way? Quite right and proper, as the world goes, but it sounds odd from the lips of one of your mother's girls."

"True, nevertheless."

A short speech, but the quiet decision with which it was uttered contrasted curiously with the young speaker. Laurie felt this instinctively, and laid himself down again, with a sense of disappointment which he could not explain. His look and silence, as well as a certain inward self-disapproval, ruffled Amy, and made her resolve to deliver her lecture without delay.

"I wish you'd do me the favor to rouse yourself a little," she said sharply.

"Do it for me, there's a dear girl."

"I could, if I tried;" and she looked as if she would like doing it in the most summary style.

"Try, then; I give you leave," returned Laurie, who enjoyed having some one to tease, after his long abstinence from his favorite pastime.

"You'd be angry in five minutes."

"I'm never angry with you. It takes two flints to make a fire: you are as cool and soft as snow."

"You don't know what I can do; snow produces a glow and a tingle, if applied rightly. Your indifference is half affectation, and a good stirring up would prove it."

"Stir away; it won't hurt me and it may amuse you, as the big man said when his little wife beat him. Regard me in the light of a husband or a carpet, and beat till you are tired, if that sort of exercise agrees with you."

Being decidedly nettled herself, and longing to see him shake off the apathy that so altered him, Amy sharpened both tongue and pencil, and began:—

"Flo and I have got a new name for you; it's 'Lazy Laurence.' How do you like it?"

She thought it would annoy him; but he only folded his arms under his head, with an imperturbable "That's not bad. Thank you, ladies."

"Do you want to know what I honestly think of you?"

"Pining to be told."

"Well, I despise you."

If she had even said "I hate you," in a petulant or coquettish tone, he would have laughed, and rather liked it; but the grave, almost sad, accent of her voice made him open his eyes, and ask quickly,—

"Why, if you please?"

"Because, with every chance for being good, useful, and happy, you are faulty, lazy, and miserable."

"Strong language, mademoiselle."

"If you like it, I'll go on."

"Pray, do; it's quite interesting."

"I thought you'd find it so; selfish people always like to talk about themselves."

"Am *I* selfish?" The question slipped out involuntarily and in a tone of surprise, for the one virtue on which he prided himself was generosity.

"Yes, very selfish," continued Amy, in a calm, cool voice, twice as effective, just then, as an angry one. "I'll show you how, for I've studied you while we have been frolicking, and I'm not at all satisfied with you. Here you have been abroad nearly six months, and done nothing but waste time and money and disappoint your friends."

"Isn't a fellow to have any pleasure after a four-years grind?"

"You don't look as if you'd had much; at any rate, you are none the better for it, as far as I can see. I said, when we first met, that you had improved. Now I take it all back, for I don't think you half so nice as when I left you at home. You have grown abominably lazy; you like gossip, and waste time on frivolous things; you are contented to be petted and admired by silly people, instead of being loved and respected by wise ones. With money, talent, position, health, and beauty,—ah, you like that, Old Vanity! but it's the truth, so I can't help saying it,—with all these splendid things to use and enjoy, you can find nothing to do but dawdle; and, instead of being the man you might and ought to be, you are only—" There she stopped, with a look that had both pain and pity in it.

"Saint Laurence on a gridiron," added Laurie, blandly finishing the sentence. But the lecture began to take effect, for there was a wide-awake sparkle in his eyes now, and a half-angry, half-injured expression replaced the former indifference.

"I supposed you'd take it so. You men tell us we are angels, and say we can make you what we will; but the instant we honestly try to do you good, you laugh at us, and won't listen, which proves how much your flattery is worth." Amy spoke bitterly, and turned her back on the exasperating martyr at her feet.

In a minute a hand came down over the page, so that she could not draw, and Laurie's voice said, with a droll imitation of a penitent child,—

"I will be good, oh, I will be good!"

But Amy did not laugh, for she was in earnest; and, tapping on the outspread hand with her pencil, said soberly,—

"Aren't you ashamed of a hand like that? It's as soft and white as a woman's, and looks as if it never did anything but wear Jouvin's best gloves, and pick flowers for ladies. You are not a dandy, thank Heaven! so I'm glad to see there are no diamonds or big seal-rings on it, only the little old one Jo gave you so long ago. Dear soul, I wish she was here to help me!"

"So do I!"

The hand vanished as suddenly as it came, and there was energy enough in the echo of her wish to suit even Amy. She glanced down at him with a new thought in her mind; but he was lying with his hat half over his face, as if for shade, and his mustache hid his mouth. She only saw his chest rise and fall, with a long breath that might have been a sigh, and the hand that wore the ring nestled down into the grass, as if to hide something too precious or too tender to be spoken of. All in a minute various hints and trifles assumed shape and significance in Amy's mind, and told her what her sister never had confided to her. She remembered that Laurie never spoke voluntarily of Jo; she recalled the shadow on his face just now, the change in his character, and the wearing of the little old ring, which was no ornament to a handsome hand. Girls are quick to read such signs and feel their eloquence. Amy had fancied that perhaps a love trouble was at the bottom of the alteration, and now she was sure of it. Her keen eyes filled, and, when she spoke again, it was in a voice that could be beautifully soft and kind when she chose to make it so.

"I know I have no right to talk so to you, Laurie; and if you weren't the sweetest-tempered fellow in the world, you'd be very angry with me. But we are all so fond and proud of you, I couldn't bear to think they should be disappointed in you at home as I have been, though, perhaps, they would understand the change better than I do."

"I think they would," came from under the hat, in a grim tone, quite as touching as a broken one.

"They ought to have told me, and not let me go blundering and scolding, when I should have been more kind and patient than ever. I never did like that Miss Randal, and now I hate her!" said artful Amy, wishing to be sure of her facts this time.

"Hang Miss Randal!" and Laurie knocked the hat off his face with a look that left no doubt of his sentiments toward that young lady.

"I beg pardon; I thought—" and there she paused diplomatically.

"No, you didn't; you knew perfectly well I never cared for any one but Jo." Laurie said that in his old, impetuous tone, and turned his face away as he spoke.

"I did think so; but as they never said anything about it, and you came away, I supposed I was mistaken. And Jo wouldn't be kind to you? Why, I was sure she loved you dearly."

"She *was* kind, but not in the right way; and it's lucky for her she didn't love me, if I'm the good-for-nothing fellow you think me. It's her fault, though, and you may tell her so."

The hard, bitter look came back again as he said that, and it troubled Amy, for she did not know what balm to apply.

"I was wrong, I didn't know. I'm very sorry I was so cross, but I can't help wishing you'd bear it better, Teddy, dear."

"Don't, that's her name for me!" and Laurie put up his hand with a quick gesture to stop the words spoken in Jo's half-kind, half-reproachful tone. "Wait till you've tried it yourself," he added, in a low voice, as he pulled up the grass by the handful.

"I'd take it manfully, and be respected if I couldn't be loved," said Amy, with the decision of one who knew nothing about it.

Now, Laurie flattered himself that he *had* borne it remarkably well, making no moan, asking no sympathy, and taking his trouble away to live it down alone. Amy's lecture put the matter in a new light, and for the first time it did look weak and selfish to lose heart at the first failure, and shut himself up in moody indifference. He felt as if suddenly shaken out of a pensive dream, and found it impossible to go to sleep again. Presently he sat up, and asked slowly,—

"Do you think Jo would despise me as you do?"

"Yes, if she saw you now. She hates lazy people. Why don't you do something splendid, and *make* her love you?"

"I did my best, but it was no use."

"Graduating well, you mean? That was no more than you ought to have done, for your grandfather's sake. It would have been shameful to fail after spending so much time and money, when every one knew you *could* do well."

"I did fail, say what you will, for Jo wouldn't love me," began Laurie, leaning his head on his hand in a despondent attitude.

"No, you didn't, and you'll say so in the end, for it did you good, and proved that you could do something if you tried. If you'd only set about another task of some sort, you'd soon be your hearty, happy self again, and forget your trouble."

"That's impossible."

"Try it and see. You needn't shrug your shoulders, and think, 'Much she knows about such things.' I don't pretend to be wise, but I *am* observing, and I see a great deal more than you'd imagine. I'm interested in other people's experiences and inconsistencies; and, though I can't explain, I remember and use them for my own benefit. Love Jo all your days, if you choose, but don't let it spoil you, for it's wicked to throw away so many good gifts because you can't have the one you want. There, I won't lecture any more, for I know you'll wake up and be a man in spite of that hardhearted girl."

Neither spoke for several minutes. Laurie sat turning the little ring on his finger, and Amy put the last touches to the hasty sketch she had been working at while she talked. Presently she put it on his knee, merely saying,—

"How do you like that?"

He looked and then he smiled, as he could not well help doing, for it was capitally done,—the long, lazy figure on the grass, with listless face, half-shut eyes, and one hand holding a cigar, from which came the little wreath of smoke that encircled the dreamer's head.

"How well you draw!" he said, with genuine surprise and pleasure at her skill, adding, with a half-laugh,—

"Yes, that's me."

"As you are: this is as you were;" and Amy laid another sketch beside the one he held.

It was not nearly so well done, but there was a life and spirit in it which atoned for many faults, and it recalled the past so vividly that a sudden change swept over the young man's face as he looked. Only a rough sketch of Laurie taming a horse; hat and coat were off, and every line of the active figure, resolute face, and commanding attitude, was full of energy and meaning. The handsome brute, just subdued, stood arching his neck under the tightly drawn rein, with one foot impatiently pawing the ground, and ears pricked up as if listening for the voice that had mastered him.

In the ruffled mane, the rider's breezy hair and erect attitude, there was a suggestion of suddenly arrested motion, of strength, courage, and youthful buoyancy, that contrasted sharply with the supine grace of the "*Dolce far niente*" sketch. Laurie said nothing; but, as his eye went from one to the other, Amy saw him flush up and fold his lips together as if he read and accepted the little lesson she had given him. That satisfied her; and, without waiting for him to speak, she said, in her sprightly way,—

"Don't you remember the day you played Rarey with Puck, and we all looked on? Meg and Beth were frightened, but Jo clapped and pranced, and I sat on the fence and drew you. I found that sketch in my portfolio the other day, touched it up, and kept it to show you."

"Much obliged. You've improved immensely since then, and I congratulate you. May I venture to suggest in 'a honeymoon Paradise' that five o'clock is the dinner-hour at your hotel?"

Laurie rose as he spoke, returned the pictures with a smile and a bow, and looked at his watch, as if to remind her that even moral lectures should have an end. He tried to resume his former easy, indifferent air, but it *was* an affectation now, for the rousing had been more efficacious than he would confess. Amy felt the shade of coldness in his manner, and said to herself,—

"Now I've offended him. Well, if it does him good, I'm glad; if it makes him hate me, I'm sorry; but it's true, and I can't take back a word of it."

They laughed and chatted all the way home; and little Baptiste, up behind, thought that monsieur and mademoiselle were in charming spirits. But both felt ill at ease; the friendly frankness was disturbed, the sunshine had a shadow over it, and despite their apparent gayety, there was a secret discontent in the heart of each.

"Shall we see you this evening, *mon frère*?" asked Amy as they parted at her aunt's door.

"Unfortunately I have an engagement. *Au revoir, mademoiselle*," and Laurie bent as if to kiss her hand, in the foreign fashion, which became him better than many men. Something in his face made Amy say quickly and warmly,—

"No; be yourself with me, Laurie, and part in the good old way. I'd rather have a hearty English hand-shake than all the sentimental salutations in France."

"Good-by, dear," and with these words, uttered in the tone she liked, Laurie left her, after a hand-shake almost painful in its heartiness.

Next morning, instead of the usual call, Amy received a note which made her smile at the beginning and sigh at the end:—

"MY DEAR MENTOR,—

"Please make my adieux to your aunt, and exult within yourself, for 'Lazy Laurence' has gone to his grandpa, like the best of boys. A pleasant winter to you, and may the gods grant you a blissful honeymoon at Valrosa! I think Fred would be benefited by a rouser. Tell him so, with my congratulations.

"Yours gratefully,

TELEMACHUS."

"Good boy! I'm glad he's gone," said Amy, with an approving smile; the next minute her face fell as she glanced about the empty room, adding, with an involuntary sigh,—

"Yes, I *am* glad, but how I shall miss him!"

# XV

## THE VALLEY OF THE SHADOW.

WHEN the first bitterness was over, the family accepted the inevitable, and tried to bear it cheerfully, helping one another by the increased affection which comes to bind households tenderly together in times of trouble. They put away their grief, and each did his or her part toward making that last year a happy one.

The pleasantest room in the house was set apart for Beth, and in it was gathered everything that she most loved,—flowers, pictures, her piano, the little work-table, and the beloved pussies. Father's best books found their way there, mother's easy-chair, Jo's desk, Amy's finest sketches; and every day Meg brought her babies on a loving pilgrimage, to make sunshine for Aunty Beth. John quietly set apart a little sum, that he might enjoy the pleasure of keeping the invalid supplied with the fruit she loved and longed for; old Hannah never wearied of concocting dainty dishes to tempt a capricious appetite, dropping tears as she worked; and from across the sea came little gifts and cheerful letters, seeming to bring breaths of warmth and fragrance from lands that know no winter.

Here, cherished like a household saint in its shrine, sat Beth, tranquil and busy as ever; for nothing could change the sweet, unselfish nature, and even while preparing to leave life, she tried to make it happier for those who should remain behind. The feeble fingers were never idle, and one of her pleasures was to make little things for the school-children daily passing to and fro,—to drop a pair of mittens from her window for a pair of purple hands, a needle-book for some small mother of many dolls, pen-wipers for young penmen toiling through forests of pot-hooks, scrap-books for picture-loving eyes, and all manner of pleasant devices, till the reluctant climbers up the ladder of learning found their way strewn with flowers, as it were, and came to regard the gentle giver as a sort of fairy godmother, who sat above there, and showered down gifts miraculously suited to their tastes and needs. If Beth had wanted any reward, she found it in the bright little faces always turned up to her window, with nods and smiles, and the droll little letters which came to her, full of blots and gratitude.

The first few months were very happy ones, and Beth often used to look round, and say "How beautiful this is!" as they all sat together in her sunny room, the babies kicking and crowing on the floor, mother and sisters working near, and father reading, in his pleasant voice, from the wise old books which seemed rich in good and comfortable words, as applicable now as when written centuries ago; a little chapel, where a paternal priest taught his flock the hard lessons all must learn, trying to show them that hope can comfort love, and faith make resignation possible. Simple sermons, that went straight to the souls of those who listened; for the father's heart was in the minister's religion, and the frequent falter in the voice gave a double eloquence to the words he spoke or read.

It was well for all that this peaceful time was given them as preparation for the sad hours to come; for, by and by, Beth said the needle was "so heavy," and put it down forever; talking wearied her, faces troubled her, pain claimed her for its own, and her tranquil spirit was sorrowfully perturbed by the ills that vexed her feeble flesh. Ah me! such heavy days, such long, long nights, such aching hearts and imploring prayers, when those who loved her best were forced to see the thin hands stretched out to them beseechingly, to hear the bitter cry, "Help me, help me!" and to feel that there was no help. A sad eclipse of the serene soul, a sharp struggle of the young life with death; but both were mercifully brief, and then, the natural rebellion over, the old peace returned more beautiful than ever. With the wreck of her frail body, Beth's soul grew strong; and, though she said little, those about her felt that she was ready, saw that the first pilgrim called was likewise the fittest, and waited with her on the shore, trying to see the Shining Ones coming to receive her when she crossed the river.

Jo never left her for an hour since Beth had said, "I feel stronger when you are here." She slept on a couch in the room, waking often to renew the fire, to feed, lift, or wait upon the patient creature who seldom asked for anything, and "tried not to be a trouble." All day she haunted the room, jealous of any other nurse, and prouder of being chosen then than of any honor her life ever brought her. Precious and helpful hours to Jo, for now her heart received the teaching that it needed; lessons in patience were so sweetly taught her that she could not fail to learn them; charity for all, the lovely spirit that can forgive and truly forget unkindness, the loyalty to duty that makes the hardest easy, and the sincere faith that fears nothing, but trusts undoubtingly.

Often, when she woke, Jo found Beth reading in her well-worn little book, heard her singing softly, to beguile the sleepless night, or saw her lean her face upon her hands, while slow tears dropped through the transparent fingers; and Jo would lie watching her, with thoughts too deep for tears, feeling that Beth, in her simple, unselfish way, was trying to wean herself from the dear old life, and fit herself for the life to come, by sacred words of comfort, quiet prayers, and the music she loved so well.

Seeing this did more for Jo than the wisest sermons, the saintliest hymns, the most fervent prayers that any voice could utter; for, with eyes made clear by many tears, and a heart softened by the tenderest sorrow, she recognized the beauty of her sister's life,—uneventful, unambitious, yet full of the genuine virtues which "smell sweet, and blossom in the dust," the self-forgetfulness that makes the humblest on earth remembered soonest in heaven, the true success which is possible to all.

One night, when Beth looked among the books upon her table, to find something to make her forget the mortal weariness that was almost as hard to bear as pain, as she turned the leaves of her old favorite Pilgrim's Progress, she found a little paper, scribbled over in Jo's hand. The name caught her eye, and the blurred look of the lines made her sure that tears had fallen on it.

"Poor Jo! she's fast asleep, so I won't wake her to ask leave; she shows me all her things, and I don't think she'll mind if I look at this," thought Beth, with a glance at her sister, who lay on the rug, with the tongs beside her, ready to wake up the minute the log fell apart.

"MY BETH.

"Sitting patient in the shadow
Till the blessed light shall come,
A serene and saintly presence
Sanctifies our troubled home.
Earthly joys and hopes and sorrows
Break like ripples on the strand
Of the deep and solemn river
Where her willing feet now stand.

"O my sister, passing from me,
Out of human care and strife,
Leave me, as a gift, those virtues
Which have beautified your life.
Dear, bequeath me that great patience
Which has power to sustain
A cheerful, uncomplaining spirit
In its prison-house of pain.

"Give me, for I need it sorely,
Of that courage, wise and sweet,
Which has made the path of duty
Green beneath your willing feet.
Give me that unselfish nature,
That with charity divine
Can pardon wrong for love's dear sake—
Meek heart, forgive me mine!

"Thus our parting daily loseth
Something of its bitter pain,

And while learning this hard lesson,
My great loss becomes my gain.
For the touch of grief will render
My wild nature more serene,
Give to life new aspirations,
A new trust in the unseen.

"Henceforth, safe across the river,
I shall see forevermore
A beloved, household spirit
Waiting for me on the shore.
Hope and faith, born of my sorrow,
Guardian angels shall become,
And the sister gone before me
By their hands shall lead me home."

Blurred and blotted, faulty and feeble, as the lines were, they brought a look of inexpressible comfort to Beth's face, for her one regret had been that she had done so little; and this seemed to assure her that her life had not been useless, that her death would not bring the despair she feared. As she sat with the paper folded between her hands, the charred log fell asunder. Jo started up, revived the blaze, and crept to the bedside, hoping Beth slept.

"Not asleep, but so happy, dear. See, I found this and read it; I knew you wouldn't care. Have I been all that to you, Jo?" she asked, with wistful, humble earnestness.

"O Beth, so much, so much!" and Jo's head went down upon the pillow, beside her sister's.

"Then I don't feel as if I'd wasted my life. I'm not so good as you make me, but I *have* tried to do right; and now, when it's too late to begin even to do better, it's such a comfort to know that some one loves me so much, and feels as if I'd helped them."

"More than any one in the world, Beth. I used to think I couldn't let you go; but I'm learning to feel that I don't lose you; that you'll be more to me than ever, and death can't part us, though it seems to."

"I know it cannot, and I don't fear it any longer, for I'm sure I shall be your Beth still, to love and help you more than ever. You must take my place, Jo, and be everything to father and mother when I'm gone. They will turn to you, don't fail them; and if it's hard to work alone, remember that I don't forget you, and that you'll be happier in doing that than writing splendid books or seeing all the world; for love is the only thing that we can carry with us when we go, and it makes the end so easy."

"I'll try, Beth;" and then and there Jo renounced her old ambition, pledged herself to a new and better one, acknowledging the poverty of other desires, and feeling the blessed solace of a belief in the immortality of love.

So the spring days came and went, the sky grew clearer, the earth greener, the flowers were up fair and early, and the birds came back in time to say good-by to Beth, who, like a tired but trustful child, clung to the hands that had led her all her life, as father and mother guided her tenderly through the Valley of the Shadow, and gave her up to God.

Seldom, except in books, do the dying utter memorable words, see visions, or depart with beatified countenances; and those who have sped many parting souls know that to most the end comes as naturally and simply as sleep. As Beth had hoped, the "tide went out easily;" and in the dark hour before the dawn, on the bosom where she had drawn her first breath, she quietly drew her last, with no farewell but one loving look, one little sigh.

With tears and prayers and tender hands, mother and sisters made her ready for the long sleep that pain would never mar again, seeing with grateful eyes the beautiful serenity that soon replaced the pathetic patience that had wrung their hearts so long, and feeling, with reverent joy, that to their darling death was a benignant angel, not a phantom full of dread.

When morning came, for the first time in many months the fire was out, Jo's place was empty, and the room was very still. But a bird sang blithely on a budding bough, close by, the snow-drops blossomed freshly at the window, and the spring sunshine streamed in like a benediction over the placid face upon the pillow,—a face so full of painless peace that those who loved it best smiled through their tears, and thanked God that Beth was well at last.

## XLI.
## LEARNING TO FORGET.

AMY'S lecture did Laurie good, though, of course, he did not own it till long afterward; men seldom do, for when women are the advisers, the lords of creation don't take the advice till they have persuaded themselves that it is just what they intended to do; then they act upon it, and, if it succeeds, they give the weaker vessel half the credit of it; if it fails, they generously give her the whole. Laurie went back to his grandfather, and was so dutifully devoted for several weeks that the old gentleman declared the climate of Nice had improved him wonderfully, and he had better try it again. There was nothing the young gentleman would have liked better, but elephants could not have dragged him back after the scolding he had received; pride forbid, and whenever the longing grew very strong, he fortified his resolution by repeating the words that had made the deepest impression, "I despise you;" "Go and do something splendid that will *make* her love you."

Laurie turned the matter over in his mind so often that he soon brought himself to confess that he *had* been selfish and lazy; but then when a man has a great sorrow, he should be indulged in all sorts of vagaries till he has lived it down. He felt that his blighted affections were quite dead now; and, though he should never cease to be a faithful mourner, there was no occasion to wear his weeds ostentatiously. Jo *wouldn't* love him, but he might *make* her respect and admire him by doing something which should prove that a girl's "No" had not spoilt his life. He had always meant to do something, and Amy's advice was quite unnecessary. He had only been waiting till the aforesaid blighted affections were decently interred; that being done, he felt that he was ready to "hide his stricken heart, and still toil on."

As Goethe, when he had a joy or a grief, put it into a song, so Laurie resolved to embalm his love-sorrow in music, and compose a Requiem which should harrow up Jo's soul and melt the heart of every hearer. Therefore the next time the old gentleman found him getting restless and moody, and ordered him off, he went to Vienna, where he had musical friends, and fell to work with the firm determination to distinguish himself. But, whether the sorrow was too vast to be embodied in music, or music too ethereal to uplift a mortal woe, he soon discovered that the Requiem was beyond him, just at present. It was evident that his mind was not in working order yet, and his ideas needed clarifying; for often in the middle of a plaintive strain, he would find himself humming a dancing tune that vividly recalled the Christmas ball at Nice, especially the stout Frenchman, and put an effectual stop to tragic composition for the time being.

Then he tried an Opera, for nothing seemed impossible in the beginning; but here, again, unforeseen difficulties beset him. He wanted Jo for his heroine, and called upon his memory to supply him with tender recollections and romantic visions of his love. But memory turned traitor; and, as if possessed by the perverse spirit of the girl, would only recall Jo's oddities, faults, and freaks, would only show her in the most unsentimental aspects,—beating mats with her head tied up in a bandanna, barricading herself with the sofa-pillow, or throwing cold water over his passion *à la* Gummidge,—and an irresistible laugh spoilt the pensive picture he was endeavoring to paint. Jo wouldn't be put into the Opera at any price, and he had to give her up with a "Bless that girl, what a torment she is!" and a clutch at his hair, as became a distracted composer.

When he looked about him for another and a less intractable damsel to immortalize in melody, memory produced one with the most obliging readiness. This phantom wore many faces, but it always had golden hair, was enveloped in a diaphanous cloud, and floated airily before his mind's eye in a pleasing chaos of roses, peacocks, white ponies, and blue ribbons. He did not give the complacent wraith any name, but he took her for his heroine, and grew quite fond of her, as well he might; for he gifted her with every gift and grace under the sun, and escorted her, unscathed, through trials which would have annihilated any mortal woman.

Thanks to this inspiration, he got on swimmingly for a time, but gradually the work lost its charm, and he forgot to compose, while he sat musing, pen in hand, or roamed about the gay city to get new ideas and refresh his mind, which seemed to be in a somewhat unsettled state that winter. He did not do much, but he thought a great deal and was conscious of a change of some sort going on in spite of himself. "It's genius simmering, perhaps. I'll let it simmer, and see what comes of it," he said, with a secret suspicion, all the while, that it wasn't genius, but something far more common. Whatever it was, it simmered to some purpose, for he grew more and more discontented with his desultory life, began to long for some real and earnest work to go at, soul and body, and finally came to the wise conclusion that every one who loved music was not a composer. Returning from one of Mozart's grand operas, splendidly performed at the Royal Theatre, he looked over his own, played a few of the best parts, sat staring up at the busts of Mendelssohn, Beethoven, and Bach, who stared benignly back again; then suddenly he tore up his music-sheets, one by one, and, as the last fluttered out of his hand, he said soberly to himself,—

"She is right! Talent isn't genius, and you can't make it so. That music has taken the vanity out of me as Rome took it out of her, and I won't be a humbug any longer. Now what shall I do?"

That seemed a hard question to answer, and Laurie began to wish he had to work for his daily bread. Now, if ever, occurred an eligible opportunity for "going to the devil," as he once forcibly expressed it, for he had plenty of money and nothing to do, and Satan is proverbially fond of providing employment for full and idle hands. The poor fellow had temptations enough from without and from within, but he withstood them pretty well; for, much as he valued liberty, he valued good faith and confidence more, so his promise to his grandfather, and his desire to be able to look honestly into the eyes of the women who loved him, and say "All's well," kept him safe and steady.

Very likely some Mrs. Grundy will observe, "I don't believe it; boys will be boys, young men must sow their wild oats, and women must not expect miracles." I dare say *you* don't, Mrs. Grundy, but it's true nevertheless. Women work a good many miracles, and I have a persuasion that they may perform even that of raising the standard of manhood by refusing to echo such sayings. Let the boys be boys, the longer the better, and let the young men sow their wild oats if they must; but mothers, sisters, and friends may help to make the crop a small one, and keep many tares from spoiling the harvest, by believing, and showing that they believe, in the possibility of loyalty to the virtues which make men manliest in good women's eyes. If it *is* a feminine delusion, leave us to enjoy it while we may, for without it half the beauty and the romance of life is lost, and sorrowful forebodings would embitter all our hopes of the brave, tender-hearted little lads, who still love their mothers better than themselves, and are not ashamed to own it.

Laurie thought that the task of forgetting his love for Jo would absorb all his powers for years; but, to his great surprise, he discovered it grew easier every day. He refused to believe it at first, got angry with himself, and couldn't understand it; but these hearts of ours are curious and contrary things, and time and nature work their will in spite of us. Laurie's heart *wouldn't* ache; the wound persisted in healing with a rapidity that astonished him, and, instead of trying to forget, he found himself trying to remember. He had not foreseen this turn of affairs, and was not prepared for it. He was disgusted with himself, surprised at his own fickleness, and full of a queer mixture of disappointment and relief that he could recover from such a tremendous blow so soon. He carefully stirred up the embers of his lost love, but they refused to burst into a blaze: there was only a comfortable glow that warmed and did him good without putting him into a fever, and he was reluctantly obliged to confess that the boyish passion was slowly subsiding into a more tranquil sentiment, very tender, a little sad and resentful still, but that was sure to pass away in time, leaving a brotherly affection which would last unbroken to the end.

As the word "brotherly" passed through his mind in one of these reveries, he smiled, and glanced up at the picture of Mozart that was before him:—

"Well, he was a great man; and when he couldn't have one sister he took the other, and was happy."

Laurie did not utter the words, but he thought them; and the next instant kissed the little old ring, saying to himself,—

"No, I won't! I haven't forgotten, I never can. I'll try again, and if that fails, why, then—"

Leaving his sentence unfinished, he seized pen and paper and wrote to Jo, telling her that he could not settle to anything while there was the least hope of her changing her mind. Couldn't she, wouldn't she, and let him come home and be happy? While waiting for an answer he did nothing, but he did it energetically, for he was in a fever of impatience. It came at last, and settled his mind effectually on one point, for Jo decidedly couldn't and wouldn't. She was wrapped up in Beth, and never wished to hear the word "love" again. Then she begged him to be happy with somebody else, but always to keep a little corner of his heart for his loving sister Jo. In a postscript she desired him not to tell Amy that Beth was worse; she was coming home in the spring, and there was no need of saddening the remainder of her stay. That would be time enough, please God, but Laurie must write to her often, and not let her feel lonely, homesick, or anxious.

"So I will, at once. Poor little girl; it will be a sad going home for her, I'm afraid;" and Laurie opened his desk, as if writing to Amy had been the proper conclusion of the sentence left unfinished some weeks before.

But he did not write the letter that day; for, as he rummaged out his best paper, he came across something which changed his purpose. Tumbling about in one part of the desk, among bills, passports, and business documents of various kinds, were several of Jo's letters, and in another compartment were three notes from Amy, carefully tied up with one of her blue ribbons, and sweetly suggestive of the little dead roses put away inside. With a half-repentant, half-amused expression, Laurie gathered up all Jo's letters, smoothed, folded, and put them neatly into a small drawer of the desk, stood a minute turning the ring thoughtfully on his finger, then slowly drew it off, laid it with the letters, locked the drawer, and went out to hear High Mass at Saint Stefan's, feeling as if there had been a funeral; and, though not overwhelmed with affliction, this seemed a more proper way to spend the rest of the day than in writing letters to charming young ladies.

The letter went very soon, however, and was promptly answered, for Amy *was* homesick, and confessed it in the most delightfully confiding manner. The correspondence flourished famously, and letters flew to and fro, with unfailing regularity, all through the early spring. Laurie sold his busts, made allumettes of his opera, and went back to Paris, hoping somebody would arrive before long. He wanted desperately to go to Nice, but would not till he was asked; and Amy would not ask him, for just then she was having little experiences of her own, which made her rather wish to avoid the quizzical eyes of "our boy."

Fred Vaughn had returned, and put the question to which she had once decided to answer "Yes, thank you;" but now she said, "No, thank you," kindly but steadily; for, when the time came, her courage failed her, and she found that something more than money and position was needed to satisfy the new longing that filled her heart so full of tender hopes and fears. The words, "Fred is a good fellow, but not at all the man I fancied you would ever like," and Laurie's face when he uttered them, kept returning to her as pertinaciously as her own did when she said in look, if not in words, "I shall marry for money." It troubled her to remember that now, she wished she could take it back, it sounded so unwomanly. She didn't want Laurie to think her a heartless, worldly creature; she didn't care to be a queen of society now half so much as she did to be a lovable woman; she was so glad he didn't hate her for the dreadful things she said, but took them so beautifully, and was kinder than ever. His letters were such a comfort, for the home letters were very irregular, and were not half so satisfactory as his when they did come. It was not only a pleasure, but a duty to answer them, for the poor fellow was forlorn, and needed petting, since Jo persisted in being stony-hearted. She ought to have made an effort, and tried to love him; it couldn't be very hard, many people would be proud and glad to have such a dear boy care for them; but Jo never would act like other girls, so there was nothing to do but be very kind, and treat him like a brother.

If all brothers were treated as well as Laurie was at this period, they would be a much happier race of beings than they are. Amy never lectured now; she asked his opinion on all subjects; she was interested in everything he did, made charming little presents for him, and sent him two letters a week, full of lively gossip, sisterly confidences, and captivating sketches of the lovely scenes about her. As few brothers are complimented by having their letters carried about in their sisters' pockets, read and reread diligently, cried over when short, kissed when long, and treasured carefully, we will not hint that Amy did any of these fond and foolish things. But she certainly did grow a little pale and pensive that spring, lost much of her relish for society, and went out sketching alone a good deal. She never had much to show when she came home, but was studying nature, I dare say, while she sat for hours, with her hands folded, on the terrace at Valrosa, or absently sketched any fancy that occurred to her,—a stalwart knight carved on a tomb, a young man asleep in the grass, with his hat over his eyes, or a curly-haired girl in gorgeous array, promenading down a ball-room on the arm of a tall gentleman, both faces being left a blur according to the last fashion in art, which was safe, but not altogether satisfactory.

Her aunt thought that she regretted her answer to Fred; and, finding denials useless and explanations impossible, Amy left her to think what she liked, taking care that Laurie should know that Fred had gone to Egypt. That was all, but he understood it, and looked relieved, as he said to himself, with a venerable air,—

"I was sure she would think better of it. Poor old fellow! I've been through it all, and I can sympathize."

With that he heaved a great sigh, and then, as if he had discharged his duty to the past, put his feet up on the sofa, and enjoyed Amy's letter luxuriously.

While these changes were going on abroad, trouble had come at home; but the letter telling that Beth was failing never reached Amy, and when the next found her, the grass was green above her sister. The sad news met her at Vevay, for the heat had driven them from Nice in May, and they had travelled slowly to Switzerland, by way of Genoa and the Italian lakes. She bore it very well, and quietly submitted to the family decree that she should not shorten her visit, for, since it was too late to say good-by to Beth, she had better stay, and let absence soften her sorrow. But her heart was very heavy; she longed to be at home, and every day looked wistfully across the lake, waiting for Laurie to come and comfort her.

He did come very soon; for the same mail brought letters to them both, but he was in Germany, and it took some days to reach him. The moment he read it, he packed his knapsack, bade adieu to his fellow-pedestrians, and was off to keep his promise, with a heart full of joy and sorrow, hope and suspense.

He knew Vevay well; and as soon as the boat touched the little quay, he hurried along the shore to La Tour, where the Carrols were living *en pension*. The *garçon* was in despair that the whole family had gone to take a promenade on the lake; but no, the blond mademoiselle might be in the chateau garden. If monsieur would give himself the pain of sitting down, a flash of time should present her. But monsieur could not wait even "a flash of time," and, in the middle of the speech, departed to find mademoiselle himself.

A pleasant old garden on the borders of the lovely lake, with chestnuts rustling overhead, ivy climbing everywhere, and the black shadow of the tower falling far across the sunny water. At one corner of the wide, low wall was a seat, and here Amy often came to read or work, or console herself with the beauty all about her. She was sitting here that day, leaning her head on her hand, with a homesick heart and heavy eyes, thinking of Beth, and wondering why Laurie did not come. She did not hear him cross the court-yard beyond, nor see him pause in the archway that led from the subterranean path into the garden. He stood a minute, looking at her with new eyes, seeing what no one had ever seen before,—the tender side of Amy's character. Everything about her mutely suggested love and sorrow,—the blotted letters in her lap, the black ribbon that tied up her hair, the womanly pain and patience in her face; even the little ebony cross at her throat seemed pathetic to Laurie, for he had given it to her, and she wore it as her only ornament. If he had any doubts about the reception she would give him, they were set at rest the minute she looked up and saw him; for, dropping everything, she ran to him, exclaiming, in a tone of unmistakable love and longing,—

"O Laurie, Laurie, I knew you'd come to me!"

I think everything was said and settled then; for, as they stood together quite silent for a moment, with the dark head bent down protectingly over the light one, Amy felt that no one could comfort and sustain her so well as Laurie, and Laurie decided that Amy was the only woman in the world who could fill Jo's place, and make him happy. He did not tell her so; but she was not disappointed, for both felt the truth, were satisfied, and gladly left the rest to silence.

In a minute Amy went back to her place; and, while she dried her tears, Laurie gathered up the scattered papers, finding in the sight of sundry well-worn letters and suggestive sketches good omens for the future. As he sat down beside her, Amy felt shy again, and turned rosy red at the recollection of her impulsive greeting.

"I couldn't help it; I felt so lonely and sad, and was so very glad to see you. It was such a surprise to look up and find you, just as I was beginning to fear you wouldn't come," she said, trying in vain to speak quite naturally.

"I came the minute I heard. I wish I could say something to comfort you for the loss of dear little Beth; but I can only feel, and—" He could not get any further, for he, too, turned bashful all of a sudden, and did not quite know what to say. He longed to lay Amy's head down on his shoulder, and tell her to have a good cry, but he did not dare; so took her hand instead, and gave it a sympathetic squeeze that was better than words.

"You needn't say anything; this comforts me," she said softly. "Beth is well and happy, and I mustn't wish her back; but I dread the going home, much as I long to see them all. We won't talk about it now, for it makes me cry, and I want to enjoy you while you stay. You needn't go right back, need you?"

"Not if you want me, dear."

"I do, so much. Aunt and Flo are very kind; but you seem like one of the family, and it would be so comfortable to have you for a little while."

Amy spoke and looked so like a homesick child, whose heart was full, that Laurie forgot his bashfulness all at once, and gave her just what she wanted,—the petting she was used to and the cheerful conversation she needed.

"Poor little soul, you look as if you'd grieved yourself half-sick! I'm going to take care of you, so don't cry any more, but come and walk about with me; the wind is too chilly for you to sit still," he said, in the half-caressing, half-commanding way that Amy liked, as he tied on her hat, drew her arm through his, and began to pace up and down the sunny walk, under the new-leaved chestnuts. He felt more at ease upon his legs; and Amy found it very pleasant to have a strong arm to lean upon, a familiar face to smile at her, and a kind voice to talk delightfully for her alone.

The quaint old garden had sheltered many pairs of lovers, and seemed expressly made for them, so sunny and secluded was it, with nothing but the tower to overlook them, and the wide lake to carry away the echo of their words, as it rippled by below. For an hour this new pair walked and talked, or rested on the wall, enjoying the sweet influences which gave such a charm to time and place; and when an unromantic dinner-bell warned them away, Amy felt as if she left her burden of loneliness and sorrow behind her in the chateau garden.

The moment Mrs. Carrol saw the girl's altered face, she was illuminated with a new idea, and exclaimed to herself, "Now I understand it all,—the child has been pining for young Laurence. Bless my heart, I never thought of such a thing!"

With praiseworthy discretion, the good lady said nothing, and betrayed no sign of enlightenment; but cordially urged Laurie to stay, and begged Amy to enjoy his society, for it would do her more good than so much solitude. Amy was a model of docility; and, as her aunt was a good deal occupied with Flo, she was left to entertain her friend, and did it with more than her usual success.

At Nice, Laurie had lounged and Amy had scolded; at Vevay, Laurie was never idle, but always walking, riding, boating, or studying, in the most energetic manner, while Amy admired everything he did, and followed his example as far and as fast as she could. He said the change was owing to the climate, and she did not contradict him, being glad of a like excuse for her own recovered health and spirits.

The invigorating air did them both good, and much exercise worked wholesome changes in minds as well as bodies. They seemed to get clearer views of life and duty up there among the everlasting hills; the fresh winds blew away desponding doubts, delusive fancies, and moody mists; the warm spring sunshine brought out all sorts of aspiring ideas, tender hopes, and happy thoughts; the lake seemed to wash away the troubles of the past, and the grand old mountains to look benignly down upon them, saying, "Little children, love one another."

In spite of the new sorrow, it was a very happy time, so happy that Laurie could not bear to disturb it by a word. It took him a little while to recover from his surprise at the rapid cure of his first, and, as he had firmly believed, his last and only love. He consoled himself for the seeming disloyalty by the thought that Jo's sister was almost the same as Jo's self, and the conviction that it would have been impossible to love any other woman but Amy so soon and so well. His first wooing had been of the tempestuous order, and he looked back upon it as if through a long vista of years, with a feeling of compassion blended with regret. He was not ashamed of it, but put it away as one of the bitter-sweet experiences of his life, for which he could be grateful when the pain was over. His second wooing he resolved should be as calm and simple as possible; there was no need of having a scene, hardly any need of telling Amy that he loved her; she knew it without words, and had given him his answer long ago. It all came about so naturally that no one could complain, and he knew that everybody would be pleased, even Jo. But when our first little passion has been crushed, we are apt to be wary and slow in making a second trial; so Laurie let the days pass, enjoying every hour, and leaving to chance the utterance of the word that would put an end to the first and sweetest part of his new romance.

He had rather imagined that the *dénouement* would take place in the chateau garden by moonlight, and in the most graceful and decorous manner; but it turned out exactly the reverse, for the matter was settled on the lake, at noonday, in a few blunt words. They had been floating about all the morning, from gloomy St. Gingolf to sunny Montreux, with the Alps of Savoy on one side, Mont St. Bernard and the Dent du Midi on the other, pretty Vevay in the valley, and Lausanne upon the hill beyond, a cloudless blue sky overhead, and the bluer lake below, dotted with the picturesque boats that look like white-winged gulls.

They had been talking of Bonnivard, as they glided past Chillon, and of Rousseau, as they looked up at Clarens, where he wrote his "Héloise." Neither had read it, but they knew it was a love-story, and each privately wondered if it was half as interesting as their own. Amy had been dabbling her hand in the water during the little pause that fell between them, and, when she looked up, Laurie was leaning on his oars, with an expression in his eyes that made her say hastily, merely for the sake of saying something,—

"You must be tired; rest a little, and let me row; it will do me good; for, since you came, I have been altogether lazy and luxurious."

"I'm not tired; but you may take an oar, if you like. There's room enough, though I have to sit nearly in the middle, else the boat won't trim," returned Laurie, as if he rather liked the arrangement.

Feeling that she had not mended matters much, Amy took the offered third of a seat, shook her hair over her face, and accepted an oar. She rowed as well as she did many other things; and, though she used both hands, and Laurie but one, the oars kept time, and the boat went smoothly through the water.

"How well we pull together, don't we?" said Amy, who objected to silence just then.

"So well that I wish we might always pull in the same boat. Will you, Amy?" very tenderly.

"Yes, Laurie," very low.

Then they both stopped rowing, and unconsciously added a pretty little *tableau* of human love and happiness to the dissolving views reflected in the lake.

---

## XVI

## ALL ALONE.

IT was easy to promise self-abnegation when self was wrapped up in another, and heart and soul were purified by a sweet example; but when the helpful voice was silent, the daily lesson over, the beloved presence gone, and nothing remained but loneliness and grief, then Jo found her promise very hard to keep. How could she "comfort father and mother," when her own heart ached with a ceaseless longing for her sister; how could she "make the house cheerful," when all its light and warmth and beauty seemed to have deserted it when Beth left the old home for the new; and where in all the world could she "find some useful, happy work to do," that would take the place of the loving service which had been its own reward? She tried in a blind, hopeless way to do her duty, secretly rebelling against it all the while, for it seemed unjust that her few joys should be lessened, her burdens made heavier, and life get harder and harder as she toiled along. Some people seemed to get all sunshine, and some all shadow; it was not fair, for she tried more than Amy to be good, but never got any reward, only disappointment, trouble, and hard work.

Poor Jo, these were dark days to her, for something like despair came over her when she thought of spending all her life in that quiet house, devoted to humdrum cares, a few small pleasures, and the duty that never seemed to grow any easier. "I can't do it. I wasn't meant for a life like this, and I know I shall break away and do something desperate if somebody don't come and help me," she said to herself, when her first efforts failed, and she fell into the moody, miserable state of mind which often comes when strong wills have to yield to the inevitable.

But some one did come and help her, though Jo did not recognize her good angels at once, because they wore familiar shapes, and used the simple spells best fitted to poor humanity. Often she started up at night, thinking Beth called her; and when the sight of the little empty bed made her cry with the bitter cry of an unsubmissive sorrow, "O Beth, come back! come back!" she did not stretch out her yearning arms in vain; for, as quick to hear her sobbing as she had been to hear her sister's faintest whisper, her mother came to comfort her, not with words only, but the patient tenderness that soothes by a touch, tears that were mute reminders of a greater grief than Jo's, and broken whispers, more eloquent than prayers, because hopeful resignation went hand-in-hand with natural sorrow. Sacred moments, when heart talked to heart in the silence of the night, turning affliction to a blessing, which chastened grief and strengthened love. Feeling this, Jo's burden seemed easier to bear, duty grew sweeter, and life looked more endurable, seen from the safe shelter of her mother's arms.

When aching heart was a little comforted, troubled mind likewise found help; for one day she went to the study, and, leaning over the good gray head lifted to welcome her with a tranquil smile, she said, very humbly,—

"Father, talk to me as you did to Beth. I need it more than she did, for I'm all wrong."

"My dear, nothing can comfort me like this," he answered, with a falter in his voice, and both arms round her, as if he, too, needed help, and did not fear to ask it.

Then, sitting in Beth's little chair close beside him, Jo told her troubles,—the resentful sorrow for her loss, the fruitless efforts that discouraged her, the want of faith that made life look so dark, and all the sad bewilderment which we call despair. She gave him entire confidence, he gave her the help she needed, and both found consolation in the act; for the time had come when they could talk together not only as father and daughter, but as man and woman, able and glad to serve each other with mutual sympathy as well as mutual love. Happy, thoughtful times there in the old study which Jo called "the church of one member," and from which she came with fresh courage, recovered cheerfulness, and a more submissive spirit; for the parents who had taught one child to meet death without fear, were trying now to teach another to accept life without despondency or distrust, and to use its beautiful opportunities with gratitude and power.

Other helps had Jo,—humble, wholesome duties and delights that would not be denied their part in serving her, and which she slowly learned to see and value. Brooms and dishcloths never could be as distasteful as they once had been, for Beth had presided over both; and something of her housewifely spirit seemed to linger round the little mop and the old brush, that was never thrown away. As she used them, Jo found herself humming the songs Beth used to hum, imitating Beth's orderly ways, and giving the little touches here and there that kept everything fresh and cosey, which was the first step toward making home happy, though she didn't know it, till Hannah said with an approving squeeze of the hand,—

"You thoughtful creter, you're determined we sha'n't miss that dear lamb ef you can help it. We don't say much, but we see it, and the Lord will bless you for't, see ef He don't."

As they sat sewing together, Jo discovered how much improved her sister Meg was; how well she could talk, how much she knew about good, womanly impulses, thoughts, and feelings, how happy she was in husband and children, and how much they were all doing for each other.

"Marriage is an excellent thing, after all. I wonder if I should blossom out half as well as you have, if I tried it?" said Jo, as she constructed a kite for Demi, in the topsy-turvy nursery.

"It's just what you need to bring out the tender, womanly half of your nature, Jo. You are like a chestnut-burr, prickly outside, but silky-soft within, and a sweet kernel, if one can only get at it. Love will make you show your heart some day, and then the rough burr will fall off."

"Frost opens chestnut-burrs, ma'am, and it takes a good shake to bring them down. Boys go nutting, and I don't care to be bagged by them," returned Jo, pasting away at the kite which no wind that blows would ever carry up, for Daisy had tied herself on as a bob.

Meg laughed, for she was glad to see a glimmer of Jo's old spirit, but she felt it her duty to enforce her opinion by every argument in her power; and the sisterly chats were not wasted, especially as two of Meg's most effective arguments were the babies, whom Jo loved tenderly. Grief is the best opener for some hearts, and Jo's was nearly ready for the bag: a little more sunshine to ripen the nut, then, not a boy's impatient shake, but a man's hand reached up to pick it gently from the burr, and find the kernel sound and sweet. If she had suspected this, she would have shut up tight, and been more prickly than ever; fortunately she wasn't thinking about herself, so, when the time came, down she dropped.

Now, if she had been the heroine of a moral story-book, she ought at this period of her life to have become quite saintly, renounced the world, and gone about doing good in a mortified bonnet, with tracts in her pocket. But, you see, Jo wasn't a heroine; she was only a struggling human girl, like hundreds of others, and she just acted out her nature, being sad, cross, listless, or energetic, as the mood suggested. It's highly virtuous to say we'll be good, but we can't do it all at once, and it takes a long pull, a strong pull, and a pull all together, before some of us even get our feet set in the right way. Jo had got so far, she was learning to do her duty, and to feel unhappy if she did not; but to do it cheerfully—ah, that was another thing! She had often said she wanted to do something splendid, no matter how hard; and now she had her wish, for what could be more beautiful than to devote her life to father and mother, trying to make home as happy to them as they had to her? And, if difficulties were necessary to increase the splendor of the effort, what could be harder for a restless, ambitious girl than to give up her own hopes, plans, and desires, and cheerfully live for others?

Providence had taken her at her word; here was the task, not what she had expected, but better, because self had no part in it: now, could she do it? She decided that she would try; and, in her first attempt, she found the helps I have suggested. Still another was given her, and she took it, not as a reward, but as a comfort, as Christian took the refreshment afforded by the little arbor where he rested, as he climbed the hill called Difficulty.

"Why don't you write? That always used to make you happy," said her mother, once, when the desponding fit overshadowed Jo.

"I've no heart to write, and if I had, nobody cares for my things."

"We do; write something for us, and never mind the rest of the world. Try it, dear; I'm sure it would do you good, and please us very much."

"Don't believe I can;" but Jo got out her desk, and began to overhaul her half-finished manuscripts.

An hour afterward her mother peeped in, and there she was, scratching away, with her black pinafore on, and an absorbed expression, which caused Mrs. March to smile, and slip away, well pleased with the success of her suggestion. Jo never knew how it happened, but something got into that story that went straight to the hearts of those who read it; for, when her family had laughed and cried over it, her father sent it, much against her will, to one of the popular magazines, and, to her utter surprise, it was not only paid for, but others requested. Letters from several persons, whose praise was honor, followed the appearance of the little story, newspapers copied it, and strangers as well as friends admired it. For a small thing it was a great success; and Jo was more astonished than when her novel was commended and condemned all at once.

"I don't understand it. What *can* there be in a simple little story like that, to make people praise it so?" she said, quite bewildered.

"There is truth in it, Jo, that's the secret; humor and pathos make it alive, and you have found your style at last. You wrote with no thought of fame or money, and put your heart into it, my daughter; you have had the bitter, now comes the sweet. Do your best, and grow as happy as we are in your success."

"If there *is* anything good or true in what I write, it isn't mine; I owe it all to you and mother and to Beth," said Jo, more touched by her father's words than by any amount of praise from the world.

So, taught by love and sorrow, Jo wrote her little stories, and sent them away to make friends for themselves and her, finding it a very charitable world to such humble wanderers; for they were kindly welcomed, and sent home comfortable tokens to their mother, like dutiful children whom good fortune overtakes.

When Amy and Laurie wrote of their engagement, Mrs. March feared that Jo would find it difficult to rejoice over it, but her fears were soon set at rest; for, though Jo looked grave at first, she took it very quietly, and was full of hopes and plans for "the children" before she read the letter twice. It was a sort of written duet, wherein each glorified the other in lover-like fashion, very pleasant to read and satisfactory to think of, for no one had any objection to make.

"You like it, mother?" said Jo, as they laid down the closely written sheets, and looked at one another.

"Yes, I hoped it would be so, ever since Amy wrote that she had refused Fred. I felt sure then that something better than what you call the 'mercenary spirit' had come over her, and a hint here and there in her letters made me suspect that love and Laurie would win the day."

"How sharp you are, Marmee, and how silent! You never said a word to me."

"Mothers have need of sharp eyes and discreet tongues when they have girls to manage. I was half afraid to put the idea into your head, lest you should write and congratulate them before the thing was settled."

"I'm not the scatter-brain I was; you may trust me, I'm sober and sensible enough for any one's *confidante* now."

"So you are, dear, and I should have made you mine, only I fancied it might pain you to learn that your Teddy loved any one else."

"Now, mother, did you really think I could be so silly and selfish, after I'd refused his love, when it was freshest, if not best?"

"I knew you were sincere then, Jo, but lately I have thought that if he came back, and asked again, you might, perhaps, feel like giving another answer. Forgive me, dear, I can't help seeing that you are very lonely, and sometimes there is a hungry look in your eyes that goes to my heart; so I fancied that your boy might fill the empty place if he tried now."

"No, mother, it is better as it is, and I'm glad Amy has learned to love him. But you are right in one thing: I *am* lonely, and perhaps if Teddy had tried again, I might have said 'Yes,' not because I love him any more, but because I care more to be loved than when he went away."

"I'm glad of that, Jo, for it shows that you are getting on. There are plenty to love you, so try to be satisfied with father and mother, sisters and brothers, friends and babies, till the best lover of all comes to give you your reward."

"Mothers are the *best* lovers in the world; but I don't mind whispering to Marmee that I'd like to try all kinds. It's very curious, but the more I try to satisfy myself with all sorts of natural affections, the more I seem to want. I'd no idea hearts could take in so many; mine is so elastic, it never seems full now, and I used to be quite contented with my family. I don't understand it."

"I do;" and Mrs. March smiled her wise smile, as Jo turned back the leaves to read what Amy said of Laurie.

"It is so beautiful to be loved as Laurie loves me; he isn't sentimental, doesn't say much about it, but I see and feel it in all he says and does, and it makes me so happy and so humble that I don't seem to be the same girl I was. I never knew how good and generous and tender he was till now, for he lets me read his heart, and I find it full of noble impulses and hopes and purposes, and am so proud to know it's mine. He says he feels as if he 'could make a prosperous voyage now with me aboard as mate, and lots of love for ballast.' I pray he may, and try to be all he believes me, for I love my gallant captain with all my heart and soul and might, and never will desert him, while God lets us be together. O mother, I never knew how much like heaven this world could be, when two people love and live for one another!"

"And that's our cool, reserved, and worldly Amy! Truly, love does work miracles. How very, very happy they must be!" And Jo laid the rustling sheets together with a careful hand, as one might shut the covers of a lovely romance, which holds the reader fast till the end comes, and he finds himself alone in the work-a-day world again.

By and by Jo roamed away upstairs, for it was rainy, and she could not walk. A restless spirit possessed her, and the old feeling came again, not bitter as it once was, but a sorrowfully patient wonder why one sister should have all she asked, the other nothing. It was not true; she knew that, and tried to put it away, but the natural craving for affection was strong, and Amy's happiness woke the hungry longing for some one to "love with heart and soul, and cling to while God let them be together."

Up in the garret, where Jo's unquiet wanderings ended, stood four little wooden chests in a row, each marked with its owner's name, and each filled with relics of the childhood and girlhood ended now for all. Jo glanced into them, and when she came to her own, leaned her chin on the edge, and stared absently at the chaotic collection, till a bundle of old exercise-books caught her eye. She drew them out, turned them over, and re-lived that pleasant winter at kind Mrs. Kirke's. She had smiled at first, then she looked thoughtful, next sad, and when she came to a little message written in the Professor's hand, her lips began to tremble, the books slid out of her lap, and she sat looking at the friendly words, as if they took a new meaning, and touched a tender spot in her heart.

"Wait for me, my friend. I may be a little late, but I shall surely come."

"Oh, if he only would! So kind, so good, so patient with me always; my dear old Fritz, I didn't value him half enough when I had him, but now how I should love to see him, for every one seems going away from me, and I'm all alone."

And holding the little paper fast, as if it were a promise yet to be fulfilled, Jo laid her head down on a comfortable rag-bag, and cried, as if in opposition to the rain pattering on the roof.

Was it all self-pity, loneliness, or low spirits? or was it the waking up of a sentiment which had bided its time as patiently as its inspirer? Who shall say?

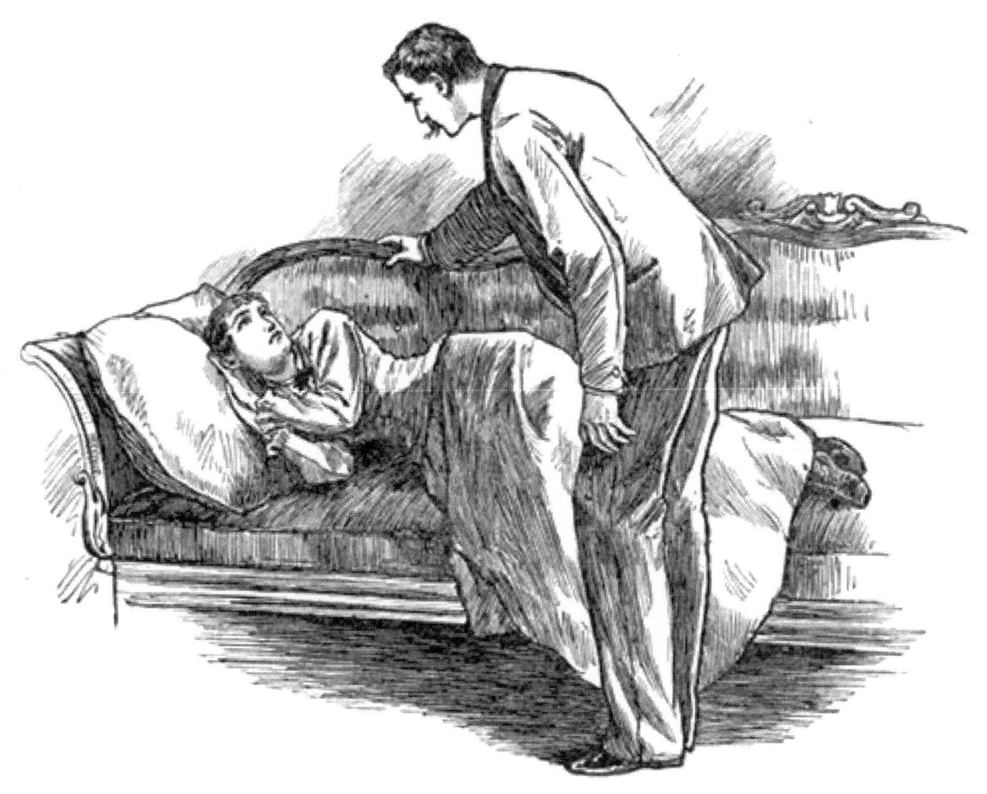

## XLIII.
## SURPRISES.

JO was alone in the twilight, lying on the old sofa, looking at the fire, and thinking. It was her favorite way of spending the hour of dusk; no one disturbed her, and she used to lie there on Beth's little red pillow, planning stories, dreaming dreams, or thinking tender thoughts of the sister who never seemed far away. Her face looked tired, grave, and rather sad; for to-morrow was her birthday, and she was thinking how fast the years went by, how old she was getting, and how little she seemed to have accomplished. Almost twenty-five, and nothing to show for it. Jo was mistaken in that; there was a good deal to show, and by and by she saw, and was grateful for it.

"An old maid, that's what I'm to be. A literary spinster, with a pen for a spouse, a family of stories for children, and twenty years hence a morsel of fame, perhaps; when, like poor Johnson, I'm old, and can't enjoy it, solitary, and can't share it, independent, and don't need it. Well, I needn't be a sour saint nor a selfish sinner; and, I dare say, old maids are very comfortable when they get used to it; but—" and there Jo sighed, as if the prospect was not inviting.

It seldom is, at first, and thirty seems the end of all things to five-and-twenty; but it's not so bad as it looks, and one can get on quite happily if one has something in one's self to fall back upon. At twenty-five, girls begin to talk about being old maids, but secretly resolve that they never will be; at thirty they say nothing about it, but quietly accept the fact, and, if sensible, console themselves by remembering that they have twenty more useful, happy years, in which they may be learning to grow old gracefully. Don't laugh at the spinsters, dear girls, for often very tender, tragical romances are hidden away in the hearts that beat so quietly under the sober gowns, and many silent sacrifices of youth, health, ambition, love itself, make the faded faces beautiful in God's sight. Even the sad, sour sisters should be kindly dealt with, because they have missed the sweetest part of life, if for no other reason; and, looking at them with compassion, not contempt, girls in their bloom should remember that they too may miss the blossom time; that rosy cheeks don't last forever, that silver threads will come in the bonnie brown hair, and that, by and by, kindness and respect will be as sweet as love and admiration now.

Gentlemen, which means boys, be courteous to the old maids, no matter how poor and plain and prim, for the only chivalry worth having is that which is the readiest to pay deference to the old, protect the feeble, and serve womankind, regardless of rank, age, or color. Just recollect the good aunts who have not only lectured and fussed, but nursed and petted, too often without thanks; the scrapes they have helped you out of, the "tips" they have given you from their small store, the stitches the patient old fingers have set for you, the steps the willing old feet have taken, and gratefully pay the dear old ladies the little attentions that women love to receive as long as they live. The bright-eyed girls are quick to see such traits, and will like you all the better for them; and if death, almost the only power that can part mother and son, should rob you of yours, you will be sure to find a tender welcome and maternal cherishing from some Aunt Priscilla, who has kept the warmest corner of her lonely old heart for "the best nevvy in the world."

Jo must have fallen asleep (as I dare say my reader has during this little homily), for suddenly Laurie's ghost seemed to stand before her,—a substantial, lifelike ghost,—leaning over her, with the very look he used to wear when he felt a good deal and didn't like to show it. But, like Jenny in the ballad,—

"She could not think it he,"

and lay staring up at him in startled silence, till he stooped and kissed her. Then she knew him, and flew up, crying joyfully,—

"O my Teddy! O my Teddy!"

"Dear Jo, you are glad to see me, then?"

"Glad! My blessed boy, words can't express my gladness. Where's Amy?"

"Your mother has got her down at Meg's. We stopped there by the way, and there was no getting my wife out of their clutches."

"Your what?" cried Jo, for Laurie uttered those two words with an unconscious pride and satisfaction which betrayed him.

"Oh, the dickens! now I've done it;" and he looked so guilty that Jo was down upon him like a flash.

"You've gone and got married!"

"Yes, please, but I never will again;" and he went down upon his knees, with a penitent clasping of hands, and a face full of mischief, mirth, and triumph.

"Actually married?"

"Very much so, thank you."

"Mercy on us! What dreadful thing will you do next?" and Jo fell into her seat, with a gasp.

"A characteristic, but not exactly complimentary, congratulation," returned Laurie, still in an abject attitude, but beaming with satisfaction.

"What can you expect, when you take one's breath away, creeping in like a burglar, and letting cats out of bags like that? Get up, you ridiculous boy, and tell me all about it."

"Not a word, unless you let me come in my old place, and promise not to barricade."

Jo laughed at that as she had not done for many a long day, and patted the sofa invitingly, as she said, in a cordial tone,—

"The old pillow is up garret, and we don't need it now; so, come and 'fess, Teddy."

"How good it sounds to hear you say 'Teddy'! No one ever calls me that but you;" and Laurie sat down, with an air of great content.

"What does Amy call you?"

"My lord."

"That's like her. Well, you look it;" and Jo's eyes plainly betrayed that she found her boy comelier than ever.

The pillow was gone, but there *was* a barricade, nevertheless,—a natural one, raised by time, absence, and change of heart. Both felt it, and for a minute looked at one another as if that invisible barrier cast a little shadow over them. It was gone directly, however, for Laurie said, with a vain attempt at dignity,—

"Don't I look like a married man and the head of a family?"

"Not a bit, and you never will. You've grown bigger and bonnier, but you are the same scapegrace as ever."

"Now, really, Jo, you ought to treat me with more respect," began Laurie, who enjoyed it all immensely.

"How can I, when the mere idea of you, married and settled, is so irresistibly funny that I can't keep sober!" answered Jo, smiling all over her face, so infectiously that they had another laugh, and then settled down for a good talk, quite in the pleasant old fashion.

"It's no use your going out in the cold to get Amy, for they are all coming up presently. I couldn't wait; I wanted to be the one to tell you the grand surprise, and have 'first skim,' as we used to say when we squabbled about the cream."

"Of course you did, and spoilt your story by beginning at the wrong end. Now, start right, and tell me how it all happened; I'm pining to know."

"Well, I did it to please Amy," began Laurie, with a twinkle that made Jo exclaim,—

"Fib number one; Amy did it to please you. Go on, and tell the truth, if you can, sir."

"Now she's beginning to marm it; isn't it jolly to hear her?" said Laurie to the fire, and the fire glowed and sparkled as if it quite agreed. "It's all the same, you know, she and I being one. We planned to come home with the Carrols, a month or more ago, but they suddenly changed their minds, and decided to pass another winter in Paris. But grandpa wanted to come home; he went to please me, and I couldn't let him go alone, neither could I leave Amy; and Mrs. Carrol had got English notions about chaperons and such nonsense, and wouldn't let Amy come with us. So I just settled the difficulty by saying, 'Let's be married, and then we can do as we like.'"

"Of course you did; you always have things to suit you."

"Not always;" and something in Laurie's voice made Jo say hastily,—

"How did you ever get aunt to agree?"

"It was hard work; but, between us, we talked her over, for we had heaps of good reasons on our side. There wasn't time to write and ask leave, but you all liked it, had consented to it by and by, and it was only 'taking Time by the fetlock,' as my wife says."

"Aren't we proud of those two words, and don't we like to say them?" interrupted Jo, addressing the fire in her turn, and watching with delight the happy light it seemed to kindle in the eyes that had been so tragically gloomy when she saw them last.

"A trifle, perhaps; she's such a captivating little woman I can't help being proud of her. Well, then, uncle and aunt were there to play propriety; we were so absorbed in one another we were of no mortal use apart, and that charming arrangement would make everything easy all round; so we did it."

"When, where, how?" asked Jo, in a fever of feminine interest and curiosity, for she could not realize it a particle.

"Six weeks ago, at the American consul's, in Paris; a very quiet wedding, of course, for even in our happiness we didn't forget dear little Beth."

Jo put her hand in his as he said that, and Laurie gently smoothed the little red pillow, which he remembered well.

"Why didn't you let us know afterward?" asked Jo, in a quieter tone, when they had sat quite still a minute.

"We wanted to surprise you; we thought we were coming directly home, at first; but the dear old gentleman, as soon as we were married, found he couldn't be ready under a month, at least, and sent us off to spend our honeymoon wherever we liked. Amy had once called Valrosa a regular honeymoon home, so we went there, and were as happy as people are but once in their lives. My faith! wasn't it love among the roses!"

Laurie seemed to forget Jo for a minute, and Jo was glad of it; for the fact that he told her these things so freely and naturally assured her that he had quite forgiven and forgotten. She tried to draw away her hand; but, as if he guessed the thought that prompted the half-involuntary impulse, Laurie held it fast, and said, with a manly gravity she had never seen in him before,—

"Jo, dear, I want to say one thing, and then we'll put it by forever. As I told you in my letter, when I wrote that Amy had been so kind to me, I never shall stop loving you; but the love is altered, and I have learned to see that it is better as it is. Amy and you change places in my heart, that's all. I think it was meant to be so, and would have come about naturally, if I had waited, as you tried to make me; but I never could be patient, and so I got a heartache. I was a boy then, headstrong and violent; and it took a hard lesson to show me my mistake. For it *was* one, Jo, as you said, and I found it out, after making a fool of myself. Upon my word, I was so tumbled up in my mind, at one time, that I didn't know which I loved best, you or Amy, and tried to love both alike; but I couldn't, and when I saw her in Switzerland, everything seemed to clear up all at once. You both got into your right places, and I felt sure that it was well off with the old love before it was on with the new; that I could honestly share my heart between sister Jo and wife Amy, and love them both dearly. Will you believe it, and go back to the happy old times when we first knew one another?"

"I'll believe it, with all my heart; but, Teddy, we never can be boy and girl again: the happy old times can't come back, and we mustn't expect it. We are man and woman now, with sober work to do, for playtime is over, and we must give up frolicking. I'm sure you feel this; I see the change in you, and you'll find it in me. I shall miss my boy, but I shall love the man as much, and admire him more, because he means to be what I hoped he would. We can't be little playmates any longer, but we will be brother and sister, to love and help one another all our lives, won't we, Laurie?"

He did not say a word, but took the hand she offered him, and laid his face down on it for a minute, feeling that out of the grave of a boyish passion, there had risen a beautiful, strong friendship to bless them both. Presently Jo said cheerfully, for she didn't want the coming home to be a sad one,—

"I can't make it true that you children are really married, and going to set up housekeeping. Why, it seems only yesterday that I was buttoning Amy's pinafore, and pulling your hair when you teased. Mercy me, how time does fly!"

"As one of the children is older than yourself, you needn't talk so like a grandma. I flatter myself I'm a 'gentleman growed,' as Peggotty said of David; and when you see Amy, you'll find her rather a precocious infant," said Laurie, looking amused at her maternal air.

"You may be a little older in years, but I'm ever so much older in feeling, Teddy. Women always are; and this last year has been such a hard one that I feel forty."

"Poor Jo! we left you to bear it alone, while we went pleasuring. You *are* older; here's a line, and there's another; unless you smile, your eyes look sad, and when I touched the cushion, just now, I found a tear on it. You've had a great deal to bear, and had to bear it all alone. What a selfish beast I've been!" and Laurie pulled his own hair, with a remorseful look.

But Jo only turned over the traitorous pillow, and answered, in a tone which she tried to make quite cheerful,—

"No, I had father and mother to help me, the dear babies to comfort me, and the thought that you and Amy were safe and happy, to make the troubles here easier to bear. I *am* lonely, sometimes, but I dare say it's good for me, and—"

"You never shall be again," broke in Laurie, putting his arm about her, as if to fence out every human ill. "Amy and I can't get on without you, so you must come and teach 'the children' to keep house, and go halves in everything, just as we used to do, and let us pet you, and all be blissfully happy and friendly together."

"If I shouldn't be in the way, it would be very pleasant. I begin to feel quite young already; for, somehow, all my troubles seemed to fly away when you came. You always were a comfort, Teddy;" and Jo leaned her head on his shoulder, just as she did years ago, when Beth lay ill, and Laurie told her to hold on to him.

He looked down at her, wondering if she remembered the time, but Jo was smiling to herself, as if, in truth, her troubles *had* all vanished at his coming.

"You are the same Jo still, dropping tears about one minute, and laughing the next. You look a little wicked now; what is it, grandma?"

"I was wondering how you and Amy get on together."

"Like angels!"

"Yes, of course, at first; but which rules?"

"I don't mind telling you that she does, now; at least I let her think so,—it pleases her, you know. By and by we shall take turns, for marriage, they say, halves one's rights and doubles one's duties."

"You'll go on as you begin, and Amy will rule you all the days of your life."

"Well, she does it so imperceptibly that I don't think I shall mind much. She is the sort of woman who knows how to rule well; in fact, I rather like it, for she winds one round her finger as softly and prettily as a skein of silk, and makes you feel as if she was doing you a favor all the while."

"That ever I should live to see you a henpecked husband and enjoying it!" cried Jo, with uplifted hands.

It was good to see Laurie square his shoulders, and smile with masculine scorn at that insinuation, as he replied, with his "high and mighty" air,—

"Amy is too well-bred for that, and I am not the sort of man to submit to it. My wife and I respect ourselves and one another too much ever to tyrannize or quarrel."

Jo liked that, and thought the new dignity very becoming, but the boy seemed changing very fast into the man, and regret mingled with her pleasure.

"I am sure of that; Amy and you never did quarrel as we used to. She is the sun and I the wind, in the fable, and the sun managed the man best, you remember."

"She can blow him up as well as shine on him," laughed Laurie. "Such a lecture as I got at Nice! I give you my word it was a deal worse than any of your scoldings,—a regular rouser. I'll tell you all about it sometime,—*she* never will, because, after telling me that she despised and was ashamed of me, she lost her heart to the despicable party and married the good-for-nothing."

"What baseness! Well, if she abuses you, come to me, and I'll defend you."

"I look as if I needed it, don't I?" said Laurie, getting up and striking an attitude which suddenly changed from the imposing to the rapturous, as Amy's voice was heard calling,—

"Where is she? Where's my dear old Jo?"

In trooped the whole family, and every one was hugged and kissed all over again, and, after several vain attempts, the three wanderers were set down to be looked at and exulted over. Mr. Laurence, hale and hearty as ever, was quite as much improved as the others by his foreign tour, for the crustiness seemed to be nearly gone, and the old-fashioned courtliness had received a polish which made it kindlier than ever. It was good to see him beam at "my children," as he called the young pair; it was better still to see Amy pay him the daughterly duty and affection which completely won his old heart; and best of all, to watch Laurie revolve about the two, as if never tired of enjoying the pretty picture they made.

The minute she put her eyes upon Amy, Meg became conscious that her own dress hadn't a Parisian air, that young Mrs. Moffat would be entirely eclipsed by young Mrs. Laurence, and that "her ladyship" was altogether a most elegant and graceful woman. Jo thought, as she watched the pair, "How well they look together! I was right, and Laurie has found the beautiful, accomplished girl who will become his home better than clumsy old Jo, and be a pride, not a torment to him." Mrs. March and her husband smiled and nodded at each other with happy faces, for they saw that their youngest had done well, not only in worldly things, but the better wealth of love, confidence, and happiness.

For Amy's face was full of the soft brightness which betokens a peaceful heart, her voice had a new tenderness in it, and the cool, prim carriage was changed to a gentle dignity, both womanly and winning. No little affectations marred it, and the cordial sweetness of her manner was more charming than the new beauty or the old grace, for it stamped her at once with the unmistakable sign of the true gentlewoman she had hoped to become.

"Love has done much for our little girl," said her mother softly.

"She has had a good example before her all her life, my dear," Mr. March whispered back, with a loving look at the worn face and gray head beside him.

Daisy found it impossible to keep her eyes off her "pitty aunty," but attached herself like a lap-dog to the wonderful châtelaine full of delightful charms. Demi paused to consider the new relationship before he compromised himself by the rash acceptance of a bribe, which took the tempting form of a family of wooden bears from Berne. A flank movement produced an unconditional surrender, however, for Laurie knew where to have him.

"Young man, when I first had the honor of making your acquaintance you hit me in the face: now I demand the satisfaction of a gentleman;" and with that the tall uncle proceeded to toss and tousle the small nephew in a way that damaged his philosophical dignity as much as it delighted his boyish soul.

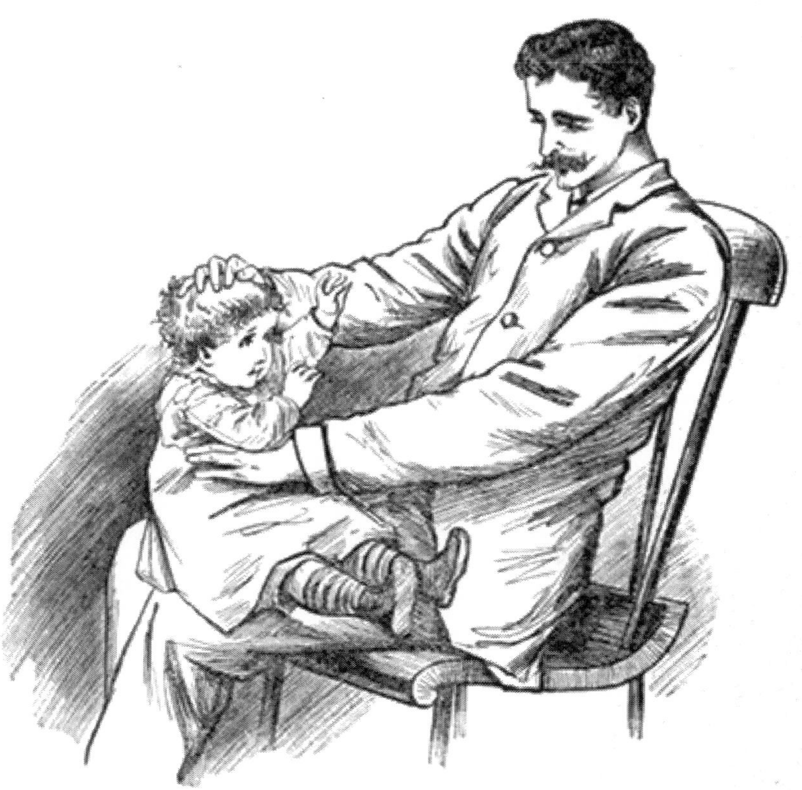

"Blest if she ain't in silk from head to foot? Ain't it a relishin' sight to see her settin' there as fine as a fiddle, and hear folks calling little Amy, Mis. Laurence?" muttered old Hannah, who could not resist frequent "peeks" through the slide as she set the table in a most decidedly promiscuous manner.

Mercy on us, how they did talk! first one, then the other, then all burst out together, trying to tell the history of three years in half an hour. It was fortunate that tea was at hand, to produce a lull and provide refreshment, for they would have been hoarse and faint if they had gone on much longer. Such a happy procession as filed away into the little dining-room! Mr. March proudly escorted "Mrs. Laurence;" Mrs. March as proudly leaned on the arm of "my son;" the old gentleman took Jo, with a whispered "You must be my girl now," and a glance at the empty corner by the fire, that made Jo whisper back, with trembling lips, "I'll try to fill her place, sir."

The twins pranced behind, feeling that the millennium was at hand, for every one was so busy with the new-comers that they were left to revel at their own sweet will, and you may be sure they made the most of the opportunity. Didn't they steal sips of tea, stuff gingerbread *ab libitum*, get a hot biscuit apiece, and, as a crowning trespass, didn't they each whisk a captivating little tart into their tiny pockets, there to stick and crumble treacherously, teaching them that both human nature and pastry are frail? Burdened with the guilty consciousness of the sequestered tarts, and fearing that Dodo's sharp eyes would pierce the thin disguise of cambric and merino which hid their booty, the little sinners attached themselves to "Dranpa," who hadn't his spectacles on. Amy, who was handed about like refreshments, returned to the parlor on Father Laurence's arm; the others paired off as before, and this arrangement left Jo companionless. She did not mind it at the minute, for she lingered to answer Hannah's eager inquiry,—

"Will Miss Amy ride in her coop (*coupé*), and use all them lovely silver dishes that's stored away over yander?"

"Shouldn't wonder if she drove six white horses, ate off gold plate, and wore diamonds and point-lace every day. Teddy thinks nothing too good for her," returned Jo with infinite satisfaction.

"No more there is! Will you have hash or fish-balls for breakfast?" asked Hannah, who wisely mingled poetry and prose.

"I don't care;" and Jo shut the door, feeling that food was an uncongenial topic just then. She stood a minute looking at the party vanishing above, and, as Demi's short plaid legs toiled up the last stair, a sudden sense of loneliness came over her so strongly that she looked about her with dim eyes, as if to find something to lean upon, for even Teddy had deserted her. If she had known what birthday gift was coming every minute nearer and nearer, she would not have said to herself, "I'll weep a little weep when I go to bed; it won't do to be dismal now." Then she drew her hand over her eyes,—for one of her boyish habits was never to know where her handkerchief was,—and had just managed to call up a smile when there came a knock at the porch-door.

She opened it with hospitable haste, and started as if another ghost had come to surprise her; for there stood a tall, bearded gentleman, beaming on her from the darkness like a midnight sun.

"O Mr. Bhaer, I *am* so glad to see you!" cried Jo, with a clutch, as if she feared the night would swallow him up before she could get him in.

"And I to see Miss Marsch,—but no, you haf a party—" and the Professor paused as the sound of voices and the tap of dancing feet came down to them.

"No, we haven't, only the family. My sister and friends have just come home, and we are all very happy. Come in, and make one of us."

Though a very social man, I think Mr. Bhaer would have gone decorously away, and come again another day; but how could he, when Jo shut the door behind him, and bereft him of his hat? Perhaps her face had something to do with it, for she forgot to hide her joy at seeing him, and showed it with a frankness that proved irresistible to the solitary man, whose welcome far exceeded his boldest hopes.

"If I shall not be Monsieur de Trop, I will so gladly see them all. You haf been ill, my friend?"

He put the question abruptly, for, as Jo hung up his coat, the light fell on her face, and he saw a change in it.

"Not ill, but tired and sorrowful. We have had trouble since I saw you last."

"Ah, yes, I know. My heart was sore for you when I heard that;" and he shook hands again, with such a sympathetic face that Jo felt as if no comfort could equal the look of the kind eyes, the grasp of the big, warm hand.

"Father, mother, this is my friend, Professor Bhaer," she said, with a face and tone of such irrepressible pride and pleasure that she might as well have blown a trumpet and opened the door with a flourish.

If the stranger had had any doubts about his reception, they were set at rest in a minute by the cordial welcome he received. Every one greeted him kindly, for Jo's sake at first, but very soon they liked him for his own. They could not help it, for he carried the talisman that opens all hearts, and these simple people warmed to him at once, feeling even the more friendly because he was poor; for poverty enriches those who live above it, and is a sure passport to truly hospitable spirits. Mr. Bhaer sat looking about him with the air of a traveller who knocks at a strange door, and, when it opens, finds himself at home. The children went to him like bees to a honey-pot; and, establishing themselves on each knee, proceeded to captivate him by rifling his pockets, pulling his beard, and investigating his watch, with juvenile audacity. The women telegraphed their approval to one another, and Mr. March, feeling that he had got a kindred spirit, opened his choicest stores for his guest's benefit, while silent John listened and enjoyed the talk, but said not a word, and Mr. Laurence found it impossible to go to sleep.

If Jo had not been otherwise engaged, Laurie's behavior would have amused her; for a faint twinge, not of jealousy, but something like suspicion, caused that gentleman to stand aloof at first, and observe the new-comer with brotherly circumspection. But it did not last long. He got interested in spite of himself, and, before he knew it, was drawn into the circle; for Mr. Bhaer talked well in this genial atmosphere, and did himself justice. He seldom spoke to Laurie, but he looked at him often, and a shadow would pass across his face, as if regretting his own lost youth, as he watched the young man in his prime. Then his eye would turn to Jo so wistfully that she would have surely answered the mute inquiry if she had seen it; but Jo had her own eyes to take care of, and, feeling that they could not be trusted, she prudently kept them on the little sock she was knitting, like a model maiden aunt.

A stealthy glance now and then refreshed her like sips of fresh water after a dusty walk, for the sidelong peeps showed her several propitious omens. Mr. Bhaer's face had lost the absent-minded expression, and looked all alive with interest in the present moment, actually young and handsome, she thought, forgetting to compare him with Laurie, as she usually did strange men, to their great detriment. Then he seemed quite inspired, though the burial customs of the ancients, to which the conversation had strayed, might not be considered an exhilarating topic. Jo quite glowed with triumph when Teddy got quenched in an argument, and thought to herself, as she watched her father's absorbed face, "How he would enjoy having such a man as my Professor to talk with every day!" Lastly, Mr. Bhaer was dressed in a new suit of black, which made him look more like a gentleman than ever. His bushy hair had been cut and smoothly brushed, but didn't stay in order long, for, in exciting moments, he rumpled it up in the droll way he used to do; and Jo liked it rampantly erect better than flat, because she thought it gave his fine forehead a Jove-like aspect. Poor Jo, how she did glorify that plain man, as she sat knitting away so quietly, yet letting nothing escape her, not even the fact that Mr. Bhaer actually had gold sleeve-buttons in his immaculate wristbands!

"Dear old fellow! He couldn't have got himself up with more care if he'd been going a-wooing," said Jo to herself; and then a sudden thought, born of the words, made her blush so dreadfully that she had to drop her ball, and go down after it to hide her face.

The manœuvre did not succeed as well as she expected, however; for, though just in the act of setting fire to a funeral-pile, the Professor dropped his torch, metaphorically speaking, and made a dive after the little blue ball. Of course they bumped their heads smartly together, saw stars, and both came up flushed and laughing, without the ball, to resume their seats, wishing they had not left them.

Nobody knew where the evening went to; for Hannah skilfully abstracted the babies at an early hour, nodding like two rosy poppies, and Mr. Laurence went home to rest. The others sat round the fire, talking away, utterly regardless of the lapse of time, till Meg, whose maternal mind was impressed with a firm conviction that Daisy had tumbled out of bed, and Demi set his night-gown afire studying the structure of matches, made a move to go.

"We must have our sing, in the good old way, for we are all together again once more," said Jo, feeling that a good shout would be a safe and pleasant vent for the jubilant emotions of her soul.

They were not *all* there. But no one found the words thoughtless or untrue; for Beth still seemed among them, a peaceful presence, invisible, but dearer than ever, since death could not break the household league that love made indissoluble. The little chair stood in its old place; the tidy basket, with the bit of work she left unfinished when the needle grew "so heavy," was still on its accustomed shelf; the beloved instrument, seldom touched now, had not been moved; and above it Beth's face, serene and smiling, as in the early days, looked down upon them, seeming to say, "Be happy. I am here."

"Play something, Amy. Let them hear how much you have improved," said Laurie, with pardonable pride in his promising pupil.

But Amy whispered, with full eyes, as she twirled the faded stool,—

"Not to-night, dear. I can't show off to-night."

But she did show something better than brilliancy or skill; for she sung Beth's songs with a tender music in her voice which the best master could not have taught, and touched the listeners' hearts with a sweeter power than any other inspiration could have given her. The room was very still, when the clear voice failed suddenly at the last line of Beth's favorite hymn. It was hard to say,—

"Earth hath no sorrow that heaven cannot heal;"

and Amy leaned against her husband, who stood behind her, feeling that her welcome home was not quite perfect without Beth's kiss.

"Now, we must finish with Mignon's song; for Mr. Bhaer sings that," said Jo, before the pause grew painful. And Mr. Bhaer cleared his throat with a gratified "Hem!" as he stepped into the corner where Jo stood, saying,—

"You will sing with me? We go excellently well together."

A pleasing fiction, by the way; for Jo had no more idea of music than a grasshopper. But she would have consented if he had proposed to sing a whole opera, and warbled away, blissfully regardless of time and tune. It didn't much matter; for Mr. Bhaer sang like a true German, heartily and well; and Jo soon subsided into a subdued hum, that she might listen to the mellow voice that seemed to sing for her alone.

"Know'st thou the land where the citron blooms,"

used to be the Professor's favorite line, for "das land" meant Germany to him; but now he seemed to dwell, with peculiar warmth and melody, upon the words,—

"There, oh there, might I with thee,
O my beloved, go!"

and one listener was so thrilled by the tender invitation that she longed to say she did know the land, and would joyfully depart thither whenever he liked.

The song was considered a great success, and the singer retired covered with laurels. But a few minutes afterward, he forgot his manners entirely, and stared at Amy putting on her bonnet; for she had been introduced simply as "my sister," and no one had called her by her new name since he came. He forgot himself still further when Laurie said, in his most gracious manner, at parting,—

"My wife and I are very glad to meet you, sir. Please remember that there is always a welcome waiting for you over the way."

Then the Professor thanked him so heartily, and looked so suddenly illuminated with satisfaction, that Laurie thought him the most delightfully demonstrative old fellow he ever met.

"I too shall go; but I shall gladly come again, if you will gif me leave, dear madame, for a little business in the city will keep me here some days."

He spoke to Mrs. March, but he looked at Jo; and the mother's voice gave as cordial an assent as did the daughter's eyes; for Mrs. March was not so blind to her children's interest as Mrs. Moffat supposed.

"I suspect that is a wise man," remarked Mr. March, with placid satisfaction, from the hearth-rug, after the last guest had gone.

"I know he is a good one," added Mrs. March, with decided approval, as she wound up the clock.

"I thought you'd like him," was all Jo said, as she slipped away to her bed.

She wondered what the business was that brought Mr. Bhaer to the city, and finally decided that he had been appointed to some great honor, somewhere, but had been too modest to mention the fact. If she had seen his face when, safe in his own room, he looked at the picture of a severe and rigid young lady, with a good deal of hair, who appeared to be gazing darkly into futurity, it might have thrown some light upon the subject, especially when he turned off the gas, and kissed the picture in the dark.

XVII

# MY LORD AND LADY.

"PLEASE, Madam Mother, could you lend me my wife for half an hour? The luggage has come, and I've been making hay of Amy's Paris finery, trying to find some things I want," said Laurie, coming in the next day to find Mrs. Laurence sitting in her mother's lap, as if being made "the baby" again.

"Certainly. Go, dear; I forget that you have any home but this," and Mrs. March pressed the white hand that wore the wedding-ring, as if asking pardon for her maternal covetousness.

"I shouldn't have come over if I could have helped it; but I can't get on without my little woman any more than a—"

"Weathercock can without wind," suggested Jo, as he paused for a simile; Jo had grown quite her own saucy self again since Teddy came home.

"Exactly; for Amy keeps me pointing due west most of the time, with only an occasional whiffle round to the south, and I haven't had an easterly spell since I was married; don't know anything about the north, but am altogether salubrious and balmy, hey, my lady?"

"Lovely weather so far; I don't know how long it will last, but I'm not afraid of storms, for I'm learning how to sail my ship. Come home, dear, and I'll find your bootjack; I suppose that's what you are rummaging after among my things. Men are *so* helpless, mother," said Amy, with a matronly air, which delighted her husband.

"What are you going to do with yourselves after you get settled?" asked Jo, buttoning Amy's cloak as she used to button her pinafores.

"We have our plans; we don't mean to say much about them yet, because we are such very new brooms, but we don't intend to be idle. I'm going into business with a devotion that shall delight grandfather, and prove to him that I'm not spoilt. I need something of the sort to keep me steady. I'm tired of dawdling, and mean to work like a man."

"And Amy, what is she going to do?" asked Mrs. March, well pleased at Laurie's decision, and the energy with which he spoke.

"After doing the civil all round, and airing our best bonnet, we shall astonish you by the elegant hospitalities of our mansion, the brilliant society we shall draw about us, and the beneficial influence we shall exert over the world at large. That's about it, isn't it, Madame Récamier?" asked Laurie, with a quizzical look at Amy.

"Time will show. Come away, Impertinence, and don't shock my family by calling me names before their faces," answered Amy, resolving that there should be a home with a good wife in it before she set up a *salon* as a queen of society.

"How happy those children seem together!" observed Mr. March, finding it difficult to become absorbed in his Aristotle after the young couple had gone.

"Yes, and I think it will last," added Mrs. March, with the restful expression of a pilot who has brought a ship safely into port.

"I know it will. Happy Amy!" and Jo sighed, then smiled brightly as Professor Bhaer opened the gate with an impatient push.

Later in the evening, when his mind had been set at rest about the bootjack, Laurie said suddenly to his wife, who was flitting about, arranging her new art treasures,—

"Mrs. Laurence."

"My lord!"

"That man intends to marry our Jo!"

"I hope so; don't you, dear?"

"Well, my love, I consider him a trump, in the fullest sense of that expressive word, but I do wish he was a little younger and a good deal richer."

"Now, Laurie, don't be too fastidious and worldly-minded. If they love one another it doesn't matter a particle how old they are nor how poor. Women *never* should marry for money—" Amy caught herself up short as the words escaped her, and looked at her husband, who replied, with malicious gravity,—

"Certainly not, though you do hear charming girls say that they intend to do it sometimes. If my memory serves me, you once thought it your duty to make a rich match; that accounts, perhaps, for your marrying a good-for-nothing like me."

"O my dearest boy, don't, don't say that! I forgot you were rich when I said 'Yes.' I'd have married you if you hadn't a penny, and I sometimes wish you *were* poor that I might show how much I love you;" and Amy, who was very dignified in public and very fond in private, gave convincing proofs of the truth of her words.

"You don't really think I am such a mercenary creature as I tried to be once, do you? It would break my heart if you didn't believe that I'd gladly pull in the same boat with you, even if you had to get your living by rowing on the lake."

"Am I an idiot and a brute? How could I think so, when you refused a richer man for me, and won't let me give you half I want to now, when I have the right? Girls do it every day, poor things, and are taught to think it is their only salvation; but you had better lessons, and, though I trembled for you at one time, I was not disappointed, for the daughter was true to the mother's teaching. I told mamma so yesterday, and she looked as glad and grateful as if I'd given her a check for a million, to be spent in charity. You are not listening to my moral remarks, Mrs. Laurence;" and Laurie paused, for Amy's eyes had an absent look, though fixed upon his face.

"Yes, I am, and admiring the dimple in your chin at the same time. I don't wish to make you vain, but I must confess that I'm prouder of my handsome husband than of all his money. Don't laugh, but your nose is *such* a comfort to me;" and Amy softly caressed the well-cut feature with artistic satisfaction.

Laurie had received many compliments in his life, but never one that suited him better, as he plainly showed, though he did laugh at his wife's peculiar taste, while she said slowly,—

"May I ask you a question, dear?"

"Of course you may."

"Shall you care if Jo does marry Mr. Bhaer?"

"Oh, that's the trouble, is it? I thought there was something in the dimple that didn't suit you. Not being a dog in the manger, but the happiest fellow alive, I assure you I can dance at Jo's wedding with a heart as light as my heels. Do you doubt it, my darling?"

Amy looked up at him, and was satisfied; her last little jealous fear vanished forever, and she thanked him, with a face full of love and confidence.

"I wish we could do something for that capital old Professor. Couldn't we invent a rich relation, who shall obligingly die out there in Germany, and leave him a tidy little fortune?" said Laurie, when they began to pace up and down the long drawing-room, arm-in-arm, as they were fond of doing, in memory of the chateau garden.

"Jo would find us out, and spoil it all; she is very proud of him, just as he is, and said yesterday that she thought poverty was a beautiful thing."

"Bless her dear heart! she won't think so when she has a literary husband, and a dozen little professors and professorins to support. We won't interfere now, but watch our chance, and do them a good turn in spite of themselves. I owe Jo for a part of my education, and she believes in people's paying their honest debts, so I'll get round her in that way."

"How delightful it is to be able to help others, isn't it? That was always one of my dreams, to have the power of giving freely; and, thanks to you, the dream has come true."

"Ah! we'll do quantities of good, won't we? There's one sort of poverty that I particularly like to help. Out-and-out beggars get taken care of, but poor gentlefolks fare badly, because they won't ask, and people don't dare to offer charity; yet there are a thousand ways of helping them, if one only knows how to do it so delicately that it does not offend. I must say, I like to serve a decayed gentleman better than a blarneying beggar; I suppose it's wrong, but I do, though it is harder."

"Because it takes a gentleman to do it," added the other member of the domestic admiration society.

"Thank you, I'm afraid I don't deserve that pretty compliment. But I was going to say that while I was dawdling about abroad, I saw a good many talented young fellows making all sorts of sacrifices, and enduring real hardships, that they might realize their dreams. Splendid fellows, some of them, working like heroes, poor and friendless, but so full of courage, patience, and ambition, that I was ashamed of myself, and longed to give them a right good lift. Those are people whom it's a satisfaction to help, for if they've got genius, it's an honor to be allowed to serve them, and not let it be lost or delayed for want of fuel to keep the pot boiling; if they haven't, it's a pleasure to comfort the poor souls, and keep them from despair when they find it out."

"Yes, indeed; and there's another class who can't ask, and who suffer in silence. I know something of it, for I belonged to it before you made a princess of me, as the king does the beggar-maid in the old story. Ambitious girls have a hard time, Laurie, and often have to see youth, health, and precious opportunities go by, just for want of a little help at the right minute. People have been very kind to me; and whenever I see girls struggling along, as we used to do, I want to put out my hand and help them, as I was helped."

"And so you shall, like an angel as you are!" cried Laurie, resolving, with a glow of philanthropic zeal, to found and endow an institution for the express benefit of young women with artistic tendencies. "Rich people have no right to sit down and enjoy themselves, or let their money accumulate for others to waste. It's not half so sensible to leave legacies when one dies as it is to use the money wisely while alive, and enjoy making one's fellow-creatures happy with it. We'll have a good time ourselves, and add an extra relish to our own pleasure by giving other people a generous taste. Will you be a little Dorcas, going about emptying a big basket of comforts, and filling it up with good deeds?"

"With all my heart, if you will be a brave St. Martin, stopping, as you ride gallantly through the world, to share your cloak with the beggar."

"It's a bargain, and we shall get the best of it!"

So the young pair shook hands upon it, and then paced happily on again, feeling that their pleasant home was more home-like because they hoped to brighten other homes, believing that their own feet would walk more uprightly along the flowery path before them, if they smoothed rough ways for other feet, and feeling that their hearts were more closely knit together by a love which could tenderly remember those less blest than they.

# XVIII

# DAISY AND DEMI.

I CANNOT feel that I have done my duty as humble historian of the March family, without devoting at least one chapter to the two most precious and important members of it. Daisy and Demi had now arrived at years of discretion; for in this fast age babies of three or four assert their rights, and get them, too, which is more than many of their elders do. If there ever were a pair of twins in danger of being utterly spoilt by adoration, it was these prattling Brookes. Of course they were the most remarkable children ever born, as will be shown when I mention that they walked at eight months, talked fluently at twelve months, and at two years they took their places at table, and behaved with a propriety which charmed all beholders. At three, Daisy demanded a "needler," and actually made a bag with four stitches in it; she likewise set up housekeeping in the sideboard, and managed a microscopic cooking-stove with a skill that brought tears of pride to Hannah's eyes, while Demi learned his letters with his grandfather, who invented a new mode of teaching the alphabet by forming the letters with his arms and legs, thus uniting gymnastics for head and heels. The boy early developed a mechanical genius which delighted his father and distracted his mother, for he tried to imitate every machine he saw, and kept the nursery in a chaotic condition, with his "sewin-sheen,"—a mysterious structure of string, chairs, clothes-pins, and spools, for wheels to go "wound and wound;" also a basket hung over the back of a big chair, in which he vainly tried to hoist his too confiding sister, who, with feminine devotion, allowed her little head to be bumped till rescued, when the young inventor indignantly remarked, "Why, marmar, dat's my lellywaiter, and me's trying to pull her up."

Though utterly unlike in character, the twins got on remarkably well together, and seldom quarrelled more than thrice a day. Of course, Demi tyrannized over Daisy, and gallantly defended her from every other aggressor; while Daisy made a galley-slave of herself, and adored her brother as the one perfect being in the world. A rosy, chubby, sunshiny little soul was Daisy, who found her way to everybody's heart, and nestled there. One of the captivating children, who seem made to be kissed and cuddled, adorned and adored like little goddesses, and produced for general approval on all festive occasions. Her small virtues were so sweet that she would have been quite angelic if a few small naughtinesses had not kept her delightfully human. It was all fair weather in her world, and every morning she scrambled up to the window in her little night-gown to look out, and say, no matter whether it rained or shone, "Oh, pitty day, oh, pitty day!" Every one was a friend, and she offered kisses to a stranger so confidingly that the most inveterate bachelor relented, and baby-lovers became faithful worshippers.

"Me loves evvybody," she once said, opening her arms, with her spoon in one hand, and her mug in the other, as if eager to embrace and nourish the whole world.

As she grew, her mother began to feel that the Dove-cote would be blest by the presence of an inmate as serene and loving as that which had helped to make the old house home, and to pray that she might be spared a loss like that which had lately taught them how long they had entertained an angel unawares. Her grandfather often called her "Beth," and her grandmother watched over her with untiring devotion, as if trying to atone for some past mistake, which no eye but her own could see.

Demi, like a true Yankee, was of an inquiring turn, wanting to know everything, and often getting much disturbed because he could not get satisfactory answers to his perpetual "What for?"

He also possessed a philosophic bent, to the great delight of his grandfather, who used to hold Socratic conversations with him, in which the precocious pupil occasionally posed his teacher, to the undisguised satisfaction of the womenfolk.

"What makes my legs go, dranpa?" asked the young philosopher, surveying those active portions of his frame with a meditative air, while resting after a go-to-bed frolic one night.

"It's your little mind, Demi," replied the sage, stroking the yellow head respectfully.

"What is a little mine?"

"It is something which makes your body move, as the spring made the wheels go in my watch when I showed it to you."

"Open me; I want to see it go wound."

"I can't do that any more than you could open the watch. God winds you up, and you go till He stops you."

"Does I?" and Demi's brown eyes grew big and bright as he took in the new thought. "Is I wounded up like the watch?"

"Yes; but I can't show you how; for it is done when we don't see."

Demi felt of his back, as if expecting to find it like that of the watch, and then gravely remarked,—

"I dess Dod does it when I's asleep."

A careful explanation followed, to which he listened so attentively that his anxious grandmother said,—

"My dear, do you think it wise to talk about such things to that baby? He's getting great bumps over his eyes, and learning to ask the most unanswerable questions."

"If he is old enough to ask the questions he is old enough to receive true answers. I am not putting the thoughts into his head, but helping him unfold those already there. These children are wiser than we are, and I have no doubt the boy understands every word I have said to him. Now, Demi, tell me where you keep your mind?"

If the boy had replied like Alcibiades, "By the gods, Socrates, I cannot tell," his grandfather would not have been surprised; but when, after standing a moment on one leg, like a meditative young stork, he answered, in a tone of calm conviction, "In my little belly," the old gentleman could only join in grandma's laugh, and dismiss the class in metaphysics.

There might have been cause for maternal anxiety, if Demi had not given convincing proofs that he was a true boy, as well as a budding philosopher; for, often, after a discussion which caused Hannah to prophesy, with ominous nods, "That child ain't long for this world," he would turn about and set her fears at rest by some of the pranks with which dear, dirty, naughty little rascals distract and delight their parents' souls.

Meg made many moral rules, and tried to keep them; but what mother was ever proof against the winning wiles, the ingenious evasions, or the tranquil audacity of the miniature men and women who so early show themselves accomplished Artful Dodgers?

"No more raisins, Demi, they'll make you sick," says mamma to the young person who offers his services in the kitchen with unfailing regularity on plum-pudding day.

"Me likes to be sick."

"I don't want to have you, so run away and help Daisy make patty-cakes."

He reluctantly departs, but his wrongs weigh upon his spirit; and, by and by, when an opportunity comes to redress them, he outwits mamma by a shrewd bargain.

"Now you have been good children, and I'll play anything you like," says Meg, as she leads her assistant cooks upstairs, when the pudding is safely bouncing in the pot.

"Truly, marmar?" asks Demi, with a brilliant idea in his well-powdered head.

"Yes, truly; anything you say," replies the short-sighted parent, preparing herself to sing "The Three Little Kittens" half a dozen times over, or to take her family to "Buy a penny bun," regardless of wind or limb. But Demi corners her by the cool reply,—

"Then we'll go and eat up all the raisins."

Aunt Dodo was chief playmate and *confidante* of both children, and the trio turned the little house topsy-turvy. Aunt Amy was as yet only a name to them, Aunt Beth soon faded into a pleasantly vague memory, but Aunt Dodo was a living reality, and they made the most of her, for which compliment she was deeply grateful. But when Mr. Bhaer came, Jo neglected her playfellows, and dismay and desolation fell upon their little souls. Daisy, who was fond of going about peddling kisses, lost her best customer and became bankrupt; Demi, with infantile penetration, soon discovered that Dodo liked to play with "the bear-man" better than she did with him; but, though hurt, he concealed his anguish, for he hadn't the heart to insult a rival who kept a mine of chocolate-drops in his waistcoat-pocket, and a watch that could be taken out of its case and freely shaken by ardent admirers.

Some persons might have considered these pleasing liberties as bribes; but Demi didn't see it in that light, and continued to patronize the "bear-man" with pensive affability, while Daisy bestowed her small affections upon him at the third call, and considered his shoulder her throne, his arm her refuge, his gifts treasures of surpassing worth.

Gentlemen are sometimes seized with sudden fits of admiration for the young relatives of ladies whom they honor with their regard; but this counterfeit philoprogenitiveness sits uneasily upon them, and does not deceive anybody a particle. Mr. Bhaer's devotion was sincere, however likewise effective,—for honesty is the best policy in love as in law; he was one of the men who are at home with children, and looked particularly well when little faces made a pleasant contrast with his manly one. His business, whatever it was, detained him from day to day, but evening seldom failed to bring him out to see—well, he always asked for Mr. March, so I suppose *he* was the attraction. The excellent papa labored under the delusion that he was, and revelled in long discussions with the kindred spirit, till a chance remark of his more observing grandson suddenly enlightened him.

Mr. Bhaer came in one evening to pause on the threshold of the study, astonished by the spectacle that met his eye. Prone upon the floor lay Mr. March, with his respectable legs in the air, and beside him, likewise prone, was Demi, trying to imitate the attitude with his own short, scarlet-stockinged legs, both grovellers so seriously absorbed that they were unconscious of spectators, till Mr. Bhaer laughed his sonorous laugh, and Jo cried out, with a scandalized face,—

"Father, father, here's the Professor!"

Down went the black legs and up came the gray head, as the preceptor said, with undisturbed dignity,—

"Good evening, Mr. Bhaer. Excuse me for a moment; we are just finishing our lesson. Now, Demi, make the letter and tell its name."

"I knows him!" and, after a few convulsive efforts, the red legs took the shape of a pair of compasses, and the intelligent pupil triumphantly shouted, "It's a We, dranpa, it's a We!"

"He's a born Weller," laughed Jo, as her parent gathered himself up, and her nephew tried to stand on his head, as the only mode of expressing his satisfaction that school was over.

"What have you been at to-day, bübchen?" asked Mr. Bhaer, picking up the gymnast.

"Me went to see little Mary."

"And what did you there?"

"I kissed her," began Demi, with artless frankness.

"Prut! thou beginnest early. What did the little Mary say to that?" asked Mr. Bhaer, continuing to confess the young sinner, who stood upon his knee, exploring the waistcoat-pocket.

"Oh, she liked it, and she kissed me, and I liked it. *Don't* little boys like little girls?" added Demi, with his mouth full, and an air of bland satisfaction.

"You precocious chick! Who put that into your head?" said Jo, enjoying the innocent revelations as much as the Professor.

"'Tisn't in mine head; it's in mine mouf," answered literal Demi, putting out his tongue, with a chocolate-drop on it, thinking she alluded to confectionery, not ideas.

"Thou shouldst save some for the little friend: sweets to the sweet, mannling;" and Mr. Bhaer offered Jo some, with a look that made her wonder if chocolate was not the nectar drunk by the gods. Demi also saw the smile, was impressed by it, and artlessly inquired,—

"Do great boys like great girls, too, 'Fessor?"

Like young Washington, Mr. Bhaer "couldn't tell a lie;" so he gave the somewhat vague reply that he believed they did sometimes, in a tone that made Mr. March put down his clothes-brush, glance at Jo's retiring face, and then sink into his chair, looking as if the "precocious chick" had put an idea into *his* head that was both sweet and sour.

Why Dodo, when she caught him in the china-closet half an hour afterward, nearly squeezed the breath out of his little body with a tender embrace, instead of shaking him for being there, and why she followed up this novel performance by the unexpected gift of a big slice of bread and jelly, remained one of the problems over which Demi puzzled his small wits, and was forced to leave unsolved forever.

## XIX

## UNDER THE UMBRELLA.

WHILE Laurie and Amy were taking conjugal strolls over velvet carpets, as they set their house in order, and planned a blissful future, Mr. Bhaer and Jo were enjoying promenades of a different sort, along muddy roads and sodden fields.

"I always do take a walk toward evening, and I don't know why I should give it up, just because I often happen to meet the Professor on his way out," said Jo to herself, after two or three encounters; for, though there were two paths to Meg's, whichever one she took she was sure to meet him, either going or returning. He was always walking rapidly, and never seemed to see her till quite close, when he would look as if his short-sighted eyes had failed to recognize the approaching lady till that moment. Then, if she was going to Meg's, he always had something for the babies; if her face was turned homeward, he had merely strolled down to see the river, and was just about returning, unless they were tired of his frequent calls.

Under the circumstances, what could Jo do but greet him civilly, and invite him in? If she *was* tired of his visits, she concealed her weariness with perfect skill, and took care that there should be coffee for supper, "as Friedrich—I mean Mr. Bhaer—doesn't like tea."

By the second week, every one knew perfectly well what was going on, yet every one tried to look as if they were stone-blind to the changes in Jo's face. They never asked why she sang about her work, did up her hair three times a day, and got so blooming with her evening exercise; and no one seemed to have the slightest suspicion that Professor Bhaer, while talking philosophy with the father, was giving the daughter lessons in love.

Jo couldn't even lose her heart in a decorous manner, but sternly tried to quench her feelings; and, failing to do so, led a somewhat agitated life. She was mortally afraid of being laughed at for surrendering, after her many and vehement declarations of independence. Laurie was her especial dread; but, thanks to the new manager, he behaved with praiseworthy propriety, never called Mr. Bhaer "a capital old fellow" in public, never alluded, in the remotest manner, to Jo's improved appearance, or expressed the least surprise at seeing the Professor's hat on the Marches' hall-table nearly every evening. But he exulted in private and longed for the time to come when he could give Jo a piece of plate, with a bear and a ragged staff on it as an appropriate coat-of-arms.

For a fortnight, the Professor came and went with lover-like regularity; then he stayed away for three whole days, and made no sign,—a proceeding which caused everybody to look sober, and Jo to become pensive, at first, and then—alas for romance!—very cross.

"Disgusted, I dare say, and gone home as suddenly as he came. It's nothing to me, of course; but I *should* think he would have come and bid us good-by, like a gentleman," she said to herself, with a despairing look at the gate, as she put on her things for the customary walk, one dull afternoon.

"You'd better take the little umbrella, dear; it looks like rain," said her mother, observing that she had on her new bonnet, but not alluding to the fact.

"Yes, Marmee; do you want anything in town? I've got to run in and get some paper," returned Jo, pulling out the bow under her chin before the glass as an excuse for not looking at her mother.

"Yes; I want some twilled silesia, a paper of number nine needles, and two yards of narrow lavender ribbon. Have you got your thick boots on, and something warm under your cloak?"

"I believe so," answered Jo absently.

"If you happen to meet Mr. Bhaer, bring him home to tea. I quite long to see the dear man," added Mrs. March.

Jo heard *that*, but made no answer, except to kiss her mother, and walk rapidly away, thinking with a glow of gratitude, in spite of her heartache,—

"How good she is to me! What *do* girls do who haven't any mothers to help them through their troubles?"

The dry-goods stores were not down among the counting-houses, banks, and wholesale warerooms, where gentlemen most do congregate; but Jo found herself in that part of the city before she did a single errand, loitering along as if waiting for some one, examining engineering instruments in one window and samples of wool in another with most unfeminine interest; tumbling over barrels, being half-smothered by descending bales, and hustled unceremoniously by busy men who looked as if they wondered "how the deuce she got there." A drop of rain on her cheek recalled her thoughts from baffled hopes to ruined ribbons; for the drops continued to fall, and, being a woman as well as a lover, she felt that, though it was too late to save her heart, she might her bonnet. Now she remembered the little umbrella, which she had forgotten to take in her hurry to be off; but regret was unavailing, and nothing could be done but borrow one or submit to a drenching. She looked up at the lowering sky, down at the crimson bow already flecked with black, forward along the muddy street, then one long, lingering look behind, at a certain grimy warehouse, with "Hoffmann, Swartz, & Co." over the door, and said to herself, with a sternly reproachful air,—

"It serves me right! What business had I to put on all my best things and come philandering down here, hoping to see the Professor? Jo, I'm ashamed of you! No, you shall *not* go there to borrow an umbrella, or find out where he is, from his friends. You shall trudge away, and do your errands in the rain; and if you catch your death and ruin your bonnet, it's no more than you deserve. Now then!"

With that she rushed across the street so impetuously that she narrowly escaped annihilation from a passing truck, and precipitated herself into the arms of a stately old gentleman, who said, "I beg pardon, ma'am," and looked mortally offended. Somewhat daunted, Jo righted herself, spread her handkerchief over the devoted ribbons, and, putting temptation behind her, hurried on, with increasing dampness about the ankles, and much clashing of umbrellas overhead. The fact that a somewhat dilapidated blue one remained stationary above the unprotected bonnet, attracted her attention; and, looking up, she saw Mr. Bhaer looking down.

"I feel to know the strong-minded lady who goes so bravely under many horse-noses, and so fast through much mud. What do you down here, my friend?"

"I'm shopping."

Mr. Bhaer smiled, as he glanced from the pickle-factory on one side, to the wholesale hide and leather concern on the other; but he only said politely,—

"You haf no umbrella. May I go also, and take for you the bundles?"

"Yes, thank you."

Jo's cheeks were as red as her ribbon, and she wondered what he thought of her; but she didn't care, for in a minute she found herself walking away arm-in-arm with her Professor, feeling as if the sun had suddenly burst out with uncommon brilliancy, that the world was all right again, and that one thoroughly happy woman was paddling through the wet that day.

"We thought you had gone," said Jo hastily, for she knew he was looking at her. Her bonnet wasn't big enough to hide her face, and she feared he might think the joy it betrayed unmaidenly.

"Did you believe that I should go with no farewell to those who haf been so heavenly kind to me?" he asked so reproachfully that she felt as if she had insulted him by the suggestion, and answered heartily,—

"No, *I* didn't; I knew you were busy about your own affairs, but we rather missed you,—father and mother especially."

"And you?"

"I'm always glad to see you, sir."

In her anxiety to keep her voice quite calm, Jo made it rather cool, and the frosty little monosyllable at the end seemed to chill the Professor, for his smile vanished, as he said gravely,—

"I thank you, and come one time more before I go."

"You *are* going, then?"

"I haf no longer any business here; it is done."

"Successfully, I hope?" said Jo, for the bitterness of disappointment was in that short reply of his.

"I ought to think so, for I haf a way opened to me by which I can make my bread and gif my Jünglings much help."

"Tell me, please! I like to know all about the—the boys," said Jo eagerly.

"That is so kind, I gladly tell you. My friends find for me a place in a college, where I teach as at home, and earn enough to make the way smooth for Franz and Emil. For this I should be grateful, should I not?"

"Indeed you should. How splendid it will be to have you doing what you like, and be able to see you often, and the boys!" cried Jo, clinging to the lads as an excuse for the satisfaction she could not help betraying.

"Ah! but we shall not meet often, I fear; this place is at the West."

"So far away!" and Jo left her skirts to their fate, as if it didn't matter now what became of her clothes or herself.

Mr. Bhaer could read several languages, but he had not learned to read women yet. He flattered himself that he knew Jo pretty well, and was, therefore, much amazed by the contradictions of voice, face, and manner, which she showed him in rapid succession that day, for she was in half a dozen different moods in the course of half an hour. When she met him she looked surprised, though it was impossible to help suspecting that she had come for that express purpose. When he offered her his arm, she took it with a look that filled him with delight; but when he asked if she missed him, she gave such a chilly, formal reply that despair fell upon him. On learning his good fortune she almost clapped her hands: was the joy all for the boys? Then, on hearing his destination, she said, "So far away!" in a tone of despair that lifted him on to a pinnacle of hope; but the next minute she tumbled him down again by observing, like one entirely absorbed in the matter,—

"Here's the place for my errands; will you come in? It won't take long."

Jo rather prided herself upon her shopping capabilities, and particularly wished to impress her escort with the neatness and despatch with which she would accomplish the business. But, owing to the flutter she was in, everything went amiss; she upset the tray of needles, forgot the silesia was to be "twilled" till it was cut off, gave the wrong change, and covered herself with confusion by asking for lavender ribbon at the calico counter. Mr. Bhaer stood by, watching her blush and blunder; and, as he watched, his own bewilderment seemed to subside, for he was beginning to see that on some occasions women, like dreams, go by contraries.

When they came out, he put the parcel under his arm with a more cheerful aspect, and splashed through the puddles as if he rather enjoyed it, on the whole.

"Should we not do a little what you call shopping for the babies, and haf a farewell feast to-night if I go for my last call at your so pleasant home?" he asked, stopping before a window full of fruit and flowers.

"What will we buy?" said Jo, ignoring the latter part of his speech, and sniffing the mingled odors with an affectation of delight as they went in.

"May they haf oranges and figs?" asked Mr. Bhaer, with a paternal air.

"They eat them when they can get them."

"Do you care for nuts?"

"Like a squirrel."

"Hamburg grapes; yes, we shall surely drink to the Fatherland in those?"

Jo frowned upon that piece of extravagance, and asked why he didn't buy a frail of dates, a cask of raisins, and a bag of almonds, and done with it? Whereat Mr. Bhaer confiscated her purse, produced his own, and finished the marketing by buying several pounds of grapes, a pot of rosy daisies, and a pretty jar of honey, to be regarded in the light of a demijohn. Then, distorting his pockets with the knobby bundles, and giving her the flowers to hold, he put up the old umbrella, and they travelled on again.

"Miss Marsch, I haf a great favor to ask of you," began the Professor, after a moist promenade of half a block.

"Yes, sir;" and Jo's heart began to beat so hard she was afraid he would hear it.

"I am bold to say it in spite of the rain, because so short a time remains to me."

"Yes, sir;" and Jo nearly crushed the small flower-pot with the sudden squeeze she gave it.

"I wish to get a little dress for my Tina, and I am too stupid to go alone. Will you kindly gif me a word of taste and help?"

"Yes, sir;" and Jo felt as calm and cool, all of a sudden, as if she had stepped into a refrigerator.

"Perhaps also a shawl for Tina's mother, she is so poor and sick, and the husband is such a care. Yes, yes, a thick, warm shawl would be a friendly thing to take the little mother."

"I'll do it with pleasure, Mr. Bhaer. I'm going very fast and he's getting dearer every minute," added Jo to herself; then, with a mental shake, she entered into the business with an energy which was pleasant to behold.

Mr. Bhaer left it all to her, so she chose a pretty gown for Tina, and then ordered out the shawls. The clerk, being a married man, condescended to take an interest in the couple, who appeared to be shopping for their family.

"Your lady may prefer this; it's a superior article, a most desirable color, quite chaste and genteel," he said, shaking out a comfortable gray shawl, and throwing it over Jo's shoulders.

"Does this suit you, Mr. Bhaer?" she asked, turning her back to him, and feeling deeply grateful for the chance of hiding her face.

"Excellently well; we will haf it," answered the Professor, smiling to himself as he paid for it, while Jo continued to rummage the counters like a confirmed bargain-hunter.

"Now shall we go home?" he asked, as if the words were very pleasant to him.

"Yes; it's late, and I'm *so* tired." Jo's voice was more pathetic than she knew; for now the sun seemed to have gone in as suddenly as it came out, the world grew muddy and miserable again, and for the first time she discovered that her feet were cold, her head ached, and that her heart was colder than the former, fuller of pain than the latter. Mr. Bhaer was going away; he only cared for her as a friend; it was all a mistake, and the sooner it was over the better. With this idea in her head, she hailed an approaching omnibus with such a hasty gesture that the daisies flew out of the pot and were badly damaged.

"This is not our omniboos," said the Professor, waving the loaded vehicle away, and stopping to pick up the poor little flowers.

"I beg your pardon, I didn't see the name distinctly. Never mind, I can walk. I'm used to plodding in the mud," returned Jo, winking hard, because she would have died rather than openly wipe her eyes.

Mr. Bhaer saw the drops on her cheeks, though she turned her head away; the sight seemed to touch him very much, for, suddenly stooping down, he asked in a tone that meant a great deal,—

"Heart's dearest, why do you cry?"

Now, if Jo had not been new to this sort of thing she would have said she wasn't crying, had a cold in her head, or told any other feminine fib proper to the occasion; instead of which that undignified creature answered, with an irrepressible sob,—

"Because you are going away."

"Ach, mein Gott, that is *so* good!" cried Mr. Bhaer, managing to clasp his hands in spite of the umbrella and the bundles. "Jo, I haf nothing but much love to gif you; I came to see if you could care for it, and I waited to be sure that I was something more than a friend. Am I? Can you make a little place in your heart for old Fritz?" he added, all in one breath.

"Oh, yes!" said Jo; and he was quite satisfied, for she folded both hands over his arm, and looked up at him with an expression that plainly showed how happy she would be to walk through life beside him, even though she had no better shelter than the old umbrella, if he carried it.

It was certainly proposing under difficulties, for, even if he had desired to do so, Mr. Bhaer could not go down upon his knees, on account of the mud; neither could he offer Jo his hand, except figuratively, for both were full; much less could he indulge in tender demonstrations in the open street, though he was near it: so the only way in which he could express his rapture was to look at her, with an expression which glorified his face to such a degree that there actually seemed to be little rainbows in the drops that sparkled on his beard. If he had not loved Jo very much, I don't think he could have done it *then*, for she looked far from lovely, with her skirts in a deplorable state, her rubber boots splashed to the ankle, and her bonnet a ruin. Fortunately, Mr. Bhaer considered her the most beautiful woman living, and she found him more "Jove-like" than ever, though his hat-brim was quite limp with the little rills trickling thence upon his shoulders (for he held the umbrella all over Jo), and every finger of his gloves needed mending.

Passers-by probably thought them a pair of harmless lunatics, for they entirely forgot to hail a 'bus, and strolled leisurely along, oblivious of deepening dusk and fog. Little they cared what anybody thought, for they were enjoying the happy hour that seldom comes but once in any life, the magical moment which bestows youth on the old, beauty on the plain, wealth on the poor, and gives human hearts a foretaste of heaven. The Professor looked as if he had conquered a kingdom, and the world had nothing more to offer him in the way of bliss; while Jo trudged beside him, feeling as if her place had always been there, and wondering how she ever could have chosen any other lot. Of course, she was the first to speak—intelligibly, I mean, for the emotional remarks which followed her impetuous "Oh, yes!" were not of a coherent or reportable character.

"Friedrich, why didn't you—"

"Ah, heaven, she gifs me the name that no one speaks since Minna died!" cried the Professor, pausing in a puddle to regard her with grateful delight.

"I always call you so to myself—I forgot; but I won't, unless you like it."

"Like it? it is more sweet to me than I can tell. Say 'thou,' also, and I shall say your language is almost as beautiful as mine."

"Isn't 'thou' a little sentimental?" asked Jo, privately thinking it a lovely monosyllable.

"Sentimental? Yes. Thank Gott, we Germans believe in sentiment, and keep ourselves young mit it. Your English 'you' is so cold, say 'thou,' heart's dearest, it means so much to me," pleaded Mr. Bhaer, more like a romantic student than a grave professor.

"Well, then, why didn't thou tell me all this sooner?" asked Jo bashfully.

"Now I shall haf to show thee all my heart, and I so gladly will, because thou must take care of it hereafter. See, then, my Jo,—ah, the dear, funny little name!—I had a wish to tell something the day I said good-by, in New York; but I thought the handsome friend was betrothed to thee, and so I spoke not. Wouldst thou have said 'Yes,' then, if I *had* spoken?"

"I don't know; I'm afraid not, for I didn't have any heart just then."

"Prut! that I do not believe. It was asleep till the fairy prince came through the wood, and waked it up. Ah, well, 'Die erste Liebe ist die beste;' but that I should not expect."

"Yes, the first love *is* the best; so be contented, for I never had another. Teddy was only a boy, and soon got over his little fancy," said Jo, anxious to correct the Professor's mistake.

"Good! then I shall rest happy, and be sure that thou givest me all. I haf waited so long, I am grown selfish, as thou wilt find, Professorin."

"I like that," cried Jo, delighted with her new name. "Now tell me what brought you, at last, just when I most wanted you?"

"This;" and Mr. Bhaer took a little worn paper out of his waistcoat-pocket.

Jo unfolded it, and looked much abashed, for it was one of her own contributions to a paper that paid for poetry, which accounted for her sending it an occasional attempt.

"How could that bring you?" she asked, wondering what he meant.

"I found it by chance; I knew it by the names and the initials, and in it there was one little verse that seemed to call me. Read and find him; I will see that you go not in the wet."

Jo obeyed, and hastily skimmed through the lines which she had christened—

"IN THE GARRET.

"Four little chests all in a row,
Dim with dust, and worn by time,
All fashioned and filled, long ago,
By children now in their prime.
Four little keys hung side by side,
With faded ribbons, brave and gay
When fastened there, with childish pride,
Long ago, on a rainy day.
Four little names, one on each lid,
Carved out by a boyish hand,
And underneath there lieth hid

Histories of the happy band
Once playing here, and pausing oft
To hear the sweet refrain,
That came and went on the roof aloft,
In the falling summer rain.

"'Meg' on the first lid, smooth and fair.
I look in with loving eyes,
For folded here, with well-known care,
A goodly gathering lies,
The record of a peaceful life,—
Gifts to gentle child and girl,
A bridal gown, lines to a wife,
A tiny shoe, a baby curl.
No toys in this first chest remain,
For all are carried away,
In their old age, to join again
In another small Meg's play.
Ah, happy mother! well I know
You hear, like a sweet refrain,
Lullabies ever soft and low
In the falling summer rain.

"'Jo' on the next lid, scratched and worn,
And within a motley store
Of headless dolls, of school-books torn,
Birds and beasts that speak no more;
Spoils brought home from the fairy ground
Only trod by youthful feet,
Dreams of a future never found,
Memories of a past still sweet;
Half-writ poems, stories wild,
April letters, warm and cold,
Diaries of a wilful child,
Hints of a woman early old;
A woman in a lonely home,
Hearing, like a sad refrain,—
'Be worthy love, and love will come,'
In the falling summer rain.

"My Beth! the dust is always swept
From the lid that bears your name,
As if by loving eyes that wept,
By careful hands that often came.
Death canonized for us one saint,
Ever less human than divine,
And still we lay, with tender plaint,
Relics in this household shrine.—
The silver bell, so seldom rung,
The little cap which last she wore,
The fair, dead Catherine that hung
By angels borne above her door;
The songs she sang, without lament,
In her prison-house of pain,
Forever are they sweetly blent
With the falling summer rain.

"Upon the last lid's polished field—
Legend now both fair and true—
A gallant knight bears on his shield,
'Amy,' in letters gold and blue.
Within lie snoods that bound her hair,
Slippers that have danced their last,
Faded flowers laid by with care,
Fans whose airy toils are past;
Gay valentines, all ardent flames,
Trifles that have borne their part
In girlish hopes and fears and shames,—
The record of a maiden heart
Now learning fairer, truer spells,
Hearing, like a blithe refrain,
The silver sound of bridal bells
In the falling summer rain.

"Four little chests all in a row,
Dim with dust, and worn by time,
Four women, taught by weal and woe
To love and labor in their prime.
Four sisters, parted for an hour,
None lost, one only gone before,
Made by love's immortal power,
Nearest and dearest evermore.
Oh, when these hidden stores of ours
Lie open to the Father's sight,
May they be rich in golden hours,
Deeds that show fairer for the light,
Lives whose brave music long shall ring,
Like a spirit-stirring strain,
Souls that shall gladly soar and sing
In the long sunshine after rain.

"J. M."

"It's very bad poetry, but I felt it when I wrote it, one day when I was very lonely, and had a good cry on a rag-bag. I never thought it would go where it could tell tales," said Jo, tearing up the verses the Professor had treasured so long.

"Let it go, it has done its duty, and I will haf a fresh one when I read all the brown book in which she keeps her little secrets," said Mr. Bhaer, with a smile, as he watched the fragments fly away on the wind. "Yes," he added earnestly, "I read that, and I think to myself, 'She has a sorrow, she is lonely, she would find comfort in true love. I haf a heart full, full for her; shall I not go and say, 'If this is not too poor a thing to gif for what I shall hope to receive, take it in Gott's name?'"

"And so you came to find that it was not too poor, but the one precious thing I needed," whispered Jo.

"I had no courage to think that at first, heavenly kind as was your welcome to me. But soon I began to hope, and then I said, 'I will haf her if I die for it,' and so I will!" cried Mr. Bhaer, with a defiant nod, as if the walls of mist closing round them were barriers which he was to surmount or valiantly knock down.

Jo thought that was splendid, and resolved to be worthy of her knight, though he did not come prancing on a charger in gorgeous array.

"What made you stay away so long?" she asked presently, finding it so pleasant to ask confidential questions and get delightful answers that she could not keep silent.

"It was not easy, but I could not find the heart to take you from that so happy home until I could haf a prospect of one to give you, after much time, perhaps, and hard work. How could I ask you to gif up so much for a poor old fellow, who has no fortune but a little learning?"

"I'm glad you *are* poor; I couldn't bear a rich husband," said Jo decidedly, adding, in a softer tone, "Don't fear poverty; I've known it long enough to lose my dread, and be happy working for those I love; and don't call yourself old,—forty is the prime of life. I couldn't help loving you if you were seventy!"

The Professor found that so touching that he would have been glad of his handkerchief, if he could have got at it; as he couldn't, Jo wiped his eyes for him, and said, laughing, as she took away a bundle or two,—

"I may be strong-minded, but no one can say I'm out of my sphere now, for woman's special mission is supposed to be drying tears and bearing burdens. I'm to carry my share, Friedrich, and help to earn the home. Make up your mind to that, or I'll never go," she added resolutely, as he tried to reclaim his load.

"We shall see. Haf you patience to wait a long time, Jo? I must go away and do my work alone. I must help my boys first, because, even for you, I may not break my word to Minna. Can you forgif that, and be happy while we hope and wait?"

"Yes, I know I can; for we love one another, and that makes all the rest easy to bear. I have my duty, also, and my work. I couldn't enjoy myself if I neglected them even for you, so there's no need of hurry or impatience. You can do your part out West, I can do mine here, and both be happy hoping for the best, and leaving the future to be as God wills."

"Ah! thou gifest me such hope and courage, and I haf nothing to gif back but a full heart and these empty hands," cried the Professor, quite overcome.

Jo never, never would learn to be proper; for when he said that as they stood upon the steps, she just put both hands into his, whispering tenderly, "Not empty now;" and, stooping down, kissed her Friedrich under the umbrella. It was dreadful, but she would have done it if the flock of draggle-tailed sparrows on the hedge had been human beings, for she was very far gone indeed, and quite regardless of everything but her own happiness. Though it came in such a very simple guise, that was the crowning moment of both their lives, when, turning from the night and storm and loneliness to the household light and warmth and peace waiting to receive them, with a glad "Welcome home!" Jo led her lover in, and shut the door.

## XX

## HARVEST TIME.

FOR a year Jo and her Professor worked and waited, hoped and loved, met occasionally, and wrote such voluminous letters that the rise in the price of paper was accounted for, Laurie said. The second year began rather soberly, for their prospects did not brighten, and Aunt March died suddenly. But when their first sorrow was over,—for they loved the old lady in spite of her sharp tongue,—they found they had cause for rejoicing, for she had left Plumfield to Jo, which made all sorts of joyful things possible.

"It's a fine old place, and will bring a handsome sum; for of course you intend to sell it," said Laurie, as they were all talking the matter over, some weeks later.

"No, I don't," was Jo's decided answer, as she petted the fat poodle, whom she had adopted, out of respect to his former mistress.

"You don't mean to live there?"

"Yes, I do."

"But, my dear girl, it's an immense house, and will take a power of money to keep it in order. The garden and orchard alone need two or three men, and farming isn't in Bhaer's line, I take it."

"He'll try his hand at it there, if I propose it."

"And you expect to live on the produce of the place? Well, that sounds paradisiacal, but you'll find it desperate hard work."

"The crop we are going to raise is a profitable one;" and Jo laughed.

"Of what is this fine crop to consist, ma'am?"

"Boys. I want to open a school for little lads,—a good, happy, homelike school, with me to take care of them, and Fritz to teach them."

"There's a truly Joian plan for you! Isn't that just like her?" cried Laurie, appealing to the family, who looked as much surprised as he.

"I like it," said Mrs. March decidedly.

"So do I," added her husband, who welcomed the thought of a chance for trying the Socratic method of education on modern youth.

"It will be an immense care for Jo," said Meg, stroking the head of her one all-absorbing son.

"Jo can do it, and be happy in it. It's a splendid idea. Tell us all about it," cried Mr. Laurence, who had been longing to lend the lovers a hand, but knew that they would refuse his help.

"I knew you'd stand by me, sir. Amy does too—I see it in her eyes, though she prudently waits to turn it over in her mind before she speaks. Now, my dear people," continued Jo earnestly, "just understand that this isn't a new idea of mine, but a long-cherished plan. Before my Fritz came, I used to think how, when I'd made my fortune, and no one needed me at home, I'd hire a big house, and pick up some poor, forlorn little lads, who hadn't any mothers, and take care of them, and make life jolly for them before it was too late. I see so many going to ruin, for want of help at the right minute; I love so to do anything for them; I seem to feel their wants, and sympathize with their troubles, and, oh, I should *so* like to be a mother to them!"

Mrs. March held out her hand to Jo, who took it, smiling, with tears in her eyes, and went on in the old enthusiastic way, which they had not seen for a long while.

"I told my plan to Fritz once, and he said it was just what he would like, and agreed to try it when we got rich. Bless his dear heart, he's been doing it all his life,—helping poor boys, I mean, not getting rich; that he'll never be; money doesn't stay in his pocket long enough to lay up any. But now, thanks to my good old aunt, who loved me better than I ever deserved, *I'm* rich, at least I feel so, and we can live at Plumfield perfectly well, if we have a flourishing school. It's just the place for boys, the house is big, and the furniture strong and plain. There's plenty of room for dozens inside, and splendid grounds outside. They could help in the garden and orchard: such work is healthy, isn't it, sir? Then Fritz can train and teach in his own way, and father will help him. I can feed and nurse and pet and scold them; and mother will be my stand-by. I've always longed for lots of boys, and never had enough; now I can fill the house full, and revel in the little dears to my heart's content. Think what luxury,—Plumfield my own, and a wilderness of boys to enjoy it with me!"

As Jo waved her hands, and gave a sigh of rapture, the family went off into a gale of merriment, and Mr. Laurence laughed till they thought he'd have an apoplectic fit.

"I don't see anything funny," she said gravely, when she could be heard. "Nothing could be more natural or proper than for my Professor to open a school, and for me to prefer to reside on my own estate."

"She is putting on airs already," said Laurie, who regarded the idea in the light of a capital joke. "But may I inquire how you intend to support the establishment? If all the pupils are little ragamuffins, I'm afraid your crop won't be profitable in a worldly sense, Mrs. Bhaer."

"Now don't be a wet-blanket, Teddy. Of course I shall have rich pupils, also,—perhaps begin with such altogether; then, when I've got a start, I can take a ragamuffin or two, just for a relish. Rich people's children often need care and comfort, as well as poor. I've seen unfortunate little creatures left to servants, or backward ones pushed forward, when it's real cruelty. Some are naughty through mismanagement or neglect, and some lose their mothers. Besides, the best have to get through the hobbledehoy age, and that's the very time they need most patience and kindness. People laugh at them, and hustle them about, try to keep them out of sight, and expect them to turn, all at once, from pretty children into fine young men. They don't complain much,—plucky little souls,—but they feel it. I've been through something of it, and I know all about it. I've a special interest in such young bears, and like to show them that I see the warm, honest, well-meaning boys' hearts, in spite of the clumsy arms and legs and the topsy-turvy heads. I've had experience, too, for haven't I brought up one boy to be a pride and honor to his family?"

"I'll testify that you tried to do it," said Laurie, with a grateful look.

"And I've succeeded beyond my hopes; for here you are, a steady, sensible business man, doing heaps of good with your money, and laying up the blessings of the poor, instead of dollars. But you are not merely a business man: you love good and beautiful things, enjoy them yourself, and let others go halves, as you always did in the old times. I *am* proud of you, Teddy, for you get better every year, and every one feels it, though you won't let them say so. Yes, and when I have my flock, I'll just point to you, and say, 'There's your model, my lads.'"

Poor Laurie didn't know where to look; for, man though he was, something of the old bashfulness came over him as this burst of praise made all faces turn approvingly upon him.

"I say, Jo, that's rather too much," he began, just in his old boyish way. "You have all done more for me than I can ever thank you for, except by doing my best not to disappoint you. You have rather cast me off lately, Jo, but I've had the best of help, nevertheless; so, if I've got on at all, you may thank these two for it;" and he laid one hand gently on his grandfather's white head, the other on Amy's golden one, for the three were never far apart.

"I do think that families are the most beautiful things in all the world!" burst out Jo, who was in an unusually uplifted frame of mind just then. "When I have one of my own, I hope it will be as happy as the three I know and love the best. If John and my Fritz were only here, it would be quite a little heaven on earth," she added more quietly. And that night, when she went to her room, after a blissful evening of family counsels, hopes, and plans, her heart was so full of happiness that she could only calm it by kneeling beside the empty bed always near her own, and thinking tender thoughts of Beth.

It was a very astonishing year altogether, for things seemed to happen in an unusually rapid and delightful manner. Almost before she knew where she was, Jo found herself married and settled at Plumfield. Then a family of six or seven boys sprung up like mushrooms, and flourished surprisingly, poor boys as well as rich; for Mr. Laurence was continually finding some touching case of destitution, and begging the Bhaers to take pity on the child, and he would gladly pay a trifle for its support. In this way the sly old gentleman got round proud Jo, and furnished her with the style of boy in which she most delighted.

Of course it was up-hill work at first, and Jo made queer mistakes; but the wise Professor steered her safely into calmer waters, and the most rampant ragamuffin was conquered in the end. How Jo did enjoy her "wilderness of boys," and how poor, dear Aunt March would have lamented had she been there to see the sacred precincts of prim, well-ordered Plumfield overrun with Toms, Dicks, and Harrys! There was a sort of poetic justice about it, after all, for the old lady had been the terror of the boys for miles round; and now the exiles feasted freely on forbidden plums, kicked up the gravel with profane boots unreproved, and played cricket in the big field where the irritable "cow with a crumpled horn" used to invite rash youths to come and be tossed. It became a sort of boys' paradise, and Laurie suggested that it should be called the "Bhaer-garten," as a compliment to its master and appropriate to its inhabitants.

It never was a fashionable school, and the Professor did not lay up a fortune; but it *was* just what Jo intended it to be,—"a happy, homelike place for boys, who needed teaching, care, and kindness." Every room in the big house was soon full; every little plot in the garden soon had its owner; a regular menagerie appeared in barn and shed, for pet animals were allowed; and, three times a day, Jo smiled at her Fritz from the head of a long table lined on either side with rows of happy young faces, which all turned to her with affectionate eyes, confiding words, and grateful hearts, full of love for "Mother Bhaer." She had boys enough now, and did not tire of them, though they were not angels, by any means, and some of them caused both Professor and Professorin much trouble and anxiety. But her faith in the good spot which exists in the heart of the naughtiest, sauciest, most tantalizing little ragamuffin gave her patience, skill, and, in time, success; for no mortal boy could hold out long with Father Bhaer shining on him as benevolently as the sun, and Mother Bhaer forgiving him seventy times seven. Very precious to Jo was the friendship of the lads; their penitent sniffs and whispers after wrong-doing; their droll or touching little confidences; their pleasant enthusiasms, hopes, and plans; even their misfortunes, for they only endeared them to her all the more. There were slow boys and bashful boys; feeble boys and riotous boys; boys that lisped and boys that stuttered; one or two lame ones; and a merry little quadroon, who could not be taken in elsewhere, but who was welcome to the "Bhaer-garten," though some people predicted that his admission would ruin the school.

Yes; Jo was a very happy woman there, in spite of hard work, much anxiety, and a perpetual racket. She enjoyed it heartily, and found the applause of her boys more satisfying than any praise of the world; for now she told no stories except to her flock of enthusiastic believers and admirers. As the years went on, two little lads of her own came to increase her happiness,—Rob, named for grandpa, and Teddy, a happy-go-lucky baby, who seemed to have inherited his papa's sunshiny temper as well as his mother's lively spirit. How they ever grew up alive in that whirlpool of boys was a mystery to their grandma and aunts; but they flourished like dandelions in spring, and their rough nurses loved and served them well.

There were a great many holidays at Plumfield, and one of the most delightful was the yearly apple-picking; for then the Marches, Laurences, Brookes, and Bhaers turned out in full force, and made a day of it. Five years after Jo's wedding, one of these fruitful festivals occurred,—a mellow October day, when the air was full of an exhilarating freshness which made the spirits rise, and the blood dance healthily in the veins. The old orchard wore its holiday attire; golden-rod and asters fringed the mossy walls; grasshoppers skipped briskly in the sere grass, and crickets chirped like fairy pipers at a feast; squirrels were busy with their small harvesting; birds twittered their adieux from the alders in the lane; and every tree stood ready to send down its shower of red or yellow apples at the first shake. Everybody was there; everybody laughed and sang, climbed up and tumbled down; everybody declared that there never had been such a perfect day or such a jolly set to enjoy it; and every one gave themselves up to the simple pleasures of the hour as freely as if there were no such things as care or sorrow in the world.

Mr. March strolled placidly about, quoting Tusser, Cowley, and Columella to Mr. Laurence, while enjoying—

"The gentle apple's winey juice."

The Professor charged up and down the green aisles like a stout Teutonic knight, with a pole for a lance, leading on the boys, who made a hook and ladder company of themselves, and performed wonders in the way of ground and lofty tumbling. Laurie devoted himself to the little ones, rode his small daughter in a bushel-basket, took Daisy up among the birds' nests, and kept adventurous Rob from breaking his neck. Mrs. March and Meg sat among the apple piles like a pair of Pomonas, sorting the contributions that kept pouring in; while Amy, with a beautiful motherly expression in her face, sketched the various groups, and watched over one pale lad, who sat adoring her with his little crutch beside him.

Jo was in her element that day, and rushed about, with her gown pinned up, her hat anywhere but on her head, and her baby tucked under her arm, ready for any lively adventure which might turn up. Little Teddy bore a charmed life, for nothing ever happened to him, and Jo never felt any anxiety when he was whisked up into a tree by one lad, galloped off on the back of another, or supplied with sour russets by his indulgent papa, who labored under the Germanic delusion that babies could digest anything, from pickled cabbage to buttons, nails, and their own small shoes. She knew that little Ted would turn up again in time, safe and rosy, dirty and serene, and she always received him back with a hearty welcome, for Jo loved her babies tenderly.

At four o'clock a lull took place, and baskets remained empty, while the apple-pickers rested, and compared rents and bruises. Then Jo and Meg, with a detachment of the bigger boys, set forth the supper on the grass, for an out-of-door tea was always the crowning joy of the day. The land literally flowed with milk and honey on such occasions, for the lads were not required to sit at table, but allowed to partake of refreshment as they liked,—freedom being the sauce best beloved by the boyish soul. They availed themselves of the rare privilege to the fullest extent, for some tried the pleasing experiment of drinking milk while standing on their heads, others lent a charm to leap-frog by eating pie in the pauses of the game, cookies were sown broadcast over the field, and apple-turnovers roosted in the trees like a new style of bird. The little girls had a private tea-party, and Ted roved among the edibles at his own sweet will.

When no one could eat any more, the Professor proposed the first regular toast, which was always drunk at such times,—"Aunt March, God bless her!" A toast heartily given by the good man, who never forgot how much he owed her, and quietly drunk by the boys, who had been taught to keep her memory green.

"Now, grandma's sixtieth birthday! Long life to her, with three times three!"

That was given with a will, as you may well believe; and the cheering once begun, it was hard to stop it. Everybody's health was proposed, from Mr. Laurence, who was considered their special patron, to the astonished guinea-pig, who had strayed from its proper sphere in search of its young master. Demi, as the oldest grandchild, then presented the queen of the day with various gifts, so numerous that they were transported to the festive scene in a wheelbarrow. Funny presents, some of them, but what would have been defects to other eyes were ornaments to grandma's,—for the children's gifts were all their own. Every stitch Daisy's patient little fingers had put into the handkerchiefs she hemmed was better than embroidery to Mrs. March; Demi's shoe-box was a miracle of mechanical skill, though the cover wouldn't shut; Rob's footstool had a wiggle in its uneven legs, that she declared was very soothing; and no page of the costly book Amy's child gave her was so fair as that on which appeared, in tipsy capitals, the words,—"To dear Grandma, from her little Beth."

During this ceremony the boys had mysteriously disappeared; and, when Mrs. March had tried to thank her children, and broken down, while Teddy wiped her eyes on his pinafore, the Professor suddenly began to sing. Then, from above him, voice after voice took up the words, and from tree to tree echoed the music of the unseen choir, as the boys sung, with all their hearts, the little song Jo had written, Laurie set to music, and the Professor trained his lads to give with the best effect. This was something altogether new, and it proved a grand success; for Mrs. March couldn't get over her surprise, and insisted on shaking hands with every one of the featherless birds, from tall Franz and Emil to the little quadroon, who had the sweetest voice of all.

After this, the boys dispersed for a final lark, leaving Mrs. March and her daughters under the festival tree.

**"Leaving Mrs. March and her daughters under the festival tree."—Page**

"I don't think I ever ought to call myself 'Unlucky Jo' again, when my greatest wish has been so beautifully gratified," said Mrs. Bhaer, taking Teddy's little fist out of the milk-pitcher, in which he was rapturously churning.

"And yet your life is very different from the one you pictured so long ago. Do you remember our castles in the air?" asked Amy, smiling as she watched Laurie and John playing cricket with the boys.

"Dear fellows! It does my heart good to see them forget business, and frolic for a day," answered Jo, who now spoke in a maternal way of all mankind. "Yes, I remember; but the life I wanted then seems selfish, lonely, and cold to me now. I haven't given up the hope that I may write a good book yet, but I can wait, and I'm sure it will be all the better for such experiences and illustrations as these;" and Jo pointed from the lively lads in the distance to her father, leaning on the Professor's arm, as they walked to and fro in the sunshine, deep in one of the conversations which both enjoyed so much, and then to her mother, sitting enthroned among her daughters, with their children in her lap and at her feet, as if all found help and happiness in the face which never could grow old to them.

"My castle was the most nearly realized of all. I asked for splendid things, to be sure, but in my heart I knew I should be satisfied, if I had a little home, and John, and some dear children like these. I've got them all, thank God, and am the happiest woman in the world;" and Meg laid her hand on her tall boy's head, with a face full of tender and devout content.

"My castle is very different from what I planned, but I would not alter it, though, like Jo, I don't relinquish all my artistic hopes, or confine myself to helping others fulfil their dreams of beauty. I've begun to model a figure of baby, and Laurie says it is the best thing I've ever done. I think so myself, and mean to do it in marble, so that, whatever happens, I may at least keep the image of my little angel."

As Amy spoke, a great tear dropped on the golden hair of the sleeping child in her arms; for her one well-beloved daughter was a frail little creature and the dread of losing her was the shadow over Amy's sunshine. This cross was doing much for both father and mother, for one love and sorrow bound them closely together. Amy's nature was growing sweeter, deeper, and more tender; Laurie was growing more serious, strong, and firm; and both were learning that beauty, youth, good fortune, even love itself, cannot keep care and pain, loss and sorrow, from the most blest; for—

"Into each life some rain must fall,
Some days must be dark and sad and dreary."

"She is growing better, I am sure of it, my dear. Don't despond, but hope and keep happy," said Mrs. March, as tender-hearted Daisy stooped from her knee, to lay her rosy cheek against her little cousin's pale one.

"I never ought to, while I have you to cheer me up, Marmee, and Laurie to take more than half of every burden," replied Amy warmly. "He never lets me see his anxiety, but is so sweet and patient with me, so devoted to Beth, and such a stay and comfort to me always, that I can't love him enough. So, in spite of my one cross, I can say with Meg, 'Thank God, I'm a happy woman.'"

"There's no need for me to say it, for every one can see that I'm far happier than I deserve," added Jo, glancing from her good husband to her chubby children, tumbling on the grass beside her. "Fritz is getting gray and stout; I'm growing as thin as a shadow, and am thirty; we never shall be rich, and Plumfield may burn up any night, for that incorrigible Tommy Bangs *will* smoke sweet-fern cigars under the bed-clothes, though he's set himself afire three times already. But in spite of these unromantic facts, I have nothing to complain of, and never was so jolly in my life. Excuse the remark, but living among boys, I can't help using their expressions now and then."

"Yes, Jo, I think your harvest will be a good one," began Mrs. March, frightening away a big black cricket that was staring Teddy out of countenance.

"Not half so good as yours, mother. Here it is, and we never can thank you enough for the patient sowing and reaping you have done," cried Jo, with the loving impetuosity which she never could outgrow.

"I hope there will be more wheat and fewer tares every year," said Amy softly. large sheaf, but I know there's room in your heart for it, Marmee dear," added Meg's tender voice.

Touched to the heart, Mrs. March could only stretch out her arms, as if to gather children and grandchildren to herself, and say, with face and voice full of motherly love, gratitude, and humility,—

"O, my girls, however long you may live, I never can wish you a greater happiness than this!"

# BOOK THREE

# LITTLE MEN

With Illustrations Reginald Birch

# CHAPTER I. NAT

"Please, sir, is this Plumfield?" asked a ragged boy of the man who opened the great gate at which the omnibus left him.

"Yes. Who sent you?"

"Mr. Laurence. I have got a letter for the lady."

"All right; go up to the house, and give it to her; she'll see to you, little chap."

The man spoke pleasantly, and the boy went on, feeling much cheered by the words. Through the soft spring rain that fell on sprouting grass and budding trees, Nat saw a large square house before him a hospitable-looking house, with an old-fashioned porch, wide steps, and lights shining in many windows. Neither curtains nor shutters hid the cheerful glimmer; and, pausing a moment before he rang, Nat saw many little shadows dancing on the walls, heard the pleasant hum of young voices, and felt that it was hardly possible that the light and warmth and comfort within could be for a homeless "little chap" like him.

"I hope the lady will see to me," he thought, and gave a timid rap with the great bronze knocker, which was a jovial griffin's head.

A rosy-faced servant-maid opened the door, and smiled as she took the letter which he silently offered. She seemed used to receiving strange boys, for she pointed to a seat in the hall, and said, with a nod:

"Sit there and drip on the mat a bit, while I take this in to missis."

Nat found plenty to amuse him while he waited, and stared about him curiously, enjoying the view, yet glad to do so unobserved in the dusky recess by the door.

The house seemed swarming with boys, who were beguiling the rainy twilight with all sorts of amusements. There were boys everywhere, "up-stairs and down-stairs and in the lady's chamber," apparently, for various open doors showed pleasant groups of big boys, little boys, and middle-sized boys in all stages of evening relaxation, not to say effervescence. Two large rooms on the right were evidently schoolrooms, for desks, maps, blackboards, and books were scattered about. An open fire burned on the hearth, and several indolent lads lay on their backs before it, discussing a new cricket-ground, with such animation that their boots waved in the air. A tall youth was practising on the flute in one corner, quite undisturbed by the racket all about him. Two or three others were jumping over the desks, pausing, now and then, to get their breath and laugh at the droll sketches of a little wag who was caricaturing the whole household on a blackboard.

In the room on the left a long supper-table was seen, set forth with great pitchers of new milk, piles of brown and white bread, and perfect stacks of the shiny gingerbread so dear to boyish souls. A flavor of toast was in the air, also suggestions of baked apples, very tantalizing to one hungry little nose and stomach.

The hall, however, presented the most inviting prospect of all, for a brisk game of tag was going on in the upper entry. One landing was devoted to marbles, the other to checkers, while the stairs were occupied by a boy reading, a girl singing a lullaby to her doll, two puppies, a kitten, and a constant succession of small boys sliding down the banisters, to the great detriment of their clothes and danger to their limbs.

So absorbed did Nat become in this exciting race, that he ventured farther and farther out of his corner; and when one very lively boy came down so swiftly that he could not stop himself, but fell off the banisters, with a crash that would have broken any head but one rendered nearly as hard as a cannon-ball by eleven years of constant bumping, Nat forgot himself, and ran up to the fallen rider, expecting to find him half-dead. The boy, however, only winked rapidly for a second, then lay calmly looking up at the new face with a surprised, "Hullo!"

"Hullo!" returned Nat, not knowing what else to say, and thinking that form of reply both brief and easy.

"Are you a new boy?" asked the recumbent youth, without stirring.

"Don't know yet."

"What's your name?"

"Nat Blake."

"Mine's Tommy Bangs. Come up and have a go, will you?" and Tommy got upon his legs like one suddenly remembering the duties of hospitality.

"Guess I won't, till I see whether I'm going to stay or not," returned Nat, feeling the desire to stay increase every moment.

"I say, Demi, here's a new one. Come and see to him;" and the lively Thomas returned to his sport with unabated relish.

At his call, the boy reading on the stairs looked up with a pair of big brown eyes, and after an instant's pause, as if a little shy, he put the book under his arm, and came soberly down to greet the new-comer, who found something very attractive in the pleasant face of this slender, mild-eyed boy.

"Have you seen Aunt Jo?" he asked, as if that was some sort of important ceremony.

"I haven't seen anybody yet but you boys; I'm waiting," answered Nat.

"Did Uncle Laurie send you?" proceeded Demi, politely, but gravely.

"Mr. Laurence did."

"He is Uncle Laurie; and he always sends nice boys."

Nat looked gratified at the remark, and smiled, in a way that made his thin face very pleasant. He did not know what to say next, so the two stood staring at one another in friendly silence, till the little girl came up with her doll in her arms. She was very like Demi, only not so tall, and had a rounder, rosier face, and blue eyes.

"This is my sister, Daisy," announced Demi, as if presenting a rare and precious creature.

The children nodded to one another; and the little girl's face dimpled with pleasure, as she said affably:

"I hope you'll stay. We have such good times here; don't we, Demi?"

"Of course, we do: that's what Aunt Jo has Plumfield for."

"It seems a very nice place indeed," observed Nat, feeling that he must respond to these amiable young persons.

"It's the nicest place in the world, isn't it, Demi?" said Daisy, who evidently regarded her brother as authority on all subjects.

"No, I think Greenland, where the icebergs and seals are, is more interesting. But I'm fond of Plumfield, and it is a very nice place to be in," returned Demi, who was interested just now in a book on Greenland. He was about to offer to show Nat the pictures and explain them, when the servant returned, saying with a nod toward the parlor-door:

"All right; you are to stop."

"I'm glad; now come to Aunt Jo." And Daisy took him by the hand with a pretty protecting air, which made Nat feel at home at once.

Demi returned to his beloved book, while his sister led the new-comer into a back room, where a stout gentleman was frolicking with two little boys on the sofa, and a thin lady was just finishing the letter which she seemed to have been re-reading.

"Here he is, aunty!" cried Daisy.

"So this is my new boy? I am glad to see you, my dear, and hope you'll be happy here," said the lady, drawing him to her, and stroking back the hair from his forehead with a kind hand and a motherly look, which made Nat's lonely little heart yearn toward her.

She was not at all handsome, but she had a merry sort of face that never seemed to have forgotten certain childish ways and looks, any more than her voice and manner had; and these things, hard to describe but very plain to see and feel, made her a genial, comfortable kind of person, easy to get on with, and generally "jolly," as boys would say. She saw the little tremble of Nat's lips as she smoothed his hair, and her keen eyes grew softer, but she only drew the shabby figure nearer and said, laughing:

"I am Mother Bhaer, that gentleman is Father Bhaer, and these are the two little Bhaers. Come here, boys, and see Nat."

The three wrestlers obeyed at once; and the stout man, with a chubby child on each shoulder, came up to welcome the new boy. Rob and Teddy merely grinned at him, but Mr. Bhaer shook hands, and pointing to a low chair near the fire, said, in a cordial voice:

"There is a place all ready for thee, my son; sit down and dry thy wet feet at once."

"Wet? So they are! My dear, off with your shoes this minute, and I'll have some dry things ready for you in a jiffy," cried Mrs. Bhaer, bustling about so energetically that Nat found himself in the cosy little chair, with dry socks and warm slippers on his feet, before he would have had time to say Jack Robinson, if he had wanted to try. He said "Thank you, ma'am," instead; and said it so gratefully that Mrs. Bhaer's eyes grew soft again, and she said something merry, because she felt so tender, which was a way she had.

"There are Tommy Bangs' slippers; but he never will remember to put them on in the house; so he shall not have them. They are too big; but that's all the better; you can't run away from us so fast as if they fitted."

"I don't want to run away, ma'am." And Nat spread his grimy little hands before the comfortable blaze, with a long sigh of satisfaction.

"That's good! Now I am going to toast you well, and try to get rid of that ugly cough. How long have you had it, dear?" asked Mrs. Bhaer, as she rummaged in her big basket for a strip of flannel.

"All winter. I got cold, and it wouldn't get better, somehow."

"No wonder, living in that damp cellar with hardly a rag to his poor dear back!" said Mrs. Bhaer, in a low tone to her husband, who was looking at the boy with a skillful pair of eyes that marked the thin temples and feverish lips, as well as the hoarse voice and frequent fits of coughing that shook the bent shoulders under the patched jacket.

"Robin, my man, trot up to Nursey, and tell her to give thee the cough-bottle and the liniment," said Mr. Bhaer, after his eyes had exchanged telegrams with his wife's.

Nat looked a little anxious at the preparations, but forgot his fears in a hearty laugh, when Mrs. Bhaer whispered to him, with a droll look:

"Hear my rogue Teddy try to cough. The syrup I'm going to give you has honey in it; and he wants some."

Little Ted was red in the face with his exertions by the time the bottle came, and was allowed to suck the spoon after Nat had manfully taken a dose and had the bit of flannel put about his throat.

These first steps toward a cure were hardly completed when a great bell rang, and a loud tramping through the hall announced supper. Bashful Nat quaked at the thought of meeting many strange boys, but Mrs. Bhaer held out her hand to him, and Rob said, patronizingly, "Don't be 'fraid; I'll take care of you."

Twelve boys, six on a side, stood behind their chairs, prancing with impatience to begin, while the tall flute-playing youth was trying to curb their ardor. But no one sat down till Mrs. Bhaer was in her place behind the teapot, with Teddy on her left, and Nat on her right.

"This is our new boy, Nat Blake. After supper you can say how do you do? Gently, boys, gently."

As she spoke every one stared at Nat, and then whisked into their seats, trying to be orderly and failing utterly. The Bhaers did their best to have the lads behave well at meal times, and generally succeeded pretty well, for their rules were few and sensible, and the boys, knowing that they tried to make things easy and happy, did their best to obey. But there are times when hungry boys cannot be repressed without real cruelty, and Saturday evening, after a half-holiday, was one of those times.

"Dear little souls, do let them have one day in which they can howl and racket and frolic to their hearts' content. A holiday isn't a holiday without plenty of freedom and fun; and they shall have full swing once a week," Mrs. Bhaer used to say, when prim people wondered why banister-sliding, pillow-fights, and all manner of jovial games were allowed under the once decorous roof of Plumfield.

It did seem at times as if the aforesaid roof was in danger of flying off, but it never did, for a word from Father Bhaer could at any time produce a lull, and the lads had learned that liberty must not be abused. So, in spite of many dark predictions, the school flourished, and manners and morals were insinuated, without the pupils exactly knowing how it was done.

Nat found himself very well off behind the tall pitchers, with Tommy Bangs just around the corner, and Mrs. Bhaer close by to fill up plate and mug as fast as he could empty them.

"Who is that boy next the girl down at the other end?" whispered Nat to his young neighbor under cover of a general laugh.

"That's Demi Brooke. Mr. Bhaer is his uncle."

"What a queer name!"

"His real name is John, but they call him Demi-John, because his father is John too. That's a joke, don't you see?" said Tommy, kindly explaining. Nat did not see, but politely smiled, and asked, with interest:

"Isn't he a very nice boy?"

"I bet you he is; knows lots and reads like any thing."

"Who is the fat one next him?"

"Oh, that's Stuffy Cole. His name is George, but we call him Stuffy 'cause he eats so much. The little fellow next Father Bhaer is his boy Rob, and then there's big Franz his nephew; he teaches some, and kind of sees to us."

"He plays the flute, doesn't he?" asked Nat as Tommy rendered himself speechless by putting a whole baked apple into his mouth at one blow.

Tommy nodded, and said, sooner than one would have imagined possible under the circumstances, "Oh, don't he, though? And we dance sometimes, and do gymnastics to music. I like a drum myself, and mean to learn as soon as ever I can."

"I like a fiddle best; I can play one too," said Nat, getting confidential on this attractive subject.

"Can you?" and Tommy stared over the rim of his mug with round eyes, full of interest. "Mr. Bhaer's got an old fiddle, and he'll let you play on it if you want to."

"Could I? Oh, I would like it ever so much. You see, I used to go round fiddling with my father, and another man, till he died."

"Wasn't that fun?" cried Tommy, much impressed.

"No, it was horrid; so cold in winter, and hot in summer. And I got tired; and they were cross sometimes; and I didn't get enough to eat." Nat paused to take a generous bite of gingerbread, as if to assure himself that the hard times were over; and then he added regretfully: "But I did love my little fiddle, and I miss it. Nicolo took it away when father died, and wouldn't have me any longer, 'cause I was sick."

"You'll belong to the band if you play good. See if you don't."

"Do you have a band here?" Nat's eyes sparkled.

"Guess we do; a jolly band, all boys; and they have concerts and things. You just see what happens to-morrow night."

After this pleasantly exciting remark, Tommy returned to his supper, and Nat sank into a blissful reverie over his full plate.

Mrs. Bhaer had heard all they said, while apparently absorbed in filling mugs, and overseeing little Ted, who was so sleepy that he put his spoon in his eye, nodded like a rosy poppy, and finally fell fast asleep, with his cheek pillowed on a soft bun. Mrs. Bhaer had put Nat next to Tommy, because that roly-poly boy had a frank and social way with him, very attractive to shy persons. Nat felt this, and had made several small confidences during supper, which gave Mrs. Bhaer the key to the new boy's character, better than if she had talked to him herself.

In the letter which Mr. Laurence had sent with Nat, he had said:

"DEAR JO: Here is a case after your own heart. This poor lad is an orphan now, sick and friendless. He has been a street-musician; and I found him in a cellar, mourning for his dead father, and his lost violin. I think there is something in him, and have a fancy that between us we may give this little man a lift. You cure his overtasked body, Fritz help his neglected mind, and when he is ready I'll see if he is a genius or only a boy with a talent which may earn his bread for him. Give him a trial, for the sake of your own boy,

"TEDDY."

"Of course we will!" cried Mrs. Bhaer, as she read the letter; and when she saw Nat she felt at once that, whether he was a genius or not, here was a lonely, sick boy who needed just what she loved to give, a home and motherly care. Both she and Mr. Bhaer observed him quietly; and in spite of ragged clothes, awkward manners, and a dirty face, they saw much about Nat that pleased them. He was a thin, pale boy, of twelve, with blue eyes, and a good forehead under the rough, neglected hair; an anxious, scared face, at times, as if he expected hard words, or blows; and a sensitive mouth that trembled when a kind glance fell on him; while a gentle speech called up a look of gratitude, very sweet to see. "Bless the poor dear, he shall fiddle all day long if he likes," said Mrs. Bhaer to herself, as she saw the eager, happy expression on his face when Tommy talked of the band.

So, after supper, when the lads flocked into the schoolroom for more "high jinks," Mrs. Jo appeared with a violin in her hand, and after a word with her husband, went to Nat, who sat in a corner watching the scene with intense interest.

"Now, my lad, give us a little tune. We want a violin in our band, and I think you will do it nicely."

She expected that he would hesitate; but he seized the old fiddle at once, and handled it with such loving care, it was plain to see that music was his passion.

"I'll do the best I can, ma'am," was all he said; and then drew the bow across the strings, as if eager to hear the dear notes again.

There was a great clatter in the room, but as if deaf to any sounds but those he made, Nat played softly to himself, forgetting every thing in his delight. It was only a simple Negro melody, such as street-musicians play, but it caught the ears of the boys at once, and silenced them, till they stood listening with surprise and pleasure. Gradually they got nearer and nearer, and Mr. Bhaer came up to watch the boy; for, as if he was in his element now, Nat played away and never minded any one, while his eyes shone, his cheeks reddened, and his thin fingers flew, as he hugged the old fiddle and made it speak to all their hearts the language that he loved.

A hearty round of applause rewarded him better than a shower of pennies, when he stopped and glanced about him, as if to say:

"I've done my best; please like it."

"I say, you do that first rate," cried Tommy, who considered Nat his protege.

"You shall be the first fiddle in my band," added Franz, with an approving smile.

Mrs. Bhaer whispered to her husband:

"Teddy is right: there's something in the child." And Mr. Bhaer nodded his head emphatically, as he clapped Nat on the shoulder, saying, heartily:

"You play well, my son. Come now and play something which we can sing."

It was the proudest, happiest minute of the poor boy's life when he was led to the place of honor by the piano, and the lads gathered round, never heeding his poor clothes, but eying him respectfully and waiting eagerly to hear him play again.

They chose a song he knew; and after one or two false starts they got going, and violin, flute, and piano led a chorus of boyish voices that made the old roof ring again. It was too much for Nat, more feeble than he knew; and as the final shout died away, his face began to work, he dropped the fiddle, and turning to the wall sobbed like a little child.

"My dear, what is it?" asked Mrs. Bhaer, who had been singing with all her might, and trying to keep little Rob from beating time with his boots.

"You are all so kind and it's so beautiful I can't help it," sobbed Nat, coughing till he was breathless.

"Come with me, dear; you must go to bed and rest; you are worn out, and this is too noisy a place for you," whispered Mrs. Bhaer; and took him away to her own parlor, where she let him cry himself quiet.

Then she won him to tell her all his troubles, and listened to the little story with tears in her own eyes, though it was not a new one to her.

"My child, you have got a father and a mother now, and this is home. Don't think of those sad times any more, but get well and happy; and be sure you shall never suffer again, if we can help it. This place is made for all sorts of boys to have a good time in, and to learn how to help themselves and be useful men, I hope. You shall have as much music as you want, only you must get strong first. Now come up to Nursey and have a bath, and then go to bed, and to-morrow we will lay some nice little plans together."

Nat held her hand fast in his, but had not a word to say, and let his grateful eyes speak for him, as Mrs. Bhaer led him up to a big room, where they found a stout German woman with a face so round and cheery that it looked like a sort of sun, with the wide frill of her cap for rays.

"This is Nursey Hummel, and she will give you a nice bath, and cut your hair, and make you all 'comfy,' as Rob says. That's the bath-room in there; and on Saturday nights we scrub all the little lads first, and pack them away in bed before the big ones get through singing. Now then, Rob, in with you."

As she talked, Mrs. Bhaer had whipped off Rob's clothes and popped him into a long bath-tub in the little room opening into the nursery.

There were two tubs, besides foot-baths, basins, douche-pipes, and all manner of contrivances for cleanliness. Nat was soon luxuriating in the other bath; and while simmering there, he watched the performances of the two women, who scrubbed, clean night-gowned, and bundled into bed four or five small boys, who, of course, cut up all sorts of capers during the operation, and kept every one in a gale of merriment till they were extinguished in their beds.

By the time Nat was washed and done up in a blanket by the fire, while Nursey cut his hair, a new detachment of boys arrived and were shut into the bath-room, where they made as much splashing and noise as a school of young whales at play.

"Nat had better sleep here, so that if his cough troubles him in the night you can see that he takes a good draught of flax-seed tea," said Mrs. Bhaer, who was flying about like a distracted hen with a large brood of lively ducklings.

Nursey approved the plan, finished Nat off with a flannel night-gown, a drink of something warm and sweet, and then tucked him into one of the three little beds standing in the room, where he lay looking like a contented mummy and feeling that nothing more in the way of luxury could be offered him. Cleanliness in itself was a new and delightful sensation; flannel gowns were unknown comforts in his world; sips of "good stuff" soothed his cough as pleasantly as kind words did his lonely heart; and the feeling that somebody cared for him made that plain room seem a sort of heaven to the homeless child. It was like a cosy dream; and he often shut his eyes to see if it would not vanish when he opened them again. It was too pleasant to let him sleep, and he could not have done so if he had tried, for in a few minutes one of the peculiar institutions of Plumfield was revealed to his astonished but appreciative eyes.

A momentary lull in the aquatic exercises was followed by the sudden appearance of pillows flying in all directions, hurled by white goblins, who came rioting out of their beds. The battle raged in several rooms, all down the upper hall, and even surged at intervals into the nursery, when some hard-pressed warrior took refuge there. No one seemed to mind this explosion in the least; no one forbade it, or even looked surprised. Nursey went on hanging up towels, and Mrs. Bhaer laid out clean clothes, as calmly as if the most perfect order reigned. Nay, she even chased one daring boy out of the room, and fired after him the pillow he had slyly thrown at her.

"Won't they hurt 'em?" asked Nat, who lay laughing with all his might.

"Oh dear, no! We always allow one pillow-fight Saturday night. The cases are changed to-morrow; and it gets up a glow after the boys' baths; so I rather like it myself," said Mrs. Bhaer, busy again among her dozen pairs of socks.

"What a very nice school this is!" observed Nat, in a burst of admiration.

"It's an odd one," laughed Mrs. Bhaer, "but you see we don't believe in making children miserable by too many rules, and too much study. I forbade night-gown parties at first; but, bless you, it was of no use. I could no more keep those boys in their beds than so many jacks in the box. So I made an agreement with them: I was to allow a fifteen-minute pillow-fight every Saturday night; and they promised to go properly to bed every other night. I tried it, and it worked well. If they don't keep their word, no frolic; if they do, I just turn the glasses round, put the lamps in safe places, and let them rampage as much as they like."

"It's a beautiful plan," said Nat, feeling that he should like to join in the fray, but not venturing to propose it the first night. So he lay enjoying the spectacle, which certainly was a lively one.

Tommy Bangs led the assailing party, and Demi defended his own room with a dogged courage fine to see, collecting pillows behind him as fast as they were thrown, till the besiegers were out of ammunition, when they would charge upon him in a body, and recover their arms. A few slight accidents occurred, but nobody minded, and gave and took sounding thwacks with perfect good humor, while pillows flew like big snowflakes, till Mrs. Bhaer looked at her watch, and called out:

"Time is up, boys. Into bed, every man jack, or pay the forfeit!"

"What is the forfeit?" asked Nat, sitting up in his eagerness to know what happened to those wretches who disobeyed this most peculiar, but public-spirited school-ma'am.

"Lose their fun next time," answered Mrs. Bhaer. "I give them five minutes to settle down, then put out the lights, and expect order. They are honorable lads, and they keep their word."

That was evident, for the battle ended as abruptly as it began a parting shot or two, a final cheer, as Demi fired the seventh pillow at the retiring foe, a few challenges for next time, then order prevailed. And nothing but an occasional giggle or a suppressed whisper broke the quiet which followed the Saturday-night frolic, as Mother Bhaer kissed her new boy and left him to happy dreams of life at Plumfield.

## CHAPTER II. THE BOYS

While Nat takes a good long sleep, I will tell my little readers something about the boys, among whom he found himself when he woke up.

To begin with our old friends. Franz was a tall lad, of sixteen now, a regular German, big, blond, and bookish, also very domestic, amiable, and musical. His uncle was fitting him for college, and his aunt for a happy home of his own hereafter, because she carefully fostered in him gentle manners, love of children, respect for women, old and young, and helpful ways about the house. He was her right-hand man on all occasions, steady, kind, and patient; and he loved his merry aunt like a mother, for such she had tried to be to him.

Emil was quite different, being quick-tempered, restless, and enterprising, bent on going to sea, for the blood of the old vikings stirred in his veins, and could not be tamed. His uncle promised that he should go when he was sixteen, and set him to studying navigation, gave him stories of good and famous admirals and heroes to read, and let him lead the life of a frog in river, pond, and brook, when lessons were done. His room looked like the cabin of a man-of-war, for every thing was nautical, military, and shipshape. Captain Kyd was his delight, and his favorite amusement was to rig up like that piratical gentleman, and roar out sanguinary sea-songs at the top of his voice. He would dance nothing but sailors' hornpipes, rolled in his gait, and was as nautical in conversation to his uncle would permit. The boys called him "Commodore," and took great pride in his fleet, which whitened the pond and suffered disasters that would have daunted any commander but a sea-struck boy.

Demi was one of the children who show plainly the effect of intelligent love and care, for soul and body worked harmoniously together. The natural refinement which nothing but home influence can teach, gave him sweet and simple manners: his mother had cherished an innocent and loving heart in him; his father had watched over the physical growth of his boy, and kept the little body straight and strong on wholesome food and exercise and sleep, while Grandpa March cultivated the little mind with the tender wisdom of a modern Pythagoras, not tasking it with long, hard lessons, parrot-learned, but helping it to unfold as naturally and beautifully as sun and dew help roses bloom. He was not a perfect child, by any means, but his faults were of the better sort; and being early taught the secret of self-control, he was not left at the mercy of appetites and passions, as some poor little mortals are, and then punished for yielding to the temptations against which they have no armor. A quiet, quaint boy was Demi, serious, yet cheery, quite unconscious that he was unusually bright and beautiful, yet quick to see and love intelligence or beauty in other children. Very fond of books, and full of lively fancies, born of a strong imagination and a spiritual nature, these traits made his parents anxious to balance them with useful knowledge and healthful society, lest they should make him one of those pale precocious children who amaze and delight a family sometimes, and fade away like hot-house flowers, because the young soul blooms too soon, and has not a hearty body to root it firmly in the wholesome soil of this world.

So Demi was transplanted to Plumfield, and took so kindly to the life there, that Meg and John and Grandpa felt satisfied that they had done well. Mixing with other boys brought out the practical side of him, roused his spirit, and brushed away the pretty cobwebs he was so fond of spinning in that little brain of his. To be sure, he rather shocked his mother when he came home, by banging doors, saying "by George" emphatically, and demanding tall thick boots "that clumped like papa's." But John rejoiced over him, laughed at his explosive remarks, got the boots, and said contentedly,

"He is doing well; so let him clump. I want my son to be a manly boy, and this temporary roughness won't hurt him. We can polish him up by and by; and as for learning, he will pick that up as pigeons do peas. So don't hurry him."

Daisy was as sunshiny and charming as ever, with all sorts of womanlinesses budding in her, for she was like her gentle mother, and delighted in domestic things. She had a family of dolls, whom she brought up in the most exemplary manner; she could not get on without her little work-basket and bits of sewing, which she did so nicely, that Demi frequently pulled out his handkerchief display her neat stitches, and Baby Josy had a flannel petticoat beautifully made by Sister Daisy. She like to quiddle about the china-closet, prepare the salt-cellars, put the spoons straight on the table; and every day went round the parlor with her brush, dusting chairs and tables. Demi called her a "Betty," but was very glad to have her keep his things in order, lend him her nimble fingers in all sorts of work, and help him with his lessons, for they kept abreast there, and had no thought of rivalry.

The love between them was as strong as ever; and no one could laugh Demi out of his affectionate ways with Daisy. He fought her battles valiantly, and never could understand why boys should be ashamed to say "right out," that they loved their sisters. Daisy adored her twin, thought "my brother" the most remarkable boy in the world, and every morning, in her little wrapper, trotted to tap at his door with a motherly "Get up, my dear, it's 'most breakfast time; and here's your clean collar."

Rob was an energetic morsel of a boy, who seemed to have discovered the secret of perpetual motion, for he never was still. Fortunately, he was not mischievous, nor very brave; so he kept out of trouble pretty well, and vibrated between father and mother like an affectionate little pendulum with a lively tick, for Rob was a chatterbox.

Teddy was too young to play a very important part in the affairs of Plumfield, yet he had his little sphere, and filled it beautifully. Every one felt the need of a pet at times, and Baby was always ready to accommodate, for kissing and cuddling suited him excellently. Mrs. Jo seldom stirred without him; so he had his little finger in all the domestic pies, and every one found them all the better for it, for they believed in babies at Plumfield.

Dick Brown, and Adolphus or Dolly Pettingill, were two eight year-olds. Dolly stuttered badly, but was gradually getting over it, for no one was allowed to mock him and Mr. Bhaer tried to cure it, by making him talk slowly. Dolly was a good little lad, quite uninteresting and ordinary, but he flourished here, and went through his daily duties and pleasures with placid content and propriety.

Dick Brown's affliction was a crooked back, yet he bore his burden so cheerfully, that Demi once asked in his queer way, "Do humps make people good-natured? I'd like one if they do." Dick was always merry, and did his best to be like other boys, for a plucky spirit lived in the feeble little body. When he first came, he was very sensitive about his misfortune, but soon learned to forget it, for no one dared remind him of it, after Mr. Bhaer had punished one boy for laughing at him.

"God don't care; for my soul is straight if my back isn't," sobbed Dick to his tormentor on that occasion; and, by cherishing this idea, the Bhaers soon led him to believe that people also loved his soul, and did not mind his body, except to pity and help him to bear it.

Playing menagerie once with the others, some one said,

"What animal will you be, Dick?"

"Oh, I'm the dromedary; don't you see the hump on my back?" was the laughing answer.

"So you are, my nice little one that don't carry loads, but marches by the elephant first in the procession," said Demi, who was arranging the spectacle.

"I hope others will be as kind to the poor dear as my boys have learned to be," said Mrs. Jo, quite satisfied with the success of her teaching, as Dick ambled past her, looking like a very happy, but a very feeble little dromedary, beside stout Stuffy, who did the elephant with ponderous propriety.

Jack Ford was a sharp, rather a sly lad, who was sent to this school, because it was cheap. Many men would have thought him a smart boy, but Mr. Bhaer did not like his way of illustrating that Yankee word, and thought his unboyish keenness and money-loving as much of an affliction as Dolly's stutter, or Dick's hump.

Ned Barker was like a thousand other boys of fourteen, all legs, blunder, and bluster. Indeed the family called him the "Blunderbuss," and always expected to see him tumble over the chairs, bump against the tables, and knock down any small articles near him. He bragged a good deal about what he could do, but seldom did any thing to prove it, was not brave, and a little given to tale-telling. He was apt to bully the small boys, and flatter the big ones, and without being at all bad, was just the sort of fellow who could very easily be led astray.

George Cole had been spoilt by an over-indulgent mother, who stuffed him with sweetmeats till he was sick, and then thought him too delicate to study, so that at twelve years old, he was a pale, puffy boy, dull, fretful, and lazy. A friend persuaded her to send him to Plumfield, and there he soon got waked up, for sweet things were seldom allowed, much exercise required, and study made so pleasant, that Stuffy was gently lured along, till he quite amazed his anxious mamma by his improvement, and convinced her that there was really something remarkable in Plumfield air.

Billy Ward was what the Scotch tenderly call an "innocent," for though thirteen years old, he was like a child of six. He had been an unusually intelligent boy, and his father had hurried him on too fast, giving him all sorts of hard lessons, keeping at his books six hours a day, and expecting him to absorb knowledge as a Strasburg goose does the food crammed down its throat. He thought he was doing his duty, but he nearly killed the boy, for a fever gave the poor child a sad holiday, and when he recovered, the overtasked brain gave out, and Billy's mind was like a slate over which a sponge has passed, leaving it blank.

It was a terrible lesson to his ambitious father; he could not bear the sight of his promising child, changed to a feeble idiot, and he sent him away to Plumfield, scarcely hoping that he could be helped, but sure that he would be kindly treated. Quite docile and harmless was Billy, and it was pitiful to see how hard he tried to learn, as if groping dimly after the lost knowledge which had cost him so much.

Day after day, he pored over the alphabet, proudly said A and B, and thought that he knew them, but on the morrow they were gone, and all the work was to be done over again. Mr. Bhaer had infinite patience with him, and kept on in spite of the apparent hopelessness of the task, not caring for book lessons, but trying gently to clear away the mists from the darkened mind, and give it back intelligence enough to make the boy less a burden and an affliction.

Mrs. Bhaer strengthened his health by every aid she could invent, and the boys all pitied and were kind to him. He did not like their active plays, but would sit for hours watching the doves, would dig holes for Teddy till even that ardent grubber was satisfied, or follow Silas, the man, from place to place seeing him work, for honest Si was very good to him, and though he forgot his letters Billy remembered friendly faces.

Tommy Bangs was the scapegrace of the school, and the most trying scapegrace that ever lived. As full of mischief as a monkey, yet so good-hearted that one could not help forgiving his tricks; so scatter-brained that words went by him like the wind, yet so penitent for every misdeed, that it was impossible to keep sober when he vowed tremendous vows of reformation, or proposed all sorts of queer punishments to be inflicted upon himself. Mr. and Mrs. Bhaer lived in a state of preparation for any mishap, from the breaking of Tommy's own neck, to the blowing up of the entire family with gunpowder; and Nursey had a particular drawer in which she kept bandages, plasters, and salves for his especial use, for Tommy was always being brought in half dead; but nothing ever killed him, and he arose from every downfall with redoubled vigor.

The first day he came, he chopped the top off one finger in the hay-cutter, and during the week, fell from the shed roof, was chased by an angry hen who tried to pick his out because he examined her chickens, got run away with, and had his ears boxed violent by Asia, who caught him luxuriously skimming a pan of cream with half a stolen pie. Undaunted, however, by any failures or rebuffs, this indomitable youth went on amusing himself with all sorts of tricks till no one felt safe. If he did not know his lessons, he always had some droll excuse to offer, and as he was usually clever at his books, and as bright as a button in composing answers when he did not know them, he go on pretty well at school. But out of school, Ye gods and little fishes! how Tommy did carouse!

He wound fat Asia up in her own clothes line against the post, and left here there to fume and scold for half an hour one busy Monday morning. He dropped a hot cent down Mary Ann's back as that pretty maid was waiting at table one day when there were gentlemen to dinner, whereat the poor girl upset the soup and rushed out of the room in dismay, leaving the family to think that she had gone mad. He fixed a pail of water up in a tree, with a bit of ribbon fastened to the handle, and when Daisy, attracted by the gay streamer, tried to pull it down, she got a douche bath that spoiled her clean frock and hurt her little feelings very much. He put rough white pebbles in the sugar-bowl when his grandmother came to tea, and the poor old lady wondered why they didn't melt in her cup, but was too polite to say anything. He passed around snuff in church so that five of the boys sneezed with such violence they had to go out. He dug paths in winter time, and then privately watered them so that people should tumble down. He drove poor Silas nearly wild by hanging his big boots in conspicuous places, for his feet were enormous, and he was very much ashamed of them. He persuaded confiding little Dolly to tie a thread to one of his loose teeth, and leave the string hanging from his mouth when he went to sleep, so that Tommy could pull it out without his feeling the dreaded operation. But the tooth wouldn't come at the first tweak, and poor Dolly woke up in great anguish of spirit, and lost all faith in Tommy from that day forth.

The last prank had been to give the hens bread soaked in rum, which made them tipsy and scandalized all the other fowls, for the respectable old biddies went staggering about, pecking and clucking in the most maudlin manner, while the family were convulsed with laughter at their antics, till Daisy took pity on them and shut them up in the hen-house to sleep off their intoxication.

These were the boys and they lived together as happy as twelve lads could, studying and playing, working and squabbling, fighting faults and cultivating virtues in the good old-fashioned way. Boys at other schools probably learned more from books, but less of that better wisdom which makes good men. Latin, Greek, and mathematics were all very well, but in Professor Bhaer's opinion, self knowledge, self-help, and self-control were more important, and he tried to teach them carefully. People shook their heads sometimes at his ideas, even while they owned that the boys improved wonderfully in manners and morals. But then, as Mrs. Jo said to Nat, "it was an odd school."

## CHAPTER III. SUNDAY

The moment the bell rang next morning Nat flew out of bed, and dressed himself with great satisfaction in the suit of clothes he found on the chair. They were not new, being half-worn garments of one of the well-to-do boys; but Mrs. Bhaer kept all such cast-off feathers for the picked robins who strayed into her nest. They were hardly on when Tommy appeared in a high state of clean collar, and escorted Nat down to breakfast.

The sun was shining into the dining-room on the well-spread table, and the flock of hungry, hearty lads who gathered round it. Nat observed that they were much more orderly than they had been the night before, and every one stood silently behind his chair while little Rob, standing beside his father at the head of the table, folded his hands, reverently bent his curly head, and softly repeated a short grace in the devout German fashion, which Mr. Bhaer loved and taught his little son to honor. Then they all sat down to enjoy the Sunday-morning breakfast of coffee, steak, and baked potatoes, instead of the bread and milk fare with which they usually satisfied their young appetites. There was much pleasant talk while the knives and forks rattled briskly, for certain Sunday lessons were to be learned, the Sunday walk settled, and plans for the week discussed. As he listened, Nat thought it seemed as if this day must be a very pleasant one, for he loved quiet, and there was a cheerful sort of hush over every thing that pleased him very much; because, in spite of his rough life, the boy possessed the sensitive nerves which belong to a music-loving nature.

"Now, my lads, get your morning jobs done, and let me find you ready for church when the 'bus comes round," said Father Bhaer, and set the example by going into the school-room to get books ready for the morrow.

Every one scattered to his or her task, for each had some little daily duty, and was expected to perform it faithfully. Some brought wood and water, brushed the steps, or ran errands for Mrs. Bhaer. Others fed the pet animals, and did chores about the barn with Franz. Daisy washed the cups, and Demi wiped them, for the twins liked to work together, and Demi had been taught to make himself useful in the little house at home. Even Baby Teddy had his small job to do, and trotted to and fro, putting napkins away, and pushing chairs into their places. For half and hour the lads buzzed about like a hive of bees, then the 'bus drove round, Father Bhaer and Franz with the eight older boys piled in, and away they went for a three-mile drive to church in town.

Because of the troublesome cough Nat prefered to stay at home with the four small boys, and spent a happy morning in Mrs. Bhaer's room, listening to the stories she read them, learning the hymns she taught them, and then quietly employing himself pasting pictures into an old ledger.

"This is my Sunday closet," she said, showing him shelves filled with picture-books, paint-boxes, architectural blocks, little diaries, and materials for letter-writing. "I want my boys to love Sunday, to find it a peaceful, pleasant day, when they can rest from common study and play, yet enjoy quiet pleasures, and learn, in simple ways, lessons more important than any taught in school. Do you understand me?" she asked, watching Nat's attentive face.

"You mean to be good?" he said, after hesitating a minute.

"Yes; to be good, and to love to be good. It is hard work sometimes, I know very well; but we all help one another, and so we get on. This is one of the ways in which I try to help my boys," and she took down a thick book, which seemed half-full of writing, and opened at a page on which there was one word at the top.

"Why, that's my name!" cried Nat, looking both surprised and interested.

"Yes; I have a page for each boy. I keep a little account of how he gets on through the week, and Sunday night I show him the record. If it is bad I am sorry and disappointed, if it is good I am glad and proud; but, whichever it is, the boys know I want to help them, and they try to do their best for love of me and Father Bhaer."

"I should think they would," said Nat, catching a glimpse of Tommy's name opposite his own, and wondering what was written under it.

Mrs. Bhaer saw his eye on the words, and shook her head, saying, as she turned a leaf,

"No, I don't show my records to any but the one to whom each belongs. I call this my conscience book; and only you and I will ever know what is to be written on the page below your name. Whether you will be pleased or ashamed to read it next Sunday depends on yourself. I think it will be a good report; at any rate, I shall try to make things easy for you in this new place, and shall be quite contented if you keep our few rules, live happily with the boys, and learn something."

"I'll try ma'am;" and Nat's thin face flushed up with the earnestness of his desire to make Mrs. Bhaer "glad and proud," not "sorry and disappointed." "It must be a great deal of trouble to write about so many," he added, as she shut her book with an encouraging pat on the shoulder.

"Not to me, for I really don't know which I like best, writing or boys," she said, laughing to see Nat stare with astonishment at the last item. "Yes, I know many people think boys are a nuisance, but that is because they don't understand them. I do; and I never saw the boy yet whom I could not get on capitally with after I had once found the soft spot in his heart. Bless me, I couldn't get on at all without my flock of dear, noisy, naughty, harum-scarum little lads, could I, my Teddy?" and Mrs. Bhaer hugged the young rogue, just in time to save the big inkstand from going into his pocket.

Nat, who had never heard anything like this before, really did not know whether Mother Bhaer was a trifle crazy, or the most delightful woman he had ever met. He rather inclined to the latter opinion, in spite of her peculiar tastes, for she had a way of filling up a fellow's plate before he asked, of laughing at his jokes, gently tweaking him by the ear, or clapping him on the shoulder, that Nat found very engaging.

"Now, I think you would like to go into the school-room and practise some of the hymns we are to sing to-night," she said, rightly guessing the thing of all others that he wanted to do.

Alone with the beloved violin and the music-book propped up before him in the sunny window, while Spring beauty filled the world outside, and Sabbath silence reigned within, Nat enjoyed an hour or two of genuine happiness, learning the sweet old tunes, and forgetting the hard past in the cheerful present.

When the church-goers came back and dinner was over, every one read, wrote letters home, said their Sunday lessons, or talked quietly to one another, sitting here and there about the house. At three o'clock the entire family turned out to walk, for all the active young bodies must have exercise; and in these walks the active young minds were taught to see and love the providence of God in the beautiful miracles which Nature was working before their eyes. Mr. Bhaer always went with them, and in his simple, fatherly way, found for his flock, "Sermons in stones, books in the running brooks, and good in everything."

Mrs. Bhaer with Daisy and her own two boys drove into town, to pay the weekly visit to Grandma, which was busy Mother Bhaer's one holiday and greatest pleasure. Nat was not strong enough for the long walk, and asked to stay at home with Tommy, who kindly offered to do the honors of Plumfield. "You've seen the house, so come out and have a look at the garden, and the barn, and the menagerie," said Tommy, when they were left alone with Asia, to see that they didn't get into mischief; for, though Tommy was one of the best-meaning boys who ever adorned knickerbockers, accidents of the most direful nature were always happening to him, no one could exactly tell how.

"What is your menagerie?" asked Nat, as they trotted along the drive that encircled the house.

"We all have pets, you see, and we keep 'em in the corn-barn, and call it the menagerie. Here you are. Isn't my guinea-pig a beauty?" and Tommy proudly presented one of the ugliest specimens of that pleasing animal that Nat ever saw.

"I know a boy with a dozen of 'em, and he said he'd give me one, only I hadn't any place to keep it, so I couldn't have it. It was white, with black spots, a regular rouser, and maybe I could get it for you if you'd like it," said Nat, feeling it would be a delicate return for Tommy's attentions.

"I'd like it ever so much, and I'll give you this one, and they can live together if they don't fight. Those white mice are Rob's, Franz gave 'em to him. The rabbits are Ned's, and the bantams outside are Stuffy's. That box thing is Demi's turtle-tank, only he hasn't begun to get 'em yet. Last year he had sixty-two, whackers some of 'em. He stamped one of 'em with his name and the year, and let it go; and he says maybe he will find it ever so long after and know it. He read about a turtle being found that had a mark on it that showed it must be hundreds of years old. Demi's such a funny chap."

"What is in this box?" asked Nat, stopping before a large deep one, half-full of earth.

"Oh, that's Jack Ford's worm-shop. He digs heaps of 'em and keeps 'em here, and when we want any to go afishing with, we buy some of him. It saves lots of trouble, only he charged too much for 'em. Why, last time we traded I had to pay two cents a dozen, and then got little ones. Jack's mean sometimes, and I told him I'd dig for myself if he didn't lower his prices. Now, I own two hens, those gray ones with top knots, first-rate ones they are too, and I sell Mrs. Bhaer the eggs, but I never ask her more than twenty-five cents a dozen, never! I'd be ashamed to do it," cried Tommy, with a glance of scorn at the worm-shop.

"Who owns the dogs?" asked Nat, much interested in these commercial transactions, and feeling that T. Bangs was a man whom it would be a privilege and a pleasure to patronize.

"The big dog is Emil's. His name is Christopher Columbus. Mrs. Bhaer named him because she likes to say Christopher Columbus, and no one minds it if she means the dog," answered Tommy, in the tone of a show-man displaying his menagerie. "The white pup is Rob's, and the yellow one is Teddy's. A man was going to drown them in our pond, and Pa Bhaer wouldn't let him. They do well enough for the little chaps, I don't think much of 'em myself. Their names are Castor and Pollux."

"I'd like Toby the donkey best, if I could have anything, it's so nice to ride, and he's so little and good," said Nat, remembering the weary tramps he had taken on his own tired feet.

"Mr. Laurie sent him out to Mrs. Bhaer, so she shouldn't carry Teddy on her back when we go to walk. We're all fond of Toby, and he's a first-rate donkey, sir. Those pigeons belong to the whole lot of us, we each have our pet one, and go shares in all the little ones as they come along. Squabs are great fun; there ain't any now, but you can go up and take a look at the old fellows, while I see if Cockletop and Granny have laid any eggs."

Nat climbed up a ladder, put his head through a trap door and took a long look at the pretty doves billing and cooing in their spacious loft. Some on their nests, some bustling in and out, and some sitting at their doors, while many went flying from the sunny housetop to the straw-strewn farmyard, where six sleek cows were placidly ruminating.

"Everybody has got something but me. I wish I had a dove, or a hen, or even a turtle, all my own," thought Nat, feeling very poor as he saw the interesting treasures of the other boys. "How do you get these things?" he asked, when he joined Tommy in the barn.

"We find 'em or buy 'em, or folks give 'em to us. My father sends me mine; but as soon as I get egg money enough, I'm going to buy a pair of ducks. There's a nice little pond for 'em behind the barn, and people pay well for duck-eggs, and the little duckies are pretty, and it's fun to see 'em swim," said Tommy, with the air of a millionaire.

Nat sighed, for he had neither father nor money, nothing in the wide world but an old empty pocketbook, and the skill that lay in his ten finger tips. Tommy seemed to understand the question and the sigh which followed his answer, for after a moment of deep thought, he suddenly broke out,

"Look here, I'll tell you what I'll do. If you will hunt eggs for me, I hate it, I'll give you one egg out of every dozen. You keep account, and when you've had twelve, Mother Bhaer will give you twenty-five cents for 'em, and then you can buy what you like, don't you see?"

"I'll do it! What a kind feller you are, Tommy!" cried Nat, quite dazzled by this brilliant offer.

"Pooh! that is not anything. You begin now and rummage the barn, and I'll wait here for you. Granny is cackling, so you're sure to find one somewhere," and Tommy threw himself down on the hay with a luxurious sense of having made a good bargain, and done a friendly thing.

Nat joyfully began his search, and went rustling from loft to loft till he found two fine eggs, one hidden under a beam, and the other in an old peck measure, which Mrs. Cockletop had appropriated.

"You may have one and I'll have the other, that will just make up my last dozen, and to-morrow we'll start fresh. Here, you chalk your accounts up near mine, and then we'll be all straight," said Tommy, showing a row of mysterious figures on the side of an old winnowing machine.

With a delightful sense of importance, the proud possessor of one egg opened his account with his friend, who laughingly wrote above the figures these imposing words,

"T. Bangs & Co."

Poor Nat found them so fascinating that he was with difficulty persuaded to go and deposit his first piece of portable property in Asia's store-room. Then they went on again, and having made the acquaintance of the two horses, six cows, three pigs, and one Alderney "Bossy," as calves are called in New England, Tommy took Nat to a certain old willow-tree that overhung a noisy little brook. From the fence it was an easy scramble into a wide niche between the three big branches, which had been cut off to send out from year to year a crowd of slender twigs, till a green canopy rustled overhead. Here little seats had been fixed, and a hollow place a closet made big enough to hold a book or two, a dismantled boat, and several half-finished whistles.

"This is Demi's and my private place; we made it, and nobody can come up unless we let 'em, except Daisy, we don't mind her," said Tommy, as Nat looked with delight from the babbling brown water below to the green arch above, where bees were making a musical murmur as they feasted on the long yellow blossoms that filled the air with sweetness.

"Oh, it's just beautiful!" cried Nat. "I do hope you'll let me up sometimes. I never saw such a nice place in all my life. I'd like to be a bird, and live here always."

"It is pretty nice. You can come if Demi don't mind, and I guess he won't, because he said last night that he liked you."

"Did he?" and Nat smiled with pleasure, for Demi's regard seemed to be valued by all the boys, partly because he was Father Bhaer's nephew, and partly because he was such a sober, conscientious little fellow.

"Yes; Demi likes quiet chaps, and I guess he and you will get on if you care about reading as he does."

Poor Nat's flush of pleasure deepened to a painful scarlet at those last words, and he stammered out,

"I can't read very well; I never had any time; I was always fiddling round, you know."

"I don't love it myself, but I can do it well enough when I want to," said Tommy, after a surprised look, which said as plainly as words, "A boy twelve years old and can't read!"

"I can read music, anyway," added Nat, rather ruffled at having to confess his ignorance.

"I can't;" and Tommy spoke in a respectful tone, which emboldened Nat to say firmly,

"I mean to study real hard and learn every thing I can, for I never had a chance before. Does Mr. Bhaer give hard lessons?"

"No; he isn't a bit cross; he sort of explains and gives you a boost over the hard places. Some folks don't; my other master didn't. If we missed a word, didn't we get raps on the head!" and Tommy rubbed his own pate as if it tingled yet with the liberal supply of raps, the memory of which was the only thing he brought away after a year with his "other master."

"I think I could read this," said Nat, who had been examining the books.

"Read a bit, then; I'll help you," resumed Tommy, with a patronizing air.

So Nat did his best, and floundered through a page with may friendly "boosts" from Tommy, who told him he would soon "go it" as well as anybody. Then they sat and talked boy-fashion about all sorts of things, among others, gardening; for Nat, looking down from his perch, asked what was planted in the many little patches lying below them on the other side of the brook.

"These are our farms," said Tommy. "We each have our own patch, and raise what we like in it, only have to choose different things, and can't change till the crop is in, and we must keep it in order all summer."

"What are you going to raise this year?"

"Wal, I cattleated to hev beans, as they are about the easiest crop a-goin'."

Nat could not help laughing, for Tommy had pushed back his hat, put his hands in his pockets, and drawled out his words in unconscious imitation of Silas, the man who managed the place for Mr. Bhaer.

"Come, you needn't laugh; beans are ever so much easier than corn or potatoes. I tried melons last year, but the bugs were a bother, and the old things wouldn't get ripe before the frost, so I didn't have but one good water and two little 'mush mellions,'" said Tommy, relapsing into a "Silasism" with the last word.

"Corn looks pretty growing," said Nat, politely, to atone for his laugh.

"Yes, but you have to hoe it over and over again. Now, six weeks' beans only have to be done once or so, and they get ripe soon. I'm going to try 'em, for I spoke first. Stuffy wanted 'em, but he's got to take peas; they only have to be picked, and he ought to do it, he eats such a lot."

"I wonder if I shall have a garden?" said Nat, thinking that even corn-hoeing must be pleasant work.

"Of course you will," said a voice from below, and there was Mr. Bhaer returned from his walk, and come to find them, for he managed to have a little talk with every one of the lads some time during the day, and found that these chats gave them a good start for the coming week.

Sympathy is a sweet thing, and it worked wonders here, for each boy knew that Father Bhaer was interested in him, and some were readier to open their hearts to him than to a woman, especially the older ones, who liked to talk over their hopes and plans, man to man. When sick or in trouble they instinctively turned to Mrs. Jo, while the little ones made her their mother-confessor on all occasions.

In descending from their nest, Tommy fell into the brook; being used to it, he calmly picked himself out and retired to the house to be dried. This left Nat to Mr. Bhaer, which was just what he wished, and, during the stroll they took among the garden plots, he won the lad's heart by giving him a little "farm," and discussing crops with him as gravely as if the food for the family depended on the harvest. From this pleasant topic they went to others, and Nat had many new and helpful thoughts put into a mind that received them as gratefully as the thirsty earth had received the warm spring rain. All supper time he brooded over them, often fixing his eyes on Mr. Bhaer with an inquiring look, that seemed to say, "I like that, do it again, sir." I don't know whether the man understood the child's mute language or not, but when the boys were all gathered together in Mrs. Bhaer's parlor for the Sunday evening talk, he chose a subject which might have been suggested by the walk in the garden.

As he looked about him Nat thought it seemed more like a great family than a school, for the lads were sitting in a wide half-circle round the fire, some on chairs, some on the rug, Daisy and Demi on the knees of Uncle Fritz, and Rob snugly stowed away in the back of his mother's easy-chair, where he could nod unseen if the talk got beyond his depth.

Every one looked quite comfortable, and listened attentively, for the long walk made rest agreeable, and as every boy there knew that he would be called upon for his views, he kept his wits awake to be ready with an answer.

"Once upon a time," began Mr. Bhaer, in the dear old-fashioned way, "there was a great and wise gardener who had the largest garden ever seen. A wonderful and lovely place it was, and he watched over it with the greatest skill and care, and raised all manner of excellent and useful things. But weeds would grow even in this fine garden; often the ground was bad and the good seeds sown in it would not spring up. He had many under gardeners to help him. Some did their duty and earned the rich wages he gave them; but others neglected their parts and let them run to waste, which displeased him very much. But he was very patient, and for thousands and thousands of years he worked and waited for his great harvest."

"He must have been pretty old," said Demi, who was looking straight into Uncle Fritz's face, as if to catch every word.

"Hush, Demi, it's a fairy story," whispered Daisy.

"No, I think it's an arrygory," said Demi.

"What is a arrygory?" called out Tommy, who was of an inquiring turn.

"Tell him, Demi, if you can, and don't use words unless you are quite sure you know what they mean," said Mr. Bhaer.

"I do know, Grandpa told me! A fable is a arrygory; it's a story that means something. My 'Story without an end' is one, because the child in it means a soul; don't it, Aunty?" cried Demi, eager to prove himself right.

"That's it, dear; and Uncle's story is an allegory, I am quite sure; so listen and see what it means," returned Mrs. Jo, who always took part in whatever was going on, and enjoyed it as much as any boy among them.

Demi composed himself, and Mr. Bhaer went on in his best English, for he had improved much in the last five years, and said the boys did it.

"This great gardener gave a dozen or so of little plots to one of his servants, and told him to do his best and see what he could raise. Now this servant was not rich, nor wise, nor very good, but he wanted to help because the gardener had been very kind to him in many ways. So he gladly took the little plots and fell to work. They were all sorts of shapes and sizes, and some were very good soil, some rather stony, and all of them needed much care, for in the rich soil the weeds grew fast, and in the poor soil there were many stones."

"What was growing in them besides the weeds, and stones?" asked Nat; so interested, he forgot his shyness and spoke before them all.

"Flowers," said Mr. Bhaer, with a kind look. "Even the roughest, most neglected little bed had a bit of heart's-ease or a sprig of mignonette in it. One had roses, sweet peas, and daisies in it," here he pinched the plump cheek of the little girl leaning on his arm. "Another had all sorts of curious plants in it, bright pebbles, a vine that went climbing up like Jack's beanstalk, and many good seeds just beginning to sprout; for, you see, this bed had been taken fine care of by a wise old man, who had worked in gardens of this sort all his life."

At this part of the "arrygory," Demi put his head on one side like an inquisitive bird, and fixed his bright eye on his uncle's face, as if he suspected something and was on the watch. But Mr. Bhaer looked perfectly innocent, and went on glancing from one young face to another, with a grave, wistful look, that said much to his wife, who knew how earnestly he desired to do his duty in these little garden plots.

"As I tell you, some of these beds were easy to cultivate, that means to take care of Daisy, and others were very hard. There was one particularly sunshiny little bed that might have been full of fruits and vegetables as well as flowers, only it wouldn't take any pains, and when the man sowed, well, we'll say melons in this bed, they came to nothing, because the little bed neglected them. The man was sorry, and kept on trying, though every time the crop failed, all the bed said, was, 'I forgot.'"

Here a general laugh broke out, and every one looked at Tommy, who had pricked up his ears at the word "melons," and hung down his head at the sound of his favorite excuse.

"I knew he meant us!" cried Demi, clapping his hands. "You are the man, and we are the little gardens; aren't we, Uncle Fritz?"

"You have guessed it. Now each of you tell me what crop I shall try to sow in you this spring, so that next autumn I may get a good harvest out of my twelve, no, thirteen, plots," said Mr. Bhaer, nodding at Nat as he corrected himself.

"You can't sow corn and beans and peas in us. Unless you mean we are to eat a great many and get fat," said Stuffy, with a sudden brightening of his round, dull face as the pleasing idea occurred to him.

"He don't mean that kind of seeds. He means things to make us good; and the weeds are faults," cried Demi, who usually took the lead in these talks, because he was used to this sort of thing, and liked it very much.

"Yes, each of you think what you need most, and tell me, and I will help you to grow it; only you must do your best, or you will turn out like Tommy's melons, all leaves and no fruit. I will begin with the oldest, and ask the mother what she will have in her plot, for we are all parts of the beautiful garden, and may have rich harvests for our Master if we love Him enough," said Father Bhaer.

"I shall devote the whole of my plot to the largest crop of patience I can get, for that is what I need most," said Mrs. Jo, so soberly that the lads fell to thinking in good earnest what they should say when their turns came, and some among them felt a twinge of remorse, that they had helped to use up Mother Bhaer's stock of patience so fast.

Franz wanted perseverance, Tommy steadiness, Ned went in for good temper, Daisy for industry, Demi for "as much wiseness as Grandpa," and Nat timidly said he wanted so many things he would let Mr. Bhaer choose for him. The others chose much the same things, and patience, good temper, and generosity seemed the favorite crops. One boy wished to like to get up early, but did not know what name to give that sort of seed; and poor Stuffy sighed out,

"I wish I loved my lessons as much as I do my dinner, but I can't."

"We will plant self-denial, and hoe it and water it, and make it grow so well that next Christmas no one will get ill by eating too much dinner. If you exercise your mind, George, it will get hungry just as your body does, and you will love books almost as much as my philosopher here," said Mr. Bhaer; adding, as he stroked the hair off Demi's fine forehead, "You are greedy also, my son, and you like to stuff your little mind full of fairy tales and fancies, as well as George likes to fill his little stomach with cake and candy. Both are bad, and I want you to try something better. Arithmetic is not half so pleasant as 'Arabian Nights,' I know, but it is a very useful thing, and now is the time to learn it, else you will be ashamed and sorry by and by."

"But, 'Harry and Lucy,' and 'Frank,' are not fairy books, and they are all full of barometers, and bricks, and shoeing horses, and useful things, and I'm fond of them; ain't I, Daisy?" said Demi, anxious to defend himself.

"So they are; but I find you reading 'Roland and Maybird,' a great deal oftener than 'Harry and Lucy,' and I think you are not half so fond of 'Frank' as you are of 'Sinbad.' Come, I shall make a little bargain with you both, George shall eat but three times a day, and you shall read but one story-book a week, and I will give you the new cricket-ground; only, you must promise to play in it," said Uncle Fritz, in his persuasive way, for Stuffy hated to run about, and Demi was always reading in play hours.

"But we don't like cricket," said Demi.

"Perhaps not now, but you will when you know it. Besides, you do like to be generous, and the other boys want to play, and you can give them the new ground if you choose."

This was taken them both on the right side, and they agreed to the bargain, to the great satisfaction of the rest.

There was a little more talk about the gardens, and then they all sang together. The band delighted Nat, for Mrs. Bhaer played the piano, Franz the flute, Mr. Bhaer a bass viol, and he himself the violin. A very simple little concert, but all seemed to enjoy it, and old Asia, sitting in the corner, joined at times with the sweetest voice of any, for in this family, master and servant, old and young, black and white, shared in the Sunday song, which went up to the Father of them all. After this they each shook hands with Father Bhaer; Mother Bhaer kissed them every one from sixteen-year-old Franz to little Rob, how kept the tip of her nose for his own particular kisses, and then they trooped up to bed.

The light of the shaded lamp that burned in the nursery shone softly on a picture hanging at the foot of Nat's bed. There were several others on the walls, but the boy thought there must be something peculiar about this one, for it had a graceful frame of moss and cones about it, and on a little bracket underneath stood a vase of wild flowers freshly gathered from the spring woods. It was the most beautiful picture of them all, and Nat lay looking at it, dimly feeling what it meant, and wishing he knew all about it.

"That's my picture," said a little voice in the room. Nat popped up his head, and there was Demi in his night-gown pausing on his way back from Aunt Jo's chamber, whither he had gone to get a cot for a cut finger.

"What is he doing to the children?" asked Nat.

"That is Christ, the Good Man, and He is blessing the children. Don't you know about Him?" said Demi, wondering.

"Not much, but I'd like to, He looks so kind," answered Nat, whose chief knowledge of the Good Man consisted in hearing His name taken in vain.

"I know all about it, and I like it very much, because it is true," said Demi.

"Who told you?"

"My Grandpa, he knows every thing, and tells the best stories in the world. I used to play with his big books, and make bridges, and railroads, and houses, when I was a little boy," began Demi.

"How old are you now?" asked Nat, respectfully.

"'Most ten."

"You know a lot of things, don't you?"

"Yes; you see my head is pretty big, and Grandpa says it will take a good deal to fill it, so I keep putting pieces of wisdom into it as fast as I can," returned Demi, in his quaint way.

Nat laughed, and then said soberly,

"Tell on, please."

And Demi gladly told on without pause or punctuation. "I found a very pretty book one day and wanted to play with it, but Grandpa said I mustn't, and showed me the pictures, and told me about them, and I liked the stories very much, all about Joseph and his bad brothers, and the frogs that came up out of the sea, and dear little Moses in the water, and ever so many more lovely ones, but I liked about the Good Man best of all, and Grandpa told it to me so many times that I learned it by heart, and he gave me this picture so I shouldn't forget, and it was put up here once when I was sick, and I left it for other sick boys to see.'"

"What makes Him bless the children?" asked Nat, who found something very attractive in the chief figure of the group.

"Because He loved them."

"Were they poor children?" asked Nat, wistfully.

"Yes, I think so; you see some haven't got hardly any clothes on, and the mothers don't look like rich ladies. He liked poor people, and was very good to them. He made them well, and helped them, and told rich people they must not be cross to them, and they loved Him dearly, dearly," cried Demi, with enthusiasm.

"Was He rich?"

"Oh no! He was born in a barn, and was so poor He hadn't any house to live in when He grew up, and nothing to eat sometimes, but what people gave Him, and He went round preaching to everybody, and trying to make them good, till the bad men killed Him."

"What for?" and Nat sat up in his bed to look and listen, so interested was he in this man who cared for the poor so much.

"I'll tell you all about it; Aunt Jo won't mind;" and Demi settled himself on the opposite bed, glad to tell his favorite story to so good a listener.

Nursey peeped in to see if Nat was asleep, but when she saw what was going on, she slipped away again, and went to Mrs. Bhaer, saying with her kind face full of motherly emotion,

"Will the dear lady come and see a pretty sight? It's Nat listening with all his heart to Demi telling the story of the Christ-child, like a little white angel as he is."

Mrs. Bhaer had meant to go and talk with Nat a moment before he slept, for she had found that a serious word spoken at this time often did much good. But when she stole to the nursery door, and saw Nat eagerly drinking in the words of his little friends, while Demi told the sweet and solemn story as it had been taught him, speaking softly as he sat with his beautiful eyes fixed on the tender face above them, her own filled with tears, and she went silently away, thinking to herself,

"Demi is unconsciously helping the poor boy better than I can; I will not spoil it by a single word."

The murmur of the childish voice went on for a long time, as one innocent heart preached that great sermon to another, and no one hushed it. When it ceased at last, and Mrs. Bhaer went to take away the lamp, Demi was gone and Nat fast asleep, lying with his face toward the picture, as if he had already learned to love the Good Man who loved little children, and was a faithful friend to the poor. The boy's face was very placid, and as she looked at it she felt that if a single day of care and kindness had done so much, a year of patient cultivation would surely bring a grateful harvest from this neglected garden, which was already sown with the best of all seed by the little missionary in the night-gown.

# CHAPTER IV. STEPPING-STONES

When Nat went into school on Monday morning, he quaked inwardly, for now he thought he should have to display his ignorance before them all. But Mr. Bhaer gave him a seat in the deep window, where he could turn his back on the others, and Franz heard him say his lessons there, so no one could hear his blunders or see how he blotted his copybook. He was truly grateful for this, and toiled away so diligently that Mr. Bhaer said, smiling, when he saw his hot face and inky fingers:

"Don't work so hard, my boy; you will tire yourself out, and there is time enough."

"But I must work hard, or I can't catch up with the others. They know heaps, and I don't know anything," said Nat, who had been reduced to a state of despair by hearing the boys recite their grammar, history, and geography with what he thought amazing ease and accuracy.

"You know a good many things which they don't," said Mr. Bhaer, sitting down beside him, while Franz led a class of small students through the intricacies of the multiplication table.

"Do I?" and Nat looked utterly incredulous.

"Yes; for one thing, you can keep your temper, and Jack, who is quick at numbers, cannot; that is an excellent lesson, and I think you have learned it well. Then, you can play the violin, and not one of the lads can, though they want to do it very much. But, best of all, Nat, you really care to learn something, and that is half the battle. It seems hard at first, and you will feel discouraged, but plod away, and things will get easier and easier as you go on."

Nat's face had brightened more and more as he listened, for, small as the list of his learning was, it cheered him immensely to feel that he had anything to fall back upon. "Yes, I can keep my temper father's beating taught me that; and I can fiddle, though I don't know where the Bay of Biscay is," he thought, with a sense of comfort impossible to express. Then he said aloud, and so earnestly that Demi heard him:

"I do want to learn, and I will try. I never went to school, but I couldn't help it; and if the fellows don't laugh at me, I guess I'll get on first rate you and the lady are so good to me."

"They shan't laugh at you; if they do, I'll I'll tell them not to," cried Demi, quite forgetting where he was.

The class stopped in the middle of 7 times 9, and everyone looked up to see what was going on.

Thinking that a lesson in learning to help one another was better than arithmetic just then, Mr. Bhaer told them about Nat, making such an interesting and touching little story out of it that the good-hearted lads all promised to lend him a hand, and felt quite honored to be called upon to impart their stores of wisdom to the chap who fiddled so capitally. This appeal established the right feeling among them, and Nat had few hindrances to struggle against, for every one was glad to give him a "boost" up the ladder of learning.

Till he was stronger, much study was not good for him, however, and Mrs. Jo found various amusements in the house for him while others were at their books. But his garden was his best medicine, and he worked away like a beaver, preparing his little farm, sowing his beans, watching eagerly to see them grow, and rejoicing over each green leaf and slender stock that shot up and flourished in the warm spring weather. Never was a garden more faithfully hoed; Mr. Bhaer really feared that nothing would find time to grow, Nat kept up such a stirring of the soil; so he gave him easy jobs in the flower garden or among the strawberries, where he worked and hummed as busily as the bees booming all about him.

"This is the crop I like best," Mrs. Bhaer used to say, as she pinched the once thin cheeks, now getting plump and ruddy, or stroked the bent shoulders that were slowly straightening up with healthful work, good food, and the absence of that heavy burden, poverty.

Demi was his little friend, Tommy his patron, and Daisy the comforter of all his woes; for, though the children were younger than he, his timid spirit found a pleasure in their innocent society, and rather shrunk from the rough sports of the elder lads. Mr. Laurence did not forget him, but sent clothes and books, music and kind messages, and now and then came out to see how his boy was getting on, or took him into town to a concert; on which occasions Nat felt himself translated into the seventh heaven of bliss, for he went to Mr. Laurence's great house, saw his pretty wife and little fairy of a daughter, had a good dinner, and was made so comfortable, that he talked and dreamed of it for days and nights afterward.

It takes so little to make a child happy that it is a pity, in a world so full of sunshine and pleasant things, that there should be any wistful faces, empty hands, or lonely little hearts. Feeling this, the Bhaers gathered up all the crumbs they could find to feed their flock of hungry sparrows, for they were not rich, except in charity. Many of Mrs. Jo's friends who had nurseries sent her they toys of which their children so soon tired, and in mending these Nat found an employment that just suited him. He was very neat and skillful with those slender fingers of his, and passed many a rainy afternoon with his gum-bottle, paint-box, and knife, repairing furniture, animals, and games, while Daisy was dressmaker to the dilapidated dolls. As fast as the toys were mended, they were put carefully away in a certain drawer which was to furnish forth a Christmas-tree for all the poor children of the neighborhood, that being the way the Plumfield boys celebrated the birthday of Him who loved the poor and blessed the little ones.

Demi was never tired of reading and explaining his favorite books, and many a pleasant hour did they spend in the old willow, revelling over "Robinson Crusoe," "Arabian Nights," "Edgeworth's Tales," and the other dear immortal stories that will delight children for centuries to come. This opened a new world to Nat, and his eagerness to see what came next in the story helped him on till he could read as well as anybody, and felt so rich and proud with his new accomplishment, that there was danger of his being as much of a bookworm as Demi.

Another helpful thing happened in a most unexpected and agreeable manner. Several of the boys were "in business," as they called it, for most of them were poor, and knowing that they would have their own way to make by and by, the Bhaers encouraged any efforts at independence. Tommy sold his eggs; Jack speculated in live stock; Franz helped in the teaching, and was paid for it; Ned had a taste for carpentry, and a turning-lathe was set up for him in which he turned all sorts of useful or pretty things, and sold them; while Demi constructed water-mills, whirligigs, and unknown machines of an intricate and useless nature, and disposed of them to the boys.

"Let him be a mechanic if he likes," said Mr. Bhaer. "Give a boy a trade, and he is independent. Work is wholesome, and whatever talent these lads possess, be it for poetry or ploughing, it shall be cultivated and made useful to them if possible."

So, when Nat came running to him one day to ask with an excited face:

"Can I go and fiddle for some people who are to have a picnic in our woods? They will pay me, and I'd like to earn some money as the other boys do, and fiddling is the only way I know how to do it."

Mr. Bhaer answered readily:

"Go, and welcome. It is an easy and a pleasant way to work, and I am glad it is offered you."

Nat went, and did so well that when he came home he had two dollars in his pocket, which he displayed with intense satisfaction, as he told how much he had enjoyed the afternoon, how kind the young people were, and how they had praised his dance music, and promised to have him again.

"It is so much nicer than fiddling in the street, for then I got none of the money, and now I have it all, and a good time besides. I'm in business now as well as Tommy and Jack, and I like it ever so much," said Nat, proudly patting the old pocketbook, and feeling like a millionaire already.

He was in business truly, for picnics were plenty as summer opened, and Nat's skill was in great demand. He was always at liberty to go if lessons were not neglected, and if the picnickers were respectable young people. For Mr. Bhaer explained to him that a good plain education is necessary for everyone, and that no amount of money should hire him to go where he might be tempted to do wrong. Nat quite agreed to this, and it was a pleasant sight to see the innocent-hearted lad go driving away in the gay wagons that stopped at the gate for him, or to hear him come fiddling home tired but happy, with his well-earned money in one pocket, and some "goodies" from the feast for Daisy or little Ted, whom he never forgot.

"I'm going to save up till I get enough to buy a violin for myself, and then I can earn my own living, can't I?" he used to say, as he brought his dollars to Mr. Bhaer to keep.

"I hope so, Nat; but we must get you strong and hearty first, and put a little more knowledge into this musical head of yours. Then Mr. Laurie will find you a place somewhere, and in a few years we will all come to hear you play in public."

With much congenial work, encouragement, and hope, Nat found life getting easier and happier every day, and made such progress in his music lessons that his teacher forgave his slowness in some other things, knowing very well that where the heart is the mind works best. The only punishment the boy ever needed for neglect of more important lessons was to hang up the fiddle and the bow for a day. The fear of losing his bosom friend entirely made him go at his books with a will; and having proved that he could master the lessons, what was the use of saying "I can't?"

Daisy had a great love of music, and a great reverence for any one who could make it, and she was often found sitting on the stairs outside Nat's door while he was practising. This pleased him very much, and he played his best for that one quiet little listener; for she never would come in, but preferred to sit sewing her gay patchwork, or tending one of her many dolls, with an expression of dreamy pleasure on her face that made Aunt Jo say, with tears in her eyes: "So like my Beth," and go softly by, lest even her familiar presence mar the child's sweet satisfaction.

Nat was very fond of Mrs. Bhaer, but found something even more attractive in the good professor, who took fatherly care of the shy feeble boy, who had barely escaped with his life from the rough sea on which his little boat had been tossing rudderless for twelve years. Some good angel must have been watching over him, for, though his body had suffered, his soul seemed to have taken little harm, and came ashore as innocent as a shipwrecked baby. Perhaps his love of music kept it sweet in spite of the discord all about him; Mr. Laurie said so, and he ought to know. However that might be, Father Bhaer took pleasure in fostering poor Nat's virtues, and in curing his faults, finding his new pupil as docile and affectionate as a girl. He often called Nat his "daughter" when speaking of him to Mrs. Jo, and she used to laugh at his fancy, for Madame liked manly boys, and thought Nat amiable but weak, though you never would have guessed it, for she petted him as she did Daisy, and he thought her a very delightful woman.

One fault of Nat's gave the Bhaers much anxiety, although they saw how it had been strengthened by fear and ignorance. I regret to say that Nat sometimes told lies. Not very black ones, seldom getting deeper than gray, and often the mildest of white fibs; but that did not matter, a lie is a lie, and though we all tell many polite untruths in this queer world of ours, it is not right, and everybody knows it.

"You cannot be too careful; watch your tongue, and eyes, and hands, for it is easy to tell, and look, and act untruth," said Mr. Bhaer, in one of the talks he had with Nat about his chief temptation.

"I know it, and I don't mean to, but it's so much easier to get along if you ain't very fussy about being exactly true. I used to tell 'em because I was afraid of father and Nicolo, and now I do sometimes because the boys laugh at me. I know it's bad, but I forget," and Nat looked much depressed by his sins.

"When I was a little lad I used to tell lies! Ach! what fibs they were, and my old grandmother cured me of it how, do you think? My parents had talked, and cried, and punished, but still did I forget as you. Then said the dear old grandmother, 'I shall help you to remember, and put a check on this unruly part,' with that she drew out my tongue and snipped the end with her scissors till the blood ran. That was terrible, you may believe, but it did me much good, because it was sore for days, and every word I said came so slowly that I had time to think. After that I was more careful, and got on better, for I feared the big scissors. Yet the dear grandmother was most kind to me in all things, and when she lay dying far away in Nuremberg, she prayed that little Fritz might love God and tell the truth."

"I never had any grandmothers, but if you think it will cure me, I'll let you snip my tongue," said Nat, heroically, for he dreaded pain, yet did wish to stop fibbing.

Mr. Bhaer smiled, but shook his head.

"I have a better way than that, I tried it once before and it worked well. See now, when you tell a lie I will not punish you, but you shall punish me."

"How?" asked Nat, startled at the idea.

"You shall ferule me in the good old-fashioned way; I seldom do it myself, but it may make you remember better to give me pain than to feel it yourself."

"Strike you? Oh, I couldn't!" cried Nat.

"Then mind that tripping tongue of thine. I have no wish to be hurt, but I would gladly bear much pain to cure this fault."

This suggestion made such an impression on Nat, that for a long time he set a watch upon his lips, and was desperately accurate, for Mr. Bhaer judged rightly, that love of him would be more powerful with Nat that fear for himself. But alas! one sad day Nat was off his guard, and when peppery Emil threatened to thrash him, if it was he who had run over his garden and broken down his best hills of corn, Nat declared he didn't, and then was ashamed to own up that he did do it, when Jack was chasing him the night before.

He thought no one would find it out, but Tommy happened to see him, and when Emil spoke of it a day or two later, Tommy gave his evidence, and Mr. Bhaer heard it. School was over, and they were all standing about in the hall, and Mr. Bhaer had just set down on the straw settee to enjoy his frolic with Teddy; but when he heard Tommy and saw Nat turn scarlet, and look at him with a frightened face, he put the little boy down, saying, "Go to thy mother, bubchen, I will come soon," and taking Nat by the hand led him into the school and shut the door.

The boys looked at one another in silence for a minute, then Tommy slipped out and peeping in at the half-closed blinds, beheld a sight that quite bewildered him. Mr. Bhaer had just taken down the long rule that hung over his desk, so seldom used that it was covered with dust.

"My eye! He's going to come down heavy on Nat this time. Wish I hadn't told," thought good-natured Tommy, for to be feruled was the deepest disgrace at this school.

"You remember what I told you last time?" said Mr. Bhaer, sorrowfully, not angrily.

"Yes; but please don't make me, I can't bear it," cried Nat, backing up against the door with both hands behind him, and a face full of distress.

"Why don't he up and take it like a man? I would," thought Tommy, though his heart beat fast at the sight.

"I shall keep my word, and you must remember to tell the truth. Obey me, Nat, take this and give me six good strokes."

Tommy was so staggered by this last speech that he nearly tumbled down the bank, but saved himself, and hung onto the window ledge, staring in with eyes as round as the stuffed owl's on the chimney-piece.

Nat took the rule, for when Mr. Bhaer spoke in that tone everyone obeyed him, and, looking as scared and guilty as if about to stab his master, he gave two feeble blows on the broad hand held out to him. Then he stopped and looked up half-blind with tears, but Mr. Bhaer said steadily:

"Go on, and strike harder."

As if seeing that it must be done, and eager to have the hard task soon over, Nat drew his sleeve across his eyes and gave two more quick hard strokes that reddened the hand, yet hurt the giver more.

"Isn't that enough?" he asked in a breathless sort of tone.

"Two more," was all the answer, and he gave them, hardly seeing where they fell, then threw the rule all across the room, and hugging the kind hand in both his own, laid his face down on it sobbing out in a passion of love, and shame, and penitence:

"I will remember! Oh! I will!"

Then Mr. Bhaer put an arm about him, and said in a tone as compassionate as it had just now been firm:

"I think you will. Ask the dear God to help you, and try to spare us both another scene like this."

Tommy saw no more, for he crept back to the hall, looking so excited and sober that the boys crowded round him to ask what was being done to Nat.

In a most impressive whisper Tommy told them, and they looked as if the sky was about to fall, for this reversing the order of things almost took their breath away.

"He made me do the same thing once," said Emil, as if confessing a crime of the deepest dye.

"And you hit him? dear old Father Bhaer? By thunder, I'd just like to see you do it now!" said Ned, collaring Emil in a fit of righteous wrath.

"It was ever so long ago. I'd rather have my head cut off than do it now," and Emil mildly laid Ned on his back instead of cuffing him, as he would have felt it his duty to do on any less solemn occasion.

"How could you?" said Demi, appalled at the idea.

"I was hopping mad at the time, and thought I shouldn't mind a bit, rather like it perhaps. But when I'd hit uncle one good crack, everything he had ever done for me came into my head all at once somehow, and I couldn't go on. No sir! If he'd laid me down and walked on me, I wouldn't have minded, I felt so mean," and Emil gave himself a good thump in the chest to express his sense of remorse for the past.

"Nat's crying like anything, and feels no end sorry, so don't let's say a word about it; will we?" said tender-hearted Tommy.

"Of course we won't, but it's awful to tell lies," and Demi looked as if he found the awfulness much increased when the punishment fell not upon the sinner, but his best Uncle Fritz.

"Suppose we all clear out, so Nat can cut upstairs if he wants to," proposed Franz, and led the way to the barn, their refuge in troublous times.

Nat did not come to dinner, but Mrs. Jo took some up to him, and said a tender word, which did him good, though he could not look at her. By and by the lads playing outside heard the violin, and said among themselves: "He's all right now." He was all right, but felt shy about going down, till opening his door to slip away into the woods, he found Daisy sitting on the stairs with neither work nor doll, only her little handkerchief in her hand, as if she had been mourning for her captive friend.

"I'm going to walk; want to come?" asked Nat, trying to look as if nothing was the matter, yet feeling very grateful for her silent sympathy, because he fancied everyone must look upon him as a wretch.

"Oh yes!" and Daisy ran for her hat, proud to be chosen as a companion by one of the big boys.

The others saw them go, but no one followed, for boys have a great deal more delicacy than they get credit for, and the lads instinctively felt that, when in disgrace, gentle little Daisy was their most congenial friend.

The walk did Nat good, and he came home quieter than usual, but looking cheerful again, and hung all over with daisy-chains made by his little playmate while he lay on the grass and told her stories.

No one said a word about the scene of the morning, but its effect was all the more lasting for that reason, perhaps. Nat tried his very best, and found much help, not only from the earnest little prayers he prayed to his Friend in heaven, but also in the patient care of the earthly friend whose kind hand he never touched without remembering that it had willingly borne pain for his sake.

# CHAPTER V. PATTYPANS

"What's the matter, Daisy?"

"The boys won't let me play with them."

"Why not?"

"They say girls can't play football."

"They can, for I've done it!" and Mrs. Bhaer laughed at the remembrance of certain youthful frolics.

"I know I can play; Demi and I used to, and have nice times, but he won't let me now because the other boys laugh at him," and Daisy looked deeply grieved at her brother's hardness of heart.

"On the whole, I think he is right, deary. It's all very well when you two are alone, but it is too rough a game for you with a dozen boys; so I'd find some nice little play for myself."

"I'm tired of playing alone!" and Daisy's tone was very mournful.

"I'll play with you by and by, but just now I must fly about and get things ready for a trip into town. You shall go with me and see mamma, and if you like you can stay with her."

"I should like to go and see her and Baby Josy, but I'd rather come back, please. Demi would miss me, and I love to be here, Aunty."

"You can't get on without your Demi, can you?" and Aunt Jo looked as if she quite understood the love of the little girl for her only brother.

"'Course I can't; we're twins, and so we love each other more than other people," answered Daisy, with a brightening face, for she considered being a twin one of the highest honors she could ever receive.

"Now, what will you do with your little self while I fly around?" asked Mrs. Bhaer, who was whisking piles of linen into a wardrobe with great rapidity.

"I don't know, I'm tired of dolls and things; I wish you'd make up a new play for me, Aunty Jo," said Daisy, swinging listlessly on the door.

"I shall have to think of a brand new one, and it will take me some time; so suppose you go down and see what Asia has got for your lunch," suggested Mrs. Bhaer, thinking that would be a good way in which to dispose of the little hindrance for a time.

"Yes, I think I'd like that, if she isn't cross," and Daisy slowly departed to the kitchen, where Asia, the black cook, reigned undisturbed.

In five minutes, Daisy was back again, with a wide-awake face, a bit of dough in her hand and a dab of flour on her little nose.

"Oh aunty! Please could I go and make gingersnaps and things? Asia isn't cross, and she says I may, and it would be such fun, please do," cried Daisy, all in one breath.

"Just the thing, go and welcome, make what you like, and stay as long as you please," answered Mrs. Bhaer, much relieved, for sometimes the one little girl was harder to amuse than the dozen boys.

Daisy ran off, and while she worked, Aunt Jo racked her brain for a new play. All of a sudden she seemed to have an idea, for she smiled to herself, slammed the doors of the wardrobe, and walked briskly away, saying, "I'll do it, if it's a possible thing!"

What it was no one found out that day, but Aunt Jo's eyes twinkled so when she told Daisy she had thought of a new play, and was going to buy it, that Daisy was much excited and asked questions all the way into town, without getting answers that told her anything. She was left at home to play with the new baby, and delight her mother's eyes, while Aunt Jo went off shopping. When she came back with all sorts of queer parcels in corners of the carry-all, Daisy was so full of curiosity that she wanted to go back to Plumfield at once. But her aunt would not be hurried, and made a long call in mamma's room, sitting on the floor with baby in her lap, making Mrs. Brooke laugh at the pranks of the boys, and all sorts of droll nonsense.

How her aunt told the secret Daisy could not imagine, but her mother evidently knew it, for she said, as she tied on the little bonnet and kissed the rosy little face inside, "Be a good child, my Daisy, and learn the nice new play aunty has got for you. It's a most useful and interesting one, and it is very kind of her to play it with you, because she does not like it very well herself."

This last speech made the two ladies laugh heartily, and increased Daisy's bewilderment. As they drove away something rattled in the back of the carriage.

"What's that?" asked Daisy, pricking up her ears.

"The new play," answered Mrs. Jo, solemnly.

"What is it made of?" cried Daisy.

"Iron, tin, wood, brass, sugar, salt, coal, and a hundred other things."

"How strange! What color is it?"

"All sorts of colors."

"Is it large?"

"Part of it is, and a part isn't."

"Did I ever see one?"

"Ever so many, but never one so nice as this."

"Oh! what can it be? I can't wait. When shall I see it?" and Daisy bounced up and down with impatience.

"To-morrow morning, after lessons."

"Is it for the boys, too?"

"No, all for you and Bess. The boys will like to see it, and want to play one part of it. But you can do as you like about letting them."

"I'll let Demi, if he wants to."

"No fear that they won't all want to, especially Stuffy," and Mrs. Bhaer's eyes twinkled more than ever as she patted a queer knobby bundle in her lap.

"Let me feel just once," prayed Daisy.

"Not a feel; you'd guess in a minute and spoil the fun."

Daisy groaned and then smiled all over her face, for through a little hole in the paper she caught a glimpse of something bright.

"How can I wait so long? Couldn't I see it today?"

"Oh dear, no! It has got to be arranged, and ever so many parts fixed in their places. I promised Uncle Teddy that you shouldn't see it till it was all in apple-pie order."

"If uncle knows about it then it must be splendid!" cried Daisy, clapping her hands; for this kind, rich, jolly uncle of hers was as good as a fairy godmother to the children, and was always planning merry surprises, pretty gifts, and droll amusements for them.

"Yes; Teddy went and bought it with me, and we had such fun in the shop choosing the different parts. He would have everything fine and large, and my little plan got regularly splendid when he took hold. You must give him your very best kiss when he comes, for he is the kindest uncle that ever went and bought a charming little coo Bless me! I nearly told you what it was!" and Mrs. Bhaer cut that most interesting word short off in the middle, and began to look over her bills, as if afraid she would let the cat out of the bag if she talked any more. Daisy folded her hands with an air of resignation, and sat quite still trying to think what play had a "coo" in it.

When they got home she eyed every bundle that was taken out, and one large heavy one, which Franz took straight upstairs and hid in the nursery, filled her with amazement and curiosity. Something very mysterious went on up there that afternoon, for Franz was hammering, and Asia trotting up and down, and Aunt Jo flying around like a will-o'-the-wisp, with all sort of things under her apron, while little Ted, who was the only child admitted, because he couldn't talk plain, babbled and laughed, and tried to tell what the "sumpin pitty" was.

All this made Daisy half-wild, and her excitement spread among the boys, who quite overwhelmed Mother Bhaer with offers of assistance, which she declined by quoting their own words to Daisy:

"Girls can't play with boys. This is for Daisy, and Bess, and me, so we don't want you." Whereupon the young gentlemen meekly retired, and invited Daisy to a game of marbles, horse, football, anything she liked, with a sudden warmth and politeness which astonished her innocent little soul.

Thanks to these attentions, she got through the afternoon, went early to bed, and next morning did her lessons with an energy which made Uncle Fritz wish that a new game could be invented every day. Quite a thrill pervaded the school-room when Daisy was dismissed at eleven o'clock, for everyone knew that now she was going to have the new and mysterious play.

Many eyes followed her as she ran away, and Demi's mind was so distracted by this event that when Franz asked him where the desert of Sahara was, he mournfully replied, "In the nursery," and the whole school laughed at him.

"Aunt Jo, I've done all my lessons, and I can't wait one single minute more!" cried Daisy, flying into Mrs. Bhaer's room.

"It's all ready, come on;" and tucking Ted under one arm, and her workbasket under the other, Aunt Jo promptly led the way upstairs.

"I don't see anything," said Daisy, staring about her as she got inside the nursery door.

"Do you hear anything?" asked Aunt Jo, catching Ted back by his little frock as he was making straight for one side of the room.

Daisy did hear an odd crackling, and then a purry little sound as of a kettle singing. These noises came from behind a curtain drawn before a deep bay window. Daisy snatched it back, gave one joyful, "Oh!" and then stood gazing with delight at what do you think?

A wide seat ran round the three sides of the window; on one side hung and stood all sorts of little pots and pans, gridirons and skillets; on the other side a small dinner and tea set; and on the middle part a cooking-stove. Not a tin one, that was of no use, but a real iron stove, big enough to cook for a large family of very hungry dolls. But the best of it was that a real fire burned in it, real steam came out of the nose of the little tea-kettle, and the lid of the little boiler actually danced a jig, the water inside bubbled so hard. A pane of glass had been taken out and replaced by a sheet of tin, with a hole for the small funnel, and real smoke went sailing away outside so naturally, that it did one's heart good to see it. The box of wood with a hod of charcoal stood near by; just above hung dust-pan, brush and broom; a little market basket was on the low table at which Daisy used to play, and over the back of her little chair hung a white apron with a bib, and a droll mob cap. The sun shone in as if he enjoyed the fun, the little stove roared beautifully, the kettle steamed, the new tins sparkled on the walls, the pretty china stood in tempting rows, and it was altogether as cheery and complete a kitchen as any child could desire.

Daisy stood quite still after the first glad "Oh!" but her eyes went quickly from one charming object to another, brightening as they looked, till they came to Aunt Jo's merry face; there they stopped as the happy little girl hugged her, saying gratefully:

"Oh aunty, it's a splendid new play! Can I really cook at the dear stove, and have parties and mess, and sweep, and make fires that truly burn? I like it so much! What made you think of it?"

"Your liking to make gingersnaps with Asia made me think of it," said Mrs. Bhaer, holding Daisy, who frisked as if she would fly. "I knew Asia wouldn't let you mess in her kitchen very often, and it wouldn't be safe at this fire up here, so I thought I'd see if I could find a little stove for you, and teach you to cook; that would be fun, and useful too. So I travelled round among the toy shops, but everything large cost too much and I was thinking I should have to give it up, when I met Uncle Teddy. As soon as he knew what I was about, he said he wanted to help, and insisted on buying the biggest toy stove we could find. I scolded, but he only laughed, and teased me about my cooking when we were young, and said I must teach Bess as well as you, and went on buying all sorts of nice little things for my 'cooking class' as he called it."

"I'm so glad you met him!" said Daisy, as Mrs. Jo stopped to laugh at the memory of the funny time she had with Uncle Teddy.

"You must study hard and learn to make all kinds of things, for he says he shall come out to tea very often, and expects something uncommonly nice."

"It's the sweetest, dearest kitchen in the world, and I'd rather study with it than do anything else. Can't I learn pies, and cake, and macaroni, and everything?" cried Daisy, dancing round the room with a new saucepan in one hand and the tiny poker in the other.

"All in good time. This is to be a useful play, I am to help you, and you are to be my cook, so I shall tell you what to do, and show you how. Then we shall have things fit to eat, and you will be really learning how to cook on a small scale. I'll call you Sally, and say you are a new girl just come," added Mrs. Jo, settling down to work, while Teddy sat on the floor sucking his thumb, and staring at the stove as if it was a live thing, whose appearance deeply interested him.

"That will be so lovely! What shall I do first?" asked Sally, with such a happy face and willing air that Aunt Jo wished all new cooks were half as pretty and pleasant.

"First of all, put on this clean cap and apron. I am rather old-fashioned, and I like my cook to be very tidy."

Sally tucked her curly hair into the round cap, and put on the apron without a murmur, though usually she rebelled against bibs.

"Now, you can put things in order, and wash up the new china. The old set needs washing also, for my last girl was apt to leave it in a sad state after a party."

Aunt Jo spoke quite soberly, but Sally laughed, for she knew who the untidy girl was who had left the cups sticky. Then she turned up her cuffs, and with a sigh of satisfaction began to stir about her kitchen, having little raptures now and then over the "sweet rolling pin," the "darling dish-tub," or the "cunning pepper-pot."

"Now, Sally, take your basket and go to market; here is the list of things I want for dinner," said Mrs. Jo, giving her a bit of paper when the dishes were all in order.

"Where is the market?" asked Daisy, thinking that the new play got more and more interesting every minute.

"Asia is the market."

Away went Sally, causing another stir in the schoolroom as she passed the door in her new costume, and whispered to Demi, with a face full of delight, "It's a perfectly splendid play!"

Old Asia enjoyed the joke as much as Daisy, and laughed jollily as the little girl came flying into the room with her cap all on one side, the lids of her basket rattling like castanets and looking like a very crazy little cook.

"Mrs. Aunt Jo wants these things, and I must have them right away," said Daisy, importantly.

"Let's see, honey; here's two pounds of steak, potatoes, squash, apples, bread, and butter. The meat ain't come yet; when it does I'll send it up. The other things are all handy."

Then Asia packed one potato, one apple, a bit of squash, a little pat of butter, and a roll, into the basket, telling Sally to be on the watch for the butcher's boy, because he sometimes played tricks.

"Who is he?" and Daisy hoped it would be Demi.

*"You'll see," was all Asia would say; and Sally went off in great spirits, singing a verse from dear Mary Howitt's sweet story in rhyme:*

*"Away went little Mabel,*
*With the wheaten cake so fine,*
*The new-made pot of butter,*
*And the little flask of wine."*

"Put everything but the apple into the store-closet for the present," said Mrs. Jo, when the cook got home.

There was a cupboard under the middle shelf, and on opening the door fresh delights appeared. One half was evidently the cellar, for wood, coal, and kindlings were piled there. The other half was full of little jars, boxes, and all sorts of droll contrivances for holding small quantities of flour, meal, sugar, salt, and other household stores. A pot of jam was there, a little tin box of gingerbread, a cologne bottle full of currant wine, and a tiny canister of tea. But the crowning charm was two doll's pans of new milk, with cream actually rising on it, and a wee skimmer all ready to skim it with. Daisy clasped her hands at this delicious spectacle, and wanted to skim it immediately. But Aunt Jo said:

"Not yet; you will want the cream to eat on your apple pie at dinner, and must not disturb it till then."

"Am I going to have pie?" cried Daisy, hardly believing that such bliss could be in store for her.

"Yes; if your oven does well we will have two pies, one apple and one strawberry," said Mrs. Jo, who was nearly as much interested in the new play as Daisy herself.

"Oh, what next?" asked Sally, all impatience to begin.

"Shut the lower draught of the stove, so that the oven may heat. Then wash your hands and get out the flour, sugar, salt, butter, and cinnamon. See if the pie-board is clean, and pare your apple ready to put in."

Daisy got things together with as little noise and spilling as could be expected, from so young a cook.

"I really don't know how to measure for such tiny pies; I must guess at it, and if these don't succeed, we must try again," said Mrs. Jo, looking rather perplexed, and very much amused with the small concern before her. "Take that little pan full of flour, put in a pinch of salt, and then rub in as much butter as will go on that plate. Always remember to put your dry things together first, and then the wet. It mixes better so."

"I know how; I saw Asia do it. Don't I butter the pie plates too? She did, the first thing," said Daisy, whisking the flour about at a great rate.

"Quite right! I do believe you have a gift for cooking, you take to it so cleverly," said Aunt Jo, approvingly. "Now a dash of cold water, just enough to wet it; then scatter some flour on the board, work in a little, and roll the paste out; yes, that's the way. Now put dabs of butter all over it, and roll it out again. We won't have our pastry very rich, or the dolls will get dyspeptic."

Daisy laughed at the idea, and scattered the dabs with a liberal hand. Then she rolled and rolled with her delightful little pin, and having got her paste ready proceeded to cover the plates with it. Next the apple was sliced in, sugar and cinnamon lavishly sprinkled over it, and then the top crust put on with breathless care.

"I always wanted to cut them round, and Asia never would let me. How nice it is to do it all my ownty donty self!" said Daisy, as the little knife went clipping round the doll's plate poised on her hand.

All cooks, even the best, meet with mishaps sometimes, and Sally's first one occurred then, for the knife went so fast that the plate slipped, turned a somersault in the air, and landed the dear little pie upside down on the floor. Sally screamed, Mrs. Jo laughed, Teddy scrambled to get it, and for a moment confusion reigned in the new kitchen.

"It didn't spill or break, because I pinched the edges together so hard; it isn't hurt a bit, so I'll prick holes in it, and then it will be ready," said Sally, picking up the capsized treasure and putting it into shape with a child-like disregard of the dust it had gathered in its fall.

"My new cook has a good temper, I see, and that is such a comfort," said Mrs. Jo. "Now open the jar of strawberry jam, fill the uncovered pie, and put some strips of paste over the top as Asia does."

"I'll make a D in the middle, and have zigzags all round, that will be so interesting when I come to eat it," said Sally, loading the pie with quirls and flourishes that would have driven a real pastry cook wild. "Now I put them in!" she exclaimed; when the last grimy knob had been carefully planted in the red field of jam, and with an air of triumph she shut them into the little oven.

"Clear up your things; a good cook never lets her utensils collect. Then pare your squash and potatoes."

"There is only one potato," giggled Sally.

"Cut it in four pieces, so it will go into the little kettle, and put the bits into cold water till it is time to cook them."

"Do I soak the squash too?"

"No, indeed! Just pare it and cut it up, and put in into the steamer over the pot. It is drier so, though it takes longer to cook."

Here a scratching at the door caused Sally to run and open it, when Kit appeared with a covered basket in his mouth.

"Here's the butcher boy!" cried Daisy, much tickled at the idea, as she relieved him of his load, whereat he licked his lips and began to beg, evidently thinking that it was his own dinner, for he often carried it to his master in that way. Being undeceived, he departed in great wrath and barked all the way downstairs, to ease his wounded feelings.

In the basket were two bits of steak (doll's pounds), a baked pear, a small cake, and paper with them on which Asia had scrawled, "For Missy's lunch, if her cookin' don't turn out well."

"I don't want any of her old pears and things; my cooking will turn out well, and I'll have a splendid dinner; see if I don't!" cried Daisy, indignantly.

"We may like them if company should come. It is always well to have something in the storeroom," said Aunt Jo, who had been taught this valuable fact by a series of domestic panics.

"Me is hundry," announced Teddy, who began to think what with so much cooking going on it was about time for somebody to eat something. His mother gave him her workbasket to rummage, hoping to keep him quiet till dinner was ready, and returned to her housekeeping.

"Put on your vegetables, set the table, and then have some coals kindling ready for the steak."

What a thing it was to see the potatoes bobbing about in the little pot; to peep at the squash getting soft so fast in the tiny steamer; to whisk open the oven door every five minutes to see how the pies got on, and at last when the coals were red and glowing, to put two real steaks on a finger-long gridiron and proudly turn them with a fork. The potatoes were done first, and no wonder, for they had boiled frantically all the while. The were pounded up with a little pestle, had much butter and no salt put in (cook forgot it in the excitement of the moment), then it was made into a mound in a gay red dish, smoothed over with a knife dipped in milk, and put in the oven to brown.

So absorbed in these last performances had Sally been, that she forgot her pastry till she opened the door to put in the potato, then a wail arose, for alas! alas! the little pies were burnt black!

"Oh, my pies! My darling pies! They are all spoilt!" cried poor Sally, wringing her dirty little hands as she surveyed the ruin of her work. The tart was especially pathetic, for the quirls and zigzags stuck up in all directions from the blackened jelly, like the walls and chimney of a house after a fire.

"Dear, dear, I forgot to remind you to take them out; it's just my luck," said Aunt Jo, remorsefully. "Don't cry, darling, it was my fault; we'll try again after dinner," she added, as a great tear dropped from Sally's eyes and sizzled on the hot ruins of the tart.

More would have followed, if the steak had not blazed up just then, and so occupied the attention of cook, that she quickly forgot the lost pastry.

"Put the meat-dish and your own plates down to warm, while you mash the squash with butter, salt, and a little pepper on the top," said Mrs. Jo, devoutly hoping that the dinner would meet with no further disasters.

The "cunning pepper-pot" soothed Sally's feelings, and she dished up her squash in fine style. The dinner was safely put upon the table; the six dolls were seated three on a side; Teddy took the bottom, and Sally the top. When all were settled, it was a most imposing spectacle, for one doll was in full ball costume, another in her night-gown; Jerry, the worsted boy, wore his red winter suit, while Annabella, the noseless darling, was airily attired in nothing but her own kid skin. Teddy, as father of the family, behaved with great propriety, for he smilingly devoured everything offered him, and did not find a single fault. Daisy beamed upon her company like the weary, warm, but hospitable hostess so often to be seen at larger tables than this, and did the honors with an air of innocent satisfaction, which we do not often see elsewhere.

The steak was so tough that the little carving-knife would not cut it; the potato did not go round, and the squash was very lumpy; but the guests appeared politely unconscious of these trifles; and the master and mistress of the house cleared the table with appetites that anyone might envy them. The joy of skimming a jug-full of cream mitigated the anguish felt for the loss of the pies, and Asia's despised cake proved a treasure in the way of dessert.

"That is the nicest lunch I ever had; can't I do it every day?" asked Daisy as she scraped up and ate the leavings all round.

"You can cook things every day after lessons, but I prefer that you should eat your dishes at your regular meals, and only have a bit of gingerbread for lunch. To-day, being the first time, I don't mind, but we must keep our rules. This afternoon you can make something for tea if you like," said Mrs. Jo, who had enjoyed the dinner-party very much, though no one had invited her to partake.

"Do let me make flapjacks for Demi, he loves them so, and it's such fun to turn them and put sugar in between," cried Daisy, tenderly wiping a yellow stain off Annabella's broken nose, for Bella had refused to eat squash when it was pressed upon her as good for "lumatism," a complaint which it is no wonder she suffered from, considering the lightness of her attire.

"But if you give Demi goodies, all the others will expect some also, and then you will have your hands full."

"Couldn't I have Demi come up to tea alone just this one time? And after that I could cook things for the others if they were good," proposed Daisy, with a sudden inspiration.

"That is a capital idea, Posy! We will make your little messes rewards for the good boys, and I don't know one among them who would not like something nice to eat more than almost anything else. If little men are like big ones, good cooking will touch their hearts and soothe their tempers delightfully," added Aunt Jo, with a merry nod toward the door, where stood Papa Bhaer, surveying the scene with a face full of amusement.

"That last hit was for me, sharp woman. I accept it, for it is true; but if I had married thee for thy cooking, heart's dearest, I should have fared badly all these years," answered the professor, laughing as he tossed Teddy, who became quite apoplectic in his endeavors to describe the feast he had just enjoyed.

Daisy proudly showed her kitchen, and rashly promised Uncle Fritz as many flapjacks as he could eat. She was just telling about the new rewards when the boys, headed by Demi, burst into the room snuffing the air like a pack of hungry hounds, for school was out, dinner was not ready, and the fragrance of Daisy's steak led them straight to the spot.

A prouder little damsel was never seen than Sally as she displayed her treasures and told the lads what was in store for them. Several rather scoffed at the idea of her cooking anything fit to eat, but Stuffy's heart was won at once. Nat and Demi had firm faith in her skill, and the others said they would wait and see. All admired the kitchen, however, and examined the stove with deep interest. Demi offered to buy the boiler on the spot, to be used in a steam-engine which he was constructing; and Ned declared that the best and biggest saucepan was just the thing to melt his lead in when he ran bullets, hatchets, and such trifles.

Daisy looked so alarmed at these proposals, that Mrs. Jo then and there made and proclaimed a law that no boy should touch, use, or even approach the sacred stove without a special permit from the owner thereof. This increased its value immensely in the eyes of the gentlemen, especially as any infringement of the law would be punished by forfeiture of all right to partake of the delicacies promised to the virtuous.

At this point the bell rang, and the entire population went down to dinner, which meal was enlivened by each of the boys giving Daisy a list of things he would like to have cooked for him as fast as he earned them. Daisy, whose faith in her stove was unlimited, promised everything, if Aunt Jo would tell her how to make them. This suggestion rather alarmed Mrs. Jo, for some of the dishes were quite beyond her skill wedding-cake, for instance, bull's-eye candy; and cabbage soup with herrings and cherries in it, which Mr. Bhaer proposed as his favorite, and immediately reduced his wife to despair, for German cookery was beyond her.

Daisy wanted to begin again the minute dinner was done, but she was only allowed to clear up, fill the kettle ready for tea, and wash out her apron, which looked as if she had a Christmas feast. She was then sent out to play till five o'clock, for Uncle Fritz said that too much study, even at cooking stoves, was bad for little minds and bodies, and Aunt Jo knew by long experience how soon new toys lose their charm if they are not prudently used.

Everyone was very kind to Daisy that afternoon. Tommy promised her the first fruits of his garden, though the only visible crop just then was pigweed; Nat offered to supply her with wood, free of charge; Stuffy quite worshipped her; Ned immediately fell to work on a little refrigerator for her kitchen; and Demi, with a punctuality beautiful to see in one so young, escorted her to the nursery just as the clock struck five. It was not time for the party to begin, but he begged so hard to come in and help that he was allowed privileges few visitors enjoy, for he kindled the fire, ran errands, and watched the progress of his supper with intense interest. Mrs. Jo directed the affair as she came and went, being very busy putting up clean curtains all over the house.

"Ask Asia for a cup of sour cream, then your cakes will be light without much soda, which I don't like," was the first order.

Demi tore downstairs, and returned with the cream, also a puckered-up face, for he had tasted it on his way, and found it so sour that he predicted the cakes would be uneatable. Mrs. Jo took this occasion to deliver a short lecture from the step-ladder on the chemical properties of soda, to which Daisy did not listen, but Demi did, and understood it, as he proved by the brief but comprehensive reply:

"Yes, I see, soda turns sour things sweet, and the fizzling up makes them light. Let's see you do it, Daisy."

"Fill that bowl nearly full of flour and add a little salt to it," continued Mrs. Jo.

"Oh dear, everything has to have salt in it, seems to me," said Sally, who was tired of opening the pill-box in which it was kept.

"Salt is like good-humor, and nearly every thing is better for a pinch of it, Posy," and Uncle Fritz stopped as he passed, hammer in hand, to drive up two or three nails for Sally's little pans to hang on.

"You are not invited to tea, but I'll give you some cakes, and I won't be cross," said Daisy, putting up her floury little face to thank him with a kiss.

"Fritz, you must not interrupt my cooking class, or I'll come in and moralize when you are teaching Latin. How would you like that?" said Mrs. Jo, throwing a great chintz curtain down on his head.

"Very much, try it and see," and the amiable Father Bhaer went singing and tapping about the house like a mammoth woodpecker.

"Put the soda into the cream, and when it 'fizzles,' as Demi says, stir it into the flour, and beat it up as hard as ever you can. Have your griddle hot, butter it well, and then fry away till I come back," and Aunt Jo vanished also.

Such a clatter as the little spoon made, and such a beating as the batter got, it quite foamed, I assure you; and when Daisy poured some on to the griddle, it rose like magic into a puffy flapjack that made Demi's mouth water. To be sure, the first one stuck and scorched, because she forgot the butter, but after that first failure all went well, and six capital little cakes were safely landed in a dish.

"I think I like maple-syrup better than sugar," said Demi, from his arm-chair where he had settled himself after setting the table in a new and peculiar manner.

"Then go and ask Asia for some," answered Daisy, going into the bath-room to wash her hands.

While the nursery was empty something dreadful happened. You see, Kit had been feeling hurt all day because he had carried meat safely and yet got none to pay him. He was not a bad dog, but he had his little faults like the rest of us, and could not always resist temptation. Happening to stroll into the nursery at that moment, he smelt the cakes, saw them unguarded on the low table, and never stopping to think of consequences, swallowed all six at one mouthful. I am glad to say that they were very hot, and burned him so badly that he could not repress a surprised yelp. Daisy heard it, ran in, saw the empty dish, also the end of a yellow tail disappearing under the bed. Without a word she seized that tail, pulled out the thief, and shook him till his ears flapped wildly, then bundled him down-stairs to the shed, where he spent a lonely evening in the coal-bin.

Cheered by the sympathy which Demi gave her, Daisy made another bowlful of batter, and fried a dozen cakes, which were even better than the others. Indeed, Uncle Fritz after eating two sent up word that he had never tasted any so nice, and every boy at the table below envied Demi at the flapjack party above.

It was a truly delightful supper, for the little teapot lid only fell off three times and the milk jug upset but once; the cakes floated in syrup, and the toast had a delicious beef-steak flavor, owing to cook's using the gridiron to make it on. Demi forgot philosophy, and stuffed like any carnal boy, while Daisy planned sumptuous banquets, and the dolls looked on smiling affably.

"Well, dearies, have you had a good time?" asked Mrs. Jo, coming up with Teddy on her shoulder.

"A very good time. I shall come again soon," answered Demi, with emphasis.

"I'm afraid you have eaten too much, by the look of that table."

"No, I haven't; I only ate fifteen cakes, and they were very little ones," protested Demi, who had kept his sister busy supplying his plate.

"They won't hurt him, they are so nice," said Daisy, with such a funny mixture of maternal fondness and housewifely pride that Aunt Jo could only smile and say:

"Well, on the whole, the new game is a success then?"

"I like it," said Demi, as if his approval was all that was necessary.

"It is the dearest play ever made!" cried Daisy, hugging her little dish-tub as she proposed to wash up the cups. "I just wish everybody had a sweet cooking stove like mine," she added, regarding it with affection.

"This play out to have a name," said Demi, gravely removing the syrup from his countenance with his tongue.

"It has."

"Oh, what?" asked both children eagerly.

"Well, I think we will call it Pattypans," and Aunt Jo retired, satisfied with the success of her last trap to catch a sunbeam.

## CHAPTER VI. A FIRE BRAND

"Please, ma'am, could I speak to you? It is something very important," said Nat, popping his head in at the door of Mrs. Bhaer's room.

It was the fifth head which had popped in during the last half-hour; but Mrs. Jo was used to it, so she looked up, and said, briskly,

"What is it, my lad?"

Nat came in, shut the door carefully behind him, and said in an eager, anxious tone,

"Dan has come."

"Who is Dan?"

"He's a boy I used to know when I fiddled round the streets. He sold papers, and he was kind to me, and I saw him the other day in town, and told him how nice it was here, and he's come."

"But, my dear boy, that is rather a sudden way to pay a visit."

"Oh, it isn't a visit; he wants to stay if you will let him!" said Nat innocently.

"Well, I don't know about that," began Mrs. Bhaer, rather startled by the coolness of the proposition.

"Why, I thought you liked to have poor boys come and live with you, and be kind to 'em as you were to me," said Nat, looking surprised and alarmed.

"So I do, but I like to know something about them first. I have to choose them, because there are so many. I have not room for all. I wish I had."

"I told him to come because I thought you'd like it, but if there isn't room he can go away again," said Nat, sorrowfully.

The boy's confidence in her hospitality touched Mrs. Bhaer, and she could not find the heart to disappoint his hope, and spoil his kind little plan, so she said,

"Tell me about this Dan."

"I don't know any thing, only he hasn't got any folks, and he's poor, and he was good to me, so I'd like to be good to him if I could."

"Excellent reasons every one; but really, Nat, the house is full, and I don't know where I could put him," said Mrs. Bhaer, more and more inclined to prove herself the haven of refuge he seemed to think her.

"He could have my bed, and I could sleep in the barn. It isn't cold now, and I don't mind, I used to sleep anywhere with father," said Nat, eagerly.

Something in his speech and face made Mrs. Jo put her hand on his shoulder, and say in her kindest tone:

"Bring in your friend, Nat; I think we must find room for him without giving him your place."

Nat joyfully ran off, and soon returned followed by a most unprepossessing boy, who slouched in and stood looking about him, with a half bold, half sullen look, which made Mrs. Bhaer say to herself, after one glance,

"A bad specimen, I am afraid."

"This is Dan," said Nat, presenting him as if sure of his welcome.

"Nat tells me you would like to come and stay with us," began Mrs. Jo, in a friendly tone.

"Yes," was the gruff reply.

"Have you no friends to take care of you?"

"No."

"Say, 'No, ma'am,'" whispered Nat.

"Shan't neither," muttered Dan.

"How old are you?"

"About fourteen."

"You look older. What can you do?"

"'Most anything."

"If you stay here we shall want you to do as the others do, work and study as well as play. Are you willing to agree to that?"

"Don't mind trying."

"Well, you can stay a few days, and we will see how we get on together. Take him out, Nat, and amuse him till Mr. Bhaer comes home, when we will settle about the matter," said Mrs. Jo, finding it rather difficult to get on with this cool young person, who fixed his big black eyes on her with a hard, suspicious expression, sorrowfully unboyish.

"Come on, Nat," he said, and slouched out again.

"Thank you, ma'am," added Nat, as he followed him, feeling without quite understanding the difference in the welcome given to him and to his ungracious friend.

"The fellows are having a circus out in the barn; don't you want to come and see it?" he asked, as they came down the wide steps on to the lawn.

"Are they big fellows?" said Dan.

"No; the big ones are gone fishing."

"Fire away, then," said Dan.

Nat led him to the great barn and introduced him to his set, who were disporting themselves among the half-empty lofts. A large circle was marked out with hay on the wide floor, and in the middle stood Demi with a long whip, while Tommy, mounted on the much-enduring Toby, pranced about the circle playing being a monkey.

"You must pay a pin apiece, or you can't see the show," said Stuffy, who stood by the wheelbarrow in which sat the band, consisting of a pocket-comb blown upon by Ned, and a toy drum beaten spasmodically by Rob.

"He's company, so I'll pay for both," said Nat, handsomely, as he stuck two crooked pins in the dried mushroom which served as money-box.

With a nod to the company they seated themselves on a couple of boards, and the performance went on. After the monkey act, Ned gave them a fine specimen of his agility by jumping over an old chair, and running up and down ladders, sailor fashion. Then Demi danced a jig with a gravity beautiful to behold. Nat was called upon to wrestle with Stuffy, and speedily laid that stout youth upon the ground. After this, Tommy proudly advanced to turn a somersault, an accomplishment which he had acquired by painful perseverance, practising in private till every joint of his little frame was black and blue. His feats were received with great applause, and he was about to retire, flushed with pride and a rush of blood to the head, when a scornful voice in the audience was heard to say,

"Ho! that ain't any thing!"

"Say that again, will you?" and Tommy bristled up like an angry turkey-cock.

"Do you want to fight?" said Dan, promptly descending from the barrel and doubling up his fists in a business-like manner.

"No, I don't;" and the candid Thomas retired a step, rather taken aback by the proposition.

"Fighting isn't allowed!" cried the others, much excited.

"You're a nice lot," sneered Dan.

"Come, if you don't behave, you shan't stay," said Nat, firing up at that insult to his friends.

"I'd like to see him do better than I did, that's all," observed Tommy, with a swagger.

"Clear the way, then," and without the slightest preparation Dan turned three somersaults one after the other and came up on his feet.

"You can't beat that, Tom; you always hit your head and tumble flat," said Nat, pleased at his friend's success.

Before he could say any more the audience were electrified by three more somersaults backwards, and a short promenade on the hands, head down, feet up. This brought down the house, and Tommy joined in the admiring cries which greeted the accomplished gymnast as he righted himself, and looked at them with an air of calm superiority.

"Do you think I could learn to do it without its hurting me very much?" Tom meekly asked, as he rubbed the elbows which still smarted after the last attempt.

"What will you give me if I'll teach you?" said Dan.

"My new jack-knife; it's got five blades, and only one is broken."

"Give it here, then."

Tommy handed it over with an affectionate look at its smooth handle. Dan examined it carefully, then putting it into his pocket, walked off, saying with a wink,

"Keep it up till you learn, that's all."

A howl of wrath from Tommy was followed by a general uproar, which did not subside till Dan, finding himself in a minority, proposed that they should play stick-knife, and whichever won should have the treasure. Tommy agreed, and the game was played in a circle of excited faces, which all wore an expression of satisfaction, when Tommy won and secured the knife in the depth of his safest pocket.

"You come off with me, and I'll show you round," said Nat, feeling that he must have a little serious conversation with his friend in private.

What passed between them no one knew, but when they appeared again, Dan was more respectful to every one, though still gruff in his speech, and rough in his manner; and what else could be expected of the poor lad who had been knocking about the world all his short life with no one to teach him any better?

The boys had decided that they did not like him, and so they left him to Nat, who soon felt rather oppressed by the responsibility, but too kind-hearted to desert him.

Tommy, however, felt that in spite of the jack-knife transaction, there was a bond of sympathy between them, and longed to return to the interesting subject of somersaults. He soon found an opportunity, for Dan, seeing how much he admired him, grew more amiable, and by the end of the first week was quite intimate with the lively Tom.

Mr. Bhaer, when he heard the story and saw Dan, shook his head, but only said quietly,

"The experiment may cost us something, but we will try it."

If Dan felt any gratitude for his protection, he did not show it, and took without thanks all that was give him. He was ignorant, but very quick to learn when he chose; had sharp eyes to watch what went on about him; a saucy tongue, rough manners, and a temper that was fierce and sullen by turns. He played with all his might, and played well at almost all the games. He was silent and gruff before grown people, and only now and then was thoroughly sociable among the lads. Few of them really liked him, but few could help admiring his courage and strength, for nothing daunted him, and he knocked tall Franz flat on one occasion with an ease that caused all the others to keep at a respectful distance from his fists. Mr. Bhaer watched him silently, and did his best to tame the "Wild Boy," as they called him, but in private the worthy man shook his head, and said soberly, "I hope the experiment will turn out well, but I am a little afraid it may cost too much."

Mrs. Bhaer lost her patience with him half a dozen times a day, yet never gave him up, and always insisted that there was something good in the lad, after all; for he was kinder to animals than to people, he liked to rove about in the woods, and, best of all, little Ted was fond of him. What the secret was no one could discover, but Baby took to him at once gabbled and crowed whenever he saw him preferred his strong back to ride on to any of the others and called him "My Danny" out of his own little head. Teddy was the only creature to whom Dan showed an affection, and this was only manifested when he thought no one else would see it; but mothers' eyes are quick, and motherly hearts instinctively divine who love their babies. So Mrs. Jo soon saw and felt that there was a soft spot in rough Dan, and bided her time to touch and win him.

But an unexpected and decidedly alarming event upset all their plans, and banished Dan from Plumfield.

Tommy, Nat, and Demi began by patronizing Dan, because the other lads rather slighted him; but soon they each felt there was a certain fascination about the bad boy, and from looking down upon him they came to looking up, each for a different reason. Tommy admired his skill and courage; Nat was grateful for past kindness; and Demi regarded him as a sort of animated story book, for when he chose Dan could tell his adventures in a most interesting way. It pleased Dan to have the three favorites like him, and he exerted himself to be agreeable, which was the secret of his success.

The Bhaers were surprised, but hoped the lads would have a good influence over Dan, and waited with some anxiety, trusting that no harm would come of it.

Dan felt they did not quite trust him, and never showed them his best side, but took a wilful pleasure in trying their patience and thwarting their hopes as far as he dared.

Mr. Bhaer did not approve of fighting, and did not think it a proof of either manliness or courage for two lads to pommel one another for the amusement of the rest. All sorts of hardy games and exercises were encouraged, and the boys were expected to take hard knocks and tumbles without whining; but black eyes and bloody noses given for the fun of it were forbidden as a foolish and a brutal play.

Dan laughed at this rule, and told such exciting tales of his own valor, and the many frays that he had been in, that some of the lads were fired with a desire to have a regular good "mill."

"Don't tell, and I'll show you how," said Dan; and, getting half a dozen of the lads together behind the barn, he gave them a lesson in boxing, which quite satisfied the ardor of most of them. Emil, however, could not submit to be beaten by a fellow younger than himself, for Emil was past fourteen and a plucky fellow, so he challenged Dan to a fight. Dan accepted at once, and the others looked on with intense interest.

What little bird carried the news to head-quarters no one ever knew, but, in the very hottest of the fray, when Dan and Emil were fighting like a pair of young bulldogs, and the others with fierce, excited faces were cheering them on, Mr. Bhaer walked into the ring, plucked the combatants apart with a strong hand, and said, in the voice they seldom heard,

"I can't allow this, boys! Stop it at once; and never let me see it again. I keep a school for boys, not for wild beasts. Look at each other and be ashamed of yourselves."

"You let me go, and I'll knock him down again," shouted Dan, sparring away in spite of the grip on his collar.

"Come on, come on, I ain't thrashed yet!" cried Emil, who had been down five times, but did not know when he was beaten.

"They are playing be gladdy what-you-call-'ems, like the Romans, Uncle Fritz," called out Demi, whose eyes were bigger than ever with the excitement of this new pastime.

"They were a fine set of brutes; but we have learned something since then, I hope, and I cannot have you make my barn a Colosseum. Who proposed this?" asked Mr. Bhaer.

"Dan," answered several voices.

"Don't you know that it is forbidden?"

"Yes," growled Dan, sullenly.

"Then why break the rule?"

"They'll all be molly-coddles, if they don't know how to fight."

"Have you found Emil a molly-coddle? He doesn't look much like one," and Mr. Bhaer brought the two face to face. Dan had a black eye, and his jacket was torn to rags, but Emil's face was covered with blood from a cut lip and a bruised nose, while a bump on his forehead was already as purple as a plum. In spite of his wounds however, he still glared upon his foe, and evidently panted to renew the fight.

"He'd make a first-rater if he was taught," said Dan, unable to withhold the praise from the boy who made it necessary for him to do his best.

"He'll be taught to fence and box by and by, and till then I think he will do very well without any lessons in mauling. Go and wash your faces; and remember, Dan, if you break any more of the rules again, you will be sent away. That was the bargain; do your part and we will do ours."

The lads went off, and after a few more words to the spectators, Mr. Bhaer followed to bind up the wounds of the young gladiators. Emil went to bed sick, and Dan was an unpleasant spectacle for a week.

But the lawless lad had no thought of obeying, and soon transgressed again.

One Saturday afternoon as a party of the boys went out to play, Tommy said,

"Let's go down to the river, and cut a lot of new fish-poles."

"Take Toby to drag them back, and one of us can ride him down," proposed Stuffy, who hated to walk.

"That means you, I suppose; well, hurry up, lazy-bones," said Dan.

Away they went, and having got the poles were about to go home, when Demi unluckily said to Tommy, who was on Toby with a long rod in his hand,

"You look like the picture of the man in the bull-fight, only you haven't got a red cloth, or pretty clothes on."

"I'd like to see one; there's old Buttercup in the big meadow, ride at her, Tom, and see her run," proposed Dan, bent on mischief.

"No, you mustn't," began Demi, who was learning to distrust Dan's propositions.

"Why not, little fuss-button?" demanded Dan.

"I don't think Uncle Fritz would like it."

"Did he ever say we must not have a bull-fight?"

"No, I don't think he ever did," admitted Demi.

"Then hold your tongue. Drive on, Tom, and here's a red rag to flap at the old thing. I'll help you to stir her up," and over the wall went Dan, full of the new game, and the rest followed like a flock of sheep; even Demi, who sat upon the bars, and watched the fun with interest.

Poor Buttercup was not in a very good mood, for she had been lately bereft of her calf, and mourned for the little thing most dismally. Just now she regarded all mankind as her enemies (and I do not blame her), so when the matadore came prancing towards her with the red handkerchief flying at the end of his long lance, she threw up her head, and gave a most appropriate "Moo!" Tommy rode gallantly at her, and Toby recognizing an old friend, was quite willing to approach; but when the lance came down on her back with a loud whack, both cow and donkey were surprised and disgusted. Toby back with a bray of remonstrance, and Buttercup lowered her horns angrily.

"At her again, Tom; she's jolly cross, and will do it capitally!" called Dan, coming up behind with another rod, while Jack and Ned followed his example.

Seeing herself thus beset, and treated with such disrespect, Buttercup trotted round the field, getting more and more bewildered and excited every moment, for whichever way she turned, there was a dreadful boy, yelling and brandishing a new and very disagreeable sort of whip. It was great fun for them, but real misery for her, till she lost patience and turned the tables in the most unexpected manner. All at once she wheeled short round, and charged full at her old friend Toby, whose conduct cut her to the heart. Poor slow Toby backed so precipitately that he tripped over a stone, and down went horse, matadore, and all, in one ignominious heap, while distracted Buttercup took a surprising leap over the wall, and galloped wildly out of sight down the road.

"Catch her, stop her, head her off! run, boys, run!" shouted Dan, tearing after her at his best pace, for she was Mr. Bhaer's pet Alderney, and if anything happened to her, Dan feared it would be all over with him. Such a running and racing and bawling and puffing as there was before she was caught! The fish-poles were left behind; Toby was trotted nearly off his legs in the chase; and every boy was red, breathless, and scared. They found poor Buttercup at last in a flower garden, where she had taken refuge, worn out with the long run. Borrowing a rope for a halter, Dan led her home, followed by a party of very sober young gentlemen, for the cow was in a sad state, having strained her shoulder jumping, so that she limped, her eyes looked wild, and her glossy coat was wet and muddy.

"You'll catch it this time, Dan," said Tommy, as he led the wheezing donkey beside the maltreated cow.

"So will you, for you helped."

"We all did, but Demi," added Jack.

"He put it into our heads," said Ned.

"I told you not to do it," cried Demi, who was most broken-hearted at poor Buttercup's state.

"Old Bhaer will send me off, I guess. Don't care if he does," muttered Dan, looking worried in spite of his words.

"We'll ask him not to, all of us," said Demi, and the others assented with the exception of Stuffy, who cherished the hope that all the punishment might fall on one guilty head. Dan only said, "Don't bother about me;" but he never forgot it, even though he led the lads astray again, as soon as the temptation came.

When Mr. Bhaer saw the animal, and heard the story, he said very little, evidently fearing that he should say too much in the first moments of impatience. Buttercup was made comfortable in her stall, and the boys sent to their rooms till supper-time. This brief respite gave them time to think the matter over, to wonder what the penalty would be, and to try to imagine where Dan would be sent. He whistled briskly in his room, so that no one should think he cared a bit; but while he waited to know his fate, the longing to stay grew stronger and stronger, the more he recalled the comfort and kindness he had known here, the hardship and neglect he had felt elsewhere. He knew they tried to help him, and at the bottom of his heart he was grateful, but his rough life had made him hard and careless, suspicious and wilful. He hated restraint of any sort, and fought against it like an untamed creature, even while he knew it was kindly meant, and dimly felt that he would be the better for it. He made up his mind to be turned adrift again, to knock about the city as he had done nearly all his life; a prospect that made him knit his black brows, and look about the cosy little room with a wistful expression that would have touched a much harder heart than Mr. Bhaer's if he had seen it. It vanished instantly, however, when the good man came in, and said in his accustomed grave way,

"I have heard all about it, Dan, and though you have broken the rules again, I am going to give you one more trial, to please Mother Bhaer."

Dan flushed up to his forehead at this unexpected reprieve, but he only said in his gruff way,

"I didn't know there was any rule about bull-fighting."

"As I never expected to have any at Plumfield, I never did make such a rule," answered Mr. Bhaer, smiling in spite of himself at the boy's excuse. Then he added gravely, "But one of the first and most important of our few laws is the law of kindness to every dumb creature on the place. I want everybody and everything to be happy here, to love and trust, and serve us, as we try to love and trust and serve them faithfully and willingly. I have often said that you were kinder to the animals than any of the other boys, and Mrs. Bhaer liked that trait in you very much, because she thought it showed a good heart. But you have disappointed us in that, and we are sorry, for we hoped to make you quite one of us. Shall we try again?"

Dan's eyes had been on the floor, and his hands nervously picking at the bit of wood he had been whittling as Mr. Bhaer came in, but when he heard the kind voice ask that question, he looked up quickly, and said in a more respectful tone than he had ever used before,

"Yes, please."

"Very well, then, we will say no more, only you will stay at home from the walk to-morrow, as the other boys will and all of you must wait on poor Buttercup till she is well again."

"I will."

"Now, go down to supper, and do your best, my boy, more for your own sake than for ours." Then Mr. Bhaer shook hands with him, and Dan went down more tamed by kindness than he would have been by the good whipping which Asia had strongly recommended.

Dan did try for a day or two, but not being used to it, he soon tired and relapsed into his old wilful ways. Mr. Bhaer was called from home on business one day, and the boys had no lessons. They liked this, and played hard till bedtime, when most of them turned in and slept like dormice. Dan, however, had a plan in his head, and when he and Nat were alone, he unfolded it.

"Look here!" he said, taking from under his bed a bottle, a cigar, and a pack of cards, "I'm going to have some fun, and do as I used to with the fellows in town. Here's some beer, I got if of the old man at the station, and this cigar; you can pay for 'em or Tommy will, he's got heaps of money and I haven't a cent. I'm going to ask him in; no, you go, they won't mind you."

"The folks won't like it," began Nat.

"They won't know. Daddy Bhaer is away, and Mrs. Bhaer's busy with Ted; he's got croup or something, and she can't leave him. We shan't sit up late or make any noise, so where's the harm?"

"Asia will know if we burn the lamp long, she always does."

"No, she won't, I've got a dark lantern on purpose; it don't give much light, and we can shut it quick if we hear anyone coming," said Dan.

This idea struck Nat as a fine one, and lent an air of romance to the thing. He started off to tell Tommy, but put his head in again to say,

"You want Demi, too, don't you?"

"No, I don't; the Deacon will rollup eyes and preach if you tell him. He will be asleep, so just tip the wink to Tom and cut back again."

Nat obeyed, and returned in a minute with Tommy half dressed, rather tousled about the head and very sleepy, but quite ready for fun as usual.

"Now, keep quiet, and I'll show you how to play a first-rate game called 'Poker,'" said Dan, as the three revellers gathered round the table, on which were set forth the bottle, the cigar, and the cards. "First we'll all have a drink, then we'll take a go at the 'weed,' and then we'll play. That's the way men do, and it's jolly fun."

The beer circulated in a mug, and all three smacked their lips over it, though Nat and Tommy did not like the bitter stuff. The cigar was worse still, but they dared not say so, and each puffed away till he was dizzy or choked, when he passed the "weed" on to his neighbor. Dan liked it, for it seemed like old times when he now and then had a chance to imitate the low men who surrounded him. He drank, and smoked, and swaggered as much like them as he could, and, getting into the spirit of the part he assumed, he soon began to swear under his breath for fear some one should hear him. "You mustn't; it's wicked to say 'Damn!'" cried Tommy, who had followed his leader so far.

"Oh, hang! don't you preach, but play away; it's part of the fun to swear."

"I'd rather say 'thunder turtles,'" said Tommy, who had composed this interesting exclamation and was very proud of it.

"And I'll say 'The Devil;' that sounds well," added Nat, much impressed by Dan's manly ways.

Dan scoffed at their "nonsense," and swore stoutly as he tried to teach them the new game.

But Tommy was very sleepy, and Nat's head began to ache with the beer and the smoke, so neither of them was very quick to learn, and the game dragged. The room was nearly dark, for the lantern burned badly; they could not laugh loud nor move about much, for Silas slept next door in the shed-chamber, and altogether the party was dull. In the middle of a deal Dan stopped suddenly, and called out, "Who's that?" in a startled tone, and at the same moment drew the slide over the light. A voice in the darkness said tremulously, "I can't find Tommy," and then there was the quick patter of bare feet running away down the entry that led from the wing to the main house.

"It's Demi! he's gone to call some one; cut into bed, Tom, and don't tell!" cried Dan, whisking all signs of the revel out of sight, and beginning to tear off his clothes, while Nat did the same.

Tommy flew to his room and dived into bed, where he lay, laughing till something burned his hand, when he discovered that he was still clutching the stump of the festive cigar, which he happened to be smoking when the revel broke up.

It was nearly out, and he was about to extinguish it carefully when Nursey's voice was heard, and fearing it would betray him if he hid it in the bed, he threw it underneath, after a final pinch which he thought finished it.

Nursey came in with Demi, who looked much amazed to see the red face of Tommy reposing peacefully upon his pillow.

"He wasn't there just now, because I woke up and could not find him anywhere," said Demi, pouncing on him.

"What mischief are you at now, bad child?" asked Nursey, with a good-natured shake, which made the sleeper open his eyes to say meekly,

"I only ran into Nat's room to see him about something. Go away, and let me alone; I'm awful sleepy."

Nursey tucked Demi in, and went off to reconnoitre, but only found two boys slumbering peacefully in Dan's room. "Some little frolic," she thought, and as there was no harm done she said nothing to Mrs. Bhaer, who was busy and worried over little Teddy.

Tommy was sleepy, and telling Demi to mind his own business and not ask questions, he was snoring in ten minutes, little dreaming what was going on under his bed. The cigar did not go out, but smouldered away on the straw carpet till it was nicely on fire, and a hungry little flame went creeping along till the dimity bedcover caught, then the sheets, and then the bed itself. The beer made Tommy sleep heavily, and the smoke stupified Demi, so they slept on till the fire began to scorch them, and they were in danger of being burned to death.

Franz was sitting up to study, and as he left the school-room he smelt the smoke, dashed up-stairs and saw it coming in a cloud from the left wing of the house. Without stopping to call any one, he ran into the room, dragged the boys from the blazing bed, and splashed all the water he could find at hand on to the flames. It checked but did not quench the fire, and the children wakened on being tumbled topsy-turvy into a cold hall, began to roar at the top of their voices. Mrs. Bhaer instantly appeared, and a minute after Silas burst out of his room shouting, "Fire!" in a tone that raised the whole house. A flock of white goblins with scared faces crowded into the hall, and for a minute every one was panic-stricken.

Then Mrs. Bhaer found her wits, bade Nursey see to the burnt boys, and sent Franz and Silas down-stairs for some tubs of wet clothes which she flung on the bed, over the carpet, and up against the curtains, now burning finely, and threatening to kindle the walls.

Most of the boys stood dumbly looking on, but Dan and Emil worked bravely, running to and fro with water from the bath-room, and helping to pull down the dangerous curtains.

The peril was soon over, and ordering the boys all back to bed, and leaving Silas to watch lest the fire broke out again, Mrs. Bhaer and Franz went to see how the poor boys got on. Demi had escaped with one burn and a grand scare, but Tommy had not only most of his hair scorched off his head, but a great burn on his arm, that made him half crazy with the pain. Demi was soon made cosy, and Franz took him away to his own bed, where the kind lad soothed his fright and hummed him to sleep as cosily as a woman. Nursey watched over poor Tommy all night, trying to ease his misery, and Mrs. Bhaer vibrated between him and little Teddy with oil and cotton, paregoric and squills, saying to herself from time to time, as if she found great amusement in the thought, "I always knew Tommy would set the house on fire, and now he has done it!"

When Mr. Bhaer got home next morning he found a nice state of things. Tommy in bed, Teddy wheezing like a little grampus, Mrs. Jo quite used up, and the whole flock of boys so excited that they all talked at once, and almost dragged him by main force to view the ruins. Under his quiet management things soon fell into order, for every one felt that he was equal to a dozen conflagrations, and worked with a will at whatever task he gave them.

There was no school that morning, but by afternoon the damaged room was put to rights, the invalids were better, and there was time to hear and judge the little culprits quietly. Nat and Tommy told their parts in the mischief, and were honestly sorry for the danger they had brought to the dear old house and all in it. But Dan put on his devil-may-care look, and would not own that there was much harm done.

Now, of all things, Mr. Bhaer hated drinking, gambling, and swearing; smoking he had given up that the lads might not be tempted to try it, and it grieved and angered him deeply to find that the boy, with whom he had tried to be most forbearing, should take advantage of his absence to introduce these forbidden vices, and teach his innocent little lads to think it manly and pleasant to indulge in them. He talked long and earnestly to the assembled boys, and ended by saying, with an air of mingled firmness and regret,

"I think Tommy is punished enough, and that scar on his arm will remind him for a long time to let these things alone. Nat's fright will do for him, for he is really sorry, and does try to obey me. But you, Dan, have been many times forgiven, and yet it does no good. I cannot have my boys hurt by your bad example, nor my time wasted in talking to deaf ears, so you can say good-bye to them all, and tell Nursey to put up your things in my little black bag."

"Oh! sir, where is he going?" cried Nat.

"To a pleasant place up in the country, where I sometimes send boys when they don't do well here. Mr. Page is a kind man, and Dan will be happy there if he chooses to do his best."

"Will he ever come back?" asked Demi.

"That will depend on himself; I hope so."

As he spoke, Mr. Bhaer left the room to write his letter to Mr. Page, and the boys crowded round Dan very much as people do about a man who is going on a long and perilous journey to unknown regions.

"I wonder if you'll like it," began Jack.

"Shan't stay if I don't," said Dan coolly.

"Where will you go?" asked Nat.

"I may go to sea, or out west, or take a look at California," answered Dan, with a reckless air that quite took away the breath of the little boys.

"Oh, don't! stay with Mr. Page awhile and then come back here; do, Dan," pleaded Nat, much affected at the whole affair.

"I don't care where I go, or how long I stay, and I'll be hanged if I ever come back here," with which wrathful speech Dan went away to put up his things, every one of which Mr. Bhaer had given him.

That was the only good-bye he gave the boys, for they were all talking the matter over in the barn when he came down, and he told Nat not to call them. The wagon stood at the door, and Mrs. Bhaer came out to speak to Dan, looking so sad that his heart smote him, and he said in a low tone,

"May I say good-bye to Teddy?"

"Yes, dear; go in and kiss him, he will miss his Danny very much."

No one saw the look in Dan's eyes as he stooped over the crib, and saw the little face light up at first sight of him, but he heard Mrs. Bhaer say pleadingly,

"Can't we give the poor lad one more trial, Fritz?" and Mr. Bhaer answer in his steady way,

"My dear, it is not best, so let him go where he can do no harm to others, while they do good to him, and by and by he shall come back, I promise you."

"He's the only boy we ever failed with, and I am so grieved, for I thought there was the making of a fine man in him, spite of his faults."

Dan heard Mrs. Bhaer sigh, and he wanted to ask for one more trial himself, but his pride would not let him, and he came out with the hard look on his face, shook hands without a word, and drove away with Mr. Bhaer, leaving Nat and Mrs. Jo to look after him with tears in their eyes.

A few days afterwards they received a letter from Mr. Page, saying that Dan was doing well, whereat they all rejoiced. But three weeks later came another letter, saying that Dan had run away, and nothing had been heard of him, whereat they all looked sober, and Mr. Bhaer said,

"Perhaps I ought to have given him another chance."

Mrs. Bhaer, however, nodded wisely and answered, "Don't be troubled, Fritz; the boy will come back to us, I'm sure of it."

But time went on and no Dan came.

# CHAPTER VII. NAUGHTY NAN

"Fritz, I've got a new idea," cried Mrs. Bhaer, as she met her husband one day after school.

"Well, my dear, what is it?" and he waited willingly to hear the new plan, for some of Mrs. Jo's ideas were so droll, it was impossible to help laughing at them, though usually they were quite sensible, and he was glad to carry them out.

"Daisy needs a companion, and the boys would be all the better for another girl among them; you know we believe in bringing up little men and women together, and it is high time we acted up to our belief. They pet and tyrannize over Daisy by turns, and she is getting spoilt. Then they must learn gentle ways, and improve their manners, and having girls about will do it better than any thing else."

"You are right, as usual. Now, who shall we have?" asked Mr. Bhaer, seeing by the look in her eye that Mrs. Jo had some one all ready to propose.

"Little Annie Harding."

"What! Naughty Nan, as the lads call her?" cried Mr. Bhaer, looking very much amused.

"Yes, she is running wild at home since her mother died, and is too bright a child to be spoilt by servants. I have had my eye on her for some time, and when I met her father in town the other day I asked him why he did not send her to school. He said he would gladly if he could find as good a school for girls as ours was for boys. I know he would rejoice to have her come; so suppose we drive over this afternoon and see about it."

"Have not you cares enough now, my Jo, without this little gypsy to torment you?" asked Mr. Bhaer, patting the hand that lay on his arm.

"Oh dear, no," said Mother Bhaer, briskly. "I like it, and never was happier than since I had my wilderness of boys. You see, Fritz, I feel a great sympathy for Nan, because I was such a naughty child myself that I know all about it. She is full of spirits, and only needs to be taught what to do with them to be as nice a little girl as Daisy. Those quick wits of hers would enjoy lessons if they were rightly directed, and what is now a tricksy midget would soon become a busy, happy child. I know how to manage her, for I remember how my blessed mother managed me, and—"

"And if you succeed half as well as she did, you will have done a magnificent work," interrupted Mr. Bhaer, who labored under the delusion that Mrs. B. was the best and most charming woman alive.

"Now, if you make fun of my plan I'll give you bad coffee for a week, and then where are you, sir?" cried Mrs. Jo, tweaking him by the ear just as if he was one of the boys.

"Won't Daisy's hair stand erect with horror at Nan's wild ways?" asked Mr. Bhaer, presently, when Teddy had swarmed up his waistcoat, and Rob up his back, for they always flew at their father the minute school was done.

"At first, perhaps, but it will do Posy good. She is getting prim and Bettyish, and needs stirring up a bit. She always has a good time when Nan comes over to play, and the two will help each other without knowing it. Dear me, half the science of teaching is knowing how much children do for one another, and when to mix them."

"I only hope she won't turn out another firebrand."

"My poor Dan! I never can quite forgive myself for letting him go," sighed Mrs. Bhaer.

At the sound of the name, little Teddy, who had never forgotten his friend, struggled down from his father's arms, and trotted to the door, looked out over the sunny lawn with a wistful face, and then trotted back again, saying, as he always did when disappointed of the longed-for sight,

"My Danny's tummin' soon."

"I really think we ought to have kept him, if only for Teddy's sake, he was so fond of him, and perhaps baby's love would have done for him what we failed to do."

"I've sometimes felt that myself; but after keeping the boys in a ferment, and nearly burning up the whole family, I thought it safer to remove the firebrand, for a time at least," said Mr. Bhaer.

"Dinner's ready, let me ring the bell," and Rob began a solo upon that instrument which made it impossible to hear one's self speak.

"Then I may have Nan, may I?" asked Mrs. Jo.

"A dozen Nans if you want them, my dear," answered Mr. Bhaer, who had room in his fatherly heart for all the naughty neglected children in the world.

When Mrs. Bhaer returned from her drive that afternoon, before she could unpack the load of little boys, without whom she seldom moved, a small girl of ten skipped out at the back of the carry-all and ran into the house, shouting,

"Hi, Daisy! where are you?"

Daisy came, and looked pleased to see her guest, but also a trifle alarmed, when Nan said, still prancing, as if it was impossible to keep still,

"I'm going to stay here always, papa says I may, and my box is coming tomorrow, all my things had to be washed and mended, and your aunt came and carried me off. Isn't it great fun?"

"Why, yes. Did you bring your big doll?" asked Daisy, hoping she had, for on the last visit Nan had ravaged the baby house, and insisted on washing Blanche Matilda's plaster face, which spoilt the poor dear's complexion for ever.

"Yes, she's somewhere round," returned Nan, with most unmaternal carelessness. "I made you a ring coming along, and pulled the hairs out of Dobbin's tail. Don't you want it?" and Nan presented a horse-hair ring in token of friendship, as they had both vowed they would never speak to one another again when they last parted.

Won by the beauty of the offering, Daisy grew more cordial, and proposed retiring to the nursery, but Nan said, "No, I want to see the boys, and the barn," and ran off, swinging her hat by one string till it broke, when she left it to its fate on the grass.

"Hullo! Nan!" cried the boys as she bounced in among them with the announcement,

"I'm going to stay."

"Hooray!" bawled Tommy from the wall on which he was perched, for Nan was a kindred spirit, and he foresaw "larks" in the future.

"I can bat; let me play," said Nan, who could turn her hand to any thing, and did not mind hard knocks.

"We ain't playing now, and our side beat without you."

"I can beat you in running, any way," returned Nan, falling back on her strong point.

"Can she?" asked Nat of Jack.

"She runs very well for a girl," answered Jack, who looked down upon Nan with condescending approval.

"Will you try?" said Nan, longing to display her powers.

"It's too hot," and Tommy languished against the wall as if quite exhausted.

"What's the matter with Stuffy?" asked Nan, whose quick eyes were roving from face to face.

"Ball hurt his hand; he howls at every thing," answered Jack scornfully.

"I don't, I never cry, no matter how I'm hurt; it's babyish," said Nan, loftily.

"Pooh! I could make you cry in two minutes," returned Stuffy, rousing up.

"See if you can."

"Go and pick that bunch of nettles, then," and Stuffy pointed to a sturdy specimen of that prickly plant growing by the wall.

Nan instantly "grasped the nettle," pulled it up, and held it with a defiant gesture, in spite of the almost unbearable sting.

"Good for you," cried the boys, quick to acknowledge courage even in one of the weaker sex.

More nettled than she was, Stuffy determined to get a cry out of her somehow, and he said tauntingly, "You are used to poking your hands into every thing, so that isn't fair. Now go and bump your head real hard against the barn, and see if you don't howl then."

"Don't do it," said Nat, who hated cruelty.

But Nan was off, and running straight at the barn, she gave her head a blow that knocked her flat, and sounded like a battering-ram. Dizzy, but undaunted, she staggered up, saying stoutly, though her face was drawn with pain,

"That hurt, but I don't cry."

"Do it again," said Stuffy angrily; and Nan would have done it, but Nat held her; and Tommy, forgetting the heat, flew at Stuffy like a little game-cock, roaring out,

"Stop it, or I'll throw you over the barn!" and so shook and hustled poor Stuffy that for a minute he did not know whether he was on his head or his heels.

"She told me to," was all he could say, when Tommy let him alone.

"Never mind if she did; it is awfully mean to hurt a little girl," said Demi, reproachfully.

"Ho! I don't mind; I ain't a little girl, I'm older than you and Daisy; so now," cried Nan, ungratefully.

"Don't preach, Deacon, you bully Posy every day of your life," called out the Commodore, who just then hove in sight.

"I don't hurt her; do I, Daisy?" and Demi turned to his sister, who was "pooring" Nan's tingling hands, and recommending water for the purple lump rapidly developing itself on her forehead.

"You are the best boy in the world," promptly answered Daisy; adding, as truth compelled her to do, "You hurt me sometimes, but you don't mean to."

"Put away the bats and things, and mind what you are about, my hearties. No fighting allowed aboard this ship," said Emil, who rather lorded it over the others.

"How do you do, Madge Wildfire?" said Mr. Bhaer, as Nan came in with the rest to supper. "Give the right hand, little daughter, and mind thy manners," he added, as Nan offered him her left.

"The other hurts me."

"The poor little hand! what has it been doing to get those blisters?" he asked, drawing it from behind her back, where she had put it with a look which made him think she had been in mischief.

Before Nan could think of any excuse, Daisy burst out with the whole story, during which Stuffy tried to hide his face in a bowl of bread and milk. When the tale was finished, Mr. Bhaer looked down the long table towards his wife, and said with a laugh in his eyes,

"This rather belongs to your side of the house, so I won't meddle with it, my dear."

Mrs. Jo knew what he meant, but she liked her little black sheep all the better for her pluck, though she only said in her soberest way,

"Do you know why I asked Nan to come here?"

"To plague me," muttered Stuffy, with his mouth full.

"To help make little gentlemen of you, and I think you have shown that some of you need it."

Here Stuffy retired into his bowl again, and did not emerge till Demi made them all laugh by saying, in his slow wondering way,

"How can she, when she's such a tomboy?"

"That's just it, she needs help as much as you, and I expect you set her an example of good manners."

"Is she going to be a little gentleman too?" asked Rob.

"She'd like it; wouldn't you, Nan?" added Tommy.

"No, I shouldn't; I hate boys!" said Nan fiercely, for her hand still smarted, and she began to think that she might have shown her courage in some wiser way.

"I am sorry you hate my boys, because they can be well-mannered, and most agreeable when they choose. Kindness in looks and words and ways is true politeness, and any one can have it if they only try to treat other people as they like to be treated themselves."

Mrs. Bhaer had addressed herself to Nan, but the boys nudged one another, and appeared to take the hint, for that time at least, and passed the butter; said "please," and "thank you," "yes, sir," and "no, ma'am," with unusual elegance and respect. Nan said nothing, but kept herself quiet and refrained from tickling Demi, though strongly tempted to do so, because of the dignified airs he put on. She also appeared to have forgotten her hatred of boys, and played "I spy" with them till dark. Stuffy was observed to offer her frequent sucks on his candy-ball during the game, which evidently sweetened her temper, for the last thing she said on going to bed was,

"When my battledore and shuttle-cock comes, I'll let you all play with 'em."

Her first remark in the morning was "Has my box come?" and when told that it would arrive sometime during the day, she fretted and fumed, and whipped her doll, till Daisy was shocked. She managed to exist, however, till five o'clock, when she disappeared, and was not missed till supper-time, because those at home thought she had gone to the hill with Tommy and Demi.

"I saw her going down the avenue alone as hard as she could pelt," said Mary Ann, coming in with the hasty-pudding, and finding every one asking, "Where is Nan?"

"She has run home, little gypsy!" cried Mrs. Bhaer, looking anxious.

"Perhaps she has gone to the station to look after her luggage," suggested Franz.

"That is impossible, she does not know the way, and if she found it, she could never carry the box a mile," said Mrs. Bhaer, beginning to think that her new idea might be rather a hard one to carry out.

"It would be like her," and Mr. Bhaer caught up his hat to go and find the child, when a shout from Jack, who was at the window, made everyone hurry to the door.

There was Miss Nan, to be sure, tugging along a very large band-box tied up in linen bag. Very hot and dusty and tired did she look, but marched stoutly along, and came puffing up to the steps, where she dropped her load with a sigh of relief, and sat down upon it, observed as she crossed her tired arms,

"I couldn't wait any longer, so I went and got it."

"But you did not know the way," said Tommy, while the rest stood round enjoying the joke.

"Oh, I found it, I never get lost."

"It's a mile, how could you go so far?"

"Well, it was pretty far, but I rested a good deal."

"Wasn't that thing very heavy?"

"It's so round, I couldn't get hold of it good, and I thought my arms would break right off."

"I don't see how the station-master let you have it," said Tommy.

"I didn't say anything to him. He was in the little ticket place, and didn't see me, so I just took it off the platform."

"Run down and tell him it is all right, Franz, or old Dodd will think it is stolen," said Mr. Bhaer, joining in the shout of laughter at Nan's coolness.

"I told you we would send for it if it did not come. Another time you must wait, for you will get into trouble if you run away. Promise me this, or I shall not dare to trust you out of my sight," said Mrs. Bhaer, wiping the dust off Nan's little hot face.

"Well, I won't, only papa tells me not to put off doing things, so I don't."

"That is rather a poser; I think you had better give her some supper now, and a private lecture by and by," said Mr. Bhaer, too much amused to be angry at the young lady's exploit.

The boys thought it "great fun," and Nan entertained them all supper-time with an account of her adventures; for a big dog had barked at her, a man had laughed at her, a woman had given her a doughnut, and her hat had fallen into the brook when she stopped to drink, exhausted with her exertion.

"I fancy you will have your hands full now, my dear; Tommy and Nan are quite enough for one woman," said Mr. Bhaer, half an hour later.

"I know it will take some time to tame the child, but she is such a generous, warm-hearted little thing, I should love her even if she were twice as naughty," answered Mrs. Jo, pointing to the merry group, in the middle of which stood Nan, giving away her things right and left, as lavishly as if the big band-box had no bottom.

It was those good traits that soon made little "Giddygaddy," as they called her, a favorite with every one. Daisy never complained of being dull again, for Nan invented the most delightful plays, and her pranks rivalled Tommy's, to the amusement of the whole school. She buried her big doll and forgot it for a week, and found it well mildewed when she dragged it up. Daisy was in despair, but Nan took it to the painter who as at work about the house, got him to paint it brick red, with staring black eyes, then she dressed it up with feathers, and scarlet flannel, and one of Ned's leaden hatchets; and in the character of an Indian chief, the late Poppydilla tomahawked all the other dolls, and caused the nursery to run red with imaginary gore. She gave away her new shoes to a beggar child, hoping to be allowed to go barefoot, but found it impossible to combine charity and comfort, and was ordered to ask leave before disposing of her clothes. She delighted the boys by making a fire-ship out of a shingle with two large sails wet with turpentine, which she lighted, and then sent the little vessel floating down the brook at dusk. She harnessed the old turkey-cock to a straw wagon, and made him trot round the house at a tremendous pace. She gave her coral necklace for four unhappy kittens, which had been tormented by some heartless lads, and tended them for days as gently as a mother, dressing their wounds with cold cream, feeding them with a doll's spoon, and mourning over them when they died, till she was consoled by one of Demi's best turtles. She made Silas tattoo an anchor on her arm like his, and begged hard to have a blue star on each cheek, but he dared not do it, though she coaxed and scolded till the soft-hearted fellow longed to give in. She rode every animal on the place, from the big horse Andy to the cross pig, from whom she was rescued with difficulty. Whatever the boys dared her to do she instantly attempted, no matter how dangerous it might be, and they were never tired of testing her courage.

Mr. Bhaer suggested that they should see who would study best, and Nan found as much pleasure in using her quick wits and fine memory as her active feet and merry tongue, while the lads had to do their best to keep their places, for Nan showed them that girls could do most things as well as boys, and some things better. There were no rewards in school, but Mr. Bhaer's "Well done!" and Mrs. Bhaer's good report on the conscience book, taught them to love duty for its own sake, and try to do it faithfully, sure sooner or later the recompense would come. Little Nan was quick to feel the new atmosphere, to enjoy it, to show that it was what she needed; for this little garden was full of sweet flowers, half hidden by the weeds; and when kind hands gently began to cultivate it, all sorts of green shoots sprung up, promising to blossom beautifully in the warmth of love and care, the best climate for young hearts and souls all the world over.

# CHAPTER VIII. PRANKS AND PLAYS

As there is no particular plan to this story, except to describe a few scenes in the life at Plumfield for the amusement of certain little persons, we will gently ramble along in this chapter and tell some of the pastimes of Mrs. Jo's boys. I beg leave to assure my honored readers that most of the incidents are taken from real life, and that the oddest are the truest; for no person, no matter how vivid an imagination he may have, can invent anything half so droll as the freaks and fancies that originate in the lively brains of little people.

Daisy and Demi were full of these whims, and lived in a world of their own, peopled with lovely or grotesque creatures, to whom they gave the queerest names, and with whom they played the queerest games. One of these nursery inventions was an invisible sprite called "The Naughty Kitty-mouse," whom the children had believed in, feared, and served for a long time. They seldom spoke of it to any one else, kept their rites as private as possible; and, as they never tried to describe it even to themselves, this being had a vague mysterious charm very agreeable to Demi, who delighted in elves and goblins. A most whimsical and tyrannical imp was the Naughty Kitty-mouse, and Daisy found a fearful pleasure in its service, blindly obeying its most absurd demands, which were usually proclaimed from the lips of Demi, whose powers of invention were great. Rob and Teddy sometimes joined in these ceremonies, and considered them excellent fun, although they did not understand half that went on.

One day after school Demi whispered to his sister, with an ominous wag of the head,

"The Kitty-mouse wants us this afternoon."

"What for?" asked Daisy, anxiously.

"A sackerryfice," answered Demi, solemnly. "There must be a fire behind the big rock at two o'clock, and we must all bring the things we like best, and burn them!" he added, with an awful emphasis on the last words.

"Oh, dear! I love the new paper dollies Aunt Amy painted for me best of any thing; must I burn them up?" cried Daisy, who never thought of denying the unseen tyrant any thing it demanded.

"Every one. I shall burn my boat, my best scrapbook, and all my soldiers," said Demi firmly.

"Well, I will; but it's too bad of Kitty-mouse to want our very nicest things," sighed Daisy.

"A sackerryfice means to give up what you are fond of, so we must," explained Demi, to whom the new idea had been suggested by hearing Uncle Fritz describe the customs of the Greeks to the big boys who were reading about them in school.

"Is Rob coming too," asked Daisy.

"Yes, and he is going to bring his toy village; it is all made of wood, you know, and will burn nicely. We'll have a grand bonfire, and see them blaze up, won't we?"

This brilliant prospect consoled Daisy, and she ate her dinner with a row of paper dolls before her, as a sort of farewell banquet.

At the appointed hour the sacrificial train set forth, each child bearing the treasures demanded by the insatiable Kitty-mouse. Teddy insisted on going also, and seeing that all the others had toys, he tucked a squeaking lamb under one arm, and old Annabella under the other, little dreaming what anguish the latter idol was to give him.

"Where are you going, my chickens?" asked Mrs. Jo, as the flock passed her door.

"To play by the big rock; can't we?"

"Yes, only don't do near the pond, and take good care of baby."

"I always do," said Daisy, leading forth her charge with a capable air.

"Now, you must all sit round, and not move till I tell you. This flat stone is an altar, and I am going to make a fire on it."

Demi then proceeded to kindle up a small blaze, as he had seen the boys do at picnics. When the flame burned well, he ordered the company to march round it three times and then stand in a circle.

"I shall begin, and as fast as my things are burnt, you must bring yours."

With that he solemnly laid on a little paper book full of pictures, pasted in by himself; this was followed by a dilapidated boat, and then one by one the unhappy leaden soldiers marched to death. Not one faltered or hung back, from the splendid red and yellow captain to the small drummer who had lost his legs; all vanished in the flames and mingled in one common pool of melted lead.

"Now, Daisy!" called the high priest of Kitty-mouse, when his rich offerings had been consumed, to the great satisfaction of the children.

"My dear dollies, how can I let them go?" moaned Daisy, hugging the entire dozen with a face full of maternal woe.

"You must," commanded Demi; and with a farewell kiss to each, Daisy laid her blooming dolls upon the coals.

"Let me keep one, the dear blue thing, she is so sweet," besought the poor little mamma, clutching her last in despair.

"More! more!" growled an awful voice, and Demi cried, "that's the Kitty-mouse! she must have every one, quick, or she will scratch us."

In went the precious blue belle, flounces, rosy hat, and all, and nothing but a few black flakes remained of that bright band.

"Stand the houses and trees round, and let them catch themselves; it will be like a real fire then," said Demi, who liked variety even in his "sackerryfices."

Charmed by this suggestion, the children arranged the doomed village, laid a line of coals along the main street, and then sat down to watch the conflagration. It was somewhat slow to kindle owing to the paint, but at last one ambitious little cottage blazed up, fired a tree of the palm species, which fell on to the roof of a large family mansion, and in a few minutes the whole town was burning merrily. The wooden population stood and stared at the destruction like blockheads, as they were, till they also caught and blazed away without a cry. It took some time to reduce the town to ashes, and the lookers-on enjoyed the spectacle immensely, cheering as each house fell, dancing like wild Indians when the steeple flamed aloft, and actually casting one wretched little churn-shaped lady, who had escaped to the suburbs, into the very heart of the fire.

The superb success of this last offering excited Teddy to such a degree, that he first threw his lamb into the conflagration, and before it had time even to roast, he planted poor Annabella on the funeral pyre. Of course she did not like it, and expressed her anguish and resentment in a way that terrified her infant destroyer. Being covered with kid, she did not blaze, but did what was worse, she squirmed. First one leg curled up, then the other, in a very awful and lifelike manner; next she flung her arms over her head as if in great agony; her head itself turned on her shoulders, her glass eyes fell out, and with one final writhe of her whole body, she sank down a blackened mass on the ruins of the town. This unexpected demonstration startled every one and frightened Teddy half out of his little wits. He looked, then screamed and fled toward the house, roaring "Marmar" at the top of his voice.

Mrs. Bhaer heard the outcry and ran to the rescue, but Teddy could only cling to her and pour out in his broken way something about "poor Bella hurted," "a dreat fire," and "all the dollies dorn." Fearing some dire mishap, his mother caught him up and hurried to the scene of action, where she found the blind worshippers of Kitty-mouse mourning over the charred remains of the lost darling.

"What have you been at? Tell me all about it," said Mrs. Jo, composing herself to listen patiently, for the culprits looked so penitent, she forgave them beforehand.

With some reluctance Demi explained their play, and Aunt Jo laughed till the tears ran down her cheeks, the children were so solemn, and the play was so absurd.

*"I thought you were too sensible to play such a silly game as this. If I had any Kitty-mouse I'd have a good one who liked you to play in safe pleasant ways, and not destroy and frighten. Just see what a ruin you have made; all Daisy's pretty dolls, Demi's soldiers, and Rob's new village beside poor Teddy's pet lamb, and dear old Annabella. I shall have to write up in the nursery the verse that used to come in the boxes of toys,*

*"The children of Holland take pleasure in making,*
*What the children of Boston take pleasure in breaking."*

"Only I shall put Plumfield instead of Boston."

"We never will again, truly, truly!" cried the repentant little sinners, much abashed at this reproof.

"Demi told us to," said Rob.

"Well, I heard Uncle tell about the Greece people, who had altars and things, and so I wanted to be like them, only I hadn't any live creatures to sackerryfice, so we burnt up our toys."

"Dear me, that is something like the bean story," said Aunt Jo, laughing again.

"Tell about it," suggested Daisy, to change the subject.

"Once there was a poor woman who had three or four little children, and she used to lock them up in her room when she went out to work, to keep them safe. On day when she was going away she said, 'Now, my dears, don't let baby fall out of window, don't play with the matches, and don't put beans up your noses.' Now the children had never dreamed of doing that last thing, but she put it into their heads, and the minute she was gone, they ran and stuffed their naughty little noses full of beans, just to see how it felt, and she found them all crying when she came home."

"Did it hurt?" asked Rob, with such intense interest that his mother hastily added a warning sequel, lest a new edition of the bean story should appear in her own family.

"Very much, as I know, for when my mother told me this story, I was so silly that I went and tried it myself. I had no beans, so I took some little pebbles, and poked several into my nose. I did not like it at all, and wanted to take them out again very soon, but one would not come, and I was so ashamed to tell what a goose I been that I went for hours with the stone hurting me very much. At last the pain got so bad I had to tell, and when my mother could not get it out the doctor came. Then I was put in a chair and held tight, Rob, while he used his ugly little pincers till the stone hopped out. Dear me! how my wretched little nose did ache, and how people laughed at me!" and Mrs. Jo shook her head in a dismal way, as if the memory of her sufferings was too much for her.

Rob looked deeply impressed and I am glad to say took the warning to heart. Demi proposed that they should bury poor Annabella, and in the interest of the funeral Teddy forgot his fright. Daisy was soon consoled by another batch of dolls from Aunt Amy, and the Naughty Kitty-mouse seemed to be appeased by the last offerings, for she tormented them no more.

"Brops" was the name of a new and absorbing play, invented by Bangs. As this interesting animal is not to be found in any Zoological Garden, unless Du Chaillu has recently brought one from the wilds of Africa, I will mention a few of its peculiar habits and traits, for the benefit of inquiring minds. The Brop is a winged quadruped, with a human face of a youthful and merry aspect. When it walks the earth it grunts, when it soars it gives a shrill hoot, occasionally it goes erect, and talks good English. Its body is usually covered with a substance much resembling a shawl, sometimes red, sometimes blue, often plaid, and, strange to say, they frequently change skins with one another. On their heads they have a horn very like a stiff brown paper lamp-lighter. Wings of the same substance flap upon their shoulders when they fly; this is never very far from the ground, as they usually fall with violence if they attempt any lofty flights. They browse over the earth, but can sit up and eat like the squirrel. Their favorite nourishment is the seed-cake; apples also are freely taken, and sometimes raw carrots are nibbled when food is scarce. They live in dens, where they have a sort of nest, much like a clothes-basket, in which the little Brops play till their wings are grown. These singular animals quarrel at times, and it is on these occasions that they burst into human speech, call each other names, cry, scold, and sometimes tear off horns and skin, declaring fiercely that they "won't play." The few privileged persons who have studied them are inclined to think them a remarkable mixture of the monkey, the sphinx, the roc, and the queer creatures seen by the famous Peter Wilkins.

This game was a great favorite, and the younger children beguiled many a rainy afternoon flapping or creeping about the nursery, acting like little bedlamites and being as merry as little grigs. To be sure, it was rather hard upon clothes, particularly trouser-knees, and jacket-elbows; but Mrs. Bhaer only said, as she patched and darned,

"We do things just as foolish, and not half so harmless. If I could get as much happiness out of it as the little dears do, I'd be a Brop myself."

Nat's favorite amusements were working in his garden, and sitting in the willow-tree with his violin, for that green nest was a fairy world to him, and there he loved to perch, making music like a happy bird. The lads called him "Old Chirper," because he was always humming, whistling, or fiddling, and they often stopped a minute in their work or play to listen to the soft tones of the violin, which seemed to lead a little orchestra of summer sounds. The birds appeared to regard him as one of themselves, and fearlessly sat on the fence or lit among the boughs to watch him with their quick bright eyes. The robins in the apple-tree near by evidently considered him a friend, for the father bird hunted insects close beside him, and the little mother brooded as confidingly over her blue eggs as if the boy was only a new sort of blackbird who cheered her patient watch with his song. The brown brook babbled and sparkled below him, the bees haunted the clover fields on either side, friendly faces peeped at him as they passed, the old house stretched its wide wings hospitably toward him, and with a blessed sense of rest and love and happiness, Nat dreamed for hours in this nook, unconscious what healthful miracles were being wrought upon him.

One listener he had who never tired, and to whom he was more than a mere schoolmate. Poor Billy's chief delight was to lie beside the brook, watching leaves and bits of foam dance by, listening dreamily to the music in the willow-tree. He seemed to think Nat a sort of angel who sat aloft and sang, for a few baby memories still lingered in his mind and seemed to grow brighter at these times. Seeing the interest he took in Nat, Mr. Bhaer begged him to help them lift the cloud from the feeble brain by this gentle spell. Glad to do any thing to show his gratitude, Nat always smiled on Billy when he followed him about, and let him listen undisturbed to the music which seemed to speak a language he could understand. "Help one another," was a favorite Plumfield motto, and Nat learned how much sweetness is added to life by trying to live up to it.

Jack Ford's peculiar pastime was buying and selling; and he bid fair to follow in the footsteps of his uncle, a country merchant, who sold a little of every thing and made money fast. Jack had seen the sugar sanded, the molasses watered, the butter mixed with lard, and things of that kind, and labored under the delusion that it was all a proper part of the business. His stock in trade was of a different sort, but he made as much as he could out of every worm he sold, and always got the best of the bargain when he traded with the boys for string, knives, fish-hooks, or whatever the article might be. The boys who all had nicknames, called him "Skinflint," but Jack did not care as long as the old tobacco-pouch in which he kept his money grew heavier and heavier.

He established a sort of auction-room, and now and then sold off all the odds and ends he had collected, or helped the lads exchange things with one another. He got bats, balls, hockey-sticks, etc., cheap, from one set of mates, furbished them up, and let them for a few cents a time to another set, often extending his business beyond the gates of Plumfield in spite of the rules. Mr. Bhaer put a stop to some of his speculations, and tried to give him a better idea of business talent than mere sharpness in overreaching his neighbors. Now and then Jack made a bad bargain, and felt worse about it than about any failure in lessons or conduct, and took his revenge on the next innocent customer who came along. His account-book was a curiosity; and his quickness at figures quite remarkable. Mr. Bhaer praised him for this, and tried to make his sense of honesty and honor as quick; and, by and by, when Jack found that he could not get on without these virtues, he owned that his teacher was right.

Cricket and football the boys had of course; but, after the stirring accounts of these games in the immortal "Tom Brown at Rugby," no feeble female pen may venture to do more than respectfully allude to them.

Emil spent his holidays on the river or the pond, and drilled the elder lads for a race with certain town boys, who now and then invaded their territory. The race duly came off, but as it ended in a general shipwreck, it was not mentioned in public; and the Commodore had serious thoughts of retiring to a desert island, so disgusted was he with his kind for a time. No desert island being convenient, he was forced to remain among his friends, and found consolation in building a boat-house.

The little girls indulged in the usual plays of their age, improving upon them somewhat as their lively fancies suggested. The chief and most absorbing play was called "Mrs. Shakespeare Smith;" the name was provided by Aunt Jo, but the trials of the poor lady were quite original. Daisy was Mrs. S. S., and Nan by turns her daughter or a neighbor, Mrs. Giddygaddy.

No pen can describe the adventures of these ladies, for in one short afternoon their family was the scene of births, marriages, deaths, floods, earthquakes, tea-parties, and balloon ascensions. Millions of miles did these energetic women travel, dressed in hats and habits never seen before by mortal eye, perched on the bed, driving the posts like mettlesome steeds, and bouncing up and down till their heads spun. Fits and fires were the pet afflictions, with a general massacre now and then by way of change. Nan was never tired of inventing fresh combinations, and Daisy followed her leader with blind admiration. Poor Teddy was a frequent victim, and was often rescued from real danger, for the excited ladies were apt to forget that he was not of the same stuff their longsuffering dolls. Once he was shut into the closet for a dungeon, and forgotten by the girls, who ran off to some out-of-door game. Another time he was half drowned in the bath-tub, playing be a "cunning little whale." And, worst of all, he was cut down just in time after being hung up for a robber.

But the institution most patronized by all was the Club. It had no other name, and it needed none, being the only one in the neighborhood. The elder lads got it up, and the younger were occasionally admitted if they behaved well. Tommy and Demi were honorary members, but were always obliged to retire unpleasantly early, owing to circumstances over which they had no control. The proceedings of this club were somewhat peculiar, for it met at all sorts of places and hours, had all manner of queer ceremonies and amusements, and now and then was broken up tempestuously, only to be re-established, however, on a firmer basis.

Rainy evenings the members met in the schoolroom, and passed the time in games: chess, morris, backgammon, fencing matches, recitations, debates, or dramatic performances of a darkly tragical nature. In summer the barn was the rendezvous, and what went on there no uninitiated mortal knows. On sultry evenings the Club adjourned to the brook for aquatic exercises, and the members sat about in airy attire, frog-like and cool. On such occasions the speeches were unusually eloquent, quite flowing, as one might say; and if any orator's remarks displeased the audience, cold water was thrown upon him till his ardor was effectually quenched. Franz was president, and maintained order admirably, considering the unruly nature of the members. Mr. Bhaer never interfered with their affairs, and was rewarded for this wise forbearance by being invited now and then to behold the mysteries unveiled, which he appeared to enjoy much.

When Nan came she wished to join the Club, and caused great excitement and division among the gentlemen by presenting endless petitions, both written and spoken, disturbing their solemnities by insulting them through the key-hole, performing vigorous solos on the door, and writing up derisive remarks on walls and fences, for she belonged to the "Irrepressibles." Finding these appeals in vain, the girls, by the advice of Mrs. Jo, got up an institution of their own, which they called the Cosy Club. To this they magnanimously invited the gentlemen whose youth excluded them from the other one, and entertained these favored beings so well with little suppers, new games devised by Nan, and other pleasing festivities, that, one by one, the elder boys confessed a desire to partake of these more elegant enjoyments, and, after much consultation, finally decided to propose an interchange of civilities.

The members of the Cosy Club were invited to adorn the rival establishment on certain evenings, and to the surprise of the gentlemen their presence was not found to be a restraint upon the conversation or amusement of the regular frequenters; which could not be said of all Clubs, I fancy. The ladies responded handsomely and hospitably to these overtures of peace, and both institutions flourished long and happily.

## CHAPTER IX. DAISY'S BALL

"Mrs. Shakespeare Smith would like to have Mr. John Brooke, Mr. Thomas Bangs, and Mr. Nathaniel Blake to come to her ball at three o'clock today.

"P.S. Nat must bring his fiddle, so we can dance, and all the boys must be good, or they cannot have any of the nice things we have cooked."

This elegant invitation would, I fear, have been declined, but for the hint given in the last line of the postscript.

"They have been cooking lots of goodies, I smelt 'em. Let's go," said Tommy.

"We needn't stay after the feast, you know," added Demi.

"I never went to a ball. What do you have to do?" asked Nat.

"Oh, we just play be men, and sit round stiff and stupid like grown-up folks, and dance to please the girls. Then we eat up everything, and come away as soon as we can."

"I think I could do that," said Nat, after considering Tommy's description for a minute.

"I'll write and say we'll come;" and Demi despatched the following gentlemanly reply,

"We will all come. Please have lots to eat. J. B. Esquire."

Great was the anxiety of the ladies about their first ball, because if every thing went well they intended to give a dinner-party to the chosen few.

"Aunt Jo likes to have the boys play with us, if they are not rough; so we must make them like our balls, then they will do them good," said Daisy, with her maternal air, as she set the table and surveyed the store of refreshments with an anxious eye.

"Demi and Nat will be good, but Tommy will do something bad, I know he will," replied Nan, shaking her head over the little cake-basket which she was arranging.

"Then I shall send him right home," said Daisy, with decision.

"People don't do so at parties, it isn't proper."

"I shall never ask him any more."

"That would do. He'd be sorry not to come to the dinner-ball, wouldn't he?"

"I guess he would! we'll have the splendidest things ever seen, won't we? Real soup with a ladle and a tureem [she meant tureen] and a little bird for turkey, and gravy, and all kinds of nice vegytubbles." Daisy never could say vegetables properly, and had given up trying.

"It is 'most three, and we ought to dress," said Nan, who had arranged a fine costume for the occasion, and was anxious to wear it.

"I am the mother, so I shan't dress up much," said Daisy, putting on a night-cap ornamented with a red bow, one of her aunt's long skirts, and a shawl; a pair of spectacles and large pocket handkerchief completed her toilette, making a plump, rosy little matron of her.

Nan had a wreath of artificial flowers, a pair of old pink slippers, a yellow scarf, a green muslin skirt, and a fan made of feathers from the duster; also, as a last touch of elegance, a smelling-bottle without any smell in it.

"I am the daughter, so I rig up a good deal, and I must sing and dance, and talk more than you do. The mothers only get the tea and be proper, you know."

A sudden very loud knock caused Miss Smith to fly into a chair, and fan herself violently, while her mamma sat bolt upright on the sofa, and tried to look quite calm and "proper." Little Bess, who was on a visit, acted the part of maid, and opened the door, saying with a smile, "Wart in, gemplemun; it's all weady."

In honor of the occasion, the boys wore high paper collars, tall black hats, and gloves of every color and material, for they were an afterthought, and not a boy among them had a perfect pair.

"Good day, mum," said Demi, in a deep voice, which was so hard to keep up that his remarks had to be extremely brief.

Every one shook hands and then sat down, looking so funny, yet so sober, that the gentlemen forgot their manners, and rolled in their chairs with laughter.

"Oh, don't!" cried Mrs. Smith, much distressed.

"You can't ever come again if you act so," added Miss Smith, rapping Mr. Bangs with her bottle because he laughed loudest.

"I can't help it, you look so like fury," gasped Mr. Bangs, with most uncourteous candor.

"So do you, but I shouldn't be so rude as to say so. He shan't come to the dinner-ball, shall he, Daisy?" cried Nan, indignantly.

"I think we had better dance now. Did you bring your fiddle, sir?" asked Mrs. Smith, trying to preserve her polite composure.

"It is outside the door," and Nat went to get it.

"Better have tea first," proposed the unabashed Tommy, winking openly at Demi to remind him that the sooner the refreshments were secured, the sooner they could escape.

"No, we never have supper first; and if you don't dance well you won't have any supper at all, not one bit, sir," said Mrs. Smith, so sternly that her wild guests saw she was not to be trifled with, and grew overwhelmingly civil all at once.

"I will take Mr. Bangs and teach him the polka, for he does not know it fit to be seen," added the hostess, with a reproachful look that sobered Tommy at once.

Nat struck up, and the ball opened with two couples, who went conscientiously through a somewhat varied dance. The ladies did well, because they liked it, but the gentlemen exerted themselves from more selfish motives, for each felt that he must earn his supper, and labored manfully toward that end. When every one was out of breath they were allowed to rest; and, indeed, poor Mrs. Smith needed it, for her long dress had tripped her up many times. The little maid passed round molasses and water in such small cups that one guest actually emptied nine. I refrain from mentioning his name, because this mild beverage affected him so much that he put cup and all into his mouth at the ninth round, and choked himself publicly.

"You must ask Nan to play and sing now," said Daisy to her brother, who sat looking very much like an owl, as he gravely regarded the festive scene between his high collars.

"Give us a song, mum," said the obedient guest, secretly wondering where the piano was.

*Miss Smith sailed up to an old secretary which stood in the room,*
*threw back the lid of the writing-desk, and sitting down before it,*
*accompanied herself with a vigor which made the old desk rattle as she*
*sang that new and lovely song, beginning*

*"Gaily the troubadour*
*Touched his guitar,*
*As he was hastening*
*Home from the war."*

The gentlemen applauded so enthusiastically that she gave them "Bounding Billows," "Little Bo-Peep," and other gems of song, till they were obliged to hint that they had had enough. Grateful for the praises bestowed upon her daughter, Mrs. Smith graciously announced,

"Now we will have tea. Sit down carefully, and don't grab."

It was beautiful to see the air of pride with which the good lady did the honors of her table, and the calmness with which she bore the little mishaps that occurred. The best pie flew wildly on the floor when she tried to cut it with a very dull knife; the bread and butter vanished with a rapidity calculated to dismay a housekeeper's soul; and, worst of all, the custards were so soft that they had to be drunk up, instead of being eaten elegantly with the new tin spoons.

I grieve to state that Miss Smith squabbled with the maid for the best jumble, which caused Bess to toss the whole dish into the air, and burst out crying amid a rain of falling cakes. She was comforted by a seat at the table, and the sugar-bowl to empty; but during this flurry a large plate of patties was mysteriously lost, and could not be found. They were the chief ornament of the feast, and Mrs. Smith was indignant at the loss, for she had made them herself, and they were beautiful to behold. I put it to any lady if it was not hard to have one dozen delicious patties (made of flour, salt, and water, with a large raisin in the middle of each, and much sugar over the whole) swept away at one fell swoop?

"You hid them, Tommy; I know you did!" cried the outraged hostess, threatening her suspected guest with the milk-pot.

"I didn't!"

"You did!"

"It isn't proper to contradict," said Nan, who was hastily eating up the jelly during the fray.

"Give them back, Demi," said Tommy.

"That's a fib, you've got them in your own pocket," bawled Demi, roused by the false accusation.

"Let's take 'em away from him. It's too bad to make Daisy cry," suggested Nat, who found his first ball more exciting than he expected.

Daisy was already weeping, Bess like a devoted servant mingled her tears with those of her mistress, and Nan denounced the entire race of boys as "plaguey things." Meanwhile the battle raged among the gentlemen, for, when the two defenders of innocence fell upon the foe, that hardened youth intrenched himself behind a table and pelted them with the stolen tarts, which were very effective missiles, being nearly as hard as bullets. While his ammunition held out the besieged prospered, but the moment the last patty flew over the parapet, the villain was seized, dragged howling from the room, and cast upon the hall floor in an ignominious heap. The conquerors then returned flushed with victory, and while Demi consoled poor Mrs. Smith, Nat and Nan collected the scattered tarts, replaced each raisin in its proper bed, and rearranged the dish so that it really looked almost as well as ever. But their glory had departed, for the sugar was gone, and no one cared to eat them after the insult offered to them.

"I guess we had better go," said Demi, suddenly, as Aunt Jo's voice was heard on the stairs.

"P'r'aps we had," and Nat hastily dropped a stray jumble that he had just picked up.

But Mrs. Jo was among them before the retreat was accomplished, and into her sympathetic ear the young ladies poured the story of their woes.

"No more balls for these boys till they have atoned for this bad behavior by doing something kind to you," said Mrs. Jo, shaking her head at the three culprits.

"We were only in fun," began Demi.

"I don't like fun that makes other people unhappy. I am disappointed in you, Demi, for I hoped you would never learn to tease Daisy. Such a kind little sister as she is to you."

"Boys always tease their sisters; Tom says so," muttered Demi.

"I don't intend that my boys shall, and I must send Daisy home if you cannot play happily together," said Aunt Jo, soberly.

At this awful threat, Demi sidled up to his sister, and Daisy hastily dried her tears, for to be separated was the worst misfortune that could happen to the twins.

"Nat was bad, too, and Tommy was baddest of all," observed Nan, fearing that two of the sinners would not get their fair share of punishment.

"I am sorry," said Nat, much ashamed.

"I ain't!" bawled Tommy through the keyhole, where he was listening with all his might.

Mrs. Jo wanted very much to laugh, but kept her countenance, and said impressively, as she pointed to the door,

"You can go, boys, but remember, you are not to speak to or play with the little girls till I give you leave. You don't deserve the pleasure, so I forbid it."

The ill-mannered young gentlemen hastily retired, to be received outside with derision and scorn by the unrepentant Bangs, who would not associate with them for at least fifteen minutes. Daisy was soon consoled for the failure of her ball, but lamented the edict that parted her from her brother, and mourned over his short-comings in her tender little heart. Nan rather enjoyed the trouble, and went about turning up her pug nose at the three, especially Tommy, who pretended not to care, and loudly proclaimed his satisfaction at being rid of those "stupid girls." But in his secret soul he soon repented of the rash act that caused this banishment from the society he loved, and every hour of separation taught him the value of the "stupid girls."

The others gave in very soon, and longed to be friends, for now there was no Daisy to pet and cook for them; no Nan to amuse and doctor them; and, worst of all, no Mrs. Jo to make home life pleasant and life easy for them. To their great affliction, Mrs. Jo seemed to consider herself one of the offended girls, for she hardly spoke to the outcasts, looked as if she did not see them when she passed, and was always too busy now to attend to their requests. This sudden and entire exile from favor cast a gloom over their souls, for when Mother Bhaer deserted them, their sun had set at noon-day, as it were, and they had no refuge left.

This unnatural state of things actually lasted for three days, then they could bear it no longer, and fearing that the eclipse might become total, went to Mr. Bhaer for help and counsel.

It is my private opinion that he had received instructions how to behave if the case should be laid before him. But no one suspected it, and he gave the afflicted boys some advice, which they gratefully accepted and carried out in the following manner:

Secluding themselves in the garret, they devoted several play-hours to the manufacture of some mysterious machine, which took so much paste that Asia grumbled, and the little girls wondered mightily. Nan nearly got her inquisitive nose pinched in the door, trying to see what was going on, and Daisy sat about, openly lamenting that they could not all play nicely together, and not have any dreadful secrets. Wednesday afternoon was fine, and after a good deal of consultation about wind and weather, Nat and Tommy went off, bearing an immense flat parcel hidden under many newspapers. Nan nearly died with suppressed curiosity, Daisy nearly cried with vexation, and both quite trembled with interest when Demi marched into Mrs. Bhaer's room, hat in hand, and said, in the politest tone possible to a mortal boy of his years,

"Please, Aunt Jo, would you and the girls come out to a surprise party we have made for you? Do it's a very nice one."

"Thank you, we will come with pleasure; only, I must take Teddy with me," replied Mrs. Bhaer, with a smile that cheered Demi like sunshine after rain.

"We'd like to have him. The little wagon is all ready for the girls; you won't mind walking just up to Pennyroyal Hill, will you Aunty?"

"I should like it exceedingly; but are you quite sure I shall not be in the way?"

"Oh, no, indeed! we want you very much; and the party will be spoilt if you don't come," cried Demi, with great earnestness.

"Thank you kindly, sir;" and Aunt Jo made him a grand curtsey, for she liked frolics as well as any of them.

"Now, young ladies, we must not keep them waiting; on with the hats, and let us be off at once. I'm all impatience to know what the surprise is."

As Mrs. Bhaer spoke every one bustled about, and in five minutes the three little girls and Teddy were packed into the "clothes-basket," as they called the wicker wagon which Toby drew. Demi walked at the head of the procession, and Mrs. Jo brought up the rear, escorted by Kit. It was a most imposing party, I assure you, for Toby had a red feather-duster in his head, two remarkable flags waved over the carriage, Kit had a blue bow on his neck, which nearly drove him wild, Demi wore a nosegay of dandelions in his buttonhole, and Mrs. Jo carried the queer Japanese umbrella in honor of the occasion.

The girls had little flutters of excitement all the way; and Teddy was so charmed with the drive that he kept dropping his hat overboard, and when it was taken from him he prepared to tumble out himself, evidently feeling that it behooved him to do something for the amusement of the party.

When they came to the hill "nothing was to be seen but the grass blowing in the wind," as the fairy books say, and the children looked disappointed. But Demi said, in his most impressive manner,

"Now, you all get out and stand still, and the surprise party with come in;" with which remark he retired behind a rock, over which heads had been bobbing at intervals for the last half-hour.

A short pause of intense suspense, and then Nat, Demi, and Tommy marched forth, each bearing a new kite, which they presented to the three young ladies. Shrieks of delight arose, but were silenced by the boys, who said, with faces brimful of merriment, "That isn't all the surprise;" and, running behind the rock, again emerged bearing a fourth kite of superb size, on which was printed, in bright yellow letters, "For Mother Bhaer."

"We thought you'd like one, too, because you were angry with us, and took the girls' part," cried all three, shaking with laughter, for this part of the affair evidently was a surprise to Mrs. Jo.

She clapped her hands, and joined in the laugh, looking thoroughly tickled at the joke.

"Now, boys, that is regularly splendid! Who did think of it?" she asked, receiving the monster kite with as much pleasure as the little girls did theirs.

"Uncle Fritz proposed it when we planned to make the others; he said you'd like it, so we made a bouncer," answered Demi, beaming with satisfaction at the success of the plot.

"Uncle Fritz knows what I like. Yes, these are magnificent kites, and we were wishing we had some the other day when you were flying yours, weren't we, girls?"

"That's why we made them for you," cried Tommy, standing on his head as the most appropriate way of expressing his emotions.

"Let us fly them," said energetic Nan.

"I don't know how," began Daisy.

"We'll show you, we want to!" cried all the boys in a burst of devotion, as Demi took Daisy's, Tommy Nan's, and Nat, with difficulty, persuaded Bess to let go her little blue one.

"Aunty, if you will wait a minute, we'll pitch yours for you," said Demi, feeling that Mrs. Bhaer's favor must not be lost again by any neglect of theirs.

"Bless your buttons, dear, I know all about it; and here is a boy who will toss up for me," added Mrs. Jo, as the professor peeped over the rock with a face full of fun.

He came out at once, tossed up the big kite, and Mrs. Jo ran off with it in fine style, while the children stood and enjoyed the spectacle. One by one all the kites went up, and floated far overhead like gay birds, balancing themselves on the fresh breeze that blew steadily over the hill. Such a merry time as they had! running and shouting, sending up the kites or pulling them down, watching their antics in the air, and feeling them tug at the string like live creatures trying to escape. Nan was quite wild with the fun, Daisy thought the new play nearly as interesting as dolls, and little Bess was so fond of her "boo tite," that she would only let it go on very short flights, preferring to hold it in her lap and look at the remarkable pictures painted on it by Tommy's dashing brush. Mrs. Jo enjoyed hers immensely, and it acted as if it knew who owned it, for it came tumbling down head first when least expected, caught on trees, nearly pitched into the river, and finally darted away to such a height that it looked a mere speck among the clouds.

By and by every one got tired, and fastening the kite-strings to trees and fences, all sat down to rest, except Mr. Bhaer, who went off to look at the cows, with Teddy on his shoulder.

"Did you ever have such a good time as this before?" asked Nat, as they lay about on the grass, nibbling pennyroyal like a flock of sheep.

"Not since I last flew a kite, years ago, when I was a girl," answered Mrs. Jo.

"I'd like to have known you when you were a girl, you must have been so jolly," said Nat.

"I was a naughty little girl, I am sorry to say."

"I like naughty little girls," observed Tommy, looking at Nan, who made a frightful grimace at him in return for the compliment.

"Why don't I remember you then, Aunty? Was I too young?" asked Demi.

"Rather, dear."

"I suppose my memory hadn't come then. Grandpa says that different parts of the mind unfold as we grow up, and the memory part of my mind hadn't unfolded when you were little, so I can't remember how you looked," explained Demi.

"Now, little Socrates, you had better keep that question for grandpa, it is beyond me," said Aunt Jo, putting on the extinguisher.

"Well, I will, he knows about those things, and you don't," returned Demi, feeling that on the whole kites were better adapted to the comprehension of the present company.

"Tell about the last time you flew a kite," said Nat, for Mrs. Jo had laughed as she spoke of it, and he thought it might be interesting.

"Oh, it was only rather funny, for I was a great girl of fifteen, and was ashamed to be seen at such a play. So Uncle Teddy and I privately made our kites, and stole away to fly them. We had a capital time, and were resting as we are now, when suddenly we heard voices, and saw a party of young ladies and gentlemen coming back from a picnic. Teddy did not mind, though he was rather a large boy to be playing with a kite, but I was in a great flurry, for I knew I should be sadly laughed at, and never hear the last of it, because my wild ways amused the neighbors as much as Nan's do us.

"'What shall I do?' I whispered to Teddy, as the voices drew nearer and nearer.

"'I'll show you,' he said, and whipping out his knife he cut the strings. Away flew the kites, and when the people came up we were picking flowers as properly as you please. They never suspected us, and we had a grand laugh over our narrow escape."

"Were the kites lost, Aunty?" asked Daisy.

"Quite lost, but I did not care, for I made up my mind that it would be best to wait till I was an old lady before I played with kites again; and you see I have waited," said Mrs. Jo, beginning to pull in the big kite, for it was getting late.

"Must we go now?"

"I must, or you won't have any supper; and that sort of surprise party would not suit you, I think, my chickens."

"Hasn't our party been a nice one?" asked Tommy, complacently.

"Splendid!" answered every one.

"Do you know why? It is because your guests have behaved themselves, and tried to make everything go well. You understand what I mean, don't you?"

"Yes'm," was all the boys said, but they stole a shamefaced look at one another, as they meekly shouldered their kites and walked home, thinking of another party where the guests had not behaved themselves, and things had gone badly on account of it.

## CHAPTER X. HOME AGAIN

July had come, and haying begun; the little gardens were doing finely and the long summer days were full of pleasant hours. The house stood open from morning till night, and the lads lived out of doors, except at school time. The lessons were short, and there were many holidays, for the Bhaers believed in cultivating healthy bodies by much exercise, and our short summers are best used in out-of-door work. Such a rosy, sunburnt, hearty set as the boys became; such appetites as they had; such sturdy arms and legs, as outgrew jackets and trousers; such laughing and racing all over the place; such antics in house and barn; such adventures in the tramps over hill and dale; and such satisfaction in the hearts of the worthy Bhaers, as they saw their flock prospering in mind and body, I cannot begin to describe. Only one thing was needed to make them quite happy, and it came when they least expected it.

One balmy night when the little lads were in bed, the elder ones bathing down at the brook, and Mrs. Bhaer undressing Teddy in her parlor, he suddenly cried out, "Oh, my Danny!" and pointed to the window, where the moon shone brightly.

"No, lovey, he is not there, it was the pretty moon," said his mother.

"No, no, Danny at a window; Teddy saw him," persisted baby, much excited.

"It might have been," and Mrs. Bhaer hurried to the window, hoping it would prove true. But the face was gone, and nowhere appeared any signs of a mortal boy; she called his name, ran to the front door with Teddy in his little shirt, and made him call too, thinking the baby voice might have more effect than her own. No one answered, nothing appeared, and they went back much disappointed. Teddy would not be satisfied with the moon, and after he was in his crib kept popping up his head to ask if Danny was not "tummin' soon."

By and by he fell asleep, the lads trooped up to bed, the house grew still, and nothing but the chirp of the crickets broke the soft silence of the summer night. Mrs. Bhaer sat sewing, for the big basket was always piled with socks, full of portentous holes, and thinking of the lost boy. She had decided that baby had been mistaken, and did not even disturb Mr. Bhaer by telling him of the child's fancy, for the poor man got little time to himself till the boys were abed, and he was busy writing letters. It was past ten when she rose to shut up the house. As she paused a minute to enjoy the lovely scene from the steps, something white caught her eye on one of the hay-cocks scattered over the lawn. The children had been playing there all the afternoon, and, fancying that Nan had left her hat as usual, Mrs. Bhaer went out to get it. But as she approached, she saw that it was neither hat nor handkerchief, but a shirt sleeve with a brown hand sticking out of it. She hurried round the hay-cock, and there lay Dan, fast asleep.

Ragged, dirty, thin, and worn-out he looked; one foot was bare, the other tied up in the old gingham jacket which he had taken from his own back to use as a clumsy bandage for some hurt. He seemed to have hidden himself behind the hay-cock, but in his sleep had thrown out the arm that had betrayed him. He sighed and muttered as if his dreams disturbed him, and once when he moved, he groaned as if in pain, but still slept on quite spent with weariness.

"He must not lie here," said Mrs. Bhaer, and stooping over him she gently called his name. He opened his eyes and looked at her, as if she was a part of his dream, for he smiled and said drowsily, "Mother Bhaer, I've come home."

The look, the words, touched her very much, and she put her hand under his head to lift him up, saying in her cordial way,

"I thought you would, and I'm so glad to see you, Dan." He seemed to wake thoroughly then, and started up looking about him as if he suddenly remembered where he was, and doubted even that kind welcome. His face changed, and he said in his old rough way,

"I was going off in the morning. I only stopped to peek in, as I went by."

"But why not come in, Dan? Didn't you hear us call you? Teddy saw, and cried for you."

"Didn't suppose you'd let me in," he said, fumbling with a little bundle which he had taken up as if going immediately.

"Try and see," was all Mrs. Bhaer answered, holding out her hand and pointing to the door, where the light shone hospitably.

With a long breath, as if a load was off his mind, Dan took up a stout stick, and began to limp towards the house, but stopped suddenly, to say inquiringly,

"Mr. Bhaer won't like it. I ran away from Page."

"He knows it, and was sorry, but it will make no difference. Are you lame?" asked Mrs. Jo, as he limped on again.

"Getting over a wall a stone fell on my foot and smashed it. I don't mind," and he did his best to hide the pain each step cost him.

Mrs. Bhaer helped him into her own room, and, once there, he dropped into a chair, and laid his head back, white and faint with weariness and suffering.

"My poor Dan! drink this, and then eat a little; you are at home now, and Mother Bhaer will take good care of you."

He only looked up at her with eyes full of gratitude, as he drank the wine she held to his lips, and then began slowly to eat the food she brought him. Each mouthful seemed to put heart into him, and presently he began to talk as if anxious to have her know all about him.

"Where have you been, Dan?" she asked, beginning to get out some bandages.

"I ran off more'n a month ago. Page was good enough, but too strict. I didn't like it, so I cut away down the river with a man who was going in his boat. That's why they couldn't tell where I'd gone. When I left the man, I worked for a couple of weeks with a farmer, but I thrashed his boy, and then the old man thrashed me, and I ran off again and walked here."

"All the way?"

"Yes, the man didn't pay me, and I wouldn't ask for it. Took it out in beating the boy," and Dan laughed, yet looked ashamed, as he glanced at his ragged clothes and dirty hands.

"How did you live? It was a long, long tramp for a boy like you."

"Oh, I got on well enough, till I hurt my foot. Folks gave me things to eat, and I slept in barns and tramped by day. I got lost trying to make a short cut, or I'd have been here sooner."

"But if you did not mean to come in and stay with us, what were you going to do?"

"I thought I'd like to see Teddy again, and you; and then I was going back to my old work in the city, only I was so tired I went to sleep on the hay. I'd have been gone in the morning, if you hadn't found me."

"Are you sorry I did?" and Mrs. Jo looked at him with a half merry, half reproachful look, as she knelt down to look at his wounded foot.

The color came up into Dan's face, and he kept his eyes fixed on his plate, as he said very low, "No, ma'am, I'm glad, I wanted to stay, but I was afraid you—"

He did not finish, for Mrs. Bhaer interrupted him by an exclamation of pity, as she saw his foot, for it was seriously hurt.

"When did you do it?"

"Three days ago."

"And you have walked on it in this state?"

"I had a stick, and I washed it at every brook I came to, and one woman gave me a rag to put on it."

"Mr. Bhaer must see and dress it at once," and Mrs. Jo hastened into the next room, leaving the door ajar behind her, so that Dan heard all that passed.

"Fritz, the boy has come back."

"Who? Dan?"

"Yes, Teddy saw him at the window, and he called to him, but he went away and hid behind the hay-cocks on the lawn. I found him there just now fast asleep, and half dead with weariness and pain. He ran away from Page a month ago, and has been making his way to us ever since. He pretends that he did not mean to let us see him, but go on to the city, and his old work, after a look at us. It is evident, however, that the hope of being taken in has led him here through every thing, and there he is waiting to know if you will forgive and take him back."

"Did he say so?"

"His eyes did, and when I waked him, he said, like a lost child, 'Mother Bhaer, I've come home.' I hadn't the heart to scold him, and just took him in like a poor little black sheep come back to the fold. I may keep him, Fritz?"

"Of course you may! This proves to me that we have a hold on the boy's heart, and I would no more send him away now than I would my own Rob."

Dan heard a soft little sound, as if Mrs. Jo thanked her husband without words, and, in the instant's silence that followed, two great tears that had slowly gathered in the boy's eyes brimmed over and rolled down his dusty cheeks. No one saw them, for he brushed them hastily away; but in that little pause I think Dan's old distrust for these good people vanished for ever, the soft spot in his heart was touched, and he felt an impetuous desire to prove himself worthy of the love and pity that was so patient and forgiving. He said nothing, he only wished the wish with all his might, resolved to try in his blind boyish way, and sealed his resolution with the tears which neither pain, fatigue, nor loneliness could wring from him.

"Come and see his foot. I am afraid it is badly hurt, for he has kept on three days through heat and dust, with nothing but water and an old jacket to bind it up with. I tell you, Fritz, that boy is a brave lad, and will make a fine man yet."

"I hope so, for your sake, enthusiastic woman, your faith deserves success. Now, I will go and see your little Spartan. Where is he?"

"In my room; but, dear, you'll be very kind to him, no matter how gruff he seems. I am sure that is the way to conquer him. He won't bear sternness nor much restraint, but a soft word and infinite patience will lead him as it used to lead me."

"As if you ever like this little rascal!" cried Mr. Bhaer, laughing, yet half angry at the idea.

"I was in spirit, though I showed it in a different way. I seem to know by instinct how he feels, to understand what will win and touch him, and to sympathize with his temptations and faults. I am glad I do, for it will help me to help him; and if I can make a good man of this wild boy, it will be the best work of my life."

"God bless the work, and help the worker!"

Mr. Bhaer spoke now as earnestly as she had done, and both came in together to find Dan's head down upon his arm, as if he was quite overcome by sleep. But he looked up quickly, and tried to rise as Mr. Bhaer said pleasantly,

"So you like Plumfield better than Page's farm. Well, let us see if we can get on more comfortably this time than we did before."

"Thanky, sir," said Dan, trying not to be gruff, and finding it easier than he expected.

"Now, the foot! Ach! this is not well. We must have Dr. Firth to-morrow. Warm water, Jo, and old linen."

Mr. Bhaer bathed and bound up the wounded foot, while Mrs. Jo prepared the only empty bed in the house. It was in the little guest-chamber leading from the parlor, and often used when the lads were poorly, for it saved Mrs. Jo from running up and down, and the invalids could see what was going on. When it was ready, Mr. Bhaer took the boy in his arms, and carried him in, helped him undress, laid him on the little white bed, and left him with another hand-shake, and a fatherly "Good-night, my son."

Dan dropped asleep at once, and slept heavily for several hours; then his foot began to throb and ache, and he awoke to toss about uneasily, trying not to groan lest any one should hear him, for he was a brave lad, and did bear pain like "a little Spartan," as Mr. Bhaer called him.

Mrs. Jo had a way of flitting about the house at night, to shut the windows if the wind grew chilly, to draw mosquito curtains over Teddy, or look after Tommy, who occasionally walked in his sleep. The least noise waked her, and as she often heard imaginary robbers, cats, and conflagrations, the doors stood open all about, so her quick ear caught the sound of Dan's little moans, and she was up in a minute. He was just giving his hot pillow a despairing thump when a light came glimmering through the hall, and Mrs. Jo crept in, looking like a droll ghost, with her hair in a great knob on the top of her head, and a long gray dressing-gown trailing behind her.

"Are you in pain, Dan?"

"It's pretty bad; but I didn't mean to wake you."

"I'm a sort of owl, always flying about at night. Yes, your foot is like fire; the bandages must be wet again," and away flapped the maternal owl for more cooling stuff, and a great mug of ice water.

"Oh, that's so nice!" sighed Dan, the wet bandages went on again, and a long draught of water cooled his thirsty throat.

"There, now, sleep your best, and don't be frightened if you see me again, for I'll slip down by and by, and give you another sprinkle."

As she spoke, Mrs. Jo stooped to turn the pillow and smooth the bed-clothes, when, to her great surprise, Dan put his arm around her neck, drew her face down to his, and kissed her, with a broken "Thank you, ma'am," which said more than the most eloquent speech could have done; for the hasty kiss, the muttered words, meant, "I'm sorry, I will try." She understood it, accepted the unspoken confession, and did not spoil it by any token of surprise. She only remembered that he had no mother, kissed the brown cheek half hidden on the pillow, as if ashamed of the little touch of tenderness, and left him, saying, what he long remembered, "You are my boy now, and if you choose you can make me proud and glad to say so."

Once again, just at dawn, she stole down to find him so fast asleep that he did not wake, and showed no sign of consciousness as she wet his foot, except that the lines of pain smoothed themselves away, and left his face quite peaceful.

The day was Sunday, and the house so still that he never waked till near noon, and, looking round him, saw an eager little face peering in at the door. He held out his arms, and Teddy tore across the room to cast himself bodily upon the bed, shouting, "My Danny's tum!" as he hugged and wriggled with delight. Mrs. Bhaer appeared next, bringing breakfast, and never seeming to see how shamefaced Dan looked at the memory of the little scene last night. Teddy insisted on giving him his "betfus," and fed him like a baby, which, as he was not very hungry, Dan enjoyed very much.

Then came the doctor, and the poor Spartan had a bad time of it, for some of the little bones in his foot were injured, and putting them to rights was such a painful job, that Dan's lips were white, and great drops stood on his forehead, though he never cried out, and only held Mrs. Jo's hand so tight that it was red long afterwards.

"You must keep this boy quiet, for a week at least, and not let him put his foot to the ground. By that time, I shall know whether he may hop a little with a crutch, or stick to his bed for a while longer," said Dr. Firth, putting up the shining instruments that Dan did not like to see.

"It will get well sometime, won't it?" he asked, looking alarmed at the word "crutches."

"I hope so;" and with that the doctor departed, leaving Dan much depressed; for the loss of a foot is a dreadful calamity to an active boy.

"Don't be troubled, I am a famous nurse, and we will have you tramping about as well as ever in a month," said Mrs. Jo, taking a hopeful view of the case.

But the fear of being lame haunted Dan, and even Teddy's caresses did not cheer him; so Mrs. Jo proposed that one or two of the boys should come in and pay him a little visit, and asked whom he would like to see.

"Nat and Demi; I'd like my hat too, there's something in it I guess they'd like to see. I suppose you threw away my bundle of plunder?" said Dan, looking rather anxious as he put the question.

"No, I kept it, for I thought they must be treasures of some kind, you took such care of them;" and Mrs. Jo brought him his old straw hat stuck full of butterflies and beetles, and a handkerchief containing a collection of odd things picked up on his way: birds' eggs, carefully done up in moss, curious shells and stones, bits of fungus, and several little crabs, in a state of great indignation at their imprisonment.

"Could I have something to put these fellers in? Mr. Hyde and I found 'em, and they are first-rate ones, so I'd like to keep and watch 'em; can I?" asked Dan, forgetting his foot, and laughing to see the crabs go sidling and backing over the bed.

"Of course you can; Polly's old cage will be just the thing. Don't let them nip Teddy's toes while I get it;" and away went Mrs. Jo, leaving Dan overjoyed to find that his treasures were not considered rubbish, and thrown away.

Nat, Demi, and the cage arrived together, and the crabs were settled in their new house, to the great delight of the boys, who, in the excitement of the performance, forgot any awkwardness they might otherwise have felt in greeting the runaway. To these admiring listeners Dan related his adventures much more fully than he had done to the Bhaers. Then he displayed his "plunder," and described each article so well, that Mrs. Jo, who had retired to the next room to leave them free, was surprised and interested, as well as amused, at their boyish chatter.

"How much the lad knows of these things! how absorbed he is in them! and what a mercy it is just now, for he cares so little for books, it would be hard to amuse him while he is laid up; but the boys can supply him with beetles and stones to any extent, and I am glad to find out this taste of his; it is a good one, and may perhaps prove the making of him. If he should turn out a great naturalist, and Nat a musician, I should have cause to be proud of this year's work;" and Mrs. Jo sat smiling over her book as she built castles in the air, just as she used to do when a girl, only then they were for herself, and now they were for other people, which is the reason perhaps that some of them came to pass in reality for charity is an excellent foundation to build anything upon.

Nat was most interested in the adventures, but Demi enjoyed the beetles and butterflies immensely, drinking in the history of their changeful little lives as if it were a new and lovely sort of fairy tale for, even in his plain way, Dan told it well, and found great satisfaction in the thought that here at least the small philosopher could learn of him. So interested were they in the account of catching a musk rat, whose skin was among the treasures, that Mr. Bhaer had to come himself to tell Nat and Demi it was time for the walk. Dan looked so wistfully after them as they ran off that Father Bhaer proposed carrying him to the sofa in the parlor for a little change of air and scene.

When he was established, and the house quiet, Mrs. Jo, who sat near by showing Teddy pictures, said, in an interested tone, as she nodded towards the treasures still in Dan's hands,

"Where did you learn so much about these things?"

"I always liked 'em, but didn't know much till Mr. Hyde told me."

"Oh, he was a man who lived round in the woods studying these things I don't know what you call him and wrote about frogs, and fishes, and so on. He stayed at Page's, and used to want me to go and help him, and it was great fun, 'cause he told me ever so much, and was uncommon jolly and wise. Hope I'll see him again sometime."

"I hope you will," said Mrs. Jo, for Dan's face had brightened up, and he was so interested in the matter that he forgot his usual taciturnity.

"Why, he could make birds come to him, and rabbits and squirrels didn't mind him any more than if he was a tree. Did you ever tickle a lizard with a straw?" asked Dan, eagerly.

"No, but I should like to try it."

"Well, I've done it, and it's so funny to see 'em turn over and stretch out, they like it so much. Mr. Hyde used to do it; and he'd make snakes listen to him while he whistled, and he knew just when certain flowers would blow, and bees wouldn't sting him, and he'd tell the wonderfullest things about fish and flies, and the Indians and the rocks."

"I think you were so fond of going with Mr. Hyde, you rather neglected Mr. Page," said Mrs. Jo, slyly.

"Yes, I did; I hated to have to weed and hoe when I might be tramping round with Mr. Hyde. Page thought such things silly, and called Mr. Hyde crazy because he'd lay hours watching a trout or a bird."

"Suppose you say lie instead of lay, it is better grammar," said Mrs. Jo, very gently; and then added, "Yes, Page is a thorough farmer, and would not understand that a naturalist's work was just as interesting, and perhaps just as important as his own. Now, Dan, if you really love these things, as I think you do, and I am glad to see it, you shall have time to study them and books to help you; but I want you to do something besides, and to do it faithfully, else you will be sorry by and by, and find that you have got to begin again."

"Yes, ma'am," said Dan, meekly, and looked a little scared by the serious tone of the last remarks, for he hated books, yet had evidently made up his mind to study anything she proposed.

"Do you see that cabinet with twelve drawers in it?" was the next very unexpected question.

Dan did see two tall old-fashioned ones standing on either side of the piano; he knew them well, and had often seen nice bits of string, nails, brown paper, and such useful matters come out of the various drawers. He nodded and smiled. Mrs. Jo went on,

"Well, don't you think those drawers would be good places to put your eggs, and stones, and shells, and lichens?"

"Oh, splendid, but you wouldn't like my things 'clutterin' round,' as Mr. Page used to say, would you?" cried Dan, sitting up to survey the old piece of furniture with sparkling eyes.

"I like litter of that sort; and if I didn't, I should give you the drawers, because I have a regard for children's little treasures, and I think they should be treated respectfully. Now, I am going to make a bargain with you, Dan, and I hope you will keep it honorably. Here are twelve good-sized drawers, one for each month of the year, and they shall be yours as fast as you earn them, by doing the little duties that belong to you. I believe in rewards of a certain kind, especially for young folks; they help us along, and though we may begin by being good for the sake of the reward, if it is rightly used, we shall soon learn to love goodness for itself."

"Do you have 'em?" asked Dan, looking as if this was new talk for him.

"Yes, indeed! I haven't learnt to get on without them yet. My rewards are not drawers, or presents, or holidays, but they are things which I like as much as you do the others. The good behavior and success of my boys is one of the rewards I love best, and I work for it as I want you to work for your cabinet. Do what you dislike, and do it well, and you get two rewards, one, the prize you see and hold; the other, the satisfaction of a duty cheerfully performed. Do you understand that?"

"Yes, ma'am."

"We all need these little helps; so you shall try to do your lessons and your work, play kindly with all the boys, and use your holidays well; and if you bring me a good report, or if I see and know it without words for I'm quick to spy out the good little efforts of my boys you shall have a compartment in the drawer for your treasures. See, some are already divided into four parts, and I will have the others made in the same way, a place for each week; and when the drawer is filled with curious and pretty things, I shall be as proud of it as you are; prouder, I think for in the pebbles, mosses, and gay butterflies, I shall see good resolutions carried out, conquered faults, and a promise well kept. Shall we do this, Dan?"

The boys answered with one of the looks which said much, for it showed that he felt and understood her wish and words, although he did not know how to express his interest and gratitude for such care and kindness. She understood the look, and seeing by the color that flushed up to his forehead that he was touched, as she wished him to be, she said no more about that side of the new plan, but pulled out the upper drawer, dusted it, and set it on two chairs before the sofa, saying briskly,

"Now, let us begin at once by putting those nice beetles in a safe place. These compartments will hold a good deal, you see. I'd pin the butterflies and bugs round the sides; they will be quite safe there, and leave room for the heavy things below. I'll give you some cotton wool, and clean paper and pins, and you can get ready for the week's work."

"But I can't go out to find any new things," said Dan, looking piteously at his foot.

"That's true; never mind, we'll let these treasures do for this week, and I dare say the boys will bring you loads of things if you ask them."

"They don't know the right sort; besides, if I lay, no, lie here all the time, I can't work and study, and earn my drawers."

"There are plenty of lessons you can learn lying there, and several little jobs of work you can do for me."

"Can I?" and Dan looked both surprised and pleased.

"You can learn to be patient and cheerful in spite of pain and no play. You can amuse Teddy for me, wind cotton, read to me when I sew, and do many things without hurting your foot, which will make the days pass quickly, and not be wasted ones."

Here Demi ran in with a great butterfly in one hand, and a very ugly little toad in the other.

"See, Dan, I found them, and ran back to give them to you; aren't they beautiful ones?" panted Demi, all out of breath.

Dan laughed at the toad, and said he had no place to put him, but the butterfly was a beauty, and if Mrs. Jo would give him a big pin, he would stick it right up in the drawer.

"I don't like to see the poor thing struggle on a pin; if it must be killed, let us put it out of pain at once with a drop of camphor," said Mrs. Jo, getting out the bottle.

"I know how to do it Mr. Hyde always killed 'em that way but I didn't have any camphor, so I use a pin," and Dan gently poured a drop on the insect's head, when the pale green wings fluttered an instant, and then grew still.

This dainty little execution was hardly over when Teddy shouted from the bedroom, "Oh, the little trabs are out, and the big one's eaten 'em all up." Demi and his aunt ran to the rescue, and found Teddy dancing excitedly in a chair, while two little crabs were scuttling about the floor, having got through the wires of the cage. A third was clinging to the top of the cage, evidently in terror of his life, for below appeared a sad yet funny sight. The big crab had wedged himself into the little recess where Polly's cup used to stand, and there he sat eating one of his relations in the coolest way. All the claws of the poor victim were pulled off, and he was turned upside down, his upper shell held in one claw close under the mouth of the big crab like a dish, while he leisurely ate out of it with the other claw, pausing now and then to turn his queer bulging eyes from side to side, and to put out a slender tongue and lick them in a way that made the children scream with laughter. Mrs. Jo carried the cage in for Dan to see the sight, while Demi caught and confined the wanderers under an inverted wash-bowl.

"I'll have to let these fellers go, for I can't keep 'em in the house," said Dan, with evident regret.

"I'll take care of them for you, if you will tell me how, and they can live in my turtle-tank just as well as not," said Demi, who found them more interesting even that his beloved slow turtles. So Dan gave him directions about the wants and habits of the crabs, and Demi bore them away to introduce them to their new home and neighbors. "What a good boy he is!" said Dan, carefully settling the first butterfly, and remembering that Demi had given up his walk to bring it to him.

"He ought to be, for a great deal has been done to make him so."

"He's had folks to tell him things, and to help him; I haven't," said Dan, with a sigh, thinking of his neglected childhood, a thing he seldom did, and feeling as if he had not had fair play somehow.

"I know it, dear, and for that reason I don't expect as much from you as from Demi, though he is younger; you shall have all the help that we can give you now, and I hope to teach you how to help yourself in the best way. Have you forgotten what Father Bhaer told you when you were here before, about wanting to be good, and asking God to help you?"

"No, ma'am," very low.

"Do you try that way still?"

"No, ma'am," lower still.

"Will you do it every night to please me?"

"Yes, ma'am," very soberly.

"I shall depend on it, and I think I shall know if you are faithful to your promise, for these things always show to people who believe in them, though not a word is said. Now here is a pleasant story about a boy who hurt his foot worse than you did yours; read it, and see how bravely he bore his troubles."

She put that charming little book, "The Crofton Boys," into his hands, and left him for an hour, passing in and out from time to time that he might not feel lonely. Dan did not love to read, but soon got so interested that he was surprised when the boys came home. Daisy brought him a nosegay of wild flowers, and Nan insisted on helping bring him his supper, as he lay on the sofa with the door open into the dining-room, so that he could see the lads at table, and they could nod socially to him over their bread and butter.

Mr. Bhaer carried him away to his bed early, and Teddy came in his night-gown to say good-night, for he went to his little nest with the birds.

"I want to say my prayers to Danny; may I?" he asked; and when his mother said, "Yes," the little fellow knelt down by Dan's bed, and folding his chubby hands, said softly,

"Pease Dod bess everybody, and hep me to be dood."

Then he went away smiling with sleepy sweetness over his mother's shoulder.

But after the evening talk was done, the evening song sung, and the house grew still with beautiful Sunday silence, Dan lay in his pleasant room wide awake, thinking new thoughts, feeling new hopes and desires stirring in his boyish heart, for two good angels had entered in: love and gratitude began the work which time and effort were to finish; and with an earnest wish to keep his first promise, Dan folded his hands together in the Darkness, and softly whispered Teddy's little prayer,

"Please God bless every one, and help me to be good."

# CHAPTER XI. UNCLE TEDDY

For a week Dan only moved from bed to sofa; a long week and a hard one, for the hurt foot was very painful at times, the quiet days were very wearisome to the active lad, longing to be out enjoying the summer weather, and especially difficult was it to be patient. But Dan did his best, and every one helped him in their various ways; so the time passed, and he was rewarded at last by hearing the doctor say, on Saturday morning,

"This foot is doing better than I expected. Give the lad the crutch this afternoon, and let him stump about the house a little."

"Hooray!" shouted Nat, and raced away to tell the other boys the good news.

Everybody was very glad, and after dinner the whole flock assembled to behold Dan crutch himself up and down the hall a few times before he settled in the porch to hold a sort of levee. He was much pleased at the interest and good-will shown him, and brightened up more and more every minute; for the boys came to pay their respects, the little girls fussed about him with stools and cushions, and Teddy watched over him as if he was a frail creature unable to do anything for himself. They were still sitting and standing about the steps, when a carriage stopped at the gate, a hat was waved from it, and with a shout of "Uncle Teddy! Uncle Teddy!" Rob scampered down the avenue as fast as his short legs would carry him. All he boys but Dan ran after him to see who should be first to open the gate, and in a moment the carriage drove up with boys swarming all over it, while Uncle Teddy sat laughing in the midst, with his little daughter on his knee.

"Stop the triumphal car and let Jupiter descend," he said, and jumping out ran up the steps to meet Mrs. Bhaer, who stood smiling and clapping her hands like a girl.

"How goes it, Teddy?"

"All right, Jo."

Then they shook hands, and Mr. Laurie put Bess into her aunt's arms, saying, as the child hugged her tight, "Goldilocks wanted to see you so much that I ran away with her, for I was quite pining for a sight of you myself. We want to play with your boys for an hour or so, and to see how 'the old woman who lived in a shoe, and had so many children she did not know what to do,' is getting on."

"I'm so glad! Play away, and don't get into mischief," answered Mrs. Jo, as the lads crowded round the pretty child, admiring her long golden hair, dainty dress, and lofty ways, for the little "Princess," as they called her, allowed no one to kiss her, but sat smiling down upon them, and graciously patting their heads with her little, white hands. They all adored her, especially Rob, who considered her a sort of doll, and dared not touch her lest she should break, but worshipped her at a respectful distance, made happy by an occasional mark of favor from her little highness. As she immediately demanded to see Daisy's kitchen, she was borne off by Mrs. Jo, with a train of small boys following.

The others, all but Nat and Demi, ran away to the menagerie and gardens to have all in order; for Mr. Laurie always took a general survey, and looked disappointed if things were not flourishing.

Standing on the steps, he turned to Dan, saying like an old acquaintance, though he had only seen him once or twice before,

"How is the foot?"

"Better, sir."

"Rather tired of the house, aren't you?"

"Guess I am!" and Dan's eyes roved away to the green hills and woods where he longed to be.

"Suppose we take a little turn before the others come back? That big, easy carriage will be quite safe and comfortable, and a breath of fresh air will do you good. Get a cushion and a shawl, Demi, and let's carry Dan off."

The boys thought it a capital joke, and Dan looked delighted, but asked, with an unexpected burst of virtue,

"Will Mrs. Bhaer like it?"

"Oh, yes; we settled all that a minute ago."

"You didn't say any thing about it, so I don't see how you could," said Demi, inquisitively.

"We have a way of sending messages to one another, without any words. It is a great improvement on the telegraph."

"I know it's eyes; I saw you lift your eyebrows, and nod toward the carriage, and Mrs. Bhaer laughed and nodded back again," cried Nat, who was quite at his ease with kind Mr. Laurie by this time.

"Right. Now them, come on," and in a minute Dan found himself settled in the carriage, his foot on a cushion on the seat opposite, nicely covered with a shawl, which fell down from the upper regions in a most mysterious manner, just when they wanted it. Demi climbed up to the box beside Peter, the black coachman. Nat sat next Dan in the place of honor, while Uncle Teddy would sit opposite, to take care of the foot, he said, but really that he might study the faces before him both so happy, yet so different, for Dan's was square, and brown, and strong, while Nat's was long, and fair, and rather weak, but very amiable with its mild eyes and good forehead.

"By the way, I've got a book somewhere here that you may like to see," said the oldest boy of the party, diving under the seat and producing a book which make Dan exclaim,

"Oh! by George, isn't that a stunner?" as he turned the leaves, and saw fine plates of butterflies, and birds, and every sort of interesting insect, colored like life. He was so charmed that he forgot his thanks, but Mr. Laurie did not mind, and was quite satisfied to see the boy's eager delight, and to hear this exclamations over certain old friends as he came to them. Nat leaned on his shoulder to look, and Demi turned his back to the horses, and let his feet dangle inside the carriage, so that he might join in the conversation.

When they got among the beetles, Mr. Laurie took a curious little object out of his vest-pocket, and laying it in the palm of his hand, said,

"There's a beetle that is thousands of years old;" and then, while the lads examined the queer stone-bug, that looked so old and gray, he told them how it came out of the wrappings of a mummy, after lying for ages in a famous tomb. Finding them interested, he went on to tell about the Egyptians, and the strange and splendid ruins they have left behind them the Nile, and how he sailed up the mighty river, with the handsome dark men to work his boat; how he shot alligators, saw wonderful beasts and birds; and afterwards crossed the desert on a camel, who pitched him about like a ship in a storm.

"Uncle Teddy tells stories 'most as well as Grandpa," said Demi, approvingly, when the tale was done, and the boys' eyes asked for more.

"Thank you," said Mr. Laurie, quite soberly, for he considered Demi's praise worth having, for children are good critics in such cases, and to suit them is an accomplishment that any one may be proud of.

"Here's another trifle or two that I tucked into my pocket as I was turning over my traps to see if I had any thing that would amuse Dan," and Uncle Teddy produced a fine arrow-head and a string of wampum.

"Oh! tell about the Indians," cried Demi, who was fond of playing wigwam.

"Dan knows lots about them," added Nat.

"More than I do, I dare say. Tell us something," and Mr. Laurie looked as interested as the other two.

"Mr. Hyde told me; he's been among 'em, and can talk their talk, and likes 'em," began Dan, flattered by their attention, but rather embarrassed by having a grown-up listener.

"What is wampum for?" asked curious Demi, from his perch.

The others asked questions likewise, and, before he knew it, Dan was reeling off all Mr. Hyde had told him, as they sailed down the river a few weeks before. Mr. Laurie listened well, but found the boy more interesting than the Indians, for Mrs. Jo had told him about Dan, and he rather took a fancy to the wild lad, who ran away as he himself had often longed to do, and who was slowly getting tamed by pain and patience.

"I've been thinking that it would be a good plan for you fellows to have a museum of your own; a place in which to collect all the curious and interesting things that you find, and make, and have given you. Mrs. Jo is too kind to complain, but it is rather hard for her to have the house littered up with all sorts of rattletraps, half-a-pint of dor-bugs in one of her best vases, for instance, a couple of dead bats nailed up in the back entry, wasps nests tumbling down on people's heads, and stones lying round everywhere, enough to pave the avenue. There are not many women who would stand that sort of thing, are there, now?"

As Mr. Laurie spoke with a merry look in his eyes, the boys laughed and nudged one another, for it was evident that some one told tales out of school, else how could he know of the existence of these inconvenient treasures.

"Where can we put them, then?" said Demi, crossing his legs and leaning down to argue the question.

"In the old carriage-house."

"But it leaks, and there isn't any window, nor any place to put things, and it's all dust and cobwebs," began Nat.

"Wait till Gibbs and I have touched it up a bit, and then see how you like it. He is to come over on Monday to get it ready; then next Saturday I shall come out, and we will fix it up, and make the beginning, at least, of a fine little museum. Every one can bring his things, and have a place for them; and Dan is to be the head man, because he knows most about such matters, and it will be quiet, pleasant work for him now that he can't knock about much."

"Won't that be jolly?" cried Nat, while Dan smiled all over his face and had not a word to say, but hugged his book, and looked at Mr. Laurie as if he thought him one of the greatest public benefactors that ever blessed the world.

"Shall I go round again, sir?" asked Peter, as they came to the gate, after two slow turns about the half-mile triangle.

"No, we must be prudent, else we can't come again. I must go over the premises, take a look at the carriage-house, and have a little talk with Mrs. Jo before I go;" and, having deposited Dan on his sofa to rest and enjoy his book, Uncle Teddy went off to have a frolic with the lads who were raging about the place in search of him. Leaving the little girls to mess up-stairs, Mrs. Bhaer sat down by Dan, and listened to his eager account of the drive till the flock returned, dusty, warm, and much excited about the new museum, which every one considered the most brilliant idea of the age.

"I always wanted to endow some sort of an institution, and I am going to begin with this," said Mr. Laurie, sitting down on a stool at Mrs. Jo's feet.

"You have endowed one already. What do you call this?" and Mrs. Jo pointed to the happy-faced lads, who had camped upon the floor about him.

"I call it a very promising Bhaer-garden, and I'm proud to be a member of it. Did you know I was the head boy in this school?" he asked, turning to Dan, and changing the subject skilfully, for he hated to be thanked for the generous things he did.

"I thought Franz was!" answered Dan, wondering what the man meant.

"Oh, dear no! I'm the first boy Mrs. Jo ever had to take care of, and I was such a bad one that she isn't done with me yet, though she has been working at me for years and years."

"How old she must be!" said Nat, innocently.

"She began early, you see. Poor thing! she was only fifteen when she took me, and I led her such a life, it's a wonder she isn't wrinkled and gray, and quite worn out," and Mr. Laurie looked up at her laughing.

"Don't Teddy; I won't have you abuse yourself so;" and Mrs. Jo stroked the curly black head at her knee as affectionately as ever, for, in spite of every thing Teddy was her boy still.

"If it hadn't been for you, there never would have been a Plumfield. It was my success with you, sir, that gave me courage to try my pet plan. So the boys may thank you for it, and name the new institution 'The Laurence Museum,' in honor of its founder, won't we, boys?" she added, looking very like the lively Jo of old times.

"We will! we will!" shouted the boys, throwing up their hats, for though they had taken them off on entering the house, according to rule, they had been in too much of a hurry to hang them up.

"I'm as hungry as a bear, can't I have a cookie?" asked Mr. Laurie, when the shout subsided and he had expressed his thanks by a splendid bow.

"Trot out and ask Asia for the gingerbread-box, Demi. It isn't in order to eat between meals, but, on this joyful occasion, we won't mind, and have a cookie all round," said Mrs. Jo; and when the box came she dealt them out with a liberal hand, every one munching away in a social circle.

Suddenly, in the midst of a bite, Mr. Laurie cried out, "Bless my heart, I forgot grandma's bundle!" and running out to the carriage, returned with an interesting white parcel, which, being opened, disclosed a choice collection of beasts, birds, and pretty things cut out of crisp sugary cake, and baked a lovely brown.

"There's one for each, and a letter to tell which is whose. Grandma and Hannah made them, and I tremble to think what would have happened to me if I had forgotten to leave them."

Then, amid much laughing and fun, the cakes were distributed. A fish for Dan, a fiddle for Nat, a book for Demi, a money for Tommy, a flower for Daisy, a hoop for Nan, who had driven twice round the triangle without stopping, a star for Emil, who put on airs because he studied astronomy, and, best of all, an omnibus for Franz, whose great delight was to drive the family bus. Stuffy got a fat pig, and the little folks had birds, and cats, and rabbits, with black currant eyes.

"Now I must go. Where is my Goldilocks? Mamma will come flying out to get her if I'm not back early," said Uncle Teddy, when the last crumb had vanished, which it speedily did, you may be sure.

The young ladies had gone into the garden, and while they waited till Franz looked them up, Jo and Laurie stood at the door talking together.

"How does little Giddy-gaddy come on?" he asked, for Nan's pranks amused him very much, and he was never tired of teasing Jo about her.

"Nicely; she is getting quite mannerly, and begins to see the error of her wild ways."

"Don't the boys encourage her in them?"

"Yes; but I keep talking, and lately she has improved much. You saw how prettily she shook hands with you, and how gentle she was with Bess. Daisy's example has its effect upon her, and I'm quite sure that a few months will work wonders."

Here Mrs. Jo's remarks were cut short by the appearance of Nan tearing round the corner at a break-neck pace, driving a mettlesome team of four boys, and followed by Daisy trundling Bess in a wheelbarrow. Hat off, hair flying, whip cracking, and barrow bumping, up they came in a cloud of dust, looking as wild a set of little hoydens as one would wish to see.

"So, these are the model children, are they? It's lucky I didn't bring Mrs. Curtis out to see your school for the cultivation of morals and manners; she would never have recovered from the shock of this spectacle," said Mr. Laurie, laughing at Mrs. Jo's premature rejoicing over Nan's improvement.

"Laugh away; I'll succeed yet. As you used to say at College, quoting some professor, 'Though the experiment has failed, the principle remains the same,'" said Mrs. Bhaer, joining in the merriment.

"I'm afraid Nan's example is taking effect upon Daisy, instead of the other way. Look at my little princess! she has utterly forgotten her dignity, and is screaming like the rest. Young ladies, what does this mean?" and Mr. Laurie rescued his small daughter from impending destruction, for the four horses were champing their bits and curvetting madly all about her, as she sat brandishing a great whip in both hands.

"We're having a race, and I beat," shouted Nan.

"I could have run faster, only I was afraid of spilling Bess," screamed Daisy.

"Hi! go long!" cried the princess, giving such a flourish with her whip that the horses ran away, and were seen no more.

"My precious child! come away from this ill-mannered crew before you are quite spoilt. Good-by, Jo! Next time I come, I shall expect to find the boys making patchwork."

"It wouldn't hurt them a bit. I don't give in, mind you; for my experiments always fail a few times before they succeed. Love to Amy and my blessed Marmee," called Mrs. Jo, as the carriage drove away; and the last Mr. Laurie saw of her, she was consoling Daisy for her failure by a ride in the wheelbarrow, and looking as if she liked it.

Great was the excitement all the week about the repairs in the carriage-house, which went briskly on in spite of the incessant questions, advice, and meddling of the boys. Old Gibbs was nearly driven wild with it all, but managed to do his work nevertheless; and by Friday night the place was all in order roof mended, shelves up, walls whitewashed, a great window cut at the back, which let in a flood of sunshine, and gave them a fine view of the brook, the meadows, and the distant hills; and over the great door, painted in red letters, was "The Laurence Museum."

All Saturday morning the boys were planning how it should be furnished with their spoils, and when Mr. Laurie arrived, bringing an aquarium which Mrs. Amy said she was tired of, their rapture was great.

The afternoon was spent in arranging things, and when the running and lugging and hammering was over, the ladies were invited to behold the institution.

It certainly was a pleasant place, airy, clean, and bright. A hop-vine shook its green bells round the open window, the pretty aquarium stood in the middle of the room, with some delicate water plants rising above the water, and gold-fish showing their brightness as they floated to and fro below. On either side of the window were rows of shelves ready to receive the curiosities yet to be found. Dan's tall cabinet stood before the great door which was fastened up, while the small door was to be used. On the cabinet stood a queer Indian idol, very ugly, but very interesting; old Mr. Laurence sent it, as well as a fine Chinese junk in full sail, which had a conspicuous place on the long table in the middle of the room. Above, swinging in a loop, and looking as if she was alive, hung Polly, who died at an advanced age, had been carefully stuffed, and was no presented by Mrs. Jo. The walls were decorated with all sorts of things. A snake's skin, a big wasp's nest, a birch-bark canoe, a string of birds' eggs, wreaths of gray moss from the South, and a bunch of cotton-pods. The dead bats had a place, also a large turtle-shell, and an ostrich-egg proudly presented by Demi, who volunteered to explain these rare curiosities to guests whenever they liked. There were so many stones that it was impossible to accept them all, so only a few of the best were arranged among the shells on the shelves, the rest were piled up in corners, to be examined by Dan at his leisure.

Every one was eager to give something, even Silas, who sent home for a stuffed wild-cat killed in his youth. It was rather moth-eaten and shabby, but on a high bracket and best side foremost the effect was fine, for the yellow glass eyes glared, and the mouth snarled so naturally, that Teddy shook in his little shoes at sight of it, when he came bringing his most cherished treasure, one cocoon, to lay upon the shrine of science.

"Isn't it beautiful? I'd no idea we had so many curious things. I gave that; don't it look well? We might make a lot by charging something for letting folks see it."

Jack added that last suggestion to the general chatter that went on as the family viewed the room.

"This is a free museum and if there is any speculating on it I'll paint out the name over the door," said Mr. Laurie, turning so quickly that Jack wished he had held his tongue.

"Hear! hear!" cried Mr. Bhaer.

"Speech! speech!" added Mrs. Jo.

"Can't, I'm too bashful. You give them a lecture yourself you are used to it," Mr. Laurie answered, retreating towards the window, meaning to escape. But she held him fast, and said, laughing as she looked at the dozen pairs of dirty hands about her,

"If I did lecture, it would on the chemical and cleansing properties of soap. Come now, as the founder of the institution, you really ought to give us a few moral remarks, and we will applaud tremendously."

Seeing that there was no way of escaping, Mr. Laurie looked up at Polly hanging overhead, seemed to find inspiration in the brilliant old bird, and sitting down upon the table, said, in his pleasant way,

"There is one thing I'd like to suggest, boys, and that is, I want you to get some good as well as much pleasure out of this. Just putting curious or pretty things here won't do it; so suppose you read up about them, so that when anybody asks questions you can answer them, and understand the matter. I used to like these things myself, and should enjoy hearing about them now, for I've forgotten all I once knew. It wasn't much, was it, Jo? Here's Dan now, full of stories about birds, and bugs, and so on; let him take care of the museum, and once a week the rest of you take turns to read a composition, or tell about some animal, mineral, or vegetable. We should all like that, and I think it would put considerable useful knowledge into our heads. What do you say, Professor?"

"I like it much, and will give the lads all the help I can. But they will need books to read up these new subjects, and we have not many, I fear," began Mr. Bhaer, looking much pleased, planning many fine lectures on geology, which he liked. "We should have a library for the special purpose."

"Is that a useful sort of book, Dan?" asked Mr. Laurie, pointing to the volume that lay open by the cabinet.

"Oh, yes! it tells all I want to know about insects. I had it here to see how to fix the butterflies right. I covered it, so it is not hurt;" and Dan caught it up, fearing the lender might think him careless.

"Give it here a minute;" and, pulling out his pencil, Mr. Laurie wrote Dan's name in it, saying, as he set the book up on one of the corner shelves, where nothing stood but a stuffed bird without a tail, "There, that is the beginning of the museum library. I'll hunt up some more books, and Demi shall keep them in order. Where are those jolly little books we used to read, Jo? 'Insect Architecture' or some such name, all about ants having battles, and bees having queens, and crickets eating holes in our clothes and stealing milk, and larks of that sort."

"In the garret at home. I'll have them sent out, and we will plunge into Natural History with a will," said Mrs. Jo, ready for any thing.

"Won't it be hard to write about such things?" asked Nat, who hated compositions.

"At first, perhaps; but you will soon like it. If you think that hard, how would you like to have this subject given to you, as it was to a girl of thirteen: A conversation between Themistocles, Aristides, and Pericles on the proposed appropriation of funds of the confederacy of Delos for the ornamentation of Athens?" said Mrs. Jo.

The boys groaned at the mere sound of the long names, and the gentlemen laughed at the absurdity of the lesson.

"Did she write it?" asked Demi, in an awe-stricken tone.

"Yes, but you can imagine what a piece of work she make of it, though she was rather a bright child."

"I'd like to have seen it," said Mr. Bhaer.

"Perhaps I can find it for you; I went to school with her," and Mrs. Jo looked so wicked that every one knew who the little girl was.

Hearing of this fearful subject for a composition quite reconciled the boys to the thought of writing about familiar things. Wednesday afternoon was appointed for the lectures, as they preferred to call them, for some chose to talk instead of write. Mr. Bhaer promised a portfolio in which the written productions should be kept, and Mrs. Bhaer said she would attend the course with great pleasure.

Then the dirty-handed society went off the wash, followed by the Professor, trying to calm the anxiety of Rob, who had been told by Tommy that all water was full of invisible pollywogs.

"I like your plan very much, only don't be too generous, Teddy," said Mrs. Bhaer, when they were left alone. "You know most of the boys have got to paddle their own canoes when they leave us, and too much sitting in the lap of luxury will unfit them for it."

"I'll be moderate, but do let me amuse myself. I get desperately tired of business sometimes, and nothing freshens me up like a good frolic with your boys. I like that Dan very much, Jo. He isn't demonstrative; but he has the eye of a hawk, and when you have tamed him a little he will do you credit."

"I'm so glad you think so. Thank you very much for your kindness to him, especially for this museum affair; it will keep him happy while he is lame, give me a chance to soften and smooth this poor, rough lad, and make him love us. What did inspire you with such a beautiful, helpful idea, Teddy?" asked Mrs. Bhaer, glancing back at the pleasant room, as she turned to leave it.

Laurie took both her hands in his, and answered, with a look that made her eyes fill with happy tears,

"Dear Jo! I have known what it is to be a motherless boy, and I never can forget how much you and yours have done for me all these years."

## CHAPTER XII. HUCKLEBERRIES

There was a great clashing of tin pails, much running to and fro, and frequent demands for something to eat, one August afternoon, for the boys were going huckleberrying, and made as much stir about it as if they were setting out to find the North West Passage.

"Now, my lads, get off as quietly as you can, for Rob is safely out of the way, and won't see you," said Mrs. Bhaer, as she tied Daisy's broad-brimmed hat, and settled the great blue pinafore in which she had enveloped Nan.

But the plan did not succeed, for Rob had heard the bustle, decided to go, and prepared himself, without a thought of disappointment. The troop was just getting under way when the little man came marching downstairs with his best hat on, a bright tin pail in his hand, and a face beaming with satisfaction.

"Oh, dear! now we shall have a scene," sighed Mrs. Bhaer, who found her eldest son very hard to manage at times.

"I'm all ready," said Rob, and took his place in the ranks with such perfect unconsciousness of his mistake, that it really was very hard to undeceive him.

"It's too far for you, my love; stay and take care of me, for I shall be all alone," began his mother.

"You've got Teddy. I'm a big boy, so I can go; you said I might when I was bigger, and I am now," persisted Rob, with a cloud beginning to dim the brightness of his happy face.

"We are going up to the great pasture, and it's ever so far; we don't want you tagging on," cried Jack, who did not admire the little boys.

"I won't tag, I'll run and keep up. O Mamma! let me go! I want to fill my new pail, and I'll bring 'em all to you. Please, please, I will be good!" prayed Robby, looking up at his mother, so grieved and disappointed that her heart began to fail her.

"But, my deary, you'll get so tired and hot you won't have a good time. Wait till I go, and then we will stay all day, and pick as many berries as you want."

"You never do go, you are so busy, and I'm tired of waiting. I'd rather go and get the berries for you all myself. I love to pick 'em, and I want to fill my new pail dreffly," sobbed Rob.

The pathetic sight of great tears tinkling into the dear new pail, and threatening to fill it with salt water instead of huckleberries, touched all the ladies present. His mother patted the weeper on his back; Daisy offered to stay home with him; and Nan said, in her decided way,

"Let him come; I'll take care of him."

"If Franz was going I wouldn't mind, for he is very careful; but he is haying with the father, and I'm not sure about the rest of you," began Mrs. Bhaer.

"It's so far," put in Jack.

"I'd carry him if I was going wish I was," said Dan, with a sigh.

"Thank you, dear, but you must take care of your foot. I wish I could go. Stop a minute, I think I can manage it after all;" and Mrs. Bhaer ran out to the steps, waving her apron wildly.

Silas was just driving away in the hay-cart, but turned back, and agreed at once, when Mrs. Jo proposed that he should take the whole party to the pasture, and go for them at five o'clock.

"It will delay your work a little, but never mind; we will pay you in huckleberry pies," said Mrs. Jo, knowing Silas's weak point.

His rough, brown face brightened up, and he said, with a cheery "Haw! haw!" "Wal now, Mis' Bhaer, if you go to bribin' of me, I shall give in right away."

"Now, boys, I have arranged it so that you can all go," said Mrs. Bhaer, running back again, much relieved, for she loved to make them happy, and always felt miserable when she had disturbed the serenity of her little sons; for she believed that the small hopes and plans and pleasures of children should be tenderly respected by grown-up people, and never rudely thwarted or ridiculed.

"Can I go?" said Dan, delighted.

"I thought especially of you. Be careful, and never mind the berries, but sit about and enjoy the lovely things which you know how to find all about you," answered Mrs. Bhaer, who remembered his kind offer to her boy.

"Me too! me too!" sung Rob, dancing with joy, and clapping his precious pail and cover like castanets.

"Yes, and Daisy and Nan must take good care of you. Be at the bars at five o'clock, and Silas will come for you all."

Robby cast himself upon his mother in a burst of gratitude, promising to bring her every berry he picked, and not eat one. Then they were all packed into the hay-cart, and went rattling away, the brightest face among the dozen being that of Rob, as he sat between his two temporary little mothers, beaming upon the whole world, and waving his best hat; for his indulgent mamma had not the heart to bereave him of it, since this was a gala-day to him.

Such a happy afternoon as they had, in spite of the mishaps which usually occur on such expeditions! Of course Tommy came to grief, tumbled upon a hornet's nest and got stung; but being used to woe, he bore the smart manfully, till Dan suggested the application of damp earth, which much assuaged the pain. Daisy saw a snake, and flying from it lost half her berries; but Demi helped her to fill up again, and discussed reptiles most learnedly the while. Ned fell out of a tree, and split his jacket down the back, but suffered no other fracture. Emil and Jack established rival claims to a certain thick patch, and while they were squabbling about it, Stuffy quickly and quietly stripped the bushes and fled to the protection of Dan, who was enjoying himself immensely. The crutch was no longer necessary, and he was delighted to see how strong his foot felt as he roamed about the great pasture, full of interesting rocks and stumps, with familiar little creatures in the grass, and well-known insects dancing in the air.

But of all the adventures that happened on this afternoon that which befell Nan and Rob was the most exciting, and it long remained one of the favorite histories of the household. Having explored the country pretty generally, torn three rents in her frock, and scratched her face in a barberry-bush, Nan began to pick the berries that shone like big, black beads on the low, green bushes. Her nimble fingers flew, but still her basket did not fill up as rapidly as she desired, so she kept wandering here and there to search for better places, instead of picking contentedly and steadily as Daisy did. Rob followed Nan, for her energy suited him better than his cousin's patience, and he too was anxious to have the biggest and best berries for Marmar.

"I keep putting 'em in, but it don't fill up, and I'm so tired," said Rob, pausing a moment to rest his short legs, and beginning to think huckleberrying was not all his fancy painted it; for the sun blazed, Nan skipped hither and thither like a grasshopper, and the berries fell out of his pail almost as fast as he put them in, because, in his struggles with the bushes, it was often upside-down.

"Last time we came they were ever so much thicker over that wall great bouncers; and there is a cave there where the boys made a fire. Let's go and fill our things quick, and then hide in the cave and let the others find us," proposed Nan, thirsting for adventures.

Rob consented, and away they went, scrambling over the wall and running down the sloping fields on the other side, till they were hidden among the rocks and underbrush. The berries were thick, and at last the pails were actually full. It was shady and cool down there, and a little spring gave the thirsty children a refreshing drink out of its mossy cup.

"Now we will go and rest in the cave, and eat our lunch," said Nan, well satisfied with her success so far.

"Do you know the way?" asked Rob.

"'Course I do; I've been once, and I always remember. Didn't I go and get my box all right?"

That convinced Rob, and he followed blindly as Nan led him over stock and stone, and brought him, after much meandering, to a small recess in the rock, where the blackened stones showed that fires had been made.

"Now, isn't it nice?" asked Nan, as she took out a bit of bread-and-butter, rather damaged by being mixed up with nails, fishhooks, stones and other foreign substances, in the young lady's pocket.

"Yes; do you think they will find us soon?" asked Rob, who found the shadowy glen rather dull, and began to long for more society.

"No, I don't; because if I hear them, I shall hide, and have fun making them find me."

"P'raps they won't come."

"Don't care; I can get home myself."

"Is it a great way?" asked Rob, looking at his little stubby boots, scratched and wet with his long wandering.

"It's six miles, I guess." Nan's ideas of distance were vague, and her faith in her own powers great.

"I think we better go now," suggested Rob, presently.

"I shan't till I have picked over my berries;" and Nan began what seemed to Rob an endless task.

"Oh, dear! you said you'd take good care of me," he sighed, as the sun seemed to drop behind the hill all of a sudden.

"Well I am taking good care of you as hard as I can. Don't be cross, child; I'll go in a minute," said Nan, who considered five-year-old Robby a mere infant compared to herself.

So little Rob sat looking anxiously about him, and waiting patiently, for, spite of some misgivings, he felt great confidence in Nan.

"I guess it's going to be night pretty soon," he observed, as if to himself, as a mosquito bit him, and the frogs in a neighboring marsh began to pipe up for the evening concert.

"My goodness me! so it is. Come right away this minute, or they will be gone," cried Nan, looking up from her work, and suddenly perceiving that the sun was down.

"I heard a horn about an hour ago; may be they were blowing for us," said Rob, trudging after his guide as she scrambled up the steep hill.

"Where was it?" asked Nan, stopping short.

"Over that way;" he pointed with a dirty little finger in an entirely wrong direction.

"Let's go that way and meet them;" and Nan wheeled about, and began to trot through the bushes, feeling a trifle anxious, for there were so many cow-paths all about she could not remember which way they came.

On they went over stock and stone again, pausing now and then to listen for the horn, which did not blow any more, for it was only the moo of a cow on her way home.

"I don't remember seeing that pile of stones do you?" asked Nan, as she sat on a wall to rest a moment and take an observation.

"I don't remember any thing, but I want to go home," and Rob's voice had a little tremble in it that made Nan put her arms round him and lift him gently down, saying, in her most capable way,

"I'm going just as fast as I can, dear. Don't cry, and when we come to the road, I'll carry you."

"Where is the road?" and Robby wiped his eyes to look for it.

"Over by that big tree. Don't you know that's the one Ned tumbled out of?"

"So it is. May be they waited for us; I'd like to ride home wouldn't you?" and Robby brightened up as he plodded along toward the end of the great pasture.

"No, I'd rather walk," answered Nan, feeling quite sure that she would be obliged to do so, and preparing her mind for it.

Another long trudge through the fast-deepening twilight and another disappointment, for when they reached the tree, they found to their dismay that it was not the one Ned climbed, and no road anywhere appeared.

"Are we lost?" quavered Rob, clasping his pail in despair.

"Not much. I don't just see which way to go, and I guess we'd better call."

So they both shouted till they were hoarse, yet nothing answered but the frogs in full chorus.

"There is another tall tree over there, perhaps that's the one," said Nan, whose heart sunk within her, though she still spoke bravely.

"I don't think I can go any more; my boots are so heavy I can't pull 'em;" and Robby sat down on a stone quite worn out.

"Then we must stay here all night. I don't care much, if snakes don't come."

"I'm frightened of snakes. I can't stay all night. Oh, dear! I don't like to be lost," and Rob puckered up his face to cry, when suddenly a thought occurred to him, and he said, in a tone of perfect confidence,

"Marmar will come and find me she always does; I ain't afraid now."

"She won't know where we are."

"She didn't know I was shut up in the ice-house, but she found me. I know she'll come," returned Robby, so trustfully, that Nan felt relieved, and sat down by him, saying, with a remorseful sigh,

"I wish we hadn't run away."

"You made me; but I don't mind much Marmar will love me just the same," answered Rob, clinging to his sheet-anchor when all other hope was gone.

"I'm so hungry. Let's eat our berries," proposed Nan, after a pause, during which Rob began to nod.

"So am I, but I can't eat mine, 'cause I told Marmar I'd keep them all for her."

"You'll have to eat them if no one comes for us," said Nan, who felt like contradicting every thing just then. "If we stay here a great many days, we shall eat up all the berries in the field, and then we shall starve," she added grimly.

"I shall eat sassafras. I know a big tree of it, and Dan told me how squirrels dig up the roots and eat them, and I love to dig," returned Rob, undaunted by the prospect of starvation.

"Yes; and we can catch frogs, and cook them. My father ate some once, and he said they were nice," put in Nan, beginning to find a spice of romance even in being lost in a huckleberry pasture.

"How could we cook frogs? we haven't got any fire."

"I don't know; next time I'll have matches in my pocket," said Nan, rather depressed by this obstacle to the experiment in frog-cookery.

"Couldn't we light a fire with a fire-fly?" asked Rob, hopefully, as he watched them flitting to and fro like winged sparks.

"Let's try;" and several minutes were pleasantly spent in catching the flies, and trying to make them kindle a green twig or two. "It's a lie to call them fire-flies when there isn't a fire in them," Nan said, throwing one unhappy insect away with scorn, though it shone its best, and obligingly walked up and down the twigs to please the innocent little experimenters.

"Marmar's a good while coming," said Rob, after another pause, during which they watched the stars overhead, smelt the sweet fern crushed under foot, and listened to the crickets' serenade.

"I don't see why God made any night; day is so much pleasanter," said Nan, thoughtfully.

"It's to sleep in," answered Rob, with a yawn.

"Then do go to sleep," said Nan, pettishly.

"I want my own bed. Oh, I wish I could see Teddy!" cried Rob, painfully reminded of home by the soft chirp of birds safe in their little nests.

"I don't believe your mother will ever find us," said Nan, who was becoming desperate, for she hated patient waiting of any sort. "It's so dark she won't see us."

"It was all black in the ice-house, and I was so scared I didn't call her, but she saw me; and she will see me now, no matter how dark it is," returned confiding Rob, standing up to peer into the gloom for the help which never failed him.

"I see her! I see her!" he cried, and ran as fast as his tired legs would take him toward a dark figure slowly approaching. Suddenly he stopped, then turned about, and came stumbling back, screaming in a great panic,

"No, it's a bear, a big black one!" and hid his face in Nan's skirts.

For a moment Nan quailed; ever her courage gave out at the thought of a real bear, and she was about to turn and flee in great disorder, when a mild "Moo!" changed her fear to merriment, as she said, laughing,

"It's a cow, Robby! the nice, black cow we saw this afternoon."

The cow seemed to feel that it was not just the thing to meet two little people in her pasture after dark, and the amiable beast paused to inquire into the case. She let them stroke her, and stood regarding them with her soft eyes so mildly, that Nan, who feared no animal but a bear, was fired with a desire to milk her.

*"Silas taught me how; and berries and milk would be so nice," she said, emptying the contents of her pail into her hat, and boldly beginning her new task, while Rob stood by and repeated, at her command, the poem from Mother Goose:*

*"Cushy cow, bonny, let down your milk,*
*Let down your milk to me,*
*And I will give you a gown of silk,*
*A gown of silk and a silver tee."*

But the immortal rhyme had little effect, for the benevolent cow had already been milked, and had only half a gill to give the thirsty children.

"Shoo! get away! you are an old cross patch," cried Nan, ungratefully, as she gave up the attempt in despair; and poor Molly walked on with a gentle gurgle of surprise and reproof.

"Each can have a sip, and then we must take a walk. We shall go to sleep if we don't; and lost people mustn't sleep. Don't you know how Hannah Lee in the pretty story slept under the snow and died?"

"But there isn't any snow now, and it's nice and warm," said Rob, who was not blessed with as lively a fancy as Nan.

"No matter, we will poke about a little, and call some more; and then, if nobody comes, we will hide under the bushes, like Hop-'o-my-thumb and his brothers."

It was a very short walk, however, for Rob was so sleepy he could not get on, and tumbled down so often that Nan entirely lost patience, being half distracted by the responsibility she had taken upon herself.

"If you tumble down again, I'll shake you," she said, lifting the poor little man up very kindly as she spoke, for Nan's bark was much worse than her bite.

"Please don't. It's my boots they keep slipping so;" and Rob manfully checked the sob just ready to break out, adding, with a plaintive patience that touched Nan's heart, "If the skeeters didn't bite me so, I could go to sleep till Marmar comes."

"Put your head on my lap, and I'll cover you up with my apron; I'm not afraid of the night," said Nan, sitting down and trying to persuade herself that she did not mind the shadow nor the mysterious rustlings all about her.

"Wake me up when she comes," said rob, and was fast asleep in five minutes with his head in Nan's lap under the pinafore.

The little girl sat for some fifteen minutes, staring about her with anxious eyes, and feeling as if each second was an hour. Then a pale light began to glimmer over the hill-top and she said to herself,

"I guess the night is over and morning is coming. I'd like to see the sun rise, so I'll watch, and when it comes up we can find our way right home."

But before the moon's round face peeped above the hill to destroy her hope, Nan had fallen asleep, leaning back in a little bower of tall ferns, and was deep in a mid-summer night's dream of fire-flies and blue aprons, mountains of huckleberries, and Robby wiping away the tears of a black cow, who sobbed, "I want to go home! I want to go home!"

While the children were sleeping, peacefully lulled by the drowsy hum of many neighborly mosquitoes, the family at home were in a great state of agitation. The hay-cart came at five, and all but Jack, Emil, Nan, and Rob were at the bars ready for it. Franz drove instead of Silas, and when the boys told him that the others were going home through the wood, he said, looking ill-pleased, "They ought to have left Rob to ride, he will be tired out by the long walk."

"It's shorter that way, and they will carry him," said Stuffy, who was in a hurry for his supper.

"You are sure Nan and Rob went with them?"

"Of course they did; I saw them getting over the wall, and sung out that it was most five, and Jack called back that they were going the other way," explained Tommy.

"Very well, pile in then," and away rattled the hay-cart with the tired children and the full pails.

Mrs. Jo looked sober when she heard of the division of the party, and sent Franz back with Toby to find and bring the little ones home. Supper was over, and the family sitting about in the cool hall as usual, when Franz came trotting back, hot, dusty, and anxious.

"Have they come?" he called out when half-way up the avenue.

"No!" and Mrs. Jo flew out of her chair looking so alarmed that every one jumped up and gathered round Franz.

"I can't find them anywhere," he began; but the words were hardly spoken when a loud "Hullo!" startled them all, and the next minute Jack and Emil came round the house.

"Where are Nan and Rob?" cried Mrs. Jo, clutching Emil in a way that caused him to think his aunt had suddenly lost her wits.

"I don't know. They came home with the others, didn't they?" he answered, quickly.

"No; George and Tommy said they went with you."

"Well, they didn't. Haven't seen them. We took a swim in the pond, and came by the wood," said Jack, looking alarmed, as well he might.

"Call Mr. Bhaer, get the lanterns, and tell Silas I want him."

That was all Mrs. Jo said, but they knew what she meant, and flew to obey her orders. In ten minutes, Mr. Bhaer and Silas were off to the wood, and Franz tearing down the road on old Andy to search the great pasture. Mrs. Jo caught up some food from the table, a little bottle of brandy from the medicine-closet, took a lantern, and bidding Jack and Emil come with her, and the rest not stir, she trotted away on Toby, never stopping for hat or shawl. She heard some one running after her, but said not a word till, as she paused to call and listen, the light of her lantern shone on Dan's face.

"You here! I told Jack to come," she said, half-inclined to send him back, much as she needed help.

"I wouldn't let him; he and Emil hadn't had any supper, and I wanted to come more than they did," he said, taking the lantern from her and smiling up in her face with the steady look in his eyes that made her feel as if, boy though he was, she had some one to depend on.

Off she jumped, and ordered him on to Toby, in spite of his pleading to walk; then they went on again along the dusty, solitary road, stopping every now and then to call and hearken breathlessly for little voices to reply.

When they came to the great pasture, other lights were already flitting to and fro like will-o'-the-wisps, and Mr. Bhaer's voice was heard shouting, "Nan! Rob! Rob! Nan!" in every part of the field. Silas whistled and roared, Dan plunged here and there on Toby, who seemed to understand the case, and went over the roughest places with unusual docility. Often Mrs. Jo hushed them all, saying, with a sob in her throat, "The noise may frighten them, let me call; Robby will know my voice;" and then she would cry out the beloved little name in every tone of tenderness, till the very echoes whispered it softly, and the winds seemed to waft it willingly; but still no answer came.

The sky was overcast now, and only brief glimpses of the moon were seen, heat-lightening darted out of the dark clouds now and then, and a faint far-off rumble as of thunder told that a summer-storm was brewing.

"O my Robby! my Robby!" mourned poor Mrs. Jo, wandering up and down like a pale ghost, while Dan kept beside her like a faithful fire-fly. "What shall I say to Nan's father if she comes to harm? Why did I ever trust my darling so far away? Fritz, do you hear any thing?" and when a mournful, "No" came back, she wrung her hands so despairingly that Dan sprung down from Toby's back, tied the bridle to the bars, and said, in his decided way,

"They may have gone down the spring I'm going to look."

He was over the wall and away so fast that she could hardly follow him; but when she reached the spot, he lowered the lantern and showed her with joy the marks of little feet in the soft ground about the spring. She fell down on her knees to examine the tracks, and then sprung up, saying eagerly,

"Yes; that is the mark of my Robby's little boots! Come this way, they must have gone on."

Such a weary search! But now some inexplicable instinct seemed to lead the anxious mother, for presently Dan uttered a cry, and caught up a little shining object lying in the path. It was the cover of the new tin pail, dropped in the first alarm of being lost. Mrs. Jo hugged and kissed it as if it were a living thing; and when Dan was about to utter a glad shout to bring the others to the spot, she stopped him, saying, as she hurried on, "No, let me find them; I let Rob go, and I want to give him back to his father all myself."

A little farther on Nan's hat appeared, and after passing the place more than once, they came at last upon the babes in the wood, both sound asleep. Dan never forgot the little picture on which the light of his lantern shone that night. He thought Mrs. Jo would cry out, but she only whispered, "Hush!" as she softly lifted away the apron, and saw the little ruddy face below. The berry-stained lips were half-open as the breath came and went, the yellow hair lay damp on the hot forehead, and both the chubby hands held fast the little pail still full.

The sight of the childish harvest, treasured through all the troubles of that night for her, seemed to touch Mrs. Jo to the heart, for suddenly she gathered up her boy, and began to cry over him, so tenderly, yet so heartily, that he woke up, and at first seemed bewildered. Then he remembered, and hugged her close, saying with a laugh of triumph,

"I knew you'd come! O Marmar! I did want you so!" For a moment they kissed and clung to one another, quite forgetting all the world; for no matter how lost and soiled and worn-out wandering sons may be, mothers can forgive and forget every thing as they fold them in their fostering arms. Happy the son whose faith in his mother remains unchanged, and who, through all his wanderings, has kept some filial token to repay her brave and tender love.

Dan meantime picked Nan out of her bush, and, with a gentleness none but Teddy ever saw in him before, he soothed her first alarm at the sudden waking, and wiped away her tears; for Nan also began to cry for joy, it was so good to see a kind face and feel a strong arm round her after what seemed to her ages of loneliness and fear.

"My poor little girl, don't cry! You are all safe now, and no one shall say a word of blame to-night," said Mrs. Jo, taking Nan into her capacious embrace, and cuddling both children as a hen might gather her lost chickens under her motherly wings.

"It was my fault; but I am sorry. I tried to take care of him, and I covered him up and let him sleep, and didn't touch his berries, though I was so hungry; and I never will do it again truly, never, never," sobbed Nan, quite lost in a sea of penitence and thankfulness.

"Call them now, and let us get home," said Mrs. Jo; and Dan, getting upon the wall, sent a joyful word "Found!" ringing over the field.

How the wandering lights came dancing from all sides, and gathered round the little group among the sweet fern bushes! Such a hugging, and kissing, and talking, and crying, as went on must have amazed the glowworms, and evidently delighted the mosquitoes, for they hummed frantically, while the little moths came in flocks to the party, and the frogs croaked as if they could not express their satisfaction loudly enough.

Then they set out for home, a queer party, for Franz rode on to tell the news; Dan and Toby led the way; then came Nan in the strong arms of Silas, who considered her "the smartest little baggage he ever saw," and teased her all the way home about her pranks. Mrs. Bhaer would let no one carry Rob but himself, and the little fellow, refreshed by sleep, sat up, and chattered gayly, feeling himself a hero, while his mother went beside him holding on to any pat of his precious little body that came handy, and never tired of hearing him say, "I knew Marmar would come," or seeing him lean down to kiss her, and put a plump berry into her mouth, "'Cause he picked 'em all for her."

The moon shone out just as they reached the avenue, and all the boys came shouting to meet them, so the lost lambs were borne in triumph and safety, and landed in the dining-room, where the unromantic little things demanded supper instead of preferring kisses and caresses. They were set down to bread and milk, while the entire household stood round to gaze upon them. Nan soon recovered her spirits, and recounted her perils with a relish now that they were all over. Rob seemed absorbed in his food, but put down his spoon all of a sudden, and set up a doleful roar.

"My precious, why do you cry?" asked his mother, who still hung over him.

"I'm crying 'cause I was lost," bawled Rob, trying to squeeze out a tear, and failing entirely.

"But you are found now. Nan says you didn't cry out in the field, and I was glad you were such a brave boy."

"I was so busy being frightened I didn't have any time then. But I want to cry now, 'cause I don't like to be lost," explained Rob, struggling with sleep, emotion, and a mouthful of bread and milk.

The boys set up such a laugh at this funny way of making up for lost time, that Rob stopped to look at them, and the merriment was so infectious, that after a surprised stare he burst out into a merry, "Ha, ha!" and beat his spoon upon the table as if he enjoyed the joke immensely.

"It is ten o'clock; into bed, every man of you," said Mr. Bhaer, looking at his watch.

"And, thank Heaven! there will be no empty ones to-night," added Mrs. Bhaer, watching, with full eyes, Robby going up in his father's arms, and Nan escorted by Daisy and Demi, who considered her the most interesting heroine of their collection.

"Poor Aunt Jo is so tired she ought to be carried up herself," said gentle Franz, putting his arm round her as she paused at the stair-foot, looking quite exhausted by her fright and long walk.

"Let's make an arm-chair," proposed Tommy.

"No, thank you, my lads; but somebody may lend me a shoulder to lean on," answered Mrs. Jo.

"Me! me!" and half-a-dozen jostled one another, all eager to be chosen, for there was something in the pale motherly face that touched the warm hearts under the round jackets.

Seeing that they considered it an honor, Mrs. Jo gave it to the one who had earned it, and nobody grumbled when she put her arm on Dan's broad shoulder, saying, with a look that made him color up with pride and pleasure,

"He found the children; so I think he must help me up."

Dan felt richly rewarded for his evening's work, not only that he was chosen from all the rest to go proudly up bearing the lamp, but because Mrs. Jo said heartily, "Good-night, my boy! God bless you!" as he left her at her door.

"I wish I was your boy," said Dan, who felt as if danger and trouble had somehow brought him nearer than ever to her.

"You shall be my oldest son," and she sealed her promise with a kiss that made Dan hers entirely.

Little Rob was all right next day, but Nan had a headache, and lay on Mother Bhaer's sofa with cold-cream upon her scratched face. Her remorse was quite gone, and she evidently thought being lost rather a fine amusement. Mrs. Jo was not pleased with this state of things, and had no desire to have her children led from the paths of virtue, or her pupils lying round loose in huckleberry fields. So she talked soberly to Nan, and tried to impress upon her mind the difference between liberty and license, telling several tales to enforce her lecture. She had not decided how to punish Nan, but one of these stories suggested a way, and as Mrs. Jo liked odd penalties, she tried it.

"All children run away," pleaded Nan, as if it was as natural and necessary a thing as measles or hooping cough.

"Not all, and some who do run away don't get found again," answered Mrs. Jo.

"Didn't you do it yourself?" asked Nan, whose keen little eyes saw some traces of a kindred spirit in the serious lady who was sewing so morally before her.

Mrs. Jo laughed, and owned that she did.

"Tell about it," demanded Nan, feeling that she was getting the upper hand in the discussion.

Mrs. Jo saw that, and sobered down at once, saying, with a remorseful shake of the head,

"I did it a good many times, and led my poor mother rather a hard life with my pranks, till she cured me."

"How?" and Nan sat up with a face full of interest.

"I had a new pair of shoes once, and wanted to show them; so, though I was told not to leave the garden, I ran away and was wandering about all day. It was in the city, and why I wasn't killed I don't know. Such a time as I had. I frolicked in the park with dogs, sailed boats in the Back Bay with strange boys, dined with a little Irish beggar-girl on salt fish and potatoes, and was found at last fast asleep on a door-step with my arms round a great dog. It was late in the evening, and I was a dirty as a little pig, and the new shoes were worn out I had travelled so far."

"How nice!" cried Nan, looking all ready to go and do it herself.

"It was not nice next day;" and Mrs. Jo tried to keep her eyes from betraying how much she enjoyed the memory of her early capers.

"Did your mother whip you?" asked Nan, curiously.

"She never whipped me but once, and then she begged my pardon, or I don't think I ever should have forgiven her, it hurt my feelings so much."

"Why did she beg your pardon? my father don't."

"Because, when she had done it, I turned round and said, 'Well, you are mad yourself, and ought to be whipped as much as me.' She looked at me a minute, then her anger all died out, and she said, as if ashamed, 'You are right, Jo, I am angry; and why should I punish you for being in a passion when I set you such a bad example? Forgive me, dear, and let us try to help one another in a better way.' I never forgot it, and it did me more good than a dozen rods."

Nan sat thoughtfully turning the little cold-cream jar for a minute, and Mrs. Jo said nothing, but let that idea get well into the busy little mind that was so quick to see and feel what went on about her.

"I like that," said Nan, presently, and her face looked less elfish, with its sharp eyes, inquisitive nose, and mischievous mouth. "What did your mother do to you when you ran away that time?"

"She tied me to the bed-post with a long string, so that I could not go out of the room, and there I stayed all day with the little worn-out shoes hanging up before me to remind me of my fault."

"I should think that would cure anybody," cried Nan, who loved her liberty above all things.

"It did cure me, and I think it will you, so I am going to try it," said Mrs. Jo, suddenly taking a ball of strong twine out of a drawer in her work-table.

Nan looked as if she was decidedly getting the worst of the argument now, and sat feeling much crestfallen while Mrs. Jo tied one end round her waist and the other to the arm of the sofa, saying, as she finished,

"I don't like to tie you up like a naughty little dog, but if you don't remember any better than a dog, I must treat you like one."

"I'd just as lief be tied up as not I like to play dog;" and Nan put on a don't-care face, and began to growl and grovel on the floor.

Mrs. Jo took no notice, but leaving a book or two and a handkerchief to hem, she went away, and left Miss Nan to her own devices. This was not agreeable, and after sitting a moment she tried to untie the cord. But it was fastened in the belt of her apron behind, so she began on the knot at the other end. It soon came loose, and, gathering it up, Nan was about to get out of the window, when she heard Mrs. Jo say to somebody as she passed through the hall,

"No, I don't think she will run away now; she is an honorable little girl, and knows that I do it to help her."

In a minute, Nan whisked back, tied herself up, and began to sew violently. Rob came in a moment after, and was so charmed with the new punishment, that he got a jump-rope and tethered himself to the other arm of the sofa in the most social manner.

"I got lost too, so I ought to be tied up as much as Nan," he explained to his mother when she saw the new captive.

"I'm not sure that you don't deserve a little punishment, for you knew it was wrong to go far away from the rest."

"Nan took me," began Rob, willing to enjoy the novel penalty, but not willing to take the blame.

"You needn't have gone. You have got a conscience, though you are a little boy, and you must learn to mind it."

"Well, my conscience didn't prick me a bit when she said 'Let's get over the wall,'" answered Rob, quoting one of Demi's expressions.

"Did you stop to see if it did?"

"No."

"Then you cannot tell."

"I guess it's such a little conscience that it don't prick hard enough for me to feel it," added Rob, after thinking the matter over for a minute.

"We must sharpen it up. It's bad to have a dull conscience; so you may stay here till dinner-time, and talk about it with Nan. I trust you both not to untie yourselves till I say the word."

"No, we won't," said both, feeling a certain sense of virtue in helping to punish themselves.

For an hour they were very good, then they grew tired of one room, and longed to get out. Never had the hall seemed so inviting; even the little bedroom acquired a sudden interest, and they would gladly have gone in and played tent with the curtains of the best bed. The open windows drove them wild because they could not reach them; and the outer world seemed so beautiful, they wondered how they ever found the heart to say it was dull. Nan pined for a race round the lawn, and Rob remembered with dismay that he had not fed his dog that morning, and wondered what poor Pollux would do. They watched the clock, and Nan did some nice calculations in minutes and seconds, while Rob learned to tell all the hours between eight and one so well that he never forgot them. It was maddening to smell the dinner, to know that there was to be succotash and huckleberry pudding, and to feel that they would not be on the spot to secure good helps of both. When Mary Ann began to set the table, they nearly cut themselves in two trying to see what meat there was to be; and Nan offered to help her make the beds, if she would only see that she had "lots of sauce on her pudding."

When the boys came bursting out of school, they found the children tugging at their halters like a pair of restive little colts, and were much edified, as well as amused, by the sequel to the exciting adventures of the night.

"Untie me now, Marmar; my conscience will prick like a pin next time, I know it will," said Rob, as the bell rang, and Teddy came to look at him with sorrowful surprise.

"We shall see," answered his mother, setting him free. He took a good run down the hall, back through the dining-room, and brought up beside Nan, quite beaming with virtuous satisfaction.

"I'll bring her dinner to her, may I?" he asked, pitying his fellow-captive.

"That's my kind little son! Yes, pull out the table, and get a chair;" and Mrs. Jo hurried away to quell the ardor of the others, who were always in a raging state of hunger at noon.

Nan ate alone, and spent a long afternoon attached to the sofa. Mrs. Bhaer lengthened her bonds so that she could look out of the window; and there she stood watching the boys play, and all the little summer creatures enjoying their liberty. Daisy had a picnic for the dolls on the lawn, so that Nan might see the fun if she could not join in it. Tommy turned his best somersaults to console her; Demi sat on the steps reading aloud to himself, which amused Nan a good deal; and Dan brought a little tree-toad to show her as the most delicate attention in his power.

But nothing atoned for the loss of freedom; and a few hours of confinement taught Nan how precious it was. A good many thoughts went through the little head that lay on the window-sill during the last quiet hour when all the children went to the brook to see Emil's new ship launched. She was to have christened it, and had depended on smashing a tiny bottle of currant-wine over the prow as it was named Josephine in honor of Mrs. Bhaer. Now she had lost her chance, and Daisy wouldn't do it half so well. Tears rose to her eyes as she remembered that it was all her own fault; and she said aloud, addressing a fat bee who was rolling about in the yellow heart of a rose just under the window,

"If you have run away, you'd better go right home, and tell your mother you are sorry, and never do so any more."

"I am glad to hear you give him such good advice, and I think he has taken it," said Mrs. Jo, smiling, as the bee spread his dusty wings and flew away.

Nan brushed off a bright drop or two that shone on the window-sill, and nestled against her friend as she took her on her knee, adding kindly for she had seen the little drops, and knew what they meant,

"Do you think my mother's cure for running away a good one?"

"Yes, ma'am," answered Nan, quite subdued by her quiet day.

"I hope I shall not have to try it again."

"I guess not;" and Nan looked up with such an earnest little face that Mrs. Jo felt satisfied, and said no more, for she liked to have her penalties do their own work, and did not spoil the effect by too much moralizing.

Here Rob appeared, bearing with infinite care what Asia called a "sarcer pie," meaning one baked in a saucer.

"It's made out of some of my berries, and I'm going to give you half at supper-time," he announced with a flourish.

"What makes you, when I'm so naughty?" asked Nan, meekly.

"Because we got lost together. You ain't going to be naughty again, are you?"

"Never," said Nan, with great decision.

"Oh, goody! now let's go and get Mary Ann to cut this for us all ready to eat; it's 'most tea time;" and Rob beckoned with the delicious little pie.

Nan started to follow, then stopped, and said,

"I forgot, I can't go."

"Try and see," said Mrs. Bhaer, who had quietly untied the cord sash while she had been talking.

Nan saw that she was free, and with one tempestuous kiss to Mrs. Jo, she was off like a humming-bird, followed by Robby, dribbling huckleberry juice as he ran.

# CHAPTER XIII. GOLDILOCKS

After the last excitement peace descended upon Plumfield and reigned unbroken for several weeks, for the elder boys felt that the loss of Nan and Rob lay at their door, and all became so paternal in their care that they were rather wearying; while the little ones listened to Nan's recital of her perils so many times, that they regarded being lost as the greatest ill humanity was heir to, and hardly dared to put their little noses outside the great gate lest night should suddenly descend upon them, and ghostly black cows come looming through the dusk.

"It is too good to last," said Mrs. Jo; for years of boy-culture had taught her that such lulls were usually followed by outbreaks of some sort, and when less wise women would have thought that the boys had become confirmed saints, she prepared herself for a sudden eruption of the domestic volcano.

One cause of this welcome calm was a visit from little Bess, whose parents lent her for a week while they were away with Grandpa Laurence, who was poorly. The boys regarded Goldilocks as a mixture of child, angel, and fairy, for she was a lovely little creature, and the golden hair which she inherited from her blonde mamma enveloped her like a shining veil, behind which she smiled upon her worshippers when gracious, and hid herself when offended. Her father would not have it cut and it hung below her waist, so soft and fine and bright, that Demi insisted that it was silk spun from a cocoon. Every one praised the little Princess, but it did not seem to do her harm, only to teach her that her presence brought sunshine, her smiles made answering smiles on other faces, and her baby griefs filled every heart with tenderest sympathy.

Unconsciously, she did her young subjects more good than many a real sovereign, for her rule was very gentle and her power was felt rather than seen. Her natural refinement made her dainty in all things, and had a good effect upon the careless lads about her. She would let no one touch her roughly or with unclean hands, and more soap was used during her visits than at any other time, because the boys considered it the highest honor to be allowed to carry her highness, and the deepest disgrace to be repulsed with the disdainful command, "Do away, dirty boy!"

Lour voices displeased her and quarrelling frightened her; so gentler tones came into the boyish voices as they addressed her, and squabbles were promptly suppressed in her presence by lookers-on if the principles could not restrain themselves. She liked to be waited on, and the biggest boys did her little errands without a murmur, while the small lads were her devoted slaves in all things. They begged to be allowed to draw her carriage, bear her berry-basket, or pass her plate at table. No service was too humble, and Tommy and Ned came to blows before they could decide which should have the honor of blacking her little boots.

Nan was especially benefited by a week in the society of a well-bred lady, though such a very small one; for Bess would look at her with a mixture of wonder and alarm in her great blue eyes when the hoyden screamed and romped; and she shrunk from her as if she thought her a sort of wild animal. Warm-hearted Nan felt this very much. She said at first, "Pooh! I don't care!" But she did care, and was so hurt when Bess said, "I love my tuzzin best, tause she is twiet," that she shook poor Daisy till her teeth chattered in her head, and then fled to the barn to cry dismally. In that general refuge for perturbed spirits she found comfort and good counsel from some source or other. Perhaps the swallows from their mud-built nests overhead twittered her a little lecture on the beauty of gentleness. However that might have been, she came out quite subdued, and carefully searched the orchard for a certain kind of early apple that Bess liked because it was sweet and small and rosy. Armed with this peace-offering, she approached the little Princess, and humbly presented it. To her great joy it was graciously accepted, and when Daisy gave Nan a forgiving kiss, Bess did likewise, as if she felt that she had been too severe, and desired to apologize. After this they played pleasantly together, and Nan enjoyed the royal favor for days. To be sure she felt a little like a wild bird in a pretty cage at first, and occasionally had to slip out to stretch her wings in a long flight, or to sing at the top of her voice, where neither would disturb the plump turtle-dove Daisy, nor the dainty golden canary Bess. But it did her good; for, seeing how every one loved the little Princess for her small graces and virtues, she began to imitate her, because Nan wanted much love, and tried hard to win it.

Not a boy in the house but felt the pretty child's influence, and was improved by it without exactly knowing how or why, for babies can work miracles in the hearts that love them. Poor Billy found infinite satisfaction in staring at her, and though she did not like it she permitted without a frown, after she had been made to understand that he was not quite like the others, and on that account must be more kindly treated. Dick and Dolly overwhelmed her with willow whistles, the only thing they knew how to make, and she accepted but never used them. Rob served her like a little lover, and Teddy followed her like a pet dog. Jack she did not like, because he was afflicted with warts and had a harsh voice. Stuffy displeased her because he did not eat tidily, and George tried hard not to gobble, that he might not disgust the dainty little lady opposite. Ned was banished from court in utter disgrace when he was discovered tormenting some unhappy field-mice. Goldilocks could never forget the sad spectacle, and retired behind her veil when he approached, waving him away with an imperious little hand, and crying, in a tone of mingled grief and anger,

"No, I tarn't love him; he tut the poor mouses' little tails off, and they queeked!"

Daisy promptly abdicated when Bess came, and took the humble post of chief cook, while Nan was first maid of honor; Emil was chancellor of the exchequer, and spent the public monies lavishly in getting up spectacles that cost whole ninepences. Franz was prime minister, and directed her affairs of state, planned royal progresses through the kingdom, and kept foreign powers in order. Demi was her philosopher, and fared much better than such gentlemen usually do among crowned heads. Dan was her standing army, and defended her territories gallantly; Tommy was court fool, and Nat a tuneful Rizzio to this innocent little Mary.

Uncle Fritz and Aunt Jo enjoyed this peaceful episode, and looked on at the pretty play in which the young folk unconsciously imitated their elders, without adding the tragedy that is so apt to spoil the dramas acted on the larger stage.

"They teach us quite as much as we teach them," said Mr. Bhaer.

"Bless the dears! they never guess how many hints they give us as to the best way of managing them," answered Mrs. Jo.

"I think you were right about the good effect of having girls among the boys. Nan has stirred up Daisy, and Bess is teaching the little bears how to behave better than we can. If this reformation goes on as it has begun, I shall soon feel like Dr. Blimber with his model young gentlemen," said Professor, laughing, as he saw Tommy not only remove his own hat, but knock off Ned's also, as they entered the hall where the Princess was taking a ride on the rocking-horse, attended by Rob and Teddy astride of chairs, and playing gallant knights to the best of their ability.

"You will never be a Blimber, Fritz, you couldn't do it if you tried; and our boys will never submit to the forcing process of that famous hot-bed. No fear that they will be too elegant: American boys like liberty too well. But good manners they cannot fail to have, if we give them the kindly spirit that shines through the simplest demeanor, making it courteous and cordial, like yours, my dear old boy."

"Tut! tut! we will not compliment; for if I begin you will run away, and I have a wish to enjoy this happy half hour to the end;" yet Mr. Bhaer looked pleased with the compliment, for it was true, and Mrs. Jo felt that she had received the best her husband could give her, by saying that he found his truest rest and happiness in her society.

"To return to the children: I have just had another proof of Goldilocks' good influence," said Mrs. Jo, drawing her chair nearer the sofa, where the Professor lay resting after a long day's work in his various gardens. "Nan hates sewing, but for love of Bess has been toiling half the afternoon over a remarkable bag in which to present a dozen of our love-apples to her idol when she goes. I praised her for it, and she said, in her quick way, 'I like to sew for other people; it is stupid sewing for myself.' I took the hint, and shall give her some little shirts and aprons for Mrs. Carney's children. She is so generous, she will sew her fingers sore for them, and I shall not have to make a task of it."

"But needlework is not a fashionable accomplishment, my dear."

"Sorry for it. My girls shall learn all I can teach them about it, even if they give up the Latin, Algebra, and half-a-dozen ologies it is considered necessary for girls to muddle their poor brains over now-a-days. Amy means to make Bess an accomplished woman, but the dear's mite of a forefinger has little pricks on it already, and her mother has several specimens of needlework which she values more than the clay bird without a bill, that filled Laurie with such pride when Bess made it."

"I also have proof of the Princess's power," said Mrs. Bhaer, after he had watched Mrs. Jo sew on a button with an air of scorn for the whole system of fashionable education. "Jack is so unwilling to be classed with Stuffy and Ned, as distasteful to Bess, that he came to me a little while ago, and asked me to touch his warts with caustic. I have often proposed it, and he never would consent; but now he bore the smart manfully, and consoles his present discomfort by hopes of future favor, when he can show her fastidious ladyship a smooth hand."

Mrs. Bhaer laughed at the story, and just then Stuffy came in to ask if he might give Goldilocks some of the bonbons his mother had sent him.

"She is not allowed to eat sweeties; but if you like to give her the pretty box with the pink sugar-rose in it, she would like it very much," said Mrs. Jo, unwilling to spoil this unusual piece of self-denial, for the "fat boy" seldom offered to share his sugar-plums.

"Won't she eat it? I shouldn't like to make her sick," said Stuffy, eyeing the delicate sweetmeat lovingly, yet putting it into the box.

"Oh, no, she won't touch it, if I tell her it is to look at, not to eat. She will keep it for weeks, and never think of tasting it. Can you do as much?"

"I should hope so! I'm ever so much older than she is," cried Stuffy, indignantly.

"Well, suppose we try. Here, put your bonbons in this bag, and see how long you can keep them. Let me count two hearts, four red fishes, three barley-sugar horses, nine almonds, and a dozen chocolate drops. Do you agree to that?" asked sly Mrs. Jo, popping the sweeties into her little spool-bag.

"Yes," said Stuffy, with a sigh; and pocketing the forbidden fruit, he went away to give Bess the present, that won a smile from her, and permission to escort her round the garden.

"Poor Stuffy's heart has really got the better of his stomach at last, and his efforts will be much encouraged by the rewards Bess gives him," said Mrs. Jo.

"Happy is the man who can put temptation in his pocket and learn self-denial from so sweet a little teacher!" added Mr. Bhaer, as the children passed the window, Stuffy's fat face full of placid satisfaction, and Goldilocks surveying her sugar-rose with polite interest, though she would have preferred a real flower with a "pitty smell."

When her father came to take her home, a universal wail arose, and the parting gifts showered upon her increased her luggage to such an extent that Mr. Laurie proposed having out the big wagon to take it into town. Every one had given her something; and it was found difficult to pack white mice, cake, a parcel of shells, apples, a rabbit kicking violently in a bag, a large cabbage for his refreshment, a bottle of minnows, and a mammoth bouquet. The farewell scene was moving, for the Princess sat upon the hall-table, surrounded by her subjects. She kissed her cousins, and held out her hand to the other boys, who shook it gently with various soft speeches, for they were taught not to be ashamed of showing their emotions.

"Come again soon, little dear," whispered Dan, fastening his best green-and-gold beetle in her hat.

"Don't forget me, Princess, whatever you do," said the engaging Tommy, taking a last stroke of the pretty hair.

"I am coming to your house next week, and then I shall see you, Bess," added Nat, as if he found consolation in the thought.

"Do shake hands now," cried Jack, offering a smooth paw.

"Here are two nice new ones to remember us by," said Dick and Dolly, presenting fresh whistles, quite unconscious that seven old ones had been privately deposited in the kitchen-stove.

"My little precious! I shall work you a book-mark right away, and you must keep it always," said Nan, with a warm embrace.

But of all the farewells, poor Billy's was the most pathetic, for the thought that she was really going became so unbearable that he cast himself down before her, hugging her little blue boots and blubbering despairingly, "Don't go away! oh, don't!" Goldilocks was so touched by this burst of feeling, that she leaned over and lifting the poor lad's head, said, in her soft, little voice,

"Don't cry, poor Billy! I will tiss you and tum adain soon."

This promise consoled Billy, and he fell back beaming with pride at the unusual honor conferred upon him.

"Me too! me too!" clamored Dick and Dolly, feeling that their devotion deserved some return. The others looked as if they would like to join in the cry; and something in the kind, merry faces about her moved the Princess to stretch out her arms and say, with reckless condescension,

"I will tiss evvybody!"

Like a swarm of bees about a very sweet flower, the affectionate lads surrounded their pretty playmate, and kissed her till she looked like a little rose, not roughly, but so enthusiastically that nothing but the crown of her hat was visible for a moment. Then her father rescued her, and she drove away still smiling and waving her hands, while the boys sat on the fence screaming like a flock of guinea-fowls, "Come back! come back!" till she was out of sight.

They all missed her, and each dimly felt that he was better for having known a creature so lovely, delicate, and sweet; for little Bess appealed to the chivalrous instinct in them as something to love, admire, and protect with a tender sort of reverence. Many a man remembers some pretty child who has made a place in his heart and kept her memory alive by the simple magic of her innocence; these little men were just learning to feel this power, and to love it for its gentle influence, not ashamed to let the small hand lead them, nor to own their loyalty to womankind, even in the bud.

# CHAPTER XIV. DAMON AND PYTHIAS

Mrs. Bhaer was right; peace was only a temporary lull, a storm was brewing, and two days after Bess left, a moral earthquake shook Plumfield to its centre.

Tommy's hens were at the bottom of the trouble, for if they had not persisted in laying so many eggs, he could not have sold them and made such sums. Money is the root of all evil, and yet it is such a useful root that we cannot get on without it any more than we can without potatoes. Tommy certainly could not, for he spent his income so recklessly, that Mr. Bhaer was obliged to insist on a savings-bank, and presented him with a private one an imposing tin edifice, with the name over the door, and a tall chimney, down which the pennies were to go, there to rattle temptingly till leave was given to open a sort of trap-door in the floor.

The house increased in weight so rapidly, that Tommy soon became satisfied with his investment, and planned to buy unheard-of treasures with his capital. He kept account of the sums deposited, and was promised that he might break the bank as soon as he had five dollars, on condition that he spent the money wisely. Only one dollar was needed, and the day Mrs. Jo paid him for four dozen eggs, he was so delighted, that he raced off to the barn to display the bright quarters to Nat, who was also laying by money for the long-desired violin.

"I wish I had 'em to put with my three dollars, then I'd soon get enough to buy my fiddle," he said, looking wistfully at the money.

"P'raps I'll lend you some. I haven't decided yet what I'll do with mine," said Tommy, tossing up his quarters and catching them as they fell.

"Hi! boys! come down to the brook and see what a jolly great snake Dan's got!" called a voice from behind the barn.

"Come on," said Tommy; and, laying his money inside the old winnowing machine, away he ran, followed by Nat.

The snake was very interesting, and then a long chase after a lame crow, and its capture, so absorbed Tommy's mind and time, that he never thought of his money till he was safely in bed that night.

"Never mind, no one but Nat knows where it is," said the easy-going lad, and fell asleep untroubled by any anxiety about his property.

Next morning, just as the boys assembled for school, Tommy rushed into the room breathlessly, demanding,

"I say, who has got my dollar?"

"What are you talking about?" asked Franz.

Tommy explained, and Nat corroborated his statement.

Every one else declared they knew nothing about it, and began to look suspiciously at Nat, who got more and more alarmed and confused with each denial.

"Somebody must have taken it," said Franz, as Tommy shook his fist at the whole party, and wrathfully declared that,

"By thunder turtles! if I get hold of the thief, I'll give him what he won't forget in a hurry."

"Keep cool, Tom; we shall find him out; thieves always come to grief," said Dan, as one who knew something of the matter.

"May be some tramp slept in the barn and took it," suggested Ned.

"No, Silas don't allow that; besides, a tramp wouldn't go looking in that old machine for money," said Emil, with scorn.

"Wasn't it Silas himself?" said Jack.

"Well, I like that! Old Si is as honest as daylight. You wouldn't catch him touching a penny of ours," said Tommy, handsomely defending his chief admirer from suspicion.

"Whoever it was had better tell, and not wait to be found out," said Demi, looking as if an awful misfortune had befallen the family.

"I know you think it's me," broke out Nat, red and excited.

"You are the only one who knew where it was," said Franz.

"I can't help it I didn't take it. I tell you I didn't I didn't!" cried Nat, in a desperate sort of way.

"Gently, gently, my son! What is all this noise about?" and Mr. Bhaer walked in among them.

Tommy repeated the story of his loss, and, as he listened, Mr. Bhaer's face grew graver and graver; for, with all their faults and follies, the lads till now had been honest.

"Take your seats," he said; and, when all were in their places, he added slowly, as his eye went from face to face with a grieved look, that was harder to bear than a storm of words,

"Now, boys, I shall ask each one of you a single question, and I want an honest answer. I am not going to try to frighten, bribe, or surprise the truth out of you, for every one of you have got a conscience, and know what it is for. Now is the time to undo the wrong done to Tommy, and set yourselves right before us all. I can forgive the yielding to sudden temptation much easier than I can deceit. Don't add a lie to the theft, but confess frankly, and we will all try to help you make us forget and forgive."

He paused a moment, and one might have heard a pin drop, the room was so still; then slowly and impressively he put the question to each one, receiving the same answer in varying tones from all. Every face was flushed and excited, so that Mr. Bhaer could not take color as a witness, and some of the little boys were so frightened that they stammered over the two short words as if guilty, though it was evident that they could not be. When he came to Nat, his voice softened, for the poor lad looked so wretched, Mr. Bhaer felt for him. He believed him to be the culprit, and hoped to save the boy from another lie, by winning him to tell the truth without fear.

"Now, my son, give me an honest answer. Did you take the money?"

"No, sir!" and Nat looked up at him imploringly.

As the words fell from his trembling lips, somebody hissed.

"Stop that!" cried Mr. Bhaer, with a sharp rap on his desk, as he looked sternly toward the corner whence the sound came.

Ned, Jack, and Emil sat there, and the first two looked ashamed of themselves, but Emil called out,

"It wasn't me, uncle! I'd be ashamed to hit a fellow when he is down."

"Good for you!" cried Tommy, who was in a sad state of affliction at the trouble his unlucky dollar had made.

"Silence!" commanded Mr. Bhaer; and when it came, he said soberly,

"I am very sorry, Nat, but evidences are against you, and your old fault makes us more ready to doubt you than we should be if we could trust you as we do some of the boys, who never fib. But mind, my child, I do not charge you with this theft; I shall not punish you for it till I am perfectly sure, nor ask any thing more about it. I shall leave it for you to settle with your own conscience. If you are guilty, come to me at any hour of the day or night and confess it, and I will forgive and help you to amend. If you are innocent, the truth will appear sooner or later, and the instant it does, I will be the first to beg your pardon for doubting you, and will so gladly do my best to clear your character before us all."

"I didn't! I didn't!" sobbed Nat, with his head down upon his arms, for he could not bear the look of distrust and dislike which he read in the many eyes fixed on him.

"I hope not." Mr. Bhaer paused a minute, as if to give the culprit, whoever he might be, one more chance. Nobody spoke, however, and only sniffs of sympathy from some of the little fellows broke the silence. Mr. Bhaer shook his head, and added, regretfully,

"There is nothing more to be done, then, and I have but one thing to say: I shall not speak of this again, and I wish you all to follow my example. I cannot expect you to feel as kindly toward any one whom you suspect as before this happened, but I do expect and desire that you will not torment the suspected person in any way, he will have a hard enough time without that. Now go to your lessons."

"Father Bhaer let Nat off too easy," muttered Ned to Emil, as they got out their books.

"Hold your tongue," growled Emil, who felt that this event was a blot upon the family honor.

Many of the boys agreed with Ned, but Mr. Bhaer was right, nevertheless; and Nat would have been wiser to confess on the spot and have the trouble over, for even the hardest whipping he ever received from his father was far easier to bear than the cold looks, the avoidance, and general suspicion that met him on all sides. If ever a boy was sent to Coventry and kept there, it was poor Nat; and he suffered a week of slow torture, though not a hand was raised against him, and hardly a word said.

That was the worst of it; if they would only have talked it out, or even have thrashed him all round, he could have stood it better than the silent distrust that made very face so terrible to meet. Even Mrs. Bhaer's showed traces of it, though her manner was nearly as kind as ever; but the sorrowful anxious look in Father Bhaer's eyes cut Nat to the heart, for he loved his teacher dearly, and knew that he had disappointed all his hopes by this double sin.

Only one person in the house entirely believed in him, and stood up for him stoutly against all the rest. This was Daisy. She could not explain why she trusted him against all appearances, she only felt that she could not doubt him, and her warm sympathy made her strong to take his part. She would not hear a word against him from any one, and actually slapped her beloved Demi when he tried to convince her that it must have been Nat, because no one else knew where the money was.

"Maybe the hens ate it; they are greedy old things," she said; and when Demi laughed, she lost her temper, slapped the amazed boy, and then burst out crying and ran away, still declaring, "He didn't! he didn't! he didn't!"

Neither aunt nor uncle tried to shake the child's faith in her friend, but only hoped her innocent instinct might prove sure, and loved her all the better for it. Nat often said, after it was over, that he couldn't have stood it, if it had not been for Daisy. When the others shunned him, she clung to him closer than ever, and turned her back on the rest. She did not sit on the stairs now when he solaced himself with the old fiddle, but went in and sat beside him, listening with a face so full of confidence and affection, that Nat forgot disgrace for a time, and was happy. She asked him to help her with her lessons, she cooked him marvelous messes in her kitchen, which he ate manfully, no matter what they were, for gratitude gave a sweet flavor to the most distasteful. She proposed impossible games of cricket and ball, when she found that he shrank from joining the other boys. She put little nosegays from her garden on his desk, and tried in every way to show that she was not a fair-weather friend, but faithful through evil as well as good repute. Nan soon followed her example, in kindness at least; curbed her sharp tongue, and kept her scornful little nose from any demonstration of doubt or dislike, which was good of Madame Giddy-gaddy, for she firmly believed that Nat took the money.

Most of the boys let him severely alone, but Dan, though he said he despised him for being a coward, watched over him with a grim sort of protection, and promptly cuffed any lad who dared to molest his mate or make him afraid. His idea of friendship was as high as Daisy's, and, in his own rough way, he lived up to it as loyally.

Sitting by the brook one afternoon, absorbed in the study of the domestic habits of water-spiders, he overheard a bit of conversation on the other side of the wall. Ned, who was intensely inquisitive, had been on tenterhooks to know certainly who was the culprit; for of late one or two of the boys had begun to think that they were wrong, Nat was so steadfast in his denials, and so meek in his endurance of their neglect. This doubt had teased Ned past bearing, and he had several times privately beset Nat with questions, regardless of Mr. Bhaer's express command. Finding Nat reading alone on the shady side of the wall, Ned could not resist stopping for a nibble at the forbidden subject. He had worried Nat for some ten minutes before Dan arrived, and the first words the spider-student heard were these, in Nat's patient, pleading voice,

"Don't, Ned! oh, don't! I can't tell you because I don't know, and it's mean of you to keep nagging at me on the sly, when Father Bhaer told you not to plague me. You wouldn't dare to if Dan was round."

"I ain't afraid of Dan; he's nothing but an old bully. Don't believe but what he took Tom's money, and you know it, and won't tell. Come, now!"

"He didn't, but, if he did, I would stand up for him, he has always been so good to me," said Nat, so earnestly that Dan forgot his spiders, and rose quickly to thank him, but Ned's next words arrested him.

"I know Dan did it, and gave the money to you. Shouldn't wonder if he got his living picking pockets before he came here, for nobody knows any thing about him but you," said Ned, not believing his own words, but hoping to get the truth out of Nat by making him angry.

He succeeded in a part of his ungenerous wish, for Nat cried out, fiercely,

"If you say that again I'll go and tell Mr. Bhaer all about it. I don't want to tell tales, but, by George! I will, if you don't let Dan alone."

"Then you'll be a sneak, as well as a liar and a thief," began Ned, with a jeer, for Nat had borne insult to himself so meekly, the other did not believe he would dare to face the master just to stand up for Dan.

What he might have added I cannot tell, for the words were hardly out of his mouth when a long arm from behind took him by the collar, and, jerking him over the wall in a most promiscuous way, landed him with a splash in the middle of the brook.

"Say that again and I'll duck you till you can't see!" cried Dan, looking like a modern Colossus of Rhodes as he stood, with a foot on either side of the narrow stream, glaring down at the discomfited youth in the water.

"I was only in fun," said Ned.

"You are a sneak yourself to badger Nat round the corner. Let me catch you at it again, and I'll souse you in the river next time. Get up, and clear out!" thundered Dan, in a rage.

Ned fled, dripping, and his impromptu sitz-bath evidently did him good, for he was very respectful to both the boys after that, and seemed to have left his curiosity in the brook. As he vanished Dan jumped over the wall, and found Nat lying, as if quite worn out and bowed down with his troubles.

"He won't pester you again, I guess. If he does, just tell me, and I'll see to him," said Dan, trying to cool down.

"I don't mind what he says about me so much, I've got used to it," answered Nat sadly; "but I hate to have him pitch into you."

"How do you know he isn't right?" asked Dan, turning his face away.

"What, about the money?" cried Nat, looking up with a startled air.

"Yes."

"But I don't believe it! You don't care for money; all you want is your old bugs and things," and Nat laughed, incredulously.

"I want a butterfly net as much as you want a fiddle; why shouldn't I steal the money for it as much as you?" said Dan, still turning away, and busily punching holes in the turf with his stick.

"I don't think you would. You like to fight and knock folks round sometimes, but you don't lie, and I don't believe you'd steal," and Nat shook his head decidedly.

"I've done both. I used to fib like fury; it's too much trouble now; and I stole things to eat out of gardens when I ran away from Page, so you see I am a bad lot," said Dan, speaking in the rough, reckless way which he had been learning to drop lately.

"O Dan! don't say it's you! I'd rather have it any of the other boys," cried Nat, in such a distressed tone that Dan looked pleased, and showed that he did, by turning round with a queer expression in his face, though he only answered,

"I won't say any thing about it. But don't you fret, and we'll pull through somehow, see if we don't."

Something in his face and manner gave Nat a new idea; and he said, pressing his hands together, in the eagerness of his appeal,

"I think you know who did it. If you do, beg him to tell, Dan. It's so hard to have 'em all hate me for nothing. I don't think I can bear it much longer. If I had any place to go to, I'd run away, though I love Plumfield dearly; but I'm not brave and big like you, so I must stay and wait till some one shows them that I haven't lied."

As he spoke, Nat looked so broken and despairing, that Dan could not bear it, and, muttered huskily,

"You won't wait long," and he walked rapidly away, and was seen no more for hours.

"What is the matter with Dan?" asked the boys of one another several times during the Sunday that followed a week which seemed as if it would never end. Dan was often moody, but that day he was so sober and silent that no one could get any thing out of him. When they walked he strayed away from the rest, and came home late. He took no part in the evening conversation, but sat in the shadow, so busy with his own thoughts that he scarcely seemed to hear what was going on. When Mrs. Jo showed him an unusually good report in the Conscience Book, he looked at it without a smile, and said, wistfully,

"You think I am getting on, don't you?"

"Excellently, Dan! and I am so pleased, because I always thought you only needed a little help to make you a boy to be proud of."

He looked up at her with a strange expression in his black eyes an expression of mingled pride and love and sorrow which she could not understand then but remembered afterward.

"I'm afraid you'll be disappointed, but I do try," he said, shutting the book with no sign of pleasure in the page that he usually liked so much to read over and talk about.

"Are you sick, dear?" asked Mrs. Jo, with her hand on his shoulder.

"My foot aches a little; I guess I'll go to bed. Good-night, mother," he added, and held the hand against his cheek a minute, then went away looking as if he had said good-bye to something dear.

"Poor Dan! he takes Nat's disgrace to heart sadly. He is a strange boy; I wonder if I ever shall understand him thoroughly?" said Mrs. Jo to herself, as she thought over Dan's late improvement with real satisfaction, yet felt that there was more in the lad than she had at first suspected.

One of things which cut Nat most deeply was an act of Tommy's, for after his loss Tommy had said to him, kindly, but firmly,

"I don't wish to hurt you, Nat, but you see I can't afford to lose my money, so I guess we won't be partners any longer;" and with that Tommy rubbed out the sign, "T. Bangs & Co."

Nat had been very proud of the "Co.," and had hunted eggs industriously, kept his accounts all straight, and had added a good sum to his income from the sale of his share of stock in trade.

"O Tom! must you?" he said, feeling that his good name was gone for ever in the business world if this was done.

"I must," returned Tommy, firmly. "Emil says that when one man 'bezzles (believe that's the word it means to take money and cut away with it) the property of a firm, the other one sues him, or pitches into him somehow, and won't have any thing more to do with him. Now you have 'bezzled my property; I shan't sue you, and I shan't pitch into you, but I must dissolve the partnership, because I can't trust you, and I don't wish to fail."

"I can't make you believe me, and you won't take my money, though I'd be thankful to give all my dollars if you'd only say you don't think I took your money. Do let me hunt for you, I won't ask any wages, but do it for nothing. I know all the places, and I like it," pleaded Nat.

But Tommy shook his head, and his jolly round face looked suspicious and hard as he said, shortly, "Can't do it; wish you didn't know the places. Mind you don't go hunting on the sly, and speculate in my eggs."

Poor Nat was so hurt that he could not get over it. He felt that he had lost not only his partner and patron, but that he was bankrupt in honor, and an outlaw from the business community. No one trusted his word, written or spoken, in spite of his efforts to redeem the past falsehood; the sign was down, the firm broken up, and he a ruined man. The barn, which was the boys' Wall Street, knew him no more. Cockletop and her sisters cackled for him in vain, and really seemed to take his misfortune to heart, for eggs were fewer, and some of the biddies retired in disgust to new nests, which Tommy could not find.

"They trust me," said Nat, when he heard of it; and though the boys shouted at the idea, Nat found comfort in it, for when one is down in the world, the confidence of even a speckled hen is most consoling.

Tommy took no new partner, however, for distrust had entered in, and poisoned the peace of his once confiding soul. Ned offered to join him, but he declined, saying, with a sense of justice that did him honor,

"It might turn out that Nat didn't take my money, and then we could be partners again. I don't think it will happen, but I will give him a chance, and keep the place open a little longer."

Billy was the only person whom Bangs felt he could trust in his shop, and Billy was trained to hunt eggs, and hand them over unbroken, being quite satisfied with an apple or a sugar-plum for wages. The morning after Dan's gloomy Sunday, Billy said to his employer, as he displayed the results of a long hunt,

"Only two."

"It gets worse and worse; I never saw such provoking old hens," growled Tommy, thinking of the days when he often had six to rejoice over. "Well, put 'em in my hat and give me a new bit of chalk; I must mark 'em up, any way."

Billy mounted a peck-measure, and looked into the top of the machine, where Tommy kept his writing materials.

"There's lots of money in here," said Billy.

"No, there isn't. Catch me leaving my cash round again," returned Tommy.

"I see 'em one, four, eight, two dollars," persisted Billy, who had not yet mastered the figures correctly.

"What a jack you are!" and Tommy hopped up to get the chalk for himself, but nearly tumbled down again, for there actually were four bright quarters in a row, with a bit of paper on them directed to "Tom Bangs," that there might be no mistake.

"Thunder turtles!" cried Tommy, and seizing them he dashed into the house, bawling wildly, "It's all right! Got my money! Where's Nat?"

He was soon found, and his surprise and pleasure were so genuine that few doubted his word when he now denied all knowledge of the money.

"How could I put it back when I didn't take it? Do believe me now, and be good to me again," he said, so imploringly, that Emil slapped him on the back, and declared he would for one.

"So will I, and I'm jolly glad it's not you. But who the dickens is it?" said Tommy, after shaking hands heartily with Nat.

"Never mind, as long as it's found," said Dan with his eyes fixed on Nat's happy face.

"Well, I like that! I'm not going to have my things hooked, and then brought back like the juggling man's tricks," cried Tommy, looking at his money as if he suspected witchcraft.

"We'll find him out somehow, though he was sly enough to print this so his writing wouldn't be known," said Franz, examining the paper.

"Demi prints tip-top," put in Rob, who had not a very clear idea what the fuss was all about.

"You can't make me believe it's him, not if you talk till you are blue," said Tommy, and the others hooted at the mere idea; for the little deacon, as they called him, was above suspicion.

Nat felt the difference in the way they spoke of Demi and himself, and would have given all he had or ever hoped to have to be so trusted; for he had learned how easy it is to lose the confidence of others, how very, very hard to win it back, and truth became to him a precious thing since he had suffered from neglecting it.

Mr. Bhaer was very glad one step had been taken in the right direction, and waited hopefully for yet further revelations. They came sooner than he expected, and in a way that surprised and grieved him very much. As they sat at supper that night, a square parcel was handed to Mrs. Bhaer from Mrs. Bates, a neighbor. A note accompanied the parcel, and, while Mr. Bhaer read it, Demi pulled off the wrapper, exclaiming, as he saw its contents,

"Why, it's the book Uncle Teddy gave Dan!"

"The devil!" broke from Dan, for he had not yet quite cured himself of swearing, though he tried very hard.

Mr. Bhaer looked up quickly at the sound. Dan tried to meet his eyes, but could not; his own fell, and he sat biting his lips, getting redder and redder till he was the picture of shame.

"What is it?" asked Mrs. Bhaer, anxiously.

"I should have preferred to talk about this in private, but Demi has spoilt that plan, so I may as well have it out now," said Mr. Bhaer, looking a little stern, as he always did when any meanness or deceit came up for judgment.

"The note is from Mrs. Bates, and she says that her boy Jimmy told her he bought this book of Dan last Saturday. She saw that it was worth much more than a dollar, and thinking there was some mistake, has sent it to me. Did you sell it, Dan?"

"Yes, sir," was the slow answer.

"Why?"

"Wanted money."

"For what?"

"To pay somebody."

"To whom did you owe it?"

"Tommy."

"Never borrowed a cent of me in his life," cried Tommy, looked scared, for he guessed what was coming now, and felt that on the whole he would have preferred witchcraft, for he admired Dan immensely.

"Perhaps he took it," cried Ned, who owed Dan a grudge for the ducking, and, being a mortal boy, liked to pay it off.

"O Dan!" cried Nat, clasping his hands, regardless of the bread and butter in them.

"It is a hard thing to do, but I must have this settled, for I cannot have you watching each other like detectives, and the whole school disturbed in this way, did you put that dollar in the barn this morning?" asked Mr. Bhaer.

Dan looked him straight in the face, and answered steadily, "Yes, I did."

A murmur went round the table, Tommy dropped his mug with a crash; Daisy cried out, "I knew it wasn't Nat;" Nan began to cry, and Mrs. Jo left the room, looking so disappointed, sorry, and ashamed that Dan could not bear it. He hid his face in his hands a moment, then threw up his head, squared his shoulders as if settling some load upon them, and said, with the dogged look, and half-resolute, half-reckless tone he had used when he first came,

"I did it; now you may do what you like to me, but I won't say another word about it."

"Not even that you are sorry?" asked Mr. Bhaer, troubled by the change in him.

"I ain't sorry."

"I'll forgive him without asking," said Tommy, feeling that it was harder somehow to see brave Dan disgraced than timid Nat.

"Don't want to be forgiven," returned Dan, gruffly.

"Perhaps you will when you have thought about it quietly by yourself, I won't tell you now how surprised and disappointed I am, but by and by I will come up and talk to you in your room."

"Won't make any difference," said Dan, trying to speak defiantly, but failing as he looked at Mr. Bhaer's sorrowful face; and, taking his words for a dismissal, Dan left the room as if he found it impossible to stay.

It would have done him good if he had stayed; for the boys talked the matter over with such sincere regret, and pity, and wonder, it might have touched and won him to ask pardon. No one was glad to find that it was he, not even Nat; for, spite of all his faults, and they were many, every one liked Dan now, because under his rough exterior lay some of the manly virtues which we most admire and love. Mrs. Jo had been the chief prop, as well as cultivator, of Dan; and she took it sadly to heart that her last and most interesting boy had turned out so ill. The theft was bad, but the lying about it, and allowing another to suffer so much from an unjust suspicion was worse; and most discouraging of all was the attempt to restore the money in an underhand way, for it showed not only a want of courage, but a power of deceit that boded ill for the future. Still more trying was his steady refusal to talk of the matter, to ask pardon, or express any remorse. Days passed; and he went about his lessons and his work, silent, grim, and unrepentant. As if taking warning by their treatment of Nat, he asked no sympathy of any one, rejected the advances of the boys, and spent his leisure hours roaming about the fields and woods, trying to find playmates in the birds and beasts, and succeeding better than most boys would have done, because he knew and loved them so well.

"If this goes on much longer, I'm afraid he will run away again, for he is too young to stand a life like this," said Mr. Bhaer, quite dejected at the failure of all his efforts.

"A little while ago I should have been quite sure that nothing would tempt him away, but now I am ready of any thing, he is so changed," answered poor Mrs. Jo, who mourned over her boy and could not be comforted, because he shunned her more than any one else, and only looked at her with the half-fierce, half-imploring eyes of a wild animal caught in a trap, when she tried to talk to him alone.

Nat followed him about like a shadow, and Dan did not repulse him as rudely as he did others, but said, in his blunt way, "You are all right; don't worry about me. I can stand it better than you did."

"But I don't like to have you all alone," Nat would say, sorrowfully.

"I like it;" and Dan would tramp away, stifling a sigh sometimes, for he was lonely.

Passing through the birch grove one day, he came up on several of the boys, who were amusing themselves by climbing up the trees and swinging down again, as they slender elastic stems bent till their tops touched the ground. Dan paused a minute to watch the fun, without offering to join in it, and as he stood there Jack took his turn. He had unfortunately chosen too large a tree; for when he swung off, it only bent a little way, and left him hanging at a dangerous height.

"Go back; you can't do it!" called Ned from below.

Jack tried, but the twigs slipped from his hands, and he could not get his legs round the trunk. He kicked, and squirmed, and clutched in vain, then gave it up, and hung breathless, saying helplessly,

"Catch me! help me! I must drop!"

"You'll be killed if you do," cried Ned, frightened out of his wits.

"Hold on!" shouted Dan; and up the tree he went, crashing his way along till he nearly reached Jack, whose face looked up at him, full of fear and hope.

"You'll both come down," said Ned, dancing with excitement on the slope underneath, while Nat held out his arms, in the wild hope of breaking the fall.

"That's what I want; stand from under," answered Dan, coolly; and, as he spoke, his added weight bent the tree many feet nearer the earth.

Jack dropped safely; but the birch, lightened of half its load, flew up again so suddenly, that Dan, in the act of swinging round to drop feet foremost, lost his hold and fell heavily.

"I'm not hurt, all right in a minute," he said, sitting up, a little pale and dizzy, as the boys gathered round him, full of admiration and alarm.

"You're a trump, Dan, and I'm ever so much obliged to you," cried Jack, gratefully.

"It wasn't any thing," muttered Dan, rising slowly.

"I say it was, and I'll shake hands with you, though you are," Ned checked the unlucky word on his tongue, and held out his hand, feeling that it was a handsome thing on his part.

"But I won't shake hands with a sneak;" and Dan turned his back with a look of scorn, that caused Ned to remember the brook, and retire with undignified haste.

"Come home, old chap; I'll give you a lift;" and Nat walked away with him leaving the others to talk over the feat together, to wonder when Dan would "come round," and to wish one and all that Tommy's "confounded money had been in Jericho before it made such a fuss."

When Mr. Bhaer came into school next morning, he looked so happy, that the boys wondered what had happened to him, and really thought he had lost his mind when they saw him go straight to Dan, and, taking him by both hands, say all in one breath, as he shook them heartily,

"I know all about it, and I beg your pardon. It was like you to do it, and I love you for it, though it's never right to tell lies, even for a friend."

"What is it?" cried Nat, for Dan said not a word, only lifted up his head, as if a weight of some sort had fallen off his back.

"Dan did not take Tommy's money;" and Mr. Bhaer quite shouted it, he was so glad.

"Who did?" cried the boys in a chorus.

Mr. Bhaer pointed to one empty seat, and every eye followed his finger, yet no one spoke for a minute, they were so surprised.

"Jack went home early this morning, but he left this behind him;" and in the silence Mr. Bhaer read the note which he had found tied to his door-handle when he rose.

"I took Tommy's dollar. I was peeking in through a crack and saw him put it there. I was afraid to tell before, though I wanted to. I didn't care so much about Nat, but Dan is a trump, and I can't stand it any longer. I never spent the money; it's under the carpet in my room, right behind the washstand. I'm awful sorry. I am going home, and don't think I shall ever come back, so Dan may have my things.

"JACK"

It was not an elegant confession, being badly written, much blotted, and very short; but it was a precious paper to Dan; and, when Mr. Bhaer paused, the boy went to him, saying, in a rather broken voice, but with clear eyes, and the frank, respectful manner they had tried to teach him,

"I'll say I'm sorry now, and ask you to forgive me, sir."

"It was a kind lie, Dan, and I can't help forgiving it; but you see it did no good," said Mr. Bhaer, with a hand on either shoulder, and a face full of relief and affection.

"It kept the boys from plaguing Nat. That's what I did it for. It made him right down miserable. I didn't care so much," explained Dan, as if glad to speak out after his hard silence.

"How could you do it? You are always so kind to me," faltered Nat, feeling a strong desire to hug his friend and cry. Two girlish performances, which would have scandalized Dan to the last degree.

"It's all right now, old fellow, so don't be a fool," he said, swallowing the lump in his throat, and laughing out as he had not done for weeks. "Does Mrs. Bhaer know?" he asked, eagerly.

"Yes; and she is so happy I don't know what she will do to you," began Mr. Bhaer, but got no farther, for here the boys came crowding about Dan in a tumult of pleasure and curiosity; but before he had answered more than a dozen questions, a voice cried out,

"Three cheers for Dan!" and there was Mrs. Jo in the doorway waving her dish-towel, and looking as if she wanted to dance a jig for joy, as she used to do when a girl.

"Now then," cried Mr. Bhaer, and led off a rousing hurrah, which startled Asia in the kitchen, and made old Mr. Roberts shake his head as he drove by, saying,

"Schools are not what they were when I was young!"

Dan stood it pretty well for a minute, but the sight of Mrs. Jo's delight upset him, and he suddenly bolted across the hall into the parlor, whither she instantly followed, and neither were seen for half an hour.

Mr. Bhaer found it very difficult to calm his excited flock; and, seeing that lessons were an impossibility for a time, he caught their attention by telling them the fine old story of the friends whose fidelity to one another has made their names immortal. The lads listened and remembered, for just then their hearts were touched by the loyalty of a humbler pair of friends. The lie was wrong, but the love that prompted it and the courage that bore in silence the disgrace which belonged to another, made Dan a hero in their eyes. Honesty and honor had a new meaning now; a good name was more precious than gold; for once lost money could not buy it back; and faith in one another made life smooth and happy as nothing else could do.

Tommy proudly restored the name of the firm; Nat was devoted to Dan; and all the boys tried to atone to both for former suspicion and neglect. Mrs. Jo rejoiced over her flock, and Mr. Bhaer was never tired of telling the story of his young Damon and Pythias.

# CHAPTER XV. IN THE WILLOW

The old tree saw and heard a good many little scenes and confidences that summer, because it became the favorite retreat of all the children, and the willow seemed to enjoy it, for a pleasant welcome always met them, and the quiet hours spent in its arms did them all good. It had a great deal of company one Saturday afternoon, and some little bird reported what went on there.

First came Nan and Daisy with their small tubs and bits of soap, for now and then they were seized with a tidy fit, and washed up all their dolls' clothes in the brook. Asia would not have them "slopping round" in her kitchen, and the bath-room was forbidden since Nan forgot to turn off the water till it overflowed and came gently dripping down through the ceiling. Daisy went systematically to work, washing first the white and then the colored things, rinsing them nicely, and hanging them to dry on a cord fastened from one barberry-bush to another, and pinning them up with a set of tiny clothes-pins Ned had turned for her. But Nan put all her little things to soak in the same tub, and then forgot them while she collected thistledown to stuff a pillow for Semiramis, Queen of Babylon, as one doll was named. This took some time, and when Mrs. Giddy-gaddy came to take out her clothes, deep green stains appeared on every thing, for she had forgotten the green silk lining of a certain cape, and its color had soaked nicely into the pink and blue gowns, the little chemises, and even the best ruffled petticoat.

"Oh me! what a mess!" sighed Nan.

"Lay them on the grass to bleach," said Daisy, with an air of experience.

"So I will, and we can sit up in the nest and watch that they don't blow away."

The Queen of Babylon's wardrobe was spread forth upon the bank, and, turning up their tubs to dry, the little washerwomen climbed into the nest, and fell to talking, as ladies are apt to do in the pauses of domestic labor.

"I'm going to have a feather-bed to go with my new pillow," said Mrs. Giddy-gaddy, as she transferred the thistledown from her pocket to her handkerchief, losing about half in the process.

"I wouldn't; Aunt Jo says feather-beds aren't healthy. I never let my children sleep on any thing but a mattress," returned Mrs. Shakespeare Smith, decidedly.

"I don't care; my children are so strong they often sleep on the floor, and don't mind it," (which was quite true). "I can't afford nine mattresses, and I like to make beds myself."

"Won't Tommy charge for the feathers?"

"May be he will, but I shan't pay him, and he won't care," returned Mrs. G., taking a base advantage of the well-known good nature of T. Bangs.

"I think the pink will fade out of that dress sooner than the green mark will," observed Mrs. S., looking down from her perch, and changing the subject, for she and her gossip differed on many points, and Mrs. Smith was a discreet lady.

"Never mind; I'm tired of dolls, and I guess I shall put them all away and attend to my farm; I like it rather better than playing house," said Mrs. G., unconsciously expressing the desire of many older ladies, who cannot dispose of their families so easily however.

"But you mustn't leave them; they will die without their mother," cried the tender Mrs. Smith.

"Let 'em die then; I'm tired of fussing over babies, and I'm going to play with the boys; they need me to see to 'em," returned the strong-minded lady.

Daisy knew nothing about women's rights; she quietly took all she wanted, and no one denied her claim, because she did not undertake what she could not carry out, but unconsciously used the all-powerful right of her own influence to win from others any privilege for which she had proved her fitness. Nan attempted all sorts of things, undaunted by direful failures, and clamored fiercely to be allowed to do every thing that the boys did. They laughed at her, hustled her out of the way, and protested against her meddling with their affairs. But she would not be quenched and she would be heard, for her will was strong, and she had the spirit of a rampant reformer. Mrs. Bhaer sympathized with her, but tired to curb her frantic desire for entire liberty, showing her that she must wait a little, learn self-control, and be ready to use her freedom before she asked for it. Nan had meek moments when she agreed to this, and the influences at work upon her were gradually taking effect. She no longer declared that she would be engine-driver or a blacksmith, but turned her mind to farming, and found in it a vent for the energy bottled up in her active little body. It did not quite satisfy her, however; for her sage and sweet marjoram were dumb things, and could not thank her for her care. She wanted something human to love, work for, and protect, and was never happier than when the little boys brought their cut fingers, bumped heads, or bruised joints for her to "mend-up." Seeing this, Mrs. Jo proposed that she should learn how to do it nicely, and Nursey had an apt pupil in bandaging, plastering, and fomenting. The boys began to call her "Dr. Giddy-gaddy," and she liked it so well that Mrs. Jo one day said to the Professor,

"Fritz, I see what we can do for that child. She wants something to live for even now, and will be one of the sharp, strong, discontented women if she does not have it. Don't let us snub her restless little nature, but do our best to give her the work she likes, and by and by persuade her father to let her study medicine. She will make a capital doctor, for she has courage, strong nerves, a tender heart, and an intense love and pity for the weak and suffering."

Mr. Bhaer smiled at first, but agreed to try, and gave Nan an herb-garden, teaching her the various healing properties of the plants she tended, and letting her try their virtues on the children in the little illnesses they had from time to time. She learned fast, remembered well, and showed a sense and interest most encouraging to her Professor, who did not shut his door in her face because she was a little woman.

She was thinking of this, as she sat in the willow that day, and when Daisy said in her gentle way,

"I love to keep house, and mean to have a nice one for Demi when we grow up and live together."

Nan replied with decision

"Well, I haven't got any brother, and I don't want any house to fuss over. I shall have an office, with lots of bottles and drawers and pestle things in it, and I shall drive round in a horse and chaise and cure sick people. That will be such fun."

"Ugh! how can you bear the bad-smelling stuff and the nasty little powders and castor-oil and senna and hive syrup?" cried Daisy, with a shudder.

"I shan't have to take any, so I don't care. Besides, they make people well, and I like to cure folks. Didn't my sage-tea make Mother Bhaer's headache go away, and my hops stop Ned's toothache in five hours? So now!"

"Shall you put leeches on people, and cut off legs and pull out teeth?" asked Daisy, quaking at the thought.

"Yes, I shall do every thing; I don't care if the people are all smashed up, I shall mend them. My grandpa was a doctor, and I saw him sew a great cut in a man's cheek, and I held the sponge, and wasn't frightened a bit, and Grandpa said I was a brave girl."

"How could you? I'm sorry for sick people, and I like to nurse them, but it makes my legs shake so I have to run away. I'm not a brave girl," sighed Daisy.

"Well, you can be my nurse, and cuddle my patients when I have given them the physic and cut off their legs," said Nan, whose practice was evidently to be of the heroic kind.

"Ship ahoy! Where are you, Nan?" called a voice from below.

"Here we are."

"Ay, ay!" said the voice, and Emil appeared holding one hand in the other, with his face puckered up as if in pain.

"Oh, what's the matter?" cried Daisy, anxiously.

"A confounded splinter in my thumb. Can't get it out. Take a pick at it, will you, Nanny?"

"It's in very deep, and I haven't any needle," said Nan, examining a tarry thumb with interest.

"Take a pin," said Emil, in a hurry.

"No, it's too big and hasn't got a sharp point."

Here Daisy, who had dived into her pocket, presented a neat little housewife with four needles in it.

"You are the Posy who always has what we want," said Emil; and Nan resolved to have a needle-book in her own pocket henceforth, for just such cases as this were always occurring in her practice.

Daisy covered her eyes, but Nan probed and picked with a steady hand, while Emil gave directions not down in any medical work or record.

"Starboard now! Steady, boys, steady! Try another tack. Heave ho! there she is!"

"Suck it," ordered the Doctor, surveying the splinter with an experienced eye.

"Too dirty," responded the patient, shaking his bleeding hand.

"Wait; I'll tie it up if you have got a handkerchief."

"Haven't; take one of those rags down there."

"Gracious! no, indeed; they are doll's clothes," cried Daisy, indignantly.

"Take one of mine; I'd like to have you," said Nan; and swinging himself down, Emil caught up the first "rag" he saw. It happened to be the frilled skirt; but Nan tore it up without a murmur; and when the royal petticoat was turned into a neat little bandage, she dismissed her patient with the command,

"Keep it wet, and let it alone; then it will heal right up, and not be sore."

"What do you charge?" asked the Commodore, laughing.

"Nothing; I keep a 'spensary; that is a place where poor people are doctored free gratis for nothing," explained Nan, with an air.

"Thank you, Doctor Giddy-gaddy. I'll always call you in when I come to grief;" and Emil departed, but looked back to say for one good turn deserves another "Your duds are blowing away, Doctor."

Forgiving the disrespectful word, "duds," the ladies hastily descended, and, gathering up their wash, retired to the house to fire up the little stove, and go to ironing.

A passing breath of air shook the old willow, as if it laughed softly at the childish chatter which went on in the nest, and it had hardly composed itself when another pair of birds alighted for a confidential twitter.

"Now, I'll tell you the secret," began Tommy, who was "swellin' wisibly" with the importance of his news.

"Tell away," answered Nat, wishing he had brought his fiddle, it was so shady and quiet here.

"Well, we fellows were talking over the late interesting case of circumstantial evidence," said Tommy, quoting at random from a speech Franz had made at the club, "and I proposed giving Dan something to make up for our suspecting him, to show our respect, and so on, you know something handsome and useful, that he could keep always and be proud of. What do you think we chose?"

"A butterfly-net; he wants one ever so much," said Nat, looking a little disappointed, for he meant to get it himself.

"No, sir; it's to be a microscope, a real swell one, that we see what-do-you-call-'ems in water with, and stars, and ant-eggs, and all sorts of games, you know. Won't it be a jolly good present?" said Tommy, rather confusing microscopes and telescopes in his remarks.

"Tip-top! I'm so glad! Won't it cost a heap, though?" cried Nat, feeling that his friend was beginning to be appreciated.

"Of course it will; but we are all going to give something. I headed the paper with my five dollars; for if it is done at all, it must be done handsome."

"What! all of it? I never did see such a generous chap as you are;" and Nat beamed upon him with sincere admiration.

"Well, you see, I've been so bothered with my property, that I'm tired of it, and don't mean to save up any more, but give it away as I go along, and then nobody will envy me, or want to steal it, and I shan't be suspecting folks and worrying about my old cash," replied Tommy, on whom the cares and anxieties of a millionaire weighed heavily.

"Will Mr. Bhaer let you do it?"

"He thought it was a first-rate plan, and said that some of the best men he knew preferred to do good with their money instead of laying it up to be squabbled over when they died."

"Your father is rich; does he do that way?"

"I'm not sure; he gives me all I want; I know that much. I'm going to talk to him about it when I go home. Anyhow, I shall set him a good example;" and Tommy was so serious, that Nat did not dare to laugh, but said, respectfully,

"You will be able to do ever so much with your money, won't you?"

"So Mr. Bhaer said, and he promised to advise me about useful ways of spending it. I'm going to begin with Dan; and next time I get a dollar or so, I shall do something for Dick, he's such a good little chap, and only has a cent a week for pocket-money. He can't earn much, you know; so I'm going to kind of see to him;" and good-hearted Tommy quite longed to begin.

"I think that's a beautiful plan, and I'm not going to try to buy a fiddle any more; I'm going to get Dan his net all myself, and if there is any money left, I'll do something to please poor Billy. He's fond of me, and though he isn't poor, he'd like some little thing from me, because I can make out what he wants better than the rest of you." And Nat fell to wondering how much happiness could be got out of his precious three dollars.

"So I would. Now come and ask Mr. Bhaer if you can't go in town with me on Monday afternoon, so you can get the net, while I get the microscope. Franz and Emil are going too, and we'll have a jolly time larking round among the shops."

The lads walked away arm-in-arm, discussing the new plans with droll importance, yet beginning already to feel the sweet satisfaction which comes to those who try, no matter how humbly, to be earthly providences to the poor and helpless, and gild their mite with the gold of charity before it is laid up where thieves cannot break through and steal.

"Come up and rest while we sort the leaves; it's so cool and pleasant here," said Demi, as he and Dan came sauntering home from a long walk in the woods.

"All right!" answered Dan, who was a boy of few words, and up they went.

"What makes birch leaves shake so much more than the others?" asked inquiring Demi, who was always sure of an answer from Dan.

"They are hung differently. Don't you see the stem where it joins the leaf is sort of pinched one way, and where it joins the twig, it is pinched another. This makes it waggle with the least bit of wind, but the elm leaves hang straight, and keep stiller."

"How curious! will this do so?" and Demi held up a sprig of acacia, which he had broken from a little tree on the lawn, because it was so pretty.

"No; that belongs to the sort that shuts up when you touch it. Draw your finger down the middle of the stem, and see if the leaves don't curl up," said Dan, who was examining a bit of mica.

Demi tried it, and presently the little leaves did fold together, till the spray showed a single instead of a double line of leaves.

"I like that; tell me about the others. What do these do?" asked Demi, taking up a new branch.

"Feed silk-worms; they live on mulberry leaves, till they begin to spin themselves up. I was in a silk-factory once, and there were rooms full of shelves all covered with leaves, and worms eating them so fast that it made a rustle. Sometimes they eat so much they die. Tell that to Stuffy," and Dan laughed, as he took up another bit of rock with a lichen on it.

"I know one thing about this mullein leaf: the fairies use them for blankets," said Demi, who had not quite given up his faith in the existence of the little folk in green.

"If I had a microscope, I'd show you something prettier than fairies," said Dan, wondering if he should ever own that coveted treasure. "I knew an old woman who used mullein leaves for a night-cap because she had face-ache. She sewed them together, and wore it all the time."

"How funny! was she your grandmother?"

"Never had any. She was a queer old woman, and lived alone in a little tumble-down house with nineteen cats. Folks called her a witch, but she wasn't, though she looked like an old rag-bag. She was real kind to me when I lived in that place, and used to let me get warm at her fire when the folks at the poorhouse were hard on me."

"Did you live in a poorhouse?"

"A little while. Never mind that I didn't mean to speak of it;" and Dan stopped short in his unusual fit of communicativeness.

"Tell about the cats, please," said Demi, feeling that he had asked an unpleasant question, and sorry for it.

"Nothing to tell; only she had a lot of 'em, and kept 'em in a barrel nights; and I used to go and tip over the barrel sometimes, and let 'em out all over the house, and then she'd scold, and chase 'em and put 'em in again, spitting and yowling like fury."

"Was she good to them?" asked Demi, with a hearty child's laugh, pleasant to hear.

"Guess she was. Poor old soul! she took in all the lost and sick cats in the town; and when anybody wanted one they went to Marm Webber, and she let 'em pick any kind and color they wanted, and only asked ninepence, she was glad to have her pussies get a good home."

"I should like to see Marm Webber. Could I, if I went to that place?"

"She's dead. All my folks are," said Dan, briefly.

"I'm sorry;" and Demi sat silent a minute, wondering what subject would be safe to try next. He felt delicate about speaking of the departed lady, but was very curious about the cats, and could not resist asking softly,

"Did she cure the sick ones?"

"Sometimes. One had a broken leg, and she tied it up to a stick, and it got well; and another had fits, and she doctored it with yarbs till it was cured. But some of 'em died, and she buried 'em; and when they couldn't get well, she killed 'em easy."

"How?" asked Demi, feeling that there was a peculiar charm about this old woman, and some sort of joke about the cats, because Dan was smiling to himself.

"A kind lady, who was fond of cats, told her how, and gave her some stuff, and sent all her own pussies to be killed that way. Marm used to put a sponge wet with ether, in the bottom of an old boot, then poke puss in head downwards. The ether put her to sleep in a jiffy, and she was drowned in warm water before she woke up."

"I hope the cats didn't feel it. I shall tell Daisy about that. You have known a great many interesting things, haven't you?" asked Demi, and fell to meditating on the vast experience of a boy who had run away more than once, and taken care of himself in a big city.

"Wish I hadn't sometimes."

"Why? Don't remembering them feel good?"

"No."

"It's very singular how hard it is to manage your mind," said Demi, clasping his hands round his knees, and looking up at the sky as if for information upon his favorite topic.

"Devilish hard no, I don't mean that;" and Dan bit his lips, for the forbidden word slipped out in spite of him, and he wanted to be more careful with Demi than with any of the other boys.

"I'll play I didn't hear it," said Demi; "and you won't do it again, I'm sure."

"Not if I can help it. That's one of the things I don't want to remember. I keep pegging away, but it don't seem to do much good;" and Dan looked discouraged.

"Yes, it does. You don't say half so many bad words as you used to; and Aunt Jo is pleased, because she said it was a hard habit to break up."

"Did she?" and Dan cheered up a bit.

"You must put swearing away in your fault-drawer, and lock it up; that's the way I do with my badness."

"What do you mean?" asked Dan, looking as if he found Demi almost as amusing as a new sort of cockchafer or beetle.

"Well, it's one of my private plays, and I'll tell you, but I think you'll laugh at it," began Demi, glad to hold forth on this congenial subject. "I play that my mind is a round room, and my soul is a little sort of creature with wings that lives in it. The walls are full of shelves and drawers, and in them I keep my thoughts, and my goodness and badness, and all sorts of things. The goods I keep where I can see them, and the bads I lock up tight, but they get out, and I have to keep putting them in and squeezing them down, they are so strong. The thoughts I play with when I am alone or in bed, and I make up and do what I like with them. Every Sunday I put my room in order, and talk with the little spirit that lives there, and tell him what to do. He is very bad sometimes, and won't mind me, and I have to scold him, and take him to Grandpa. He always makes him behave, and be sorry for his faults, because Grandpa likes this play, and gives me nice things to put in the drawers, and tells me how to shut up the naughties. Hadn't you better try that way? It's a very good one;" and Demi looked so earnest and full of faith, that Dan did not laugh at his quaint fancy, but said, soberly,

"I don't think there is a lock strong enough to keep my badness shut up. Any way my room is in such a clutter I don't know how to clear it up."

"You keep your drawers in the cabinet all spandy nice; why can't you do the others?"

"I ain't used to it. Will you show me how?" and Dan looked as if inclined to try Demi's childish way of keeping a soul in order.

"I'd love to, but I don't know how, except to talk as Grandpa does. I can't do it good like him, but I'll try."

"Don't tell any one; only now and then we'll come here and talk things over, and I'll pay you for it by telling all I know about my sort of things. Will that do?" and Dan held out his big, rough hand.

Demi gave his smooth, little hand readily, and the league was made; for in the happy, peaceful world where the younger boy lived, lions and lambs played together, and little children innocently taught their elders.

"Hush!" said Dan, pointing toward the house, as Demi was about to indulge in another discourse on the best way of getting badness down, and keeping it down; and peeping from their perch, they saw Mrs. Jo strolling slowly along, reading as she went, while Teddy trotted behind her, dragging a little cart upside down.

"Wait till they see us," whispered Demi, and both sat still as the pair came nearer, Mrs. Jo so absorbed in her book that she would have walked into the brook if Teddy had not stopped her by saying,

"Marmar, I wanter fis."

Mrs. Jo put down the charming book which she had been trying to read for a week, and looked about her for a fishing-pole, being used to making toys out of nothing. Before she had broken one from the hedge, a slender willow bough fell at her feet; and, looking up, she saw the boys laughing in the nest.

"Up! up!" cried Teddy, stretching his arms and flapping his skirts as if about to fly.

"I'll come down and you come up. I must go to Daisy now;" and Demi departed to rehearse the tale of the nineteen cats, with the exciting boot-and-barrel episodes.

Teddy was speedily whisked up; and then Dan said, laughing, "Come, too; there's plenty of room. I'll lend you a hand."

Mrs. Jo glanced over her shoulder, but no one was in sight; and rather liking the joke of the thing, she laughed back, saying, "Well, if you won't mention it, I think I will;" and with two nimble steps was in the willow.

"I haven't climbed a tree since I was married. I used to be very fond of it when I was a girl," she said, looking well-pleased with her shady perch.

"Now, you read if you want to, and I'll take care of Teddy," proposed Dan, beginning to make a fishing-rod for impatient Baby.

"I don't think I care about it now. What were you and Demi at up here?" asked Mrs. Jo, thinking, from the sober look on Dan's face, that he had something on his mind.

"Oh! we were talking. I'd been telling him about leaves and things, and he was telling me some of his queer plays. Now, then, Major, fish away;" and Dan finished off his work by putting a big blue fly on the bent pin which hung at the end of the cord he had tied to the willow-rod.

Teddy leaned down from the tree, and was soon wrapt up in watching for the fish which he felt sure would come. Dan held him by his little petticoats, lest he should take a "header" into the brook, and Mrs. Jo soon won him to talk by doing so herself.

"I am so glad you told Demi about 'leaves and things;' it is just what he needs; and I wish you would teach him, and take him to walk with you."

"I'd like to, he is so bright; but—"

"But what?"

"I didn't think you'd trust me."

"Why not?"

"Well, Demi is so kind of precious, and so good, and I'm such a bad lot, I thought you'd keep him away from me."

"But you are not a 'bad lot,' as you say; and I do trust you, Dan, entirely, because you honestly try to improve, and do better and better every week."

"Really?" and Dan looked up at her with the cloud of despondency lifting from his face.

"Yes; don't you feel it?"

"I hoped so, but I didn't know."

"I have been waiting and watching quietly, for I thought I'd give you a good trial first; and if you stood it, I would give you the best reward I had. You have stood it well; and now I'm going to trust not only Demi, but my own boy, to you, because you can teach them some things better than any of us."

"Can I?" and Dan looked amazed at the idea.

"Demi has lived among older people so much that he needs just what you have knowledge of common things, strength, and courage. He thinks you are the bravest boy he ever saw, and admires your strong way of doing things. Then you know a great deal about natural objects, and can tell him more wonderful tales of birds, and bees, and leaves, and animals, than his story-books give him; and, being true, these stories will teach and do him good. Don't you see now how much you can help him, and why I like to have him with you?"

"But I swear sometimes, and might tell him something wrong. I wouldn't mean to, but it might slip out, just as 'devil' did a few minutes ago," said Dan, anxious to do his duty, and let her know his shortcomings.

"I know you try not to say or do any thing to harm the little fellow, and here is where I think Demi will help you, because he is so innocent and wise in his small way, and has what I am trying to give you, dear, good principles. It is never too early to try and plant them in a child, and never too late to cultivate them in the most neglected person. You are only boys yet; you can teach one another. Demi will unconsciously strengthen your moral sense, you will strengthen his common sense, and I shall feel as if I had helped you both."

Words could not express how pleased and touched Dan was by this confidence and praise. No one had ever trusted him before, no one had cared to find out and foster the good in him, and no one had suspected how much there was hidden away in the breast of the neglected boy, going fast to ruin, yet quick to feel and value sympathy and help. No honor that he might earn hereafter would ever be half so precious as the right to teach his few virtues and small store of learning to the child whom he most respected; and no more powerful restraint could have been imposed upon him than the innocent companion confided to his care. He found courage now to tell Mrs. Jo of the plan already made with Demi, and she was glad that the first step had been so naturally taken. Every thing seemed to be working well for Dan, and she rejoiced over him, because it had seemed a hard task, yet, working on with a firm belief in the possibility of reformation in far older and worse subjects than he, there had come this quick and hopeful change to encourage her. He felt that he had friends now and a place in the world, something to live and work for, and, though he said little, all that was best and bravest in a character made old by a hard experience responded to the love and faith bestowed on him, and Dan's salvation was assured.

Their quiet talk was interrupted by a shout of delight from Teddy, who, to the surprise of every one, did actually catch a trout where no trout had been seen for years. He was so enchanted with his splendid success that he insisted on showing his prize to the family before Asia cooked it for supper; so the three descended and went happily away together, all satisfied with the work of that half hour.

Ned was the next visitor to the tree, but he only made a short stay, sitting there at his ease while Dick and Dolly caught a pailful of grasshoppers and crickets for him. He wanted to play a joke on Tommy, and intended to tuck up a few dozen of the lively creatures in his bed, so that when Bangs got in he would speedily tumble out again, and pass a portion of the night in chasing "hopper-grasses" round the room. The hunt was soon over, and having paid the hunters with a few peppermints apiece Ned retired to make Tommy's bed.

For an hour the old willow sighed and sung to itself, talked with the brook, and watched the lengthening shadows as the sun went down. The first rosy color was touching its graceful branches when a boy came stealing up the avenue, across the lawn, and, spying Billy by the brook-side, went to him, saying, in a mysterious tone,

"Go and tell Mr. Bhaer I want to see him down here, please. Don't let any one hear."

Billy nodded and ran off, while the boy swung himself up into the tree, and sat there looking anxious, yet evidently feeling the charm of the place and hour. In five minutes, Mr. Bhaer appeared, and, stepping up on the fence, leaned into the nest, saying, kindly,

"I am glad to see you, Jack; but why not come in and meet us all at once?"

"I wanted to see you first, please, sir. Uncle made me come back. I know I don't deserve any thing, but I hope the fellows won't be hard upon me."

Poor Jack did not get on very well, but it was evident that he was sorry and ashamed, and wanted to be received as easily as possible; for his Uncle had thrashed him well and scolded him soundly for following the example he himself set. Jack had begged not to be sent back, but the school was cheap, and Mr. Ford insisted, so the boy returned as quietly as possible, and took refuge behind Mr. Bhaer.

"I hope not, but I can't answer for them, though I will see that they are not unjust. I think, as Dan and Nat have suffered so much, being innocent, you should suffer something, being guilty. Don't you?" asked Mr. Bhaer, pitying Jack, yet feeling he deserved punishment for a fault which had so little excuse.

"I suppose so, but I sent Tommy's money back, and I said I was sorry, isn't that enough?" said Jack, rather sullenly; for the boy who could do so mean a thing was not brave enough to bear the consequences well.

"No; I think you should ask pardon of all three boys, openly and honestly. You cannot expect them to respect and trust you for a time, but you can live down this disgrace if you try, and I will help you. Stealing and lying are detestable sins, and I hope this will be a lesson to you. I am glad you are ashamed, it is a good sign; bear it patiently, and do your best to earn a better reputation."

"I'll have an auction, and sell off all my goods dirt cheap," said Jack, showing his repentance in the most characteristic way.

"I think it would be better to give them away, and begin on a new foundation. Take 'Honesty is the best policy' for your motto, and live up to it in act, and word, and thought, and though you don't make a cent of money this summer, you will be a rich boy in the autumn," said Mr. Bhaer, earnestly.

It was hard, but Jack consented, for he really felt that cheating didn't pay, and wanted to win back the friendship of the boys. His heart clung to his possessions, and he groaned inwardly at the thought of actually giving away certain precious things. Asking pardon publicly was easy compared to this; but then he began to discover that certain other things, invisible, but most valuable, were better property than knives, fish-hooks, or even money itself. So he decided to buy up a little integrity, even at a high price, and secure the respect of his playmates, though it was not a salable article.

"Well, I'll do it," he said, with a sudden air of resolution, which pleased Mr. Bhaer.

"Good! and I'll stand by you. Now come and begin at once."

And Father Bhaer led the bankrupt boy back into the little world, which received him coldly at first, but slowly warmed to him, when he showed that he had profited by the lesson, and was sincerely anxious to go into a better business with a new stock-in-trade.

# CHAPTER XVI. TAMING THE COLT

"What in the world is that boy doing?" said Mrs. Jo to herself, as she watched Dan running round the half-mile triangle as if for a wager. He was all alone, and seemed possessed by some strange desire to run himself into a fever, or break his neck; for, after several rounds, he tried leaping walls, and turning somersaults up the avenue, and finally dropped down on the grass before the door as if exhausted.

"Are you training for a race, Dan?" asked Mrs. Jo, from the window where she sat.

He looked up quickly, and stopped panting to answer, with a laugh,

"No; I'm only working off my steam."

"Can't you find a cooler way of doing it? You will be ill if you tear about so in such warm weather," said Mrs. Jo, laughing also, as she threw him out a great palm-leaf fan.

"Can't help it. I must run somewhere," answered Dan, with such an odd expression in his restless eyes, that Mrs. Jo was troubled, and asked, quickly,

"Is Plumfield getting too narrow for you?"

"I wouldn't mind if it was a little bigger. I like it though; only the fact is the devil gets into me sometimes, and then I do want to bolt."

The words seemed to come against his will, for he looked sorry the minute they were spoken, and seemed to think he deserved a reproof for his ingratitude. But Mrs. Jo understood the feeling, and though sorry to see it, she could not blame the boy for confessing it. She looked at him anxiously, seeing how tall and strong he had grown, how full of energy his face was, with its eager eyes and resolute mouth; and remembering the utter freedom he had known for years before, she felt how even the gentle restraint of this home would weigh upon him at times when the old lawless spirit stirred in him. "Yes," she said to herself, "my wild hawk needs a larger cage; and yet, if I let him go, I am afraid he will be lost. I must try and find some lure strong enough to keep him safe."

"I know all about it," she added, aloud. "It is not 'the devil,' as you call it, but the very natural desire of all young people for liberty. I used to feel just so, and once, I really did think for a minute that I would bolt."

"Why didn't you?" said Dan, coming to lean on the low window-ledge, with an evident desire to continue the subject.

"I knew it was foolish, and love for my mother kept me at home."

"I haven't got any mother," began Dan.

"I thought you had now," said Mrs. Jo, gently stroking the rough hair off his hot forehead.

"You are no end good to me, and I can't ever thank you enough, but it just isn't the same, is it?" and Dan looked up at her with a wistful, hungry look that went to her heart.

"No, dear, it is not the same, and never can be. I think an own mother would have been a great deal to you. But as that cannot be, you must try to let me fill her place. I fear I have not done all I ought, or you would not want to leave me," she added, sorrowfully.

"Yes, you have!" cried Dan, eagerly. "I don't want to go, and I won't go, if I can help it; but every now and then I feel as if I must burst out somehow. I want to run straight ahead somewhere, to smash something, or pitch into somebody. Don't know why, but I do, and that's all about it."

Dan laughed as he spoke, but he meant what he said, for he knit his black brows, and brought down his fist on the ledge with such force, that Mrs. Jo's thimble flew off into the grass. He brought it back, and as she took it she held the big, brown hand a minute, saying, with a look that showed the words cost her something,

"Well, Dan, run if you must, but don't run very far; and come back to me soon, for I want you very much."

He was rather taken aback by this unexpected permission to play truant, and somehow it seemed to lessen his desire to go. He did not understand why, but Mrs. Jo did, and, knowing the natural perversity of the human mind, counted on it to help her now. She felt instinctively that the more the boy was restrained the more he would fret against it; but leave him free, and the mere sense of liberty would content him, joined to the knowledge that his presence was dear to those whom he loved best. It was a little experiment, but it succeeded, for Dan stood silent a moment, unconsciously picking the fan to pieces and turning the matter over in his mind. He felt that she appealed to his heart and his honor, and owned that he understood it by saying presently, with a mixture of regret and resolution in his face,

"I won't go yet awhile, and I'll give you fair warning before I bolt. That's fair, isn't it?"

"Yes, we will let it stand so. Now, I want to see if I can't find some way for you to work off your steam better than running about the place like a mad dog, spoiling my fans, or fighting with the boys. What can we invent?" and while Dan tried to repair the mischief he had done, Mrs. Jo racked her brain for some new device to keep her truant safe until he had learned to love his lessons better.

"How would you like to be my express-man?" she said, as a sudden thought popped into her head.

"Go into town, and do the errands?" asked Dan, looking interested at once.

"Yes; Franz is tired of it, Silas cannot be spared just now, and Mr. Bhaer has no time. Old Andy is a safe horse, you are a good driver, and know your way about the city as well as a postman. Suppose you try it, and see if it won't do most as well to drive away two or three times a week as to run away once a month."

"I'd like it ever so much, only I must go alone and do it all myself. I don't want any of the other fellows bothering round," said Dan, taking to the new idea so kindly that he began to put on business airs already.

"If Mr. Bhaer does not object you shall have it all your own way. I suppose Emil will growl, but he cannot be trusted with horses, and you can. By the way, to-morrow is market-day, and I must make out my list. You had better see that the wagon is in order, and tell Silas to have the fruit and vegetables ready for mother. You will have to be up early and get back in time for school, can you do that?"

"I'm always an early bird, so I don't mind," and Dan slung on his jacket with despatch.

"The early bird got the worm this time, I'm sure," said Mrs. Jo, merrily.

"And a jolly good worm it is," answered Dan, as he went laughing away to put a new lash to the whip, wash the wagon, and order Silas about with all the importance of a young express-man.

"Before he is tired of this I will find something else and have it ready when the next restless fit comes on," said Mrs. Jo to herself, as she wrote her list with a deep sense of gratitude that all her boys were not Dans.

Mr. Bhaer did not entirely approve of the new plan, but agreed to give it a trial, which put Dan on his mettle, and caused him to give up certain wild plans of his own, in which the new lash and the long hill were to have borne a part. He was up and away very early the next morning, heroically resisting the temptation to race with the milkmen going into town. Once there, he did his errands carefully, to Mr. Bhaer's surprise and Mrs. Jo's great satisfaction. The Commodore did growl at Dan's promotion, but was pacified by a superior padlock to his new boat-house, and the thought that seamen were meant for higher honors than driving market-wagons and doing family errands. So Dan filled his new office well and contentedly for weeks, and said no more about bolting. But one day Mr. Bhaer found him pummelling Jack, who was roaring for mercy under his knee.

"Why, Dan, I thought you had given up fighting," he said, as he went to the rescue.

"We ain't fighting, we are only wrestling," answered Dan, leaving off reluctantly.

"It looks very much like it, and feels like it, hey, Jack?" said Mr. Bhaer, as the defeated gentleman got upon his legs with difficulty.

"Catch me wrestling with him again. He's most knocked my head off," snarled Jack, holding on to that portion of his frame as if it really was loose upon his shoulders.

"The fact is, we began in fun, but when I got him down I couldn't help pounding him. Sorry I hurt you, old fellow," explained Dan, looking rather ashamed of himself.

"I understand. The longing to pitch into somebody was so strong you couldn't resist. You are a sort of Berserker, Dan, and something to tussle with is as necessary to you as music is to Nat," said Mr. Bhaer, who knew all about the conversation between the boy and Mrs. Jo.

"Can't help it. So if you don't want to be pounded you'd better keep out of the way," answered Dan, with a warning look in his black eyes that made Jack sheer off in haste.

"If you want something to wrestle with, I will give you a tougher specimen than Jack," said Mr. Bhaer; and, leading the way to the wood-yard, he pointed out certain roots of trees that had been grubbed up in the spring, and had been lying there waiting to be split.

"There, when you feel inclined to maltreat the boys, just come and work off your energies here, and I'll thank you for it."

"So I will;" and, seizing the axe that lay near Dan hauled out a tough root, and went at it so vigorously, that the chips flew far and wide, and Mr. Bhaer fled for his life.

To his great amusement, Dan took him at his word, and was often seen wrestling with the ungainly knots, hat and jacket off, red face, and wrathful eyes; for he got into royal rages over some of his adversaries, and swore at them under his breath till he had conquered them, when he exulted, and marched off to the shed with an armful of gnarled oak-wood in triumph. He blistered his hands, tired his back, and dulled the axe, but it did him good, and he got more comfort out of the ugly roots than any one dreamed, for with each blow he worked off some of the pent-up power that would otherwise have been expended in some less harmless way.

"When this is gone I really don't know what I shall do," said Mrs. Jo to herself, for no inspiration came, and she was at the end of her resources.

But Dan found a new occupation for himself, and enjoyed it some time before any one discovered the cause of his contentment. A fine young horse of Mr. Laurie's was kept at Plumfield that summer, running loose in a large pasture across the brook. The boys were all interested in the handsome, spirited creature, and for a time were fond of watching him gallop and frisk with his plumey tail flying, and his handsome head in the air. But they soon got tired of it, and left Prince Charlie to himself. All but Dan, he never tired of looking at the horse, and seldom failed to visit him each day with a lump of sugar, a bit of bread, or an apple to make him welcome. Charlie was grateful, accepted his friendship, and the two loved one another as if they felt some tie between them, inexplicable but strong. In whatever part of the wide field he might be, Charlie always came at full speed when Dan whistled at the bars, and the boy was never happier than when the beautiful, fleet creature put its head on his shoulder, looking up at him with fine eyes full of intelligent affection.

"We understand one another without any palaver, don't we, old fellow?" Dan would say, proud of the horse's confidence, and, so jealous of his regard, that he told no one how well the friendship prospered, and never asked anybody but Teddy to accompany him on these daily visits.

Mr. Laurie came now and then to see how Charlie got on, and spoke of having him broken to harness in the autumn.

"He won't need much taming, he is such a gentle, fine-tempered brute. I shall come out and try him with a saddle myself some day," he said, on one of these visits.

"He lets me put a halter on him, but I don't believe he will bear a saddle even if you put it on," answered Dan, who never failed to be present when Charlie and his master met.

"I shall coax him to bear it, and not mind a few tumbles at first. He has never been harshly treated, so, though he will be surprised at the new performance, I think he won't be frightened, and his antics will do no harm."

"I wonder what he would do," said Dan to himself, as Mr. Laurie went away with the Professor, and Charlie returned to the bars, from which he had retired when the gentlemen came up.

A daring fancy to try the experiment took possession of the boy as he sat on the topmost rail with the glossy back temptingly near him. Never thinking of danger, he obeyed the impulse, and while Charlie unsuspectingly nibbled at the apple he held, Dan quickly and quietly took his seat. He did not keep it long, however, for with an astonished snort, Charlie reared straight up, and deposited Dan on the ground. The fall did not hurt him, for the turf was soft, and he jumped up, saying, with a laugh,

"I did it anyway! Come here, you rascal, and I'll try it again."

But Charlie declined to approach, and Dan left him resolving to succeed in the end; for a struggle like this suited him exactly. Next time he took a halter, and having got it on, he played with the horse for a while, leading him to and fro, and putting him through various antics till he was a little tired; then Dan sat on the wall and gave him bread, but watched his chance, and getting a good grip of the halter, slipped on to his back. Charlie tried the old trick, but Dan held on, having had practice with Toby, who occasionally had an obstinate fit, and tried to shake off his rider. Charlie was both amazed and indignant; and after prancing for a minute, set off at a gallop, and away went Dan heels over head. If he had not belonged to the class of boys who go through all sorts of dangers unscathed, he would have broken his neck; as it was, he got a heavy fall, and lay still collecting his wits, while Charlie tore round the field tossing his head with every sign of satisfaction at the discomfiture of his rider. Presently it seemed to occur to him that something was wrong with Dan, and, being of a magnanimous nature, he went to see what the matter was. Dan let him sniff about and perplex himself for a few minutes; then he looked up at him, saying, as decidedly as if the horse could understand,

"You think you have beaten, but you are mistaken, old boy; and I'll ride you yet see if I don't."

He tried no more that day, but soon after attempted a new method of introducing Charlie to a burden. He strapped a folded blanket on his back, and then let him race, and rear, and roll, and fume as much as he liked. After a few fits of rebellion Charlie submitted, and in a few days permitted Dan to mount him, often stopped short to look round, as if he said, half patiently, half reproachfully, "I don't understand it, but I suppose you mean no harm, so I permit the liberty."

Dan patted and praised him, and took a short turn every day, getting frequent falls, but persisting in spite of them, and longing to try a saddle and bridle, but not daring to confess what he had done. He had his wish, however, for there had been a witness of his pranks who said a good word for him.

"Do you know what that chap has ben doin' lately?" asked Silas of his master, one evening, as he received his orders for the next day.

"Which boy?" said Mr. Bhaer, with an air of resignation, expecting some sad revelation.

"Dan, he's ben a breaking the colt, sir, and I wish I may die if he ain't done it," answered Silas, chuckling.

"How do you know?"

"Wal, I kinder keep an eye on the little fellers, and most gen'lly know what they're up to; so when Dan kep going off to the paster, and coming home black and blue, I mistrusted that suthing was goin' on. I didn't say nothin', but I crep up into the barn chamber, and from there I see him goin' through all manner of games with Charlie. Blest if he warn't throwed time and agin, and knocked round like a bag o' meal. But the pluck of that boy did beat all, and he 'peared to like it, and kep on as ef bound to beat."

"But, Silas, you should have stopped it the boy might have been killed," said Mr. Bhaer, wondering what freak his irrepressibles would take into their heads next.

"S'pose I oughter; but there warn't no real danger, for Charlie ain't no tricks, and is as pretty a tempered horse as ever I see. Fact was, I couldn't bear to spile sport, for ef there's any thing I do admire it's grit, and Dan is chock full on 't. But now I know he's hankerin' after a saddle, and yet won't take even the old one on the sly; so I just thought I'd up and tell, and may be you'd let him try what he can do. Mr. Laurie won't mind, and Charlie's all the better for 't."

"We shall see;" and off went Mr. Bhaer to inquire into the matter.

Dan owned up at once, and proudly proved that Silas was right by showing off his power over Charlie; for by dint of much coaxing, many carrots, and infinite perseverance, he really had succeeded in riding the colt with a halter and blanket. Mr. Laurie was much amused, and well pleased with Dan's courage and skill, and let him have a hand in all future performances; for he set about Charlie's education at once, saying that he was not going to be outdone by a slip of a boy. Thanks to Dan, Charlie took kindly to the saddle and bridle when he had once reconciled himself to the indignity of the bit; and after Mr. Laurie had trained him a little, Dan was permitted to ride him, to the great envy and admiration of the other boys.

"Isn't he handsome? and don't he mind me like a lamb?" said Dan one day as he dismounted and stood with his arm round Charlie's neck.

"Yes, and isn't he a much more useful and agreeable animal than the wild colt who spent his days racing about the field, jumping fences, and running away now and then?" asked Mrs. Bhaer from the steps where she always appeared when Dan performed with Charlie.

"Of course he is. See he won't run away now, even if I don't hold him, and he comes to me the minute I whistle; I have tamed him well, haven't I?" and Dan looked both proud and pleased, as well he might, for, in spite of their struggles together, Charlie loved him better than his master.

"I am taming a colt too, and I think I shall succeed as well as you if I am as patient and persevering," said Mrs. Jo, smiling so significantly at him, that Dan understood and answered, laughing, yet in earnest,

"We won't jump over the fence and run away, but stay and let them make a handsome, useful span of us, hey, Charlie?"

## CHAPTER XVII. COMPOSITION DAY

"Hurry up, boys, it's three o'clock, and Uncle Fritz likes us to be punctual, you know," said Franz one Wednesday afternoon as a bell rang, and a stream of literary-looking young gentlemen with books and paper in their hands were seen going toward the museum.

Tommy was in the school-room, bending over his desk, much bedaubed with ink, flushed with the ardor of inspiration, and in a great hurry as usual, for easy-going Bangs never was ready till the very last minute. As Franz passed the door looking up laggards, Tommy gave one last blot and flourish, and departed out the window, waving his paper to dry as he went. Nan followed, looking very important, with a large roll in her hand, and Demi escorted Daisy, both evidently brimful of some delightful secret.

The museum was all in order, and the sunshine among the hop-vines made pretty shadows on the floor as it peeped through the great window. On one side sat Mr. and Mrs. Bhaer, on the other was a little table on which the compositions were laid as soon as read, and in a large semicircle sat the children on camp-stools which occasionally shut up and let the sitter down, thus preventing any stiffness in the assembly. As it took too much time to have all read, they took turns, and on this Wednesday the younger pupils were the chief performers, while the elder ones listened with condescension and criticised freely.

"Ladies first; so Nan may begin," said Mr. Bhaer, when the settling of stools and rustling of papers had subsided.

Nan took her place beside the little table, and, with a preliminary giggle, read the following interesting essay on,

"THE SPONGE

"The sponge, my friends, is a most useful and interesting plant. It grows on rocks under the water, and is a kind of sea-weed, I believe. People go and pick it and dry it and wash it, because little fish and insects live in the holes of the sponge; I found shells in my new one, and sand. Some are very fine and soft; babies are washed with them. The sponge has many uses. I will relate some of them, and I hope my friends will remember what I say. One use is to wash the face; I don't like it myself, but I do it because I wish to be clean. Some people don't, and they are dirty." Here the eye of the reader rested sternly upon Dick and Dolly, who quailed under it, and instantly resolved to scrub themselves virtuously on all occasions. "Another use is to wake people up; I allude to boys par-tic-u-lar-ly." Another pause after the long word to enjoy the smothered laugh that went round the room. "Some boys do not get up when called, and Mary Ann squeezes the water out of a wet sponge on their faces, and it makes them so mad they wake up." Here the laugh broke out, and Emil said, as if he had been hit,

"Seems to me you are wandering from the subject."

"No, I ain't; we are to write about vegetables or animals, and I'm doing both: for boys are animals, aren't they?" cried Nan; and, undaunted by the indignant "No!" shouted at her, she calmly proceeded,

"One more interesting thing is done with sponges, and this is when doctors put ether on it, and hold it to people's noses when they have teeth out. I shall do this when I am bigger, and give ether to the sick, so they will go to sleep and not feel me cut off their legs and arms."

"I know somebody who killed cats with it," called out Demi, but was promptly crushed by Dan, who upset his camp-stool and put a hat over his face.

"I will not be interruckted," said Nan, frowning upon the unseemly scrimmagers. Order was instantly restored, and the young lady closed her remarks as follows:

"My composition has three morals, my friends." Somebody groaned, but no notice was taken of the insult. "First, is keep your faces clean second, get up early third, when the ether sponge is put over your nose, breathe hard and don't kick, and your teeth will come out easy. I have no more to say." And Miss Nan sat down amid tumultuous applause.

"That is a very remarkable composition; its tone is high, and there is a good deal of humor in it. Very well done, Nan. Now, Daisy," and Mr. Bhaer smiled at one young lady as he beckoned the other.

Daisy colored prettily as she took her place, and said, in her modest little voice,

"I'm afraid you won't like mine; it isn't nice and funny like Nan's. But I couldn't do any better."

"We always like yours, Posy," said Uncle Fritz, and a gentle murmur from the boys seemed to confirm the remark. Thus encouraged, Daisy read her little paper, which was listened to with respectful attention.

"THE CAT

"The cat is a sweet animal. I love them very much. They are clean and pretty, and catch rats and mice, and let you pet them, and are fond of you if you are kind. They are very wise, and can find their way anywhere. Little cats are called kittens, and are dear things. I have two, named Huz and Buz, and their mother is Topaz, because she has yellow eyes. Uncle told me a pretty story about a man named Ma-ho-met. He had a nice cat, and when she was asleep on his sleeve, and he wanted to go away, he cut off the sleeve so as not to wake her up. I think he was a kind man. Some cats catch fish."

"So do I!" cried Teddy, jumping up eager to tell about his trout.

"Hush!" said his mother, setting him down again as quickly as possible, for orderly Daisy hated to be "interruckted," as Nan expressed it.

"I read about one who used to do it very slyly. I tried to make Topaz, but she did not like the water, and scratched me. She does like tea, and when I play in my kitchen she pats the teapot with her paw, till I give her some. She is a fine cat, she eats apple-pudding and molasses. Most cats do not."

"That's a first-rater," called out Nat, and Daisy retired, pleased with the praise of her friend.

"Demi looks so impatient we must have him up at once or he won't hold out," said Uncle Fritz, and Demi skipped up with alacrity.

"Mine is a poem!" he announced in a tone of triumph, and read his first effort in a loud and solemn voice:

*"I write about the butterfly,*
*It is a pretty thing;*
*And flies about like the birds,*
*But it does not sing.*
*"First it is a little grub,*
*And then it is a nice yellow cocoon,*

*And then the butterfly*
*Eats its way out soon.*
*"They live on dew and honey,*
*They do not have any hive,*
*They do not sting like wasps, and bees, and hornets,*
*And to be as good as they are we should strive.*
*"I should like to be a beautiful butterfly,*
*All yellow, and blue, and green, and red;*
*But I should not like*
*To have Dan put camphor on my poor little head."*

This unusual burst of genius brought down the house, and Demi was obliged to read it again, a somewhat difficult task, as there was no punctuation whatever, and the little poet's breath gave out before he got to the end of some of the long lines.

"He will be a Shakespeare yet," said Aunt Jo, laughing as if she would die, for this poetic gem reminded her of one of her own, written at the age of ten, and beginning gloomily,

*"I wish I had a quiet tomb,*
*Beside a little rill;*
*Where birds, and bees, and butterflies,*
*Would sing upon the hill."*

"Come on, Tommy. If there is as much ink inside your paper as there is outside, it will be a long composition," said Mr. Bhaer, when Demi had been induced to tear himself from his poem and sit down.

"It isn't a composition, it's a letter. You see, I forgot all about its being my turn till after school, and then I didn't know what to have, and there wasn't time to read up; so I thought you wouldn't mind my taking a letter that I wrote to my Grandma. It's got something about birds in it, so I thought it would do."

With this long excuse, Tommy plunged into a sea of ink and floundered through, pausing now and then to decipher one of his own flourishes.

"MY DEAR GRANDMA, I hope you are well. Uncle James sent me a pocket rifle. It is a beautiful little instrument of killing, shaped like this [Here Tommy displayed a remarkable sketch of what looked like an intricate pump, or the inside of a small steam-engine] 44 are the sights; 6 is a false stock that fits in at A; 3 is the trigger, and 2 is the cock. It loads at the breech, and fires with great force and straightness. I am going out shooting squirrels soon. I shot several fine birds for the museum. They had speckled breasts, and Dan liked them very much. He stuffed them tip-top, and they sit on the tree quite natural, only one looks a little tipsy. We had a Frenchman working here the other day, and Asia called his name so funnily that I will tell you about it. His name was Germain: first she called him Jerry, but we laughed at her, and she changed it to Jeremiah; but ridicule was the result, so it became Mr. Germany; but ridicule having been again resumed, it became Garrymon, which it has remained ever since. I do not write often, I am so busy; but I think of you often, and sympathize with you, and sincerely hope you get on as well as can be expected without me. Your affectionate grandson,

"THOMAS BUCKMINSTER BANGS.

"P.S.? If you come across any postage-stamps, remember me.

"N.B. Love to all, and a great deal to Aunt Almira. Does she make any nice plum-cakes now?

"P.S.? Mrs. Bhaer sends her respects.

"P.S.? And so would Mr. B, if he knew I was in act to write.

"N.B. Father is going to give me a watch on my birthday. I am glad as at present I have no means of telling time, and am often late at school.

"P.S.? I hope to see you soon. Don't you wish to send for me?

"T. B. B."

As each postscript was received with a fresh laugh from the boys, by the time he came to the sixth and last, Tommy was so exhausted that he was glad to sit down and wipe his ruddy face.

"I hope the dear old lady will live through it," said Mr. Bhaer, under cover of the noise.

"We won't take any notice of the broad hint given in that last P.S. The letter will be quite as much as she can bear without a visit from Tommy," answered Mrs. Jo, remembering that the old lady usually took to her bed after a visitation from her irrepressible grandson.

"Now, me," said Teddy, who had learned a bit of poetry, and was so eager to say it that he had been bobbing up and down during the reading, and could no longer be restrained.

"I'm afraid he will forget it if he waits; and I have had a deal of trouble teaching him," said his mother.

Teddy trotted to the rostrum, dropped a curtsey and nodded his head at the same time, as if anxious to suit every one; then, in his baby voice, and putting the emphasis on the wrong words, he said his verse all in one breath:

*"Little drops of water,*
*Little drains of sand,*
*Mate a might okum (ocean),*
*And a peasant land.*
*"Little words of kindness,*
*Pokin evvy day,*
*Make a home a hebbin,*
*And hep us on a way."*

Clapping his hands at the end, he made another double salutation, and then ran to hide his head in his mother's lap, quite overcome by the success of his "piece," for the applause was tremendous.

Dick and Dolly did not write, but were encouraged to observe the habits of animals and insects, and report what they saw. Dick liked this, and always had a great deal to say; so, when his name was called, he marched up, and, looking at the audience with his bright confiding eyes, told his little story so earnestly that no one smiled at his crooked body, because the "straight soul" shone through it beautifully.

"I've been watching dragonflies, and I read about them in Dan's book, and I'll try and tell you what I remember. There's lots of them flying round on the pond, all blue, with big eyes, and sort of lace wings, very pretty. I caught one, and looked at him, and I think he was the handsomest insect I ever saw. They catch littler creatures than they are to eat, and have a queer kind of hook thing that folds up when they ain't hunting. It likes the sunshine, and dances round all day. Let me see! what else was there to tell about? Oh, I know! The eggs are laid in the water, and go down to the bottom, and are hatched in the mud. Little ugly things come out of 'em; I can't say the name, but they are brown, and keep having new skins, and getting bigger and bigger. Only think! it takes them two years to be a dragonfly! Now this is the curiousest part of it, so you listen tight, for I don't believe you know it. When it is ready it knows somehow, and the ugly, grubby thing climbs up out of the water on a flag or a bulrush, and bursts open its back."

"Come, I don't believe that," said Tommy, who was not an observant boy, and really thought Dick was "making up."

"It does burst open its back, don't it?" and Dick appealed to Mr. Bhaer, who nodded a very decided affirmative, to the little speaker's great satisfaction.

"Well, out comes the dragonfly, all whole, and he sits in the sun sort of coming alive, you know; and he gets strong, and then he spreads his pretty wings, and flies away up in the air, and never is a grub any more. That's all I know; but I shall watch and try to see him do it, for I think it's splendid to turn into a beautiful dragonfly, don't you?"

Dick had told his story well, and, when he described the flight of the new-born insect, had waved his hands, and looked up as if he saw, and wanted to follow it. Something in his face suggested to the minds of the elder listeners the thought that some day little Dick would have his wish, and after years of helplessness and pain would climb up into the sun some happy day, and, leaving his poor little body behind him, find a new lovely shape in a fairer world than this. Mrs. Jo drew him to her side, and said, with a kiss on his thin cheek,

"That is a sweet little story, dear, and you remembered it wonderfully well. I shall write and tell your mother all about it;" and Dick sat on her knee, contentedly smiling at the praise, and resolving to watch well, and catch the dragonfly in the act of leaving its old body for the new, and see how he did it. Dolly had a few remarks to make upon the "Duck," and made them in a sing-song tone, for he had learned it by heart, and thought it a great plague to do it at all.

"Wild ducks are hard to kill; men hide and shoot at them, and have tame ducks to quack and make the wild ones come where the men can fire at them. They have wooden ducks made too, and they sail round, and the wild ones come to see them; they are stupid, I think. Our ducks are very tame. They eat a great deal, and go poking round in the mud and water. They don't take good care of their eggs, but them spoil, and—"

"Mine don't!" cried Tommy.

"Well, some people's do; Silas said so. Hens take good care of little ducks, only they don't like to have them go in the water, and make a great fuss. But the little ones don't care a bit. I like to eat ducks with stuffing in them and lots of apple-sauce."

"I have something to say about owls," began Nat, who had carefully prepared a paper upon this subject with some help from Dan.

"Owls have big heads, round eyes, hooked bills, and strong claws. Some are gray, some white, some black and yellowish. Their feathers are very soft, and stick out a great deal. They fly very quietly, and hunt bats, mice, little birds, and such things. They build nests in barns, hollow trees, and some take the nests of other birds. The great horned owl has two eggs bigger than a hen's and reddish brown. The tawny owl has five eggs, white and smooth; and this is the kind that hoots at night. Another kind sounds like a child crying. They eat mice and bats whole, and the parts that they cannot digest they make into little balls and spit out."

"My gracious! how funny!" Nan was heard to observe.

"They cannot see by day; and if they get out into the light, they go flapping round half blind, and the other birds chase and peck at them, as if they were making fun. The horned owl is very big, 'most as big as the eagle. It eats rabbits, rats, snakes, and birds; and lives in rocks and old tumble-down houses. They have a good many cries, and scream like a person being choked, and say, 'Waugh O! waugh O!' and it scares people at night in the woods. The white owl lives by the sea, and in cold places, and looks something like a hawk. There is a kind of owl that makes holes to live in like moles. It is called the burrowing owl, and is very small. The barn-owl is the commonest kind; and I have watched one sitting in a hole in a tree, looking like a little gray cat, with one eye shut and the other open. He comes out at dusk, and sits round waiting for the bats. I caught one, and here he is."

With that Nat suddenly produced from inside his jacket a little downy bird, who blinked and ruffled his feathers, looking very plump and sleepy and scared.

"Don't touch him! He is going to show off," said Nat, displaying his new pet with great pride. First he put a cocked hat on the bird's head, and the boys laughed at the funny effect; then he added a pair of paper spectacles, and that gave the owl such a wise look that they shouted with merriment. The performance closed with making the bird angry, and seeing him cling to a handkerchief upside down, pecking and "clucking," as Rob called it. He was allowed to fly after that, and settled himself on the bunch of pine-cones over the door, where he sat staring down at the company with an air of sleepy dignity that amused them very much.

"Have you anything for us, George?" asked Mr. Bhaer, when the room was still again.

"Well, I read and learned ever so much about moles, but I declare I've forgotten every bit of it, except that they dig holes to live in, that you catch them by pouring water down, and that they can't possibly live without eating very often;" and Stuffy sat down, wishing he had not been too lazy to write out his valuable observations, for a general smile went round when he mentioned the last of the three facts which lingered in his memory.

"Then we are done for to-day," began Mr. Bhaer, but Tommy called out in a great hurry,

"No we ain't. Don't you know? We must give the thing;" and he winked violently as he made an eye-glass of his fingers.

"Bless my heart, I forgot! Now is your time, Tom;" and Mr. Bhaer dropped into his seat again, while all the boys but Dan looked mightily tickled at something.

Nat, Tommy, and Demi left the room, and speedily returned with a little red morocco box set forth in state on Mrs. Jo's best silver salver. Tommy bore it, and, still escorted by Nat and Demi, marched up to unsuspecting Dan, who stared at them as if he thought they were going to make fun of him. Tommy had prepared an elegant and impressive speech for the occasion, but when the minute came, it all went out of his head, and he just said, straight from his kindly boyish heart,

"Here, old fellow, we all wanted to give you something to kind of pay for what happened awhile ago, and to show how much we liked you for being such a trump. Please take it, and have a jolly good time with it."

Dan was so surprised he could only get as red as the little box, and mutter, "Thanky, boys!" as he fumbled to open it. But when he saw what was inside, his face lighted up, and he seized the long desired treasure, saying so enthusiastically that every one was satisfied, though is language was anything but polished,

"What a stunner! I say, you fellows are regular bricks to give me this; it's just what I wanted. Give us your paw, Tommy."

Many paws were given, and heartily shaken, for the boys were charmed with Dan's pleasure, and crowded round him to shake hands and expatiate on the beauties of their gift. In the midst of this pleasant chatter, Dan's eye went to Mrs. Jo, who stood outside the group enjoying the scene with all her heart.

"No, I had nothing to do with it. The boys got it up all themselves," she said, answering the grateful look that seemed to thank her for that happy moment. Dan smiled, and said, in a tone that only she could understand,

"It's you all the same;" and making his way through the boys, he held out his hand first to her and then to the good Professor, who was beaming benevolently on his flock.

He thanked them both with the silent, hearty squeeze he gave the kind hands that had held him up, and led him into the safe refuge of a happy home. Not a word was spoken, but they felt all he would say, and little Teddy expressed his pleasure for them as he leaned from his father's arm to hug the boy, and say, in his baby way,

"My dood Danny! everybody loves him now."

"Come here, show off your spy-glass, Dan, and let us see some of your magnified pollywogs and annymalcumisms as you call 'em," said Jack, who felt so uncomfortable during this scene that he would have slipped away if Emil had not kept him.

"So I will, take a squint at that and see what you think of it," said Dan, glad to show off his precious microscope.

He held it over a beetle that happened to be lying on the table, and Jack bent down to take his squint, but looked up with an amazed face, saying,

"My eye! what nippers the old thing has got! I see now why it hurts so confoundedly when you grab a dorbug and he grabs back again."

"He winked at me," cried Nan, who had poked her head under Jack's elbow and got the second peep.

Every one took a look, and then Dan showed them the lovely plumage on a moth's wing, the four feathery corners to a hair, the veins on a leaf, hardly visible to the naked eye, but like a thick net through the wonderful little glass; the skin on their own fingers, looking like queer hills and valleys; a cobweb like a bit of coarse sewing silk, and the sting of a bee.

"It's like the fairy spectacles in my story-book, only more curious," said Demi, enchanted with the wonders he saw.

"Dan is a magician now, and he can show you many miracles going on all round you; for he has two things needful patience and a love of nature. We live in a beautiful and wonderful world, Demi, and the more you know about it the wiser and the better you will be. This little glass will give you a new set of teachers, and you may learn fine lessons from them if you will," said Mr. Bhaer, glad to see how interested the boys were in the matter.

"Could I see anybody's soul with this microscope if I looked hard?" asked Demi, who was much impressed with the power of the bit of glass.

"No, dear; it's not powerful enough for that, and never can be made so. You must wait a long while before your eyes are clear enough to see the most invisible of God's wonders. But looking at the lovely things you can see will help you to understand the lovelier things you can not see," answered Uncle Fritz, with his hand on the boy's head.

"Well, Daisy and I both think that if there are any angels, their wings look like that butterfly's as we see it through the glass, only more soft and gold."

"Believe it if you like, and keep your own little wings as bright and beautiful, only don't fly away for a long time yet."

"No, I won't," and Demi kept his word.

"Good-by, my boys; I must go now, but I leave you with our new Professor of Natural History;" and Mrs. Jo went away well pleased with that composition day.

# CHAPTER XVIII. CROPS

The gardens did well that summer, and in September the little crops were gathered in with much rejoicing. Jack and Ned joined their farms and raised potatoes, those being a good salable article. They got twelve bushels, counting little ones and all, and sold them to Mr. Bhaer at a fair price, for potatoes went fast in that house. Emil and Franz devoted themselves to corn, and had a jolly little husking in the barn, after which they took their corn to the mill, and came proudly home with meal enough to supply the family with hasty-pudding and Johnny-cake for a lone time. They would not take money for their crop; because, as Franz said, "We never can pay Uncle for all he has done for us if we raised corn for the rest of our days."

Nat had beans in such abundance that he despaired of ever shelling them, till Mrs. Jo proposed a new way, which succeeded admirably. The dry pods were spread upon the barn-floor, Nat fiddled, and the boys danced quadrilles on them, till they were thrashed out with much merriment and very little labor.

Tommy's six weeks' beans were a failure; for a dry spell early in the season hurt them, because he gave them no water; and after that he was so sure that they could take care of themselves, he let the poor things struggle with bugs and weeds till they were exhausted and died a lingering death. So Tommy had to dig his farm over again, and plant peas. But they were late; the birds ate many; the bushes, not being firmly planted, blew down, and when the poor peas came at last, no one cared for them, as their day was over, and spring-lamb had grown into mutton. Tommy consoled himself with a charitable effort; for he transplanted all the thistles he could find, and tended them carefully for Toby, who was fond of the prickly delicacy, and had eaten all he could find on the place. The boys had great fun over Tom's thistle bed; but he insisted that it was better to care for poor Toby than for himself, and declared that he would devote his entire farm next year to thistles, worms, and snails, that Demi's turtles and Nat's pet owl might have the food they loved, as well as the donkey. So like shiftless, kind-hearted, happy-go-lucky Tommy!

*Demi had supplied his grandmother with lettuce all summer, and in the autumn sent his grandfather a basket of turnips, each one scrubbed up till it looked like a great white egg. His Grandma was fond of salad, and one of his Grandpa's favorite quotations was,*

*"Lucullus, whom frugality could charm,*
*Ate roasted turnips at the Sabine farm."*

Therefore these vegetable offerings to the dear domestic god and goddess were affectionate, appropriate, and classical.

Daisy had nothing but flowers in her little plot, and it bloomed all summer long with a succession of gay or fragrant posies. She was very fond of her garden, and delved away in it at all hours, watching over her roses, and pansies, sweet-peas, and mignonette, as faithfully and tenderly as she did over her dolls or her friends. Little nosegays were sent into town on all occasions, and certain vases about the house were her especial care. She had all sorts of pretty fancies about her flowers, and loved to tell the children the story of the pansy, and show them how the step-mother-leaf sat up in her green chair in purple and gold; how the two own children in gay yellow had each its little seat, while the step children, in dull colors, both sat on one small stool, and the poor little father in his red nightcap, was kept out of sight in the middle of the flower; that a monk's dark face looked out of the monk's-hood larkspur; that the flowers of the canary-vine were so like dainty birds fluttering their yellow wings, that one almost expected to see them fly away, and the snapdragons that went off like little pistol-shots when you cracked them. Splendid dollies did she make out of scarlet and white poppies, with ruffled robes tied round the waist with grass blade sashes, and astonishing hats of coreopsis on their green heads. Pea-pod boats, with rose-leaf sails, received these flower-people, and floated them about a placid pool in the most charming style; for finding that there were no elves, Daisy made her own, and loved the fanciful little friends who played their parts in her summer-life.

Nan went in for herbs, and had a fine display of useful plants, which she tended with steadily increasing interest and care. Very busy was she in September cutting, drying, and tying up her sweet harvest, and writing down in a little book how the different herbs are to be used. She had tried several experiments, and made several mistakes; so she wished to be particular lest she should give little Huz another fit by administering wormwood instead of catnip.

Dick, Dolly, and Rob each grubbed away on his small farm, and made more stir about it than all the rest put together. Parsnips and carrots were the crops of the two D.'s; and they longed for it to be late enough to pull up the precious vegetables. Dick did privately examine his carrots, and plant them again, feeling that Silas was right in saying it was too soon for them yet.

Rob's crop was four small squashes and one immense pumpkin. It really was a "bouncer," as every one said; and I assure you that two small persons could sit on it side by side. It seemed to have absorbed all the goodness of the little garden, and all the sunshine that shone down on it, and lay there a great round, golden ball, full of rich suggestions of pumpkin-pies for weeks to come. Robby was so proud of his mammoth vegetable that he took every one to see it, and, when frosts began to nip, covered it up each night with an old bedquilt, tucking it round as if the pumpkin was a well-beloved baby. The day it was gathered he would let no one touch it but himself, and nearly broke his back tugging it to the barn in his little wheelbarrow, with Dick and Dolly harnessed in front to give a heave up the path. His mother promised him that the Thanksgiving-pies should be made from it, and hinted vaguely that she had a plan in her head which would cover the prize pumpkin and its owner with glory.

Poor Billy had planted cucumbers, but unfortunately hoed them up and left the pig-weed. This mistake grieved him very much for ten minutes, then he forgot all about it, and sowed a handful of bright buttons which he had collected, evidently thinking in his feeble mind that they were money, and would come up and multiply, so that he might make many quarters, as Tommy did. No one disturbed him, and he did what he liked with his plot, which soon looked as if a series of small earthquakes had stirred it up. When the general harvest-day came, he would have had nothing but stones and weeds to show, if kind old Asia had not hung half-a-dozen oranges on the dead tree he stuck up in the middle. Billy was delighted with his crop; and no one spoiled his pleasure in the little miracle which pity wrought for him, by making withered branches bear strange fruit.

Stuffy had various trials with his melons; for, being impatient to taste them, he had a solitary revel before they were ripe, and made himself so ill, that for a day or two it seemed doubtful if he would ever eat any more. But he pulled through it, and served up his first cantaloupe without tasting a mouthful himself. They were excellent melons, for he had a warm slope for them, and they ripened fast. The last and best were lingering on the vines, and Stuffy had announced that he should sell them to a neighbor. This disappointed the boys, who had hoped to eat the melons themselves, and they expressed their displeasure in a new and striking manner. Going one morning to gaze upon the three fine watermelons which he had kept for the market, Stuffy was horrified to find the word "PIG" cut in white letters on the green rind, staring at him from every one. He was in a great rage, and flew to Mrs. Jo for redress. She listened, condoled with him, and then said,

"If you want to turn the laugh, I'll tell you how, but you must give up the melons."

"Well, I will; for I can't thrash all the boys, but I'd like to give them something to remember, the mean sneaks," growled Stuff, still in a fume.

Now Mrs. Jo was pretty sure who had done the trick, for she had seen three heads suspiciously near to one another in the sofa-corner the evening before; and when these heads had nodded with chuckles and whispers, this experienced woman knew mischief was afoot. A moonlight night, a rustling in the old cherry-tree near Emil's window, a cut on Tommy's finger, all helped to confirm her suspicions; and having cooled Stuffy's wrath a little, she bade him bring his maltreated melons to her room, and say not a word to any one of what had happened. He did so, and the three wags were amazed to find their joke so quietly taken. It spoilt the fun, and the entire disappearance of the melons made them uneasy. So did Stuffy's good-nature, for he looked more placid and plump than ever, and surveyed them with an air of calm pity that perplexed them very much.

At dinner-time they discovered why; for then Stuffy's vengeance fell upon them, and the laugh was turned against them. When the pudding was eaten, and the fruit was put on, Mary Ann re-appeared in a high state of giggle, bearing a large watermelon; Silas followed with another; and Dan brought up the rear with a third. One was placed before each of the three guilty lads; and they read on the smooth green skins this addition to their own work, "With the compliments of the PIG." Every one else read it also, and the whole table was in a roar, for the trick had been whispered about; so every one understood the sequel. Emil, Ned, and Tommy did not know where to look, and had not a word to say for themselves; so they wisely joined in the laugh, cut up the melons, and handed them round, saying, what all the rest agreed to, that Stuffy had taken a wise and merry way to return good for evil.

Dan had no garden, for he was away or lame the greater part of the summer; so he had helped Silas wherever he could, chopped wood for Asia, and taken care of the lawn so well, that Mrs. Jo always had smooth paths and nicely shaven turf before her door.

When the others got in their crops, he looked sorry that he had so little to show; but as autumn went on, he bethought himself of a woodland harvest which no one would dispute with him, and which was peculiarly his own. Every Saturday he was away alone to the forests, fields, and hills, and always came back loaded with spoils; for he seemed to know the meadows where the best flag-root grew, the thicket where the sassafras was spiciest, the haunts where the squirrels went for nuts, the white oak whose bark was most valuable, and the little gold-thread vine that Nursey liked to cure the canker with. All sorts of splendid red and yellow leaves did Dan bring home for Mrs. Jo to dress her parlor with, graceful-seeded grasses, clematis tassels, downy, soft, yellow wax-work berries, and mosses, red-brimmed, white, or emerald green.

"I need not sigh for the woods now, because Dan brings the woods to me," Mrs. Jo used to say, as she glorified the walls with yellow maple boughs and scarlet woodbine wreaths, or filled her vases with russet ferns, hemlock sprays full of delicate cones, and hardy autumn flowers; for Dan's crop suited her well.

The great garret was full of the children's little stores and for a time was one of the sights of the house. Daisy's flower seeds in neat little paper bags, all labelled, lay in a drawer of a three-legged table. Nan's herbs hung in bunches against the wall, filling the air with their aromatic breath. Tommy had a basket of thistle-down with the tiny seeds attached, for he meant to plant them next year, if they did not all fly away before that time. Emil had bunches of pop-corn hanging there to dry, and Demi laid up acorns and different sorts of grain for the pets. But Dan's crop made the best show, for fully one half of the floor was covered with the nuts he brought. All kinds were there, for he ranged the woods for miles round, climbed the tallest trees, and forced his way into the thickest hedges for his plunder. Walnuts, chestnuts, hazelnuts, and beechnuts lay in separate compartments, getting brown, and dry, and sweet, ready for winter revels.

There was one butternut-tree on the place, and Rob and Teddy called it theirs. It bore well this year, and the great dingy nuts came dropping down to hide among the dead leaves, where the busy squirrels found them better than the lazy Bhaers. Their father had told them (the boys, not the squirrels) they should have the nuts if they would pick them up, but no one was to help. It was easy work, and Teddy liked it, only he soon got tired, and left his little basket half full for another day. But the other day was slow to arrive, and, meantime, the sly squirrels were hard at work, scampering up and down the old elm-trees stowing the nuts away till their holes were full, then all about the crotches of the boughs, to be removed at their leisure. Their funny little ways amused the boys, till one day Silas said,

"Hev you sold them nuts to the squirrels?"

"No," answered Rob, wondering what Silas meant.

"Wal, then, you'd better fly round, or them spry little fellers won't leave you none."

"Oh, we can beat them when we begin. There are such lots of nuts we shall have a plenty."

"There ain't many more to come down, and they have cleared the ground pretty well, see if they hain't."

Robby ran to look, and was alarmed to find how few remained. He called Teddy, and they worked hard all one afternoon, while the squirrels sat on the fence and scolded.

"Now, Ted, we must keep watch, and pick up just as fast as they fall, or we shan't have more than a bushel, and every one will laugh at us if we don't."

"The naughty quillies tarn't have 'em. I'll pick fast and run and put 'em in the barn twick," said Teddy, frowning at little Frisky, who chattered and whisked his tail indignantly.

That night a high wind blew down hundreds of nuts, and when Mrs. Jo came to wake her little sons, she said, briskly,

"Come, my laddies, the squirrels are hard at it, and you will have to work well to-day, or they will have every nut on the ground."

"No, they won't," and Robby tumbled up in a great hurry, gobbled his breakfast, and rushed out to save his property.

Teddy went too, and worked like a little beaver, trotting to and fro with full and empty baskets. Another bushel was soon put away in the corn-barn, and they were scrambling among the leaves for more nuts when the bell rang for school.

"O father! let me stay out and pick. Those horrid squirrels will have my nuts if you don't. I'll do my lessons by and by," cried Rob, running into the school-room, flushed and tousled by the fresh cold wind and his eager work.

"If you had been up early and done a little every morning there would be no hurry now. I told you that, Rob, and you never minded. I cannot have the lessons neglected as the work has been. The squirrels will get more than their share this year, and they deserve it, for they have worked best. You may go an hour earlier, but that is all," and Mr. Bhaer led Rob to his place where the little man dashed at his books as if bent on making sure of the precious hour promised him.

It was almost maddening to sit still and see the wind shaking down the last nuts, and the lively thieves flying about, pausing now and then to eat one in his face, and flirt their tails, as if they said, saucily, "We'll have them in spite of you, lazy Rob." The only thing that sustained the poor child in this trying moment was the sight of Teddy working away all alone. It was really splendid the pluck and perseverance of the little lad. He picked and picked till his back ached; he trudged to and fro till his small legs were tired; and he defied wind, weariness, and wicked "quillies," till his mother left her work and did the carrying for him, full of admiration for the kind little fellow who tried to help his brother. When Rob was dismissed, he found Teddy reposing in the bushel-basket quite used up, but unwilling to quit the field; for he flapped his hat at the thieves with one grubby little hand, while he refreshed himself with the big apple held in the other.

Rob fell to work and the ground was cleared before two o'clock, the nuts safely in the corn-barn loft, and the weary workers exulted in their success. But Frisky and his wife were not to be vanquished so easily; and when Rob went up to look at his nuts a few days later he was amazed to see how many had vanished. None of the boys could have stolen them, because the door had been locked; the doves could not have eaten them, and there were no rats about. There was great lamentation among the young Bhaers till Dick said,

"I saw Frisky on the roof of the corn-barn, may be he took them."

"I know he did! I'll have a trap, and kill him dead," cried Rob, disgusted with Frisky's grasping nature.

"Perhaps if you watch, you can find out where he puts them, and I may be able to get them back for you," said Dan, who was much amused by the fight between the boys and squirrels.

So Rob watched and saw Mr. and Mrs. Frisky drop from the drooping elm boughs on to the roof of the corn-barn, dodge in at one of the little doors, much to the disturbance of the doves, and come out with a nut in each mouth. So laden they could not get back the way they came, but ran down the low roof, along the wall, and leaping off at a corner they vanished a minute and re-appeared without their plunder. Rob ran to the place, and in a hollow under the leaves he found a heap of the stolen property hidden away to be carried off to the holes by and by.

"Oh, you little villains! I'll cheat you now, and not leave one," said Rob. So he cleared the corner and the corn-barn, and put the contested nuts in the garret, making sure that no broken window-pane could anywhere let in the unprincipled squirrels. They seemed to feel that the contest was over, and retired to their hole, but now and then could not resist throwing down nut-shells on Rob's head, and scolding violently as if they could not forgive him nor forget that he had the best of the battle.

Father and Mother Bhaer's crop was of a different sort, and not so easily described; but they were satisfied with it, felt that their summer work had prospered well, and by and by had a harvest that made them very happy.

## CHAPTER XIX. JOHN BROOKE

"Wake up, Demi, dear! I want you."

"Why, I've just gone to bed; it can't be morning yet;" and Demi blinked like a little owl as he waked from his first sound sleep.

"It's only ten, but your father is ill, and we must go to him. O my little John! my poor little John!" and Aunt Jo laid her head down on the pillow with a sob that scared sleep from Demi's eyes and filled his heart with fear and wonder; for he dimly felt why Aunt Jo called him "John," and wept over him as if some loss had come that left him poor. He clung to her without a word, and in a minute she was quite steady again, and said, with a tender kiss as she saw his troubled face,

"We are going to say good-by to him, my darling, and there is no time to lose; so dress quickly and come to me in my room. I must go to Daisy."

"Yes, I will;" and when Aunt Jo was gone, little Demi got up quietly, dressed as if in a dream, and leaving Tommy fast asleep went away through the silent house, feeling that something new and sorrowful was going to happen something that set him apart from the other boys for a time, and made the world seem as dark and still and strange as those familiar rooms did in the night. A carriage sent by Mr. Laurie stood before the door. Daisy was soon ready, and the brother and sister held each other by the hand all the way into town, as they drove swiftly and silently with aunt and uncle through the shadowy roads to say good-by to father.

None of the boys but Franz and Emil knew what had happened, and when they came down next morning, great was their wonderment and discomfort, for the house seemed forlorn without its master and mistress. Breakfast was a dismal meal with no cheery Mrs. Jo behind the teapots; and when school-time came, Father Bhaer's place was empty. They wandered about in a disconsolate kind of way for an hour, waiting for news and hoping it would be all right with Demi's father, for good John Brooke was much beloved by the boys. Ten o'clock came, and no one arrived to relieve their anxiety. They did not feel like playing, yet the time dragged heavily, and they sat about listless and sober. All at once, Franz got up, and said, in his persuasive way,

"Look here, boys! let's go into school and do our lessons just as if Uncle was here. It will make the day go faster, and will please him, I know."

"But who will hear us say them?" asked Jack.

"I will; I don't know much more than you do, but I'm the oldest here, and I'll try to fill Uncle's place till he comes, if you don't mind."

Something in the modest, serious way Franz said this impressed the boys, for, though the poor lad's eyes were red with quiet crying for Uncle John in that long sad night, there was a new manliness about him, as if he had already begun to feel the cares and troubles of life, and tried to take them bravely.

"I will, for one," and Emil went to his seat, remembering that obedience to his superior officer is a seaman's first duty.

The others followed; Franz took his uncle's seat, and for an hour order reigned. Lessons were learned and said, and Franz made a patient, pleasant teacher, wisely omitting such lessons as he was not equal to, and keeping order more by the unconscious dignity that sorrow gave him than by any words of his own. The little boys were reading when a step was heard in the hall, and every one looked up to read the news in Mr. Bhaer's face as he came in. The kind face told them instantly that Demi had no father now, for it was worn and pale, and full of tender grief, which left him no words with which to answer Rob, as he ran to him, saying, reproachfully,

"What made you go and leave me in the night, papa?"

The memory of the other father who had left his children in the night, never to return, made Mr. Bhaer hold his own boy close, and, for a minute, hide his face in Robby's curly hair. Emil laid his head down on his arms, Franz, went to put his hand on his uncle's shoulder, his boyish face pale with sympathy and sorrow, and the others sat so still that the soft rustle of the falling leaves outside was distinctly heard.

Rob did not clearly understand what had happened, but he hated to see papa unhappy, so he lifted up the bent head, and said, in his chirpy little voice,

"Don't cry, mein Vater! we were all so good, we did our lessons, without you, and Franz was the master."

Mr. Bhaer looked up then, tried to smile, and said in a grateful tone that made the lads feel like saints, "I thank you very much, my boys. It was a beautiful way to help and comfort me. I shall not forget it, I assure you."

"Franz proposed it, and was a first-rate master, too," said Nat; and the others gave a murmur of assent most gratifying to the young dominie.

Mr. Bhaer put Rob down, and, standing up, put his arm round his tall nephew's shoulder, as he said, with a look of genuine pleasure,

"This makes my hard day easier, and gives me confidence in you all. I am needed there in town, and must leave you for some hours. I thought to give you a holiday, or send some of you home, but if you like to stay and go on as you have begun, I shall be glad and proud of my good boys."

"We'll stay;" "We'd rather;" "Franz can see to us;" cried several, delighted with the confidence shown in them.

"Isn't Marmar coming home?" asked Rob, wistfully; for home without "Marmar" was the world without the sun to him.

"We shall both come to-night; but dear Aunt Meg needs Mother more than you do now, and I know you like to lend her for a little while."

"Well, I will; but Teddy's been crying for her, and he slapped Nursey, and was dreadful naughty," answered Rob, as if the news might bring mother home.

"Where is my little man?" asked Mr. Bhaer.

"Dan took him out, to keep him quiet. He's all right now," said Franz, pointing to the window, through which they could see Dan drawing baby in his little wagon, with the dogs frolicking about him.

"I won't see him, it would only upset him again; but tell Dan I leave Teddy in his care. You older boys I trust to manage yourselves for a day. Franz will direct you, and Silas is here to over see matters. So good-by till to-night."

"Just tell me a word about Uncle John," said Emil, detaining Mr. Bhaer, as he was about hurrying away again.

"He was only ill a few hours, and died as he has lived, so cheerfully, so peacefully, that it seems a sin to mar the beauty of it with any violent or selfish grief. We were in time to say good-by: and Daisy and Demi were in his arms as he fell asleep on Aunt Meg's breast. No more now, I cannot bear it," and Mr. Bhaer went hastily away quite bowed with grief, for in John Brooke he had lost both friend and brother, and there was no one left to take his place.

All that day the house was very still; the small boys played quietly in the nursery; the others, feeling as if Sunday had come in the middle of the week, spent it in walking, sitting in the willow, or among their pets, all talking much of "Uncle John," and feeling that something gentle, just, and strong, had gone out of their little world, leaving a sense of loss that deepened every hour. At dusk, Mr. and Mrs. Bhaer came home alone, for Demi and Daisy were their mother's best comfort now, and could not leave her. Poor Mrs. Jo seemed quite spent, and evidently needed the same sort of comfort, for her first words, as she came up the stairs, were, "Where is my baby?"

"Here I is," answered a little voice, as Dan put Teddy into her arms, adding, as she hugged him close, "My Danny tooked tare of me all day, and I was dood."

Mrs. Jo turned to thank the faithful nurse, but Dan was waving off the boys, who had gathered in the hall to meet her, and was saying, in a low voice, "Keep back; she don't want to be bothered with us now."

"No, don't keep back. I want you all. Come in and see me, my boys. I've neglected you all day," and Mrs. Jo held out her hands to them as they gathered round and escorted her into her own room, saying little, but expressing much by affectionate looks and clumsy little efforts to show their sorrow and sympathy.

"I am so tired, I will lie here and cuddle Teddy, and you shall bring me in some tea," she said, trying to speak cheerfully for their sakes.

A general stampede into the dining-room followed, and the supper-table would have been ravaged if Mr. Bhaer had not interfered. It was agreed that one squad should carry in the mother's tea, and another bring it out. The four nearest and dearest claimed the first honor, so Franz bore the teapot, Emil the bread, Rob the milk, and Teddy insisted on carrying the sugar basin, which was lighter by several lumps when it arrived than when it started. Some women might have found it annoying at such a time to have boys creaking in and out, upsetting cups and rattling spoons in violent efforts to be quiet and helpful; but it suited Mrs. Jo, because just then her heart was very tender; and remembering that many of her boys were fatherless or motherless, she yearned over them, and found comfort in their blundering affection. It was the sort of food that did her more good than the very thick bread-and-butter that they gave her, and the rough Commodore's broken whisper,

"Bear up, Aunty, it's a hard blow; but we'll weather it somehow;" cheered her more than the sloppy cup he brought her, full of tea as bitter as if some salt tear of his own had dropped into it on the way. When supper was over, a second deputation removed the tray; and Dan said, holding out his arms for sleepy little Teddy,

"Let me put him to bed, you're so tired, Mother."

"Will you go with him, lovey?" asked Mrs. Jo of her small lord and master, who lay on her arm among the sofa-pillows.

"Torse I will;" and he was proudly carried off by his faithful bearer.

"I wish I could do something," said Nat, with a sigh, as Franz leaned over the sofa, and softly stroked Aunt Jo's hot forehead.

"You can, dear. Go and get your violin, and play me the sweet little airs Uncle Teddy sent you last. Music will comfort me better than any thing else to-night."

Nat flew for his fiddle, and, sitting just outside her door, played as he had never done before, for now his heart was in it, and seemed to magnetize his fingers. The other lads sat quietly upon the steps, keeping watch that no new-comer should disturb the house; Franz lingered at his post; and so, soothed, served, and guarded by her boys, poor Mrs. Jo slept at last, and forgot her sorrow for an hour.

Two quiet days, and on the third Mr. Bhaer came in just after school, with a note in his hand, looking both moved and pleased.

"I want to read you something, boys," he said; and as they stood round him he read this:

"DEAR BROTHER FRITZ, I hear that you do not mean to bring your flock today, thinking that I may not like it. Please do. The sight of his friends will help Demi through the hard hour, and I want the boys to hear what father says of my John. It will do them good, I know. If they would sing one of the sweet old hymns you have taught them so well, I should like it better than any other music, and feel that it was beautifully suited to the occasion. Please ask them, with my love.

"MEG."

"Will you go?" and Mr. Bhaer looked at the lads, who were greatly touched by Mrs. Brooke's kind words and wishes.

"Yes," they answered, like one boy; and an hour later they went away with Franz to bear their part in John Brooke's simple funeral.

The little house looked as quiet, sunny, and home-like as when Meg entered it as a bride, ten years ago, only then it was early summer, and rose blossomed everywhere; now it was early autumn, and dead leaves rustled softly down, leaving the branches bare. The bride was a widow now; but the same beautiful serenity shone in her face, and the sweet resignation of a truly pious soul made her presence a consolation to those who came to comfort her.

"O Meg! how can you bear it so?" whispered Jo, as she met them at the door with a smile of welcome, and no change in her gentle manner, except more gentleness.

"Dear Jo, the love that has blest me for ten happy years supports me still. It could not die, and John is more my own than ever," whispered Meg; and in her eyes the tender trust was so beautiful and bright, that Jo believed her, and thanked God for the immortality of love like hers.

They were all there father and mother, Uncle Teddy, and Aunt Amy, old Mr. Laurence, white-haired and feeble now, Mr. and Mrs. Bhaer, with their flock, and many friends, come to do honor to the dead. One would have said that modest John Brooke, in his busy, quiet, humble life, had had little time to make friends; but now they seemed to start up everywhere, old and young, rich and poor, high and low; for all unconsciously his influence had made itself widely felt, his virtues were remembered, and his hidden charities rose up to bless him. The group about his coffin was a far more eloquent eulogy than any Mr. March could utter. There were the rich men whom he had served faithfully for years; the poor old women whom he cherished with his little store, in memory of his mother; the wife to whom he had given such happiness that death could not mar it utterly; the brothers and sisters in whose hearts he had made a place for ever; the little son and daughter, who already felt the loss of his strong arm and tender voice; the young children, sobbing for their kindest playmate, and the tall lads, watching with softened faces a scene which they never could forget. A very simple service, and very short; for the fatherly voice that had faltered in the marriage-sacrament now failed entirely as Mr. March endeavored to pay his tribute of reverence and love to the son whom he most honored. Nothing but the soft coo of Baby Josy's voice up-stairs broke the long hush that followed the last Amen, till, at a sign from Mr. Bhaer, the well-trained boyish voices broke out in a hymn, so full of lofty cheer, that one by one all joined in it, singing with full hearts, and finding their troubled spirits lifted into peace on the wings of that brave, sweet psalm.

As Meg listened, she felt that she had done well; for not only did the moment comfort her with the assurance that John's last lullaby was sung by the young voices he loved so well, but in the faces of the boys she saw that they had caught a glimpse of the beauty of virtue in its most impressive form, and that the memory of the good man lying dead before them would live long and helpfully in their remembrance. Daisy's head lay in her lap, and Demi held her hand, looking often at her, with eyes so like his father's, and a little gesture that seemed to say, "Don't be troubled, mother; I am here;" and all about her were friends to lean upon and love; so patient, pious Meg put by her heavy grief, feeling that her best help would be to live for others, as her John had done.

That evening, as the Plumfield boys sat on the steps, as usual, in the mild September moonlight, they naturally fell to talking of the event of the day.

Emil began by breaking out, in his impetuous way, "Uncle Fritz is the wisest, and Uncle Laurie the jolliest, but Uncle John was the best; and I'd rather be like him than any man I ever saw."

"So would I. Did you hear what those gentlemen said to Grandpa to-day? I would like to have that said of me when I was dead;" and Franz felt with regret that he had not appreciated Uncle John enough.

"What did they say?" asked Jack, who had been much impressed by the scenes of the day.

"Why, one of the partners of Mr. Laurence, where Uncle John has been ever so long, was saying that he was conscientious almost to a fault as a business man, and above reproach in all things. Another gentleman said no money could repay the fidelity and honesty with which Uncle John had served him, and then Grandpa told them the best of all. Uncle John once had a place in the office of a man who cheated, and when this man wanted uncle to help him do it, uncle wouldn't, though he was offered a big salary. The man was angry and said, 'You will never get on in business with such strict principles;' and uncle answered back, 'I never will try to get on without them,' and left the place for a much harder and poorer one."

"Good!" cried several of the boys warmly, for they were in the mood to understand and value the little story as never before.

"He wasn't rich, was he?" asked Jack.

"No."

"He never did any thing to make a stir in the world, did he?"

"No."

"He was only good?"

"That's all;" and Franz found himself wishing that Uncle John had done something to boast of, for it was evident that Jack was disappointed by his replies.

"Only good. That is all and every thing," said Mr. Bhaer, who had overheard the last few words, and guessed what was going on the minds of the lads.

"Let me tell you a little about John Brooke, and you will see why men honor him, and why he was satisfied to be good rather than rich or famous. He simply did his duty in all things, and did it so cheerfully, so faithfully, that it kept him patient and brave, and happy through poverty and loneliness and years of hard work. He was a good son, and gave up his own plans to stay and live with his mother while she needed him. He was a good friend, and taught Laurie much beside his Greek and Latin, did it unconsciously, perhaps, by showing him an example of an upright man. He was a faithful servant, and made himself so valuable to those who employed him that they will find it hard to fill his place. He was a good husband and father, so tender, wise, and thoughtful, that Laurie and I learned much of him, and only knew how well he loved his family, when we discovered all he had done for them, unsuspected and unassisted."

Mr. Bhaer stopped a minute, and the boys sat like statues in the moonlight until he went on again, in a subdued, but earnest voice: "As he lay dying, I said to him, 'Have no care for Meg and the little ones; I will see that they never want.' Then he smiled and pressed my hand, and answered, in his cheerful way, 'No need of that; I have cared for them.' And so he had, for when we looked among his papers, all was in order, not a debt remained; and safely put away was enough to keep Meg comfortable and independent. Then we knew why he had lived so plainly, denied himself so many pleasures, except that of charity, and worked so hard that I fear he shortened his good life. He never asked help for himself, though often for others, but bore his own burden and worked out his own task bravely and quietly. No one can say a word of complaint against him, so just and generous and kind was he; and now, when he is gone, all find so much to love and praise and honor, that I am proud to have been his friend, and would rather leave my children the legacy he leaves his than the largest fortune ever made. Yes! Simple, generous goodness is the best capital to found the business of this life upon. It lasts when fame and money fail, and is the only riches we can take out of this world with us. Remember that, my boys; and if you want to earn respect and confidence and love follow in the footsteps of John Brooke."

When Demi returned to school, after some weeks at home, he seemed to have recovered from his loss with the blessed elasticity of childhood, and so he had in a measure; but he did not forget, for his was a nature into which things sank deeply, to be pondered over, and absorbed into the soil where the small virtues were growing fast. He played and studied, worked and sang, just as before, and few suspected any change; but there was one and Aunt Jo saw it for she watched over the boy with her whole heart, trying to fill John's place in her poor way. He seldom spoke of his loss, but Aunt Jo often heard a stifled sobbing in the little bed at night; and when she went to comfort him, all his cry was, "I want my father! oh, I want my father!" for the tie between the two had been a very tender one, and the child's heart bled when it was broken. But time was kind to him, and slowly he came to feel that father was not lost, only invisible for a while, and sure to be found again, well and strong and fond as ever, even though his little son should see the purple asters blossom on his grave many, many times before they met. To this belief Demi held fast, and in it found both help and comfort, because it led him unconsciously through a tender longing for the father whom he had seen to a childlike trust in the Father whom he had not seen. Both were in heaven, and he prayed to both, trying to be good for love of them.

The outward change corresponded to the inward, for in those few weeks Demi seemed to have grown tall, and began to drop his childish plays, not as if ashamed of them, as some boys do, but as if he had outgrown them, and wanted something manlier. He took to the hated arithmetic, and held on so steadily that his uncle was charmed, though he could not understand the whim, until Demi said,

"I am going to be a bookkeeper when I grow up, like papa, and I must know about figures and things, else I can't have nice, neat ledgers like his."

At another time he came to his aunt with a very serious face, and said

"What can a small boy do to earn money?"

"Why do you ask, my deary?"

"My father told me to take care of mother and the little girls, and I want to, but I don't know how to begin."

"He did not mean now, Demi, but by and by, when you are large."

"But I wish to begin now, if I can, because I think I ought to make some money to buy things for the family. I am ten, and other boys no bigger than I earn pennies sometimes."

"Well, then, suppose you rake up all the dead leaves and cover the strawberry bed. I'll pay you a dollar for the job," said Aunt Jo.

"Isn't that a great deal? I could do it in one day. You must be fair, and no pay too much, because I want to truly earn it."

"My little John, I will be fair, and not pay a penny too much. Don't work too hard; and when that is done I will have something else for you to do," said Mrs. Jo, much touched by his desire to help, and his sense of justice, so like his scrupulous father.

When the leaves were done, many barrowloads of chips were wheeled from the wood to the shed, and another dollar earned. Then Demi helped cover the schoolbooks, working in the evenings under Franz's direction, tugging patiently away at each book, letting no one help, and receiving his wages with such satisfaction that the dingy bills became quite glorified in his sight.

"Now, I have a dollar for each of them, and I should like to take my money to mother all myself, so she can see that I have minded my father."

So Demi made a duteous pilgrimage to his mother, who received his little earnings as a treasure of great worth, and would have kept it untouched, if Demi had not begged her to buy some useful thing for herself and the women-children, whom he felt were left to his care.

This made him very happy, and, though he often forgot his responsibilities for a time, the desire to help was still there, strengthening with his years. He always uttered the words "my father" with an air of gentle pride, and often said, as if he claimed a title full of honor, "Don't call me Demi any more. I am John Brooke now." So, strengthened by a purpose and a hope, the little lad of ten bravely began the world, and entered into his inheritance, the memory of a wise and tender father, the legacy of an honest name.

# CHAPTER XX. ROUND THE FIRE

With the October frosts came the cheery fires in the great fireplaces; and Demi's dry pine-chips helped Dan's oak-knots to blaze royally, and go roaring up the chimney with a jolly sound. All were glad to gather round the hearth, as the evenings grew longer, to play games, read, or lay plans for the winter. But the favorite amusement was story-telling, and Mr. and Mrs. Bhaer were expected to have a store of lively tales always on hand. Their supply occasionally gave out, and then the boys were thrown upon their own resources, which were not always successful. Ghost-parties were the rage at one time; for the fun of the thing consisted in putting out the lights, letting the fire die down, and then sitting in the dark, and telling the most awful tales they could invent. As this resulted in scares of all sorts among the boys, Tommy's walking in his sleep on the shed roof, and a general state of nervousness in the little ones, it was forbidden, and they fell back on more harmless amusements.

One evening, when the small boys were snugly tucked in bed, and the older lads were lounging about the school-room fire, trying to decide what they should do, Demi suggested a new way of settling the question.

Seizing the hearth-brush, he marched up and down the room, saying, "Row, row, row;" and when the boys, laughing and pushing, had got into line, he said, "Now, I'll give you two minutes to think of a play." Franz was writing, and Emil reading the Life of Lord Nelson, and neither joined the party, but the others thought hard, and when the time was up were ready to reply.

"Now, Tom!" and the poker softly rapped him on the head.

"Blind-man's Buff."

"Jack!"

"Commerce; a good round game, and have cents for the pool."

"Uncle forbids our playing for money. Dan, what do you want?"

"Let's have a battle between the Greeks and Romans."

"Stuffy?"

"Roast apples, pop corn, and crack nuts."

"Good! good!" cried several; and when the vote was taken, Stuffy's proposal carried the day.

Some went to the cellar for apples, some to the garret for nuts, and others looked up the popper and the corn.

"We had better ask the girls to come in, hadn't we?" said Demi, in a sudden fit of politeness.

"Daisy pricks chestnuts beautifully," put in Nat, who wanted his little friend to share the fun.

"Nan pops corn tip-top, we must have her," added Tommy.

"Bring in your sweethearts then, we don't mind," said Jack, who laughed at the innocent regard the little people had for one another.

"You shan't call my sister a sweetheart; it is so silly!" cried Demi, in a way that made Jack laugh.

"She is Nat's darling, isn't she, old chirper?"

"Yes, if Demi don't mind. I can't help being fond of her, she is so good to me," answered Nat, with bashful earnestness, for Jack's rough ways disturbed him.

"Nan is my sweetheart, and I shall marry her in about a year, so don't you get in the way, any of you," said Tommy, stoutly; for he and Nan had settled their future, child-fashion, and were to live in the willow, lower down a basket for food, and do other charmingly impossible things.

Demi was quenched by the decision of Bangs, who took him by the arm and walked him off to get the ladies. Nan and Daisy were sewing with Aunt Jo on certain small garments, for Mrs. Carney's newest baby.

"Please, ma'am, could you lend us the girls for a little while? We'll be very careful of them," said Tommy, winking one eye to express apples, snapping his fingers to signify pop-corn, and gnashing his teeth to convey the idea of nut-cracking.

The girls understood this pantomime at once, and began to pull of their thimbles before Mrs. Jo could decide whether Tommy was going into convulsions or was brewing some unusual piece of mischief. Demi explained with elaboration, permission was readily granted, and the boys departed with their prize.

"Don't you speak to Jack," whispered Tommy, as he and Nan promenaded down the hall to get a fork to prick the apples.

"Why not?"

"He laughs at me, so I don't wish you to have any thing to do with him."

"Shall, if I like," said Nan, promptly resenting this premature assumption of authority on the part of her lord.

"Then I won't have you for my sweetheart."

"I don't care."

"Why, Nan, I thought you were fond of me!" and Tommy's voice was full of tender reproach.

"If you mind Jack's laughing I don't care for you one bit."

"Then you may take back your old ring; I won't wear it any longer;" and Tommy plucked off a horsehair pledge of affection which Nan had given him in return for one made of a lobster's feeler.

"I shall give it to Ned," was her cruel reply; for Ned liked Mrs. Giddy-gaddy, and had turned her clothespins, boxes, and spools enough to set up housekeeping with.

Tommy said, "Thunder turtles!" as the only vent equal to the pent-up anguish of the moment, and, dropping Nan's arm, retired in high dudgeon, leaving her to follow with the fork, a neglect which naughty Nan punished by proceeding to prick his heart with jealousy as if it were another sort of apple.

The hearth was swept, and the rosy Baldwins put down to roast. A shovel was heated, and the chestnuts danced merrily upon it, while the corn popped wildly in its wire prison. Dan cracked his best walnuts, and every one chattered and laughed, while the rain beat on the window-pane and the wind howled round the house.

"Why is Billy like this nut?" asked Emil, who was frequently inspired with bad conundrums.

"Because he is cracked," answered Ned.

"That's not fair; you mustn't make fun of Billy, because he can't hit back again. It's mean," cried Dan, smashing a nut wrathfully.

"To what family of insects does Blake belong?" asked peacemaker Franz, seeing that Emil looked ashamed and Dan lowering.

"Gnats," answered Jack.

"Why is Daisy like a bee?" cried Nat, who had been wrapt in thought for several minutes.

"Because she is queen of the hive," said Dan.

"No."

"Because she is sweet."

"Bees are not sweet."

"Give it up."

"Because she makes sweet things, is always busy, and likes flowers," said Nat, piling up his boyish compliments till Daisy blushed like a rosy clover.

"Why is Nan like a hornet?" demanded Tommy, glowering at her, and adding, without giving any one time to answer, "Because she isn't sweet, makes a great buzzing about nothing, and stings like fury."

"Tommy's mad, and I'm glad," cried Ned, as Nan tossed her head and answered quickly,

"What thing in the china-closet is Tom like?"

"A pepper pot," answered Ned, giving Nan a nut meat with a tantalizing laugh that made Tommy feel as if he would like to bounce up like a hot chestnut and hit somebody.

Seeing that ill-humor was getting the better of the small supply of wit in the company, Franz cast himself into the breach again.

"Let's make a law that the first person who comes into the room shall tell us a story. No matter who it is, he must do it, and it will be fun to see who comes first."

The others agreed, and did not have to wait long, for a heavy step soon came clumping through the hall, and Silas appeared, bearing an armful of wood. He was greeted by a general shout, and stood staring about him with a bewildered grin on his big red face, till Franz explained the joke.

"Sho! I can't tell a story," he said, putting down his load and preparing to leave the room. But the boys fell upon him, forced him into a seat, and held him there, laughing, and clamoring for their story, till the good-natured giant was overpowered.

"I don't know but jest one story, and that's about a horse," he said, much flattered by the reception he received.

"Tell it! tell it!" cried the boys.

"Wal," began Silas, tipping his chair back against the wall, and putting his thumbs in the arm-holes of his waistcoat, "I jined a cavalry regiment durin' the war, and see a consid'able amount of fightin'. My horse, Major, was a fust-rate animal, and I was as fond on him as ef he'd ben a human critter. He warn't harnsome, but he was the best-tempered, stiddyest, lovenest brute I ever see. I fust battle we went into, he gave me a lesson that I didn't forgit in a hurry, and I'll tell you how it was. It ain't no use tryin' to picter the noise and hurry, and general horridness of a battle to you young fellers, for I ain't no words to do it in; but I'm free to confess that I got so sort of confused and upset at the fust on it, that I didn't know what I was about. We was ordered to charge, and went ahead like good ones, never stoppin' to pick up them that went down in the scrimmage. I got a shot in the arm, and was pitched out of the saddle don't know how, but there I was left behind with two or three others, dead and wounded, for the rest went on, as I say. Wal, I picked myself up and looked round for Major, feeling as ef I'd had about enough for that spell. I didn't see him nowhere, and was kinder walking back to camp, when I heard a whinny that sounded nateral. I looked round, and there was Major stopping for me a long way off, and lookin' as ef he didn't understand why I was loiterin' behind. I whistled, and he trotted up to me as I'd trained him to do. I mounted as well as I could with my left arm bleedin' and was for going on to camp, for I declare I felt as sick and wimbly as a woman; folks often do in their fust battle. But, no sir! Major was the bravest of the two, and he wouldn't go, not a peg; he jest rared up, and danced, and snorted, and acted as ef the smell of powder and the noise had drove him half wild. I done my best, but he wouldn't give in, so I did; and what do you think that plucky brute done? He wheeled slap round, and galloped back like a hurricane, right into the thickest of the scrimmage!"

"Good for him!" cried Dan excitedly, while the other boys forgot apples and nuts in their interest.

"I wish I may die ef I warn't ashamed of myself," continued Silas, warming up at the recollection of that day. "I was mad as a hornet, and I forgot my waound, and jest pitched in, rampagin' raound like fury till there come a shell into the midst of us, and in bustin' knocked a lot of us flat. I didn't know nothin' for a spell, and when I come-to, the fight was over just there, and I found myself layin' by a wall of poor Major long-side wuss wounded than I was. My leg was broke, and I had a ball in my shoulder, but he, poor old feller! was all tore in the side with a piece of that blasted shell."

"O Silas! what did you do?" cried Nan, pressing close to him with a face full of eager sympathy and interest.

"I dragged myself nigher, and tried to stop the bleedin' with sech rags as I could tear off of me with one hand. But it warn't no use, and he lay moanin' with horrid pain, and lookin' at me with them lovin' eyes of his, till I thought I couldn't bear it. I give him all the help I could, and when the sun got hotter and hotter, and he began to lap out his tongue, I tried to get to a brook that was a good piece away, but I couldn't do it, being stiff and faint, so I give it up and fanned him with my hat. Now you listen to this, and when you hear folks comin' down on the rebs, you jest remember what one on 'em did, and give him credit of it. I poor feller in gray laid not fur off, shot through the lungs and dyin' fast. I'd offered him my handkerchief to keep the sun off his face, and he'd thanked me kindly, for in sech times as that men don't stop to think on which side they belong, but jest buckle-to and help one another. When he see me mournin' over Major and tryin' to ease his pain, he looked up with his face all damp and white with sufferin', and sez he, 'There's water in my canteen; take it, for it can't help me,' and he flung it to me. I couldn't have took it ef I hadn't had a little brandy in a pocket flask, and I made him drink it. It done him good, and I felt as much set up as if I'd drunk it myself. It's surprisin' the good sech little things do folks sometime;" and Silas paused as if he felt again the comfort of that moment when he and his enemy forgot their feud, and helped one another like brothers.

"Tell about Major," cried the boys, impatient for the catastrophe.

"I poured the water over his poor pantin' tongue, and ef ever a dumb critter looked grateful, he did then. But it warn't of much use, for the dreadful waound kep on tormentin' him, till I couldn't bear it any longer. It was hard, but I done it in mercy, and I know he forgive me."

"What did you do?" asked Emil, as Silas stopped abruptly with a loud "hem," and a look in his rough face that made Daisy go and stand by him with her little hand on his knee.

"I shot him."

Quite a thrill went through the listeners as Silas said that, for Major seemed a hero in their eyes, and his tragic end roused all their sympathy.

"Yes, I shot him, and put him out of his misery. I patted him fust, and said, 'Good-by;' then I laid his head easy on the grass, give a last look into his lovin' eyes, and sent a bullet through his head. He hardly stirred, I aimed so true, and when I seen him quite still, with no more moanin' and pain, I was glad, and yet wal, I don't know as I need by ashamed on't I jest put my arms raound his neck and boo-hooed like a great baby. Sho! I didn't know I was sech a fool;" and Silas drew his sleeve across his eyes, as much touched by Daisy's sob, as by the memory of faithful Major.

No one spoke for a minute, because the boys were as quick to feel the pathos of the little story as tender-hearted Daisy, though they did not show it by crying.

"I'd like a horse like that," said Dan, half-aloud.

"Did the rebel man die, too?" asked Nan, anxiously.

"Not then. We laid there all day, and at night some of our fellers came to look after the missing ones. They nat'rally wanted to take me fust, but I knew I could wait, and the rebel had but one chance, maybe, so I made them carry him off right away. He had jest strength enough to hold out his hand to me and say, 'Thanky, comrade!' and them was the last words he spoke, for he died an hour after he got to the hospital-tent."

"How glad you must have been that you were kind to him!" said Demi, who was deeply impressed by this story.

"Wal, I did take comfort thinkin' of it, as I laid there alone for a number of hours with my head on Major's neck, and see the moon come up. I'd like to have buried the poor beast decent, but it warn't possible; so I cut off a bit of his mane, and I've kep it ever sence. Want to see it, sissy?"

"Oh, yes, please," answered Daisy, wiping away her tears to look.

Silas took out an old "wallet" as he called his pocket-book, and produced from an inner fold a bit of brown paper, in which was a rough lock of white horse-hair. The children looked at it silently, as it lay in the broad palm, and no one found any thing to ridicule in the love Silas bore his good horse Major.

"That is a sweet story, and I like it, though it did make me cry. Thank you very much, Si," and Daisy helped him fold and put away his little relic; while Nan stuffed a handful of pop-corn into his pocket, and the boys loudly expressed their flattering opinions of his story, feeling that there had been two heroes in it.

He departed, quite overcome by his honors, and the little conspirators talked the tale over, while they waited for their next victim. It was Mrs. Jo, who came in to measure Nan for some new pinafores she was making for her. They let her get well in, and then pounced upon her, telling her the law, and demanding the story. Mrs. Jo was very much amused at the new trap, and consented at once, for the sound of happy voices had been coming across the hall so pleasantly that she quite longed to join them, and forget her own anxious thoughts of Sister Meg.

"Am I the first mouse you have caught, you sly pussies-in-boots?" she asked, as she was conducted to the big chair, supplied with refreshments, and surrounded by a flock of merry-faced listeners.

They told her about Silas and his contribution, and she slapped her forehead in despair, for she was quite at her wits' end, being called upon so unexpectedly for a brand new tale.

"What shall I tell about?" she said.

"Boys," was the general answer.

"Have a party in it," said Daisy.

"And something good to eat," added Stuffy.

"That reminds me of a story, written years ago, by a dear old lady. I used to be very fond of it, and I fancy you will like it, for it has both boys, and 'something good to eat' in it."

"What is it called?" asked Demi.

"'The Suspected Boy.'"

Nat looked up from the nuts he was picking, and Mrs. Jo smiled at him, guessing what was in his mind.

"Miss Crane kept a school for boys in a quiet little town, and a very good school it was, of the old-fashioned sort. Six boys lived in her house, and four or five more came in from the town. Among those who lived with her was one named Lewis White. Lewis was not a bad boy, but rather timid, and now and then he told a lie. One day a neighbor sent Miss Crane a basket of gooseberries. There were not enough to go round, so kind Miss Crane, who liked to please her boys, went to work and made a dozen nice little gooseberry tarts."

"I'd like to try gooseberry tarts. I wonder if she made them as I do my raspberry ones," said Daisy, whose interest in cooking had lately revived.

"Hush," said Nat, tucking a plump pop-corn into her mouth to silence her, for he felt a particular interest in this tale, and thought it opened well.

"When the tarts were done, Miss Crane put them away in the best parlor closet, and said not a word about them, for she wanted to surprise the boys at tea-time. When the minute came and all were seated at table, she went to get her tarts, but came back looking much troubled, for what do you think had happened?"

"Somebody had hooked them!" cried Ned.

"No, there they were, but some one had stolen all the fruit out of them by lifting up the upper crust and then putting it down after the gooseberry had been scraped out."

"What a mean trick!" and Nan looked at Tommy, as if to imply that he would do the same.

"When she told the boys her plan and showed them the poor little patties all robbed of their sweetness, the boys were much grieved and disappointed, and all declared that they knew nothing about the matter. 'Perhaps the rats did it,' said Lewis, who was among the loudest to deny any knowledge of the tarts. 'No, rats would have nibbled crust and all, and never lifted it up and scooped out the fruit. Hands did that,' said Miss Crane, who was more troubled about the lie that some one must have told than about her lost patties. Well, they had supper and went to bed, but in the night Miss Crane heard some one groaning, and going to see who it was she found Lewis in great pain. He had evidently eaten something that disagreed with him, and was so sick that Miss Crane was alarmed, and was going to send for the doctor, when Lewis moaned out, 'It's the gooseberries; I ate them, and I must tell before I die,' for the thought of a doctor frightened him. 'If that is all, I'll give you an emetic and you will soon get over it,' said Miss Crane. So Lewis had a good dose, and by morning was quite comfortable. 'Oh, don't tell the boys; they will laugh at me so,' begged the invalid. Kind Miss Crane promised not to, but Sally, the girl, told the story, and poor Lewis had no peace for a long time. His mates called him Old Gooseberry, and were never tired of asking him the price of tarts."

"Served him right," said Emil.

"Badness always gets found out," added Demi, morally.

"No, it don't," muttered Jack, who was tending the apples with great devotion, so that he might keep his back to the rest and account for his red face.

"Is that all?" asked Dan.

"No, that is only the first part; the second part is more interesting. Some time after this a peddler came by one day and stopped to show his things to the boys, several of whom bought pocket-combs, jew's-harps, and various trifles of that sort. Among the knives was a little white-handled penknife that Lewis wanted very much, but he had spent all his pocket-money, and no one had any to lend him. He held the knife in his hand, admiring and longing for it, till the man packed up his goods to go, then he reluctantly laid it down, and the man went on his way. The next day, however, the peddler returned to say that he could not find that very knife, and thought he must have left it at Miss Crane's. It was a very nice one with a pearl handle, and he could not afford to lose it. Every one looked, and every one declared they knew nothing about it. 'This young gentleman had it last, and seemed to want it very much. Are you quite sure you put it back?' said the man to Lewis, who was much troubled at the loss, and vowed over and over again that he did return it. His denials seemed to do no good, however, for every one was sure he had taken it, and after a stormy scene Miss Crane paid for it, and the man went grumbling away."

"Did Lewis have it?" cried Nat, much excited.

"You will see. Now poor Lewis had another trial to bear, for the boys were constantly saying, 'Lend me your pearl-handled knife, Gooseberry,' and things of that sort, till Lewis was so unhappy he begged to be sent home. Miss Crane did her best to keep the boys quiet, but it was hard work, for they would tease, and she could not be with them all the time. That is one of the hardest things to teach boys; they won't 'hit a fellow when he is down,' as they say, but they will torment him in little ways till he would thank them to fight it out all round."

"I know that," said Dan.

"So do I," added Nat, softly.

Jack said nothing, but he quite agreed; for he knew that the elder boys despised him, and let him alone for that very reason.

"Do go on about poor Lewis, Aunt Jo. I don't believe he took the knife, but I want to be sure," said Daisy, in great anxiety.

"Well, week after week went on and the matter was not cleared up. The boys avoided Lewis, and he, poor fellow, was almost sick with the trouble he had brought upon himself. He resolved never to tell another lie, and tried so hard that Miss Crane pitied and helped him, and really came at last to believe that he did not take the knife. Two months after the peddler's first visit, he came again, and the first thing he said was,

"'Well, ma'am, I found that knife after all. It had slipped behind the lining of my valise, and fell out the other day when I was putting in a new stock of goods. I thought I'd call and let you know, as you paid for it, and maybe would like it, so here it is.'"

"The boys had all gathered round, and at these words they felt much ashamed, and begged Lewis' pardon so heartily that he could not refuse to give it. Miss Crane presented the knife to him, and he kept it many years to remind him of the fault that had brought him so much trouble."

"I wonder why it is that things you eat on the sly hurt you, and don't when you eat them at table," observed Stuffy, thoughtfully.

"Perhaps your conscience affects your stomach," said Mrs. Jo, smiling at his speech.

"He is thinking of the cucumbers," said Ned, and a gale of merriment followed the words, for Stuffy's last mishap had been a funny one.

He ate two large cucumbers in private, felt very ill, and confided his anguish to Ned, imploring him to do something. Ned good-naturedly recommended a mustard plaster and a hot flat iron to the feet; only in applying these remedies he reversed the order of things, and put the plaster on the feet, the flat iron on the stomach, and poor Stuffy was found in the barn with blistered soles and a scorched jacket.

"Suppose you tell another story, that was such an interesting one," said Nat, as the laughter subsided.

Before Mrs. Jo could refuse these insatiable Oliver Twists, Rob walked into the room trailing his little bed-cover after him, and wearing an expression of great sweetness as he said, steering straight to his mother as a sure haven of refuge,

"I heard a great noise, and I thought sumfin dreffle might have happened, so I came to see."

"Did you think I would forget you, naughty boy?" asked his mother, trying to look stern.

"No; but I thought you'd feel better to see me right here," responded the insinuating little party.

"I had much rather see you in bed, so march straight up again, Robin."

"Everybody that comes in here has to tell a story, and you can't so you'd better cut and run," said Emil.

"Yes, I can! I tell Teddy lots of ones, all about bears and moons, and little flies that say things when they buzz," protested Rob, bound to stay at any price.

"Tell one now, then, right away," said Dan, preparing to shoulder and bear him off.

"Well, I will; let me fink a minute," and Rob climbed into his mother's lap, where he was cuddled, with the remark

"It is a family failing, this getting out of bed at wrong times. Demi used to do it; and as for me, I was hopping in and out all night long. Meg used to think the house was on fire, and send me down to see, and I used to stay and enjoy myself, as you mean to, my bad son."

"I've finked now," observed Rob, quite at his ease, and eager to win the entree into this delightful circle.

Every one looked and listened with faces full of suppressed merriment as Rob, perched on his mother's knee and wrapped in the gay coverlet, told the following brief but tragic tale with an earnestness that made it very funny:

"Once a lady had a million children, and one nice little boy. She went up-stairs and said, 'You mustn't go in the yard.' But he wented, and fell into the pump, and was drowned dead."

"Is that all?" asked Franz, as Rob paused out of breath with this startling beginning.

"No, there is another piece of it," and Rob knit his downy eyebrows in the effort to evolve another inspiration.

"What did the lady do when he fell into the pump?" asked his mother, to help him on.

"Oh, she pumped him up, and wrapped him in a newspaper, and put him on a shelf to dry for seed."

A general explosion of laughter greeted this surprising conclusion, and Mrs. Jo patted the curly head, as she said, solemnly,

"My son, you inherit your mother's gift of story-telling. Go where glory waits thee."

"Now I can stay, can't I? Wasn't it a good story?" cried Rob, in high feather at his superb success.

"You can stay till you have eaten these twelve pop-corns," said his mother, expecting to see them vanish at one mouthful.

But Rob was a shrewd little man, and got the better of her by eating them one by one very slowly, and enjoying every minute with all his might.

"Hadn't you better tell the other story, while you wait for him?" said Demi, anxious that no time should be lost.

"I really have nothing but a little tale about a wood-box," said Mrs. Jo, seeing that Rob had still seven corns to eat.

"Is there a boy in it?"

"It is all boy."

"Is it true?" asked Demi.

"Every bit of it."

"Goody! tell on, please."

"James Snow and his mother lived in a little house, up in New Hampshire. They were poor, and James had to work to help his mother, but he loved books so well he hated work, and just wanted to sit and study all day long."

"How could he! I hate books, and like work," said Dan, objecting to James at the very outset.

"It takes all sorts of people to make a world; workers and students both are needed, and there is room for all. But I think the workers should study some, and the students should know how to work if necessary," answered Mrs. Jo, looking from Dan to Demi with a significant expression.

"I'm sure I do work," and Demi showed three small hard spots in his little palm, with pride.

"And I'm sure I study," added Dan, nodding with a groan toward the blackboard full of neat figures.

"See what James did. He did not mean to be selfish, but his mother was proud of him, and let him do as he liked, working by herself that he might have books and time to read them. One autumn James wanted to go to school, and went to the minister to see if he would help him, about decent clothes and books. Now the minister had heard the gossip about James's idleness, and was not inclined to do much for him, thinking that a boy who neglected his mother, and let her slave for him, was not likely to do very well even at school. But the good man felt more interested when he found how earnest James was, and being rather an odd man, he made this proposal to the boy, to try now sincere he was.

"'I will give you clothes and books on one condition, James.'

"'What is that, sir?' and the boy brightened up at once.

"'You are to keep your mother's wood-box full all winter long, and do it yourself. If you fail, school stops.' James laughed at the queer condition and readily agreed to it, thinking it a very easy one.

"He began school, and for a time got on capitally with the wood-box, for it was autumn, and chips and brushwood were plentiful. He ran out morning and evening and got a basket full, or chopped up the cat sticks for the little cooking stove, and as his mother was careful and saving, the task was not hard. But in November the frost came, the days were dull and cold, and wood went fast. His mother bought a load with her own earnings, but it seemed to melt away, and was nearly gone, before James remembered that he was to get the next. Mrs. Snow was feeble and lame with rheumatism, and unable to work as she had done, so James had to put down the books, and see what he could do.

"It was hard, for he was going on well, and so interested in his lessons that he hated to stop except for food and sleep. But he knew the minister would keep his word, and much against his will James set about earning money in his spare hours, lest the wood-box should get empty. He did all sorts of things, ran errands, took care of a neighbor's cow, helped the old sexton dust and warm the church on Sundays, and in these ways got enough to buy fuel in small quantities. But it was hard work; the days were short, the winter was bitterly cold, and precious time went fast, and the dear books were so fascinating, that it was sad to leave them, for dull duties that never seemed done.

"The minister watched him quietly, and seeing that he was in earnest helped him without his knowledge. He met him often driving the wood sleds from the forest, where the men were chopping and as James plodded beside the slow oxen, he read or studied, anxious to use every minute. 'The boy is worth helping, this lesson will do him good, and when he has learned it, I will give him an easier one,' said the minister to himself, and on Christmas eve a splendid load of wood was quietly dropped at the door of the little house, with a new saw and a bit of paper, saying only,

"'The Lord helps those who help themselves.'

"Poor James expected nothing, but when he woke on that cold Christmas morning, he found a pair of warm mittens, knit by his mother, with her stiff painful fingers. This gift pleased him very much, but her kiss and tender look as she called him her 'good son,' was better still. In trying to keep her warm, he had warmed his own heart, you see, and in filling the wood-box he had also filled those months with duties faithfully done. He began to see this, to feel that there was something better than books, and to try to learn the lessons God set him, as well as those his school-master gave.

"When he saw the great pile of oak and pine logs at his door, and read the little paper, he knew who sent it, and understood the minister's plan; thanked him for it, and fell to work with all his might. Other boys frolicked that day, but James sawed wood, and I think of all the lads in the town the happiest was the one in the new mittens, who whistled like a blackbird as he filled his mother's wood-box."

"That's a first rater!" cried Dan, who enjoyed a simple matter-of-face story better than the finest fairy tale; "I like that fellow after all."

"I could saw wood for you, Aunt Jo!" said Demi, feeling as if a new means of earning money for his mother was suggested by the story.

"Tell about a bad boy. I like them best," said Nan.

"You'd better tell about a naughty cross-patch of a girl," said Tommy, whose evening had been spoilt by Nan's unkindness. It made his apple taste bitter, his pop-corn was insipid, his nuts were hard to crack, and the sight of Ned and Nan on one bench made him feel his life a burden.

But there were no more stories from Mrs. Jo, for on looking down at Rob he was discovered to be fast asleep with his last corn firmly clasped in his chubby hand. Bundling him up in his coverlet, his mother carried him away and tucked him up with no fear of his popping out again.

"Now let's see who will come next," said Emil, setting the door temptingly ajar.

*Mary Ann passed first, and he called out to her, but Silas had warned her, and she only laughed and hurried on in spite of their enticements. Presently a door opened, and a strong voice was heard humming in the hall,*

*"Ich weiss nicht was soll es bedeuten*
*Dass ich so traurig bin."*

"It's Uncle Fritz; all laugh loud and he will be sure to come in," said Emil.

A wild burst of laughter followed, and in came Uncle Fritz, asking, "What is the joke, my lads?"

"Caught! caught! you can't go out till you've told a story," cried the boys, slamming the door.

"So! that is the joke then? Well, I have no wish to go, it is so pleasant here, and I pay my forfeit at once," which he did by sitting down and beginning instantly,

"A long time ago your Grandfather, Demi, went to lecture in a great town, hoping to get some money for a home for little orphans that some good people were getting up. His lecture did well, and he put a considerable sum of money in his pocket, feeling very happy about it. As he was driving in a chaise to another town, he came to a lonely bit of road, late in the afternoon, and was just thinking what a good place it was for robbers when he saw a bad-looking man come out of the woods in front of him and go slowly along as if waiting till he came up. The thought of the money made Grandfather rather anxious, and at first he had a mind to turn round and drive away. But the horse was tired, and then he did not like to suspect the man, so he kept on, and when he got nearer and saw how poor and sick and ragged the stranger looked, his heart reproached him, and stopping, he said in a kind voice,

"'My friend, you look tired; let me give you a lift.' The man seemed surprised, hesitated a minute, and then got in. He did not seem inclined to talk, but Grandfather kept on in his wise, cheerful way, speaking of what a hard year it had been, how much the poor had suffered, and how difficult it was to get on sometimes. The man slowly softened a little, and won by the kind chat, told his story. How he had been sick, could get no work, had a family of children, and was almost in despair. Grandfather was so full of pity that he forgot his fear, and, asking the man his name, said he would try to get him work in the next town, as he had friends there. Wishing to get at pencil and paper to write down the address, Grandfather took out his plump pocket-book, and the minute he did so, the man's eye was on it. Then Grandfather remembered what was in it and trembled for his money, but said quietly,

"'Yes, I have a little sum here for some poor orphans. I wish it was my own, I would so gladly give you some of it. I am not rich, but I know many of the trials of the poor; this five dollars is mine, and I want to give it to you for your children.'

"The hard, hungry look in the man's eyes changed to a grateful one as he took the small sum, freely given, and left the orphans' money untouched. He rode on with Grandfather till they approached the town, then he asked to be set down. Grandpa shook hands with him, and was about to drive on, when the man said, as if something made him, 'I was desperate when we met, and I meant to rob you, but you were so kind I couldn't do it. God bless you, sir, for keeping me from it!'"

"Did Grandpa ever see him again?" asked Daisy, eagerly.

"No; but I believe the man found work, and did not try robbery any more."

"That was a curious way to treat him; I'd have knocked him down," said Dan.

"Kindness is always better than force. Try it and see," answered Mr. Bhaer, rising.

"Tell another, please," cried Daisy.

"You must, Aunt Jo did," added Demi.

"Then I certainly won't, but keep my others for next time. Too many tales are as bad as too many bonbons. I have paid my forfeit and I go," and Mr. Bhaer ran for his life, with the whole flock in full pursuit. He had the start, however, and escaped safely into his study, leaving the boys to go rioting back again.

They were so stirred up by the race that they could not settle to their former quiet, and a lively game of Blindman's Buff followed, in which Tommy showed that he had taken the moral of the last story to heart, for, when he caught Nan, he whispered in her ear, "I'm sorry I called you a cross-patch."

Nan was not to be outdone in kindness, so, when they played "Button, button, who's got the button?" and it was her turn to go round, she said, "Hold fast all I give you," with such a friendly smile at Tommy, that he was not surprised to find the horse-hair ring in his hand instead of the button. He only smiled back at her then, but when they were going to bed, he offered Nan the best bite of his last apple; she saw the ring on his stumpy little finger, accepted the bite, and peace was declared. Both were ashamed of the temporary coldness, neither was ashamed to say, "I was wrong, forgive me," so the childish friendship remained unbroken, and the home in the willow lasted long, a pleasant little castle in the air.

# CHAPTER XXI. THANKSGIVING

This yearly festival was always kept at Plumfield in the good old-fashioned way, and nothing was allowed to interfere with it. For days beforehand, the little girls helped Asia and Mrs. Jo in store-room and kitchen, making pies and puddings, sorting fruit, dusting dishes, and being very busy and immensely important. The boys hovered on the outskirts of the forbidden ground, sniffing the savory odors, peeping in at the mysterious performances, and occasionally being permitted to taste some delicacy in the process of preparation.

Something more than usual seemed to be on foot this year, for the girls were as busy up-stairs as down, so were the boys in school-room and barn, and a general air of bustle pervaded the house. There was a great hunting up of old ribbons and finery, much cutting and pasting of gold paper, and the most remarkable quantity of straw, gray cotton, flannel, and big black beads, used by Franz and Mrs. Jo. Ned hammered at strange machines in the workshop, Demi and Tommy went about murmuring to themselves as if learning something. A fearful racket was heard in Emil's room at intervals, and peals of laughter from the nursery when Rob and Teddy were sent for and hidden from sight whole hours at a time. But the thing that puzzled Mr. Bhaer the most was what became of Rob's big pumpkin. It had been borne in triumph to the kitchen, where a dozen golden-tinted pies soon after appeared. It would not have taken more than a quarter of the mammoth vegetable to make them, yet where was the rest? It disappeared, and Rob never seemed to care, only chuckled when it was mentioned, and told his father, "To wait and see," for the fun of the whole thing was to surprise Father Bhaer at the end, and not let him know a bit about what was to happen.

He obediently shut eyes, ears, and mouth, and went about trying not to see what was in plain sight, not to hear the tell-tale sounds that filled the air, not to understand any of the perfectly transparent mysteries going on all about him. Being a German, he loved these simple domestic festivals, and encouraged them with all his heart, for they made home so pleasant that the boys did not care to go elsewhere for fun.

When at last the day came, the boys went off for a long walk, that they might have good appetites for dinner; as if they ever needed them! The girls remained at home to help set the table, and give last touches to various affairs which filled their busy little souls with anxiety. The school-room had been shut up since the night before, and Mr. Bhaer was forbidden to enter it on pain of a beating from Teddy, who guarded the door like a small dragon, though he was dying to tell about it, and nothing but his father's heroic self-denial in not listening, kept him from betraying a grand secret.

"It's all done, and it's perfectly splendid," cried Nan, coming out at last with an air of triumph.

"The you know goes beautifully, and Silas knows just what to do now," added Daisy, skipping with delight at some unspeakable success.

"I'm blest if it ain't the 'cutest thing I ever see, them critters in particular," said Silas, who had been let into the secret, went off laughing like a great boy.

"They are coming; I hear Emil roaring 'Land lubbers lying down below,' so we must run and dress," cried Nan, and up-stairs they scampered in a great hurry.

The boys came trooping home with appetites that would have made the big turkey tremble, if it had not been past all fear. They also retired to dress; and for half-an-hour there was a washing, brushing, and prinking that would have done any tidy woman's heart good to see. When the bell rang, a troop of fresh-faced lads with shiny hair, clean collars, and Sunday jackets on, filed into the dining-room, where Mrs. Jo, in her one black silk, with a knot of her favorite white chrysanthemums in her bosom, sat at the head of the table, "looking splendid," as the boys said, whenever she got herself up. Daisy and Nan were as gay as a posy bed in their new winter dresses, with bright sashes and hair ribbons. Teddy was gorgeous to behold in a crimson merino blouse, and his best button boots, which absorbed and distracted him as much as Mr. Toot's wristbands did on one occasion.

As Mr. and Mrs. Bhaer glanced at each other down the long table, with those rows of happy faces on either side, they had a little thanksgiving all to themselves, and without a word, for one heart said to the other,

"Our work has prospered, let us be grateful and go on."

The clatter of knives and forks prevented much conversation for a few minutes, and Mary Ann with an amazing pink bow in her hair "flew round" briskly, handing plates and ladling out gravy. Nearly every one had contributed to the feast, so the dinner was a peculiarly interesting ones to the eaters of it, who beguiled the pauses by remarks on their own productions.

"If these are not good potatoes I never saw any," observed Jack, as he received his fourth big mealy one.

"Some of my herbs are in the stuffing of the turkey, that's why it's so nice," said Nan, taking a mouthful with intense satisfaction.

"My ducks are prime any way; Asia said she never cooked such fat ones," added Tommy.

"Well, our carrots are beautiful, ain't they, and our parsnips will be ever so good when we dig them," put in Dick, and Dolly murmured his assent from behind the bone he was picking.

"I helped make the pies with my pumpkin," called out Robby, with a laugh which he stopped by retiring into his mug.

"I picked some of the apples that the cider is made of," said Demi.

"I raked the cranberries for the sauce," cried Nat.

"I got the nuts," added Dan, and so it went on all round the table.

"Who made up Thanksgiving?" asked Rob, for being lately promoted to jacket and trousers he felt a new and manly interest in the institutions of his country.

"See who can answer that question," and Mr. Bhaer nodded to one or two of his best history boys.

"I know," said Demi, "the Pilgrims made it."

"What for?" asked Rob, without waiting to learn who the Pilgrims were.

"I forget," and Demi subsided.

"I believe it was because they were starved once, and so when they had a good harvest, they said, 'We will thank God for it,' and they had a day and called it Thanksgiving," said Dan, who liked the story of the brave men who suffered so nobly for their faith.

"Good! I didn't think you would remember any thing but natural history," and Mr. Bhaer tapped gently on the table as applause for his pupil.

Dan looked pleased; and Mrs. Jo said to her son, "Now do you understand about it, Robby?"

"No, I don't. I thought pil-grins were a sort of big bird that lived on rocks, and I saw pictures of them in Demi's book."

"He means penguins. Oh, isn't he a little goosey!" and Demi laid back in his chair and laughed aloud.

"Don't laugh at him, but tell him all about it if you can," said Mrs. Bhaer, consoling Rob with more cranberry sauce for the general smile that went round the table at his mistake.

"Well, I will;" and, after a pause to collect his ideas, Demi delivered the following sketch of the Pilgrim Fathers, which would have made even those grave gentlemen smile if they could have heard it.

"You see, Rob, some of the people in England didn't like the king, or something, so they got into ships and sailed away to this country. It was all full of Indians, and bears, and wild creatures, and they lived in forts, and had a dreadful time."

"The bears?" asked Robby, with interest.

"No; the Pilgrims, because the Indians troubled them. They hadn't enough to eat, and they went to church with guns, and ever so many died, and they got out of the ships on a rock, and it's called Plymouth Rock, and Aunt Jo saw it and touched it. The Pilgrims killed all the Indians, and got rich; and hung the witches, and were very good; and some of the greatest great-grandpas came in the ships. One was the Mayflower; and they made Thanksgiving, and we have it always, and I like it. Some more turkey, please."

"I think Demi will be an historian, there is such order and clearness in his account of events;" and Uncle Fritz's eyes laughed at Aunt Jo, as he helped the descendant of the Pilgrims to his third bit of turkey.

"I thought you must eat as much as ever you could on Thanksgiving. But Franz says you mustn't even then;" and Stuffy looked as if he had received bad news.

"Franz is right, so mind your knife and fork, and be moderate, or else you won't be able to help in the surprise by and by," said Mrs. Jo.

"I'll be careful; but everybody does eat lots, and I like it better than being moderate," said Stuffy, who leaned to the popular belief that Thanksgiving must be kept by coming as near apoplexy as possible, and escaping with merely a fit of indigestion or a headache.

"Now, my 'pilgrims' amuse yourselves quietly till tea-time, for you will have enough excitement this evening," said Mrs. Jo, as they rose from the table after a protracted sitting, finished by drinking every one's health in cider.

"I think I will take the whole flock for a drive, it is so pleasant; then you can rest, my dear, or you will be worn out this evening," added Mr. Bhaer; and as soon as coats and hats could be put on, the great omnibus was packed full, and away they went for a long gay drive, leaving Mrs. Jo to rest and finish sundry small affairs in peace.

An early and light tea was followed by more brushing of hair and washing of hands; then the flock waited impatiently for the company to come. Only the family was expected; for these small revels were strictly domestic, and such being the case, sorrow was not allowed to sadden the present festival. All came; Mr. and Mrs. March, with Aunt Meg, so sweet and lovely, in spite of her black dress and the little widow's cap that encircled her tranquil face. Uncle Teddy and Aunt Amy, with the Princess looking more fairy-like than ever, in a sky-blue gown, and a great bouquet of hot-house flowers, which she divided among the boys, sticking one in each button-hole, making them feel peculiarly elegant and festive. One strange face appeared, and Uncle Teddy led the unknown gentleman up to the Bhaers, saying,

"This is Mr. Hyde; he has been inquiring about Dan, and I ventured to bring him to-night, that he might see how much the boy has improved."

The Bhaers received him cordially, for Dan's sake, pleased that the lad had been remembered. But, after a few minutes' chat, they were glad to know Mr. Hyde for his own sake, so genial, simple, and interesting was he. It was pleasant to see the boy's face light up when he caught sight of his friend; pleasanter still to see Mr. Hyde's surprise and satisfaction in Dan's improved manners and appearance, and pleasantest of all to watch the two sit talking in a corner, forgetting the differences of age, culture, and position, in the one subject which interested both, as man and boy compared notes, and told the story of their summer life.

"The performance must begin soon, or the actors will go to sleep," said Mrs. Jo, when the first greetings were over.

So every one went into the school-room, and took seats before a curtain made of two bed-covers. The children had already vanished; but stifled laughter, and funny little exclamations from behind the curtain, betrayed their whereabouts. The entertainment began with a spirited exhibition of gymnastics, led by Franz. The six elder lads, in blue trousers and red shirts, made a fine display of muscle with dumb-bells, clubs, and weights, keeping time to the music of the piano, played by Mrs. Jo behind the scenes. Dan was so energetic in this exercise, that there was some danger of his knocking down his neighbors, like so many nine-pins, or sending his bean-bags whizzing among the audience; for he was excited by Mr. Hyde's presence, and a burning desire to do honor to his teachers.

"A fine, strong lad. If I go on my trip to South America, in a year or two, I shall be tempted to ask you to lend him to me, Mr. Bhaer," said Mr. Hyde, whose interest in Dan was much increased by the report he had just heard of him.

"You shall have him, and welcome, though we shall miss our young Hercules very much. It would do him a world of good, and I am sure he would serve his friend faithfully."

Dan heard both question and answer, and his heart leaped with joy at the thought of travelling in a new country with Mr. Hyde, and swelled with gratitude for the kindly commendation which rewarded his efforts to be all these friends desired to see him.

After the gymnastics, Demi and Tommy spoke the old school dialogue, "Money makes the mare go." Demi did very well, but Tommy was capital as the old farmer; for he imitated Silas in a way that convulsed the audience, and caused Silas himself to laugh so hard that Asia had to slap him on the back, as they stood in the hall enjoying the fun immensely.

Then Emil, who had got his breath by this time, gave them a sea-song in costume, with a great deal about "stormy winds," "lee shores," and a rousing chorus of "Luff, boys, luff," which made the room ring; after which Ned performed a funny Chinese dance, and hopped about like a large frog in a pagoda hat. As this was the only public exhibition ever held at Plumfield, a few exercises in lightning-arithmetic, spelling, and reading were given. Jack quite amazed the public by his rapid calculations on the blackboard. Tommy won in the spelling match, and Demi read a little French fable so well that Uncle Teddy was charmed.

"Where are the other children?" asked every one as the curtain fell, and none of the little ones appeared.

"Oh, that is the surprise. It's so lovely, I pity you because you don't know it," said Demi, who had gone to get his mother's kiss, and stayed by her to explain the mystery when it should be revealed.

Goldilocks had been carried off by Aunt Jo, to the great amazement of her papa, who quite outdid Mr. Bhaer in acting wonder, suspense, and wild impatience to know "what was going to happen."

At last, after much rustling, hammering, and very audible directions from the stage manager, the curtain rose to soft music, and Bess was discovered sitting on a stool beside a brown paper fire-place. A dearer little Cinderella was never seen; for the gray gown was very ragged, the tiny shoes all worn, the face so pretty under the bright hair, and the attitude so dejected, it brought tears, as well as smiles, to the fond eyes looking at the baby actress. She sat quite still, till a voice whispered, "Now!" then she sighed a funny little sigh, and said, "Oh I wish I tood go to the ball!" so naturally, that her father clapped frantically, and her mother called out, "Little darling!" These highly improper expressions of feeling caused Cinderella to forget herself, and shake her head at them, saying, reprovingly, "You mustn't 'peak to me."

Silence instantly prevailed, and three taps were heard on the wall. Cinderella looked alarmed, but before she could remember to say, "What is dat?" the back of the brown paper fire-place opened like a door, and, with some difficulty, the fairy godmother got herself and her pointed hat through. It was Nan, in a red cloak, a cap, and a wand, which she waved as she said decidedly,

"You shall go to the ball, my dear."

"Now you must pull and show my pretty dress," returned Cinderella, tugging at her brown gown.

"No, no; you must say, 'How can I go in my rags?'" said the godmother in her own voice.

"Oh yes, so I mus';" and the Princess said it, quite undisturbed by her forgetfulness.

"I change your rags into a splendid dress, because you are good," said the godmother in her stage tones; and deliberately unbuttoning the brown pinafore, she displayed a gorgeous sight.

The little Princess really was pretty enough to turn the heads of any number of small princes, for her mamma had dressed her like a tiny court lady, in a rosy silk train with satin under-skirt, and bits of bouquets here and there, quite lovely to behold. The godmother put a crown, with pink and white feathers drooping from it, on her head, and gave her a pair of silver paper slippers, which she put on, and then stood up, lifting her skirts to show them to the audience, saying, with pride, "My dlass ones, ain't they pitty?"

She was so charmed with them, that she was with difficulty recalled to her part, and made to say,

"But I have no toach, Dodmother."

"Behold it!" and Nan waved her wand with such a flourish, that she nearly knocked off the crown of the Princess.

Then appeared the grand triumph of the piece. First, a rope was seen to flap on the floor, to tighten with a twitch as Emil's voice was heard to say, "Heave, ahoy!" and Silas's gruff one to reply, "Stiddy, now, stiddy!" A shout of laughter followed, for four large gray rats appeared, rather shaky as to their legs, and queer as to their tails, but quite fine about the head, where black beads shone in the most lifelike manner. They drew, or were intended to appear as if they did, a magnificent coach made of half the mammoth pumpkin, mounted on the wheels of Teddy's wagon, painted yellow to match the gay carriage. Perched on a seat in front sat a jolly little coachman in a white cotton-wool wig, cocked hat, scarlet breeches, and laced coat, who cracked a long whip and jerked the red reins so energetically, that the gray steeds reared finely. It was Teddy, and he beamed upon the company so affably that they gave him a round all to himself; and Uncle Laurie said, "If I could find as sober a coachman as that one, I would engage him on the spot." The coach stopped, the godmother lifted in the Princess, and she was trundled away in state, kissing her hand to the public, with her glass shoes sticking up in front, and her pink train sweeping the ground behind, for, elegant as the coach was, I regret to say that her Highness was rather a tight fit.

The next scene was the ball, and here Nan and Daisy appeared as gay as peacocks in all sorts of finery. Nan was especially good as the proud sister, and crushed many imaginary ladies as she swept about the palace-hall. The Prince, in solitary state upon a somewhat unsteady throne, sat gazing about him from under an imposing crown, as he played with his sword and admired the rosettes in his shoes. When Cinderella came in he jumped up, and exclaimed, with more warmth than elegance,

"My gracious! who is that?" and immediately led the lady out to dance, while the sisters scowled and turned up their noses in the corner.

The stately jig executed by the little couple was very pretty, for the childish faces were so earnest, the costumes so gay, and the steps so peculiar, that they looked like the dainty quaint figures painted on a Watteau fan. The Princess's train was very much in her way, and the sword of Prince Rob nearly tripped him up several times. But they overcame these obstacles remarkably well, and finished the dance with much grace and spirit, considering that neither knew what the other was about.

"Drop your shoe," whispered Mrs. Jo's voice as the lady was about to sit down.

"Oh, I fordot!" and, taking off one of the silvery slippers, Cinderella planted it carefully in the middle of the stage, said to Rob, "Now you must try and tatch me," and ran away, while the Prince, picking up the shoe, obediently trotted after her.

The third scene, as everybody knows, is where the herald comes to try on the shoe. Teddy, still in coachman's dress, came in blowing a tin fish-horn melodiously, and the proud sisters each tried to put on the slipper. Nan insisted on playing cut off her toe with a carving-knife, and performed that operation so well that the herald was alarmed, and begged her to be "welly keerful." Cinderella then was called, and came in with the pinafore half on, slipped her foot into the slipper, and announced, with satisfaction,

"I am the Pinsiss."

Daisy wept, and begged pardon; but Nan, who liked tragedy, improved upon the story, and fell in a fainting-fit upon the floor, where she remained comfortably enjoying the rest of the play. It was not long, for the Prince ran in, dropped upon his knees, and kissed the hand of Goldilocks with great ardor, while the herald blew a blast that nearly deafened the audience. The curtain had no chance to fall, for the Princess ran off the stage to her father, crying, "Didn't I do well?" while the Prince and herald had a fencing-match with the tin horn and wooden sword.

"It was beautiful!" said every one; and, when the raptures had a little subsided, Nat came out with his violin in his hand.

"Hush! hush!" cried all the children, and silence followed, for something in the boy's bashful manner and appealing eyes make every one listen kindly.

The Bhaers thought he would play some of the old airs he knew so well, but, to their surprise, they heard a new and lovely melody, so softly, sweetly played, that they could hardly believe it could be Nat. It was one of those songs without words that touch the heart, and sing of all tender home-like hopes and joys, soothing and cheering those who listen to its simple music. Aunt Meg leaned her head on Demi's shoulder, Grandmother wiped her eyes, and Mrs. Jo looked up at Mr. Laurie, saying, in a choky whisper,

"You composed that."

"I wanted your boy to do you honor, and thank you in his own way," answered Laurie, leaning down to answer her.

When Nat made his bow and was about to go, he was called back by many hands, and had to play again. He did so with such a happy face, that it was good to see him, for he did his best, and gave them the gay old tunes that set the feet to dancing, and made quietude impossible.

"Clear the floor!" cried Emil; and in a minute the chairs were pushed back, the older people put safely in corners and the children gathered on the stage.

"Show your manners!" called Emil; and the boys pranced up to the ladies, old and young; with polite invitations to "tread the mazy," as dear Dick Swiveller has it. The small lads nearly came to blows for the Princess, but she chose Dick, like a kind, little gentlewoman as she was, and let him lead her proudly to her place. Mrs. Jo was not allowed to decline; and Aunt Amy filled Dan with unspeakable delight by refusing Franz and taking him. Of course Nan and Tommy, Nat and Daisy paired off, while Uncle Teddy went and got Asia, who was longing to "jig it," and felt much elated by the honor done her. Silas and Mary Ann had a private dance in the hall; and for half-an-hour Plumfield was at its merriest.

The party wound up with a grand promenade of all the young folks, headed by the pumpkin-coach with the Princess and driver inside, and the rats in a wildly frisky state.

While the children enjoyed this final frolic, the elders sat in the parlor looking on as they talked together of the little people with the interest of parents and friends.

"What are you thinking of, all by yourself, with such a happy face, sister Jo?" asked Laurie, sitting down beside her on the sofa.

"My summer's work, Teddy, and amusing myself by imagining the future of my boys," she answered, smiling as she made room for him.

"They are all to be poets, painters, and statesmen, famous soldiers, or at least merchant princes, I suppose."

"No, I am not as aspiring as I once was, and I shall be satisfied if they are honest men. But I will confess that I do expect a little glory and a career for some of them. Demi is not a common child, and I think he will blossom into something good and great in the best sense of the word. The others will do well, I hope, especially my last two boys, for, after hearing Nat play to-night, I really think he has genius."

"Too soon to say; talent he certainly has, and there is no doubt that the boy can soon earn his bread by the work he loves. Build him up for another year or so, and then I will take him off your hands, and launch him properly."

"That is such a pleasant prospect for poor Nat, who came to me six months ago so friendless and forlorn. Dan's future is already plain to me. Mr. Hyde will want him soon, and I mean to give him a brave and faithful little servant. Dan is one who can serve well if the wages are love and confidence, and he has the energy to carve out his own future in his own way. Yes, I am very happy over our success with these boys one so weak, and one so wild; both so much better now, and so full of promise."

"What magic did you use, Jo?"

"I only loved them, and let them see it. Fritz did the rest."

"Dear soul! you look as if 'only loving' had been rather hard work sometimes," said Laurie, stroking her thin cheek with a look of more tender admiration than he had ever given her as a girl.

"I'm a faded old woman, but I'm a very happy one; so don't pity me, Teddy;" and she glanced about the room with eyes full of a sincere content.

"Yes, your plan seems to work better and better every year," he said, with an emphatic nod of approval toward the cheery scene before him.

"How can it fail to work well when I have so much help from you all?" answered Mrs. Jo, looking gratefully at her most generous patron.

"It is the best joke of the family, this school of yours and its success. So unlike the future we planned for you, and yet so suited to you after all. It was a regular inspiration, Jo," said Laurie, dodging her thanks as usual.

"Ah! but you laughed at it in the beginning, and still make all manner of fun of me and my inspirations. Didn't you predict that having girls with the boys would be a dead failure? Now see how well it works;" and she pointed to the happy group of lads and lassies dancing, singing, and chattering together with every sign of kindly good fellowship.

"I give in, and when my Goldilocks is old enough I'll send her to you. Can I say more than that?"

"I shall be so proud to have your little treasure trusted to me. But really, Teddy, the effect of these girls has been excellent. I know you will laugh at me, but I don't mind, I'm used to it; so I'll tell you that one of my favorite fancies is to look at my family as a small world, to watch the progress of my little men, and, lately, to see how well the influence of my little women works upon them. Daisy is the domestic element, and they all feel the charm of her quiet, womanly ways. Nan is the restless, energetic, strong-minded one; they admire her courage, and give her a fair chance to work out her will, seeing that she has sympathy as well as strength, and the power to do much in their small world. Your Bess is the lady, full of natural refinement, grace, and beauty. She polishes them unconsciously, and fills her place as any lovely woman may, using her gentle influence to lift and hold them above the coarse, rough things of life, and keep them gentlemen in the best sense of the fine old word."

"It is not always the ladies who do that best, Jo. It is sometimes the strong brave woman who stirs up the boy and makes a man of him;" and Laurie bowed to her with a significant laugh.

"No; I think the graceful woman, whom the boy you allude to married, has done more for him than the wild Nan of his youth; or, better still, the wise, motherly woman who watched over him, as Daisy watches over Demi, did more to make him what he is;" and Jo turned toward her mother, who sat a little apart with Meg, looking so full of the sweet dignity and beauty of old age, that Laurie gave her a glance of filial respect and love as he replied, in serious earnest,

"All three did much for him, and I can understand how well these little girls will help your lads."

"Not more than the lads help them; it is mutual, I assure you. Nat does much for Daisy with his music; Dan can manage Nan better than any of us; and Demi teaches your Goldilocks so easily and well that Fritz calls them Roger Ascham and Lady Jane Grey. Dear me! if men and women would only trust, understand, and help one another as my children do, what a capital place the world would be!" and Mrs. Jo's eyes grew absent, as if she was looking at a new and charming state of society in which people lived as happily and innocently as her flock at Plumfield.

"You are doing your best to help on the good time, my dear. Continue to believe in it, to work for it, and to prove its possibility by the success of her small experiment," said Mr. March, pausing as he passed to say an encouraging word, for the good man never lost his faith in humanity, and still hoped to see peace, good-will, and happiness reign upon the earth.

"I am not so ambitious as that, father. I only want to give these children a home in which they can be taught a few simple things which will help to make life less hard to them when they go out to fight their battles in the world. Honesty, courage, industry, faith in God, their fellow-creatures, and themselves; that is all I try for."

"That is every thing. Give them these helps, then let them go to work out their life as men and women; and whatever their success or failure is, I think they will remember and bless your efforts, my good son and daughter."

The Professor had joined them, and as Mr. March spoke he gave a hand to each, and left them with a look that was a blessing. As Jo and her husband stood together for a moment talking quietly, and feeling that their summer work had been well done if father approved, Mr. Laurie slipped into the hall, said a word to the children, and all of a sudden the whole flock pranced into the room, joined hands and danced about Father and Mother Bhaer, singing blithely,

*"Summer days are over,*
*Summer work is done;*
*Harvests have been gathered*
*Gayly one by one.*
*Now the feast is eaten,*
*Finished is the play;*
*But one rite remains for*
*Our Thanksgiving-day.*
*"Best of all the harvest*
*In the dear God's sight,*
*Are the happy children*
*In the home to-night;*
*And we come to offer*
*Thanks where thanks are due,*
*With grateful hearts and voices,*
*Father, mother, unto you."*

With the last words the circle narrowed till the good Professor and his wife were taken prisoner by many arms, and half hidden by the bouquet of laughing young faces which surrounded them, proving that one plant had taken root and blossomed beautifully in all the little gardens. For love is a flower that grows in any soil, works its sweet miracles undaunted by autumn frost or winter snow, blooming fair and fragrant all the year, and blessing those who give and those who receive.

END

# BOOK FOUR

# JO'S BOYS AND HOW THEY TURNED OUT.

# A SEQUEL TO "LITTLE MEN."

# CHAPTER 1. TEN YEARS LATER

'If anyone had told me what wonderful changes were to take place here in ten years, I wouldn't have believed it,' said Mrs Jo to Mrs Meg, as they sat on the piazza at Plumfield one summer day, looking about them with faces full of pride and pleasure.

'This is the sort of magic that money and kind hearts can work. I am sure Mr Laurence could have no nobler monument than the college he so generously endowed; and a home like this will keep Aunt March's memory green as long as it lasts,' answered Mrs Meg, always glad to praise the absent.

'We used to believe in fairies, you remember, and plan what we'd ask for if we could have three wishes. Doesn't it seem as if mine had been really granted at last? Money, fame, and plenty of the work I love,' said Mrs Jo, carelessly rumpling up her hair as she clasped her hands over her head just as she used to do when a girl.

'I have had mine, and Amy is enjoying hers to her heart's content. If dear Marmee, John, and Beth were here, it would be quite perfect,' added Meg, with a tender quiver in her voice; for Marmee's place was empty now.

Jo put her hand on her sister's, and both sat silent for a little while, surveying the pleasant scene before them with mingled sad and happy thoughts.

It certainly did look as if magic had been at work, for quiet Plumfield was transformed into a busy little world. The house seemed more hospitable than ever, refreshed now with new paint, added wings, well-kept lawn and garden, and a prosperous air it had not worn when riotous boys swarmed everywhere and it was rather difficult for the Bhaers to make both ends meet. On the hill, where kites used to be flown, stood the fine college which Mr Laurence's munificent legacy had built. Busy students were going to and fro along the paths once trodden by childish feet, and many young men and women were enjoying all the advantages that wealth, wisdom, and benevolence could give them.

Just inside the gates of Plumfield a pretty brown cottage, very like the Dovecote, nestled among the trees, and on the green slope westward Laurie's white-pillared mansion glittered in the sunshine; for when the rapid growth of the city shut in the old house, spoilt Meg's nest, and dared to put a soap-factory under Mr Laurence's indignant nose, our friends emigrated to Plumfield, and the great changes began.

These were the pleasant ones; and the loss of the dear old people was sweetened by the blessings they left behind; so all prospered now in the little community, and Mr Bhaer as president, and Mr March as chaplain of the college, saw their long-cherished dream beautifully realized. The sisters divided the care of the young people among them, each taking the part that suited her best. Meg was the motherly friend of the young women, Jo the confidante and defender of all the youths, and Amy the lady Bountiful who delicately smoothed the way for needy students, and entertained them all so cordially that it was no wonder they named her lovely home Mount Parnassus, so full was it of music, beauty, and the culture hungry young hearts and fancies long for.

The original twelve boys had of course scattered far and wide during these years, but all that lived still remembered old Plumfield, and came wandering back from the four quarters of the earth to tell their various experiences, laugh over the pleasures of the past, and face the duties of the present with fresh courage; for such home-comings keep hearts tender and hands helpful with the memories of young and happy days. A few words will tell the history of each, and then we can go on with the new chapter of their lives.

Franz was with a merchant kinsman in Hamburg, a man of twenty-six now, and doing well. Emil was the jolliest tar that ever 'sailed the ocean blue'. His uncle sent him on a long voyage to disgust him with this adventurous life; but he came home so delighted with it that it was plain this was his profession, and the German kinsman gave him a good chance in his ships; so the lad was happy. Dan was a wanderer still; for after the geological researches in South America he tried sheep-farming in Australia, and was now in California looking up mines. Nat was busy with music at the Conservatory, preparing for a year or two in Germany to finish him off. Tom was studying medicine and trying to like it. Jack was in business with his father, bent on getting rich. Dolly was in college with Stuffy and Ned reading law.

Poor little Dick was dead, so was Billy; and no one could mourn for them, since life would never be happy, afflicted as they were in mind and body.

Rob and Teddy were called the 'Lion and the Lamb'; for the latter was as rampant as the king of beasts, and the former as gentle as any sheep that ever baaed. Mrs Jo called him 'my daughter', and found him the most dutiful of children, with plenty of manliness underlying the quiet manners and tender nature. But in Ted she seemed to see all the faults, whims, aspirations, and fun of her own youth in a new shape. With his tawny locks always in wild confusion, his long legs and arms, loud voice, and continual activity, Ted was a prominent figure at Plumfield. He had his moods of gloom, and fell into the Slough of Despond about once a week, to be hoisted out by patient Rob or his mother, who understood when to let him alone and when to shake him up. He was her pride and joy as well as torment, being a very bright lad for his age, and so full of all sorts of budding talent, that her maternal mind was much exercised as to what this remarkable boy would become.

Demi had gone through College with honour, and Mrs Meg had set her heart on his being a minister—picturing in her fond fancy the first sermon her dignified young parson would preach, as well as the long, useful, and honoured life he was to lead. But John, as she called him now, firmly declined the divinity school, saying he had had enough of books, and needed to know more of men and the world, and caused the dear woman much disappointment by deciding to try a journalist's career. It was a blow; but she knew that young minds cannot be driven, and that experience is the best teacher; so she let him follow his own inclinations, still hoping to see him in the pulpit. Aunt Jo raged when she found that there was to be a reporter in the family, and called him 'Jenkins' on the spot. She liked his literary tendencies, but had reason to detest official Paul Prys, as we shall see later. Demi knew his own mind, however, and tranquilly carried out his plans, unmoved by the tongues of the anxious mammas or the jokes of his mates. Uncle Teddy encouraged him, and painted a splendid career, mentioning Dickens and other celebrities who began as reporters and ended as famous novelists or newspaper men.

The girls were all flourishing. Daisy, as sweet and domestic as ever, was her mother's comfort and companion. Josie at fourteen was a most original young person, full of pranks and peculiarities, the latest of which was a passion for the stage, which caused her quiet mother and sister much anxiety as well as amusement. Bess had grown into a tall, beautiful girl looking several years older than she was, with the same graceful ways and dainty tastes which the little Princess had, and a rich inheritance of both the father's and mother's gifts, fostered by every aid love and money could give. But the pride of the community was naughty Nan; for, like so many restless, wilful children, she was growing into a woman full of the energy and promise that suddenly blossoms when the ambitious seeker finds the work she is fitted to do well. Nan began to study medicine at sixteen, and at twenty was getting on bravely; for now, thanks to other intelligent women, colleges and hospitals were open to her. She had never wavered in her purpose from the childish days when she shocked Daisy in the old willow by saying: 'I don't want any family to fuss over. I shall have an office, with bottles and pestle things in it, and drive round and cure folks.' The future foretold by the little girl the young woman was rapidly bringing to pass, and finding so much happiness in it that nothing could win her from the chosen work. Several worthy young gentlemen had tried to make her change her mind and choose, as Daisy did, 'a nice little house and family to take care of'. But Nan only laughed, and routed the lovers by proposing to look at the tongue which spoke of adoration, or professionally felt the pulse in the manly hand offered for her acceptance. So all departed but one persistent youth, who was such a devoted Traddles it was impossible to quench him.

This was Tom, who was as faithful to his child sweetheart as she to her 'pestle things', and gave a proof of fidelity that touched her very much. He studied medicine for her sake alone, having no taste for it, and a decided fancy for a mercantile life. But Nan was firm, and Tom stoutly kept on, devoutly hoping he might not kill many of his fellow-beings when he came to practise. They were excellent friends, however, and caused much amusement to their comrades, by the vicissitudes of this merry love-chase.

Both were approaching Plumfield on the afternoon when Mrs Meg and Mrs Jo were talking on the piazza. Not together; for Nan was walking briskly along the pleasant road alone, thinking over a case that interested her, and Tom was pegging on behind to overtake her, as if by accident, when the suburbs of the city were past—a little way of his, which was part of the joke.

Nan was a handsome girl, with a fresh colour, clear eye, quick smile, and the self-poised look young women with a purpose always have. She was simply and sensibly dressed, walked easily, and seemed full of vigour, with her broad shoulders well back, arms swinging freely, and the elasticity of youth and health in every motion. The few people she met turned to look at her, as if it was a pleasant sight to see a hearty, happy girl walking countryward that lovely day; and the red-faced young man steaming along behind, hat off and every tight curl wagging with impatience, evidently agreed with them.

Presently a mild 'Hallo!' was borne upon the breeze, and pausing, with an effort to look surprised that was an utter failure, Nan said affably:

'Oh, is that you, Tom?'

'Looks like it. Thought you might be walking out today'; and Tom's jovial face beamed with pleasure.

'You knew it. How is your throat?' asked Nan in her professional tone, which was always a quencher to undue raptures.

'Throat? Oh, ah! yes, I remember. It is well. The effect of that prescription was wonderful. I'll never call homoeopathy a humbug again.'

'You were the humbug this time, and so were the unmedicated pellets I gave you. If sugar or milk can cure diphtheria in this remarkable manner, I'll make a note of it. O Tom, Tom, will you never be done playing tricks?'

'O Nan, Nan, will you never be done getting the better of me?' And the merry pair laughed at one another just as they did in the old times, which always came back freshly when they went to Plumfield.

'Well, I knew I shouldn't see you for a week if I didn't scare up some excuse for a call at the office. You are so desperately busy all the time I never get a word,' explained Tom.

'You ought to be busy too, and above such nonsense. Really, Tom, if you don't give your mind to your lectures, you'll never get on,' said Nan soberly.

'I have quite enough of them as it is,' answered Tom with an air of disgust. 'A fellow must lark a bit after dissecting corpuses all day. I can't stand it long at a time, though some people seem to enjoy it immensely.'

'Then why not leave it, and do what suits you better? I always thought it a foolish thing, you know,' said Nan, with a trace of anxiety in the keen eyes that searched for signs of illness in a face as ruddy as a Baldwin apple.

'You know why I chose it, and why I shall stick to it if it kills me. I may not look delicate, but I've a deep-seated heart complaint, and it will carry me off sooner or later; for only one doctor in the world can cure it, and she won't.'

There was an air of pensive resignation about Tom that was both comic and pathetic; for he was in earnest, and kept on giving hints of this sort, without the least encouragement.

Nan frowned; but she was used to it, and knew how to treat him.

'She is curing it in the best and only way; but a more refractory patient never lived. Did you go to that ball, as I directed?'

'I did.'

'And devote yourself to pretty Miss West?'

'Danced with her the whole evening.'

'No impression made on that susceptible organ of yours?'

'Not the slightest. I gaped in her face once, forgot to feed her, and gave a sigh of relief when I handed her over to her mamma.'

'Repeat the dose as often as possible, and note the symptoms. I predict that you'll "cry for it" by and by.'

'Never! I'm sure it doesn't suit my constitution.'

'We shall see. Obey orders!' sternly.

'Yes, Doctor,' meekly.

Silence reigned for a moment; then, as if the bone of contention was forgotten in the pleasant recollections called up by familiar objects, Nan said suddenly:

'What fun we used to have in that wood! Do you remember how you tumbled out of the big nut-tree and nearly broke your collar-bones?'

'Don't I! and how you steeped me in wormwood till I was a fine mahogany colour, and Aunt Jo wailed over my spoilt jacket,' laughed Tom, a boy again in a minute.

'And how you set the house afire?'

'And you ran off for your band-box?'

'Do you ever say "Thunder-turtles" now?'

'Do people ever call you "Giddy-gaddy"?'

'Daisy does. Dear thing, I haven't seen her for a week.'

'I saw Demi this morning, and he said she was keeping house for Mother Bhaer.'

'She always does when Aunt Jo gets into a vortex. Daisy is a model housekeeper; and you couldn't do better than make your bow to her, if you can't go to work and wait till you are grown up before you begin lovering.'

'Nat would break his fiddle over my head if I suggested such a thing. No, thank you. Another name is engraved upon my heart as indelibly as the blue anchor on my arm. "Hope" is my motto, and "No surrender", yours; see who will hold out longest.'

'You silly boys think we must pair off as we did when children; but we shall do nothing of the kind. How well Parnassus looks from here!' said Nan, abruptly changing the conversation again.

'It is a fine house; but I love old Plum best. Wouldn't Aunt March stare if she could see the changes here?' answered Tom, as they both paused at the great gate to look at the pleasant landscape before them.

A sudden whoop startled them, as a long boy with a wild yellow head came leaping over a hedge like a kangaroo, followed by a slender girl, who stuck in the hawthorn, and sat there laughing like a witch. A pretty little lass she was, with curly dark hair, bright eyes, and a very expressive face. Her hat was at her back, and her skirts a good deal the worse for the brooks she had crossed, the trees she had climbed, and the last leap, which added several fine rents.

'Take me down, Nan, please. Tom, hold Ted; he's got my book, and I will have it,' called Josie from her perch, not at all daunted by the appearance of her friends.

Tom promptly collared the thief, while Nan picked Josie from among the thorns and set her on her feet without a word of reproof; for having been a romp in her own girlhood, she was very indulgent to like tastes in others. 'What's the matter, dear?' she asked, pinning up the longest rip, while Josie examined the scratches on her hands. 'I was studying my part in the willow, and Ted came slyly up and poked the book out of my hands with his rod. It fell in the brook, and before I could scrabble down he was off. You wretch, give it back this moment or I'll box your ears,' cried Josie, laughing and scolding in the same breath.

Escaping from Tom, Ted struck a sentimental attitude, and with tender glances at the wet, torn young person before him, delivered Claude Melnotte's famous speech in a lackadaisical way that was irresistibly funny, ending with 'Dost like the picture, love?' as he made an object of himself by tying his long legs in a knot and distorting his face horribly.

The sound of applause from the piazza put a stop to these antics, and the young folks went up the avenue together very much in the old style when Tom drove four in hand and Nan was the best horse in the team. Rosy, breathless, and merry, they greeted the ladies and sat down on the steps to rest, Aunt Meg sewing up her daughter's rags while Mrs Jo smoothed the Lion's mane, and rescued the book. Daisy appeared in a moment to greet her friend, and all began to talk.

'Muffins for tea; better stay and eat 'em; Daisy's never fail,' said Ted hospitably.

'He's a judge; he ate nine last time. That's why he's so fat,' added Josie, with a withering glance at her cousin, who was as thin as a lath.

'I must go and see Lucy Dove. She has a whitlow, and it's time to lance it. I'll tea at college,' answered Nan, feeling in her pocket to be sure she had not forgotten her case of instruments.

'Thanks, I'm going there also. Tom Merryweather has granulated lids, and I promised to touch them up for him. Save a doctor's fee and be good practice for me. I'm clumsy with my thumbs,' said Tom, bound to be near his idol while he could.

'Hush! Daisy doesn't like to hear you saw-bones talk of your work. Muffins suit us better'; and Ted grinned sweetly, with a view to future favours in the eating line.

'Any news of the Commodore?' asked Tom.

'He is on his way home, and Dan hopes to come soon. I long to see my boys together, and have begged the wanderers to come to Thanksgiving, if not before,' answered Mrs Jo, beaming at the thought.

'They'll come, every man of them, if they can. Even Jack will risk losing a dollar for the sake of one of our jolly old dinners,' laughed Tom.

'There's the turkey fattening for the feast. I never chase him now, but feed him well; and he's "swellin' wisibly", bless his drumsticks!' said Ted, pointing out the doomed fowl proudly parading in a neighbouring field.

'If Nat goes the last of the month we shall want a farewell frolic for him. I suppose the dear old Chirper will come home a second Ole Bull,' said Nan to her friend.

A pretty colour came into Daisy's cheek, and the folds of muslin on her breast rose and fell with a quick breath; but she answered placidly: 'Uncle Laurie says he has real talent, and after the training he will get abroad he can command a good living here, though he may never be famous.'

'Young people seldom turn out as one predicts, so it is of little use to expect anything,' said Mrs Meg with a sigh. 'If our children are good and useful men and women, we should be satisfied; yet it's very natural to wish them to be brilliant and successful.'

'They are like my chickens, mighty uncertain. Now, that fine-looking cockerel of mine is the stupidest one of the lot, and the ugly, long-legged chap is the king of the yard, he's so smart; crows loud enough to wake the Seven Sleepers; but the handsome one croaks, and is no end of a coward. I get snubbed; but you wait till I grow up, and then see'; and Ted looked so like his own long-legged pet that everyone laughed at his modest prediction.

'I want to see Dan settled somewhere. "A rolling stone gathers no moss", and at twenty-five he is still roaming about the world without a tie to hold him, except this'; and Mrs Meg nodded towards her sister.

'Dan will find his place at last, and experience is his best teacher. He is rough still, but each time he comes home I see a change for the better, and never lose my faith in him. He may never do anything great, or get rich; but if the wild boy makes an honest man, I'm satisfied,' said Mrs Jo, who always defended the black sheep of her flock.

'That's right, mother, stand by Dan! He's worth a dozen Jacks and Neds bragging about money and trying to be swells. You see if he doesn't do something to be proud of and take the wind out of their sails,' added Ted, whose love for his 'Danny' was now strengthened by a boy's admiration for the bold, adventurous man.

'Hope so, I'm sure. He's just the fellow to do rash things and come to glory—climbing the Matterhorn, taking a "header" into Niagara, or finding a big nugget. That's his way of sowing wild oats, and perhaps it's better than ours,' said Tom thoughtfully; for he had gained a good deal of experience in that sort of agriculture since he became a medical student.

'Much better!' said Mrs Jo emphatically. 'I'd rather send my boys off to see the world in that way than leave them alone in a city full of temptations, with nothing to do but waste time, money, and health, as so many are left. Dan has to work his way, and that teaches him courage, patience, and self-reliance. I don't worry about him as much as I do about George and Dolly at college, no more fit than two babies to take care of themselves.'

'How about John? He's knocking round town as a newspaper man, reporting all sorts of things, from sermons to prize-fights,' asked Tom, who thought that sort of life would be much more to his own taste than medical lectures and hospital wards.

'Demi has three safeguards—good principles, refined tastes, and a wise mother. He won't come to harm, and these experiences will be useful to him when he begins to write, as I'm sure he will in time,' began Mrs Jo in her prophetic tone; for she was anxious to have some of her geese turn out swans.

'Speak of Jenkins, and you'll hear the rustling of his paper,' cried Tom, as a fresh-faced, brown-eyed young man came up the avenue, waving a newspaper over his head.

'Here's your Evening Tattler! Latest Edition! Awful murder! Bank clerk absconded! Powder-mill explosion, and great strike of the Latin School boys!' roared Ted, going to meet his cousin with the graceful gait of a young giraffe.

'The Commodore is in, and will cut his cable and run before the wind as soon as he can get off,' called Demi, with 'a nice derangement of nautical epitaphs', as he came up smiling over his good news.

Everyone talked together for a moment, and the paper passed from hand to hand that each eye might rest on the pleasant fact that the Brenda, from Hamburg, was safe in port.

'He'll come lurching out by tomorrow with his usual collection of marine monsters and lively yarns. I saw him, jolly and tarry and brown as a coffee-berry. Had a good run, and hopes to be second mate, as the other chap is laid up with a broken leg,' added Demi.

'Wish I had the setting of it,' said Nan to herself, with a professional twist of her hand.

'How's Franz?' asked Mrs Jo.

'He's going to be married! There's news for you. The first of the flock, Aunty, so say good-bye to him. Her name is Ludmilla Heldegard Blumenthal; good family, well-off, pretty, and of course an angel. The dear old boy wants Uncle's consent, and then he will settle down to be a happy and an honest burgher. Long life to him!'

'I'm glad to hear it. I do so like to settle my boys with a good wife and a nice little home. Now, if all is right, I shall feel as if Franz was off my mind,' said Mrs Jo, folding her hands contentedly; for she often felt like a distracted hen with a large brood of mixed chickens and ducks upon her hands.

'So do I,' sighed Tom, with a sly glance at Nan. 'That's what a fellow needs to keep him steady; and it's the duty of nice girls to marry as soon as possible, isn't it, Demi?'

'If there are enough nice fellows to go round. The female population exceeds the male, you know, especially in New England; which accounts for the high state of culture we are in, perhaps,' answered John, who was leaning over his mother's chair, telling his day's experiences in a whisper.

'It is a merciful provision, my dears; for it takes three or four women to get each man into, through, and out of the world. You are costly creatures, boys; and it is well that mothers, sisters, wives, and daughters love their duty and do it so well, or you would perish off the face of the earth,' said Mrs Jo solemnly, as she took up a basket filled with dilapidated hose; for the good Professor was still hard on his socks, and his sons resembled him in that respect.

'Such being the case, there is plenty for the "superfluous women" to do, in taking care of these helpless men and their families. I see that more clearly every day, and am very glad and grateful that my profession will make me a useful, happy, and independent spinster.'

Nan's emphasis on the last word caused Tom to groan, and the rest to laugh.

'I take great pride and solid satisfaction in you, Nan, and hope to see you very successful; for we do need just such helpful women in the world. I sometimes feel as if I've missed my vocation and ought to have remained single; but my duty seemed to point this way, and I don't regret it,' said Mrs Jo, folding a large and very ragged blue sock to her bosom.

'Neither do I. What should I ever have done without my dearest Mum?' added Ted, with a filial hug which caused both to disappear behind the newspaper in which he had been mercifully absorbed for a few minutes.

'My darling boy, if you would wash your hands semi-occasionally, fond caresses would be less disastrous to my collar. Never mind, my precious touslehead, better grass stains and dirt than no cuddlings at all'; and Mrs Jo emerged from that brief eclipse looking much refreshed, though her back hair was caught in Ted's buttons and her collar under one ear.

Here Josie, who had been studying her part at the other end of the piazza, suddenly burst forth with a smothered shriek, and gave Juliet's speech in the tomb so effectively that the boys applauded, Daisy shivered, and Nan murmured: 'Too much cerebral excitement for one of her age.'

'I'm afraid you'll have to make up your mind to it, Meg. That child is a born actress. We never did anything so well, not even the Witch's Curse,' said Mrs Jo, casting a bouquet of many-coloured socks at the feet of her flushed and panting niece, when she fell gracefully upon the door-mat.

'It is a sort of judgement upon me for my passion for the stage when a girl. Now I know how dear Marmee felt when I begged to be an actress. I never can consent, and yet I may be obliged to give up my wishes, hopes, and plans again.'

There was an accent of reproach in his mother's voice, which made Demi pick up his sister with a gentle shake, and the stern command to 'drop that nonsense in public'.

'Drop me, Minion, or I'll give you the Maniac Bride, with my best Ha-ha!' cried Josie, glaring at him like an offended kitten. Being set on her feet, she made a splendid courtesy, and dramatically proclaiming, 'Mrs Woffington's carriage waits,' swept down the steps and round the corner, trailing Daisy's scarlet shawl majestically behind her.

'Isn't she great fun? I couldn't stop in this dull place if I hadn't that child to make it lively for me. If ever she turns prim, I'm off; so mind how you nip her in the bud,' said Teddy, frowning at Demi, who was now writing out shorthand notes on the steps.

'You two are a team, and it takes a strong hand to drive you, but I rather like it. Josie ought to have been my child, and Rob yours, Meg. Then your house would have been all peace and mine all Bedlam. Now I must go and tell Laurie the news. Come with me, Meg, a little stroll will do us good'; and sticking Ted's straw hat on her head, Mrs Jo walked off with her sister, leaving Daisy to attend to the muffins, Ted to appease Josie, and Tom and Nan to give their respective patients a very bad quarter of an hour.

## CHAPTER 2. PARNASSUS

It was well named; and the Muses seemed to be at home that day, for as the newcomers went up the slope appropriate sights and sounds greeted them. Passing an open window, they looked in upon a library presided over by Clio, Calliope, and Urania; Melpomene and Thalia were disporting themselves in the hall, where some young people were dancing and rehearsing a play; Erato was walking in the garden with her lover, and in the music-room Phoebus himself was drilling a tuneful choir.

A mature Apollo was our old friend Laurie, but comely and genial as ever; for time had ripened the freakish boy into a noble man. Care and sorrow, as well as ease and happiness, had done much for him; and the responsibility of carrying out his grandfather's wishes had been a duty most faithfully performed. Prosperity suits some people, and they blossom best in a glow of sunshine; others need the shade, and are the sweeter for a touch of frost. Laurie was one of the former sort, and Amy was another; so life had been a kind of poem to them since they married—not only harmonious and happy, but earnest, useful, and rich in the beautiful benevolence which can do so much when wealth and wisdom go hand in hand with charity. Their house was full of unostentatious beauty and comfort, and here the art-loving host and hostess attracted and entertained artists of all kinds. Laurie had music enough now, and was a generous patron to the class he most liked to help. Amy had her proteges among ambitious young painters and sculptors, and found her own art double dear as her daughter grew old enough to share its labours and delights with her; for she was one of those who prove that women can be faithful wives and mothers without sacrificing the special gift bestowed upon them for their own development and the good of others.

Her sisters knew where to find her, and Jo went at once to the studio, where mother and daughter worked together. Bess was busy with the bust of a little child, while her mother added the last touches to a fine head of her husband. Time seemed to have stood still with Amy, for happiness had kept her young and prosperity given her the culture she needed. A stately, graceful woman, who showed how elegant simplicity could be made by the taste with which she chose her dress and the grace with which she wore it. As someone said: 'I never know what Mrs Laurence has on, but I always receive the impression that she is the best-dressed lady in the room.'

It was evident that she adored her daughter, and well she might; for the beauty she had longed for seemed, to her fond eyes at least, to be impersonated in this younger self. Bess inherited her mother's Diana-like figure, blue eyes, fair skin, and golden hair, tied up in the same classic knot of curls. Also—ah! never-ending source of joy to Amy—she had her father's handsome nose and mouth, cast in a feminine mould. The severe simplicity of a long linen pinafore suited her; and she worked away with the entire absorption of the true artist, unconscious of the loving eyes upon her, till Aunt Jo came in exclaiming eagerly:

'My dear girls, stop your mud-pies and hear the news!'

Both artists dropped their tools and greeted the irrepressible woman cordially, though genius had been burning splendidly and her coming spoilt a precious hour. They were in the full tide of gossip when Laurie, who had been summoned by Meg, arrived, and sitting down between the sisters, with no barricade anywhere, listened with interest to the news of Franz and Emil.

'The epidemic has broke out, and now it will rage and ravage your flock. Be prepared for every sort of romance and rashness for the next ten years, Jo. Your boys are growing up and will plunge headlong into a sea of worse scrapes than any you have had yet,' said Laurie, enjoying her look of mingled delight and despair.

'I know it, and I hope I shall be able to pull them through and land them safely; but it's an awful responsibility, for they will come to me and insist that I can make their poor little loves run smoothly. I like it, though, and Meg is such a mush of sentiment she revels in the prospect,' answered Jo, feeling pretty easy about her own boys, whose youth made them safe for the present.

'I'm afraid she won't revel when our Nat begins to buzz too near her Daisy. Of course you see what all that means? As musical director I am also his confidante, and would like to know what advice to give,' said Laurie soberly.

'Hush! you forget that child,' began Jo, nodding towards Bess, who was at work again.

'Bless you! she's in Athens, and doesn't hear a word. She ought to leave off, though, and go out. My darling, put the baby to sleep, and go for a run. Aunt Meg is in the parlour; go and show her the new pictures till we come,' added Laurie, looking at his tall girl as Pygmalion might have looked at Galatea; for he considered her the finest statue in the house.

'Yes, papa; but please tell me if it is good'; and Bess obediently put down her tools, with a lingering glance at the bust.

'My cherished daughter, truth compels me to confess that one cheek is plumper than the other; and the curls upon its infant brow are rather too much like horns for perfect grace; otherwise it rivals Raphael's Chanting Cherubs, and I'm proud of it.'

Laurie was laughing as he spoke; for these first attempts were so like Amy's early ones, it was impossible to regard them as soberly as the enthusiastic mamma did.

'You can't see beauty in anything but music,' answered Bess, shaking the golden head that made the one bright spot in the cool north lights of the great studio.

'Well, I see beauty in you, dear. And if you are not art, what is? I wish to put a little more nature into you, and get you away from this cold clay and marble into the sunshine, to dance and laugh as the others do. I want a flesh-and-blood girl, not a sweet statue in a grey pinafore, who forgets everything but her work.' As he spoke, two dusty hands came round his neck, and Bess said earnestly, punctuating her words with soft touches of her lips:

'I never forget you, papa; but I do want to do something beautiful that you may be proud of me by and by. Mamma often tells me to stop; but when we get in here we forget there is any world outside, we are so busy and so happy. Now I'll go and run and sing, and be a girl to please you.' And throwing away the apron, Bess vanished from the room, seeming to take all the light with her.

'I'm glad you said that. The dear child is too much absorbed in her artistic dreams for one so young. It is my fault; but I sympathize so deeply in it all, I forget to be wise,' sighed Amy, carefully covering the baby with a wet towel.

'I think this power of living in our children is one of the sweetest things in the world; but I try to remember what Marmee once said to Meg—that fathers should have their share in the education of both girls and boys; so I leave Ted to his father all I can, and Fritz lends me Rob, whose quiet ways are as restful and good for me as Ted's tempests are for his father. Now I advise you, Amy, to let Bess drop the mud-pies for a time, and take up music with Laurie; then she won't be one-sided, and he won't be jealous.'

'Hear, hear! A Daniel—a very Daniel!' cried Laurie, well pleased. 'I thought you'd lend a hand, Jo, and say a word for me. I am a little jealous of Amy, and want more of a share in my girl. Come, my lady, let me have her this summer, and next year, when we go to Rome, I'll give her up to you and high art. Isn't that a fair bargain?'

'I agree; but in trying your hobby, nature, with music thrown in, don't forget that, though only fifteen, our Bess is older than most girls of that age, and cannot be treated like a child. She is so very precious to me, I feel as if I wanted to keep her always as pure and beautiful as the marble she loves so well.'

Amy spoke regretfully as she looked about the lovely room where she had spent so many happy hours with this dear child of hers.

'"Turn and turn about is fair play", as we used to say when we all wanted to ride on Ellen Tree or wear the russet boots,' said Jo briskly; 'so you must share your girl between you, and see who will do the most for her.'

'We will,' answered the fond parents, laughing at the recollections Jo's proverb brought up to them.

'How I did use to enjoy bouncing on the limbs of that old apple-tree! No real horse ever gave me half the pleasure or the exercise,' said Amy, looking out of the high window as if she saw the dear old orchard again and the little girls at play there.

'And what fun I had with those blessed boots!' laughed Jo. 'I've got the relics now. The boys reduced them to rags; but I love them still, and would enjoy a good theatrical stalk in them if it were possible.'

'My fondest memories twine about the warming-pan and the sausage. What larks we had! And how long ago it seems!' said Laurie, staring at the two women before him as if he found it hard to realize that they ever had been little Amy and riotous Jo.

'Don't suggest that we are growing old, my Lord. We have only bloomed; and a very nice bouquet we make with our buds about us,' answered Mrs Amy, shaking out the folds of her rosy muslin with much the air of dainty satisfaction the girl used to show in a new dress.

'Not to mention our thorns and dead leaves,' added Jo, with a sigh; for life had never been very easy to her, and even now she had her troubles both within and without.

'Come and have a dish of tea, old dear, and see what the young folks are about. You are tired, and want to be "stayed with flagons and comforted with apples",' said Laurie, offering an arm to each sister, and leading them away to afternoon tea, which flowed as freely on Parnassus as the nectar of old.

They found Meg in the summer-parlour, an airy and delightful room, full now of afternoon sunshine and the rustle of trees; for the three long windows opened on the garden. The great music-room was at one end, and at the other, in a deep alcove hung with purple curtains, a little household shrine had been made. Three portraits hung there, two marble busts stood in the corners, and a couch, an oval table, with its urn of flowers, were the only articles of furniture the nook contained. The busts were John Brooke and Beth—Amy's work—both excellent likenesses, and both full of the placid beauty which always recalls the saying, that 'Clay represents life; plaster, death; marble, immortality'. On the right, as became the founder of the house, hung the portrait of Mr Laurence, with its expression of mingled pride and benevolence, as fresh and attractive as when he caught the girl Jo admiring it. Opposite was Aunt March—a legacy to Amy—in an imposing turban, immense sleeves, and long mittens decorously crossed on the front of her plum-coloured satin gown. Time had mellowed the severity of her aspect; and the fixed regard of the handsome old gentleman opposite seemed to account for the amiable simper on lips that had not uttered a sharp word for years.

In the place of honour, with the sunshine warm upon it, and a green garland always round it, was Marmee's beloved face, painted with grateful skill by a great artist whom she had befriended when poor and unknown. So beautifully lifelike was it that it seemed to smile down upon her daughters, saying cheerfully:

'Be happy; I am with you still.'

The three sisters stood a moment looking up at the beloved picture with eyes full of tender reverence and the longing that never left them; for this noble mother had been so much to them that no one could ever fill her place. Only two years since she had gone away to live and love anew, leaving such a sweet memory behind her that it was both an inspiration and a comforter to all the household. They felt this as they drew closer to one another, and Laurie put it into words as he said earnestly:

'I can ask nothing better for my child than that she may be a woman like our mother. Please God, she shall be, if I can do it; for I owe the best I have to this dear saint.'

Just then a fresh voice began to sing 'Ave Maria' in the music-room, and Bess unconsciously echoed her father's prayer for her as she dutifully obeyed his wishes. The soft sound of the air Marmee used to sing led the listeners back into the world again from that momentary reaching after the loved and lost, and they sat down together near the open windows enjoying the music, while Laurie brought them tea, making the little service pleasant by the tender care he gave to it.

Nat came in with Demi, soon followed by Ted and Josie, the Professor and his faithful Rob, all anxious to hear more about 'the boys'. The rattle of cups and tongues grew brisk, and the setting sun saw a cheerful company resting in the bright room after the varied labours of the day.

Professor Bhaer was grey now, but robust and genial as ever; for he had the work he loved, and did it so heartily that the whole college felt his beautiful influence. Rob was as much like him as it was possible for a boy to be, and was already called the 'young Professor', he so adored study and closely imitated his honoured father in all ways.

'Well, heart's dearest, we go to have our boys again, all two, and may rejoice greatly,' said Mr Bhaer, seating himself beside Jo with a beaming face and a handshake of congratulation.

'Oh, Fritz, I'm so delighted about Emil, and if you approve about Franz also. Did you know Ludmilla? Is it a wise match?' asked Mrs Jo, handing him her cup of tea and drawing closer, as if she welcomed her refuge in joy as well as sorrow.

'It all goes well. I saw the Madchen when I went over to place Franz. A child then, but most sweet and charming. Blumenthal is satisfied, I think, and the boy will be happy. He is too German to be content away from Vaterland, so we shall have him as a link between the new and the old, and that pleases me much.'

'And Emil, he is to be second mate next voyage; isn't that fine? I'm so happy that both your boys have done well; you gave up so much for them and their mother. You make light of it, dear, but I never forget it,' said Jo, with her hand in his as sentimentally as if she was a girl again and her Fritz had come a-wooing.

He laughed his cheery laugh, and whispered behind her fan: 'If I had not come to America for the poor lads, I never should have found my Jo. The hard times are very sweet now, and I bless Gott for all I seemed to lose, because I gained the blessing of my life.'

'Spooning! spooning! Here's an awful flirtation on the sly,' cried Teddy, peering over the fan just at that interesting moment, much to his mother's confusion and his father's amusement; for the Professor never was ashamed of the fact that he still considered his wife the dearest woman in the world. Rob promptly ejected his brother from one window, to see him skip in at the other, while Mrs Jo shut her fan and held it ready to rap her unruly boy's knuckles if he came near her again.

Nat approached in answer to Mr Bhaer's beckoning teaspoon, and stood before them with a face full of the respectful affection he felt for the excellent man who had done so much for him.

'I have the letters ready for thee, my son. They are two old friends of mine in Leipzig, who will befriend thee in that new life. It is well to have them, for thou wilt be heartbroken with Heimweh at the first, Nat, and need comforting,' said the Professor, giving him several letters.

'Thanks, sir. Yes, I expect to be pretty lonely till I get started, then my music and the hope of getting on will cheer me up,' answered Nat, who both longed and dreaded to leave all these friends behind him and make new ones.

He was a man now; but the blue eyes were as honest as ever, the mouth still a little weak, in spite of the carefully cherished moustache over it, and the broad forehead more plainly than ever betrayed the music-loving nature of the youth. Modest, affectionate, and dutiful, Nat was considered a pleasant though not a brilliant success by Mrs Jo. She loved and trusted him, and was sure he would do his best, but did not expect that he would be great in any way, unless the stimulus of foreign training and self-dependence made him a better artist and a stronger man than now seemed likely.

'I've marked all your things—or rather, Daisy did—and as soon as your books are collected, we can see about the packing,' said Mrs Jo, who was so used to fitting boys off for all quarters of the globe that a trip to the North Pole would not have been too much for her.

Nat grew red at mention of that name—or was it the last glow of sunset on his rather pale cheek?—and his heart beat happily at the thought of the dear girl working Ns and Bs on his humble socks and handkerchiefs; for Nat adored Daisy, and the cherished dream of his life was to earn a place for himself as a musician and win this angel for his wife. This hope did more for him than the Professor's counsels, Mrs Jo's care, or Mr Laurie's generous help. For her sake he worked, waited, and hoped, finding courage and patience in the dream of that happy future when Daisy should make a little home for him and he fiddle a fortune into her lap. Mrs Jo knew this; and though he was not exactly the man she would have chosen for her niece, she felt that Nat would always need just the wise and loving care Daisy could give him, and that without it there was danger of his being one of the amiable and aimless men who fail for want of the right pilot to steer them safely through the world. Mrs Meg decidedly frowned upon the poor boy's love, and would not hear of giving her dear girl to any but the best man to be found on the face of the earth. She was very kind, but as firm as such gentle souls can be; and Nat fled for comfort to Mrs Jo, who always espoused the interests of her boys heartily. A new set of anxieties was beginning now that the aforesaid boys were growing up, and she foresaw no end of worry as well as amusement in the love-affairs already budding in her flock. Mrs Meg was usually her best ally and adviser, for she loved romances as well now as when a blooming girl herself. But in this case she hardened her heart, and would not hear a word of entreaty. 'Nat was not man enough, never would be, no one knew his family, a musician's life was a hard one; Daisy was too young, five or six years hence when time had proved both perhaps. Let us see what absence will do for him.' And that was the end of it, for when the maternal Pelican was roused she could be very firm, though for her precious children she would have plucked her last feather and given the last drop of her blood.

Mrs Jo was thinking of this as she looked at Nat while he talked with her husband about Leipzig, and she resolved to have a clear understanding with him before he went; for she was used to confidences, and talked freely with her boys about the trials and temptations that beset all lives in the beginning, and so often mar them, for want of the right word at the right moment.

This is the first duty of parents, and no false delicacy should keep them from the watchful care, the gentle warning, which makes self-knowledge and self-control the compass and pilot of the young as they leave the safe harbour of home.

'Plato and his disciples approach,' announced irreverent Teddy, as Mr March came in with several young men and women about him; for the wise old man was universally beloved, and ministered so beautifully to his flock that many of them thanked him all their lives for the help given to both hearts and souls.

Bess went to him at once; for since Marmee died, Grandpapa was her special care, and it was sweet to see the golden head bend over the silver one as she rolled out his easy-chair and waited on him with tender alacrity.

'Aesthetic tea always on tap here, sir; will you have a flowing bowl or a bit of ambrosia?' asked Laurie, who was wandering about with a sugar-basin in one hand and a plate of cake in the other; for sweetening cups and feeding the hungry was work he loved.

'Neither, thanks; this child has taken care of me'; and Mr March turned to Bess, who sat on one arm of his chair, holding a glass of fresh milk.

'Long may she live to do it, sir, and I be here to see this pretty contradiction of the song that "youth and age cannot live together"!' answered Laurie, smiling at the pair. '"Crabbed age", papa; that makes all the difference in the world,' said Bess quickly; for she loved poetry, and read the best.

*'Wouldst thou see fresh roses grow*
*In a reverend bed of snow?'*

quoted Mr March, as Josie came and perched on the other arm, looking like a very thorny little rose; for she had been having a hot discussion with Ted, and had got the worst of it.

'Grandpa, must women always obey men and say they are the wisest, just because they are the strongest?' she cried, looking fiercely at her cousin, who came stalking up with a provoking smile on the boyish face that was always very comical atop of that tall figure.

'Well, my dear, that is the old-fashioned belief, and it will take some time to change it. But I think the woman's hour has struck; and it looks to me as if the boys must do their best, for the girls are abreast now, and may reach the goal first,' answered Mr March, surveying with paternal satisfaction the bright faces of the young women, who were among the best students in the college.

'The poor little Atalantas are sadly distracted and delayed by the obstacles thrown in their way—not golden apples, by any means—but I think they will stand a fair chance when they have learned to run better,' laughed Uncle Laurie, stroking Josie's breezy hair, which stood up like the fur of an angry kitten.

'Whole barrels of apples won't stop me when I start, and a dozen Teds won't trip me up, though they may try. I'll show him that a woman can act as well, if not better, than a man. It has been done, and will be again; and I'll never own that my brain isn't as good as his, though it may be smaller,' cried the excited young person.

'If you shake your head in that violent way you'll addle what brains you have got; and I'd take care of 'em, if I were you,' began teasing Ted.

'What started this civil war?' asked Grandpapa, with a gentle emphasis on the adjective, which caused the combatants to calm their ardour a little.

'Why, we were pegging away at the Iliad and came to where Zeus tells Juno not to inquire into his plans or he'll whip her, and Jo was disgusted because Juno meekly hushed up. I said it was all right, and agreed with the old fellow that women didn't know much and ought to obey men,' explained Ted, to the great amusement of his hearers.

'Goddesses may do as they like, but those Greek and Trojan women were poor-spirited things if they minded men who couldn't fight their own battles and had to be hustled off by Pallas, and Venus, and Juno, when they were going to get beaten. The idea of two armies stopping and sitting down while a pair of heroes flung stones at one another! I don't think much of your old Homer. Give me Napoleon or Grant for my hero.'

Josie's scorn was as funny as if a humming-bird scolded at an ostrich, and everyone laughed as she sniffed at the immortal poet and criticized the gods.

'Napoleon's Juno had a nice time; didn't she? That's just the way girls argue—first one way and then the other,' jeered Ted.

'Like Johnson's young lady, who was "not categorical, but all wiggle-waggle",' added Uncle Laurie, enjoying the battle immensely.

'I was only speaking of them as soldiers. But if you come to the woman side of it, wasn't Grant a kind husband and Mrs Grant a happy woman? He didn't threaten to whip her if she asked a natural question; and if Napoleon did do wrong about Josephine, he could fight, and didn't want any Minerva to come fussing over him. They were a stupid set, from dandified Paris to Achilles sulking in his ships, and I won't change my opinion for all the Hectors and Agamemnons in Greece,' said Josie, still unconquered.

'You can fight like a Trojan, that's evident; and we will be the two obedient armies looking on while you and Ted have it out,' began Uncle Laurie, assuming the attitude of a warrior leaning on his spear.

'I fear we must give it up, for Pallas is about to descend and carry off our Hector,' said Mr March, smiling, as Jo came to remind her son that suppertime was near.

'We will fight it out later when there are no goddesses to interfere,' said Teddy, as he turned away with unusual alacrity, remembering the treat in store.

'Conquered by a muffin, by Jove!' called Josie after him, exulting in an opportunity to use the classical exclamation forbidden to her sex.

But Ted shot a Parthian arrow as he retired in good order by replying, with a highly virtuous expression:

'Obedience is a soldier's first duty.'

Bent on her woman's privilege of having the last word, Josie ran after him, but never uttered the scathing speech upon her lips, for a very brown young man in a blue suit came leaping up the steps with a cheery 'Ahoy! ahoy! where is everybody?'

'Emil! Emil!' cried Josie, and in a moment Ted was upon him, and the late enemies ended their fray in a joyful welcome to the newcomer.

Muffins were forgotten, and towing their cousin like two fussy little tugs with a fine merchantman, the children returned to the parlour, where Emil kissed all the women and shook hands with all the men except his uncle; him he embraced in the good old German style, to the great delight of the observers.

'Didn't think I could get off today, but found I could, and steered straight for old Plum. Not a soul there, so I luffed and bore away for Parnassus, and here is every man Jack of you. Bless your hearts, how glad I am to see you all!' exclaimed the sailor boy, beaming at them, as he stood with his legs apart as if he still felt the rocking deck under his feet.

'You ought to "shiver your timbers", not "bless our hearts", Emil; it's not nautical at all. Oh, how nice and shippy and tarry you do smell!' said Josie, sniffing at him with great enjoyment of the fresh sea odours he brought with him. This was her favourite cousin, and she was his pet; so she knew that the bulging pockets of the blue jacket contained treasures for her at least.

'Avast, my hearty, and let me take soundings before you dive,' laughed Emil, understanding her affectionate caresses, and holding her off with one hand while with the other he rummaged out sundry foreign little boxes and parcels marked with different names, and handed them round with appropriate remarks, which caused much laughter; for Emil was a wag.

'There's a hawser that will hold our little cock-boat still about five minutes,' he said, throwing a necklace of pretty pink coral over Josie's head; 'and here's something the mermaids sent to Undine,' he added, handing Bess a string of pearly shells on a silver chain.

I thought Daisy would like a fiddle, and Nat can find her a beau,' continued the sailor, with a laugh, as he undid a dainty filigree brooch in the shape of a violin.

'I know she will, and I'll take it to her,' answered Nat, as he vanished, glad of an errand, and sure that he could find Daisy though Emil had missed her.

Emil chuckled, and handed out a quaintly carved bear whose head opened, showing a capacious ink-stand. This he presented, with a scrape, to Aunt Jo.

'Knowing your fondness for these fine animals, I brought this one to your pen.'

'Very good, Commodore! Try again,' said Mrs Jo, much pleased with her gift, which caused the Professor to prophesy 'works of Shakespeare' from its depths, so great would be the inspiration of the beloved bruin.

'As Aunt Meg will wear caps, in spite of her youth, I got Ludmilla to get me some bits of lace. Hope you'll like 'em'; and out of a soft paper came some filmy things, one of which soon lay like a net of snowflakes on Mrs Meg's pretty hair.

'I couldn't find anything swell enough for Aunt Amy, because she has everything she wants, so I brought a little picture that always makes me think of her when Bess was a baby'; and he handed her an oval ivory locket, on which was painted a goldenhaired Madonna, with a rosy child folded in her blue mantle.

'How lovely!' cried everyone; and Aunt Amy at once hung it about her neck on the blue ribbon from Bess's hair, charmed with her gift; for it recalled the happiest year of her life.

'Now, I flatter myself I've got just the thing for Nan, neat but not gaudy, a sort of sign you see, and very appropriate for a doctor,' said Emil, proudly displaying a pair of lava earrings shaped like little skulls.

'Horrid!' And Bess, who hated ugly things, turned her eyes to her own pretty shells.

'She won't wear earrings,' said Josie.

'Well, she'll enjoy punching your ears then. She's never so happy as when she's overhauling her fellow creatures and going for 'em with a knife,' answered Emil, undisturbed. 'I've got a lot of plunder for you fellows in my chest, but I knew I should have no peace till my cargo for the girls was unloaded. Now tell me all the news.' And, seated on Amy's best marbletopped table, the sailor swung his legs and talked at the rate of ten knots an hour, till Aunt Jo carried them all off to a grand family tea in honour of the Commodore.

# CHAPTER 3. JO'S LAST SCRAPE

The March family had enjoyed a great many surprises in the course of their varied career, but the greatest of all was when the Ugly Duckling turned out to be, not a swan, but a golden goose, whose literary eggs found such an unexpected market that in ten years Jo's wildest and most cherished dream actually came true. How or why it happened she never clearly understood, but all of a sudden she found herself famous in a small way, and, better still, with a snug little fortune in her pocket to clear away the obstacles of the present and assure the future of her boys.

It began during a bad year when everything went wrong at Plumfield; times were hard, the school dwindled, Jo overworked herself and had a long illness; Laurie and Amy were abroad, and the Bhaers too proud to ask help even of those as near and dear as this generous pair. Confined to her room, Jo got desperate over the state of affairs, till she fell back upon the long-disused pen as the only thing she could do to help fill up the gaps in the income. A book for girls being wanted by a certain publisher, she hastily scribbled a little story describing a few scenes and adventures in the lives of herself and sisters, though boys were more in her line, and with very slight hopes of success sent it out to seek its fortune.

Things always went by contraries with Jo. Her first book, laboured over for years, and launched full of the high hopes and ambitious dreams of youth, foundered on its voyage, though the wreck continued to float long afterward, to the profit of the publisher at least. The hastily written story, sent away with no thought beyond the few dollars it might bring, sailed with a fair wind and a wise pilot at the helm into public favour, and came home heavily laden with an unexpected cargo of gold and glory.

A more astonished woman probably never existed than Josephine Bhaer when her little ship came into port with flags flying, cannon that had been silent before now booming gaily, and, better than all, many kind faces rejoicing with her, many friendly hands grasping hers with cordial congratulations. After that it was plain sailing, and she merely had to load her ships and send them off on prosperous trips, to bring home stores of comfort for all she loved and laboured for.

The fame she never did quite accept; for it takes very little fire to make a great deal of smoke nowadays, and notoriety is not real glory. The fortune she could not doubt, and gratefully received; though it was not half so large a one as a generous world reported it to be. The tide having turned continued to rise, and floated the family comfortably into a snug harbour where the older members could rest secure from storms, and whence the younger ones could launch their boats for the voyage of life.

All manner of happiness, peace, and plenty came in those years to bless the patient waiters, hopeful workers, and devout believers in the wisdom and justice of Him who sends disappointment, poverty, and sorrow to try the love of human hearts and make success the sweeter when it comes. The world saw the prosperity, and kind souls rejoiced over the improved fortunes of the family; but the success Jo valued most, the happiness that nothing could change or take away, few knew much about.

It was the power of making her mother's last years happy and serene; to see the burden of care laid down for ever, the weary hands at rest, the dear face untroubled by any anxiety, and the tender heart free to pour itself out in the wise charity which was its delight. As a girl, Jo's favourite plan had been a room where Marmee could sit in peace and enjoy herself after her hard, heroic life. Now the dream had become a happy fact, and Marmee sat in her pleasant chamber with every comfort and luxury about her, loving daughters to wait on her as infirmities increased, a faithful mate to lean upon, and grand-children to brighten the twilight of life with their dutiful affection. A very precious time to all, for she rejoiced as only mothers can in the good fortunes of their children. She had lived to reap the harvest she sowed; had seen prayers answered, hopes blossom, good gifts bear fruit, peace and prosperity bless the home she had made; and then, like some brave, patient angel, whose work was done, turned her face heavenward, glad to rest.

This was the sweet and sacred side of the change; but it had its droll and thorny one, as all things have in this curious world of ours. After the first surprise, incredulity, and joy, which came to Jo, with the ingratitude of human nature, she soon tired of renown, and began to resent her loss of liberty. For suddenly the admiring public took possession of her and all her affairs, past, present, and to come. Strangers demanded to look at her, question, advise, warn, congratulate, and drive her out of her wits by well-meant but very wearisome attentions. If she declined to open her heart to them, they reproached her; if she refused to endow her pet charities, relieve private wants, or sympathize with every ill and trial known to humanity, she was called hard-hearted, selfish, and haughty; if she found it impossible to answer the piles of letters sent her, she was neglectful of her duty to the admiring public; and if she preferred the privacy of home to the pedestal upon which she was requested to pose, 'the airs of literary people' were freely criticized.

She did her best for the children, they being the public for whom she wrote, and laboured stoutly to supply the demand always in the mouths of voracious youth—'More stories; more right away!' Her family objected to this devotion at their expense, and her health suffered; but for a time she gratefully offered herself up on the altar of juvenile literature, feeling that she owed a good deal to the little friends in whose sight she had found favour after twenty years of effort.

But a time came when her patience gave out; and wearying of being a lion, she became a bear in nature as in name, and returning to her den, growled awfully when ordered out. Her family enjoyed the fun, and had small sympathy with her trials, but Jo came to consider it the worse scrape of her life; for liberty had always been her dearest possession, and it seemed to be fast going from her. Living in a lantern soon loses its charm, and she was too old, too tired, and too busy to like it. She felt that she had done all that could reasonably be required of her when autographs, photographs, and autobiographical sketches had been sown broadcast over the land; when artists had taken her home in all its aspects, and reporters had taken her in the grim one she always assumed on these trying occasions; when a series of enthusiastic boarding-schools had ravaged her grounds for trophies, and a steady stream of amiable pilgrims had worn her doorsteps with their respectful feet; when servants left after a week's trial of the bell that rang all day; when her husband was forced to guard her at meals, and the boys to cover her retreat out of back windows on certain occasions when enterprising guests walked in unannounced at unfortunate moments.

A sketch of one day may perhaps explain the state of things, offer some excuse for the unhappy woman, and give a hint to the autograph-fiend now rampant in the land; for it is a true tale.

'There ought to be a law to protect unfortunate authors,' said Mrs Jo one morning soon after Emil's arrival, when the mail brought her an unusually large and varied assortment of letters. 'To me it is a more vital subject than international copyright; for time is money, peace is health, and I lose both with no return but less respect for my fellow creatures and a wild desire to fly into the wilderness, since I cannot shut my doors even in free America.'

'Lion-hunters are awful when in search of their prey. If they could change places for a while it would do them good; and they'd see what bores they were when they "do themselves the honour of calling to express their admiration of our charming work",' quoted Ted, with a bow to his parent, now frowning over twelve requests for autographs.

'I have made up my mind on one point,' said Mrs Jo with great firmness. 'I will not answer this kind of letter. I've sent at least six to this boy, and he probably sells them. This girl writes from a seminary, and if I send her one all the other girls will at once write for more. All begin by saying they know they intrude, and that I am of course annoyed by these requests; but they venture to ask because I like boys, or they like the books, or it is only one. Emerson and

Whittier put these things in the wastepaper-basket; and though only a literary nursery-maid who provides moral pap for the young, I will follow their illustrious example; for I shall have no time to eat or sleep if I try to satisfy these dear unreasonable children'; and Mrs Jo swept away the entire batch with a sigh of relief.

'I'll open the others and let you eat your breakfast in peace, liebe Mutter,' said Rob, who often acted as her secretary. 'Here's one from the South'; and breaking an imposing seal, he read:

'MADAM, As it has pleased Heaven to bless your efforts with a large fortune, I feel no hesitation in asking you to supply funds to purchase a new communion-service for our church. To whatever denomination you belong, you will of course respond with liberality to such a request,

'Respectfully yours,

'MRS X.Y. ZAVIER'

'Send a civil refusal, dear. All I have to give must go to feed and clothe the poor at my gates. That is my thank-offering for success. Go on,' answered his mother, with a grateful glance about her happy home.

'A literary youth of eighteen proposes that you put your name to a novel he has written; and after the first edition your name is to be taken off and his put on. There's a cool proposal for you. I guess you won't agree to that, in spite of your soft-heartedness towards most of the young scribblers.'

'Couldn't be done. Tell him so kindly, and don't let him send the manuscript. I have seven on hand now, and barely time to read my own,' said Mrs Jo, pensively fishing a small letter out of the slop-bowl and opening it with care, because the down-hill address suggested that a child wrote it.

'I will answer this myself. A little sick girl wants a book, and she shall have it, but I can't write sequels to all the rest to please her. I should never come to an end if I tried to suit these voracious little Oliver Twists, clamouring for more. What next, Robin?'

'This is short and sweet.

'DEAR MRS BHAER, I am now going to give you my opinion of your works. I have read them all many times, and call them first-rate. Please go ahead.

'Your admirer,

'BILLY BABCOCK'

'Now that is what I like. Billy is a man of sense and a critic worth having, since he had read my works many times before expressing his opinion. He asks for no answer, so send my thanks and regards.'

'Here's a lady in England with seven girls, and she wishes to know your views upon education. Also what careers they shall follow the oldest being twelve. Don't wonder she's worried,' laughed Rob.

'I'll try to answer it. But as I have no girls, my opinion isn't worth much and will probably shock her, as I shall tell her to let them run and play and build up good, stout bodies before she talks about careers. They will soon show what they want, if they are let alone, and not all run in the same mould.'

'Here's a fellow who wants to know what sort of a girl he shall marry, and if you know of any like those in your stories.'

'Give him Nan's address, and see what he'll get,' proposed Ted, privately resolving to do it himself if possible.

'This is from a lady who wants you to adopt her child and lend her money to study art abroad for a few years. Better take it, and try your hand at a girl, mother.'

'No, thank you, I will keep to my own line of business. What is that blotted one? It looks rather awful, to judge by the ink,' asked Mrs Jo, who beguiled her daily task by trying to guess from the outside what was inside her many letters. This proved to be a poem from an insane admirer, to judge by its incoherent style.

*'TO J.M.B.*

*'Oh, were I a heliotrope,*

*I would play poet,*
*And blow a breeze of fragrance*
*To you; and none should know it.*

*'Your form like the stately elm*
*When Phoebus gilds the morning ray;*
*Your cheeks like the ocean bed*
*That blooms a rose in May.*

*'Your words are wise and bright,*
*I bequeath them to you a legacy given;*
*And when your spirit takes its flight,*
*May it bloom aflower in heaven.*

*'My tongue in flattering language spoke,*
*And sweeter silence never broke*
*in busiest street or loneliest glen.*
*I take you with the flashes of my pen.*

*'Consider the lilies, how they grow;*
*They toil not, yet are fair,*
*Gems and flowers and Solomon's seal.*
*The geranium of the world is J. M. Bhaer.*

*'JAMES'*

While the boys shouted over this effusion—which is a true one—their mother read several liberal offers from budding magazines for her to edit them gratis; one long letter from a young girl inconsolable because her favourite hero died, and 'would dear Mrs Bhaer rewrite the tale, and make it end good?' another from an irate boy denied an autograph, who darkly foretold financial ruin and loss of favour if she did not send him and all other fellows who asked autographs, photographs, and auto-biographical sketches; a minister wished to know her religion; and an undecided maiden asked which of her two lovers she should marry. These samples will suffice to show a few of the claims made on a busy woman's time, and make my readers pardon Mrs Jo if she did not carefully reply to all.

'That job is done. Now I will dust a bit, and then go to my work. I'm all behind-hand, and serials can't wait; so deny me to everybody, Mary. I won't see Queen Victoria if she comes today.' And Mrs Bhaer threw down her napkin as if defying all creation.

'I hope the day will go well with thee, my dearest,' answered her husband, who had been busy with his own voluminous correspondence. 'I will dine at college with Professor Plock, who is to visit us today. The Junglings can lunch on Parnassus; so thou shalt have a quiet time.' And smoothing the worried lines out of her forehead with his good-bye kiss, the excellent man marched away, both pockets full of books, an old umbrella in one hand, and a bag of stones for the geology class in the other.

'If all literary women had such thoughtful angels for husbands, they would live longer and write more. Perhaps that wouldn't be a blessing to the world though, as most of us write too much now,' said Mrs Jo, waving her feather duster to her spouse, who responded with flourishes of the umbrella as he went down the avenue.

Rob started for school at the same time, looking so much like him with his books and bag and square shoulders and steady air that his mother laughed as she turned away, saying heartily: 'Bless both my dear professors, for better creatures never lived!'

Emil was already gone to his ship in the city; but Ted lingered to steal the address he wanted, ravage the sugar-bowl, and talk with 'Mum'; for the two had great larks together. Mrs Jo always arranged her own parlour, refilled her vases, and gave the little touches that left it cool and neat for the day. Going to draw down the curtain, she beheld an artist sketching on the lawn, and groaned as she hastily retired to the back window to shake her duster.

At that moment the bell rang and the sound of wheels was heard in the road.

'I'll go; Mary lets 'em in'; and Ted smoothed his hair as he made for the hall.

'Can't see anyone. Give me a chance to fly upstairs,' whispered Mrs Jo, preparing to escape. But before she could do so, a man appeared at the door with a card in his hand. Ted met him with a stern air, and his mother dodged behind the window-curtains to bide her time for escape.

'I am doing a series of articles for the Saturday Tattler, and I called to see Mrs Bhaer the first of all,' began the newcomer in the insinuating tone of his tribe, while his quick eyes were taking in all they could, experience having taught him to make the most of his time, as his visits were usually short ones.

'Mrs Bhaer never sees reporters, sir.'

'But a few moments will be all I ask,' said the man, edging his way farther in.

'You can't see her, for she is out,' replied Teddy, as a backward glance showed him that his unhappy parent had vanished—through the window, he supposed, as she sometimes did when hard bestead.

'Very sorry. I'll call again. Is this her study? Charming room!' And the intruder fell back on the parlour, bound to see something and bag a fact if he died in the attempt. 'It is not,' said Teddy, gently but firmly backing him down the hall, devoutly hoping that his mother had escaped round the corner of the house.

'If you could tell me Mrs Bhaer's age and birthplace, date of marriage, and number of children, I should be much obliged,' continued the unabashed visitor as he tripped over the door-mat.

'She is about sixty, born in Nova Zembla, married just forty years ago today, and has eleven daughters. Anything else, sir?' And Ted's sober face was such a funny contrast to his ridiculous reply that the reporter owned himself routed, and retired laughing just as a lady followed by three beaming girls came up the steps.

'We are all the way from Oshkosh, and couldn't go home without seein' dear Aunt Jo. My girls just admire her works, and lot on gettin' a sight of her. I know it's early; but we are goin' to see Holmes and Longfeller, and the rest of the celebrities, so we ran out here fust thing. Mrs Erastus Kingsbury Parmalee, of Oshkosh, tell her. We don't mind waitin'; we can look round a spell if she ain't ready to see folks yet.'

All this was uttered with such rapidity that Ted could only stand gazing at the buxom damsels, who fixed their six blue eyes upon him so beseechingly that his native gallantry made it impossible to deny them a civil reply at least.

'Mrs Bhaer is not visible today—out just now, I believe; but you can see the house and grounds if you like,' he murmured, falling back as the four pressed in gazing rapturously about them.

'Oh, thank you! Sweet, pretty place I'm sure! That's where she writes, ain't it? Do tell me if that's her picture! Looks just as I imagined her!'

With these remarks the ladies paused before a fine engraving of the Hon. Mrs Norton, with a pen in her hand and a rapt expression of countenance, likewise a diadem and pearl necklace.

Keeping his gravity with an effort, Teddy pointed to a very bad portrait of Mrs Jo, which hung behind the door, and afforded her much amusement, it was so dismal, in spite of a curious effect of light upon the end of the nose and cheeks as red as the chair she sat in.

'This was taken for my mother; but it is not very good,' he said, enjoying the struggles of the girls not to look dismayed at the sad difference between the real and the ideal. The youngest, aged twelve, could not conceal her disappointment, and turned away, feeling as so many of us have felt when we discover that our idols are very ordinary men and women.

'I thought she'd be about sixteen and have her hair braided in two tails down her back. I don't care about seeing her now,' said the honest child, walking off to the hall door, leaving her mother to apologize, and her sisters to declare that the bad portrait was 'perfectly lovely, so speaking and poetic, you know, 'specially about the brow'.

'Come girls, we must be goin', if we want to get through today. You can leave your albums and have them sent when Mrs Bhaer has written a sentiment in 'em. We are a thousand times obliged. Give our best love to your ma, and tell her we are so sorry not to see her.' Just as Mrs. Erastus Kingsbury Parmalee uttered the words her eye fell upon a middle-aged woman in a large checked apron, with a handkerchief tied over her head, busily dusting an end room which looked like a study.

'One peep at her sanctum since she is out,' cried the enthusiastic lady, and swept across the hall with her flock before Teddy could warn his mother, whose retreat had been cut off by the artist in front, the reporter at the back of the house—for he hadn't gone and the ladies in the hall.

'They've got her!' thought Teddy, in comical dismay. 'No use for her to play housemaid since they've seen the portrait.'

Mrs Jo did her best, and being a good actress, would have escaped if the fatal picture had not betrayed her. Mrs Parmalee paused at the desk, and regardless of the meerschaum that lay there, the man's slippers close by, and a pile of letters directed to 'Prof. F. Bhaer', she clasped her hands, exclaiming impressively: 'Girls, this is the spot where she wrote those sweet, those moral tales which have thrilled us to the soul! Could I—ah, could I take one morsel of paper, an old pen, a postage stamp even, as a memento of this gifted woman?'

'Yes'm, help yourselves,' replied the maid, moving away with a glance at the boy, whose eyes were now full of merriment he could not suppress.

The oldest girl saw it, guessed the truth, and a quick look at the woman in the apron confirmed her suspicion. Touching her mother, she whispered: 'Ma, it's Mrs Bhaer herself. I know it is.'

'No? yes? it is! Well, I do declare, how nice that is!' And hastily pursuing the unhappy woman, who was making for the door, Mrs Parmalee cried eagerly:

'Don't mind us! I know you're busy, but just let me take your hand and then we'll go.'

Giving herself up for lost, Mrs Jo turned and presented her hand like a tea-tray, submitting to have it heartily shaken, as the matron said, with somewhat alarming hospitality:

'If ever you come to Oshkosh, your feet won't be allowed to touch the pavement; for you'll be borne in the arms of the populace, we shall be so dreadful glad to see you.'

Mentally resolving never to visit that effusive town, Jo responded as cordially as she could; and having written her name in the albums, provided each visitor with a memento, and kissed them all round, they at last departed, to call on 'Longfeller, Holmes, and the rest'—who were all out, it is devoutly to be hoped.

'You villain, why didn't you give me a chance to whip away? Oh, my dear, what fibs you told that man! I hope we shall be forgiven our sins in this line, but I don't know what is to become of us if we don't dodge. So many against one isn't fair play.' And Mrs Jo hung up her apron in the hall closet, with a groan at the trials of her lot.

'More people coming up the avenue! Better dodge while the coast is clear! I'll head them off!' cried Teddy, looking back from the steps, as he was departing to school.

Mrs Jo flew upstairs, and having locked her door, calmly viewed a young ladies' seminary camp on the lawn, and being denied the house, proceed to enjoy themselves by picking the flowers, doing up their hair, eating lunch, and freely expressing their opinion of the place and its possessors before they went.

A few hours of quiet followed, and she was just settling down to a long afternoon of hard work, when Rob came home to tell her that the Young Men's Christian Union would visit the college, and two or three of the fellows whom she knew wanted to pay their respects to her on the way.

'It is going to rain, so they won't come, I dare say; but father thought you'd like to be ready, in case they do call. You always see the boys, you know, though you harden your heart to the poor girls,' said Rob, who had heard from his brother about the morning visitations.

'Boys don't gush, so I can stand it. The last time I let in a party of girls one fell into my arms and said, "Darling, love me!" I wanted to shake her,' answered Mrs Jo, wiping her pen with energy.

'You may be sure the fellows won't do it, but they will want autographs, so you'd better be prepared with a few dozen,' said Rob, laying out a quire of notepaper, being a hospitable youth and sympathizing with those who admired his mother.

'They can't outdo the girls. At X College I really believe I wrote three hundred during the day I was there, and I left a pile of cards and albums on my table when I came away. It is one of the most absurd and tiresome manias that ever afflicted the world.'

Nevertheless Mrs Jo wrote her name a dozen times, put on her black silk, and resigned herself to the impending call, praying for rain, however, as she returned to her work.

The shower came, and feeling quite secure, she rumpled up her hair, took off her cuffs, and hurried to finish her chapter; for thirty pages a day was her task, and she liked to have it well done before evening. Josie had brought some flowers for the vases, and was just putting the last touches when she saw several umbrellas bobbing down the hill.

'They are coming, Aunty! I see uncle hurrying across the field to receive them,' she called at the stair-foot.

'Keep an eye on them, and let me know when they enter the avenue. It will take but a minute to tidy up and run down,' answered Mrs Jo, scribbling away for dear life, because serials wait for no man, not even the whole Christian Union en masse.

'There are more than two or three. I see half a dozen at least,' called sister Ann from the hall door. 'No! a dozen, I do believe; Aunty, look out; they are all coming! What shall we do?' And Josie quailed at the idea of facing the black throng rapidly approaching.

'Mercy on us, there are hundreds! Run and put a tub in the back entry for their umbrellas to drip into. Tell them to go down the hall and leave them, and pile their hats on the table; the tree won't hold them all. No use to get mats; my poor carpets!' And down went Mrs Jo to prepare for the invasion, while Josie and the maids flew about dismayed at the prospect of so many muddy boots.

On they came, a long line of umbrellas, with splashed legs and flushed faces underneath; for the gentlemen had been having a good time all over the town, undisturbed by the rain. Professor Bhaer met them at the gate, and was making a little speech of welcome, when Mrs Jo, touched by their bedraggled state, appeared at the door, beckoning them in. Leaving their host to orate bareheaded in the wet, the young men hastened up the steps, merry, warm, and eager, clutching off their hats as they came, and struggling with their umbrellas, as the order was passed to march in and stack arms.

Tramp, tramp, tramp, down the hall went seventy-five pairs of boots; soon seventy-five umbrellas dripped sociably in the hospitable tub, while their owners swarmed all over the lower part of the house; and seventy-five hearty hands were shaken by the hostess without a murmur, though some were wet, some very warm, and nearly all bore trophies of the day's ramble. One impetuous party flourished a small turtle as he made his compliments; another had a load of sticks cut from noted spots; and all begged for some memento of Plumfield. A pile of cards mysteriously appeared on the table, with a written request for autographs; and despite her morning vow, Mrs Jo wrote everyone, while her husband and boys did the honours of the house.

Josie fled to the back parlour, but was discovered by exploring youths, and mortally insulted by one of them, who innocently inquired if she was Mrs Bhaer. The reception did not last long, and the end was better than the beginning; for the rain ceased, and a rainbow shone beautifully over them as the good fellows stood upon the lawn singing sweetly for a farewell. A happy omen, that bow of promise arched over the young heads, as if Heaven smiled upon their union, and showed them that above the muddy earth and rainy skies the blessed sun still shone for all. Three cheers, and then away they went, leaving a pleasant recollection of their visit to amuse the family as they scraped the mud off the carpets with shovels and emptied the tub half-full of water.

'Nice, honest, hard-working fellows, and I don't begrudge my half-hour at all; but I must finish, so don't let anyone disturb me till tea-time,' said Mrs Jo, leaving Mary to shut up the house; for papa and the boys had gone off with the guests, and Josie had run home to tell her mother about the fun at Aunt Jo's.

Peace reigned for an hour, then the bell rang and Mary came giggling up to say: 'A queer kind of a lady wants to know if she can catch a grasshopper in the garden.'

'A what?' cried Mrs Jo, dropping her pen with a blot; for of all the odd requests ever made, this was the oddest.

'A grasshopper, ma'am. I said you was busy, and asked what she wanted, and says she: "I've got grasshoppers from the grounds of several famous folks, and I want one from Plumfield to add to my collection." Did you ever?' And Mary giggled again at the idea.

'Tell her to take all there are and welcome. I shall be glad to get rid of them; always bouncing in my face and getting in my dress,' laughed Mrs Jo.

Mary retired, to return in a moment nearly speechless with merriment.

'She's much obliged, ma'am, and she'd like an old gown or a pair of stockings of yours to put in a rug she's making. Got a vest of Emerson's, she says, and a pair of Mr. Holmes's trousers, and a dress of Mrs Stowe's. She must be crazy!'

'Give her that old red shawl, then I shall make a gay show among the great ones in that astonishing rug. Yes, they are all lunatics, these lion-hunters; but this seems to be a harmless maniac, for she doesn't take my time, and gives me a good laugh,' said Mrs Jo, returning to her work after a glance from the window, which showed her a tall, thin lady in rusty black, skipping wildly to and fro on the lawn in pursuit of the lively insect she wanted.

No more interruptions till the light began to fade, then Mary popped her head in to say a gentleman wished to see Mrs Bhaer, and wouldn't take no for an answer.

'He must. I shall not go down. This has been an awful day, and I won't be disturbed again,' replied the harassed authoress, pausing in the midst of the grand finale of her chapter.

'I told him so, ma'am; but he walked right in as bold as brass. I guess he's another crazy one, and I declare I'm 'most afraid of him, he's so big and black, and cool as cucumbers, though I will say he's good-looking,' added Mary, with a simper; for the stranger had evidently found favour in her sight despite his boldness.

'My day has been ruined, and I will have this last half-hour to finish. Tell him to go away; I won't go down,' cried Mrs Jo, fiercely.

Mary went; and listening, in spite of herself, her mistress heard first a murmur of voices, then a cry from Mary, and remembering the ways of reporters, also that her maid was both pretty and timid, Mrs Bhaer flung down her pen and went to the rescue. Descending with her most majestic air she demanded in an awe-inspiring voice, as she paused to survey the somewhat brigandish intruder, who seemed to be storming the staircase which Mary was gallantly defending:

'Who is this person who insists on remaining when I have declined to see him?'

'I'm sure I don't know, ma'am. He won't give no name, and says you'll be sorry if you don't see him,' answered Mary, retiring flushed and indignant from her post.

'Won't you be sorry?' asked the stranger, looking up with a pair of black eyes full of laughter, the flash of white teeth through a long beard, and both hands out as he boldly approached the irate lady.

Mrs Jo gave one keen look, for the voice was familiar; then completed Mary's bewilderment by throwing both arms round the brigand's neck, exclaiming joyfully: 'My dearest boy, where did you come from?'

'California, on purpose to see you, Mother Bhaer. Now won't you be sorry if I go away?' answered Dan, with a hearty kiss.

'To think of my ordering you out of the house when I've been longing to see you for a year,' laughed Mrs Jo, and she went down to have a good talk with her returned wanderer, who enjoyed the joke immensely.

# CHAPTER 4. DAN

Mrs Jo often thought that Dan had Indian blood in him, not only because of his love of a wild, wandering life, but his appearance; for as he grew up, this became more striking. At twenty-five he was very tall, with sinewy limbs, a keen, dark face, and the alert look of one whose senses were all alive; rough in manner, full of energy, quick with word and blow, eyes full of the old fire, always watchful as if used to keep guard, and a general air of vigour and freshness very charming to those who knew the dangers and delights of his adventurous life. He was looking his best as he sat talking with 'Mother Bhaer', one strong brown hand in hers, and a world of affection in his voice as he said:

'Forget old friends! How could I forget the only home I ever knew? Why, I was in such a hurry to come and tell my good luck that I didn't stop to fix up, you see; though I knew you'd think I looked more like a wild buffalo than ever,' with a shake of his shaggy black head, a tug at his beard, and a laugh that made the room ring.

'I like it; I always had a fancy for banditti—and you look just like one. Mary, being a newcomer, was frightened at your looks and manners. Josie won't know you, but Ted will recognize his Danny in spite of the big beard and flowing mane. They will all be here soon to welcome you; so before they come tell me more about yourself. Why, Dan, dear! it's nearly two years since you were here! Has it gone well with you?' asked Mrs Jo, who had been listening with maternal interest to his account of life in California, and the unexpected success of a small investment he had made.

'First-rate! I don't care for the money, you know. I only want a trifle to pay my way—rather earn as I go, and not be bothered with the care of a lot. It's the fun of the thing coming to me, and my being able to give away, that I like. No use to lay up; I shan't live to be old and need it,—my sort never do,' said Dan, looking as if his little fortune rather oppressed him.

'But if you marry and settle somewhere, as I hope you will, you must have something to begin with, my son. So be prudent and invest your money; don't give it away, for rainy days come to all of us, and dependence would be very hard for you to bear,' answered Mrs Jo with a sage air, though she liked to see that the money-making fever had not seized her lucky boy yet.

Dan shook his head, and glanced about the room as if he already found it rather confined and longed for all out-of-doors again.

'Who would marry a jack-o'-lantern like me? Women like a steady-going man; I shall never be that.'

'My dear boy, when I was a girl I liked just such adventurous fellows as you are. Anything fresh and daring, free and romantic, is always attractive to us womenfolk. Don't be discouraged; you'll find an anchor some day, and be content to take shorter voyages and bring home a good cargo.'

'What should you say if I brought you an Indian squaw some day?' asked Dan, with a glimmer of mischief in the eyes that rested on a marble bust of Galatea gleaming white and lovely in the corner.

'Welcome her heartily, if she was a good one. Is there a prospect of it?' and Mrs Jo peered at him with the interest which even literary ladies take in love affairs.

'Not at present, thank you. I'm too busy "to gallivant", as Ted calls it. How is the boy?' asked Dan, skilfully turning the conversation, as if he had had enough of sentiment.

Mrs Jo was off at once, and expatiated upon the talents and virtues of her sons till they came bursting in and fell upon Dan like two affectionate young bears, finding a vent for their joyful emotions in a sort of friendly wrestling-match; in which both got worsted, of course, for the hunter soon settled them. The Professor followed, and tongues went like mill-clappers while Mary lighted up and cook devoted herself to an unusually good supper, instinctively divining that this guest was a welcome one.

After tea Dan was walking up and down the long rooms as he talked, with occasional trips into the hall for a fresher breath of air, his lungs seeming to need more than those of civilized people. In one of these trips he saw a white figure framed in the dark doorway, and paused to look at it. Bess paused also, not recognizing her old friend, and quite unconscious of the pretty picture she made standing, tall and slender, against the soft gloom of the summer night, with her golden hair like a halo round her head, and the ends of a white shawl blown out like wings by the cool wind sweeping through the hail. 'Is it Dan?' she asked, coming in with a gracious smile and outstretched hand.

'Looks like it; but I didn't know you, Princess. I thought it was a spirit,' answered Dan, looking down at her with a curious softness and wonder in his face.

'I've grown very much, but two years have changed you entirely'; and Bess looked up with girlish pleasure at the picturesque figure before her—for it was a decided contrast to the well-dressed people about her.

Before they could say more, Josie rushed in, and, forgetfull of the newly acquired dignity of her teens, let Dan catch her up and kiss her like a child. Not till he set her down did he discover she also was changed, and exclaimed in comic dismay:

'Hallo! Why, you are growing up too! What am I going to do, with no young one to play with? Here's Ted going it like a beanstalk, and Bess a young lady, and even you, my mustard-seed, letting down your frocks and putting on airs.'

The girls laughed, and Josie blushed as she stared at the tall man, conscious that she had leaped before she looked. They made a pretty contrast, these two young cousins—one as fair as a lily, the other a little wild rose. And Dan gave a nod of satisfaction as he surveyed them; for he had seen many bonny girls in his travels, and was glad that these old friends were blooming so beautifully.

'Here! we can't allow any monopoly of Dan!' called Mrs Jo. 'Bring him back and keep an eye on him, or he will be slipping off for another little run of a year or two before we have half seen him.'

Led by these agreeable captors, Dan returned to the parlour to receive a scolding from Josie for getting ahead of all the other boys and looking like a man first.

'Emil is older; but he's only a boy, and dances jigs and sings sailor songs just as he used to. You look about thirty, and as big and black as a villain in a play. Oh, I've got a splendid idea! You are just the thing for Arbaces in The Last Days of Pompeii. We want to act it; have the lion and the gladiators and the eruption. Tom and Ted are going to shower bushels of ashes down and roll barrels of stones about. We wanted a dark man for the Egyptian; and you will be gorgeous in red and white shawls. Won't he, Aunt Jo?'

This deluge of words made Dan clap his hands over his ears; and before Mrs Bhaer could answer her impetuous niece the Laurences, with Meg and her family, arrived, soon followed by Tom and Nan, and all sat down to listen to Dan's adventures—told in brief yet effective manner, as the varying expressions of interest, wonder, merriment, and suspense painted on the circle of faces round him plainly showed. The boys all wanted to start at once for California and make fortunes; the girls could hardly wait for the curious and pretty things he had picked up for them in his travels; while the elders rejoiced heartily over the energy and good prospects of their wild boy.

'Of course you will want to go back for another stroke of luck; and I hope you will have it. But speculation is a dangerous game, and you may lose all you've won,' said Mr Laurie, who had enjoyed the stirring tale as much as any of the boys, and would have liked to rough it with Dan as well as they.

'I've had enough of it, for a while at least; too much like gambling. The excitement is all I care for, and it isn't good for me. I have a notion to try farming out West. It's grand on a large scale; and I feel as if steady work would be rather jolly after loafing round so long. I can make a beginning, and you can send me your black sheep to stock my place with. I tried sheep-farming in Australia, and know something about black ones, any way.'

A laugh chased away the sober look in Dan's face as he ended; and those who knew him best guessed that he had learned a lesson there in San Francisco, and dared not try again.

'That is a capital idea, Dan!' cried Mrs Jo, seeing great hope in this desire to fix himself somewhere and help others. 'We shall know where you are, and can go and see you, and not have half the world between us. I'll send my Ted for a visit. He's such a restless spirit, it would do him good. With you he would be safe while he worked off his surplus energies and learned a wholesome business.'

'I'll use the "shubble and de hoe" like a good one, if I get a chance out there; but the Speranza mines sound rather jollier,' said Ted, examining the samples of ore Dan had brought for the Professor.

'You go and start a new town, and when we are ready to swarm we will come out and settle there. You will want a newspaper very soon, and I like the idea of running one myself much better than grinding away as I do now,' observed Demi, panting to distinguish himself in the journalistic line.

'We could easily plant a new college there. These sturdy Westerners are hungry for learning, and very quick to see and choose the best,' added ever-young Mr March, beholding with his prophetic eye many duplicates of their own flourishing establishment springing up in the wide West.

'Go on, Dan. It is a fine plan, and we will back you up. I shouldn't mind investing in a few prairies and cowboys myself,' said Mr Laurie, always ready to help the lads to help themselves, both by his cheery words and ever-open purse.

'A little money sort of ballasts a fellow, and investing it in land anchors him—for a while, at least. I'd like to see what I can do, but I thought I'd consult you before I decided. Have my doubts about it suiting me for many years; but I can cut loose when I'm tired,' answered Dan, both touched and pleased at the eager interest of these friends in his plans.

'I know you won't like it. After having the whole world to roam over, one farm will seem dreadfully small and stupid,' said Josie, who much preferred the romance of the wandering life which brought her thrilling tales and pretty things at each return.

'Is there any art out there?' asked Bess, thinking what a good study in black and white Dan would make as he stood talking, half turned from the light.

'Plenty of nature, dear; and that is better. You will find splendid animals to model, and scenery such as you never saw in Europe to paint. Even prosaic pumpkins are grand out there. You can play Cinderella in one of them, Josie, when you open your theatre in Dansville,' said Mr Laurie, anxious that no cold water should be thrown on the new plan.

Stage-struck Josie was caught at once, and being promised all the tragic parts on the yet unbuilt stage, she felt a deep interest in the project and begged Dan to lose no time in beginning his experiment. Bess also confessed that studies from nature would be good for her, and wild scenery improve her taste, which might grow over-nice if only the delicate and beautiful were set before her.

'I speak for the practice of the new town,' said Nan, always eager for fresh enterprises. 'I shall be ready by the time you get well started—towns grow so fast out there.'

'Dan isn't going to allow any woman under forty in his place. He doesn't like them, 'specially young and pretty ones,' put in Tom, who was raging with jealousy, because he read admiration for Nan in Dan's eyes.

'That won't affect me, because doctors are exceptions to all rules. There won't be much sickness in Dansville, everyone will lead such active, wholesome lives, and only energetic young people will go there. But accidents will be frequent, owing to wild cattle, fast riding, Indian scrimmages, and the recklessness of Western life. That will just suit me. I long for broken bones, surgery is so interesting and I get so little here,' answered Nan, yearning to put out her shingle and begin.

'I'll have you, Doctor, and be glad of such a good sample of what we can do in the East. Peg away, and I'll send for you as soon as I have a roof to cover you. I'll scalp a few red fellows or smash up a dozen or so of cowboys for your special benefit,' laughed Dan, well pleased with the energy and fine physique which made Nan a conspicuous figure among other girls.

'Thanks. I'll come. Would you just let me feel your arm? Splendid biceps! Now, boys, see here: this is what I call muscle.' And Nan delivered a short lecture with Dan's sinewy arm to illustrate it. Tom retired to the alcove and glowered at the stars, while he swung his own right arm with a vigour suggestive of knocking someone down.

'Make Tom sexton; he'll enjoy burying the patients Nan kills. He's trying to get up the glum expression proper to the business. Don't forget him, Dan,' said Ted, directing attention to the blighted being in the corner.

But Tom never sulked long, and came out from his brief eclipse with the cheerful proposition:

'Look here, we'll get the city to ship out to Dansville all the cases of yellow fever, smallpox, and cholera that arrive; then Nan will be happy and her mistakes won't matter much with emigrants and convicts.'

'I should advise settling near Jacksonville, or some such city, that you might enjoy the society of cultivated persons. The Plato Club is there, and a most ardent thirst for philosophy. Everything from the East is welcomed hospitably, and new enterprises would flourish in such kindly soil,' observed Mr March, mildly offering a suggestion, as he sat among the elders enjoying the lively scene.

The idea of Dan studying Plato was very funny; but no one except naughty Ted smiled, and Dan made haste to unfold another plan seething in that active brain of his.

'I'm not sure the farming will succeed, and have a strong leaning towards my old friends the Montana Indians. They are a peaceful tribe, and need help awfully; hundreds have died of starvation because they don't get their share. The Sioux are fighters, thirty thousand strong, so Government fears 'em, and gives 'em all they want. I call that a damned shame!' Dan stopped short as the oath slipped out, but his eyes flashed, and he went on quickly: 'It is just that, and I won't beg pardon. If I'd had any money when I was there I'd have given every cent to those poor devils, cheated out of everything, and waiting patiently, after being driven from their own land to places where nothing will grow. Now, honest agents could do much, and I've a feeling that I ought to go and lend a hand. I know their lingo, and I like 'em. I've got a few thousands, and I ain't sure I have any right to spend it on myself and settle down to enjoy it. Hey?'

Dan looked very manly and earnest as he faced his friends, flushed and excited by the energy of his words; and all felt that little thrill of sympathy which links hearts together by the tie of pity for the wronged.

'Do it, do it!' cried Mrs Jo, fired at once; for misfortune was much more interesting to her than good luck.

'Do it, do it!' echoed Ted, applauding as if at a play, 'and take me along to help. I'm just raging to get among those fine fellows and hunt.'

'Let us hear more and see if it is wise,' said Mr Laurie, privately resolving to people his as yet unbought prairies with Montana Indians, and increase his donations to the society that sent missionaries to this much wronged people.

Dan plunged at once into the history of what he saw among the Dakotas, and other tribes in the Northwest, telling of their wrongs, patience, and courage as if they were his brothers.

'They called me Dan Fire Cloud, because my rifle was the best they ever saw. And Black Hawk was as good a friend as a fellow would want; saved my life more than once, and taught me just what will be useful if I go back. They are down on their luck, now, and I'd like to pay my debts.'

By this time everyone was interested, and Dansville began to lose its charm. But prudent Mr Bhaer suggested that one honest agent among many could not do much, and noble as the effort would be, it was wiser to think over the matter carefully, get influence and authority from the right quarters, and meantime look at lands before deciding.

'Well, I will. I'm going to take a run to Kansas and see how that promises. Met a fellow in 'Frisco who'd been there, and he spoke well of it. The fact is, there's so much to be done every where that I don't know where to catch on, and half wish I hadn't any money,' answered Dan, knitting his brows in the perplexity all kind souls feel when anxious to help at the great task of the world's charity.

'I'll keep it for you till you decide. You are such an impetuous lad you'll give it to the first beggar that gets hold of you. I'll turn it over while you are prospecting, and hand it back when you are ready to invest, shall I?' asked Mr Laurie, who had learned wisdom since the days of his own extravagant youth.

'Thanky, sir, I'd be glad to get rid of it. You just hold on till I say the word; and if anything happens to me this time, keep it to help some other scamp as you helped me. This is my will, and you all witness it. Now I feel better.'

And Dan squared his shoulders as if relieved of a burden, after handing over the belt in which he carried his little fortune.

No one dreamed how much was to happen before Dan came to take his money back, nor how nearly that act was his last will and testament; and while Mr Laurie was explaining how he would invest it, a cheery voice was heard singing:

*'Oh, Peggy was a jolly lass,*
*Ye heave ho, boys, ye heave ho!*
*She never grudged her Jack a glass,*
*Ye heave ho, boys, ye heave ho!*
*And when he sailed the raging main,*
*She faithful was unto her swain,*
*Ye heave ho, boys, ye heave ho!'*

Emil always announced his arrival in that fashion, and in a moment he came hurrying in with Nat, who had been giving lessons in town all day. It was good to see the latter beam at his friend as he nearly shook his hand off; better still to see how Dan gratefully remembered all he owed Nat, and tried to pay the debt in his rough way; and best of all to hear the two travellers compare notes and reel off yarns to dazzle the land-lubbers and home-keepers.

After this addition the house would not contain the gay youngsters, so they migrated to the piazza and settled on the steps, like a flock of night-loving birds. Mr March and the Professor retired to the study, Meg and Amy went to look after the little refection of fruit and cake which was to come, and Mrs Jo and Mr Laurie sat in the long window listening to the chat that went on outside.

'There they are, the flower of our flock!' she said, pointing to the group before them. 'The others are dead or scattered, but these seven boys and four girls are my especial comfort and pride. Counting Alice Heath, my dozen is made up, and my hands are full trying to guide these young lives as far as human skill can do it.'

'When we remember how different they are, from what some of them came, and the home influences about others, I think we may feel pretty well satisfied so far,' answered Mr Laurie soberly, as his eyes rested on one bright head among the black and brown ones, for the young moon shone alike on all.

'I don't worry about the girls; Meg sees to them, and is so wise and patient and tender they can't help doing well; but my boys are more care every year, and seem to drift farther away from me each time they go,' sighed Mrs Jo. 'They will grow up, and I can only hold them by one little thread, which may snap at any time, as it has with Jack and Ned. Dolly and George still like to come back, and I can say my word to them; and dear old Franz is too true ever to forget his own. But the three who are soon going out into the world again I can't help worrying about. Emil's good heart will keep him straight, I hope, and

*'"A sweet little cherub sits up aloft,*
*To look out for the life of poor Jack."'*

Nat is to make his first flight, and he's weak in spite of your strengthening influence; and Dan is still untamed. I fear it will take some hard lesson to do that.'

'He's a fine fellow, Jo, and I almost regret this farming project. A little polish would make a gentleman of him, and who knows what he might become here among us,' answered Mr Laurie, leaning over Mrs Bhaer's chair, just as he used to do years ago when they had mischievous secrets together.

'It wouldn't be safe, Teddy. Work and the free life he loves will make a good man of him, and that is better than any amount of polish, with the dangers an easy life in a city would bring him. We can't change his nature—only help it to develop in the right direction. The old impulses are there, and must be controlled, or he will go wrong. I see that; but his love for us is a safeguard, and we must keep a hold on him till he is older or has a stronger tie to help him.'

Mrs Jo spoke earnestly, for, knowing Dan better than anyone else, she saw that her colt was not thoroughly broken yet, and feared while she hoped, knowing that life would always be hard for one like him. She was sure that before he went away again, in some quiet moment he would give her a glimpse of his inner self, and then she could say the word of warning or encouragement that he needed. So she bided her time, studying him meanwhile, glad to see all that was promising, and quick to detect the harm the world was doing him. She was very anxious to make a success of her 'firebrand' because others predicted failure; but having learned that people cannot be moulded like clay, she contented herself with the hope that this neglected boy might become a good man, and asked no more. Even that was much to expect, so full was he of wayward impulses, strong passions, and the lawless nature born in him. Nothing held him but the one affection of his life—the memory of Plumfield, the fear of disappointing these faithful friends, the pride, stronger than principle, that made him want to keep the regard of the mates who always had admired and loved him in spite of all his faults.

'Don't fret, old dear; Emil is one of the happy-go-lucky sort who always fall on their legs. I'll see to Nat, and Dan is in a good way now. Let him take a look at Kansas, and if the farm plan loses its charm, he can fall back on poor Lo, and really do good out there. He's unusually fitted for that peculiar task and I hope he'll decide to do it. Fighting oppressors, and befriending the oppressed will keep those dangerous energies of his busy, and the life will suit him better than sheep-folds and wheat-fields.'

'I hope so. What is that?' and Mrs Jo leaned forward to listen, as exclamations from Ted and Josie caught her ear.

'A mustang! a real, live one; and we can ride it. Dan, you are a first-class trump!' cried the boy.

'A whole Indian dress for me! Now I can play Namioka, if the boys act Metamora,' added Josie, clapping her hands.

'A buffalo's head for Bess! Good gracious, Dan, why did you bring such a horrid thing as that to her?' asked Nan.

'Thought it would do her good to model something strong and natural. She'll never amount to anything if she keeps on making namby-pamby gods and pet kittens,' answered irreverent Dan, remembering that when he was last here Bess was vibrating distractedly between a head of Apollo and her Persian cat as models.

'Thank you; I'll try it, and if I fail we can put the buffalo up in the hall to remind us of you,' said Bess, indignant at the insult offered the gods of her idolatry, but too well bred to show it except in her voice, which was as sweet and as cold as ice-cream.

'I suppose you won't come out to see our new settlement when the rest do? Too rough for you?' asked Dan, trying to assume the deferential air all the boys used when addressing their Princess.

'I am going to Rome to study for years. All the beauty and art of the world is there, and a lifetime isn't long enough to enjoy it,' answered Bess.

'Rome is a mouldy old tomb compared to the "Garden of the gods" and my magnificent Rockies. I don't care a hang for art; nature is as much as I can stand, and I guess I could show you things that would knock your old masters higher than kites. Better come, and while Josie rides the horses you can model 'em. If a drove of a hundred or so of wild ones can't show you beauty, I'll give up,' cried Dan, waxing enthusiastic over the wild grace and vigour which he could enjoy but had no power to describe.

'I'll come some day with papa, and see if they are better than the horses of St Mark and those on Capitol Hill. Please don't abuse my gods, and I will try to like yours,' said Bess, beginning to think the West might be worth seeing, though no Raphael or Angelo had yet appeared there.

'That's a bargain! I do think people ought to see their own country before they go scooting off to foreign parts, as if the new world wasn't worth discovering,' began Dan, ready to bury the hatchet.

'It has some advantages, but not all. The women of England can vote, and we can't. I'm ashamed of America that she isn't ahead in all good things,' cried Nan, who held advanced views on all reforms, and was anxious about her rights, having had to fight for some of them.

'Oh, please don't begin on that. People always quarrel over that question, and call names, and never agree. Do let us be quiet and happy tonight,' pleaded Daisy, who hated discussion as much as Nan loved it.

'You shall vote as much as you like in our new town, Nan; be mayor and aldermen, and run the whole concern. It's going to be as free as air, or I can't live in it,' said Dan, adding, with a laugh, 'I see Mrs Giddygaddy and Mrs Shakespeare Smith don't agree any better than they used to.'

'If everyone agreed, we should never get on. Daisy is a dear, but inclined to be an old fogy; so I stir her up; and next fall she will go and vote with me. Demi will escort us to do the one thing we are allowed to do as yet.'

'Will you take 'em, Deacon?' asked Dan, using the old name as if he liked it. 'It works capitally in Wyoming.'

'I shall be proud to do it. Mother and the aunts go every year, and Daisy will come with me. She is my better half still; and I don't mean to leave her behind in anything,' said Demi, with an arm round his sister of whom he was fonder than ever.

Dan looked at them wistfully, thinking how sweet it must be to have such a tie; and his lonely youth seemed sadder than ever as he recalled its struggles. A gusty sigh from Tom made sentiment impossible, as he said pensively:

'I always wanted to be a twin. It's so sociable and so cosy to have someone glad to lean on a fellow and comfort him, if other girls are cruel.'

As Tom's unrequited passion was the standing joke of the family, this allusion produced a laugh, which Nan increased by whipping out a bottle of Nux, saying, with her professional air:

'I knew you ate too much lobster for tea. Take four pellets, and your dyspepsia will be all right. Tom always sighs and is silly when he's overeaten.'

'I'll take 'em. These are the only sweet things you ever give me.' And Tom gloomily crunched his dose.

'"Who can minister to a mind diseased, or pluck out a rooted sorrow?" quoted Josie tragically from her perch on the railing.

'Come with me, Tommy, and I'll make a man of you. Drop your pills and powders, and cavort round the world a spell, and you'll soon forget you've got a heart, or a stomach either,' said Dan, offering his one panacea for all ills.

'Ship with me, Tom. A good fit of seasickness will set you up, and a stiff north-easter blow your blue-devils away. Come along as surgeon—easy berth, and no end of larks.'

*'"And if your Nancy frowns, my lad,*
*And scorns a jacket blue,*
*Just hoist your sails for other ports,*
*And find a maid more true."'*

added Emil, who had a fragment of song to cheer every care and sorrow, and freely offered them to his friends.

'Perhaps I'll think of it when I've got my diploma. I'm not going to grind three mortal years and have nothing to show for it. Till then,—'

'I'll never desert Mrs Micawber,' interrupted Teddy, with a gurgling sob. Tom immediately rolled him off the step into the wet grass below; and by the time this slight skirmish was over, the jingle of teaspoons suggested refreshments of a more agreeable sort. In former times the little girls waited on the boys, to save confusion; now the young men flew to serve the ladies, young and old; and that slight fact showed plainly how the tables were turned by time. And what a pleasant arrangement it was! Even Josie sat still, and let Emil bring her berries; enjoying her young lady-hood, till Ted stole her cake, when she forgot manners, and chastised him with a rap on the knuckles. As guest of honour, Dan was only allowed to wait on Bess, who still held the highest place in this small world. Tom carefully selected the best of everything for Nan, to be crushed by the remark:

'I never eat at this hour; and you will have a nightmare if you do.'

So, dutifully curbing the pangs of hunger, he gave the plate to Daisy, and chewed rose-leaves for his supper.

When a surprising quantity of wholesome nourishment had been consumed, someone said, 'Let's sing!' and a tuneful hour followed. Nat fiddled, Demi piped, Dan strummed the old banjo, and Emil warbled a doleful ballad about the wreck of the Bounding Betsey; then everybody joined in the old songs till there was very decidedly 'music in the air'; and passers-by said, as they listened smiling: 'Old Plum is gay tonight!'

When all had gone Dan lingered on the piazza, enjoying the balmy wind that blew up from the hayfields, and brought the breath of flowers from Parnassus; and as he leaned there romantically in the moonlight, Mrs Jo came to shut the door.

'Dreaming dreams, Dan?' she asked, thinking the tender moment might have come. Imagine the shock when, instead of some interesting confidence or affectionate word, Dan swung round, saying bluntly:

'I was wishing I could smoke.'

Mrs Jo laughed at the downfall of her hopes, and answered kindly:

'You may, in your room; but don't set the house afire.'

Perhaps Dan saw a little disappointment in her face, or the memory of the sequel of that boyish frolic touched his heart; for he stooped and kissed her, saying in a whisper: 'Good night, mother.' And Mrs Jo was half satisfied.

# CHAPTER 5. VACATION

Everyone was glad of a holiday next morning, and all lingered over the breakfast-table, till Mrs Jo suddenly exclaimed:

'Why, there's a dog!' And on the threshold of the door appeared a great deer-hound, standing motionless, with his eyes fixed on Dan.

'Hallo, old boy! Couldn't you wait till I came for you? Have you cut away on the sly? Own up now, and take your whipping like a man,' said Dan, rising to meet the dog, who reared on his hind legs to look his master in the face and bark as if uttering an indignant denial of any disobedience.

'All right; Don never lies.' And Dan gave the tall beast a hug, adding as he glanced out of the window, where a man and horse were seen approaching:

'I left my plunder at the hotel over night, not knowing how I should find you. Come out and see Octoo, my mustang; she's a beauty.' And Dan was off, with the family streaming after him, to welcome the newcomer.

They found her preparing to go up the steps in her eagerness to reach her master, to the great dismay of the man, who was holding her back.

'Let her come,' called Dan; 'she climbs like a cat and jumps like a deer. Well, my girl, do you want a gallop?' he asked, as the pretty creature clattered up to him and whinnied with pleasure as he rubbed her nose and slapped her glossy flank.

'That's what I call a horse worth having,' said Ted, full of admiration and delight; for he was to have the care of her during Dan's absence.

'What intelligent eyes! She looks as if she would speak,' said Mrs Jo.

'She talks like a human in her way. Very little that she don't know. Hey, old Lass?' and Dan laid his cheek to hers as if the little black mare was very dear to him.

'What does "Octoo" mean?' asked Rob.

'Lightning; she deserves it, as you'll see. Black Hawk gave her to me for my rifle, and we've had high times together out yonder. She's saved my life more than once. Do you see that scar?'

Dan pointed to a small one, half hidden by the long mane; and standing with his arm about Octoo's neck, he told the story of it.

'Black Hawk and I were after buffalo one time, but didn't find 'em as soon as we expected; so our food gave out, and there we were a hundred miles from Red Deer River, where our camp was. I thought we were done for, but my brave pal says: "Now I'll show you how we can live till we find the herds." We were unsaddling for the night by a little pond; there wasn't a living creature in sight anywhere, not even a bird, and we could see for miles over the prairies. What do you think we did?' And Dan looked into the faces round him.

'Ate worms like the Australian fellows,' said Rob. 'Boiled grass or leaves,' added Mrs Jo.

'Perhaps filled the stomach with clay, as we read of savages doing?' suggested Mr Bhaer.

'Killed one of the horses,' cried Ted, eager for bloodshed of some sort.

'No; but we bled one of them. See, just here; filled a tin cup, put some wild sage leaves in it, with water, and heated it over a fire of sticks. It was good, and we slept well.'

'I guess Octoo didn't.' And Josie patted the animal, with a face full of sympathy.

'Never minded it a bit. Black Hawk said we could live on the horses several days and still travel before they felt it. But by another morning we found the buffalo, and I shot the one whose head is in my box, ready to hang up and scare brats into fits. He's a fierce old fellow, you bet.'

'What is this strap for?' asked Ted, who was busily examining the Indian saddle, the single rein and snaffle, with lariat, and round the neck the leather band he spoke of.

'We hold on to that when we lie along the horse's flank farthest from the enemy, and fire under the neck as we gallop round and round. I'll show you.' And springing into the saddle, Dan was off down the steps, tearing over the lawn at a great pace, sometimes on Octoo's back, sometimes half hidden as he hung by stirrup and strap, and sometimes off altogether, running beside her as she loped along, enjoying the fun immensely; while Don raced after, in a canine rapture at being free again and with his mates.

It was a fine sight—the three wild things at play, so full of vigour, grace, and freedom, that for the moment the smooth lawn seemed a prairie; and the spectators felt as if this glimpse of another life made their own seem rather tame and colourless.

'This is better than a circus!' cried Mrs Jo, wishing she were a girl again, that she might take a gallop on this chained lightning of a horse. 'I foresee that Nan will have her hands full setting bones, for Ted will break every one of his trying to rival Dan.'

'A few falls will not harm, and this new care and pleasure will be good for him in all ways. But I fear Dan will never follow a plough after riding a Pegasus like that,' answered Mr Bhaer, as the black mare leaped the gate and came flying up the avenue, to stop at a word and stand quivering with excitement, while Dan swung himself off and looked up for applause.

He received plenty of it, and seemed more pleased for his pet's sake than for his own. Ted clamoured for a lesson at once, and was soon at ease in the queer saddle, finding Octoo gentle as a lamb, as he trotted away to show off at college. Bess came hastening down the hill, having seen the race from afar; and all collected on the piazza while Dan 'yanked' the cover off the big box the express had 'dumped' before the door—to borrow his own words.

Dan usually travelled in light marching order, and hated to have more luggage than he could carry in his well-worn valise. But now that he had a little money of his own, he had cumbered himself with a collection of trophies won by his bow and spear, and brought them home to bestow upon his friends.

'We shall be devoured with moths,' thought Mrs Jo, as the shaggy head appeared, followed by a wolf-skin rug for her feet, a bear-skin ditto for the Professor's study, and Indian garments bedecked with foxes' tails for the boys.

All nice and warm for a July day, but received with delight nevertheless. Ted and Josie immediately 'dressed up', learned the war-whoop, and proceeded to astonish their friends by a series of skirmishes about the house and grounds, with tomahawks and bows and arrows, till weariness produced a lull.

Gay birds' wings, plumy pampas grass, strings of wampum, and pretty work in beads, bark, and feathers, pleased the girls. Minerals, arrow-heads, and crude sketches interested the Professor; and when the box was empty, Dan gave Mr Laurie, as his gift, several plaintive Indian songs written on birch-bark.

'We only want a tent over us to be quite perfect. I feel as if I ought to give you parched corn and dried meat for dinner, my braves. Nobody will want lamb and green peas after this splendid pow-wow,' said Mrs Jo, surveying the picturesque confusion of the long hall, where people lay about on the rugs, all more or less bedecked with feathers, moccasins, or beads.

'Moose noses, buffalo tongues, bear steaks, and roasted marrow-bones would be the thing, but I don't mind a change; so bring on your baa-baa and green meat,' answered Dan from the box, where he sat in state like a chief among his tribe, with the great hound at his feet.

The girls began to clear up, but made little headway; for everything they touched had a story, and all were thrilling, comical, or wild; so they found it hard to settle to their work, till Dan was carried off by Mr Laurie.

This was the beginning of the summer holiday, and it was curious to see what a pleasant little stir Dan's and Emil's coming made in the quiet life of the studious community; for they seemed to bring a fresh breeze with them that enlivened everyone. Many of the collegians remained during vacation; and Plumfield and Parnassus did their best to make these days pleasant for them, since most came from distant States, were poor, and had few opportunities but this for culture or amusement. Emil was hail-fellow-well-met with men and maids, and went rollicking about in true sailor fashion; but Dan stood rather in awe of the 'fair girl-graduates', and was silent when among them, eyeing them as an eagle might a flock of doves. He got on better with the young men, and was their hero at once. Their admiration for his manly accomplishments did him good; because he felt his educational defects keenly, and often wondered if he could find anything in books to satisfy him as thoroughly as did the lessons he was learning from Nature's splendidly illustrated volume. In spite of his silence, the girls found out his good qualities, and regarded 'the Spaniard', as they named him, with great favour; for his black eyes were more eloquent than his tongue, and the kind creatures tried to show their friendly interests in many charming ways.

He saw this, and endeavoured to be worthy of it—curbing his free speech, toning down his rough manners, and watching the effect of all he said and did, anxious to make a good impression. The social atmosphere warmed his lonely heart, the culture excited him to do his best, and the changes which had taken place during his absence, both in himself and others, made the old home seem like a new world. After the life in California, it was sweet and restful to be here, with these familiar faces round him, helping him to forget much that he regretted, and to resolve to deserve more entirely the confidence of these good fellows, the respect of these innocent girls.

So there was riding, rowing, and picnicking by day, music, dancing, and plays by night; and everyone said there had not been so gay a vacation for years. Bess kept her promise, and let the dust gather on her beloved clay while she went pleasuring with her mates or studied music with her father, who rejoiced over the fresh roses in her cheeks and the laughter which chased away the dreamy look she used to wear. Josie quarrelled less with Ted; for Dan had a way of looking at her which quelled her instantly, and had almost as good an effect upon her rebellious cousin. But Octoo did even more for the lively youth, who found that her charms entirely eclipsed those of the bicycle which had been his heart's delight before. Early and late he rode this untiring beast, and began to gain flesh—to the great joy of his mother, who feared that her beanstalk was growing too fast for health.

Demi, finding business dull, solaced his leisure by photographing everybody he could induce to sit or stand to him, producing some excellent pictures among many failures; for he had a pretty taste in grouping, and endless patience. He might be said to view the world through the lens of his camera, and seemed to enjoy himself very much squinting at his fellow beings from under a bit of black cambric. Dan was a treasure to him; for he took well, and willingly posed in his Mexican costume, with horse and hound, and all wanted copies of these effective photographs. Bess, also, was a favourite sitter; and Demi received a prize at the Amateur Photographic Exhibition for one of his cousin with all her hair about her face, which rose from the cloud of white lace draping the shoulders. These were freely handed round by the proud artist; and one copy had a tender little history yet to be told.

Nat was snatching every minute he could get with Daisy before the long parting; and Mrs Meg relented somewhat, feeling sure that absence would quite cure this unfortunate fancy. Daisy said little; but her gentle face was sad when she was alone, and a few quiet tears dropped on the handkerchiefs she marked so daintily with her own hair. She was sure Nat would not forget her; and life looked rather forlorn without the dear fellow who had been her friend since the days of patty-pans and confidences in the willow-tree. She was an old-fashioned daughter, dutiful and docile, with such love and reverence for her mother that her will was law; and if love was forbidden, friendship must suffice. So she kept her little sorrow to herself, smiled cheerfully at Nat, and made his last days of home-life very happy with every comfort and pleasure she could give, from sensible advice and sweet words to a well-filled work-bag for his bachelor establishment and a box of goodies for the voyage.

Tom and Nan took all the time they could spare from their studies to enjoy high jinks at Plumfield with their old friends; for Emil's next voyage was to be a long one, Nat's absence was uncertain, and no one ever knew when Dan would turn up again. They all seemed to feel that life was beginning to grow serious; and even while they enjoyed those lovely summer days together they were conscious that they were children no longer, and often in the pauses of their fun talked soberly of their plans and hopes, as if anxious to know and help one another before they drifted farther apart on their different ways.

A few weeks were all they had; then the Brenda was ready, Nat was to sail from New York, and Dan went along to see him off; for his own plans fermented in his head, and he was eager to be up and doing. A farewell dance was given on Parnassus in honour of the travellers, and all turned out in their best array and gayest spirits. George and Dolly came with the latest Harvard airs and graces, radiant to behold, in dress-suits and 'crushed hats', as Josie called the especial pride and joy of their boyish souls. Jack and Ned sent regrets and best wishes, and no one mourned their absence; for they were among what Mrs Jo called her failures. Poor Tom got into trouble, as usual, by deluging his head with some highly scented preparation in the vain hope of making his tight curls lie flat and smooth, as was the style. Unhappily, his rebellious crop only kinked the closer, and the odour of many barbers' shops clung to him in spite of his frantic efforts to banish it. Nan wouldn't allow him near her, and flapped her fan vigorously whenever he was in sight; which cut him to the heart, and made him feel like the Peri shut out from Paradise. Of course his mates jeered at him, and nothing but the unquenchable jollity of his nature kept him from despair.

Emil was resplendent in his new uniform, and danced with an abandon which only sailors know. His pumps seemed to be everywhere, and his partners soon lost breath trying to keep up with him; but the girls all declared he steered like an angel, and in spite of his pace no collisions took place; so he was happy, and found no lack of damsels to ship with him.

Having no dress-suit, Dan had been coaxed to wear his Mexican costume, and feeling at ease in the many-buttoned trousers, loose jacket, and gay sash, flung his serape over his shoulder with a flourish and looked his best, doing great execution with his long spurs, as he taught Josie strange steps or rolled his black eyes admiringly after certain blonde damsels whom he dared not address.

The mammas sat in the alcove, supplying pins, smiles, and kindly words to all, especially the awkward youths new to such scenes, and the bashful girls conscious of faded muslins and cleaned gloves. It was pleasant to see stately Mrs Amy promenade on the arm of a tall country boy, with thick boots and a big forehead, or Mrs Jo dance like a girl with a shy fellow whose arms went like pump-handles, and whose face was scarlet with confusion and pride at the honour of treading on the toes of the president's wife. Mrs Meg always had room on her sofa for two or three girls, and Mr Laurie devoted himself to these plain, poorly dressed damsels with a kindly grace that won their hearts and made them happy. The good Professor circulated like refreshments, and his cheerful face shone on all alike, while Mr March discussed Greek comedy in the study with such serious gentlemen as never unbent their mighty minds to frivolous joys.

The long music-room, parlour, hall, and piazza were full of white-gowned maidens with attendant shadows; the air was full of lively voices, and hearts and feet went lightly together as the home band played vigorously, and the friendly moon did her best to add enchantment to the scene.

'Pin me up, Meg; that dear Dunbar boy has nearly rent me "in sunder", as Mr Peggotty would say. But didn't he enjoy himself, bumping against his fellow men and swinging me round like a mop. On these occasions I find that I'm not as young as I was, nor as light of foot. In ten years more we shall be meal-bags, sister; so be resigned.' And Mrs Jo subsided into a corner, much dishevelled by her benevolent exertions.

'I know I shall be stout; but you won't keep still long enough to get much flesh on your bones, dear; and Amy will always keep her lovely figure. She looks about eighteen tonight, in her white gown and roses,' answered Meg, busily pinning up one sister's torn frills, while her eyes fondly followed the other's graceful movements; for Meg still adored Amy in the old fashion.

It was one of the family jokes that Jo was getting fat, and she kept it up, though as yet she had only acquired a matronly outline, which was very becoming. They were laughing over the impending double chins, when Mr Laurie came off duty for a moment.

'Repairing damages as usual, Jo? You never could take a little gentle exercise without returning in rags. Come and have a quiet stroll with me and cool off before supper. I've a series of pretty tableaux to show you while Meg listens to the raptures of lisping Miss Carr, whom I made happy by giving her Demi for a partner.'

As he spoke, Laurie led Jo to the music-room, nearly empty now after a dance which sent the young people into garden and hall. Pausing before the first of the four long windows that opened on a very wide piazza, he pointed to a group outside, saying: 'The name of this is "Jack Ashore".'

A pair of long, blue legs, ending in very neat pumps, hung from the veranda roof among the vines; and roses, gathered by unseen hands, evidently appertaining to aforesaid legs, were being dropped into the laps of several girls perched like a flock of white birds on the railing below; while a manly voice 'fell like a falling star', as it sung this pensive ditty to a most appreciative audience:

*MARY'S DREAM*

*The moon had climbed the eastern hill*
*Which rises o'er the sands of Dee,*
*And from its highest summit shed*
*A silver light on tower and tree,*
*When Mary laid her down to sleep*
*(Her thoughts on Sandy far at sea);*
*When soft and low a voice was heard,*
*Saying, 'Mary, weep no more for me.'*

*She from her pillow gently raised*
*Her head, to see who there might be,*
*And saw young Sandy, shivering stand*
*With visage pale and hollow e'e.*
*'Oh Mary dear, cold is my clay;*
*It lies beneath the stormy sea;*
*Far, far from thee, I sleep in death.*
*Dear Mary, weep no more for me.*

*'Three stormy nights and stormy days*
*We tossed upon the raging main.*
*And long we strove our bark to save;*
*But all our striving was in vain.*
*E'en then, when terror chilled my blood,*
*My heart was filled with love of thee.*
*The storm is past, and I'm at rest;*
*So, Mary, weep no more for me.*

*'Oh maiden dear, yourself prepare;*
*We soon shall meet upon that shore*
*Where love is free from doubt and care,*
*And you and I shall part no more.'*
*Loud crew the cock, the shadow fled;*
*No more her Sandy did she see;*
*But soft the passing spirit said,*
*'Sweet Mary, weep no more for me.'*

'The constant jollity of that boy is worth a fortune to him. He'll never sink with such a buoyant spirit to keep him afloat through life,' said Mrs Jo, as the roses were tossed back with much applause when the song ended.

'Not he; and it's a blessing to be grateful for, isn't it? We moody people know its worth. Glad you like my first tableau. Come and see number two. Hope it isn't spoilt; it was very pretty just now. This is "Othello telling his adventures to Desdemona".'

The second window framed a very picturesque group of three. Mr March in an arm-chair, with Bess on a cushion at his feet, was listening to Dan, who, leaning against a pillar, was talking with unusual animation. The old man was in shadow, but little Desdemona was looking up with the moonlight full upon her into young Othello's face, quite absorbed in the story he was telling so well. The gay drapery over Dan's shoulder, his dark colouring, and the gesture of his arm made the picture very striking, and both spectators enjoyed it with silent pleasure, till Mrs Jo said in a quick whisper:

'I'm glad he's going away. He's too picturesque to have here among so many romantic girls. Afraid his "grand, gloomy, and peculiar" style will be too much for our simple maids.'

'No danger; Dan is in the rough as yet, and always will be, I fancy; though he is improving in many ways. How well Queenie looks in that soft light!'

'Dear little Goldilocks looks well everywhere.' And with a backward glance full of pride and fondness, Mrs Jo went on. But that scene returned to her long afterward and her own prophetic words also.

Number three was a tragical tableau at first sight; and Mr Laurie stifled a laugh as he whispered 'The Wounded Knight', pointing to Tom with his head enveloped in a large handkerchief, as he knelt before Nan, who was extracting a thorn or splinter from the palm of his hand with great skill, to judge from the patient's blissful expression of countenance.

'Do I hurt you?' she asked, turning the hand to the moonlight for a better view.

'Not a bit; dig away; I like it,' answered Tom, regardless of his aching knees and the damage done to his best trousers.

'I won't keep you long.'

'Hours, if you please. Never so happy as here.'

Quite unmoved by this tender remark, Nan put on a pair of large, round-eyed glasses, saying in a matter-of-fact tone: 'Now I see it. Only a splinter, and there it is.

'My hand is bleeding; won't you bind it up?' asked Tom, wishing to prolong the situation.

'Nonsense; suck it. Only take care of it tomorrow if you dissect. Don't want any more blood-poisoning.'

'That was the only time you were kind to me. Wish I'd lost my arm.'

'I wish you'd lost your head; it smells more like turpentine and kerosene than ever. Do take a run in the garden and air it.'

Fearing to betray themselves by laughter, the watchers went on, leaving the Knight to rush away in despair, and the Lady to bury her nose in the cup of a tall lily for refreshment.

'Poor Tom, his fate is a hard one, and he's wasting his time! Do advise him to quit philandering and go to work, Jo.'

'I have, Teddy, often; but it will take some great shock to make that boy wise. I wait with interest to see what it will be. Bless me! what is all this?'

She might well ask; for on a rustic stool stood Ted trying to pose on one foot, with the other extended, and both hands waving in the air. Josie, with several young mates, was watching his contortions with deep interest as they talked about 'little wings', 'gilded wire twisted', and a 'cunning skull-cap'.

'This might be called "Mercury Trying to Fly",' said Mr Laurie, as they peeped through the lace curtains.

'Bless the long legs of that boy! how does he expect to manage them? They are planning for the Owlsdark Marbles, and a nice muddle they will make of my gods and goddesses with no one to show them how,' answered Mrs Jo, enjoying this scene immensely. 'Now, he's got it!' 'That's perfectly splendid!' 'See how long you can keep so!' cried the girls, as Ted managed to maintain his equilibrium a moment by resting one toe on the trellis. Unfortunately this brought all his weight on the other foot; the straw seat of the stool gave way, and the flying Mercury came down with a crash, amid shrieks of laughter from the girls. Being accustomed to ground and lofty tumbling, he quickly recovered himself, and hopped gaily about, with one leg through the stool as he improvised a classic jig.

'Thanks for four nice little pictures. You have given me an idea, and I think some time we will get up regular tableaux of this sort and march our company round a set of dissolving views. New and striking; I'll propose it to our manager and give you all the glory,' said Mrs Jo, as they strolled towards the room whence came the clash of glass and china, and glimpses of agitated black coats.

Let us follow the example of our old friends and stroll about among the young people, eavesdropping, so gathering up various little threads to help in the weaving of the story. George and Dolly were at supper, and having served the ladies in their care stood in a corner absorbing nourishment of all kinds with a vain attempt to conceal hearty appetites under an air of elegant indifference.

'Good spread, this; Laurence does things in style. First-rate coffee, but no wine, and that's a mistake,' said Stuffy, who still deserved his name, and was a stout youth with a heavy eye and bilious complexion.

'Bad for boys, he says. Jove! wish he could see us at some of our wines. Don't we just "splice the main brace" as Emil says,' answered Dolly, the dandy, carefully spreading a napkin over the glossy expanse of shirt-front whereon a diamond stud shone like a lone star. His stutter was nearly outgrown; but he, as well as George, spoke in the tone of condescension, which, with the blase airs they assumed, made a very funny contrast to their youthful faces and foolish remarks. Good-hearted little fellows both, but top-heavy with the pride of being Sophs and the freedom that college life gave them.

'Little Jo is getting to be a deuced pretty girl, isn't she?' said George, with a long sigh of satisfaction as his first mouthful of ice went slowly down his throat.

'H'm—well, fairish. The Princess is rather more to my taste. I like 'em blonde and queenly and elegant, don't you know.'

'Yes, Jo is too lively; might as well dance with a grasshopper. I've tried her, and she's one too many for me. Miss Perry is a nice, easy-going girl. Got her for the german.'

'You'll never be a dancing man. Too lazy. Now I'll undertake to steer any girl and dance down any fellow you please. Dancing's my forte.' And Dolly glanced from his trim feet to his flashing gem with the defiant air of a young turkey-cock on parade.

'Miss Grey is looking for you. Wants more grub. Just see if Miss Nelson's plate is empty, there's a good fellow. Can't eat ice in a hurry.' And George remained in his safe corner, while Dolly struggled through the crowd to do his duty, coming back in a fume, with a splash of salad dressing on his coat-cuff.

'Confound these country chaps! they go blundering round like so many dor-bugs, and make a deuce of a mess. Better stick to books and not try to be society men. Can't do it. Beastly stain. Give it a rub, and let me bolt a mouthful, I'm starved. Never saw girls eat such a lot. It proves that they ought not to study so much. Never liked co-ed,' growled Dolly, much ruffled in spirit.

'So they do. 'Tisn't ladylike. Ought to be satisfied with an ice and a bit of cake, and eat it prettily. Don't like to see a girl feed. We hard-working men need it, and, by Jove, I mean to get some more of that meringue if it's not all gone. Here, waiter! bring along that dish over there, and be lively,' commanded Stuffy, poking a young man in a rather shabby dress-suit, who was passing with a tray of glasses.

His order was obeyed promptly; but George's appetite was taken away the next moment by Dolly's exclaiming, as he looked up from his damaged coat, with a scandalized face:

'You've put your foot in it now, old boy! that's Morton, Mr Bhaer's crack man. Knows everything, no end of a "dig", and bound to carry off all the honours. You won't hear the last of it in a hurry.' And Dolly laughed so heartily that a spoonful of ice flew upon the head of a lady sitting below him, and got him into a scrape also.

Leaving them to their despair, let us listen to the whispered chat of two girls comfortably seated in a recess waiting till their escorts were fed.

'I do think the Laurences give lovely parties. Don't you enjoy them?' asked the younger, looking about her with the eager air of one unused to this sort of pleasure.

'Very much, only I never feel as if I was dressed right. My things seemed elegant at home, and I thought I'd be over over-dressed if anything; but I look countrified and dowdy here. No time or money to change now, even if I knew how to do it,' answered the other, glancing anxiously at her bright pink silk grown, trimmed with cheap lace.

'You must get Mrs Brooke to tell you how to fix your things. She was very kind to me. I had a green silk, and it looked so cheap and horrid by the side of the nice dresses here I felt regularly unhappy about it, and asked her how much a dress like one Mrs Laurence had would cost. That looked so simple and elegant I thought it wouldn't be costly; but it was India mull and Valenciennes lace, so, of course, I couldn't have it. Then Mrs Brooke said: "Get some muslin to cover the green silk, and wear hops or some white flowers, instead of pink, in your hair, and you will have a pretty suit." Isn't it lovely and becoming?' And Miss Burton surveyed herself with girlish satisfaction; for a little taste had softened the harsh green, and hop-bells became her red hair better than roses.

'It's sweet: I've been admiring it. I'll do mine so and ask about my purple one. Mrs Brooke has helped me to get rid of my headaches, and Mary Clay's dyspepsia is all gone since she gave up coffee and hot bread.'

'Mrs Laurence advised me to walk and run and use the gymnasium to cure my round shoulders and open my chest, and I'm a much better figure than I was.'

'Did you know that Mr Laurence pays all Amelia Merrill's bills? Her father failed, and she was heartbroken at having to leave college; but that splendid man just stepped in and made it all right.' 'Yes, and Professor Bhaer has several of the boys down at his house evenings to help them along so they can keep up with the rest; and Mrs Bhaer took care of Charles Mackey herself when he had a fever last year. I do think they are the best and kindest people in the world.'

'So do I, and my time here will be the happiest and most useful years of my life.'

And both girls forgot their gowns and their suppers for a moment to look with grateful, affectionate eyes at the friends who tried to care for bodies and for souls as well as minds.

Now come to a lively party supping on the stairs, girls like foam at the top, and a substratum of youths below, where the heaviest particles always settle. Emil, who never sat if he could climb or perch, adorned the newel-post; Tom, Nat, Demi, and Dan were camped on the steps, eating busily, as their ladies were well served and they had earned a moment's rest, which they enjoyed with their eyes fixed on the pleasing prospect above them.

'I'm so sorry the boys are going. It will be dreadfully dull without them. Now they have stopped teasing and are polite, I really enjoy them,' said Nan, who felt unusually gracious tonight as Tom's mishap kept him from annoying her.

'So do I; and Bess was mourning about it today, though as a general thing she doesn't like boys unless they are models of elegance. She has been doing Dan's head, and it is not quite finished. I never saw her so interested in any work, and it's very well done. He is so striking and big he always makes me think of the Dying Gladiator or some of those antique creatures. There's Bess now. Dear child, how sweet she looks tonight!' answered Daisy, waving her hand as the Princess went by with Grandpa on her arm.

'I never thought he would turn out so well. Don't you remember how we used to call him "the bad boy" and be sure he would become a pirate or something awful because he glared at us and swore sometimes? Now he is the handsomest of all the boys, and very entertaining with his stories and plans. I like him very much; he's so big and strong and independent. I'm tired of mollycoddles and book-worms,' said Nan in her decided way.

'Not handsomer that Nat!' cried loyal Daisy, contrasting two faces below, one unusually gay, the other sentimentally sober even in the act of munching cake. 'I like Dan, and am glad he is doing well; but he tires me, and I'm still a little afraid of him. Quiet people suit me best.'

'Life is a fight, and I like a good soldier. Boys take things too easily, don't see how serious it all is and go to work in earnest. Look at that absurd Tom, wasting his time and making an object of himself just because he can't have what he wants, like a baby crying for the moon. I've no patience with such nonsense,' scolded Nan, looking down at the jovial Thomas, who was playfully putting macaroons in Emil's shoes, and trying to beguile his exile as best he could.

'Most girls would be touched by such fidelity. I think it's beautiful,' said Daisy behind her fan; for other girls sat just below.

'You are a sentimental goose and not a judge. Nat will be twice the man when he comes back after his trip. I wish Tom was going with him. My idea is that if we girls have any influence we should use it for the good of these boys, and not pamper them up, making slaves of ourselves and tyrants of them. Let them prove what they can do and be before they ask anything of us, and give us a chance to do the same. Then we know where we are, and shall not make mistakes to mourn over all our lives.'

'Hear, hear!' cried Alice Heath, who was a girl after Nan's own heart, and had chosen a career, like a brave and sensible young woman. 'Only give us a chance, and have patience till we can do our best. Now we are expected to be as wise as men who have had generations of all the help there is, and we scarcely anything. Let us have equal opportunities, and in a few generations we will see what the judgement is. I like justice, and we get very little of it.'

'Still shouting the battle-cry of freedom?' asked Demi, peering through the banisters at this moment. 'Up with your flag! I'll stand by and lend a hand if you want it. With you and Nan to lead the van, I think you won't need much help.'

'You are a great comfort, Demi, and I'll call on you in all emergencies; for you are an honest boy, and don't forget that you owe much to your mother and your sisters and your aunts,' continued Nan. 'I do like men who come out frankly and own that they are not gods. How can we think them so when such awful mistakes are being made all the time by these great creatures? See them sick, as I do, then you know them.'

'Don't hit us when we are down; be merciful, and set us up to bless and believe in you evermore,' pleaded Demi from behind the bars.

'We'll be kind to you if you will be just to us. I don't say generous, only just. I went to a suffrage debate in the Legislature last winter; and of all the feeble, vulgar twaddle I ever heard, that was the worst; and those men were our representatives. I blushed for them, and the wives and mothers. I want an intelligent man to represent me, if I can't do it myself, not a fool.'

'Nan is on the stump. Now we shall catch it,' cried Tom, putting up an umbrella to shield his unhappy head; for Nan's earnest voice was audible, and her indignant eye happened to rest on him as she spoke.

'Go on, go on! I'll take notes, and put in "great applause" liberally,' added Demi, producing his ball-book and pencil, with his Jenkins air.

Daisy pinched his nose through the bars, and the meeting was rather tumultuous for a moment, for Emil called: 'Avast, avast, here's a squall to wind'ard'; Tom applauded wildly; Dan looked up as if the prospect of a fight, even with words, pleased him, and Nat went to support Demi, as his position seemed to be a good one. At this crisis, when everyone laughed and talked at once, Bess came floating through the upper hall and looked down like an angel of peace upon the noisy group below, as she asked, with wondering eyes and smiling lips:

'What is it?'

'An indignation meeting. Nan and Alice are on the rampage, and we are at the bar to be tried for our lives. Will Your Highness preside and judge between us?' answered Demi, as a lull at once took place; for no one rioted in the presence of the Princess.

'I'm not wise enough. I'll sit here and listen. Please go on.' And Bess took her place above them all as cool and calm as a little statue of Justice, with fan and nosegay in place of sword and scales.

'Now, ladies, free your minds, only spare us till morning; for we've got a german to dance as soon as everyone is fed, and Parnassus expects every man to do his duty. Mrs President Giddy-gaddy has the floor,' said Demi, who liked this sort of fun better than the very mild sort of flirtation which was allowed at Plumfield, for the simple reason that it could not be entirely banished, and is a part of all education, co- or otherwise.

'I have only one thing to say, and it is this,' began Nan soberly, though her eyes sparkled with a mixture of fun and earnestness. 'I want to ask every boy of you what you really think on this subject. Dan and Emil have seen the world and ought to know their own minds. Tom and Nat have had five examples before them for years. Demi is ours and we are proud of him. So is Rob. Ted is a weathercock, and Dolly and George, of course, are fogies in spite of the Annex, and girls at Girton going ahead of the men. Commodore, are you ready for the question?'

'Ay, ay, skipper.'

'Do you believe in Woman's Suffrage?'

'Bless your pretty figger head! I do, and I'll ship a crew of girls any time you say so. Aren't they worse than a press-gang to carry a fellow out of his moorings? Don't we all need one as pilot to steer us safe to port? and why shouldn't they share our mess afloat and ashore since we are sure to be wrecked without 'em?'

'Good for you, Emil! Nan will take you for first mate after that handsome speech,' said Demi, as the girls applauded, and Tom glowered. 'Now, Dan, you love liberty so well yourself, are you willing we should have it?'

'All you can get, and I'll fight any man who's mean enough to say you don't deserve it.'

This brief and forcible reply delighted the energetic President, and she beamed upon the member from California, as she said briskly:

'Nat wouldn't dare to say he was on the other side even if he were, but I hope he has made up his mind to pipe for us, at least when we take the field, and not be one of those who wait till the battle is won, and then beat the drums and share the glory.'

Mrs Giddy-gaddy's doubts were most effectually removed, and her sharp speech regretted, as Nat looked up blushing, but with a new sort of manliness in face and manner, saying, in a tone that touched them all:

'I should be the most ungrateful fellow alive if I did not love, honour, and serve women with all my heart and might, for to them I owe everything I am or ever shall be.'

Daisy clapped her hands, and Bess threw her bouquet into Nat's lap, while the other girls waved their fans, well pleased; for real feeling made his little speech eloquent.

'Thomas B. Bangs, come into court, and tell the truth, the whole truth, and nothing but the truth, if you can,' commanded Nan, with a rap to call the meeting to order.

Tom shut the umbrella, and standing up raised his hand, saying solemnly:

'I believe in suffrage of all kinds. I adore all women, and will die for them at any moment if it will help the cause.'

'Living and working for it is harder, and therefore more honourable. Men are always ready to die for us, but not to make our lives worth having. Cheap sentiment and bad logic. You will pass, Tom, only don't twaddle. Now, having taken the sense of the meeting we will adjourn, as the hour for festive gymnastics has arrived. I am glad to see that old Plum has given six true men to the world, and hope they will continue to be staunch to her and the principles she has taught them, wherever they may go. Now, girls, don't sit in draughts, and, boys, beware of ice-water when you are warm.'

With this characteristic close Nan retired from office, and the girls went to enjoy one of the few rights allowed them.

# CHAPTER 6. LAST WORDS

The next day was Sunday, and a goodly troop of young and old set forth to church.—some driving, some walking, all enjoying the lovely weather and the happy quietude which comes to refresh us when the work and worry of the week are over. Daisy had a headache; and Aunt Jo remained at home to keep her company, knowing very well that the worst ache was in the tender heart struggling dutifully against the love that grew stronger as the parting drew nearer.

'Daisy knows my wishes, and I trust her. You must keep an eye on Nat, and let him clearly understand that there is to be no "lovering", or I shall forbid the letter-writing. I hate to seem cruel, but it is too soon for my dear girl to bind herself in any way,' said Mrs Meg, as she rustled about in her best grey silk, while waiting for Demi, who always escorted his pious mother to church as a peace-offering for crossing her wishes in other things.

'I will, dear; I'm lying in wait for all three boys today, like an old spider; and I will have a good talk with each. They know I understand them, and they always open their hearts sooner or later. You look like a nice, plump little Quakeress, Meg; and no one will believe that big boy is your son,' added Mrs Jo, as Demi came in shining with Sunday neatness, from his well-blacked boots to his smooth brown head.

'You flatter me, to soften my heart toward your boy. I know your ways, Jo, and I don't give in. Be firm, and spare me a scene by and by. As for John, as long as he is satisfied with his old mother, I don't care what people think,' answered Mrs Meg, accepting with a smile the little posy of sweet peas and mignonette Demi brought her.

Then, having buttoned her dove-coloured gloves with care, she took her son's arm and went proudly away to the carriage, where Amy and Bess waited, while Jo called after them, just as Marmee used to do:

'Girls, have you got nice pocket-handkerchiefs?' They all smiled at the familiar words, and three white banners waved as they drove away, leaving the spider to watch for her first fly. She did not wait long. Daisy was lying down with a wet cheek on the little hymnbook out of which she and Nat used to sing together; so Mrs Jo strolled about the lawn, looking very like a wandering mushroom with her large buff umbrella.

Dan had gone for a ten-mile stroll; and Nat was supposed to have accompanied him, but presently came sneaking back, unable to tear himself away from the Dovecote or lose a moment of nearness to his idol that last day. Mrs Jo saw him at once, and beckoned him to a rustic seat under the old elm, where they could have their confidences undisturbed, and both keep an eye on a certain white-curtained window, half hidden in vines.

'Nice and cool here. I'm not up to one of Dan's tramps today—it's so warm, and he goes so like a steam-engine. He headed for the swamp where his pet snakes used to live, and I begged to be excused,' said Nat, fanning himself with his straw hat, though the day was not oppressive.

'I'm glad you did. Sit and rest with me, and have one of our good old talks. We've both been so busy lately, I feel as if I didn't half know your plans; and I want to,' answered Mrs Jo, feeling sure that though they might start with Leipzig they would bring up at Plumfield.

'You are very kind, and there's nothing I'd like better. I don't realize I'm going so far—suppose I shan't till I get afloat. It's a splendid start, and I don't know how I can ever thank Mr Laurie for all he's done, or you either,' added Nat, with a break in his voice; for he was a tender-hearted fellow, and never forgot a kindness.

'You can thank us beautifully by being and doing all we hope and expect of you, my dear. In the new life you are going to there will be a thousand trials and temptations, and only your own wit and wisdom to rely on. That will be the time to test the principles we have tried to give you, and see how firm they are. Of course, you will make mistakes—we all do; but don't let go of your conscience and drift along blindly. Watch and pray, dear Nat; and while your hand gains skill, let your head grow wiser, and keep your heart as innocent and warm as it is now.'

'I'll try, Mother Bhaer, my very best to be a credit to you. I know I shall improve in my music—can't help it there; but I never shall be very wise, I'm afraid. As for my heart, you know, I leave it behind me in good keeping.'

As he spoke, Nat's eyes were fixed on the window with a look of love and longing that made his quiet face both manly and sad—plainly showing how strong a hold this boyish affection had upon him.

'I want to speak of that; and I know you will forgive what seems hard, because I do most heartily sympathize with you,' said Mrs Jo, glad to have her say.

'Yes, do talk about Daisy! I think of nothing but leaving and losing her. I have no hope—I suppose it is too much to ask; only I can't help loving her, wherever I am!' cried Nat, with a mixture of defiance and despair in his face that rather startled Mrs Jo.

'Listen to me and I'll try to give you both comfort and good advice. We all know that Daisy is fond of you, but her mother objects, and being a good girl she tries to obey. Young people think they never can change, but they do in the most wonderful manner, and very few die of broken hearts.' Mrs Jo smiled as she remembered another boy whom she had once tried to comfort, and then went soberly on while Nat listened as if his fate hung upon her lips.

'One of two things will happen. You will find someone else to love, or, better still, be so busy and happy in your music that you will be willing to wait for time to settle the matter for you both. Daisy will perhaps forget when you are gone, and be glad you are only friends. At any rate it is much wiser to have no promises made; then both are free, and in a year or two may meet to laugh over the little romance nipped in the bud.'

'Do you honestly think that?' asked Nat, looking at her so keenly that the truth had to come; for all his heart was in those frank blue eyes of his.

'No, I don't!' answered Mrs Jo. 'Then if you were in my place, what would you do?' he added, with a tone of command never heard in his gentle voice before.

'Bless me! the boy is in dead earnest, and I shall forget prudence in sympathy I'm afraid,' thought Mrs Jo, surprised and pleased by the unexpected manliness Nat showed.

'I'll tell you what I should do. I'd say to myself:

"I'll prove that my love is strong and faithful, and make Daisy's mother proud to give her to me by being not only a good musician but an excellent man, and so command respect and confidence. This I will try for; and if I fail, I shall be the better for the effort, and find comfort in the thought that I did my best for her sake."'

'That is what I meant to do. But I wanted a word of hope to give me courage,' cried Nat, firing up as if the smouldering spark was set ablaze by a breath of encouragement. 'Other fellows, poorer and stupider than I, have done great things and come to honour. Why may not I, though I'm nothing now? I know Mrs Brooke remembers what I came from, but my father was honest though everything went wrong; and I have nothing to be ashamed of though I was a charity boy. I never will be ashamed of my people or myself, and I'll make other folks respect me if I can.'

'Good! that's the right spirit, Nat. Hold to it and make yourself a man. No one will be quicker to see and admire the brave work than my sister Meg. She does not despise your poverty or your past; but mothers are very tender over their daughters, and we Marches, though we have been poor, are, I confess, a little proud of our good family. We don't care for money; but a long line of virtuous ancestors is something to desire and to be proud of.'

'Well, the Blakes are a good lot. I looked 'em up, and not one was ever in prison, hanged, or disgraced in any way. We used to be rich and honoured years ago, but we've died out and got poor, and father was a street musician rather than beg; and I'll be one again before I'll do the mean things some men do and pass muster.'

Nat was so excited that Mrs Jo indulged in a laugh to calm him, and both went on more quietly.

'I told my sister all that and it pleased her. I am sure if you do well these next few years that she will relent and all be happily settled, unless that wonderful change, which you don't believe possible, should occur. Now, cheer up; don't be lackadaisical and blue. Say good-bye cheerfully and bravely, show a manly front, and leave a pleasant memory behind you. We all wish you well and hope much for you. Write to me every week and I'll send a good, gossipy answer. Be careful what you write to Daisy; don't gush or wail, for sister Meg will see the letters; and you can help your cause very much by sending sensible, cheery accounts of your life to us all.'

'I will; I will; it looks brighter and better already, and I won't lose my one comfort by any fault of my own. Thank you so much, Mother Bhaer, for taking my side. I felt so ungrateful and mean and crushed when I thought you all considered me a sneak who had no business to love such a precious girl as Daisy. No one said anything, but I knew how you felt, and that Mr Laurie sent me off partly to get me out of the way. Oh dear, life is pretty tough sometimes, isn't it?' And Nat took his head in both hands as if it ached with the confusion of hopes and fears, passions and plans that proved boyhood was past and manhood had begun.

'Very tough, but it is that very struggle with obstacles which does us good. Things have been made easy for you in many ways, but no one can do everything. You must paddle your own canoe now, and learn to avoid the rapids and steer straight to the port you want to reach. I don't know just what your temptations will be for you have no bad habits and seem to love music so well, nothing can lure you from it. I only hope you won't work too hard.'

'I feel as if I could work like a horse, I'm so eager to get on; but I'll take care. Can't waste time being sick, and you've given me doses enough to keep me all right, I guess.' Nat laughed as he remembered the book of directions Mrs Jo had written for him to consult on all occasions.

She immediately added some verbal ones on the subject of foreign messes, and having mounted one of her pet hobbies, was in full gallop when Emil was seen strolling about on the roof of the old house, that being his favourite promenade; for there he could fancy himself walking the deck, with only blue sky and fresh air about him.

'I want a word with the Commodore, and up there we shall be nice and quiet. Go and play to Daisy: it will put her to sleep and do you both good. Sit in the porch, so I can keep an eye on you as I promised'; and with a motherly pat on the shoulder Mrs Jo left Nat to his delightful task and briskly ascended to the house-top, not up the trellis as of old but by means of the stairs inside.

Emerging on the platform she found Emil cutting his initials afresh in the wood-work and singing 'Pull for the Shore', like the tuneful mariner he was.

'Come aboard and make yourself at home, Aunty,' he said, with a playful salute. 'I'm just leaving a P.P.C. in the old place, so when you fly up here for refuge you'll remember me.'

'Ah, my dear, I'm not likely to forget you. It doesn't need E. B. H. cut on all the trees and railings to remind me of my sailor boy'; and Mrs Jo took the seat nearest the blue figure astride the balustrade, not quite sure how to begin the little sermon she wanted to preach.

'Well, you don't pipe your eye and look squally when I sheer off as you used to, and that's a comfort. I like to leave port in fair weather and have a jolly send-off all round. Specially this time, for it will be a year or more before we drop anchor here again,' answered Emil, pushing his cap back, and glancing about him as if he loved old Plum and would be sorry never to see it any more.

'You have salt water enough without my adding to it. I'm going to be quite a Spartan mother, and send my sons to battle with no wailing, only the command:

"With your shield or on it",' said Mrs Jo cheerfully, adding after a pause: 'I often wish I could go too, and some day I will, when you are captain and have a ship of your own—as I've no doubt you will before long, with Uncle Herman to push you on.'

'When I do I'll christen her the Jolly Jo and take you as first mate. It would be regular larks to have you aboard, and I'd be a proud man to carry you round the world you've wanted to see so long and never could,' answered Emil, caught at once by this splendid vision.

'I'll make my first voyage with you and enjoy myself immensely in spite of seasickness and all the stormy winds that blow. I've always thought I'd like to see a wreck, a nice safe one with all saved after great danger and heroic deeds, while we clung like Mr Pillicoddy to main-top jibs and lee scuppers.'

'No wrecks yet, ma'am, but we'll try to accommodate customers. Captain says I'm a lucky dog and bring fair weather, so we'll save the dirty weather for you if you want it,' laughed Emil, digging at the ship in full sail which he was adding to his design.

'Thanks, I hope you will. This long voyage will give you new experiences, and being an officer, you will have new duties and responsibilities. Are you ready for them? You take everything so gaily, I've been wondering if you realized that now you will have not only to obey but to command also, and power is a dangerous thing. Be careful that you don't abuse it or let it make a tyrant of you.'

'Right you are, ma'am. I've seen plenty of that, and have got my bearings pretty well, I guess. I shan't have very wide swing with Peters over me, but I'll see that the boys don't get abused when he's bowsed up his jib. No right to speak before, but now I won't stand it.'

'That sounds mysteriously awful; could I ask what nautical torture "bowsing jibs" is?' asked Mrs Jo, in a tone of deep interest.

'Getting drunk. Peters can hold more grog than any man I ever saw; he keeps right side up, but is as savage as a norther, and makes things lively all round. I've seen him knock a fellow down with a belaying pin, and couldn't lend a hand. Better luck now, I hope.' And Emil frowned as if he already trod the quarter-deck, lord of all he surveyed.

'Don't get into trouble, for even Uncle Herman's favour won't cover insubordination, you know. You have proved yourself a good sailor; now be a good officer, which is a harder thing, I fancy. It takes a fine character to rule justly and kindly; you will have to put by your boyish ways and remember your dignity. That will be excellent training for you, Emil, and sober you down a bit. No more skylarking except here, so mind your ways, and do honour to your buttons,' said Mrs Jo, tapping one of the very bright brass ones that ornamented the new suit Emil was so proud of.

'I'll do my best. I know my time for skirmshander (chaff) is over, and I must steer a straighter course; but don't you fear, Jack ashore is a very different craft from what he is with blue water under his keel. I had a long talk with Uncle last night and got my orders; I won't forget 'em nor all I owe him. As for you, I'll name my first ship as I say, and have your bust for the figurehead, see if I don't,' and Emil gave his aunt a hearty kiss to seal the vow, which proceeding much amused Nat, playing softly in the porch of the Dovecote.

'You do me proud, Captain. But, dear, I want to say one thing and then I'm done; for you don't need much advice of mine after my good man has spoken. I read somewhere that every inch of rope used in the British Navy has a strand of red in it, so that wherever a bit of it is found it is known. That is the text of my little sermon to you. Virtue, which means honour, honesty, courage, and all that makes character, is the red thread that marks a good man wherever he is. Keep that always and everywhere, so that even if wrecked by misfortune, that sign shall still be found and recognized. Yours is a rough life, and your mates not all we could wish, but you can be a gentleman in the true sense of the word; and no matter what happens to your body, keep your soul clean, your heart true to those who love you, and do your duty to the end.'

As she spoke Emil had risen and stood listening with his cap off and a grave, bright look as if taking orders from a superior officer; when she ended, he answered briefly, but heartily:

'Please God, I will!'

'That's all; I have little fear for you, but one never knows when or how the weak moment may come, and sometimes a chance word helps us, as so many my dear mother spoke come back to me now for my own comfort and the guidance of my boys,' said Mrs Jo, rising; for the words had been said and no more were needed.

'I've stored 'em up and know where to find 'em when wanted. Often and often in my watch I've seen old Plum, and heard you and Uncle talking so plainly, I'd have sworn I was here. It is a rough life, Aunty, but a wholesome one if a fellow loves it as I do, and has an anchor to windward as I have. Don't worry about me, and I'll come home next year with a chest of tea that will cheer your heart and give you ideas enough for a dozen novels. Going below? All right, steady in the gangway! I'll be along by the time you've got out the cake-box. Last chance for a good old lunch ashore.'

Mrs Jo descended laughing, and Emil finished his ship whistling cheerfully, neither dreaming when and where this little chat on the house-top would return to the memory of one of them.

Dan was harder to catch, and not until evening did a quiet moment come in that busy family; when, while the rest were roaming about, Mrs Jo sat down to read in the study, and presently Dan looked in at the window.

'Come and rest after your long tramp; you must be tired,' she called, with an inviting nod towards the big sofa where so many boys had reposed—as much as that active animal ever does.

'Afraid I shall disturb you'; but Dan looked as if he wanted to stay his restless feet somewhere.

'Not a bit; I'm always ready to talk, shouldn't be a woman if I were not,' laughed Mrs Jo, as Dan swung himself in and sat down with an air of contentment very pleasant to see.

'Last day is over, yet somehow I don't seem to hanker to be off. Generally, I'm rather anxious to cut loose after a short stop. Odd, ain't it?' asked Dan, gravely picking grass and leaves out of his hair and beard; for he had been lying on the grass, thinking many thoughts in the quiet summer night.

'Not at all; you are beginning to get civilized. It's a good sign, and I'm glad to see it,' answered Mrs Jo promptly. 'You've had your swing, and want a change. Hope the farming will give it to you, though helping the Indians pleases me more: it is so much better to work for others than for one's self alone.'

'So 'tis,' assented Dan heartily. 'I seem to want to root somewhere and have folks of my own to take care of. Tired of my own company, I suppose, now I've seen so much better. I'm a rough, ignorant lot, and I've been thinking maybe I've missed it loafing round creation, instead of going in for education as the other chaps did. Hey?'

He looked anxiously at Mrs Jo; and she tried to hide the surprise this new outburst caused her; for till now Dan had scorned books and gloried in his freedom.

'No; I don't think so in your case. So far I'm sure the free life was best. Now that you are a man you can control that lawless nature better; but as a boy only great activity and much adventure could keep you out of mischief. Time is taming my colt, you see, and I shall yet be proud of him, whether he makes a pack-horse of himself to carry help to the starving or goes to ploughing as Pegasus did.'

Dan liked the comparison, and smiled as he lounged in the sofa-corner, with the new thoughtfulness in his eyes.

'Glad you think so. The fact is it's going to take a heap of taming to make me go well in harness anywhere. I want to, and I try now and then, but always kick over the traces and run away. No lives lost yet; but I shouldn't wonder if there was some time, and a general smash-up.'

'Why, Dan, did you have any dangerous adventures during this last absence? I fancied so, but didn't ask before, knowing you'd tell me if I could help in any way. Can I?' And Mrs Jo looked anxiously at him; for a sudden lowering expression had come into his face, and he leaned forward as if to hide it.

'Nothing very bad; but 'Frisco isn't just a heaven on earth, you know, and it's harder to be a saint there than here,' he answered slowly; then, as if he had made up his mind to "fess', as the children used to say, he sat up, and added rapidly, in a half-defiant, half-shamefaced way, 'I tried gambling, and it wasn't good for me.'

'Was that how you made your money?'

'Not a penny of it! That's all honest, if speculation isn't a bigger sort of gambling. I won a lot; but I lost or gave it away, and cut the whole concern before it got the better of me.'

'Thank heaven for that! Don't try it again; it may have the terrible fascination for you it has for so many. Keep to your mountains and prairies, and shun cities, if these things tempt you, Dan. Better lose your life than your soul, and one such passion leads to worse sins, as you know better than I.'

Dan nodded, and seeing how troubled she was, said, in a lighter tone, though still the shadow of that past experience remained:

'Don't be scared; I'm all right now; and a burnt dog dreads the fire. I don't drink, or do the things you dread; don't care for 'em; but I get excited, and then this devilish temper of mine is more than I can manage. Fighting a moose or a buffalo is all right; but when you pitch into a man, no matter how great a scamp he is, you've got to look out. I shall kill someone some day; that's all I'm afraid of. I do hate a sneak!' And Dan brought his fist down on the table with a blow that made the lamp totter and the books skip.

'That always was your trial, Dan, and I can sympathize with you; for I've been trying to govern my own temper all my life, and haven't learnt yet,' said Mrs Jo, with a sigh. 'For heaven's sake, guard your demon well, and don't let a moment's fury ruin all your life. As I said to Nat, watch and pray, my dear boy. There is no other help or hope for human weakness but God's love and patience.'

Tears were in Mrs Jo's eyes as she spoke; for she felt this deeply, and knew how hard a task it is to rule these bosom sins of ours. Dan looked touched, also uncomfortable, as he always did when religion of any sort was mentioned, though he had a simple creed of his own, and tried to live up to it in his blind way.

'I don't do much praying; don't seem to come handy to me; but I can watch like a redskin, only it's easier to mount guard over a lurking grizzly than my own cursed temper. It's that I'm afraid of, if I settle down. I can get on with wild beasts first-rate; but men rile me awfully, and I can't take it out in a free fight, as I can with a bear or a wolf. Guess I'd better head for the Rockies, and stay there a spell longer—till I'm tame enough for decent folks, if I ever am.' And Dan leaned his rough head on his hands in a despondent attitude.

'Try my sort of help, and don't give up. Read more, study a little, and try to meet a better class of people, who won't "rile", but soothe and strengthen you. We don't make you savage, I'm sure; for you have been as meek as a lamb, and made us very happy.'

'Glad of it; but I've felt like a hawk in a hen-house all the same, and wanted to pounce and tear more than once. Not so much as I used, though,' added Dan, after a short laugh at Mrs Jo's surprised face. 'I'll try your plan, and keep good company this bout if I can; but a man can't pick and choose, knocking about as I do.'

'Yes, you can this time; for you are going on a peaceful errand and can keep clear of temptation if you try. Take some books and read; that's an immense help; and books are always good company if you have the right sort. Let me pick out some for you.' And Mrs Jo made a bee-line to the well-laden shelves, which were the joy of her heart and the comfort of her life.

'Give me travels and stories, please; don't want any pious works, can't seem to relish 'em, and won't pretend I do,' said Dan, following to look over her head with small favour at the long lines of well-worn volumes.

Mrs Jo turned short round, and putting a hand on either broad shoulder, looked him in the eye, saying soberly:

'Now, Dan, see here; never sneer at good things or pretend to be worse than you are. Don't let false shame make you neglect the religion without which no man can live. You needn't talk about it if you don't like, but don't shut your heart to it in whatever shape it comes. Nature is your God now; she has done much for you; let her do more, and lead you to know and love a wiser and more tender teacher, friend, and comforter than she can ever be. That is your only hope; don't throw it away, and waste time; for sooner or later you will feel the need of Him, and He will come to you and hold you up when all other help fails.'

Dan stood motionless, and let her read in his softened eyes the dumb desire that lived in his heart, though he had no words to tell it, and only permitted her to catch a glimpse of the divine spark which smoulders or burns clearly in every human soul. He did not speak; and glad to be spared some answer which should belie his real feelings, Mrs Jo hastened to say, with her most motherly smile:

'I saw in your room the little Bible I gave you long ago; it was well worn outside, but fresh within, as if not much read. Will you promise me to read a little once a week, dear, for my sake? Sunday is a quiet day everywhere, and this book is never old nor out of place. Begin with the stories you used to love when I told them to you boys. David was your favourite, you remember? Read him again; he'll suit you even better now, and you'll find his sins and repentance useful reading till you come to the life and work of a diviner example than he. You will do it, for love of mother Bhaer, who always loved her "firebrand" and hoped to save him?'

'I will,' answered Dan, with a sudden brightening of face that was like a sunburst through a cloud, full of promise though so short-lived and rare.

Mrs Jo turned at once to the books and began to talk of them, knowing well that Dan would not hear any more just then. He seemed relieved; for it was always hard for him to show his inner self, and he took pride in hiding it as an Indian does in concealing pain or fear.

'Hallo, here's old Sintram! I remember him; used to like him and his tantrums, and read about 'em to Ted. There he is riding ahead with Death and the Devil alongside.'

As Dan looked at the little picture of the young man with horse and hound going bravely up the rocky defile, accompanied by the companions who ride beside most men through this world, a curious impulse made Mrs Jo say quickly:

'That's you, Dan, just you at this time! Danger and sin are near you in the life you lead; moods and passions torment you; the bad father left you to fight alone, and the wild spirit drives you to wander up and down the world looking for peace and self-control. Even the horse and hound are there, your Octoo and Don, faithful friends, unscared by the strange mates that go with you. You have not got the armour yet, but I'm trying to show you where to find it. Remember the mother Sintram loved and longed to find, and did find when his battle was bravely fought, his reward well earned? You can recollect your mother; and I have always felt that all the good qualities you possess come from her. Act out the beautiful old story in this as in the other parts, and try to give her back a son to be proud of.'

Quite carried away by the likeness of the quaint tale to Dan's life and needs, Mrs Jo went on pointing to the various pictures which illustrated it, and when she looked up was surprised to see how struck and interested he seemed to be. Like all people of his temperament he was very impressionable, and his life among hunters and Indians had made him superstitious; he believed in dreams, liked weird tales, and whatever appealed to the eye or mind, vividly impressed him more than the wisest words. The story of poor, tormented Sintram came back clearly as he looked and listened, symbolizing his secret trials even more truly than Mrs Jo knew; and just at that moment this had an effect upon him that never was forgotten. But all he said was:

'Small chance of that. I don't take much stock in the idea of meeting folks in heaven. Guess mother won't remember the poor little brat she left so long ago; why should she?'

'Because true mothers never forget their children; and I know she was one, from the fact that she ran away from the cruel husband, to save her little son from bad influences. Had she lived, life would have been happier for you, with this tender friend to help and comfort you. Never forget that she risked everything for your sake, and don't let it be in vain.'

Mrs Jo spoke very earnestly, knowing that this was the one sweet memory of Dan's early life, and glad to have recalled it at this moment; for suddenly a great tear splashed down on the page where Sintram kneels at his mother's feet, wounded, but victorious over sin and death. She looked up, well pleased to have touched Dan to the heart's core, as that drop proved; but a sweep of the arm brushed away the tell-tale, and his beard hid the mate to it, as he shut the book, saying with a suppressed quiver in his strong voice:

'I'll keep this, if nobody wants it. I'll read it over, and maybe it will do me good. I'd like to meet her anywhere, but don't believe I ever shall.'

'Keep it and welcome. My mother gave it to me; and when you read it try to believe that neither of your mothers will ever forget you.'

Mrs Jo gave the book with a caress; and simply saying: 'Thanks; good night,' Dan thrust it into his pocket, and walked straight away to the river to recover from this unwonted mood of tenderness and confidence.

Next day the travellers were off. All were in good spirits, and a cloud of handkerchiefs whitened the air as they drove away in the old bus, waving their hats to everyone and kissing their hands, especially to mother Bhaer, who said in her prophetic tone as she wiped her eyes, when the familiar rumble died away:

'I have a feeling that something is going to happen to some of them, and they will never come back to me, or come back changed. Well, I can only say, God be with my boys!'

And He was.

# CHAPTER 7. THE LION AND THE LAMB

When the boys were gone a lull fell upon Plumfield, and the family scattered to various places for brief outings, as August had come and all felt the need of change. The Professor took Mrs Jo to the mountains. The Laurences were at the seashore, and there Meg's family and the Bhaer boys took turns to visit, as someone must always be at home to keep things in order.

Mrs Meg, with Daisy, was in office when the events occurred which we are about to relate. Rob and Ted were just up from Rocky Nook, and Nan was passing a week with her friend as the only relaxation she allowed herself. Demi was off on a run with Tom, so Rob was man of the house, with old Silas as general overseer. The sea air seemed to have gone to Ted's head, for he was unusually freakish, and led his gentle aunt and poor Rob a life of it with his pranks. Octoo was worn out with the wild rides he took, and Don openly rebelled when ordered to leap and show off his accomplishments; while the girls at college were both amused and worried by the ghosts who haunted the grounds at night, the unearthly melodies that disturbed their studious hours, and the hairbreadth escapes of this restless boy by flood and field and fire. Something happened at length which effectually sobered Ted and made a lasting impression on both the boys; for sudden danger and a haunting fear turned the Lion into a lamb and the Lamb into a lion, as far as courage went.

On the first of September—the boys never forgot the date—after a pleasant tramp and good luck with their fishing, the brothers were lounging in the barn; for Daisy had company, and the lads kept out of the way.

'I tell you what it is, Bobby, that dog is sick. He won't play, nor eat, nor drink, and acts queerly. Dan will kill us if anything happens to him,' said Ted, looking at Don, who lay near his kennel resting a moment after one of the restless wanderings which kept him vibrating between the door of Dan's room and the shady corner of the yard, where his master had settled him with an old cap to guard till he came back.

'It's the hot weather, perhaps. But I sometimes think he's pining for Dan. Dogs do, you know, and the poor fellow has been low in his mind ever since the boys went. Maybe something has happened to Dan. Don howled last night and can't rest. I've heard of such things,' answered Rob thoughtfully.

'Pooh! he can't know. He's cross. I'll stir him up and take him for a run. Always makes me feel better. Hi, boy! wake up and be jolly'; and Ted snapped his fingers at the dog, who only looked at him with grim indifference.

'Better let him alone. If he isn't right tomorrow, we'll take him to Dr Watkins and see what he says.' And Rob went on watching the swallows as he lay in the hay polishing up some Latin verses he had made.

The spirit of perversity entered into Ted, and merely because he was told not to tease Don he went on doing it, pretending that it was for the dog's good. Don took no heed of his pats, commands, reproaches, or insults, till Ted's patience gave out; and seeing a convenient switch near by he could not resist the temptation to conquer the great hound by force, since gentleness failed to win obedience. He had the wisdom to chain Don up first; for a blow from any hand but his master's made him savage, and Ted had more than once tried the experiment, as the dog remembered. This indignity roused Don and he sat up with a growl. Rob heard it, and seeing Ted raise the switch, ran to interfere, exclaiming:

'Don't touch him! Dan forbade it! Leave the poor thing in peace; I won't allow it.'

Rob seldom commanded, but when he did Master Ted had to give in. His temper was up, and Rob's masterful tone made it impossible to resist one cut at the rebellious dog before he submitted. Only a single blow, but it was a costly one; for as it fell, the dog sprang at Ted with a snarl, and Rob, rushing between the two, felt the sharp teeth pierce his leg. A word made Don let go and drop remorsefully at Rob's feet, for he loved him and was evidently sorry to have hurt his friend by mistake. With a forgiving pat Rob left him, to limp to the barn followed by Ted, whose wrath was changed to shame and sorrow when he saw the red drops on Rob's sock and the little wounds in his leg.

'I'm awfully sorry. Why did you get in the way? Here, wash it up, and I'll get a rag to tie on it,' he said quickly filling a sponge with water and pulling out a very demoralized handkerchief. Rob usually made light of his own mishaps and was over ready to forgive if others were to blame; but now he sat quite still, looking at the purple marks with such a strange expression on his white face that Ted was troubled, though he added with a laugh: 'Why, you're not afraid of a little dig like that, are you, Bobby?'

'I am afraid of hydrophobia. But if Don is mad I'd rather be the one to have it,' answered Rob, with a smile and a shiver.

At that dreadful word Ted turned whiter than his brother, and, dropping sponge and handkerchief, stared at him with a frightened face, whispering in a tone of despair:

'Oh, Rob, don't say it! What shall we do, what shall we do?'

'Call Nan; she will know. Don't scare Aunty, or tell a soul but Nan; she's on the back piazza; get her out here as quick as you can. I'll wash it till she comes. Maybe it's nothing; don't look so staggered, Ted. I only thought it might be, as Don is queer.'

Rob tried to speak bravely; but Ted's long legs felt strangely weak as he hurried away, and it was lucky he met no one, for his face would have betrayed him. Nan was swinging luxuriously in a hammock, amusing herself with a lively treatise on croup, when an agitated boy suddenly clutched her, whispering, as he nearly pulled her overboard:

'Come to Rob in the barn! Don's mad and he's bitten him, and we don't know what to do; it's all my fault; no one must know. Oh, do be quick!'

Nan was on her feet at once, startled, but with her wits about her, and both were off without more words as they dodged round the house where unconscious Daisy chatted with her friends in the parlour and Aunt Meg peacefully took her afternoon nap upstairs.

Rob was braced up, and was as calm and steady as ever when they found him in the harness-room, whither he had wisely retired, to escape observation. The story was soon told, and after a look at Don, now in his kennel, sad and surly, Nan said slowly, with her eye on the full water-pan:

'Rob, there is one thing to do for the sake of safety, and it must be done at once. We can't wait to see if Don is—sick—or to go for a doctor. I can do it, and I will; but it is very painful, and I hate to hurt you, dear.'

A most unprofessional quiver got into Nan's voice as she spoke, and her keen eyes dimmed as she looked at the two anxious young faces turned so confidingly to her for help.

'I know, burn it; well, do it, please; I can bear it. But Ted better go away,' said Rob, with a firm setting of his lips, and a nod at his afflicted brother.

'I won't stir; I can stand it if he can, only it ought to be me!' cried Ted, with a desperate effort not to cry, so full of grief and fear and shame was he that it seemed as if he couldn't bear it like a man.

'He'd better stay and help; do him good,' answered

Nan sternly, because, her heart was faint within her, knowing as she did all that might be in store for both poor boys. 'Keep quiet; I'll be back in a minute,' she added, going towards the house, while her quick mind hastily planned what was best to be done.

It was ironing day, and a hot fire still burned in the empty kitchen, for the maids were upstairs resting. Nan put a slender poker to heat, and as she sat waiting for it, covered her face with her hands, asking help in this sudden need for strength, courage, and wisdom; for there was no one else to call upon, and young as she was, she knew what was to be done if she only had the nerve to do it. Any other patient would have been calmly interesting, but dear, good Robin, his father's pride, his mother's comfort, everyone's favourite and friend, that he should be in danger was very terrible; and a few hot tears dropped on the well-scoured table as Nan tried to calm her trouble by remembering how very likely it was to be all a mistake, a natural but vain alarm.

'I must make light of it, or the boys will break down, and then there will be a panic. Why afflict and frighten everyone when all is in doubt? I won't. I'll take Rob to Dr Morrison at once, and have the dog man see Don. Then, having done all we can, we will either laugh at our scare—if it is one—or be ready for whatever comes. Now for my poor boy.'

Armed with the red-hot poker, a pitcher of ice-water, and several handkerchiefs from the clotheshorse, Nan went back to the barn ready to do her best in this her most serious 'emergency case'. The boys sat like statues, one of despair, the other of resignation; and it took all Nan's boasted nerve to do her work quickly and well.

'Now, Rob, only a minute, then we are safe. Stand by, Ted; he may be a bit faintish.'

Rob shut his eyes, clinched his hands, and sat like a hero. Ted knelt beside him, white as a sheet, and as weak as a girl; for the pangs of remorse were rending him, and his heart failed at the thought of all this pain because of his wilfulness. It was all over in a moment, with only one little groan; but when Nan looked to her assistant to hand the water, poor Ted needed it the most, for he had fainted away, and lay on the floor in a pathetic heap of arms and legs.

Rob laughed, and, cheered by that unexpected sound, Nan bound up the wound with hands that never trembled, though great drops stood on her forehead; and she shared the water with patient number one before she turned to patient number two. Ted was much ashamed, and quite broken in spirit, when he found how he had failed at the critical moment, and begged them not to tell, as he really could not help it; then by way of finishing his utter humiliation, a burst of hysterical tears disgraced his manly soul, and did him a world of good.

'Never mind, never mind, we are all right now, and no one need be the wiser,' said Nan briskly, as poor Ted hiccoughed on Rob's shoulder, laughing and crying in the most tempestuous manner, while his brother soothed him, and the young doctor fanned both with Silas's old straw hat.

'Now, boys, listen to me and remember what I say. We won't alarm anyone yet, for I've made up my mind our scare is all nonsense. Don was out lapping the water as I came by, and I don't believe he's mad any more than I am. Still, to ease our minds and compose our spirits, and get our guilty faces out of sight for a while, I think we had better drive into town to my old friend Dr Morrison, and let him just take a look at my work, and give us some quieting little dose; for we are all rather shaken by this flurry. Sit still, Rob; and Ted, you harness up while I run and get my hat and tell Aunty to excuse me to Daisy. I don't know those Penniman girls, and she will be glad of our room at tea, and we'll have a cosy bite at my house, and come home as gay as larks.'

Nan talked on as a vent for the hidden emotions which professional pride would not allow her to show, and the boys approved her plan at once; for action is always easier than quiet waiting. Ted went staggering away to wash his face at the pump, and rub some colour into his cheeks before he harnessed the horse. Rob lay tranquilly on the hay, looking up at the swallows again as he lived through some very memorable moments. Boy as he was, the thought of death coming suddenly to him, and in this way, might well make him sober; for it is a very solemn thing to be arrested in the midst of busy life by the possibility of the great change. There were no sins to be repented of, few faults, and many happy, dutiful years to remember with infinite comfort. So Rob had no fears to daunt him, no regrets to sadden, and best of all, a very strong and simple piety to sustain and cheer him.

'Mein Vater,' was his first thought; for Rob was very near the Professor's heart, and the loss of his eldest would have been a bitter blow. These words, whispered with a tremble of the lips that had been so firm when the hot iron burned, recalled that other Father who is always near, always tender and helpful; and, folding his hands, Rob said the heartiest little prayer he ever prayed, there on the hay, to the soft twitter of the brooding birds. It did him good; and wisely laying all his fear and doubt and trouble in God's hand, the boy felt ready for whatever was to come, and from that hour kept steadily before him the one duty that was plain—to be brave and cheerful, keep silent, and hope for the best.

Nan stole her hat, and left a note on Daisy's pincushion, saying she had taken the boys to drive, and all would be out of the way till after tea. Then she hurried back and found her patients much better, the one for work, the other for rest. In they got, and, putting Rob on the back seat with his leg up drove away, looking as gay and care-free as if nothing had happened.

Dr Morrison made light of the affair, but told Nan she had done right; and as the much-relieved lads went downstairs, he added in a whisper: 'Send the dog off for a while, and keep your eye on the boy. Don't let him know it, and report to me if anything seems wrong. One never knows in these cases. No harm to be careful.'

Nan nodded, and feeling much relieved now that the responsibility was off her shoulders, took the lads to Dr Watkins, who promised to come out later and examine Don. A merry tea at Nan's house, which was kept open for her all summer, did them good, and by the time they got home in the cool of the evening no sign of the panic remained but Ted's heavy eyes, and a slight limp when Rob walked. As the guests were still chattering on the front piazza they retired to the back, and Ted soothed his remorseful soul by swinging Rob in the hammock, while Nan told stories till the dog man arrived.

He said Don was a little under the weather, but no more mad than the grey kitten that purred round his legs while the examination went on.

'He wants his master, and feels the heat. Fed too well, perhaps. I'll keep him a few weeks and send him home all right,' said Dr Watkins, as Don laid his great head in his hand, and kept his intelligent eyes on his face, evidently feeling that this man understood his trials, and knew what to do for him.

So Don departed without a murmur, and our three conspirators took counsel together how to spare the family all anxiety, and give Rob the rest his leg demanded. Fortunately, he always spent many hours in his little study, so he could lie on the sofa with a book in his hand as long as he liked, without exciting any remark. Being of a quiet temperament, he did not worry himself or Nan with useless fears, but believed what was told him, and dismissing all dark possibilities, went cheerfully on his way, soon recovering from the shock of what he called 'our scare'.

But excitable Ted was harder to manage, and it took all Nan's wit and wisdom to keep him from betraying the secret; for it was best to say nothing and spare all discussion of the subject for Rob's sake. Ted's remorse preyed upon him, and having no 'Mum' to confide in, he was very miserable. By day he devoted himself to Rob, waiting on him, talking to him, gazing anxiously at him, and worrying the good fellow very much; though he wouldn't own it, since Ted found comfort in it. But at night, when all was quiet, Ted's lively imagination and heavy heart got the better of him, and kept him awake, or set him walking in his sleep. Nan had her eye on him, and more than once administered a little dose to give him a rest, read to him, scolded him, and when she caught him haunting the house in the watches of the night, threatened to lock him up if he did not stay in his bed. This wore off after a while; but a change came over the freakish boy, and everyone observed it, even before his mother returned to ask what they had done to quench the Lion's spirits. He was gay, but not so heedless; and often when the old wilfulness beset him, he would check it sharply, look at Rob, and give up, or stalk away to have his sulk out alone. He no longer made fun of his brother's old-fashioned ways and bookish tastes, but treated him with a new and very marked respect, which touched and pleased modest Rob, and much amazed all observers. It seemed as if he felt that he owed him reparation for the foolish act that might have cost him his life; and love being stronger than will, Ted forgot his pride, and paid his debt like an honest boy.

'I don't understand it,' said Mrs Jo, after a week of home life, much impressed by the good behaviour of her younger son. 'Ted is such a saint, I'm afraid we are going to lose him. Is it Meg's sweet influence, or Daisy's fine cooking, or the pellets I catch Nan giving him on the sly? Some witchcraft has been at work during my absence, and this will-o'-the-wisp is so amiable, quiet, and obedient, I don't know him.'

'He is growing up, heart's-dearest, and being a precocious plant, he begins to bloom early. I also see a change in my Robchen. He is more manly and serious than ever, and is seldom far from me, as if his love for the old papa was growing with his growth. Our boys will often surprise us in this way, Jo, and we can only rejoice over them and leave them to become what Gott pleases.'

As the Professor spoke, his eyes rested proudly on the brothers, who came walking up the steps together, Ted's arm over Rob's shoulder as he listened attentively to some geological remarks Rob was making on a stone he held. Usually, Ted made fun of such tastes, and loved to lay boulders in the student's path, put brickbats under his pillow, gravel in his shoes, or send parcels of dirt by express to 'Prof. R. M. Bhaer'. Lately, he had treated Rob's hobbies respectfully, and had begun to appreciate the good qualities of this quiet brother whom he had always loved but rather undervalued, till his courage under fire won Ted's admiration, and made it impossible to forget a fault, the consequences of which might have been so terrible. The leg was still lame, though doing well, and Ted was always offering an arm as support, gazing anxiously at his brother, and trying to guess his wants; for regret was still keen in Ted's soul, and Rob's forgiveness only made it deeper. A fortunate slip on the stairs gave Rob an excuse for limping, and no one but Nan and Ted saw the wound; so the secret was safe up to this time.

'We are talking about you, my lads. Come in and tell us what good fairy has been at work while we were gone. Or is it because absence sharpens our eyes, that we find such pleasant changes when we come back?' said Mrs Jo, patting the sofa on either side, while the Professor forgot his piles of letters to admire the pleasing prospect of his wife in a bower of arms, as the boys sat down beside her, smiling affectionately, but feeling a little guilty; for till now 'Mum' and 'Vater' knew every event in their boyish lives.

'Oh, it's only because Bobby and I have been alone so much; we are sort of twins. I stir him up a bit, and he steadies me a great deal. You and father do the same, you know. Nice plan. I like it'; and Ted felt that he had settled the matter capitally.

'Mother won't thank you for comparing yourself to her, Ted. I'm flattered at being like father in any way. I try to be,' answered Rob, as they laughed at Ted's compliment.

'I do thank him, for it's true; and if you, Robin, do half as much for your brother as Papa has for me, your life won't be a failure,' said Mrs Jo heartily. 'I'm very glad to see you helping one another. It's the right way, and we can't begin too soon to try to understand the needs, virtues, and failings of those nearest us. Love should not make us blind to faults, nor familiarity make us too ready to blame the shortcomings we see. So work away, my sonnies, and give us more surprises of this sort as often as you like.'

'The liebe Mutter has said all. I too am well pleased at the friendly brother-warmth I find. It is good for everyone; long may it last!' and Professor Bhaer nodded at the boys, who looked gratified, but rather at a loss how to respond to these flattering remarks.

Rob wisely kept silent, fearing to say too much; but Ted burst out, finding it impossible to help telling something:

'The fact is I've been finding out what a brave good chap Bobby is, and I'm trying to make up for all the bother I've been to him. I knew he was awfully wise, but I thought him rather soft, because he liked books better than larks, and was always fussing about his conscience. But I begin to see that it isn't the fellows who talk the loudest and show off best that are the manliest. No, sir! quiet old Bob is a hero and a trump, and I'm proud of him; so would you be if you knew all about it.'

Here a look from Rob brought Ted up with a round turn; he stopped short, grew red, and clapped his hand on his mouth in dismay.

'Well, are we not to "know all about it"?' asked Mrs Jo quickly; for her sharp eye saw signs of danger and her maternal heart felt that something had come between her and her sons. 'Boys,' she went on solemnly, 'I suspect that the change we talk about is not altogether the effect of growing up, as we say. It strikes me that Ted has been in mischief and Rob has got him out of some scrape; hence the lovely mood of my bad boy and the sober one of my conscientious son, who never hides anything from his mother.'

Rob was as red as Ted now, but after a moment's hesitation he looked up and answered with an air of relief:

'Yes, mother, that's it; but it's all over and no harm done, and I think we'd better let it be, for a while at least. I did feel guilty to keep anything from you, but now you know so much I shall not worry and you needn't either. Ted's sorry, I don't mind, and it has done us both good.'

Mrs Jo looked at Ted, who winked hard but bore the look like a man; then she turned to Rob, who smiled at her so cheerfully that she felt reassured; but something in his face struck her, and she saw what it was that made him seem older, graver, yet more lovable than ever. It was the look pain of mind, as well as body, brings, and the patience of a sweet submission to some inevitable trial. Like a flash she guessed that some danger had been near her boy, and the glances she had caught between the two lads and Nan confirmed her fears.

'Rob, dear, you have been ill, hurt, or seriously troubled by Ted? Tell me at once; I will not have any secrets now. Boys sometimes suffer all their lives from neglected accidents or carelessness. Fritz, make them speak out!'

Mr Bhaer put down his papers and came to stand before them, saying in a tone that quieted Mrs Jo, and gave the boys courage:

'My sons, give us the truth. We can bear it; do not hold it back to spare us. Ted knows we forgive much because we love him, so be frank, all two.'

Ted instantly dived among the sofa pillows and kept there, with only a pair of scarlet ears visible, while Rob in a few words told the little story, truthfully, but as gently as he could, hastening to add the comfortable assurance that Don was not mad, the wound nearly well, and no danger would ever come of it.

But Mrs Jo grew so pale he had to put his arms about her, and his father turned and walked away, exclaiming: 'Ach Himmel!' in a tone of such mingled pain, relief, and gratitude, that Ted pulled an extra pillow over his head to smother the sound. They were all right in a minute; but such news is always a shock, even if the peril is past, and Mrs Jo hugged her boy close till his father came and took him away, saying with a strong shake of both hands and a quiver in his voice:

'To be in danger of one's life tries a man's mettle, and you bear it well; but I cannot spare my good boy yet; thank Gott, we keep him safe!'

A smothered sound, between a choke and a groan, came from under the pillows, and the writhing of Ted's long legs so plainly expressed despair that his mother relented towards him, and burrowing till she found a tousled yellow head, pulled it out and smoothed it, exclaiming with an irrepressible laugh, though her cheeks were wet with tears:

'Come and be forgiven, poor sinner! I know you have suffered enough, and I won't say a word; only if harm had come to Rob you would have made me more miserable than yourself. Oh, Teddy, Teddy, do try to cure that wilful spirit of yours before it is too late!'

'Oh, Mum, I do try! I never can forget this—I hope it's cured me; if it hasn't, I am afraid I ain't worth saving,' answered Ted, pulling his own hair as the only way of expressing his deep remorse.

'Yes, you are, my dear; I felt just so at fifteen when Amy was nearly drowned, and Marmee helped me as I'll help you. Come to me, Teddy, when the evil one gets hold of you, and together we'll rout him. Ah, me! I've had many a tussle with that old Apollyon, and often got worsted, but not always. Come under my shield, and we'll fight till we win.'

No one spoke for a minute as Ted and his mother laughed and cried in one handkerchief, and Rob stood with his father's arm round him so happy that all was told and forgiven, though never to be forgotten; for such experiences do one good, and knit hearts that love more closely together.

Presently Ted rose straight up and going to his father, said bravely and humbly:

'I ought to be punished. Please do it; but first say you forgive me, as Rob does.'

'Always that, mein Sohn, seventy time seven, if needs be, else I am not worthy the name you give me. The punishment has come; I can give no greater. Let it not be in vain. It will not with the help of the mother and the All Father. Room here for both, always!'

The good Professor opened his arms and embraced his boys like a true German, not ashamed to express by gesture or by word the fatherly emotions an American would have compressed into a slap on the shoulder and a brief 'All right'.

Mrs Jo sat and enjoyed the prospect like a romantic soul as she was, and then they had a quiet talk together, saying freely all that was in their hearts, and finding much comfort in the confidence which comes when love casts out fear. It was agreed that nothing be said except to Nan, who was to be thanked and rewarded for her courage, discretion, and fidelity.

'I always knew that girl had the making of a fine woman in her, and this proves it. No panics and shrieks and faintings and fuss, but calm sense and energetic skill. Dear child, what can I give or do to show my gratitude?' said Mrs Jo enthusiastically.

'Make Tom clear out and leave her in peace,' suggested Ted, almost himself again, though a pensive haze still partially obscured his native gaiety.

'Yes, do! he frets her like a mosquito. She forbade him to come out here while she stayed, and packed him off with Demi. I like old Tom, but he is a regular noodle about Nan,' added Rob, as he went away to help his father with the accumulated letters.

'I'll do it!' said Mrs Jo decidedly. 'That girl's career shall not be hampered by a foolish boy's fancy. In a moment of weariness she may give in, and then it's all over. Wiser women have done so and regretted it all their lives. Nan shall earn her place first, and prove that she can fill it; then she may marry if she likes, and can find a man worthy of her.'

But Mrs Jo's help was not needed; for love and gratitude can work miracles, and when youth, beauty, accident, and photography are added, success is sure; as was proved in the case of the unsuspecting but too susceptible Thomas.

# CHAPTER 8. JOSIE PLAYS MERMAID

While the young Bhaers were having serious experiences at home, Josie was enjoying herself immensely at Rocky Nook; for the Laurences knew how to make summer idleness both charming and wholesome. Bess was very fond of her little cousin; Mrs Amy felt that whether her niece was an actress or not she must be a gentlewoman, and gave her the social training which marks the well-bred woman everywhere; while Uncle Laurie was never happier than when rowing, riding, playing, or lounging with two gay girls beside him. Josie bloomed like a wild flower in this free life, Bess grew rosy, brisk, and merry, and both were great favourites with the neighbours, whose villas were by the shore or perched on the cliffs along the pretty bay.

One crumpled rose-leaf disturbed Josie's peace, one baffled wish filled her with a longing which became a mania, and kept her as restless and watchful as a detective with a case to 'work up'. Miss Cameron, the great actress, had hired one of the villas and retired thither to rest and 'create' a new part for next season. She saw no one but a friend or two, had a private beach, and was invisible except during her daily drive, or when the opera-glasses of curious gazers were fixed on a blue figure disporting itself in the sea. The Laurences knew her, but respected her privacy, and after a call left her in peace till she expressed a wish for society—a courtesy which she remembered and repaid later, as we shall see.

But Josie was like a thirsty fly buzzing about a sealed honey-pot, for this nearness to her idol was both delightful and maddening. She pined to see, hear, talk with, and study this great and happy woman who could thrill thousands by her art, and win friends by her virtue, benevolence, and beauty. This was the sort of actress the girl meant to be, and few could object if the gift was really hers; for the stage needs just such women to purify and elevate the profession which should teach as well as amuse. If kindly Miss Cameron had known what passionate love and longing burned in the bosom of the little girl whom she idly observed skipping over the rocks, splashing about the beach, or galloping past her gate on a Shetland pony, she would have made her happy by a look or a word. But being tired with her winter's work and busy with her new part, the lady took no more notice of this young neighbour than of the sea-gulls in the bay or the daisies dancing in the fields. Nosegays left on her doorstep, serenades under her garden-wall, and the fixed stare of admiring eyes were such familiar things that she scarcely minded them; and Josie grew desperate when all her little attempts failed.

'I might climb that pine-tree and tumble off on her piazza roof, or get Sheltie to throw me just at her gate and be taken in fainting. It's no use to try to drown myself when she is bathing. I can't sink, and she'd only send a man to pull me out. What can I do? I will see her and tell her my hopes and make her say I can act some day. Mamma would believe her; and if—oh, if she only would let me study with her, what perfect joy that would be!'

Josie made these remarks one afternoon as she and Bess prepared for a swim, a fishing party having prevented their morning bathe.

'You must bide your time, dear, and not be so impatient. Papa promised to give you a chance before the season is over, and he always manages things nicely. That will be better than any queer prank of yours,' answered Bess, tying her pretty hair in a white net to match her suit, while Josie made a little lobster of herself in scarlet.

'I hate to wait; but I suppose I must. Hope she will bathe this afternoon, though it is low tide. She told Uncle she should have to go in then because in the morning people stared so and went on her beach. Come and have a good dive from the big rock. No one round but nurses and babies, so we can romp and splash as much as we like.'

Away they went to have a fine time; for the little bay was free from other bathers, and the babies greatly admired their aquatic gymnastics, both being expert swimmers.

As they sat dripping on the big rock Josie suddenly gave a clutch that nearly sent Bess overboard, as she cried excitedly:

'There she is! Look! coming to bathe. How splendid! Oh, if she only would drown a little and let me save her! or even get her toe nipped by a crab; anything so I could go and speak!'

'Don't seem to look; she comes to be quiet and enjoy herself. Pretend we don't see her, that's only civil,' answered Bess, affecting to be absorbed in a white-winged yacht going by.

'Let's carelessly float that way as if going for seaweed on the rocks. She can't mind if we are flat on our backs, with only our noses out. Then when we can't help seeing her, we'll swim back as if anxious to retire. That will impress her, and she may call to thank the very polite young ladies who respect her wishes,' proposed Josie, whose lively fancy was always planning dramatic situations.

Just as they were going to slip from their rock, as if Fate relented at last, Miss Cameron was seen to beckon wildly as she stood waist-deep in the water, looking down. She called to her maid, who seemed searching along the beach for something, and not finding what she sought, waved a towel towards the girls as if summoning them to help her.

'Run, fly! she wants us, she wants us!' cried Josie, tumbling into the water like a very energetic turtle, and swimming away in her best style towards this long desired haven of joy. Bess followed more slowly, and both came panting and smiling up to Miss Cameron, who never lifted her eyes, but said in that wonderful voice of hers:

'I've dropped a bracelet. I see it, but can't get it. Will the little boy find me a long stick? I'll keep my eye on it, so the water shall not wash it away.'

'I'll dive for it with pleasure; but I'm not a boy,' answered Josie, laughing as she shook the curly head which at a distance had deceived the lady.

'I beg your pardon. Dive away, child; the sand is covering it fast. I value it very much. Never forgot to take it off before.'

'I'll get it!' and down went Josie, to come up with a handful of pebbles, but no bracelet.

'It's gone; never mind—my fault,' said Miss Cameron, disappointed, but amused at the girl's dismay as she shook the water out of her eyes and gasped bravely:

'No, it isn't. I'll have it, if I stay down all night!' and with one long breath Josie dived again, leaving nothing but a pair of agitated feet to be seen.

'I'm afraid she will hurt herself,' said Miss Cameron, looking at Bess, whom she recognized by her likeness to her mother.

'Oh, no; Josie is a little fish. She likes it'; and Bess smiled happily at this wonderful granting of her cousin's desire.

'You are Mr Laurence's daughter, I think? How d'ye do, dear? Tell papa I'm coming to see him soon. Too tired before. Quite savage. Better now. Ah! here's our pearl of divers. What luck?' she asked, as the heels went down and a dripping head came up.

Josie could only choke and splutter at first, being half strangled; but though her hands had failed again, her courage had not; and with a resolute shake of her wet hair, a bright look at the tall lady, and a series of puffs to fill her lungs, she said calmly:

'"Never give up" is my motto. I'm going to get it, if I go to Liverpool for it! Now, then!' and down went the mermaid quite out of sight this time, groping like a real lobster at the bottom of the sea.

'Plucky little girl! I like that. Who is she?' asked the lady, sitting down on a half-covered stone to watch her diver, since the bracelet was lost sight of.

Bess told her, adding, with the persuasive smile of her father: 'Josie longs to be an actress, and has waited for a month to see you. This is a great happiness for her.'

'Bless the child! why didn't she come and call? I'd have let her in; though usually I avoid stage-struck girls as I do reporters,' laughed Miss Cameron.

There was no time for more; a brown hand, grasping the bracelet, rose out of the sea, followed by a purple face as Josie came up so blind and dizzy she could only cling to Bess, half drowned but triumphant.

Miss Cameron drew her to the rock where she sat, and pushing the hair out of her eyes, revived her with a hearty 'Bravo! bravo!' which assured the girl that her first act was a hit. Josie had often imagined her meeting with the great actress—the dignity and grace with which she would enter and tell her ambitious hopes, the effective dress she would wear, the witty things she would say, the deep impression her budding genius would make. But never in her wildest moments had she imagined an interview like this; scarlet, sandy, streaming, and speechless she leaned against the illustrious shoulder, looking like a beautiful seal as she blinked and wheezed till she could smile joyfully and exclaim proudly:

'I did get it! I'm so glad!'

'Now get your breath, my dear; then I shall be glad also. It was very nice of you to take all that trouble for me. How shall I thank you?' asked the lady, looking at her with the beautiful eyes that could say so many things without words.

Josie clasped her hands with a wet spat which rather destroyed the effect of the gesture, and answered in a beseeching tone that would have softened a far harder heart than Miss Cameron's:

'Let me come and see you once—only once! I want you to tell me if I can act; you will know. I'll abide by what you say; and if you think I can—by and by, when I've studied very hard—I shall be the happiest girl in the world. May I?'

'Yes; come tomorrow at eleven. We'll have a good talk; you shall show me what you can do, and I'll give you my opinion. But you won't like it.'

'I will, no matter if you tell me I'm a fool. I want it settled; so does mamma. I'll take it bravely if you say no; and if you say yes, I'll never give up till I've done my best—as you did.'

'Ah, my child, it's a weary road, and there are plenty of thorns among the roses when you've won them. I think you have the courage, and this proves that you have perseverance. Perhaps you'll do. Come, and we'll see.'

Miss Cameron touched the bracelet as she spoke, and smiled so kindly that impetuous Josie wanted to kiss her; but wisely refrained, though her eyes were wet with softer water than any in the sea as she thanked her.

'We are keeping Miss Cameron from her bath, and the tide is going out. Come, Josie,' said thoughtful Bess, fearing to outstay their welcome.

'Run over the beach and get warm. Thank you very much, little mermaid. Tell papa to bring his daughter to see me any time. Good-bye'; and with a wave of her hand the tragedy queen dismissed her court, but remained on her weedy throne watching the two lithe figures race over the sand with twinkling feet till they were out of sight. Then, as she calmly bobbed up and down in the water, she said to herself: 'The child has a good stage face, vivid, mobile; fine eyes, abandon, pluck, will. Perhaps she'll do. Good stock—talent in the family. We shall see.'

Of course Josie never slept a wink, and was in a fever of joyful excitement next day. Uncle Laurie enjoyed the episode very much, and Aunt Amy looked out her most becoming white dress for the grand occasion; Bess lent her most artistic hat, and Josie ranged the wood and marsh for a bouquet of wild roses, sweet white azalea, ferns, and graceful grasses, as the offering of a very grateful heart.

At ten she solemnly arrayed herself, and then sat looking at her neat gloves and buckled shoes till it was time to go, growing pale and sober with the thought that her fate was soon to be decided; for, like all young people she was sure that her whole life could be settled by one human creature, quite forgetting how wonderfully Providence trains us by disappointment, surprises us with unexpected success, and turns our seeming trials into blessings.

'I will go alone: we shall be freer so. Oh, Bess, pray that she may tell me rightly! So much depends on that! Don't laugh, uncle! It is a very serious moment for me. Miss Cameron knows that, and will tell you so. Kiss me, Aunt Amy, since mamma isn't here. If you say I look nice, I'm quite satisfied. Good-bye.' And with a wave of the hand as much like her model's as she could make it, Josie departed, looking very pretty and feeling very tragical.

Sure now of admittance, she boldly rang at the door which excluded so many, and being ushered into a shady parlour, feasted her eyes upon several fine portraits of great actors while she waited. She had read about most of them, and knew their trials and triumphs so well that she soon forgot herself, and tried to imitate Mrs Siddons as Lady Macbeth, looking up at the engraving as she held her nosegay like the candle in the sleep-walking scene, and knit her youthful brows distressfully while murmuring the speech of the haunted queen. So busy was she that Miss Cameron watched her for several minutes unseen, then startled her by suddenly sweeping in with the words upon her lips, the look upon her face, which made that one of her greatest scenes.

'I never can do it like that; but I'll keep trying, if you say I may,' cried Josie, forgetting her manners in the intense interest of the moment.

'Show me what you can do,' answered the actress, wisely plunging into the middle of things at once, well knowing that no common chat would satisfy this very earnest little person.

'First let me give you these. I thought you'd like wild things better than hot-house flowers; and I loved to bring them, as I'd no other way to thank you for your great kindness to me,' said Josie, offering her nosegay with a simple warmth that was very sweet.

'I do love them best, and keep my room full of the posies some good fairy hangs on my gate. Upon my word, I think I've found the fairy out—these are so like,' she added quickly, as her eye went from the flowers in her hand to others that stood near by, arranged with the same taste.

Josie's blush and smile betrayed her before she said, with a look full of girlish adoration and humility: 'I couldn't help it; I admire you so much. I know it was a liberty; but as I couldn't get in myself, I loved to think my posies pleased you.'

Something about the child and her little offering touched the woman, and, drawing Josie to her, she said, with no trace of actress in face or voice:

'They did please me, dear, and so do you. I'm tired of praise; and love is very sweet, when it is simple and sincere like this.'

Josie remembered to have heard, among many other stories, that Miss Cameron lost her lover years ago, and since had lived only for art. Now she felt that this might have been true; and pity for the splendid, lonely life made her face very eloquent, as well as grateful. Then, as if anxious to forget the past, her new friend said, in the commanding way that seemed natural to her:

'Let me see what you can do. Juliet, of course. All begin with that. Poor soul, how she is murdered!'

Now, Josie had intended to begin with Romeo's much-enduring sweetheart, and follow her up with Bianca, Pauline, and several of the favourite idols of stage-struck girls; but being a shrewd little person, she suddenly saw the wisdom of Uncle Laurie's advice, and resolved to follow it. So instead of the rant Miss Cameron expected, Josie gave poor Ophelia's mad scene, and gave it very well, having been trained by the college professor of elocution and done it many times. She was too young, of course, but the white gown, the loose hair, the real flowers she scattered over the imaginary grave, added to the illusion; and she sung the songs sweetly, dropped her pathetic curtsies, and vanished behind the curtain that divided the rooms with a backward look that surprised her critical auditor into a quick gesture of applause. Cheered by that welcome sound, Josie ran back as a little hoyden in one of the farces she had often acted, telling a story full of fun and naughtiness at first, but ending with a sob of repentance and an earnest prayer for pardon.

'Very good! Try again. Better than I expected,' called the voice of the oracle.

Josie tried Portia's speech, and recited very well, giving due emphasis to each fine sentence. Then, unable to refrain from what she considered her greatest effort, she burst into Juliet's balcony scene, ending with the poison and the tomb. She felt sure that she surpassed herself, and waited for applause. A ringing laugh made her tingle with indignation and disappointment, as she went to stand before Miss Cameron, saying in a tone of polite surprise:

'I have been told that I did it very well. I'm sorry you don't think so.'

'My dear, it's very bad. How can it help being so? What can a child like you know of love and fear and death? Don't try it yet. Leave tragedy alone till you are ready for it.'

'But you clapped Ophelia.'

'Yes, that was very pretty. Any clever girl can do it effectively. But the real meaning of Shakespeare is far above you yet, child. The comedy bit was best. There you showed real talent. It was both comic and pathetic. That's art. Don't lose it. The Portia was good declamation. Go on with that sort of thing; it trains the voice—teaches shades of expression. You've a good voice and natural grace—great helps both, hard to acquire.'

'Well, I'm glad I've got something,' sighed Josie, sitting meekly on a stool, much crestfallen, but not daunted yet, and bound to have her say out.

'My dear little girl, I told you that you would not like what I should say to you; yet I must be honest if I would really help you. I've had to do it for many like you; and most of them have never forgiven me, though my words have proved true, and they are what I advised them to be—good wives and happy mothers in quiet homes. A few have kept on, and done fairly well. One you will hear of soon, I think; for she has talent, indomitable patience, and mind as well as beauty. You are too young to show to which class you belong. Geniuses are very rare, and even at fifteen seldom give much promise of future power.'

'Oh, I don't think I'm a genius!' cried Josie, growing calm and sober as she listened to the melodious voice and looked into the expressive face that filled her with confidence, so strong, sincere, and kindly was it. 'I only want to find out if I have talent enough to go on, and after years of study to be able to act well in any of the good plays people never tire of seeing. I don't expect to be a Mrs Siddons or a Miss Cameron, much as I long to be; but it does seem as if I had something in me which can't come out in any way but this. When I act I'm perfectly happy. I seem to live, to be in my own world, and each new part is a new friend. I love Shakespeare, and am never tired of his splendid people. Of course, I don't understand it all; but it's like being alone at night with the mountains and the stars, solemn and grand, and I try to imagine how it will look when the sun comes up, and all is glorious and clear to me. I can't see, but I feel the beauty, and long to express it.'

As she spoke with the most perfect self-forgetfulness Josie was pale with excitement, her eyes shone, her lips trembled, and all her little soul seemed trying to put into words the emotions that filled it to overflowing. Miss Cameron understood, felt that this was something more than a girlish whim; and when she answered there was a new tone of sympathy in her voice, a new interest in her face, though she wisely refrained from saying all she thought, well knowing what splendid dreams young people build upon a word, and how bitter is the pain when the bright bubbles burst.

'If you feel this, I can give you no better advice than to go on loving and studying our great master,' she said slowly; but Josie caught the changed tone, and felt, with a thrill of joy, that her new friend was speaking to her now as to a comrade. 'It is an education in itself, and a lifetime is not long enough to teach you all his secret. But there is much to do before you can hope to echo his words. Have you the patience, courage, strength, to begin at the beginning, and slowly, painfully, lay the foundation for future work? Fame is a pearl many dive for and only a few bring up. Even when they do, it is not perfect, and they sigh for more, and lose better things in struggling for them.'

The last words seemed spoken more to herself than to her hearer, but Josie answered quickly, with a smile and an expressive gesture:

'I got the bracelet in spite of all the bitter water in my eyes.'

'You did! I don't forget it. A good omen. We will accept it.'

Miss Cameron answered the smile with one that was like sunshine to the girl, and stretched her white hands as if taking some invisible gift. Then added in a different tone, watching the effect of her words on the expressive face before her:

'Now you will be disappointed, for instead of telling you to come and study with me, or go and act in some second-rate theatre at once, I advise you to go back to school and finish your education. That is the first step, for all accomplishments are needed, and a single talent makes a very imperfect character. Cultivate mind and body, heart and soul, and make yourself an intelligent, graceful, beautiful, and healthy girl. Then, at eighteen or twenty, go into training and try your powers. Better start for the battle with your arms in order, and save the hard lesson which comes when we rush on too soon. Now and then genius carries all before it, but not often. We have to climb slowly, with many slips and falls. Can you wait as well as work?'

'I will!'

'We shall see. It would be pleasant to me to know that when I quit the stage I leave behind me a well-trained, faithful, gifted comrade to more than fill my place, and carry on what I have much at heart—the purification of the stage. Perhaps you are she; but remember, mere beauty and rich costumes do not make an actress, nor are the efforts of a clever little girl to play great characters real art. It is all dazzle and sham, and a disgrace and disappointment now. Why will the public be satisfied with opera bouffe, or the trash called society plays when a world of truth and beauty, poetry and pathos lies waiting to be interpreted and enjoyed?'

Miss Cameron had forgotten to whom she spoke, and walked to and fro, full of the noble regret all cultivated people feel at the low state of the stage nowadays.

'That's what Uncle Laurie says; and he and Aunt Jo try to plan plays about true and lovely things—simple domestic scenes that touch people's hearts, and make them laugh and cry and feel better. Uncle says that sort is my style, and I must not think of tragedy. But it's so much nicer to sweep about in crowns and velvet trains than to wear everyday clothes, and just be myself, though it is so easy.'

'Yet that is high art, child, and what we need for a time till we are ready for the masters. Cultivate that talent of yours. It is a special gift, this power to bring tears and smiles, and a sweeter task to touch the heart than to freeze the blood or fire the imagination. Tell your uncle he is right, and ask your aunt to try a play for you. I'll come and see it when you are ready.'

'Will you? Oh! will you? We are going to have some at Christmas, with a nice part for me. A simple little thing, but I can do it, and should be so proud, so happy to have you there.'

Josie rose as she spoke, for a glance at the clock showed her that her call was a long one; and hard as it was to end this momentous interview, she felt that she must go. Catching up her hat she went to Miss Cameron, who stood looking at her so keenly that she felt as transparent as a pane of glass, and coloured prettily as she looked up, saying, with a grateful little tremor in her voice:

'I can never thank you for this hour and all you have told me. I shall do just what you advise, and mamma will be very glad to see me settled at my books again. I can study now with all my heart, because it is to help me on; and I won't hope too much, but work and wait, and try to please you, as the only way to pay my debt.'

'That reminds me that I have not paid mine. Little friend, wear this for my sake. It is fit for a mermaid, and will remind you of your first dive. May the next bring up a better jewel, and leave no bitter water on your lips!'

As she spoke, Miss Cameron took from the lace at her throat a pretty pin of aquamarine, and fastened it like an order on Josie's proud bosom; then lifting the happy little face, she kissed it very tenderly, and watched it go smiling away with eyes that seemed to see into a future full of the trials and the triumphs which she knew so well.

Bess expected to see Josie come flying in, all raptures and excitement, or drowned in tears of disappointment, but was surprised at the expression of calm content and resolution which she wore. Pride and satisfaction, and a new feeling of responsibility both sobered and sustained her, and she felt that any amount of dry study and long waiting would be bearable, if in the glorious future she could be an honour to her profession and a comrade to the new friend whom she already adored with girlish ardour.

She told her little story to a deeply interested audience, and all felt that Miss Cameron's advice was good. Mrs Amy was relieved at the prospect of delay; for she did not want her niece to be an actress and hoped the fancy would die out.

Uncle Laurie was full of charming plans and prophecies and wrote one of his most delightful notes to thank their neighbour for her kindness; while Bess, who loved art of all kinds, fully sympathized with her cousin's ambitious hopes, only wondering why she preferred to act out her visions rather than embody them in marble.

That first interview was not the last; for Miss Cameron was really interested, and had several memorable conversations with the Laurences, while the girls sat by, drinking in every word with the delight all artists feel in their own beautiful world, and learning to see how sacred good gifts are, how powerful, and how faithfully they should be used for high ends, each in its own place helping to educate, refine, and refresh.

Josie wrote reams to her mother; and when the visit ended rejoiced her heart by bringing her a somewhat changed little daughter, who fell to work at the once-detested books with a patient energy which surprised and pleased everyone. The right string had been touched, and even French exercises and piano practice became endurable, since accomplishments would be useful by and by; dress, manners, and habits were all interesting now, because 'mind and body, heart and soul, must be cultivated', and while training to become an 'intelligent, graceful, healthy girl', little Josie was unconsciously fitting herself to play her part well on whatever stage the great Manager might prepare for her.

## CHAPTER 9. THE WORM TURNS

Two very superior bicycles went twinkling up the road to Plumfield one September afternoon, bearing two brown and dusty riders evidently returning from a successful run, for though their legs might be a trifle weary, their faces beamed as they surveyed the world from their lofty perches with the air of calm content all wheelmen wear after they have learned to ride; before that happy period anguish of mind and body is the chief expression of the manly countenance.

'Go ahead and report, Tom; I'm due here. See you later,' said Demi, swinging himself down at the door of the Dovecote.

'Don't peach, there's a good fellow. Let me have it out with Mother Bhaer first,' returned Tom, wheeling in at the gate with a heavy sigh.

Demi laughed, and his comrade went slowly up the avenue, devoutly hoping that the coast was clear; for he was the bearer of tidings which would, he thought, convulse the entire family with astonishment and dismay.

To his great joy Mrs Jo was discovered alone in a grove of proof-sheets, which she dropped, to greet the returning wanderer cordially. But after the first glance she saw that something was the matter, recent events having made her unusually sharp-eyed and suspicious.

'What is it now, Tom?' she asked, as he subsided into an easy-chair with a curious expression of mingled fear, shame, amusement, and distress in his brick-red countenance.

'I'm in an awful scrape, ma'am.'

'Of course; I'm always prepared for scrapes when you appear. What is it? Run over some old lady who is going to law about it?' asked Mrs Jo cheerfully.

'Worse than that,' groaned Tom.

'Not poisoned some trusting soul who asked you to prescribe, I hope?'

'Worse than that.'

'You haven't let Demi catch any horrid thing and left him behind, have you?'

'Worse even than that.'

'I give it up. Tell me quick; I hate to wait for bad news.'

Having got his listener sufficiently excited, Tom launched his thunderbolt in one brief sentence, and fell back to watch the effect.

'I'm engaged!'

Mrs Jo's proof-sheets flew wildly about as she clasped her hands, exclaiming in dismay:

'If Nan has yielded, I'll never forgive her!'

'She hasn't; it's another girl.'

Tom's face was so funny as he said the words, that it was impossible to help laughing; for he looked both sheepish and pleased, besides very much perplexed and worried.

'I'm glad, very glad indeed! Don't care who it is; and I hope you'll be married soon. Now tell me all about it,' commanded Mrs Jo, so much relieved that she felt ready for anything.

'What will Nan say?' demanded Tom, rather taken aback at this view of his predicament.

'She will be rejoiced to get rid of the mosquito who has plagued her so long. Don't worry about Nan. Who is this "other girl"?'

'Demi hasn't written about her?'

'Only something about your upsetting a Miss West down at Quitno; I thought that was scrape enough.'

'That was only the beginning of a series of scrapes. Just my luck! Of course after sousing the poor girl I had to be attentive to her, hadn't I? Everyone seemed to think so, and I couldn't get away, and so I was lost before I knew it. It's all Demi's fault, he would stay there and fuss with his old photos, because the views were good and all the girls wanted to be taken. Look at these, will you, ma'am? That's the way we spent our time when we weren't playing tennis'; and Tom pulled a handful of pictures from his pocket, displaying several in which he was conspicuous, either holding a sun-umbrella over a very pretty young lady on the rocks, reposing at her feet in the grass, or perched on a piazza railing with other couples in seaside costumes and effective attitudes.

'This is she of course?' asked Mrs Jo, pointing to the much-ruffled damsel with the jaunty hat, coquettish shoes, and racquet in her hand.

'That's Dora. Isn't she lovely?' cried Tom, forgetting his tribulations for a moment and speaking with lover-like ardour.

'Very nice little person to look at. Hope she is not a Dickens Dora? That curly crop looks like it.'

'Not a bit; she's very smart; can keep house, and sew, and do lots of things, I assure you, ma'am. All the girls like her, and she's sweet-tempered and jolly, and sings like a bird, and dances beautifully, and loves books. Thinks yours are splendid, and made me talk about you no end.'

'That last sentence is to flatter me and win my help to get you out of the scrape. Tell me first how you got in'; and Mrs Jo settled herself to listen with interest, never tired of boys' affairs.

Tom gave his head a rousing rub all over to clear his wits, and plunged into his story with a will.

'Well, we've met her before, but I didn't know she was there. Demi wanted to see a fellow, so we went, and finding it nice and cool rested over Sunday. Found some pleasant people and went out rowing; I had Dora, and came to grief on a confounded rock. She could swim, no harm done, only the scare and the spoilt gown. She took it well, and we got friendly at once—couldn't help it, scrambling into that beast of a boat while the rest laughed at us. Of course we had to stay another day to see that Dora was all right. Demi wanted to. Alice Heath is down there and two other girls from our college, so we sort of lingered along, and Demi kept taking pictures, and we danced, and got into a tennis tournament; and that was as good exercise as wheeling, we thought. Fact is, tennis is a dangerous game, ma'am. A great deal of courting goes on in those courts, and we fellows find that sort of "serving" mighty agreeable, don't you know?'

'Not much tennis in my day, but I understand perfectly,' said Mrs Jo, enjoying it all as much as Tom did.

'Upon my word, I hadn't the least idea of being serious,' he continued slowly, as if this part of his tale was hard to tell; 'but everyone else spooned, so I did. Dora seemed to like it and expect it, and of course I was glad to be agreeable. She thought I amounted to something, though Nan does not, and it was pleasant to be appreciated after years of snubbing. Yes, it was right down jolly to have a sweet girl smile at you all day, and blush prettily when you said a neat thing to her, and look glad when you came, sorry when you left, and admire all you did, and make you feel like a man and act your best. That's the sort of treatment a fellow enjoys and ought to get if he behaves himself; not frowns and cold shoulders year in and year out, and made to look like a fool when he means well, and is faithful, and has loved a girl ever since he was a boy. No, by Jove, it's not fair, and I won't stand it!'

Tom waxed warm and eloquent as he thought over his wrongs, and bounced up to march about the room, wagging his head and trying to feel aggrieved as usual, but surprised to find that his heart did not ache a bit.

'I wouldn't. Drop the old fancy, for it was nothing more, and take up the new one, if it is genuine. But how came you to propose, Tom, as you must have done to be engaged?' asked Mrs Jo, impatient for the crisis of the tale.

'Oh, that was an accident. I didn't mean it at all; the donkey did it, and I couldn't get out of the scrape without hurting Dora's feelings, you see,' began Tom, seeing that the fatal moment had come.

'So there were two donkeys in it, were there?' said Mrs Jo, foreseeing fun of some sort.

'Don't laugh! It sounds funny, I know; but it might have been awful,' answered Tom darkly, though a twinkle of the eye showed that his love trials did not quite blind him to the comic side of the adventure.

'The girls admired our new wheels, and of course we liked to show off. Took 'em to ride, and had larks generally. Well, one day, Dora was on behind, and we were going nicely along a good bit of road, when a ridiculous old donkey got right across the way. I thought he'd move, but he didn't, so I gave him a kick; he kicked back, and over we went in a heap, donkey and all. Such a mess! I thought only of Dora, and she had hysterics; at least, she laughed till she cried, and that beast brayed, and I lost my head. Any fellow would, with a poor girl gasping in the road, and he wiping her tears and begging pardon, not knowing whether her bones were broken or not. I called her my darling, and went on like a fool in my flurry, till she grew calmer, and said, with such a look: "I forgive you, Tom. Pick me up, and let us go on again."

'Wasn't that sweet now, after I'd upset her for the second time? It touched me to the heart; and I said I'd like to go on for ever with such an angel to steer for, and—well I don't know what I did say; but you might have knocked me down with a feather when she put her arm round my neck and whispered: "Tom, dear, with you I'm not afraid of any lions in the path." She might have said donkeys; but she was in earnest, and she spared my feelings. Very nice of the dear girl; but there I am with two sweethearts on my hands, and in a deuce of a scrape.'

Finding it impossible to contain herself another moment, Mrs Jo laughed till the tears ran down her cheeks at this characteristic episode; and after one reproachful look, which only added to her merriment, Tom burst into a jolly roar that made the room ring.

'Tommy Bangs! Tommy Bangs! who but you could ever get into such a catastrophe?' said Mrs Jo, when she recovered her breath.

'Isn't it a muddle all round, and won't everyone chaff me to death about it? I shall have to quit old Plum for a while,' answered Tom, as he mopped his face, trying to realize the full danger of his position.

'No, indeed; I'll stand by you, for I think it the best joke of the season. But tell me how things ended. Is it really serious, or only a summer flirtation? I don't approve of them, but boys and girls will play with edged tools and cut their fingers.'

'Well, Dora considers herself engaged, and wrote to her people at once. I couldn't say a word when she took it all in solemn earnest and seemed so happy. She's only seventeen, never liked anyone before, and is sure all will be all right; as her father knows mine, and we are both well off. I was so staggered that I said:

'"Why, you can't love me really when we know so little of one another?" But she answered right out of her tender little heart: "Yes, I do, dearly, Tom; you are so gay and kind and honest, I couldn't help it." Now, after that what could I do but go ahead and make her happy while I stayed, and trust to luck to straighten the snarl out afterwards?'

'A truly Tomian way of taking things easy. I hope you told your father at once.'

'Oh yes, I wrote off and broke it to him in three lines. I said: "Dear Father, I'm engaged to Dora West, and I hope she will suit the family. She suits me tip-top. Yours ever, Tom." He was all right, never liked Nan, you know; but Dora will suit him down to the ground.' And Tom looked entirely satisfied with his own tact and taste.

'What did Demi say to this rapid and funny lovemaking? Wasn't he scandalized?' asked Mrs Jo, trying not to laugh again as she thought of the unromantic spectacle of donkey, bicycle, boy, and girl all in the dust together.

'Not a bit. He was immensely interested and very kind; talked to me like a father; said it was a good thing to steady a fellow, only I must be honest with her and myself and not trifle a moment. Demi is a regular Solomon, especially when he is in the same boat,' answered Tom, looking wise.

'You don't mean—?' gasped Mrs Jo, in sudden alarm at the bare idea of more love-affairs just yet.

'Yes, I do, please, ma'am; it's a regular sell all the way through, and I owe Demi one for taking me into temptation blindfold. He said he went to Quitno to see Fred Wallace, but he never saw the fellow. How could he, when Wallace was off in his yacht all the time we were there? Alice was the real attraction, and I was left to my fate, while they were maundering round with that old camera. There were three donkeys in this affair, and I'm not the worst one, though I shall have to bear the laugh. Demi will look innocent and sober, and no one will say a word to him.'

'The midsummer madness has broken out, and no one knows who will be stricken next. Well, leave Demi to his mother, and let us see what you are going to do, Tom.'

'I don't know exactly; it's awkward to be in love with two girls at once. What do you advise?'

'A common-sense view of the case, by all means. Dora loves you and thinks you love her. Nan does not care for you, and you only care for her as a friend, though you have tried to do more. It is my opinion, Tom, that you love Dora, or are on the way to it; for in all these years I've never seen you look or speak about Nan as you do about Dora. Opposition has made you obstinately cling to her till accident has shown you a more attractive girl. Now, I think you had better take the old love for a friend, the new one for a sweetheart, and in due time, if the sentiment is genuine, marry her.'

If Mrs Jo had any doubts about the matter, Tom's face would have proved the truth of her opinion; for his eyes shone, his lips smiled, and in spite of dust and sunburn a new expression of happiness quite glorified him as he stood silent for a moment, trying to understand the beautiful miracle which real love works when it comes to a young man's heart.

'The fact is I meant to make Nan jealous, for she knows Dora, and I was sure would hear of our doings. I was tired of being walked on, and I thought I'd try to break away and not be a bore and a laughing-stock any more,' he said slowly, as if it relieved him to pour out his doubts and woes and hopes and joys to his old friend. 'I was regularly astonished to find it so easy and so pleasant. I didn't mean to do any harm, but drifted along beautifully, and told Demi to mention things in his letters to Daisy, so Nan might know. Then I forgot Nan altogether, and saw, heard, felt, cared for no one but Dora, till the donkey—bless his old heart!—pitched her into my arms and I found she loved me. Upon my soul, I don't see why she should! I'm not half good enough.'

'Every honest man feels that when an innocent girl puts her hand in his. Make yourself worthy of her, for she isn't an angel, but a woman with faults of her own for you to bear, and forgive, and you must help one another,' said Mrs Jo, trying to realize that this sober youth was her scapegrace Tommy.

'What troubles me is that I didn't mean it when I began, and was going to use the dear girl as an instrument of torture for Nan. It wasn't right, and I don't deserve to be so happy. If all my scrapes ended as well as this, what a state of bliss I should be in!' and Tom beamed again at the rapturous prospect.

'My dear boy, it is not a scrape, but a very sweet experience suddenly dawning upon you,' answered Mrs Jo, speaking very soberly; for she saw he was in earnest. 'Enjoy it wisely and be worthy of it, for it is a serious thing to accept a girl's love and trust, and let her look up to you for tenderness and truth in return. Don't let little Dora look in vain, but be a man in all things for her sake, and make this affection a blessing to you both.'

'I'll try. Yes, I do love her, only I can't believe it just yet. Wish you knew her. Dear little soul, I long to see her already! She cried when we parted last night and I hated to go.' Tom's hand went to his cheek as if he still felt the rosy little seal Dora had set upon his promise not to forget her, and for the first time in his happy-go-lucky life Tommy Bangs understood the difference between sentiment and sentimentality. The feeling recalled Nan, for he had never known that tender thrill when thinking of her, and the old friendship seemed rather a prosaic affair beside this delightful mingling of romance, surprise, love, and fun. 'I declare, I feel as if a weight was off me, but what the dickens will Nan say when she knows it!' he exclaimed with a chuckle.

'Knows what?' asked a clear voice that made both start and turn, for there was Nan calmly surveying them from the doorway.

Anxious to put Tom out of suspense and see how Nan would take the news, Mrs Jo answered quickly:

'Tom's engagement to Dora West.'

'Really?' and Nan looked so surprised that Mrs Jo was afraid she might be fonder of her old playmate than she knew; but her next words set the fear at rest, and made everything comfortable and merry at once.

'I knew my prescription would work wonders if he only took it long enough. Dear old Tom, I'm so glad. Bless you! bless you!' And she shook both his hands with hearty affection.

'It was an accident, Nan. I didn't mean to, but I'm always getting into messes, and I couldn't seem to get out of this any other way. Mother Bhaer will tell you all about it. I must go and make myself tidy. Going to tea with Demi. See you later.'

Stammering, blushing, and looking both sheepish and gratified, Tom suddenly bolted, leaving the elder lady to enlighten the younger at length, and have another laugh over this new sort of courtship, which might well be called accidental. Nan was deeply interested, for she knew Dora, thought her a nice little thing, and predicted that in time she would make Tom an excellent wife, since she admired and 'appreciated' him so much.

'I shall miss him of course, but it will be a relief to me and better for him; dangling is so bad for a boy. Now he will go into business with his father and do well, and everyone be happy. I shall give Dora an elegant family medicine-chest for a wedding-present, and teach her how to use it. Tom can't be trusted, and is no more fit for the profession than Silas.'

The latter part of this speech relieved Mrs Jo's mind, for Nan had looked about her as if she had lost something valuable when she began; but the medicine-chest seemed to cheer her, and the thought of Tom in a safe profession was evidently a great comfort.

'The worm has turned at last, Nan, and your bond-man is free. Let him go, and give your whole mind to your work; for you are fitted for the profession, and will be an honour to it by and by,' she said approvingly.

'I hope so. That reminds me—measles are in the village, and you had better tell the girls not to call where there are children. It would be bad to have a run of them just as term begins. Now I'm off to Daisy. Wonder what she will say to Tom. Isn't he great fun?' And Nan departed, laughing over the joke with such genuine satisfaction that it was evident no sentimental regrets disturbed her 'maiden meditation, fancy-free'.

'I shall have my eye on Demi, but won't say a word. Meg likes to manage her children in her own way, and a very good way it is. But the dear Pelican will be somewhat ruffled if her boy has caught the epidemic which seems to have broken out among us this summer.'

Mrs Jo did not mean the measles, but that more serious malady called love, which is apt to ravage communities, spring and autumn, when winter gaiety and summer idleness produce whole bouquets of engagements, and set young people to pairing off like the birds. Franz began it, Nat was a chronic and Tom a sudden case; Demi seemed to have the symptoms; and worst of all, her own Ted had only the day before calmly said to her: 'Mum, I think I should be happier if I had a sweetheart, like the other boys.' If her cherished son had asked her for dynamite to play with, she would hardly have been more startled, or have more decidedly refused the absurd request.

'Well, Barry Morgan said I ought to have one and offered to pick me out a nice one among our set. I asked Josie first, and she hooted at the idea, so I thought I'd let Barry look round. You say it steadies a fellow, and I want to be steady,' explained Ted in a serious tone, which would have convulsed his parent at any other time.

'Good lack! What are we coming to in this fast age when babes and boys make such demands and want to play with one of the most sacred things in life?' exclaimed Mrs Jo, and having in a few words set the matter in its true light, sent her son away to wholesome baseball and Octoo for a safe sweetheart.

Now, here was Tom's bomb-shell to explode in their midst, carrying widespread destruction, perhaps; for though one swallow does not make a summer, one engagement is apt to make several, and her boys were, most of them, at the inflammable age when a spark ignites the flame, which soon flickers and dies out, or burns warm and clear for life. Nothing could be done about it but to help them make wise choices, and be worthy of good mates. But of all the lessons Mrs Jo had tried to teach her boys, this great one was the hardest; for love is apt to make lunatics of even saints and sages, so young people cannot be expected to escape the delusions, disappointments, and mistakes, as well as the delights, of this sweet madness.

'I suppose it is inevitable, since we live in America, so I won't borrow trouble, but hope that some of the new ideas of education will produce a few hearty, happy, capable, and intelligent girls for my lads. Lucky for me that I haven't the whole twelve on my hands, I should lose my wits if I had, for I foresee complications and troubles ahead worse than Tom's boats, bicycles, donkeys, and Doras,' meditated Mrs Jo, as she went back to her neglected proof-sheets.

Tom was quite satisfied with the tremendous effect his engagement produced in the little community at Plumfield.

'It was paralysing,' as Demi said; and astonishment left most of Tom's mates little breath for chaff. That he, the faithful one, should turn from the idol to strange goddesses, was a shock to the romantic and a warning to the susceptible. It was comical to see the airs our Thomas put on; for the most ludicrous parts of the affair were kindly buried in oblivion by the few who knew them, and Tom burst forth as a full-blown hero who had rescued the maiden from a watery grave, and won her gratitude and love by his daring deed. Dora kept the secret, and enjoyed the fun when she came to see Mother Bhaer and pay her respects to the family generally. Everyone liked her at once, for she was a gay and winning little soul; fresh, frank, and so happy, it was beautiful to see her innocent pride in Tom, who was a new boy, or man rather; for with this change in his life a great change took place in him. Jolly he would always be, and impulsive, but he tried to become all that Dora believed him, and his best side came uppermost for everyday wear. It was surprising to see how many good traits Tom had; and his efforts to preserve the manly dignity belonging to his proud position as an engaged man was very comical. So was the entire change from his former abasement and devotion to Nan to a somewhat lordly air with his little betrothed; for Dora made an idol of him, and resented the idea of a fault or a flaw in her Tom. This new state of things suited both, and the once blighted being bloomed finely in the warm atmosphere of appreciation, love, and confidence. He was very fond of the dear girl, but meant to be a slave no longer, and enjoyed his freedom immensely, quite unconscious that the great tyrant of the world had got hold of him for life.

To his father's satisfaction he gave up his medical studies, and prepared to go into business with the old gentleman, who was a flourishing merchant, ready now to make the way smooth and smile upon his marriage with Mr West's well-endowed daughter. The only thorn in Tom's bed of roses was Nan's placid interest in his affairs, and evident relief at his disloyalty. He did not want her to suffer, but a decent amount of regret at the loss of such a lover would have gratified him; a slight melancholy, a word of reproach, a glance of envy as he passed with adoring Dora on his arm, seemed but the fitting tribute to such years of faithful service and sincere affection. But Nan regarded him with a maternal sort of air that nettled him very much, and patted Dora's curly head with a worldlywise air worthy of the withered spinster, Julia Mills, in David Copperfield.

It took some time to get the old and the new emotions comfortably adjusted, but Mrs Jo helped him, and Mr Laurie gave him some wise advice upon the astonishing gymnastic feats the human heart can perform, and be all the better for it if it only held fast to the balancing-pole of truth and common sense. At last our Tommy got his bearings, and as autumn came on Plumfield saw but little of him; for his new lode star was in the city, and business kept him hard at work. He was evidently in his right place now, and soon throve finely, to his father's great contentment; for his jovial presence pervaded the once quiet office like a gale of fresh wind, and his lively wits found managing men and affairs much more congenial employment than studying disease, or playing unseemly pranks with skeletons.

Here we will leave him for a time and turn to the more serious adventures of his mates, though this engagement, so merrily made, was the anchor which kept our mercurial Tom happy, and made a man of him.

# CHAPTER 10. DEMI SETTLES

'Mother, can I have a little serious conversation with you?' asked Demi one evening, as they sat together enjoying the first fire of the season, while Daisy wrote letters upstairs and Josie was studying in the little library close by.

'Certainly, dear. No bad news, I hope?' and Mrs Meg looked up from her sewing with a mixture of pleasure and anxiety on her motherly face; for she dearly loved a good talk with her son, and knew that he always had something worth telling.

'It will be good news for you, I think,' answered Demi, smiling as he threw away his paper and went to sit beside her on the little sofa which just held two.

'Let me hear it, then, at once.'

'I know you don't like the reporting, and will be glad to hear that I have given it up.'

'I am very glad! It is too uncertain a business, and there is no prospect of getting on for a long time. I want you settled in some good place where you can stay, and in time make money. I wish you liked a profession; but as you don't, any clean, well-established business will do.'

'What do you say to a railroad office?'

'I don't like it. A noisy, hurried kind of place, I know, with all sorts of rough men about. I hope it isn't that, dear?'

'I could have it; but does book-keeping in a wholesale leather business please you better?'

'No; you'll get round-shouldered writing at a tall desk; and they say, once a book-keeper always a book-keeper.'

'How does a travelling agent suit your views?'

'Not at all; with all those dreadful accidents, and the exposure and bad food as you go from place to place, you are sure to get killed or lose your health.'

'I could be private secretary to a literary man; but the salary is small, and may end any time.'

'That would be better, and more what I want. It isn't that I object to honest work of any kind; but I don't want my son to spend his best years grubbing for a little money in a dark office, or be knocked about in a rough-and-tumble scramble to get on. I want to see you in some business where your tastes and talents can be developed and made useful; where you can go on rising, and in time put in your little fortune and be a partner; so that your years of apprenticeship will not be wasted, but fit you to take your place among the honourable men who make their lives and work useful and respected. I talked it all over with your dear father when you were a child; and if he had lived he would have shown you what I mean, and helped you to be what he was.'

Mrs Meg wiped away a quiet tear as she spoke; for the memory of her husband was a very tender one, and the education of his children had been a sacred task to which she gave all her heart and life, and so far she had done wonderfully well—as her good son and loving daughters tried to prove. Demi's arm was round her now, as he said, in a voice so like his father's that it was the sweetest music to her ear:

'Mother dear, I think I have got just what you want for me; and it shall not be my fault if I don't become the man you hope to see me. Let me tell you all about it. I didn't say anything till it was sure because it would only worry you; but Aunt Jo and I have been on the look-out for it some time, and now it has come. You know her publisher, Mr Tiber, is one of the most successful men in the business; also generous, kind, and the soul of honour—as his treatment of Aunty proves. Well, I've rather hankered for that place; for I love books, and as I can't make them I'd like to publish them. That needs some literary taste and judgement, it brings you in contact with fine people, and is an education in itself. Whenever I go into that large, handsome room to see Mr Tiber for Aunt Jo, I always want to stay; for it's lined with books and pictures, famous men and women come and go, and Mr Tiber sits at his desk like a sort of king, receiving his subjects; for the greatest authors are humble to him, and wait his Yes or No with anxiety. Of course I've nothing to do with all that, and may never have; but I like to see it, and the atmosphere is so different from the dark offices and hurly-burly of many other trades, where nothing but money is talked about, that it seems another world, and I feel at home in it. Yes, I'd rather beat the door-mats and make fires there than be head clerk in the great hide and leather store at a big salary.' Here Demi paused for breath; and Mrs Meg, whose face had been growing brighter and brighter, exclaimed eagerly:

'Just what I should like! Have you got it? Oh, my dear boy! your fortune is made if you go to that well-established and flourishing place, with those good men to help you along!'

'I think I have, but we mustn't be too sure of anything yet. I may not suit; I'm only on trial, and must begin at the beginning and work my way up faithfully. Mr Tiber was very kind, and will push me on as fast as is fair to the other fellows, and as I prove myself fit to go up. I'm to begin the first of next month in the book-room, filling orders; and I go round and get orders, and do various other things of the sort. I like it. I am ready to do anything about books, if it's only to dust them,' laughed Demi, well pleased with his prospects, for, after trying various things, he seemed at last to have found the sort of work he liked, and a prospect that was very inviting to him.

'You inherit that love of books from grandpa; he can't live without them. I'm glad of it. Tastes of that kind show a refined nature, and are both a comfort and a help all one's life. I am truly glad and grateful, John, that at last you want to settle, and have got such an entirely satisfactory place. Most boys begin much earlier; but I don't believe in sending them out to face the world so young, just when body and soul need home care and watchfulness. Now you are a man, and must begin your life for yourself. Do your best, and be as honest, useful, and happy as your father, and I won't care about making a fortune.'

'I'll try, mother. Couldn't have a better chance; for Tiber & Co. treat their people like gentlemen, and pay generously for faithful work. Things are done in a businesslike way there, and that suits me. I hate promises that are not kept, and shiftless or tyrannical ways anywhere. Mr Tiber said: "This is only to teach you the ropes, Brooke; I shall have other work for you by and by." Aunty told him I had done book notices, and had rather a fancy for literature; so though I can't produce any "works of Shakespeare", as she says, I may get up some little things later. If I don't, I think it a very honourable and noble profession to select and give good books to the world; and I'm satisfied to be a humble helper in the work.'

'I'm glad you feel so. It adds so much to one's happiness to love the task one does. I used to hate teaching; but housekeeping for my own family was always sweet, though much harder in many ways. Isn't Aunt Jo pleased about all this?' asked Mrs Meg, already seeing in her mind's eye a splendid sign with 'Tiber, Brooke & Co.' over the door of a famous publishing house.

'So pleased that I could hardly keep her from letting the cat out of the bag too soon. I've had so many plans, and disappointed you so often, I wanted to be very sure this time. I had to bribe Rob and Ted to keep her at home tonight till I'd told my news, she was eager to rush down and tell you herself. The castles that dear woman has built for me would fill all Spain, and have kept us jolly while we waited to know our fate. Mr Tiber doesn't do things in a hurry; but when he makes up his mind, you are all right; and I feel that I am fairly launched.'

'Bless you, dear, I hope so! It is a happy day for me, because I've been so anxious lest, with all my care, I have been too easy and indulgent, and my boy, with his many good gifts, might fritter his time away in harmless but unsatisfactory things. Now I am at ease about you. If only Daisy can be happy, and Josie give up her dream, I shall be quite contented.'

Demi let his mother enjoy herself for a few minutes, while he smiled over a certain little dream of his own, not ready yet for the telling; then he said, in the paternal tone which he unconsciously used when speaking of his sisters:

'I'll see to the girls; but I begin to think grandpa is right in saying we must each be what God and nature makes us. We can't change it much—only help to develop the good and control the bad elements in us. I have fumbled my way into my right place at last, I hope. Let Daisy be happy in her way, since it is a good and womanly one. If Nat comes home all right, I'd say: "Bless you, my children," and give them a nest of their own. Then you and I will help little Jo to find out if it is to be "All the world's a stage" or "Home, sweet home", for her.'

'I suppose we must, John; but I can't help making plans, and hoping they will come to pass. I see that Daisy is bound up in Nat; and if he is worthy of her I shall let them be happy in their own way, as my parents let me. But Josie will be a trial, I foresee; and much as I love the stage, and always did, I don't see how I can ever let my little girl be an actress, though she certainly has great talent for it.'

'Whose fault is that?' asked Demi, smiling, as he remembered his mother's early triumphs and unquenchable interest in the dramatic efforts of the young people round her.

'Mine, I know. How could it be otherwise when I acted Babes in the Wood with you and Daisy before you could speak, and taught Josie to declaim Mother Goose in her cradle. Ah, me! the tastes of the mother come out in her children, and she must atone for them by letting them have their own way, I suppose.' And Mrs Meg laughed, even while she shook her head over the undeniable fact that the Marches were a theatrical family.

'Why not have a great actress of our name, as well as an authoress, a minister, and an eminent publisher? We don't choose our talents, but we needn't hide them in a napkin because they are not just what we want. I say, let Jo have her way, and do what she can. Here am I to take care of her; and you can't deny you'd enjoy fixing her furbelows, and seeing her shine before the footlights, where you used to long to be. Come, mother, better face the music and march gaily, since your wilful children will "gang their ain gait".'

'I don't see but I must, and "leave the consequences to the Lord", as Marmee used to say when she had to decide, and only saw a step of the road. I should enjoy it immensely, if I could only feel that the life would not hurt my girl, and leave her unsatisfied when it was too late to change; for nothing is harder to give up than the excitements of that profession. I know something of it; and if your blessed father had not come along, I'm afraid I should have been an actress in spite of Aunt March and all our honoured ancestors.'

'Let Josie add new honour to the name, and work out the family talent in its proper place. I'll play dragon to her, and you play nurse, and no harm can come to our little Juliet, no matter how many Romeos spoon under her balcony. Really, ma'am, opposition comes badly from an old lady who is going to wring the hearts of our audience in the heroine's part in Aunty's play next Christmas. It's the most pathetic thing I ever saw, mother; and I'm sorry you didn't become an actress, though we should be nowhere if you had.'

Demi was on his legs now, with his back to the fire, in the lordly attitude men like to assume when things go well with them, or they want to lay down the law on any subject.

Mrs Meg actually blushed at her son's hearty praise, and could not deny that the sound of applause was as sweet now as when she played the Witch's Curse and The Moorish Maiden's Vow long years ago.

'It's perfectly absurd for me to do it, but I couldn't resist when Jo and Laurie made the part for me, and you children were to act in it. The minute I get on the old mother's dress I forget myself and feel the same thrill at the sound of the bell that I used to feel when we got up plays in the garret. If Daisy would only take the daughter's part it would be so complete; for with you and Josie I am hardly acting, it is all so real.'

'Especially the hospital scene, where you find the wounded son. Why, mother, do you know when we did that at last rehearsal my face was wet with real tears as you cried over me. It will bring down the house; but don't forget to wipe 'em off, or I shall sneeze,' said Demi, laughing at the recollection of his mother's hit.

'I won't; but it almost broke my heart to see you so pale and dreadful. I hope there will never be another war in my time, for I should have to let you go; and I never want to live through the same experience we had with father.'

'Don't you think Alice does the part better than Daisy would? Daisy hasn't a bit of the actress in her, and Alice puts life into the dullest words she speaks. I think the Marquise is just perfect in our piece,' said Demi, strolling about the room as if the warmth of the fire sent a sudden colour to his face.

'So do I. She is a dear girl, and I'm proud and fond of her. Where is she tonight?'

'Pegging away at her Greek, I suppose. She usually is in the evening. More's the pity,' added Demi, in a low tone, as he stared intently at the book-case, though he couldn't read a title.

'Now, there is a girl after my own heart. Pretty, well-bred, well-educated, and yet domestic, a real companion as well as help-meet for some good and intelligent man. I hope she will find one.'

'So do I,' muttered Demi.

Mrs Meg had taken up her work again, and was surveying a half-finished buttonhole with so much interest that her son's face escaped her eye. He shed a beaming smile upon the rows of poets, as if even in their glass prison they could sympathize and rejoice with him at the first rosy dawn of the great passion which they knew so well. But Demi was a wise youth, and never leaped before looking carefully. He hardly knew his own heart yet, and was contented to wait till the sentiment, the fluttering of those folded wings he began to feel, should escape from the chrysalis and be ready to soar away in the sunshine to seek and claim its lovely mate. He had said nothing; but the brown eyes were eloquent, and there was an unconscious underplot to all the little plays he and Alice Heath acted so well together. She was busy with her books, bound to graduate with high honours, and he was trying to do the same in that larger college open to all, and where each man has his own prize to win or lose. Demi had nothing but himself to offer and, being a modest youth, considered that a poor gift till he had proved his power to earn his living, and the right to take a woman's happiness into his keeping.

No one guessed that he had caught the fever except sharp-eyed Josie, and she, having a wholesome fear of her brother—who could be rather awful when she went too far—wisely contented herself with watching him like a little cat, ready to pounce on the first visible sign of weakness. Demi had taken to playing pensively upon his flute after he was in his room for the night, making this melodious friend his confidante, and breathing into it all the tender hopes and fears that filled his heart. Mrs Meg, absorbed in domestic affairs, and Daisy, who cared for no music but Nat's violin, paid no heed to these chamber concerts, but Josie always murmured to herself, with a naughty chuckle, 'Dick Swiveller is thinking of his Sophy Wackles,' and bided her time to revenge certain wrongs inflicted upon her by Demi, who always took Daisy's side when she tried to curb the spirits of her unruly little sister.

This evening she got her chance, and made the most of it. Mrs Meg was just rounding off her buttonhole, and Demi still strolling restlessly about the room, when a book was heard to slam in the study, followed by an audible yawn and the appearance of the student looking as if sleep and a desire for mischief were struggling which should be master.

'I heard my name; have you been saying anything bad about me?' she demanded, perching on the arm of an easychair.

Her mother told the good news, over which Josie duly rejoiced, and Demi received her congratulations with a benignant air which made her feel that too much satisfaction was not good for him, and incited her to put a thorn into his bed of roses at once.

'I caught something about the play just now, and I want to tell you that I'm going to introduce a song into my part to liven it up a bit. How would this do?' and seating herself at the piano she began to sing to these words the air of 'Kathleen Mavourneen':

*'Sweetest of maidens, oh, how can I tell*
*The love that transfigures the whole earth to me?*
*The longing that causes my bosom to swell,*
*When I dream of a life all devoted to thee?'*

She got no further, for Demi, red with wrath, made a rush at her, and the next moment a very agile young person was seen dodging round tables and chairs with the future partner of Tiber & Co. in hot pursuit. 'You monkey, how dare you meddle with my papers?' cried the irate poet, making futile grabs at the saucy girl, who skipped to and fro, waving a bit of paper tantalizingly before him.

'Didn't; found it in the big "Dic". Serves you right if you leave your rubbish about. Don't you like my song? It's very pretty.'

'I'll teach you one that you won't like if you don't give me my property.'

'Come and get it if you can'; and Josie vanished into the study to have out her squabble in peace, for Mrs Meg was already saying:

'Children, children! don't quarrel.'

The paper was in the fire by the time Demi arrived and he at once calmed down, seeing that the bone of contention was out of the way.

'I'm glad it's burnt; I don't care for it, only some verse I was trying to set to music for one of the girls. But I'll trouble you to let my papers alone, or I shall take back the advice I gave mother tonight about allowing you to act as much as you like.'

Josie was sobered at once by this dire threat, and in her most wheedling tone begged to know what he had said. By way of heaping coals of fire on her head he told her, and this diplomatic performance secured him an ally on the spot.

'You dear old boy! I'll never tease you again though you moon and spoon both day and night. If you stand by me, I'll stand by you and never say a word. See here! I've got a note for you from Alice. Won't that be a peace-offering and soothe your little feelings?'

Demi's eyes sparkled as Josie held up a paper cocked hat, but as he knew what was probably in it, he took the wind out of Josie's sails, and filled her with blank astonishment by saying carelessly:

'That's nothing; it's only to say whether she will go to the concert with us tomorrow night. You can read it if you like.'

With the natural perversity of her sex Josie ceased to be curious the moment she was told to read it, and meekly handed it over; but she watched Demi as he calmly read the two lines it contained and then threw it into the fire. 'Why, Jack, I thought you'd treasure every scrap the "sweetest maid" touched. Don't you care for her?'

'Very much; we all do; but "mooning and spooning", as you elegantly express it, is not in my line. My dear little girl, your plays make you romantic, and because Alice and I act lovers sometimes you take it into your silly head that we are really so. Don't waste time hunting mares nests, but attend to your own affairs and leave me to mine. I forgive you, but don't do it again; it's bad taste, and tragedy queens don't romp.'

The last cut finished Josie; she humbly begged pardon and went off to bed, while Demi soon followed, feeling that he had not only settled himself but his too inquisitive little sister also. But if he had seen her face as she listened to the soft wailing of his flute he would not have been so sure, for she looked as cunning as a magpie as she said, with a scornful sniff: 'Pooh, you can't deceive me; I know Dick is serenading Sophy Wackles.'

## CHAPTER 11. EMIL'S THANKSGIVING

The Brenda was scudding along with all sail set to catch the rising wind, and everyone on board was rejoicing, for the long voyage was drawing towards an end.

'Four weeks more, Mrs Hardy, and we'll give you a cup of tea such as you never had before,' said second mate Hoffmann, as he paused beside two ladies sitting in a sheltered corner of the deck.

'I shall be glad to get it, and still gladder to put my feet on solid ground,' answered the elder lady, smiling; for our friend Emil was a favourite, as well he might be, since he devoted himself to the captain's wife and daughter, who were the only passengers on board.

'So shall I, even if I have to wear a pair of shoes like Chinese junks. I've tramped up and down the deck so much, I shall be barefooted if we don't arrive soon,' laughed Mary, the daughter, showing two shabby little boots as she glanced up at the companion of these tramps, remembering gratefully how pleasant he had made them.

'Don't think there are any small enough in China,' answered Emil, with a sailor's ready gallantry, privately resolving to hunt up the handsomest shoes he could find the moment he landed.

'I don't know what you would have done for exercise, dear, if Mr Hoffmann had not made you walk every day. This lazy life is bad for young people, though it suits an old body like me well enough in calm weather. Is this likely to be a gale, think ye?' added Mrs Hardy, with an anxious glance at the west, where the sun was setting redly.

'Only a capful of wind, ma'am, just enough to send us along lively,' answered Emil, with a comprehensive glance aloft and alow.

'Please sing, Mr Hoffmann, it's so pleasant to have music at this time. We shall miss it very much when we get ashore,' said Mary, in a persuasive tone which would have won melody from a shark, if such a thing were possible.

Emil had often blessed his one accomplishment during these months, for it cheered the long days, and made the twilight hour his happiest time, wind and weather permitting. So now he gladly tuned his pipe, and leaning on the taffrail near the girl, watched the brown locks blowing in the wind as he sang her favourite song:

*'Give me freshening breeze, my boys,*
*A white and swelling sail,*
*A ship that cuts the dashing waves,*
*And weathers every gale.*
*What life is like a sailor's life,*
*So free, so bold, so brave?*
*His home the ocean's wide expanse,*
*A coral bed his grave.'*

Just as the last notes of the clear, strong voice died away, Mrs Hardy suddenly exclaimed: 'What's that?' Emil's quick eye saw at once the little puff of smoke coming up a hatchway where no smoke should be, and his heart seemed to stand still for an instant as the dread word 'Fire!' flashed through his mind. Then he was quite steady, and strolled away saying quietly:

'Smoking not allowed there, I'll go and stop it.' But the instant he was out of sight his face changed, and he leaped down the hatchway, thinking, with a queer smile on his lips: 'If we are afire, shouldn't wonder if I did make a coral bed my grave!'

He was gone a few minutes, and when he came up, half stifled with smoke, he was as white as a very brown man could be, but calm and cool as he went to report to the captain.

'Fire in the hold, sir.'

'Don't frighten the women,' was Captain Hardy's first order; then both be stirred themselves to discover how strong the treacherous enemy was, and to rout it if possible.

The Brenda's cargo was a very combustible one, and in spite of the streams of water poured into the hold it was soon evident that the ship was doomed. Smoke began to ooze up between the planks everywhere, and the rising gale soon fanned the smouldering fire to flames that began to break out here and there, telling the dreadful truth too plainly for anyone to hide. Mrs Hardy and Mary bore the shock bravely when told to be ready to quit the ship at a minute's notice; the boats were hastily prepared, and the men worked with a will to batten down every loophole whence the fire might escape. Soon the poor Brenda was a floating furnace, and the order to 'Take to the boats!' came for all. The women first, of course, and it was fortunate that, being a merchantman, there were no more passengers on board, so there was no panic, and one after the other the boats pushed off. That in which the women were lingered near, for the brave captain would be the last to leave his ship.

Emil stayed by him till ordered away, and reluctantly obeyed; but it was well for him he went, for just as he had regained the boat, rocking far below, half hidden by a cloud of smoke, a mast, undermined by the fire now raging in the bowels of the ship, fell with a crash, knocking Captain Hardy overboard. The boat soon reached him as he floated out from the wreck, and Emil sprung into the sea to rescue him, for he was wounded and senseless. This accident made it necessary for the young man to take command, and he at once ordered the men to pull for their lives, as an explosion might occur at any moment.

The other boats were out of danger and all lingered to watch the splendid yet awesome spectacle of the burning ship alone on the wide sea, reddening the night and casting a lurid glare upon the water, where floated the frail boats filled with pale faces, all turned for a last look at the fated Brenda, slowly settling to her watery grave. No one saw the end, however, for the gale soon swept the watchers far away and separated them, some never to meet again till the sea gives up its dead.

The boat whose fortunes we must follow was alone when dawn came up, showing these survivors all the dangers of their situation. Food and water had been put in, and such provision for comfort and safety as time allowed; but it was evident that with a badly wounded man, two women, and seven sailors, their supply would not last long, and help was sorely needed. Their only hope was in meeting a ship, although the gale, which had raged all night, had blown them out of their course. To this hope all clung, and wiled away the weary hours, watching the horizon and cheering one another with prophecies of speedy rescue.

Second mate Hoffmann was very brave and helpful, though his unexpected responsibility weighed heavily on his shoulders; for the captain's state seemed desperate, the poor wife's grief wrung his heart, and the blind confidence of the young girl in his power to save them made him feel that no sign of doubt or fear must lessen it. The men did their part readily now, but Emil knew that if starvation and despair made brutes of them, his task might be a terrible one. So he clutched his courage with both hands, kept up a manly front, and spoke so cheerily of their good chances, that all instinctively turned to him for guidance and support.

The first day and night passed in comparative comfort, but when the third came, things looked dark and hope began to fail. The wounded man was delirious, the wife worn out with anxiety and suspense, the girl weak for want of food, having put away half her biscuit for her mother, and given her share of water to wet her father's feverish lips. The sailors ceased rowing and sat grimly waiting, openly reproaching their leader for not following their advice, others demanding more food, all waxing dangerous as privation and pain brought out the animal instincts lurking in them. Emil did his best, but mortal man was helpless there, and he could only turn his haggard face from the pitiless sky, that dropped no rain for their thirst, to the boundless sea where no sail appeared to gladden their longing eyes. All day he tried to cheer and comfort them, while hunger gnawed, thirst parched, and growing fear lay heavy at his heart. He told stories to the men, implored them to bear up for the helpless women's sake, and promised rewards if they would pull while they had strength to regain the lost route, as nearly as he could make it out, and increase their chance of rescue. He rigged an awning of sailcloth over the suffering man and tended him like a son, comforted the wife, and tried to make the pale girl forget herself, by singing every song he knew or recounting his adventures by land and sea, till she smiled and took heart; for all ended well.

The fourth day came and the supply of food and water was nearly gone. Emil proposed to keep it for the sick man and the women, but two of the men rebelled, demanding their share. Emil gave up his as an example, and several of the good fellows followed it, with the quiet heroism which so often crops up in rough but manly natures. This shamed the others, and for another day an ominous peace reigned in that little world of suffering and suspense. But during the night, while Emil, worn out with fatigue, left the watch to the most trustworthy sailor, that he might snatch an hour's rest, these two men got at the stores and stole the last of the bread and water, and the one bottle of brandy, which was carefully hoarded to keep up their strength and make the brackish water drinkable. Half mad with thirst, they drank greedily and by morning one was in a stupor, from which he never woke; the other so crazed by the strong stimulant, that when Emil tried to control him, he leaped overboard and was lost. Horror-stricken by this terrible scene, the other men were submissive henceforth, and the boat floated on and on with its sad freight of suffering souls and bodies.

Another trial came to them that left all more despairing than before. A sail appeared, and for a time a frenzy of joy prevailed, to be turned to bitterest disappointment when it passed by, too far away to see the signals waved to them or hear the frantic cries for help that rang across the sea. Emil's heart sank then, for the captain seemed dying, and the women could not hold out much longer. He kept up till night came; then in the darkness, broken only by the feeble murmuring of the sick man, the whispered prayers of the poor wife, the ceaseless swash of waves, Emil hid his face, and had an hour of silent agony that aged him more than years of happy life could have done. It was not the physical hardship that daunted him, though want and weakness tortured him; it was his dreadful powerlessness to conquer the cruel fate that seemed hanging over them. The men he cared little for, since these perils were but a part of the life they chose; but the master he loved, the good woman who had been so kind to him, the sweet girl whose winsome presence had made the long voyage so pleasant for them all—if he could only save these dear and innocent creatures from a cruel death, he felt that he could willingly give his life for them.

As he sat there with his head in his hands, bowed down by the first great trial of his young life, the starless sky overhead, the restless sea beneath, and all around him suffering, for which he had no help, a soft sound broke the silence, and he listened like one in a dream. It was Mary singing to her mother, who lay sobbing in her arms, spent with this long anguish. A very faint and broken voice it was, for the poor girl's lips were parched with thirst; but the loving heart turned instinctively to the great Helper in this hour of despair, and He heard her feeble cry. It was a sweet old hymn often sung at Plumfield; and as he listened, all the happy past came back so clearly that Emil forgot the bitter present, and was at home again. His talk on the housetop with Aunt Jo seemed but yesterday, and, with a pang of self-reproach, he thought:

'The scarlet strand! I must remember it, and do my duty to the end. Steer straight, old boy; and if you can't come into port, go down with all sail set.'

Then, as the soft voice crooned on to lull the weary woman to a fitful sleep, Emil for a little while forgot his burden in a dream of Plumfield. He saw them all, heard the familiar voices, felt the grip of welcoming hands, and seemed to say to himself: 'Well, they shall not be ashamed of me if I never see them any more.'

A sudden shout startled him from that brief rest, and a drop on his forehead told him that the blessed rain had come at last, bringing salvation with it; for thirst is harder to bear than hunger, heat, or cold. Welcomed by cries of joy, all lifted up their parched lips, held out their hands, and spread their garments to catch the great drops that soon came pouring down to cool the sick man's fever, quench the agony of thirst, and bring refreshment to every weary body in the boat. All night it fell, all night the castaways revelled in the saving shower, and took heart again, like dying plants revived by heaven's dew. The clouds broke away at dawn, and Emil sprung up, wonderfully braced and cheered by those hours of silent gratitude for this answer to their cry for help. But this was not all; as his eye swept the horizon, clear against the rosy sky shone the white sails of a ship, so near that they could see the pennon at her mast-head and black figures moving on the deck.

One cry broke from all those eager throats, and rang across the sea, as every man waved hat or handkerchief and the women stretched imploring hands towards this great white angel of deliverance coming down upon them as if the fresh wind filled every sail to help her on.

No disappointment now; answering signals assured them of help; and in the rapture of that moment the happy women fell on Emil's neck, giving him his reward in tears and blessings as their grateful hearts overflowed. He always said that was the proudest moment of his life, as he stood there holding Mary in his arms; for the brave girl, who had kept up so long, broke down then, and clung to him half fainting; while her mother busied herself about the invalid, who seemed to feel the joyful stir, and gave an order, as if again on the deck of his lost ship.

It was soon over; and then all were safely aboard the good Urania, homeward bound. Emil saw his friends in tender hands, his men among their mates, and told the story of the wreck before he thought of himself. The savoury odour of the soup, carried by to the cabin for the ladies, reminded him that he was starving, and a sudden stagger betrayed his weakness. He was instantly borne away, to be half killed by kindness, and being fed, clothed, and comforted, was left to rest. Just as the surgeon left the state-room, he asked in his broken voice: 'What day is this? My head is so confused, I've lost my reckoning.'

'Thanksgiving Day, man! And we'll give you a regular New England dinner, if you'll eat it,' answered the surgeon heartily.

But Emil was too spent to do anything, except lie still and give thanks, more fervently and gratefully than ever before, for the blessed gift of life, which was the sweeter for a sense of duty faithfully performed.

# CHAPTER 12. DAN'S CHRISTMAS

Where was Dan? In prison. Alas for Mrs Jo! how her heart would have ached if she had known that while old Plum shone with Christmas cheer her boy sat alone in his cell, trying to read the little book she gave him, with eyes dimmed now and then by the hot tears no physical suffering had ever wrung from him, and longing with a homesick heart for all that he had lost.

Yes, Dan was in prison; but no cry for help from him as he faced the terrible strait he was in with the dumb despair of an Indian at the stake; for his own bosom sin had brought him there, and this was to be the bitter lesson that tamed the lawless spirit and taught him self-control.

The story of his downfall is soon told; for it came, as so often happens, just when he felt unusually full of high hopes, good resolutions, and dreams of a better life. On his journey he met a pleasant young fellow, and naturally felt an interest in him, as Blair was on his way to join his elder brothers on a ranch in Kansas. Card-playing was going on in the smoking-car, and the lad—for he was barely twenty—tired with the long journey, beguiled the way with such partners as appeared, being full of spirits, and a little intoxicated with the freedom of the West. Dan, true to his promise, would not join, but watched with intense interest the games that went on, and soon made up his mind that two of the men were sharpers anxious to fleece the boy, who had imprudently displayed a well-filled pocket-book. Dan always had a soft spot in his heart for any younger, weaker creature whom he met, and something about the lad reminded him of Teddy; so he kept an eye on Blair, and warned him against his new friends.

Vainly, of course; for when all stopped overnight in one of the great cities, Dan missed the boy from the hotel whither he had taken him for safe-keeping; and learning who had come for him, went to find him, calling himself a fool for his pains, yet unable to leave the confiding boy to the dangers that surrounded him.

He found him gambling in a low place with the men, who were bound to have his money; and by the look of relief on Blair's anxious face when he saw him Dan knew without words that things were going badly with him, and he saw the peril too late.

'I can't come yet—I've lost; it's not my money; I must get it back, or I dare not face my brothers,' whispered the poor lad, when Dan begged him to get away without further loss. Shame and fear made him desperate; and he played on, sure that he could recover the money confided to his care. Seeing Dan's resolute face, keen eye, and travelled air, the sharpers were wary, played fair, and let the boy win a little; but they had no mind to give up their prey, and finding that Dan stood sentinel at the boy's back, an ominous glance was exchanged between them, which meant:

'We must get this fellow out of the way.'

Dan saw it, and was on his guard; for he and Blair were strangers, evil deeds are easily done in such places, and no tales told. But he would not desert the boy, and still kept watch of every card till he plainly detected false play, and boldly said so. High words passed, Dan's indignation overcame his prudence; and when the cheat refused to restore his plunder with insulting words and drawn pistol, Dan's hot temper flashed out, and he knocked the man down with a blow that sent him crashing head first against a stove, to roll senseless and bleeding to the floor. A wild scene followed, but in the midst of it Dan whispered to the boy: 'Get away, and hold your tongue. Don't mind me.'

Frightened and bewildered, Blair quitted the city at once, leaving Dan to pass the night in the lock-up, and a few days later to stand in court charged with manslaughter; for the man was dead. Dan had no friends, and having once briefly told the story, held his peace, anxious to keep all knowledge of this sad affair from those at home. He even concealed his name—giving that of David Kent, as he had done several times before in emergencies. It was all over very soon; but as there were extenuating circumstances his sentence was a year in prison, with hard labour.

Dazed by the rapidity with which this horrible change in his life came upon him, Dan did not fully realize it till the iron door clanged behind him and he sat alone in a cell as narrow, cold, and silent as a tomb. He knew that a word would bring Mr Laurie to help and comfort him; but he could not bear to tell of this disgrace, or see the sorrow and the shame it would cause the friends who hoped so much for him.

'No,' he said, clenching his fist, 'I'll let them think me dead first. I shall be if I am kept here long'; and he sprang up to pace the stone floor like a caged lion, with a turmoil of wrath and grief, rebellion and remorse, seething in heart and brain, till he felt as if he should go mad and beat upon the walls that shut him away from the liberty which was his life. For days he suffered terribly, then worn out, sank into a black melancholy sadder to see than his excitement.

The warden of this prison was a rough man who had won the ill will of all by unnecessary harshness, but the chaplain was full of sympathy, and did his hard duty faithfully and tenderly. He laboured with poor Dan, but seemed to make no impression, and was forced to wait till work had soothed the excited nerves and captivity tamed the proud spirit that would suffer but not complain.

Dan was put in the brush-shop, and feeling that activity was his only salvation, worked with a feverish energy that soon won the approval of the master and the envy of less skilful mates. Day after day he sat in his place, watched by an armed overseer, forbidden any but necessary words, no intercourse with the men beside him, no change but from cell to shop, no exercise but the dreary marches to and fro, each man's hand on the other's shoulder keeping step with the dreary tramp so different from the ringing tread of soldiers. Silent, gaunt, and grim, Dan did his daily task, ate his bitter bread, and obeyed commands with a rebellious flash of the eye, that made the warden say:

'That's a dangerous man. Watch him. He'll break out some day.'

There were others more dangerous than he, because older in crime and ready for any desperate outbreak to change the monotony of long sentences. These men soon divined Dan's mood, and in the mysterious way convicts invent, managed to convey to him before a month was over that plans were being made for a mutiny at the first opportunity. Thanksgiving Day was one of the few chances for them to speak together as they enjoyed an hour of freedom in the prison yard. Then all would be settled and the rash attempt made if possible, probably to end in bloodshed and defeat for most, but liberty for a few. Dan had already planned his own escape and bided his time, growing more and more moody, fierce, and rebellious, as loss of liberty wore upon soul and body; for this sudden change from his free, healthy life to such a narrow, gloomy, and miserable one, could not but have a terrible effect upon one of Dan's temperament and age.

He brooded over his ruined life, gave up all his happy hopes and plans, felt that he could never face dear old Plumfield again, or touch those friendly hands, with the stain of blood upon his own. He did not care for the wretched man whom he had killed, for such a life was better ended, he thought; but the disgrace of prison would never be wiped out of his memory, though the cropped hair would grow again, the grey suit easily be replaced, and the bolts and bars left far behind.

'It's all over with me; I've spoilt my life, now let it go. I'll give up the fight and get what pleasure I can anywhere, anyhow. They shall think me dead and so still care for me, but never know what I am. Poor Mother Bhaer! she tried to help me, but it's no use; the firebrand can't be saved.'

And dropping his head in his hands as he sat on his low bed, Dan would mourn over all he had lost in tearless misery, till merciful sleep would comfort him with dreams of the happy days when the boys played together, or those still later and happier ones when all smiled on him, and Plumfield seemed to have gained a new and curious charm.

There was one poor fellow in Dan's shop whose fate was harder than his, for his sentence expired in the spring, but there was little hope of his living till that time; and the coldest-hearted man pitied poor Mason as he sat coughing his life away in that close place and counting the weary days yet to pass before he could see his wife and little child again. There was some hope that he might be pardoned out, but he had no friends to bestir themselves in the matter, and it was evident that the great Judge's pardon would soon end his patient pain for ever.

Dan pitied him more than he dared to show, and this one tender emotion in that dark time was like the little flower that sprung up between the stones of the prison yard and saved the captive from despair, in the beautiful old story. Dan helped Mason with his work when he was too feeble to finish his task, and the grateful look that thanked him was a ray of sunshine to cheer his cell when he was alone. Mason envied the splendid health of his neighbour, and mourned to see it wasting there. He was a peaceful soul and tried, as far as a whispered word or warning glance could do it, to deter Dan from joining the 'bad lot', as the rebels were called. But having turned his face from the light, Dan found the downward way easy, and took a grim satisfaction in the prospect of a general outbreak during which he might revenge himself upon the tyrannical warden, and strike a blow for his own liberty, feeling that an hour of insurrection would be a welcome vent for the pent-up passions that tormented him. He had tamed many a wild animal, but his own lawless spirit was too much for him, till he found the curb that made him master of himself.

The Sunday before Thanksgiving, as he sat in chapel, Dan observed several guests in the seats reserved for them, and looked anxiously to see if any familiar face was there; for he had a mortal fear that someone from home would suddenly confront him. No, all were strangers, and he soon forgot them in listening to the chaplain's cheerful words, and the sad singing of many heavy hearts. People often spoke to the convicts, so it caused no surprise when, on being invited to address them, one of the ladies rose and said she would tell them a little story; which announcement caused the younger listeners to pack up their ears, and even the older ones to look interested; for any change in their monotonous life was welcome.

The speaker was a middle-aged woman in black, with a sympathetic face, eyes full of compassion, and a voice that seemed to warm the heart, because of certain motherly tones in it. She reminded Dan of Mrs Jo, and he listened intently to every word, feeling that each was meant for him, because by chance, they came at the moment when he needed a softening memory to break up the ice of despair which was blighting all the good impulses of his nature.

It was a very simple little story, but it caught the men's attention at once, being about two soldiers in a hospital during the late war, both badly wounded in the right arm, and both anxious to save these breadwinners and go home unmaimed. One was patient, docile, and cheerfully obeyed orders, even when told that the arm must go. He submitted and after much suffering recovered, grateful for life, though he could fight no more. The other rebelled, would listen to no advice, and having delayed too long, died a lingering death, bitterly regretting his folly when it was too late. 'Now, as all stories should have a little moral, let me tell you mine,' added the lady, with a smile, as she looked at the row of young men before her, sadly wondering what brought them there.

'This is a hospital for soldiers wounded in life's battle; here are sick souls, weak wills, insane passions, blind consciences, all the ills that come from broken laws, bringing their inevitable pain and punishment with them, There is hope and help for every one, for God's mercy is infinite and man's charity is great; but penitence and submission must come before the cure is possible. Pay the forfeit manfully, for it is just; but from the suffering and shame wring new strength for a nobler life. The scar will remain, but it is better for a man to lose both arms than his soul; and these hard years, instead of being lost, may be made the most precious of your lives, if they teach you to rule yourselves. O friends, try to outlive the bitter past, to wash the sin away, and begin anew. If not for your own sakes, for that of the dear mothers, wives, and children, who wait and hope so patiently for you. Remember them, and do not let them love and long in vain. And if there be any here so forlorn that they have no friend to care for them, never forget the Father whose arms are always open to receive, forgive, and comfort His prodigal sons, even at the eleventh hour.' There the little sermon ended; but the preacher of it felt that her few hearty words had not been uttered in vain, for one boy's head was down, and several faces wore the softened look which told that a tender memory was touched. Dan was forced to set his lips to keep them steady, and drop his eyes to hide the sudden dew that dimmed them when waiting, hoping friends were spoken of. He was glad to be alone in his cell again, and sat thinking deeply, instead of trying to forget himself in sleep. It seemed as if those words were just what he needed to show him where he stood and how fateful the next few days might be to him. Should he join the 'bad lot', and perhaps add another crime to the one already committed, lengthen the sentence already so terrible to bear, deliberately turn his back on all that was good, and mar the future that might yet be redeemed? Or should he, like the wiser man in the story, submit, bear the just punishment, try to be better for it; and though the scar would remain, it might serve as a reminder of a battle not wholly lost, since he had saved his soul though innocence was gone? Then he would dare go home, perhaps, confess, and find fresh strength in the pity and consolation of those who never gave him up.

Good and evil fought for Dan that night as did the angel and the devil for Sintram, and it was hard to tell whether lawless nature or loving heart would conquer. Remorse and resentment, shame and sorrow, pride and passion, made a battle-field of that narrow cell, and the poor fellow felt as if he had fiercer enemies to fight now than any he had met in all his wanderings. A little thing turned the scale, as it so often does in these mysterious hearts of ours, and a touch of sympathy helped Dan decide the course which would bless or ban his life.

In the dark hour before the dawn, as he lay wakeful on his bed, a ray of light shone through the bars, the bolts turned softly, and a man came in. It was the good chaplain, led by the same instinct that brings a mother to her sick child's pillow; for long experience as nurse of souls had taught him to see the signs of hope in the hard faces about him, and to know when the moment came for a helpful word and the cordial of sincere prayer that brings such comfort and healing to tried and troubled hearts. He had been to Dan before at unexpected hours, but always found him sullen, indifferent, or rebellious, and had gone away to patiently bide his time. Now it had come; a look of relief was in the prisoner's face as the light shone on it, and the sound of a human voice was strangely comfortable after listening to the whispers of the passions, doubts, and fears which had haunted the cell for hours, dismaying Dan by their power, and showing him how much he needed help to fight the good fight, since he had no armour of his own.

'Kent, poor Mason has gone. He left a message for you, and I felt impelled to come and give it now, because I think you were touched by what we heard today, and in need of the help Mason tried to give you,' said the chaplain, taking the one seat and fixing his kind eyes on the grim figure in the bed.

'Thank you, sir, I'd like to hear it,' was all Dan's answer; but he forgot himself in pity for the poor fellow dead in prison, with no last look at wife or child.

He went suddenly, but remembered you, and begged me to say these words: "Tell him not to do it, but to hold on, do his best, and when his time is out go right to Mary, and she'll make him welcome for my sake. He's got no friends in these parts and will feel lonesome, but a woman's always safe and comfortable when a fellow's down on his luck. Give him my love and good-bye for he was kind to me, and God will bless him for it." Then he died quietly, and tomorrow will go home with God's pardon, since man's came too late.'

Dan said nothing, but laid his arm across his face and lay quite still. Seeing that the pathetic little message had done its work even better than he hoped, the chaplain went on, unconscious how soothing his paternal voice was to the poor prisoner who longed to 'go home', but felt he had forfeited the right.

'I hope you won't disappoint this humble friend whose last thought was for you. I know that there is trouble brewing, and fear that you may be tempted to lend a hand on the wrong side. Don't do it, for the plot will not succeed—it never does—and it would be a pity to spoil your record which is fair so far. Keep up your courage, my son, and go out at the year's end better, not worse, for this hard experience. Remember a grateful woman waits to welcome and thank you if you have no friends of your own; if you have, do your best for their sake, and let us ask God to help you as He only can.'

Then waiting for no answer the good man prayed heartily, and Dan listened as he never had before; for the lonely hour, the dying message, the sudden uprising of his better self, made it seem as if some kind angel had come to save and comfort him. After that night there was a change in Dan, though no one knew it but the chaplain; for to all the rest he was the same silent, stern, unsocial fellow as before, and turning his back on the bad and the good alike, found his only pleasure in the books his friend brought him. Slowly, as the steadfast drop wears away the rock, the patient kindness of this man won Dan's confidence, and led by him he began to climb out of the Valley of Humiliation towards the mountains, whence, through the clouds, one can catch glimpses of the Celestial City whither all true pilgrims sooner or later turn their wistful eyes and stumbling feet. There were many back-slidings, many struggles with Giant Despair and fiery Apollyon, many heavy hours when life did not seem worth living and Mason's escape the only hope. But through all, the grasp of a friendly hand, the sound of a brother's voice, the unquenchable desire to atone for the past by a better future, and win the right to see home again, kept poor Dan to his great task as the old year drew to its end, and the new waited to turn another leaf in the book whose hardest lesson he was learning now.

At Christmas he yearned so for Plumfield that he devised a way to send a word of greeting to cheer their anxious hearts, and comfort his own. He wrote to Mary Mason, who lived in another State, asking her to mail the letter he enclosed. In it he merely said he was well and busy, had given up the farm, and had other plans which he would tell later; would not be home before autumn probably, nor write often, but was all right, and sent love and merry Christmas to everyone.

Then he took up his solitary life again, and tried to pay his forfeit manfully.

# CHAPTER 13. NAT'S NEW YEAR

'I don't expect to hear from Emil yet, and Nat writes regularly, but where is Dan? Only two or three postals since he went. Such an energetic fellow as he is could buy up all the farms in Kansas by this time,' said Mrs Jo one morning when the mail came in and no card or envelope bore Dan's dashing hand.

'He never writes often, you know, but does his work and then comes home. Months and years seem to mean little to him, and he is probably prospecting in the wilderness, forgetful of time,' answered Mr Bhaer, deep in one of Nat's long letters from Leipzig.

'But he promised he would let me know how he got on, and Dan keeps his word if he can. I'm afraid something has happened to him'; and Mrs Jo comforted herself by patting Don's head, as he came at the sound of his master's name to look at her with eyes almost human in their wistful intelligence.

'Don't worry, Mum dear, nothing ever happens to the old fellow. He'll turn up all right, and come stalking in some day with a gold-mine in one pocket and a prairie in the other, as jolly as a grig,' said Ted, who was in no haste to deliver Octoo to her rightful owner.

'Perhaps he has gone to Montana and given up the farm plan. He seemed to like Indians best, I thought'; and Rob went to help his mother with her pile of letters and his cheerful suggestions.

'I hope so, it would suit him best. But I am sure he would have told us his change of plan and sent for some money to work with. No, I feel in my prophetic bones that something is wrong,' said Mrs Jo, looking as solemn as Fate in a breakfast-cap.

'Then we shall hear; ill news always travels fast. Don't borrow trouble, Jo, but hear how well Nat is getting on. I'd no idea the boy would care for anything but music. My good friend Baumgarten has launched him well, and it will do him good if he lose not his head. A good lad, but new to the world, and Leipzig is full of snares for the unwary. Gott be with him!'

The Professor read Nat's enthusiastic account of certain literary and musical parties he had been to, the splendours of the opera, the kindness of his new friends, the delight of studying under such a master as Bergmann, his hopes of rapid gain, and his great gratitude to those who had opened this enchanted world to him.

'That, now, is satisfactory and comfortable. I felt that Nat had unsuspected power in him before he went away; he was so manly and full of excellent plans,' said Mrs Jo, in a satisfied tone.

'We shall see. He will doubtless get his lesson and be the better for it. That comes to us all in our young days. I hope it will not be too hard for our good Jungling,' answered the Professor, with a wise smile, remembering his own student life in Germany.

He was right; and Nat was already getting his lesson in life with a rapidity which would have astonished his friends at home. The manliness over which Mrs Jo rejoiced was developing in unexpected ways, and quiet Nat had plunged into the more harmless dissipations of the gay city with all the ardour of an inexperienced youth taking his first sip of pleasure. The entire freedom and sense of independence was delicious, for many benefits began to burden him, and he longed to stand on his own legs and make his own way. No one knew his past here; and with a well-stocked wardrobe, a handsome sum at his banker's, and the best teacher in Leipzig, he made his debut as a musical young gentleman, presented by the much-respected Professor Bhaer and the wealthy Mr Laurence, who had many friends glad to throw open their houses to his protege. Thanks to these introductions, his fluent German, modest manners, and undeniable talent, the stranger was cordially welcomed, and launched at once into a circle which many an ambitious young man strove in vain to enter.

All this rather turned Nat's head; and as he sat in the brilliant opera-house, chatted among the ladies at some select coffee-party, or whisked an eminent professor's amiable daughter down the room, trying to imagine she was Daisy, he often asked himself if this gay fellow could be the poor homeless little Street musician who once stood waiting in the rain at the gates of Plumfield. His heart was true, his impulses good, and his ambitions high; but the weak side of his nature came uppermost here; vanity led him astray, pleasure intoxicated him, and for a time he forgot everything but the delights of this new and charming life. Without meaning to deceive, he allowed people to imagine him a youth of good family and prospects; he boasted a little of Mr Laurie's wealth and influence, of Professor Bhaer's eminence, and the flourishing college at which he himself had been educated. Mrs Jo was introduced to the sentimental Frauleins who read her books, and the charms and virtues of his own dear Madchen confided to sympathetic mammas. All these boyish boastings and innocent vanities were duly circulated among the gossips, and his importance much increased thereby, to his surprise and gratification, as well as some shame.

But they bore fruit that was bitter in the end; for, finding that he was considered one of the upper class, it very soon became impossible for him to live in the humble quarters he had chosen, or to lead the studious, quiet life planned for him. He met other students, young officers, and gay fellows of all sorts, and was flattered at being welcomed among them; though it was a costly pleasure, and often left a thorn of regret to vex his honest conscience. He was tempted to take better rooms in a more fashionable street, leaving good Frau Tetzel to lament his loss, and his artist neighbour, Fraulein Vogelstein, to shake her grey ringlets and predict his return, a sadder and a wiser man.

The sum placed at his disposal for expenses and such simple pleasures as his busy life could command seemed a fortune to Nat, though it was smaller than generous Mr Laurie first proposed. Professor Bhaer wisely counselled prudence, as Nat was unused to the care of money, and the good man knew the temptations that a well-filled purse makes possible at this pleasure-loving age. So Nat enjoyed his handsome little apartment immensely, and insensibly let many unaccustomed luxuries creep in. He loved his music and never missed a lesson; but the hours he should have spent in patient practice were too often wasted at theatre, ball, beer-garden, or club—doing no harm beyond that waste of precious time, and money not his own; for he had no vices, and took his recreation like a gentleman, so far. But slowly a change for the worse was beginning to show itself, and he felt it. These first steps along the flowery road were downward, not upward; and the constant sense of disloyalty which soon began to haunt him made Nat feel, in the few quiet hours he gave himself, that all was not well with him, spite of the happy whirl in which he lived.

'Another month, and then I will be steady,' he said more than once, trying to excuse the delay by the fact that all was new to him, that his friends at home wished him to be happy, and that society was giving him the polish he needed. But as each month slipped away it grew harder to escape; he was inevitably drawn on, and it was so easy to drift with the tide that he deferred the evil day as long as possible. Winter festivities followed the more wholesome summer pleasures, and Nat found them more costly; for the hospitable ladies expected some return from the stranger; and carriages, bouquets, theatre tickets, and all the little expenses a young man cannot escape at such times, told heavily on the purse which seemed bottomless at first. Taking Mr Laurie for his model, Nat became quite a gallant, and was universally liked; for through all the newly acquired airs and graces the genuine honesty and simplicity of his character plainly shone, winning confidence and affection from all who knew him.

Among these was a certain amiable old lady with a musical daughter—well-born but poor, and very anxious to marry the aforesaid daughter to some wealthy man. Nat's little fictions concerning his prospects and friends charmed the gnadige Frau as much as his music and devoted manners did the sentimental Minna. Their quiet parlour seemed homelike and restful to Nat, when tired of gayer scenes; and the motherly interest of the elder lady was sweet and comfortable to him; while the tender blue eyes of the pretty girl were always so full of welcome when he came, of regret when he left, and of admiration when he played to her, that he found it impossible to keep away from this attractive spot. He meant no harm, and feared no danger, having confided to the Frau Mamma that he was betrothed; so he continued to call, little dreaming what ambitious hopes the old lady cherished, nor the peril there was in receiving the adoration of a romantic German girl, till it was too late to spare her pain and himself great regret.

Of course some inkling of these new and agreeable experiences got into the voluminous letters he never was too gay, too busy, or too tired to write each week; and while Daisy rejoiced over his happiness and success, and the boys laughed at the idea of 'old Chirper coming out as a society man', the elders looked sober, and said among themselves:

'He is going too fast; he must have a word of warning, or trouble may come.'

But Mr Laurie said: 'Oh, let him have his fling; he's been dependent and repressed long enough. He can't go far with the money he has, and I've no fear of his getting into debt. He's too timid and too honest to be reckless. It is his first taste of freedom; let him enjoy it, and he'll work the better by and by; I know—and I'm sure I'm right.'

So the warnings were very gentle, and the good people waited anxiously to hear more of hard study, and less of 'splendid times'. Daisy sometimes wondered, with a pang of her faithful heart, if one of the charming Minnas, Hildegardes, and Lottchens mentioned were not stealing her Nat away from her; but she never asked, always wrote calmly and cheerfully, and looked in vain for any hint of change in the letters that were worn out with much reading.

Month after month slipped away, till the holidays came with gifts, good wishes, and brilliant festivities. Nat expected to enjoy himself very much, and did at first; for a German Christmas is a spectacle worth seeing. But he paid dearly for the abandon with which he threw himself into the gaieties of that memorable week; and on New Year's Day the reckoning came. It seemed as if some malicious fairy had prepared the surprises that arrived, so unwelcome were they, so magical the change they wrought, turning his happy world into a scene of desolation and despair as suddenly as a transformation at the pantomime.

The first came in the morning when, duly armed with costly bouquets and bon-bons, he went to thank Minna and her mother for the braces embroidered with forget-me-nots and the silk socks knit by the old lady's nimble fingers, which he had found upon his table that day. The Frau Mamma received him graciously; but when he asked for the daughter the good lady frankly demanded what his intentions were, adding that certain gossip which had reached her ear made it necessary for him to declare himself or come no more, as Minna's peace must not be compromised.

A more panic-stricken youth was seldom seen than Nat as he received this unexpected demand. He saw too late that his American style of gallantry had deceived the artless girl, and might be used with terrible effect by the artful mother, if she chose to do it. Nothing but the truth could save him, and he had the honour and honesty to tell it faithfully. A sad scene followed; for Nat was obliged to strip off his fictitious splendour, confess himself only a poor student, and humbly ask pardon for the thoughtless freedom with which he had enjoyed their too confiding hospitality. If he had any doubts of Frau Schomburg's motives and desires, they were speedily set at rest by the frankness with which she showed her disappointment, the vigour with which she scolded him, and the scorn with which she cast him off when her splendid castles in the air collapsed.

The sincerity of Nat's penitence softened her a little and she consented to a farewell word with Minna, who had listened at the keyhole, and was produced drenched in tears, to fall on Nat's bosom, crying: 'Ah, thou dear one, never can I forget thee, though my heart is broken!'

This was worse than the scolding; for the stout lady also wept, and it was only after much German gush and twaddle that he escaped, feeling like another Werther; while the deserted Lotte consoled herself with the bonbons, her mother with the more valuable gifts.

The second surprise arrived as he dined with Professor Baumgarten. His appetite had been effectually taken away by the scene of the morning, and his spirits received another damper when a fellow student cheerfully informed him that he was about to go to America, and should make it his agreeable duty to call on the 'lieber Herr Professor Bhaer', to tell him how gaily his protege was disporting himself at Leipzig. Nat's heart died within him as he imagined the effect these glowing tales would have at Plumfield—not that he had wilfully deceived them, but in his letters many things were left untold; and when Carlsen added, with a friendly wink, that he would merely hint at the coming betrothal of the fair Minna and his 'heart's friend', Nat found himself devoutly hoping that this other inconvenient heart's friend might go to the bottom of the sea before he reached Plumfield to blast all his hopes by these tales of a mis-spent winter. Collecting his wits, he cautioned Carlsen with what he flattered himself was Mephistophelian art, and gave him such confused directions that it would be a miracle if he ever found Professor Bhaer. But the dinner was spoilt for Nat, and he got away as soon as possible, to wander disconsolately about the streets, with no heart for the theatre or the supper he was to share with some gay comrades afterwards. He comforted himself a little by giving alms to sundry beggars, making two children happy with gilded gingerbread, and drinking a lonely glass of beer, in which he toasted his Daisy and wished himself a better year than the last had been.

Going home at length, he found a third surprise awaiting him in the shower of bills which had descended upon him like a snowstorm, burying him in an avalanche of remorse, despair, and self-disgust. These bills were so many and so large that he was startled and dismayed; for, as Mr Bhaer wisely predicted, he knew little about the value of money. It would take every dollar at the bankers to pay them all at once, and leave him penniless for the next six months, unless he wrote home for more. He would rather starve than do that; and his first impulse was to seek help at the gaming-table, whither his new friends had often tempted him. But he had promised Mr Bhaer to resist what then had seemed an impossible temptation; and now he would not add another fault to the list already so long. Borrow he would not, nor beg. What could he do? For these appalling bills must be paid, and the lessons go on; or his journey was an ignominious failure. But he must live meantime. And how? Bowed down with remorse for the folly of these months, he saw too late whither he was drifting, and for hours paced up and down his pretty rooms, floundering in a Slough of Despond, with no helping hand to pull him out—at least he thought so till letters were brought in, and among fresh bills lay one well-worn envelope with an American stamp in the corner.

Ah, how welcome it was! how eagerly he read the long pages full of affectionate wishes from all at home! For everyone had sent a line, and as each familiar name appeared, his eyes grew dimmer and dimmer till, as he read the last—'God bless my boy! Mother Bhaer'—he broke down; and laying his head on his arms, blistered the paper with a rain of tears that eased his heart and washed away the boyish sins that now lay so heavy on his conscience.

'Dear people, how they love and trust me! And how bitterly they would be disappointed if they knew what a fool I've been! I'll fiddle in the streets again before I'll ask for help from them!' cried Nat, brushing away the tears of which he was ashamed, although he felt the good they had done.

Now he seemed to see more clearly what to do; for the helping hand had been stretched across the sea, and Love, the dear Evangelist, had lifted him out of the slough and shown him the narrow gate, beyond which deliverance lay. When the letter had been reread, and one corner where a daisy was painted, passionately kissed, Nat felt strong enough to face the worst and conquer it. Every bill should be paid, every salable thing of his own sold, these costly rooms given up; and once back with thrifty Frau Tetzel, he would find work of some sort by which to support himself, as many another student did. He must give up the new friends, turn his back on the gay life, cease to be a butterfly, and take his place among the grubs. It was the only honest thing to do, but very hard for the poor fellow to crush his little vanities, renounce the delights so dear to the young, own his folly, and step down from his pedestal to be pitied, laughed at, and forgotten.

It took all Nat's pride and courage to do this, for his was a sensitive nature; esteem was very precious to him, failure very bitter, and nothing but the inborn contempt for meanness and deceit kept him from asking help or trying to hide his need by some dishonest device. As he sat alone that night, Mr Bhaer's words came back to him with curious clearness, and he saw himself a boy again at Plumfield, punishing his teacher as a lesson to himself, when timidity had made him lie.

'He shall not suffer for me again, and I won't be a sneak if I am a fool. I'll go and tell Professor Baumgarten all about it and ask his advice. I'd rather face a loaded cannon; but it must be done. Then I'll sell out, pay my debts, and go back where I belong. Better be an honest pauper than a jackdaw among peacocks'; and Nat smiled in the midst of his trouble, as he looked about him at the little elegancies of his room, remembering what he came from.

He kept his word manfully, and was much comforted to find that his experience was an old story to the professor, who approved his plan, thinking wisely that the discipline would be good for him, and was very kind in offering help and promising to keep the secret of his folly from his friend Bhaer till Nat had redeemed himself.

The first week of the new year was spent by our prodigal in carrying out his plan with penitent dispatch, and his birthday found him alone in the little room high up at Frau Tetzel's, with nothing of his former splendour, but sundry unsalable keepsakes from the buxom maidens, who mourned his absence deeply. His male friends had ridiculed, pitied, and soon left him alone, with one or two exceptions, who offered their purses generously and promised to stand by him. He was lonely and heavy-hearted, and sat brooding over his small fire as he remembered the last New Year's Day at Plumfield, when at this hour he was dancing with his Daisy.

A tap at the door roused him, and with a careless 'Herein', he waited to see who had climbed so far for his sake. It was the good Frau proudly bearing a tray, on which stood a bottle of wine and an astonishing cake bedecked with sugar-plums of every hue, and crowned with candles. Fraulein Vogelstein followed, embracing a blooming rose-tree, above which her grey curls waved and her friendly face beamed joyfully as she cried:

'Dear Herr Blak, we bring you greetings and a little gift or two in honour of this ever-to-be-remembered day. Best wishes! and may the new year bloom for you as beautifully as we your heart-warm friends desire.'

'Yes, yes, in truth we do, dear Herr,' added Frau Tetzel. 'Eat of this with-joy-made Kuchen, and drink to the health of the far-away beloved ones in the good wine.'

Amused, yet touched by the kindness of the good souls, Nat thanked them both, and made them stay to enjoy the humble feast with him. This they gladly did, being motherly women full of pity for the dear youth, whose straits they knew, and having substantial help to offer, as well as kind words and creature comforts.

Frau Tetzel, with some hesitation, mentioned a friend of hers who, forced by illness to leave his place in the orchestra of a second-rate theatre, would gladly offer it to Nat, if he could accept so humble a position. Blushing and toying with the roses like a shy girl, good old Vogelstein asked if in his leisure moments he could give English lessons in the young ladies' school where she taught painting, adding that a small but certain salary would be paid him.

Gratefully Nat accepted both offers, finding it less humiliating to be helped by women than by friends of his own sex. This work would support him in a frugal way, and certain musical drudgery promised by his master assured his own teaching. Delighted with the success of their little plot, these friendly neighbours left him with cheery words, warm hand-grasps, and faces beaming with feminine satisfaction at the hearty kiss Nat put on each faded cheek, as the only return he could make for all their helpful kindness.

It was strange how much brighter the world looked after that; for hope was a better cordial than the wine, and good resolutions bloomed as freshly as the little rose-tree that filled the room with fragrance, as Nat woke the echoes with the dear old airs, finding now as always his best comforter in music, to whom henceforth he swore to be a more loyal subject.

## CHAPTER 14. PLAYS AT PLUMFIELD

As it is as impossible for the humble historian of the March family to write a story without theatricals in it as for our dear Miss Yonge to get on with less than twelve or fourteen children in her interesting tales, we will accept the fact, and at once cheer ourselves after the last afflicting events, by proceeding to the Christmas plays at Plumfield; for they influence the fate of several of our characters, and cannot well be skipped.

When the college was built Mr Laurie added a charming little theatre which not only served for plays, but declamations, lectures, and concerts. The drop-curtain displayed Apollo with the Muses grouped about him; and as a compliment to the donor of the hall the artist had given the god a decided resemblance to our friend, which was considered a superb joke by everyone else. Home talent furnished stars, stock company, orchestra, and scene painter; and astonishing performances were given on this pretty little stage.

Mrs Jo had been trying for some time to produce a play which should be an improvement upon the adaptations from the French then in vogue, curious mixtures of fine toilettes, false sentiment, and feeble wit, with no touch of nature to redeem them. It was easy to plan plays full of noble speeches and thrilling situations, but very hard to write them; so she contented herself with a few scenes of humble life in which the comic and pathetic were mingled; and as she fitted her characters to her actors, she hoped the little venture would prove that truth and simplicity had not entirely lost their power to charm. Mr Laurie helped her, and they called themselves Beaumont and Fletcher, enjoying their joint labour very much; for Beaumont's knowledge of dramatic art was of great use in curbing Fletcher's too-aspiring pen, and they flattered themselves that they had produced a neat and effective bit of work as an experiment.

All was ready now; and Christmas Day was much enlivened by last rehearsals, the panics of timid actors, the scramble for forgotten properties, and the decoration of the theatre. Evergreen and holly from the woods, blooming plants from the hothouse on Parnassus, and flags of all nations made it very gay that night in honour of the guests who were coming, chief among them, Miss Cameron, who kept her promise faithfully. The orchestra tuned their instruments with unusual care, the scene-shifters set their stage with lavish elegance, the prompter heroically took his seat in the stifling nook provided for him, and the actors dressed with trembling hands that dropped the pins, and perspiring brows whereon the powder wouldn't stick. Beaumont and Fletcher were everywhere, feeling that their literary reputation was at stake; for sundry friendly critics were invited, and reporters, like mosquitoes, cannot be excluded from any earthly scene, be it a great man's death-bed or a dime museum.

'Has she come?' was the question asked by every tongue behind the curtain; and when Tom, who played an old man, endangered his respectable legs among the footlights to peep, announced that he saw Miss Cameron's handsome head in the place of honour, a thrill pervaded the entire company, and Josie declared with an excited gasp that she was going to have stage fright for the first time in her life.

'I'll shake you if you do,' said Mrs Jo, who was in such a wild state of dishevelment with her varied labours that she might have gone on as Madge Wildlife, without an additional rag or crazy elf-lock.

'You'll have time to get your wits together while we do our piece. We are old stagers and calm as clocks,' answered Demi, with a nod towards Alice, ready in her pretty dress and all her properties at hand.

But both clocks were going rather faster than usual, as heightened colour, brilliant eyes, and a certain flutter under the laces and velvet coat betrayed. They were to open the entertainment with a gay little piece which they had played before and did remarkably well. Alice was a tall girl, with dark hair and eyes, and a face which intelligence, health, and a happy heart made beautiful. She was looking her best now, for the brocades, plumes, and powder of the Marquise became her stately figure; and Demi in his court suit, with sword, three-cornered hat, and white wig, made as gallant a Baron as one would wish to see. Josie was the maid, and looked her part to the life, being as pretty, pert, and inquisitive as any French soubrette. These three were all the characters; and the success of the piece depended on the spirit and skill with which the quickly changing moods of the quarrelsome lovers were given, their witty speeches made to tell, and by-play suited to the courtly period in which the scene was laid.

Few would have recognized sober John and studious Alice in the dashing gentleman and coquettish lady, who kept the audience laughing at their caprices; while they enjoyed the brilliant costumes, and admired the ease and grace of the young actors. Josie was a prominent figure in the plot, as she listened at keyholes, peeped into notes, and popped in and out at all the most inopportune moments, with her nose in the air, her hands in her apron-pockets, and curiosity pervading her little figure from the topmost bow of her jaunty cap to the red heels of her slippers. All went smoothly; and the capricious Marquise, after tormenting the devoted Baron to her heart's content, owned herself conquered in the war of wits, and was just offering the hand he had fairly won, when a crash startled them, and a heavily decorated side-scene swayed forward, ready to fall upon Alice. Demi saw it and sprung before her to catch and hold it up, standing like a modern Samson with the wall of a house on his back. The danger was over in a moment, and he was about to utter his last speech, when the excited young scene-shifter, who had flown up a ladder to repair the damage, leaned over to whisper 'All right', and release Demi from his spread-eagle attitude: as he did so, a hammer slipped out of his pocket, to fall upon the upturned face below, inflicting a smart blow and literally knocking the Baron's part out of his head.

'A quick curtain,' robbed the audience of a pretty little scene not down on the bill; for the Marquise flew to staunch the blood with a cry of alarm: 'Oh! John, you are hurt! Lean on me'—which John gladly did for a moment, being a trifle dazed yet quite able to enjoy the tender touch of the hands busied about him and the anxiety of the face so near his own; for both told him something which he would have considered cheaply won by a rain of hammers and the fall of the whole college on his head.

Nan was on the spot in a moment with the case that never left her pocket; and the wound was neatly plastered up by the time Mrs Jo arrived, demanding tragically:

'Is he too much hurt to go on again? If he is, my play is lost!'

'I'm all the fitter for it, Aunty; for here's a real instead of a painted wound. I'll be ready; don't worry about me.' And catching up his wig, Demi was off, with only a very eloquent look of thanks to the Marquise, who had spoilt her gloves for his sake, but did not seem to mind it at all, though they reached above her elbows, and were most expensive.

'How are your nerves, Fletcher?' asked Mr Laurie as they stood together during the breathless minute before the last bell rings.

'About as calm as yours, Beaumont,' answered Mrs Jo, gesticulating wildly to Mrs Meg to set her cap straight.

'Bear up, partner! I'll stand by you whatever comes!'

'I feel that it ought to go; for, though it's a mere trifle, a good deal of honest work and truth have gone into it. Doesn't Meg look the picture of a dear old country woman?'

She certainly did, as she sat in the farmhouse kitchen by a cheery fire, rocking a cradle and darning stockings, as if she had done nothing else all her life. Grey hair, skilfully drawn lines on the forehead, and a plain gown, with cap, little shawl, and check apron, changed her into a comfortable, motherly creature who found favour the moment the curtain went up and discovered her rocking, darning, and crooning an old song. In a short soliloquy about Sam, her boy, who wanted to enlist; Dolly, her discontented little daughter, who longed for city ease and pleasures; and poor 'Elizy', who had married badly, and came home to die, bequeathing her baby to her mother, lest its bad father should claim it, the little story was very simply opened, and made effective by the real boiling of the kettle on the crane, the ticking of a tall clock, and the appearance of a pair of blue worsted shoes which waved fitfully in the air to the soft babble of a baby's voice. Those shapeless little shoes won the first applause; and Mr Laurie, forgetting elegance in satisfaction, whispered to his coadjutor:

'I thought the baby would fetch them!'

'If the dear thing won't squall in the wrong place, we are saved. But it is risky. Be ready to catch it if all Meg's cuddlings prove in vain,' answered Mrs Jo, adding, with a clutch at Mr Laurie's arm as a haggard face appeared at the window:

'Here's Demi! I hope no one will recognize him when he comes on as the son. I'll never forgive you for not doing the villain yourself.'

'Can't run the thing and act too. He's capitally made up, and likes a bit of melodrama.'

'This scene ought to have come later; but I wanted to show that the mother was the heroine as soon as possible. I'm tired of love-sick girls and runaway wives. We'll prove that there's romance in old women also. Now he's coming!'

And in slouched a degraded-looking man, shabby, unshaven, and evil-eyed, trying to assume a masterful air as he dismayed the tranquil old woman by demanding his child. A powerful scene followed; and Mrs Meg surprised even those who knew her best by the homely dignity with which she at first met the man she dreaded; then, as he brutally pressed his claim, she pleaded with trembling voice and hands to keep the little creature she had promised the dying mother to protect; and when he turned to take it by force, quite a thrill went through the house as the old woman sprung to snatch it from the cradle, and holding it close, defied him in God's name to tear it from that sacred refuge. It was really well done; and the round of applause that greeted the fine tableau of the indignant old woman, the rosy, blinking baby clinging to her neck, and the daunted man who dared not execute his evil purpose with such a defender for helpless innocence, told the excited authors that their first scene was a hit.

The second was quieter, and introduced Josie as a bonny country lass setting the supper-table in a bad humour. The pettish way in which she slapped down the plates, hustled the cups, and cut the big brown loaf, as she related her girlish trials and ambitions, was capital. Mrs Jo kept her eye on Miss Cameron, and saw her nod approval several times at some natural tone or gesture, some good bit of by-play or a quick change of expression in the young face, which was as variable as an April day. Her struggle with the toasting-fork made much merriment; so did her contempt for the brown sugar, and the relish with which she sweetened her irksome duties by eating it; and when she sat, like Cinderella, on the hearth, tearfully watching the flames dance on the homely room, a girlish voice was heard to exclaim impulsively:

'Poor little thing! she ought to have some fun!'

The old woman enters; and mother and daughter have a pretty scene, in which the latter coaxes and threatens, kisses and cries, till she wins the reluctant consent of the former to visit a rich relation in the city; and from being a little thunder-cloud Dolly becomes bewitchingly gay and good, as soon as her wilful wish is granted. The poor old soul has hardly recovered from this trial when the son enters, in army blue, tells he has enlisted and must go. That is a hard blow; but the patriotic mother bears it well, and not till the thoughtless young folks have hastened away to tell their good news elsewhere does she break down. Then the country kitchen becomes pathetic as the old mother sits alone mourning over her children, till the grey head is hidden in the hands as she kneels down by the cradle to weep and pray, with only Baby to comfort her fond and faithful heart.

Sniffs were audible all through the latter part of this scene; and when the curtain fell, people were so busy wiping their eyes that for a moment they forgot to applaud. That silent moment was more flattering than noise; and as Mrs Jo wiped the real tears off her sister's face, she said as solemnly as an unconscious dab of rouge on her nose permitted:

'Meg, you have saved my play! Oh, why aren't you a real actress, and I a real playwright?'

'Don't gush now, dear, but help me dress Josie; she's in such a quiver of excitement, I can't manage her, and this is her best scene, you know.'

So it was; for her aunt had written it especially for her, and little Jo was happy in a gorgeous dress, with a train long enough to satisfy her wildest dreams. The rich relation's parlour was in festival array, and the country cousin sails in, looking back at her sweeping flounces with such artless rapture that no one had the heart to laugh at the pretty jay in borrowed plumes. She has confidences with herself in the mirror, from which it is made evident that she had discovered all is not gold that glitters, and has found greater temptations than those a girlish love of pleasure, luxury, and flattery bring her. She is sought by a rich lover; but her honest heart resists the allurements he offers, and in its innocent perplexity wishes 'mother' was there to comfort and counsel.

A gay little dance, in which Dora, Nan, Bess, and several of the boys took part, made a good background for the humble figure of the old woman in her widow's bonnet, rusty shawl, big umbrella, and basket. Her naive astonishment, as she surveys the spectacle, feels the curtains, and smooths her old gloves during the moment she remains unseen, was very good; but Josie's unaffected start when she sees her, and the cry: 'Why, there's mother!' was such a hearty little bit of nature, it hardly needed the impatient tripping over her train as she ran into the arms that seemed now to be her nearest refuge.

The lover plays his part; and ripples of merriment greeted the old woman's searching questions and blunt answers during the interview which shows the girl how shallow his love is, and how near she had been to ruining her life as bitterly as poor 'Elizy' did. She gives her answer frankly, and when they are alone, looks from her own bedizened self to the shabby dress, work-worn hands, and tender face, crying with a repentant sob and kiss: 'Take me home, mother, and keep me safe. I've had enough of this!'

'That will do you good, Maria; don't forget it,' said one lady to her daughter as the curtain went down; and the girl answered: 'Well, I'm sure I don't see why it's touching; but it is,' as she spread her lace handkerchief to dry.

Tom and Nan came out strong in the next scene; for it was a ward in an army hospital, and surgeon and nurse went from bed to bed, feeling pulses, administering doses, and hearing complaints with an energy and gravity which convulsed the audience. The tragic element, never far from the comic at such times and places, came in when, while they bandaged an arm, the doctor told the nurse about an old woman who was searching through the hospital for her son, after days and nights on battlefields, through ambulances, and among scenes which would have killed most women.

'She will be here directly, and I dread her coming, for I'm afraid the poor lad who has just gone is her boy. I'd rather face a cannon than these brave women, with their hope and courage and great sorrow,' says the surgeon.

'Ah, these poor mothers break my heart!' adds the nurse, wiping her eyes on her big apron; and with the words Mrs Meg came in.

There was the same dress, the basket and umbrella, the rustic speech, the simple manners; but all were made pathetic by the terrible experience which had changed the tranquil old woman to that haggard figure with wild eyes, dusty feet, trembling hands, and an expression of mingled anguish, resolution, and despair which gave the homely figure a tragic dignity and power that touched all hearts. A few broken words told the story of her vain search, and then the sad quest began again. People held their breath as, led by the nurse, she went from bed to bed, showing in her face the alternations of hope, dread, and bitter disappointment as each was passed. On a narrow cot was a long figure covered with a sheet, and here she paused to lay one hand on her heart and one on her eyes, as if to gather courage to look at the nameless dead. Then she drew down the sheet, gave a long shivering sigh of relief, saying softly:

'Not my son, thank God! but some mother's boy.' And stooping down, she kissed the cold forehead tenderly.

Somebody sobbed there, and Miss Cameron shook two tears out of her eyes, anxious to lose no look or gesture as the poor soul, nearly spent with the long strain, struggled on down the long line. But her search was happily ended for, as if her voice had roused him from his feverish sleep, a gaunt, wild-eyed man sat up in his bed, and stretching his arms to her, cried in a voice that echoed through the room:

'Mother, mother! I knew you'd come to me!'

She did go to him, with a cry of love and joy that thrilled every listener, as she gathered him in her arms with the tears and prayers and blessing such as only a fond and faithful old mother could give.

The last scene was a cheerful contrast to this; for the country kitchen was bright with Christmas cheer, the wounded hero, with black patch and crutches well displayed, sat by the fire in the old chair whose familiar creak was soothing to his ear; pretty Dolly was stirring about, gaily trimming dresser, settle, high chimney-piece, and old-fashioned cradle with mistletoe and holly; while the mother rested beside her son, with that blessed baby on her knee. Refreshed by a nap and nourishment, this young actor now covered himself with glory by his ecstatic prancings, incoherent remarks to the audience, and vain attempts to get to the footlights, as he blinked approvingly at these brilliant toys. It was good to see Mrs Meg pat him on the back, cuddle the fat legs out of sight, and appease his vain longings with a lump of sugar, till Baby embraced her with a grateful ardour that brought him a round of applause all for his little self.

A sound of singing outside disturbs the happy family, and, after a carol in the snowy moonlight, a flock of neighbours troop in with Christmas gifts and greetings. Much by-play made this a lively picture; for Sam's sweetheart hovered round him with a tenderness the Marquise did not show the Baron; and Dolly had a pretty bit under the mistletoe with her rustic adorer, who looked so like Ham Peggotty in his cowhide boots, rough jacket, and dark beard and wig, that no one would have recognized Ted but for the long legs, which no extent of leather could disguise. It ended with a homely feast, brought by the guests; and as they sat round the table covered with doughnuts and cheese, pumpkin-pie, and other delicacies, Sam rises on his crutches to propose the first toast, and holding up his mug of cider, says, with a salute, and a choke in his voice: 'Mother, God bless her!' All drink it standing, Dolly with her arm round the old woman's neck, as she hides her happy tears on her daughter's breast; while the irrepressible baby beat rapturously on the table with a spoon, and crowed audibly as the curtain went down.

They had it up again in a jiffy to get a last look at the group about that central figure, which was showered with bouquets, to the great delight of the infant Roscius; till a fat rosebud hit him on the nose, and produced the much-dreaded squall, which, fortunately, only added to the fun at that moment.

'Well, that will do for a beginning,' said Beaumont, with a sigh of relief, as the curtain descended for the last time, and the actors scattered to dress for the closing piece.

'As an experiment, it is a success. Now we can venture to begin our great American drama,' answered Mrs Jo, full of satisfaction and grand ideas for the famous play—which, we may add, she did not write that year, owing to various dramatic events in her own family.

The Owlsdark Marbles closed the entertainment, and, being something new, proved amusing to this very indulgent audience. The gods and goddesses on Parnassus were displayed in full conclave; and, thanks to Mrs Amy's skill in draping and posing, the white wigs and cotton-flannel robes were classically correct and graceful, though sundry modern additions somewhat marred the effect, while adding point to the showman's learned remarks. Mr Laurie was Professor Owlsdark in cap and gown; and, after a high-flown introduction, he proceeded to exhibit and explain his marbles. The first figure was a stately Minerva; but a second glance produced a laugh, for the words 'Women's Rights' adorned her shield, a scroll bearing the motto 'Vote early and often' hung from the beak of the owl perched on her lance, and a tiny pestle and mortar ornamented her helmet. Attention was drawn to the firm mouth, the piercing eye, the awe-inspiring brow, of the strong-minded woman of antiquity, and some scathing remarks made upon the degeneracy of her modern sisters who failed to do their duty. Mercury came next, and was very fine in his airy attitude, though the winged legs quivered as if it was difficult to keep the lively god in his place. His restless nature was dilated upon, his mischievous freaks alluded to, and a very bad character given to the immortal messenger-boy; which delighted his friends and caused the marble nose of the victim to curl visibly with scorn when derisive applause greeted a particularly hard hit. A charming little Hebe stood next, pouring nectar from a silver teapot into a blue china tea-cup. She also pointed a moral; for the Professor explained that the nectar of old was the beverage which cheers but does not inebriate, and regretted that the excessive devotion of American women to this classic brew proved so harmful, owing to the great development of brain their culture produced. A touch at modern servants, in contrast to this accomplished table-girl, made the statue's cheeks glow under the chalk, and brought her a hearty round as the audience recognized Dolly and the smart soubrette.

Jove in all his majesty followed, as he and his wife occupied the central pedestals in the half-circle of immortals. A splendid Jupiter, with hair well set up off the fine brow, ambrosial beard, silver thunderbolts in one hand, and a well-worn ferule in the other. A large stuffed eagle from the museum stood at his feet; and the benign expression of his august countenance showed that he was in a good humour—as well he might be, for he was paid some handsome compliments upon his wise rule, the peaceful state of his kingdom, and the brood of all-accomplished Pallases that yearly issued from his mighty brain. Cheers greeted this and other pleasant words, and caused the thunderer to bow his thanks; for 'Jove nods', as everyone knows, and flattery wins the heart of gods and men.

Mrs Juno, with her peacocks, darning-needle, pen, and cooking-spoon, did not get off so easily; for the Professor was down on her with all manner of mirth-provoking accusations, criticisms, and insults even. He alluded to her domestic infelicity, her meddlesome disposition, sharp tongue, bad temper, and jealousy, closing, however, with a tribute to her skill in caring for the wounds and settling the quarrels of belligerent heroes, as well as her love for youths in Olympus and on earth. Gales of laughter greeted these hits, varied by hisses from some indignant boys, who would not bear, even in joke, any disrespect to dear Mother Bhaer, who, however, enjoyed it all immensely, as the twinkle in her eye and the irrepressible pucker of her lips betrayed.

A jolly Bacchus astride of his cask took Vulcan's place, and appeared to be very comfortable with a beer-mug in one hand, a champagne bottle in the other, and a garland of grapes on his curly head. He was the text of a short temperance lecture, aimed directly at a row of smart young gentlemen who lined the walls of the auditorium. George Cole was seen to dodge behind a pillar at one point, Dolly nudged his neighbour at another, and there was laughter all along the line as the Professor glared at them through his big glasses, and dragged their bacchanalian orgies to the light and held them up to scorn.

Seeing the execution he had done, the learned man turned to the lovely Diana, who stood as white and still as the plaster stag beside her, with sandals, bow, and crescent; quite perfect, and altogether the best piece of statuary in the show. She was very tenderly treated by the paternal critic who, merely alluding to her confirmed spinsterhood, fondness for athletic sports, and oracular powers, gave a graceful little exposition of true art and passed on to the last figure.

This was Apollo in full fig, his curls skilfully arranged to hide a well-whitened patch over the eye, his handsome legs correctly poised, and his gifted fingers about to draw divine music from the silvered gridiron which was his lyre. His divine attributes were described, as well as his little follies and failings, among which were his weakness for photography and flute-playing, his attempts to run a newspaper, and his fondness for the society of the Muses; which latter slap produced giggles and blushes among the girl-graduates, and much mirth among the stricken youths; for misery loves company, and after this they began to rally.

Then, with a ridiculous conclusion, the Professor bowed his thanks; and after several recalls the curtain fell, but not quickly enough to conceal Mercury, wildly waving his liberated legs, Hebe dropping her teapot, Bacchus taking a lovely roll on his barrel, and Mrs Juno rapping the impertinent Owlsdark on the head with Jove's ruler.

While the audience filed out to supper in the hall, the stage was a scene of dire confusion as gods and goddesses, farmers and barons, maids and carpenters, congratulated one another on the success of their labours. Assuming various costumes, actors and actresses soon joined their guests, to sip bounteous draughts of praise with their coffee, and cool their modest blushes with ice-cream. Mrs Meg was a proud and happy woman when Miss Cameron came to her as she sat by Josie, with Demi serving both, and said, so cordially that it was impossible to doubt the sincerity of her welcome words:

'Mrs Brooke, I no longer wonder where your children get their talent. I make my compliments to the Baron and next summer you must let me have little "Dolly" as a pupil when we are at the beach.'

One can easily imagine how this offer was received, as well as the friendly commendation bestowed by the same kind critic on the work of Beaumont and Fletcher, who hastened to explain that this trifle was only an attempt to make nature and art go hand in hand, with little help from fine writing or imposing scenery. Everybody was in the happiest mood, especially 'little Dolly', who danced like a will-o'-the-wisp with light-footed Mercury and Apollo as he promenaded with the Marquise on his arm, who seemed to have left her coquetry in the green room with her rouge.

When all was over, Mrs Juno said to Jove, to whose arm she clung as they trudged home along the snowy paths: 'Fritz dear, Christmas is a good time for new resolutions, and I've made one never to be impatient or fretful with my beloved husband again. I know I am, though you won't own it; but Laurie's fun had some truth in it, and I felt hit in a tender spot. Henceforth I am a model wife, else I don't deserve the dearest, best man ever born'; and being in a dramatic mood, Mrs Juno tenderly embraced her excellent Jove in the moonlight, to the great amusement of sundry lingerers behind them.

So all three plays might be considered successes, and that merry Christmas night a memorable one in the March family; for Demi got an unspoken question answered, Josie's fondest wish was granted, and, thanks to Professor Owlsdark's jest, Mrs Jo made Professor Bhaer's busy life quite a bed of roses by the keeping of her resolution. A few days later she had her reward for this burst of virtue in Dan's letter, which set her fears at rest and made her very happy, though she was unable to tell him so, because he sent her no address.

## CHAPTER 15. WAITING

'My wife, I have bad news for thee,' said Professor Bhaer, coming in one day early in January.

'Please tell it at once. I can't bear to wait, Fritz,' cried Mrs Jo, dropping her work and standing up as if to take the shot bravely.

'But we must wait and hope, heart's-dearest. Come and let us bear it together. Emil's ship is lost, and as yet no news of him.'

It was well Mr Bhaer had taken his wife into his strong arms, for she looked ready to drop, but bore up after a moment, and sitting by her good man, heard all that there was to tell. Tidings had been sent to the shipowners at Hamburg by some of the survivors, and telegraphed at once by Franz to his uncle. As one boat-load was safe, there was hope that others might also escape, though the gale had sent two to the bottom. A swift-sailing steamer had brought these scanty news, and happier ones might come at any hour; but kind Franz had not added that the sailors reported the captain's boat as undoubtedly wrecked by the falling mast, since the smoke hid its escape, and the gale soon drove all far asunder. But this sad rumour reached Plumfield in time; and deep was the mourning for the happyhearted Commodore, never to come singing home again. Mrs Jo refused to believe it, stoutly insisting that Emil would outlive any storm and yet turn up safe and gay. It was well she clung to this hopeful view, for poor Mr Bhaer was much afflicted by the loss of his boy, because his sister's sons had been his so long he scarcely knew a different love for his very own. Now was a chance for Mrs Juno to keep her word; and she did, speaking cheerily of Emil, even when hope waxed faint and her heart was heavy. If anything could comfort the Bhaers for the loss of one boy, it would have been the affection and sorrow shown by all the rest. Franz kept the cable busy with his varying messages, Nat sent loving letters from Leipzig, and Tom harassed the shipping agents for news. Even busy Jack wrote them with unusual warmth; Dolly and George came often, bearing the loveliest flowers and the daintiest bon-bons to cheer Mrs Bhaer and sweeten Josie's grief; while good-hearted Ned travelled all the way from Chicago to press their hands and say, with a tear in his eye: 'I was so anxious to hear all about the dear old boy, I couldn't keep away.'

'That's right comfortable, and shows me that if I didn't teach my boys anything else, I did give them the brotherly love that will make them stand by one another all their lives,' said Mrs Jo, when he had gone.

Rob answered reams of sympathizing letters, which showed how many friends they had; and the kindly praises of the lost man would have made Emil a hero and a saint, had they all been true. The elders bore it quietly, having learned submission in life's hard school; but the younger people rebelled; some hoped against hope and kept up, others despaired at once, and little Josie, Emil's pet cousin and playmate, was so broken-hearted nothing could comfort her. Nan dosed in vain, Daisy's cheerful words went by like the wind, and Bess's devices to amuse her all failed utterly. To cry in mother's arms and talk about the wreck, which haunted her even in her sleep, was all she cared to do; and Mrs Meg was getting anxious when Miss Cameron sent Josie a kind note bidding her learn bravely her first lesson in real tragedy, and be like the self-sacrificing heroines she loved to act. That did the little girl good, and she made an effort in which Teddy and Octoo helped her much; for the boy was deeply impressed by this sudden eclipse of the firefly whose light and life all missed when they were gone, and lured her out every day for long drives behind the black mare, who shook her silvery bells till they made such merry music Josie could not help listening to it, and whisked her over the snowy roads at a pace which set the blood dancing in her veins and sent her home strengthened and comforted by sunshine, fresh air, and congenial society—three aids young sufferers seldom can resist.

As Emil was helping nurse Captain Hardy, safe and well, aboard the ship, all this sorrow would seem wasted; but it was not, for it drew many hearts more closely together by a common grief, taught some patience, some sympathy, some regret for faults that lie heavy on the conscience when the one sinned against is gone, and all of them the solemn lesson to be ready when the summons comes. A hush lay over Plumfield for weeks, and the studious faces on the hill reflected the sadness of those in the valley. Sacred music sounded from Parnassus to comfort all who heard; the brown cottage was beseiged with gifts for the little mourner, and Emil's flag hung at half-mast on the roof where he last sat with Mrs Jo.

So the weeks went heavily by till suddenly, like a thunderbolt out of a clear sky, came the news, 'All safe, letters on the way.' Then up went the flag, out rang the college bells, bang went Teddy's long-unused cannon, and a chorus of happy voices cried 'Thank God', as people went about, laughing, crying, and embracing one another in a rapture of delight. By and by the longed-for letters came, and all the story of the wreck was told; briefly by Emil, eloquently by Mrs Hardy, gratefully by the captain, while Mary added a few tender words that went straight to their hearts and seemed the sweetest of all. Never were letters so read, passed round, admired, and cried over as these; for Mrs Jo carried them in her pocket when Mr Bhaer did not have them in his, and both took a look at them when they said their prayers at night. Now the Professor was heard humming like a big bee again as he went to his classes, and the lines smoothed out of Mother Bhaer's forehead, while she wrote this real story to anxious friends and let her romances wait. Now messages of congratulation flowed in, and beaming faces showed everywhere. Rob amazed his parents by producing a poem which was remarkably good for one of his years, and Demi set it to music that it might be sung when the sailor boy returned. Teddy stood on his head literally, and tore about the neighbourhood on Octoo, like a second Paul Revere—only his tidings were good. But best of all, little Josie lifted up her head as the snowdrops did, and began to bloom again, growing tall and quiet, with the shadow of past sorrow to tone down her former vivacity and show that she had learned a lesson in trying to act well her part on the real stage, where all have to take their share in the great drama of life.

Now another sort of waiting began; for the travellers were on their way to Hamburg, and would stay there awhile before coming home, as Uncle Hermann owned the Brenda, and the captain must report to him. Emil must remain to Franz's wedding, deferred till now because of the season of mourning, so happily ended. These plans were doubly welcome and pleasant after the troublous times which went before, and no spring ever seemed so beautiful as this one; for, as Teddy put it:

*'Now is the winter of our discontent*
*Made glorious by these sons of Bhaer!'*

Franz and Emil being regarded in the light of elder brothers by the real 'sons of Bhaer'.

There was great scrubbing and dusting among the matrons as they set their houses in order not only for Class Day, but to receive the bride and groom, who were to come to them for the honeymoon trip. Great plans were made, gifts prepared, and much joy felt at the prospect of seeing Franz again; though Emil, who was to accompany them, would be the greater hero. Little did the dear souls dream what a surprise was in store for them, as they innocently laid their plans and wished all the boys could be there to welcome home their eldest and their Casablanca.

While they wait and work so happily, let us see how our other absent boys are faring as they too wait and work and hope for better days. Nat was toiling steadily along the path he had wisely chosen, though it was by no means strewn with flowers—quite thorny was it, in fact, and hard to travel, after the taste of ease and pleasure he had got when nibbling at forbidden fruit. But his crop of wild oats was a light one, and he resolutely reaped what he had sowed, finding some good wheat among the tares. He taught by day; he fiddled night after night in the dingy little theatre, and he studied so diligently that his master was well pleased, and kept him in mind as one to whom preferment was due, if any chance occurred. Gay friends forgot him; but the old ones stood fast, and cheered him up when Heimweh and weariness made him sad. As spring came on things mended—expenses grew less, work pleasanter, and life more bearable than when wintry storms beat on his thinly clad back, and frost pinched the toes that patiently trudged in old boots. No debts burdened him; the year of absence was nearly over; and if he chose to stay, Herr Bergmann had hopes for him that would bring independence for a time at least. So he walked under the lindens with a lighter heart, and in the May evenings went about the city with a band of strolling students, making music before houses where he used to sit as guest. No one recognized him in the darkness, though old friends often listened to the band; and once Minna threw him money, which he humbly received as part of his penance, being morbid on the subject of his sins.

His reward came sooner than he expected, and was greater than he deserved, he thought, though his heart leaped with joy when his master one day informed him that he was chosen, with several other of his most promising pupils, to join the musical society which was to take part in the great festival in London the next July. Here was not only honour for the violinist but happiness for the man, as it brought him nearer home, and would open a chance of further promotion and profit in his chosen profession.

'Make thyself useful to Bachmeister there in London with thy English, and if all goes well with him, he will be glad to take thee to America, whither he goes in the early autumn for winter concerts. Thou hast done well these last months, and I have hopes of thee.'

As the great Bergmann seldom praised his pupils, these words filled Nat's soul with pride and joy, and he worked yet more diligently than before to fulfil his master's prophecy. He thought the trip to England happiness enough, but found room for more when, early in June, Franz and Emil paid him a flying visit, bringing all sorts of good news, kind wishes, and comfortable gifts for the lonely fellow, who could have fallen on their necks and cried like a girl at seeing his old mates again. How glad he was to be found in his little room busy at his proper work, not living like an idle gentleman on borrowed money! How proud he was to tell his plans, assure them that he had no debts, and receive their praises for his improvement in music, their respect for his economy and steadfastness in well-doing! How relieved when, having honestly confessed his shortcomings, they only laughed, and owned that they also had known like experiences, and were the wiser for them. He was to go to the wedding late in June, and join his comrades in London. As best man, he could not refuse the new suit Franz insisted on ordering for him; and a cheque from home about that time made him feel like a millionaire—and a happy one; for this was accompanied by such kind letters full of delight in his success, he felt that he had earned it, and waited for his joyful holiday with the impatience of a boy.

Dan meantime was also counting the weeks till August, when he would be free. But neither marriage-bells nor festival music awaited him; no friends would greet him as he left the prison; no hopeful prospect lay before him; no happy home-going was to be his. Yet his success was far greater than Nat's, though only God and one good man saw it. It was a hard-won battle; but he would never have to fight so terrible a one again; for though enemies would still assail from within and from without, he had found the little guide-book that Christian carried in his bosom, and Love, Penitence, and Prayer, the three sweet sisters, had given him the armour which would keep him safe. He had not learned to wear it yet, and chafed against it, though he felt its value, thanks to the faithful friend who had stood by him all that bitter year.

Soon he was to be free again, worn and scarred in the fray, but out among men in the blessed sun and air. When he thought of it Dan felt as if he could not wait, but must burst that narrow cell and fly away, as the caddis-worms he used to watch by the brookside shed their stony coffins, to climb the ferns and soar into the sky. Night after night he lulled himself to sleep with planning how, when he had seen Mary Mason according to his promise, he would steer straight for his old friends, the Indians, and in the wilderness hide his disgrace and heal his wounds. Working to save the many would atone for the sin of killing one, he thought; and the old free life would keep him safe from the temptations that beset him in cities.

'By and by, when I'm all right again, and have something to tell that I'm not ashamed of, I'll go home,' he said, with a quicker beat of the impetuous heart that longed to be there so intensely, he found it as hard to curb as one of his unbroken horses on the plains. 'Not yet. I must get over this first. They'd see and smell and feel the prison taint on me, if I went now, and I couldn't look them in the face and hide the truth. I can't lose Ted's love, Mother Bhaer's confidence, and the respect of the girls, for they did respect my strength, anyway; but now they wouldn't touch me.' And poor Dan looked with a shudder at the brown fist he clenched involuntarily as he remembered what it had done since a certain little white hand had laid in it confidingly. 'I'll make 'em proud of me yet; and no one shall ever know of this awful year. I can wipe it out, and I will, so help me God!' And the clenched hand was held up as if to take a solemn oath that this lost year should yet be made good, if resolution and repentance could work the miracle.

## CHAPTER 16. IN THE TENNIS-COURT

Athletic sports were in high favour at Plumfield; and the river where the old punt used to wabble about with a cargo of small boys, or echo to the shrill screams of little girls trying to get lilies, now was alive with boats of all kinds, from the slender wherry to the trim pleasure-craft, gay with cushions, awnings, and fluttering pennons. Everyone rowed, and the girls as well as the youths had their races, and developed their muscles in the most scientific manner. The large, level meadow near the old willow was now the college playground, and here baseball battles raged with fury, varied by football, leaping, and kindred sports fitted to split the fingers, break the ribs, and strain the backs of the too ambitious participants. The gentler pastimes of the damsels were at a safe distance from this Champ de Mars; croquet mallets clicked under the elms that fringed the field, rackets rose and fell energetically in several tennis-courts, and gates of different heights were handy to practise the graceful bound by which every girl expected to save her life some day when the mad bull, which was always coming but never seemed to arrive, should be bellowing at her heels.

One of these tennis grounds was called 'Jo's Court', and here the little lady ruled like a queen; for she was fond of the game, and being bent on developing her small self to the highest degree of perfection, she was to be found at every leisure moment with some victim hard at it. On a certain pleasant Saturday afternoon she had been playing with Bess and beating her; for, though more graceful, the Princess was less active than her cousin, and cultivated her roses by quieter methods.

'Oh dear! you are tired, and every blessed boy is at that stupid baseball match. 'What shall I do?' sighed Josie, pushing back the great red hat she wore, and gazing sadly round her for more worlds to conquer.

'I'll play presently, when I'm a little cooler. But it is dull work for me, as I never win,' answered Bess, fanning herself with a large leaf.

Josie was about to sit down beside her on the rustic seat and wait, when her quick eye saw afar off two manly forms arrayed in white flannel; their blue legs seemed bearing them towards the battle going on in the distance; but they never reached the fray; for with a cry of joy, Jo raced away to meet them, bent on securing this heaven-sent reinforcement. Both paused as she came flying up, and both raised their hats; but oh, the difference there was in the salutes! The stout youth pulled his off lazily and put it on again at once, as if glad to get the duty over; the slender being, with the crimson tie, lifted his with a graceful bend, and held it aloft while he accosted the rosy, breathless maid, thus permitting her to see his raven locks smoothly parted, with one little curl upon the brow. Dolly prided himself upon that bow, and practised it before his glass, but did not bestow it upon all alike, regarding it as a work of art, fit only for the fairest and most favoured of his female admirers; for he was a pretty youth, and fancied himself an Adonis.

Eager Josie evidently did not appreciate the honour he did her, for with a nod she begged them both to 'come along and play tennis, not go and get all hot and dirty with the boys'. These two adjectives won the day; for Stuffy was already warmer than he liked to be, and Dolly had on a new suit which he desired to keep immaculate as long as possible, conscious that it was very becoming.

'Charmed to oblige,' answered the polite one, with another bend.

'You play, I'll rest,' added the fat boy, yearning for repose and gentle converse with the Princess in the cooling shade.

'Well, you can comfort Bess, for I've beaten her all to bits and she needs amusing. I know you've got something nice in your pocket, George; give her some, and 'Dolphus can have her racket. Now then, fly round'; and driving her prey before her, Josie returned in triumph to the court.

Casting himself ponderously upon the bench, which creaked under his weight, Stuffy—as we will continue to call him, though no one else dared to use the old name now—promptly produced the box of confectionery, without which he never travelled far, and regaled Bess with candied violets and other dainties, while Dolly worked hard to hold his own against a most accomplished antagonist. He would have beaten her if an unlucky stumble, which produced an unsightly stain upon the knee of those new shorts, had not distracted his mind and made him careless. Much elated at her victory, Josie permitted him to rest, and offered ironical consolation for the mishap which evidently weighed upon his mind.

'Don't be an old Betty; it can be cleaned. You must have been a cat in some former state, you are so troubled about dirt; or a tailor, and lived for clothes.'

'Come now, don't hit a fellow when he is down,' responded Dolly from the grass where he and Stuffy now lay to make room for both girls on the seat. One handkerchief was spread under him, and his elbow leaned upon another, while his eyes were sadly fixed upon the green and brown spot which afflicted him. 'I like to be neat; don't think it civil to cut about in old shoes and grey flannel shirts before ladies. Our fellows are gentlemen, and dress as such,' he added, rather nettled at the word 'tailor'; for he owed one of those too attractive persons an uncomfortably big bill.

'So are ours; but good clothes alone don't make a gentleman here. We require a good deal more,' flashed Josie, in arms at once to defend her college. 'You will hear of some of the men in "old boots and grey flannel" when you and your fine gentlemen are twiddling your ties and scenting your hair in obscurity. I like old boots and wear them, and I hate dandies; don't you, Bess?'

'Not when they are kind to me, and belong to our old set,' answered Bess, with a nod of thanks to Dolly, who was carefully removing an inquisitive caterpillar from one of her little russet shoes.

'I like a lady who is always polite, and doesn't snap a man's head off if he has a mind of his own; don't you, George?' asked Dolly, with his best smile for Bess and a Harvard stare of disapprobation for Josie.

A tranquil snore was Stuffy's sole reply, and a general laugh restored peace for the moment. But Josie loved to harass the lords of creation who asserted themselves too much, and bided her time for another attack till she had secured more tennis. She got another game; for Dolly was a sworn knight of dames, so he obeyed her call, leaving Bess to sketch George as he lay upon his back, his stout legs crossed, and his round red face partially eclipsed by his hat. Josie got beaten this time and came back rather cross, so she woke the peaceful sleeper by tickling his nose with a straw till he sneezed himself into a sitting posture, and looked wrathfully about for 'that confounded fly'.

'Come, sit up and let us have a little elegant conversation; you "howling swells" ought to improve our minds and manners, for we are only poor "country girls in dowdy gowns and hats",' began the gad-fly, opening the battle with a sly quotation from one of Dolly's unfortunate speeches about certain studious damsels who cared more for books than finery.

'I didn't mean you! Your gowns are all right, and those hats the latest thing out,' began poor 'Dolphus, convicting himself by the incautious exclamation.

'Caught you that time; I thought you fellows were all gentlemen, civil as well as nice. But you are always sneering at girls who don't dress well and that is a very unmanly thing to do; my mother said so'; and Josie felt that she had dealt a shrewd blow at the elegant youth who bowed at many shrines if they were well-decorated ones.

'Got you there, old boy, and she's right. You never hear me talk about clothes and such twaddle,' said Stuffy, suppressing a yawn, and feeling for another bon-bon wherewith to refresh himself.

'You talk about eating, and that is even worse for a man. You will marry a cook and keep a restaurant some day,' laughed Josie, down on him at once.

This fearful prediction kept him silent for several moments; but Dolly rallied, and wisely changing the subject, carried war into the enemy's camp.

'As you wanted us to improve your manners, allow me to say that young ladies in good society don't make personal remarks or deliver lectures. Little girls who are not out do it, and think it witty; but I assure you it's not good form.'

Josie paused a moment to recover from the shock of being called 'a little girl', when all the honours of her fourteenth birthday were fresh upon her; and Bess said, in the lofty tone which was infinitely more crushing than Jo's impertinence:

'That is true; but we have lived all our lives with superior people, so we have no society talk like your young ladies. We are so accustomed to sensible conversation, and helping one another by telling our faults, that we have no gossip to offer you.'

When the Princess reproved, the boys seldom resented it; so Dolly held his peace, and Josie burst out, following her cousin's lead, which she thought a happy one:

'Our boys like to have us talk with them, and take kindly any hints we give. They don't think they know everything and are quite perfect at eighteen, as I've observed the Harvard men do, especially the very young ones.'

Josie took immense satisfaction in that return shot; and Dolly showed that he was hit, by the nettled tone in which he answered, with a supercilious glance at the hot, dusty, and noisy crowd on the baseball ground: 'The class of fellows you have here need all the polish and culture you can give them; and I'm glad they get it. Our men are largely from the best families all over the country, so we don't need girls to teach us anything.'

'It's a pity you don't have more of such "fellows" as ours. They value and use well what college gives them, and aren't satisfied to slip through, getting all the fun they can and shirking the work. Oh, I've heard you "men" talk, and heard your fathers say they wish they hadn't wasted time and money just that you might say you'd been through college. As for the girls, you'll be much better off in all ways when they do get in, and keep you lazy things up to the mark, as we do here.'

'If you have such a poor opinion of us, why do you wear our colour?' asked Dolly, painfully conscious that he was not improving the advantages his Alma Mater offered him, but bound to defend her.

'I don't; my hat is scarlet, not crimson. Much you know about a colour,' scoffed Josie.

'I know that a cross cow would soon set you scampering, if you flaunted that red tile under her nose,' retorted Dolly.

'I'm ready for her. Can your fine young ladies do this? or you either?' and burning to display her latest accomplishment, Josie ran to the nearest gate, put one hand on the top rail, and vaulted over as lightly as a bird.

Bess shook her head, and Stuffy languidly applauded; but Dolly scorning to be braved by a girl, took a flying leap and landed on his feet beside Josie, saying calmly: 'Can you do that?'

'Not yet; but I will by and by.'

As his foe looked a little crestfallen, Dolly relented, and affably added sundry feats of a like nature, quite unconscious that he had fallen into a dreadful snare; for the dull red paint on the gate, not being used to such vigorous handling, came off in streaks upon his shoulders when he turned a backward swing and came up smiling, to be rewarded with the aggravating remark:

'If you want to know what crimson is, look at your back; it's nicely stamped on and won't wash out, I think.'

'The deuce it won't!' cried Dolly, trying to get an impossible view, and giving it up in great disgust.

'I guess we'd better be going, Dolf,' said peaceable Stuffy, feeling that it would be wise to retreat before another skirmish took place, as his side seemed to be getting the worst of it.

'Don't hurry, I beg; stay and rest; you must need it after the tremendous amount of brain work you've done this week. It is time for our Greek. Come, Bess. Good afternoon, gentlemen.' And, with a sweeping courtesy, Josie led the way, with her hat belligerently cocked up, and her racket borne like a triumphal banner over one shoulder; for having had the last word, she felt that she could retire with the honours of war.

Dolly gave Bess his best bow, with the chill on; and Stuffy subsided luxuriously, with his legs in the air, murmuring in a dreamy tone:

'Little Jo is as cross as two sticks today. I'm going in for another nap: too hot to play anything.'

'So it is. Wonder if Spitfire was right about these beastly spots?' And Dolly sat down to try dry cleansing with one of his handkerchiefs. 'Asleep?' he asked, after a few moments of this cheerful occupation, fearing that his chum might be too comfortable when he was in a fume himself.

'No. I was thinking that Jo wasn't far wrong about shirking. 'Tis a shame to get so little done, when we ought to be grinding like Morton and Torry and that lot. I never wanted to go to college; but my governor made me. Much good it will do either of us!' answered Stuffy, with a groan; for he hated work, and saw two more long years of it before him.

'Gives a man prestige, you know. No need to dig. I mean to have a gay old time, and be a "howling swell", if I choose. Between you and me though, it would be no end jolly to have the girls along. Study be hanged! But if we've got to turn the grindstone, it would be mighty nice to have some of the little dears to lend a hand. Wouldn't it now?'

'I'd like three this minute—one to fan me, one to kiss me, and one to give me some iced lemonade!' sighed Stuffy, with a yearning glance towards the house, whence no succour appeared.

'How would root-beer do?' asked a voice behind them, which made Dolly spring to his feet and Stuffy roll over like a startled porpoise.

Sitting on the stile that crossed the wall near by was Mrs Jo, with two jugs slung over her shoulder by a strap, several tin mugs in her hand, and an old-fashioned sun-bonnet on her head.

'I knew the boys would be killing themselves with ice-water; so I strolled down with some of my good, wholesome beer. They drank like fishes. But Silas was with me; so my cruse still holds out. Have some?'

'Yes, thanks, very much. Let us pour it.' And Dolly held the cup while Stuffy joyfully filled it; both very grateful, but rather afraid she had heard what went before the wish she fulfilled.

She proved that she had by saying, as they stood drinking her health, while she sat between them, looking like a middle-aged vivandiere, with her jugs and mugs:

'I was glad to hear you say you would like to have girls at your college; but I hope you will learn to speak more respectfully of them before they come; for that will be the first lesson they will teach you.'

'Really, ma'am, I was only joking,' began Stuffy, gulping down his beer in a hurry.

'So was I. I'm sure I—I'm devoted to 'em,' stuttered Dolly, panic-stricken; for he saw that he was in for a lecture of some sort.

'Not in the right way. Frivolous girls may like to be called "little dears" and things of that sort; but the girls who love study wish to be treated like reasonable beings, not dolls to flirt with. Yes, I'm going to preach; that's my business; so stand up and take it like men.'

Mrs Jo laughed; but she was in earnest; for by various hints and signs during the past winter she knew that the boys were beginning to 'see life' in the way she especially disapproved. Both were far from home, had money enough to waste, and were as inexperienced, curious, and credulous as most lads of their age. Not fond of books, therefore without the safeguard which keeps many studious fellows out of harm; one self-indulgent, indolent, and so used to luxury that pampering of the senses was an easy thing; the other vain, as all comely boys are, full of conceit, and so eager to find favour in the eyes of his comrades that he was ready for anything which would secure it. These traits and foibles made both peculiarly liable to the temptations which assail pleasure-loving and weak-willed boys. Mrs Jo knew them well, and had dropped many a warning word since they went to college; but till lately they seemed not to understand some of her friendly hints; now she was sure they would, and meant to speak out: for long experience with boys made her both bold and skilful in handling some of the dangers usually left to silence, till it is too late for anything but pity and reproach.

'I'm going to talk to you like a mother, because yours are far away; and there are things that mothers can manage best, if they do their duty,' she solemnly began from the depths of the sunbonnet.

'Great Scott! We're in for it now!' thought Dolly, in secret dismay; while Stuffy got the first blow by trying to sustain himself with another mug of beer.

'That won't hurt you; but I must warn you about drinking other things, George. Overeating is an old story; and a few more fits of illness will teach you to be wise. But drinking is a more serious thing, and leads to worse harm than any that can afflict your body alone. I hear you talk about wines as if you knew them and cared more for them than a boy should; and several times I've heard jokes that meant mischief. For heaven's sake, don't begin to play with this dangerous taste "for fun", as you say, or because it's the fashion, and the other fellows do. Stop at once, and learn that temperance in all things is the only safe rule.'

'Upon my honour, I only take wine and iron. I need a tonic, mother says, to repair the waste of brain-tissue while I'm studying,' protested Stuffy, putting down the mug as if it burnt his fingers.

'Good beef and oatmeal will repair your tissues much better than any tonic of that sort. Work and plain fare are what you want; and I wish I had you here for a few months out of harm's way. I'd Banting you, and fit you to run without puffing, and get on without four or five meals a day. What an absurd hand that is for a man! You ought to be ashamed of it!' And Mrs Jo caught up the plump fist, with deep dimples at each knuckle, which was fumbling distressfully at the buckle of the belt girt about a waist far too large for a youth of his age.

'I can't help it—we all grow fat; it's in the family,' said Stuffy in self-defence.

'All the more reason you should live carefully. Do you want to die early, or be an invalid all your life?'

'No, ma'am!'

Stuffy looked so scared that Mrs Jo could not be hard upon his budding sins, for they lay at his overindulgent mother's door line in a great measure; so she softened the tone of her voice, and added, with a little slap on the fat hand, as she used to do when it was small enough to pilfer lumps of sugar from her bowl:

'Then be careful; for a man writes his character in his face; and you don't want gluttony and intemperance in yours, I know.'

'I'm sure I don't! Please make out a wholesome bill of fare, and I'll stick to it, if I can. I am getting stout, and I don't like it; and my liver's torpid, and I have palpitations and headache. Overwork, mother says; but it may be overeating.' And Stuffy gave a sigh of mingled regret for the good things he renounced, and relief as he finished loosening his belt as soon as his hand was free.

'I will; follow it, and in a year you'll be a man and not a meal-bag. Now, Dolly'; and Mrs Jo turned to the other culprit, who shook in his shoes and wished he hadn't come.

'Are you studying French as industriously as you were last winter?'

'No ma'am; I don't care for it—that is, I, I'm busy with G-Greek just now,' answered Dolly, beginning bravely, quite in the dark as to what that odd question meant till a sudden memory made him stutter and look at his shoes with deep interest.

'Oh, he doesn't study it; only reads French novels and goes to the theatre when the opera bouffe is here,' said Stuffy, innocently confirming Mrs Jo's suspicions.

'So I understood; and that is what I want to speak about. Ted had a sudden desire to learn French in that way, from something you said, Dolly; so I went myself, and was quite satisfied that it was no place for a decent boy. Your men were out in full force; and I was glad to see that some of the younger ones looked as ashamed as I felt. The older fellows enjoyed it, and when we came out were waiting to take those painted girls to supper. Did you ever go with them?'

'Once.'

'Did you like it?'

'No 'm; I—I came away early,' stammered Dolly, with a face as red as his splendid tie.

'I'm glad you have not lost the grace of blushing yet; but you will soon, if you keep up this sort of study and forget to be ashamed. The society of such women will unfit you for that of good ones, and lead you into trouble and sin and shame. Oh, why don't the city fathers stop that evil thing, when they know the harm it does? It made my heart ache to see those boys, who ought to be at home and in their beds, going off for a night of riot which would help to ruin some of them for ever.'

The youths looked scared at Mrs Jo's energetic protest against one of the fashionable pleasures of the day, and waited in conscience-stricken silence—Stuffy glad that he never went to those gay suppers, and Dolly deeply grateful that he 'came away early'. With a hand on either shoulder, and all the terrors smoothed from her brow, Mrs Jo went on in her most motherly tone, anxious to do for them what no other woman would, and do it kindly:

'My dear boys, if I didn't love you, I would not say these things. I know they are not pleasant; but my conscience won't let me hold my peace when a word may keep you from two of the great sins that curse the world and send so many young men to destruction. You are just beginning to feel the allurement of them, and soon it will be hard to turn away. Stop now, I beg of you, and not only save yourselves but help others by a brave example. Come to me if things worry you; don't be afraid or ashamed; I have heard many sadder confessions than any you are ever likely to bring me, and been able to comfort many poor fellows, gone wrong for want of a word in time. Do this, and you will be able to kiss your mothers with clean lips, and by and by have the right to ask innocent girls to love you.'

'Yes'm, thank you. I suppose you're right; but it's pretty hard work to toe the mark when ladies give you wine and gentlemen take their daughters to see Aimee,' said Dolly, foreseeing tribulations ahead though he knew it was time to 'pull up'.

'So it is; but all the more honour to those who are brave and wise enough to resist public opinion, and the easy-going morals of bad or careless men and women. Think of the persons whom you respect most, and in imitating them you will secure the respect of those who look up to you. I'd rather my boys should be laughed at and cold-shouldered by a hundred foolish fellows than lose what, once gone, no power can give them back—innocence and self-respect. I don't wonder you find it "hard to toe the mark", when books, pictures, ball-rooms, theatres, and streets offer temptations; yet you can resist, if you try. Last winter Mrs Brooke used to worry about John's being out so late reporting; but when she spoke to him about the things he must see and hear on his way to and fro from the office at midnight, he said in his sober way, "I know what you mean, mother; but no fellow need to go wrong unless he wants to."

'That's like the Deacon!' exclaimed Stuffy, with an approving smile on his fat face.

'I'm glad you told me that. He's right; and it's because he doesn't want to go wrong we all respect him so,' added Dolly, looking up now with an expression which assured his Mentor that the right string had been touched, and a spirit of emulation roused, more helpful, perhaps, than any words of hers. Seeing this, she was satisfied, and said, as she prepared to leave the bar before which her culprits had been tried and found guilty, but recommended to mercy:

'Then be to others what John is to you—a good example. Forgive me for troubling you, my dear lads, and remember my little preachment. I think it will do you good, though I may never know it. Chance words spoken in kindness often help amazingly; and that's what old people are here for—else their experience is of little use. Now, come and find the young folk. I hope I shall never have to shut the gates of Plumfield upon you, as I have on some of your "gentlemen". I mean to keep my boys and girls safe if I can, and this a wholesome place where the good old-fashioned virtues are lived and taught.'

Much impressed by that dire threat, Dolly helped her from her perch with deep respect; and Stuffy relieved her of her empty jugs, solemnly vowing to abstain from all fermented beverages except root-beer, as long as feeble flesh could hold out. Of course they made light of 'Mother Bhaer's lecture' when they were alone—that was to be expected of 'men of our class' but in their secret souls they thanked her for giving their boyish consciences a jog, and more than once afterward had cause to remember gratefully that half-hour in the tennis court.

# CHAPTER 17. AMONG THE MAIDS

Although this story is about Jo's boys, her girls cannot be neglected, because they held a high place in this little republic, and especial care was taken to fit them to play their parts worthily in the great republic which offered them wider opportunities and more serious duties. To many the social influence was the better part of the training they received; for education is not confined to books, and the finest characters often graduate from no college, but make experience their master, and life their book. Others cared only for the mental culture, and were in danger of over-studying, under the delusion which pervades New England that learning must be had at all costs, forgetting that health and real wisdom are better. A third class of ambitious girls hardly knew what they wanted, but were hungry for whatever could fit them to face the world and earn a living, being driven by necessity, the urgency of some half-conscious talent, or the restlessness of strong young natures to break away from the narrow life which no longer satisfied.

At Plumfield all found something to help them; for the growing institution had not yet made its rules as fixed as the laws of the Medes and Persians, and believed so heartily in the right of all sexes, colours, creeds, and ranks to education, that there was room for everyone who knocked, and a welcome to the shabby youths from up country, the eager girls from the West, the awkward freedman or woman from the South, or the well-born student whose poverty made this college a possibility when other doors were barred. There still was prejudice, ridicule, neglect in high places, and prophecies of failure to contend against; but the Faculty was composed of cheerful, hopeful men and women who had seen greater reforms spring from smaller roots, and after stormy seasons blossom beautifully, to add prosperity and honour to the nation. So they worked on steadily and bided their time, full of increasing faith in their attempt as year after year their numbers grew, their plans succeeded, and the sense of usefulness in this most vital of all professions blessed them with its sweet rewards.

Among the various customs which had very naturally sprung up was one especially useful and interesting to 'the girls', as the young women liked to be called. It all grew out of the old sewing hour still kept up by the three sisters long after the little work-boxes had expanded into big baskets full of household mending. They were busy women, yet on Saturdays they tried to meet in one of the three sewing-rooms; for even classic Parnassus had its nook where Mrs Amy often sat among her servants, teaching them to make and mend, thereby giving them a respect for economy, since the rich lady did not scorn to darn her hose, and sew on buttons. In these household retreats, with books and work, and their daughters by them, they read and sewed and talked in the sweet privacy that domestic women love, and can make so helpful by a wise mixture of cooks and chemistry, table linen and theology, prosaic duties and good poetry.

Mrs Meg was the first to propose enlarging this little circle; for as she went her motherly rounds among the young women she found a sad lack of order, skill, and industry in this branch of education. Latin, Greek, the higher mathematics, and science of all sorts prospered finely; but the dust gathered on the work-baskets, frayed elbows went unheeded, and some of the blue stockings sadly needed mending. Anxious lest the usual sneer at learned women should apply to 'our girls', she gently lured two or three of the most untidy to her house, and made the hour so pleasant, the lesson so kindly, that they took the hint, were grateful for the favour, and asked to come again. Others soon begged to make the detested weekly duty lighter by joining the party, and soon it was a privilege so much desired that the old museum was refitted with sewing-machines, tables, rocking-chair, and a cheerful fireplace, so that, rain or shine, the needles might go on undisturbed.

Here Mrs Meg was in her glory, and stood wielding her big shears like a queen as she cut out white work, fitted dresses, and directed Daisy, her special aide, about the trimming of hats, and completing the lace and ribbon trifles which add grace to the simplest costume and save poor or busy girls so much money and time. Mrs Amy contributed taste, and decided the great question of colours and complexions; for few women, even the most learned, are without that desire to look well which makes many a plain face comely, as well as many a pretty one ugly for want of skill and knowledge of the fitness of things. She also took her turn to provide books for the readings, and as art was her forte she gave them selections from Ruskin, Hamerton, and Mrs Jameson, who is never old. Bess read these aloud as her contribution, and Josie took her turn at the romances, poetry, and plays her uncles recommended. Mrs Jo gave little lectures on health, religion, politics, and the various questions in which all should be interested, with copious extracts from Miss Cobbe's Duties of Women, Miss Brackett's Education of American Girls, Mrs Duffy's No Sex in Education, Mrs Woolson's Dress Reform, and many of the other excellent books wise women write for their sisters, now that they are waking up and asking: 'What shall we do?'

It was curious to see the prejudices melt away as ignorance was enlightened, indifference change to interest, and intelligent minds set thinking, while quick wits and lively tongues added spice to the discussions which inevitably followed. So the feet that wore the neatly mended hose carried wiser heads than before, the pretty gowns covered hearts warmed with higher purposes, and the hands that dropped the thimbles for pens, lexicons, and celestial globes, were better fitted for life's work, whether to rock cradles, tend the sick, or help on the great work of the world.

One day a brisk discussion arose concerning careers for women. Mrs Jo had read something on the subject and asked each of the dozen girls sitting about the room, what she intended to do on leaving college. The answers were as usual: 'I shall teach, help mother, study medicine, art,' etc.; but nearly all ended with:

'Till I marry.'

'But if you don't marry, what then?' asked Mrs Jo, feeling like a girl again as she listened to the answers, and watched the thoughtful, gay, or eager faces.

'Be old maids, I suppose. Horrid, but inevitable, since there are so many superfluous women,' answered a lively lass, too pretty to fear single blessedness unless she chose it.

'It is well to consider that fact, and fit yourselves to be useful, not superfluous women. That class, by the way, is largely made up of widows, I find; so don't consider it a slur on maidenhood.'

'That's a comfort! Old maids aren't sneered at half as much as they used to be, since some of them have grown famous and proved that woman isn't a half but a whole human being, and can stand alone.'

'Don't like it all the same. We can't all be like Miss Nightingale, Miss Phelps, and the rest.'

So what can we do but sit in a corner and look on?' asked a plain girl with a dissatisfied expression.

'Cultivate cheerfulness and content, if nothing else. But there are so many little odd jobs waiting to be done that nobody need "sit idle and look on", unless she chooses,' said Mrs Meg, with a smile, laying on the girl's head the new hat she had just trimmed.

'Thank you very much. Yes, Mrs Brooke, I see; it's a little job, but it makes me neat and happy—and grateful,' she added, looking up with brighter eyes as she accepted the labour of love and the lesson as sweetly as they were given.

'One of the best and most beloved women I know has been doing odd jobs for the Lord for years, and will keep at it till her dear hands are folded in her coffin. All sorts of things she does—picks up neglected children and puts them in safe homes, saves lost girls, nurses poor women in trouble, sews, knits, trots, begs, works for the poor day after day with no reward but the thanks of the needy, the love and honour of the rich who make Saint Matilda their almoner. That's a life worth living; and I think that quiet little woman will get a higher seat in Heaven than many of those of whom the world has heard.'

'I know it's lovely, Mrs Bhaer; but it's dull for young folks. We do want a little fun before we buckle to,' said a Western girl with a wide-awake face.

'Have your fun, my dear; but if you must earn your bread, try to make it sweet with cheerfulness, not bitter with the daily regret that it isn't cake. I used to think mine was a very hard fate because I had to amuse a somewhat fretful old lady; but the books I read in that lonely library have been of immense use to me since, and the dear old soul bequeathed me Plumfield for my "cheerful service and affectionate care". I didn't deserve it, but I did use to try to be jolly and kind, and get as much honey out of duty as I could, thanks to my dear mother's help and advice.'

'Gracious! if I could earn a place like this, I'd sing all day and be an angel; but you have to take your chance, and get nothing for your pains, perhaps. I never do,' said the Westerner, who had a hard time with small means and large aspirations.

'Don't do it for the reward; but be sure it will come, though not in the shape you expect. I worked hard for fame and money one winter; but I got neither, and was much disappointed. A year afterwards I found I had earned two prizes: skill with my pen, and Professor Bhaer.'

Mrs Jo's laugh was echoed blithely by the girls, who liked to have these conversations enlivened by illustrations from life.

'You are a very lucky woman,' began the discontented damsel, whose soul soared above new hats, welcome as they were, but did not quite know where to steer.

'Yet her name used to be "Luckless Jo", and she never had what she wanted till she had given up hoping for it,' said Mrs Meg.

'I'll give up hoping, then, right away, and see if my wishes will come. I only want to help my folks, and get a good school.'

'Take this proverb for your guide: "Get the distaff ready, and the Lord will send the flax",' answered Mrs Jo.

'We'd better all do that, if we are to be spinsters,' said the pretty one, adding gaily, 'I think I should like it, on the whole—they are so independent. My Aunt Jenny can do just what she likes, and ask no one's leave; but Ma has to consult Pa about everything. Yes, I'll give you my chance, Sally, and be a "superfluum", as Mr Plock says.'

'You'll be one of the first to go into bondage, see if you aren't. Much obliged, all the same.'

'Well, I'll get my distaff ready, and take whatever flax the Fates send—single, or double-twisted, as the powers please.'

'That is the right spirit, Nelly. Keep it up, and see how happy life will be with a brave heart, a willing hand, and plenty to do.'

'No one objects to plenty of domestic work or fashionable pleasure, I find; but the minute we begin to study, people tell us we can't bear it, and warn us to be very careful. I've tried the other things, and got so tired I came to college; though my people predict nervous exhaustion and an early death. Do you think there is any danger?' asked a stately girl, with an anxious glance at the blooming face reflected in the mirror opposite.

'Are you stronger or weaker than when you came two years ago, Miss Winthrop?'

'Stronger in body, and much happier in mind. I think I was dying of ennui; but the doctors called it inherited delicacy of constitution. That is why mamma is so anxious, and I wish not to go too fast.'

'Don't worry, my dear; that active brain of yours was starving for good food; it has plenty now, and plain living suits you better than luxury and dissipation. It is all nonsense about girls not being able to study as well as boys. Neither can bear cramming; but with proper care both are better for it; so enjoy the life your instinct led you to, and we will prove that wise headwork is a better cure for that sort of delicacy than tonics, and novels on the sofa, where far too many of our girls go to wreck nowadays. They burn the candle at both ends; and when they break down they blame the books, not the balls.'

'Dr Nan was telling me about a patient of hers who thought she had heart-complaint, till Nan made her take off her corsets, stopped her coffee and dancing all night, and made her eat, sleep, walk, and live regularly for a time; and now she's a brilliant cure. Common sense versus custom, Nan said.'

'I've had no headaches since I came here, and can do twice as much studying as I did at home. It's the air, I think, and the fun of going ahead of the boys,' said another girl, tapping her big forehead with her thimble, as if the lively brain inside was in good working order and enjoyed the daily gymnastics she gave it.

'Quality, not quantity, wins the day, you know. Our brains may be smaller, but I don't see that they fall short of what is required of them; and if I'm not mistaken, the largest-headed man in our class is the dullest,' said Nelly, with a solemn air which produced a gale of merriment; for all knew that the young Goliath she mentioned had been metaphorically slain by this quick-witted David on many a battle-field, to the great disgust of himself and his mates.

'Mrs Brooke, do I gauge on the right or the wrong side?' asked the best Greek scholar of her class, eyeing a black silk apron with a lost expression.

'The right, Miss Pierson; and leave a space between the tucks; it looks prettier so.'

'I'll never make another; but it will save my dresses from ink-stains, so I'm glad I've got it'; and the erudite Miss Pierson laboured on, finding it a harder task than any Greek root she ever dug up.

'We paper-stainers must learn how to make shields, or we are lost. I'll give you a pattern of the pinafore I used to wear in my "blood-and-thunder days", as we call them,' said Mrs Jo, trying to remember what became of the old tin-kitchen which used to hold her works.

'Speaking of writers reminds me that my ambition is to be a George Eliot, and thrill the world! It must be so splendid to know that one has such power, and to hear people own that one possesses a "masculine intellect"! I don't care for most women's novels, but hers are immense; don't you think so, Mrs Bhaer?' asked the girl with the big forehead, and torn braid on her skirt.

'Yes; but they don't thrill me as little Charlotte Bronte's books do. The brain is there, but the heart seems left out. I admire, but I don't love, George Eliot; and her life is far sadder to me than Miss Bronte's, because, in spite of the genius, love, and fame, she missed the light without which no soul is truly great, good, or happy.'

'Yes'm, I know; but still it's so romantic and sort of new and mysterious, and she was great in one sense. Her nerves and dyspepsia do rather destroy the illusion; but I adore famous people and mean to go and see all I can scare up in London some day.'

'You will find some of the best of them busy about just the work I recommend to you; and if you want to see a great lady, I'll tell you that Mrs Laurence means to bring one here today. Lady Abercrombie is lunching with her, and after seeing the college is to call on us. She especially wanted to see our sewing-school, as she is interested in things of this sort, and gets them up at home.'

'Bless me! I always imagined lords and ladies did nothing but ride round in a coach and six, go to balls, and be presented to the Queen in cocked hats, and trains and feathers,' exclaimed an artless young person from the wilds of Maine, whither an illustrated paper occasionally wandered.

'Not at all; Lord Abercrombie is over here studying up our American prison system, and my lady is busy with the schools—both very high-born, but the simplest and most sensible people I've met this long time. They are neither of them young nor handsome, and dress plainly; so don't expect anything splendid. Mr Laurence was telling me last night about a friend of his who met my lord in the hall, and owing to a rough greatcoat and a red face, mistook him for a coachman, and said: "Now, my man, what do you want here?" Lord Abercrombie mildly mentioned who he was, and that he had come to dinner. And the poor host was much afflicted, saying afterward: "Why didn't he wear his stars and garters? then a fellow would know he was a lord."'

The girls laughed again, and a general rustle betrayed that each was prinking a bit before the titled guest arrived. Even Mrs Jo settled her collar, and Mrs Meg felt if her cap was right, while Bess shook out her curls and Josie boldly consulted the glass; for they were women, in spite of philosophy and philanthropy.

'Shall we all rise?' asked one girl, deeply impressed by the impending honour.

'It would be courteous.'

'Shall we shake hands?'

'No, I'll present you en masse, and your pleasant faces will be introduction enough.'

'I wish I'd worn my best dress. Ought to have told us,' whispered Sally.

'Won't my folks be surprised when I tell them we have had a real lady to call on us?' said another.

'Don't look as if you'd never seen a gentlewoman before, Milly. We are not all fresh from the wilderness,' added the stately damsel who, having Mayflower ancestors, felt that she was the equal of all the crowned heads of Europe.

'Hush, she's coming! Oh, my heart, what a bonnet!' cried the gay girl in a stage whisper; and every eye was demurely fixed upon the busy hands as the door opened to admit Mrs Laurence and her guest.

It was rather a shock to find, after the general introduction was over, that this daughter of a hundred earls was a stout lady in a plain gown, and a rather weather-beaten bonnet, with a bag of papers in one hand and a note-book in the other. But the face was full of benevolence, the sonorous voice very kind, the genial manners very winning, and about the whole person an indescribable air of high breeding which made beauty of no consequence, costume soon forgotten, and the moment memorable to the keen-eyed girls whom nothing escaped.

A little chat about the rise, growth, and success of this particular class, and then Mrs Jo led the conversation to the English lady's work, anxious to show her pupils how rank dignifies labour, and charity blesses wealth.

It was good for these girls to hear of the evening-schools supported and taught by women whom they knew and honoured; of Miss Cobbe's eloquent protest winning the protection of the law for abused wives; Mrs Butler saving the lost; Mrs Taylor, who devoted one room in her historic house to a library for the servants; Lord Shaftesbury, busy with his new tenement-houses in the slums of London; of prison reforms; and all the brave work being done in God's name by the rich and great for the humble and the poor. It impressed them more than many quiet home lectures would have done, and roused an ambition to help when their time should come, well knowing that even in glorious America there is still plenty to be done before she is what she should be—truly just, and free, and great. They were also quick to see that Lady Abercrombie treated all there as her equals, from stately Mrs Laurence, to little Josie, taking notes of everything and privately resolving to have some thick-soled English boots as soon as possible. No one would have guessed that she had a big house in London, a castle in Wales, and a grand country seat in Scotland, as she spoke of Parnassus with admiration, Plumfield as a 'dear old home', and the college as an honour to all concerned in it. At that, of course, every head went up a little, and when my lady left, every hand was ready for the hearty shake the noble Englishwoman gave them, with words they long remembered:

'I am very pleased to see this much-neglected branch of a woman's education so well conducted here, and I have to thank my friend Mrs Laurence for one of the most charming pictures I've seen in America—Penelope among her maids.'

A group of smiling faces watched the stout boots trudge away, respectful glances followed the shabby bonnet till it was out of sight, and the girls felt a truer respect for their titled guest than if she had come in the coach and six, with all her diamonds on.

'I feel better about the "odd jobs" now. I only wish I could do them as well as Lady Abercrombie does,' said one.

'I thanked my stars my buttonholes were nice, for she looked at them and said: "Quite workmanlike, upon my word," added another, feeling that her gingham gown had come to honour.

'Her manners were as sweet and kind as Mrs Brooke's. Not a bit stiff or condescending, as I expected. I see now what you meant, Mrs Bhaer, when you said once that well-bred people were the same all the world over.'

Mrs Meg bowed her thanks for the compliment, and Mrs Bhaer said:

'I know them when I see them, but never shall be a model of deportment myself. I'm glad you enjoyed the little visit. Now, if you young people don't want England to get ahead of us in many ways, you must bestir yourselves and keep abreast; for our sisters are in earnest, you see, and don't waste time worrying about their sphere, but make it wherever duty calls them.'

'We will do our best, ma'am,' answered the girls heartily, and trooped away with their work-baskets, feeling that though they might never be Harriet Martineaus, Elizabeth Brownings, or George Eliots, they might become noble, useful, and independent women, and earn for themselves some sweet title from the grateful lips of the poor, better than any a queen could bestow.

## CHAPTER 18. CLASS DAY

The clerk of the weather evidently has a regard for young people, and sends sunshine for class days as often as he can. An especially lovely one shone over Plumfield as this interesting anniversary came round, bringing the usual accompaniments of roses, strawberries, white-gowned girls, beaming youths, proud friends, and stately dignitaries full of well-earned satisfaction with the yearly harvest. As Laurence College was a mixed one, the presence of young women as students gave to the occasion a grace and animation entirely wanting where the picturesque half of creation appear merely as spectators. The hands that turned the pages of wise books also possessed the skill to decorate the hall with flowers; eyes tired with study shone with hospitable warmth on the assembling guests; and under the white muslins beat hearts as full of ambition, hope, and courage as those agitating the broadcloth of the ruling sex.

College Hill, Parnassus, and old Plum swarmed with cheery faces, as guests, students, and professors hurried to and fro in the pleasant excitement of arriving and receiving. Everyone was welcomed cordially, whether he rolled up in a fine carriage, or trudged afoot to see the good son or daughter come to honour on the happy day that rewarded many a mutual sacrifice. Mr Laurie and his wife were on the reception committee, and their lovely house was overflowing. Mrs Meg, with Daisy and Jo as aides, was in demand among the girls, helping on belated toilettes, giving an eye to spreads, and directing the decorations. Mrs Jo had her hands full as President's lady, and the mother of Ted; for it took all the power and skill of that energetic woman to get her son into his Sunday best.

Not that he objected to be well arrayed; far from it; he adored good clothes, and owing to his great height already revelled in a dress-suit, bequeathed him by a dandy friend. The effect was very funny; but he would wear it in spite of the jeers of his mates, and sighed vainly for a beaver, because his stern parent drew the line there. He pleaded that English lads of ten wore them and were 'no end nobby'; but his mother only answered, with a consoling pat of the yellow mane:

'My child, you are absurd enough now; if I let you add a tall hat, Plumfield wouldn't hold either of us, such would be the scorn and derision of all beholders. Content yourself with looking like the ghost of a waiter, and don't ask for the most ridiculous head-gear in the known world.'

Denied this noble badge of manhood, Ted soothed his wounded soul by appearing in collars of an amazing height and stiffness, and ties which were the wonder of all female eyes. This freak was a sort of vengeance on his hard-hearted mother; for the collars drove the laundress to despair, never being just right, and the ties required such art in the tying that three women sometimes laboured long before—like Beau Brummel—he turned from a heap of 'failures' with the welcome words: 'That will do.' Rob was devoted on these trying occasions, his own toilet being distinguished only by its speed, simplicity, and neatness. Ted was usually in a frenzy before he was suited, and roars, whistles, commands, and groans were heard from the den wherein the Lion raged and the Lamb patiently toiled. Mrs Jo bore it till boots were hurled and a rain of hair-brushes set in, then, fearing for the safety of her eldest, she would go to the rescue, and by a wise mixture of fun and authority finally succeed in persuading Ted that he was 'a thing of beauty', if not 'a joy for ever'. At last he would stalk majestically forth, imprisoned in collars compared to which those worn by Dickens's afflicted Biler were trifles not worth mentioning. The dresscoat was a little loose in the shoulders, but allowed a noble expanse of glossy bosom to be seen, and with a delicate handkerchief negligently drooping at the proper angle, had a truly fine effect. Boots that shone, and likewise pinched, appeared at one end of the 'long, black clothes-pin'—as Josie called him—and a youthful but solemn face at the other, carried at an angle which, if long continued, would have resulted in spinal curvature. Light gloves, a cane, and—oh, bitter drop in the cup of joy!—an ignominious straw hat, not to mention a choice floweret in the buttonhole, and a festoon of watchguard below, finished off this impressive boy.

'How's that for style?' he asked, appearing to his mother and cousins whom he was to escort to the hall on this particular occasion.

A shout of laughter greeted him, followed by exclamations of horror; for he had artfully added the little blond moustache he often wore when acting. It was very becoming, and seemed the only balm to heal the wound made by the loss of the beloved hat.

'Take it off this moment, you audacious boy! What would your father say to such a prank on this day when we must all behave our best?' said Mrs Jo, trying to frown, but privately thinking that among the many youths about her none were so beautiful and original as her long son.

'Let him wear it, Aunty; it's so becoming. No one will ever guess he isn't eighteen at least,' cried Josie, to whom disguise of any sort was always charming.

'Father won't observe it; he'll be absorbed in his big-wigs and the girls. No matter if he does, he'll enjoy the joke and introduce me as his oldest son. Rob is nowhere when I'm in full fig'; and Ted took the stage with a tragic stalk, like Hamlet in a tail-coat and choker.

'My son, obey me!' and when Mrs Jo spoke in that tone her word was law. Later, however, the moustache appeared, and many strangers firmly believed that there were three young Bhaers. So Ted found one ray of joy to light his gloom.

Mr Bhaer was a proud and happy man when, at the appointed hour, he looked down upon the parterre of youthful faces before him, thinking of the 'little gardens' in which he had hopefully and faithfully sowed good seed years ago, and from which this beautiful harvest seemed to have sprung. Mr March's fine old face shone with the serenest satisfaction, for this was the dream of his life fulfilled after patient waiting; and the love and reverence in the countenances of the eager young men and women looking up at him plainly showed that the reward he coveted was his in fullest measure. Laurie always effaced himself on these occasions as much as courtesy would permit; for everyone spoke gratefully in ode, poem, and oration of the founder of the college and noble dispenser of his beneficence. The three sisters beamed with pride as they sat among the ladies, enjoying, as only women can, the honour done the men they loved; while 'the original Plums', as the younger ones called themselves, regarded the whole affair as their work, receiving the curious, admiring, or envious glances of strangers with a mixture of dignity and delight rather comical to behold.

The music was excellent, and well it might be when Apollo waved the baton. The poems were—as usual on such occasions—of varied excellence, as the youthful speakers tried to put old truths into new words, and made them forceful by the enthusiasm of their earnest faces and fresh voices. It was beautiful to see the eager interest with which the girls listened to some brilliant brother-student, and applauded him with a rustle as of wind over a bed of flowers. It was still more significant and pleasant to watch the young men's faces when a slender white figure stood out against the background of black-coated dignitaries, and with cheeks that flushed and paled, and lips that trembled till earnest purpose conquered maiden fear, spoke to them straight out of a woman's heart and brain concerning the hopes and doubts, the aspirations and rewards all must know, desire, and labour for. This clear, sweet voice seemed to reach and rouse all that was noblest in the souls of these youths, and to set a seal upon the years of comradeship which made them sacred and memorable for ever.

Alice Heath's oration was unanimously pronounced the success of the day; for without being flowery or sentimental, as is too apt to be the case with these first efforts of youthful orators, it was earnest, sensible, and so inspiring that she left the stage in a storm of applause, the good fellows being as much fired by her stirring appeal to 'march shoulder to shoulder', as if she had chanted the 'Marseillaise' then and there. One young man was so excited that he nearly rushed out of his seat to receive her as she hastened to hide herself among her mates, who welcomed her with faces full of tender pride and tearful eye. A prudent sister detained him, however, and in a moment he was able to listen with composure to the President's remarks.

They were worth listening to, for Mr Bhaer spoke like a father to the children whom he was dismissing to the battle of life; and his tender, wise, and helpful words lingered in their hearts long after the praise was forgotten. Then came other exercises peculiar to Plumfield, and the end. Why the roof did not fly off when the sturdy lungs of the excited young men pealed out the closing hymn will for ever be a mystery; but it remained firm, and only the fading garlands vibrated as the waves of music rolled up and died away, leaving sweet echoes to haunt the place for another year.

Dinners and spreads consumed the afternoon, and at sunset came a slight lull as everyone sought some brief repose before the festivities of the evening began. The President's reception was one of the enjoyable things in store, also dancing on Parnassus, and as much strolling, singing, and flirting, as could be compressed into a few hours by youths and maidens just out of school.

Carriages were rolling about, and gay groups on piazzas, lawns, and window-seats idly speculated as to who the distinguished guests might be. The appearance of a very dusty vehicle loaded with trunks at Mr Bhaer's hospitably open door caused much curious comment among the loungers, especially as two rather foreign-looking gentlemen sprang out, followed by two young ladies, all four being greeted with cries of joy and much embracing by the Bhaers. Then they all disappeared into the house, the luggage followed, and the watchers were left to wonder who the mysterious strangers were, till a fair collegian declared that they must be the Professor's nephews, one of whom was expected on his wedding journey.

She was right; Franz proudly presented his blonde and buxom bride, and she was hardly kissed and blessed when Emil led up his bonny English Mary, with the rapturous announcement:

'Uncle, Aunt Jo, here's another daughter! Have you room for my wife, too?'

There could be no doubt of that; and Mary was with difficulty rescued from the glad embraces of her new relatives, who, remembering all the young pair had suffered together, felt that this was the natural and happy ending of the long voyage so perilously begun.

'But why not tell us, and let us be ready for two brides instead of one?' asked Mrs Jo, looking as usual rather demoralizing in a wrapper and crimping-pins, having rushed down from her chamber, where she was preparing for the labours of the evening.

'Well, I remembered what a good joke you all considered Uncle Laurie's marriage, and I thought I'd give you another nice little surprise,' laughed Emil. 'I'm off duty, and it seemed best to take advantage of wind and tide, and come along as convoy to the old boy here. We hoped to get in last night, but couldn't fetch it, so here we are in time for the end of the jollification, anyway.'

'Ah, my sons, it is too feeling-full to see you both so happy and again in the old home. I haf no words to outpour my gratitude, and can only ask of the dear Gott in Himmel to bless and keep you all,' cried Professor Bhaer, trying to gather all four into his arms at once, while tears rolled down his cheeks, and his English failed him.

An April shower cleared the air and relieved the full hearts of the happy family; then of course everyone began to talk—Franz and Ludmilla in German with uncle, Emil and Mary with the aunts; and round this group gathered the young folk, clamouring to hear all about the wreck, and the rescue, and the homeward voyage. It was a very different story from the written one; and as they listened to Emil's graphic words, with Mary's soft voice breaking in now and then to add some fact that brought out the courage, patience, and self-sacrifice he so lightly touched upon, it became a solemn and pathetic thing to see and hear these happy creatures tell of that great danger and deliverance.

'I never hear the patter of rain now that I don't want to say my prayers; and as for women, I'd like to take my hat off to every one of 'em, for they are braver than any man I ever saw,' said Emil, with the new gravity that was as becoming to him as the new gentleness with which he treated everyone.

'If women are brave, some men are as tender and self-sacrificing as women. I know one who in the night slipped his share of food into a girl's pocket, though starving himself, and sat for hours rocking a sick man in his arms that he might get a little sleep. No, love, I will tell, and you must let me!' cried Mary, holding in both her own the hand he laid on her lips to silence her.

'Only did my duty. If that torment had lasted much longer I might have been as bad as poor Barry and the boatswain. Wasn't that an awful night?' And Emil shuddered as he recalled it.

'Don't think of it, dear. Tell about the happy days on the Urania, when papa grew better and we were all safe and homeward bound,' said Mary, with the trusting look and comforting touch which seemed to banish the dark and recall the bright side of that terrible experience.

Emil cheered up at once, and sitting with his arm about his 'dear lass', in true sailor fashion told the happy ending of the tale.

'Such a jolly old time as we had at Hamburg! Uncle Hermann couldn't do enough for the captain, and while mamma took care of him, Mary looked after me. I had to go into dock for repairs; fire hurt my eyes, and watching for a sail and want of sleep made 'em as hazy as a London fog. She was pilot and brought me in all right, you see, only I couldn't part company, so she came aboard as first mate, and I'm bound straight for glory now.'

'Hush! that's silly, dear,' whispered Mary, trying in her turn to stop him, with English shyness about tender topics. But he took the soft hand in his, and proudly surveying the one ring it wore, went on with the air of an admiral aboard his flagship.

'The captain proposed waiting a spell; but I told him we weren't like to see any rougher weather than we'd pulled through together, and if we didn't know one another after such a year as this, we never should. I was sure I shouldn't be worth my pay without this hand on the wheel; so I had my way, and my brave little woman has shipped for the long voyage. God bless her!'

'Shall you really sail with him?' asked Daisy, admiring her courage, but shrinking with cat-like horror from the water.

'I'm not afraid,' answered Mary, with a loyal smile. 'I've proved my captain in fair weather and in foul, and if he is ever wrecked again, I'd rather be with him than waiting and watching ashore.'

'A true woman, and a born sailor's wife! You are a happy man, Emil, and I'm sure this trip will be a prosperous one,' cried Mrs Jo, delighted with the briny flavour of this courtship. 'Oh, my dear boy, I always felt you'd come back, and when everyone else despaired I never gave up, but insisted that you were clinging to the main-top jib somewhere on that dreadful sea'; and Mrs Jo illustrated her faith by grasping Emil with a truly Pillycoddian gesture.

'Of course I was!' answered Emil heartily; 'and my "main-top jib" in this case was the thought of what you and Uncle said to me. That kept me up; and among the million thoughts that came to me during those long nights none was clearer than the idea of the red strand, you remember—English navy, and all that. I liked the notion, and resolved that if a bit of my cable was left afloat, the red stripe should be there.'

'And it was, my dear, it was! Captain Hardy testifies to that, and here is your reward'; and Mrs Jo kissed Mary with a maternal tenderness which betrayed that she liked the English rose better than the blue-eyed German Kornblumen, sweet and modest though it was.

Emil surveyed the little ceremony with complacency, saying, as he looked about the room which he never thought to see again: 'Odd, isn't it, how clearly trifles come back to one in times of danger? As we floated there, half-starved, and in despair, I used to think I heard the bells ringing here, and Ted tramping downstairs, and you calling, "Boys, boys, it's time to get up!" I actually smelt the coffee we used to have, and one night I nearly cried when I woke from a dream of Asia's ginger cookies. I declare, it was one of the bitterest disappointments of my life to face hunger with that spicy smell in my nostrils. If you've got any, do give me one!'

A pitiful murmur broke from all the aunts and cousins, and Emil was at once borne away to feast on the desired cookies, a supply always being on hand. Mrs Jo and her sister joined the other group, glad to hear what Franz was saying about Nat.

'The minute I saw how thin and shabby he was, I knew that something was wrong; but he made light of it, and was so happy over our visit and news that I let him off with a brief confession, and went to Professor Baumgarten and Bergmann. From them I learned the whole story of his spending more money than he ought and trying to atone for it by unnecessary work and sacrifice. Baumgarten thought it would do him good, so kept his secret till I came. It did him good, and he's paid his debts and earned his bread by the sweat of his brow, like an honest fellow.'

'I like that much in Nat. It is, as I said, a lesson, and he learns it well. He proves himself a man, and has deserved the place Bergmann offers him,' said Mr Bhaer, looking well pleased as Franz added some facts already recorded.

'I told you, Meg, that he had good stuff in him, and love for Daisy would keep him straight. Dear lad, I wish I had him here this moment!' cried Mrs Jo, forgetting in delight the doubts and anxieties which had troubled her for months past.

'I am very glad, and suppose I shall give in as I always do, especially now that the epidemic rages so among us. You and Emil have set all their heads in a ferment, and Josie will be demanding a lover before I can turn round,' answered Mrs Meg, in a tone of despair.

But her sister saw that she was touched by Nat's trials, and hastened to add the triumphs, that the victory might be complete, for success is always charming.

'This offer of Herr Bergmann is a good one, isn't it?' she asked, though Mr Laurie had already satisfied her on that point when Nat's letter brought the news.

'Very fine in every way. Nat will get capital drill in Bachmeister's orchestra, see London in a delightful way, and if he suits come home with them, well started among the violins. No great honour, but a sure thing and a step up. I congratulated him, and he was very jolly over it, saying, like the true lover he is: "Tell Daisy; be sure and tell her all about it." I'll leave that to you, Aunt Meg, and you can also break it gently to her that the old boy had a fine blond beard. Very becoming; hides his weak mouth, and gives a noble air to his big eyes and "Mendelssohnian brow", as a gushing girl called it. Ludmilla has a photo of it for you.'

This amused them; and they listened to many other interesting bits of news which kind Franz, even in his own happiness, had not forgotten to remember for his friend's sake. He talked so well, and painted Nat's patient and pathetic shifts so vividly, that Mrs Meg was half won; though if she had learned of the Minna episode and the fiddling in beer-gardens and streets, she might not have relented so soon. She stored up all she heard, however, and, womanlike, promised herself a delicious talk with Daisy, in which she would allow herself to melt by degrees, and perhaps change the doubtful 'We shall see' to a cordial 'He has done well; be happy, dear'.

In the midst of this agreeable chat the sudden striking of a clock recalled Mrs Jo from romance to reality, and she exclaimed, with a clutch at her crimping-pins:

'My blessed people, you must eat and rest; and I must dress, or receive in this disgraceful rig. Meg, will you take Ludmilla and Mary upstairs and see to them? Franz knows the way to the dining-room. Fritz, come with me and be made tidy, for what with heat and emotion, we are both perfect wrecks.'

## CHAPTER 19. WHITE ROSES

While the travellers refreshed, and Mrs President struggled into her best gown, Josie ran into the garden to gather flowers for the brides. The sudden arrival of these interesting beings had quite enchanted the romantic girl, and her head was full of heroic rescues, tender admiration, dramatic situations, and feminine wonder as to whether the lovely creatures would wear their veils or not. She was standing before a great bush of white roses, culling the most perfect for the bouquets which she meant to tie with the ribbon festooned over her arm, and lay on the toilette tables of the new cousins, as a delicate attention. A step startled her, and looking up she saw her brother coming down the path with folded arms, bent head, and the absent air of one absorbed in deep thought.

'Sophy Wackles,' said the sharp child, with a superior smile, as she sucked her thumb just pricked by a too eager pull at the thorny branches.

'What are you at here, Mischief?' asked Demi, with an Irvingesque start, as he felt rather than saw a disturbing influence in his day-dream.

'Getting flowers for "our brides". Don't you wish you had one?' answered Josie, to whom the word 'mischief' suggested her favourite amusement.

'A bride or a flower?' asked Demi calmly, though he eyed the blooming bush as if it had a sudden and unusual interest for him.

'Both; you get the one, and I'll give you the other.'

'Wish I could!' and Demi picked a little bud, with a sigh that went to Josie's warm heart.

'Why don't you, then? It's lovely to see people so happy. Now's a good time to do it if you ever mean to. She will be going away for ever soon.'

'Who?' and Demi pulled a half-opened bud, with a sudden colour in his own face; which sign of confusion delighted little Jo.

'Don't be a hypocrite. You know I mean Alice. Now, Jack, I'm fond of you, and want to help; it's so interesting—all these lovers and weddings and things, and we ought to have our share. So you take my advice and speak up like a man, and make sure of Alice before she goes.'

Demi laughed at the seriousness of the small girl's advice; but he liked it, and showed that it suited him by saying blandly, instead of snubbing her as usual:

'You are very kind, child. Since you are so wise, could you give me a hint how I'd better 'speak up', as you elegantly express it?'

'Oh, well, there are various ways, you know. In plays the lovers go down on their knees; but that's awkward when they have long legs. Ted never does it well, though I drill him for hours. You could say, "Be mine, be mine!" like the old man who threw cucumbers over the wall to Mrs Nickleby, if you want to be gay and easy; or you could write a poetical pop. You've tried it, I dare say.'

'But seriously, Jo, I do love Alice, and I think she knows it. I want to tell her so; but I lose my head when I try, and don't care to make a fool of myself. Thought you might suggest some pretty way; you read so much poetry and are so romantic.'

Demi tried to express himself clearly, but forgot his dignity and his usual reserve in the sweet perplexity of his love, and asked his little sister to teach him how to put the question which a single word can answer. The arrival of his happy cousins had scattered all his wise plans and brave resolutions to wait still longer. The Christmas play had given him courage to hope, and the oration today had filled him with tender pride; but the sight of those blooming brides and beaming grooms was too much for him, and he panted to secure his Alice without an hour's delay. Daisy was his confidante in all things but this; a brotherly feeling of sympathy had kept him from telling her his hopes, because her own were forbidden. His mother was rather jealous of any girl he admired; but knowing that she liked Alice, he loved on and enjoyed his secret alone, meaning soon to tell her all about it.

Now suddenly Josie and the rose-bush seemed to suggest a speedy end to his tender perplexities; and he was moved to accept her aid as the netted lion did that of the mouse.

'I think I'll write,' he was slowly beginning, after a pause during which both were trying to strike out a new and brilliant idea.

'I've got it! perfectly lovely! just suit her, and you too, being a poet!' cried Josie, with a skip.

'What is it? Don't be ridiculous, please,' begged the bashful lover, eager, but afraid of this sharp-tongued bit of womanhood.

'I read in one of Miss Edgeworth's stories about a man who offers three roses to his lady—a bud, a half-blown, and a full-blown rose. I don't remember which she took; but it's a pretty way; and Alice knows about it because she was there when we read it. Here are all kinds; you've got the two buds, pick the sweetest rose you can find, and I'll tie them up and put them in her room. She is coming to dress with Daisy, so I can do it nicely.'

Demi mused a moment with his eyes on the bridal bush, and a smile came over his face so unlike any it had ever worn before, that Josie was touched, and looked away as if she had no right to see the dawn of the great passion which, while it lasts, makes a young man as happy as a god.

'Do it,' was all he said, and gathered a full-blown rose to finish his floral love-message.

Charmed to have a finger in this romantic pie, Josie tied a graceful bow of ribbon about the stems, and finished her last nosegay with much content, while Demi wrote upon a card:

DEAR ALICE, You know what the flowers mean. Will you wear one, or all tonight, and make me still prouder, fonder, and happier than I am?

Yours entirely,

JOHN

Offering this to his sister, he said in a tone that made her feel the deep importance of her mission:

'I trust you, Jo. This means everything to me. No jokes, dear, if you love me.'

Josie's answer was a kiss that promised all things; and then she ran away to do her 'gentle spiriting', like Ariel, leaving Demi to dream among the roses like Ferdinand.

Mary and Ludmilla were charmed with their bouquets; and the giver had the delight of putting some of the flowers into the dark hair and the light as she played maid at the toilettes of 'our brides', which consoled her for a disappointment in the matter of veils.

No one helped Alice dress; for Daisy was in the next room with her mother; and not even their loving eyes saw the welcome which the little posy received, nor the tears and smiles and blushes that came and went as she read the note and pondered what answer she should give. There was no doubt about the one she wished to give; but duty held her back; for at home there was an invalid mother and an old father. She was needed there, with all the help she could now bring by the acquirements four years of faithful study had given her. Love looked very sweet, and a home of her own with John a little heaven on earth; but not yet. And she slowly laid away the full-blown rose as she sat before the mirror, thinking over the great question of her life.

Was it wise and kind to ask him to wait, to bind him by any promise, or even to put into words the love and honour she felt for him? No; it would be more generous to make the sacrifice alone, and spare him the pain of hope deferred. He was young; he would forget; and she would do her duty better, perhaps, if no impatient lover waited for her. With eyes that saw but dimly, and a hand that lingered on the stem he had stripped of thorns, she laid the half-blown flower by the rose, and asked herself if even the little bud might be worn. It looked very poor and pale beside the others; yet being in the self-sacrificing mood which real love brings, she felt that even a small hope was too much to give, if she could not follow it up with more.

As she sat looking sadly down on the symbols of an affection that grew dearer every moment, she listened half unconsciously to the murmur of voices in the adjoining room. Open windows, thin partitions, and the stillness of summer twilight made it impossible to help hearing, and in a few moments more she could not refrain; for they were talking of John.

'So nice of Ludmilla to bring us all bottles of real German cologne! Just what we need after this tiring day! Be sure John has his! He likes it so!'

'Yes, mother. Did you see him jump up when Alice ended her oration? He'd have gone to her if I hadn't held him back. I don't wonder he was pleased and proud. I spoilt my gloves clapping, and quite forgot my dislike of seeing women on platforms, she was so earnest and unconscious and sweet after the first moment.'

'Has he said anything to you, dear?'

'No; and I guess why. The kind boy thinks it would make me unhappy. It wouldn't. But I know his ways; so I wait, and hope all will go well with him.'

'It must. No girl in her senses would refuse our John, though he isn't rich, and never will be. Daisy, I've been longing to tell you what he did with his money. He told me last night, and I've had no time since to tell you. He sent poor young Barton to the hospital, and kept him there till his eyes were saved—a costly thing to do. But the man can work now and care for his old parents. He was in despair, sick and poor, and too proud to beg; and our dear boy found it out, and took every penny he had, and never told even his mother till she made him.'

Alice did not hear what Daisy answered, for she was busy with her own emotions—happy ones now, to judge from the smile that shone in her eyes and the decided gesture with which she put the little bud in her bosom, as if she said: 'He deserves some reward for that good deed, and he shall have it.'

Mrs Meg was speaking, and still of John, when she could hear again:

'Some people would call it unwise and reckless, when John has so little; but I think his first investment a safe and good one, for "he who giveth to the poor lendeth to the Lord"; and I was so pleased and proud, I wouldn't spoil it by offering him a penny.'

'It is his having nothing to offer that keeps him silent, I think. He is so honest, he won't ask till he has much to give. But he forgets that love is everything. I know he's rich in that; I see and feel it; and any woman should be glad to get it.'

'Right, dear. I felt just so, and was willing to work and wait with and for my John.'

'So she will be, and I hope they will find it out. But she is so dutiful and good, I'm afraid she won't let herself be happy. You would like it, mother?'

'Heartily; for a better, nobler girl doesn't live. She is all I want for my son; and I don't mean to lose the dear, brave creature if I can help it. Her heart is big enough for both love and duty; and they can wait more happily if they do it together—for wait they must, of course.'

'I'm so glad his choice suits you, mother, and he is spared the saddest sort of disappointment.'

Daisy's voice broke there; and a sudden rustle, followed by a soft murmur, seemed to tell that she was in her mother's arms, seeking and finding comfort there.

Alice heard no more, and shut her window with a guilty feeling but a shining face; for the proverb about listeners failed here, and she had learned more than she dared to hope. Things seemed to change suddenly; she felt that her heart was large enough for both love and duty; she knew now that she would be welcomed by mother and sister; and the memory of Daisy's less happy fate, Nat's weary probation, the long delay, and possible separation for ever—all came before her so vividly that prudence seemed cruelty; self-sacrifice, sentimental folly; and anything but the whole truth, disloyalty to her lover. As she thought thus, the half-blown rose went to join the bud; and then, after a pause, she slowly kissed the perfect rose, and added it to the tell-tale group, saying to herself with a sort of sweet solemnity, as if the words were a vow:

'I'll love and work and wait with and for my John.'

It was well for her that Demi was absent when she stole down to join the guests who soon began to flow through the house in a steady stream. The new brightness which touched her usually thoughtful face was easily explained by the congratulations she received as orator, and the slight agitation observable, when a fresh batch of gentlemen approached soon passed, as none of them noticed the flowers she wore over a very happy heart. Demi meantime was escorting certain venerable personages about the college, and helping his grandfather entertain them with discussion of the Socratic method of instruction, Pythagoras, Pestalozzi, Froebel, and the rest, whom he devoutly wished at the bottom of the Red Sea, and no wonder, for his head and his heart were full of love and roses, hopes and fears. He piloted the 'potent, grave, and reverend seigniors' safely down to Plumfield at last, and landed them before his uncle and aunt Bhaer, who were receiving in state, the one full of genuine delight in all men and things, the other suffering martyrdom with a smile, as she stood shaking hand after hand, and affecting utter unconsciousness of the sad fact that ponderous Professor Plock had camped upon the train of her state and festival velvet gown.

With a long sigh of relief Demi glanced about him for the beloved girl. Most persons would have looked some time before any particular angel could be discovered among the white-robed throng in parlours, hall, and study; but his eye went—like the needle to the pole—to the corner where a smooth dark head, with its braided crown, rose like a queen's, he thought, above the crowd which surrounded her. Yes, she has a flower at her throat; one, two, oh, blessed sight! he saw it all across the room, and gave a rapturous sigh which caused Miss Perry's frizzled crop to wave with a sudden gust. He did not see the rose, for it was hidden by a fold of lace; and it was well, perhaps, that bliss came by instalments, or he might have electrified the assembled multitude by flying to his idol, there being no Daisy to clutch him by the coat-tail. A stout lady, thirsting for information, seized him at that thrilling moment, and he was forced to point out celebrities with a saintly patience which deserved a better reward than it received; for a certain absence of mind and incoherence of speech at times caused the ungrateful dowager to whisper to the first friend she met after he had escaped:

'I saw no wine at any of the spreads; but it is plain that young Brooke has had too much. Quite gentlemanly, but evidently a trifle intoxicated, my dear.'

Ah, so he was! but with a diviner wine than any that ever sparkled at a class-day lunch, though many collegians know the taste of it; and when the old lady was disposed of, he gladly turned to find the young one, bent on having a single word. He saw her standing by the piano now, idly turning over music as she talked with several gentlemen. Hiding his impatience under an air of scholastic repose, Demi hovered near, ready to advance when the happy moment came, wondering meantime why elderly persons persisted in absorbing young ones instead of sensibly sitting in corners with their contemporaries. The elderly persons in question retired at length, but only to be replaced by two impetuous youths who begged Miss Heath to accompany them to Parnassus and join the dance. Demi thirsted for their blood, but was appeased by hearing George and Dolly say, as they lingered a moment after her refusal:

'Really, you know, I'm quite converted to co-education and almost wish I'd remained here. It gives a grace to study, a sort of relish even to Greek to see charming girls at it,' said Stuffy, who found the feast of learning so dry, any sauce was welcome; and he felt as if he had discovered a new one.

'Yes, by Jove! we fellows will have to look out or you'll carry off all the honours. You were superb today, and held us all like magic, though it was so hot there, I really think I couldn't have stood it for anyone else,' added Dolly, labouring to be gallant and really offering a touching proof of devotion; for the heat melted his collar, took the curl out of his hair, and ruined his gloves.

'There is room for all; and if you will leave us the books, we will cheerfully yield the baseball, boating, dancing, and flirting, which seem to be the branches you prefer,' answered Alice sweetly.

'Ah, now you are too hard upon us! We can't grind all the time and you ladies don't seem to mind taking a turn at the two latter "branches" you mention,' returned Dolly, with a glance at George which plainly said, 'I had her there.'

'Some of us do in our first years. Later we give up childish things, you see. Don't let me keep you from Parnassus'; and a smiling nod dismissed them, smarting under the bitter consciousness of youth.

'You got it there, Doll. Better not try to fence with these superior girls. Sure to be routed, horse, foot, and dragoons,' said Stuffy, lumbering away, somewhat cross with too many spreads.

'So deuced sarcastic! Don't believe she's much older than we are. Girls grow up quicker, so she needn't put on airs and talk like a grandmother,' muttered Dolly, feeling that he had sacrificed his kids upon the altar of an ungrateful Pallas.

'Come along and let's find something to eat. I'm faint with so much talking. Old Plock cornered me and made my head spin with Kant and Hegel and that lot.'

'I promised Dora West I'd give her a turn. Must look her up; she's a jolly little thing, and doesn't bother about anything but keeping in step.'

And arm in arm the boys strolled away, leaving Alice to read music as diligently as if society had indeed no charms for her. As she bent to turn a page, the eager young man behind the piano saw the rose and was struck speechless with delight. A moment he gazed, then hastened to seize the coveted place before a new detachment of bores arrived.

'Alice, I can't believe it—did you understand—how shall I ever thank you?' murmured Demi, bending as if he, too, read the song, not a note or word of which did he see, however.

'Hush! not now. I understood—I don't deserve it—we are too young, we must wait, but—I'm very proud and happy, John!'

What would have happened after that tender whisper I tremble to think, if Tom Bangs had not come bustling up, with the cheerful remark:

'Music? just the thing. People are thinning out, and we all want a little refreshment. My brain fairly reels with the 'ologies and 'isms I've heard discussed tonight. Yes, give us this; sweet thing! Scotch songs are always charming.'

Demi glowered; but the obtuse boy never saw it, and Alice, feeling that this would be a safe vent for sundry unruly emotions, sat down at once, and sang the song which gave her answer better than she could have done:

*BIDE A WEE*

*'The puir auld folk at home, ye mind,*
*Are frail and failing sair;*
*And weel I ken they'd miss me, lad,*
*Gin I come hame nae mair.*
*The grist is out, the times are hard,*
*The kine are only three;*
*I canna leave the auld folk now.*
*We'd better bide a wee.*

*'I fear me sair they're failing baith;*
*For when I sit apart,*
*They talk o' Heaven so earnestly,*
*It well nigh breaks my heart.*
*So, laddie, dinna urge me now,*

*It surely winna be;*
*I canna leave the auld folk yet.*
*We'd better bide a wee.'*

The room was very still before the first verse ended; and Alice skipped the next, fearing she could not get through; for John's eyes were on her, showing that he knew she sang for him and let the plaintive little ballad tell what her reply must be. He took it as she meant it, and smiled at her so happily that her heart got the better of her voice, and she rose abruptly, saying something about the heat.

'Yes, you are tired; come out and rest, my dearest'; and with a masterful air Demi took her into the starlight, leaving Tom to stare after them winking as if a sky-rocket had suddenly gone off under his nose.

'Bless my soul! the Deacon really meant business last summer and never told me. Won't Dora laugh?' And Tom departed in hot haste to impart and exult over his discovery.

What was said in the garden was never exactly known; but the Brooke family sat up very late that night, and any curious eye at the window would have seen Demi receiving the homage of his womankind as he told his little romance. Josie took great credit to herself in the matter, insisting that she had made the match; Daisy was full of the sweetest sympathy and joy, and Mrs Meg so happy that when Jo had gone to dream of bridal veils, and Demi sat in his room blissfully playing the air of 'Bide a Wee', she had her talk about Nat, ending with her arms round her dutiful daughter and these welcome words as her reward:

'Wait till Nat comes home, and then my good girl shall wear white roses too.'

## CHAPTER 20. LIFE FOR LIFE

The summer days that followed were full of rest and pleasure for young and old, as they did the honours of Plumfield to their happy guests. While Franz and Emil were busy with the affairs of Uncle Hermann and Captain Hardy, Mary and Ludmilla made friends everywhere; for, though very unlike, both were excellent and charming girls. Mrs Meg and Daisy found the German bride a Hausfrau after their own hearts, and had delightful times learning new dishes, hearing about the semi-yearly washes and the splendid linen-room at Hamburg, or discussing domestic life in all its branches. Ludmilla not only taught, but learned, many things, and went home with many new and useful ideas in her blonde head.

Mary had seen so much of the world that she was unusually lively for an English girl; while her various accomplishments made her a most agreeable companion. Much good sense gave her ballast; and the late experiences of danger and happiness added a sweet gravity at times, which contrasted well with her natural gaiety. Mrs Jo was quite satisfied with Emil's choice, and felt sure this true and tender pilot would bring him safe to port through fair or stormy weather. She had feared that Franz would settle down into a comfortable, moneymaking burgher, and be content with that; but she soon saw that his love of music and his placid Ludmilla put much poetry into his busy life, and kept it from being too prosaic. So she felt at rest about these boys, and enjoyed their visit with real, maternal satisfaction; parting with them in September most regretfully, yet hopefully, as they sailed away to the new life that lay before them.

Demi's engagement was confided to the immediate family only, as both were pronounced too young to do anything but love and wait. They were so happy that time seemed to stand still for them, and after a blissful week they parted bravely—Alice to home duties, with a hope that sustained and cheered her through many trials; and John to his business, full of a new ardour which made all things possible when such a reward was offered.

Daisy rejoiced over them, and was never tired of hearing her brother's plans for the future. Her own hope soon made her what she used to be—a cheery, busy creature, with a smile, kind word, and helping hand for all; and as she went singing about the house again, her mother felt that the right remedy for past sadness had been found. The dear Pelican still had doubts and fears, but kept them wisely to herself, preparing sundry searching tests to be applied when

Nat came home, and keeping a sharp eye on the letters from London; for some mysterious hint had flown across the sea, and Daisy's content seemed reflected in Nat's present cheerful state of mind.

Having passed through the Werther period, and tried a little Faust—of which experience he spoke to his Marguerite as if it had included an acquaintance with Mephistopheles, Blocksburg, and Auerbach's wine-cellar—he now felt that he was a Wilhelm Meister, serving his apprenticeship to the great masters of life. As she knew the truth of his small sins and honest repentance, Daisy only smiled at the mixture of love and philosophy he sent her, knowing that it was impossible for a young man to live in Germany without catching the German spirit.

'His heart is all right; and his head will soon grow clear when he gets out of the fog of tobacco, beer, and metaphysics he's been living in. England will wake up his common sense, and good salt air blow his little follies all away,' said Mrs Jo, much pleased with the good prospects of her violinist—whose return was delayed till spring, to his private regret, but professional advancement.

Josie had a month with Miss Cameron at the seaside, and threw herself so heartily into the lesson given her that her energy, promise, and patience laid the foundation of a friendship which was of infinite value to her in the busy, brilliant years to come; for little Jo's instincts were right; and the dramatic talent of the Marches was to blossom by and by into an actress, virtuous, and beloved.

Tom and his Dora were peacefully ambling altar-ward; for Bangs senior was so afraid his son would change his mind again and try a third profession, that he gladly consented to an early marriage, as a sort of anchor to hold the mercurial Thomas fast. Aforesaid Thomas could not complain of cold shoulders now; for Dora was a most devoted and adoring little mate, and made life so pleasant to him that his gift for getting into scrapes seemed lost, and he bade fair to become a thriving man, with undeniable talent for the business he had chosen.

'We shall be married in the autumn, and live with my father for a while. The governor is getting on, you know, and my wife and I must look after him. Later we shall have an establishment of our own,' was a favourite speech of his about this time, and usually received with smiles; for the idea of Tommy Bangs at the head of an 'establishment' was irresistibly funny to all who knew him.

Things were in this flourishing condition, and Mrs Jo was beginning to think her trials were over for that year, when a new excitement came. Several postal cards had arrived at long intervals from Dan, who gave them 'Care of M. Mason, etc.', as his address. By this means he was able to gratify his longing for home news, and to send brief messages to quiet their surprise at his delay in settling. The last one, which came in September, was dated 'Montana', and simply said:

Here at last, trying mining again; but not going to stay long. All sorts of luck. Gave up the farm idea. Tell plans soon. Well, busy, and very happy. D. K.

If they had known what the heavy dash under 'happy' meant, that postal would have been a very eloquent bit of pasteboard; for Dan was free, and had gone straight away to the liberty he panted for. Meeting an old friend by accident, he obliged him at a pinch by acting as overseer for a time, finding the society even of rough miners very sweet, and something in the muscular work wonderfully pleasant, after being cooped up in the brush-shop so long. He loved to take a pick and wrestle with rock and earth till he was weary—which was very soon; for that year of captivity had told upon his splendid physique. He longed to go home, but waited week after week to get the prison taint off him and the haggard look out of his face. Meanwhile he made friends of masters and men; and as no one knew his story, he took his place again in the world gratefully and gladly—with little pride now, and no plans but to do some good somewhere, and efface the past.

Mrs Jo was having a grand clearing-out of her desk one October day, while the rain poured outside, and peace reigned in her mansion. Coming across the postals, she pondered over them, and then put them carefully away in the drawer labelled 'Boys' Letters', saying to herself, as she bundled eleven requests for autographs into the waste-paper basket:

'It is quite time for another card, unless he is coming to tell his plans. I'm really curious to know what he has been about all this year, and how he's getting on now.'

That last wish was granted within an hour; for Ted came rushing in, with a newspaper in one hand, a collapsed umbrella in the other, and a face full of excitement, announcing, all in one breathless jumble:

'Mine caved in—twenty men shut up—no way out—wives crying—water rising—Dan knew the old shaft—risked his life—got 'em out—most killed—papers full of it—I knew he'd be a hero—hurray for old Dan!'

'What? Where? When? Who? Stop roaring, and let me read!' commanded his mother, entirely bewildered.

Relinquishing the paper, Ted allowed her to read for herself, with frequent interruptions from him—and Rob, who soon followed, eager for the tale. It was nothing new; but courage and devotion always stir generous hearts, and win admiration; so the account was both graphic and enthusiastic; and the name of Daniel Kean, the brave man who saved the lives of others at the risk of his own, was on many lips that day. Very proud were the faces of these friends as they read how their Dan was the only one who, in the first panic of the accident, remembered the old shaft that led into the mine—walled up, but the only hope of escape, if the men could be got out before the rising water drowned them; how he was lowered down alone, telling the others to keep back till he saw if it was safe; how he heard the poor fellows picking desperately for their lives on the other side, and by knocks and calls guided them to the right spot; then headed the rescue party, and working like a hero, got the men out in time. On being drawn up last of all, the worn rope broke, and he had a terrible fall, being much hurt, but was still alive. How the grateful women kissed his blackened face and bloody hands, as the men bore him away in triumph, and the owners of the mine promised a handsome reward, if he lived to receive it!

'He must live; he shall, and come home to be nursed as soon as he can stir, if I go and bring him myself! I always knew he'd do something fine and brave, if he didn't get shot or hung for some wild prank instead,' cried Mrs Jo, much excited.

'Do go, and take me with you, Mum. I ought to be the one, Dan's so fond of me and I of him,' began Ted, feeling that this would be an expedition after his own heart.

Before his mother could reply, Mr Laurie came in, with almost as much noise and flurry as Teddy the second, exclaiming as he waved the evening paper:

'Seen the news, Jo? What do you think? Shall I go off at once, and see after that brave boy?'

'I wish you would. But the thing may not be all true—rumour lies so. Perhaps a few hours will bring an entirely new version of the story.'

'I've telephoned to Demi for all he can find out; and if it's true, I'll go at once. Should like the trip. If he's able, I'll bring him home; if not, I'll stay and see to him. He'll pull through. Dan will never die of a fall on his head. He's got nine lives, and not lost half of them yet.'

'If you go, uncle, mayn't I go with you? I'm just spoiling for a journey; and it would be such larks to go out there with you, and see the mines and Dan, and hear all about it, and help. I can nurse. Can't I, Rob?' cried Teddy, in his most wheedlesome tones.

'Pretty well. But if mother can't spare you, I'm ready if uncle needs anyone,' answered Rob, in his quiet way, looking much fitter for the trip than excitable Ted.

'I can't spare either of you. My boys get into trouble, unless I keep them close at home. I've no right to hold the others; but I won't let you out of my sight, or something will happen. Never saw such a year, with wrecks and weddings and floods and engagements, and every sort of catastrophe!' exclaimed Mrs Jo.

'If you deal in girls and boys, you must expect this sort of thing, ma'am. The worst is over, I hope, till these lads begin to go off. Then I'll stand by you; for you'll need every kind of support and comfort, specially if Ted bolts early,' laughed Mr Laurie, enjoying her lamentations.

'I don't think anything can surprise me now; but I am anxious about Dan, and feel that someone had better go to him. It's a rough place out there, and he may need careful nursing. Poor lad, he seems to get a good many hard knocks! But perhaps he needs them as "a mellerin' process", as Hannah used to say.'

'We shall hear from Demi before long, and then I'll be off.' With which cheerful promise Mr Laurie departed; and Ted, finding his mother firm, soon followed, to coax his uncle to take him.

Further inquiry confirmed and added interest to the news. Mr Laurie was off at once; and Ted went into town with him, still vainly imploring to be taken to his Dan. He was absent all day; but his mother said, calmly:

'Only a fit of the sulks because he is thwarted. He's safe with Tom or Demi, and will come home hungry and meek at night. I know him.'

But she soon found that she could still be surprised; for evening brought no Ted, and no one had seen him. Mr Bhaer was just setting off to find his lost son, when a telegram arrived, dated at one of the way-stations on Mr Laurie's route:

*Found Ted in the cars. Take him along. Write tomorrow.*

*T. LAURENCE*

'Ted bolted sooner than you expected, mother. Never mind—uncle will take good care of him, and Dan be very glad to see him,' said Rob, as Mrs Jo sat, trying to realize that her youngest was actually on his way to the wild West.

'Disobedient boy! He shall be severely punished, if I ever get him again. Laurie winked at this prank; I know he did. Just like him. Won't the two rascals have a splendid time? Wish I was with them! Don't believe that crazy boy took even a night-gown with him, or an overcoat. Well, there will be two patients for us to nurse when they get back, if they ever do. Those reckless express trains always go down precipices, and burn up, or telescope. Oh! my Ted, my precious boy, how can I let him go so far away from me?'

And mother-like, Mrs Jo forgot the threatened chastisement in tender lamentations over the happy scapegrace, now whizzing across the continent in high feather at the success of his first revolt. Mr Laurie was much amused at his insisting that those words, 'when Ted bolts', put the idea into his head; and therefore the responsibility rested upon his shoulders. He assumed it kindly from the moment he came upon the runaway asleep in a car, with no visible luggage but a bottle of wine for Dan and a blacking-brush for himself; and as Mrs Jo suspected, the 'two rascals' did have a splendid time. Penitent letters arrived in due season, and the irate parents soon forgot to chide in their anxiety about Dan, who was very ill, and did not know his friends for several days. Then he began to mend; and everyone forgave the bad boy when he proudly reported that the first conscious words Dan said were: 'Hallo, Ted!' with a smile of pleasure at seeing a familiar face bent over him.

'Glad he went, and I won't scold any more. Now, what shall we put in the box for Dan?' And Mrs Jo worked off her impatience to get hold of the invalid by sending comforts enough for a hospital.

Cheering accounts soon began to come, and at length Dan was pronounced able to travel, but seemed in no haste to go home, though never tired of hearing his nurses talk of it.

'Dan is strangely altered,' wrote Laurie to Jo; 'not by this illness alone, but by something which has evidently gone before. I don't know what, and leave you to ask; but from his ravings when delirious I fear he has been in some serious trouble the past year. He seems ten years older, but improved, quieter, and so grateful to us. It is pathetic to see the hunger in his eyes as they rest on Ted, as if he couldn't see enough of him. He says Kansas was a failure, but can't talk much; so I bide my time. The people here love him very much, and he cares for that sort of thing now; used to scorn any show of emotion, you know; now he wants everyone to think well of him, and can't do enough to win affection and respect. I may be all wrong. You will soon find out. Ted is in clover, and the trip has done him a world of good. Let me take him to Europe when we go? Apron-strings don't agree with him any better than they did with me when I proposed to run away to Washington with you some century ago. Aren't you sorry you didn't?'

This private letter set Mrs Jo's lively fancy in a ferment, and she imagined every known crime, affliction, and complication which could possibly have befallen Dan. He was too feeble to be worried with questions now, but she promised herself most interesting revelations when she got him safe at home; for the 'firebrand' was her most interesting boy. She begged him to come, and spent more time in composing a letter that should bring him, than she did over the most thrilling episodes in her 'works'.

No one but Dan saw the letter; but it did bring him, and one November day Mr Laurie helped a feeble man out of a carriage at the door of Plumfield, and Mother Bhaer received the wanderer like a recovered son; while Ted, in a disreputable-looking hat and an astonishing pair of boots, performed a sort of war-dance round the interesting group.

'Right upstairs and rest; I'm nurse now, and this ghost must eat before he talks to anyone,' commanded Mrs Jo, trying not to show how shocked she was at this shorn and shaven, gaunt and pallid shadow of the stalwart man she parted with.

He was quite content to obey, and lay on the long lounge in the room prepared for him, looking about as tranquilly as a sick child restored to its own nursery and mother's arms, while his new nurse fed and refreshed him, bravely controlling the questions that burned upon her tongue. Being weak and weary, he soon fell asleep; and then she stole away to enjoy the society of the 'rascals', whom she scolded and petted, pumped and praised, to her heart's content.

'Jo, I think Dan has committed some crime and suffered for it,' said Mr Laurie, when Ted had departed to show his boots and tell glowing tales of the dangers and delights of the miners' life to his mates. 'Some terrible experience has come to the lad, and broken his spirit. He was quite out of his head when we arrived, and I took the watching, so I heard more of those sad wanderings than anyone else. He talked of the "warden", some trail, a dead man, and Blair and Mason, and would keep offering me his hand, asking me if I would take it and forgive him. Once, when he was very wild, I held his arms, and he quieted in a moment, imploring me not to "put the handcuffs on". I declare, it was quite awful sometimes to hear him in the night talk of old Plum and you, and beg to be let out and go home to die.'

'He isn't going to die, but live to repent of anything he may have done; so don't harrow me up with these dark hints, Teddy. I don't care if he's broken the Ten Commandments, I'll stand by him, and so will you, and we'll set him on his feet and make a good man of him yet. I know he's not spoilt, by the look in his poor face. Don't say a word to anyone, and I'll have the truth before long,' answered Mrs Jo, still loyal to her bad boy, though much afflicted by what she had heard.

For some days Dan rested, and saw few people; then good care, cheerful surroundings, and the comfort of being at home began to tell, and he seemed more like himself, though still very silent as to his late experiences, pleading the doctor's orders not to talk much. Everyone wanted to see him; but he shrank from any but old friends, and 'wouldn't lionize worth a cent', Ted said, much disappointed that he could not show off his brave Dan.

'Wasn't a man there who wouldn't have done the same, so why make a row over me?' asked the hero, feeling more ashamed than proud of the broken arm, which looked so interesting in a sling.

'But isn't it pleasant to think that you saved twenty lives, Dan, and gave husbands, sons, and fathers back to the women who loved them?' asked Mrs Jo one evening as they were alone together after several callers had been sent away.

'Pleasant! it's all that kept me alive, I do believe; yes, I'd rather have done it than be made president or any other big bug in the world. No one knows what a comfort it is to think I've saved twenty men to more than pay for—' There Dan stopped short, having evidently spoken out of some strong emotion to which his hearer had no key.

'I thought you'd feel so. It is a splendid thing to save life at the risk of one's own, as you did, and nearly lose it,' began Mrs Jo, wishing he had gone on with that impulsive speech which was so like his old manner.

'"He that loseth his life shall gain it",' muttered Dan, staring at the cheerful fire which lighted the room, and shone on his thin face with a ruddy glow.

Mrs Jo was so startled at hearing such words from his lips that she exclaimed joyfully:

'Then you did read the little book I gave you, and kept your promise?'

'I read it a good deal after a while. I don't know much yet, but I'm ready to learn; and that's something.'

'It's everything. Oh, my dear, tell me about it! I know something lies heavy on your heart; let me help you bear it, and so make the burden lighter.'

'I know it would; I want to tell; but some things even you couldn't forgive; and if you let go of me, I'm afraid I can't keep afloat.'

'Mothers can forgive anything! Tell me all, and be sure that I will never let you go, though the whole world should turn from you.'

Mrs Jo took one of the big wasted hands in both of hers and held it fast, waiting silently till that sustaining touch warmed poor Dan's heart, and gave him courage to speak. Sitting in his old attitude, with his head in his hands, he slowly told it all, never once looking up till the last words left his lips.

'Now you know; can you forgive a murderer, and keep a jail-bird in your house?'

Her only answer was to put her arms about him, and lay the shorn head on her breast, with eyes so full of tears they could but dimly see the hope and fear that made his own so tragical.

That was better than any words; and poor Dan clung to her in speechless gratitude, feeling the blessedness of mother love—that divine gift which comforts, purifies, and strengthens all who seek it. Two or three great, bitter drops were hidden in the little woollen shawl where Dan's cheek rested, and no one ever knew how soft and comfortable it felt to him after the hard pillows he had known so long. Suffering of both mind and body had broken will and pride, and the lifted burden brought such a sense of relief that he paused a moment to enjoy it in dumb delight.

'My poor boy, how you have suffered all this year, when we thought you free as air! Why didn't you tell us, Dan, and let us help you? Did you doubt your friends?' asked Mrs Jo, forgetting all other emotions in sympathy, as she lifted up the hidden face, and looked reproachfully into the great hollow eyes that met her own frankly now.

'I was ashamed. I tried to bear it alone rather than shock and disappoint you, as I know I have, though you try not to show it. Don't mind; I must get used to it'; and Dan's eyes dropped again as if they could not bear to see the trouble and dismay his confession painted on his best friend's face.

'I am shocked and disappointed by the sin, but I am also very glad and proud and grateful that my sinner has repented, atoned, and is ready to profit by the bitter lesson. No one but Fritz and Laurie need ever know the truth; we owe it to them, and they will feel as I do,' answered Mrs Jo, wisely thinking that entire frankness would be a better tonic than too much sympathy.

'No, they won't; men never forgive like women. But it's right. Please tell 'em for me, and get it over. Mr Laurence knows it, I guess. I blabbed when my wits were gone; but he was very kind all the same. I can bear their knowing; but oh, not Ted and the girls!' Dan clutched her arm with such an imploring face that she hastened to assure him no one should know except the two old friends, and he calmed down as if ashamed of his sudden panic.

'It wasn't murder, mind you, it was in self-defence; he drew first, and I had to hit him. Didn't mean to kill him; but it doesn't worry me as much as it ought, I'm afraid. I've more than paid for it, and such a rascal is better out of the world than in it, showing boys the way to hell. Yes, I know you think that's awful in me; but I can't help it. I hate a scamp as I do a skulking coyote, and always want to get a shot at 'em. Perhaps it would have been better if he had killed me; my life is spoilt.'

All the old prison gloom seemed to settle like a black cloud on Dan's face as he spoke, and Mrs Jo was frightened at the glimpse it gave her of the fire through which he had passed to come out alive, but scarred for life. Hoping to turn his mind to happier things, she said cheerfully:

'No, it isn't; you have learned to value it more and use it better for this trial. It is not a lost year, but one that may prove the most helpful of any you ever know. Try to think so, and begin again; we will help, and have all the more confidence in you for this failure. We all do the same and struggle on.'

'I never can be what I was. I feel about sixty, and don't care for anything now I've got here. Let me stay till I'm on my legs, then I'll clear out and never trouble you any more,' said Dan despondently.

'You are weak and low in your mind; that will pass, and by and by you will go to your missionary work among the Indians with all the old energy and the new patience, self-control, and knowledge you have gained. Tell me more about that good chaplain and Mary Mason and the lady whose chance word helped you so much. I want to know all about the trials of my poor boy.'

Won by her tender interest, Dan brightened up and talked on till he had poured out all the story of that bitter year, and felt better for the load he lifted off.

If he had known how it weighed upon his hearer's heart, he would have held his peace; but she hid her sorrow till she had sent him to bed, comforted and calm; then she cried her heart out, to the great dismay of Fritz and Laurie, till they heard the tale and could mourn with her; after which they all cheered up and took counsel together how best to help this worst of all the 'catastrophes' the year had brought them.

# CHAPTER 21. ASLAUGA'S KNIGHT

It was curious to see the change which came over Dan after that talk. A weight seemed off his mind; and though the old impetuous spirit flashed out at times, he seemed intent on trying to show his gratitude and love and honour to these true friends by a new humility and confidence very sweet to them, very helpful to him. After hearing the story from Mrs Jo, the Professor and Mr Laurie made no allusion to it beyond the hearty hand-grasp, the look of compassion, the brief word of good cheer in which men convey sympathy, and a redoubled kindness which left no doubt of pardon. Mr Laurie began at once to interest influential persons in Dan's mission, and set in motion the machinery which needs so much oiling before anything can be done where Government is concerned. Mr Bhaer, with the skill of a true teacher, gave Dan's hungry mind something to do, and helped him understand himself by carrying on the good chaplain's task so paternally that the poor fellow often said he felt as if he had found a father. The boys took him to drive, and amused him with their pranks and plans; while the women, old and young, nursed and petted him till he felt like a sultan with a crowd of devoted slaves, obedient to his lightest wish. A very little of this was enough for Dan, who had a masculine horror of 'molly-coddling', and so brief an acquaintance with illness that he rebelled against the doctor's orders to keep quiet; and it took all Mrs Jo's authority and the girls' ingenuity to keep him from leaving his sofa long before strained back and wounded head were well. Daisy cooked for him; Nan attended to his medicines; Josie read aloud to while away the long hours of inaction that hung so heavily on his hands; while Bess brought all her pictures and casts to amuse him, and, at his special desire, set up a modelling-stand in his parlour and began to mould the buffalo head he gave her. Those afternoons seemed the pleasantest part of his day; and Mrs Jo, busy in her study close by, could see the friendly trio and enjoy the pretty pictures they made. The girls were much flattered by the success of their efforts, and exerted themselves to be very entertaining, consulting Dan's moods with the feminine tact most women creatures learn before they are out of pinafores. When he was gay, the room rang with laughter; when gloomy, they read or worked in respectful silence till their sweet patience cheered him up again; and when in pain they hovered over him like 'a couple of angels', as he said. He often called Josie 'little mother', but Bess was always 'Princess'; and his manner to the two cousins was quite different. Josie sometimes fretted him with her fussy ways, the long plays she liked to read, and the maternal scoldings she administered when he broke the rules; for having a lord of creation in her power was so delightful to her that she would have ruled him with a rod of iron if he had submitted. To Bess, in her gentler ministrations, he never showed either impatience or weariness, but obeyed her least word, exerted himself to seem well in her presence, and took such interest in her work that he lay looking at her with unwearied eyes; while Josie read to him in her best style unheeded.

Mrs Jo observed this, and called them 'Una and the Lion', which suited them very well, though the lion's mane was shorn, and Una never tried to bridle him. The elder ladies did their part in providing delicacies and supplying all his wants; but Mrs Meg was busy at home, Mrs Amy preparing for the trip to Europe in the spring, and Mrs Jo hovering on the brink of a 'vortex'—for the forthcoming book had been sadly delayed by the late domestic events. As she sat at her desk, settling papers or meditatively nibbling her pen while waiting for the divine afflatus to descend upon her, she often forgot her fictitious heroes and heroines in studying the live models before her, and thus by chance looks, words, and gestures discovered a little romance unsuspected by anyone else.

The portiere between the rooms was usually drawn aside, giving a view of the group in the large bay-window—Bess at one side, in her grey blouse, busy with her tools; Josie at the other side with her book; and between, on the long couch, propped with many cushions, lay Dan in a many-hued eastern dressing-gown presented by Mr Laurie and worn to please the girls, though the invalid much preferred an old jacket 'with no confounded tail to bother over'. He faced Mrs Jo's room, but never seemed to see her, for his eyes were on the slender figure before him, with the pale winter sunshine touching her golden head, and the delicate hands that shaped the clay so deftly. Josie was just visible, rocking violently in a little chair at the head of the couch, and the steady murmur of her girlish voice was usually the only sound that broke the quiet of the room, unless a sudden discussion arose about the book or the buffalo.

Something in the big eyes, bigger and blacker than ever in the thin white face, fixed, so steadily on one object, had a sort of fascination for Mrs Jo after a time, and she watched the changes in them curiously; for Dan's mind was evidently not on the story, and he often forgot to laugh or exclaim at the comic or exciting crises. Sometimes they were soft and wistful, and the watcher was very glad that neither damsel caught that dangerous look for when they spoke it vanished; sometimes it was full of eager fire, and the colour came and went rebelliously, in spite of his attempt to hide it with an impatient gesture of hand or head; but oftenest it was dark, and sad, and stern, as if those gloomy eyes looked out of captivity at some forbidden light or joy. This expression came so often that it worried Mrs Jo, and she longed to go and ask him what bitter memory overshadowed those quiet hours. She knew that his crime and its punishment must lie heavy on his mind; but youth, and time, and new hopes would bring comfort, and help to wear away the first sharpness of the prison brand. It lifted at other times, and seemed almost forgotten when he joked with the boys, talked with old friends, or enjoyed the first snows as he drove out every fair day. Why should the shadow always fall so darkly on him in the society of these innocent and friendly girls? They never seemed to see it, and if either looked or spoke, a quick smile came like a sunburst through the clouds to answer them. So Mrs Jo went on watching, wondering, and discovering, till accident confirmed her fears.

Josie was called away one day, and Bess, tired of working, offered to take her place if he cared for more reading.

'I do; your reading suits me better than Jo's. She goes so fast my stupid head gets in a muddle and soon begins to ache. Don't tell her; she's a dear little soul, and so good to sit here with a bear like me.'

The smile was ready as Bess went to the table for a new book, the last story being finished.

'You are not a bear, but very good and patient, we think. It is always hard for a man to be shut up, mamma says, and must be terrible for you, who have always been so free.'

If Bess had not been reading titles she would have seen Dan shrink as if her last words hurt him. He made no answer; but other eyes saw and understood why he looked as if he would have liked to spring up and rush away for one of his long races up the hill, as he used to do when the longing for liberty grew uncontrollable. Moved by a sudden impulse, Mrs Jo caught up her work-basket and went to join her neighbours, feeling that a non-conductor might be needed; for Dan looked like a thundercloud full of electricity.

'What shall we read, Aunty? Dan doesn't seem to care. You know his taste; tell me something quiet and pleasant and short. Josie will be back soon,' said Bess, still turning over the books piled on the centre-table.

Before Mrs Jo could answer, Dan pulled a shabby little volume from under his pillow, and handing it to her said: 'Please read the third one; it's short and pretty—I'm fond of it.' The book opened at the right place, as if the third story had been often read, and Bess smiled as she saw the name.

'Why, Dan, I shouldn't think you'd care for this romantic German tale. There is fighting in it; but it is very sentimental, if I remember rightly.'

'I know it; but I've read so few stories, I like the simple ones best. Had nothing else to read sometimes; I guess I know it all by heart, and never seem to be tired of those fighting fellows, and the fiends and angels and lovely ladies. You read "Aslauga's Knight", and see if you don't like it. Edwald was rather too soft for my fancy; but Froda was first-rate and the spirit with the golden hair always reminded me of you.'

As Dan spoke Mrs Jo settled herself where she could watch him in the glass, and Bess took a large chair facing him, saying, as she put up her hands to retie the ribbon that held the cluster of thick, soft curls at the back of her head:

'I hope Aslauga's hair wasn't as troublesome as mine, for it's always tumbling down. I'll be ready in a minute.'

'Don't tie it up; please let it hang. I love to see it shine that way. It will rest your head, and be just right for the story, Goldilocks,' pleaded Dan, using the childish name and looking more like his boyish self than he had done for many a day.

Bess laughed, shook down her pretty hair, and began to read, glad to hide her face a little; for compliments made her shy, no matter who paid them. Dan listened intently on; and Mrs Jo, with eyes that went often from her needle to the glass, could see, without turning, how he enjoyed every word as if it had more meaning for him than for the other listeners. His face brightened wonderfully, and soon wore the look that came when anything brave or beautiful inspired and touched his better self. It was Fouque's charming story of the knight Froda, and the fair daughter of Sigurd, who was a sort of spirit, appearing to her lover in hours of danger and trial, as well as triumph and joy, till she became his guide and guard, inspiring him with courage, nobleness, and truth, leading him to great deeds in the field, sacrifices for those he loved, and victories over himself by the gleaming of her golden hair, which shone on him in battle, dreams, and perils by day and night, till after death he finds the lovely spirit waiting to receive and to reward him.

Of all the stories in the book this was the last one would have supposed Dan would like best, and even Mrs Jo was surprised at his perceiving the moral of the tale through the delicate imagery and romantic language by which it was illustrated. But as she looked and listened she remembered the streak of sentiment and refinement which lay concealed in Dan like the gold vein in a rock, making him quick to feel and to enjoy fine colour in a flower, grace in an animal, sweetness in women, heroism in men, and all the tender ties that bind heart to heart; though he was slow to show it, having no words to express the tastes and instincts which he inherited from his mother. Suffering of soul and body had tamed his stronger passions, and the atmosphere of love and pity now surrounding him purified and warmed his heart till it began to hunger for the food neglected or denied so long. This was plainly written in his too expressive face, as, fancying it unseen, he let it tell the longing after beauty, peace, and happiness embodied for him in the innocent fair girl before him.

The conviction of this sad yet natural fact came to Mrs Jo with a pang, for she felt how utterly hopeless such a longing was; since light and darkness were not farther apart than snow-white Bess and sin-stained Dan. No dream of such a thing disturbed the young girl, as her entire unconsciousness plainly showed. But how long would it be before the eloquent eyes betrayed the truth? And then what disappointment for Dan, what dismay for Bess, who was as cool and high and pure as her own marbles, and shunned all thought of love with maidenly reserve.

'How hard everything is made for my poor boy! How can I spoil his little dream, and take away the spirit of good he is beginning to love and long for? When my own dear lads are safely settled I'll never try another, for these things are heart-breaking, and I can't manage any more,' thought Mrs Jo, as she put the lining into Teddy's coat-sleeve upside down, so perplexed and grieved was she at this new catastrophe.

The story was soon done, and as Bess shook back her hair, Dan asked as eagerly as a boy:

'Don't you like it?'

'Yes, it's very pretty, and I see the meaning of it; but Undine was always my favourite.'

'Of course, that's like you—lilies and pearls and souls and pure water. Sintram used to be mine; but I took a fancy to this when I was—ahem—rather down on my luck one time, and it did me good, it was so cheerful and sort of spiritual in its meaning, you know.'

Bess opened her blue eyes in wonder at this fancy of Dan's for anything 'spiritual'; but she only nodded, saying: 'Some of the little songs are sweet and might be set to music.'

Dan laughed; 'I used to sing the last one to a tune of my own sometimes at sunset:

*"'Listening to celestial lays,*
*Bending thy unclouded gaze*
*On the pure and living light,*
*Thou art blest, Aslauga's Knight!"*

'And I was,' he added, under his breath, as he glanced towards the sunshine dancing on the wall.

'This one suits you better now'; and glad to please him by her interest, Bess read in her soft voice:

*"'Healfast, healfast, ye hero wounds;*
*O knight, be quickly strong!*
*Beloved strife*
*For fame and life,*
*Oh, tarry not too long!"'*

'I'm no hero, never can be, and "fame and life" can't do much for me. Never mind, read me that paper, please. This knock on the head has made a regular fool of me.'

Dan's voice was gentle; but the light was gone out of his face now, and he moved restlessly as if the silken pillows were full of thorns. Seeing that his mood had changed, Bess quietly put down the book, took up the paper, and glanced along the columns for something to suit him.

'You don't care for the money market, I know, nor musical news. Here's a murder; you used to like those; shall I read it? One man kills another—,'

'No!'

Only a word, but it gave Mrs Jo a thrill, and for a moment she dared not glance at the tell-tale mirror. When she did Dan lay motionless with one hand over his eyes, and Bess was happily reading the art news to ears that never heard a word. Feeling like a thief who has stolen something very precious, Mrs Jo slipped away to her study, and before long Bess followed to report that Dan was fast asleep.

Sending her home, with the firm resolve to keep her there as much as possible, Mother Bhaer had an hour of serious thought all alone in the red sunset; and when a sound in the next room led her there, she found that the feigned sleep had become real repose; for Dan lay breathing heavily, with a scarlet spot on either cheek, and one hand clinched on his broad breast. Yearning over him with a deeper pity than ever before, she sat in the little chair beside him, trying to see her way out of this tangle, till his hand slipped down, and in doing so snapped a cord he wore about his neck and let a small case drop to the floor.

Mrs Jo picked it up, and as he did not wake, sat looking at it, idly wondering what charm it held; for the case was of Indian workmanship and the broken cord, of closely woven grass, sweet scented and pale yellow.

'I won't pry into any more of the poor fellow's secrets. I'll mend and put it back, and never let him know I've seen his talisman.'

As she spoke she turned the little wallet to examine the fracture, and a card fell into her lap. It was a photograph, cut to fit its covering, and two words were written underneath the face, 'My Aslauga'. For an instant Mrs Jo fancied that it might be one of herself, for all the boys had them; but as the thin paper fell away, she saw the picture Demi took of Bess that happy summer day. There was no doubt now, and with a sigh she put it back, and was about to slip it into Dan's bosom so that not even a stitch should betray her knowledge, when as she leaned towards him, she saw that he was looking straight at her with an expression that surprised her more than any of the strange ones she had ever seen in that changeful face before.

'Your hand slipped down; it fell; I was putting it back,' explained Mrs Jo, feeling like a naughty child caught in mischief.

'You saw the picture?'

'Yes.'

'And know what a fool I am?'

'Yes, Dan, and am so grieved—'

'Don't worry about me. I'm all right—glad you know, though I never meant to tell you. Of course it is only a crazy fancy of mine, and nothing can ever come of it. Never thought there would. Good Lord! what could that little angel ever be to me but what she is—a sort of dream of all that's sweet and good?'

More afflicted by the quiet resignation of his look and tone than by the most passionate ardour, Mrs Jo could only say, with a face full of sympathy:

'It is very hard, dear, but there is no other way to look at it. You are wise and brave enough to see that, and to let the secret be ours alone.'

'I swear I will! not a word nor a look if I can help it. No one guesses, and if it troubles no one, is there any harm in my keeping this, and taking comfort in the pretty fancy that kept me sane in that cursed place?'

Dan's face was eager now, and he hid away the little worn case as if defying any hand to take it from him. Anxious to know everything before giving counsel or comfort, Mrs Jo said quietly:

'Keep it, and tell me all about the "fancy". Since I have stumbled on your secret, let me know how it came, and how I can help to make it lighter to bear.'

'You'll laugh; but I don't mind. You always did find out our secrets and give us a lift. Well, I never cared much for books, you know; but down yonder when the devil tormented me I had to do something or go stark mad, so I read both the books you gave me. One was beyond me, till that good old man showed me how to read it; but the other, this one, was a comfort, I tell you. It amused me, and was as pretty as poetry. I liked 'em all, and most wore out Sintram. See how used up he is! Then I came to this, and it sort of fitted that other happy part of my life, last summer—here.'

Dan stopped a moment as the words lingered on his lips; then, with a long breath, went on, as if it was hard to lay bare the foolish little romance he had woven about a girl, a picture, and a child's story there in the darkness of the place which was as terrible to him as Dante's Inferno, till he found his Beatrice.

'I couldn't sleep, and had to think about something, so I used to fancy I was Folko, and see the shining of Aslauga's hair in the sunset on the wall, the gum of the watchman's lamp, and the light that came in at dawn. My cell was high. I could see a bit of sky; sometimes there was a star in it, and that was most as good as a face. I set great store by that patch of blue, and when a white cloud went by, I thought it was the prettiest thing in all this world. I guess I was pretty near a fool; but those thoughts and things helped me through, so they are all solemn true to me, and I can't let them go. The dear shiny head, the white gown, the eyes like stars, and sweet, calm ways that set her as high above me as the moon in heaven. Don't take it away! it's only a fancy, but a man must love something, and I'd better love a spirit like her than any of the poor common girls who would care for me.'

The quiet despair in Dan's voice pierced Mrs Jo to the heart; but there was no hope and she gave none. Yet she felt that he was right, and that his hapless affection might do more to uplift and purify him than any other he might know. Few women would care to marry Dan now, except such as would hinder, not help, him in the struggle which life would always be to him; and it was better to go solitary to his grave than become what she suspected his father had been—a handsome, unprincipled, and dangerous man, with more than one broken heart to answer for.

'Yes, Dan, it is wise to keep this innocent fancy, if it helps and comforts you, till something more real and possible comes to make you happier. I wish I could give you any hope; but we both know that the dear child is the apple of her father's eye, the pride of her mother's heart, and that the most perfect lover they can find will hardly seem to them worthy of their precious daughter. Let her remain for you the high, bright star that leads you up and makes you believe in heaven.' Mrs Jo broke down there; it seemed so cruel to destroy the faint hope Dan's eyes betrayed, that she could not moralize when she thought of his hard life and lonely future. Perhaps it was the wisest thing she could have done, for in her hearty sympathy he found comfort for his own loss, and very soon was able to speak again in the manly tone of resignation to the inevitable that showed how honest was his effort to give up everything but the pale shadow of what, for another, might have been a happy possibility.

They talked long and earnestly in the twilight; and this second secret bound them closer than the first; for in it there was neither sin nor shame—only the tender pain and patience which has made saints and heroes of far worse men than our poor Dan. When at length they rose at the summons of a bell, all the sunset glory had departed, and in the wintry sky there hung one star, large, soft, and clear, above a snowy world. Pausing at the window before she dropped the curtains, Mrs Jo said cheerfully:

'Come and see how beautiful the evening star is, since you love it so.' And as he stood behind her, tall and pale, like the ghost of his former self, she added softly: 'And remember, dear, if the sweet girl is denied you, the old friend is always here—to love and trust and pray for you.'

This time she was not disappointed; and had she asked any reward for many anxieties and cares, she received it when Dan's strong arm came round her, as he said, in a voice which showed her that she had not laboured in vain to pluck her firebrand from the burning:

'I never can forget that; for she's helped to save my soul, and make me dare to look up there and say:

"God bless her!"'

# CHAPTER 22. POSITIVELY LAST APPEARANCE

'Upon my word, I feel as if I lived in a powder-magazine, and don't know which barrel will explode next, and send me flying,' said Mrs Jo to herself next day, as she trudged up to Parnassus to suggest to her sister that perhaps the most charming of the young nurses had better return to her marble gods before she unconsciously added another wound to those already won by the human hero. She told no secrets; but a hint was sufficient; for Mrs Amy guarded her daughter as a pearl of great price, and at once devised a very simple means of escape from danger. Mr Laurie was going to Washington on Dan's behalf, and was delighted to take his family with him when the idea was carelessly suggested. So the conspiracy succeeded finely; and Mrs Jo went home, feeling more like a traitor than ever. She expected an explosion; but Dan took the news so quietly, it was plain that he cherished no hope; and Mrs Amy was sure her romantic sister had been mistaken. If she had seen Dan's face when Bess went to say good-bye, her maternal eye would have discovered far more than the unconscious girl did. Mrs Jo trembled lest he should betray himself; but he had learned self-control in a stern school, and would have got through the hard moment bravely, only, when he took both hands, saying heartily:

'Good-bye, Princess. If we don't meet again, remember your old friend Dan sometimes,' she, touched by his late danger and the wistful look he wore, answered with unusual warmth: 'How can I help it, when you make us all so proud of you? God bless your mission, and bring you safely home to us again!'

As she looked up at him with a face full of frank affection and sweet regret, all that he was losing rose so vividly before him that Dan could not resist the impulse to take the 'dear goldy head' between his hands and kiss it, with a broken 'Good-bye'; then hurried back to his room, feeling as if it were the prison-cell again, with no glimpse of heaven's blue to comfort him.

This abrupt caress and departure rather startled Bess; for she felt with a girl's quick instinct that there was something in that kiss unknown before, and looked after him with sudden colour in her cheeks and new trouble in her eyes. Mrs Jo saw it, and fearing a very natural question answered it before it was put.

'Forgive him, Bess. He has had a great trouble, and it makes him tender at parting with old friends; for you know he may never come back from the wild world he is going to.'

'You mean the fall and danger of death?' asked Bess, innocently.

'No, dear; a greater trouble than that. But I cannot tell you any more—except that he has come through it bravely; so you may trust and respect him, as I do.'

'He has lost someone he loved. Poor Dan! We must be very kind to him.'

Bess did not ask the question, but seemed content with her solution of the mystery—which was so true that Mrs Jo confirmed it by a nod, and let her go away believing that some tender loss and sorrow wrought the great change all saw in Dan, and made him so slow to speak concerning the past year.

But Ted was less easily satisfied, and this unusual reticence goaded him to desperation. His mother had warned him not to trouble Dan with questions till he was quite well; but this prospect of approaching departure made him resolve to have a full, clear, and satisfactory account of the adventures which he felt sure must have been thrilling, from stray words Dan let fall in his fever. So one day when the coast was clear, Master Ted volunteered to amuse the invalid, and did so in the following manner:

'Look here, old boy, if you don't want me to read, you've got to talk, and tell me all about Kansas, and the farms, and that part. The Montana business I know, but you seem to forget what went before. Brace up, and let's have it,' he began, with an abruptness which roused Dan from a brown study most effectually.

'No, I don't forget; it isn't interesting to anyone but myself. I didn't see any farms—gave it up,' he said slowly.

'Why?'

'Other things to do.'

'What?'

'Well, brush-making for one thing.'

'Don't chaff a fellow. Tell true.'

'I truly did.'

'What for?'

'To keep out of mischief, as much as anything.'

'Well, of all the queer things—and you've done a lot—that's the queerest,' cried Ted, taken aback at this disappointing discovery. But he didn't mean to give up yet, and began again.

'What mischief, Dan?'

'Never you mind. Boys shouldn't bother.'

'But I do want to know, awfully, because I'm your pal, and care for you no end. Always did. Come, now, tell me a good yarn. I love scrapes. I'll be mum as an oyster if you don't want it known.'

'Will you?' and Dan looked at him, wondering how the boyish face would change if the truth were suddenly told him.

'I'll swear it on locked fists, if you like. I know it was jolly, and I'm aching to hear.'

'You are as curious as a girl. More than some—Josie and—and Bess never asked a question.'

'They don't care about rows and things; they liked the mine business, heroes, and that sort. So do I, and I'm as proud as Punch over it; but I see by your eyes that there was something else before that, and I'm bound to find out who Blair and Mason are, and who was hit and who ran away, and all the rest of it.'

'What!' cried Dan, in a tone that made Ted jump.

'Well, you used to mutter about 'em in your sleep, and Uncle Laurie wondered. So did I; but don't mind, if you can't remember, or would rather not.'

'What else did I say? Queer, what stuff a man will talk when his wits are gone.'

'That's all I heard; but it seemed interesting, and I just mentioned it, thinking it might refresh your memory a bit,' said Teddy, very politely; for Dan's frown was heavy at that moment.

It cleared off at this reply, and after a look at the boy squirming with suppressed impatience in his chair, Dan made up his mind to amuse him with a game of cross-purposes and half-truths, hoping to quench his curiosity, and so get peace.

'Let me see; Blair was a lad I met in the cars, and Mason a poor fellow who was in a—well, a sort of hospital where I happened to be. Blair ran off to his brothers, and I suppose I might say Mason was hit, because he died there. Does that suit you?'

'No, it doesn't. Why did Blair run? and who hit the other fellow? I'm sure there was a fight somewhere, wasn't there?'

'Yes!

'I guess I know what it was about.'

'The devil, you do! Let's hear you guess. Must be amusing,' said Dan, affecting an ease he did not feel.

Charmed to be allowed to free his mind, Ted at once unfolded the boyish solution of the mystery which he had been cherishing, for he felt that there was one somewhere.

'You needn't say yes, if I guess right and you are under oath to keep silent. I shall know by your face, and never tell. Now see if I'm not right. Out there they have wild doings, and it's my belief you were in some of 'em. I don't mean robbing mails, and KluKluxing, and that sort of thing; but defending the settlers, or hanging some scamp, or even shooting a few, as a fellow must sometimes, in self-defence. Ah, ha! I've hit it, I see. Needn't speak; I know the flash of your old eye, and the clench of your big fist.' And Ted pranced with satisfaction.

'Drive on, smart boy, and don't lose the trail,' said Dan, finding a curious sense of comfort in some of these random words, and longing, but not daring, to confirm the true ones. He might have confessed the crime, but not the punishment that followed, the sense of its disgrace was still so strong upon him.

'I knew I should get it; can't deceive me long,' began Ted, with such an air of pride Dan could not help a short laugh.

'It's a relief, isn't it, to have it off your mind? Now, just confide in me and it's all safe, unless you've sworn not to tell.'

'I have.'

'Oh, well, then don't'; and Ted's face fell, but he was himself again in a moment and said, with the air of a man of the world: 'It's all right—I understand—honour binds—silence to death, etc. Glad you stood by your mate in the hospital. How many did you kill?'

'Only one.'

'Bad lot, of course?'

'A damned rascal.'

'Well, don't look so fierce; I've no objection. Wouldn't mind popping at some of those bloodthirsty blackguards myself. Had to dodge and keep quiet after it, I suppose.'

'Pretty quiet for a long spell.'

'Got off all right in the end, and headed for your mines and did that jolly brave thing. Now, I call that decidedly interesting and capital. I'm glad to know it; but I won't blab.'

'Mind you don't. Look here. Ted, if you'd killed a man, would it trouble you—a bad one, I mean?'

The lad opened his mouth to say, 'Not a bit,' but checked that answer as if something in Dan's face made him change his mind. 'Well, if it was my duty in war or self-defence, I suppose I shouldn't; but if I'd pitched into him in a rage, I guess I should be very sorry. Shouldn't wonder if he sort of haunted me, and remorse gnawed me as it did Aram and those fellows. You don't mind, do you? It was a fair fight, wasn't it?'

'Yes, I was in the right; but I wish I'd been out of it. Women don't see it that way, and look horrified at such things. Makes it hard; but it don't matter.'

'Don't tell 'em; then they can't worry,' said Ted, with the nod of one versed in the management of the sex.

'Don't intend to. Mind you keep your notions to yourself, for some of 'em are wide of the mark. Now you may read if you like'; and there the talk ended; but Ted took great comfort in it, and looked as wise as an owl afterwards.

A few quiet weeks followed, during which Dan chafed at the delay; and when at length word came that his credentials were ready, he was eager to be off, to forget a vain love in hard work, and live for others, since he might not for himself.

So one wild March morning our Sintram rode away, with horse and hound, to face again the enemies who would have conquered him, but for Heaven's help and human pity.

'Ah, me! it does seem as if life was made of partings, and they get harder as we go on,' sighed Mrs Jo, a week later, as she sat in the long parlour at Parnassus one evening, whither the family had gone to welcome the travellers back.

'And meetings too, dear; for here we are, and Nat is on his way at last. Look for the silver lining, as Marmee used to say, and be comforted,' answered Mrs Amy, glad to be at home and find no wolves prowling near her sheepfold.

'I've been so worried lately, I can't help croaking. I wonder what Dan thought at not seeing you again? It was wise; but he would have enjoyed another look at home faces before he went into the wilderness,' said Mrs Jo regretfully.

'Much better so. We left notes and all we could think of that he might need, and slipped away before he came. Bess really seemed relieved; I'm sure I was'; and Mrs Amy smoothed an anxious line out of her white forehead, as she smiled at her daughter, laughing happily among her cousins.

Mrs Jo shook her head as if the silver lining of that cloud was hard to find; but she had no time to croak again, for just then Mr Laurie came in looking well pleased at something.

'A new picture has arrived; face towards the music-room, good people, and tell me how you like it. I call it "Only a fiddler", after Andersen's story. What name will you give it?'

As he spoke he threw open the wide doors, and just beyond they saw a young man standing, with a beaming face, and a violin in his hand. There was no doubt about the name to this picture, and with the cry 'Nat! Nat!' there was a general uprising. But Daisy reached him first, and seemed to have lost her usual composure somewhere on the way, for she clung to him, sobbing with the shock of a surprise and joy too great for her to bear quietly. Everything was settled by that tearful and tender embrace, for, though Mrs Meg speedily detached her daughter, it was only to take her place; while Demi shook Nat's hand with brotherly warmth, and Josie danced round them like Macbeth's three witches in one, chanting in her most tragic tones:

'Chirper thou wast; second violin thou art; first thou shalt be. Hail, all hail!'

This caused a laugh, and made things gay and comfortable at once. Then the usual fire of questions and answers began, to be kept up briskly while the boys admired Nat's blond beard and foreign clothes, the girls his improved appearance—for he was ruddy with good English beef and beer, and fresh with the sea-breezes which had blown him swiftly home—and the older folk rejoiced over his prospects. Of course all wanted to hear him play; and when tongues tired, he gladly did his best for them, surprising the most critical by his progress in music even more than by the energy and self-possession which made a new man of bashful Nat. By and by when the violin—that most human of all instruments—had sung to them the loveliest songs without words, he said, looking about him at these old friends with what Mr Bhaer called a 'feeling-full' expression of happiness and content:

'Now let me play something that you will all remember though you won't love it as I do'; and standing in the attitude which Ole Bull has immortalized, he played the street melody he gave them the first night he came to Plumfield. They remembered it, and joined in the plaintive chorus, which fitly expressed his own emotions:

*'Oh my heart is sad and weary*
*Everywhere I roam,*
*Longing for the old plantation*
*And for the old folks at home.'*

'Now I feel better,' said Mrs Jo, as they all trooped down the hill soon after. 'Some of our boys are failures, but I think this one is going to be a success, and patient Daisy a happy girl at last. Nat is your work, Fritz, and I congratulate you heartily.'

'Ach, we can but sow the seed and trust that it falls on good ground. I planted, perhaps, but you watched that the fowls of the air did not devour it, and brother Laurie watered generously; so we will share the harvest among us, and be glad even for a small one, heart's-dearest.'

'I thought the seed had fallen on very stony ground with my poor Dan; but I shall not be surprised if he surpasses all the rest in the real success of life, since there is more rejoicing over one repentant sinner than many saints,' answered Mrs Jo, still clinging fast to her black sheep although a whole flock of white ones trotted happily before her.

It is a strong temptation to the weary historian to close the present tale with an earthquake which should engulf Plumfield and its environs so deeply in the bowels of the earth that no youthful Schliemann could ever find a vestige of it. But as that somewhat melodramatic conclusion might shock my gentle readers, I will refrain, and forestall the usual question, 'How did they end?' by briefly stating that all the marriages turned out well. The boys prospered in their various callings; so did the girls, for Bess and Josie won honours in their artistic careers, and in the course of time found worthy mates. Nan remained a busy, cheerful, independent spinster, and dedicated her life to her suffering sisters and their children, in which true woman's work she found abiding happiness. Dan never married, but lived, bravely and usefully, among his chosen people till he was shot defending them, and at last lay quietly asleep in the green wilderness he loved so well, with a lock of golden hair upon his breast, and a smile on his face which seemed to say that Aslauga's Knight had fought his last fight and was at peace. Stuffy became an alderman, and died suddenly of apoplexy after a public dinner. Dolly was a society man of mark till he lost his money, when he found congenial employment in a fashionable tailoring establishment. Demi became a partner, and lived to see his name above the door, and Rob was a professor at Laurence College; but Teddy eclipsed them all by becoming an eloquent and famous clergyman, to the great delight of his astonished mother. And now, having endeavoured to suit everyone by many weddings, few deaths, and as much prosperity as the eternal fitness of things will permit, let the music stop, the lights die out, and the curtain fall for ever on the March family. END

Made in the USA
Monee, IL
31 March 2024